THE ASCENT OF WONDER

THE ASCENT OF WONDER

The Evolution of Hard SF

Edited by

DAVID G. HARTWELL AND KATHRYN CRAMER

An *Orbit* Book

First published in the United States by Tor Books in 1994
First published in Great Britain by Orbit in 1994

A CIP catalogue record for this book is available from the British Library.

ISBN 1 85723 271 2

Printed and bound in Great Britain by
BPC Hazell Books Ltd
A member of
The British Printing Company Ltd

Orbit
A Division of
Little, Brown and Company (UK)
Brettenham House
Lancaster Place
London WC2E 7EN

Copyright Acknowledgments

Acknowledgments

We would like to thank a number of people who have helped make this book possible. It has taken more than six years of research and writing to do this book, and was more dependent on the support of others than is usual in an anthology. In roughly chronological order, then, thanks:

to John Cramer, for collaborative help in many ways; to Gregory Benford, for his informed discussion and for irritating remarks; to Ralph Arnote and Linda Quinton for planning advice; to Susan Ann Protter, for patience and hard work; to Tom Doherty, who supports hard sf; to John Jarrold, who also supports hard sf, for his enthusiasm; to Abner Stein, for being there;

to James M. Young, for use of his library and for discussion; to Samuel R. Delany, for cheerful support and much discussion; to Tom Maddox, for the MLA panel; to John M. Ford, for discussion and for advice on the organization of the table of contents; to Hal Clement and the late Gerald Feinberg, for the interview; to Frank M. Robinson for his xeroxes;

to Donald G. Keller, for patient nit-picking and tireless persistence; to Patrick Nielsen Hayden, for Donald G. Keller; to Colin Murray for his patience. And finally, to all those who contributed to the ongoing discussion of hard sf in the pages of *The New York Review of Science Fiction* for six years.

Kathryn Cramer
David G. Hartwell

To Kathryn, for Big Ideas.

—D.H.

For David, who kept this project going when I was tired, and for my father, John Cramer, who let me run around the nuclear physics laboratory as a child.

—K.C.

Contents

Introductions

REAL SCIENCE, IMAGINARY WORLDS

Gregory Benford

The great simplicity of science will only be seen when we understand its strangeness.

—John Wheeler

I have found that "hard" science fiction writers share a camaraderie that is unusual even for their close-knit genre.

In my experience, writers of "the hard stuff" produce more collaborations than other types of science fiction authors, they hold in common the internationalist idealism of scientific bodies, and in their free trading of ideas often behave like scientists. Modern science itself shares many hard sf genre features—steadily, communally developed ideas; a "family" feeling; and open discourse, especially in a time when papers in scientific, learned journals can have fifty authors.

Hardness in fiction—fidelity to facts, whether in sf or in a police procedural novel—is a cultivated taste. In a nation of declining science-related skills, written hard sf may reach a shrinking audience, though its taste for high-tech imagery may continue to be widely influential. The principal contribution of the visual arts to hard sf has been in concrete backgrounds, from the serene surfaces of *2001: A Space Odyssey* to the cluttered techno-trashscapes of *Blade Runner*. The hard sf aesthetic goals may still occupy the center of the field—though much recent sf has returned to the old styles, in which scientific accuracy and worldview are subordinated to conventional literary virtues of character or plot, style or setting. Alas, in this sense hard sf may be a paradigm more often honored in the breach than not.

Still, seeking its cachet, some have tried to appropriate the hard sf name for any narrative which nods however slightly toward science at all. (J. G. Ballard, Ursula K. LeGuin and Gene Wolfe, for example, do not feature on the hard sf fan's list, but they have been enlisted in the corps by some.) Fresh writers slinging tough prose are almost routinely blurbed as purveying a new kind of hard sf. This, too, is an indirect tribute to its slow, silent success.

We can describe hard science fiction as that variety—a quite small fraction—which highly prizes faithfulness to the physical facts of the universe, while building upon them to realize new fictional worlds. But how crucial should this be—that is, how central is science to science fiction?

Many think it's peripheral. They could easily argue that, after all, science stands for Truth in our culture, the way of knowing which knocked over conventional religion in the nineteenth century. Meanwhile, fiction really describes events which didn't happen. Fiction is (let's be frank) *lies*—beautiful lies, maybe, intoxicating, uplifting, enormously suggestive—but lies, nonetheless. So "science fiction" is a contradiction. Is it Lies about the Truth? Or the deeper Truth about Lies?

Probably neither. Yet the most simon-pure breed, that based on the physical sciences, strikes many more as the true core of the field. It yields the central images (spaceship, glittering future city, time machine, alien world) upon which the rest of science fiction (sf) feeds. The gritty detail, classically clean geometries and realism of the "hard" variety informs many films. It often seems more worldly and less wishful than the "soft" fiction based on the social sciences.

It sticks to the *facts*—unless some crucial new experiment or discovery changes those—but can play fast and loose with *theory* as it likes. It's important that any new scientific theory must explain the facts we already know, though it can twist your head around to do the job. Einstein's explanation of gravity as warped space-time doesn't sound like Newton's forces acting at a distance—but they both explain the same elliptical orbits and falling apples, with Einstein winning in the fifth decimal place.

Our century has been a playground for physics, which with electronics, the atom, and the rocket, has remade the world. Because physics makes the most precise predictions, hard sf often uses it to anchor speculations. Astronomy provides the largest possible landscape for adventures, often action-filled, but also for cosmic perspectives, a hallmark. Maybe some of all this authority will rub off.

Science fiction arose in a time affected by science's unsettling revelations about ourselves, about our position in the natural order—and by relentless technology, science's burly handmaiden. Sf has tried to grapple with ideas which disturb our sense of being at home in the world. While botany, or human anatomy, or zoology do not really separate us from our common world, physics, chemistry, and especially astronomy certainly do. This alienation may be why these latter sciences turn up so much in hard sf, as it struggles with the emotions they kindle. Advances in genetics shall soon lead to bioengineering, effectively alienating us from our bodies, making us see ourselves and nature even more as machines—so hard sf has lately drawn this area into its province. Many stories expend a lot of effort trying to offset or reconcile with these poisoned gifts.

KEEPING THE NET UP

Robert Frost remarked that free verse was like playing tennis with the net down. At first maybe a netless game seems fresh, exciting—but soon nobody wants to watch you play. Hard sf plays with the net of scientific fact up and strung as tight as the story allows.

H. G. Wells admonished writers to make one assumption, as fantastic as we like, and then explore it remorselessly. A world of infinite possibilities is boring because there can be no suspense. If you write a sonnet with, say, seventeen lines, you haven't written a good or bad one—you haven't written a sonnet at all. The same way the iron rules of the sonnet can force excellence within a narrow frame, paying attention to scientific accuracy can force coherence on fiction. This aesthetic is central to hard sf.

Such a sense comes freighted with ideology present in American sf from the beginning. In the late 1920s, the legendary editor Hugo Gernsback did not require that every bit of information in a story adhere to known facts or laws; in the first issue of *Amazing Stories* he featured Jules Verne's *Off on a Comet*, in which Gernsback said, "the author abandons his usual scrupulously scientific attitude and gives his fancy freer rein." In explaining Wells's *The Time Machine* he said, "Remember, these stories are fictional, and while the science in them must have some touch of verisimilitude, the whole fabric would lose interest, if it hadn't elasticity enough in it to be stretchable." He numbered the pages of *Amazing Stories* by the volume, not merely within each issue, deliberately copying scientific journals. Later he even argued that detailed inventions in sf stories should in principle be patented—life imitating art.

Gernsbackian invention was gadget-oriented. Sf did not often venture beyond the solar system until E. E. Smith's *The Skylark of Space*, which used an interstellar backdrop for awe, with minimal science. The sheer wonder of such vast spaces seemed to inspire pulp, gaudy pulp adventure until the 1950s, when Hal Clement's landmark *Mission of Gravity* seemed like a gust of fresh air. Its detailed descriptions of a high-gravity planet and its insectlike natives were meticulous and well argued. This novel may mark the true beginning of hard sf as a recognized subgenre, though the term itself doesn't seem to have come into use until the middle 1960s, perhaps in reaction to the New Wave literary movement. (Though the New Wave was important in opening the field to wider influences, its greatest effect may have been to make hard sf into a recognized opposite.) Clement's bizarre but scientifically plausible world is a raw setting in which the protagonists struggle upward against great weight, a reflection of the sometimes grim but usually hopeful tone of hard sf.

Much of the charm of Frank Herbert's hugely successful *Dune*, written several years after *Mission of Gravity*, lies in its working out of the implications of life on a desert planet. Herbert used massive research to buttress his imagination, and the book compels us because the consequences of the rigorous environment, as the plot unveils them, seem logical and *right*. Fred Pohl's *Gateway*—a New Wave–influenced novel with futuristic psychotherapy and *angst* as a frame—uses stellar astronomy, scrupulously rendered. Except for some super-strong materials to wire it all together, Larry Niven's *Ringworld* conforms to physics as we now know it. It follows a band of explorers who trek across an immense ring which circles a star, spinning to create centrifugal "gravity." The ring is so immense it can harbor life across a surface many times larger than the area of Earth. Making this all work is great fun, with ideas unveiled by plot turns at a smooth pace. The sheer size of everything overwhelms the reader, but the game is played straight and true, no cards up the sleeve.

Well, almost. I noticed, along with many others, that the ring had a distressing property—shove it sideways and it coasts into its star. This instability can be righted by installing attitude jets on the outer rim. Niven didn't know this, but he added the jets to his sequel—a good example of holding true to the ideas of contemporary physics.

The crucial opening assumption can be pretty fanciful, though. Suppose Earth has been immersed in a medium which dumbed down all species, as in Poul Anderson's *Brain Wave*. What would happen when we got suddenly smarter—and so did the animals, including Rover and Puss? In *Shield* Anderson asks, What happens if somebody invents a perfect defensive screen against all weapons, making Jeffersonian individualism a hard fact? Or suppose there is a gene which confers immortality against disease and aging—though not against, say, being crushed by a landslide? Near immortals would be very different people. Anderson's *The Boat of a Million Years* follows a handful of these developing oddities through ancient history up to the present, then beyond. Most specialists on aging believe it arises as a side effect of relentless natural selection for reproductive efficiency in younger years, a menu of traits which make for more and better children but take their toll in the end. Given that one gene, though, Anderson's logic proceeds smoothly to a grand finale.

Robert Heinlein's "It's Great to be Back" is a bit more subtle in its delivery, following tourists from the moon on a visit to Earth, and inverting all the supposedly irksome aspects of living in "space" into virtues. Once the situation is clear, the surprises follow reasonably. Part of the pleasure comes from watching an artist work with as few props as possible. Heinlein's "By His Bootstraps" examines time travel—a far more fanciful notion than a moon colony—in all its overlapping paradoxes, turning the plot on its head in strictly logical fashion. Time travel is an idea that brings into play immense possibilities, but it lies at the margin of hard sf. Are paradoxes inevitable—or can you really shoot your grandfather and still survive? There is a considerable body of sophisticated theoretical research devoted to probing whether physics can in principle exclude time travel, and the jury—after many physics papers about faster-than-light particles (tachyons) and wormholes in space-time—is still out. Nearly all physicists are very doubtful.

The urge to visit the past is so compelling, most time-travel stories concern it, rather than trips to the future, as in H. G. Wells's *The Time Machine*, the first notable use of the idea. An appetite for such vistas lures many hard sf writers to it such as Isaac Asimov (*The End of Eternity*) and Poul Anderson (*The Time Patrol*).

Sf can reach even further afield than time travel and keep its credentials. Asimov used his broad knowledge of science to make an apparent impossibility—element plutonium 186—become real, by inventing a scientifically plausible method of connecting parallel universes. *The Gods Themselves* is his most scientifically oriented novel, producing the "feel" of hard sf through meticulous logic. His *Foundation* series, on the other hand, envisions social science as hard as physics, capable of making exact predictions—but somehow, the "hard" effect is less telling than in *The Gods Themselves*.

The drone of meticulous explanation appears often, almost like a bizarre fetish—because the authors want to retain the authority of nonfiction, its touchstones of an external (though provisional) truth. Thus the writer may stretch a quantitative point for dramatic effect, but not commit the unpardonable sin of lying—giving scientific misinformation to the reader. This sets tensions afoot in the plot, from the peculiar difficulty and excitement of building narrative suspense.

Rigor can have other drawbacks. Stories can turn on whether a match will stay lit in an orbiting spacecraft (convection of hot smoke away from the flame depends on hot air being lighter; Hal Clement, "Fireproof"). This sets up a tension between narrative drama and fidelity to facts. Most writers feel that scientific errors or finessed facts should be at least invisible to the lay reader—remembering, though, that the best reader is sophisticated and not easily fooled. They love to catch each other in oversights. (Heinlein once skewered me about the freezing point of methane, and I was mortified.) They even show off a bit by pioneering, rationalizing territory previously regarded as the province of fantasy. In "Magic, Inc." Heinlein treated magic as a technology with rules as strict as a chess game. Larry Niven followed with stories in which magic (mana) was simply a natural resource, used up in ancient times (*The Time of the Warlock*), leaving us with merely the scientific laws we know now.

BEING THERE

To get the science right, you have to know the scientists, too. This is an aspect of *verisimilitude*—imbuing fantastic events with convincing detail. Piling on well-worked-out nuances derived from the science and technology. C. S. Lewis termed this "realism of presentation," as in his *Out of the Silent Planet*; in its simplest form it uses names, geography, maps, titles of nobility, etc. Fantasy shares this trait, as in Tolkien, but the distinctive hard sf method is to fix upon a few surprising but logical consequences of the scientific facts. The most unexpected, the better. The moon colonists in Heinlein's "The Menace from Earth" notice that their low gravity allows people to fly in pressurized domes—creating a tourist industry. In *The Rolling Stones* Heinlein's savvy traders deduce that Martian gravity and sandy soil will make bicycles a thrifty, overlooked method of transport. They make a killing, like many self-sufficient hard sf heroes.

Getting the voice right is essential. Fred Pohl's "Day Million" is a frustrated rant, expressing the author's despair at ever conveying to his reader how wondrously different the far future will be—yet it tries anyway, with compact expository lumps like grumpy professorial lectures. This is one of the voices of hard sf itself, trying to punch through humanist complacency about the supposed centrality of human perspectives and comforts. Tom Godwin's "The Cold Equations" also hammers relentlessly (and melodramatically), invoking the constraints of gravity, orbital mechanics, and fuel levels. These two stories talk across the rapid social evolution between Godwin's (1954) and Pohl's (1966). Godwin used the indifference of the universe to frame a morality tale in which a woman suffers because she tries to use her innocence to avoid responsibility. Pohl doesn't personify human insularity in a woman, but in the reader himself—and ends by directly addressing that reader, assumed to be a callow young man, indeed, perhaps even the techno-weenie some see as the hard-core hard sf audience.

The most important voice to get right is the style of scientists themselves. This demands considerable craft; scientists at work are usually less interesting than watching paint dry. James Gunn's *The Listeners* opens each portion with lengthy quotations from the scientific literature, with radio astronomers debating the philosophy of listening for extraterrestrial intelligence. Fred Hoyle's *The Black Cloud* uses crisp, though long, arguments between astronomers, complete with equations. They try to cope with an immense, super-intelligent plasma cloud which swoops out of interstellar space and envelops the entire inner solar system. The astronomers are sharply rendered, shrinking the huge perspectives down to clashes of style and personality. Outside their observatories and conference rooms, the rest of humanity panics, resorting to religious frenzy and misled by dull-witted politicians who pay little attention to the scientists (a favorite Hoyle theme). Much sf struggles to reduce the vast canvas of astronomy to human scale by rendering the scientists in detail—jargon, warts and all.

Science can make the world seem surreal, a symptom of culture lagging behind technological reality; Blake's dread "satanic mills" may still seem ugly to us, but no longer bizarre. This is the problem with using current emblematic objects, as J. G. Ballard does with abandoned Cape Canaveral launch pads and traffic islands. Declaring this way that "modernity" ends in unreal landscapes fixes the author in the moment, tied to aesthetic attitudes which date quickly. Hard sf has a more flinty view of external artifacts, often taking them matter-of-factly, though occasional hints show them to be anything but, as in Alfred Bester's "The Pi Man," which uses typographical tricks to suggest interior and exterior landscapes.

PALE IMMENSITIES

In works such as *2001: A Space Odyssey*, Stanley Kubrick's fruitful collaboration with Arthur C. Clarke, hard sf symbolism dominates other fictional elements. Since the eighteenth century, science has been widely seen as a better way to understand our world than either myth or religion—two elements which, used at face value in fantastic fiction, typically yield fantasy. Hard sf can stand for a universe which cares nothing for us, yet furnishes wondrous perspectives, like an immense cathedral of an unfathomable alien faith.

In Poul Anderson's *Tau Zero* a runaway starship cannot brake itself and so must accelerate forever, leaving our galaxy, boosting ever closer to the unreachable speed of light. As relativity theory dictates, time slows onboard while the universe outside expands, galaxies age, and finally the expansion halts and an inevitable contraction begins. Against this exterior majesty Anderson contrasts the petty wrangles and sexual misadventures of the crew trapped in a cramped human vessel, responding only fitfully to the massive perspectives they witness. They pass through the inward collapse of the universe, through to the rebirth, scrapping and struggling all the way. (I was struck by this myself in writing "Relativistic Effects.") Anderson achieved this effect by using a technique of Olaf Stapledon. His first chapter covers a few hours, the second a few days, the third several weeks—a logarithmic progression in time. Each chapter has about the same wordage, which allows the reader enough time to get used to this new time span, then whisks her up another order of magnitude. New perspectives demand new literary techniques.

The hard sf symbolism of H. G. Wells's crab scuttling across a worn red beach at the end of time announced that the young genre could talk about the biggest of questions. Immensity comes naturally to astronomers, who daily deal with events and distances which we literally cannot comprehend except through mathematical notation. Even missions to our outer planets take a working scientist's lifetime for their planning, launch and rendezvous. Everywhere, as science pushes on, time and space transcend our ready perceptions. With a taste for the huge, novels such as Stanislaw Lem's *Solaris* portray alien intelligences which are literally enormous (in this case, a planet-covering ocean which doesn't fit Darwinian ideas, to say the least). Lem's career has often dealt with science's limitations as hopelessly human-centered, with no true credentials to talk about the world as it truly is—a posture owing much to the philosopher David Hume.

A favorite device casting human mortality against the inexorable laws of the universe appears in Arthur Clarke's "Transit of Earth." Here the doomed astronaut witnesses the uncaring clockwork precision of planetary orbits, communicating his awe and dread back to people comfortably safe. This motif contrasts human social insulation with the intellectual distance assumed in the physical and biological sciences. This method appears in James Gunn's "Cave of Night" and Clarke has used it many times, notably in a story with an astronaut who seems doomed to crash back onto the moon in a spent rocket, and radios good-bye to his wife on Earth—but manages a solution at the last minute, a more typically pulp ending. Both "Transit of Earth" and Tom Godwin's "The Cold Equations" profit from not attempting a pleasant finish, remorselessly sticking with the assumptions of the story, belying the commonplace that hard sf is invariably optimistic and that humans always win. The impersonality of the universe ultimately stands for its authority.

Immensity has a beauty all its own, one of the clichés of the field. The beautiful often demands the cultivated exclusion of natural forces, so artifacts emerge cool and serene, as in *2001*. The horrific is then the repressed return of those forces, the breakdown, as in so many disaster novels.

In contrast, we meet the very small in Paul Preuss's *Broken Symmetries* (particle physics and its milieu) and James Blish's "Surface Tension." Whatever the symbol—giant quasisexual spacecraft, divine aliens, Edenlike planets—many writers seem to be searching for a sense of strangeness. Robert Forward's *Dragon's Egg* explores life on a neutron star, with gravity so strong the atmosphere is an inch high. Conventional literature occasionally embraces the strange, as in William Golding's *The Inheritors*, about Neanderthal and Cro-Magnon, and Richard Adams's *The Plague Dogs* with its passages told from the point of view of dogs.

Yet all this rational hardness gives over frequently to mysticism. Edgar Allan Poe's "A Descent into the Maelström" uses a natural, though exotic, phenomenon to reveal the arabesques of reality. His hero escapes by solving his problem rationally, and the experience unsettles his worldview. Similarly, in Clarke's "The Nine Billion Names of God," efficiencies in computation cause God to sound the universe's last trumpet call. Hard sf is not truly opposed to theology; the concrete whipsaws us against the ineffable.

Awe can arise naturally from as simple a childhood question as, If the sun was an orange and the Earth a pea, how big would the solar system be? (About a mile.) While Darwin won the battle with religion in the nineteenth century, spirituality isn't organized religion; in fact, often they conflict. Transcendental beauty and awe are always with us in literature, from Lucretius' observation that exquisitely interconnected nature yields inexpressible joy. Sometimes this corkscrews into sf heroes who become the Messiah (*Dune, Stranger in a Strange Land*). At its best it gives vistas beyond conventional literature, as in the images of ascending into new states in Clarke's *Childhood's End* and Greg Bear's *Blood Music*.

These novels echo the grand master of hard sf transcendentalism, Olaf Stapledon. From his first work, *Last and First Men*, through *Star Maker* and *Sirius*, he gave us cool condensates of pure imagination, uncluttered by the apparatus of novels—characters and incidents, talk and action—yet quite fictional. His imagination moved with a grave solemnity, seldom granting a nod toward the everyday. Stapledon had digested Darwin-Wallace evolution, together with the just-emerging view of stars, too, as evolutionary. With graceful cadence, he paired the progression of intelligence as another element in the natural scheme, with the lives of stars from early compression to fiery death throes, the slow massive workings of red giants and white dwarves—anthropomorphic names for vast, imponderable energies. Cosmic evolution from brute matter, up through stellar element-building, through simple primordial chemistry and into blossoming life, is a far more beautiful image than the popular view of evolution. Stapledon anticipated this in the 1930s, blending the nineteenth-century flavor of Schopenhauer's philosophy of being with Spengler's clockworky cyclic history into a vision of man as "a fledgling caught in a brush fire"—certainly not the expansive, humanistic "measure of all things."

At times Stapledon seemed one of those "intellects vast and cool and unsympathetic" in H. G. Wells's unforgettable description of the Martians of *The War of the Worlds*, the grandest nineteenth-century hard sf novel. Stapledon directly inherited much in method and manner from Wells. Other British thinkers such as J. D. Bernal and Fred Hoyle follow this tradition. (Jules Verne became the forefather of the other face of hard sf, twentieth-century optimistic technophilia.) Brian Aldiss termed Stapledon's work "great classical ontological epic prose poems." Yet against this sober canvas, the largest ever constructed in fiction, *Last and First Men* concludes that "Man himself, at the very least, is music, a brave theme that makes music also of its vast accompaniment, its matrix of storms and stars."

This mirrors the tension in hard sf between its inhuman landscapes which dwarf us, and the fictional demand that makes people, especially their emotions, central. Stapledon's solution, fiction without people in the foreground, was extreme—and has outlasted innumerable works of humanistic merit.

INTERSECTIONS

How does hard sf sit in the recent cataloging of literature by critics—structuralist, postmodern, deconstructionist, etc.? To many sf writers, "postmodern" is simply a signature of exhaustion. Its typical apparatus—self-reference, heavy dollops of obligatory irony, self-conscious use of older genre devices, pastiche and parody—betrays lack of invention. Some deconstructionists have attacked science itself as mere rhetoric, not an ordering of nature, seeking to reduce it to the status of the ultimately arbitrary humanities. Hard sf types find this attack on empiricism an old song with new lyrics, quite retro.

At the core of hard sf lies the experience of science, which conventional fiction mostly ignores—though as J. G. Ballard remarked, the trouble with sf is often that it is not a literature won from experience. This means that hard sf is finally hostile to recent fashions in criticism, for it values its empirical ground. Deconstructionism's stress on contradictory or self-contained internal differences in texts, rather than their link to reality, often merely leads to literature seen as empty word games. Postmodernism seems to most hard sf writers as fiction about media-saturated cultures, with the attention span of MTV, and not about the deeper facets which make that culture—particularly, not about the implications of science seen up close. Thus hard sf focuses on minimally characterized figures acting against a landscape of universal, scientific truths. Postmodernist literary theorists have embraced some sf authors who display a conspicuous stylistic gloss—Ballard, William Gibson—because they write primarily about the surfaces of the technosphere now enveloping us. This places these writers at the edge for hard sf, for the "info-universe" immersing us stems directly from advanced technology—though they often don't fathom the underlying ideas which produce the shiny technical skins. In the end, technology fiction (as Sturgeon termed it) is not necessarily hard sf.

"Cyberspace" is a realm inside computer spaces, which characters can inhabit. In Vernor Vinge's pioneering *True Names* and Charles Platt's *The Silicon Man* the atmospheric weirdness dominates the mood. More often cyberspace is a magical realm with a high-tech sheen, as in Gibson's *Neuromancer*. Depicting computer-saturated futures is difficult if you actually don't have a clue how computers work—but it can make compelling reading, as in Gibson's "Johnny Mnemonic." Still relevant are earlier, thoughtful stories, such as Asimov's "The Last Word" and Gordon Dickson's "Computers Don't Argue."

The hard sf physical aesthetic was exported from the subgenre into the stylish sets of 1956's film *Forbidden Planet*, then most powerfully in *2001*. Films became exporters themselves of such informed imagery with *Tron* and especially *Blade Runner*, the cultural sources for the later "cyberpunk" literary fashions. A central moment in the full version of *Blade Runner* is a detailed discussion of why the short-lived "replicants" can't be given longer lives—not gobbledegook, but a plausible, albeit highly technical, reason. In a film short on dialogue, this is a remarkable tip of the hat to hardness.

Paralleling this concern with style, science fantasy uses the trappings of hard sf—spaceships, jargon, high-tech ornaments—awash in the devices and thought-patterns of fantasy. Galactic cultures coexist with feudal planets, complete with their swords, queens, and quests. A near neighbor to this is hard sf, though—techno-empire sf, such as Larry Niven and Jerry Pournelle's *The Mote in God's Eye*. The science is right and the action supports conflict and military virtues as eternal features—plausible assumptions, alas.

Like other subgenres of fantastic literature, hard sf works in part because it is an ongoing discussion. Its authors speak of "playing the game"—getting striking, surprising but physically plausible scenes into their work, and being able to defend their extravagances with "hard" scientific arguments, even calculations. This resembles the pleasures of police procedural novels and classic puzzle mystery stories, with their meticulous accuracy of method and logic. Genre readers immerse themselves in a system of thought, so that each fresh book or story is a further exploration of that system, mental play illuminated by all the reader has discovered before. Science and technology are more complex systems than crime or international intrigue or westerns or romances, affording both wider and odder pleasures.

The flip side of this is a daunting genre vernacular, making works somewhat unintelligible to the newcomer until he learns the ropes. With learned genre competency come the pleasures of cross-talk—the books speak to each other in an ongoing debate over big issues, such as our place in creation, the nature of consensual reality, etc. Both readers and writers form a kind of "virtual club" which inspires real feelings of companionship and loyalty.

So George Zebrowski's *Macrolife* speaks to Stapledon and Clarke and Aldiss; Joe Haldeman's *The Forever War* and Harry Harrison's *Bill, the Galactic Hero* answer Heinlein's *Starship Troopers*; Clarke and Charles Sheffield publish novels in the same year about building towers from Earth to high orbit; David Brin's *Earth* reflects the early ecological themes of George Stewart's *Earth Abides* and John Brunner's *Stand on Zanzibar*. The "young adult" novel of emergence has been dominated by sf, from the groundbreaking series of Robert Heinlein (starting with *Rocket Ship Galileo*), up to Charles Sheffield's Godspeed in 1993, which clearly descends from the Heinlein approach. The mathematical lattices of computer intelligences inform Rudy Rucker's *White Light* and William Gibson's *Neuromancer* series, the concepts evolving through Greg Bear's *Queen of Angels* and Charles Platt's *The Silicon Man* to Greg Egan's short stories. John Varley's *Steel Beach* and Allen Steele's *Lunar Descent* take up from Heinlein's sense of the future as a frontier, rewarding hard-nosed realism with head-spinning possibilities. Ben Bova's *Mars*, Jack Williamson's *Beachhead*, Kim Stanley Robinson's *Red Mars*, and Allen Steele's *Labyrinth of Night*, all published in 1992, speak to Arthur Clarke's 1951 *Sands of Mars*. My *Jupiter Project* is a "prequel" to Heinlein's *Farmer in the Sky*, as my *Against Infinity* is a sequel, and the fictional possibilities of the moons of the outer system are further developed in *Iris* by William Barton and Michael Capobianco, and in several Jeffrey Carver novels (particularly *Neptune Crossing*). Michael P. Kube-McDowell's *The Quiet Pools*, Roger MacBride Allen's *Ring of Charon*, Vernor Vinge's *A Fire Upon the Deep*, Iain M. Banks's *Consider Phlebas* series and Thomas McDonough's *The Architechts of Hyperspace* glance over their shoulders at galaxy-spanning epics of A. E. van Vogt, E. E. Smith, and Jack Williamson. The long perspectives in time of Anderson's *The Boat of a Million Years* achieve a lofty yet warmly human view, as Brian Aldiss did in his Helliconia trilogy. World-builders, from the planet-planners like Joan Slonczewski's *A Door Into Ocean* and Sheila Finch's *The Garden of the Shaped*, through the jarring pastorals in Paul J. McAuley's *Of the Fall*, to the weird science of Stephen Baxter's *Raft*—all offer alternatives and replies to a tradition begun by *Mission of Gravity*.

This contrasts strongly with "serious" fiction—more accurately described, in my eyes, as merely solemn—which proceeds from canonical classics that supposedly stand outside of time, deserving awe, great and intact by themselves. Genres are more like immense discussions, with ideas developed, traded, varied; players ring changes on each other—a steppin'-out jazz band, not a solo concert in a plush auditorium. I suspect readers of "serious" fiction are probably more likely to blame themselves if they find a book from the approved canon boring; a genre reader blames the writer.

Hard sf mirrors science itself in the importance of cross-talk. Science continually reconstructs itself in overlapping, complex dialogs. This is a better picture of how scientists actually work than the oversimplified paradigm-shift model allows. Genres do this, and hard sf even more so. In this sense it is the core of sf itself because its very sociology reflects that of science as a profession.

Faking the science dooms a hard sf writer among both colleagues and fans. It's a violation of the sacred game. Genre pleasures are many, but this quality of shared values within an ongoing discussion may be the most powerful, enlisting lifelong devotion in its fans. In contrast to the Grand Canon view, genre-reading satisfactions are a striking facet of modern democratic ("pop") culture, an ongoing party, carried out against the cool, austere landscapes of modern science.

ON SCIENCE AND SCIENCE FICTION

Kathryn Cramer

M. C. Escher remarked in his essay "The Impossible" that "whoever wants to portray something that does not exist has to obey certain rules." The majority of science fiction stories are not plausible extrapolations upon our current situation, using available information; rather they are impossible Escheresque objects which use the principles of science in much the same way that Escher used rules of geometric symmetry—the rules give form to the impossible imaginative content.

All sf about the future, no matter how rigorously constructed, must build its future from fragments of the past and present. The futures we construct are as much a part of the present as we ourselves are; although they will never really be the future, they can represent it. Sf allows us to understand and experience *our* past, present, and future in terms of an imagined future. Like the conventions of perspective in drawing, which allow us to extrapolate railroads from two convergent lines crossed by a lot of parallel line segments, the conventions of sf allow us to imagine a physical world beyond the frame of the scenes described.

There has been a persistent view that hard sf is somehow the core and center of the sf field; that all other sf orbits around this center; and that the characteristic of this core is a particular attitude toward science and technology. What we habitually call hard sf is more precisely technophilic sf, which Poul Anderson described in the seventies: "Science, technology, material achievement, and the rest are basically good. In them lies a necessary if not sufficient condition for the improvement of man's lot, even his mental and spiritual lot." He also differentiated the hard sf story from other varieties of sf: "A hard science story bases itself upon real, present-day science or technology and carries these further with a minimum of imaginary forces, materials, or laws of nature." One is more likely to identify a story as hard sf—regardless of the amount of actual science it contains—if the narrative voice is pragmatic, deterministic, and matter-of-fact about the many high-tech artifacts among which the story takes place, and if the future (or clearly alternate present or past) in which the protagonist lives is primarily the result of significant technological change from the here and now. Through repetition we have come to identify this narrative voice as "futuristic."

Like utopian fiction, science fiction grew out of the desire to create and predict the possibility of a better world. In sf, this better world will be created and predicted through science and technology: scientific exploration and technological innovation are political acts leading to world salvation. But without the tradition of the folktale, sf, if it existed at all, would be a literature of didactic tracts, blueprints for "utopia." Fortunately, the enlightened, rationalistic, utopian impulse collided with the irrational, romantic, fanciful folk storytelling tradition.

In addition to its connection to the folktale, sf has another important connection to preliterate culture. Before the Reformation, when only the clergy were allowed to read the Bible, the laity looked to religious art not for representations of daily reality, but for revelations of the principles underlying reality—to discover the sacred texts. Sf is the religious art of science. While people who can read today are of course as entitled to read scientific texts as they are to read the Bible, the habits of "reading" religious art have carried forward to the way we read sf. We read sf not for representations of our daily lives, but for revelation of the principles behind everyday experience—the cosmic order. As young teenagers we may have read science fiction to learn about science itself. As adults, we probably know much of the science already, perhaps better than some of the sf authors whose works we read, but science linked to storytelling gives us an emotional experience difficult to replicate while confronting mundane reality alone, without the company of a book.

Since the founding of the science-fiction field in the 1920s, science has been the guiding force of science fiction, and to some extent science fiction has been able to reciprocate. Could there have been a space program without science fiction? While the robots that make cars in Japanese factories bear precious little resemblance to those in *I, Robot*, they might not now exist were it not for Isaac Asimov and company. Several generations of scientists and engineers have grown up reading sf, learning that there is such a thing as science, and if they work hard in school they can play too—science fiction influenced the career choices of such scientists as Carl Sagan and the late Gerald Feinberg. A number of sf readers turned scientist have later in life become science-fiction writers: Fred Hoyle, Gene Wolfe, John Cramer, Carl Sagan, Joan Slonczewski, Robert L. Forward, and Donald Kingsbury, just to name a few. Despite this connection between science and sf, the nature of this connection remains largely unexplored.

The early defense of sf emphasized the wonders of science and the sensation that they arouse in the reader. At its best, science fiction tends to be about the emotional experience of discovering what is true, often represented by scientific discoveries of great consequence. In traditional hard sf, the story is to be taken very literally, insisting on it more strongly than any other kind of English-language fiction.

However over the last couple of decades too little attention has been paid to those virtues that science fiction derives from its unique relationship with science. During this time, the relationship between science and science fiction has been deemphasized in favor of the relationship between science fiction and literature. By now a significant portion of the field's practitioners prefer to call sf "speculative fiction," because the social position of a futurist is more desirable than that of a science-fiction writer. From this view, speculative fiction, which addresses not just the past and present, but also the glorious, mysterious future, is a much broader field than "mainstream" (the sf world's dismissive term for nonscience fiction) set in the currently known or historically known world, usually involving only those characters and situations that we conceive of as appropriate to a realistic account. Thus defined, mainstream is a subset of science fiction, and the greats of literature are, intentionally or not, merely speculative fiction writers without much talent for speculation.

John W. Campbell promoted this view of sf. But when it is stripped of Campbell's technologically oriented futurism it takes on a different meaning: Science is marginalized in favor of social extrapolation. While the prose style of the average science-fiction story has improved, many of the best writers have been distracted from the task of working out their own syntheses of science and fiction, and so it goes: Out go the paragraphs giving clear evidence that the writer spent all day calculating the nature and quality of eclipses on a planet with five moons, and in come paragraphs of carefully observed description of the protagonist's moods, signifying the writer's sincere obeisance to the conservative but currently fashionable belief that all good stories are "character-driven."

Hard sf also interacts with the technologies and accompanying institutions that produce and distribute it. In the twenty years since the death of John W. Campbell, much has happened to obscure his technophilic vision of science fiction. The hard sf attitude became a salable commodity on its own, separable from scientific content. Particularly during the Reagan years, hard sf evolved into right-wing power fantasies about military hardware, tales of men killing things with big machines, fantasies that had very little to do with scientific thought or theory.

In that era, the majority of the most talented younger sf writers were quite uninterested in writing about science, precisely because what was generally perceived as hard sf was rapidly degenerating into political allegory. In the midst of this, many writers were still writing good hard sf: Isaac Asimov, Arthur C. Clarke, Charles Sheffield, Joe Haldeman, Donald Kingsbury, Gregory Benford, Greg Bear, Paul Preuss, and Joan Slonczewski. Simultaneously, certain of the cyberpunk writers—Bruce Sterling, William Gibson, and Rudy Rucker—were bending certain tropes of hard sf to their postmodern project. A number of good hard-sf stories have appeared in the past few years by such writers as Geoffrey Landis, Connie Willis, George Alec Effinger, and Lois McMaster Bujold.

The 1983 Eaton Conference on hard sf brought together literary critics and "writer/scientists" Robert L. Forward, David Brin, and Gregory Benford. They discussed many aspects of the affect of hard science fiction, but judging by the published proceedings of the conference, some basic connections between science and fiction remained obscure. In the proceedings of the conference and elsewhere, I have noticed certain rhetorical patterns in the claims hard sf writers make for hard sf. Whenever possible, they minimize the differences between very hard science fiction and science itself. For example, David Brin, in his essay "Running Out of Speculative Niches: A Crisis for Hard SF?" astutely observes that in a hard sf story, " 'science' itself . . . is a major character." He goes on to describe how something rather like peer review transpires among hard sf writers. While this sort of interactive reading occurs among hard sf writers and among writers in other genres and subgenres, the general drift of Brin's essay in the Eaton Conference Proceedings—and for that matter Forward's, entitled "When Science Writes the Fiction," and Benford's, entitled "Is There a Technological Fix for the Human Condition?"—is that science and hard sf are very similar. This perception of the similarity of science and hard sf is manifest in Benford's definition of hard sf in that essay:

> My minimum definition of hard sf demands that it highly prize fidelity to the physical facts of the universe, while constructing a new objective "reality" within a fictional matrix. It is not enough to merely use science as integral to the narrative. . . . Sf must use science in a speculative fashion. The physical sciences are the most capable of detailed prediction (and thus falsification by experiment), so they are perceived in fiction as more reliable indicators of future possibilities, or stable grounds for orderly speculation.

This view of the relationship between hard sf and science is oversimplified and omits certain important distinctions: As mathematician Jules-Henri Poincaré pointed out, only a small minority of the human race experiences mathematics pleasurably. So, while mathematics is the bones holding up the scientific animal, the science must be "de-boned" before it can be used in fiction, because the majority of readers, even hard sf readers, will tolerate very few equations in a work of fiction. Even the anthology *Mathenauts*, edited by Rudy Rucker, contains, by my count, only four equations, and of those, none are beyond the ken of a high-school freshman.

Although some hard sf writers take the same attitude as Leonardo da Vinci—who claimed in his essay "On Painting and Science" that "No human inquiry can call itself a true science if it is not confirmed by mathematical proofs"—and expect that the scientifically literate reader will whip out her calculator and discover that all the math behind appearances works out, as often as not it doesn't. In this sense science and hard sf are very different.

Hard science fiction is a lively and diverse literature that attempts to evoke the power and wonder of science, to articulate the sensation of discovering the true and the real. Stories like "The Singing Diamond" by Robert L. Forward and "Surface Tension" by James Blish hit the reader with a shotgun blast of ideas; at the right moment, under the right circumstances, reading a story like that can capture the feeling of making a major discovery.

Hard science fiction is about the aesthetics of knowledge, even knowledge of the most disturbing, overwhelming kind—that which is bigger than one's loving or hating it. In Philip Latham's "The Xi Effect," Edgar Allan Poe's "A Descent into the Maelström," and Arthur C. Clarke's "Transit of Earth" this knowledge is deadly, but its revelation is numinous. Hard sf is at its core beyond questions of optimism and pessimism, beyond questions of technology and application. Hard sf recognizes wonder as the finest human emotion.

As most sf readers already know, hard sf has an identifiable feel, a particular kind of narrative voice, the right attitude. This attitude is respectful of the principles underlying the practice of science, not unlike the reverence one should display when entering a chapel. A rationalist cosmology accompanies this attitude: a cosmology based on the belief that the literal facts of a situation are more important than any interpretation. The antimysticism of hard sf is a point of pride for sf writers (and scientists of similar mindset) who see science as a replacement for religion and superstition.

In his essay on metaphor, entitled "On Truth and Falsity in their Extramoral Sense," the philosopher Friedrich Nietzsche describes what he feels to be the literal, factual, nonmetaphorical situation of humanity, which might easily serve as a description of the hard sf cosmography:

> In some remote corner of the universe, effused into innumerable solar-systems, there was once a star upon which clever animals invented cognition. It was the haughtiest, most mendacious moment in the history of this world, but yet only a moment. After Nature had taken breath awhile the star congealed and the clever animals had to die.

The lifespan of our sun is but the briefest moment in the history of the universe; everything we value will vanish soon unless we spread ourselves across the universe, or unless there have been, are, or will be other intelligent life-forms out there. Hard sf writers try to find a way out of this dilemma. Hard sf uses the rules of a deterministic universe to show us that our fate is not yet sealed. As Hal Clement remarked in conversation, in hard sf, the universe itself is the antagonist.

Hard sf's problem-solving attitude toward our inevitable extinction has three corollaries: (1) no precondition of viable intelligent life is irreplaceable, given enough scientific knowledge; (2) the replacement of things needed to sustain life is necessary, desirable, and promotes the long-term survival of our species; (3) the scientific should replace the unscientific. Nietzsche's pronouncement that "the clever animals had to die" is a depressing thought for the realist; but for the hard sf rationalist, it is an exciting challenge! Hard sf's strong connection to physics—one of the last systems of classical idealism to retain its intellectual validity—allows hard sf to continue to take on the most all-encompassing aspect of the human condition, our survival as a species. The technophilic wing of the science-fiction community treasures the thought that because of our interest in and enthusiasm for technological innovation, we may just be the next stage of human evolution.

This notion leads to one of hard sf's paradoxes: If our faith in science replaces religious faith, science is co-opted into becoming a religion, which, of course, would be unscientific. The work of Arthur C. Clarke best shows the tension between science and religion within hard sf: Some editions of his novel *Childhood's End* carried the disclaimer that the opinions in the book were "not those of the author." His story "The Star" also shows this tension: The story "explains" the Star of Bethlehem in hard sf terms, a scientific and technological notion replaces a religious one; yet, were it not for Christianity, this replacement would lack meaning.

The primacy of the sense of wonder in science fiction poses a direct challenge to religion: Does the wonder of science and the natural world as experienced through science fiction replace religious awe? It is perhaps no coincidence that a similar controversy has emerged in the New Age movement over whether or not true enlightenment can be attained through the use of meditation machines—are electric revelations authentic? If not, how can we tell the difference? The idea that in the future better and more scientific things will replace all the things we currently need and use—a cosmic belief in an ever-improving standard of living—constitutes what I call the *replacement principle* of sf.

In this book, the replacement principle is strongly in evidence. Robert Heinlein's "It's Great to Be Back" expresses this idea in strong terms: A family returning to Earth after years of living on the Moon discovers that their nostalgia for the lushness of Earth and the richness of its societies was misguided sentimentality. Frederik Pohl's "Day Million" describes a society in which most of what we know has been replaced by something more futuristic, but he makes less attempt at salesmanship. While atomic light bulbs no longer seem like such a good idea, the notions of living in an L5 colony, traveling to another planet, and communicating with an extraterrestrial intelligence still enchant us. If "slow glass" as described in Bob Shaw's "Light of Other Days" were commercially available, many of us would buy it. And we remain fascinated by such technologies as cloning (see Ursula K. Le Guin's "Nine Lives") and time travel (see Ian Watson's "The Very Slow Time Machine").

The big ideas of hard science fiction are more ambitious than the creation of any single device. Hard sf shows us many alternate places to live: space stations, other planets, undersea communities, and so on. Hard sf takes the position that we should have the knowledge and technology to create, from the building blocks of the universe, everything we need to have rich and happy lives, so as to end our childlike dependence on the earth and what nature gives us.

Though some hard sf writers claim that their future worlds and situations never violate physical law, and therefore just might happen, most sf scenarios are at least implausible, often wildly so, and many are outright impossible. The long-standing controversy over whether sf writers should use faster-than-light (FTL) travel in their stories exposes the various conflicting demands upon the writer. Because of sf's utopian goal of saving humanity from extinction, it is a game that must be played by the rules; it will do no good to beg for favors from the uncaring universe. Eliminating FTL from possibility does rather limit our options: we're all dressed up with no place to go. And yet, we must become a self-made species, become the fittest, so we can survive the inevitable death of our sun.

Writing stories within the rules of the universe as we know it and yet discovering fantastic possibilities of new ways of life is the central endeavor of the hard sf writer. Physical law tells us that many things are impossible given existing technology, but the ever-expanding frontier of scientific knowledge shows us how to do many things of which we would never have dreamed. Sf represents what the future could be like, although we know that the actual future will look nothing like it, and when we meet it we may not recognize it.

HARD SCIENCE FICTION

David G. Hartwell

When we read a work of fiction, we test its details against our experience of the nuances and gestures of everyday life. Appearances are at issue when we investigate and assess the value of a literary text. We consider the text authentic if it matches what we observe—or, in fictional circumstances, could observe—when we look at the world around us. But in the case of science fiction this test does not entirely apply. We must take the seemingly unreal setting and the element of science in the fiction into account.

When we read a work of sf, we also test it against our scientific and technical knowledge. Scientific principles operating behind imaginary—rather than everyday—experience are at issue. The attitude that underpins science fiction is that there is a reality beyond appearances which is knowable through science.

There is a particular variety of science fiction, commonly called "hard" sf, that emphasizes the rigorous nature of our relation to this reality behind experience. Other sf (even such classics as Walter M. Miller's A Canticle for Leibowitz*), while it usually takes this into account, emphasizes our experience of the nature of human behavior and is more nearly, but not entirely, testable in the ordinary way we read.*

I. THE PLEASURES AND PROBLEMS OF HARD SF

This anthology presents examples of the way science functions in science fiction throughout the history and development of the genre—from Poe and Verne and Hawthorne and Wells to the giants of today—focusing primarily upon the type known as "hard science fiction." Oddly enough, this is the first anthology ever to set out to do this ambitious task. All others have chosen more limited themes or specific images: stories of immortality, or space travel, or time travel, of mutation, of black holes, of other dimensions—*The Science Fiction Weight-Loss Book* appeared in the early 1980s. Perhaps this is because there is a general prejudice among readers who never read science fiction against science in general—science is not fun for them—and so it has been traditional for anthologists to emphasize the fictional fun. But not only is the science in science fiction the foundation of science-fictional delights and entertainments, it is in fact chief among those delights. We believe that this needs to be said strongly now, at this precise historic moment in the evolution of sf.

Hard sf is about the beauty of truth. It is a metaphorical or symbolic representation of the wonder at the perception of truth that is experienced at the moment of scientific discovery. The eureka. There are a number of ways this is done in hard sf. The crucial moment may in fact come early in the story and the rest of the story scientific discovery. The eureka. There are a number of ways this is done in hard sf. The crucial moment may in fact come early in the story and the rest of the story may simply require a character (and the reader) to respond to the impact of the discovery. Or it may come at the climax, or there may be several or a number of these moments in a hard sf story (and this is the kind of story, such as Hal Clement's *Mission of Gravity*, or Gregory Benford's *Timescape*, or Robert L. Forward's *Dragon's Egg*) that is seen by readers as a milestone or classic.

Hard sf is, then, about the emotional experience of describing and confronting what is scientifically true. We may compare both the nonrealistic aspects of hard sf and the realistic elements (such as the way the characters experience the hypothetical reality) to our personal experiences of perceived or consensus reality and have our perceptions of reality illuminated by contrast. This is as true of J. G. Ballard's "Cage of Sand" as it is of Isaac Asimov's "Waterclap." The hypothetical experiences are the ones that are particularly illuminating to a reader of hard sf.

Hard sf feels authentic to experienced readers when the way things work in the story is scientifically plausible—in the place and time the story is set. For example: In the event that there were an ellipsoid planet like Hal Clement's Mesklin, inhabited by an intelligent alien race, then if humans were to visit they might plausibly find that gravity, geology, chemistry, and the alien race itself resembled, with some precision and in some detail, Clement's description of this hypothetical place—according to what we know of astronomy, physics, chemistry, and biology at present.

Hard sf relies, at some point in the story, on expository prose rather than literary prose, prose aimed at describing the nature of its particular reality. The reality that is the case is usually not literally true, but, at the same time, adheres to the principles by which science describes what is known. Originally this exposition was merely a device for achieving verisimilitude (in Poe), as it still is often in nongenre writing, but by the advent of 1920s "scientifiction" it had become of central interest, and by the 1940s, the essential point or turning point of a science-fiction story.

Because hard sf is a literary form demanding of both its writers and its readers significant amounts of scientific knowledge as well as previous reading in the genre, it has continued to yield a disproportionate number of the central images common to all forms of science fiction, and to generate new translations of scientific ideas into literary contexts, through which they can then become the devices and ultimately the clichés of many other stories. Stories such as Clifford D. Simak's "Desertion" and James Blish's "Surface Tension," in which humanity is physically transformed to live in alien environments, contain the seeds of many other stories in the genre. If it served no other functions, these would still preserve its critical importance.

It is a commonly held opinion of the writers who write hard sf and the perception of the readers who prefer to read it, that hard sf is the core of all science fiction as well as a body of works set apart from the large body of run-of-the-mill sf throughout the modern period. Its heroic figures are H. G. Wells, Robert A. Heinlein, John W. Campbell, Arthur C. Clarke, Isaac Asimov, Larry Niven, Poul Anderson, and Gregory Benford. Hard sf is sf with "the right stuff."

However, hard science fiction is an acquired taste and a special pleasure. Devoted readers of hard sf know the real thing when they see it, the way readers of poetry are able to distinguish real poetry from greeting-card versifying: by the way in which the text fulfills an implied contract between writer and reader. Even work by a great poet which is (arguably) imperfectly executed can nevertheless be important and influential. "The Lake Isle of Innisfree" by William Butler Yeats, with its "purple noon," might serve as example. Or, in descending order, much of

Rudyard Kipling's or Robert W. Service's poetry. Nevertheless we know it as authentic, the real thing.

An essential condition of this recognition (of "the right stuff") is experience gained from reading in the genre. (We acknowledge the difficulty of using the word *genre* to describe both poetry and science fiction, but intend to use it to refer to any body of literature with distinct reader expectations and reading protocols that distinguish that body from other genres.) Also useful is technical knowledge of the rules by which the particular literary game is usually played. In the case of hard science fiction, one must be able to summon up a basic knowledge of the scientific laws and principles by which our contemporary world is believed to operate. Sad to say, this last condition prevents enjoyment of the work by many otherwise educated and experienced readers, but it is our hope in compiling this anthology to have provided enough of a spectrum of striking imagery, startling and innovative ideas, and a generally high level of literary execution in the fiction that most readers of contemporary fiction new to hard science fiction will survive the initial shock to their habitual reading protocols and experience the excitement of this vigorous, lively, and influential branch of science fiction.

The primary pleasures of hard science fiction do not reside in its stylistic effects. One can summarize a hard sf story and communicate its essential spark without reference to its execution. It is normally a conservative literature, traditionally told in clear journalistic prose, eschewing consciously literary effects: the prose of scientific description. Historically, this is one of the main techniques for achieving verisimilitude in a literature which is in fact radically distanced from the here and now in a majority of the stories. It is also an advantage for the main body of writers and readers, who come from a scientific or technological background and often read and write mostly in this prose style. Many of them harbor a deep suspicion of the self-consciously literary, together with an ingrained belief in the efficacy of scientific know-how to solve problems in the real world (and in any imaginable world). This last assumption underlies all hard science fiction. Even those stories that appear to be antithetical to this attitude or written in conscious reaction to it (Ballard's "Cage of Sand" and Godwin's "The Cold Equations" respectively) take this attitude as their starting point.

The experience of reading all science fiction generates a feeling of radical distance or escape from the real world, but paradoxically the experience of reading hard science fiction adds to that a need to bring external knowledge to the story, knowledge that exists only in the real world and is accessible to the reader through education and general knowledge of science. Hard sf uses spectacular images envisioned according to plausible scientific extrapolation in order to isolate us from ordinary life and confront us with the ideal universe of science. This isolation can produce extraordinary intellectual and emotional effects, as in Arthur C. Clarke's "The Star" (with its vision of the dead solar system after a supernova linked to the birth of Christ) or Rudy Rucker's "Ms. Found in a Copy of *Flatland*" (in which the central character is literally trapped in a two-dimensional universe).

Hard sf, then, always depends upon scientific knowledge external to the story. "Inconstant Moon" by Larry Niven, for instance, depends for its finest moment upon basic knowledge of the relative position of the Earth, the Moon and the Sun in the solar system: high-school astronomy. "Stop Evolution in Its Tracks!" by John Sladek is funny only if you know the most basic facts of evolutionary biology. "Chromatic Aberration" by John M. Ford is based on the theory of paradigm shifts—without knowledge of said theory, it is still a creditable emulation of magic realism but not recognizably hard sf.

Science fiction as a whole comes in many varieties, but overall it tends to depend more on a knowledge of the body of hard science fiction written over the past few decades than upon science. Sf as a whole ranges from Brian Aldiss, Michael Moorcock, or Ray Bradbury, brilliantly literate at their best, to a spectrum of journeyman works by category writers. Ordinary science-fiction adventure in particular—the works of Jack Vance serve as a distinguished example—tends to exist *only* in reference to earlier sf. It could arguably not exist without the tropes and cliché locutions (spaceship, time machine, space warp, blaster) developed with rigorous logic and strict adherence to scientific principles in past hard sf stories. Even Bradbury's classic *Martian Chronicles* take place on the sandy, habitable Mars of earlier sf writers, not the known planet of the time Bradbury wrote them (the late 1940s and early 1950s).

And even though interstellar travel may have been invented in the creaky, visionary space adventures of E. E. ("Doc") Smith, Ph.D., hard sf writers then went to work on the problems his inventions presented and used his devices in other stories wherein they were reconceived with plausible scientific rationales. The hard sf discussions that took place in the stories, in frequent speculative nonfiction articles and in the letter columns of the sf magazines, from the late 1920s to the present, have been the forum for establishing and maintaining standards of plausibility in hard sf and in all sf. One sense in which hard science fiction is the core of the whole genre is that the rest of the literature is in this real sense secondary to it, existing primarily in implied reference to its prior logical developments, ideas, specialized terms, all assumed by writers as known and familiar to the genre audience.

Texts in all genres fulfill an implied contract between writer and reader: This story will exist within the recognizable boundaries of the genre conventions and will deliver the pleasures expected of a text in this genre. Since genres are by nature interactive, in the sense that writers read in the genre and readers, in addition, interact with the writers (who are public figures—and in the science fiction field, with its fanzines and hundreds of conventions a year, this interaction is frequent and constant), the re-use of good ideas, with innovative variations, is common. One might compare this to the way sonnetteers in literary history gained reputation by innovation within the form, or more recently, mystery writers became the darling of genre connoisseurs by building a better locked-room story. Thus Hal Clement's *Mission of Gravity* generates a whole body of "world-building" fiction over several decades, which includes Frank Herbert's *Dune*, Anne McCaffrey's "Weyr Search," and Larry Niven's *Ringworld*.

In reading hard sf you are participating in an experience that involves you in a tension between the story's radical distance from the real world and its similarity to real world scientific principles upon which the imagined world also operates, and through which the imagined characters perceive their experience. James Blish's "Surface Tension," for instance, in which tiny genetically engineered descendants of humans living in a large mud puddle on an alien planet develop enough scientific knowledge to build a wooden spaceship in which to explore the airy spaces above the surface of their puddle-world, is a paradigm. This tension generates in experienced readers an intense involvement in the innovative content (ideas) of the fiction, since the new and different ideas are still familiar through being based on known principles. The elements of fiction (story, characterization, plot, thematics, etc.) draw you in emotionally while the necessity of applying knowledge of science distances you intellectually—asking you, at the same time, to become emotionally involved in the problems of the characters in the fiction and to follow and understand, in an intellectual sense, the scientific grounding of the fiction. Hard sf, then, requires a double consciousness in readers, an intense involvement coupled paradoxically with (at least at the crucial points of exposition) great aesthetic distance.

Sf readers nevertheless expect to be surprised at some point by a sudden perception of connection to things they know or observe in daily life. If the revelation is of the inner life, as in Daniel Keyes's well-known *Flowers for Algernon*, then the story is not hard sf; if the revelation is of the functioning of the laws of nature, as in Arthur C. Clarke's "Transit of Earth," or Isaac Asimov's "Waterclap," then the story is hard sf. In a hard sf story, the expectation is both escape and surprise: The conjunction between them should delight and inform our view of the nature of reality.

Hard sf achieves its characteristic affect essentially through informing, by being, in fact, didactic. One is taken a great distance in time and space only to learn something possibly or plausibly true in the here and now. To a greater or lesser extent most science fiction escapes the limits of a real world to somewhere else in time and space, a setting radically distanced—not days or weeks in the future, but hundreds or thousands or millions of years; not in another country, but far away in space. But hard science fiction uses the distance to bring us home again in an apparently intellectual way, not usually through insight into human character but through insight into the mechanics of the universe, true in all times and places. Thus a story such as Larry Niven's "The Hole Man" teaches us little about the character of scientists but a lot about its idea, the nature, and possible misuse, of a tiny black hole; James Blish's "Beep" opens up a myriad of possibilities for new levels of complex information transfer; Hilbert Schenck's "The Morphology of the Kirkham Wreck" gives us information about hurricanes worthy of comparison to the didactic chapters of Herman Melville's *Moby-Dick*.

Furthermore, the world of the hard sf story is deterministic, ruled by scientific law: It is inimical to anyone who does not know said law or how to figure it out—scientific method, facts. This is the world of Ballard as well as the world of Clement. "Somebody had asked me," said Clement in a recent interview, "why I didn't have bad entities—villains—in my stories, generally speaking, and my point was that the universe was a perfectly adequate villain!" The universe is enough of an antagonist. So it follows that the villains of hard sf pervert science, or are ignorant of it. The assumption that knowledge is good is essential to the hard sf affect, even when it is being undercut, as in Kate Wilhelm's "The Planners," or Vernor Vinge's "Bookworm, Run."

Because human characters nearly always survive in the face of an environment that is inherently inhuman, hard sf gained a reputation for optimism. (But "The Cold Equations," in which a responsible space pilot is forced to kill a sweet and ignorant stowaway because otherwise the mathematics of space travel say that all will die, is a title freighted with deep and complex meaning for the hard sf reader—it symbolizes the cold, inexorable, inhuman forces of universal law.)

Traditionally—although this was not so much a conscious literary strategy as a response to pulp magazine publishing and editing, which dictated that central characters be heroic or likable or both, and get on with the action of the story—there is not fully rounded characterization in hard sf because that would reduce the impact of the general (mankind versus the universal) structure that underlies all hard sf. In a hard sf story, the universe is external to character and the character must interact with that universe, and in so doing, achieves or validates his identity. Hard sf characters tend not to achieve validation through gaining knowledge of their own inner life but rather through action in the external environment. Knowing oneself, or feeling better about oneself, is far secondary to having accomplished something important (such as saving a life, or the world) for the sf protagonist.

The external universe in all sf is distanced from the here and now in part to emphasize that this fiction is not about the specific human condition of any individual today, but about a bigger, wider view of all humanity. Robert A. Heinlein plays sophisticated games with ordinary people in extraordinary circumstances in "It's Great to Be Back," as does Gregory Benford in "Relativistic Effects." But the characters in both stories are relatively flat (vs. rounded) and represent or symbolize ordinary people, Everyman. Thus the human condition in hypothetical circumstances is illuminated. It is frequently a surprising literary experience, and one of the ordinary pleasures of all sf.

The characters in hard sf, regardless of their individuality, have something of the Everyman about them. Sometimes they have to get past their own psychology to survive, or survive precisely because of their psychological quirks, but traditionally they act upon the environment and affect it. The implication is that any other man (who knows what the character knows) would do precisely the same. Hard sf tries to have it both ways: The character is at the same time exceptional (described and portrayed as a unique individual) and typical (acts and solves the problem using reason and knowledge).

This is another of the qualities of hard sf that puts it at the core of the sf genre: It is only truly of interest to people with faith in science, faith that knowledge has meaning. Faith tells them that the universe is ultimately knowable and that human problems (the human condition) are solvable through science and technology; that although science can be misused, if used properly it will lead to the improvement of the human condition, implicitly to heaven on earth. This faith in improvement in the long run (combining images of evolution with the idea of progress) is a kind of bedrock Darwinism that underlies scientific and engineering culture in the western world in this century. Science fiction is one of the most interesting and eloquent expressions of this faith. Look for a moment at the titles of some of the classic novels: *Men like Gods; Childhood's End; Mission of Gravity; The Stars My Destination*; and at the themes of immortality and transcendence that underlie so very much of the literature. Hard sf is a dream of winning against the house, beating the ultimate laws of the universe that constrain us and finally kill us, at least before the end of time. Hard sf validates this belief system in a way that other literature does not.

As Karl Poppers said of philosophical Marxism, it is a system that cannot be disproved by any conceivable historical event, even the end of the entire universe (which has been transcended in many stories, for instance Poul Anderson's classic novel *Tau Zero*, or James Blish's *The Triumph of Time*). It has frequently been noted that science fiction is often about catastrophes, nuclear or cosmic, but almost always then about a small band of hardy survivors. Science fiction affirms the future. Human life, albeit often transformed, persists in science fiction in spite of the inimical universe. The optimism is, however, more cosmic than individual. Compare H. G. Wells's *The War of the Worlds* (in which the Martian victory is stopped by disease, not the actions of inferior humanity—nature rights the balance) to Thomas M. Disch's *The Genocides* (wherein superior alien invaders win, and the hardy survivors are reduced to the status of vermin living inside huge alien farm plants, until they wander off to die as pests—nature doesn't right any balances) for an eloquent contrast in affect and attitude between hard sf and its postgothic opposite. Belief—individuals die, the race lives on—vs. unbelief—given the circumstances, everyone dies.

The whole argument might then seem a distraction blinding us to the real issue of affect and faith versus ironic distance and individual failure. The body of hard sf makes readers take the god's-eye view. This is the ultimate meaning behind the aspect of hard sf that requires great aesthetic distance. Hard sf is in fact at base a Neoplatonic literature, referring implicitly or explicitly to the forms behind external reality, which the readers are expected to know of and identify as the laws and principles of science and mathematics. And believe in.

II. HISTORY AND DEVELOPMENT: THE PERSISTENCE OF THE ANTI-MODERN

In the early years of this century a perceived divide developed between high art and popular culture under pressure from the Modernist movement. Sf fell into the paraliterary or popular category, particularly since there was a long and bitter aesthetic battle between H. G. Wells (whose work is a major repository of ideas and techniques for all writers in the sf genre) and Henry James that for all practical purposes Wells lost—becoming the most popular and successful writer of his era at the price of losing literary influence and prestige to James. All this is well-known literary history. The other principal sources for the new genre were pulp fiction and boys' books, low-class popular origins indeed. The case of science fiction is, however, complex and rather more interesting than has usually been credited.

In the Modernist era, rather than remaining merely low art, sf evolved in opposition to the Modernist aesthetic of style as information and came to privilege innovation in the content rather then in style. Hard sf, at least from the time of science fiction's gentrification in the 1920s as a separate and self-conscious body of fiction with a separate audience, might best be seen as anti-Modern (or as the pop culture shadow of the continuing Realism of Dreiser, with his chemical theories of human behavior, or the pulp shadow of Ezra Pound's utopianism). Modernism was rationalist and scientific in its attitude and method, but it generally averted its gaze from technological knowledge. The Jamesian aesthetic was embodied in the phrase "art for art's sake." The concerns of the scientific community interested in problem solving, reproducible results and methods, clarity and logic and the nature of external reality, the world of action, cause and effect, the whole external universe, became the meat of science fiction.

Science fiction arose and thrived by validating this technological culture, by addressing its concerns and manifesting its values. Poe, Verne, and Wells all affirmed science as our essential hold on external reality, as giving us rules by which to interact and live. Their attitude differed from the earlier Gothic attitude toward science in literature, as represented by Hawthorne (and Mary Shelley, and later Stevenson), in that their point was what science could reveal and/or do, not particularly about human character but about humanity's relation to the universe.

Early in his career, Wells identified himself as writing in the genre of "Scientific Romance." Hawthorne, too, exercised much effort to establish that he was a Romancer, not a novelist. Although there is a specific distinction from other Romances (as revelations of character) that Wells was affirming, still both writers felt a difference from the novel as it was understood in their day. The practitioners of proto-science fiction felt for decades a sense of being in opposition to fashionable art and literary forms. Not until the creation of the sf genre in 1926, out of the materials and conventions of the earlier genre of Scientific Romance, did the actual genre coalesce and begin to take form. The Wellsian stream persisted well into the 1930s and beyond, as the "literary" (e.g., Zamyatin, Huxley, Stapledon, Orwell) form of which the "low art" pulp genre was the paraliterary shadow. It was not until the 1940s that all the strains blended.

It is only a start, however, to observe the influence of Poe, Verne, and Wells (and the later philosophical novels of Olaf Stapledon) on the founding of the science-fiction genre. Hugo Gernsback had the inspiration to put them all cheek-by-jowl in one publication and call it "scientifiction." He described it as part "charming Romance" and part "scientific fact" in the founding issue of *Amazing Stories* (April 1926), the first genre magazine. Genre definition, however, began to reach a level of clarity and consensus only with the advent of John W. Campbell, Jr., more than a decade later.

Campbell was *the* editor of Modern science fiction. When in the later 1930s he took the helm of *Astounding Stories*, the highest-paying market for sf, he set about establishing a model for sf through a process that Alexei and Cory Panshin have elucidated in their award-winning study, *The World Beyond the Hill*: Campbell wrote editorials that pointed to stories written by L. Sprague de Camp (and in part conceived in discussion with Campbell) as examples of what he wanted science fiction to be. Campbell had already established a reputation as a popular space-adventure writer and had then begun to experiment with more ambitious hard sf under a pseudonym (Don A. Stuart). So his aesthetic position had both literary authority and economic force on writers. In this manner, Campbell privileged what came to be known as hard sf as the only true, pure, and real science fiction—all the rest, he later maintained, is fantasy.

What he in fact did was set up a class system within the science-fiction field that reflected the worldview of U.S. technological culture in that period in opposition to the dominant literary culture. It was a thinly veiled version of the Social Darwinism exemplified in Wells's "The Land Ironclads" and Kipling's "With the Night Mail," with scientists and engineers, the people who know and can manipulate the physical universe, at the top. The values of this system derived from the axiom that knowledge is power and that the only real knowledge is scientific knowledge.

At the top of the scientific hierarchy are physics, chemistry, and astronomy, whose knowledge and laws are mathematically verifiable. On the next level are the biological sciences, because they are in part descriptive or impure (dealing with living creatures); then the social sciences—anthropology, economics, political science, and experimental psychology. All of these are the meat of hard science fiction. But below them, one finds the humanities: theology, philosophy—and clinical psychology(!)—to which Modern science fiction is opposed (although it was always fair game to try to invent a way to reform these disciplines into true sciences—which led, among other things, to Scientology). In general, hard sf still disdains theology, politics, and Modern art in all its manifestations.

Campbellian sf privileges the outer life over the inner life, skills over feelings. Thought is associated with action. Intensity is generated through the macrocosmic or microcosmic scale of the settings that lend importance to the action of the stories. It also privileges exposition as a primary element of the fiction and therefore privileges the third-person past tense as the dominant mode of hard sf (following the practice and influence of H. G. Wells and Kipling) because it allows for ease of exposition, and for the omniscient narrative voice that speaks for the values of the Campbellian system. All sf today is still more often told in the third person than other contemporary fiction.

Campbell's own technological optimism (he was educated at M.I.T. and Duke University in engineering) led him to extend the domain of science over all literature. He often argued that science fiction is larger (better) than all other literature because its domain, all times and places in the universe, is larger. True science can predict events in the real world in Campbell's system, and he encouraged his writers to attempt to predict real inventions, real science, and future events. In this way, science fiction would become more like science. Although

Damon Knight, the leading sf critic of the 1950s, pointed out that including prediction in the aesthetic was absurd, leading to the logical necessity of waiting until the end of time to judge the relative merits of sf literature, Campbell collected examples of successful predictions to enforce his point. Most writers did not take him entirely seriously, but many readers of *Astounding* did, and in his heyday looked for story elements to come true in their lifetimes.

Character, in this literature, is in a sense only a series of conventional stock characters with minor variations, meant to display the natural superiority of intelligence over irrationality and emotions. Generally the central characters of hard science fiction are winners (the competent man, the engineer, the scientist, the good soldier, the man who transcends his circumstances, the inventor—the "Heinlein individual" who was for decades the model for the Modern sf hero). One needs to know no more than the basic qualities the author has presented of the character of, for instance, the surviving clone in Ursula K. Le Guin's "Nine Lives" or the nun in Poul Anderson's "Kyrie" for each story to achieve full impact. What happens is more important, even in these two stories that are richer, deeper in characterization than most hard sf.

What has been most undervalued by observers of sf is that it invents hypothetical human experiences and privileges them over real experiences. While these experiences may be interpreted metaphorically (the interaction between a human and an alien as a metaphor for a sexist or racist encounter, for example), sometimes with depth and richness, still there is a literal hypothetical experience that must be taken into consideration to read the experience as an sf reader. Thus "Dolphin's Way" by Gordon R. Dickson requires an adjustment of our perception of humanity's position in the natural world; Frederik Pohl's "Day Million" confronts us with the true strangeness of a far future environment; and David Brin's "What Continues, What Fails" forces us to reconsider what is eternal versus what changes both in human nature and in the universe.

Hard sf embodies the fantasies of empowerment of the scientific and technological culture of the modern era and validates its faith in scientific knowledge as dominant over other ways of knowing. During the height of Campbell's reign in the forties and fifties, a lot of it was also xenophobic, elitist, racist, and psychologically naive. For the most part, that is not the literature we still read from that period today, but strains of it persist. Consider Raymond F. Jones's "The Person from Porlock" or James P. Hogan's "Making Light" as having grown out of Campbell's social and political attitudes. The influence for good and ill of Rudyard Kipling's jingoism (both in his proto-science fiction, such as "With the Night Mail," and his other poetry and fiction) on Campbell, Robert A. Heinlein and other masters of the Campbellian "Golden Age" should not be ignored in considering the later evolution of hard sf.

All that having been said, many of the best writers, for instance Heinlein, Sturgeon, and Simak, either broke with Campbell quite early or often wrote in reaction to his dominant views. Others, such as Pohl, Kornbluth, and Bester, had to wait to flourish for a decade or more until the 1950s, when other markets appeared to publish new styles and approaches. This aggregation of fiction was called "speculative fiction" in its day by Judith Merril, Damon Knight, and other powerful critics and editors (who were also sf writers) and was happily, and sometimes blindly, published in all the other sf magazines, and by the newly formed paperback book publishers of the day, as science fiction. It was at that moment in the late fifties that the term *hard sf* was coined by P. Schuyler Miller in his book review column in *Astounding*.

The last year that Campbell's magazine won the popular vote for the Hugo Award as best sf magazine of the year was 1965, the year the serial publication of Frank Herbert's *Dune* ended. After that came the revolutionary spirit of the New Wave, which got all the media attention for the rest of the decade, in both its British and American forms reacting strongly against Campbell, *Analog*, and the traditions of science fiction, especially hard science fiction. Everyone had agreed that poorly written and conceived sf in the pulp adventure tradition was obsolete, at least since the advent of Campbell in 1937. In the late sixties and early seventies, a serious attempt was made to declare all hard sf before about 1965 as literary history, no longer a living part of the genre, and the hard sf enterprise as dead.

This literary political tack did not entirely fail. Campbell's prestige and influence was diminished, and hard science fiction became only one variety of a larger genre body, still called science fiction but with less genre coherence than ever. This is the situation that stabilized in the 1970s and lasts into the 1990s. But while the social and political attitudes of Campbell began to lose their hold in the fifties, the idea that science used in the Campbellian way was the ideal of hard sf never disappeared. It is still evident in, for instance, recent stories that concentrate entirely on presenting neat ideas, such as Robert L. Forward's "The Singing Diamond."

The advent of J. G. Ballard and of Brian W. Aldiss at the end of the fifties can be seen in retrospect as the first harbinger of the return of the Hawthornian (Aldiss was later to characterize himself and all sf as Mary Shelleyan) gothic mode, concerned with the inner life of character, as an influence on sf. Ballard's first story, "Prima Belladonna," is a recasting of Hawthorne's "Rappaccini's Daughter."

The implied argument of the Ballardian stream of hard sf, written in reaction to the main tradition, is: Campbellian hard sf said that if you know, you may survive; Ballard says, knowing is not enough to survive. Ballard is medically trained, clinically detached. His characters live ordinary lives in extraordinary landscapes. Even when they are scientists, they tend to be obsessives fixated upon their own inner lives. Ballard's stories thus feel radically different from other hard sf, even when he uses science rigorously.

The situation now is that hard sf has been removed from the center of attention in the sf field by a number of forces including literary fashion, competing modes, and marketing. Yet in the past decade, hard sf has never been more popular and has in addition become more self-conscious of the "specialness" of its nature and of its literary position as the generator of paradigms, tropes, and conventions for the genre. Such leading younger writers as Greg Bear, Gregory Benford, and David Brin have become vigorous defenders of hard sf. The most recent reformers of hard sf, the cyberpunks (most especially Bruce Sterling and William Gibson), have attempted a fusion of the Gothic mode, with its stylistic sophistication and *noir* atmosphere, and the heavily technological concerns and essential metaphysic of hard sf. The fallout from the work of, in particular, Sterling (see *Mirrorshades: The Cyberpunk Anthology*, with its polemical introduction) and Gibson (whose novel, *Neuromancer*, is the primary cyberpunk literary text), who adulate respectively Brian Aldiss and J. G. Ballard, has yet to become clear. But their work has been instrumental in bringing the argument about hard sf to the forefront, and cyberpunk is always referred to in discussions of contemporary hard sf, if only to deny that the movement has any lasting effect.

Today, the main body of science fiction results from a mixture of literary influences (having more or less absorbed the Wellsian and integrated many of the techniques of the Modernists) and paraliterary or extraliterary influences (films, works in the genre and preserves its position as the repository of new ideas and images drawn from new science and technology. And it retains its anti-Modernist spirit. It is still sf with "the right stuff." The best of it is still a model to which the rest of the genre may aspire.

III. CODA: ATTITUDES

Wonderful, often seemingly magical things are presented to the reader in science fiction, then rationalized and made plausible. Scientific principles are meaningless unless grounded in examples. And science fiction exists to give them a context in which they can mean intensely for sensitive and knowledgeable readers. Hard sf is merely a special case, in which the standards of rigor through which the demands of plausibility are met are foregrounded in the fiction and are therefore higher. Anne McCaffrey, for instance, is proud that her world of Pern was carefully designed in the best hard sf tradition (and in editorial correspondence with Campbell). It allows her to make "Weyr Search" mean more to genre readers.

The whole genre of sf is set up to permit the suspension of disbelief in experienced readers in works of fiction that exist in times and places that are not real and we know it (the future, the past, distanced in time and space). Yet for the duration of the experiment, the rigorous boundaries of the story are observed and the reader must experience the story as superficially literally true to life in that world which is not ours. This is as true of a story such as "The Planners," set in a laboratory of the day after tomorrow, as it is of Frederik Pohl's "Day Million," set in the distant future.

One can observe constant challenges both from within and from outside the sf field to hard sf, and enduring disagreements as to whether any new variety "belongs." The Ballardian strain is still quite controversial in some quarters because it has the wrong attitude.

Perhaps in the end the value of this anthology is to present the materials both in the center and on the edges of the argument, showing the evolution of texts and attitudes over the decades, from the days in which Jules Verne claimed that H. G. Wells's work was worthless because Wells invented such things as time machines and antigravity devices, to the claims of the cyberpunks of the 1980s, "radical reformers of hard sf"—as Bruce Sterling announced in his introduction to *Mirrorshades*. The science, and the use of science, in fiction has always been a central issue, as it is in this book.

Part One

NINE LIVES

Ursula K. Le Guin

Ursula K. Le Guin is one of the reigning masters of science fiction, winner of many Hugo and Nebula Awards (most recently, *Tehanu: The Last Book of Earthsea* won the 1991 Nebula award for best novel), author of *The Left Hand of Darkness* (1969), *The Dispossessed* (1974), *Always Coming Home* (1985), and other innovative science fiction novels and stories. She also wrote the modern classic of fantasy, *The Earthsea Trilogy*, and a number of provocative essays on sf and fantasy. A fantasist, a feminist, a literate and humane writer, Le Guin has often been portrayed as having left science fiction for greener pastures, although sf has always been only one of her major modes. In a recent interview, Le Guin said:

"I hope I've never been, and am never perceived as being in any way 'anti-science' in my work. Confusion often arises concerning what science and technology are. For example, I thought *Always Coming Home* was a rather interesting work in the technological mode; I had tried to think out carefully and consistently a highly refined, thoroughly useful, aesthetically gratifying technology for my invented society of the Valley. Being an anthropologist's daughter, I think of technology as encompassing everything a society makes and uses in the material sphere. However, a lot of people now use 'technology' simply to mean extremely high-tech inventions that are predicated on and depend on an enormous global network of intense exploitation of all natural resources, including an exploited working class, mostly in the Third World. Technology in this sense doesn't strike me as having much of a future, I must admit."

Her essay, "On Theme," written to accompany "Nine Lives" in Robin Scott Wilson's anthology *Those Who Can*, describes how reading about early experiments in cloning generated the main idea: exploring the human implications of what was at the time a biological experiment in reproducing carrots. Le Guin magnifies the meaning of the idea and investigates its rich possibilities by extrapolating it into a future in which it has larger scale, broader, bigger implications, in her words sounding "the great bells of love and death." Le Guin uses technological extrapolation here to explore the relationship between individual identity and personal uniqueness, postulating a protagonist who is not unique and who must confront both the problems of being *alone* and of *being* alone. Inverting the supernatural story of the doppelgänger, Le Guin shows us how uncanny it is *not* to meet ourselves at every turn.

Le Guin's influence on hard science fiction over recent decades has been evident in its movement toward deeper and richer characterization. This story is perhaps her most famous.

She was alive inside, but dead outside, her face a black and dun net of wrinkles, tumors, cracks. She was bald and blind. The tremors that crossed Libra's face were mere quiverings of corruption: underneath, in the black corridors, the halls beneath the skin, there were crepitations in darkness, ferments, chemical nightmares that went on for centuries. "Oh the damned flatulent planet," Pugh murmured as the dome shook and a boil burst a kilometer to the southwest, spraying silver pus across the sunset. The sun had been setting for the last two days. "I'll be glad to see a human face."

"Thanks," said Martin.

"Yours is human to be sure," said Pugh, "but I've seen it so long I can't see it."

Radvid signals cluttered the communicator which Martin was operating, faded, returned as face and voice. The face filled the screen, the nose of an Assyrian king, the eyes of a samurai, skin bronze, eyes the color of iron: young, magnificent. "Is that what human beings look like?" said Pugh with awe. "I'd forgotten."

"Shut up, Owen, we're on."

"Libra Exploratory Mission Base, come in please, this is *Passerine* launch."

"Libra here. Beam fixed. Come on down, launch."

"Expulsion in seven E-seconds. Hold on." The screen blanked and sparkled.

"Do they all look like that? Martin, you and I are uglier men than I thought."

"Shut up, Owen. . . ."

For twenty-two minutes Martin followed the landing-craft down by signal and then through the cleared dome they saw it, small star in the blood-colored east, sinking. It came down neat and quiet, Libra's thin atmosphere carrying little sound. Pugh and Martin closed the headpieces of their imsuits, zipped out of the dome airlocks, and ran with soaring strides, Nijinsky and Nureyev, toward the boat. Three equipment modules came floating down at four-minute intervals from each other and hundred-meter intervals east of the boat. "Come on out," Martin said on his suit radio, "we're waiting at the door."

"Come on in, the methane's fine," said Pugh.

The hatch opened. The young man they had seen on the screen came out with one athletic twist and leaped down onto the shaky dust and clinkers of Libra. Martin shook his hand, but Pugh was staring at the hatch, from which another young man emerged with the same neat twist and jump, followed by a young woman who emerged with the same neat twist, ornamented with a wriggle, and a jump. They were all tall, with bronze skin, black hair, high-bridged noses, epicanthic fold, the same face. They all had the same face. The fourth was emerging from the hatch with a neat twist and jump. "Martin bach," said Pugh, "we've got a clone."

"Right," said one of them, "we're a tenclone. John Chow's the name. You're Lieutenant Martin?"

"I'm Owen Pugh."

"Alvaro Guillen Martin," said Martin, formal, bowing slightly. Another girl was out, the same beautiful face; Martin stared at her and his eye rolled like a nervous pony's. Evidently he had never given any thought to cloning, and was suffering technological shock. "Steady," Pugh said in the Argentine dialect, "it's only excess twins." He stood close by Martin's elbow. He was glad himself of the contact.

It is hard to meet a stranger. Even the greatest extravert meeting even the meekest stranger knows a certain dread, though he may not know he knows it. Will he make a fool of me wreck my image of myself invade me destroy me change me? Will he be different from me? Yes, that he will. There's the terrible thing: the strangeness of the stranger.

After two years on a dead planet, and the last half year isolated as a team of two, oneself and one other, after that it's even harder to meet a stranger, however welcome he may be. You're out of the habit of difference, you've lost the touch; and so the fear revives, the primitive anxiety, the old dread.

The clone, five males and five females, had got done in a couple of minutes what a man might have got done in twenty: greeted Pugh and Martin, had a glance at Libra, unloaded the boat, made ready to go. They went, and the dome filled with them, a hive of golden bees. They hummed and buzzed quietly, filled up all silences, all spaces with a honey-brown swarm of human presence. Martin looked bewilderedly at the long-limbed girls, and they smiled at him, three at once. Their smile was gentler than that of the boys, but no less radiantly self-possessed.

"Self-possessed," Owen Pugh murmured to his friend, "that's it. Think of it, to be oneself ten times over. Nine seconds for every motion, nine ayes on every vote. It would be glorious!" But Martin was asleep. And the John Chows had all gone to sleep at once. The dome was filled with their quiet breathing. They were young, they didn't snore. Martin sighed and snored, his Hershey-bar-colored face relaxed in the dim afterglow of Libra's primary, set at last. Pugh had cleared the dome and stars looked in, Sol among them, a great company of lights, a clone of splendors. Pugh slept and dreamed of a one-eyed giant who chased him through the shaking halls of Hell.

From his sleeping-bag Pugh watched the clone's awakening. They all got up within one minute except for one pair, a boy and a girl, who lay snugly tangled and still sleeping in one bag. As Pugh saw this there was a shock like one of Libra's earthquakes inside him, a very deep tremor. He was not aware of this, and in fact thought he was pleased at the sight; there was no other such comfort on this dead hollow world; more power to them, who made love. One of the others stepped on the pair. They woke and the girl sat up flushed and sleepy, with bare golden breasts. One of her sisters murmured something to her; she shot a glance at Pugh and disappeared in the sleeping-bag, followed by a giant giggle, from another direction a fierce stare, from still another direction a voice: "Christ, we're used to having a room to ourselves. Hope you don't mind, Captain Pugh."

"It's a pleasure," Pugh said half-truthfully. He had to stand up then, wearing only the shorts he slept in, and he felt like a plucked rooster, all white scrawn and pimples. He had seldom envied Martin's compact brownness so much. The United Kingdom had come through the Great Famines well, losing less than half its population: a record achieved by rigorous food-control. Black-marketeers and hoarders had been executed. Crumbs had been shared. Where in richer lands most had died and a few had thriven, in Britain fewer died and none throve. They all got lean. Their sons were lean, their grandsons lean, small, brittle-boned, easily infected. When civilization became a matter of standing in lines, the British had kept queue, and so had replaced the survival of the fittest with the survival of the fair-minded. Owen Pugh was a scrawny little man. All the same, he was there.

At the moment he wished he wasn't.

At breakfast a John said, "Now if you'll brief us, Captain Pugh—"

"Owen, then."

"Owen, we can work out our schedule. Anything new on the mine since your last report to your Mission? We saw your reports when *Passerine* was orbiting Planet V, where they are now."

Martin did not answer, though the mine was his discovery and project, and Pugh had to do his best. It was hard to talk to them. The same faces, each with the same expression of intelligent interest, all leaned toward him across the table at almost the same angle. They all nodded together.

Over the Exploitation Corps insignia on their tunics each had a nameband, first name John and last name Chow of course, but the middle names different. The men were Aleph, Kaph, Yod, Gimel, and Samedh; the women Sadhe, Daleth, Zayin, Beth, and Resh. Pugh tried to use the names but gave it up at once; he could not even tell sometimes which one had spoken, for the voices were all alike.

Martin buttered and chewed his toast, and finally interrupted: "You're a team. Is that it?"

"Right," said two Johns.

"God, what a team! I hadn't seen the point. How much do you each know what the others are thinking?"

"Not at all, properly speaking," replied one of the girls, Zayin. The others watched her with the proprietary, approving look they had. "No ESP, nothing fancy. But we think alike. We have exactly the same equipment. Given the same stimulus, the same problem, we're likely to be coming up with the same reactions and solutions at the same time. Explanations are easy—don't even have to make them, usually. We seldom misunderstand each other. It does facilitate our working as a team."

"Christ yes," said Martin. "Pugh and I have spent seven hours out of ten for six months misunderstanding each other. Like most people. What about emergencies, are you as good at meeting the unexpected problem as a nor . . . an unrelated team?"

"Statistics so far indicate that we are," Zayin answered readily. Clones must be trained, Pugh thought, to meet questions, to reassure and reason. All they said had the slightly bland and stilted quality of answers furnished to the Public. "We can't brainstorm as singletons can, we as a team don't profit from the interplay of varied minds; but we have a compensatory advantage. Clones are drawn from the best human material, individuals of IIQ 99th percentile, Genetic Constitution alpha double A, and so on. We have more to draw on than most individuals do."

"And it's multiplied by a factor of ten. Who is—who was John Chow?"

"A genius surely," Pugh said politely. His interest in cloning was not so new and avid as Martin's.

"Leonardo Complex type," said Yod. "Biomath, also a cellist, and an undersea hunter, and interested in structural engineering problems, and so on. Died before he'd worked out his major theories."

"Then you each represent a different facet of his mind, his talents?"

"No," said Zayin, shaking her head in time with several others. "We share the basic equipment and tendencies, of course, but we're all engineers in Planetary Exploitation. A later clone can be trained to develop other aspects of the basic equipment. It's all training; the genetic substance is identical. We *are* John Chow. But we were differently trained."

Martin looked shell-shocked. "How old are you?"

"Twenty-three."

"You say he died young— Had they taken germ cells from him beforehand or something?"

Gimel took over: "He died at twenty-four in an aircar crash. They couldn't save the brain, so they took some intestinal cells and cultured them for cloning. Reproductive cells aren't used for cloning since they have only half the chromosomes. Intestinal cells happen to be easy to despecialize and reprogram for total growth."

"All chips off the old block," Martin said valiantly. "But how can . . . some of you be women . . . ?"

Beth took over: "It's easy to program half the clonal mass back to the female.

Just delete the male gene from half the cells and they revert to the basic, that is, the female. It's trickier to go the other way, have to hook in artificial Y chromosomes. So they mostly clone from males, since clones function best bisexually."

Gimel again: "They've worked these matters of technique and function out carefully. The taxpayer wants the best for his money, and of course clones are expensive. With the cell-manipulations, and the incubation in Ngama Placentae, and the maintenance and training of the foster-parent groups, we end up costing about three million apiece."

"For your next generation," Martin said, still struggling, "I suppose you . . . you breed?"

"We females are sterile," said Beth with perfect equanimity; "you remember that the Y chromosome was deleted from our original cell. The males can interbreed with approved singletons, if they want to. But to get John Chow again as often as they want, they just reclone a cell from this clone."

Martin gave up the struggle. He nodded and chewed cold toast. "Well," said one of the Johns, and all changed mood, like a flock of starlings that change course in one wingflick, following a leader so fast that no eye can see which leads. They were ready to go. "How about a look at the mine? Then we'll unload the equipment. Some nice new models in the roboats; you'll want to see them. Right?" Had Pugh or Martin not agreed they might have found it hard to say so. The Johns were polite but unanimous; their decisions carried. Pugh, Commander of Libra Base 2, felt a qualm. Could he boss around this superman-woman-entity-of-ten? and a genius at that? He stuck close to Martin as they suited for outside. Neither said anything.

Four apiece in the three large jetsleds, they slipped off north from the dome, over Libra's dun rugose skin, in starlight.

"Desolate," one said.

It was a boy and girl with Pugh and Martin. Pugh wondered if these were the two that had shared a sleeping-bag last night. No doubt they wouldn't mind if he asked them. Sex must be as handy as breathing, to them. Did you two breathe last night?

"Yes," he said, "it is desolate."

"This is our first time Off, except training on Luna." The girl's voice was definitely a bit higher and softer.

"How did you take the big hop?"

"They doped us. I wanted to experience it." That was the boy; he sounded wistful. They seemed to have more personality, only two at a time. Did repetition of the individual negate individuality?

"Don't worry," said Martin, steering the sled, "you can't experience no-time because it isn't there."

"I'd just like to once," one of them said. "So we'd know."

The Mountains of Merioneth showed leprotic in starlight to the east, a plume of freezing gas trailed silvery from a vent-hole to the west, and the sled tilted groundward. The twins braced for the stop at one moment, each with a slight protective gesture to the other. Your skin is my skin, Pugh thought, but literally, no metaphor. What would it be like, then, to have someone as close to you as that? Always to be answered when you spoke, never to be in pain alone. Love your neighbor as you love yourself. . . . That hard old problem was solved. The neighbor was the self: the love was perfect.

And here was Hellmouth, the mine.

Pugh was the Exploratory Mission's ET geologist, and Martin his technician and cartographer; but when in the course of a local survey Martin had discovered the U-mine, Pugh had given him full credit, as well as the onus of prospecting the lode and planning the Exploitation Team's job. These kids had been sent out from Earth years before Martin's reports got there, and had not known what their job would be until they got here. The Exploitation Corps simply sent out teams regularly and blindly as a dandelion sends out its seeds, knowing there would be a job for them on Libra or the next planet out or one they hadn't even heard about yet. The Government wanted uranium too urgently to wait while reports drifted home across the light-years. The stuff was like gold, old-fashioned but essential, worth mining extraterrestrially and shipping interstellar. Worth its weight in people, Pugh thought sourly, watching the tall young men and women go one by one, glimmering in starlight, into the black hole Martin had named Hellmouth.

As they went in their homeostatic forehead-lamps brightened. Twelve nodding gleams ran along the moist, wrinkled walls. Pugh heard Martin's radiation counter peeping twenty to the dozen up ahead. "Here's the drop-off," said Martin's voice in the suit intercom, drowning out the peeping and the dead silence that was around them. "We're in a side-fissure; this is the main vertical vent in front of us." The black void gaped, its far side not visible in the headlamp beams. "Last vulcanism seems to have been a couple of thousand years ago. Nearest fault is twenty-eight kilos east, in the Trench. This region seems to be as safe seismically as anything in the area. The big basalt-flow overhead stabilizes all these substructures, so long as it remains stable itself. Your central lode is thirty-six meters down and runs in a series of five bubble-caverns northeast. It is a lode, a pipe of very high-grade ore. You saw the percentage figures, right? Extraction's going to be no problem. All you've got to do is get the bubbles topside."

"Take off the lid and let 'em float up." A chuckle. Voices began to talk, but they were all the same voice and the suit radio gave them no location in space. "Open the thing right up. —Safer that way. —But it's a solid basalt roof, how thick, ten meters here? —Three to twenty, the report said. —Blow good ore all over the lot. —Use this access we're in, straighten it a bit and run slider-rails for the robos. —Import burros. —Have we got enough propping material? —What's your estimate of total payload mass, Martin?"

"Say over five million kilos and under eight."

"Transport will be here in ten E-months. —It'll have to go pure. —No, they'll have the mass problem in NAFAL shipping licked by now; remember it's been sixteen years since we left Earth last Tuesday. —Right, they'll send the whole lot back and purify it in Earth orbit. —Shall we go down, Martin?"

"Go on. I've been down."

The first one—Aleph? (Heb., the ox, the leader)—swung onto the ladder and down; the rest followed. Pugh and Martin stood at the chasm's edge. Pugh set his intercom to exchange only with Martin's suit, and noticed Martin doing the same. It was a bit wearing, this listening to one person think aloud in ten voices, or was it one voice speaking the thoughts of ten minds?

"A great gut," Pugh said, looking down into the black pit, its veined and warted walls catching stray gleams of headlamps far below. "A cow's bowel. A bloody great constipated intestine."

Martin's counter peeped like a lost chicken. They stood inside the epileptic planet, breathing oxygen from tanks, wearing suits impermeable to corrosives and harmful radiations, resistant to a two-hundred-degree range of temperatures, tear-proof, and as shock-resistent as possible given the soft vulnerable stuff inside.

"Next hop," Martin said, "I'd like to find a planet that has nothing whatever to exploit."

"You found this."

"Keep me home next time."

Pugh was pleased. He had hoped Martin would want to go on working with him, but neither of them was used to talking much about their feelings, and he had hesitated to ask. "I'll try that," he said.

"I hate this place. I like caves, you know. It's why I came in here. Just spelunking. But this one's a bitch. Mean. You can't ever let down in here. I guess this lot can handle it, though. They know their stuff."

"Wave of the future, whatever," said Pugh.

The wave of the future came swarming up the ladder, swept Martin to the entrance, gabbled at and around him: "Have we got enough material for supports? —If we convert one of the extractor-servos to anneal, yes. —Sufficient if we miniblast? —Kaph can calculate stress."

Pugh had switched his intercom back to receive them; he looked at them, so many thoughts jabbering in an eager mind, and at Martin standing silent among them, and at Hellmouth, and the wrinkled plain. "Settled! How does that strike you as a preliminary schedule, Martin?"

"It's your baby," Martin said.

Within five E-days, the Johns had all their material and equipment unloaded and operating, and were starting to open up the mine. They worked with total efficiency. Pugh was fascinated and frightened by their effectiveness, their confidence, their independence. He was no use to them at all. A clone, he thought, might indeed be the first truly stable, self-reliant human being. Once adult it would need nobody's help. It would be sufficient to itself physically, sexually, emotionally, intellectually. Whatever he did, any member of it would always receive the support and approval of his peers, his other selves. Nobody else was needed.

Two of the clone stayed in the dome doing calculations and paperwork, with frequent sled-trips to the mine for measurements and tests. They were the mathematicians of the clone, Zayin and Kaph. That is, as Zayin explained, all ten had had thorough mathematical training from age three to twenty-one, but from twenty-one to twenty-three she and Kaph had gone on with math while the others intensified other specialties, geology, mining engineering, electronic engineering, equipment robotics, applied atomics, and so on. "Kaph and I feel," she said, "that we're the element of the clone closest to what John Chow was in his singleton lifetime. But of course he was principally in biomath, and they didn't take us far in that."

"They needed us most in this field," Kaph said, with the patriotic priggishness they sometimes evinced.

Pugh and Martin soon could distinguish this pair from the others, Zayin by gestalt, Kaph only by a discolored left fourth fingernail, got from an ill-aimed hammer at the age of six. No doubt there were many such differences, physical and psychological, among them; nature might be identical, nurture could not be. But the differences were hard to find. And part of the difficulty was that they really never talked to Pugh and Martin. They joked with them, were polite, got along fine. They gave nothing. It was nothing one could complain about; they were very pleasant, they had the standardized American friendliness. "Do you come from Ireland, Owen?"

"Nobody comes from Ireland, Zayin."

"There are lots of Irish-Americans."

"To be sure, but no more Irish. A couple of thousand in all the island, the last I knew. They didn't go in for birth-control, you know, so the food ran out. By the Third Famine there were no Irish left at all but the priesthood, and they were all celibate, or nearly all."

Zayin and Kaph smiled stiffly. They had no experience of either bigotry or irony. "What are you then, ethnically?" Kaph asked, and Pugh replied, "A Welshman."

"Is it Welsh that you and Martin speak together?"

None of your business, Pugh thought, but said, "No, it's his dialect, not mine: Argentinean. A descendent of Spanish."

"You learned it for private communication?"

"Whom had we here to be private from? It's just that sometimes a man likes to speak his native language."

"Ours is English," Kaph said unsympathetically. Why should they have sympathy? That's one of the things you give because you need it back.

"Is Wells quaint?" asked Zayin.

"Wells? Oh, Wales, it's called. Yes. Wales is quaint." Pugh switched on his rock-cutter, which prevented further conversation by a synapse-destroying whine, and while it whined he turned his back and said a profane word in Welsh.

That night he used the Argentine dialect for private communication. "Do they pair off in the same couples, or change every night?"

Martin looked surprised. A prudish expression, unsuited to his features, appeared for a moment. It faded. He too was curious. "I think it's random."

"Don't whisper, man, it sounds dirty. I think they rotate."

"On a schedule?"

"So nobody gets omitted."

Martin gave a vulgar laugh and smothered it. "What about us? Aren't we omitted?"

"That doesn't occur to them."

"What if I proposition one of the girls?"

"She'd tell the others and they'd decide as a group."

"I am not a bull," Martin said, his dark, heavy face heating up. "I will not be judged—"

"Down, down, *machismo*," said Pugh. "Do you mean to proposition one?"

Martin shrugged, sullen. "Let 'em have their incest."

"Incest is it, or masturbation?"

"I don't care, if they'd do it out of earshot!"

The clone's early attempts at modesty had soon worn off, unmotivated by any deep defensiveness of self or awareness of others. Pugh and Martin were daily deeper swamped under the intimacies of its constant emotional-sexual-mental interchange: swamped yet excluded.

"Two months to go," Martin said one evening.

"To what?" snapped Pugh. He was edgy lately and Martin's sullenness got on his nerves.

"To relief."

In sixty days the full crew of their Exploratory Mission were due back from their survey of the other planets of the system. Pugh was aware of this.

"Crossing off the days on your calendar?" he jeered.

"Pull yourself together, Owen."

"What do you mean?"

"What I say."

They parted in contempt and resentment.

Pugh came in after a day alone on the Pampas, a vast lava-plain the nearest edge of which was two hours south by jet. He was tired, but refreshed by solitude. They were not supposed to take long trips alone, but lately had often done so. Martin stooped under bright lights, drawing one of his elegant, masterly charts: this one was of the whole face of Libra, the cancerous face. The dome was otherwise empty, seeming dim and large as it had before the clone came. "Where's the golden horde?"

Martin grunted ignorance, crosshatching. He straightened his back to glance around at the sun, which squatted feebly like a great red toad on the eastern plain, and at the clock, which said 18:45. "Some big quakes today," he said, returning to his map. "Feel them down there? Lots of crates were falling around. Take a look at the seismo."

The needle jigged and wavered on the roll. It never stopped dancing here. The roll had recorded five quakes of major intensity back in mid-afternoon; twice the needle had hopped off the roll. The attached computer had been activated to emit a slip reading, "Epicenter 61′ N by 4′24″ E."

"Not in the Trench this time."

"I thought I felt a bit different from usual. Sharper."

"In Base One I used to lie awake all night feeling the ground jump. Queer how you get used to things."

"Go spla if you didn't. What's for dinner?"

"I thought you'd have cooked it."

"Waiting for the clone."

Feeling put upon, Pugh got out a dozen dinnerboxes, stuck two in the Instobake, pulled them out. "All right, here's dinner."

"Been thinking," Martin said, coming to the table. "What if some clone cloned itself? Illegally. Made a thousand duplicates—ten thousand. Whole army. They could make a tidy power-grab, couldn't they?"

"But how many millions did this lot cost to rear? Artificial placentae and all that. It would be hard to keep secret, unless they had a planet to themselves. . . . Back before the Famines when Earth had national governments, they talked about that: clone your best soldiers, have whole regiments of them. But the food ran out before they could play that game."

They talked amicably, as they used to do.

"Funny," Martin said, chewing. "They left early this morning, didn't they?"

"All but Kaph and Zayin. They thought they'd get the first payload aboveground today. What's up?"

"They weren't back for lunch."

"They won't starve, to be sure."

"They left at seven."

"So they did." Then Pugh saw it. The air-tanks held eight hours' supply.

"Kaph and Zayin carried out spare cans when they left. Or they've got a heap out there."

"They did, but they brought the whole lot in to recharge." Martin stood up, pointing to one of the stacks of stuff that cut the dome into rooms and alleys.

"There's an alarm signal on every imsuit."

"It's not automatic."

Pugh was tired and still hungry. "Sit down and eat, man. That lot can look after themselves."

Martin sat down, but did not eat. "There was a big quake, Owen. The first one. Big enough, it scared me."

After a pause Pugh sighed and said, "All right."

Unenthusiastically, they got out the two-man sled that was always left for them, and headed it north. The long sunrise covered everything in poisonous red Jell-O. The horizontal light and shadow made it hard to see, raised walls of fake iron ahead of them through which they slid, turned the convex plain beyond Hellmouth into a great dimple full of bloody water. Around the tunnel entrance a wilderness of machinery stood, cranes and cables and servos and wheels and diggers and robocarts and sliders and control-huts, all slanting and bulking incoherently in the red light. Martin jumped from the sled, ran into the mine. He came out again, to Pugh. "Oh God, Owen, it's down," he said. Pugh went in and saw, five meters from the entrance, the shiny, moist, black wall that ended the tunnel. Newly exposed to air, it looked organic, like visceral tissue. The tunnel entrance, enlarged by blasting and double-tracked for robocarts, seemed unchanged until he noticed thousands of tiny spiderweb cracks in the walls. The floor was wet with some sluggish fluid.

"They were inside," Martin said.

"They may be still. They surely had extra air-cans—"

"Look, Owen, look at the basalt flow, at the roof; don't you see what the quake did, look at it."

The low hump of land that roofed the caves still had the unreal look of an optical illusion. It had reversed itself, sunk down, leaving a vast dimple or pit. When Pugh walked on it he saw that it too was cracked with many tiny fissures. From some a whitish gas was seeping, so that the sunlight on the surface of the gas-pool was shafted as if by the waters of a dim red lake.

"The mine's not on the fault. There's no fault here!"

Pugh came back to him quickly. "No, there's no fault, Martin. Look, they surely weren't all inside together."

Martin followed him and searched among the wrecked machines dully, then actively. He spotted the airsled. It had come down heading south, and struck at an angle in a pothole of colloidal dust. It had carried two riders. One was half sunk in the dust, but his suit-meters registered normal functioning; the other hung strapped onto the tilted sled. Her imsuit had burst open on the broken legs, and the body was frozen hard as any rock. That was all they found. As both regulation and custom demanded, they cremated the dead at once with the laser-guns they carried by regulation and had never used before. Pugh, knowing he was going to be sick, wrestled the survivor onto the two-man sled and sent Martin off to the dome with him. Then he vomited, and flushed the waste out of his suit, and finding one four-man sled undamaged followed after Martin, shaking as if the cold of Libra had got through to him.

The survivor was Kaph. He was in deep shock. They found a swelling on the occiput that might mean concussion, but no fracture was visible.

Pugh brought two glasses of food-concentrate and two chasers of aquavit. "Come on," he said. Martin obeyed, drinking off the tonic. They sat down on crates near the cot and sipped the aquavit.

Kaph lay immobile, face like beeswax, hair bright black to the shoulders, lips stiffly parted for faintly gasping breaths.

"It must have been the first shock, the big one," Martin said. "It must have slid the whole structure sideways. Till it fell in on itself. There must be gas layers in the lateral rocks, like those formations in the Thirty-first Quadrant. But there wasn't any sign—" As he spoke the world slid out from under them. Things leaped and clattered, hopped and jigged, shouted Ha! Ha! Ha! "It was like this at fourteen hours," said Reason shakily in Martin's voice, amidst the unfastening and ruin of the world. But Unreason sat up, as the tumult lessened and things ceased dancing, and screamed aloud.

Pugh leaped across his spilled aquavit and held Kaph down. The muscular body flailed him off. Martin pinned the shoulders down. Kaph screamed, struggled, choked; his face blackened. "Oxy," Pugh said, and his hand found the right needle in the medical kit as if by homing instinct; while Martin held the mask he stuck the needle home to the vagus nerve, restoring Kaph to life.

"Didn't know you knew that stunt," Martin said, breathing hard.

"The Lazarus Jab; my father was a doctor. It doesn't often work," Pugh said. "I want that drink I spilled. Is the quake over? I can't tell."

"Aftershocks. It's not just you shivering."

"Why did he suffocate?"

"I don't know, Owen. Look in the book."

Kaph was breathing normally and his color was restored, only his lips were still darkened. They poured a new shot of courage and sat down by him again with their medical guide. "Nothing about cyanosis or asphyxiation under 'shock' or 'concussion.' He can't have breathed in anything with his suit on. I don't know. We'd get as much good out of *Mother Mog's Home Herbalist*. . . . 'Anal Hemorrhoids,' fy!" Pugh pitched the book to a crate-table. It fell short, because either Pugh or the table was still unsteady.

"Why didn't he signal?"

"Sorry?"

"The eight inside the mine never had time. But he and the girl must have been outside. Maybe she was in the entrance, and got hit by the first slide. He must have been outside, in the control-hut maybe. He ran in, pulled her out, strapped her onto the sled, started for the dome. And all that time never pushed the panic button in his imsuit. Why not?"

"Well, he'd had that whack on his head. I doubt he ever realized the girl was dead. He wasn't in his senses. But if he had been I don't know if he'd have thought to signal us. They looked to one another for help."

Martin's face was like an Indian mask, grooves at the mouth-corners, eyes of dull coal. "That's so. What must he have felt, then, when the quake came and he was outside, alone—"

In answer Kaph screamed.

He came up off the cot in the heaving convulsions of one suffocating, knocked Pugh right down with his flailing arm, staggered into a stack of crates and fell to the floor, lips blue, eyes white. Martin dragged him back onto the cot and gave him a whiff of oxygen, then knelt by Pugh, who was just sitting up, and wiped at his cut cheekbone. "Owen, are you all right, are you going to be all right, Owen?"

"I think I am," Pugh said. "Why are you rubbing that on my face?"

It was a short length of computer-tape, now spotted with Pugh's blood. Martin dropped it. "Thought it was a towel. You clipped your cheek on that box there."

"Is he out of it?"

"Seems to be."

They stared down at Kaph lying stiff, his teeth a white line inside dark parted lips.

"Like epilepsy. Brain damage maybe?"

"What about shooting him full of meprobamate?"

Pugh shook his head. "I don't know what's in that shot I already gave him for shock. Don't want to overdose him."

"Maybe he'll sleep it off now."

"I'd like to myself. Between him and the earthquake I can't seem to keep on my feet."

"You got a nasty crack there. Go on, I'll sit up a while."

Pugh cleaned his cut cheek and pulled off his shirt, then paused.

"Is there anything we ought to have done—have tried to do—"

"They're all dead," Martin said heavily, gently.

Pugh lay down on top of his sleeping-bag, and one instant later was wakened by a hideous, sucking, struggling noise. He staggered up, found the needle, tried three times to jab it in correctly and failed, began to massage over Kaph's heart. "Mouth-to-mouth," he said, and Martin obeyed. Presently Kaph drew a harsh breath, his heartbeat steadied, his rigid muscles began to relax.

"How long did I sleep?"

"Half an hour."

They stood up sweating. The ground shuddered, the fabric of the dome sagged and swayed. Libra was dancing her awful polka again, her Totentanz. The sun, though rising, seemed to have grown larger and redder; gas and dust must have been stirred up in the feeble atmosphere.

"What's wrong with him, Owen?"

"I think he's dying with them."

"Them— But they're dead, I tell you."

"Nine of them. They're all dead, they were crushed or suffocated. They were all him, he is all of them. They died, and now he's dying their deaths one by one."

"Oh pity of God," said Martin.

The next time was much the same. The fifth time was worse, for Kaph fought and raved, trying to speak but getting no words out, as if his mouth were stopped with rocks or clay. After that the attacks grew weaker, but so did he. The eighth seizure came at about four-thirty; Pugh and Martin worked till five-thirty doing all they could to keep life in the body that slid without protest into death. They kept him, but Martin said, "The next will finish him." And it did; but Pugh breathed his own breath into the inert lungs, until he himself passed out.

He woke. The dome was opaqued and no light on. He listened and heard the breathing of two sleeping men. He slept, and nothing woke him till hunger did.

The sun was well up over the dark plains, and the planet had stopped dancing. Kaph lay asleep. Pugh and Martin drank tea and looked at him with proprietary triumph.

When he woke Martin went to him: "How do you feel, old man?" There was no answer. Pugh took Martin's place and looked into the brown, dull eyes that gazed toward but not into his own. Like Martin he quickly turned away. He heated food-concentrate and brought it to Kaph. "Come on, drink."

He could see the muscles in Kaph's throat tighten. "Let me die," the young man said.

"You're not dying."

Kaph spoke with clarity and precision: "I am nine-tenths dead. There is not enough of me left alive."

That precision convinced Pugh, and he fought the conviction. "No," he said, peremptorily. "They are dead. The others. Your brothers and sisters. You're not them, you're alive. You are John Chow. Your life is in your own hands."

The young man lay still, looking into a darkness that was not there.

Martin and Pugh took turns taking the Exploitation hauler and a spare set of robos over to Hellmouth to salvage equipment and protect it from Libra's sinister atmosphere, for the value of the stuff was, literally, astronomical. It was slow work for one man at a time, but they were unwilling to leave Kaph by himself. The one left in the dome did paperwork, while Kaph sat or lay and stared into his darkness, and never spoke. The days went by silent.

The radio spat and spoke: the Mission calling from ship. "We'll be down on Libra in five weeks, Owen. Thirty-four E-days nine hours I make it as of now. How's tricks in the old dome?"

"Not good, chief. The Exploit team were killed, all but one of them, in the mine. Earthquake. Six days ago."

The radio crackled and sang starsong. Sixteen seconds lag each way; the ship was out around Planet 11 now. "Killed, all but one? You and Martin were unhurt?"

"We're all right, chief."

Thirty-two seconds.

"*Passerine* left an Exploit team out here with us. I may put them on the Hellmouth project then, instead of the Quadrant Seven project. We'll settle that when we come down. In any case you and Martin will be relieved at Dome Two. Hold tight. Anything else?"

"Nothing else."

Thirty-two seconds.

"Right then. So long, Owen."

Kaph had heard all this, and later on Pugh said to him, "The chief may ask you to stay here with the other Exploit team. You know the ropes here." Knowing the exigencies of Far Out Life, he wanted to warn the young man. Kaph made no answer. Since he had said, "There is not enough of me left alive," he had not spoken a word.

"Owen," Martin said on suit intercom, "he's spla. Insane. Psycho."

"He's doing very well for a man who's died nine times."

"Well? Like a turned-off android is well? The only emotion he has left is hate. Look at his eyes."

"That's not hate, Martin. Listen, it's true that he has, in a sense, been dead. I cannot imagine what he feels. But it's not hatred. He can't even see us. It's too dark."

"Throats have been cut in the dark. He hates us because we're not Aleph and Yod and Zayin."

"Maybe. But I think he's alone. He doesn't see us or hear us, that's the truth. He never had to see anyone else before. He never was alone before. He had himself to see, talk with, live with, nine other selves all his life. He doesn't know how you go it alone. He must learn. Give him time."

Martin shook his heavy head. "Spla," he said. "Just remember when you're alone with him that he could break your neck one-handed."

"He could do that," said Pugh, a short, soft-voiced man with a scarred cheekbone; he smiled. They were just outside the dome airlock, programming one of the servos to repair a damaged hauler. They could see Kaph sitting inside the great half-egg of the dome like a fly in amber.

"Hand me the insert pack there. What makes you think he'll get any better?"

"He has a strong personality, to be sure."

"Strong? Crippled. Nine-tenths dead, as he put it."

"But he's not dead. He's a live man: John Kaph Chow. He had a jolly queer upbringing, but after all every boy has got to break free of his family. He will do it."

"I can't see it."

"Think a bit, Martin bach. What's this cloning for? To repair the human race. We're in a bad way. Look at me. My IIQ and GC are half this John Chow's. Yet they wanted me so badly for the Far Out Service that when I volunteered they took me and fitted me out with an artificial lung and corrected my myopia. Now if there were enough good sound lads about would they be taking one-lunged shortsighted Welshmen?"

"Didn't know you had an artificial lung."

"I do then. Not tin, you know. Human, grown in a tank from a bit of somebody; cloned, if you like. That's how they make replacement-organs, the same general idea as cloning, but bits and pieces instead of whole people. It's my own lung now, whatever. But what I am saying is this; there are too many like me these days and not enough like John Chow. They're trying to raise the level of the human genetic pool, which is a mucky little puddle since the population crash. So then if a man is cloned, he's a strong and clever man. It's only logic, to be sure."

Martin grunted; the servo began to hum.

Kaph had been eating little; he had trouble swallowing his food, choking on it, so that he would give up trying after a few bites. He had lost eight or ten kilos. After three weeks or so, however, his appetite began to pick up, and one day he began to look through the clone's possessions, the sleeping-bags, kits, papers which Pugh had stacked neatly in a far angle of a packing-crate alley. He sorted, destroyed a heap of papers and oddments, made a small packet of what remained, then relapsed into his walking coma.

Two days later he spoke. Pugh was trying to correct a flutter in the tape-player, and failing; Martin had the jet out, checking their maps of the Pampas. "Hell and damnation!" Pugh said, and Kaph said in a toneless voice, "Do you want me to do that?"

Pugh jumped, controlled himself, and gave the machine to Kaph. The young man took it apart, put it back together, and left it on the table.

"Put on a tape," Pugh said with careful casualness, busy at another table.

Kaph put on the topmost tape, a chorale. He lay down on his cot. The sound of a hundred human voices singing together filled the dome. He lay still, his face blank.

In the next days he took over several routine jobs, unasked. He undertook nothing that wanted initiative, and if asked to do anything he made no response at all.

"He's doing well," Pugh said in the dialect of Argentina.

"He's not. He's turning himself into a machine. Does what he's programmed to do, no reaction to anything else. He's worse off than when he didn't function at all. He's not human any more."

Pugh sighed. "Well, good night," he said in English. "Good night, Kaph."

"Good night," Martin said; Kaph did not.

Next morning at breakfast Kaph reached across Martin's plate for the toast. "Why don't you ask for it?" Martin said with the geniality of repressed exasperation. "I can pass it."

"I can reach it," Kaph said in his flat voice.

"Yes, but look. Asking to pass things, saying good night or hello, they're not important, but all the same when somebody says something a person ought to answer. . . ."

The young man looked indifferently in Martin's direction; his eyes still did not seem to see clear through to the person he looked toward. "Why should I answer?"

"Because somebody has said something to you."

"Why?"

Martin shrugged and laughed. Pugh jumped up and turned on the rock-cutter.

Later on he said, "Lay off that, please, Martin."

"Manners are essential in small isolated crews, some kind of manners, whatever you work out together. He's been taught that, everybody in Far Out knows it. Why does he deliberately flout it?"

"Do you tell yourself good night?"

"So?"

"Don't you see Kaph's never known anyone but himself?"

Martin brooded and then broke out, "Then by God this cloning business is all wrong. It won't do. What are a lot of duplicate geniuses going to do for us when they don't even know we exist?"

Pugh nodded. "It might be wiser to separate the clones and bring them up with others. But they make such a grand team this way."

"Do they? I don't know. If this lot had been ten average inefficient ET engineers, would they all have been in the same place at the same time? Would they all have got killed? What if, when the quake came and things started caving in, what if all those kids ran the same way, farther into the mine, maybe, to save the one that was farthest in? Even Kaph was outside and went in. . . . It's hypothetical. But I keep thinking, out of ten ordinary confused guys, more might have got out."

"I don't know. It's true that identical twins tend to die at about the same time, even when they have never seen each other. Identity and death, it is very strange. . . ."

The days went on, the red sun crawled across the dark sky, Kaph did not speak when spoken to, Pugh and Martin snapped at each other more frequently each day. Pugh complained of Martin's snoring. Offended, Martin moved his cot clear across the dome and also ceased speaking to Pugh for some while. Pugh whistled Welsh dirges until Martin complained, and then Pugh stopped speaking for a while.

The day before the Mission ship was due, Martin announced he was going over to Merioneth.

"I thought at least you'd be giving me a hand with the computer to finish the rock-analyses," Pugh said, aggrieved.

"Kaph can do that. I want one more look at the Trench. Have fun," Martin added in dialect, and laughed, and left.

"What is that language?"

"Argentinean. I told you that once, didn't I?"

"I don't know." After a while the young man added, "I have forgotten a lot of things, I think."

"It wasn't important, to be sure," Pugh said gently, realizing all at once how important this conversation was. "Will you give me a hand running the computer, Kaph?"

He nodded.

Pugh had left a lot of loose ends, and the job took them all day. Kaph was a good co-worker, quick and systematic, much more so than Pugh himself. His flat voice, now that he was talking again, got on the nerves; but it didn't matter, there was only this one day left to get through and then the ship would come, the old crew, comrades and friends.

During tea-break Kaph said, "What will happen if the Explorer ship crashes?"

"They'd be killed."

"To you, I mean."

"To us? We'd radio SOS all signals, and live on half rations till the rescue cruiser from Area Three Base came. Four and a half E-years away it is. We have life-support here for three men for, let's see maybe between four and five years. A bit tight, it would be."

"Would they send a cruiser for three men?"

"They would."

Kaph said no more.

"Enough cheerful speculations," Pugh said cheerfully, rising to get back to work. He slipped sideways and the chair avoided his hand; he did a sort of half-pirouette and fetched up hard against the dome-hide. "My goodness," he said, reverting to his native idiom, "what is it?"

"Quake," said Kaph.

The teacups bounced on the table with a plastic cackle, a litter of papers slid off a box, the skin of the dome swelled and sagged. Underfoot there was a huge noise, half sound half shaking, a subsonic boom.

Kaph sat unmoved. An earthquake does not frighten a man who died in an earthquake.

Pugh, white-faced, wiry black hair sticking out, a frightened man, said, "Martin is in the Trench."

"What trench?"

"The big fault line. The epicenter for the local quakes. Look at the seismograph." Pugh struggled with the stuck door of a still-jittering locker.

"Where are you going?"

"After him."

"Martin took the jet. Sleds aren't safe to use during quakes. They go out of control."

"For God's sake, man, shut up."

Kaph stood up, speaking in a flat voice as usual. "It's unnecessary to go out after him now. It's taking an unnecessary risk."

"If his alarm goes off, radio me," Pugh said, shut the headpiece of his suit, and ran to the lock. As he went out Libra picked up her ragged skirts and danced a bellydance from under his feet clear to the red horizon.

Inside the dome, Kaph saw the sled go up, tremble like a meteor in the dull red daylight, and vanish to the northeast. The hide of the dome quivered; the earth coughed. A vent south of the dome belched up a slow-flowing bile of black gas.

A bell shrilled and a red light flashed on the central control board. The sign under the light read Suit Two and scribbled under that, A.G.M. Kaph did not turn the signal off. He tried to radio Martin, then Pugh, but got no reply from either.

When the aftershocks decreased he went back to work, and finished up Pugh's job. It took him about two hours. Every half hour he tried to contact Suit One, and got no reply, then Suit Two and got no reply. The red light had stopped flashing after an hour.

It was dinnertime. Kaph cooked dinner for one, and ate it. He lay down on his cot.

The aftershocks had ceased except for faint rolling tremors at long intervals. The sun hung in the west, oblate, pale-red, immense. It did not sink visibly. There was no sound at all.

Kaph got up and began to walk about the messy, half-packed-up, overcrowded, empty dome. The silence continued. He went to the player and put on the first tape that came to hand. It was pure music, electronic, without harmonies, without voices. It ended. The silence continued.

Pugh's uniform tunic, one button missing, hung over a stack of rock-samples. Kaph stared at it a while.

The silence continued.

The child's dream: There is no one else alive in the world but me. In all the world.

Low, north of the dome, a meteor flickered.

Kaph's mouth opened as if he were trying to say something, but no sound came. He went hastily to the north wall and peered out into the gelatinous red light.

The little star came in and sank. Two figures blurred the airlock. Kaph stood close beside the lock as they came in. Martin's imsuit was covered with some kind of dust so that he looked raddled and warty like the surface of Libra. Pugh had him by the arm.

"Is he hurt?"

Pugh shucked his suit, helped Martin peel off his. "Shaken up," he said, curt.

"A piece of cliff fell onto the jet," Martin said, sitting down at the table and waving his arms. "Not while I was in it, though. I was parked, see, and poking about that carbon-dust area when I felt things humping. So I went out onto a nice bit of early igneous I'd noticed from above, good footing and out from under the cliffs. Then I saw this bit of the planet fall off onto the flyer, quite a sight it was, and after a while it occurred to me the spare aircans were in the flyer, so I leaned on the panic button. But I didn't get any radio reception, that's always happening here during quakes, so I didn't know if the signal was getting through either. And things went on jumping around and pieces of the cliff coming off. Little rocks flying around, and so dusty you couldn't see a meter ahead. I was really beginning to wonder what I'd do for breathing in the small hours, you know, when I saw old Owen buzzing up the Trench in all that dust and junk like a big ugly bat—"

"Want to eat?" said Pugh.

"Of course I want to eat. How'd you come through the quake here, Kaph? No damage? It wasn't a big one actually, was it, what's the seismo say? My trouble was I was in the middle of it. Old Epicenter Alvaro. Felt like Richter Fifteen there—total destruction of planet—"

"Sit down," Pugh said. "Eat."

After Martin had eaten a little his spate of talk ran dry. He very soon went off to his cot, still in the remote angle where he had removed it when Pugh complained of his snoring. "Good night, you one-lunged Welshman," he said across the dome.

"Good night."

There was no more out of Martin. Pugh opaqued the dome, turned the lamp down to a yellow glow less than a candle's light, and sat doing nothing, saying nothing, withdrawn.

The silence continued.

"I finished the computations."

Pugh nodded thanks.

"The signal from Martin came through, but I couldn't contact you or him."

Pugh said with effort, "I should not have gone. He had two hours of air left even with only one can. He might have been heading home when I left. This way we were all out of touch with one another. I was scared."

The silence came back, punctuated now by Martin's long, soft snores.

"Do you love Martin?"

Pugh looked up with angry eyes: "Martin is my friend. We've worked together, he's a good man." He stopped. After a while he said, "Yes, I love him. Why did you ask that?"

Kaph said nothing, but he looked at the other man. His face was changed, as if he were glimpsing something he had not seen before; his voice too was changed. "How can you . . . ? How do you . . . ?"

But Pugh could not tell him. "I don't know," he said, "it's practice, partly. I don't know. We're each of us alone, to be sure. What can you do but hold your hand out in the dark?"

Kaph's strange gaze dropped, burned out by its own intensity.

"I'm tired," Pugh said. "That was ugly, looking for him in all that black dust and muck, and mouths opening and shutting in the ground. . . . I'm going to bed. The ship will be transmitting to us by six or so." He stood up and stretched.

"It's a clone," Kaph said. "The other Exploit team they're bringing with them."

"Is it, then?"

"A twelveclone. They came out with us on the *Passerine*."

Kaph sat in the small yellow aura of the lamp seeming to look past it at what he feared: the new clone, the multiple self of which he was not part. A lost piece of a broken set, a fragment, inexpert at solitude, not knowing even how you go about giving love to another individual, now he must face the absolute, closed self-sufficiency of the clone of twelve; that was a lot to ask of the poor fellow, to be sure. Pugh put a hand on his shoulder in passing. "The chief won't ask you to stay here with a clone. You can go home. Or since you're Far Out maybe you'll come on farther out with us. We could use you. No hurry deciding. You'll make out all right."

Pugh's quiet voice trailed off. He stood unbuttoning his coat, stooped a little with fatigue. Kaph looked at him and saw the thing he had never seen before: saw him: Owen Pugh, the other, the stranger who held his hand out in the dark.

"Good night," Pugh mumbled, crawling into his sleeping-bag and half asleep already, so that he did not hear Kaph reply after a pause, repeating, across darkness, benediction.

LIGHT OF OTHER DAYS

Bob Shaw

Bob Shaw is the author of a significant body of successful science fiction novels and stories and is one of the leading science fiction personalities in the United Kingdom. Perhaps his most famous novel is *Orbitsville* (1975), a spectacular vision of a complex artificial habitat comparable to Larry Niven's *Ringworld* (1970). But his most famous single story is "Light of Other Days," containing his powerfully evocative invention of "slow glass," later used in several other stories that all together form his book, *Other Days, Other Eyes* (1972). One might compare the story to Isaac Asimov's "The Dead Past" in its investigation of the human meaning of our individual life experiences. But Shaw's plausible construction, so simple and logical on the surface, teases the reader with the idea that it might really work.

From Newton's *Optics*, which had such a profound effect on art and science in the eighteenth century, to the present, that branch of physics has had a continuing impact on visual and literary art. Shaw extrapolates "slow glass" from the indices of refraction of glass and crystal, and from the simple fact that all of our sensory input is delayed by a tiny interval. In *Remembrance of Things Past,* Marcel Proust's central character becomes a writer by learning to represent life through reflection. Shaw's slow glass can recall images of the past, allowing Shaw to show the consequences of attaining the state to which Proust's protagonist aspires—through the imagery of hard science fiction, Shaw binds the fact of the speed of light to our most intimate experiences.

Years ago, in a class taught at Stevens Institute of Technology, Samuel R. Delany had to explain to a student who had done the math proving that slow glass didn't work, that it was science fiction, not fact; if it did work, then the story would no longer be sf but merely literary realism. It is the rigor with which the conceit is plausibly depicted that underpins the imaginative force of all hard science fiction—particularly "Light of Other Days." It is an interesting contrast to the jammed-with-ideas-and-wonderful-gadgets hard sf of, say, Robert L. Forward, in which no one idea, but rather the constant introduction of new ideas and things, carries the story. Here Shaw presents the "one big idea" story in its classic form. All other details of setting that ground the world of the story and make it distinct from the present world are made secondary by Shaw, so that the central image and idea is foregrounded and highlighted, its surprising implications and deep complexities investigated.

Leaving the village behind, we followed the heady sweeps of the road up into a land of slow glass.

I had never seen one of the farms before and at first found them slightly eerie—

an effect heightened by imagination and circumstance. The car's turbine was pulling smoothly and quietly in the damp air so that we seemed to be carried over the convolutions of the road in a kind of supernatural silence. On our right the mountain sifted down into an incredibly perfect valley of timeless pine, and everywhere stood the great frames of slow glass, drinking light. An occasional flash of afternoon sunlight on their wind bracing created an illusion of movement, but in fact the frames were deserted. The rows of windows had been standing on the hillside for years, staring into the valley, and men only cleaned them in the middle of the night when their human presence would not matter to the thirsty glass.

They were fascinating, but Selina and I didn't mention the windows. I think we hated each other so much we both were reluctant to sully anything new by drawing it into the nexus of our emotions. The holiday, I had begun to realize, was a stupid idea in the first place. I had thought it would cure everything, but, of course, it didn't stop Selina being pregnant and, worst still, it didn't even stop her being angry about being pregnant.

Rationalizing our dismay over her condition, we had circulated the usual statements to the effect that we would have *liked* having children—but later on, at the proper time. Selina's pregnancy had cost us her well-paid job and with it the new house we had been negotiating and which was far beyond the reach of my income from poetry. But the real source of our annoyance was that we were face to face with the realization that people who say they want children later always mean they want children never. Our nevers were thrumming with the knowledge that we, who had thought ourselves so unique, had fallen into the same biological trap as every mindless rutting creature which ever existed.

The road took us along the southern slopes of Ben Cruachan until we began to catch glimpses of the gray Atlantic far ahead. I had just cut our speed to absorb the view better when I noticed the sign spiked to a gatepost. It said: "SLOW GLASS—QUALITY HIGH, PRICES LOW—J. R. HAGAN." On an impulse I stopped the car on the verge, wincing slightly as tough grasses whipped noisily at the bodywork.

"Why have we stopped?" Selina's neat, smoke-silver head turned in surprise.

"Look at that sign. Let's go up and see what there is. The stuff might be reasonably priced out here."

Selina's voice was pitched high with scorn as she refused, but I was too taken with my idea to listen. I had an illogical conviction that doing something extravagant and crazy would set us right again.

"Come on," I said, "the exercise might do us some good. We've been driving too long anyway."

She shrugged in a way that hurt me and got out of the car. We walked up a path made of irregular, packed clay steps nosed with short lengths of sapling. The path curved through trees which clothed the edge of the hill and at its end we found a low farmhouse. Beyond the little stone building tall frames of slow glass gazed out toward the voice-stilling sight of Cruachan's ponderous descent toward the waters of Loch Linnhe. Most of the panes were perfectly transparent but a few were dark, like panels of polished ebony.

As we approached the house through a neat cobbled yard a tall middle-aged man in ash-colored tweeds arose and waved to us. He had been sitting on the low rubble wall which bounded the yard, smoking a pipe and staring toward the house. At the front window of the cottage a young woman in a tangerine dress stood with a small boy in her arms, but she turned uninterestedly and moved out of sight as we drew near.

"Mr. Hagan?" I guessed.

"Correct. Come to see some glass, have you? Well, you've come to the right place." Hagan spoke crisply, with traces of the pure highland which sounds so much like Irish to the unaccustomed ear. He had one of those calmly dismayed faces one finds on elderly road menders and philosophers.

"Yes," I said. "We're on holiday. We saw your sign."

Selina, who usually has a natural fluency with strangers, said nothing. She was looking toward the now empty window with what I thought was a slightly puzzled expression.

"Up from London, are you? Well, as I said, you've come to the right place—and at the right time, too. My wife and I don't see many people this early in the season."

I laughed. "Does that mean we might be able to buy a little glass without mortgaging our home?"

"Look at that now," Hagan said, smiling helplessly. "I've thrown away any advantage I might have had in the transaction. Rose, that's my wife, says I never learn. Still, let's sit down and talk it over." He pointed at the rubble wall, then glanced doubtfully at Selina's immaculate blue skirt. "Wait till I fetch a rug from the house." Hagan limped quickly into the cottage, closing the door behind him.

"Perhaps it wasn't such a marvelous idea to come up here," I whispered to Selina, "but you might at least be pleasant to the man. I think I can smell a bargain."

"Some hope," she said with deliberate coarseness. "Surely even you must have noticed that ancient dress his wife is wearing! He won't give much away to strangers."

"Was that his wife?"

"Of course that was his wife."

"Well, well," I said, surprised. "Anyway, try to be civil with him. I don't want to be embarrassed."

Selina snorted, but she smiled whitely when Hagan reappeared and I relaxed a little. Strange how a man can love a woman and yet at the same time pray for her to fall under a train.

Hagan spread a tartan blanket on the wall and we sat down, feeling slightly self-conscious at having been translated from our city-oriented lives into a rural tableau. On the distant slate of the loch, beyond the watchful frames of slow glass, a slow-moving steamer drew a white line toward the south. The boisterous mountain air seemed almost to invade our lungs, giving us more oxygen than we required.

"Some of the glass farmers around here," Hagan began, "give strangers, such as yourselves, a sales talk about how beautiful the autumn is in this part of Argyll. Or it might be the spring, or the winter. I don't do that—any fool knows that a place which doesn't look right in summer never looks right. What do you say?"

I nodded compliantly.

"I want you just to take a good look out toward Mull, Mr. . . ."

"Garland."

". . . Garland. That's what you're buying if you buy my glass, and it never looks better than it does at this minute. The glass is in perfect phase, none of it is less than ten years thick—and a four-foot window will cost you two hundred pounds."

"*Two hundred!*" Selina was shocked. "That's as much as they charge at the Scenedow shop in Bond Street."

Hagan smiled patiently, then looked closely at me to see if I knew enough about slow glass to appreciate what he had been saying. His price had been much higher than I had hoped—but *ten years thick*! The cheap glass one found in places like the

Vistaplex and Pane-o-rama stores usually consisted of a quarter of an inch of ordinary glass faced with a veneer of slow glass perhaps only ten or twelve months thick.

"You don't understand, darling," I said, already determined to buy. "This glass will last ten years and it's in phase."

"Doesn't that only mean it keeps time?"

Hagan smiled at her again, realizing he had no further necessity to bother with me. "Only, you say! Pardon me, Mrs. Garland, but you don't seem to appreciate the miracle, the genuine honest-to-goodness miracle, of engineering precision needed to produce a piece of glass in phase. When I say the glass is ten years thick it means it takes light ten years to pass through it. In effect, each one of those panes is ten light-years thick—more than twice the distance to the nearest star—so a variation in actual thickness of only a millionth of an inch would . . ."

He stopped talking for a moment and sat quietly looking toward the house. I turned my head from the view of the Loch and saw the young woman standing at the window again. Hagan's eyes were filled with a kind of greedy reverence which made me feel uncomfortable and at the same time convinced me Selina had been wrong. In my experience husbands never looked at wives that way—at least, not at their own.

The girl remained in view for a few seconds, dress glowing warmly, then moved back into the room. Suddenly I received a distinct, though inexplicable, impression she was blind. My feeling was that Selina and I were perhaps blundering through an emotional interplay as violent as our own.

"I'm sorry," Hagan continued; "I thought Rose was going to call me for something. Now, where was I, Mrs. Garland? Ten light-years compressed into a quarter of an inch means . . ."

I ceased to listen, partly because I was already sold, partly because I had heard the story of slow glass many times before and had never yet understood the principles involved. An acquaintance with scientific training had once tried to be helpful by telling me to visualize a pane of slow glass as a hologram which did not need coherent light from a laser for the reconstitution of its visual information, and in which every photon of ordinary light passed through a spiral tunnel coiled outside the radius of capture of each atom in the glass. This gem of, to me, incomprehensibility not only told me nothing, it convinced me once again that a mind as nontechnical as mine should concern itself less with causes than effects.

The most important effect, in the eyes of the average individual, was that light took a long time to pass through a sheet of slow glass. A new piece was always jet black because nothing had yet come through, but one could stand the glass beside, say, a woodland lake until the scene emerged, perhaps a year later. If the glass was then removed and installed in a dismal city flat, the flat would—for that year—appear to overlook the woodland lake. During the year it wouldn't be merely a very realistic but still picture—the water would ripple in sunlight, silent animals would come to drink, birds would cross the sky, night would follow day, season would follow season. Until one day, a year later, the beauty held in the subatomic pipelines would be exhausted and the familiar gray cityscape would reappear.

Apart from its stupendous novelty value, the commercial success of slow glass was founded on the fact that having a scenedow was the exact emotional equivalent of owning land. The meanest cave dweller could look out on misty parks—and who was to say they weren't his? A man who really owns tailored gardens and estates doesn't spend his time proving his ownership by crawling on his ground, feeling, smelling, tasting it. All he receives from the land are light patterns, and with scenedows those patterns could be taken into coal mines, submarines, prison cells.

On several occasions I have tried to write short pieces about the enchanted crystal but, to me, the theme is so ineffably poetic as to be, paradoxically, beyond the reach of poetry—mine, at any rate. Besides, the best songs and verse had already been written, with prescient inspiration, by men who had died long before slow glass was discovered. I had no hope of equaling, for example, Moore with his:

Oft in the stilly night,
Ere slumber's chain has bound me,
Fond Memory brings the light
Of other days around me . . .

It took only a few years for slow glass to develop from a scientific curiosity to a sizable industry. And much to the astonishment of us poets—those of us who remain convinced that beauty lives though lilies die—the trappings of that industry were no different from those of any other. There were good scenedows which cost a lot of money, and there were inferior scenedows which cost rather less. The thickness, measured in years, was an important factor in the cost but there was also the question of *actual* thickness, or phase.

Even with the most sophisticated engineering techniques available thickness control was something of a hit-and-miss affair. A coarse discrepancy could mean that a pane intended to be five years thick might be five and a half, so that light which entered in summer emerged in winter; a fine discrepancy could mean that noon sunshine emerged at midnight. These incompatibilities had their peculiar charm—many night workers, for example, liked having their own private time zones—but, in general, it cost more to buy scenedows which kept closely in step with real time.

Selina still looked unconvinced when Hagan had finished speaking. She shook her head almost imperceptibly and I knew he had been using the wrong approach. Quite suddenly the pewter helmet of her hair was disturbed by a cool gust of wind, and huge clean tumbling drops of rain began to spang round us from an almost cloudless sky.

"I'll give you a check now," I said abruptly, and saw Selina's green eyes triangulate angrily on my face. "You can arrange delivery?"

"Aye, delivery's no problem," Hagan said, getting to his feet. "But wouldn't you rather take the glass with you?"

"Well, yes—if you don't mind." I was shamed by his readiness to trust my scrip.

"I'll unclip a pane for you. Wait here. It won't take long to slip it into a carrying frame." Hagan limped down the slope towards the seriate windows, through some of which the view towards Linnhe was sunny, while others were cloudy and a few pure black.

Selina drew the collar of her blouse closed at her throat. "The least he could have done was invite us inside. There can't be so many fools passing through that he can afford to neglect them."

I tried to ignore the insult and concentrated on writing the check. One of the outsized drops broke across my knuckles, splattering the pink paper.

"All right," I said, "let's move in under the eaves till he gets back." *You worm,* I thought as I felt the whole thing go completely wrong. *I just had to be a fool to marry you. A prize fool, a fool's fool—and now that you've trapped part of me inside you I'll never ever, never ever,* never ever *get away.*

Feeling my stomach clench itself painfully, I ran behind Selina to the side of the cottage. Beyond the window the neat living room, with its coal fire, was empty but the child's toys were scattered on the floor. Alphabet blocks and a wheelbarrow the exact color of freshly pared carrots. As I stared in, the boy came running from the other room and began kicking the blocks. He didn't notice me. A few moments later the young woman entered the room and lifted him, laughing easily and wholeheartedly as she swung the boy under her arm. She came to the window as she had done earlier. I smiled self-consciously, but neither she nor the child responded.

My forehead prickled icily. *Could they both be blind?* I sidled away.

Selina gave a little scream and I spun towards her.

"The rug!" she said. "It's getting soaked."

She ran across the yard in the rain, snatched the reddish square from the dappling wall and ran back, toward the cottage door. Something heaved convulsively in my subconscious.

"Selina," I shouted. "Don't open it!"

But I was too late. She had pushed open the latched wooden door and was standing, hand over mouth, looking into the cottage. I moved close to her and took the rug from her unresisting fingers.

As I was closing the door I let my eyes traverse the cottage's interior. The neat living room in which I had just seen the woman and child was, in reality, a sickening clutter of shabby furniture, old newspapers, cast-off clothing and smeared dishes. It was damp, stinking and utterly deserted. The only object I recognized from my view through the window was the little wheelbarrow, paintless and broken.

I latched the door firmly and ordered myself to forget what I had seen. Some men who live alone are good housekeepers; others just don't know how.

Selina's face was white. "I don't understand. I don't understand it."

"Slow glass works both ways," I said gently. "Light passes out of a house, as well as in."

"You mean . . . ?"

"I don't know. It isn't our business. Now steady up—Hagan's coming back with our glass." The churning in my stomach was beginning to subside.

Hagan came into the yard carrying an oblong, plastic-covered frame. I held the check out to him, but he was staring at Selina's face. He seemed to know immediately that our uncomprehending fingers had rummaged through his soul. Selina avoided his gaze. She was old and ill-looking, and her eyes stared determinedly toward the nearing horizon.

"I'll take the rug from you, Mr. Garland," Hagan finally said. "You shouldn't have troubled yourself over it."

"No trouble. Here's the check."

"Thank you." He was still looking at Selina with a strange kind of supplication. "It's been a pleasure to do business with you."

"The pleasure was mine," I said with equal, senseless formality. I picked up the heavy frame and guided Selina toward the path which led to the road. Just as we reached the head of the now slippery steps Hagan spoke again.

"Mr. Garland!"

I turned unwillingly.

"It wasn't my fault," he said steadily. "A hit-and-run driver got them both, down on the Oban road six years ago. My boy was only seven when it happened. I'm entitled to keep something."

I nodded wordlessly and moved down the path, holding my wife close to me, treasuring the feel of her arms locked around me. At the bend I looked back through the rain and saw Hagan sitting with squared shoulders on the wall where we had first seen him.

He was looking at the house, but I was unable to tell if there was anyone at the window.

RAPPACCINI'S DAUGHTER

Nathaniel Hawthorne

Nathaniel Hawthorne, one of the great nineteenth-century American writers, was the principal conduit of Gothic science into American literature in the generation after Charles Brockden Brown, and remains secondary only to Mary Shelley (in *Frankenstein* [1818] and *The Last Man* [1826]) and Edgar Allan Poe as an influence on the Gothic elements that endure in science fiction to this day. "Rappaccini's Daughter," a masterpiece of the American short story, is one of the founding documents in the depiction of the doctor and scientist as devoted to (and sometimes perverted by) science and the quest for knowledge.

A scientist who "cares more for science than for mankind" has come up with a novel solution to keeping his daughter pure: because of an ingenious biochemical innovation, any man who touches Rappaccini's daughter without his approval will die. The story explores life in this parental garden of Eden when a handsome young man who falls in love with Rappaccini's daughter becomes a pawn in the rivalry between two ambitious scientists.

This is a tale of chemistry and medicine, love and poison, set in Italy, traditionally the land of evil poisoners and wellspring of distinguished physicians. It harks back to Elizabethan drama and folktale, and leads forward to the Faustian image of the mad scientist—who sacrifices moral virtue on the altar of knowledge—perhaps our primary modern version of original sin. It is in constant competition throughout the history and development of the literature with the Promethean image of the scientist as benign inventor, whose devotion to knowledge benefits humanity and whose devices better human life. This Faustian-Gothic strain, with its echoes of the sublime, is persistent in twentieth-century science fiction (Leslie Fiedler and Brian Aldiss both consider it characteristic of the genre) and re-emerges, full-blown, in the early work of J. G. Ballard (especially in "Prima Belladonna") and Aldiss. It is antithetical in imagery and in affect to the ideal of hard science fiction from Verne and most of Wells through Campbell's Modern sf. Yet this Gothic strain is always there in a significant number of works, casting a shadow of catastrophe and apocalypse over hard sf, from Wells's "The Star" to Fred Hoyle's *The Black Cloud* (1957) and James Tiptree, Jr.'s "The Psychologist Who Wouldn't Do Awful Things to Rats."

A young man, named Giovanni Guasconti, came, very long ago, from the more southern region of Italy, to pursue his studies at the University of Padua. Giovanni, who had but a scanty supply of gold ducats in his pocket, took lodgings in a high and gloomy chamber of an old edifice which looked not unworthy to have been the palace of a Paduan noble, and which, in fact, exhibited over its entrance the armorial bearings of a family long since extinct. The young stranger, who was not unstudied in the great poem of his country, recollected that one of the ancestors of this family, and perhaps an occupant of this very mansion, had been pictured by Dante as a partaker of the immortal agonies of his Inferno. These reminiscences and associations, together with the tendency to heartbreak natural to a young man for the first time out of his native sphere, caused Giovanni to sigh heavily as he looked around the desolate and ill-furnished apartment.

"Holy Virgin, signor!" cried old Dame Lisabetta, who, won by the youth's remarkable beauty of person, was kindly endeavoring to give the chamber a habitable air, "what a sigh was that to come out of a young man's heart! Do you find this old mansion gloomy? For the love of Heaven, then, put your head out of the window, and you will see as bright sunshine as you have left in Naples."

Guasconti mechanically did as the old woman advised, but could not quite agree with her that the Paduan sunshine was as cheerful as that of southern Italy. Such as it was, however, it fell upon a garden beneath the window and expended its fostering influences on a variety of plants, which seemed to have been cultivated with exceeding care.

"Does this garden belong to the house?" asked Giovanni.

"Heaven forbid, signor, unless it were fruitful of better pot herbs than any that grow there now," answered old Lisabetta. "No; that garden is cultivated by the own hands of Signor Giacomo Rappaccini, the famous doctor, who, I warrant him, has been heard of as far as Naples. It is said that he distils these plants into medicines that are as potent as a charm. Oftentimes you may see the signor doctor at work, and perchance the signora, his daughter, too, gathering the strange flowers that grow in the garden."

The old woman had now done what she could for the aspect of the chamber; and, commending the young man to the protection of the saints, took her departure.

Giovanni still found no better occupation than to look down into the garden beneath his window. From its appearance, he judged it to be one of those botanic gardens which were of earlier date in Padua than elsewhere in Italy or in the world. Or, not improbably, it might once have been the pleasure-place of an opulent family; for there was the ruin of a marble fountain in the centre, sculptured with rare art, but so wofully shattered that it was impossible to trace the original design from the chaos of remaining fragments. The water, however, continued to gush and sparkle into the sunbeams as cheerfully as ever. A little gurgling sound ascended to the young man's window and made him feel as if the fountain were an immortal spirit, that sung its song unceasingly and without heeding the vicissitudes around it, while one century imbodied it in marble and another scattered the perishable garniture on the soil. All about the pool into which the water subsided grew various plants, that seemed to require a plentiful supply of moisture for the nourishment of gigantic leaves, and, in some instances, flowers gorgeously magnificent. There was one shrub in particular, set in a marble vase in the midst of the pool, that bore a profusion of purple blossoms, each of which had the lustre and richness of a gem; and the whole together made a show so resplendent that it seemed enough to illuminate the garden, even had there been no sunshine. Every portion of the soil was peopled with plants and herbs, which, if less beautiful, still bore tokens of assiduous care, as if all had their individual virtues, known to the scientific mind that fostered them. Some were placed in urns, rich with old carving, and others in common garden pots; some crept serpent-like along the ground or climbed on high, using whatever means of ascent was offered them. One plant had wreathed itself round a statue of Vertumnus, which was thus quite veiled and shrouded in a drapery of hanging foliage, so happily arranged that it might have served a sculptor for a study.

While Giovanni stood at the window he heard a rustling behind a screen of leaves, and became aware that a person was at work in the garden. His figure soon emerged into view, and showed itself to be that of no common laborer, but a tall, emaciated, sallow, and sickly-looking man, dressed in a scholar's garb of black. He was beyond the middle term of life, with gray hair, a thin, gray beard, and a face singularly marked with intellect and cultivation, but which could never, even in his more youthful days, have expressed much warmth of heart.

Nothing could exceed the intentness with which this scientific gardener examined every shrub which grew in his path: it seemed as if he was looking into their inmost nature, making observations in regard to their creative essence, and discovering why one leaf grew in this shape and another in that, and wherefore such and such flowers differed among themselves in hue and perfume. Nevertheless, in spite of this deep intelligence on his part, there was no approach to intimacy between himself and these vegetable existences. On the contrary, he avoided their actual touch or the direct inhaling of their odors with a caution that impressed Giovanni most disagreeably; for the man's demeanor was that of one walking among malignant influences, such as savage beasts, or deadly snakes, or evil spirits, which, should he allow them one moment of license, would wreak upon him some terrible fatality. It was strangely frightful to the young man's imagination to see this air of insecurity in a person cultivating a garden, that most simple and innocent of human toils, and which had been alike the joy and labor of the unfallen parents of the race. Was this garden, then, the Eden of the present world? And this man, with such a perception of harm in what his own hands caused to grow,—was he the Adam?

The distrustful gardener, while plucking away the dead leaves or pruning the too luxuriant growth of the shrubs, defended his hands with a pair of thick gloves. Nor were these his only armor. When, in his walk through the garden, he came to the magnificent plant that hung its purple gems beside the marble fountain, he placed a kind of mask over his mouth and nostrils, as if all this beauty did but conceal a deadlier malice; but, finding his task still too dangerous, he drew back, removed the mask, and called loudly, but in the infirm voice of a person affected with inward disease,—

"Beatrice! Beatrice!"

"Here am I, my father. What would you?" cried a rich and youthful voice from the window of the opposite house—a voice as rich as a tropical sunset, and which made Giovanni, though he knew not why, think of deep hues of purple or crimson and of perfumes heavily delectable. "Are you in the garden?"

"Yes, Beatrice," answered the gardener; "and I need your help."

Soon there emerged from under a sculptured portal the figure of a young girl, arrayed with as much richness of taste as the most splendid of the flowers, beautiful as the day, and with a bloom so deep and vivid that one shade more would have been too much. She looked redundant with life, health, and energy; all of which attributes were bound down and compressed, as it were, and girdled tensely, in their luxuriance, by her virgin zone. Yet Giovanni's fancy must have grown morbid while he looked down into the garden; for the impression which the fair stranger made upon him was as if here were another flower, the human sister of those vegetable ones, as beautiful as they, more beautiful than the richest of them, but still to be touched only with a glove, nor to be approached without a mask. As Beatrice came down the garden path, it was observable that she handled and inhaled the odor of several of the plants which her father had most sedulously avoided.

"Here, Beatrice," said the latter, "see how many needful offices require to be done to our chief treasure. Yet, shattered as I am, my life might pay the penalty of approaching it so closely as circumstances demand. Henceforth, I fear, this plant must be consigned to your sole charge."

"And gladly will I undertake it," cried again the rich tones of the young lady, as she bent towards the magnificent plant and opened her arms as if to embrace it. "Yes, my sister, my splendor, it shall be Beatrice's task to nurse and serve thee; and thou shalt reward her with thy kisses and perfumed breath, which to her is as the breath of life."

Then, with all the tenderness in her manner that was so strikingly expressed in her words, she busied herself with such attentions as the plant seemed to require; and Giovanni, at his lofty window, rubbed his eyes, and almost doubted whether it were a girl tending her favorite flower, or one sister performing the duties of affection to another. The scene soon terminated. Whether Dr. Rappaccini had finished his labors in the garden, or that his watchful eye had caught the stranger's face, he now took his daughter's arm and retired. Night was already closing in; oppressive exhalations seemed to proceed from the plants and steal upward past the open window; and Giovanni, closing the lattice, went to his couch and dreamed of a rich flower and beautiful girl. Flower and maiden were different, and yet the same, and fraught with some strange peril in either shape.

But there is an influence in the light of morning that tends to rectify whatever errors of fancy, or even of judgment, we may have incurred during the sun's decline, or among the shadows of the night, or in the less wholesome glow of moonshine. Giovanni's first movement, on starting from sleep, was to throw open the window and gaze down into the garden which his dreams had made so fertile of mysteries. He was surprised, and a little ashamed, to find how real and matter-of-fact an affair it proved to be, in the first rays of the sun which gilded the dewdrops that hung upon leaf and blossom, and, while giving a brighter beauty to each rare flower, brought every thing within the limits of ordinary experience. The young man rejoiced that, in the heart of the barren city, he had the privilege of overlooking this spot of lovely and luxuriant vegetation. It would serve, he said to himself, as a symbolic language to keep him in communion with Nature. Neither the sickly and thoughtworn Dr. Giacomo Rappaccini, it is true, nor his brilliant daughter, were now visible; so that Giovanni could not determine how much of the singularity which he attributed to both was due to their own qualities and how much to his wonder-working fancy; but he was inclined to take a most rational view of the whole matter.

In the course of the day he paid his respects to Signor Pietro Baglioni, professor of medicine in the university, a physician of eminent repute, to whom Giovanni had brought a letter of introduction. The professor was an elderly personage, apparently of genial nature and habits that might almost be called jovial. He kept the young man to dinner, and made himself very agreeable by the freedom and liveliness of his conversation, especially when warmed by a flask or two of Tuscan wine. Giovanni, conceiving that men of science, inhabitants of the same city, must needs be on familiar terms with one another, took an opportunity to mention the name of Dr. Rappaccini. But the professor did not respond with so much cordiality as he had anticipated.

"Ill would it become a teacher of the divine art of medicine," said Professor Pietro Baglioni, in answer to a question of Giovanni, "to withhold due and well-considered praise of a physician so eminently skilled as Rappaccini; but, on the other hand, I should answer it but scantily to my conscience were I to permit a worthy youth like yourself, Signor Giovanni, the son of an ancient friend, to imbibe erroneous ideas respecting a man who might hereafter chance to hold your life and death in his hands. The truth is, our worshipful Dr. Rappaccini has as much science as any member of the faculty—with perhaps one single exception—in Padua, or all Italy; but there are certain grave objections to his professional character."

"And what are they?" asked the young man.

"Has my friend Giovanni any disease of body or heart, that he is so inquisitive about physicians?" said the professor, with a smile. "But as for Rappaccini, it is said of him—and I, who know the man well, can answer for its truth—that he cares infinitely more for science than for mankind. His patients are interesting to him only as subjects for some new experiment. He would sacrifice human life, his own among the rest, or whatever else was dearest to him, for the sake of adding so much as a grain of mustard seed to the great heap of his accumulated knowledge."

"Methinks he is an awful man indeed," remarked Guasconti, mentally recalling the cold and purely intellectual aspect of Rappaccini. "And yet, worshipful professor, is it not a noble spirit? Are there many men capable of so spiritual a love of science?"

"God forbid," answered the professor, somewhat testily; "at least, unless they take sounder views of the healing art than those adopted by Rappaccini. It is his theory that all medicinal virtues are comprised within those substances which we term vegetable poisons. These he cultivates with his own hands, and is said even to have produced new varieties of poison, more horribly deleterious than Nature, without the assistance of this learned person, would ever have plagued the world withal. That the signor doctor does less mischief than might be expected with such dangerous substances, is undeniable. Now and then, it must be owned, he has effected, or seemed to effect, a marvellous cure; but, to tell you my private mind, Signor Giovanni, he should receive little credit for such instances of success,—they being probably the work of chance,—but should be held strictly accountable for his failures, which may justly be considered his own work."

The youth might have taken Baglioni's opinions with many grains of allowance had he known that there was a professional warfare of long continuance between him and Dr. Rappaccini, in which the latter was generally thought to have gained the advantage. If the reader be inclined to judge for himself, we refer him to certain black-letter tracts on both sides, preserved in the medical department of the University of Padua.

"I know not, most learned professor," returned Giovanni, after musing on what had been said of Rappaccini's exclusive zeal for science,—"I know not how dearly this physician may love his art; but surely there is one object more dear to him. He has a daughter."

"Aha!" cried the professor, with a laugh. "So now our friend Giovanni's secret is out. You have heard of this daughter, whom all the young men in Padua are wild about, though not half a dozen have ever had the good hap to see her face. I know little of the Signora Beatrice save that Rappaccini is said to have instructed her deeply in his science, and that, young and beautiful as fame reports her, she is already qualified to fill a professor's chair. Perchance her father destines her for mine! Other absurd rumors there be, not worth talking about or listening to. So now, Signor Giovanni, drink off your glass of lachryma."

Guasconti returned to his lodgings somewhat heated with the wine he had quaffed, and which caused his brain to swim with strange fantasies in reference to Dr. Rappaccini and the beautiful Beatrice. On his way, happening to pass by a florist's, he bought a fresh bouquet of flowers.

Ascending to his chamber, he seated himself near the window, but within the shadow thrown by the depth of the wall, so that he could look down into the garden with little risk of being discovered. All beneath his eye was a solitude. The strange plants were basking in the sunshine, and now and then nodding gently to one another, as if in acknowledgment of sympathy and kindred. In the midst, by the shattered fountain, grew the magnificent shrub, with its purple gems clustering all over it; they glowed in the air, and gleamed back again out of the depths of the pool, which thus seemed to overflow with colored radiance from the rich reflection that was steeped in it. At first, as we have said, the garden was a solitude. Soon, however,—as Giovanni had half hoped, half feared, would be the case,—a figure appeared beneath the antique sculptured portal, and came down between the rows of plants, inhaling their various perfumes as if she were one of those beings of old classic fable that lived upon sweet odors. On again beholding Beatrice, the young man was even startled to perceive how much her beauty exceeded his recollection of it; so brilliant, so vivid, was its character, that she glowed amid the sunlight, and, as Giovanni whispered to himself, positively illuminated the more shadowy intervals of the garden path. Her face being now more revealed than on the former occasion, he was struck by its expression of simplicity and sweetness—qualities that had not entered into his idea of her character, and which made him ask anew what manner of mortal she might be. Nor did he fail again to observe, or imagine, an analogy between the beautiful girl and the gorgeous shrub that hung its gemlike flowers over the fountain—a resemblance which Beatrice seemed to have indulged a fantastic humor in heightening, both by the arrangement of her dress and the selection of its hues.

Approaching the shrub, she threw open her arms, as with a passionate ardor, and drew its branches into an intimate embrace—so intimate that her features were hidden in its leafy bosom and her glistening ringlets all intermingled with the flowers.

"Give me thy breath, my sister," exclaimed Beatrice; "for I am faint with common air. And give me this flower of thine, which I separate with gentlest fingers from the stem and place it close beside my heart."

With these words the beautiful daughter of Rappaccini plucked one of the richest blossoms of the shrub, and was about to fasten it in her bosom. But now, unless Giovanni's draughts of wine had bewildered his senses, a singular incident occurred. A small orange-colored reptile, of the lizard or chameleon species, chanced to be creeping along the path, just at the feet of Beatrice. It appeared to Giovanni,—but, at the distance from which he gazed, he could scarcely have seen any thing so minute,—it appeared to him, however, that a drop or two of moisture from the broken stem of the flower descended upon the lizard's head. For an instant the reptile contorted itself violently, and then lay motionless in the sunshine. Beatrice observed this remarkable phenomenon, and crossed herself, sadly, but without surprise; nor did she therefore hesitate to arrange the fatal flower in her bosom. There it blushed, and almost glimmered with the dazzling effect of a precious stone, adding to her dress and aspect the one appropriate charm which nothing else in the world could have supplied. But Giovanni, out of the shadow of his window, bent forward and shrank back, and murmured and trembled.

"Am I awake? Have I my senses?" said he to himself. "What is this being? Beautiful shall I call her, or inexpressibly terrible?"

Beatrice now strayed carelessly through the garden, approaching closer beneath Giovanni's window, so that he was compelled to thrust his head quite out of its concealment in order to gratify the intense and painful curiosity which she excited. At this moment there came a beautiful insect over the garden wall: it had, perhaps, wandered through the city, and found no flowers or verdure among those antique haunts of men until the heavy perfumes of Dr. Rappaccini's shrubs had lured it from afar. Without alighting on the flowers, this winged brightness seemed to be attracted by Beatrice, and lingered in the air and fluttered about her head. Now, here it could not be but that Giovanni Guasconti's eyes deceived him. Be that as it might, he fancied that, while Beatrice was gazing at the insect with childish delight, it grew faint and fell at her feet; its bright wings shivered; it was dead—from no cause that he could discern, unless it were the atmosphere of her breath. Again Beatrice crossed herself and sighed heavily as she bent over the dead insect.

An impulsive movement of Giovanni drew her eyes to the window. There she beheld the beautiful head of the young man—rather a Grecian than an Italian head, with fair, regular features, and a glistening of gold among his ringlets—gazing down upon her like a being that hovered in mid air. Scarcely knowing what he did, Giovanni threw down the bouquet which he had hitherto held in his hand.

"Signora," said he, "there are pure and healthful flowers. Wear them for the sake of Giovanni Guasconti."

"Thanks, signor," replied Beatrice, with her rich voice, that came forth as it were like a gush of music, and with a mirthful expression half childish and half womanlike. "I accept your gift, and would fain recompense it with this precious purple flower; but, if I toss it into the air, it will not reach you. So Signor Guasconti must even content himself with my thanks."

She lifted the bouquet from the ground, and then, as if inwardly ashamed at having stepped aside from her maidenly reserve to respond to a stranger's greeting, passed swiftly homeward through the garden. But, few as the moments were, it seemed to Giovanni, when she was on the point of vanishing beneath the sculptured portal, that his beautiful bouquet was already beginning to wither in her grasp. It was an idle thought; there could be no possibility of distinguishing a faded flower from a fresh one at so great a distance.

For many days after this incident the young man avoided the window that looked into Dr. Rappaccini's garden, as if something ugly and monstrous would have blasted his eyesight had he been betrayed into a glance. He felt conscious of having put himself, to a certain extent, within the influence of an unintelligible power by the communication which he had opened with Beatrice. The wisest course would have been, if his heart were in any real danger, to quit his lodgings and Padua itself at once; the next wiser, to have accustomed himself, as far as possible, to the familiar and daylight view of Beatrice—thus bringing her rigidly and systematically within the limits of ordinary experience. Least of all, while avoiding her sight, ought Giovanni to have remained so near this extraordinary being that the proximity and possibility even of intercourse should give a kind of substance and reality to the wild vagaries which his imagination ran riot continually in producing. Guasconti had not a deep heart—or, at all events, its depths were not sounded now; but he had a quick fancy, and an ardent southern temperament, which rose every instant to a higher fever pitch. Whether or no Beatrice possessed those terrible attributes, that fatal breath, the affinity with those so beautiful and deadly flowers which were indicated by what Giovanni had witnessed, she had at least instilled a fierce and subtle poison into his system. It was not love, although her rich beauty was a madness to him; nor horror, even while he fancied her spirit to be imbued with the same baneful essence that seemed to pervade her physical frame; but a wild offspring of both love and horror that had each parent in it, and burned like one and shivered like the other. Giovanni knew not what to dread; still less did he know what to hope; yet hope and dread kept a continual warfare in his breast, alternately vanquishing one another and starting up afresh to renew the contest. Blessed are all simple emotions, be they dark or bright! It is the lurid intermixture of the two that produces the illuminating blaze of the infernal regions.

Sometimes he endeavored to assuage the fever of his spirit by a rapid walk through the streets of Padua or beyond its gates: his footsteps kept time with the throbbings of his brain, so that the walk was apt to accelerate itself to a race. One day he found himself arrested; his arm was seized by a portly personage, who had turned back on recognizing the young man and expended much breath in overtaking him.

"Signor Giovanni! Stay, my young friend!" cried he. "Have you forgotten me? That might well be the case if I were as much altered as yourself."

It was Baglioni, whom Giovanni had avoided ever since their first meeting, from a doubt that the professor's sagacity would look too deeply into his secrets. Endeavoring to recover himself, he stared forth wildly from his inner world into the outer one and spoke like a man in a dream.

"Yes; I am Giovanni Guasconti. You are Professor Pietro Baglioni. Now let me pass!"

"Not yet, not yet, Signor Giovanni Guasconti," said the professor, smiling, but at the same time scrutinizing the youth with an earnest glance. "What! did I grow up side by side with your father? and shall his son pass me like a stranger in these old streets of Padua? Stand still, Signor Giovanni; for we must have a word or two before we part."

"Speedily, then, most worshipful professor, speedily," said Giovanni, with feverish impatience. "Does not your worship see that I am in haste?"

Now, while he was speaking there came a man in black along the street, stooping and moving feebly like a person in inferior health. His face was all overspread with a most sickly and sallow hue, but yet so pervaded with an expression of piercing and active intellect that an observer might easily have overlooked the merely physical attributes and have seen only this wonderful energy. As he passed, this person exchanged a cold and distant salutation with Baglioni, but fixed his eyes upon Giovanni with an intentness that seemed to bring out whatever was within him worthy of notice. Nevertheless, there was a peculiar quietness in the look, as if taking merely a speculative, not a human, interest in the young man.

"It is Dr. Rappaccini!" whispered the professor when the stranger had passed. "Has he ever seen your face before?"

"Not that I know," answered Giovanni, starting at the name.

"He *has* seen you! he must have seen you!" said Baglioni, hastily. "For some purpose or other, this man of science is making a study of you. I know that look of his! It is the same that coldly illuminates his face as he bends over a bird, a mouse, or a butterfly; which, in pursuance of some experiment, he has killed by the perfume of a flower; a look as deep as Nature itself, but without Nature's warmth of love. Signor Giovanni, I will stake my life upon it, you are the subject of one of Rappaccini's experiments!"

"Will you make a fool of me?" cried Giovanni, passionately. "*That*, signor professor, were an untoward experiment."

"Patience! patience!" replied the imperturbable professor. "I tell thee, my poor Giovanni, that Rappaccini has a scientific interest in thee. Thou hast fallen into fearful hands! And the Signora Beatrice,—what part does she act in this mystery?"

But Guasconti, finding Baglioni's pertinacity intolerable, here broke away, and was gone before the professor could again seize his arm. He looked after the young man intently and shook his head.

"This must not be," said Baglioni to himself. "The youth is the son of my old friend, and shall not come to any harm from which the arcana of medical science can preserve him. Besides, it is too insufferable an impertinence in Rappaccini thus to snatch the lad out of my own hands, as I may say, and make use of him for his infernal experiments. This daughter of his! It shall be looked to. Perchance, most learned Rappaccini, I may foil you where you little dream of it!"

Meanwhile Giovanni had pursued a circuitous route, and at length found himself at the door of his lodgings. As he crossed the threshold he was met by old Lisabetta, who smirked and smiled, and was evidently desirous to attract his attention; vainly, however, as the ebullition of his feelings had momentarily subsided into a cold and dull vacuity. He turned his eyes full upon the withered face that was puckering itself into a smile, but seemed to behold it not. The old dame, therefore, laid her grasp upon his cloak.

"Signor! signor!" whispered she, still with a smile over the whole breadth of her visage, so that it looked not unlike a grotesque carving in wood, darkened by centuries. "Listen, signor! There is a private entrance into the garden!"

"What do you say?" exclaimed Giovanni, turning quickly about, as if an inanimate thing should start into feverish life. "A private entrance into Dr. Rappaccini's garden?"

"Hush! hush! not so loud!" whispered Lisabetta, putting her hand over his mouth. "Yes; into the worshipful doctor's garden, where you may see all his fine shrubbery. Many a young man in Padua would give gold to be admitted among those flowers."

Giovanni put a piece of gold into her hand.

"Show me the way," said he.

A surmise, probably excited by his conversation with Baglioni, crossed his mind, that this interposition of old Lisabetta might perchance be connected with the intrigue, whatever were its nature, in which the professor seemed to suppose that Dr. Rappaccini was involving him. But such a suspicion, though it disturbed Giovanni, was inadequate to restrain him. The instant that he was aware of the possibility of approaching Beatrice, it seemed an absolute necessity of his existence to do so. It mattered not whether she were angel or demon; he was irrevocably within her sphere, and must obey the law that whirled him onward, in everlessening circles, towards a result which he did not attempt to foreshadow; and yet, strange to say, there came across him a sudden doubt whether this intense interest on his part were not delusory; whether it were really of so deep and positive a nature as to justify him in now thrusting himself into an incalculable position; whether it were not merely the fantasy of a young man's brain, only slightly or not at all connected with his heart.

He paused, hesitated, turned half about, but again went on. His withered guide led him along several obscure passages, and finally undid a door, through which, as it was opened, there came the sight and sound of rustling leaves, with the broken sunshine glimmering among them. Giovanni stepped forth, and, forcing himself through the entanglement of a shrub that wreathed its tendrils over the hidden entrance, stood beneath his own window in the open area of Dr. Rappaccini's garden.

How often is it the case that, when impossibilities have come to pass and dreams have condensed their misty substance into tangible realities, we find ourselves calm, and even coldly self-possessed, amid circumstances which it would have been a delirium of joy or agony to anticipate! Fate delights to thwart us thus. Passion will choose his own time to rush upon the scene, and lingers sluggishly behind when an appropriate adjustment of events would seem to summon his appearance. So was it now with Giovanni. Day after day his pulses had throbbed with feverish blood at the improbable idea of an interview with Beatrice, and of standing with her, face to face, in this very garden, basking in the Oriental sunshine of her beauty, and snatching from her full gaze the mystery which he deemed the riddle of his own existence. But now there was a singular and untimely equanimity within his breast. He threw a glance around the garden to discover if Beatrice or her father were present, and, perceiving that he was alone, began a critical observation of the plants.

The aspect of one and all of them dissatisfied him; their gorgeousness seemed fierce, passionate, and even unnatural. There was hardly an individual shrub which a wanderer, straying by himself through a forest, would not have been startled to find growing wild, as if an unearthly face had glared at him out of the thicket. Several also would have shocked a delicate instinct by an appearance of artificialness indicating that there had been such commixture, and, as it were, adultery of various vegetable species, that the production was no longer of God's making, but the monstrous offspring of man's depraved fancy, glowing with only an evil mockery of beauty. They were probably the result of experiment, which in one or two cases had succeeded in mingling plants individually lovely into a compound possessing the questionable and ominous character that distinguished the whole growth of the garden. In fine, Giovanni recognized but two or three plants in the collection, and those of a kind that he well knew to be poisonous. While busy with these contemplations he heard the rustling of a silken garment, and, turning, beheld Beatrice emerging from beneath the sculptured portal.

Giovanni had not considered with himself what should be his deportment; whether he should apologize for his intrusion into the garden, or assume that he was there with the privity at least, if not by the desire, of Dr. Rappaccini or his daughter; but Beatrice's manner placed him at his ease, though leaving him still in doubt by what agency he had gained admittance. She came lightly along the path and met him near the broken fountain. There was surprise in her face, but brightened by a simple and kind expression of pleasure.

"You are a connoisseur in flowers, signor," said Beatrice, with a smile, alluding to the bouquet which he had flung her from the window. "It is no marvel, therefore, if the sight of my father's rare collection has tempted you to take a nearer view. If he were here, he could tell you many strange and interesting facts as to the nature and habits of these shrubs; for he has spent a lifetime in such studies, and this garden is his world."

"And yourself, lady," observed Giovanni, "if fame says true,—you likewise are deeply skilled in the virtues indicated by these rich blossoms and these spicy perfumes. Would you deign to be my instructress, I should prove an apter scholar than if taught by Signor Rappaccini himself."

"Are there such idle rumors?" asked Beatrice, with the music of a pleasant laugh. "Do people say that I am skilled in my father's science of plants? What a jest is there! No; though I have grown up among these flowers, I know no more of them than their hues and perfume; and sometimes methinks I would fain rid myself of even that small knowledge. There are many flowers here, and those not the least brilliant, that shock and offend me when they meet my eye. But pray, signor, do not believe these stories about my science. Believe nothing of me save what you see with your own eyes."

"And must I believe all that I have seen with my own eyes?" asked Giovanni, pointedly, while the recollection of former scenes made him shrink. "No, signora; you demand too little of me. Bid me believe nothing save what comes from your own lips."

It would appear that Beatrice understood him. There came a deep flush to her cheek; but she looked full into Giovanni's eyes, and responded to his gaze of uneasy suspicion with a queenlike haughtiness.

"I do so bid you, signor," she replied. "Forget whatever you may have fancied in regard to me. If true to the outward senses, still it may be false in its essence; but the words of Beatrice Rappaccini's lips are true from the depths of the heart outward. Those you may believe."

A fervor glowed in her whole aspect and beamed upon Giovanni's consciousness like the light of truth itself; but while she spoke there was a fragrance in the atmosphere around her, rich and delightful, though evanescent, yet which the young man, from an indefinable reluctance, scarcely dared to draw into his lungs. It might be the odor of the flowers. Could it be Beatrice's breath which thus embalmed her words with a strange richness, as if by steeping them in her heart? A faintness passed like a shadow over Giovanni and flitted away; he seemed to gaze through the beautiful girl's eyes into her transparent soul, and felt no more doubt or fear.

The tinge of passion that had colored Beatrice's manner vanished; she became gay, and appeared to derive a pure delight from her communion with the youth not unlike what the maiden of a lonely island might have felt conversing with a voyager from the civilized world. Evidently her experience of life had been confined within the limits of that garden. She talked now about matters as simple as the daylight or summer clouds, and now asked questions in reference to the city, or Giovanni's distant home, his friends, his mother, and his sisters—questions indicating such seclusion, and such lack of familiarity with modes and forms, that Giovanni responded as if to an infant. Her spirit gushed out before him like a fresh rill that was just catching its first glimpse of the sunlight and wondering at the reflections of earth and sky which were flung into its bosom. There came thoughts, too, from a deep source, and fantasies of a gemlike brilliancy, as if diamonds and rubies sparkled upward among the bubbles of the fountain. Ever and anon there gleamed across the young man's mind a sense of wonder that he should be walking side by side with the being who had so wrought upon his imagination, whom he had idealized in such hues of terror, in whom he had positively witnessed such manifestations of dreadful attributes—that he should be conversing with Beatrice like a brother, and should find her so human and so maidenlike. But such reflections were only momentary; the effect of her character was too real not to make itself familiar at once.

In this free intercourse they had strayed through the garden, and now, after many turns among its avenues, were come to the shattered fountain, beside which grew the magnificent shrub, with its treasury of glowing blossoms. A fragrance was diffused from it which Giovanni recognized as identical with that which he had attributed to Beatrice's breath, but incomparably more powerful. As her eyes fell upon it, Giovanni beheld her press her hand to her bosom as if her heart were throbbing suddenly and painfully.

"For the first time in my life," murmured she, addressing the shrub, "I had forgotten thee."

"I remember, signora," said Giovanni, "that you once promised to reward me with one of these living gems for the bouquet which I had the happy boldness to fling to your feet. Permit me now to pluck it as a memorial of this interview."

He made a step towards the shrub with extended hand; but Beatrice darted forward, uttering a shriek that went through his heart like a dagger. She caught his hand and drew it back with the whole force of her slender figure. Giovanni felt her touch thrilling through his fibres. "Touch it not!" exclaimed she, in a voice of agony. "Not for thy life! It is fatal!"

Then, hiding her face, she fled from him and vanished beneath the sculptured portal. As Giovanni followed her with his eyes, he beheld the emaciated figure and pale intelligence of Dr. Rappaccini, who had been watching the scene, he knew not how long, within the shadow of the entrance.

No sooner was Guasconti alone in his chamber than the image of Beatrice came back to his passionate musings, invested with all the witchery that had been gathering around it ever since his first glimpse of her, and now likewise imbued with a tender warmth of girlish womanhood. She was human; her nature was endowed with all gentle and feminine qualities; she was worthiest to be worshipped; she was capable, surely, on her part, of the height and heroism of love. Those tokens which he had hitherto considered as proofs of a frightful peculiarity in her physical and moral system were now either forgotten or by the subtle sophistry of passion transmitted into a golden crown of enchantment, rendering Beatrice the more admirable by so much as she was the more unique. Whatever had looked ugly was now beautiful; or, if incapable of such a change, it stole away and hid itself among those shapeless half ideas which throng the dim region beyond the daylight of our perfect consciousness. Thus did he spend the night, nor fell asleep until the dawn had begun to awake the slumbering flowers in Dr. Rappaccini's garden, whither Giovanni's dreams doubtless led him. Up rose the sun in his due season, and, flinging his beams upon the young man's eyelids, awoke him to a sense of pain. When thoroughly aroused, he became sensible of a burning and tingling agony in his hand—in his right hand—the very hand which Beatrice had grasped in her own when he was on the point of plucking one of the gemlike flowers. On the back of that hand there was now a purple print like that of four small fingers, and the likeness of a slender thumb upon his wrist.

O, how stubbornly does love,—or even that cunning semblance of love which flourishes in the imagination, but strikes no depth of root into the heart,—how stubbornly does it hold its faith until the moment comes when it is doomed to vanish into thin mist! Giovanni wrapped a handkerchief about his hand and wondered what evil thing had stung him, and soon forgot his pain in a revery of Beatrice.

After the first interview, a second was in the inevitable course of what we call fate. A third; a fourth; and a meeting with Beatrice in the garden was no longer an incident in Giovanni's daily life, but the whole space in which he might be said to live; for the anticipation and memory of that ecstatic hour made up the remainder. Nor was it otherwise with the daughter of Rappaccini. She watched for the youth's appearance and flew to his side with confidence as unreserved as if they had been playmates from early infancy—as if they were such playmates still. If, by any unwonted chance, he failed to come at the appointed moment, she stood beneath the window and sent up the rich sweetness of her tones to float around him in his chamber and echo and reverberate throughout his heart: "Giovanni! Giovanni! Why tarriest thou? Come down!" And down he hastened into that Eden of poisonous flowers.

But, with all this intimate familiarity, there was still a reserve in Beatrice's demeanor, so rigidly and invariably sustained that the idea of infringing it scarcely occurred to his imagination. By all appreciable signs, they loved; they had looked love with eyes that conveyed the holy secret from the depths of one soul into the depths of the other, as if it were too sacred to be whispered by the way; they had even spoken love in those gushes of passion when their spirits darted forth in articulated breath like tongues of long hidden flame; and yet there had been no seal of lips, no clasp of hands, nor any slightest caress such as love claims and hallows. He had never touched one of the gleaming ringlets of her hair; her garment—so marked was the physical barrier between them—had never been waved against him by a breeze. On the few occasions when Giovanni had seemed tempted to overstep the limit, Beatrice grew so sad, so stern, and withal wore such a look of desolate separation, shuddering at itself, that not a spoken word was requisite to repel him. At such time he was startled at the horrible suspicions that rose, monsterlike, out of the caverns of his heart and stared him in the face; his love grew thin and faint as the morning mist; his doubts alone had substance. But, when Beatrice's face brightened again after the momentary shadow, she was transformed at once from the mysterious, questionable being whom he had watched with so much awe and horror; she was now the beautiful and unsophisticated girl whom he felt that his spirit knew with a certainty beyond all other knowledge.

A considerable time had now passed since Giovanni's last meeting with Baglioni. One morning, however, he was disagreeably surprised by a visit from the professor, whom he had scarcely thought of for whole weeks, and would willingly have forgotten still longer. Given up as he had long been to a pervading excitement, he could tolerate no companions except upon condition of their perfect sympathy with his present state of feeling. Such sympathy was not to be expected from Professor Baglioni.

The visitor chatted carelessly for a few moments about the gossip of the city and the university, and then took up another topic.

"I have been reading an old classic author lately," said he, "and met with a story that strangely interested me. Possibly you may remember it. It is of an Indian prince, who sent a beautiful woman as a present to Alexander the Great. She was as lovely as the dawn and gorgeous as the sunset; but what especially distinguished her was a certain rich perfume in her breath—richer than a garden of Persian roses. Alexander, as was natural to a youthful conqueror, fell in love at first sight with this magnificent stranger; but a certain sage physician, happening to be present, discovered a terrible secret in regard to her."

"And what was that?" asked Giovanni, turning his eyes downward to avoid those of the professor.

"That this lovely woman," continued Baglioni, with emphasis, "had been nourished with poisons from her birth upward, until her whole nature was so imbued with them that she herself had become the deadliest poison in existence. Poison was her element of life. With that rich perfume of her breath she blasted the very air. Her love would have been poison—her embrace death. Is not this a marvellous tale?"

"A childish fable," answered Giovanni, nervously starting from his chair. "I marvel how your worship finds time to read such nonsense among your graver studies."

"By the by," said the professor, looking uneasily about him, "what singular fragrance is this in your apartment? Is it the perfume of your gloves? It is faint, but delicious; and yet, after all, by no means agreeable. Were I to breathe it long, methinks it would make me ill. It is like the breath of a flower; but I see no flowers in the chamber."

"Nor are there any," replied Giovanni, who had turned pale as the professor spoke; "nor, I think, is there any fragrance except in your worship's imagination. Odors, being a sort of element combined of the sensual and the spiritual, are apt to deceive us in this manner. The recollection of a perfume, the bare idea of it, may easily be mistaken for a present reality."

"Ay; but my sober imagination does not often play such tricks," said Baglioni; "and, were I to fancy any kind of odor, it would be that of some vile apothecary drug, wherewith my fingers are likely enough to be imbued. Our worshipful friend Rappaccini, as I have heard, tinctures his medicaments with odors richer than those of Araby. Doubtless, likewise, the fair and learned Signora Beatrice would minister to her patients with draughts as sweet as a maiden's breath; but woe to him that sips them!"

Giovanni's face evinced many contending emotions. The tone in which the professor alluded to the pure and lovely daughter of Rappaccini was a torture to his soul; and yet the intimation of a view of her character, opposite to his own, gave instantaneous distinctness to a thousand dim suspicions, which now grinned at him like so many demons. But he strove hard to quell them and to respond to Baglioni with a true lover's perfect faith.

"Signor professor," said he, "you were my father's friend; perchance, too, it is your purpose to act a friendly part towards his son. I would fain feel nothing towards you save respect and deference; but I pray you to observe, signor, that there is one subject on which we must not speak. You know not the Signora Beatrice. You cannot, therefore, estimate the wrong—the blasphemy, I may even say—that is offered to her character by a light or injurious word."

"Giovanni! my poor Giovanni!" answered the professor, with a calm expression of pity, "I know this wretched girl far better than yourself. You shall hear the truth in respect to the poisoner Rappaccini and his poisonous daughter; yes, poisonous as she is beautiful. Listen; for, even should you do violence to my gray hairs, it shall not silence me. That old fable of the Indian woman has become a truth by the deep and deadly science of Rappaccini and in the person of the lovely Beatrice."

Giovanni groaned and hid his face.

"Her father," continued Baglioni, "was not restrained by natural affection from offering up his child in this horrible manner as the victim of his insane zeal for science; for, let us do him justice, he is as true a man of science as ever distilled his own heart in an alembic. What, then, will be your fate? Beyond a doubt you are selected as the material of some new experiment. Perhaps the result is to be death; perhaps a fate more awful still. Rappaccini, with what he calls the interest of science before his eyes, will hesitate at nothing."

"It is a dream," muttered Giovanni to himself; "surely it is a dream."

"But," resumed the professor, "be of good cheer, son of my friend. It is not yet too late for the rescue. Possibly we may even succeed in bringing back this miserable child within the limits of ordinary nature, from which her father's madness has estranged her. Behold this little silver vase! It was wrought by the hands of the renowned Benvenuto Cellini, and is well worthy to be a love gift to the fairest dame in Italy. But its contents are invaluable. One little sip of this antidote would have rendered the most virulent poisons of the Borgias innocuous. Doubt not that it will be as efficacious against those of Rappaccini. Bestow the vase, and the precious liquid within it, on your Beatrice, and hopefully await the result."

Baglioni laid a small, exquisitely wrought silver vial on the table and withdrew, leaving what he had said to produce its effect upon the young man's mind.

"We will thwart Rappaccini yet," thought he, chuckling to himself, as he descended the stairs; "but, let us confess the truth of him, he is a wonderful man—a wonderful man indeed; a vile empiric, however, in his practice, and therefore not to be tolerated by those who respect the good old rules of the medical profession."

Throughout Giovanni's whole acquaintance with Beatrice, he had occasionally, as we have said, been haunted by dark surmises as to her character; yet so thoroughly had she made herself felt by him as a simple, natural, most affectionate, and guileless creature, that the image now held up by Professor Baglioni looked as strange and incredible as if it were not in accordance with his own original conception. True, there were ugly recollections connected with his first glimpses of the beautiful girl; he could not quite forget the bouquet that withered in her grasp, and the insect that perished amid the sunny air, by no ostensible agency save the fragrance of her breath. These incidents, however, dissolving in the pure light of her character, had no longer the efficacy of facts, but were acknowledged as mistaken fantasies, by whatever testimony of the senses they might appear to be substantiated. There is something truer and more real than what we can see with the eyes and touch with the finger. On such better evidence had Giovanni founded his confidence in Beatrice, though rather by the necessary force of her high attributes than by any deep and generous faith on his part. But now his spirit was incapable of sustaining itself at the height to which the early enthusiasm of passion had exalted it; he fell down, grovelling among earthly doubts, and defiled therewith the pure whiteness of Beatrice's image. Not that he gave her up; he did but distrust. He resolved to institute some decisive test that should satisfy him, once for all, whether there were those dreadful peculiarities in her physical nature which could not be supposed to exist without some corresponding monstrosity of soul. His eyes, gazing down afar, might have deceived him as to the lizard, the insect, and the flowers; but if he could witness, at the distance of a few paces, the sudden blight of one fresh and healthful flower in Beatrice's hand, there would be room for no further question. With this idea he hastened to the florist's and purchased a bouquet that was still gemmed with the morning dewdrops.

It was now the customary hour of his daily interview with Beatrice. Before descending into the garden, Giovanni failed not to look at his figure in the mirror—a vanity to be expected in a beautiful young man, yet, as displaying itself at that troubled and feverish moment, the token of a certain shallowness of feeling and insincerity of character. He did gaze, however, and said to himself that his features had never before possessed so rich a grace, nor his eyes such vivacity, nor his cheeks so warm a hue of superabundant life.

"At least," thought he, "her poison has not yet insinuated itself into my system. I am no flower to perish in her grasp."

With that thought he turned his eyes on the bouquet, which he had never once laid aside from his hand. A thrill of indefinable horror shot through his frame on perceiving that those dewy flowers were already beginning to droop; they wore the aspect of things that had been fresh and lovely yesterday. Giovanni grew white as marble, and stood motionless before the mirror, staring at his own reflection there as at the likeness of something frightful. He remembered Baglioni's remark about the fragrance that seemed to pervade the chamber. It must have been the poison in his breath! Then he shuddered—shuddered at himself. Recovering from his stupor, he began to watch with curious eye a spider that was busily at work hanging its web from the antique cornice of the apartment, crossing and recrossing the artful system of interwoven lines—as vigorous and active a spider as ever dangled from an old ceiling. Giovanni bent towards the insect, and emitted a deep, long breath. The spider suddenly ceased its toil; the web vibrated with a tremor originating in the body of the small artisan. Again Giovanni sent forth a breath, deeper, longer, and imbued with a venomous feeling out of his heart: he knew not whether he were wicked, or only desperate. The spider made a convulsive gripe with his limbs and hung dead across the window.

"Accursed! accursed!" muttered Giovanni, addressing himself. "Hast thou grown so poisonous that this deadly insect perishes by thy breath?"

At that moment a rich, sweet voice came floating up from the garden.

"Giovanni! Giovanni! It is past the hour! Why tarriest thou? Come down!"

"Yes," muttered Giovanni again. "She is the only being whom my breath may not slay! Would that it might!"

He rushed down, and in an instant was standing before the bright and loving eyes of Beatrice. A moment ago his wrath and despair had been so fierce that he could have desired nothing so much as to wither her by a glance; but with her actual presence there came influences which had too real an existence to be at once shaken off; recollections of the delicate and benign power of her feminine nature, which had so often enveloped him in a religious calm; recollections of many a holy and passionate outgush of her heart, when the pure fountain had been unsealed from its depths and made visible in its transparency to his mental eye; recollections which, had Giovanni known how to estimate them, would have assured him that all this ugly mystery was but an earthly illusion, and that, whatever mist of evil might seem to have gathered over her, the real Beatrice was a heavenly angel. Incapable as he was of such high faith, still her presence had not utterly lost its magic. Giovanni's rage was quelled into an aspect of sullen insensibility. Beatrice, with a quick spiritual sense, immediately felt that there was a gulf of blackness between them which neither he nor she could pass. They walked on together, sad and silent, and came thus to the marble fountain and to its pool of water on the ground, in the midst of which grew the shrub that bore gemlike blossoms. Giovanni was affrighted at the eager enjoyment—the appetite, as it were—with which he found himself inhaling the fragrance of the flowers.

"Beatrice," asked he, abruptly, "whence came this shrub?"

"My father created it," answered she, with simplicity.

"Created it! created it!" repeated Giovanni. "What mean you, Beatrice?"

"He is a man fearfully acquainted with the secrets of Nature," replied Beatrice; "and, at the hour when I first drew breath, this plant sprang from the soil, the offspring of his science, of his intellect, while I was but his earthly child. Approach it not!" continued she, observing with terror that Giovanni was drawing nearer to the shrub. "It has qualities that you little dream of. But I, dearest Giovanni,—I grew up and blossomed with the plant and was nourished with its breath. It was my sister, and I loved it with a human affection; for, alas!—hast thou not suspected it?—there was an awful doom."

Here Giovanni frowned so darkly upon her that Beatrice paused and trembled. But her faith in his tenderness reassured her, and made her blush that she had doubted for an instant.

"There was an awful doom," she continued, "the effect of my father's fatal love of science, which estranged me from all society of my kind. Until Heaven sent thee, dearest Giovanni, O, how lonely was thy poor Beatrice!"

"Was it a hard doom?" asked Giovanni, fixing his eyes upon her.

"Only of late have I known how hard it was," answered she, tenderly. "O, yes; but my heart was torpid, and therefore quiet."

Giovanni's rage broke forth from his sullen gloom like a lightning flash out of a dark cloud.

"Accursed one!" cried he, with venomous scorn and anger. "And, finding thy solitude wearisome, thou hast severed me likewise from all the warmth of life and enticed me into thy region of unspeakable horror!"

"Giovanni!" exclaimed Beatrice, turning her large bright eyes upon his face. The force of his words had not found its way into her mind; she was merely thunderstruck.

"Yes, poisonous thing!" repeated Giovanni, beside himself with passion. "Thou hast done it! Thou hast blasted me! Thou hast filled my veins with poison! Thou hast made me as hateful, as ugly, as loathsome and deadly a creature as thyself—a world's wonder of hideous monstrosity! Now, if our breath be happily as fatal to ourselves as to all others, let us join our lips in one kiss of unutterable hatred, and so die!"

"What has befallen me?" murmured Beatrice, with a low moan out of her heart. "Holy Virgin, pity me, a poor heart-broken child!"

"Thou,—dost thou pray?" cried Giovanni, still with the same fiendish scorn. "Thy very prayers, as they come from thy lips, taint the atmosphere with death. Yes, yes; let us pray! Let us to church and dip our fingers in the holy water at the portal! They that come after us will perish as by a pestilence! Let us sign crosses in the air! It will be scattering curses abroad in the likeness of holy symbols!"

"Giovanni," said Beatrice, calmly, for her grief was beyond passion, "why dost thou join thyself with me thus in those terrible words? I, it is true, am the horrible thing thou namest me. But thou,—what hast thou to do, save with one other shudder at my hideous misery to go forth out of the garden and mingle with thy race, and forget that there ever crawled on earth such a monster as poor Beatrice?"

"Dost thou pretend ignorance?" asked Giovanni, scowling upon her. "Behold! this power have I gained from the pure daughter of Rappaccini."

There was a swarm of summer insects flitting through the air in search of the food promised by the flower odors of the fatal garden. They circled round Giovanni's head, and were evidently attracted towards him by the same influence which had drawn them for an instant within the sphere of several of the shrubs. He sent forth a breath among them, and smiled bitterly at Beatrice as at least a score of the insects fell dead upon the ground.

"I see it! I see it!" shrieked Beatrice. "It is my father's fatal science! No, no, Giovanni; it was not I! Never! never! I dreamed only to love thee and be with thee a little time, and so to let thee pass away, leaving but thine image in mine heart; for, Giovanni, believe it, though my body be nourished with poison, my spirit is God's creature, and craves love as its daily food. But my father,—he has united us in this fearful sympathy. Yes; spurn me, tread upon me, kill me! O, what is death after such words as thine? But it was not I. Not for a world of bliss would I have done it."

Giovanni's passion had exhausted itself in its outburst from his lips. There now came across him a sense, mournful, and not without tenderness, of the intimate and peculiar relationship between Beatrice and himself. They stood, as it were, in an utter solitude, which would be made none the less solitary by the densest throng of human life. Ought not, then, the desert of humanity around them to press this insulated pair closer together? If they should be cruel to one another, who was there to be kind to them? Besides, thought Giovanni, might there not still be a hope of his returning within the limits of ordinary nature, and leading Beatrice, the redeemed Beatrice, by the hand? O, weak, and selfish, and unworthy spirit, that could dream of an earthly union and earthly happiness as possible, after such deep love had been so bitterly wronged as was Beatrice's love by Giovanni's blighting words! No, no; there could be no such hope. She must pass heavily, with that broken heart, across the borders of Time—she must bathe her hurts in some fount of paradise, and forget her grief in the light of immortality, and *there* be well.

But Giovanni did not know it.

"Dear Beatrice," said he, approaching her, while she shrank away as always at his approach, but now with a different impulse, "dearest Beatrice, our fate is not yet so desperate. Behold! there is a medicine, potent, as a wise physician has assured me, and almost divine in its efficacy. It is composed of ingredients the most opposite to those by which thy awful father has brought this calamity upon thee and me. It is distilled of blessed herbs. Shall we not quaff it together, and thus be purified from evil?"

"Give it me!" said Beatrice, extending her hand to receive the little silver vial which Giovanni took from his bosom. She added, with a peculiar emphasis, "I will drink; but do thou await the result."

She put Baglioni's antidote to her lips; and, at the same moment, the figure of Rappaccini emerged from the portal and came slowly towards the marble fountain. As he drew near, the pale man of science seemed to gaze with a triumphant expression at the beautiful youth and maiden, as might an artist who should spend his life in achieving a picture or a group of statuary and finally be satisfied with his success. He paused; his bent form grew erect with conscious power; he spread out his hands over them in the attitude of a father imploring a blessing upon his children; but those were the same hands that had thrown poison into the stream of their lives. Giovanni trembled. Beatrice shuddered nervously, and pressed her hand upon her heart.

"My daughter," said Rappaccini, "thou art no longer lonely in the world. Pluck one of those precious gems from thy sister shrub and bid thy bridegroom wear it in his bosom. It will not harm him now. My science and the sympathy between thee and him have so wrought within his system that he now stands apart from common men, as thou dost, daughter of my pride and triumph, from ordinary women. Pass on, then, through the world, most dear to one another and dreadful to all besides!"

"My father," said Beatrice, feebly,—and still as she spoke she kept her hand upon her heart,—"wherefore didst thou inflict this miserable doom upon thy child?"

"Miserable!" exclaimed Rappaccini. "What mean you, foolish girl? Dost thou deem it misery to be endowed with marvellous gifts against which no power nor strength could avail an enemy—misery, to be able to quell the mightiest with a breath—misery, to be as terrible as thou art beautiful? Wouldst thou, then, have preferred the condition of a weak woman, exposed to all evil and capable of none?"

"I would fain have been loved, not feared," murmured Beatrice, sinking down upon the ground. "But now it matters not. I am going, father, where the evil which thou hast striven to mingle with my being will pass away like a dream—like the fragrance of these poisonous flowers, which will no longer taint my breath among the flowers of Eden. Farewell, Giovanni! Thy words of hatred are like lead within my heart; but they, too, will fall away as I ascend. O, was there not, from the first, more poison in thy nature than in mine?"

To Beatrice,—so radically had her earthly part been wrought upon by Rappaccini's skill,—as poison had been life, so the powerful antidote was death; and thus the poor victim of man's ingenuity and of thwarted nature, and of the fatality that attends all such efforts of perverted wisdom, perished there, at the feet of her father and Giovanni. Just at that moment Professor Pietro Baglioni looked forth from the window, and called loudly, in a tone of triumph mixed with horror, to the thunder-stricken man of science,—

"Rappaccini! Rappaccini! and is *this* the upshot of your experiment?"

THE STAR

Arthur C. Clarke

Arthur C. Clarke is a giant of Modern sf; his novels and stories characterize the genre for many readers: he is the lyric master of astronomical vistas and technological innovations. His devotion to science and technological optimism is legendary in the field. His achievements include collaboration with Stanley Kubrick on the film masterpiece *2001: A Space Odyssey* (1968); novels such as *Prelude to Space* (1951), *Childhood's End* (1953), *The City and the Stars* (1956), *The Deep Range* (1957), *Rendezvous With Rama* (1973), and more than a dozen others.

Clarke's international reputation was first founded on the nonfiction popular science best-sellers *Interplanetary Flight* and *The Exploration of Space* in the early 1950s, and his first major award, from UNESCO, was for popular science writing. His science fiction, technologically and scientifically accurate, is often wedded to metaphysical speculation with such power that, with Bradbury, Heinlein, Herbert, and Asimov, he has remained at the top of the pantheon of sf writers since the fifties.

Among his famous short stories, such as "The Nine Billion Names of God" and "A Meeting with Medusa," "The Star" is still arguably his best. A story of astronomy, space technology, and physics, it creates a speculative scenario—which could be true—extrapolating from our present knowledge of how the universe works that collides explosively with the deeply felt religious faith of millions of civilized and educated people. This is hard sf on the grand scale.

It is three thousand light-years to the Vatican. Once, I believed that space could have no power over faith, just as I believed that the heavens declared the glory of God's handiwork. Now I have seen that handiwork, and my faith is sorely troubled. I stare at the crucifix that hangs on the cabin wall above the Mark VI Computer, and for the first time in my life I wonder if it is no more than an empty symbol.

I have told no one yet, but the truth cannot be concealed. The facts are there for all to read, recorded on the countless miles of magnetic tape and the thousands of photographs we are carrying back to Earth. Other scientists can interpret them as easily as I can, and I am not one who would condone that tampering with the truth which often gave my order a bad name in the olden days.

The crew are already sufficiently depressed: I wonder how they will take this ultimate irony. Few of them have any religious faith, yet they will not relish using this final weapon in their campaign against me—that private, good-natured, but fundamentally serious, war which lasted all the way from Earth. It amused them to have a Jesuit as chief astrophysicist: Dr. Chandler, for instance, could never get over it (why are medical men such notorious atheists?). Sometimes he would meet me on the observation deck, where the lights are always low so that the stars shine with undiminished glory. He would come up to me in the gloom and stand staring out of the great oval port, while the heavens crawled slowly around us as the ship turned end over end with the residual spin we had never bothered to correct.

"Well, Father," he would say at last, "it goes on forever and forever, and perhaps *Something* made it. But how you can believe that Something has a special interest in us and our miserable little world—that just beats me." Then the argument would start, while the stars and nebulae would swing around us in silent, endless arcs beyond the flawlessly clear plastic of the observation port.

It was, I think, the apparent incongruity of my position that caused most amusement to the crew. In vain I would point to my three papers in the *Astrophysical Journal*, my five in the *Monthly Notices of the Royal Astronomical Society*. I would remind them that my order has long been famous for its scientific works. We may be few now, but ever since the eighteenth century we have made contributions to astronomy and geophysics out of all proportion to our numbers. Will my report on the Phoenix Nebula end our thousand years of history? It will end, I fear, much more than that.

I do not know who gave the nebula its name, which seems to me a very bad one. If it contains a prophecy, it is one that cannot be verified for several billion years. Even the word nebula is misleading: this is a far smaller object than those stupendous clouds of mist—the stuff of unborn stars—that are scattered throughout the length of the Milky Way. On the cosmic scale, indeed, the Phoenix Nebula is a tiny thing—a tenuous shell of gas surrounding a single star.

Or what is left of a star . . .

The Rubens engraving of Loyola seems to mock me as it hangs there above the spectrophotometer tracings. What would *you*, Father, have made of this knowledge that has come into my keeping, so far from the little world that was all the universe you knew? Would your faith have risen to the challenge, as mine has failed to do?

You gaze into the distance, Father, but I have traveled a distance beyond any that you could have imagined when you founded our order a thousand years ago. No other survey ship has been so far from Earth: we are at the very frontiers of the explored universe. We set out to reach the Phoenix Nebula, we succeeded, and we are homeward bound with our burden of knowledge. I wish I could lift that burden from my shoulders, but I call to you in vain across the centuries and the light-years that lie between us.

On the book you are holding the words are plain to read. AD MAIOREM DEI GLORIAM, the message runs, but it is a message I can no longer believe. Would you still believe it, if you could see what we have found?

We knew, of course, what the Phoenix Nebula was. Every year, in our galaxy alone, more than a hundred stars explode, blazing for a few hours or days with thousands of times their normal brilliance before they sink back into death and obscurity. Such are the ordinary novae—the commonplace disasters of the universe. I have recorded the spectrograms and light curves of dozens since I started working at the Lunar Observatory.

But three or four times in every thousand years occurs something beside which even a nova pales into total insignificance.

When a star becomes a *supernova*, it may for a little while outshine all the massed suns of the galaxy. The Chinese astronomers watched this happen in A.D. 1054, not knowing what it was they saw. Five centuries later, in 1572, a supernova blazed in Cassiopeia so brilliantly that it was visible in the daylight sky. There have been three more in the thousand years that have passed since then.

Our mission was to visit the remnants of such a catastrophe, to reconstruct the events that led up to it, and, if possible, to learn its cause. We came slowly in through the concentric shells of gas that had been blasted out six thousand years before, yet were expanding still. They were immensely hot, radiating even now with a fierce violet light, but were far too tenuous to do us any damage. When the star had exploded, its outer layers had been driven upward with such speed that they had escaped completely from its gravitational field. Now they formed a hollow shell large enough to engulf a thousand solar systems, and at its center burned the tiny, fantastic object which the star had now become—a White Dwarf, smaller than the Earth, yet weighing a million times as much.

The glowing gas shells were all around us, banishing the normal night of interstellar space. We were flying into the center of a cosmic bomb that had detonated millennia ago and whose incandescent fragments were still hurtling apart. The immense scale of the explosion, and the fact that the debris already covered a volume of space many billions of miles across, robbed the scene of any visible movement. It would take decades before the unaided eye could detect any motion in these tortured wisps and eddies of gas, yet the sense of turbulent expansion was overwhelming.

We had checked our primary drive hours before, and were drifting slowly toward the fierce little star ahead. Once it had been a sun like our own, but it had squandered in a few hours the energy that should have kept it shining for a million years. Now it was a shrunken miser, hoarding its resources as if trying to make amends for its prodigal youth.

No one seriously expected to find planets. If there had been any before the explosion, they would have been boiled into puffs of vapor, and their substance lost in the greater wreckage of the star itself. But we made the automatic search, as we always do when approaching an unknown sun, and presently we found a single small world circling the star at an immense distance. It must have been the Pluto of this vanished solar system, orbiting on the frontiers of the night. Too far from the central sun ever to have known life, its remoteness had saved it from the fate of all its lost companions.

The passing fires had seared its rocks and burned away the mantle of frozen gas that must have covered it in the days before the disaster. We landed, and we found the Vault.

Its builders had made sure that we should. The monolithic marker that stood above the entrance was now a fused stump, but even the first long-range photographs told us that here was the work of intelligence. A little later we detected the continent-wide pattern of radio-activity that had been buried in the rock. Even if the pylon above the Vault had been destroyed, this would have remained, an immovable and all but eternal beacon calling to the stars. Our ship fell toward this gigantic bull's-eye like an arrow into its target.

The pylon must have been a mile high when it was built, but now it looked like a candle that had melted down into a puddle of wax. It took us a week to drill through the fused rock, since we did not have the proper tools for a task like this. We were astronomers, not archaeologists, but we could improvise. Our original purpose was forgotten: this lonely monument, reared with such labor at the greatest possible distance from the doomed sun, could have only one meaning. A civilization that knew it was about to die had made its last bid for immortality.

It will take us generations to examine all the treasures that were placed in the Vault. They had plenty of time to prepare, for their sun must have given its first warnings many years before the final detonation. Everything that they wished to preserve, all the fruit of their genius, they brought here to this distant world in the days before the end, hoping that some other race would find it and that they would not be utterly forgotten. Would we have done as well, or would we have been too lost in our own misery to give thought to a future we could never see or share?

If only they had had a little more time! They could travel freely enough between the planets of their own sun, but they had not yet learned to cross the interstellar gulfs, and the nearest solar system was a hundred light-years away. Yet even had they possessed the secret of the Transfinite Drive, no more than a few millions could have been saved. Perhaps it was better thus.

Even if they had not been so disturbingly human as their sculpture shows, we could not have helped admiring them and grieving for their fate. They left thousands of visual records and the machines for projecting them, together with elaborate pictorial instructions from which it will not be difficult to learn their written language. We have examined many of these records, and brought to life for the first time in six thousand years the warmth and beauty of a civilization that in many ways must have been superior to our own. Perhaps they only showed us the best, and one can hardly blame them. But their worlds were very lovely, and their cities were built with a grace that matches anything of man's. We have watched them at work and play, and listened to their musical speech sounding across the centuries. One scene is still before my eyes—a group of children on a beach of strange blue sand, playing in the waves as children play on Earth. Curious whiplike trees line the shore, and some very large animal is wading in the shadows yet attracting no attention at all.

And sinking into the sea, still warm and friendly and life-giving, is the sun that will soon turn traitor and obliterate all this innocent happiness.

Perhaps if we had not been so far from home and so vulnerable to loneliness, we should not have been so deeply moved. Many of us had seen the ruins of ancient civilizations on other worlds, but they had never affected us so profoundly. This tragedy was unique. It is one thing for a race to fail and die, as nations and cultures have done on Earth. But to be destroyed so completely in the full flower of its achievement, leaving no survivors—how could that be reconciled with the mercy of God?

My colleagues have asked me that, and I have given what answers I can. Perhaps you could have done better, Father Loyola, but I have found nothing in the *Exercitia Spiritualia* that helps me here. They were not an evil people: I do not know what gods they worshiped, if indeed they worshiped any. But I have looked back at them across the centuries, and have watched while the loveliness they used their last strength to preserve was brought forth again into the light of their shrunken sun. They could have taught us much: why were they destroyed?

I know the answers that my colleagues will give when they get back to Earth. They will say that the universe has no purpose and no plan, that since a hundred suns explode every year in our galaxy, at this very moment some race is dying in the depths of space. Whether that race has done good or evil during its lifetime will make no difference in the end: there is no divine justice, for there is no God.

Yet, of course, what we have seen proves nothing of the sort. Anyone who argues thus is being swayed by emotion, not logic. God has no need to justify His actions to man. He who built the universe can destroy it when He chooses. It is arrogance—it is perilously near blasphemy—for us to say what He may or may not do.

This I could have accepted, hard though it is to look upon whole worlds and peoples thrown into the furnace. But there comes a point when even the deepest faith must falter, and now, as I look at the calculations lying before me, I know I have reached that point at last.

We could not tell, before we reached the nebula, how long ago the explosion took place. Now, from the astronomical evidence and the record in the rocks of that one surviving planet, I have been able to date it very exactly. I know in what year the light of this colossal conflagration reached our Earth. I know how brilliantly the supernova whose corpse now dwindles behind our speeding ship once shone in terrestrial skies. I know how it must have blazed low in the east before sunrise, like a beacon in that oriental dawn.

There can be no reasonable doubt: the ancient mystery is solved at last. Yet, oh God, there were so many stars you could have used. What was the need to give these people to the fire, that the symbol of their passing might shine above Bethlehem?

PROOF

Hal Clement

Hal Clement is the pen name of Harry Clement Stubbs, a retired schoolteacher who began writing science fiction in the 1940s and who devoted himself to the creation of cleverly imagined and thoroughly worked out environments elsewhere in space. Clement has said that one of his early models was the pulp sf of J. Lewis Burtt, B.Sc., writer of heavily expository science wonder stories filled with mind-boggling ideas such as "The Never-Dying Light" (an alien leader, Adman, bringing settlers to Earth from a dying planet), "When the Meteor Struck" (Earth saved from destruction and huge engineering feats performed by benign star-travelers), and "The White Dwarf" (ingenious scientists moving Earth and Venus nearer to the collapsing, cooling Sol) in the mid-1930s in *Amazing Stories*. Early Clement was one of the principal conduits of this super science into Campbell's Golden Age in short fiction.

His mastery of the astronomy, physics and chemistry in stories set in space and on other worlds became famous with the publication of the *Astounding* serial, "Heavy Planet" (*Mission of Gravity*, 1954), but especially with the immediately subsequent publication of a nonfiction article in the same magazine, detailing the process by which he had figured out the physics, astronomy, and biochemistry of the world of Mesklin. With the publication of the book and article he gained a worldwide reputation as a quintessential hard science fiction writer whose works in later years more or less defined the term. When the Russian sf writer Arkady Strugatsky visited the west for the first time, to attend a science fiction convention, the one writer he most wanted to meet was Hal Clement.

With the publication of *Mission of Gravity*, Clement in effect redefined the game of hard sf as an exercise in interrelating the sciences to achieve a created world that would plausibly withstand rigorous examination from many angles. Of such conceptual breakthroughs are scientific revolutions accomplished, and this was a revolution in science fiction, a slow and subtle one that took more than a decade to take hold. Robert A. Heinlein remained the defining icon of hard sf for at least another decade, but sf was evolving into a field of novelists, not short-story writers, as the paperback book became the primary market, and novel length offered writers enough scope to build worlds. Thus the game of hard sf became one best played by the writers of novels, or series of stories or novels. From Frank Herbert's Dune World and Anne McCaffrey's Pern to Brian W. Aldiss's Helliconia (this last created with the help of teams of scientists), the world-building aspect of hard science fiction has been foregrounded in the hard sf novel over the decades since *Mission of Gravity*, and Clement's influence grows in importance. Even in works that are not hard sf, the worldbuilding background of much sf written since has been richer and more plausible; the general effect has been to emphasize the interrelatedness of the hard sciences in sf and to deemphasize engineering problems (the staple of much Golden Age fiction) and the Heinleinesque evolutionary themes.

"Proof," first published in 1942 in *Astounding*, and Clement's first published story, is exemplary in several ways. Its derivation is as abstract as Flatland (the two-dimensional world in which the classic novel by Edwin Abbott is set) and other mathematical fictions that invent concrete images to embody theoretical concepts. It builds a consistent and detailed world for its characters to operate in, a world radically distanced from our own by its physical nature but also clearly, through our knowledge of science, connected to it: it is plausible. It takes a god's-eye point of view, with which the reader is to identify (rather than identifying with any of the characters more than provisionally). Most of the story is exposition, but clothed in intriguing images. Clement's work is presently the most influential model for hard science fiction writers.

Kron held his huge freighter motionless, feeling forward for outside contact. The tremendous interplay of magnetic and electrostatic fields just beyond the city's edge was as clearly perceptible to his senses as the city itself—a mile-wide disk ringed with conical field towers, stretching away behind and to each side. The ship was poised between two of the towers; immediately behind it was the field from which Kron had just taken off. The area was covered with cradles of various forms—cup-shaped receptacles which held city craft like Kron's own; long, boat-shaped hollows wherein reposed the cigarlike vessels which plied between the cities; and towering skeleton frameworks which held upright the slender double cones that hurtled across the dark, lifeless regions between stars.

Beyond the landing field was the city proper; the surface of the disk was covered with geometrically shaped buildings—cones, cylinders, prisms, and hemispheres, jumbled together.

Kron could "see" all this as easily as a human being in an airplane can see New York; but no human eyes could have perceived this city, even if a man could have existed anywhere near it. The city, buildings and all, glowed a savage, white heat; and about and beyond it—a part of it, to human eyes—raged the equally dazzling, incandescent gases of the solar photosphere.

The freighter was preparing to launch itself into that fiery ocean; Kron was watching the play of the artificial reaction fields that supported the city, preparatory to plunging through them at a safe moment.

There was considerable risk of being flattened against the edge of the disk if an inauspicious choice was made, but Kron was an experienced flier, and slipped past the barrier with a sudden, hurtling acceleration that would have pulped any body of flesh and bone. The outer fringe of the field flung the globe sharply downward; then it was free, and the city was dwindling above them.

Kron and four others remained at their posts; the rest of the crew of thirty relaxed, their spherical bodies lying passive in the cuplike rests distributed through the ship, bathing in the fierce radiance on which those bodies fed, and which was continually streaming from a three-inch spheroid at the center of the craft. That an artificial source of energy should be needed in such an environment may seem strange, but to these creatures the outer layers of the Sun were far more inhospitable to life than is the stratosphere of Earth to human beings.

They had evolved far down near the solar core, where pressures and temperatures were such that matter existed in the "collapsed" state characteristic of the entire mass of white dwarf stars. Their bodies were simply constructed: a matrix of close-packed electrons—really an unimaginably dense electrostatic field, possessing quasi-solid properties—surrounded a core of neutrons, compacted to the ultimate degree.

Radiation of sufficient energy, falling on the "skin," was stabilized, altered to the pattern and structure of neutrons; the tiny particles of neutronium which resulted were borne along a circulatory system—of magnetic fields, instead of blood—to the nucleus, where it was stored.

The race had evolved to the point where no material appendages were needed. Projected beams and fields of force were their limbs, powered by the annihilation of some of their own neutron substance. Their strange senses gave them awareness not only of electromagnetic radiation, permitting them to "see" in a more or less normal fashion, but also of energies still undreamed of by human scientists. Kron, now hundreds of miles below the city, was still dimly aware of its location, though radio waves, light and gamma rays were all hopelessly fogged in the clouds of free electrons. At his goal, far down in the solar interior, "seeing" conditions would be worse—anything more than a few hundred yards distant would be quite indetectable even to him.

Poised beside Kron, near the center of the spheroidal Sunship, was another being. Its body was ovoid in shape, like that of the Solarian, but longer and narrower, while the ends were tipped with pyramidal structures of neutronium, which projected through the "skin." A second, fainter static aura outside the principal surface enveloped the creature; and as the crew relaxed in their cups, a beam of energy from this envelope impinged on Kron's body. It carried a meaning, transmitting a clear thought from one being to the other.

"I still find difficulty in believing my senses," stated the stranger. "My own worlds revolve about another which is somewhat similar to this; but such a vast and tenuous atmosphere is most unlike conditions at home. Have you ever been away from Sol?"

"Yes," replied Kron, "I was once on the crew of an interstellar projectile. I have never seen your star, however; my acquaintance with it is entirely through hearsay. I am told it consists almost entirely of collapsed matter, like the core of our own; but there is practically no atmosphere. Can this be so? I should think, at the temperature necessary for life, gases would break free of the core and form an envelope."

"They tend to do so, of course," returned the other, "but our surface gravity is immeasurably greater than anything you have here; even your core pull is less, since it is much less dense than our star. Only the fact that our worlds are small, thus causing a rapid diminution of gravity as one leaves them, makes it possible to get a ship away from them at all; atoms, with only their original velocities, remain within a few miles of the surface.

"But you remind me of my purpose on this world—to check certain points of a new theory concerning the possible behavior of aggregations of normal atoms. That was why I arranged a trip on your flier; I have to make density, pressure, temperature, and a dozen other kinds of measurements at a couple of thousand different levels, in your atmosphere. While I'm doing it, would you mind telling me why you make these regular trips—and why, for that matter, you live so far above your natural level? I should think you would find life easier below, since there would be no need to remain in sealed buildings or to expend such a terrific amount of power in supporting your cities."

Kron's answer was slow.

"We make the journeys to obtain neutronium. It is impossible to convert enough power from the immediate neighborhood of the cities to support them; we must descend periodically for more, even though our converters take so much as to lower the solar temperature considerably for thousands of miles around each city.

"The trips are dangerous—you should have been told that. We carry a crew of thirty, when two would be enough to man this ship, for we must fight, as well as fly. You spoke truly when you said that the lower regions of Sol are our natural home; but for aeons we have not dared to make more than fleeting visits, to steal the power which is life to us.

"Your little worlds have been almost completely subjugated by your people, Sirian; they never had life forms sufficiently powerful to threaten seriously your domination. But Sol, whose core alone is far larger than the Sirius B pair, did develop such creatures. Some are vast, stupid, slow-moving, or immobile; others are semi-intelligent, and rapid movers; all are more than willing to ingest the ready-compacted neutronium of another living being."

Kron's tale was interrupted for a moment, as the Sirian sent a ray probing out through the ship's wall, testing the physical state of the inferno beyond. A record was made, and the Solarian resumed.

"We, according to logical theory, were once just such a race—of small intelligence, seeking the needs of life among a horde of competing organisms. Our greatest enemy was a being much like ourselves in size and power—just slightly superior in both ways. We were somewhat ahead in intelligence, and I suppose we owe them some thanks—with out the competition they provided, we should not have been forced to develop our minds to their present level. We learned to cooperate in fighting them, and from that came the discovery that many of us together could handle natural forces that a single individual could not even approach, and survive. The creation of force effects that had no counterpart in Nature was the next step; and, with the understanding of them, our science grew.

"The first cities were of neutronium, like those of today, but it was necessary to stabilize the neutrons with fields of energy; at core temperature, as you know, neutronium is a gas. The cities were spherical and much smaller than our present ones. For a long time, we managed to defend them.

"But our enemies evolved, too; not in intelligence, but in power and fecundity. With overspecialization of their physical powers, their mentalities actually degenerated; they became little more than highly organized machines, driven, by an age-old enmity toward our race, to seek us out and destroy us. Their new powers at last enabled them to neutralize, by brute force, the fields which held our cities in shape; and then it was that, from necessity, we fled to the wild, inhospitable upper regions of Sol's atmosphere. Many cities were destroyed by the enemy before a means of supporting them was devised; many more fell victims to forces which we generated, without being able to control, in the effort. The dangers of our present-day trips seem trivial beside those our ancestors braved, in spite of the fact that ships not infrequently fail to return from their flights. Does that answer your question?"

The Sirian's reply was hesitant. "I guess it does. You of Sol must have developed far more rapidly than we, under that drive; your science, I know, is superior to ours in certain ways, although it was my race which first developed space flight."

"You had greater opportunities in that line," returned Kron. "Two small stars, less than a diameter apart, circling a larger one at a distance incomparably smaller than the usual interstellar interval, provided perfect ground for experimental flights; between your world and mine, even radiation requires some hundred and thirty rotations to make the journey, and even the nearest other star is almost half as far.

"But enough of this—history is considered by too many to be a dry subject. What brings you on a trip with a power flier? You certainly have not learned anything yet which you could not have been told in the city."

During the conversation, the Sirian had periodically tested the atmosphere beyond the hull. He spoke rather absently, as though concentrating on something other than his words.

"I would not be too sure of that, Solarian. My measurements are of greater delicacy than we have ever before achieved. I am looking for a very special effect, to substantiate or disprove an hypothesis which I have recently advanced—much to the detriment of my prestige. If you are interested, I might explain: laugh afterward if you care to—you will not be the first.

"The theory is simplicity itself. It has occurred to me that matter—ordinary substances like iron and calcium—might actually take on solid form, like neutronium, under the proper conditions. The normal gas, you know, consists of minute particles traveling with considerable speed in all directions. There seems to be no way of telling whether or not these atoms exert appreciable forces on one another; but it seems to me that if they were brought closely enough together, or slowed down sufficiently, some such effects might be detected."

"How, and why?" asked Kron. "If the forces are there, why should they not be detectable under ordinary conditions?"

"Tiny changes in velocity due to mutual attraction or repulsion would scarcely be noticed when the atomic speeds are of the order of hundreds of kilometers per second," returned the Sirian. "The effects I seek to detect are of a different nature. Consider, please. We know the sizes of the various atoms, from their radiations. We also know that, under normal conditions, a given mass of any particular gas fills a certain volume. If, however, we surround this gas with an impenetrable container and exert pressure, that volume decreases. We would expect that decrease to be proportional to the pressure, except for an easily determined constant due to the size of the atoms, if no interatomic forces existed; to detect such forces, I am making a complete series of pressure-density tests, more delicate than any heretofore, from the level of your cities down to the neutron core of your world.

"If we could reduce the kinetic energy of the atoms—slow down their motions of translation—the task would probably be simpler; but I see no way to accomplish that. Perhaps, if we could negate nearly all of that energy, the interatomic forces would actually hold the atoms in definite relative positions, approximating the solid state. It was that somewhat injudicious and perhaps too imaginative suggestion which caused my whole idea to be ridiculed on Sirius."

The ship dropped several hundred miles in the few seconds before Kron answered; since gaseous friction is independent of change in density, the high pressures of the regions being penetrated would be no bar to high speed of flight. Unfortunately, the viscosity of a gas does increase directly as the square root of its temperature; and at the lower levels of the Sun, travel would be slow.

"Whether or not our scientists will listen to you, I cannot say," said Kron finally. "Some of them are a rather imaginative crowd, I guess, and none of them will ignore any data you may produce.

"I do not laugh, either. My reason will certainly interest you, as your theory intrigues me. It is the first time anyone has accounted even partly for the things that happened to us on one of my flights."

The other members of the crew shifted slightly on their cradles; a ripple of interest passed through them, for all had heard rumors and vague tales of Kron's time in the space carrier fleets. The Sirian settled himself more comfortably; Kron dimmed the central globe of radiance a trifle, for the outside temperature was now considerably higher, and began the tale.

"This happened toward the end of my career in space. I had made many voyages with the merchant and passenger vessels, had been promoted from the lowest ranks, through many rotations, to the post of independent captain. I had my own cruiser—a special long-period explorer, owned by the Solarian government. She was shaped like our modern interstellar carriers, consisting of two cones, bases together, with the field ring just forward of their meeting point. She was larger than most, being designed to carry fuel for exceptionally long flights.

"Another cruiser, similar in every respect, was under the command of a comrade of mine, named Akro; and the two of us were commissioned to transport a party of scientists and explorers to the then newly discovered Fourth System, which lies, as you know, nearly in the plane of the solar equator, but about half again as distant as Sirius.

"We made good time, averaging nearly half the speed of radiation, and reached the star with a good portion of our hulls still unconsumed. We need not have worried about that, in any case; the star was denser even than the Sirius B twins, and neutronium was very plentiful. I restocked at once, plating my inner walls with the stuff until they had reached their original thickness, although experience indicated that the original supply was ample to carry us back to Sol, to Sirius, or to Procyon B.

"Akro, at the request of the scientists, did not refuel. Life was present on the star, as it seems to be on all stars where the atomic velocities and the density are high enough; and the biologists wanted to bring back specimens. That meant that room would be needed, and if Akro replated his walls to normal thickness, that room would be lacking—as I have mentioned, these were special long-range craft, and a large portion of their volume consisted of available neutronium.

"So it happened that the other ship left the Fourth System with a low, but theoretically sufficient, stock of fuel, and half a dozen compartments filled with specimens of alien life. I kept within detection distance at all times, in case of trouble, for some of those life forms were as dangerous as those of Sol, and, like them, all consumed neutronium. They had to be kept well under control to safeguard the very walls of the ship, and it is surprisingly difficult to make a wild beast, surrounded by food, stay on short rations.

"Some of the creatures proved absolutely unmanageable; they had to be destroyed. Others were calmed by lowering the atomic excitation of their compartments, sending them into a stupor; but the scientists were reluctant to try that in most cases, since not all of the beings could stand such treatment.

"So, for nearly four hundred solar rotations, Akro practically fought his vessel across space—fought successfully. He managed on his own power until we were within a few hundred diameters of Sol; but I had to help him with the landing—or try to, for the landing was never made.

"It may seem strange, but there is a large volume of space in the neighborhood of this Sun which is hardly ever traversed. The normal landing orbit arches high over one of the poles of rotation, enters atmosphere almost tangentially somewhere between that pole and the equator, and kills as much as remains of the ship's velocity in the outer atmospheric layers. There is a minimum of magnetic interference that way, since the flier practically coasts along the lines of force of the solar magnetic field.

"As a result, few ships pass through the space near the plane of the solar equator. One or two may have done so before us, and I know of several that searched the region later; but none encountered the thing which we found.

"About the time we would normally have started correcting our orbits for a tangential landing, Akro radiated me the information that he could not possibly control his ship any farther with the power still available to him. His walls were already so thin that radiation loss, ordinarily negligible, was becoming a definite menace to his vessel. All his remaining energy would have to be employed in keeping the interior of his ship habitable.

"The only thing I could do was to attach our ships together with an attractor beam, and make a nearly perpendicular drop to Sol. We would have to take our chances with magnetic and electrostatic disturbances in the city-supporting fields which cover so much of the near-equatorial zones, and try to graze the nucleus of the Sun instead of its outer atmosphere, so that Akro could replenish his rapidly failing power.

"Akro's hull was radiating quite perceptibly now; it made an easy target for an attractor. We connected without difficulty, and our slightly different linear velocities caused us to revolve slowly about each other, pivoting on the center of mass of our two ships. I cut off my driving fields, and we fell spinning toward Sol.

"I was becoming seriously worried about Akro's chances of survival. The now-alarming energy loss through his almost consumed hull threatened to exhaust his supply long before we reached the core; and we were still more than a hundred diameters out. I could not give him any power; we were revolving about each other at a distance of about one-tenth of a solar diameter. To lessen that distance materially would increase our speed of revolution to a point where the attractor could not overcome centrifugal force; and I had neither power nor time to perform the delicate job of exactly neutralizing our rotary momentum without throwing us entirely off course. All we could do was hope.

"We were somewhere between one hundred and one hundred and fifty diameters out when there occurred the most peculiar phenomenon I have ever encountered. The plane of revolution of our two ships passed near Sol, but was nearly perpendicular to the solar equator; at the time of which I speak, Akro's ship was almost directly between my flier and the Sun. Observations had just shown that we were accelerating Sunward at an unexpectedly high pace, when a call came from Akro.

" 'Kron! I am being pulled away from your attractor! There is a large mass somewhere near, for the pull is gravitational, but it emits no radiation that I can detect. Increase your pull, if you can; I cannot possibly free myself alone.'

"I did what I could, which was very little. Since we did not know the location of the disturbing dark body, it was impossible to tell just what I should do to avoid bringing my own or Akro's vessel too close. I think now that if I had released him immediately he would have swung clear, for the body was not large, I believe. Unfortunately, I did the opposite, and nearly lost my own ship as well. Two of my crew were throwing as much power as they could convert and handle into the attractor, and trying to hold it on the still easily visible hull of Akro's ship; but the motions of the latter were so peculiar that aiming was a difficult task. They held the ship as long as we could see it; but quite suddenly the radiations by means of which we perceived the vessel faded out, and before we could find a band which would get through, the sudden cessation of our centripetal acceleration told us that the beam had slipped from its target.

"We found that electromagnetic radiations of wave lengths in the octave above H-alpha would penetrate the interference, and Akro's hull was leaking energy enough to radiate in that band. When we found him, however, we could scarcely believe our senses; his velocity was now nearly at right angles to his former course, and his hull radiation had become far weaker. What terrific force had caused this acceleration, and what strange field was blanketing the radiation, were questions none of us could answer.

"Strain as we might, not one of us could pick up an erg of radiant energy that might emanate from the thing that had trapped Akro. We could only watch, and endeavor to plot his course relative to our own, at first. Our ships were nearing each other rapidly, and we were attempting to determine the time and distance of closest approach, when we were startled by the impact of a communicator beam. Akro was alive! The beam was weak, very weak, showing what an infinitesimal amount of power he felt he could spare. His words were not encouraging.

" 'Kron! You may as well cut your attractor, if you are still trying to catch me. No power that I dare apply seems to move me perceptibly in any direction from this course. We are all badly shocked, for we hit something that felt almost solid. The walls, even, are strained, and may go at any time.'

" 'Can you perceive anything around you?' I returned. 'You seem to us to be alone in space, though something is absorbing most of your radiated energy. There must be energies in the cosmos of which we have never dreamed, simply because they did not affect our senses. What do your scientists say?'

" 'Very little,' was the answer. 'They have made a few tests, but they say that anything they project is absorbed without reradiating anything useful. We seem to be in a sort of energy vacuum—it takes everything and returns nothing.'

"This was the most alarming item yet. Even in free space, we had been doubtful of Akro's chances of survival; now they seemed reduced to the ultimate zero.

"Meanwhile, our ships were rapidly approaching each other. As nearly as my navigators could tell, both vessels were pursuing almost straight lines in space. The lines were nearly perpendicular but did not lie in a common plane; their minimum distance apart was about one one-thousandth of a solar diameter. His velocity seemed nearly constant, while I was accelerating Sunward. It seemed that we would reach the near-intersection point almost simultaneously, which meant that my ship was certain to approach the energy vacuum much too closely. I did not dare to try to pull Akro free with an attractor; it was only too obvious that such an attempt could only end in disaster for both vessels. If he could not free himself, he was lost.

"We could only watch helplessly as the point of light marking the position of Akro's flier swept closer and closer. At first, as I have said, it seemed perfectly free in space; but as we looked, the region around it began to radiate feebly. There was nothing recognizable about the vibrations, simply a continuous spectrum, cut off by some interference just below the H-alpha wave length and, at the other end, some three octaves higher. As the emission grew stronger, the visible region around the stranded ship grew larger, fading into nothingness at the edges. Brighter and broader the patch of radiance grew, as we swept toward it."

That same radiance was seriously inconveniencing Gordon Aller, who was supposed to be surveying for a geological map of northern Australia. He was camped by the only water hole in many miles, and had stayed up long after dark preparing his cameras, barometer, soil kit, and other equipment for the morrow's work.

The arrangement of instruments completed, he did not at once retire to his blankets. With his back against a smooth rock, and a short, blackened pipe clenched in his teeth, he sat for some time, pondering. The object of his musing does not matter to us; though his eyes were directed heavenward, he was sufficiently accustomed to the southern sky to render it improbable that he was paying much attention to its beauties.

However that may be, his gaze was suddenly attracted to the zenith. He had often seen stars which appeared to move when near the edge of his field of vision—it is a common illusion; but this one continued to shift as he turned his eyes upward.

Not far from Achernar was a brilliant white point, which brightened as Aller watched it. It was moving slowly northward, it seemed; but only a moment was needed for the man to realize that the slowness was illusory. The thing was slashing almost vertically downward at an enormous speed, and must strike Earth not far from his camp.

Aller was not an astronomer and had no idea of astronomical distances or speeds. He may be forgiven for thinking of the object as traveling perhaps as fast as a modern fighting plane, and first appearing at a height of two or three miles. The natural conclusion from this belief was that the crash would occur within a few hundred feet of the camp. Aller paled; he had seen pictures of the Devil's Pit in Arizona.

Actually, of course, the meteor first presented itself to his gaze at a height of some eighty miles, and was then traveling at a rate of many miles per second relative to Earth. At that speed, the air presented a practically solid obstacle to its flight, and the object was forced to a fairly constant velocity of ten or twelve hundred yards a second while still nearly ten miles from Earth's surface. It was at that point that Aller's eyes caught up with, and succeeded in focusing upon, the celestial visitor.

That first burst of light had been radiated by the frightfully compressed and heated air in front of the thing; as the original velocity departed, so did the dazzling light. Aller got a clear view of the meteor at a range of less than five miles, for perhaps ten seconds before the impact. It was still incandescent, radiating a bright cherry-red; this must have been due to the loss from within, for so brief a contact even with such highly heated air could not have warmed the Sunship's neutronium walls a measurable fraction of a degree.

Aller felt the ground tremble as the vessel struck. A geyser of earth, barely visible in the reddish light of the hull, spouted skyward, to fall back seconds later with a long-drawn-out rumble. The man stared at the spot, two miles away, which was still giving off a faint glow. Were "shooting stars" as regularly shaped as that? He had seen a smooth, slender body, more than a hundred feet in length, apparently composed of two cones of unequal length, joined together at the bases. Around the longer cone, not far from the point of juncture, was a thick bulging ring; no further details were visible at the distance from which he had observed. Aller's vague recollections of meteorites, seen in various museums, brought images of irregular, clinkerlike objects before his mind's eye. What, then, could this thing be?

He was not imaginative enough to think for a moment of any possible extraterrestrial source for an aircraft; when it did occur to him that the object was of artificial origin, he thought more of some experimental machine produced by one of the more progressive Earth nations.

At the thought, Aller strapped a first-aid kit to his side and set out toward the crater, in the face of the obvious fact that nothing human could possibly have survived such a crash. He stumbled over the uneven terrain for a quarter of a mile and then stopped on a small rise of ground to examine more closely the site of the wreck.

The glow should have died by this time, for Aller had taken all of ten minutes to pick his way those few hundred yards; but the dull-red light ahead had changed to a brilliant orange radiance against which the serrated edges of the pit were clearly sillhouetted. No flames were visible; whence came the increasing heat? Aller attempted to get closer, but a wave of frightfully hot air blistered his face and hands and drove him back. He took up a station near his former camp, and watched.

If the hull of the flier had been anywhere near its normal thickness, the tremendous mass of neutronium would have sunk through the hardest of rocks as though they were liquid. There was, however, scarcely more than a paper thickness of the substance at any part of the walls; and an upthrust of adamantine volcanic rock not far beneath the surface of the desert proved thick enough to absorb the Sunship's momentum and to support its still enormous weight. Consequently, the ship was covered only by a thin layer of powdered rock which had fallen back into the crater. The disturbances arising from the now extremely rapid loss of energy from Akro's ship were, as a result, decidedly visible from the surface.

The hull, though thin, was still intact; but its temperature was now far above the melting point of the surrounding rocks. The thin layer of pulverized material above the ship melted and flowed away almost instantly, permitting free radiation to the air above; and so enormous is the specific heat of neutronium that no perceptible lowering of hull temperature occurred.

Aller, from his point of observation, saw the brilliant fan of light that sprang from the pit as the flier's hull was exposed—the vessel itself was invisible to him, since he was only slightly above the level of the crater's mouth. He wondered if the impact of the "meteor" had released some pent-up volcanic energy, and began to doubt, quite justifiably, if he was at a safe distance. His doubts vanished and were replaced by certainty as the edges of the crater began to glow dull red, then bright orange, and slowly subsided out of sight. He began packing the most valuable items of his equipment, while a muted, continuous roaring and occasional heavy thuds from the direction of the pit admonished him to hasten.

When he straightened up, with the seventy-pound pack settled on his shoulders, there was simply a lake of lava where the crater had been. The fiery area spread even as he watched; and without further delay he set off on his own back trail. He could see easily by the light diffused from the inferno behind him; and he made faily good time, considering his burden and the fact that he had not slept since the preceding night.

The rock beneath Akro's craft was, as we have said, extremely hard. Since there was relatively free escape upward for the constantly liberated energy, this stratum melted very slowly, gradually letting the vessel sink deeper into the earth. What would have happened if Akro's power supply had been greater is problematical; Aller can tell us only that some five hours after the landing, as he was resting for a few moments near the top of a rocky hillock, the phenomenon came to a cataclysmic end.

A quivering of the earth beneath him caused the surveyor to look back toward his erstwhile camp. The lake of lava, which by this time was the better part of a mile in breadth, seemed curiously agitated. Aller, from his rather poor vantage point, could see huge bubbles of pasty lava hump themselves up and burst, releasing brilliant clouds of vapor. Each cloud illuminated earth and sky before cooling to invisibility, so that the effect was somewhat similar to a series of lightning flashes.

For a short time—certainly no longer than a quarter of a minute—Aller was able to watch as the activity increased. Then a particularly violent shock almost flung him from the hilltop, and at nearly the same instant the entire volume of molten rock fountained skyward. For an instant it seemed to hang there, a white, raging pillar of liquid and gas; then it dissolved, giving way before the savage thrust of the suddenly released energy below. A tongue of radiance, of an intensity indescribable in mere words, stabbed upward, into and through the lava, volatilizing instantly. A dozen square miles of desert glowed white, then an almost invisible violet, and disappeared in superheated gas. Around the edges of this region, great gouts of lava and immense fragments of solid rock were hurled to all points of the compass.

Radiation exerts pressure; at the temperature found in the cores of stars, that pressure must be measured in thousands of tons per square inch. It was this thrust, rather than the by no means negligible gas pressure of the boiling lava, which wrought most of the destruction.

Aller saw little of what occurred. When the lava was hurled upward, he had flung an arm across his face to protect his eyes from the glare. That act unquestionably saved his eyesight as the real flash followed; as it was, his body was seared and blistered through his clothing. The second, heavier, shock knocked his feet from under him, and he half crawled, half rolled down to the comparative shelter of the little hill. Even here, gusts of hot air almost cooked him; only the speed with which the phenomenon ended saved his life.

Within minutes, both the temblors and hot winds had ceased; and he crawled painfully to the hilltop again to gaze wonderingly at the five-mile-wide crater, ringed by a pile of tumbled, still-glowing rock fragments.

Far beneath that pit, shards of neutronium, no more able to remain near the surface than the steel pieces of a wrecked ocean vessel can float on water, were sinking through rock and metal to a final resting place at Earth's heart.

"The glow spread as we watched, still giving no clue to the nature of the substance radiating it," continued Kron. "Most of it seemed to originate between us and Akro's ship; Akro himself said that but little energy was being lost on the far side. His messages, during that last brief period as we swept by our point of closest approach, were clear—so clear that we could almost see, as he did, the tenuous light beyond the ever-thinning walls of his ship; the light that represented but a tiny percentage of the energy being sucked from the hull surface.

"We saw, as though with his own senses, the tiny perforation appear near one end of the ship; saw it extend, with the speed of thought, from one end of the hull to the other, permitting the free escape of all the energy in a single instant; and, from our point of vantage, saw the glowing area where the ship had been suddenly brightened, blazing for a moment almost as brightly as a piece of Sun matter.

"In that moment, every one of us saw the identifying frequencies as the heat from Akro's disrupted ship raised the substance which had trapped him to an energy level which permitted atomic radiation. Every one of us recognized the spectra of iron, of calcium, of carbon and silicon and a score of the other elements—Sirian, I tell you that that 'trapping field' was *matter*—matter in such a state that it could not radiate, and could offer resistance to other bodies in exactly the fashion of a solid. I thought, and have always thought, that some strange field of force held the atoms in their 'solid' positions; you have convinced me that I was wrong. The 'field' was the sum of the interacting atomic forces which you are trying to detect. The energy level of that material body was so low that those forces were able to act without interference. The condition you could not conceive of reaching artificially actually exists in Nature!"

"You go too fast, Kron," responded the Sirian. "Your first idea is far more likely to be the true one. The idea of unknown radiant or static force fields is easy to grasp; the one you propose in its place defies common sense. My theories called for some such conditions as you described, granted the one premise of a sufficiently low energy level; but a place in the real Universe so devoid of energy as to absorb that of a well-insulated interstellar flier is utterly inconceivable. I have assumed your tale to be true as to details, though you offer neither witnesses nor records to support it; but I seem to have heard that you have somewhat of a reputation as an entertainer, and you seem quick-witted enough to have woven such a tale on the spot, purely from the ideas I suggested. I compliment you on the tale, Kron; it was entrancing; but I seriously advise you not to make anything more out of it. Shall we leave it at that, my friend?"

"As you will," replied Kron.

IT'S GREAT TO BE BACK

Robert A. Heinlein

Robert A. Heinlein was generally regarded as the best science fiction writer working in the field between 1939 and his death in 1988. His early works, particularly the stories and novels in his "Future History" series, collected in *The Man Who Sold the Moon* (1950), *The Green Hills of Earth* (1951), *Revolt in 2100* (1953) and others, are one of the principal pipelines through which the literary techniques developed by H. G. Wells in his early novels and stories (especially *When the Sleeper Wakes* [1899]) for portraying the world of the future as palpably different from the world of the present flowed into the tropes and conventions of Modern science fiction. His first novel in book form, *Beyond This Horizon* (1942 serial, 1948 hardcover), was widely considered as the single best Modern science fiction novel from the time of its serial appearance until the mid-1950s. Locutions from that work, such as "the door dilated," became paradigms of technique for most other sf writers of the period.

Heinlein was one of the few Golden Age writers who identified emotionally with the Cambellian prescription that good science fiction should attempt to be predictive. Heinlein had a knack for prophetic utterance in his work and felt pleased and proud when devices described in his work, the manipulator devices which compensate for the congenital weakness of the central character of his novella, "Waldo" (1942), were invented in the real world (to handle radioactive material at a distance by a human operator) and named "waldoes." Of all the Campbell discoveries of the Golden Age, Robert A. Heinlein was the most popular.

Ironically, after World War II, Heinlein only wrote a few stories for Campbell, breaking into the slick fiction markets and hardcover publishing (notably beginning a series of young adult sf novels for Scribners, and publishing adult sf with Doubleday, while all the specialty sf presses vied to reprint his classic work from his prewar flowering). There was no question in the 1950s that Heinlein was the dean of science fiction writers, in the decade in which most of his influential juveniles were published (from *Farmer in the Sky* [1950] to *Have Space Suit—Will Travel* [1958]); four major adult SF novels were written (*The Puppet Masters*, 1951; *Double Star*, 1956; *The Door into Summer*, 1957; and *Starship Troopers*, 1959—this last originally drafted as one of the juveniles); and every piece of sf he had written in the previous decade was collected and reprinted. And as an active member of the sf community, Heinlein defended the special virtues of science fiction and of science-fiction readers as the avant-garde of the human race, those who stand for science, reason, change, progress, the future. His prestige was second only to Campbell's, and by the early sixties his influence was perhaps even stronger, when he published the most popular of all his novels, *Stranger in a Strange Land* (1961) and in 1966, *The Moon is a Harsh Mistress*, perhaps the pinnacle of his hard sf novels.

Ironically, since it is principally social satire and not hard sf, *Stranger* became his most popular work, read by millions in the two decades after its publication.

It signaled a move away from hard sf in his later works, into speculative fiction on a broader scale than his hard sf and attained worldwide popularity extending far outside the sf genre. He is still considered the greatest master of hard science fiction, which he always defended as the only true and real science fiction. For the next twenty years, although his in-genre prestige slipped somewhat under the pressure of new styles of sf introduced in the New Wave period and due to the more overt political agendas of his later works, Heinlein remained the single most influential hard science fiction writer, both upon readers and on their ideas of the nature of hard sf, and upon his peers and younger writers. This was true even though nearly all of the younger generations of genre writers, starting in the mid-sixties, began to look to others (for example Alfred Bester, Theodore Sturgeon, Philip K. Dick) as their models, turning away from hard sf.

The affect of hard science fiction is, then, to a certain extent the affect of Robert A. Heinlein, ex-navy officer and gentleman, engineer and commercial writer, libertarian anarchist, intellectual pioneer, patriot. He was devoted until his death to the Social Darwinist position that the evolution of humanity demands and depends upon the exploration of space. Most of the character types common in hard science fiction, including the pioneer/explorer, the good manager, the inventor/entrepreneur, the visionary businessman, the military officer with a technical education, the hard-boiled high-tech woman, and many others, were popularized, if not developed, by Heinlein. He also claimed to have recognized the principal innovation of sf as literature, the new archetypal story of "the man who learned better." To say that Heinlein influenced hard sf is, perhaps, to understate: hard science fiction from the late thirties to the early eighties is Heinleinesque fiction. The only other writers of comparable direct influence in this century are H. G. Wells and Olaf Stapledon (and Stapledon's influence is nowhere near so direct, a distant third). His literary techniques and attitudes are only in the eighties and nineties beginning to seem peripheral to the main course of hard sf now, to the majority of contemporary writers, if not readers, a process that has taken two decades to jell.

"It's Great to Be Back" is a virtuoso example of Heinlein at work. It's a sales pitch for the future in space, witty, ironic, slick extrapolation, involving the reader in a story that confirms what all superior intelligences (such as the reader) already know, that the future in space is better for you, unless you are an ignorant, lazy, evolutionary reject. Hard science fiction is a literature of, and for, survivors.

Home—back to Earth again! Josephine MacRae's heart was pounding. She said, "Hurry up, Allan!" and fidgeted while her husband checked over the apartment. Earth-Moon freight rates made it silly to ship their belongings; except for the bag he carried, they had converted everything to cash. Satisfied, he joined her at the lift; they went on up to the administration level and there to a door marked: Luna City Community Association—*Anna Stone, Service Manager.*

Miss Stone accepted their apartment keys grimly. "Mr. and Mrs. MacRae. So you're actually leaving us?"

Josephine bristled. "Think we'd change our minds?"

The manager shrugged. "No. I knew nearly three years ago that you would go back—from your complaints."

"By my comp— Miss Stone, I don't blame you personally, but this pressurized rabbit warren would try the patience of a—"

"Take it easy, Jo!" her husband cautioned her.

Josephine flushed. "Sorry, Miss Stone."

"Never mind. We just see things differently. I was here when Luna City was three air-sealed Quonset huts, with tunnels you had to crawl through." She stuck out a square hand. "I honestly hope you'll enjoy being groundhogs. Hot jets, good luck and safe landing."

Back in the lift, Josephine sputtered, " 'Groundhogs' indeed! Just because we prefer fresh air and our own native planet—"

"You use the term," Allan pointed out.

"But I use it about people who have never been off Terra."

"We've both said more than once that we wished we had had sense enough never to have left Earth. We're groundhogs at heart, Jo."

"Yes, but—Allan, you're being obnoxious. This is the happiest day of my life. Aren't you glad to be going home? Aren't you?"

"Sure I am. It'll be great to be back. Golf. Skiing."

"And opera. Real live grand opera. Allan, we've simply got to have a week or two in Manhattan before going to the country."

"I thought you wanted to feel rain on your face?"

"I want that too. I want it all at once, and I can't wait. Oh, darling, it's like getting out of jail." She clung to him.

He unwound her as the lift stopped. "Don't blubber."

"Allan, you're a beast," she said dreamily. "I'm so happy."

In bankers' row, the clerk in Trans-America had their transfer of account ready. "Going home, eh? I envy you. Hunting, fishing."

"Surf bathing is more my style. And sailing."

"I," said Jo, "simply want to see green trees and blue sky."

The clerk nodded. "I know. Well, have fun. Are you taking three months or six?"

"We're not coming back," Allan stated flatly. "Three years of living like a fish in an aquarium is enough."

"So?" The clerk's face became impassive. "Well, hot jets."

"Thanks." They went on up to subsurface and took the crosstown slidewalk out to the rocket port. Its tunnel broke surface at one point, becoming a pressurized shed; a window on the west looked out on the surface of the Moon, and, beyond the hills, the Earth.

The sight of it, great and green and bountiful, against black lunar sky and harsh, unwinking stars, brought quick tears to Jo's eyes. Home—that lovely planet was hers! Allan looked at it more casually, noting the Greenwich. The sunrise line had just touched South America—must be about eight-twenty; better hurry.

They stepped off the slidewalk into the arms of waiting friends. "Hey, you lugs are late! The Gremlin blasts off in seven minutes."

"But we aren't going in it," MacRae answered. "No, siree."

"What? Not going? Did you change your minds?"

Josephine laughed. "Pay no attention to him, Jack. We're going in the express instead. So we've got twenty minutes yet."

"Well! A couple of rich tourists, eh?"

"Oh, the extra fare isn't bad. Why make two changes and sweat out a week in space?" She rubbed her bare middle significantly.

"She can't take free flight, Jack," her husband explained.

"Well, neither can I; I was sick the whole trip out. Still, I don't think you'll be sick, Jo. You're used to Moon weight now."

"Maybe," she agreed, "but there is a lot of difference between one sixth gravity and no gravity."

Jack Crail's wife cut in, "Josephine MacRae, are you going to risk your life in an atomic-powered ship?"

"Why not, darling? You work in an atomics laboratory!"

"It's not the same thing. In the lab we take precautions. The Commerce Commission should never have licensed the expresses."

"Now, Emma," Crail objected, "they've worked the bugs out of those ships."

"Humph! I may be old-fashioned, but I'll go back the way I came, via Terminal and Supra-New-York, in good old reliable fuel rockets."

"Never mind," Allan interrupted. "It's done, and we've got to get over to the express-launching site. Good-by, everybody! It's been grand knowing you. If you come back to God's country, look us up."

"Good-by, Jo. . . . Good-by, Allan!" "Give my regards to Broadway!" "Be sure to write!" "Aloha, hot jets!"

They showed their tickets, entered the air lock and climbed into the pressurized shuttle used between Leyport proper and the express-launching site.

"Hang on, folks," the driver called back over his shoulder; Jo and Allan hurriedly settled into the cushions. The lock opened to the airless tunnel ahead. Six minutes later they climbed out twenty miles away, beyond the hills shielding Luna City's roof from the radioactive splash of the express.

In the Sparrowhawk they shared a compartment with a missionary family. The Reverend Doctor Simmons seemed to want to explain why he was traveling in luxury. "It's for the child," he told them, as his wife strapped their baby girl into a small acceleration couch rigged between her parents' couches. They all strapped down at the warning siren. Jo felt her heart begin to pound. At last—at long last!

The jets took hold, mashing them into the cushions. Jo had not known she could feel so heavy—much worse than the trip out. The baby cried all through acceleration, in wordless terror and discomfort. After a weary time they were suddenly weightless, as the ship went into free flight. When the terrible binding weight was free of her chest, Jo's heart felt as light as her body. Allan threw off his upper strap. "How do you feel, kid?"

"Oh, I feel fine!" Jo unstrapped and faced him. Then she hiccuped. "That is, I think I do."

Five minutes later she was not in doubt; she merely wished to die. Allan swam out of the compartment and located the ship's surgeon, who gave her a hypo. Allan waited until the drug had made her more comfortable, then left for the lounge to try his own cure for spacesickness—Mothersill's Seasick Remedy washed down with champagne. Presently he regretted having mixed them.

Little Gloria Simmons was not spacesick. She thought being weightless was fun, and went bouncing off floor plate, overhead and bulkhead like a dimpled balloon. Jo feebly considered strangling the child, if she floated within reach, but it was too much effort.

Deceleration, logy as it made them feel, was welcome relief after nausea—except to little Gloria. She cried again, while her mother tried to explain. Her father prayed. After a long, long time came a slight jar and the sound of the siren.

Jo managed to raise her head. "What's the matter? Is there an accident?"

"I don't think so. I think we've landed."

"We can't have! We're still braking—I'm heavy as lead."

Allan grinned feebly. "So am I. Earth gravity, remember?"

The baby continued to cry.

They said good-by to the missionary family and staggered out of the ship, supporting each other.

"It can't be just the gravity," Jo protested. "I've taken earth-normal weight in the centrifuge at the Y, back home—I mean back in Luna City. We're weak from spacesickness."

Allan steadied himself. "That's it. No food for two days."

"Allan, didn't you eat anything either?"

"No. Not permanently, so to speak. Are you hungry?"

"Starving."

"How about dinner at Keen's Chop House?"

"Wonderful. Oh, Allan, we're back!" Her tears started again.

After chuting down the Hudson Valley and into Grand Central Station, they glimpsed the Simmonses again. While waiting at the dock for their bag, Jo saw the reverend doctor climb heavily out of a tube capsule, carrying his daughter and followed by his wife. He set the child down carefully. She stood for a moment, trembling on her pudgy legs, then collapsed to the dock. She lay there, crying thinly.

A spaceman—a pilot, by his uniform—stopped and looked pityingly at the child. "Born in the Moon?" he asked.

"Uh? What? Why, yes, she was, sir."

"Pick her up and carry her. She'll have to learn to walk all over again." The spaceman shook his head sadly and glided away.

Simmons looked still more troubled, then sat down on the dock beside his child, careless of the dirt. Jo felt too weak to help. She looked around for Allan, but he was busy; their bag had arrived. He started to pick it up, then felt suddenly silly. It seemed nailed to the dock. He knew what was in it—rolls of microfilm and color film, souvenirs, toilet articles, irreplaceables—fifty pounds of mass. It couldn't weigh what it seemed to. But it did. He had forgotten what fifty pounds weigh on Earth.

"Porter, mister?" The speaker was gray-haired and thin, but he scooped the bag up casually.

Allan called,"Come along, Jo," and followed him sheepishly.

The porter slowed to match his labored steps. "Just down from the Moon?" he asked. "You got a reservation?"

"Why, no."

"Stick with me. I got a friend on the desk at the Commodore." He led them to the Concourse slidewalk and into the hotel.

They were too weary to dine out; Allan had dinner sent up. Afterward, Jo fell asleep in a hot tub and he had trouble getting her out and into bed—she liked the support the water gave her.

She woke up, struggling, about four in the morning. "Allan!"

"Huh? What's the matter?" He fumbled for the light switch.

"Uh . . . nothing, I guess. I dreamt I was back in the ship. The jets had run away with her. What makes it so stuffy? My head is splitting."

"Huh? It can't be stuffy. This joint is air-conditioned." He sniffed the air. "I've got a headache too," he admitted.

"Well, do something. Open a window."

He stumbled up and did so, shivered when the outer air hit him, and hurried back to bed. He was wondering whether he could get to sleep with the roar of the city pouring in through the open window, when his wife spoke again, "Allan, I'm cold. May I crawl in with you?"

The sunlight streamed in the window, warm and mellow. When it touched his eyes, he woke and found his wife awake beside him.

She sighed and snuggled. "Oh, darling, look! Blue sky! We're home. I'd forgotten how lovely it is."

"It's great to be back, all right." He threw off the covers.

Jo squealed and jerked them back. "Don't do that!"

"Huh?"

"Mamma's great big boy is going to climb out and close that window while mamma stays under the covers."

"Well, all right." He found he could walk more easily, but it was good to get back into bed. Once there, he faced the telephone and shouted at it, "Service!"

"Order, please," it answered in a sweet contralto.

"Orange juice and coffee for two—extra coffee—six eggs, scrambled medium, and whole-wheat toast. And please send up a *Times* and *The Saturday Evening Post.*"

The delivery cupboard buzzed while he was shaving. He answered it and served Jo in bed. Breakfast over, he put down his paper and said, "Can you pull your nose out of that magazine?"

"Glad to. The darn thing is too big and heavy to hold."

"Why don't you have the *stat* edition mailed to you from Luna City? Wouldn't cost more than eight or nine times as much."

"Don't be silly. What's on your mind?"

"Climb out of that frowsty little nest and we'll go shopping."

"Unh-uh. No. I am not going outdoors in a moonsuit."

"'Fraid of being stared at? Getting prudish in your old age?"

"No, me lord; I simply refuse to expose myself in six ounces of nylon. I want some warm clothes." She squirmed farther under the covers.

"The perfect pioneer woman. Going to have fitters sent up?"

"We can't afford that—not while we're living on our savings. Look, you're going anyway. Buy me any old rag, so long as it's warm."

MacRae looked stubborn. "I've tried shopping for you before."

"Just this once, please. Run over to Saks and pick out a street dress in a blue wool jersey, size twelve. And a pair of nylons."

"Well, all right."

"That's a lamb. I won't be loafing; I have a list as long as your arm of people I've promised to call up, look up, have lunch with."

He shopped for himself first; his sensible shorts and singlet felt as inadequate as a straw hat in a snowstorm. It was really quite balmy, but it seemed cold after Luna City's unfailing seventy-two degrees. He stayed underground mostly or stuck to the roofed-over stretch of Fifth Avenue. He suspected that the salesmen were outfitting him in clothes that made him look like a yokel. But they were warm. They were also heavy, adding to the pain in his chest and making him even more unsteady. He wondered when he would regain his ground legs.

A motherly saleswoman took care of Jo's order and sold him a warm cape for her as well. He headed back, stumbling under his load, and trying futilely to flag a ground taxi. Everyone seemed in such a hurry!

He got back, aching all over and thinking about a hot bath. He did not get it; Jo had a visitor. "Mrs. Appleby, my husband. . . . Allan, this is Emma Crail's mother."

"Oh, how do you do, doctor—or should it be professor?"

"Mister."

"When I heard you were in town I just couldn't wait to hear all about my poor darling. How is she? Does she look well? These modern girls—I've told her time and time again that she must get outdoors. I walk in the park every day, and look at me. She sent me a picture—I have it here somewhere; at least I think so—and she doesn't look a bit well, undernourished. Those synthetic foods—"

"She doesn't eat synthetic foods, Mrs. Appleby."

"—must be quite impossible, I'm sure, not to mention the taste. What were you saying?"

"Your daughter doesn't live on synthetic foods," Allan repeated. "Fresh fruits and vegetables are one thing we have almost too much of in Luna City. The air-conditioning plant, you know."

"That's just what I was saying. I confess I don't see just how you get food out of air-conditioning machinery on the Moon—"

"In the Moon, Mrs. Appleby."

"—but it can't be healthy. Our air conditioner is always breaking down and making the most horrible smells. Simply ghastly, my dears. You'd think they could build a simple little thing like an air conditioner so that—"

"Mrs. Appleby," MacRae said desperately, "the air-conditioning plant in Luna City is a hydroponic farm, tanks of green growing plants. The plants take carbon dioxide out of the air and put oxygen back in."

"But— Are you quite sure, doctor? I'm sure Emma said—"

"Quite sure."

"Well, I don't pretend to understand these things; I'm the artistic type. Poor Herbert often said— Herbert was Emma's father; simply wrapped up in his engineering, though I always saw to it that he heard good music and saw the reviews of the best books. Emma takes after her father, I'm afraid. I do wish she would give up that silly work. Hardly the thing for a lady, do you think, Mrs. MacRae? All those atoms and neuters and things floating around in the air. I read all about it in the Science Made Simple column in the—"

"She's quite good at it and she seems to like it."

"Well, perhaps that's the important thing—to be happy in what you do, no matter how silly. But I worry about the child, buried away from civilization, no one of her own sort to talk with, no theaters, no cultural life, no society."

"Luna City has stereo transcriptions of every successful Broadway play." Jo's voice had a slight edge.

"Oh! Really? But it's not just the plays, my dear; it's the society of gentle folk. Now, when I was a girl, my parents—"

Allan butted in, "One o'clock. Have you had lunch, my dear?"

Mrs. Appleby sat up with a jerk. "Oh, heavenly days! I simply must fly. My dress designer—a tyrant, but a genius. I'll give you her address. It's been charming, my dears, and I can't thank you too much for telling me all about my poor child. I do wish she would be sensible like you two; I'm always ready to make a home for her—and her husband, for that matter. Do come and see me often. I love to talk to people who've been on the Moon."

"In the Moon."

"It makes me feel closer to my darling. Good-by, then."

When the door closed behind her, Jo said, "Allan, I need a drink."

"I'll join you."

Jo cut her shopping short; it was too tiring.

By four o'clock they were driving in Central Park, enjoying the autumn scenery to the lazy clop-clop of horses' hoofs. The helicopters, the pigeons, the streak in the sky where the Antipodes rocket had passed, made a scene idyllic in beauty and serenity.

Jo whispered huskily, "Isn't it lovely?"

"Sure is. Say, did you notice they've torn up Forty-second Street again?"

Back in their room, Jo collapsed on her bed, while Allan took off his shoes. He sat rubbing his feet, and remarked, "I'm going barefooted all evening. Golly, how my feet hurt!"

"So do mine. But we're going to your father's, my sweet."

"Huh? Oh, damn, I forgot. Jo, whatever possessed you? Call him up and postpone it. We're still half dead from the trip."

"But, Allan, he's invited a lot of your friends."

"Balls of fire and cold mush! I haven't any real friends in New York. Make it next week."

" 'Next week.' H'm'm—look, Allan; let's go to the country right away." Jo's parents had left her a tiny, wornout farm in Connecticut.

"What happened to your yen for plays and music?"

"I'll show you." She went to the window, open since noon. "Look at that window sill." She drew their initials in the grime. "Allan, this city is filthy."

"You can't expect ten million people not to kick up dust."

"Luna City was never like this. I could wear a white outfit there till I got tired of it. Here one wouldn't last a day."

"Luna City has a roof, and precipitrons in every air duct."

"Well, Manhattan ought to have! I either freeze or smother."

"You wanted to feel rain on your face."

"Don't be tiresome. I want it out in the clean, green country."

"Okay. I want to start my book anyhow. I'll call your agent."

"I called this morning. We can move in any time."

It was a stand-up supper at his father's house, though Jo sat down and let food be fetched. Allan, as guest of honor, had to stay on his aching feet. His father led him to the buffet. "Here, son, try this goose liver. It should go well after a diet of green cheese."

Allan agreed that it was good.

"See here, son, you really ought to tell these folks about your trip."

"No speeches, dad. Let 'em read the *National Geographic*."

"Nonsense!" He turned around. . . . "Quiet, everybody! Allan is going to tell us how the Lunatics live."

Allan bit his lip. To be sure, the citizens of Luna City used that term to each other, but it did not sound the same here. "Oh, shucks, I haven't anything to say. Go on and eat."

"You talk, we'll eat."

"Tell about Looney City."

"Did you see the Man in the Moon?"

"Go on, what's it like to live on the Moon?"

"Not 'on the Moon'; in the Moon."

"What's the difference?"

"Why, none, I guess." There was no way to explain why Moon colonists emphasized that they lived under the surface, but it irritated him the way "Frisco" irritates a San Franciscan. " 'In the Moon' is the way we say it. We don't spend much time on the surface, except the staff at Shapley Observatory, and the prospectors, and so forth. The living quarters are underground, naturally."

"Why 'naturally'? Afraid of meteors?"

"No more than you are afraid of lightning. We go underground for insulation against heat and cold and as support for pressure sealing. Both are cheaper and easier underground. The soil is easy to work and its pores act like vacuum in a vacuum jug. It *is vacuum*."

"But, Mr. MacRae," a serious-looking lady inquired, "doesn't it hurt your ears to live under pressure?"

Allan fanned the air. "It's the same here—fifteen pounds."

She looked puzzled. "I suppose so, but it's hard to imagine. It would terrify me to be sealed up in a cave. Suppose it blew out?"

"Fifteen pounds of pressure is no problem; engineers work in thousands of pounds per square inch. Anyhow, Luna City is compartmented like a ship. The Dutch live behind dikes; down South they have levees. Subways, ocean liners, aircraft—they're all artificial ways to live. Luna City seems strange just because it's far away."

She shivered. "It scares me."

A pretentious little man pushed his way forward. "Mr. MacRae, granted that it is nice for science and all that, why should taxpayers' money be wasted on a colony on the Moon?"

"You seem to have answered yourself," Allan told him slowly.

"Then how do you justify it? Tell me that, sir."

"It doesn't need justifying; the Luna colony has paid its cost many times over. The Lunar companies are all paying propositions. Artemis Mines, Spaceways, Spaceways Provisioning Corporation, Diana Recreations, Electronics Research Company, Lunar Bio Labs, not to mention all of Rutherford—look 'em up. I'll admit the Cosmic Research Project nicks the taxpayer a little, since it's a joint enterprise of the Harriman Foundation and the Government."

"Then you admit it. It's the principle of the thing."

Allan's feet were hurting him very badly. "What principle? Historically, research has always paid off. Take it up with your senator." He turned his back and looked for more goose liver.

A man touched him on the arm; Allan recognized an old schoolmate. "Allan, congratulations on ticking off old Beetle. He's been needing it; I think he's some sort of a radical."

Allan grinned. "I shouldn't have lost my temper."

"A good job you did. Say, Allan, I'm taking a couple of out-of-town buyers around to the hot spots tomorrow night. Come along."

"Thanks a lot, but we're going out in the country."

"Oh, you mustn't miss this party. After all, you've been buried on the Moon; you need relaxation after all that monotony."

Allan felt his cheeks getting warm. "Thanks just the same, but— Ever seen the Earth-View Room in Hotel Moon Haven?"

"No. Plan to take the trip when I've made my pile, of course."

"Well, there's a night club! Ever see a dancer leap thirty feet into the air and do slow rolls? Or a juggler work in low gravity? Ever try a lunacy cocktail?" Jo caught his eye across the room. "Er—excuse me, old man. My wife wants me." As he turned away he added, "Moon Haven itself isn't just a spacemen's dive, by the way; it's recommended by the Duncan Hines Association."

Jo was very pale. "Darling, you've got to get me out of here. I'm suffocating. I'm really ill."

"Suits." They made their excuses.

Jo woke up with a stuffy cold, so they took a cab directly to her country place.

There were low-lying clouds under them, but the weather was fine above. The sunshine and the drowsy beat of the rotors regained for them the joy of homecoming.

Allan broke the lazy reverie. "Here's a funny thing, Jo. You couldn't hire me to go back to the Moon, but last night I found myself defending the Loonies every time I opened my mouth."

She nodded. "I know. Honest to heaven, some people act as if the Earth were flat. Some of them don't really believe in anything, and some are so matter-of-fact that you know they don't really understand—and I don't know which sort annoys me the more."

It was foggy when they landed, but the house was clean, the agent had laid a fire and stocked the refrigerator. In ten minutes they were sipping hot punch and baking the weariness from their bones.

"This," said Allan, stretching, "is okay. It really is great to be back."

"Uh-huh. All except the new highway." They could hear the big Diesels growling on the grade, fifty yards from their door.

"Forget it. Turn your back and you're looking into the woods."

They soon had their ground legs well enough to enjoy little walks in the woods during a long, warm Indian summer. Allan worked on the results of three years' research, preparatory to starting his book. Jo helped him with the statistical work, got reacquainted with the delights of cooking, daydreamed and rested.

It was on the day of the first frost that the toilet stopped up. The village plumber did not show up until the next day. Meanwhile they resorted to a drafty, spider-infested little building of another era, still standing out beyond the woodpile.

The plumber was not encouraging. "New septic tank. New sile pipe. Pay you to get new fixtures. Five, six hundred dollars. Have to calculate."

"That's all right," Allan told him. "Can you start today?"

The man laughed. "I can see plainly, mister, that you don't know what it is to get materials and labor today. Next spring, maybe."

"That's impossible, man. Never mind the cost. Get it done."

The native shrugged. "Sorry not to oblige you. Good day."

When he left, Jo exploded, "Allan, he doesn't want to help us."

"Well, maybe. I'll try for help from Norwalk or even from the city. You can't trudge through snow out to that Iron Maiden all winter."

"I hope not."

"You must not. You've had one cold." He stared morosely at the fire. "I suppose I brought it on by my misplaced sense of humor."

"What do you mean?"

"Well, you know we've taken a lot of kidding ever since it got around that we were colonials. Harmless, but some of it rankled. You remember I went into the village alone last Saturday?"

"Yes. What happened?"

"They started in on me in the barbershop. I let it ride at first, then the worm turned. I pitched some double-talk about the Moon—corny old stuff like the vacuum worms and petrified air. When they finally realized I was ribbing them, nobody laughed. Our rustic sanitary engineer was in the group. I'm sorry."

"Don't be." She kissed him. "I'm glad you paid them back."

The plumber from Norwalk was helpful, but rain, and then sleet, slowed the work. They both caught colds. On the ninth miserable day, Allan was working at his desk when he heard Jo come in the back door, returning from shopping. Presently he became aware that she had not come in to say "Hello." He went to investigate.

He found her slumped on a kitchen chair, crying quietly. "Darling," he said urgently, "honey baby, whatever is the matter?"

She looked up. "I did't bead to led you doe."

"Blow your nose. Then wipe your eyes. What do you mean, 'you didn't mean to let me know'? What happened?"

She let it out, punctuated by sniffles. First, the grocer had said he had no cleansing tissues; then, when she had pointed to them, had stated that they were sold. Finally, he had mentioned "bringing in outside labor and taking the bread out of the mouths of honest folk."

Jo had blown up and had rehashed the incident of Allan and the barbershop wits. The grocer had simply grown more stiff. "'Lady,' he said to me, 'I don't know or care whether you and your husband have been to the Moon. I don't take much stock in such things. In any case, I don't need your trade.' Oh, Allan, I'm so unhappy."

"Not so unhappy as he's going to be! Where's my hat?"

"Allan, you're not leaving this house! I won't have you fighting!"

"I won't have him bullying you."

"He won't again. Oh, my dear, I've tried so hard, but I can't stand it here. It's not just the villagers; it's the cold and the cockroaches and always having a runny nose. I'm tired out and my feet hurt all the time." She started to cry again.

"There, there! We'll leave, honey. We'll go to Florida. I'll finish my book while you lie in the sun."

"Oh, I don't want to go to Florida. I want to go home!"

"Huh? You mean . . . back to Luna City?"

"Yes. Oh, dearest, I know you don't want to, but I can't help it. I could put up with the dirt and cold and the comic-strip plumbing, but it's not being understood that gets me. These groundhogs don't know anything."

He grinned at her. "Keep sending, Kid; I'm on your frequency."

"Allan!"

He nodded. "I found out I was a Loony at heart quite a while ago, but I was afraid to tell you. My feet hurt, too, and I'm sick of being treated like a freak. I've tried to be tolerant, but I can't stand groundhogs. I miss the civilized folks in dear old Luna."

She nodded. "I guess it's prejudice, but I feel the same way."

"It's not prejudice. Be honest. What does it take to get to Luna City?"

"A ticket."

"Smarty pants! Not as a tourist, but to get a job there. You know the answer: Intelligence. It costs a lot to send a man to the Moon and more to keep him there. To pay off, he has to be worth a lot. High I.Q., good compatibility index, superior education—everything that makes a person pleasant and interesting to have around. We're spoiled; the human cussedness that groundhogs take for granted, we now find intolerable, because Loonies are different. The fact that Luna City is the most comfortable environment that man ever built for himself is unimportant; it's people who count. Let's go home."

He went to the phone—an antique, speech-only rig—and called the Foundation's New York office. While he waited, truncheon-like receiver to his ear, she said, "Suppose they won't have us?"

"That's what worries me." They knew that the Lunar enterprises rarely rehired personnel who had once quit; the physical examination was rumored to be much harder to pass the second time.

"Hello? Foundation? May I speak to the recruiting office? Hello. I *can't* turn on my view plate; this instrument is a hangover from the dark ages. This is Allan MacRae, physical chemist. Contract Number One-three-four-oh-seven-two-nine. And Josephine MacRae, One-three-four-oh-seven-three-oh. We want to sign up again. I said we want to sign up again. . . . Okay, I'll wait."

"Pray, darling, pray!"

"I'm praying. . . . How's that? My appointment's still vacant? Fine, fine! How about my wife?" He listened with a worried look; Jo held her breath. Then he cupped the speaker. "Hey, Jo, your job's filled. They offer you an interim job as a junior accountant."

"Tell 'em, 'Yes!' "

"That'll be fine. When can we take our exams? . . . Swell. Thanks! Good-by." He hung up and turned to his wife. "Physical and psycho as soon as we like; professional exams waived."

"What are we waiting for?"

"Nothing." He dialed the Norwalk Copter Service. "Can you send a cab? . . . Good grief, don't you have radar? Okay, g'by!" He snorted. "Grounded by the weather. I'll call New York for a modern cab."

Ninety minutes later they landed on top of Harriman Tower.

The psychologist was cordial. "We'll get this over before you have your chests thumped. Sit down. Tell me about yourselves." He drew them out skillfully. "I see. Did you get the plumbing repaired?"

"Well, it was being fixed."

"I can sympathize with your foot trouble, Mrs. MacRae; my arches always bother me here. That's the real reason, isn't it?"

"Oh, no!"

"Now, Mrs. MacRae—"

"Really it's not—truly. I want people to talk to who know what I mean. I'm homesick for my own sort. I want to go home, and I've got to have this job to do it. I'll steady down, I know I will."

The doctor looked grave. "How about you, Mr. MacRae?"

"Well, it's about the same story. I've been trying to write a book, but I can't work. I'm homesick. I want to go back."

Doctor Feldman suddenly smiled. "It won't be too difficult."

"You mean we're in? If we pass the physical?"

"Never mind that; your discharge examinations are recent enough. Of course, you'll go out to Arizona for reconditioning and quarantine. Maybe you're wondering why it's been so easy, when it's supposed to be so hard. It's simple: we don't want people lured back by the high pay. We do want people who will be happy and as permanent as possible. Now that you're 'Moonstruck,' we want you back." He got up and stuck out his hand.

Back in the Commodore that night, Jo was struck by a thought. "Allan, do you suppose we could get our own apartment back?"

"I don't know. We could send a radio. . . . No! We'll telephone."

It took ten minutes to put the call through. Miss Stone's face softened a little when she recognized them.

"Miss Stone, we're coming home!"

There was the usual three-second lag, then, "Yes, I know. It came over the tape twenty minutes ago."

"Oh. Say, Miss Stone, is our old flat vacant?" They waited.

"I've held it; I knew you'd come back. Welcome home, Loonies."

When the screen cleared, Jo said, "Allan, how did she know?"

"Does it matter? We're in, kid! Members of the lodge."

"I guess you're right. . . . Oh, Allan, look!" She had stepped to the window; scudding clouds had just uncovered the Moon. It was three days old and *Mare Fecunditatis*—the roll of hair at the back of the Lady in the Moon's head—was cleared by the sunrise line. Near the right-hand edge of that great, dark sea was a tiny spot, visible only to their inner eyes—Luna City.

The crescent hung, serene and silvery, over the tall buildings. "Darling, isn't it beautiful?"

"Certainly is. It'll be great to be back. Don't get your nose all runny."

PROCREATION

Gene Wolfe

Gene Wolfe is a retired engineer and technical editor with an interest in abnormal psychology. He came to prominence in the field through his short fiction which appeared in many volumes of the original anthology series *Orbit* in the late sixties and early seventies. *Orbit*'s editorial position in the sf field emphasized the stylistic accomplishments of its writers and deemphasized the scientific and technological grounding of the stories—when the stories had any—introducing higher literary standards into a field already in ferment from the controversies surrounding the New Wave of the 1960s. So Wolfe's initial reputation was as a writer far removed from hard sf traditions. "I was getting started in the mid-sixties (my first sale came in 1965). . . . What happened was that editors stopped buying that type of story, save from established hard sf writers. Sf's direction is determined not by what writers want to write or by what readers want to read, but by what editors want to buy."

By the early eighties it had become obvious that a substantial amount of his fiction was indeed based on innovative science and technology used metaphorically. Characteristically, however, the science and technology were in some fashion concealed while the literary artifice was strikingly evident. Wolfe's first mature book, *The Fifth Head of Cerberus*, set on an alien planet, featured robots, colonists, a mysterious alien race. But it was constructed with so much sophisticated literary ambiguity that it was not apprehended as hard sf.

Like Theodore Sturgeon's, Wolfe's stories are widely admired for literary craftsmanship. The most extreme case of this is his masterpiece to date, the four-volume *The Book of the New Sun*, set in the far distant future on an Earth grown old with the passage of eons, with a sun in need of renewal. Strange technologies abound, but the affect is of fantasy (especially since the characters do not understand the science of their world), and it marked the beginning of nearly a decade in which much of Wolfe's fiction was fantasy (such as *Soldier of the Mist*, 1986) or horror (much of his short fiction), not sf. Yet his science fiction, like Ballard's or Le Guin's, is deeply indebted to science and richly embedded with technology.

This story was sparked in part by a technical paper in *Physics Letters* entitled "The Creation of Universes Out of Nothing" which discussed how our universe might have been produced by quantum tunneling. In Wolfe's hands, this becomes a literary conceit. Such is his stature in the genre that Wolfe's impact on the uses of science in science fiction is beginning to exert a transforming power on other writers (see Michael Swanwick's recent novel, *Stations of the Tide*). The hard sf of the next generation may reject his style—or be changed by it.

I CREATION

1 August, Monday. Had a flash of insight today. Had been mulling over Gott's (Harvard) notion that the universe contains just one magnetic monopole—because that's its seed, the same way each raindrop holds just one dust particle. (Means the guys at Berkeley and U. of Houston are wrong about catching them in their balloon over Nebraska, of course.) Why not make one in the accelerator? Because you can't move anything that heavy; monopoles should be ten billion times (or so) the mass of a hydrogen atom. Flash of insight: To make industrial diamonds, you get the pressure with an explosion. Why not use an electrical discharge? Had some time on the accelerator, tried it. Nothing. Shot electrons at Nothing to see if they were attracted or repelled. Got electrons, a few positrons. Probably equipment glitch.

2 August, Tuesday. Anomaly in target. Took it out of accelerator, washed it, scrubbed with pumice, etc., still no good. Put it under scope. Dark spot of water and cleanser that won't wipe off. Heavy stuff seems to be settling out.

3 August, Wednesday. Told Sis, Martha, How'd you like to say, "My brother (husband) the Nobel Laureate?" Martha: "Gene, you're crazy, heard you talk before, etc." Sis interested. (What I expected from both, in other words.) Told her about it—found monopole, made microverse, Gott right. Drove to lab. The microverse seems pyramidal. Strange. Tilted it, water flowed as by gravity, leaving some solids dry. Gravity interuniversal. Wanted to phone John Cramer about it, but he's off Gastprofessoring in West Berlin. Had to lecture, didn't get much done.

4 August, Thursday. Rigged up light in lab so I can switch it on to study microverse. It's no longer pyramidal, cubical now and bigger. Which only means it's gone from four angles to eight. No doubt it'll continue until it approximates a sphere, if I let it. Funny to think how I've written about this odd particle or that (like the monopole) existing "in some strange corner of the universe," without guessing it might be true. (Special properties at corners?) Anyway, it seems no matter how big it gets, it takes up no "Room," not being in our universe at all. When I measure the target with calipers, it's the right size still. But ruler enters the microverse and loses a little length, making it appear the target has grown. (N.B. Remember to write on concept of "Room" for *Physical Review* C.)

5 August, Friday. Introduced cellular material (scrapings) from the apple Sis put in my lunch. Astounding results. Green matter spread over all inorganic stuff above water. (That's been growing itself, I think; it seems to be expanding with the microverse, though not as fast.) Went over to Biology and bummed tissue samples from rabbits, mice, and so forth, and put them in. Nothing—they seem to have died.

6 August, Saturday. It seems I was wrong about the animal tissue. Today I saw a couple of little things darting around and one or two swimming. They seem large for microorganisms; wanted to catch some and bring them back, but they were too fast for me. What's more surprising, the vegetable matter has turned itself into club moss, or something of the kind. With my good glass, I can even see spore pods hanging from the branches. Fascinating! Wanted to do the animal tissue thing again, but had tossed out the cultures. Scraped my wrist and put the scrapings in. They grew too. Caught the little critter before he got too lively and scraped *him*. Put him back. Soon running around as good as ever, and the tissue I had taken from him became another, much the same.

7 August, Sunday. Decided not to go to the campus today, though I knew it would mean (as it did) Martha would nag me about church. Slept late, watched baseball on TV. Got to talking about the microverse with Sis, and she wanted to

tell the "people" about us. Silly, but she was so fired up I couldn't refuse to help her. She made little drawings on a sheet of paper so it could be folded to make a booklet, beginning with the arc discharge and ending with me watching the Yankees drop one to the Angels. We went over to the campus and reduced it half a dozen times on the good copier, and she folded it up. Maybe I shouldn't say it here, but I don't think I've ever felt prouder in my life than when I showed her the microverse—she was that thrilled. (She's already talking about putting in a few cells of her own.) But when I used the glass myself, why horrors! The critters were eating the spore pods or whatever they are. I want to have a better look at those, so I began casting about for a way of scaring them off. There was a fruit fly circling the apple core in my wastebasket, and I caught it and put it in. It worked like a charm, and off they scampered. Sis said we ought to title her book, but we couldn't think of anything appropriate. After a lot of talk, we just wrote our names, "Gene" and "Sis," on the cover and dropped it in.

II RE-CREATION

1 September, Thursday. Completed turnover of the new universe to the Astronomy Department today. As I told Dr. Ramakrishna, we will eventually have to draw some sort of line between their claims to new universe and ours. Anyway, it certainly appears that Gene-eration (as I've christened it) has moved into theirs. They say it's already outside the orbit of Pluto and headed in the direction of Vega; there's a red shift too. (Dr. Ramakrishna suggested it be called "Ramajetta." I treated that as a joke, and intend to continue to do so.) Now back to work on my article for *Physical Review C*.

2 September, Friday. Received a most disturbing airmail letter from Dr. Cramer in West Germany. He points out that if my experiment created only a single monopole, then it created a net magnetic charge. (Which he calls a "no-no." He's always kidding. But about this?) To paraphrase Cramer: If Gene-eration was seeded by a *north* monopole, then there must also be a *south* monopole floating around somewhere. And that must have seeded *another* universe—call it "Sis-eration" after Sis, who was my sounding board for the first one. That's particularly apt because "sis" is a simple palindrome, read backward the same as forward, and Cramer actually goes so far as to suggest that time might run backward in Sis-eration, so that it was destroyed at the moment Gene-ration was created. If Cramer's right, Sis-eration obviously doesn't grow as fast as Gene-eration. Which may make it even more valuable. I'll have a good look for it tomorrow.

3 September, Saturday. No classes today, so I was able to go over the lab with a fine-tooth comb looking for Sis-eration. Started with the accelerator target where I found Gene-eration and worked out from there—nothing. But see here: there's only one monopole in our universe. After all, I've *proved* that Gott (Harvard) was right about it being the seed of our universe. So it *is* a net magnetic charge—so far as our universe is concerned. Aha, Cramer, I've got you! Sis-eration is mythical, the Atlantis of physics.

4 September, Sunday. No reason to go to the campus today, so I didn't. Went to church with Martha and got to musing during the sermon. Don't know what to call it—a waking dream. Anyway, while I was sitting there studying the grain in the oak pew in front of me, I remembered that yesterday while I was shaving I had a vision. It started with one of those little vagrant spots that cross my eye sometimes. (I think the biologists call them "floaters" and say they're single body cells.) Anyway, the thing was right in the middle of my eye when I was trying to scrape

that tough bit under my nose. It interfered with my vision, and somehow, I suppose because I unconsciously linked not seeing with darkness, I wanted more light. Then it happened. I *saw* what Ramakrishna and his gang call the Big Bang. I *saw* that primordial supersun the old philosophers called the Ylem—saw it open like a milkweed pod and scatter the galaxies. And then it was gone. But here's the part that scares me: I swear I've never thought about that vision from yesterday morning until I was sitting in church today. My subconscious must have decided it was irrational and blocked it out completely. God, what a frightening thought! If I've got a censorship mechanism like that, what else have I lost because of it?

5 September, Monday. Spent most of my day musing at my desk, I'm afraid. Replaying the vision of Saturday morning in my memory. The way the Ylem acted and *why* it acted like that. It's always been assumed that matter and antimatter were created in equal amounts—parity seems to require it. And it's *also* been assumed that when an atom met an anti-atom, they returned to energy again. *Therefore* there was some kind of segregation principle at work that put all the matter to the right (let's say) and all the antimatter to the left—because if they were mixed together, they'd eliminate each other perfectly. *But* that segregation principle is a violation of parity itself. It's God, or Maxwell's Demon, or some such, looking at each little atom and saying, "You sit in smoking, you in nonsmoking, you in smoking." And so on. But suppose it wasn't really like that at all? Suppose those atoms were much more stable than we think? Two atoms meet, and each has a dense, high-energy core of protons (or antiprotons) and neutrons. But far outside those cores each has the classical valence shells of electrons (or positrons), stuff that's much more diffuse and has much less mass and consequently much less energy. Now suppose that only those outer electron shells react—the atoms bounce violently apart, and deprived of their outer shells decay to simpler elements. But of course when an atom meets another of the same matter, there's no bounce. Do the atoms tend to segregate *themselves*? You bet! What's more, here's an explanation for one of the oldest mysteries of astrophysics: Why is there so much hydrogen and so little of anything else?

6 September, Tuesday. Ramakrishna called to tell me that Gene-eration (that's what he called it) has shifted into the infrared. I thought, okay, if you're a nice guy, I'm a nice guy. So I said, "Dr. Ramakrishna, I want you to stop thinking about the Big Bang. Think about the Big Blossom instead. Think of that primeval fireball unfolding and scattering out stuff that slowly picks up speed." He wanted to call me a damn fool politely, but his English isn't good enough. I told him, "Trust me," and hung up. Wonder if anybody's gotten the Nobel for physics twice. N.B. Look it up.

7 September, Wednesday. It's only 6:00 A.M., and I don't usually write this journal so early, but I can't sleep. Last evening, as I was getting ready to go to bed, I remembered—No, I can't write it. Suppose somebody (Martha) finds this? I'd be locked away. Remembered something, a visit to Sis-eration, I couldn't possibly have forgotten, *but that I've never remembered before*. My God, the continents rising from the water like whales. Cramer's right—I just didn't understand him. It was created when I performed my experiment, and it's propagating through our past. What will it do to us? Got to talk this over with Sis. But I can't—what if I'm really crazy?

III THE SISTER'S ACCOUNT

My brother and I were never ordinary children. We shared a secret, though it was not until we were both nearly grown that we understood just how extraordinary a secret it was. TV assured us that other children were transported to strange places—Dorothy to Oz, Wendy and her brothers to Never-Never Land. Why then shouldn't Gene and I find ourselves in a place equally strange, though somewhat less interesting?

The first time, we were on a camping trip; and because we were a few hundred miles from home, we believed for a long time afterward that unless we left home it wouldn't happen at all.

And yet that first time was not terribly interesting, and only a little frightening. We were camping in the Sierras. Mom and Dad were setting up the tent and Barque was superintending the job from the vantage of a fallen log. We were given a water can and told where the spring was.

It wasn't. We stood shivering in country of brown sand and tan and red stones. The towering Sierras were gone, but pinnacles of stone that seemed very high to us (as high, that is to say, as large trees) cast shadows that stretched for miles across the sand. Dark though the sky was, it was not dark with cloud, and no bird flew there.

It seemed to us that we walked forever; no doubt it was really three miles or so. Then there was a beach where glassy waves raised by the cold, thin wind crashed on the sand, sweeping it forward and back as I had swept the floor the year before in kindergarten, when I was too young to know that the broom had to be lifted after each stroke.

"Look!" I called to Gene. "There they are!" And I could see the tent quite clearly in the lifted surface of every wave, with Dad coming out of it and Barque yapping under his feet, just as if I were seeing the same picture again and again in the TVs in a department store. I ran forward, Dad picked me up, and a minute later Gene was there too.

We told Mom and Dad all about it, of course. Mom decided there was a little patch of desert nearby. Dad said that was completely impossible, as of course it was. He took us to the spring, and we found our footprints in the soft soil near the water. But all the footprints pointed away from the tent, as though we had walked into the spring and swum into the earth. Dad was something of a woodsman, and he was frightened by that. He frightened us too by making us promise not to tell Mom. After that we never told anyone.

The second time, we were at the beach raiding the tide pools for our high-school biology class. The waves reminded me of that first experience, but there had been a storm far out in the Pacific, and they were dark and opaquely green. We had not talked about the desert for a long time, but I called Gene over and asked if he couldn't see something—trees, it seemed to me—beyond the bottom of the pool I'd found.

It was just such a forest as you see in the pictures in old books, the trees ten feet across, wrapped in moss, each sleeping in its own wisp of night. A door opened in the tenth we passed, and a dark man led us down into his underground home, where his shy and lovely wife nursed their child.

The man and woman fed us nuts and mushrooms, the boiled fiddleheads of ferns, and bread made without wheat; they talked to us with many gestures and drew pictures of trees and deer on paper that was white again each time the dark man turned it over. We understood very little of what they said, but now I think they were trying to explain that they lived beneath the ground so that the trees and the deer, who could not, might live above it; and that there were many, many such families.

At last the child fell asleep, and the dark woman opened a crumpled little mirror for us so it was as large and smooth as a pier glass. In it we saw ourselves, and beyond ourselves the ocean; and in a moment its spray was in our faces.

Gene and I talked about it for a long time that night, and we decided (or rather, he decided) that there was too much danger. We had been lucky thus far; but we could not hope to be lucky always. We thought we had seen two different worlds. Perhaps we had.

After that he tried to forget, and I believe he succeeded. I went only once more, when Gene had married and it was clear I never would. I stood before the vanity in my bedroom and looked beyond my reflected face and saw the sea.

At first I thought it the same world we had visited when we were children, because it was a landscape of stones and dust, but now the sun was hot, and there was kelp on the beach and a thousand tiny crabs. I sat on a boulder for a while, thinking and looking out at the water, never seeing a sail or a gull. And I understood as I sat there that all three had been one world, and that in my own short life I had seen its senility and its flower, and now I saw its beginning.

I had carried a mirror with me, having learned something at least from the beautiful, dark woman who had been so much younger than I now was; but there was no need of it. The shore held many pools, and each showed me my bed, the coverlet neatly spread for the repose of my rag doll.

Beyond it, my closet door stood open, with tiny silver fish swimming among my coats and dresses. I reached for one, but in my hand it became a wisp of embroidered scarf.

This afternoon, I found a letter on Gene's desk from his friend Dr. Cramer, who is teaching for a year in West Germany. It said: "Congratulations on your creation of the monopole! But I have a slight quibble. You didn't mention it, but you must surely have made a pair, a 'north' monopole and a 'south' monopole. Otherwise you would have created a net magnetic charge, which is a no-no. So you must have *two* universes (for the price of one). The one you describe must be like ours, but the other should contain antimatter and have time running in reverse."

I believe that Dr. Cramer is correct; and since you had Gene's account of the first, you should have mine of the second. It is gone now, so that when I stand before my mirror, I see only my own face.

Or perhaps that second universe was ours, and it is we who are gone, leaving as our only trace these words upon a printed page.

MIMSY WERE THE BOROGOVES

Henry Kuttner and C. L. Moore

In the late 1940s at the height of the Golden Age, the fans attending a world science fiction convention voted for Henry Kuttner over Asimov, Heinlein, Sturgeon, Van Vogt, and all the others as the world's best science fiction writer. By that time it was an open secret that Kuttner (and his pseudonyms, Lewis Padgett and Lawrence O'Donnell) was three of the most popular living sf writers. And he was married to C. L. Moore, another of the finest sf writers of the day. Their collaborative works (all their stories under whatever byline were jointly created—the Padgett name was used for stories that were more strongly Kuttner's) set the highest standard of literary quality in science fiction of the forties. To other writers, he was the craftsman par excellence. Several volumes of Kuttner/Moore short fiction appeared in hardcover in the late forties and early fifties, including *A Gnome There Was* (1950), *Tomorrow and Tomorrow and The Fairy Chessmen* (1951), *Robots Have No Tails* (1952), *Mutant* (1953), *No Boundaries* (1955), as well as the novel *Fury* (1950). But they turned to mystery and detective novels at that time and returned to graduate school to pursue an education interrupted by the Great Depression, writing little sf or fantasy in the fifties before Kuttner's sudden death at age 42 in 1958, months before he was to be guest of honor at that year's world sf convention. Moore stopped writing science fiction after Kuttner's death.

Kuttner's prestige among sf writers has diminished only with the younger generation of the eighties and nineties, who do not remember the Kuttners as the source of science fiction's concern for cultural reverberations and literary values (not generally things associated with forties sf or Campbell-era fiction). His mastery of the clichés and conventions of magazine sf remains unsurpassed, lending his fiction a characteristic genre sf atmosphere. Kuttner charms us with the surprising, sometimes crazy worlds of the future. The tinge of the absurd that colors much of his best work, his fascination with gadgets and delight in invention still keep his reputation alive among sf readers, but his books are now hard to find.

"Mimsy Were the Borogoves" is one of his genre masterpieces, in which he alludes to Lewis Carroll (and invokes Carroll's play with mathmatical logic) as he parodies the advanced theories of child psychologists and the educational toy industry. If geometric sense is really learned by children at an early age by interacting with the world, most especially with their toys, what if they got toys from the fourth dimension? Mathmatical hard sf is the lighthearted penumbra of hard science fiction, more often humorous, nearly always with an aspect of intellectual game-playing (which lends a human warmth to the abstract). It is a small and scarce subcategory of science fiction. Readers looking for this special pleasure are referred to the anthology *Mathenauts*, edited by Rudy Rucker, or the classic *Fantastica Mathematica*, edited by Clifton Fadiman.

There's no use trying to describe either Unthahorsten or his surroundings, because, for one thing, a good many million years had passed since 1942 Anno Domini, and, for another, Unthahorsten wasn't on Earth, technically speaking. He was doing the equivalent of standing in the equivalent of a laboratory. He was preparing to test his time machine.

Having turned on the power, Unthahorsten suddenly realized that the Box was empty. Which wouldn't do at all. The device needed a control, a three-dimensional solid which would react to the conditions of another age. Otherwise Unthahorsten couldn't tell, on the machine's return, where and when it had been. Whereas a solid in the Box would automatically be subject to the entropy and cosmic ray bombardment of the other era, and Unthahorsten could measure the changes, both qualitative and quantitative, when the machine returned. The Calculators could then get to work and, presently, tell Unthahorsten that the Box had briefly visited 1,000,000 A.D., 1,000 A.D., or 1 A.D., as the case might be.

Not that it mattered, except to Unthahorsten. But he was childish in many respects.

There was little time to waste. The Box was beginning to glow and shiver. Unthahorsten stared around wildly, fled into the next glossatch, and groped in a storage bin there. He came up with an armful of peculiar-looking stuff. Uh-huh. Some of the discarded toys of his son Snowen, which the boy had brought with him when he had passed over from Earth, after mastering the necessary technique. Well, Snowen needed this junk no longer. He was conditioned, and had put away childish things. Besides, though Unthahorsten's wife kept the toys for sentimental reasons, the experiment was more important.

Unthahorsten left the glossatch and dumped the assortment into the Box, slamming the cover shut just before the warning signal flashed. The Box went away. The manner of its departure hurt Unthahorsten's eyes.

He waited.

And he waited.

Eventually he gave up and built another time machine, with identical results. Snowen hadn't been annoyed by the loss of his old toys, nor had Snowen's mother, so Unthahorsten cleaned out the bin and dumped the remainder of his son's childhood relics in the second time machine's Box.

According to his calculations, this one should have appeared on Earth, in the latter part of the nineteenth century, A.D. If that actually occurred, the device remained there.

Disgusted, Unthahorsten decided to make no more time machines. But the mischief had been done. There were two of them, and the first—

Scott Paradine found it while he was playing hooky from the Glendale Grammar School. There was a geography test that day, and Scott saw no sense in memorizing place names—which in 1942 was a fairly sensible theory. Besides, it was the sort of warm spring day, with a touch of coolness in the breeze, which invited a boy to lie down in a field and stare at the occasional clouds till he fell asleep. Nuts to geography! Scott dozed.

About noon he got hungry, so his stocky legs carried him to a nearby store. There he invested his small hoard with penurious care and a sublime disregard for his gastric juices. He went down by the creek to feed.

Having finished his supply of cheese, chocolate, and cookies, and having drained the soda-pop bottle to its dregs, Scott caught tadpoles and studied them with a certain amount of scientific curiosity. He did not persevere. Something tumbled down the bank and thudded into the muddy ground near the water, so Scott, with a wary glance around, hurried to investigate.

It was a box. It was, in fact, the Box. The gadgetry hitched to it meant little to Scott, though he wondered why it was so fused and burnt. He pondered. With his jackknife he pried and probed, his tongue sticking out from a corner of his mouth— Hm-m-m. Nobody was around. Where had the box come from? Somebody must have left it here, and sliding soil had dislodged it from its precarious perch.

"That's a helix," Scott decided, quite erroneously. It was helical, but it wasn't a helix, because of the dimensional warp involved. Had the thing been a model airplane, no matter how complicated, it would have held few mysteries to Scott. As it was, a problem was posed. Something told Scott that the device was a lot more complicated than the spring motor he had deftly dismantled last Friday.

But no boy has ever left a box unopened, unless forcibly dragged away. Scott probed deeper. The angles on this thing were funny. Short circuit, probably. That was why—*uh*! The knife slipped. Scott sucked his thumb and gave vent to experienced blasphemy.

Maybe it was a music box.

Scott shouldn't have felt depressed. The gadgetry would have given Einstein a headache and driven Steinmetz raving mad. The trouble was, of course, that the box had not yet completely entered the space-time continuum where Scott existed, and therefore it could not be opened. At any rate, not till Scott used a convenient rock to hammer the helical non-helix into a more convenient position.

He hammered it, in fact, from its contact point with the fourth dimension, releasing the space-time torsion it had been maintaining. There was a brittle snap. The box jarred slightly, and lay motionless, no longer only partially in existence. Scott opened it easily now.

The soft, woven helmet was the first thing that caught his eye, but he discarded that without much interest. It was just a cap. Next he lifted a square, transparent crystal block, small enough to cup in his palm—much too small to contain the maze of apparatus within it. In a moment Scott had solved that problem. The crystal was a sort of magnifying glass, vastly enlarging the things inside the block. Strange things they were, too. Miniature people, for example—

They moved. Like clockwork automatons, though much more smoothly. It was rather like watching a play. Scott was interested in their costumes, but fascinated by their actions. The tiny people were deftly building a house. Scott wished it would catch fire, so he could see the people put it out.

Flames licked up from the half-completed structure. The automatons, with a great deal of odd apparatus, extinguished the blaze.

It didn't take Scott long to catch on. But he was a little worried. The manikins would obey his thoughts. By the time he discovered that, he was frightened, and threw the cube from him.

Halfway up the bank, he reconsidered and returned. The crystal block lay partly in the water, shining in the sun. It was a toy; Scott sensed that, with the unerring instinct of a child. But he didn't pick it up immediately. Instead, he returned to the box and investigated its remaining contents.

He found some really remarkable gadgets. The afternoon passed all too quickly. Scott finally put the toys back in the box and lugged it home, grunting and puffing. He was quite red-faced by the time he arrived at the kitchen door.

His find he hid at the back of a closet in his own room upstairs. The crystal cube he slipped into his pocket, which already bulged with string, a coil of wire, two pennies, a wad of tinfoil, a grimy defense stamp, and a chunk of feldspar.

Emma, Scott's two-year-old sister, waddled unsteadily in from the hall and said hello.

"Hello, Slug," Scott nodded, from his altitude of seven years and some months. He patronized Emma shockingly, but she didn't know the difference. Small, plump, and wide-eyed, she flopped down on the carpet and stared dolefully at her shoes.

"Tie 'em, Scotty, please?"

"Sap," Scott told her kindly, but knotted the laces. "Dinner ready yet?"

Emma nodded.

"Let's see your hands." For a wonder they were reasonably clean, though probably not aseptic. Scott regarded his own paws thoughtfully and, grimacing, went to the bathroom, where he made a sketchy toilet. The tadpoles had left traces.

Dennis Paradine and his wife Jane were having a cocktail before dinner, downstairs in the living room. He was a youngish, middle-aged man with gray-shot hair and a thinnish, prim-mouthed face; he taught philosophy at the university. Jane was small, neat, dark, and very pretty. She sipped her Martini and said:

"New shoes. Like 'em?"

"Here's to crime," Paradine muttered absently. "Huh? Shoes? Not now. Wait till I've finished this. I had a bad day."

"Exams?"

"Yeah. Flaming youth aspiring toward manhood. I hope they die. In considerable agony. *Insh'Allah!*"

"I want the olive," Jane requested.

"I know," Paradine said despondently. "It's been years since I've tasted one myself. In a Martini, I mean. Even if I put six of 'em in your glass, you're still not satisfied."

"I want yours. Blood brotherhood. Symbolism. That's why."

Paradine regarded his wife balefully and crossed his long legs. "You sound like one of my students."

"Like that hussy Betty Dawson, perhaps?" Jane unsheathed her nails. "Does she still leer at you in that offensive way?"

"She does. The child is a neat psychological problem. Luckily she isn't mine. If she were—" Paradine nodded significantly. "Sex consciousness and too many movies. I suppose she still thinks she can get a passing grade by showing me her knees. Which are, by the way, rather bony."

Jane adjusted her skirt with an air of complacent pride. Paradine uncoiled himself and poured fresh Martinis. "Candidly, I don't see the point of teaching those apes philosophy. They're all at the wrong age. Their habit-patterns, their methods of thinking, are already laid down. They're horribly conservative, not that they'd admit it. The only people who can understand philosophy are mature adults or kids like Emma and Scotty."

"Well, don't enroll Scotty in your course," Jane requested. "He isn't ready to be a *Philosophiae Doctor*. I hold no brief for child geniuses, especially when it's my son."

"Scotty would probably be better at it than Betty Dawson," Paradine grunted.

" 'He died an enfeebled old dotard at five,' " Jane quoted dreamily. "I want your olive."

"Here. By the way, I like the shoes."

"Thank you. Here's Rosalie. Dinner?"

"It's all ready, Miz Pa'dine," said Rosalie, hovering. "I'll call Miss Emma 'n' Mista' Scotty."

"I'll get 'em." Paradine put his head into the next room and roared, "Kids! Come and get it!"

Small feet scuttered down the stairs. Scott dashed into view, scrubbed and shining, a rebellious cowlick aimed at the zenith. Emma pursued, levering herself carefully down the steps. Halfway she gave up the attempt to descend upright and reversed, finishing the task monkey-fashion, her small behind giving an impression of marvelous diligence upon the work in hand. Paradine watched, fascinated by the spectacle, till he was hurled back by the impact of his son's body.

"Hi, dad!" Scott shrieked.

Paradine recovered himself and regarded Scott with dignity. "Hi, yourself. Help me in to dinner. You've dislocated at least one of my hip joints."

But Scott was already tearing into the next room, where he stepped on Jane's new shoes in an ecstasy of affection, burbled an apology, and rushed off to find his place at the dinner table. Paradine cocked up an eyebrow as he followed, Emma's pudgy hand desperately gripping his forefinger.

"Wonder what the young devil's been up to?"

"No good, probably," Jane sighed. "Hello, darling. Let's see your ears."

"They're *clean*. Mickey licked 'em."

"Well, that Airedale's tongue is far cleaner than your ears," Jane pondered, making a brief examination. "Still, as long as you can hear, the dirt's only superficial."

"Fisshul?"

"Just a little, that means." Jane dragged her daughter to the table and inserted her legs into a high chair. Only lately had Emma graduated to the dignity of dining with the rest of the family, and she was, as Paradine remarked, all eat up with pride by the prospect. Only babies spilled food, Emma had been told. As a result, she took such painstaking care in conveying her spoon to her mouth that Paradine got the jitters whenever he watched.

"A conveyer belt would be the thing for Emma," he suggested, pulling out a chair for Jane. "Small buckets of spinach arriving at her face at stated intervals."

Dinner proceeded uneventfully until Paradine happened to glance at Scott's plate. "Hello, there. Sick? Been stuffing yourself at lunch?"

Scott thoughtfully examined the food still left before him. "I've had all I need, dad," he explained.

"You usually eat all you can hold, and a great deal more," Paradine said. "I know growing boys need several tons of foodstuff a day, but you're below par tonight. Feel O.K.?"

"Uh-huh. Honest, I've had all I need."

"All you *want?*"

"Sure. I eat different."

"Something they taught you at school?" Jane inquired.

Scott shook his head solemnly.

"Nobody taught me. I found it out myself. I use spit."

"Try again," Paradine suggested. "It's the wrong word."

"Uh . . . s-saliva. Hm-m-m?"

"Uh-huh. More pepsin? Is there pepsin in the salivary juices, Jane? I forget."

"There's poison in mine," Jane remarked. "Rosalie's left lumps in the mashed potatoes again."

But Paradine was interested. "You mean you're getting everything possible out of your food—no wastage—and eating less?"

Scott thought that over. "I guess so. It's not just the sp . . . saliva. I sort of measure how much to put in my mouth at once, and what stuff to mix up. I dunno. I just do it."

"Hm-m-m," said Paradine, making a note to check up later. "Rather a revolutionary idea." Kids often get screwy notions, but this one might not be so far off the beam. He pursed his lips. "Eventually I suppose people will eat quite differently—I mean the *way* they eat, as well as what. What they eat, I mean. Jane, our son shows signs of becoming a genius."

"Oh?"

"It's a rather good point in dietetics he just made. Did you figure it out yourself, Scott?"

"Sure," the boy said, and really believed it.

"Where'd you get the idea?"

"Oh, I—" Scott wriggled. "I dunno. It doesn't mean much, I guess."

Paradine was unreasonably disappointed. "But surely—"

"S-s-s-spit!" Emma shrieked, overcome by a sudden fit of badness. "*Spit!*" She attempted to demonstrate, but succeeded only in dribbling into her bib.

With a resigned air Jane rescued and reproved her daughter, while Paradine eyed Scott with rather puzzled interest. But it was not till after dinner, in the living room, that anything further happened.

"Any homework?"

"N-no," Scott said, flushing guiltily. To cover his embarrassment he took from his pocket a gadget he had found in the box, and began to unfold it. The result resembled a tesseract, strung with beads. Paradine didn't see it at first, but Emma did. She wanted to play with it.

"No. Lay off, Slug," Scott ordered. "You can watch me." He fumbled with the beads, making soft, interested noises. Emma extended a fat forefinger and yelped.

"Scotty," Paradine said warningly.

"I didn't hurt her."

"Bit me. It did," Emma mourned.

Paradine looked up. He frowned, staring. What in—

"Is that an abacus?" he asked. "Let's see it, please."

Somewhat unwillingly Scott brought the gadget across to his father's chair. Paradine blinked. The "abacus," unfolded, was more than a foot square, composed of thin, rigid wires that interlocked here and there. On the wires the colored beads were strung. They could be slid back and forth, and from one support to another, even at the points of jointure. But—a pierced bead couldn't cross *interlocking* wires—

So, apparently, they weren't pierced. Paradine looked closer. Each small sphere had a deep groove running around it, so that it could be revolved and slid along the wire at the same time. Paradine tried to pull one free. It clung as though magnetically. Iron? It looked more like plastic.

The framework itself— Paradine wasn't a mathematician. But the angles formed by the wires were vaguely shocking, in their ridiculous lack of Euclidean logic. They were a maze. Perhaps that's what the gadget was—a puzzle.

"Where'd you get this?"

"Uncle Harry gave it to me," Scott said on the spur of the moment. "Last Sunday, when he came over." Uncle Harry was out of town, a circumstance Scott well knew. At the age of seven, a boy soon learns that the vagaries of adults follow a certain definite pattern, and that they are fussy about the donors of gifts. Moreover, Uncle Harry would not return for several weeks; the expiration of that period was unimaginable to Scott, or, at least, the fact that his lie would ultimately be discovered meant less to him than the advantages of being allowed to keep the toy.

Paradine found himself growing slightly confused as he attempted to manipulate the beads. The angles were vaguely illogical. It was like a puzzle. This red bead, if slid along *this* wire to *that* junction, should reach *there*—but it didn't. A maze, odd, but no doubt instructive. Paradine had a well-founded feeling that he'd have no patience with the thing himself.

Scott did, however, retiring to a corner and sliding beads around with much fumbling and grunting. The beads *did* sting, when Scott chose the wrong ones or tried to slide them in the wrong direction. At last he crowed exultantly.

"I did it, dad!"

"Eh? What? Let's see." The device looked exactly the same to Paradine, but Scott pointed and beamed.

"I made it disappear."

"It's still there."

"That blue bead. It's gone now."

Paradine didn't believe that, so he merely snorted. Scott puzzled over the framework again. He experimented. This time there were no shocks, even slight. The abacus had showed him the correct method. Now it was up to him to do it on his own. The bizarre angles of the wires seemed a little less confusing now, somehow.

It was a most instructive toy—

It worked, Scott thought, rather like the crystal cube. Reminded of that gadget, he took it from his pocket and relinquished the abacus to Emma, who was struck dumb with joy. She fell to work sliding the beads, this time without protesting against the shocks—which, indeed, were very minor—and, being imitative, she managed to make a bead disappear almost as quickly as had Scott. The blue bead reappeared—but Scott didn't notice. He had forethoughtfully retired into an angle of the chesterfield with an overstuffed chair and amused himself with the cube.

There were little people inside the thing, tiny manikins much enlarged by the magnifying properties of the crystal, and they moved, all right. They built a house. It caught fire, with realistic-seeming flames, and stood by waiting. Scott puffed urgently. "Put it *out*!"

But nothing happened. Where was that queer fire engine, with revolving arms, that had appeared before? Here it was. It came sailing into the picture and stopped. Scott urged it on.

This was fun. Like putting on a play, only more real. The little people did what Scott told them, inside of his head. If he made a mistake, they waited till he'd found the right way. They even posed new problems for him—

The cube, too, was a most instructive toy. It was teaching Scott, with alarming rapidity—and teaching him very entertainingly. But it gave him no really new knowledge as yet. He wasn't ready. Later—later—

Emma grew tired of the abacus and went in search of Scott. She couldn't find him, even in his room, but once there the contents of the closet intrigued her. She discovered the box. It contained treasure-trove—a doll, which Scott had already noticed but discarded with a sneer. Squealing, Emma brought the doll downstairs, squatted in the middle of the floor, and began to take it apart.

"Darling! What's that?"

"Mr. Bear!"

Obviously it wasn't Mr. Bear, who was blind, earless, but comforting in his soft fatness. But all dolls were named Mr. Bear to Emma.

Jane Paradine hesitated. "Did you take that from some other little girl?"

"I didn't. She's mine."

Scott came out from his hiding place, thrusting the cube into his pocket. "Uh—that's from Uncle Harry."

"Did Uncle Harry give that to you, Emma?"

"He gave it to me for Emma," Scott put in hastily, adding another stone to his foundation of deceit. "Last Sunday."

"You'll break it, dear."

Emma brought the doll to her mother. "She comes apart. See?"

"Oh? It . . . *ugh*!" Jane sucked in her breath. Paradine looked up quickly.

"What's up?"

She brought the doll over to him, hesitated, and then went into the dining room, giving Paradine a significant glance. He followed, closing the door. Jane had already placed the doll on the cleared table.

"This isn't very nice, is it, Denny?"

"Hm-m-m." It was rather unpleasant, at first glance. One might have expected an anatomical dummy in a medical school, but a child's doll—

The thing came apart in sections, skin, muscles, organs, miniature but quite perfect, as far as Paradine could see. He was interested. "Dunno. Such things haven't the same connotations to a kid—"

"Look at that liver. Is it a liver?"

"Sure. Say, I . . . this is funny."

"What?"

"It isn't anatomically perfect, after all." Paradine pulled up a chair. "The digestive tract's too short. No large intestine. No appendix, either."

"Should Emma have a thing like this?"

"I wouldn't mind having it myself," Paradine said. "Where on earth did Harry pick it up? No, I don't see any harm in it. Adults are conditioned to react unpleasantly to innards. Kids don't. They figure they're solid inside, like a potato. Emma can get a sound working knowledge of physiology from this doll."

"But what are those? Nerves?"

"No, these are the nerves. Arteries here; veins here. Funny sort of aorta—" Paradine looked baffled. "That . . . what's Latin for network? Anyway . . . huh? *Rita? Rata?*"

"*Rales*," Jane suggested at random.

"That's a sort of breathing," Paradine said crushingly. "I can't figure out what this luminous network of stuff is. It goes all through the body, like nerves."

"Blood."

"Nope. Not circulatory, not neural—funny! It seems to be hooked up with the lungs."

They became engrossed, puzzling over the strange doll. It was made with remarkable perfection of detail, and that in itself was strange, in view of the physiological variation from the norm. "Wait'll I get that Gould," Paradine said, and presently was comparing the doll with anatomical charts. He learned little, except to increase his bafflement.

But it was more fun than a jigsaw puzzle.

Meanwhile, in the adjoining room, Emma was sliding the beads to and fro in the abacus. The motions didn't seem so strange now. Even when the beads vanished. She could almost follow that new direction—almost—

Scott panted, staring into the crystal cube and mentally directing, with many false starts, the building of a structure somewhat more complicated than the one which had been destroyed by fire. He, too, was learning—being conditioned—

• • •

Paradine's mistake, from a completely anthropomorphic standpoint, was that he didn't get rid of the toys instantly. He did not realize their significance, and, by the time he did, the progression of circumstances had got well under way. Uncle Harry remained out of town, so Paradine couldn't check with him. Too, the midterm exams were on, which meant arduous mental effort and complete exhaustion at night; and Jane was slightly ill for a week or so. Emma and Scott had free rein with the toys.

"What," Scott asked his father one evening, "is a wabe, dad?"

"Wave?"

He hesitated. "I . . . don't *think* so. Isn't wabe right?"

"Wab is Scot for web. That it?"

"I don't see how," Scott muttered, and wandered off, scowling, to amuse himself with the abacus. He was able to handle it quite deftly now. But, with the instinct of children for avoiding interruptions, he and Emma usually played with the toys in private. Not obviously, of course—but the more intricate experiments were never performed under the eye of an adult.

Scott was learning fast. What he now saw in the crystal cube had little relationship to the original simple problems. But they were fascinatingly technical. Had Scott realized that his education was being guided and supervised—though merely mechanically—he would probably have lost interest. As it was, his initiative was never quashed.

Abacus, cube, doll—and other toys the children found in the box—

Neither Paradine nor Jane guessed how much of an effect the contents of the time machine were having on the kids. How could they? Youngsters are instinctive dramatists, for purposes of self-protection. They have not yet fitted themselves to the exigencies—to them partially inexplicable—of a mature world. Moreover, their lives are complicated by human variables. They are told by one person that playing in the mud is permissible, but that, in their excavations, they must not uproot flowers or small trees. Another adult vetoes mud *per se*. The Ten Commandments are not carved on stone; they vary, and children are helplessly dependent on the caprice of those who give them birth and feed and clothe them. And tyrannize. The young animal does not resent that benevolent tyranny, for it is an essential part of nature. He is, however, an individualist, and maintains his integrity by a subtle, passive fight.

Under the eyes of an adult he changes. Like an actor on-stage, when he remembers, he strives to please, and also to attract attention to himself. Such attempts are not unknown to maturity. But adults are less obvious—to other adults.

It is difficult to admit that children lack subtlety. Children are different from the mature animal because they think in another way. We can more or less easily pierce the pretenses they set up—but they can do the same to us. Ruthlessly a child can destroy the pretenses of an adult. Iconoclasm is their prerogative.

Foppishness, for example. The amenities of social intercourse, exaggerated not quite to absurdity. The gigolo—

"Such *savoir faire*! Such punctilious courtesy!" The dowager and the blond young thing are often impressed. Men have less pleasant comments to make. But the child goes to the root of the matter.

"You're *silly*!"

How can an immature human understand the complicated system of social relationships? He can't. To him, an exaggeration of natural courtesy is silly. In his functional structure of life-patterns, it is rococo. He is an egotistic little animal, who cannot visualize himself in the position of another—certainly not an adult.

A self-contained, almost perfect natural unit, his wants supplied by others, the child is much like a unicellular creature floating in the blood stream, nutriment carried to him, waste products carried away—

From the standpoint of logic, a child is rather horribly perfect. A baby may be even more perfect, but so alien to an adult that only superficial standards of comparison apply. The thought processes of an infant are completely unimaginable. But babies think, even before birth. In the womb they move and sleep, not entirely through instinct. We are conditioned to react rather peculiarly to the idea that a nearly-viable embryo may think. We are surprised, shocked into laughter, and repelled. Nothing human is alien.

But a baby is not human. An embryo is far less human.

That, perhaps, was why Emma learned more from the toys than did Scott. He could communicate his thoughts, of course; Emma could not, except in cryptic fragments. The matter of the scrawls, for example—

Give a young child pencil and paper, and he will draw something which looks different to him than to an adult. The absurd scribbles have little resemblance to a fire engine, but it *is* a fire engine, to a baby. Perhaps it is even three-dimensional. Babies think differently and see differently.

Paradine brooded over that, reading his paper one evening and watching Emma and Scott communicate. Scott was questioning his sister. Sometimes he did it in English. More often he had resource to gibberish and sign language. Emma tried to reply, but the handicap was too great.

Finally Scott got pencil and paper. Emma liked that. Tongue in cheek, she laboriously wrote a message. Scott took the paper, examined it, and scowled.

"That isn't right, Emma," he said.

Emma nodded vigorously. She seized the pencil again and made more scrawls. Scott puzzled for a while, finally smiled rather hesitantly, and got up. He vanished into the hall. Emma returned to the abacus.

Paradine rose and glanced down at the paper, with some mad thought that Emma might abruptly have mastered calligraphy. But she hadn't. The paper was covered with meaningless scrawls, of a type familiar to any parent. Paradine pursed his lips.

It might be a graph showing the mental variations of a manic-depressive cockroach, but probably wasn't. Still, it no doubt had meaning to Emma. Perhaps the scribble represented Mr. Bear.

Scott returned, looking pleased. He met Emma's gaze and nodded. Paradine felt a twinge of curiosity.

"Secrets?"

"Nope. Emma . . . uh . . . asked me to do something for her."

"Oh." Paradine, recalling instances of babies who had babbled in unknown tongues and baffled linguists, made a note to pocket the paper when the kids had finished with it. The next day he showed the scrawl to Elkins at the university. Elkins had a sound working knowledge of many unlikely languages, but he chuckled over Emma's venture into literature.

"Here's a free translation, Dennis. Quote. I don't know what this means, but I kid the hell out of my father with it. Unquote."

The two men laughed and went off to their classes. But later Paradine was to remember the incident. Especially after he met Holloway. Before that, however, months were to pass, and the situation to develop even further toward its climax.

Perhaps Paradine and Jane had evinced too much interest in the toys. Emma and Scott took to keeping them hidden, playing with them only in private. They never did it overtly, but with a certain unobtrusive caution. Nevertheless, Jane especially was somewhat troubled.

She spoke to Paradine about it one evening. "That doll Harry gave Emma."

"Yeah?"

"I was downtown today and tried to find out where it came from. No soap."

"Maybe Harry bought it in New York."

Jane was unconvinced. "I asked them about the other things, too. They showed me their stock—Johnsons' a big store, you know. But there's nothing like Emma's abacus."

"Hm-m-m." Paradine wasn't much interested. They had tickets for a show that night, and it was getting late. So the subject was dropped for the nonce.

Later it cropped up again, when a neighbor telephoned Jane.

"Scotty's never been like that, Denny. Mrs. Burns said he frightened the devil out of her Francis."

"Francis? A little fat bully of a punk, isn't he? Like his father. I broke Burns' nose for him once, when we were sophomores."

"Stop boasting and listen," Jane said, mixing a highball. "Scott showed Francis something that scared him. Hadn't you better—"

"I suppose so." Paradine listened. Noises in the next room told him the whereabouts of his son. "Scotty!"

"Bang," Scott said, and appeared smiling. "I killed 'em all. Space pirates. You want me, dad?"

"Yes. If you don't mind leaving the space pirates unburied for a few minutes. What did you do to Francis Burns?"

Scott's blue eyes reflected incredible candor. "Huh?"

"Try hard. You can remember, I'm sure."

"Uh. Oh, that. I didn't do nothing."

"Anything," Jane corrected absently.

"Anything. Honest. I just let him look into my television set, and it . . . it scared him."

"Television set?"

Scott produced the crystal cube. "It isn't really that. See?"

Paradine examined the gadget, startled by the magnification. All he could see, though, was a maze of meaningless colored designs.

"Uncle Harry—"

Paradine reached for the telephone. Scott gulped. "Is . . . is Uncle Harry back in town?"

"Yeah."

"Well, I gotta take a bath." Scott headed for the door. Paradine met Jane's gaze and nodded significantly.

Harry was home, but disclaimed all knowledge of the peculiar toys. Rather grimly, Paradine requested Scott to bring down from his room all of the playthings. Finally they lay in a row on the table, cube, abacus, doll, helmetlike cap, several other mysterious contraptions. Scott was cross-examined. He lied valiantly for a time, but broke down at last and bawled, hiccuping his confession.

"Get the box these things came in," Paradine ordered. "Then head for bed."

"Are you . . . *hup!* . . . gonna punish me, daddy?"

"For playing hooky and lying, yes. You know the rules. No more shows for two weeks. No sodas for the same period."

Scott gulped. "You gonna keep my things?"

"I don't know yet."

"Well . . . g'night, daddy. G'night, mom."

After the small figure had gone upstairs, Paradine dragged a chair to the table and carefully scrutinized the box. He poked thoughtfully at the fused gadgetry. Jane watched.

"What is it, Denny?"

"Dunno. Who'd leave a box of toys down by the creek?"

"It might have fallen out of a car."

"Not at that point. The road doesn't hit the creek north of the railroad trestle. Empty lots—nothing else." Paradine lit a cigarette. "Drink, honey?"

"I'll fix it." Jane went to work, her eyes troubled. She brought Paradine a glass and stood behind him, ruffling his hair with her fingers. "Is anything wrong?"

"Of course not. Only—where did these toys come from?"

"Johnsons' didn't know, and they get their stock from New York."

"I've been checking up, too," Paradine admitted. "That doll"—he poked it—"rather worried me. Custom jobs, maybe, but I wish I knew who'd made 'em."

"A psychologist? That abacus—don't they give people tests with such things?"

Paradine snapped his fingers. "Right! And say! There's a guy going to speak at the university next week, fellow named Holloway, who's a child psychologist. He's a big shot, with quite a reputation. He might know something about it."

"Holloway? I don't—"

"Rex Holloway. He's . . . hm-m-m! He doesn't live far from here. Do you suppose he might have had these things made himself?"

Jane was examining the abacus. She grimaced and drew back. "If he did, I don't like him. But see if you can find out, Denny."

Paradine nodded. "I shall."

He drank his highball, frowning. He was vaguely worried. But he wasn't scared—yet.

Rex Holloway was a fat, shiny man, with a bald head and thick spectacles, above which his thick, black brows lay like bushy caterpillars. Paradine brought him home to dinner one night a week later. Holloway did not appear to watch the children, but nothing they did or said was lost on him. His gray eyes, shrewd and bright, missed little.

The toys fascinated him. In the living room the three adults gathered around the table, where the playthings had been placed. Holloway studied them carefully as he listened to what Jane and Paradine had to say. At last he broke his silence.

"I'm glad I came here tonight. But not completely. This is very disturbing, you know."

"Eh?" Paradine stared, and Jane's face showed her consternation. Holloway's next words did not calm them.

"We are dealing with madness."

He smiled at the shocked looks they gave him. "All children are mad, from an adult viewpoint. Ever read Hughes' 'High Wind in Jamaica'?"

"I've got it." Paradine secured the little book from its shelf. Holloway extended a hand, took it, and flipped the pages till he had found the place he wanted. He read aloud:

" 'Babies of course are not human—they are animals, and have a very ancient and ramified culture, as cats have, and fishes, and even snakes; the same in kind as these, but much more complicated and vivid, since babies are, after all, one of the most developed species of the lower vertebrates. In short, babies have minds which work in terms and categories of their own which cannot be translated into the terms and categories of the human mind.' "

Jane tried to take that calmly, but couldn't. "You don't mean that Emma—"

"Could you think like your daughter?" Holloway asked. "Listen: 'One can no more think like a baby than one can think like a bee.' "

Paradine mixed drinks. Over his shoulder he said, "You're theorizing quite a bit, aren't you? As I get it, you're implying that babies have a culture of their own, even a high standard of intelligence."

"Not necessarily. There's no yardstick, you see. All I say is that babies think in other ways than we do. Not necessarily *better*—that's a question of relative values. But with a different manner of extension—" He sought for words, grimacing.

"Fantasy," Paradine said, rather rudely, but annoyed because of Emma. "Babies don't have different senses from ours."

"Who said they did?" Holloway demanded. "They use their minds in a different way, that's all. But it's quite enough!"

"I'm trying to understand," Jane said slowly. "All I can think of is my Mixmaster. It can whip up batter and potatoes, but it can squeeze oranges, too."

"Something like that. The brain's a colloid, a very complicated machine. We don't know much about its potentialities. We don't even know how much it can grasp. But it *is* known that the mind becomes conditioned as the human animal matures. It follows certain familiar theorems, and all thought thereafter is pretty well based on patterns taken for granted. Look at this." Holloway touched the abacus. "Have you experimented with it?"

"A little," Paradine said.

"But not much. Eh?"

"Well—"

"Why not?"

"It's pointless," Paradine complained. "Even a puzzle has to have some logic. But those crazy angles—"

"Your mind has been conditioned to Euclid," Holloway said. "So this—thing—bores us, and seems pointless. But a child knows nothing of Euclid. A different sort of geometry from ours wouldn't impress him as being illogical. He believes what he sees."

"Are you trying to tell me that this gadget's got a fourth-dimensional extension?" Paradine demanded.

"Not visually, anyway," Holloway denied. "All I say is that our minds, conditioned to Euclid, can see nothing in this but an illogical tangle of wires. But a child—especially a baby—might see more. Not at first. It'd be a puzzle, of course. Only a child wouldn't be handicapped by too many preconceived ideas."

"Hardening of the thought-arteries," Jane interjected.

Paradine was not convinced. "Then a baby could work calculus better than Einstein? No, I don't mean that. I can see your point, more or less clearly. Only—"

"Well, look. Let's suppose there are two kinds of geometry—we'll limit it, for the sake of the example. Our kind, Euclidean, and another, which we'll call *x*. *X* hasn't much relationship to Euclid. It's based on different theorems. Two and two needn't equal four in it; they could equal y_2, or they might not even *equal*. A baby's mind is not yet conditioned, except by certain questionable factors of heredity and environment. Start the infant on Euclid—"

"Poor kid," Jane said.

Holloway shot her a quick glance. "The basis of Euclid. Alphabet blocks. Math, geometry, algebra—they come much later. We're familiar with that development. On the other hand, start the baby with the basic principles of our *x* logic."

"Blocks? What kind?"

Holloway looked at the abacus. "It wouldn't make much sense to us. But we've been conditioned to Euclid."

Paradine poured himself a stiff shot of whiskey. "That's pretty awful. You're not limiting to math."

"Right! I'm not limiting it at all. How can I? I'm not conditioned to *x* logic."

"There's the answer," Jane said, with a sigh of relief. "Who is? It'd take such a person to make the sort of toys you apparently think these are."

Holloway nodded, his eyes, behind the thick lenses, blinking. "Such people may exist."

"Where?"

"They might prefer to keep hidden."

"Supermen?"

"I wish I knew. You see, Paradine, we've got yardstick trouble again. By our standards these people might seem super-doopers in certain respects. In others they might seem moronic. It's not a quantitative difference; it's qualitative. They *think* different. And I'm sure we can do things they can't."

"Maybe they wouldn't want to," Jane said.

Paradine tapped the fused gadgetry on the box. "What about this? It implies—"

"A purpose, sure."

"Transportation?"

"One thinks of that first. If so, the box might have come from anywhere."

"Where—things are—*different*?" Paradine asked slowly.

"Exactly. In space, or even time. I don't know; I'm a pyschologist. Unfortunately I'm conditioned to Euclid, too."

"Funny place it must be," Jane said. "Denny, get rid of those toys."

"I intend to."

Holloway picked up the crystal cube. "Did you question the children much?"

Paradine said, "Yeah. Scott said there were people in that cube when he first looked. I asked him what was in it now."

"What did he say?" The psychologist's eyes widened.

"He said they were building a place. His exact words. I asked him who—people? But he couldn't explain."

"No, I suppose not," Holloway muttered. "It must be progressive. How long have the children had these toys?"

"About three months, I guess."

"Time enough. The perfect toy, you see, is both instructive and mechanical. It should do things, to interest a child, and it should teach, preferably unobtrusively. Simple problems at first. Later—"

"X logic," Jane said, white-faced.

Paradine cursed under his breath. "Emma and Scott are perfectly normal!"

"Do you know how their minds work—now?"

Holloway didn't pursue the thought. He fingered the doll. "It would be interesting to know the conditions of the place where these things came from. Induction doesn't help a great deal, though. Too many factors are missing. We can't visualize a world based on the *x* factor—environment adjusted to minds thinking in *x* patterns. This luminous network inside the doll. It could be anything. It could exist inside us, though we haven't discovered it yet. When we find the right stain—" He shrugged. "What do you make of this?"

It was a crimson globe, two inches in diameter, with a protruding knob upon its surface.

"What could anyone make of it?"

"Scott? Emma?"

"I hadn't even seen it till about three weeks ago. Then Emma started to play with it." Paradine nibbled his lip. "After that, Scott got interested."

"Just what do they do?"

"Hold it up in front of them and move it back and forth. No particular pattern of motion."

"No Euclidean pattern," Holloway corrected. "At first they couldn't understand the toy's purpose. They had to be educated up to it."

"That's horrible," Jane said.

"Not to them. Emma is probably quicker at understanding *x* than is Scott, for her mind isn't yet conditioned to this environment."

Paradine said, "But I can remember plenty of things I did as a child. Even as a baby."

"Well?"

"Was I—mad—then?"

"The things you don't remember are the criterion of your madness," Holloway retorted. "But I use the word 'madness' purely as a convenient symbol for the variation from the known human norm. The arbitrary standard of sanity."

Jane put down her glass. "You've said that induction was difficult, Mr. Holloway. But it seems to me you're making a great deal of it from very little. After all, these toys—"

"I *am* a psychologist, and I've specialized in children. I'm not a layman. These toys mean a great deal to me, chiefly because they mean so little."

"You might be wrong."

"Well, I rather hope I am. I'd like to examine the children."

Jane rose in arms. "How?"

After Holloway had explained, she nodded, though still a bit hesitantly. "Well, that's all right. But they're not guinea pigs."

The psychologist patted the air with a plump hand. "My dear girl! I'm not a Frankenstein. To me the individual is the prime factor—naturally, since I work with minds. If there's anything wrong with the youngsters, I want to cure them."

Paradine put down his cigarette and slowly watched blue smoke spiral up, wavering in an unfelt draft. "Can you give a prognosis?"

"I'll try. That's all I can say. If the undeveloped minds have been turned into the *x* channel, it's necessary to divert them back. I'm not saying that's the wisest thing to do, but it probably is from our standards. After all, Emma and Scott will have to live in this world."

"Yeah. Yeah. I can't believe there's much wrong. They seem about average, thoroughly normal."

"Superficially they may seem so. They've no reason for acting abnormally, have they? And how can you tell if they—think differently?"

"I'll call 'em," Paradine said.

"Make it informal, then. I don't want them to be on guard."

Jane nodded toward the toys. Holloway said, "Leave the stuff there, eh?"

But the psychologist, after Emma and Scott were summoned, made no immediate move at direct questioning. He managed to draw Scott unobtrusively into the conversation, dropping key words now and then. Nothing so obvious as a word-association test—co-operation is necessary for that.

The most interesting development occurred when Holloway took up the abacus. "Mind showing me how this works?"

Scott hesitated. "Yes, sir. Like this—" He slid a bead deftly through the maze, in a tangled course, so swiftly that no one was quite sure whether or not it ultimately vanished. It might have been merely legerdemain. Then, again—

Holloway tried. Scott watched, wrinkling his nose.

"That right?"

"Uh-huh. It's gotta go *there*—"

"Here? Why?"

"Well, that's the only way to make it work."

But Holloway was conditioned to Euclid. There was no apparent reason why the bead should slide from this particular wire to the other. It looked like a random factor. Also, Holloway suddenly noticed, this wasn't the path the bead had taken previously, when Scott had worked the puzzle. At least, as well as he could tell.

"Will you show me again?"

Scott did, and twice more, on request. Holloway blinked through his glasses. Random, yes. And a variable. Scott moved the bead along a different course each time.

Somehow, none of the adults could tell whether or not the bead vanished. If they had expected to see it disappear, their reactions might have been different.

In the end nothing was solved. Holloway, as he said good night, seemed ill at ease.

"May I come again?"

"I wish you would," Jane told him. "Any time. You still think—"

He nodded. "The children's minds are not reacting normally. They're not dull at all, but I've the most extraordinary impression that they arrive at conclusions in a way we don't understand. As though they used algebra while we used geometry. The same conclusion, but a different method of reaching it."

"What about the toys?" Paradine asked suddenly.

"Keep them out of the way. I'd like to borrow them, if I may—"

That night Paradine slept badly. Holloway's parallel had been ill-chosen. It led to disturbing theories. The *x* factor— The children were using the equivalent of algebraic reasoning, while adults used geometry.

Fair enough. Only—

Algebra can give you answers that geometry cannot, since there are certain terms and symbols which cannot be expressed geometrically. Suppose *x* logic showed conclusions inconceivable to an adult mind?

"Damn!" Paradine whispered. Jane stirred beside him.

"Dear? Can't you sleep either?"

"No." He got up and went into the next room. Emma slept peacefully as a cherub, her fat arm curled around Mr. Bear. Through the open doorway Paradine could see Scott's dark head motionless on the pillow.

Jane was beside him. He slipped his arm around her.

"Poor little people," she murmured. "And Holloway called them mad. I think we're the ones who are crazy, Dennis."

"Uh-huh. We've got jitters."

Scott stirred in his sleep. Without awakening, he called what was obviously a question, though it did not seem to be in any particular language. Emma gave a little mewling cry that changed pitch sharply.

She had not wakened. The children lay without stirring.

But Paradine thought, with a sudden sickness in his middle, it was exactly as though Scott had asked Emma something, and she had replied.

Had their minds changed so that even—sleep—was different to them?

He thrust the thought away. "You'll catch cold. Let's get back to bed. Want a drink?"

"I think I do," Jane said, watching Emma. Her hand reached out blindly toward the child; she drew it back. "Come on. We'll wake the kids."

They drank a little brandy together, but said nothing. Jane cried in her sleep, later.

• • •

Scott was not awake, but his mind worked in slow, careful building. Thus—

"They'll take the toys away. The fat man . . . listava dangerous maybe. But the Ghoric direction won't show . . . evankrus dun-hasn't-them. Intransdection . . . bright and shiny. Emma. She's more khopranik-high now than . . . I still don't see how to . . . thavarar lixery dist—"

A little of Scott's thoughts could still be understood. But Emma had become conditioned to *x* much faster.

She was thinking, too.

Not like an adult or a child. Not even like a human. Except, perhaps, a human of a type shockingly unfamiliar to *genus homo.*

Sometimes Scott himself had difficulty in following her thoughts.

If it had not been for Holloway, life might have settled back into an almost normal routine. The toys were no longer active reminders. Emma still enjoyed her dolls and sand pile, with a thoroughly explicable delight. Scott was satisfied with baseball and his chemical set. They did everything other children did, and evinced few, if any, flashes of abnormality. But Holloway seemed to be an alarmist.

He was having the toys tested, with rather idiotic results. He drew endless charts and diagrams, corresponded with mathematicians, engineers, and other psychologists, and went quietly crazy trying to find rhyme or reason in the construction of the gadgets. The box itself, with its cryptic machinery, told nothing. Fusing had melted too much of the stuff into slag. But the toys—

It was the random element that baffled investigation. Even that was a matter of semantics. For Holloway was convinced that it wasn't really random. There just weren't enough known factors. No adult could work the abacus, for example. And Holloway thoughtfully refrained from letting a child play with the thing.

The crystal cube was similarly cryptic. It showed a mad pattern of colors, which sometimes moved. In this it resembled a kaleidoscope. But the shifting of balance and gravity didn't affect it. Again the random factor.

Or, rather, the unknown. The *x* pattern. Eventually Paradine and Jane slipped back into something like complacence, with a feeling that the children had been cured of their mental quirk, now that the contributing cause had been removed. Certain of the actions of Emma and Scott gave them every reason to quit worrying.

For the kids enjoyed swimming, hiking, movies, games, the normal functional toys of this particular time-sector. It was true that they failed to master certain rather puzzling mechanical devices which involved some calculation. A three-dimensional jigsaw globe Paradine had picked up, for example. But he found that difficult himself.

Once in a while there were lapses. Scott was hiking with his father one Saturday afternoon, and the two had paused at the summit of a hill. Beneath them a rather lovely valley was spread.

"Pretty, isn't it?" Paradine remarked.

Scott examined the scene gravely. "It's all wrong," he said.

"Eh?"

"I dunno."

"What's wrong about it?"

"Gee—" Scott lapsed into puzzled silence. "I dunno."

The children had missed their toys, but not for long. Emma recovered first, though Scott still moped. He held unintelligible conversations with his sister, and studied meaningless scrawls she drew on paper he supplied. It was almost as though he was consulting her, anent difficult problems beyond his grasp.

If Emma understood more, Scott had more real intelligence, and manipulatory skill as well. He built a gadget with his Meccano set, but was dissatisfied. The apparent cause of his dissatisfaction was exactly why Paradine was relieved when he viewed the structure. It was the sort of thing a normal boy would make, vaguely reminiscent of a cubistic ship.

It was a bit too normal to please Scott. He asked Emma more questions, though in private. She thought for a time, and then made more scrawls with an awkwardly clutched pencil.

"Can you read that stuff?" Jane asked her son one morning.

"Not read it, exactly. I can tell what she means. Not all the time, but mostly."

"Is it writing?"

"N-no. It doesn't mean what it *looks* like."

"Symbolism," Paradine suggested over his coffee.

Jane looked at him, her eyes widening. "Denny—"

He winked and shook his head. Later, when they were alone, he said, "Don't let Holloway upset you. I'm not implying that the kids are corresponding in an unknown tongue. If Emma draws a squiggle and says it's a flower, that's an arbitrary rule—Scott remembers that. Next time she draws the same sort of squiggle, or tries to—well!"

"Sure," Jane said doubtfully. "Have you noticed Scott's been doing a lot of reading lately?"

"I noticed. Nothing unusual, though. No Kant or Spinoza."

"He browses, that's all."

"Well, so did I, at his age," Paradine said, and went off to his morning classes. He lunched with Holloway, which was becoming a daily habit, and spoke of Emma's literary endeavors.

"Was I right about symbolism, Rex?"

The psychologist nodded. "Quite right. Our own language is nothing but arbitrary symbolism now. At least in its application. Look here." On his napkin he drew a very narrow ellipse. "What's that?"

"You mean what does it represent?"

"Yes. What does it suggest to you? It could be a crude representation of—what?"

"Plenty of things," Paradine said. "Rim of a glass. A fried egg. A loaf of French bread. A cigar."

Holloway added a little triangle to his drawing, apex joined to one end of the ellipse. He looked up at Paradine.

"A fish," the latter said instantly.

"Our familiar symbol for a fish. Even without fins, eyes or mouth, it's recognizable, because we've been conditioned to identify this particular shape with our mental picture of a fish. The basis of a rebus. A symbol, to us, means a lot more than what we actually see on paper. What's in your mind when you look at this sketch?"

"Why—a fish."

"Keep going. What do you visualize—everything!"

"Scales," Paradine said slowly, looking into space. "Water. Foam. A fish's eye. The fins. The colors."

"So the symbol represents a lot more than just the abstract idea *fish*. Note the connotation's that of a noun, not a verb. It's harder to express actions by symbolism, you know. Anyway—reverse the process. Suppose you want to make a symbol for some concrete noun, say *bird*. Draw it."

Paradine drew two connected arcs, concavities down.

"The lowest common denominator," Holloway nodded. "The natural tendency is to simplify. Especially when a child is seeing something for the first time and has few standards of comparison. He tries to identify the new thing with what's already familiar to him. Ever notice how a child draws the ocean?" He didn't wait for an answer; he went on.

"A series of jagged points. Like the oscillating line on a seismograph. When I first saw the Pacific, I was about three. I remember it pretty clearly. It looked—tilted. A flat plain, slanted at an angle. The waves were regular triangles, apex upward. Now I didn't *see* them stylized that way, but later, remembering, I had to find some familiar standard of comparison. Which is the only way of getting any conception of an entirely new thing. The average child tries to draw these regular triangles, but his co-ordination's poor. He gets a seismograph pattern."

"All of which means what?"

"A child sees the ocean. He stylizes it. He draws a certain definite pattern, symbolic, to him, of the sea. Emma's scrawls may be symbols, too. I don't mean that the world looks different to her—brighter, perhaps, and sharper, more vivid and with a slackening of perception above her eye level. What I do mean is that her thought-processes are different, that she translates what she sees into abnormal symbols."

"You still believe—"

"Yes, I do. Her mind has been conditioned unusually. It may be that she breaks down what she sees into simple, obvious patterns—and realizes a significance to those patterns that we can't understand. Like the abacus. She saw a pattern in that, though to us it was completely random."

Paradine abruptly decided to taper off these luncheon engagements with Holloway. The man was an alarmist. His theories were growing more fantastic than ever, and he dragged in anything, applicable or not, that would support them.

Rather sardonically he said, "Do you mean Emma's communicating with Scott in an unknown language?"

"In symbols for which she hasn't any words. I'm sure Scott understands a great deal of those—scrawls. To him, an isosceles triangle may represent any factor, though probably a concrete noun. Would a man who knew nothing of algebra understand what H_2O meant? Would he realize that the symbol could evoke a picture of the ocean?"

Paradine didn't answer. Instead, he mentioned to Holloway Scott's curious remark that the landscape, from the hill, had looked all wrong. A moment later, he was inclined to regret his impulse, for the psychologist was off again.

"Scott's thought-patterns are building up to a sum that doesn't equal this world. Perhaps he's subconsciously expecting to see the world where those toys came from."

Paradine stopped listening. Enough was enough. The kids were getting along all right, and the only remaining disturbing factor was Holloway himself. That night, however, Scott evinced an interest, later significant, in eels.

There was nothing apparently harmful in natural history. Paradine explained about eels.

"But where do they lay their eggs? Or do they?"

"That's still a mystery. Their spawning grounds are unknown. Maybe the Sargasso Sea, or the deeps, where the pressure can help them force the young out of their bodies."

"Funny," Scott said, thinking deeply.

"Salmon do the same thing, more or less. They go up rivers to spawn." Paradine went into detail. Scott was fascinated.

"But that's *right*, dad. They're born in the river, and when they learn how to swim, they go down to the sea. And they come back to lay their eggs, huh?"

"Right."

"Only they wouldn't *come* back," Scott pondered. "They'd just send their eggs—"

"It'd take a very long ovipositor," Paradine said, and vouchsafed some well-chosen remarks upon oviparity.

His son wasn't entirely satisfied. Flowers, he contended, sent their seeds long distances.

"They don't guide them. Not many find fertile soil."

"Flowers haven't got brains, though. Dad, why do people live *here*?"

"Glendale?"

"No—*here*. This whole place. It isn't all there is, I bet."

"Do you mean the other planets?"

Scott was hesitant. "This is only—part—of the big place. It's like the river where the salmon go. Why don't people go on down to the ocean when they grow up?"

Paradine realized that Scott was speaking figuratively. He felt a brief chill. The—ocean?

The young of the species are not conditioned to live in the completer world of their parents. Having developed sufficiently, they enter that world. Later they breed. The fertilized eggs are buried in the sand, far up the river, where later they hatch.

And they learn. Instinct alone is fatally slow. Especially in the case of a specialized genus, unable to cope even with this world, unable to feed or drink or survive, unless someone has foresightedly provided for those needs.

The young, fed and tended, would survive. There would be incubators and robots. They would survive, but they would not know how to swim downstream, to the vaster world of the ocean.

So they must be taught. They must be trained and conditioned in many ways.

Painlessly, subtly, unobtrusively. Children love toys that do things—and if those toys teach at the same time—

In the latter half of the nineteenth century an Englishman sat on a grassy bank near a stream. A very small girl lay near him, staring up at the sky. She had discarded a curious toy with which she had been playing, and now was murmuring a wordless little song, to which the man listened with half an ear.

"What was that, my dear?" he asked at last.

"Just something I made up, Uncle Charles."

"Sing it again." He pulled out a notebook.

The girl obeyed.

"Does it mean anything?"

She nodded. "Oh, yes. Like the stories I tell you, you know."

"They're wonderful stories, dear."

"And you'll put them in a book some day?"

"Yes, but I must change them quite a lot, or no one would understand. But I don't think I'll change your little song."

"You mustn't. If you did, it wouldn't mean anything."

"I won't change the stanza, anyway," he promised. "Just what does it mean?"

"It's the way out, I think," the girl said doubtfully. "I'm not sure yet. My magic toys told me."

"I wish I knew what London shop sold those marvelous toys!"

"Mamma bought them for me. She's dead. Papa doesn't care."

She lied. She had found the toys in a box one day, as she played by the Thames. And they were indeed wonderful.

Her little song— Uncle Charles thought it didn't mean anything. (He wasn't her real uncle, she parenthesized. But he was nice.) The song meant a great deal. It was the way. Presently she would do what it said, and then—

But she was already too old. She never found the way.

Paradine had dropped Holloway. Jane had taken a dislike to him, naturally enough, since what she wanted most of all was to have her fears calmed. Since Scott and Emma acted normally now, Jane felt satisfied. It was partly wishful-thinking, to which Paradine could not entirely subscribe.

Scott kept bringing gadgets to Emma for her approval. Usually she'd shake her head. Sometimes she would look doubtful. Very occasionally she would signify agreement. Then there would be an hour of laborious, crazy scribbling on scraps of note paper, and Scott, after studying the notations, would arrange and rearrange his rocks, bits of machinery, candle ends, and assorted junk. Each day the maid cleaned them away, and each day Scott began again.

He condescended to explain a little to his puzzled father, who could see no rhyme or reason in the game.

"But why this pebble right here?"

"It's hard and round, dad. It *belongs* there."

"So is this one hard and round."

"Well, that's got vaseline on it. When you get that far, you can't *see* just a hard round thing."

"What comes next? This candle?"

Scott looked disgusted. "That's toward the end. The iron ring's next."

It was, Paradine thought, like a Scout trail through the woods, markers in a labyrinth. But here again was the random factor. Logic halted—familiar logic—at Scott's motives in arranging the junk as he did.

Paradine went out. Over his shoulder he saw Scott pull a crumpled piece of paper and a pencil from his pocket, and head for Emma, who was squatted in a corner thinking things over.

Well—

Jane was lunching with Uncle Harry, and, on this hot Sunday afternoon there was little to do but read the papers. Paradine settled himself in the coolest place he could find, with a Collins, and lost himself in the comic strips.

An hour later a clatter of feet upstairs roused him from his doze. Scott's voice was crying exultantly, "This is it, Slug! Come on—"

Paradine stood up quickly, frowning. As he went into the hall the telephone began to ring. Jane had promised to call—

His hand was on the receiver when Emma's faint voice squealed with excitement. Paradine grimaced. What the devil was going on upstairs?

Scott shrieked, "Look out! This way!"

Paradine, his mouth working, his nerves ridiculously tense, forgot the phone and raced up the stairs. The door of Scott's room was open.

The children were vanishing.

They went in fragments, like thick smoke in a wind, or like movement in a distorting mirror. Hand in hand they went, in a direction Paradine could not understand, and as he blinked there on the threshold, they were gone.

"Emma!" he said, dry-throated. "*Scotty!*"

On the carpet lay a pattern of markers, pebbles, an iron ring—junk. A random pattern. A crumpled sheet of paper blew toward Paradine.

He picked it up automatically.

"Kids. Where are you? Don't hide—

"Emma! SCOTTY!"

Downstairs the telephone stopped its shrill, monotonous ringing. Paradine looked at the paper he held.

It was a leaf torn from a book. There were interlineations and marginal notes, in Emma's meaningless scrawl. A stanza of verse had been so underlined and scribbled over that it was almost illegible, but Paradine was thoroughly familiar with "Through the Looking Glass." His memory gave him the words—

'Twas brillig, and the slithy toves
Did gyre and gimbel in the wabe.
All mimsy were the borogoves,
And the mome raths outgrabe.

Idiotically he thought: Humpty Dumpty explained it. A wabe is the plot of grass around a sundial. A sundial. Time— It has something to do with time. A long time ago Scotty asked me what a wabe was. Symbolism.

'Twas brillig—

A perfect mathematical formula, giving all the conditions, in symbolism the children had finally understood. The junk on the floor. The toves had to be made slithy—vaseline?—and they had to be placed in a certain relationship, so that they'd gyre and gimbel.

Lunacy!

But it had not been lunacy to Emma and Scott. They thought differently. They used *x* logic. Those notes Emma had made on the page—she'd translated Carroll's words into symbols both she and Scott could understand.

The random factor had made sense to the children. They had fulfilled the conditions of the time-space equation. *And the mome raths outgrabe—*

Paradine made a rather ghastly little sound, deep in his throat. He looked at the crazy pattern on the carpet. If he could follow it, as the kids had done— But he couldn't. The pattern was senseless. The random factor defeated him. He was conditioned to Euclid.

Even if he went insane, he still couldn't do it. It would be the wrong kind of lunacy.

His mind had stopped working now. But in a moment the stasis of incredulous horror would pass— Paradine crumpled the page in his fingers. "Emma, Scotty," he called in a dead voice, as though he could expect no response.

Sunlight slanted through the open windows, brightening the golden pelt of Mr. Bear. Downstairs the ringing of the telephone began again.

DAVY JONES' AMBASSADOR

Raymond Z. Gallun

In the era of Gernsbackian science fiction, young Raymond Z. Gallun was one of the big name writers. He first began publishing science fiction as a teenager; by 1935, the date of "Davy Jones' Ambassador" in *Astounding Stories*, he was one of the experienced writers in a genre not yet ten years old. Like the "locked-room" mystery, the "first contact" (with an alien being) tale has become a special pleasure for sf readers—another example in sf is the "time paradox" story. Gallun's innovation was to locate the story not in outer space but at the bottom of the Atlantic Ocean (as James White did later in his novel *The Watch Below*).

"Back in 1935, I couldn't find a statement anywhere about what the water pressure at the bottom of the ocean actually was. So I calculated the weight of a column of water one square inch in a cross section, and two-and-a-half miles high. I added a little for the salt content. The result was too much for me to believe, so I cut it back some. Actually I was close to right in the first place." Those were the days when accuracy to known science was established as part of the aesthetic goal of science fiction, laying the groundwork for Campbell's Golden Age. "The more important purpose," says Gallun, "was to portray, with some semblance of truth, the first meeting of two totally different sentient creatures from vastly different environments." Aliens under the oceans are a central element still in the eighties, in Gregory Benford's "Swarmer Skimmer." But it was Gallun and his peers in the late twenties and early thirties who first claimed and settled the territory for science fiction. Sea monsters have never been the same.

Like Poe's "A Descent into the Maelström," this is a sea story told by a sailor. At one point, his behavior is inspired by a volume of Kipling's poetry. But the visions of undersea creatures and the portrayal of the alien scientist are all Gallun. This is an early, influential hard sf story by a writer who is still publishing in the field in the nineties.

I

It didn't look like a jet of water at all. It seemed too rigid, like a rod of glass; and it spattered over the instruments with a brittle, jingling sound, for such was the effect of the pressure behind it: more than four thousand pounds per square inch—the weight of nearly two and a half miles of black ocean.

Cliff Rodney, hunched in the pilot seat, stared at the widening stream. It made him see how good a thing life was, and how empty and drab the alternative was going to be. Cliff Rodney was young; he did not wish to die.

A few seconds ago all had been normal aboard the bathyspheric submarine.

The velvet darkness of the depths, visible beyond the massive ports of the craft, had inspired awe in him, as it always would in human hearts; but to Cliff it had become familiar. The same was true of the schools of phosphorescent fish shining foggily through the gloom, and of the swarms of nether-world horrors that had darted in the bright golden path of the search beam.

Clifford Rodney, during his explorations, had grown accustomed to these elements of the deep-sea environment, until they had assumed an aspect that was almost friendly.

But the illusion that it was safe here had been abruptly broken. Sinuous, rusty shadows, which bore a suggestion of menace that was new to him, had surged toward the submarine from out of the surrounding murk and ooze.

Attenuated, spidery crustaceans with long feelers had burrowed into the shelter of the mud beneath them. Little fish, some of them equipped with lamplike organs, some blind and lightless, all of them at once dreadful and comic with their needle-fanged jaws and grotesque heads, had scattered in terror.

Bulbous medusæ, contracting and expanding their umbrella-shaped bodies, had swum hurriedly away. Even the pallid anemones had displayed defensive attitudes in the guarded contraction of their flowerlike crowns.

With canny craft the unknowns had avoided the search beam. Cliff had glimpsed only the swift motion of monstrous, armored limbs, and the baneful glitter of great eyes. Then the blow had fallen, like that of a battering ram. It had struck the forward observation port with a grinding concussion.

A crack, looking like a twisted ribbon of silver, had appeared in the thick, vitreous substance of the pane. From it, water had begun to spurt in a slender, unstanchable shaft that grew ominously as the sea spread the edges of the crevice wider and wider apart.

Automatically Cliff had done what he could. He had set the vertical screws of his craft churning at top speed to raise it toward the surface. But, in a moment, the blades had met with fierce resistance, as though clutched and held. The motors had refused to turn. The submarine had sunk back into the muck of the Atlantic's bed. An S O S was the last resort.

Cliff had sent it out quickly, knowing that though it would be picked up by the *Etruria*, the surface ship that served as his base of operations, nothing could be done to help him. He had reached the end of his resources:

Now, there was a breathless pause. The blackness without was inky. Cliff continued to gaze impotently at that slim cylinder of water. Ricocheting bits of it struck him, stinging fiercely, but he did not heed. It fascinated him, making him forget, almost, how it had all happened. His mind was blurred so that it conceived odd notions.

Pretty, the way that jet of water broke apart when it hit the bright metal of the instruments. You wouldn't think that it was dangerous. Flying droplets scattered here and there like jewels, each of them glinting in the shaded glow of the light bulbs. And the sounds they made resembled the chucklings of elves and fairies.

A small creature of the depths, sucked through the breach, burst with a dull plop as the pressure of its normal habitat was removed.

He and that creature had much in common, Rodney thought. Both were pawns which chance had elected to annihilate. Only he was a man; men boasted of their control over natural forces. And he himself was a blatant and ironic symbol of that boast: They had sent him here in the belief that even the bed of the Atlantic might soon yield to human dominance!

The submarine gave a gentle lurch. The youth's eyes sharpened to a keener focus. A yard beyond the fractured port a pair of orbs hung suspended. Beneath them was a fleshy beak that opened and closed as the creature sucked water through its gills. Black, whiplike tentacles swarmed around it like the hairs of a Gorgon beard. And the flesh of the monster was transparent. Cliff could see the throbbing outlines of its vital organs.

Nothing unusual here—just another devil of the depths. So Cliff Rodney would have thought had it not been for certain suggestive impressions that touched lightly on his blurred faculties. That beaked mouth was vacuously empty of expression, but the great limpid orbs were keen. The tentacles clutched a little rod, pointed at one end as a goad would be. The impression was fleeting. With a ripple of finny members the horror disappeared from view.

"That rod," Cliff muttered aloud, "I wonder if that thing made it!"

He felt a cold twinge, that was an expression of many emotions, ripple over his flesh. He moved quickly, his booted feet sloshing in the water that was now six inches deep within the stout hull of the submarine. He turned a switch; the lights winked out. It was best to be concealed in darkness.

Once more the bathyspheric submarine rocked. Then it was whirled completely over. Cliff Rodney tumbled from the pilot chair. Icy fluid cascaded around him as his body struck the hard steel of the craft's interior.

He managed to protect his head with his arms, but contact with the metal sent a numbing, aching shock through his flesh. Electricity; it could not have been anything else. He tried to curse, but the result was only a ragged gasp. Clinging desperately to the sunset edge of oblivion, he fell back among his instruments.

Impressions were very dim after that. The submarine was being towed somewhere by something. Water continued to pour into the hull, making a confused babble of sound. Rodney lay in the growing pool, the briny stuff bitter on his lips. Too near stunned to master his limbs, he rolled about the inundated floor.

With each eccentric motion of the craft, churning water slapped viciously against his face. He choked and coughed. If only he could keep his nose above the flood and breathe!

In some foggy recess of his mind he wondered why he was fighting for life, when the broken port alone was enough to doom him. Was instinct, or some deeper, more reasoned urge responsible? Cliff did not know, but for a fleeting instant the blank look of pain on his face was punctuated by a grim smile.

He was not the mythical iron man; he was a median of strengths and weaknesses as are most humans. And, among humans, courage is almost as cheap as it is glorious.

Cliff could still hear the swish of great flippers shearing the sea beyond the eighteen-inch shell of the submarine. Harsh to his submerged ears, it was the last impression he received when consciousness faded out.

II

Reawakening was slow agony. He had been half-drowned. When his brain was clear enough for him to take stock of his surroundings he did not immediately note any remarkable change.

He was still within the stout little undersea boat that had brought him to the depths. The vessel was nearly two thirds full of brine, but by luck his body had been thrown over a metal brace, and for part of the time his head had been supported above the flood.

No more water was entering the hull through the eroded crevice in the window. In fact there was no motion at all, and except for a distant, pulsating hiss, the stillness was tomblike.

The air was heavy and oppressive. It reeked with a fetid stench that was almost unbearable. Mingled with the odor was a faint pungence of chlorine, doubtless brought about by the electrolysis of sea water where it had penetrated some minor fault in the insulation of the submarine's electrical equipment. A gray luminescence seeped through the ports, lighting up the interior of the vessel dimly.

Soaked, dazed, battered, and chilled to the bone, Cliff struggled to the fractured window. There was air beyond it, not water. He had not extinguished the searchlight, and it still burned, for the storage cells that supplied current had been well protected against mishap.

There was no need to waste power to produce light here. A faint but adequate radiance seemed to come from the curving walls of the chamber in which the submarine had been docked. Cliff switched off the beam.

Groping down under the water, he found a lever and tugged at it. A valve opened, and the brine began to drain out of the submarine. The gurgling sound it made was harsh to his ears. Evidently the atmospheric pressure here was far above normal.

Next, he unfastened the hatch above his head, and hoisted its ponderous weight. Wearily he clambered through the opening and dropped down beside his craft.

The room was elliptical, domed, and bare of any furnishings. Its largest diameter was perhaps thirty-five feet, twice the length of the submarine. Puddles dotted the floor, and the walls were beaded with moisture which showed plainly that the place had been flooded recently. At opposite points there had been circular openings in the walls, one much larger than the other. Both were blocked now by great plugs of a translucent, amorphous material.

Cliff had two immediate urges: One was to get a better idea of where he was; the other was to find, if possible, a means of allaying his discomfort.

He started his investigations with the larger of the two plugs. It was held in place by a tough, glutinous cement, still sticky to the touch. From beyond it came a distant murmur of the sea. This, then, was the way by which the submarine had entered the chamber.

After the entrance had been sealed the water had been drawn off by some means through the several drains in the floor. The stream from the valve in the side of the submarine still gurgled into them, pumped away, perhaps, by some hidden mechanism. So much was clear.

Cliff's attention wandered to the walls, in quest of some explanation of the phosphorescence that came from them. Their surface was hard and smooth like that of glass, but the substance that composed them was not glass. It had a peculiar, milky opalescent sheen, like mother-of-pearl. Squinting, he tried to peer through the cloudy, semitransparent material.

At a depth of a few inches little specks of fire flitted. They were tiny, self-luminous marine animals. Beyond the swarming myriads of them was another shell, white and opaque. He understood. The chamber was double-walled. There was water between the walls, and in it those minute light-giving organisms were imprisoned for the purpose of supplying illumination.

It was a simple bit of inventive ingenuity, but not one which men would be likely to make use of. In fact there was nothing about his new surroundings that was not at least subtly different from any similar thing that human beings would produce.

The glass of the domed chamber was not glass. It seemed to be nearer to the substance that composes the inner portion of a mollusk's shell, and yet it had apparently been made in one piece, for there was no visible evidence of joints where separate parts of the dome might have been fastened together. The blocks that sealed the openings in the walls were almost equally strange. Among men they would surely have been made of metal.

Clifford Rodney became more and more aware of the fact that he had come in contact with a civilization and science more fantastic than that of Mars or Venus could ever be. Those planets were worlds of air, as was the Earth he knew, while this was a world of water. Environment here presented handicaps and possibly offered advantages which might well have turned the sea folk's path of advancement in a direction utterly different from that followed by mankind.

Continuing his investigations, Cliff discovered that the air under the dome was admitted through four pipelike tubes which penetrated the double walls of his prison; but, of course, he could not discover where they originated. The air came through those tubes in rhythmic, hissing puffs, and escaped, he supposed, down the drains through which the water had been drawn, since there was no other outlet in evidence.

He wondered how the rancid stuff had been produced, and how his hosts had even known that he needed gaseous oxygen to breathe. He wondered whether they could have any conception of the place whence he had come. To them a land of sunshine must be as ungraspable as a region of the fourth dimension!

He remembered the electric shock that had almost stunned him at the time of his capture. Electricity was produced here then. But how? As yet he had not so much as glimpsed a scrap of metal in his new surroundings.

Cliff shuddered, nor was the dank, bitter cold alone responsible. He could realize clearer than before that beyond the barriers that protected him was a realm of pressure and darkness and water with which his own normal environment had few things in common.

Belatedly it occurred to him that he was being watched by the curious of Submarinia. Standing now in the center of the slippery floor, he scanned the dome above him for evidence that his logic was correct. It was. Spaced evenly around the arching roof, more than halfway toward its central axis, was a ring of circular areas more transparent than the surrounding texture of the double walls.

Though not easily discernible at a casual glance, they were plain enough to him now. Through each, a pair of huge, glowing eyes and a Gorgon mass of black tentacles was visible. The ovoid bodies of the creatures were silhouetted against a nebulous luminescence originating from some unknown source beyond them.

The gaze of those monsters seemed cool and interested and intense, though Clifford Rodney felt that one could never be sure of what emotions, if any, their vacuous, beaked lips and limpid eyes betrayed. It would be difficult indeed to forget that they were completely inhuman.

Cliff's reaction was a kind of terror; though the only outward evidences of it were the strained hollows that came suddenly into his cheeks; still, the realization of his position thudded with ghastly weight into his mind. To those sea beings he was doubtless like a simple amœba beneath a microscope, a specimen to be observed and studied!

Then his sense of humor rescued him. He chuckled half-heartedly through chattering teeth. At least no man had ever before been in a situation quite as novel as this. It was one which a scientist, eager to learn new things, should appreciate. Besides, perhaps now he could bring the adventure to a head.

He waved his arms toward the pairs of eyes that gazed steadily at him. "Hello!" he shouted. "What in the name of good manners are you trying to do to me? Get me out of here!"

They couldn't understand him, but anyway they could see by his gestures that he had discovered them, and that he was insisting on some sort of attention. Cliff Rodney was cold, and half-choked by the rancid air.

Things had to happen soon, or his stamina would be worn down and he would no longer be in a position to see them happen. The dank, frigid chill was the worst. The air would not have been so bad if it had not been for the retch-provoking stench that impregnated it. If he only had a dry cigarette and a match, it would help a lot.

That was a funny thought—a cigarette and a match! Had he expected these ovoid beings to supply him with such luxuries?

However, since there was no one else to whom he might appeal for help, he continued to shout epithets and pleas, and to flail his arms until he was nearly spent with the effort.

Yet, the sea people gave no evidence of special response. The vital organs throbbed within their transparent bodies, tympanic membranes beneath their beaked mouths vibrated, perhaps transmitting to the water around them signals of a kind of vocal speech, inaudible to him, of course; and their tentacles scurried over the outer surfaces of the spy windows, producing a noise such as a mouse scampering inside a box might make, but Cliff saw no promise in their evident interest.

Every few minutes, one pair of eyes would turn away from a window, and another pair would take its place. The ovoids were managing the scrutiny of him just as humans would manage a show featuring a freak. He could imagine them out there waiting in line for a chance to see him. It was funny, but it was ghastly too.

Exhausted, he gave up. Probably they couldn't help him anyway. If he only had something dry to keep the chill away from his shivering flesh!

Hopefully he scrambled up the side of the submarine and lowered himself through the hatch. There was a little electric heater there, but a brief examination of it confirmed his well-founded suspicions. Soaked with brine, its coils were shorted and it refused to work. He had no means of drying it out sufficiently, and so he turned on the search beam. If he crouched against the lamp, he might capture a little heat.

He climbed out of the dripping, disordered interior. Before dropping to the floor of the domed chamber he stood on tiptoe on the curved back of the submarine and attempted to peer through one of the spy windows in the rotunda over his head.

Even now the mystery of what lay beyond the glowing walls of the room beneath the sea could fascinate him. But his vantage point was not quite high enough, nor was there any easy means to make it higher. He saw only a flicker of soft, greenish light beyond the motionless, ovoid shape that occupied the window.

He slid weakly off the submarine and pressed his body against the lens of the searchlight. The rays warmed him a little—a very little—enough to tantalize him with the thought that such a thing as warmth really existed.

He thought of exercise as a means to start his sluggish blood circulating faster; he even made an effort to put the thought into execution by shaking his arms and stamping his feet. But he felt too far gone to keep up the exertion. His head slumped against the mounting of the searchlight.

Some minutes later, a throbbing radiance caused him to look up. At one of the spy windows was a creature different from the sea people. Its body was flat, and as pallid as a mushroom.

It was shaped curiously like an oak leaf with curled edges. Its mouth was a slit at the anterior extremity of its queer form. On either side of it were pulsing gill openings, and above were beady eyes supported on stalky members. From the thin edges of the creature's body, long, slender filaments projected, glinting like new-drawn copper wire. And the flesh of the thing glowed intermittently like a firefly.

After several seconds this phenomenon ceased, and another far more startling one took its place. The creature turned its dorsal surface toward the window.

Then it was as though some invisible hand and brush were printing a message in letters of fire on the pallid hide of the monster. They were old, familiar letters spelling out English words. One by one they appeared, traced with swift and practiced accuracy until the message was complete:

> I am far away, man; but I am coming. I wish to write with you. Do not die yet. Wait until I arrive.
>
> THE STUDENT.

If Clifford Rodney had been himself, his consternation at this odd note and the outlandish means of its transmission would have been greater, and his analysis of the phenomena involved would have been more keen. As matters were, he was still able to discern the shadows of the causes underlying the enigma.

This was the subsea version of wireless. He was too tired to construct a theory of its principle; he only glanced at the fine filaments projecting from the body of the creature that had served as an agent of the miracle, and dismissed the vague germ of an idea that had oozed unbidden into his sluggish mind.

Even though this was a science completely inhuman, still it was self-evident that there were logical explanations. At present Cliff didn't care particularly whether he ever learned them. Nor did he ponder for long the riddle of how this distant spokesman of the ovoids was able to write English. Somewhere there must be a simple answer.

However, the wording of the message, strikingly demonstrating the broad physical and psychological differences between his kind and the unknowns, won somewhat more attention from him. It was "I wish to write with you," instead of "I wish to speak with you." The ovoid tympanums, vibrating in water, could not produce or convey to him the sounds of human speech.

"Do not die yet. Wait until I arrive." Did those two simple commands express naïve brutality or— Cliff scarcely knew how to think the thought. No human being would have expressed an idea of that sort with such guileless frankness. The meaning, of course, was perfectly clear; and Cliff knew that he had been afforded a glimpse into a mind differing radically from those of men.

"The Student." That at least had a familiar aspect. Because of the way the message was signed, the anger and depression which it aroused in him subsided.

The lettering vanished from the flat back of the creature which had been the means of conveying to Cliff Rodney the first expression of subsea thought. Another fire-traced message appeared, letter by letter:

> We have waited too long for the arrival of one of you, man. We must learn more about your kind before you die. All in our power has been done for you. If you require more, perhaps it is beyond the small sealed exit. Unseal it. Live until I come.
>
> THE STUDENT.

Rodney cursed and shook his fist feebly at the messenger. Nevertheless, hope gave him fresh energy. He proceeded to obey the suggestion. Returning to the submarine he procured a heavy knife, extinguished the search beam for economy, and came forth again to attack the smaller door.

The cement here was thoroughly hard, glassy; but tough and elastic rather than brittle. Cliff worked at it fiercely, digging out the gummy stuff with the point of his knife. For a time it seemed that the stubborn block would never yield; but at length, when his expiring energies were all but burned up, and little specks of blackness flitted before his vision, success came.

The plug of amorphous material toppled from the opening and thudded resoundingly to the floor. For a minute young Rodney lay exhausted beside it, a rustle in his ears that he knew was not the distant whisper of the ocean.

Then, rested a bit, he crept through the opening. He was too dazed to be very conscious of the things around him. The character of the chamber was much the same as that of the one he had just quitted, except that it was larger, and the floor was a much more elongated oval. It had the same kind of pearly, phosphorescent dome equipped with spy windows.

Even now the windows were being occupied by the grotesque forms of the sea people, eager to observe the fresh reactions of their strange captive. The air, though, was drier, for the place had not recently been flooded, and it was musty with the odor of ancient decay, like that of a tomb.

The floor was piled high with a numerous assortment of things—every one of them of human origin. Cliff let his eyes wander over the array. There was a generator, part of a ship's turbine, several life preservers, a fire extinguisher, books, tattered and pulped by sea water and pressure, rugs, and so forth. There were even two human figures.

They were propped on a dilapidated divan, and were fully clothed. Whoever had placed them there had apparently made some attempt to arrange them naturally.

Cliff Rodney came closer to examine them. One had been a man, the other a woman. Their flesh was gone, their faces were only skeleton masks. The woman's dress had once been white and beautiful, but it was just a mottled, gray rag now. Yet, the diamond pendant at her throat still gleamed as brightly as ever. The pair clutched each other with a fierceness that was still apparent. Perhaps they had died in each other's arms like that long ago. A grim tragedy of the Atlantic—

Rodney's reactions were not quite normal. He felt sick. "Damn museum!" he grumbled in a sort of inane disgust. "Damn stinky museum of Davy Jones!" He choked and sneezed.

The haze of his numbed faculties was not so dense that it obscured the animal urge to seek comfort, however. He picked up a heavy rug which, though rotted and odorous, was fairly dry.

He stripped off his soaked garments, and wrapped himself in the rug. Tearing up a book and heaping the fragments into a pile with the intention of making a fire, was quite natural and automatic. So was locating his cigarette lighter and attempting to make it work. Here, though, he struck a snag. Sparks flew, but the wick was too wet to burn.

Out of his angry chagrin an inspiration was born. He unscrewed the cap from the fuel container, poured a few drops of benzine onto the paper, and applied the sparks direct. The tinder flared up merrily, and grotesque shadows leaped about the walls of the eerie chamber. Delighted, Cliff huddled down beside the blaze, absorbing its welcome heat.

Only once did he glance at the ovoids watching him. He could not have guessed what wonder his activities provoked in the minds of those strange people of the depths.

"Go to hell!" he called to them in dismissal.

The air didn't smell so bad with the smoke in it. As the embers began to die, Clifford Rodney drew the carpet tighter about him and sprawled on the pavement. Worn out, he was quickly asleep.

III

Through the gloom of the bottoms, seven slim shapes were speeding. They were neither crustaceans nor sharklike elasmobranchs; they bore some of the characteristics of both.

Their bodies were protected by horny armor, and were tapered in such a manner as to suggest the lines of a torpedo, a comparison that was heightened by the waspish air of concentrated power about them. Rows of flippers along their flanks churned the dark water, sending them swiftly on their way. Folded carefully against their bellies were pairs of huge claws resembling the pinchers of a crawfish, though much larger. Projecting like swollen cheeks on either side of their heads were protuberances of modified muscle—their most effective weapons.

These monstrous creations were not entirely the product of nature. The knowledge of a gifted people working on their kind for ages had achieved a miracle, making of them efficient, dependable, fighting machines.

They swam in a military formation. The largest individual of the group formed its center. Above, below, ahead, behind, and on either side—one in each position—the others swam. There was a reason. Every now and then schools of small, devil-fanged fish would glide out of the darkness to attack the cavalcade. The nearest members of the escort would leap to meet them.

For an instant, many fierce little teeth would try to penetrate the tough shells of the fighters. Then the latter would strike back, invisibly, except for a momentary flicker of lavender sparks around their snouts. The attacking fish would stiffen and go drifting limply into the darkness again, dead or stunned.

The fighters were protecting their master, he who had named himself "The Student." He rode the central individual of the formation, suckerlike cups on the ventral surface of his body clinging to its back. He had flattened himself against his mount to minimize the surge of water that swept past him. His eyes peered ahead with an expectant glitter.

He changed position only to trace queer symbols, with a goad of glassy material, on the flesh of the fragile messenger that clung beside him, and to scan the phosphorescent replies to his queries, that came in return. But within him, dread and eagerness were mingled. He had received the call that he had both hoped for and feared. And he was responding.

Out of the murk and ooze that blanketed the sea floor ahead, an emerald glow arose like some infernal dawn. The cavalcade continued to speed on its way, and the radiance brightened.

A broad depression in the bottoms emerged from the fog of suspended mud, gray like tarnished silver. Above it swarmed myriads of minute, luminous animals, forming an immense canopy of green light, limned against the blackness of the depths. That canopy looked as though it had been placed there for a purpose.

To paint the scene beneath, would have challenged the genius of Gustave Doré. It was as abhorrent as the visions of a mad demon; still it possessed elements of majesty and beauty.

A city was there in the hollow—a city or a colony. The seven fighters were moving close above it now. The valley was pitted by countless small openings, arranged edge to edge after the fashion of the cells of a honeycomb. Into them and from them, ovoids swam, going about whatever business was theirs. Here and there, queer structures of a pearly, translucent material reared twisted spires that seemed to wriggle with the motion of the water.

Monsters were everywhere, vague in the shifting shadows. Scores of types were represented, each type seemingly stranger than its associates. All of the monsters were busy, guided in their activities by alert ovoids that hung in the water, goads poised, flippers stirring idly.

Some of the monsters wallowed in the muck, digging with broad, spatulate members. Wormlike in form, pallid and smooth, one knew that their purpose in life was to dig, and nothing else.

Others kneaded their bloated, shapeless bodies, forming elfin creations around them, seemingly from their own substance. Some fanned the water with long, flattened limbs, perhaps performing a function akin to ventilation. Others—they were fighters like The Student's escort—guarded the colony, swimming steadily back and forth.

And so it went. Each of the horrors followed the vocation for which it was intended. Each was a robot, a machine of living flesh, capable of some special function.

A man would have been held spellbound by this teeming, alien activity; but The Student scarcely noticed it at all. Everything—the lights, the motion, the whispering, slithering sounds that found their way to his auditory organs—held the familiarity of life-long experience, of home.

His gaze, though, wandered intently across the valley to the place where the gutted hull of an ocean liner sprawled half over on its side, its form almost obscured by the dusky murk of the depths.

Slim ribbons that had the appearance of vegetation streamed up from it, waving like banners. They were not vegetation, though they were alive. There were no plants here, away from the sunshine; and the fauna of this world was dependent for its sustenance upon organic débris settling from above, where there was sunlight, where chlorophyll could act, and where both fauna and flora could exist.

Always the wrecks of upper-world ships had interested The Student, as something from another planet would interest us. He had rummaged through their slimy interiors, examining and exploring this and that.

Of all their wondrous contents, books had fascinated him the most. With a zeal and care and love that an archeologist would understand, he had made copies of those fragile, water-soaked storehouses of knowledge, tracing the still legible parts of them on a parchment that could withstand the action of the sea.

He had studied the queer symbol groups they bore; he had discovered the value of the dictionary. And as the Rosetta Stone had been the key to Egyptian hieroglyphics, so the dictionary had been his means of solving the riddle of mankind's literature.

There was another thing that won a brief glance from The Student, as he guided his mount and escort toward the concourse of ovoids that had collected around the structures which housed the reason for his coming.

On a low rise a circular vat, filled with living protoplasm, squatted. Above it two crudely hammered bars of iron converged together. Between their adjacent ends blue sparks purred. The apparatus was a recent development which would have startled the wise inventors who had contributed so much to another culture.

With a thrusting motion The Student hurled himself from the back of the fighter. The flippers along his sides took hold of the water with powerful sweeps.

The crowd made a lane for him as he approached. Tympanic voices buzzed around him, questioning, demanding; yet, he paid no heed.

IV

The Student reached a spy window in the dome, looked down. The man was there, sprawled motionless amid the relics of his civilization. A piece of ragged fabric wrapped his pallid body.

Revulsion, fear, hope, and anxiety were not beyond The Student's understanding, and he felt them all now.

Was the prisoner dead? Was all that had been promised to end in disappointment? Paradoxically The Student would have been more at ease if such were the case. There is no harm in an enemy whose vital functions have stopped. Yet The Student himself did not live for peace and security alone. The boon of existence had many meanings.

He moved to a window in the smaller dome, and surveyed the bathyspheric submarine, marveling at the smooth, metal hull, and the precise perfection of each detail. No ovoid could fabricate such wonders.

Patiently he waited until the buzzing tympanic voice of the throng about him impinged on his sense organs, telling him that the time had arrived.

Coolly The Student returned to the window of the museum chamber. The man was awake. He stood unsteadily in the center of the floor, the rug still wrapped around him and his eyes turned upward.

Two peoples, two cultures, two backgrounds, two histories, and two points of view were face to face at last, ready for whatever might come of the meeting. The bizarre stood versus the bizarre from opposite angles. Between them the abyss was wide. Was there—could there be—any sympathy to bridge it?

It was up to The Student to open negotiations, and he did not hesitate, for he had planned well. From a pouch, which was a natural part of him, he removed a stylus of chalky material. Then, concentrating on what he had learned during his years of study, he printed a command on the pane of the window: "You made fire, man. Make it again."

He traced the letters in reverse, so that they would appear normally to the being inside the dome.

The prisoner seemed uncertain for a brief spell; then he obeyed. Paper, a daub of liquid from what appeared to be a tiny black box, a swift movement, sparks, and finally—flame! The man held up the blazing paper for his visitor to see.

The Student watched the phenomenon of rapid oxidation, drinking in the marvel of it until the flame was burned out. The water had washed the chalky letters from the window. He traced another message: "Fire gives you metals, machines, power—everything you have?"

If, before it had happened, Clifford Rodney had had an opportunity to construct a mental picture of what this meeting would be like, he would no doubt have expected to be amazed. But he could not have conceived beforehand an adequate idea of his own wonder. Tangible truth was so much more startling than a bare thought could be.

Here was a thing which bore many of the outward characteristics of the marine animals with which he was acquainted—pulsing gills, stirring flippers—organs used in a medium which must ever be foreign to those forms of life that live in air and sunshine.

There was even in the visage of the thing—if visage it might be called—a deceptive look of vacuity which only the cool glitter of the great eyes denied. And yet, clutched in the being's tentacles was a crayon, with which it was writing in English, words that displayed a considerable knowledge of human attainments!

Cliff almost forgot that he himself was a delver after hidden facts. Then his own calm purpose conquered. His sleep had refreshed him; and though he felt stiff, sore, and uncomfortable, he could still respond to the appeal of an enigma.

He looked about for some means to answer. His attention was drawn to a small area of unencumbered floor, on which a thin layer of sea sand had been deposited. With a finger he traced words in it: "Yes. Fire brought us out of the Stone Age, and kept us going since. You got it right, friend. How?"

And the swift-moving tentacles traced a reply: "I have translated books—men's books. I have read of fire. But we have never produced fire. We might produce fire from electric sparks—soon."

Rodney looked with a quizzical awe at the gleaming orbs of the ovoid. Behind them, he knew, was a brilliant brain, whose brilliance had perhaps been augmented by the very handicaps which it had faced and overcome. The truth concealed behind this intriguing statement was already dimly formulated in his mind. Now he might clear up the matter completely.

He smoothed out the sand and printed another message: "You have electricity, glass, and a kind of wireless—still, no fire. It is too wet here for fire; but how did you do it all? And you write like a man—how?"

The Student chose to answer the last question first. "I mimic the writing of men," he printed. "I must—so men understand. Glass, electricity, wireless, and other things, come from animals. Nearly everything comes from animals. We have made the animals so. We have developed the useful characteristics of the animals—great care, selection, breeding, crossbreeding—a long time—ages."

It was a confirmation of the vague theory that Cliff had formulated. Handicapped by the impossibility of fire in their normal environment, the sea folk's advancement had followed another path. Controlled evolution was what it amounted to.

Cliff remembered what miracles men such as Luther Burbank had achieved with plants—changing them, improving them. And to a lesser extent, similar marvels had been achieved with animals. Here in the depths of the Atlantic the same science had been used for ages!

Without visible excitement Cliff traced another note in the sand: "Electricity from living flesh, from modified muscle as in the electric eel or the torpedo? Glass from— Tell me!"

And on the spy window the answer appeared: "Yes. Glass from animal—from mollusk—deposited and grown as a mollusk's shell is deposited and grown. And it is formed as we wish. Electricity from modified muscle, as in the electric eel or the torpedo. I have read of them. We have animals like them—but larger. The animals fight for us, kill with electricity. And we have—electric batteries—metal from the ships. Rods—protoplasm—"

The Student's black tentacles switched and hesitated uncertainly as he groped for words that would express his thoughts to this strange monstrosity of another realm.

But Clifford Rodney had captured enough of his meaning to make a guess. "You mean," he wrote, "that you have developed a way of producing a steady current of electricity from a form of living protoplasm? A sort of isolated electric organ with metal details and grids to draw off the power?"

"Yes."

Cliff thought it over, briefly but intensely. Such protoplasm would need only food to keep it active, and it could probably obtain food from the organic dust in the sea water around it.

"Splendid!" he printed. "And the wireless, the radio beast—tell me about it!"

The Student concentrated all his powers on the task of formulating an adequate response. Slowly, hesitantly, now, he began to trace it out; for he was thinking almost in an alien plane, working with words and ideas subtly different from his own. To make the man understand, he had to choose phrases and expressions from the books he had read.

"It is the same," he inscribed. "A characteristic developed to usefulness. Long ago we studied these animals. We discovered that they could—communicate—through—over great distances. We increased—improved this power by—by—"

"By choosing those individuals in which the power was strongest, for breeding purposes, and in turn selecting those of their offspring and the descendants of their offspring in which the characteristics you desired to emphasize were most prominent," Cliff prompted. "Thus the abilities of these messenger creatures were gradually improved. Right?"

"Yes. Right," The Student printed. "Now, we make marks on the flesh of a messenger creature. The irritation produces stimuli—a sequence of stimuli through nerves of skin, through brain, through—communicating organs. Other creatures, far off, pick up the impulses. Again there is a sequence of stimuli—communicating organs, nerves of skin, luminous cells of skin. The luminous cells which—which—"

Cliff had followed the strange explanation keenly, and now his own quick analytical powers grasped the idea which The Student was trying to express.

"The result is that the luminous cells in the skin of the receiving animals, corresponding in position to the luminous cells in the skin of the transmitting animal, are stimulated so that they emit light. Thus the symbols are made visible on the hide of the receiving messenger, just as they were originally traced. Is that correct?"

"Correct," the ovoid printed.

"There are entomologists who have suggested that certain insects have the power to communicate over distances like that," Cliff answered, "the cockroach, for instance. Their antennæ are supposed to be miniature wireless sets, or something."

The Student did not offer to reply to this immediately, and so Rodney scratched one word in the sand. It was "Wait." For a minute or two he was busy piling odds and ends of wreckage beneath the spy window. Then, equipped with a piece of board, and a pencil taken from his discarded clothing, he scrambled to the top.

V

For the first time, he viewed the colony of the ovoids, the green canopy of luminous organisms, the hordes of sea people, the welter of infernal activity, the protoplasmic battery sparking on its isolated knoll, the moving shadows of robot beings, and the alert fighters that patrolled the outskirts of the city, where light and darkness met, like enemies holding each other in deadlock.

And the greatest of these miracles was this devil who called himself The Student, and who had now backed off in revulsion at Cliff's approach.

But there were matters still to be investigated more closely. Dimly visible against the outer walls of the dome was a great shapeless mass that expanded and contracted as if it were breathing. Above the thing, and projecting from the dome like a canopy, was a curious curved shell of pearly, vitreous material.

His deductive faculties keyed up, Cliff was almost certain that he understood the function of the arrangement. With his pencil he traced two questions on the board he held: "You know chemistry, physics, what oxygen and nitrogen are?"

"Yes. I have learned from research. I have learned from men's books," The Student replied, conquering his revulsion.

"You know that the air bladders of fish are filled with a mixture of oxygen and nitrogen?" Cliff asked. "You know that these gases are derived from the blood through the capillaries that line the air bladders, and that this oxygen and nitrogen is drawn originally from the oxygen and nitrogen dissolved in sea water, by means of the gills?"

"Yes."

"Then," Rodney went on, "the air in this place comes from animals too! That creature out there under that roof arrangement—it has gills which take the gases from the sea water and deliver them into the blood stream.

"Part of the oxygen is used to keep the creature alive, of course; but another part of it, together with the nitrogen, is discharged through the walls of capillaries as an actual, free gas, just as a portion of the oxygen and nitrogen in the blood of a fish is discharged into its hydrostatic organ or air bladder! The roof arrangement probably collects it in some way, and delivers it here to me!"

"That is correct," The Student printed. "Several animals work to give you air. Something new—ages to produce."

"Ages all right," Cliff breathed fervently. "I can well believe it!" He had spoken aloud.

But he was not finished yet. His face was flushed with eagerness, and his pulses were pounding. He had another question to print: "How is the water kept out of here? Nothing of flesh could prevent it from entering when the pressure is so great."

"There our skill failed," The Student responded. "We used the skill of men. We made pumps from parts of ships, and from materials which were our own. Air is pumped into the domes and from the domes—and water, when necessary."

The black tendrils withdrew from the window. Transparent lids flickered over the ovoid's great eyes. The transparent body swayed languorously, reminding Cliff of the first sting ray he had seen in an aquarium when he was a child.

It was clear at last, this alien science. Low down beyond the window, and against the shell of the dome, he glimpsed vague motion, where a monster toiled, swinging the lever of a rusty mechanism back and forth. The machine was a pump. Its operator was forcing to him the air which those other monsters produced. And beyond extended the murky, unbelievable reality of this submarine world.

"It is all glorious," Cliff printed in tribute, "even beautiful, almost—your achievements, your ways of doing things!"

The Student's tentacles stirred uneasily, but he made no reply.

A climax had been reached and passed. Rodney's enthusiasm began to cool a little, leaving him to become more cognizant of his own position. He thought of people and friends that he had known, and experiences he had enjoyed. The thoughts made him feel very cold and lonely.

His pencil scratched in the silence. "What are you going to do with me?" he was demanding.

"Keep you," was the response.

"Until I rot?"

"Until you rot."

It was a simple statement, devoid of either malice or compassion. Yet it was loaded with a dread significance. It meant staying here in this awful place, dying of starvation, perhaps, if the icy dankness didn't get him.

It meant death in any event; probably it meant madness. There would be ovoid eyes watching him, studying him; there would be ovoid beaks opening and closing vacuously—crazy, wonderful things everywhere, but only his submarine, and the depressing relics in the museum, familiar!

They had conversed, The Student and he. They had been almost friends. But beneath their apparently amicable attitudes toward each other had lain mistrust, broadened and deepened by the fact that they had so very little in common. Cliff saw it now.

Fury smoldered within him, but he held it in check.

He tossed aside the board, which was too covered with messages to be of any further use, and selected in its stead the pulped remnants of a book from the stack of things which supported him close to the spy window.

On one of the illegible pages he printed a note and held it up for the ovoid to see: "I know a better way for you to learn about my mind. Why not establish friendly relations with the world above? Certainly we have many things that you could use. And you have many things that we could use."

"No!" The Student's slender, boneless limbs seemed to jerk with emphasis as they traced the word and repeated it. "No!"

"It will happen anyway," Cliff promised. "Soon my people will come in machines of steel. They will make you understand what is best."

"Men coming here will not return," The Student answered.

And Clifford Rodney, remembering his own capture, and seeing now the waspish fighters patrolling the city of the ovoids, had no reason to doubt the weight of the statement. The sea people could protect themselves in their native element.

"You fear us? You mistrust us?" Cliff wanted to know.

The response was frank: "Yes."

"There is no reason."

To this The Student offered nothing.

Cliff tried a new angle, printing swiftly: "What do you know of the place we live in, really—sun, stars, planets, day, night? You have read of such things, no doubt. Wouldn't you like to see them? They are beautiful!"

"Beautiful?" The Student questioned. "Beautiful to you. To me—to us—horrible. The sun, the great dazzling light—it is horrible—and the heat, and the emptiness of air. They make me afraid. But they are wonderful—interesting, very interesting."

Some emotion seemed to stir the nameless soul of the ovoid, making him hesitant and uncertain.

Clifford Rodney thought he glimpsed a shadow of hope. He scarcely understood why he argued; whether he had some dim idea that he might save himself, or whether he was trying to advance the cause of mankind in its demand for expansion into alien realms.

Perhaps he was urging this queer intelligence of the deeps only because it is in the nature of any strong, healthy-minded youth to fight even the most adverse circumstance.

"You are interested, but you are afraid," he wrote. "Why don't you give your interest the chance it deserves? Why don't you—" He hesitated, not knowing quite what he wished to say. "Why don't you try to make contact with my people?"

For a flickering instant The Student paused, in a way that betrayed some hidden process within him. Then his decision seemed to come. "The world of men is the world of men," he printed. "The world of the sea is our world."

Further urgings on Cliff's part met only with flat refusal. He desisted at last, feeling oddly like a salesman, who, through a slip in technique, has lost a sale. But that comparison could not be true either. He felt that The Student's obstinacy was too deep-seated to be overcome by mere salesmanship.

Dejectedly he watched the chalky words of the ovoid's last rebuff being washed from the window by the ocean.

Then those black tendrils holding the crayon went to work once more. "You wish to escape," they printed, "it would be interesting, man, to watch you trying to escape."

Startled, Cliff wondered what bizarre mental process had given birth to these statements. Hope was resurrected.

"I cannot escape," he printed warily. "A glass port of my submarine needs repairing, for one thing. I have no materials."

"We will give you materials," was the astounding assertion.

"Eh?" the man said aloud, before he remembered that the ovoid could not hear his words, or understand them if he had been able to. "I could not get out of these domes anyway," he wrote. "It is useless."

Cliff Rodney was trying to make a subtle suggestion, in the hope that his unfathomable jailer would offer him a chance for freedom.

"Men have many tricks," The Student responded. "Watching you make use of tricks will be very interesting. We will learn much. Men have powerful explosives."

"I have no explosives!" Cliff insisted truthfully. A feeling of exasperation was rising within him.

"Men have many tricks," the ovoid repeated.

It was a tribute, nothing less; a tribute of mingled awe and mistrust, which the people of the depths felt for the people of the upper air. It was an example of other-world minds at work.

"You expect me to escape?" Cliff demanded.

"You will not escape," was the answer. "This is a test of your powers—a test of men's powers—an experiment. If you escape from the domes you shall be recaptured. We understand caution, man."

Thus Rodney's hopes were broken. But before this message had faded from the spy window, he wrote on a page of the tattered book an acceptance of the challenge: "Good! Get the materials you promised, and go to the devil!"

"Materials shall come," was the reply. "Go to the devil."

Breaking off the conversation thus, The Student wheeled in the water. His silvery fins flashed, and he vanished amid the throng of nightmare watchers.

Cliff wondered in a detached way what emotion, if any, had prompted the ovoid to repeat his angry epithet. Was it fury, amusement, some feeling beyond human conception, or just another bit of mimicry? Cliff didn't know; and because he didn't, the skin at the back of his neck tightened unpleasantly.

VI

The Student was out there among his fellows, giving orders in buzzing, tympanic tones, and preparing for the test. None could see the turmoil inside his brain—fear pitted against intense eagerness and interest.

He had made no decisions yet, nor would the decision he had in mind be sanctioned by his people. And it is certain, too, that he had no sympathy for the man who had fallen into his clutches, nor any desire to help him win his way to freedom.

Clifford Rodney did not immediately climb down from his position atop the wreckage he had piled up. Instead he remained by the window, looking out, for no particular reason. The only sound, the gentle, pulsing hiss of air being forced into his prison, had a monotonous effect that was more oppressive than absolute silence.

The weird colony wasn't so very different, though, from the cities at home, if you allowed your eyes to sort of blur out of focus; if you didn't see that sunken liner with the wispy ribbons trailing up from it, or the twisted architecture, or the inhabitants. The moving lights made you think of gay places and of gay music and people. One corner of his mouth drew back thoughtfully.

He could see that his chance of getting out of this mess was practically nil: In the first place, he had not the ghost of an idea how he might escape from the two domes. And if he did manage to break free from them, those armored fighters would bar his way. Their great claws would grip the submarine while they discharged their bolts of electric force. The metal hull would protect him to some extent, but not sufficiently, as he knew from experience.

More conscious than ever of the aches in his body, his loneliness and dejection, he looked down at his feet absently. Under them were books. He toed one. Its gilt title was almost obliterated, but he still could make it out—Kipling's "Barrack Room Ballads."

There was a friendliness in those dim, familiar words, and he chuckled a bit. Funny to think of an ovoid intellect trying to read and understand the poems in that volume—"Danny Deever," "Mandalay"! "If" was one of Kipling's works too: "If you can keep your head—"

Cliff smiled ruefully. Anyway he couldn't go wrong by attempting to improve matters a little.

He cast a final glance through the spy window. The ovoid crowd was growing thicker, anticipating activity. Behind them the fighters were gathering in the dusky shadows. In their claws some of them clutched massive bars of some material—rams, no doubt. Probably it had been one of those rams that had broken the port of his submarine.

Still garmented in the tattered carpet, he started in by setting his craft in order as best he could; straightening a warped propeller blade, draining water out of machines and instruments, and repairing those that were broken, whenever it was possible. At least, he had cloth and paper from the museum to help him mop up the wetness of everything.

The radio was a tangle, but he had hope of fixing it some way so that, by means of its beam, he could get a word up to the boys aboard the *Etruria*, on the surface. They couldn't help him, of course; they could only watch and wait.

Several hours must have passed without incident. While he worked, Cliff kept a close lookout for some sign of The Student. When it came, it was not delivered by the wizard of the deeps in person, but through the proxy of a messenger beast. The oak-leaf body of the creature wavered before a window, and on its hide luminous words appeared: "Food is coming through an air tube. Eat."

Cliff waited. From one of the air passages that entered the chamber, a mass of albuminous substance was blown, and it plopped to the floor. It looked like white of egg. Cliff touched a finger to it, and tasted the adhering dab.

No doubt it was from the body of some specialized marine animal. Probably it was very nourishing, and though it hardly excited Cliff's appetite, he realized that a man might train himself to relish such fare. At present, however, he preferred the brine-soaked chocolate and other food articles that he had brought with him on his adventure.

The messenger now exhibited another message: "Cement for port of the submarine, through same tube."

Its manner of arrival was similar to that of the food. A great lump of clear, firm jelly, probably also the product of a subsea creature.

Rodney gathered it up. As he carried it, a thin film of the substance hardened to glassy consistency on his hands, as collodion would do. He applied the jelly to the submarine's fractured port, inside and out, pressing it as firmly as he could. It would take some time for the cement to set.

He returned his attention to the radio transmitter, but only for a moment. Out of some inner well of his consciousness, the faint shadow of an idea had appeared.

He clambered from the submarine, and with a knife proceeded to dig the cement from around the huge, glassy plug that kept out the sea, just as he had done before with the smaller plug that had sealed the entrance dome from the museum.

He worked entirely around the circular mass, loosening the adhesive substance as deeply as he could probe with his blade. No seepage of sea water appeared. The great block was intended to open outwardly. It was very thick, and beyond it, holding it shut, was the weight of the Atlantic.

But Clifford Rodney's plan was maturing. His efforts were not entirely useless. Undoubtedly that external door was not as firmly placed as it had previously been.

Cliff felt that he might yet demonstrate his ability to get out of the domes, though once beyond them, he could find no glimmer of reason to expect that he could elude the circle of horror that awaited him, even for a few seconds. He could only try to do his best, not so much in the expectation of escape, but to keep his energies busy.

Conscious that his every move was watched with absorbing interest by the ovoid audience at the spy windows, he rummaged in the museum, finding there some wire and strips of metal. These he brought back beside the submarine.

The drinking-water container of his craft was glass-lined. He unfastened it from its mounting, bashed in the top, and added to its contents a small amount of acid from his batteries. Then he carried it up through the hatch and set it on the floor of the chamber.

Into the water, at opposite sides of the container, he placed upright strips of metal to act as electrodes. To each of these he fastened wires, and attached their opposite ends to the powerful storage batteries of the submarine.

Next, with paper and other refuse, he plugged the air tubes and drains of the two domes. Then he closed the switch, sending current through the apparatus he had just constructed.

There was a hiss as of a caldron boiling as the electricity went through the water in the container, splitting it up into the elemental gases that composed it. Free oxygen and hydrogen bubbled away from the electrodes, mixing with the air of the domes.

This crude process of electrolysis was only the beginning. From the museum Cliff collected all the combustible materials he could find, and carried them into the chamber of the submarine—books, wood, a few scraps of celluloid, hard rubber, and so forth. Then, with a little of the glassy cement that remained, he sealed the block that had separated the two domes, back into place.

There was another matter. For a few seconds it puzzled him, but finally a solution came. With wrenches he unbolted the heavy glass lens of the submarine's searchlight. Carefully he tapped the incandescent bulb beneath, breaking it, but leaving the delicate tungsten filaments undamaged. Against them he placed a wad of paper, daubed with the remaining benzine of his cigarette lighter.

So far, so good. He investigated the electrolysis apparatus again, shutting off the current for a moment while he scraped away the interfering bubbles that had collected on the crude electrodes.

Satisfied that his preparations were as complete as they could be made for the present, he shut himself inside the submarine and continued to work on the radio. After perhaps an hour of fussing and tampering, he believed that he might get a code message up to the *Etruria.*

He was almost ready, but there was one thing more. Aboard the craft there were ten flasks of compressed oxygen. Opening the valves of nine of these, he tossed them through the hatch, retaining only one for breathing purposes.

While their contents soughed away he disconnected the electrolysis wires and closed the heavy steel door over his head. Working the key of the radio, he flashed out his appeal:

> Rodney calling S. S. *Etruria.* . . . Rodney calling S. S. *Etruria.* . . . Captured by deep-sea creatures. . . . Trying to escape. . . . Get position and stand by to help. . . .

He repeated the communication several times. If it were received, it would be simple for his confreres to calculate his position from the direction the waves came in. They'd be waiting to pick him up. He even chuckled ruefully at the thought.

Through the ports he could see that the ovoids had moved back from the spy windows of the dome, anticipating danger; but their forms, and the forms of their fighters still hovered tensely in the luminescent haze of the ocean bed. He could not see many from his unfavorable position, but doubtless they were above and all around the dome, waiting for him to make a move!

VII

Cliff forced himself to forget these unnerving thoughts. His hand touched the searchlight switch. His face was grim as he directed his gaze through another port toward the great, circular block that kept out the sea.

"Any one of three things can happen," he muttered: "The force can be insufficient, in which case what I have done won't accomplish anything at all—I'll still be locked in this dome. Or it can be too great, forcing out that plug all at once and letting the water in here all at once, to smash this steel coffin—all at once. Or it can be just right, admitting the ocean gradually enough so that this old tub can stand the strain."

Even the stout steel hull couldn't withstand the sudden thrust of the pressure of the deeps, he knew. Its position would be something like that of a nut under the blow of a hammer.

Cliff didn't want to give himself time to think. He closed the switch. Almost immediately there was a flash of red, as the hot filaments of the searchlight ignited the benzine-soaked paper that was in contact with them.

The flame spread through the dome in a wave of orange, as the hydrogen in the air burned. The sound which penetrated the thick shell of the craft was not the concussion of an explosion. Rather, it was a whispering, soughing roar; for the weight of the sea without was too vast for this feeble beginning of chemical forces to combat.

However, the reserves now came into action. Immersed in a highly oxygenated atmosphere under pressure, the paraphernalia from the museum took fire, and, though damp, rapidly became an inferno of incandescence that threw off enormous volumes of gas, expanding irresistibly with heat.

His heart thumping, Rodney kept his eyes glued to the great block which he hoped to dislodge. Stubbornly it continued to stand its ground, unmoved. He gritted his teeth as if, by sheer force of will, he sought to move the insensate thing that barred his way.

Moments passed. There was a snap like a muffled rifle shot. The block jerked, shuddered. Around its rim a curtain of glass appeared—no—not glass—water, screaming like a concourse of mad devils. The flood rolled over the floor, found the fire, and burst into steam, the pressure of which added to the titanic forces combating the titanic weight of the deeps.

More moments—the chamber was half full of water. Then, with a sort of majestic resignation, the plug yielded, folding outward like a dying colossus. The ocean was in then, swiftly—so swiftly that a living eye could not capture its movements. The thud of it was heavier than a clap of thunder.

The submarine bobbed in the maelstrom like a bit of flotsam. But its hull held, even though it was flung repeatedly against the walls of the dome.

A minute went by before Clifford Rodney was able to do anything. He picked himself up from the place where he had been hurled, and scrambled to the controls. He could see the opening which led from his prison. The motors throbbed and the submarine turned, heading through the still surging water.

It did get clear of the dome. Cliff almost thought he had a chance. Maybe the confusion produced in the vicinity by the suction when the sea had entered the dome, had unnerved the ovoids momentarily.

He set the vertical screws spinning. Their lift wasn't very good. They had been damaged again. It was hardly remarkable after the way the little ship had been bounced around.

Cliff looked up through a ceiling port. Six fighters were pouncing down upon him, their hinged claws spread wide, their long, armored forms ghostly in the shadows. Others were approaching from all directions, accompanied by a horde of ovoids.

A seventh had joined the six now. Rodney had not seen it dart up from the deep muck of the bottoms, where it had lain, hidden even to the people of the depths. It bore a strange, glassy object of considerable size. Without much attention the man wondered what it might be.

"All right," he muttered, "you win! I hope you enjoyed the show!"

The fighters were upon him. He could hear the scrape of their claws against metal. Clouds of black stuff, like the ink of a squid, surrounded the submarine, hiding everything from view. He was still rising though—rather rapidly, he thought. In a moment the electric bolts would stun him.

Upward and upward he went. Cliff began to be puzzled. He detected scraping noises that he could not interpret. He must have advanced half a mile toward the surface since the start. It was all very odd.

There was a jolt. The climb became halting and erratic. The motors labored doggedly.

The water cleared. Cliff could make out schools of phosphorescent fish, hanging in the darkness like scattered galaxies. He was alone, far above the bottoms. There were no fighters around him, though he thought he glimpsed dim shapes vanishing beneath. They could not endure the reduced pressure that existed here.

Matters were better, far better, than he had dared to expect—mysteriously so. Now if the vertical screws continued to function at all— The submarine appeared to be badly damaged. It seemed clumsy, heavy.

Cliff came into a region of deep bluish light, beautiful as some fairy-peopled realm of infinity. Not long thereafter the bathyspheric craft broke through the sunlighted surface of the Atlantic. Cliff opened the valves of a pressure tank, inflating the bellows like water wings which supported the heavy submarine when it was on the surface.

How had this all happened? There was still the mystery. He almost forgot that he must gradually reduce the pressure around him, to avoid the "bends."

At length he opened the hatch and crawled out onto the rounded top of the undersea boat. An egg-shaped object was fastened to the metal shell just behind the hatch. Rodney approached it, unable yet to fathom its nature. Glassy cement, like that with which he had recently become acquainted, held the thing in place.

It was a massive object, six feet through at its greatest diameter. It was made of the same material as the domes, except that this substance was darker, perhaps to shield what it covered from the fierce sun.

Rodney peered into the semitransparent depths of the object, discerning there a huddled form enveloped in a milky, semiliquid film. The form was delicate; vital organs pulsed visibly beneath its skin. It had flippers, and masses of black tendrils. Its beaked mouth opened and closed, giving it an air of vacuous solemnity, but its eyes were keen. Its tentacles clutched a white crayon. It was The Student!

Clifford Rodney's mind was a whirl as he sought to solve the riddle. Then, since no other means of printing a message was available, he traced words with a finger on the wet surface of the oval object:

"You helped me—how?"

The Student's tendrils trembled as he printed the answer on the inside of his protecting shell: "I helped you. The six fighters, and the seventh, were mine. They did not attack you. Concealed by the liquid that darkens the sea, they raised your submarine upward.

"They attached me to the submarine. They raised it as far as they could climb. It was a trick to outwit my people. They forbid traffic with the upper world. They are afraid. I was afraid, but at last I chose. While you prepared for the test an idea came. I used it, outwitting my people. I am afraid. But I am glad."

Rodney was lost in the fantastic wonder of it all. "Thank you, my friend!" he printed.

The Student plied his crayon again: "Friend? No. I am not your friend. What I did, I did for myself."

"Then why in reason's name are you here?" Cliff printed. "Men will put you in an aquarium, and stare at and study you!"

"Good," was the response, "I am glad. Men study me. I study them. Good. That is why I came: to see the accomplishments of men, to see the stars, to see the planets. Now I see the sun and sky—dreadful but interesting—very interesting. Good."

"Good if you don't smother before you can be transferred to a suitable aquarium," Rodney traced.

"I am safe here," the ovoid answered with a nervous flurry of tendrils. "The pressure is normal. There is much oxygen in the fluid which surrounds me. But do what you must, man. I am waiting."

Cliff was accustomed enough to the situation by now to grin down at the great dark egg. Mixed with his awe there was a curious inner warmth. Man and ovoid were different in form and mind; perhaps real sympathy between them was impossible. But Cliff had found a tangible similarity.

In this sullen devil of the depths eagerness to know the unknown had battled fear, and had won. The Student had placed himself, without defense, in the power of the unknown. It took guts to do that, courage—

Young Rodney thought of many things as he looked out over the water in search of signs of rescue. A ship was approaching. It was near enough so that he could recognize it as the *Etruria*.

"The boys'll probably call you Davy Jones' ambassador or something," he said banteringly, addressing the ovoid. "I hope you're sport enough to take it, old socks!"

But The Student wouldn't have listened even if he were able. His eyes were drinking in the miracle of the approaching ship.

THE LIFE AND TIMES OF MULTIVAC

Isaac Asimov

Isaac Asimov's body of work is part of the essential corpus of hard science fiction. As a teenager in the 1930s he was one of the first generation of science fiction fans who became a science fiction writer. He was a leading light of Campbell's *Astounding* in the forties with his robot stories, embodying his famous "Three Laws," collected in 1950 as *I, Robot*, as well as his *Foundation* series, later published in the 1960s as *The Foundation Trilogy*. All the while he was progressing through college and graduate school, finally attaining his Ph.D. in biochemistry and a tenured teaching position at Boston University School of Medicine. At the height of his powers and popularity in sf, he turned to writing popular science essays and books in the late fifties and became the greatest living writer in that field of the second half of the twentieth century. Immensely prolific, he had published more than 400 books, most of them nonfiction, before his death in 1992.

Asimov was a rationalist and a true believer in science as a way of knowing, and that attitude permeated his writing and emanated from his personal affect. He was an indefatigable public figure in the science fiction world throughout his adult life, a charismatic center of attention. A protégé of John W. Campbell (whom at least until the 1950s he used to visit weekly whenever possible for editorial sessions), Asimov was devoted to hard science fiction, generous in his praise of other hard science fiction writers, and always careful to distinguish hard sf from other varieties.

Over several decades, Asimov wrote a number of stories about supercomputers (not always the same one) named Multivac. "The Machine That Won the War" (1961), for instance, is a clever Asimovian retelling of the folktale of John Henry and the steam drill, the legend of the man who beat the machine. It is a hard-science allegory of thinking men and thinking machines that underscores the limits of technology without undermining the basic technological optimism of sf. It is also an interesting counterpoint to Asimov's "The Last Question," an earlier Multivac story, and a more serious (and uncharacteristically metaphysical) consideration of humanity's relation to machines. As is this story.

"The Life and Times of Multivac" was written in 1973 at the request of *The New York Times Magazine* for a science fiction story about humans and machines. Asimov constructed a provocative intellectual situation using conventional materials and raised the stakes by invoking free will versus determinism, achieving in the end both a solved problem and another, posed, problem. It is interesting to note that Asimov's original title for the story was "Mathematical Games." It is in one sense a rethinking of "The Machine That Won the War," but with significantly less technological optimism and more sophisticated execution.

But no matter how intellectual and abstract the problem, an individual human can take action using knowledge of science (and math) in the external world to solve it. This is the belief which was integral to Asimov's life and writing, the faith of hard sf.

The whole world was interested. The whole world could watch. If anyone wanted to know how many did watch, Multivac could have told them. The great computer Multivac kept track—as it did of everything.

Multivac was the judge in this particular case, so coldly objective and purely upright that there was no need of prosecution or defense. There was only the accused, Simon Hines, and the evidence, which consisted, in part, of Ronald Bakst.

Bakst watched, of course. In his case, it was compulsory. He would rather it were not. In his tenth decade, he was showing signs of age and his rumpled hair was distinctly gray.

Noreen was not watching. She had said at the door, "If we had a friend left—" She paused, then added, "Which I doubt!" and left.

Bakst wondered if she would come back at all, but at the moment, it didn't matter.

Hines had been an incredible idiot to attempt actual action, as though one could think of walking up to a Multivac outlet and smashing it—as though he didn't know a world-girdling computer, *the* world-girdling Computer (capital letter, please) with millions of robots at its command, couldn't protect itself. And even if the outlet had been smashed, what would that have accomplished?

And Hines did it in Bakst's physical presence, too!

He was called, precisely on schedule—"Ronald Bakst will give evidence now."

Multivac's voice was beautiful, with a beauty that never quite vanished no matter how often it was heard. Its timbre was neither quite male nor, for that matter, female, and it spoke in whatever language its hearer understood best.

"I am ready to give evidence," Bakst said.

There was no way to say anything but what he had to say. Hines could not avoid conviction. In the days when Hines would have had to face his fellow human beings, he would have been convicted more quickly and less fairly—and would have been punished more crudely.

Fifteen days passed, days during which Bakst was quite alone. Physical aloneness was not a difficult thing to envisage in the world of Multivac. Hordes had died in the days of the great catastrophes and it had been the computers that had saved what was left and directed the recovery—and improved their own designs till all were merged into Multivac—and the five million human beings were left on Earth to live in perfect comfort.

But those five million were scattered and the chances of one seeing another outside the immediate circle, except by design, was not great. No one was designing to see Bakst, not even by television.

For the time, Bakst could endure the isolation. He buried himself in his chosen way—which happened to be, these last twenty-three years, the designing of mathematical games. Every man and woman on Earth could develop a way of life to self-suit, provided always that Multivac, weighing all of human affairs with perfect skill, did not judge the chosen way to be subtractive to human happiness.

But what could be subtractive in mathematical games? It was purely abstract—pleased Bakst—harmed no one else.

He did not expect the isolation to continue. The Congress would not isolate him permanently without a trial—a different kind of trial from that which Hines had experienced, of course, one without Multivac's tyranny of absolute justice.

Still, he was relieved when it ended, and pleased that it was Noreen coming back that ended it. She came trudging over the hill toward him and he started toward her, smiling. It had been a successful five-year period during which they had been together. Even the occasional meetings with her two children and two grandchildren had been pleasant.

He said, "Thank you for being back."

She said, "I'm not back." She looked tired. Her brown hair was windblown, her prominent cheeks a trifle rough and sunburned.

Bakst pressed the combination for a light lunch and coffee. He knew what she liked. She didn't stop him, and though she hesitated for a moment, she ate.

She said, "I've come to talk to you. The Congress sent me."

"The Congress!" he said. "Fifteen men and women—counting me. Self-appointed and helpless."

"You didn't think so when you were a member."

"I've grown older. I've learned."

"At least you've learned to betray your friends."

"There was no betrayal. Hines tried to damage Multivac; a foolish, impossible thing for him to try."

"You accused him."

"I had to. Multivac knew the facts without my accusation, and without my accusation, I would have been an accessory. Hines would not have gained, but I would have lost."

"Without a human witness, Multivac would have suspended sentence."

"Not in the case of an anti-Multivac act. This wasn't a case of illegal parenthood or life-work without permission. I couldn't take the chance."

"So you let Simon be deprived of all work permits for two years."

"He deserved it."

"A consoling thought. You may have lost the confidence of the Congress, but you have gained the confidence of Multivac."

"The confidence of Multivac is important in the world as it is," said Bakst seriously. He was suddenly conscious of not being as tall as Noreen.

She looked angry enough to strike him; her lips pressed whitely together. But then she had passed her eightieth birthday—no longer young—the habit of non-violence was too ingrained. . . . Except for fools like Hines.

"Is that all you have to say, then?" she said.

"There could be a great deal to say. Have you forgotten? Have you all forgotten? Do you remember how it once was? Do you remember the Twentieth Century? We live long now; we live securely now; we live happily now."

"We live worthlessly now."

"Do you want to go back to what the world was like once?"

Noreen shook her head violently. "Demon tales to frighten us. We have learned our lesson. With the help of Multivac we have come through—but we don't need that help any longer. Further help will soften us to death. Without Multivac, *we* will run the robots, *we* will direct the farms and mines and factories."

"How well?"

"Well enough. Better, with practice. We need the stimulation of it in any case or we will all die."

Bakst said, "We have our work, Noreen; whatever work we choose."

"Whatever we choose, as long as it's unimportant, and even that can be taken away at will—as with Hines. And what's your work, Ron? Mathematical games? Drawing lines on paper? Choosing number combinations?"

Bakst's hand reached out to her, almost pleadingly. "That can be important. It is not nonsense. Don't underestimate—" He paused, yearning to explain but not quite knowing how he could, safely. He said, "I'm working on some deep problems in combinatorial analysis based on gene patterns that can be used to—"

"To amuse you and a few others. Yes, I've heard you talk about your games. You will decide how to move from A to B in a minimum number of steps and that will teach you how to go from womb to grave in a minimum number of risks and we will all thank Multivac as we do so."

She stood up. "Ron, you will be tried. I'm sure of it. *Our* trial. And you will be dropped. Multivac will protect you against physical harm, but you know it will not force us to see you, speak to you, or have anything to do with you. You will find that without the stimulation of human interaction, you will not be able to think—or to play your games. Goodbye."

"Noreen! Wait!"

She turned at the door. "Of course, you will have Multivac. You can talk to Multivac, Ron."

He watched her dwindle as she walked down the road through the parklands kept green, and ecologically healthy, by the unobtrusive labors of quiet, single-minded robots one scarcely ever saw.

He thought: Yes, I will have to talk to Multivac.

Multivac had no particular home any longer. It was a global presence knit together by wire, optical fiber, and microwave. It had a brain divided into a hundred subsidiaries but acting as one. It had its outlets everywhere and no human being of the five million was far from one.

There was time for all of them, since Multivac could speak to all individually at the same time and not lift its mind from the greater problems that concerned it.

Bakst had no illusions as to its strength. What was its incredible intricacy but a mathematical game that Bakst had come to understand over a decade ago? He knew the manner in which the connecting links ran from continent to continent in a huge network whose analysis could form the basis of a fascinating game. How do you arrange the network so that the flow of information never jams? How do you arrange the switching points? Prove that no matter what the arrangement, there is always at least one point which, on disconnection—

Once Bakst had learned the game, he had dropped out of the Congress. What could they do but talk and of what use was that? Multivac indifferently permitted talk of any kind and in any depth precisely because it was unimportant. It was only acts that Multivac prevented, diverted, or punished.

And it was Hines's act that was bringing on the crisis; and before Bakst was ready for it, too.

Bakst had to hasten now, and he applied for an interview with Multivac without any degree of confidence in the outcome.

Questions could be asked of Multivac at any time. There were nearly a million outlets of the type that had withstood Hines's sudden attack into which, or near which, one could speak. Multivac would answer.

An *interview* was another matter. It required time; it required privacy; most of all it required Multivac's judgment that it was necessary. Although Multivac had capacities that not all the world's problems consumed, it had grown chary, somehow, of its time. Perhaps that was the result of its ever-continuing self-improvement. It was becoming constantly more aware of its own worth and less likely to bear trivialities with patience.

Bakst had to depend on Multivac's good will. His leaving of the Congress, all his actions since, even the bearing of evidence against Hines, had been to gain that good will. Surely it was the key to success in this world.

He would have to assume the good will. Having made the application, he at once traveled to the nearest substation by air. Nor did he merely send his image.

He wanted to be there in person; somehow he felt his contact with Multivac would be closer in that way.

The room was almost as it might be if there were to be a human conference planned over closed multivision. For one flash-by moment, Bakst thought Multivac might assume an imaged human form and join him—the brain made flesh.

It did not, of course. There was the soft, whispering chuckle of Multivac's unceasing operations; something always and forever present in Multivac's presence; and over it, now, Multivac's voice.

It was not the usual voice of Multivac. It was a still, small voice, beautiful and insinuating, almost in his ear.

"Good day, Bakst. You are welcome. Your fellow human beings disapprove of you."

Multivac always comes to the point, thought Bakst. He said, "It does not matter, Multivac. What counts is that I accept your decisions as for the good of the human species. You were designed to do so in the primitive versions of yourself and—"

"And my self-designs have continued this basic approach. If *you* understand this, why do so many human beings fail to understand it? I have not yet completed the analysis of that phenomenon."

"I have come to you with a problem," said Bakst.

Multivac said, "What is it?"

Bakst said, "I have spent a great deal of time on mathematical problems inspired by the study of genes and their combinations. I cannot find the necessary answers and home-computerization is of no help."

There was an odd clicking and Bakst could not repress a slight shiver at the sudden thought that Multivac might be avoiding a laugh. It was a touch of the human beyond what even he was ready to accept. The voice was in his other ear and Multivac said:

"There are thousands of different genes in the human cell. Each gene has an average of perhaps fifty variations in existence and uncounted numbers that have never been in existence. If we were to attempt to calculate all possible combinations, the mere listing of them at my fastest speed, if steadily continued, would, in the longest possible lifetime of the Universe, achieve but an infinitesimal fraction of the total."

Bakst said, "A complete listing is not needed. That is the point of my game. Some combinations are more probable than others and by building probability upon probability, we can cut the task enormously. It is the manner of achieving this building of probability upon probability that I ask you to help me with."

"It would still take a great deal of my time. How could I justify this to myself?"

Bakst hesitated. No use in trying a complicated selling job. With Multivac, a straight line was the shortest distance between two points.

He said, "An appropriate gene combination might produce a human being more content to leave decisions to you, more willing to believe in your resolve to make men happy, more anxious to *be* happy. I cannot find the proper combination, but you might, and with guided genetic engineering—"

"I see what you mean. It is—good. I will devote some time to it."

Bakst found it difficult to hitch into Noreen's private wavelength. Three times the connection broke away. He was not surprised. In the last two months, there had been an increasing tendency for technology to slip in minor ways—never for long, never seriously—and he greeted each occasion with a somber pleasure.

This time it held. Noreen's face showed, holographically three-dimensional. It flickered a moment, but it held.

"I'm returning your call," said Bakst, dully impersonal.

"For a while it seemed impossible to get you," said Noreen. "Where have you been?"

"Not hiding. I'm here, in Denver."

"Why in Denver?"

"The world is my oyster, Noreen. I may go where I please."

Her face twitched a little. "And perhaps find it empty everywhere. We are going to try you, Ron."

"Now?"

"Now!"

"And here?"

"And here!"

Volumes of space flickered into different glitters on either side of Noreen, and further away, and behind. Bakst looked from side to side, counting. There were fourteen, six men, eight women. He knew every one of them. They had been good friends once, not so long ago.

To either side and beyond the simulacra was the wild background of Colorado on a pleasant summer day that was heading toward its end. There had been a city here once named Denver. The site still bore the name though it had been cleared, as most of the city sites had been. . . . He could count ten robots in sight, doing whatever it was robots did.

They were maintaining the ecology, he supposed. He knew no details, but Multivac did, and it kept fifty million robots all over the Earth in efficient order.

Behind Bakst was one of the converging grids of Multivac, almost like a small fortress of self-defense.

"Why now?" he asked. "And why here?"

Automatically he turned to Eldred. She was the oldest of them and the one with authority—if a human being could be said to have authority.

Eldred's dark-brown face looked a little weary. The years showed, all sixscore of them, but her voice was firm and incisive. "Because we have the final fact now. Let Noreen tell you. She knows best."

Bakst's eyes shifted to Noreen. "Of what crime am I accused?"

"Let us play no games, Ron. There are no crimes under Multivac except to strike for freedom and it is your human crime that you have committed no crime under Multivac. For that we will judge whether any human being alive wants your company any longer, wants to hear your voice, be aware of your presence, or respond to you in any way."

"Why am I threatened with isolation then?"

"You have betrayed all human beings."

"How?"

"Do you deny that you seek to breed mankind into subservience to Multivac?"

"Ah!" Bakst folded his arms across his chest. "You found out quickly, but then you had only to ask Multivac."

Noreen said, "Do you deny that you asked for help in the genetic engineering of a strain of humanity designed to accept slavery under Multivac without question?"

"I suggested the breeding of a more contented humanity. Is this a betrayal?"

Eldred intervened. She said, "We don't want your sophistry, Ron. We know it by heart. Don't tell us once again that Multivac cannot be withstood, that there is no use in struggling, that we have gained security. What you call security, the rest of us call slavery."

Bakst said, "Do you proceed now to judgment, or am I allowed a defense?"

"You heard Eldred," said Noreen. "We know your defense."

"We all heard Eldred," said Bakst, "but no one has heard me. What she says is my defense is not my defense."

There was a silence as the images glanced right and left at each other. Eldred said, "Speak!"

Bakst said, "I asked Multivac to help me solve a problem in the field of mathematical games. To gain his interest, I pointed out that it was modeled on gene combinations and that a solution might help in designing a gene combination that would leave man no worse off than he is now in any respect and yet breed into him a cheerful acceptance of Multivac's direction, and acquiescence in his decisions."

"So we have said," said Eldred.

"It was only on those terms that Multivac would have accepted the task. Such a new breed is clearly desirable for mankind by Multivac's standards, and by Multivac's standards he must labor toward it. And the desirability of the end will lure him on to examine greater and greater complications of a problem whose endlessness is beyond what even he can handle. You all witness that."

Noreen said, "Witness what?"

"Haven't you had trouble reaching me? In the last two months, hasn't each of you noticed small troubles in what has always gone smoothly? . . . You are silent. May I accept that as an affirmative?"

"If so, what then?"

Bakst said, "Multivac has been placing all his spare circuits on the problem. He has been slowly pushing the running of the world toward rather a skimpy minimum of his efforts, since nothing, by his own sense of ethics, must stand in the way of human happiness and there can be no greater increase in that happiness than to accept Multivac."

Noreen said, "What does all this mean? There is still enough in Multivac to run the world—and us—and if this is done at less than full efficiency, that would only add temporary discomfort to our slavery. Only temporary, because it won't last long. Sooner or later, Multivac will decide the problem is insoluble, or will solve it, and in either case, his distraction will end. In the latter case, slavery will become permanent and irrevocable."

"But for now he is distracted," said Bakst, "and we can even talk like this—most dangerously—without his noticing. Yet I dare not risk doing so for long, so please understand me quickly.

"I have another mathematical game—the setting up of networks on the model of Multivac. I have been able to demonstrate that no matter how complicated and redundant the network is, there must be at least one place into which all the currents can funnel under particular circumstances. There will always be the fatal apopletic stroke if that one place is interfered with, since it will induce overloading elsewhere which will break down and induce overloading elsewhere—and so on indefinitely till all breaks down."

"Well?"

"And this is the point. Why else have I come to Denver? And Multivac knows it, too, and this point is guarded electronically and robotically to the extent that it cannot be penetrated."

"Well?"

"But Multivac is distracted, and Multivac trusts me. I have labored hard to gain that trust, at the cost of losing all of you, since only with trust is there the possibility of betrayal. If any of you tried to approach this point, Multivac might rouse himself even out of his present distraction. If Multivac were not distracted, he would not allow even me to approach. But he *is* distracted, and it *is* I!"

Bakst was moving toward the converging grid in a calm saunter, and the fourteen images, keyed to him, moved along as well. The soft susurrations of a busy Multivac center were all about them.

Bakst said, "Why attack an invulnerable opponent? Make him vulnerable first, and then—"

Bakst fought to stay calm, but it all depended on this now. Everything! With a sharp yank, he uncoupled a joint. (If he had only had still more time to make more certain.)

He was not stopped—and as he held his breath, he became aware of the ceasing of noise, the ending of whisper, the closing down of Multivac. If, in a moment, that soft noise did not return, then he had had the right key point, and no recovery would be possible. If he were not quickly the focus of approaching robots—

He turned in the continuing silence. The robots in the distance were working still. None were approaching.

Before him, the images of the fourteen men and women of the Congress were still there and each seemed to be stupefied at the sudden enormous thing that had happened.

Bakst said, "Multivac is shut down, burnt out. It can't be rebuilt." He felt almost drunk at the sound of what he was saying. "I have worked toward this since I left you. When Hines attacked, I feared there might be other such efforts, that Multivac would double his guard, that even I— I had to work quickly— I wasn't sure—" He was gasping, but forced himself steady, and said solemnly, "I have given us our freedom."

And he paused, aware at last of the gathering weight of the silence. Fourteen images stared at him, without any of them offering a word in response.

Bakst said sharply, "You have talked of freedom. You *have* it!"

Then, uncertainly, he said, "Isn't that what you want?"

THE SINGING DIAMOND

Robert L. Forward

Robert L. Forward is a Ph.D. who has specialized in gravitational physics; until his early retirement he was employed for most of his career as a researcher in industry. Flamboyant, self-confident in the manner of physicists (who know that they are the ones who know how the universe really works), and full of speculative ideas, Forward influenced both Larry Niven's and Jerry Pournelle's hard sf in the 1970s, through friendly conversations. ". . . I received a call from Dr. Robert Forward of Hughes Research Laboratories. Bob Forward [was] their genius in charge of far-out research. He had already invented a mass detector and was at work on other marvels. His call was to say that he'd read 'He Fell into a Dark Hole' and would like to meet the author," said Jerry Pournelle. "The result of the phone call was a visit to Forward's laboratories, where we saw marvels indeed. Naturally, I took along my partner, Larry Niven." He was their connection at the Jet Propulsion Laboratory, in Southern California, where all the sf writers went to watch the news from space during the launches and the flybys.

Then it occurred to Forward that he could do it himself, and he wrote the novel *Dragon's Egg* (1980), hard sf in the tradition of Hal Clement that made him world-famous with his first book. He followed that with a few short stories and other novels, including *The Flight of the Dragonfly* (1984), and a series of Rocheworld sequels using an interesting astronomical anomaly as a setting; *Martian Rainbow* (1991); *Timemaster* (1992); and *Camelot 30K* (1993). He has also written over one hundred popular science articles and two books, *Mirror Matter: Pioneering Antimatter Physics* (1988) and *Future Magic* (1988), in addition to his many professional publications.

Like James P. Hogan and David Brin, who both broke into the field as hard sf writers at about the same time, he is known as an idea man. In hard sf terms, that means his stories are filled with neat ideas and images based on scientific concepts and imagined conditions. It also often indicates a superficial or merely conventional command of the tools of fiction writing. The striking ideas are the central, sometimes only, interest. Physics, astronomy, and space technology are Forward's playgrounds, and he is generally at his best in Hal Clement territory, describing carefully conceived alien settings and beings in the clear, unornamented prose of science writing.

"The Singing Diamond" is a conventional hard sf short story, of the variety of a shotgun blast of ideas, compressed into a few pages. The wonderful ideas are the whole point, the foreground interest for the hard sf reader. The fiction exists to display them.

My asteroid was singing. Alone, but safe in my ship, I heard the multitude of voices coming through the rock. They were an angel chorus in a fluid tongue, strange but beautiful.

I followed the source of the sound, stereo headphones connected to a pair of sonar microphones buried in the crust. The voices were moving slowly through the solid stone. They suddenly stopped, cut off in the middle of a tremulous crescendo. I took off the earphones, looked up from the sonar screen, and peered out the port at the black void around me. I could see nothing. I would have thought my ears were playing tricks on me if I had not seen the unusual fuzzy ball on the three-dimensional display of the sonar mapper.

I stopped the pinger that was sending short bursts of sound down into the asteroid I had captured and waited while the last few pulses echoed back from within the body of almost pure metallic ore. This find would bring me a fortune once I surveyed it and got it back to the processing plant.

Most rock-hoppers are content to set up the sonar mapper on a potential claim and let the computer do the job of determining whether there is enough metal in the rock to justify dragging it in. But I always liked to work along with the computer, watching the reflections on the screen and listening to the quality of the echoes. By now my ears were so well trained I could almost tell the nickel content of an inclusion by the "accent" it put on the returning sound. But this time my ears had heard something coming from the solid rock that had not been put there by the pinger.

I had the computer play back its memory, and again I heard the eerie voices, like a chorus of sirens calling me to leave my ship and penetrate into their dense home. I was sure now that the music was real, since the computer had heard it too. I replayed the data again and found that the sound had started on one side of the asteroid, traveled right through the center in a straight line, and then had gone out the other side. I had a hunch, and 90 minutes later was waiting, earphones on, when the singing started again. This time the voices started at a different position on the surface of the asteroid, but as before, they slowly traveled in a straight line, right through the exact center of the rock and out the other side. A quick session with the computer verified my hunch. Whatever was doing the singing was orbiting the asteroid, but instead of circling about it like a moon, the orbit went back and forth right through the dense nickel-iron core!

My first thought was that the weak gravity field of the asteroid had trapped a miniature black hole. The singing would be caused by stresses in the metal ore from the intense gravitational field of the moving point of warped space. But then I realized the asteroid was too tiny, only a few hundred meters across, to have captured a black hole.

The computer did more work. It determined the orbital parameters and predicted where the singers would next intersect the surface of my slowly revolving rock. I was outside, waiting at that point, when it came.

For a long time I could see nothing. Then, high above me, there was a cloud of little sun specks—falling toward me. The glittering spots in the cloud moved in rapid swirls that were too fast to follow, and the cloud seemed to pulsate, changing in size and shape. Sometimes it collapsed into an intense concentration that was almost too small to see, only to expand later into a glittering ball as big as my helmet. Inexorably, the gravity of the asteroid pulled the swarm of star-midges down toward me. They were getting close. I tried to move back out of their path, but in my excitement I had floated upward in the weak gravity, and my magnetic boots were useless. Twisting my body around, I tried to dodge, but the cloud of light spots expanded just as it passed me, I screamed and blanked out as my right leg burst into pain. I felt as if I had stepped into a swarm of army ants.

• • •

I woke, the emergency beeper shouting in my ear. My leg ached, and my air was low. Detached, I looked down at the agony below my knee to see fine jets of vapor shooting out from hundreds of tiny holes in my boot. Fortunately, most of the holes seemed to be clogged with frozen balls of reddish stuff. My numbed brain refused to recognize the substance.

Using my hands, I dragged myself across the surface to my ship and carefully pulled my suit off. Insult was added to injury as the suit's Sani-Seal extracted a few red hairs as I peeled it off. I looked carefully at my leg. The tiny holes had stopped bleeding, so I was in no immediate danger. I just hurt a lot.

For the next few days I let my leg heal while I listened to the music. I know that I was imagining it, but the beautiful voices now seemed to have a tinge of menace to them. The computer carefully monitored the motion of the swarm. It returned every 93 minutes, the normal time of close orbit around an asteroid with such a high density. Once, I had to move the ship to keep it away from the singing swarm as it came up out of the rock underneath.

After I could move around again, I experimented. Tracking the swarm as it went upward away from the surface, I used the mass detector on it at the top of its trajectory. The collection of nearly invisible specks weighed 80 kilos—as much as I did in my space suit!

I put a thin sheet of foil underneath the swarm as it fell and later examined the myriad tiny holes under a microscope. The aluminum had been penetrated many hundreds of times by each of the specks as they swirled about in the slowly falling cloud. Whatever they were, they were about the size of a speck of dust. I finally counted the midges by tracing the streaks on a print made with my instacamera. There were over one thousand of them.

I was stumped. What was I going to do? No matter how valuable the asteroid was to me, I could not drag it back to the processing plant with its deadly hornet's nest swirling about it.

I thought about pushing the asteroid out from under the cloud, but my small ship was not going to move a 20-million-ton chunk of rock at anything like the acceleration needed. I would have to get rid of the stinging swarm in some way, but how do you trap something that travels through solid iron like it isn't there? Besides, it could be that the tiny star specks themselves were worth more than the ball of ore that they orbited.

I finally gave up and called for help. "Belt Traffic Control, this is 'Red' Vengeance in The Billionaire. I have a problem. Would you please patch the following message to Belt Science Authority?" I then gave a detailed description of what I had been able to learn about my tiny pests. I signed off and started lunch. It was nearly 20 light-minutes to the Belt Traffic Control station.

In two weeks a few of the small cadre of scientists who were allowed to live out in the Belt were there, cluttering up my rock with their instruments. They couldn't learn much more with their gadgets than I did with my camera and aluminum foil. The specks were tiny and very dense. No one could think of any way to trap them.

I was ready to abandon my claim and leave a fortune and its buzzing poltergeist to the scientists when I remembered the Belt Facility for Dangerous Experiments. The major activity was a high-current particle accelerator designed to produce the antihydrogen that filled the "water torch" engines used in deep space. At each refueling I would watch apprehensively as electric fields and laser beams carefully shepherded a few grams of frozen antimatter into my engine room. There, each grain annihilated would heat many tons of water into a blazing exhaust.

However, antimatter has other uses, and nearby a group made exotic materials by explosive-forming. I went to them with my problem. Soon I had a bemused entourage of high-powered brains trying to think of ways to stop my irresistible objects. We were relaxing with drink squeezers in the facetiously named BOOM! room, which overlooked the distant explosive-forming test site. I dressed for the occasion in an emerald-green bodysuit that I had chosen to match my eyes, and a diaphanous skirt that required dexterity to keep it looking properly arranged in free fall. I wore my one luxury, an uncirculated solid-gold Spanish doubloon.

While the discussions were going on, news arrived from the contingent still observing my find. The specks were still moving too fast to take close-up pictures with the cameras available, but at least the size and density of the specks had been determined. They were dense, but not of nuclear density, only about a million times greater than the density of water.

"Our bodies are one thousand times more dense than air, and we can move through that with ease," I said. "So, at a density ratio of a million to one, my leg was like a vacuum to them! No wonder they can go through solid iron like it isn't even there!"

"Although the asteroid's iron can't stop the swarm, its gravity does hold them," said one scientist. He pulled out a card computer and started scratching with his fingernail on the pliable input-output surface. We clustered around, holding position by whatever handhold was available, and watched as his crude scratchings were replaced by a computer-generated picture of a flat disc with curved arrows pointing smoothly in toward its two faces.

"What is it?" I asked.

"Flypaper," he said, looking up at me floating above him. "Or, for your problem, Red—gnat paper."

His thick fingers scratched some more calculations, this time in pure math. I followed them without too much trouble. There were no pictures to give me any clues, but it was obvious from the symbols that he was merely applying Newton's Law of Gravity to a disc instead of to the usual sphere.

"We can make the flypaper with the explosive-forming techniques we have developed," he said, "but to keep it from decomposing, we are going to have to contain it in a pressure capsule."

The process looks deceptively simple when one looks out through the eyes of an auto-robot. You merely take a large rotating asteroid as big as an office building and hit it from all sides with a spray of antimatter. When the shock wave passes, you have a small, rapidly spinning plate of glowing decomposed matter that is trying desperately to regain its former bulk. Before it does, you hit it from 12 sides with a carefully arranged set of accurately cut chunks of nickel-iron lined with pure carbon. In the split-nanosecond that the configuration is compressed together into an elastically rebounding supersolid, you coat it heavily with another layer of antimatter and let it cool for a week.

The auto-robots brought it to us—still warm. It was a diamond—with a flaw. Right in the center of the barrel-size crystal was a thick sheet of highly reflecting metal.

"What is that?" I asked the one who had arranged the fireworks display.

"The original asteroid, Miss Vengeance," he replied. "All four million tons of it. It has been compressed into a thin disc of ultradense matter and surrounded by diamond to keep it from expanding back into normal matter. There is your flypaper; let's go use it."

The disc was 30 centimeters across and only a centimeter thick, but it took a large space-tug to heave that ultraheavy pancake griddle into an orbit that would reach my claim and its singing hangers-on. Once it was there, it was delicate work getting the sluggish plate placed in the path of the glittering cloud that still bounced back and forth through my property every 93 minutes. Finally the task was accomplished. Passing slowly through the diamond casing as if it were not there, the scintillating sparks floated upward toward the metal disc—and stuck.

"They stopped!" I shouted in amazement.

"Of course," said a metallic voice over my suit speaker. "They ran into something that was denser than they are, and its gravitational field is strong enough to hold them on its surface."

"Something that dense must be a billion g's," I said.

"I wish it were," said the voice. "I would have liked to have made the gravity stronger so I could be sure we would hold on to the specks once we had stopped them. With the limited facilities we have at the test site, the most matter we can compress at one time is four million tons. That disc has a gravitational field of only one g on each side."

After watching for a while, I saw that the tiny specks were not going to be able to leave the surface of their flat-world prison. I conquered my fear and let my helmet rest against the outside of the diamond casing that encapsulated the shiny disc and its prisoners.

The diamond was singing.

The voices I remembered were there, but they were different from the wild, free-swirling chorus that still haunted me from our first meeting. The singing now seemed constrained and flat.

I laughed at my subconscious double pun and pulled back to let the scientists have their prize. They hauled the crystalline cask away with the space tug, and I returned to the difficult months-long task of getting my asteroid back to the processing station.

I made a fortune. Even my trained ear had underestimated the nickel content. When payoff time came, I knew that from then on every expedition I made out into the belt was for fun and gravy, for all the money I would ever need for a decent retirement nest egg was in solid credits in the Bank of Outer Belt.

With no more financial worries, I began to take an interest in my little beasties—for that is what they were. The high-speed cameras had been able to determine that their complex motion was not due to random natural laws but was caused by the deliberate motion of each of the spots with respect to the others. A few frames had even shown some of the tiny specks in the process of emitting a little jet of gamma-ray exhaust in order to change its course to meet with another speck for a fraction of a microsecond. Then, many revolutions and many milliseconds later, each of the two specks that had previously met would release another tiny speck, which joined the great swarm in its seemingly random motion.

The most significant frame from the high-speed cameras, however, is the one that I have blown up into a holopicture over the head of my bunk. I didn't think that you could create a decent three-dimensional likeness of someone using only 1000 points of light, but it is me, all right. Everyone recognizes it instantly—aristocratic nose, bobbed hair, helmet, mike, freckles, and all the rest.

But that is all the beasties have ever done in the way of communication. For years the scientists have tried to get some other response from them, but the specks just ignore their efforts. I guess that when you live a trillion times faster than someone else, even a short dialogue seems to drag on forever and just isn't worth the effort. The scientists even took the diamond down to Earth and tried to build a superfast robot as a translator. Now, after years of examination and fruitless attempts to communicate, we finally were able to place the diamond in the San-San Zoo.

The specks, which used to be plastered to one side of the dense disc, are free now that they are on Earth. The one-g upward pull of the underside of the disc is exactly canceled by the one-g downward pull of the Earth. The specks seem to be perfectly happy. They could easily leave the gravity-free region under the disc, but they don't seem to want to. Their cloud stays a compact sphere just below their antigravity ceiling. They continue with their complex intermingling, swirling behavior, passing easily through the ultrahard diamond that holds up their four-million-ton roof.

When I was a young girl at Space Polytech, I dreamed that when I got rich I would spend my latter years reveling in the vacation spots around the world and throughout the solar system, but now I don't want to. Sometimes I can stand it for a whole month—but then I just have to go back and hear my diamond sing.

DOWN & OUT ON ELLFIVE PRIME

Dean Ing

Dean Ing is an engineer turned writer, now principally in the best-selling subcategory of "techno-thrillers," whose science fiction of the seventies and early eighties epitomizes the high-tech, Campbellian, problem-solving mode of hard science fiction in direct descent from Robert A. Heinlein's *Astounding* stories of the forties and Poul Anderson's of the fifties (for instance "The Man Who Counts" [1958], later in book form as *War of the Wing-Men*). This strain of hard sf is about men in science-fictional environments who use their wits and knowledge to find a way, especially to build a way, out of their predicaments—sometimes by using their superior managerial skills. This strain is specifically in opposition to the space adventure or science fantasy story in which the hero wins through because he is tough and smart and possesses military virtues (although there are many mixed examples of hard sf adventure). It privileges scientific and technological knowledge over bravery and strength. Two stereotypical characters usually appear, the free man (pioneer/outsider/freelancer/con-man) and the good manager (often a character in the story but sometimes represented by the narrative voice/persona), and although the free man always wins, good management triumphs (it is a win-win scenario). This form is a parable that reconciles the free man and society.

Hard science fiction admires a good boss, just as it does a good scientist or engineer, knowing that on some level the builders and creators are self-absorbed, if not selfish, and that someone must impose limits on them so that a social structure can exist, but without restricting their freedom. This is the utopian dream of the scientific and engineering community, the dream of the ideal administrator who would interface between them and the rest of society so that they need not yield to the necessity of learning how to be socially adjusted adults among normal people. Their creative freedom, often indistinguishable from adolescent rebellion, requires a parental figure to react against and to take care of them in emergencies.

"Down & Out on Ellfive Prime" is a story of space pioneers on the new frontier taming a hostile environment that threatens their survival. It is a utopian allegory, of the lineage of Heinlein's "It's Great to Be Back," envisioning a better society on the future frontier. It is also an interesting contrast to George Turner's "In a Petri Dish Upstairs," which portrays some of the darker sides of the space-colony enterprise.

Responding to Almquist's control, the little utility tug wafted from the North dock port and made its gentle pirouette. Ellfive Prime Colony seemed to fall away. Two hundred thousand kilometers distant, blue-white Earth swam into view: cradle of mankind, cage for too many. Almquist turned his long body in its cushions and managed an obligatory smile over frown lines. "If that won't make you homesick, Mr. Weston, nothing will."

The fat man grunted, looking not at the planet he had deserted but at something much nearer. From the widening of Weston's eyes, you could tell it was something big, closing fast. Torin Almquist knew what it was; he eased the tug out, watching his radar, to give Weston the full benefit of it.

When the tip of the great solar mirror swept past, Weston blanched and cried out. For an instant, the view port was filled with cables and the mirror pivot mechanism. Then once again there was nothing but Earth and sharp pinpricks of starlight. Weston turned toward the engineering manager, wattles at his jawline trembling. "Stupid bastard," he grated. "If that'll be your standard joke on new arrivals, you must cause a lot of coronaries."

Abashed, disappointed: "A mirror comes by every fourteen seconds, Mr. Weston. I thought you'd enjoy it. You asked to see the casting facility, and this is where you can see it best. Besides, if you were retired as a heart case, I'd know it." *And the hell with you,* he added silently. Almquist retreated into an impersonal spiel he knew by heart, moving the tug back to gain a panorama of the colony with its yellow legend, *L-5′*, proud and unnecessary on the hull. He moved the controls gently, the blond hairs on his forearm masking the play of tendons within.

The colony hung below them, a vast shining melon the length of the new Hudson River Bridge and nearly a kilometer thick. Another of its three mirror strips, anchored near the opposite South end cap of Ellfive Prime and spread like curved petals toward the sun, hurtled silently past the view port. Almquist kept talking. ". . . Prime was the second industrial colony in space, dedicated in 2007. These days it's a natural choice for a retirement community. A fixed population of twenty-five hundred—plus a few down-and-out bums hiding here and there. Nowhere near as big a place as Orbital General's new industrial colony out near the asteroid belt."

Almquist droned on, backing the tug farther away. Beyond the South end cap, a tiny mote sparkled in the void, and Weston squinted, watching it. "The first Ellfive was a General Dynamics–Lever Brothers project in close orbit, but it got snuffed by the Chinese in 2012, during the war."

"I was only a cub then," Weston said, relaxing a bit. "This colony took some damage too, didn't it?"

Almquist glanced at Weston, who looked older despite his bland flesh. Well, living Earthside with seven billion people tended to age you. "The month I was born," Almquist nodded, "a nuke was intercepted just off the centerline of Ellfive Prime. Thermal shock knocked a tremendous dimple in the hull; from inside, of course, it looked like a dome poking up through the soil south of center."

Weston clapped pudgy hands, a gesture tagging him as neo-Afrikaner. "That'll be the hill, then. The one with the pines and spruce, near Hilton Prime?"

A nod. "Stress analysts swore they could leave the dimple if they patched the hull around it. Cheapest solution—and for once, a pretty one. When they finished bringing new lunar topsoil and distributing it inside, they saw there was enough dirt on the slope for spruce and ponderosa pine roots. To balance thousands of tons of new processed soil, they built a blister out on the opposite side of the hull and moved some heavy hardware into it."

The fat man's gaze grew condescending as he saw the great metal blister roll into view like a tumor on the hull. "Looks slapdash," he said.

"Not really; they learned from DynLever's mistakes. The first Ellfive colony was a cylinder, heavier than an ellipsoid like ours." Almquist pointed through the view port. "DynLever designed for a low ambient pressure without much nitrogen in the cylinder and raised hell with water transpiration and absorption in a lot of trees they tried to grow around their living quarters. I'm no botanist, but I know Ellfive Prime has an Earthside ecology—the same air you'd breathe in Peru, only cleaner. We don't coddle our grass and trees, and we grow all our crops right in the North end cap below us."

Something new and infinitely pleasing shifted Weston's features. "You used to have an external crop module to feed fifty thousand people, back when this colony was big in manufacturing—"

"Sold it," Almquist put in. "Detached the big rig and towed it out to a belt colony when I was new here. We didn't really need it anymore—"

Weston returned the interruption pointedly: "You didn't let me finish. I put that deal over. OrbGen made a grand sum on it—which is why the wife and I can retire up here. One hand washes the other, eh?"

Almquist said something noncommittal. He had quit wondering why he disliked so many newcomers. He *knew* why. It was a sling-cast irony that he, Ellfive Prime's top technical man, did not have enough rank in OrbGen to be slated for colony retirement. Torin Almquist might last as Civil Projects Manager for another ten years, if he kept a spotless record. Then he would be Earthsided in the crowds and smog and would eat fish cakes for the rest of his life. Unlike his ex-wife, who had left him to teach in a belt colony so that she would never have to return to Earth. And who could blame her? *Shit*.

"I beg your pardon?"

"Sorry; I was thinking. You wanted to see the high-g casting facility? It's that sphere strapped on to the mirror that's swinging toward us. It's moving over two hundred meters per second, a lot faster than the colony floor, being a kilometer and a half out from the spin axis. So at the mirror tip, instead of pulling around one standard g, they're pulling over three g's. Nobody spends more than an hour there. We balance the sphere with storage masses on the other mirror tips."

Restive, only half-interested: "Why? It doesn't look very heavy."

"It isn't," Almquist conceded, "but Ellfive Prime has to be balanced just so if she's going to spin on center. That's why they filled that blister with heavy stored equipment opposite the hill—though a few tons here and there don't matter."

Weston wasn't listening. "I keep seeing something like barn doors flipping around, past the other end, ah, end cap." He pointed. Another brief sparkle. "There," he said.

Almquist's arm tipped the control stick, and the tug slid farther from the colony's axis of rotation. "Stacking mirror cells for shipment," he explained. "We still have slag left over from a nitrogen-rich asteroid they towed here in the old days. Fused into plates, the slag makes good protection against solar flares. With a mirror face, it can do double duty. We're bundling up a pallet load, and a few cargo men are out there in P-suits—pressure suits. They—"

Weston would never know, and have cared less, what Almquist had started to say. The colony manager clapped the fingers of his free hand against the wireless speaker in his left ear. His face stiffened with zealot intensity. Fingers flickering to the console as the tug rolled and accelerated, Almquist began to speak into his throat mike—something about a Code Three. Weston knew something was being kept from him. He didn't like it and said so. Then he said so again.

". . . happened before," Almquist was saying to someone, "but this time you keep him centered, Radar Prime. I'll haul him in myself. Just talk him out of a panic; you know the drill. Please be quiet, Mr. Weston," he added in a too-polite aside.

"Don't patronize me," Weston spat. "Are we in trouble?"

"I'm swinging around the hull; give me a vector," Almquist continued, and Weston felt his body sag under acceleration. "Are you in voice contact?" Pause. "Doesn't he acknowledge? He's on a work-crew-scrambler circuit, but you can patch me in. Do it."

"You're treating me like a child."

"If you don't shut up, Weston, I *will*. Oh, hell, it's easier to humor you." He flicked a toggle, and the cabin speaker responded.

". . . be okay. I have my explosive riveter," said an unfamiliar voice; adult male, thinned and tightened by tension. "Starting to retro-fire now."

Almquist counted aloud at the muffled sharp bursts. "Not too fast, Versky," he cautioned. "You overheat a rivet gun, and the whole load could detonate."

"Jeez, I'm cartwheeling," Versky cut in. "Hang tight, guys." More bursts, now a staccato hammer. Versky's monologue gave no sign that he had heard Almquist, had all the signs of impending panic.

"Versky, listen to me. Take your goddamn finger off the trigger. We have you on radar. Relax. This is Torin Almquist, Versky. I say again—"

But he didn't. Far beyond, streaking out of the ecliptic, a brief nova flashed against the stars. The voice was cut off instantly. Weston saw Almquist's eyes blink hard, and in that moment the manager's face seemed aged by compassion and hopelessness. Then, very quietly: "Radar Prime, what do you have on scope?"

"Nothing but confetti, Mr. Almquist. Going everywhere at once."

"Should I pursue?"

"Your option, sir."

"And your responsibility."

"Yes, sir. No, don't pursue. Sorry."

"Not your fault. I want reports from you and Versky's cargo-team leader with all possible speed." Almquist flicked toggles with delicate savagery, turned his little vessel around, arrowed back to the dock port. Glancing at Weston, he said, "A skilled cargo man named Yves Versky. Experienced man; should've known better. He floated into a mirror support while horsing those slag cells around and got grazed by it. Batted him hell to breakfast." Then, whispering viciously to himself, "God*damn* those big rivet guns. They can't be used like control jets. Versky knew that."

Then, for the first time, Weston realized what he had seen. A man in a pressure suit had just been blown to small pieces before his eyes. It would make a lovely anecdote over sherry, Weston decided.

Even if Almquist had swung past the external hull blister he would have failed to see, through a darkened view port, the two shabby types looking out. Nobody had official business in the blister. The younger man grimaced nervously, heavy cords bunching at his neck. He was half a head taller than his companion. "What d'you think, Zen?"

The other man yielded a lopsided smile. "Sounds good." He unplugged a pocket communicator from the wall and stuffed it into his threadbare coverall, then leaned forward at the view port. His chunky, muscular torso and short legs ill-matched the extraordinary arms that reached halfway to his knees, giving him the look of a tall dwarf. "I think they bought it, Yves."

"What if they didn't?"

Zen swung around, now grinning outright, and regarded Yves Versky through a swatch of brown hair that was seldom cut. "Hey, do like boss Almquist told you: Relax! They *gotta* buy it."

"I don't follow you."

"Then you'd better learn to. Look, if they recover any pieces, they'll find human flesh. How can they know it was a poor rummy's body thawed after six months in deep freeze? And if they *did* decide it's a scam, they'd have to explain how we planted him in your P-suit. And cut him loose from the blister, when only a few people are supposed to have access here; *and* preset the audio tape and the explosive, *and* coaxed a decent performance out of a lunk like you, *and*," he spread his apelike arms wide, his face comically ugly in glee, "nobody can afford to admit there's a scam counterculture on Ellfive Prime. All the way up to Torin Almquist there'd be just too much egg on too many faces. It ain't gonna happen, Versky."

The hulking cargo man found himself infected by the grin, but: "I wonder how long it'll be before *I* see another egg."

Zen snorted, "First time you lug a carton of edible garbage out of Hilton Prime, me lad. Jean Neruda's half-blind; when you put on the right coverall, he won't know he has an extra in his recycling crew, and after two days you won't mind pickin' chicken out of the slop. Just sit tight in your basement hidey-hole when you're off duty for a while. Stay away from crews that might recognize you until your beard grows. And keep your head shaved like I told you."

Versky heaved a long sigh, sweeping a hand over his newly bald scalp. "You'll drop in on me? I need a lot of tips on the scam life. And—and I don't know how to repay you."

"A million ways. I'll think of a few, young fella. And sure, you'll see me—whenever I like."

Versky chuckled at the term *young fella.* He knew Zen might be in his forties, but he seemed younger. Versky followed his mentor to the air lock into the colony hull. "Well, just don't forget your friend in the garbage business," he urged, fearful of his unknown future.

Zen paused in the conduit that snaked beneath the soil of Ellfive Prime. "Friendship," he half-joked, "varies directly with mutual benefit and inversely with guilt. Put another way," he said, lapsing into scam language as he trotted toward the South end cap, "a friend who's willing to be understood is a joy. One that demands understanding is a pain in the ass."

"You think too much," Versky laughed. They moved softly now, approaching an entry to the hotel basement.

Zen glanced through the spy hole, paused before punching the wall in the requisite place. "Just like you work too much." He flashed his patented gargoyle grin. "Trust me. Give your heart a rest."

Versky, much too tall for his borrowed clothing, inflated his barrel chest in challenge. "Do I *look* like a heart murmur?"

A shrug. "You did to OrbGen's doctors, rot their souls—which is why you were due to be Earthsided next week. Don't lay that on *me*, ol' scam; I'm the one who's reprieved you to a low-g colony, if you'll just stay in low-g areas near the end caps." He opened the door.

Versky saw the hand signal and whispered, "I got it: Wait thirty seconds." He chuckled again. "Sometimes I think you should be running this colony."

Zen slipped through, left the door nearly closed, waited until Versky had moved near the slit. "In some ways," he stage-whispered back, "I do." Wink. Then he scuttled away.

At mid-morning the next day, Almquist arranged the accident report and its supporting documents into a neat sequence across his video console. Slouching behind his desk with folded arms, he regarded the display for a moment before lifting his eyes. "What've I forgot, Emory?"

Emory Reina cocked his head sparrowlike at the display. Almquist gnawed a cuticle, watching the soulful Reina's eyes dart back and forth in sober scrutiny. "It's all there," was Reina's verdict. "The only safety infraction was Versky's, I think."

"You mean the tether he should've worn?"

A nod; Reina started to speak but thought better of it, the furrows dark on his olive face.

"Spit it out, dammit," Almquist goaded. Reina usually thought a lot more than he talked, a trait Almquist valued in his assistant manager.

"I am wondering," the little Brazilian said, "if it was really accidental." Their eyes locked again, held for a long moment. "Ellfive Prime has been orbiting for fifty years. Discounting early casualties throughout the war, the colony has had twenty-seven fatal mishaps among OrbGen employees. Fourteen of them occurred during the last few days of the victim's tour on the colony."

"That's hard data?"

Another nod.

"You're trying to say they're suicides."

"I am trying not to think so." A devout Catholic, Reina spoke hesitantly.

Maybe he's afraid God is listening. I wish I thought He would. "Can't say I'd blame some of them," Almquist said aloud, remembering. "But not Yves Versky. Too young, too much to live for."

"You must account for my pessimism," Reina replied.

"It's what we pay you for," Almquist said, trying in vain to make it airy. "Maybe the insurance people could convince OrbGen to sweeten the Earthside trip for returning people. It might be cheaper in the long run."

Emory Reina's face said that was bloody likely. "After I send a repair crew to fix the drizzle from that rain pipe, I could draft a suggestion from you to the insurance group," was all he said.

"Do that." Almquist turned his attention to the desk console. As Reina padded out of the low Center building into its courtyard, the manager committed the accident report to memory storage, then paused. His fingers twitched nervously over his computer-terminal keyboard. Oh, yes, he'd forgotten something, all right. Conveniently.

In moments, Almquist had queried Prime memory for an accident report ten years past. It was an old story in more ways than one. Philip Elroy Hazen: technical editor, born 14 September 2014, arrived on L-5′ for first tour to write modification work orders 8 May 2039. Earthsided on 10 May 2041; a standard two-year tour for those who were skilled enough to qualify. A colony tour did not imply any other bonus: The tour *was* the bonus. It worked out very well for the owning conglomerates that controlled literally everything on their colonies. Almquist's mouth twitched: *well, maybe not literally* . . .

Hazen had wangled a second tour to the colony on 23 February 2045, implying that he'd been plenty good at his work. Fatal injury accident report filed 20 February 2047.

Uh-*huh*; uh-*huh*! Yes, by God, there was a familiar ring to it: a malf in Hazen's radio while he was suited up, doing one last check on a modification to the casting facility. Flung off the tip of the mirror and—*Jesus, what a freakish way to go*—straight into a mountain of white-hot slag that had radiated like a dying sun near a temporary processing module outside the colony hull. No recovery attempted; why sift ashes?

Phil Hazen; Zen, they'd called him. The guy they used to say needed rollerskates on his hands; but that was envy talking. Almquist had known Zen slightly, and the guy was an absolute terror at sky-bike racing along the zero-g axis of the colony. Built his own tri-wing craft, even gave it a Maltese cross, scarlet polymer wingskin, and a funny name. The *Red Baron* had looked like a joke, just what Zen had counted on. He'd won a year's pay before other sky bikers realized it wasn't a streak of luck.

Hazen had always made his luck. With his sky bike—it was with young seasoned spruce and the foam polymer, fine engineering and better craftsmanship, all disguised to lure the suckers. And all without an engineering degree. Zen had just picked up expertise, never seeming to work at it.

And when his luck ran out, it was—Almquist checked the display—only days before he was slated for Earthside. Uh-*huh*!

Torin Almquist knew about the shadowy wraiths who somehow dropped from sight on the colony, to be caught later or to die for lack of medical attention or, in a few cases, to find some scam—some special advantage—to keep them hidden on Ellfive Prime. He'd been sure Zen was a survivor, no matter what the accident report said. What was the phrase? *A scam, not a bum*; being on the scam wasn't quite the same. A scam wasn't down and out of resources; he was down and out of sight. Maybe the crafty Zen had engineered another fatality that wasn't fatal.

Almquist hadn't caught anyone matching the description of Zen. (Almost, but not quite.) He thought about young Yves Versky, whose medical report hadn't been all that bad, then considered Versky's life expectancy on the colony versus his chances Earthside. Versky had been a sharp hard worker too. Almquist leaned back in his chair again and stared at his display. He had no way of knowing that Reina's rain-pipe crew was too late to ward off disaster.

A rain pipe had been leaking long before Grounds Maintenance realized they had a problem. Rain was a simple matter on Ellfive Prime: You built a web of pipes with spray nozzles that ran the length of the colony. From ground level the pipes were nearly invisible, thin lines connected by crosspieces in a great cylindrical net surrounding the colony's zero-g axis. Gravity loading near the axis was so slight that the rain pipes could be anchored lightly.

Yet now and then, a sky biker would pedal foolishly from the zero-g region or would fail to compensate for the gentle rolling movement generated by the air itself. That was when the rain pipes saved somebody's bacon and on rare occasions suffered a kink. At such times, Almquist was tempted to press for the outlawing of sky bikes until the rabid sports association could raise money for a safety net to protect people and pipes alike. But the cost would have been far too great: It would have amounted to a flat prohibition of sky bikes.

The problem had started a month earlier with a mild collision between a sky bike and a crosspiece. The biker got back intact, but the impact popped a kink on the underside of the attached rain pipe. The kink could not be seen from the colony's axis. It might possibly have been spotted from floor level with a good, powerful telescope.

Inspection crews used safety tethers, which loaded the rain pipe just enough to close the crack while the inspector passed. Then the drizzle resumed for as long as the rain continued. Thereafter, the thrice-weekly afternoon rain from that pipe had been lessened in a line running from Ellfive Prime's Hilton Hotel, past the prized hill, over the colony's one shallow lake, to work-staff apartments that stretched from the lake to the North end cap, where crops were grown. Rain was lessened, that is, everywhere but over the pine-covered hill directly below the kink. Total rainfall was unchanged; but the hill got three times its normal moisture, which gradually soaked down through a forty-year accumulation of ponderosa needles and humus, into the soil below.

In this fashion the hill absorbed one hundred thousand kilograms too much water in a month. A little water percolated back to the creek and the lake it fed. Some of it was still soaking down through the humus overburden. And much of it—far too much—was held by the underlying slope soil, which was gradually turning to ooze. The extra mass had already caused a barely detectable shift in the colony's spin axis. Almquist had his best troubleshooter, Lee Shumway, quietly checking the hull for a structural problem near the hull blister.

Suzanne Nagel was a lissome widow whose second passion was for her sky bike. She had been idling along in zero-g, her chain-driven propeller a soft whirr behind her, when something obscured her view of the hill far below. She kept staring at it until she was well beyond the leak, then realized the obstruction was a spray of water. Suzy sprint-pedaled the rest of the way to the end cap, and five minutes later the rains were canceled by Emory Reina.

Thanks to Suzy Nagel's stamina, the slope did not collapse that day. But working from inspection records, Reina tragically assumed that the leak had been present for perhaps three days instead of a month. The hill needed something—a local vibration, for example—to begin the mud slide that could abruptly displace up to two hundred thousand tons of mass downslope. Which would inevitably bring on the nightmare more feared than meteorites by every colony manager: spinquake. Small meteorites could only damage a colony, but computer simulations had proved that if the spin axis shifted suddenly a spinquake could crack a colony like an egg.

The repair crew was already in place high above when Reina brought his electrabout three-wheeler to a halt near a path that led up to the pines. His belt-comm set allowed direct contact with the crew and instant access to all channels, including his private scrambler to Torin Almquist.

"I can see the kink on your video," Reina told the crew leader, studying his belt-slung video. "Sleeve it and run a pressure check. We can be thankful that a leak that large was not over Hilton Prime," he added, laughing. The retired OrbGen executives who luxuriated in the hotel would have screamed raw murder, of course. And the leak would have been noticed.

Scanning the dwarf apple trees at the foot of the slope, Reina's gaze moved to the winding footpath. In the forenoon quietude, he could hear distant swimmers cavorting in the slightly reduced gravity of the Hilton pool near the South end cap. But somewhere above him on the hill, a large animal thrashed clumsily through the pines. It wasn't one of the half-tame deer; only maladroit humans made that much commotion on Ellfive Prime. Straining to locate the hiker, Reina saw the leaning trees. He blinked. No trick of eyesight; they were really leaning. Then he saw the long shallow mud slide, no more than a portent of its potential, that covered part of the footpath. For perhaps five seconds, his mind grasping the implication of what he saw, Reina stood perfectly still. His mouth hung open.

In deadly calm, coding the alarm on his scrambler circuit: "Torin, Emory Reina. I have a Code Three on the hill. And," he swallowed hard, "potential Code One. I say again, Code One; mud slides on the main-path side of the hill. Over." Then Reina began to shout toward the pines.

Code Three was bad enough: a life in danger. Code Two was more serious still, implying an equipment malfunction that could affect many lives. Code One was reserved for colony-wide disaster. Reina's voice shook. He had never called a Code One before.

• • •

During the half-minute it took for Almquist to race from a conference to his office, Reina's shouts flushed not one but two men from the hillside. The first, a heavy individual in golf knickers, identified himself testily as Voerster Weston. He stressed that he was not accustomed to peremptory demands from an overall-clad worker. The second man emerged far to Reina's right but kept hidden in a stand of mountain laurel, listening, surmising, sweating.

Reina's was the voice of sweet reason. "If you want to live, Mr. Weston, please lie down where you are. Slowly. The trees below you are leaning outward, and they were not that way yesterday."

"Damnation, I know that much," Weston howled; "that's what I was looking at. Do you know how wet it is up here? I will not lie down on this muck!"

The man in the laurels made a snap decision, cursed, and stood up. "If you don't, two-belly, I'll shoot you here and now," came the voice of Philip Elroy Hazen. Zen had one hand thrust menacingly into a coverall pocket. He was liberally smeared with mud, and his aspect was not pleasant.

"O *demonio*, another one," Reina muttered. The fat man saw himself flanked, believed Zen's implied lie about a weapon, and carefully levered himself down to the blanket of pine needles. At this moment Torin Almquist answered the Mayday.

There was no way to tell how much soil might slide, but through staccato interchanges Emory Reina described the scene better than his video could show it. Almquist was grim. "We're already monitoring an increase in the off-center spin, Emory; not a severe shift, but it could get to be. Affirmative on that potential Code One. I'm sending a full emergency crew to the blister, now that we know where to start."

Reina thought for a moment, glumly pleased that neither man on the slope had moved. "I believe we can save these two by lowering a safety sling from my crew. They are directly overhead. Concur?"

An instant's pause. "Smart, Emory. And you get your butt out of there. Leave the electrabout, man, just *go*!"

"With respect, I cannot. Someone must direct the sling deployment from here."

"It's your bacon. I'll send another crew to you."

"Volunteers only," Reina begged, watching the slope. For the moment it seemed firm. Yet a bulge near cosmetically placed slag boulders suggested a second mass displacement. Reina then explained their predicament to the men on the slope, to ensure their compliance.

"It's worse than that," Zen called down. "There was a dugout over there," he pointed to the base of a boulder, "where a woman was living. She's buried, I'm afraid."

Reina shook his head sadly, using his comm set to his work crew. Over four hundred meters above, men were lashing tether lines from crosspieces to distribute the weight of a sling. Spare tethers could be linked by carabiners to make a lifeline reaching to the colony floor. The exercise was familiar to the crew, but only as a drill until now. And they would be hoisting, not lowering.

Diametrically opposite from the hill, troubleshooters converged on the blister where the colony's long-unused reactor and coolant tanks were stored. Their job was simple—in principle.

The reactor subsystems had been designed as portable elements, furnished with lifting and towing lugs. The whole reactor system weighed nearly ten thousand tons, including coolant tanks. Since the blister originally had been built around the stored reactor elements to balance the hill mass, Almquist needed only to split the blister open to space, then lower the reactor elements on quartz cables. As the mass moved out of the blister and away from the hull, it would increase in apparent weight, balancing the downward flow of mud across the hull. Almquist was lucky in one detail: The reactor was not in line with the great solar-mirror strips. Elements could be lowered a long way while repairs were carried out to redistribute the soil.

Almquist marshaled forces from his office. He heard the colony-wide alarm whoop its signal, watched monitors as the colony staff and two thousand other residents hurried toward safety in end-cap domes. His own P-suit, ungainly and dust-covered, hung in his apartment ten paces away. There was no time to fetch it while he was at his post. *Never again*, he promised himself. He divided his attention among monitors showing the evacuation, the blister team, and the immediate problem above Emory Reina.

Reina was optimistic as the sling snaked down. "South a bit," he urged into his comm set, then raised his voice. "Mr. Weston, a sling is above you, a little north. Climb in and buckle the harness. They will reel you in."

"Now, steady as she goes," Reina said, then, "Stop." The sling collapsed on the turf near the fat man. Reina, fearful that the mud-covered stranger might lose heart, called to assure him that the sling would return.

"I'll take my chances here," Zen called back. The sling could mean capture. The fat man did not understand that any better than Reina did.

Voerster Weston paused halfway into his harness, staring up. Suddenly he was scrambling away from it, tripping in the sling, mindless with the fear of rising into a synthetic sky. Screaming, he fled down the slope. And brought part of it with him.

Reina saw apple trees churning toward him in time to leap atop his electrabout and kept his wits enough to grab branches as the first great wave slid from the slope. He saw Weston disappear in two separate upheavals, swallowed under the mud slide he had provoked. Mauled by hardwood, mired to his knees, Reina spat blood and turf. He hauled one leg free, then the other, pulling at tree limbs. The second man, he saw, had slithered against a thick pine and was now trying to climb it.

Still calm, voice indistinct through his broken jaw, Reina redirected the sling crew. The sling harness bounced upslope near the second man. "Take the sling," Reina bawled.

Now Reina's whole world shuddered. It was a slow, perceptible motion, each displacement of mud worsening the off-center rotation and slight acceleration changes that could bring more mud that could bring worse. . . . Reina forced his mind back to the immediate problem. He could not see himself at its focus.

Almquist felt the tremors, saw what had to be done. "Emory, I'm sending your relief crew back. Shumway's in the blister. They don't have time to cut the blister now; they'll have to blow it open. You have about three minutes to get to firm ground. Then you run like hell to South end cap."

"As soon as this man is in the sling," Reina mumbled. Zen had already made his decision, seeing the glistening ooze that had buried the fat man.

"Now! Right fucking *now*," Almquist pleaded. "I can't delay it a millisecond. When Shumway blows the blister open it'll be a sudden shake, Emory. You know what that means?"

Reina did. The sharp tremor would probably bring the entire middle of the slope thundering down. Even if the reactor could be lowered in minutes, it would take only seconds for the muck to engulf him. Reina began to pick his way backward across fallen apple trees, wondering why his left arm had an extra bend above the wrist. He kept a running fire of instructions to the rain-pipe crew as Zen untangled the sling harness. Reina struggled toward safety in pain, patience, reluctance. And far too slowly.

"He is buckled in," Reina announced. His last words were, "Haul away." He saw the mud-spattered Zen begin to rise, swinging in a broad arc, and they exchanged "OK" hand signals before Reina gave full attention to his own escape. He had just reached the edge of firm ground when Lee Shumway, moving with incredible speed in a full P-suit, ducked through a blister airlock and triggered the charges.

The colony floor bucked once, throwing Reina off stride. He fell on his fractured ulna, rolled, opened his mouth—perhaps to moan, perhaps to pray. His breath was bottled by mud as he was flung beneath a viscous gray tide that rolled numberless tons of debris over him.

The immense structure groaned, but held. Zen swayed sickeningly as Ellfive Prime shook around him. He saw Reina die, watched helplessly as a retiree home across the valley sagged and collapsed. Below him, a covey of Quetzal birds burst from the treetops like jeweled scissors in flight. As he was drawn higher he could see more trees slide.

The damage worsened; too many people had been too slow. The colony was rattling everything that would rattle. Now it was all rattling louder. Somewhere, a shrill whistle keened as precious air and more precious water vapor rushed toward a hole in the sunlight windows.

When the shouts above him became louder than the carnage below, Zen began to hope. Strong arms reached for his and moments later he was attached to another tether. "I can make it from here," he said, calling his thanks back as he hauled himself toward the end-cap braces.

A crew man with a video comm set thrust it toward Zen as he neared a ladder. "It's for you," he said, noncommittal.

For an instant, an eon, Zen's body froze, though he continued to waft nearer. Then he shrugged and took the comm set as though it were ticking. He saw a remembered face in the video. Wrapping an arm around the ladder, he nodded to the face. "Don Bellows here," he said innocently.

Pause, then a snarl: "You wouldn't believe my mixed emotions when I recognized you on the monitor. Well, *Mister* Bellows, Adolf Hitler here." Almquist went on, "Or you'll think so damned quick unless you're in my office as fast as your knuckles will carry you."

The crew man was looking away, but he was tense. He knew. Zen cleared his throat for a whine. "I'm scared—"

"You've been dead for ten years, Hazen. How can you be scared? Frazer there will escort you; his instructions are to brain you if he has to. I have sweeping powers right now. Don't con me and don't argue; I need you right here, right now."

By the time Zen reached the terraces with their felled, jumbled crops, the slow shakes had subsided. They seemed to diminish to nothing as he trotted, the rangy Frazer in step behind, to an abandoned electrabout. Damage was everywhere, yet the silence was oppressive. A few electrical fires were kindling in apartments as they moved toward the Colony Center building. Some fires would be out, others out of control, in minutes. The crew man gestured Zen through the courtyard and past two doors. Torin Almquist stood looming over his console display, ignoring huge shards of glass that littered his carpet.

Almquist adjusted a video monitor. "Thanks, Frazer; would you wait in the next room?" The crew man let his face complain of his idleness but complied silently. Without glancing from the monitors, Almquist transfixed the grimy Zen. "If I say the word, you're a dead man. If I say a different word, you go Earthside in manacles. You're still here only because I wanted you here all the time, just in case I ever needed you. Well, I need you now. If you hadn't been dropped into my lap we'd have found you on a Priority One. Never doubt that.

"If I say a third word, you get a special assistant's slot—I can swing that—for as long as I'm here. All I'm waiting for is one word from *you*. If it's a lie, you're dead meat. Will you help Ellfive Prime? Yes or no?"

Zen considered his chances. Not past that long-legged Frazer. They could follow him on monitors for some distance anyhow unless he had a head start. "Given the right conditions," Zen hazarded.

Almquist's head snapped up. "My best friend just died for you, against my better judgment. *Yes or no.*"

"Yes. I owe you nothin', but I owe him somethin'."

Back to the monitors, speaking to Zen: "Lee Shumway's crew has recovered our mass balance, and they can do it again if necessary. I doubt there'll be more mud slides, though; five minutes of spinquakes should've done it all."

Zen moved to watch over the tall man's bare arms. Two crews could be seen from a utility tug monitor, rushing to repair window leaks where water vapor had crystallized in space as glittering fog. The colony's external heat radiator was in massive fragments, and the mirrors were jammed in place. It was going to get hot in Ellfive Prime. "How soon will we get help from other colonies?"

Almquist hesitated. Then, "We won't, unless we fail to cope. OrbGen is afraid some other corporate pirate will claim salvage rights. And when you're on my staff, everything I tell you is privileged data."

"You think the danger is over?"

"Over?" Almquist barked a laugh that threatened to climb out of control. He ticked items off on his fingers. "We're losing water vapor; we have to mask mirrors and repair the radiator, or we fry; half our crops are ruined and food stores may not last; and most residents are hopeless clods who have no idea how to fend for themselves. *Now* d'you see why I diverted searches when I could've taken you twice before?"

Zen's mouth was a cynical curve.

Almquist: "Once when you dragged a kid from the lake filters I could've had you at the emergency room." Zen's eyebrows lifted in surprised agreement. "And once when a waiter realized you were scamming food from the Hilton service elevator."

"That was somebody else, you weren't even close. But okay, you've been a real sweetheart. Why?"

"Because you've learned to live outside the system! Food, shelter, medical help, God knows what else; you have another system that hardly affects mine, and now we're going to teach your tricks to the survivors. This colony is going to make it. You were my experimental group, Zen. You just didn't know it." He rubbed his chin reflectively. "By the way, how many guys are on the scam? Couple of dozen?" An optimist, Torin Almquist picked what he considered a high figure.

A chuckle. "Couple of hundred, you mean." Zen saw slack-jawed disbelief and went on: "They're not all guys. A few growing families. There's Wandering Mary, Maria Polyakova; our only registered nurse, but I found her dugout full of mud this morning. I hope she was sleepin' out."

"Can you enlist their help? If they don't help, this colony can still die. The computer says it will, as things stand now. It'll be close, but we won't make it. How'd you like to take your chances with a salvage crew?"

"Not a chance. But I can't help just standing here swappin' wind with you."

"Right." Eyes bored into Zen's, assessing him. The thieves' argot, the be-damned-to-you gaze, suggested a man who was more than Hazen *had* been. "I'll give you a temporary pass. See you here tomorrow morning; for now, look the whole colony over, and bring a list of problems and solutions as you see 'em."

Zen turned to leave, then looked back. "You're really gonna let me just walk right out." A statement of wonder, and of fact.

"Not without this," Almquist said, scribbling on a plastic chit. He thrust it toward Zen. "Show it to Frazer."

Inspecting the cursive scrawl: "Doesn't look like much."

"*Más que nada*," Almquist smiled, then looked quickly away as his face fell. *Better than nothing*; his private joke with Emory Reina. He glanced at the retreating Zen and rubbed his forehead. Grief did funny things to people's heads. To deny a death you won't accept, you invest his character in another man. Not very smart when the other man might betray you for the sheer fun of it. Torin Almquist massaged his temples and called Lee Shumway. They still had casualties to rescue.

Zen fought a sense of unreality as he moved openly in broad daylight. Everyone was lost in his own concerns. Zen hauled one scam from his plastic bubble under the lake surface, half dead in stagnant air after mud from the creek swamped his air exchanger. An entire family of scams, living as servants in the illegal basement they had excavated for a resident, had been crushed when the foundation collapsed.

But he nearly wept to find Wandering Mary safe in a secret conduit, tending to a dozen wounded scams. He took notes as she told him where her curative herbs were planted and how to use them. The old girl flatly refused to leave her charges, her black eyes flashing through wisps of gray hair, and Zen promised to send food.

The luck of Sammy the Touch was holding strong. The crop compost heap that covered his half-acre foam shell seemed to insulate it from ground shock as well. Sammy patted his little round tummy, always a cheerful sign, as he ushered Zen into the bar where, on a good night, thirty scams might be gathered. If Zen was the widest-ranging scam on Ellfive Prime, Sammy the Touch was the most secure.

Zen accepted a glass of potato vodka—Sammy was seldom *that* easy a touch—and allowed a parody of the truth to be drawn from him. He'd offered his services to an assistant engineer, he said, in exchange for unspecified future privileges. Sammy either bought the story or took a lease on it. He responded after some haggling with the promise of a hundred kilos of "medicinal" alcohol and half his supply of bottled methane. Both were produced from compost precisely under the noses of the crop crew, and both were supplied on credit. Sammy also agreed to provision the hidden infirmary of Wandering Mary. Zen hugged the embarrassed Sammy and exited through one of the conduits, promising to pick up the supplies later.

Everywhere he went, Zen realized, the scams were coping better than legal residents. He helped a startlingly handsome middle-aged blonde douse the remains of her smoldering wardrobe. Her apartment complex had knelt into its courtyard and caught fire.

"I'm going to freeze tonight," Suzy Nagel murmured philosophically.

He eyed her skimpy costume and doubted it. Besides, the temperature was slowly climbing, and there wouldn't *be* any night until the solar mirrors could be pivoted again. There were other ways to move the colony to a less reflective position, but he knew Almquist would try the direct solutions first.

Farmer Brown—no one knew his original name—wore his usual stolen agronomy-crew coverall as he hawked his pack load of vegetables among residents in the low-rent area. He had not assessed all the damage to his own crops, tucked and espaliered into corners over five square kilometers of the colony. Worried as he was, he had time to hear a convincing story. "Maybe I'm crazy to compete against myself," he told Zen, "but you got a point. If a salvage outfit takes over, it's kaymag." KMAG: Kiss my ass good-bye. "I'll sell you seeds, even breeding pairs of hamsters, but don't ask me to face the honchos in person. You remember about the vigilantes, ol' scam."

Zen nodded. He gave no thought to the time until a long shadow striped a third of the colony floor. One of the mirrors had been coaxed into pivoting. Christ, he was tired—but why not? It would have been dark long before, on an ordinary day. He sought his sleeping quarters in Jean Neruda's apartment, hoping Neruda wouldn't insist on using Zen's eyesight to fill out receipts. Their arrangement was a comfortable quid pro quo, but please, thought Zen, not tonight!

He found a more immediate problem than receipts. Yves Versky slumped, trembling, in the shambles of Neruda's place, holding a standard emergency oxygen mask over the old man's face. The adjoining office had lost one wall in the spinquake, moments after the recycling crew ran for end-cap domes.

"I had to hole up here," Versky gasped, exhausted. "Didn't know where else to go. Neruda wouldn't leave either. Then the old fool smelled smoke and dumped his goldfish bowl on a live power line. Must've blown half the circuits in his body." Like a spring-wound toy, Versky's movements and voice diminished. "Took me two hours of mouth-to-mouth before he was breathing steady, Zen. Boy, have I got a headache."

Versky fell asleep holding the mask in place. Zen could infer the rest. Neruda, unwilling to leave familiar rooms in his advancing blindness. Versky, unwilling to abandon a life, even that of a half-electrocuted, crotchety old man. Yet Neruda was right to stay put: Earthside awaited the OrbGen employee whose eyes failed.

Zen lowered the inert Versky to the floor, patted the big man's shoulder. More than unremitting care, he had shown stamina and first-aid expertise. Old Neruda awoke once, half-manic, half-just disoriented. Zen nursed him through it with surface awareness. On another level he was cataloguing items for Almquist, for survivors, for Ellfive Prime.

And on the critical level a voice in him jeered, *bullshit: For yourself*. Not because Almquist or Reina had done him any favors, but because Torin Almquist was right. The colony manager could find him eventually; maybe it was better to rejoin the system now, on good terms. Besides, as the only man who could move between the official system and the scam counterculture, he could really wheel and deal. It might cause some hard feelings in the conduits, but . . . Zen sighed, and slept. Poorly.

It was two days before Zen made every contact he needed, two more when Almquist announced that Ellfive Prime would probably make it. The ambient temperature had stabilized. Air and water losses had ceased. They did not have enough stored food to provide three thousand daily calories per person beyond twenty days, but crash courses in multicropping were suddenly popular, and some immature crops could be eaten.

"It'd help if you could coax a few scams into instructing," Almquist urged as he slowed to match Zen's choppy pace. They turned from the damaged crop terraces toward the Center.

"Unnn-likely," Zen intoned. "We still talk about wartime, when vigilantes tried to clean us out. They ushered a couple of nice people out of airlocks, naked, which we think was a little brusque. Leave it alone; it's working."

A nod. "Seems to be. But I have doubts about the maturing rates of your seeds. Why didn't my people know about those hybrid daikon radishes and tomatoes?"

"You were after long-term yield," Zen shrugged. "This hot weather will ripen the stuff faster, too. We've been hiding a dozen short-term crops under your nose, including dandelions better than spinach. Like hamster haunch is better'n rabbit, and a lot quicker to grow."

Almquist could believe the eighteen-day gestation period, but was astonished at the size of the breeding stock. "You realize your one-kilo hamsters could be more pet than protein?"

"Not in our economy," Zen snorted. "It's hard to be sentimental when you're down and out. Or stylish either." He indicated his frayed coverall. "By the time the rag man gets this, it won't yield three meters of dental floss."

Almquist grinned for the first time in many days. What his new assistant had forgotten in polite speech, he made up in the optimism of a young punk. He corrected himself: an *old* punk. "You know what hurts? You're nearly my age and look ten years younger. How?"

It wasn't a specific exercise, Zen explained. It was attitude. "You're careworn," he sniffed. "Beat your brains out for idling plutocrats fifty weeks a year and then wonder why you age faster than I do." Wondering headshake.

They turned toward the Center courtyard. Amused, Almquist said, "You're a plutocrat?"

"Ain't racin' my motors. Look at all the Indians who used to live past a hundred. A Blackfoot busted his ass like I do, maybe ten or twenty weeks a year. They weren't dumb; just scruffy."

Almquist forgot his retort; his desk console was flashing for attention. Zen wandered out of the office, returning with two cups of scam "coffee." Almquist sipped it between calls, wondering if it was really brewed from ground dandelion root, considering how this impudent troll was changing his life, could change it further.

Finally he sat back. "You heard OrbGen's assessment," he sighed. "I'm a Goddamned hero, for now. Don't ask me about next year. If they insist on making poor Emory a sacrificial goat to feed ravening stockholders, I can't help it."

Impassive: "Sure you could. You just let 'em co-opt you." Zen sighed, then released a sad troglodyte's smile. "Like you co-opted me."

"I can unco-opt. Nothing's permanent."

"You said it, bubba."

Almquist took a long breath, then cantilevered a forefinger in warning. "Watch your tongue, Hazen. When I pay your salary, you pay some respect." He saw the sullen look in Zen's eyes and bored in. "Or would you rather go on the scam again and get Earthsided the first chance I get? I haven't *begun* to co-opt you yet," he glowered. "I have to meet with the Colony Council in five minutes—to explain a lot of things, including you. When I get back, I want a map of those conduits the scams built, to the best of your knowledge."

A flood of ice washed through Zen's veins. Staring over the cup of coffee that shook in his hands: "You *know* I can't do that."

Almquist paused in the doorway, his expression smug. "You know the alternative Think about it," he said, and turned and walked out.

When Torin Almquist returned, his wastebasket was overturned on his desk. A ripe odor wrinkled his nose for him even before he saw what lay atop the wastebasket like an offering on a pedestal: a lavish gift of human excrement. His letter opener~~, an antique, pro~~truded from the turd. It skewered a plastic chit, Zen's pass. On the chit, in draftsman's neat printing, full caps: I THOUGHT ABOUT IT.

Well, you sure couldn't mistake his answer, Almquist reflected as he dumped the offal into his toilet. Trust Zen to make the right decision.

Which way had he gone? Almquist could only guess at the underground warrens built during the past fifty years, but chose not to guess. He also knew better than to mention Zen to the Colony Council. The manager felt a twinge of guilt at the choice, truly no choice at all, that he had forced on Zen—but there was no other way.

If Zen knew the whole truth, he might get careless, and a low profile was vital for the scams. The setup benefited all of Ellfive Prime. Who could say when the colony might once more need the counterculture and its primitive ways?

And that meant Zen had to disappear again, genuinely down and out of reach. If Almquist himself didn't know exactly where the scams hid, he couldn't tell OrbGen even under drugs. And he didn't intend to tell. Sooner or later OrbGen would schedule Torin Almquist for permanent Earthside rotation, and when that day came he might need help in his own disappearance. *That* would be the time to ferret out a secret conduit, to contact Zen. The scams could use an engineering manager who knew the official system inside out.

Almquist grinned to himself and brewed a cup of dandelion coffee. Best to get used to the stuff now, he reasoned; it would be a staple after he retired, down and out on Ellfive Prime.

SEND ME A KISS BY WIRE

Hilbert Schenck

Hilbert Schenck's stories are rich in the characterization of scientists doing the sometimes frustrating daily work that leads to sudden moments of discovery and, perhaps, transcendence. Schenck is a professor of engineering specializing in the ocean, and his characters are rarely far from water; his tales usually deal with the shores, the currents, the storms, the creatures of the sea, particularly of the New England seacoast. His stories often contain blistering satires on academic life, as here in this story.

Harking back to the traditions of the sea story (of Melville and Conrad) and to Jules Verne's imaginary voyages, "Send Me a Kiss by Wire" is a story of adventure, exploration, and zoology. It is an interesting contrast in its depiction of sea creatures to Dickson's "Dolphin's Way," on one hand, and "Davy Jones' Ambassador" on the other, using no overt science-fictional inventions, concentrating entirely on accuracy and the hard sf affect. What if the legendary sea monster were real? Here is a hardheaded, hard-nosed contemporary scientific expedition, with a veneer of calm over barely suppressed intellectual excitement. This is science fiction as the shadow of the hard-boiled, romantic, heroic adventure—disguised as daily work. And the point of it all is a moment of revelation: The legend is revealed as a real natural wonder.

This moment of discovery after exploration is one of the goals of science and the scientist. Sf stories such as this one reaffirm that such a desire as this underpins science. Look for the phrase, "what is the price of true wonder." Then consider for a moment the dying spaceman stories of the 1950s, in which death is the price of the moment of discovery, as sincere salesmanship for space travel. Wonder is worth any price in hard sf.

I

The big *Challenger* auditorium was already jam-packed when Dr. Walter Bascom, dean of the Oceanography School, pushed through the milling crowds of students, staff, and press people looking for seats. Way down front, surrounded by his usual entourage of vice-presidents and main-campus deans, the ancient university provost, Jacob Holley, instantly spotted Bascom and gave a large and commanding wave in his direction. The small dean, exhausted from a month's cruise following North Atlantic currents, his thin face stiff and icy, pushed into the provost's row while nodding at, or tersely greeting, various important academic bureaucrats. The provost had managed to move some less vital functionary from the seat at his right, and as the dean settled down into it, the gaunt, lantern-jawed Yankee gave Bascom a robotlike smile and muttered, "Wonderful thing. Just what the place needed,

Walter, money and fame," in a voice that the engineering faculty described as a "talking live-steam leak."

Holley's iron-hard face reflected no warmth onto this verbal praise, for he had recognized in Dean Bascom's tight expression a decided lack of sympathy with the proceedings in the auditorium. Bascom turned in his seat to face the taller provost, and though his voice was very quiet, it had the sharp edge of an ice sheet snapping apart. "Whom do we get to fight with this creature, Jacob?" he said. "Fraternity pledges? All our assistant professors in jogging shorts?"

Holley's lined face became, if possible, even craggier, and his voice was now the thin hiss of an annoyed snake. "Walter, this so-called State of the Union and its huge and valuable university are *dead-broke*! If, in order to catch the attention of the state legislature, it becomes necessary to feed to your wife's monster the half a dozen or so virgins among our ten thousand co-eds, then it will be done—instantly! Do you understand that, Walter?"

Dean Bascom, managing to actually outhiss the provost, pressed his lips into an invisible line. "Virgins, Jacob, are exactly what we *ain't*!" he retorted.

To a couple of nearby wire-service reporters, this intense and highly charged exchange was simply mysterious, but to the university officials sitting around the provost, catching a word here and there, the problem was clear.

Dean Bascom, a most eligible faculty bachelor for many years, had finally married Dr. Emily Orton, a full professor of biological oceanography in his school. Less than a year later, Emily Bascom had organized a "World Record Octopus Derby" in conjunction with the Saturday afternoon TV show *Wide Sporting World*. Scuba divers in Alaska and Puget Sound were recruited in droves, and the animals were attracted from their caves and grottoes by a water-soluble chemical, pararitalitic acid, which Emily had discovered exercised both an attractive and narcotic effect on octopuses.

Unfortunately, the 102-pound world-record octopus was matched in an underwater wrestling contest against a huge scuba-diving pro football player. When it became obvious that the hulking diver was being strangled and would surely drown, over a dozen curare darts fired from three different gas guns were required to subdue and finally to stun the strong, fierce animal, all of this photographed by several underwater camera teams. This Clyde Beatty ending to the octopus project, even though much had been learned about the species, had amused the world oceanographic community, dismayed several environmental groups, and enraged Dean Bascom, who had been assured by both the TV people and his wife that the broadcast material would be educational and scholarly.

"O.K., O.K.," called out a large middle-aged woman from the platform up front. "Some of you will have to sit on the floor, I guess. Please, let's get going."

Dr. Emily Bascom's round, cheerful face scanned the choked, noisy auditorium, and when she saw her husband down front with the main-campus crowd, she smiled and gave him a small, tentative wave, which he did not return.

Her expression tightened a bit, and now she shook her arms impatiently. "Please, can I douse the lights? We've got to start!" she shouted.

The lights dimmed and went out, and Emily Bascom's loud, clear voice dropped into its lecturing tones. "Here's the film that started all of this. It was taken twelve days ago off the stern of an oil-search vessel, *Sonic Hunter*, by a young Japanese crewman who just happened to have a loaded super-eight camera in his duffel when the episode started. Thank heaven he remembered he had it!"

The big color image was jerky and grainy, and at first all they could see was a calm blue sea with two stanchions and the horizontal parts of a ship's rail in the foreground. But then, far in the distance, there was a sense of disturbance in the water.

"The *Hunter* was towing a one-hundred-foot-long acoustic pulse generator at the end of six hundred feet of line," she explained. "This is new sub-bottom profiling equipment, and I can't say any more about it other than that it sends down a series of quite sophisticated, shaped sonic pulses to penetrate the sea bottom. Echoes are received by transducers set in the bottom of *Sonic Hunter*'s hull."

Suddenly everyone in the room gave a gasp, for the amateur cameraman had finally remembered his zoom lens, and as the image was quickly and jerkily enlarged, a now clearly seen, long, whippy *something* rose out of the water, followed by several more. These lashed about in the air, making white splashes as they struck the blue sea surface.

"I've studied blowups of these movie frames," said Emily Bascom, "and we're definitely looking at a huge *Architeuthis*, a giant squid. Evidently the creature was attracted and brought up by the acoustic pulses from the towed sound generator."

She gave her audience a reassuring nod. "Now that isn't as weird as it sounds, although nobody ever thought about squids using such classy acoustics. But some fin whales definitely speak through the deep sound channel to contact each other over distances greater than a thousand miles."

The TV producer, his many assistants, plus other important network people sat in a large clot down front next to the university administrators, and now the thickly bearded, white-leather-shoed producer waved a hand. "What are these animals doing all this talking for, Dr. Bascom?" he asked in a smooth voice.

The large woman gave the whole room a wide, round smile. "Oh, the tender passion, of course," she said quickly. "They're just seeking a special friend in a big, lonely world."

But now the audience gasped again, for whereas the arms of the creature had seemed to flop and move about quite languidly for a while, they now began to wave vigorously and with what was clearly a great deal more excitement.

"Somebody on the *Hunter* realized that the signal they were generating had probably brought the thing up, so they shut it off. That was a mistake," laughed Dr. Bascom, and they saw that the squid's arms were getting larger as it moved rapidly and thrashingly toward the stern of the survey vessel along the towline.

"It evidently mistook that thick towline for a friendly tentacle," said Dr. Bascom, "so it moved along the line looking for where the noise went. When it got about fifty yards back, the captain lost his nerve."

As she said this, they saw waves begin to form against the creature's wildly waving arms while a wide, foaming wake suddenly appeared in the center of the picture. The agitation in the water began to get smaller, and in a few moments the image of the creatuare's arms had become so small that only a spot of white-water confusion showed on the wide, calm sea surface.

"The *Hunter*'s skipper went full speed ahead, and the line towing the signal generator—and now also towing our large, agitated friend—simply broke under the strain." Dr. Bascom shrugged. "That's the last they saw of either the squid or their hundred-thousand-dollar acoustic toy."

She turned the room light up a bit and motioned for a slide projection. "O.K., our TV friends—" she gestured toward the large group—"were contacted by the oil-survey company and flew to meet the boat in Dakar. They brought back the film you just saw, some shots of the crewmen telling their stories, plus an agreement that nobody on the boat will say anything about this until they dock in the U.S., which happens today. Tonight the network will air the first of its specials on *Architeuthis*, including this film and a discussion of our hunt for the animal."

She pointed up at a projected side view of a giant squid with various dimensioned arrows superimposed on the image. "We figured out from the camera optics, and what we knew about the location of the sound generator in relation to the stern of the vessel, how big those arms and tentacles are.

"Most Teuthologists"—Dr. Bascom paused, then interjected with a grin. "That's the name for us crazies who like to fondle squid, octopuses, and cuttlefish—set the upper limit on *Architeuthis* at about 1,000 pounds, with a total length of maybe 60 feet. This big boy is in a whole other class. From the scaled measurements, we estimate his weight will be a hefty 25 *tons*, and his total length will go way over 200 feet. Now the blue whale still holds the title for bulk, about 180 tons, but this animal wins any length sweepstakes hands down. Nothing living and moving, now or then, has ever been as long as he is. The largest blue whale was less than 120 feet overall."

She touched the big image with a long pointer. "Those arms, and there are eight of them, are a solid 6 feet across at the root and about 40 feet long. The two longer tentacles, which *Architeuthis* uses to catch its prey, are over 130 feet long in this specimen, a structural miracle even for a water creature. The suckers at the club end of those tentacles and arms are over 8 inches in diameter. Even the biggest sperm whale or the most violent great white shark would have a helluva fight with this fellow!"

As she paused for breath, the TV producer gestured at the slide. "How do you know it's a boy, Dr. Bascom?" he asked in a casual tone.

Emily Bascom directed her pointer at two of the arms. "In the film blowups, we can see that the creature has two hectocotylized arms, that is, specialized arms without suckers. When a male squid hugs his lady-love, he uses these two arms to make the adjustments. Otherwise, those eight-inch raspy suckers would chop her into fillets."

The producer chuckled briefly at this, then pointed with a languid hand at the image. "So, can I assume that tubular thing poking out of the—what is it, the 'mantle'?—is the thing's sex organ, its penis?"

Emily Bascom's cheerful, pleasant expression became a bit harder. "Some people have claimed that, but I'm not sure it's an intromissive organ. Since nobody has ever had a live male and female together in an aquarium, their mating methods remain speculation," she said in a stiff voice.

A silence fell over the auditorium as the producer peered in apparent puzzlement up at the high ceiling. The network's large, fleshy vice-president for contract and legal matters, sitting next to him, finally turned and said in a clear voice, "Intromission is what us legal types call 'penetration,' Harry. What we used to call 'getting in' when we were fourteen."

The producer continued staring at the ceiling. "I was a choirboy when I was fourteen, Ben," he said loftily. "I didn't use phrases of that sort." This was followed by sniggers from the other TV people and laughter from the students and most of the faculty.

The producer now turned a more alert gaze back to the projected slide. "How long would that, uh, possibly intromissive organ be, Dr. Bascom?" he said.

Emily Bascom's eyes were now quite thin and her voice was tight, but she took a breath and shrugged. "Oh, three hundred centimeters, about ten feet, I guess." she answered.

The producer sat up a bit straighter. "That would be some sort of zoological record, wouldn't it? Ten feet?"

Dr. Bascom put her hands on her hips and faced him. "Look!" she said fiercely. "This creature has eyes that are over three feet in diameter, real eyes that it sees with! That and those forty-meter tentacles are the great miracles of this thing, not some stupid sex organ that nobody knows a damn thing about!"

But the producer had relaxed back into his chair, and his smile was both broad and comfortable. "Think of that, Ben," he said in an awed, wondering voice, "ten feet long. I foresee quite an audience share with this series."

The large lawyer half-frowned in what was obviously a mock concern. "Harry, I hope you're going to keep this a family show?" he said in a tone of complete insincerity.

The auditorium again filled with laughter, but the frost surrounding Dean Bascom's stiff, small form was now so chill that even the provost twisted uncomfortably. Holley half-waved, half-pointed at Emily Bascom. "Dr. Bascom," he said loudly, "would you tell us something about the financing of this research effort?"

The woman snapped her fingers for a new slide. "The network is chartering *Glomar Explorer* for us. As some of you know"—and she pointed up at the side view of a large motor ship—"this vessel has a center well and lowerable platform half its length. As you see, the cage will be suspended beneath *Glomar*'s platform, and we'll use another oil boomer to try and coax the squid inside." She paused, then nodded at the contract lawyer. "Mr. Bernstein, would you like to spell out the money stuff for Dr. Holley?"

"Just a tad under five million for the whole thing," said the paunchy lawyer in an almost-bored voice. "Two of that for refit and charter of *Glomar*, another one-five to Perry Subs for hire of their *Gemini* photo-sub pair, the mother ship, staff, and pilots. The remainder goes to you people for your time, project management, and overhead." He paused, then added in a silky tone, "Over one million for overhead, sir."

The dean had turned again toward the provost. "Even our co-eds won't be big enough for it, Jacob," he said in a frozen whisper. "What about finding a female elephant in rut and cramming her into an oversized scuba set?"

The provost did not find this suggestion amusing. He leaned menacingly toward the small dean. "A million dollars is a lot of money, Walter, even when you said it fast," he gritted back, but the dean made no answer, and the auditorium was now alive with excited questions from the faculty and press people.

II

The flotilla that finally gathered in the mid-Atlantic three weeks later was the largest ever assembled to study a single species. In addition to the *Glomar* and its gigantic, hastily constructed cage held by cables under its center well was the somewhat smaller *Mother Gemini* catamaran support vessel, mounting a midget two-man sub on the stern of each hull. The Coast Guard had provided a big offshore cutter, the *Dauntless*, for helicopter support off her own large stern platform, while the navy, thanks to a letter from the White House, sent its most advanced remote-sensing vessel, *Argus*.

The first three days were rough and blowy, and everyone rushed around in agitated concern for the huge, fragile cage drawn tight against rolling *Glomar*'s bottom. But then the South Atlantic weather turned fair and quiet, and the convoy put down its lure and steamed at a leisurely five knots, waiting for a strike.

Emily and her husband shared a table with the *Glomar*'s captain and chief engineering officer, but they spoke only on project matters and each had a separate stateroom. After the weather turned pleasant and the hunt began in earnest, Emily waited until her husband stood alone on the fantail, then approached him with a large but fragile smile.

"Walter," she said earnestly, "there was no other way to do this. And if we don't get to understand these animals right now, the oil boomers may confuse and finish off whatever few of them are left." She peered at him directly, but his face remained stiff.

"Circuses should stay under tents," said the dean in a bitter voice, and when this caused his wife's big face to droop, he gestured defensively. "Look, Emily, the beasts and the fish are innocent, don't you know that? What they do is God's will alone. They can't know sin and they don't know lust as we do. All this suggestive coarse stuff isn't just scientifically abominable, it's plain *stupid*, too!"

But Emily Bascom had made the conciliation efforts, and now her eyes shot angry fire and she set her big jaw. "As if that gigantic, beautiful animal gave one damn about what you think!" she snarled at him. "You really should have been a priest instead of an oceanographer, Walter. Then you could tell *everybody* just how to act. . . ."

This hurtful exchange was suddenly ended by a series of shrill shrieks from *Argus*'s steam whistle. Both Bascoms turned on their heels and ran headlong down two ladders and forward to *Glomar*'s operations room. Others were running in, too, and Emily had to shoulder her way to the main communications console and seize a microphone.

"What's happening, *Argus*?" she said in a rush.

"We have a target," responded the *Argus* Ops room. "Moving target! Bearing: two-three-five; true range: thirty-six hundred meters; depth: fourteen hundred meters. Mark! We've got a first track. It's heading right for us. Total velocity about one meter a second, and it's rising at about half that. We're trying to access it now with a laser. Hang on!"

Emily pressed the *BRIDGE* button on her mike. "Captain Jorgenson," she said, "start to slow us up. I want us at dead slow in ten minutes, but don't do anything abrupt."

"Aye, Professor Bascom," came the reply, "I'll ease her back."

"*Mother Gemini!* This is Bascom. Launch! Launch! We have an approaching target!" she said over the microwave intership link.

"We loaded our crews when we heard the *Argus* message, Dr. Bascom. We're lifting the boats now," came the answer as *Mother Gemini*'s deck force swarmed around the two chrome-yellow subs and the A-frames began hefting the boats up off their cradles.

"Can we get a laser image, Commander?" said Emily in a tense and quiet voice.

A uniformed officer, the liaison representative from *Argus*, squinted at the snow-filled screens. "They're trying, Dr. Bascom. It's a long ways off yet. Wait . . . wait . . . there's something!"

"We're focused," came an excited voice from *Argus*. "You can see it! Center screen on A channel!"

Everyone in the room left their consoles and gathered behind Emily Bascom and the tall officer, every eye intent on a tiny blob in the center of a flickering TV monitor screen.

"Can you harden that image up?" said Dr. Bascom to *Argus*, peering with fixed, narrowed eyes.

"If we enhance it any more, we'll lose it completely," came the voice. "Let me just try a shorter focus space. . . ."

"Ahhh. . . ." came from every person in the room as the tiny blot on the screen resolved, ever so slightly, into a sharper blot with a sense of arms, now and then rippling at its edge.

A pool reporter stood on tiptoes, staring in wonder at the image. "That thing is two miles away and almost a mile down?" he breathed in wonder. "How in hell can you do that?"

The officer shrugged. "We're generating a thirty-megawatt blue-green laser pulse, maybe a nanosecond long. The light pulse is thin and short, like a pencil, when it leaves the projector sticking down underneath *Argus*, but it gets all smeared and scattered as it travels down into the turbid water, and finally illuminates a small bit of that target animal. But we keep the receiving photocells shut off until the undisturbed part of the original light pulse has been reflected back to *Argus* from the target, then we turn on the receiver for a nanosecond. It's called 'range-gating,' and it prevents the smeared, confused part of the light pulse from getting into our reception system. The beam is a small spot, so we have to scan the target, like a TV raster. We're assembling about one image per second now."

"*Mother Gemini*," said a tense Emily Bascom, "let me talk to your submarine pilots, please."

"Talk away, Dr. Bascom," came a voice from the speaker. "We're in the water and heading for the cage."

"No lights! No lights yet, you understand?" she said quickly. "And no high-level acoustics. Lay back from that cage until we get him inside. I'll tell you when to turn on the lights. We don't want to spook him with the strobes."

"Understood. Affirmative, Dr. Bascom," came the answer.

Now the room was utterly silent as they watched the tiny rippling image grow and fill out into what was obviously a purposefully jetting *Architeuthis* of awesome size.

"Slower, Captain Jorgenson," said Emily Bascom sharply. "We'll lose the *Gemini* twins. Easy!"

The naval officer from *Argus* frowned, then turned to Emily. "As the visual field enlarges, our image-assembly time is going to get pretty long, Dr. Bascom. We figure over a minute for one complete frame by the time that thing reaches the cage. What about the side-scan sonar? We can get a continuous high-res. moving image with acoustics when it's within a thousand yards or so."

Emily Bascom nodded. "We'll chance it. I don't think the side-scan acoustics will spook him. The pulse format from that oil boomer that he's responding to is totally different."

"Give us a ten-meter grid on that target, *Argus*," said the officer, and when the grid lines were superimposed over the image of the squid, Emily saw that this was probably the same big male that had come up to the *Hunter*'s signals. On it came, growing in size and detail.

She spoke into the mike. "*Argus*, let's try the side-scan now. Hold your power level as low as possible. Go!"

At once the acoustic projector located in a keel-mounted bubble on *Argus*'s hull began to scan the creature with a tight sonic signal. This picture was far more detailed than the one given by the optical laser, and another gasp went up as the writhing arms and a gigantic, round eyehole suddenly showed on the TV monitor, spookily white against the dark, no-return image of the water.

Even the TV producer was awed by the obvious strangeness of the creature. "Ben," he said to the lawyer in a whisper, "imagine reeling that thing in off Montauk!"

"When you put five million bucks on the hook," said the overweight, grinning lawyer, "it's amazing what you reel in."

Argus was running to port and a bit ahead of *Glomar*, so that the sonar framing geometry was showing the rear edge of the cage. "Here he comes. . . ." said everybody together in a kind of sigh.

Sure enough, the gigantic animal, slowing a bit, rose into the cage and threw out two thick arms to grasp the long, bulbous acoustic signal generator suspended in the center.

A peering Emily Bascom leaned forward. "O.K.," she said softly, as though she feared she might frighten the huge creature, "start closing up the cage."

The *Glomar* crewman in charge of the cage door winches began to lift the suspended door up to cover the open cage bottom. "Now," said Emily in a tight and breathless voice, "You! *Geminis*! Light him up!"

The *Gemini* boats were, at best, fraternal twins, looking very different from each other in both side and plan views. *Gemini One* was a thin, graceful submarine with two big navigation domes and a battery of optical and television cameras grouped in her transparent nose. *Gemini Two* was much bigger and fatter. She mounted four long arms that could be swung out to form a large underwater cross that held an array of xenon strobe lamps. *Gemini Two* contained a two-hundred-horsepower diesel generator set fed by a towed, two-pipe snorkel to power these lights. The strobes were flashed twenty-four times a second to match the image rate of the three-thousand-line TV scan of the *Gemini One* cameras. The lights were so intense, so unimaginably bright, that to viewers on *Glomar*'s deck and up in the small photo helicopters, it seemed as though a sudden and unending explosion of fearsome magnitude were continuously happening underwater alongside *Glomar*.

In the Ops rooms, the biggest TV monitor presented them with a brilliant full-color underwater picture of the male *Architeuthis*, and the whispers were stilled, for the vast animal was utterly visible in a totally detailed image. Its huge left eye peered unblinking and implacable at the sudden bright light, but its arms still rippled and fondled the signal generator while its tentacles, too long to be fully imaged by even the widest-angle lens on the closing *Gemini* twins, snaked in and out of the picture.

The cold, unblinking eyes of the cuttlefish and the squid, plus their sharp beaks, have always suggested to students of the ocean a kind of zoological epiphany for the alien ferocity possible in the great deeps of the planet, but it was evident from its motions that this creature was patiently seeking some configuration or relationship with the bulbous sound generator that eluded it. There was no sense of fierceness in these stroking and waverings, only puzzlement and a sense of some impatience.

Walter Bascom had been silently watching all this, standing at the back of the crowd around the TV monitor. "Poor, lonely bastard!" he said in a low voice to no one in particular.

And Emily, her great triumph now before them all in stunning, three-thousand-line color, felt it all spoil and turn sour as she stared at the huge, agitated creature attempting to turn an unyielding oil boomer into something very different. If he was all that was left of them, the very last of such an awesome clan, they were too late, and everything was futile and stupid. Emily Bascom stared down at her hands and blinked. How many years, she wondered, had this huge creature been searching for its moment of satisfaction?

"Target! *Close* target! Look! MY GOD!" came the sudden near screams from both *Argus* and *Mother Gemini*, and at that instant on the screens they all saw something shadowy, vast beyond imagination, hugely rising behind the cage and the bewildered, fondling male squid. At that moment *Glomar* gave a decided shudder, followed by a fearsome series of crashes and rending noises.

"ANOTHER SQUID!" came the simultaneous transmissions from all the ships and aircraft of the fleet as two great, muscular arms, each thicker than a Greyhound bus and longer than a city block, snapped around *Glomar*'s midsection and began to vigorously squeeze and shake the nine-thousand-ton vessel.

Several people in the Ops room fell down at that point, while others wildly grabbed at each other or the equipment rack handles to stay on their feet. "Open that cage!" shouted Emily Bascom into the mike. "Shut off the boomer signal! Quick!"

The mounting noises of *Glomar*'s destruction masked most of this final command, for the new arrival had seized the hull in four or five of its massive arms and was now applying its huge, horny beak to the hull plates. When a large vessel is torpedoed or smashed apart by gunfire, her breaking-up noises are often lost in the sounds of fire and explosions, but what the people on *Glomar* always remembered about those next few minutes was the deafening, fearful noises of a steel ship being torn, rent, and smashed by a totally silent and ferociously active adversary.

To their eternal credit (and the enrichment of everyone connected to Perry Subs, Inc., which had cleverly held out for a half-interest in all the film and tape taken from the boats), the two *Gemini* pilots and their crews not only kept the strobes and cameras going, but began maneuvering to get a large field of view. And what the astounded viewers on the other ships now saw was a female *Architeuthis* of a size wholly beyond speculation, over twice as long as the still-oblivious male and an order of magnitude heavier.

She was indeed the great kraken of Norwegian legend, but far, far larger even than that shadowy wonder. Nothing in the ocean would stand against this gigantic queen of deeps and darkness. Nothing, even at the peak of the dinosaur age, in or out of the water, could match her musculature. In a single stroke of a single tentacle, she could turn the head of the oldest and strongest sperm whale to bloody mush or smash a four-ton white shark in half. Her anger was as ponderous and monumental as her body, and she realized at once that her smaller consort was somehow bewitched and trapped by a large, hostile floating creature, *Glomar Explorer*.

Discovering that her fierce beak was having problems penetrating the lower hull plates of the vessel, the squid began a series of smashing blows on the deckhouses and upper works with her various arms and tentacles. These appendages, weighing between twenty and thirty tons each, were lifted out of the water over the listing vessel and brought down clublike at high speed. The first full smash, striking aft of the stack and with a shock that shook everyone aboard off their feet, almost broke *Glomar* in two. Fortunately, everyone belowdecks made a dash for the life jackets and the open air at the first series of crashes, so that no one remained in the flattened compartments and sheared, jagged steel that had once been the ship's center cabins. The squid now found she could get her ten-foot beak into the shattered-steel confusion of *Glomar*'s midsection, and commenced a terrifying series of rippings and rendings. The Ops room people had dashed up two stairways and out onto the forecastle deck by the bow, and now they stared back, dazed and open-mouthed, at a shambles of smashed lifeboats and crushed cabins.

"How in God's name can it rip steel like that with a beak of bone!" screamed the TV producer at the shocked, sagging faces around him.

Walter Bascom, who was carefully tying on a big cork life jacket, turned and gave him a thin smile. "The same way a karate chop goes through a brick: with plenty of momentum and plenty of will!"

The gigantic squid found this slashing and biting entirely too slow to satisfy her vast irritation, and she now struck the stern a mighty double blow that broke it away completely. The *Glomar*, which was already listing heavily to port, now began to go down by the stern like a rock, her bow tilting and rising rapidly. The creature interpreted all movement as challenge from her enemy, and loosed her final, most terrible stroke at the rising bow, catching the vessel just in front of the bridge. The stunning, thunderous shock threw everyone clustered up at the bow into the water, some with life jackets and some without, and as the partly dismembered *Glomar* settled rapidly, the rest of the crew and staff jumped desperately from the tilting sides and rails and paddled away to escape the suction of the sinking wreckage.

Walter Bascom had been standing close to the impact point of this final devastating blow, and as he was catapulted off the slanting deck, his lower right leg was struck and deeply slashed by a tilting, ripped deck plate. The pain had that sudden and complete authority that told the dean that he was grievously hurt. After a gasp at the initial shock of the cold water, he doubled over and put both his hands around his right calf. The entire back of his right leg from ankle to knee was cut loose, hanging, and his chill hands felt how warm the pumping blood seemed in the cold water. He gripped tightly with his hands to hold his leg together and slow that flowing warmth.

At the first sight of the squid's flailing arms, both *Dauntless* and *Argus* had stopped and launched several power lifeboats, and these now chugged stoutly toward the devastated *Glomar* and the raging squid. The two TV helicopters were far too small to take even one person aboard, but *Dauntless* carried an eight-passenger rescue machine, and this was started and lifted into the air at about the same time that *Glomar*'s stern was sheared off. It was obvious to the officers on both ships that the people shaken off the bow were in the most danger, and so the Coast Guard machine made straight for them, settling down in the middle of a cluster of heads.

Walter Bascom struggled to reach the helicopter's port pontoon, where a young crewman crouched and held out a hand to help him up. "I've got a cut leg, son. I'm bleeding," he said weakly to the boy.

"I'll get you up, sir! Just give me your hand!" shouted the crewman, but then several things happened at once: Off to starboard of the helicopter, no more than twenty yards away, a broad island of gray, scarred flesh and seething malevolence emerged, dripping and ponderous, and in the middle of that gray mountain of squid mantle was a monster eye, rising through the interface, an orange, baleful harvest moon of hostility. Seeing the helicopter and assuming its connection with the shattered *Glomar*, the creature struck at the machine with one of her arms.

The animal's bifurcated vision, with half the eyeball in the water and the other half in the air, confused the squid, and her first gigantic attempt at flyswatting went wild by ten yards or so. The splash from that nearby stroke nearly swamped the helicopter and stalled both its engines.

Walter Bascom had been distracted from the awesomely emerging squid by a thin cry for help some distance away. He saw it was Emily and that she was waving one hand in obvious distress. "Help me!" he heard his wife cry. "I don't have a life jacket!"

"Quick!" said the Coast Guardsman. "That thing is after *us*!"

Walter Bascom turned, let go of his leg, and began to swim toward his wife. "Get out of here!" he shouted back at the helicopter, "I can support her with my jacket!"

A second arm was emerging from the water about forty yards off, and the pilot desperately cranked his blades around, his starters whining, until the soaked engines finally caught, and the big machine began to skitter uncertainly across the sea surface. Sensing that with a downward stroke, she would probably miss such an evasive target, the squid rounded on the helicopter with a third arm. The arm left the water in a low hissing arc of foam and spray and caught the staggering machine much as a batter will occasionally catch a baseball bouncing off home plate and golf it up into the centerfield stands.

The big machine was instantly changed into a disintegrating mass of black shapes flying up and out amongst fiercely roaring arcs of flaming gasoline. To the squid, this explosive reaction to her blow was only more defiance and more challenge. Few living things ever completely forget or ignore the possibility of escape when a struggle becomes too uncertain or protracted, but the first part of the flight/fight reaction had atrophied in the ganglia of this immense creature, and she now began to jet toward the flames and figures in the water, her two arms poised for striking while her huge beak snapped open and shut so loudly in her red rage that the *Gemini* pilots claimed later they could hear these fierce clicks over the noise of *Gemini Two*'s roaring diesel.

Walter Bascom reached his wife and drew her shivering arms around him. "Hold on, Emily," he said. "This thing will keep us both up. It's only Sea State Two."

"Oh, look!" she gasped, and the dean saw over them a four-hundred-foot-long tentacle rising to join the waving arms, rising endlessly out of the water like a gathering waterspout, like the big atomic funnel over Bikini.

The dean felt his warm life running out into the cool water, and he put his arms around his wife. This was a very calm way to go, he thought, really very painless. "'Bye, 'bye, Emily," he said. "I can't say it hasn't been exciting."

To a peering Emily Bascom, the view showed only ruin and disaster in every direction: the *Glomar* rolling over slowly for her final dive to the bottom; raging gasoline fires and dismaying black shapes floating all around them; and, worst of all, *Dauntless*, an angry white mother goose coming to save her brood of lifeboats, her siren screaming, was digging her heels in on a tight, high-thrust turn toward them while on her forward deck her gunners had the canvas off the 4.3-inch rifle and were desperately elevating the weapon to try a shot at one of the huge arms that quivered, cobralike, above the scene.

Tears came to Emily's eyes, and her head fell forward against her husband in dismay and defeat. "You were right, Walter. This was a lousy idea," she said in a small, shivering voice.

But the light-headed dean, woozily cheerful from the wound shock and the numbing water, just shook his head. "No, no, Emily. What is the price of true wonder, anyway? It's everything, Emily, *everything*!"

That was all that the dean was able to say, and he slipped down and down into a velvety, pain-free blackness. Yet it seemed to Walter Bascom that this darkness inverted and bloomed and filled with a bright, clear light, so that he floated no longer in an ocean of dark water but now in an ocean of pure, sweet illumination. Around him swam the great creatures of the planet, no longer scarred and fierce, but made perfect and beautiful; washed in the Blood of the Lamb.

"Come, Walter," said Saint Francis, taking his hand, "come and meet my friends," and the dean filled with a joy greater than any he could ever remember.

III

Walter Bascom opened his eyes and knew at once that he was in the ship's dispensary bed. He looked to his right and saw another neat cot containing a quiet figure obscured by bandages and I.V. tubes. On the wall was a fire-hose reel stenciled *Dauntless*, CG 582. He looked to his left and saw a pert, redheaded nurse with "U.S. Coast Guard" across her cap and lieutenant (jg) bars on her open collars, seated and staring wanly at him. "How do you feel, Dr. Bascom?" she said.

"Weak," said the dean. "Did I lose my leg?"

The nurse shook her head, smiling. "Goodness, no! That wasn't the problem. You lost most of your blood out there in the water. We really pumped you up, Dr. Bascom. We went into both arms at once."

"What about my wife's pets?" asked the dean, and when he saw the young woman did not understand him, added: "The squid—uh—I mean squids?"

Her eyes sparkled. "My, that was something else, wasn't it! I've watched those movies three times already. Well, after she just *totaled* our helicopter, everybody thought you and your wife would be clobbered next. And they didn't dare shoot at her head—well, I mean 'mantle'—'cause you were so close to her. But just when it seemed like she would flatten you with one of those gigantic, absolutely *humongous* arms, the smaller squid finally got out of his cage and swam underneath her. The *Geminis* got pictures of all that. It's sort of sweet, actually. And the moment he touched her, well, she just lost interest in us completely and sank right straight down, with him doing his stuff, I suppose, and they finally disappeared from the laser picture somewhere down near the bottom."

"It was a lady squid, then?" said the dean, feeling quite cheerful in spite of his throbbing leg.

She nodded positively. "Oh, yes. Your wife says the pictures clearly show that. Imagine, getting that angry because we attracted her friend."

"Well, you know all that stuff about a 'woman scorned'?" said the dean with a sudden grin.

But the nurse took this comment seriously and shook her head in determination. "Maybe we shouldn't have been meddling with such a big sort of life," she said in a firm tone.

She paused to give him a pretty, if rueful, smile. "I shouldn't say that, I suppose, working for the Coast Guard and all, but I think it's *right* she came and got him, even if all that awful stuff had to happen."

"I couldn't agree more," said the dean with a wider grin. "Why, I've always been partial to huge, dominating ladies myself!"

The compartment door, which had been ajar, now opened fully and Emily Bascom stepped in over the sill. "Huge, dominating *women* is really better than huge, dominating *ladies* nowadays, Walter," she said in a soft voice, "but thank you for coming to save me and risking your neck to do it. We all sweated you out for a few hours, me most of all."

THE XI EFFECT

Philip Latham

Philip Latham was the pseudonym of one of the most distinguished American astronomers, Robert S. Richardson, who under his own name wrote popular science books and articles including a number of articles published in *Astounding*. From the flamboyant, apocalyptic astronomical fiction of Camille Flammarion in the late nineteenth century to the works of Fred Hoyle and Gregory Benford, working astronomers and astrophysicists have contributed stories of broad scope and cosmic speculation to the development of hard sf. Astronomical, is after all, a synonym for the very large, in number or scale. Cosmology and astronomy are primary repositories of images for the science fiction genre (as was nature for the Romantic poets). And of course it is the astronomers who investigate the environments that are the literal settings of much sf. But it is also the teasing, ambiguous border between the physical and the metaphysical that astronomical sf often confronts, that underpins much hard sf and gives depth and emotional force to the cold and the distant.

This particular story is a good-humored portrayal of astronomers at work. It shows the connection of rarefied scientific theory to the experimental and practical concerns of everyday human life and portrays vividly the meaning of physical constants—all through a series of images that transform the theoretical and abstract realm of cosmology and astrophysics into the visual. It climaxes with a vision of the end of the world—sudden, cold, immense. It is the immediate ancestor of Godwin's "The Cold Equations" and Arthur C. Clarke's "The Star," as an allegory of the cold, inhuman operation of the laws of the universe, and a worthy companion piece to Isaac Asimov's apocalyptic "Nightfall." It is also an interesting contrast to John M. Ford's "Chromatic Aberrations" and Bob Shaw's "Light of Other Days" in its use of light and color physics. There are few more powerful images in sf of theoretical physics replacing superstition than the juxtaposition at the climax of "The Xi Effect"—and no more powerful evocations of cosmic doom. As Hal Clement said, "the universe is antagonist enough."

For a week the team of Stoddard and Arnold had met with nothing but trouble in their solar infra-red exploration program. First the lead sulfide photo-conductive cell had refused to function. Next an electrical storm—practically unknown in September—had put a crimp in the power line to the mountain observatory. And now for some wholly inexplicable reason the automatic recorder stubbornly refused to register a single quantum of radiation beyond 20,000 Å.

"Here's the end of the atmospheric carbon dioxide band at sixteen thousand," said Arnold, indicating a point on their last record sheet. "You can see everything's all right out to there. But beyond twenty thousand we aren't getting a thing."

Stoddard grunted, "That's what comes of our big economy drive. Trying to cut expenses by buying from the dime store." He walked over to the spectrometer and regarded it gloomily. It was the product of his own mind, an impressive series of slits and parabolic mirrors fed by a beam of sunlight from the top of the tower. When the optical setup was in perfect adjustment the apparatus would bring just the desired band of infra-red radiation onto the sensitive surface of the photoconductive cell. But obviously all was not in perfect adjustment.

"Maybe it's in the amplifier this time," Arnold suggested hopefully.

"Well, that's the only part of this contraption that hasn't balked on us so far," said Stoddard. "Suppose you look it over while I check the cell again."

For the next hour the astronomers probed the interior of the spectrometer as intently as two surgeons performing an exploratory laparotomy, passing tools back and forth and generally anticipating each other's wants with scarcely a word spoken. For fifteen years they had thus worked together, one of the oddest-looking scientific teams at the Western Institute of Technology, but one that had also proven itself amazingly productive. Stoddard at forty had the general shape of an old-fashioned beer barrel, with big hands, big feet, and a big protruding stomach. His half-closed eyes gave him a perpetually sleepy expression, a highly effective mask for one of the keenest minds in the business. Arnold, although nearly as old as his partner, somehow still gave the impression of youth. He was small and slight with an eager boyish expression that often caused visitors to mistake him for a graduate student embarking on his first research problem. Stoddard was the practical man of the firm who designed the apparatus for their various investigations and took the bulk of the observations. Arnold was the one who reduced the observations and discussed their theoretical significance.

"Find anything wrong?" Stoddard inquired at length, straightening up and replacing the cover that housed the cell assembly.

"Nothing worth mentioning," said Arnold. "Think there's time for another run?"

"Yeah, I guess so. Put the sun back on the slit and we'll take another crack at her anyhow."

But the second run proved no better than the first; in fact, if anything the cutoff occurred a trifle farther in toward the violet than before.

"I might as well take the whole works down to the laboratory for a complete overhaul," Stoddard declared, looking at his brainchild as if he would like to heave it over the side of the mountain. He watched a cloud drift lazily across the disk of the sun projected against the slit. "Get any weather predictions on the radio this morning?"

Arnold gave him a quizzical glance. "Haven't you heard yet? All the radio stations have been dead for more than a week."

"What's the matter with 'em?"

"Well, it's really quite mysterious. Last Monday KLX faded out right in the middle of a program, and then stations farther up the dial began to be hit one after the other. For a while all you could get were the amateurs and the police department. Now they're dead, too."

Stoddard, who regarded the radio as one of the major threats to his peace of mind, took the news philosophically. "Well, I'm glad to hear we aren't the only ones having trouble these days. But I'll bet my wife was sore when she couldn't hear what happened to Priscilla Lane, Private Secretary, last night."

Stoddard was in his laboratory in the basement of the Astrophysics Building at Western Tech hard at work on the wiring diagram for the amplifier system when Arnold came breezing in, his bright young face aglow with enthusiasm.

"Guess what?" he exclaimed. "Friedmann's in town. He's agreed to give a talk this afternoon in Dickinson Hall on his theory of the Xi effect. You know Friedmann, don't you?"

Stoddard shook his head. "Never heard of him."

Arnold hooked one leg over the corner of the desk. "Well, in my opinion he's the foremost cosmologist in the world today. He had so much trouble getting published at first that his reputation isn't as big as it should be. Everybody thought his first paper was written by some crank until Eddington saw it and recognized its value immediately. Now Friedmann won't send his articles to any of the regular journals. You've got to dig his stuff out of all sorts of queer places, like the *Proceedings of the Geophysical Society of Venezuela* or the *Annals of the Portuguese Meteorological Union*."

"I know how he feels," said Stoddard sympathetically.

"Well, I thought we should hear him because his theory might possibly have some bearing on our infra-red observations last week."

"Think I could understand him if I did hear him?"

"Oh, probably not, but then that goes for a lot of the rest of us, too."

Stoddard reached for the wiring diagram. "Well, I'll see if I can manage it. But you know what I think of these high-powered theoretical fellows."

Arnold laughed. "I've been briefed on that before." He got up and started for the door. "Room 201 at four-thirty. I'll save a seat for you."

The meeting was already in progress when Stoddard opened the door and slipped to his seat without creating any more commotion than a horse backing into a stall. As usual, the front rows were occupied by the hardened campaigners among the faculty, the grizzled veterans of a thousand seminars: Fosberg and Ballantyne from the math department, Blacker and Tinsdale from the radiation laboratory, and Denning the nuclear physicist. The remainder of the audience in the rear was composed of a miscellaneous rabble of graduate students and professors from neighbouring institutions of learning and culture.

"Who's ahead?" asked Stoddard, sinking into the chair beside his partner.

"You should have heard Friedmann put old Blacker in his place a minute ago," Arnold whispered with evident relish. "He sure slapped him down plenty that time."

To Stoddard, all theoretical physicists were strange creatures far removed from the rest of mankind. It was his experience that they could be divided with remarkable uniformity into two types, A and B. A typical specimen of Type A, for example, is mentally accessible only with the greatest difficulty. As a general rule, he moves through life with the vague detached air of a confirmed somnambulist. Should you summon the courage to ask his opinion on a paper, he regards it with much the same expression of critical disapproval that a secondhand car dealer instinctively assumes when inspecting a battered automobile brought in for sale. Everything is in a pretty bad state. It is possible, however, that a little progress may be made along the following lines, et cetera. A pure Type B, on the other hand, gives the impression of being always on the point of boiling over. He trembles with suppressed excitement. One of his former pupils has just proposed a theory that constitutes a tremendous advance. Where there was only darkness before now all is sunshine and light. As soon as a few odds and ends are cleared up the whole problem will be practically solved, et cetera, et cetera.

Stoddard classified Friedmann as predominantly Type A with a few overtones of Type B thrown in. He was a tall, thin man of about thirty, with sharp angular features, and a way of looking at you as if his eyes were focused on a point ten feet behind your back. His voice was dry and flat with the barest trace of foreign accent.

Stoddard had not listened for more than five minutes before he began to experience the same sense of bewilderment that little Dorothy must have felt on her first trip to the land of Oz. As nearly as he could gather, Friedmann considered the familiar everyday world to constitute merely a tiny corner or "clot" in a vastly higher order of space-time or "Xi space." Ordinarily, events in the Xi space are on too gross a scale to exert a sensible effect on the fine-grained clot space. On rare occasions, however, a clot might be seriously disturbed by events of an exceptional nature in the Xi space, in somewhat the same way that the atoms on the surface of a stick of amber may be disturbed by rubbing it vigorously. When events in the super-cosmos happen to intrude upon an individual clot extraordinary results ensue; for example, angular momentum is not strictly conserved, and Hamilton's equations require modification, to mention only a few.

"Thus for a properly oriented observer the universe must at all times have a radius equal to tau times the velocity of light," said Friedmann, by way of conclusion. "Hence, if tau increases uniformly we must of necessity have the expanding universe as shown by the general recession of the extragalactic nebulae.

"But this increase in tau time is not really uniform but a statistical effect. Local fluctuations in the Xi space may attain such magnitude as to become distinctly perceptible in clot space. Evidence for the Xi effect in our vicinity is shown by the behavior of the Andromeda nebula, which instead of sharing in the general recession is approaching the Earth at three hundred kilometers per second. Again, certain anomalies in the motion of the inner planets, notably the secular variation in the node of Venus,[1] clearly indicate encroachment of the Xi effect within the confines of our own solar system. Further anomalies of increasing magnitude may be anticipated."

With curt nod he gathered together his papers and sat down abruptly, scarcely bothering to acknowledge the prolonged applause from the student section. The secretary of the Astronomy and Physics Club thanked Dr. Friedmann for his address which he was sure they had all enjoyed, and inquired if there were any questions. This announcement was followed by the customary minute of awkward silence. Finally the spell was broken by Fosberg, an authority on the theory of numbers and uncrowned king of the faculty's eccentric characters.

"As I get it, this postulated Xi effect started a shrinkage in our sector about ten-to-the-ninth years ago. Now then, I've just been doing some figuring on the back of this envelope and if I haven't made a mistake the present diameter of the solar system out to Pluto is 3.2×10^8 kilometers, or about two hundred million miles. Is that right?" Everyone looked expectantly at the speaker.

"I work entirely with the generalized formulae; never with numerical values," Friedmann replied with cold dignity. "However, I do not question the accuracy of Dr. Fosberg's arithmetic. Naturally the shrinkage would be quite imperceptible with

[1]The outstanding difference between gravitational theory and observation is the well-known discrepancy of 43″ per century in the motion of the perihelion of Mercury. Einstein's explanation of this discrepancy was considered a triumph for relativity.

The next largest difference between gravitational theory and observation is the secular variation of 13″ per century in the node of Venus, which has not been explained by relativity. See *Journal of the Optical Society of America*, vol. 30, p. 225, 1930.

ordinary measuring rods. It would be necessary to make some observation involving explicitly the velocity of light."

"I'm willing to grant you that," Fosberg returned, "but aren't you going to get into serious trouble with the law of gravitation due to all this shrinkage? Why, in a few more years the congestion in the solar system will be worse than the campus parking problem!" It was a remark that was always good for a laugh and one of the principal reasons he had asked the question in the first place.

"The gravitational difficulties that so worry Dr. Fosberg do not follow as a necessary consequence," said Friedmann, entirely unruffled. "As I have demonstrated, the laws of Newtonian mechanics may fail to hold even as a first approximation. At these extreme limits, however, the integration of the equations becomes quite insuperable by ordinary methods. One of my pupils at the University of Pennsylvania plans to explore these regions next year with the EDVAC."

Fosberg wagged his bald head. "Just the same all this crowding together still worries me," he declared. "And I don't like the idea of being reduced to the size of a microcosmic midget either."

Friedmann's shrug plainly indicated that it was a matter of complete indifference to him if Fosberg were reduced to the dimensions of a neutrino, and as there were no more questions, the meeting broke up. Stoddard, who had grown thoroughly bored with the whole proceedings, made a bolt for the door but Arnold was only a few lengths behind.

"Wasn't Friedmann good," he demanded. "Don't you think it's the most satisfying cosmological theory you ever heard?"

"No doubt about it," said Stoddard, continuing on down the hall.

"You know, I was thinking," Arnold went on, falling into step beside him, "why couldn't we test the Xi effect ourselves?"

"Test it ourselves!"

"Why not? After all, it shouldn't be too difficult. As Friedmann said, we would only need to make some observation that depends explicitly on the velocity of light."

Stoddard snorted. "Bet he's never made a bona fide observation in his whole life."

They stopped on the steps outside Dickinson Hall before wending their separate ways homeward. The sun had set and a slight breeze was beginning to stir the leaves of the giant oak tree at the entrance.

"Well, the next time you're in my office we'll have a long talk about it," said Stoddard, edging down the steps. "But right now I've got to get home for dinner."

"The observation would consist simply in determining whether some distant event occurred at the time predicted," Arnold mused. "Let's see, what would be the easiest thing to observe?"

At that instant his eye was attracted to a star faintly visible near the eastern horizon. "I've got it!" he cried. "We could observe an eclipse of one of Jupiter's satellites. If the solar system has really shrunk as much as the Xi effect predicts, it should occur way ahead of time."

"You mean do a kind of repeat on Roemer's work," said Stoddard, "only with a light time corresponding to the whole distance to Jupiter instead of the diameter of the Earth's orbit?"

"Exactly!"

Stoddard could feel the net closing around him. He knew that once his partner in crime became infatuated with an idea it was useless to try to discourage him. "Well, I guess we've looked for less hopeful things. Only I can't seem to remember what they were."

"Listen," said Arnold, his eyes shining, "is there a class at the ten-inch tonight?"

Stoddard considered. "This is Wednesday, isn't it? Nope, don't think there will be one."

"Then what's to stop us from making the observation right now—tonight?"

"Nothing, so far as I know, except maybe a nice thick fog." He heaved a sigh of resignation. "Come on, let's take a look at the *Ephemeris*. Maybe there *aren't* any eclipses tonight."

But the *American Ephemeris* said otherwise. An occultation of Jupiter I was scheduled for Thursday, October 5th, at four hours eight minutes and ten seconds of Greenwich Civil Time.

Arnold was delighted. "I'll meet you at the ten-inch at seven-fifteen tonight. O.K.?"

"O.K."

"We can stop in at my house for a drink afterward."

"We'll probably need one," was Stoddard's grim comment, "after we find out how much the universe has shrunk."

The lamp over the desk threw grotesque shadows around the circular room making the telescope and pier look like some giant insect flattened against the curving walls of the dome. At that moment, however, Stoddard was in no mood to appreciate the projective geometry of shadow pictures. Like all other manually operated observatory domes in the world, the one on the ten-inch at Western Tech opened only with the utmost reluctance. At length in response to an effort worthy of superman, Stoddard forced the shutter back revealing the constellation of Cygnus sprawling across the meridian. Breathing heavily, he turned the dome until Jupiter came into the center of the opening, a gleaming yellow stoplight among the faint stars of Aquarius. Then swinging the telescope around on the pier as if it were an antiaircraft gun, he sighted along the tube until the planet came darting into the field of view.

"How's the seeing?" asked Arnold, a formless black shape by the desk. He twisted the shade over the lamp until the light illuminated the chronometer and pad of paper at his elbow but left the end of the telescope in shadow.

Stoddard gave the focusing screw another touch. "Not so good," he muttered. Removing the eyepiece from the end of the telescope he substituted a longer one in its place from the box beside him. "There—that's better."

"How do the satellites look?"

"Well, just about the way the *Ephemeris* predicted. Callisto and Ganymede are over on the west. Europa's about a diameter of Jupiter to the east. Io doesn't seem to be anywhere around."

He lowered the seat on the observing platform a couple of notches thus enabling him to look into the telescope with less strain on his vertebrae. "Wait a minute—caught a glimpse of her at the limb just then."

Arnold shot a glance at the chronometer. "Gosh, don't tell me it's going into occultation already!"

"Well, it sure looks like it."

"But it can't be that much ahead of time."

"Why not? That's what you were hoping for, wasn't it? Keep an eye on the chronometer, anyhow. I'll give you the time as close as I can in this bum seeing."

For several minutes the dome was silent except for the steady ticking of the chronometer and the low hum of traffic from Los Feliz Boulevard far below. Stoddard concentrated his every faculty on the tiny point of light projecting from the planet's disk. Sometimes he felt sure it must be gone only to have it flash into view again.

He waited until it had remained out of sight for an unusually long interval. "All right, get ready," he warned. "Now!"

"Seven-thirty-three-zero-zero," said Arnold, writing down the numbers at the top of the record sheet. Stoddard rose painfully from his cramped position at the end of the telescope and began cautiously exercising one leg. His partner continued figuring busily for another five minutes. Presently he leaned back and began tapping the desk thoughtfully with the tip of his pencil.

"What's the answer?" said Stoddard, limping across the room.

"Well, according to these figures," Arnold replied, speaking with elaborate casualness, "the occultation occurred just thirty-five minutes and ten seconds ahead of time."

For a moment neither spoke. Then Stoddard let out a belly laugh that shattered the peaceful calm that had hitherto enveloped Observatory Hill. "That puts Jupiter right in our back-yard. It's so close the light gets here in nothing flat."

Arnold gazed up at the planet riding so serenely among the stars. There were Vega and Altair over in the west, with Cygnus flying close behind, and the great square of Pegasus wheeling upward in the north, precisely as he had seen them a thousand times before. Could it be possible that some catastrophe from Outside had warped their little corner of space until the giant Jupiter had been brought to what would once have been an arm's length, so close you might have reached out and seized it between your thumb and forefinger like a cherry? As a boy he had loved to read tales of time travel and flights to other planets, and the feeling that something transcendental was lurking around the corner had never entirely left him. In their seminars they talked of world lines and a space of n dimensions but did any of them really believe it? Now perhaps it was here at last. He shivered in the damp night air. The ocean breeze blowing in through the dome certainly felt real enough.

Mechanically he began helping Stoddard put the telescope to bed for the night, replacing the cap on the objective and swinging the telescope over the polar axis, where he clamped it in declination.

"What do you say we go down in the darkroom for a smoke?" said Stoddard, when everything was ship-shape. "I'd like to take a look at those figures of yours myself."

The darkroom in the basement below was a welcome relief from the windy dome. Stoddard threw off his jacket, pulled a stool up to the bench that ran down one side of the room, and began stoking his pipe from a can of tobacco in one of the drawers. Not until this operation was completed to his entire satisfaction, and the bowl glowing brightly, did he turn his attention to Arnold's reduction. Then with exasperating deliberation he started checking off the figures, pausing occasionally between puffs to compare them with those in the *Ephemeris*. Arnold leaned against the wall watching him nervously.

"Well, I can't seem to find anything wrong," he admitted grudgingly, "but, of course, that doesn't mean it's right, either."

Taking careful aim, he blew a smoke ring at the girl on the calendar over the sink, watching it swirl around her plunging neckline with moody satisfaction. "A dozen times in my life I've got results almost as crazy as this one. Every time I couldn't help saying to myself, 'Stoddard, maybe you've discovered something at last. Maybe you've stumbled onto something big.' So far I've never made a single scientific discovery.

"Now you take this observation tonight. Sure, it would be exciting to suppose the solar system has shrunk to the size of a dime, but first I want to be absolutely sure there isn't some perfectly natural commonplace explanation. It's a depressing fact that most of the exciting results a scientist gets can eventually be traced to errors of observation. Think of all the times Mira Ceti at maximum has been mistaken for a nova."

"Everybody knows that," Arnold objected. "But where's the chance for error in this observation? It's so simple."

"Maybe not so simple as you think. Remember the seeing was terrible. That time I gave you might have been off by a couple of minutes—maybe more."

"That still leaves thirty minutes to explain."

"All right. Now the question is how much faith can we put in the *Ephemeris*? It wouldn't surprise me if the predicted time itself was way off."

"As much as that?"

"Well, I know the predictions for Jupiter's four great satellites are based on Sampson's tables of 1910, and they certainly must require some kind of correction by this time. I don't know how often the Naval Observatory checks up on things like that. But until we do know—and have a lot more observations—we really don't know a thing."

"O.K., O.K.," said Arnold impatiently. "All the same, I still think it's a whale of an error."

"It's a king size one, I'll admit," said Stoddard, relighting his pipe. "And now there's something I wish you'd explain to me. After all that palaver this afternoon I still don't understand how this so-called Xi effect ties in with our infra-red observations."

Arnold reached for the pencil and a pad of yellow scratch paper. "Assume that this line represents the boundary of our local universe or 'clot,' " he said, drawing an irregular closed figure with a dot near the center. "According to Friedmann, occasionally some disturbance in the outer super-cosmos or Xi space becomes sufficiently violent to affect a particular clot. Now there are several things that can happen as a result, but by far the most probable is that the clot will begin to shrink, very slowly at first and then more rapidly. But for a long time nobody would be aware of the shrinkage because everything within the clot shrinks in proportion, with one exception. That exception is the wave length of electromagnetic radiation.

"Suppose the boundary has shrunk until it has an average radius of a thousand kilometers." He drew a line from the central dot to a point on the boundary. "Obviously nothing can exist within the boundary bigger than the boundary itself. Therefore, this means that all electromagnetic radiation exceeding a thousand kilometers is eliminated. That accounts for the fade-out in radio transmission. As the boundary continues to shrink shorter wave lengths keep being cut out all the time."

"I think I'm beginning to get it," said Stoddard, studying the diagram. "We didn't get any transmission beyond twenty thousand angstroms because there wasn't any radiation to transmit."

"That's it! Our universe only had a diameter of twenty thousand angstroms. All radiation of longer wave length was cut out."

"About one ten-thousandth of an inch," said Stoddard, doing some fast mental arithmetic. He chuckled. "No wonder old Fosberg was worried!"

"You see the Xi effect does give a consistent explanation of all the phenomena," said Arnold triumphantly. "In any case, we can't be in doubt much longer."

"How's that?"

"Why, because the universe will have shrunk so much the optical spectrum will be affected. The landscape will change color."

"Well, maybe you're right," Stoddard agreed reluctantly, "but so far everything looks just the same to me as it always has." Absently he began doodling a series of circles and squares across Arnold's diagram. "What I wish," he said with a yawn, "is that somebody would find a way to shorten the time from one pay day till the next."

Arnold waved his arms in a helpless gesture and walked to the end of the room. Stoddard sat motionless as if half asleep. Presently he took a brief case from one of the drawers and began exploring its contents. "Here're those snapshots we took at the zoo the other day," he said. "Haven't had time to develop 'em yet."

His partner eyed the rolls of film without interest. "My wife was asking about them at dinner. She wants to see that one where she's feeding the eagle."

"If you want to wait, I can develop 'em now."

Arnold glanced at his wrist watch. "Sure, go ahead. It's only eight-thirty."

Stoddard turned off the overhead light plunging the little room into total darkness. Arnold could hear him searching for the switch that operated the safe-light, but when he snapped it on there was no result. He snapped it several times but still without result.

"Globe's probably burnt out," said Arnold.

Stoddard jerked the screen back revealing the light inside burning brightly. "Now what?" he muttered.

They stood staring at the light in puzzled silence. Suddenly Arnold leaned forward, his face tense in the white glare from the lamp.

"Stoddard."

"Yeah?"

"*Put the screen back over the lamp.*"

His partner hesitated then obediently shoved the screen back in place until not a chink of white light was visible. Gradually as their eyes gained sensitivity in the dark the oblong shape of the safety screen became faintly visible.

But the screen was no longer ruby red. It was a dull colorless gray.

No scientific theory ever became accepted as fact so quickly as Friedmann's theory of the Xi effect, but then no other theory before ever had such a convincing array of scientific evidence to support it. The change in the tint of the landscape that Arnold had foreseen eventually developed but for several weeks it was too slight to be readily obvious. The effect was the same as if everyone had gone color-blind to an effective wave length of about 6500 Å. It was disconcerting to find that your hedge of geraniums was black instead of scarlet, and the absence of stoplights was nearly disastrous. Some women became violently hysterical when they first beheld the inky fluid oozing from their veins. But after the novelty had worn off the public soon lost interest. They had lived through the invasion from Mars, the flying saucers, and other scientific gags, and doubtless in time this, too, would pass. Besides, how could you expect people to work up any enthusiasm over something when they weren't even sure how to pronounce it?

But as orange and yellow followed red into the gray there came a change in the public attitude, a kind of half-credulous belief mingled with misgiving and dismay. Men still laughed and joked about the Xi effect over their old-fashioneds at the country club, but just when everybody was feeling happy and secure again someone was sure to spoil it all. "You know this thing may turn out to be more serious than we think," he would say. "I've got a nephew teaches out at the university. Hasn't got a dime but smart as the devil. Well, he told me confidentially it's getting worse instead of better. No telling where it may end, in fact."

Rather curiously, women had much more awareness of the Xi effect than men, for it struck at their most vulnerable point—their appearance. Golden hair could turn gray in a matter of weeks. A complexion drained of its warm flesh tints looked dead. Cosmetics were of no avail against it. For of what use was lipstick if it only turned the lips from gray to black? Or of rouge if it left only deeper shadows on the cheeks? The radiant beauty of a short time past anxiously examining her face in her mirror at night might see an old woman staring back at her out of the glass. Deaths from sleeping pills became a commonplace.

Not until late in November, however, did the situation reach such a critical stage that government officials felt compelled to recognize the Xi effect as a definite world menace. Previously its encroachment had been dismissed by the ingenious process of studiously minimizing its existence. It was true that the papers printed the censored reports from scientific institutions but always under captions that were misleading and with the significant news buried near the bottom of the column. A few scientists who refused to be muzzled soon found themselves out of a job or called up before an investigating committee.

Eventually, however, the clamor became so loud that announcement was made of a series of mass meetings to be held across the country in which all the facts insofar as they were known would be discussed without reservation. The first in the series was scheduled for the Los Angeles Coliseum for Monday, November 27th, with the great Dr. Friedmann as the feature speaker of the evening. Public sentiment changed almost overnight. The personal appearance of Friedmann alone did much to restore confidence. He was the fellow who had discovered this Xi effect, wasn't he? Well, then, he could probably control it, too. Man had never met a problem that man was unable to solve.

By the evening of the 27th public curiosity over what Friedmann would say had been excited to such a degree, that it was necessary to keep the man's whereabouts a profound secret to prevent him from being mobbed on sight. By five o'clock every street leading toward the coliseum was blocked solid with cars for miles around, and by seven o'clock more than a hundred thousand people had jammed themselves into the vast structure, while thousands more milled around the walls outside seeking entrance. Although the Los Angeles Police Department had every man available on duty in addition to two hundred special officers hired from outlying districts, they were able to maintain order only with considerable difficulty. An attitude of reckless abandon was manifest even among ordinary well-behaved individuals. It was a holiday crowd without the holiday spirit.

"I'm not at all sure Friedmann is the best man to talk to these people tonight," said Arnold, standing up and gazing uneasily around him at the throngs still climbing up and down the aisles in search of seats. "They've come here confidently expecting to be told something that sounds nice and reassuring and instead Friedmann will simply hand them the hard cold facts. We scientists have known the truth for weeks and had a chance to become reconciled to it. But what about the average man whose cosmic outlook is limited to his job and the mortgage on his home out in Brentwood?"

"Be quite a blow to 'em probably," said Stoddard, biting into his hot dog. "Trouble with these theoretical fellows is they act as if the Xi effect had been invented for the sole purpose of letting them test out all their screwy ideas on nuclear structure."

Arnold sat down and began studying his program. "I see Atchison Kane is going to speak, too."

"Atchison Kane. Who's he?"

"Shakespearian actor," Arnold replied. Long ago he had become accustomed to his partner's splendid state of isolation from the world of the stage and screen. "Made a big hit in 'Richard the Third' recently. I heard him at the Philharmonic last August."

"That so?" said Stoddard. For the tenth time he looked at the great clock over the archway at the east entrance. "What's holding up the procession, anyhow? They were supposed to kick-off half an hour ago."

Others besides Stoddard were getting impatient. So far the crowd had been fairly well-behaved but now it was growing decidedly restless. Someone yelled, "We want Friedmann!" and in an instant thousands of voices were repeating the words over and over in a kind of savage chant. When this failed to produce results, a mob of boys acting as if upon signal, leaped over the parapet onto the field toward the speakers' stand. Before the police could intervene they began tearing down the decorations and smashing the chairs and railing. The dozen or so officers in the vicinity were overwhelmed at first but reinforcements soon gained the upper hand. The crowd was delighted, following every incident of the struggle with fascinated attention. Several men were knocked down and trampled in the melee, or sent reeling from the battle bleeding from lacerations around the head. Suddenly a great shout went up. The speakers surrounded by a husky squad of police were spotted emerging from the south entrance. Interest in the fight evaporated immediately. The floodlights were dimmed and an expectant hush fell over the assemblage.

After the usual preliminaries, to which no one paid the slightest attention, the chairman of the National Scientific Security Council finally got around to introducing the main speaker.

"In the brief span that this committee has been in existence, citizens from all parts of the southland have been besieging us with questions concerning this effect which has been uppermost in the thoughts of each and every one of us during these last troubled days. Unfortunately, no funds were appropriated for the purpose of answering these questions. And yet as representatives of the people we felt in all sincerity that they could not and must not be ignored."

The burst of applause at this point forced him to halt briefly until quiet reigned again and he was able to gather himself together for another effort.

"In view of this situation, my colleagues and I, after due deliberation, have asked our distinguished speaker if in lieu of a formal address he would consent to answer a set of representative questions selected by the committee. To this request I am happy to say that our speaker has most willingly and graciously given his consent.

"And now without further ado, it is my great pleasure and privilege this evening to present to you a man who I am sure needs no introduction from me, that renowned scientist and scholar, Dr. Karl Gustav Friedmann."

From the uproarious applause that greeted Friedmann as he stepped to the front of the platform, it might have been supposed that he had discovered another Santa Claus instead of an effect that was relentlessly extinguishing the light of the world. He shook hands with the chairman, bowed a few degrees in the general direction of the crowd, and then stood quietly waiting for the tumult to subside. The chairman nervously riffled through the cards in his hand, selected one, and peered at it through his bifocals.

"Our first question is from a housewife in Long Beach," he announced. "She says, 'My husband has lost his job as a radio salesman on account of the Xi effect. How soon will it be over so he can go back to work again?' "

Friedmann's voice was as unemotional as if he were lecturing half a dozen sleepy students rather than a crowd of a hundred thousand that were hanging on his every word. "I think that question may be answered by reading a message from the National Bureau of Standards which was handed to me as I entered the coliseum here tonight. Here is the message: 'Spectroscopic laboratory reports sudden marked acceleration Xi effect. Cutoff 5500 at 0000GCT.' Now in plain language what does this mean? It means that at four o'clock this afternoon the extinction of radiation extended nearly to the green." He hesitated. "I regret to inform the lady that her husband will never be able to return to his work. Why? Because so little while is left to us that no time remains for either work or play."

An excited uneasy murmur swept around the coliseum that rose to a sharp peak then hastily died away as the chairman selected another card. "Our second question is from a man in Pomona who signs himself 'Taxpayer.' His letter is too long to read in full so that I must confine myself to his inquiry at the end. 'If scientists knew light was going to be extinguished, then why didn't they get busy and do something about it a long time ago? The government makes me pay taxes so scientists can sit in their laboratories and hatch these wild theories. But when danger comes along they're just as helpless as the rest of us.' "

The letter provoked a good deal of laughter mingled with a surprising amount of handclapping. The humor of the situation, however, was wholly lost on Friedmann. "What would Mr. Taxpayer have the scientists do?" he demanded in a voice that was openly contemptuous. "Does he think they deliberately create the lightning that destroys a tree? Or the earthquake that engulfs a city? Well, I can assure him that these are nothing compared to the force that threatens us now. But before he criticizes science let him first learn something about it—go back to grammar school or read some little children's book."

There was a timid scattering of applause that was soon drowned in a chorus of boos and catcalls from all sides. One could sense the rising tide of resentment and frustration underneath.

"What did I tell you?" Arnold shouted. "They aren't going to take it."

Stoddard hunched down farther in his seat. "If you ask me all hell's going to break loose here in another minute."

Two members of the committee could be seen apparently expostulating with Friedmann, who stood listening to them indifferently with folded arms. The chairman was doing his best to restore order but it was nearly a minute before he was able to proceed. "Quiet please. Quiet," he entreated. "We have many more questions on the program of vital interest which I am sure you are all anxious to hear. Now here is one from a schoolteacher in Lynwood which goes straight to the point. 'Dear Dr. Friedmann, can you tell us what course of events we may expect from the Xi effect in the immediate future?' "

"There can be no doubt as to the course of events up to a certain point," Friedmann replied, speaking more slowly than usual and evidently weighing his words with care. "Beyond that point there is no knowledge, only speculation and conjecture.

"But in the immediate future the course of events is very clear. The extinction of radiation will continue at a rapidly increasing pace. Soon the world will be completely devoid of the quality of radiation that excites the sensation of visible light. As it disappears, the sensation will be similar to that of watching a scene in a play in which the lights are gradually dimmed until finally the stage and players are utterly blotted out."

There was so much noise now that Arnold was able to hear only with the greatest difficulty. Some people stood yelling and shaking their fists at Friedmann while others shouted for them to sit down and let him proceed.

"After the visible radiation there remains the spectrum of the X-radiation and gamma rays," Friedmann continued, apparently unmindful that he had lost his audience. "Especially significant will be the nature of the reaction upon cosmic rays, a subject upon which scientists have been wholly unable to agree. At present there is no hope of securing records of this vitally important phenomenon. Furthermore, there is no hope——"

A whiskey bottle crashed against the stand showering Friedmann with glass. Another followed and another until the air was filled with them. A dozen fights were in progress within the coliseum while without a mob was attempting to break through the gate at the east entrance. In the distance could be heard the rising wail of police sirens.

Suddenly the floodlights blinked, wavered uncertainly, then slowly faded out to a chorus of anguished wails and frantic howls for lights. Whether the fade-out was by accident or intent the result was the same. A terrified panic-stricken hush descended upon the multitude.

It was at that instant a new voice was heard in the darkness; a voice calm and powerful, yet withal tender and reassuring.

"*The Lord is my Shepherd; I shall not want.*"

In the dim light men and women looked at each other fearful and bewildered, as if a miracle were about to happen.

Again the voice came crying in the darkness. "*He maketh me to lie down in green pastures; He leadeth me beside the still waters.*"

Arnold grabbed his partner by the shoulder. "It's Atchison Kane! If he can hold this crowd tonight, he's a wonder."

Men who were shouting and cursing a moment before now stood awed and irresolute. Here and there a few were beginning to kneel while others sobbed openly and unashamed.

"*He restoreth my soul; He leadeth me in the paths of righteousness for His name's sake.*"

Many were beginning to repeat the familiar words after him. Now the voice swelled to a mighty climax in its message of faith and hope,

"*Yea, though I walk through the valley of the shadow of death I will fear no evil——*"

And then more softly,

"*For Thou art with me; Thy rod and Thy staff they comfort me——*"

From directly behind Arnold there came a woman's shriek with piercing intensity. It was a shriek filled with despair. A shriek that meant something was terribly wrong. Others around her began shouting and screaming too, pointing toward the great archway at the east entrance.

The low fog that had hung over the city all evening had broken momentarily revealing the rising moon. But it was a moon that no one there had ever seen before, a moon out of a nightmare, swollen and elongated as if viewed through a cylindrical lens. But even more unnatural than its shape was its *color*—a deep transparent blue.

Arnold was so intent upon the moon that he scarcely noticed when the floodlights came on again. Gradually he became aware of some change in the aspect of the coliseum itself; there seemed to be a soft waviness spreading everywhere, warping some portions of the scene but leaving others untouched, like gelatine melting and flowing down a photographic plate. His eyes were unable to bring the mass of humanity banked against the opposite wall of the coliseum into sharp focus. The tiers of seats kept blurring and shimmering as if the light were coming from a great distance through layers of heated air.

With a sickening sensation he perceived that the distortion in space-time was beginning to affect objects right around him. The faces were undergoing some subtle alteration, noticeable particularly in the irregular position of the mouth with respect to the nose and eyes together with an apparent thickening and bending of the jaw and forehead, such as he had once seen in patients whose bony structure had undergone prolonged softening from osteitis deformans.

The night was deepening rapidly now, closing in like the folds of a vast purple curtain. Simultaneously people were gripped by that primitive wholly unreasoning fear that is felt at a total solar eclipse the instant before totality, when the shadow of the moon suddenly looms on the horizon advancing with terrifying speed. Men and women clung to each other or ran frantically this way and that as if by fleeing they could escape a fate from which no escape was possible.

Stoddard and Arnold sat huddled together watching the groping figures grow dimmer and dimmer until the last ray of light was extinguished in the dense impenetrable blackness. But hours later they knew from the sound of voices and the pressure of hands and bodies, that thousands were still crouching in their seats waiting hopefully for the light that had always returned.

Arnold dozing against Stoddard's shoulder found himself repeating a phrase from Friedmann's last remark: "There is no hope—— There is no hope——"

A DESCENT INTO THE MAELSTRÖM

Edgar Allan Poe

Edgar Allan Poe, poet, writer, and critic, is the progenitor of the use of contemporary science as a literary device to enhance verisimilitude in fiction and thereby encourage the willing suspension of disbelief in readers; he directly presages Jules Verne (who worshiped his stories). He has therefore some claim to being the literary founder of science fiction. There is a substantial collection of his works, *The Science Fiction of Edgar Allan Poe* (1976), that presents the case well. He is also the principal inventor of the mystery and detective-story genre (the Mystery Writers of America named their "Edgar" Award for him), and of what has come to be called the horror-fiction genre (virtually all current practitioners have been directly influenced by the works of Poe). Although during his lifetime he was considered by many to be a genius, his work received mixed reviews. His literary reputation was severely damaged in the nineteenth century by an obituary written by his literary executor, Rufus Wilmot Griswold, published in the *Home Journal*:

> EDGAR ALLAN POE is dead. He died in Baltimore on Sunday, October 7th. The announcement will startle many, but few will be grieved by it.

It goes on to say such things as ". . . with a *single glass* of wine, his whole nature was reversed, the demon became uppermost, and, though none of the usual signs of intoxication were visible, his *will* was palpably insane."

Many others, from Henry James to the present, have tried to dismiss Poe or denigrate his achievements, but he remains a giant of American (and world) literature. Still, today, in part because of Poe's role in the founding of these three kinds of category fiction, adverse critiques of Poe have become part of the mechanism for retaining the high culture/popular culture split in American literature, despite his status as a canonical author.

This story, of a man caught by an enormous natural force who uses his knowledge of science to escape death, is an exemplar of the rigorous methodology of hard science fiction at its best. It is also worth noting that it is a sea story. Sea stories have a very long history, dating back to Homer's *Odyssey* and before. Because of this, sea stories have a highly codified interpretive framework—all the elements of sea voyages have a conventional meaning, sometimes allegorical. On the other hand, since throughout the history of sea stories, real people have made real sea voyages, returning with marvelous tales of their adventures, sea stories insist upon their literal level, despite the conventional meaning of virtually every element of the sea story.

This story is then a founding document of the whole science fiction approach and attitude of the Golden Age. Its vision of a great dangerous natural object, the whirlpool, is perhaps the ancestor of such 'black-hole' stories as Poul Anderson's "Kyrie."

> The ways of God in Nature, as in Providence, are not as *our* ways; nor are the models that we frame any way commensurate to the vastness, profundity, and unsearchableness of His works, *which have a depth in them greater than the well of Democritus.*
>
> —JOSEPH GLANVILLE

We had now reached the summit of the loftiest crag. For some minutes the old man seemed too much exhausted to speak.

"Not long ago," said he at length, "and I could have guided you on this route as well as the youngest of my sons; but, about three years past, there happened to me an event such as never happened before to mortal man—or at least such as no man ever survived to tell of—and the six hours of deadly terror which I then endured have broken me up body and soul. You suppose me a *very* old man—but I am not. It took less than a single day to change these hairs from a jetty black to white, to weaken my limbs, and to unstring my nerves, so that I tremble at the least exertion, and am frightened at a shadow. Do you know I can scarcely look over this little cliff without getting giddy?"

The "little cliff," upon whose edge he had so carelessly thrown himself down to rest that the weightier portion of his body hung over it, while he was only kept from falling by the tenure of his elbow on its extreme and slippery edge—this "little cliff" arose, a sheer unobstructed precipice of black shining rock, some fifteen or sixteen hundred feet from the world of crags beneath us. Nothing would have tempted me to within half a dozen yards of its brink. In truth so deeply was I excited by the perilous position of my companion, that I fell at full length upon the ground, clung to the shrubs around me, and dared not even glance upward at the sky—while I struggled in vain to divest myself of the idea that the very foundations of the mountain were in danger from the fury of the winds. It was long before I could reason myself into sufficient courage to sit up and look out into the distance.

"You must get over these fancies," said the guide, "for I have brought you here that you might have the best possible view of the scene of that event I mentioned—and to tell you the whole story with the spot just under your eye.

"We are now," he continued, in that particularizing manner which distinguished him—"we are now close upon the Norwegian coast—in the sixty-eighth degree of latitude—in the great province of Nordland—and in the dreary district of Lofoden. The mountain upon whose top we sit is Helseggen, the Cloudy. Now raise yourself up a little higher—hold on to the grass if you feel giddy—so—and look out beyond the belt of vapor beneath us, into the sea."

I looked dizzily, and beheld a wide expanse of ocean, whose waters wore so inky a hue as to bring at once to my mind the Nubian geographer's account of the *Mare Tenebrarum*. A panorama more deplorably desolate no human imagination can conceive. To the right and left, as far as the eye could reach, there lay outstretched, like ramparts of the world, lines of horridly black and beetling cliff, whose character of gloom was but the more forcibly illustrated by the surf which reared high up against it its white and ghastly crest, howling and shrieking for ever. Just opposite the promontory upon whose apex we were placed, and at a distance of some five or six miles out at sea, there was visible a small, bleak-looking island; or, more properly, its position was discernible through the wilderness of surge in which it was enveloped. About two miles nearer the land, arose another of smaller size, hideously craggy and barren, and encompassed at various intervals by a cluster of dark rocks.

The appearance of the ocean, in the space between the more distant island and the shore, had something very unusual about it. Although, at the time, so strong a gale was blowing landward that a brig in the remote offing lay to under a double-reefed try-sail, and constantly plunged her whole hull out of sight, still there was here nothing like a regular swell, but only a short, quick, angry cross dashing of water in every direction—as well in the teeth of the wind as otherwise. Of foam there was little except in the immediate vicinity of the rocks.

"The island in the distance," resumed the old man, "is called by the Norwegians Vurrgh. The one midway is Moskoe. That a mile to the northward is Ambaaren. Yonder are Iflesen, Hoeyholm, Kieldholm, Suarven, and Buckholm. Farther off—between Moskoe and Vurrgh—are Otterholm, Flimen, Sandflesen, and Skarholm. These are the true names of the places—but why it has been thought necessary to name them at all, is more than either you or I can understand. Do you hear any thing? Do you see any change in the water?"

We had now been about ten minutes upon the top of Helseggen, to which we had ascended from the interior of Lofoden, so that we had caught no glimpse of the sea until it had burst upon us from the summit. As the old man spoke, I became aware of a loud and gradually increasing sound, like the moaning of a vast herd of buffaloes upon an American prairie; and at the same moment I perceived that what seamen term the *chopping* character of the ocean beneath us, was rapidly changing into a current which set to the eastward. Even while I gazed, this current acquired a monstrous velocity. Each moment added to its speed—to its headlong impetuosity. In five minutes the whole sea, as far as Vurrgh, was lashed into ungovernable fury; but it was between Moskoe and the coast that the main uproar held its sway. Here the vast bed of the waters, seamed and scarred into a thousand conflicting channels, burst suddenly into phrensied convulsion—heaving, boiling, hissing—gyrating in gigantic and innumerable vortices, and all whirling and plunging on to the eastward with a rapidity which water never elsewhere assumes except in precipitous descents.

In a few minutes more, there came over the scene another radical alteration. The general surface grew somewhat more smooth, and the whirlpools, one by one, disappeared, while prodigious streaks of foam became apparent where none had been seen before. These streaks, at length, spreading out to a great distance, and entering into combination, took unto themselves the gyratory motion of the subsided vortices, and seemed to form the germ of another more vast. Suddenly—very suddenly—this assumed a distinct and definite existence, in a circle of more than half a mile in diameter. The edge of the whirl was represented by a broad belt of gleaming spray; but no particle of this slipped into the mouth of the terrific funnel, whose interior, as far as the eye could fathom it, was a smooth, shining, and jet-black wall of water, inclined to the horizon at an angle of some forty-five degrees, speeding dizzily round and round with a swaying and sweltering motion, and sending forth to the winds an appalling voice, half shriek, half roar, such as not even the mighty cataract of Niagara ever lifts up in its agony to Heaven.

The mountain trembled to its very base, and the rock rocked. I threw myself upon my face, and clung to the scant herbage in an excess of nervous agitation.

"This," said I at length, to the old man—"this *can* be nothing else than the great whirlpool of the Maelström."

"So it is sometimes termed," said he. "We Norwegians call it the Moskoe-ström, from the island of Moskoe in the midway."

The ordinary accounts of this vortex had by no means prepared me for what I saw. That of Jonas Ramus, which is perhaps the most circumstantial of any, cannot impart the faintest conception either of the magnificence, or of the horror of the scene—or of the wild bewildering sense of *the novel* which confounds the beholder. I am not sure from what point of view the writer in question surveyed it, nor at what time; but it could neither have been from the summit of Helseggen, nor during a storm. There are some passages of his description, nevertheless, which may be quoted for their details, although their effect is exceedingly feeble in conveying an impression of the spectacle.

"Between Lofoden and Moskoe," he says, "the depth of the water is between thirty-six and forty fathoms; but on the other side, toward Ver (Vurrgh) this depth decreases so as not to afford a convenient passage for a vessel, without the risk of splitting on the rocks, which happens even in the calmest weather. When it is flood, the stream runs up the country between Lofoden and Moskoe with a boisterous rapidity; but the roar of its impetuous ebb to the sea is scarce equalled by the loudest and most dreadful cataracts; the noise being heard several leagues off, and the vortices or pits are of such an extent and depth, that if a ship comes within its attraction, it is inevitably absorbed and carried down to the bottom, and there beat to pieces against the rocks; and when the water relaxes, the fragments thereof are thrown up again. But these intervals of tranquillity are only at the turn of the ebb and flood, and in calm weather, and last but a quarter of an hour, its violence gradually returning. When the stream is most boisterous, and its fury heightened by a storm, it is dangerous to come within a Norway mile of it. Boats, yachts, and ships have been carried away by not guarding against it before they were within its reach. It likewise happens frequently, that whales come too near the stream, and are overpowered by its violence; and then it is impossible to describe their howlings and bellowings in their fruitless struggles to disengage themselves. A bear once, attempting to swim from Lofoden to Moskoe, was caught by the stream and borne down, while he roared terribly, so as to be heard on shore. Large stocks of firs and pine trees, after being absorbed by the current, rise again broken and torn to such a degree as if bristles grew upon them. This plainly shows the bottom to consist of craggy rocks, among which they are whirled to and fro. This stream is regulated by the flux and reflux of the sea—it being constantly high and low water every six hours. In the year 1645, early in the morning of Sexagesima Sunday, it raged with such noise and impetuosity that the very stones of the houses on the coast fell to the ground."

In regard to the depth of the water, I could not see how this could have been ascertained at all in the immediate vicinity of the vortex. The "forty fathoms" must have reference only to portions of the channel close upon the shore either of Moskoe or Lofoden. The depth in the centre of the Moskoe-ström must be immeasurably greater; and no better proof of this fact is necessary than can be obtained from even the side-long glance into the abyss of the whirl which may be had from the highest crag of Helseggen. Looking down from this pinnacle upon the howling Phlegethon below, I could not help smiling at the simplicity with which the honest Jonas Ramus records, as a matter difficult of belief, the anecdotes of the whales and the bears; for it appeared to me, in fact, a self-evident thing, that the largest ships of the line in existence, coming within the influence of that deadly attraction, could resist it as little as a feather the hurricane, and must disappear bodily and at once.

The attempts to account for the phenomenon—some of which, I remember, seemed to me sufficiently plausible in perusal—now wore a very different and unsatisfactory aspect. The idea generally received is that this, as well as three smaller vortices among the Feroe islands, "have no other cause than the collision of waves rising and falling, at flux and reflux, against a ridge of rocks and shelves, which confines the water so that it precipitates itself like a cataract; and thus the higher the flood rises, the deeper must the fall be, and the natural result of all is a whirlpool or vortex, the prodigious suction of which is sufficiently known by lesser experiments."—These are the words of the Encyclopædia Britannica. Kircher and others imagine that in the centre of the channel of the Maelström is an abyss penetrating the globe, and issuing in some very remote part—the Gulf of Bothnia being somewhat decidedly named in one instance. This opinion, idle in itself, was the one to which, as I gazed, my imagination most readily assented; and, mentioning it to the guide, I was rather surprised to hear him say that, although it was the view almost universally entertained of the subject by the Norwegians, it nevertheless was not his own. As to the former notion he confessed his inability to comprehend it; and here I agreed with him—for, however conclusive on paper, it becomes altogether unintelligible, and even absurd, amid the thunder of the abyss.

"You have had a good look at the whirl now," said the old man, "and if you will creep round this crag, so as to get in its lee, and deaden the roar of the water, I will tell you a story that will convince you I ought to know something of the Moskoe-ström."

I placed myself as desired, and he proceeded.

"Myself and my two brothers once owned a schooner-rigged smack of about seventy tons burthen, with which we were in the habit of fishing among the islands beyond Moskoe, nearly to Vurrgh. In all violent eddies at sea there is good fishing, at proper opportunities, if one has only the courage to attempt it; but among the whole of the Lofoden coastmen, we three were the only ones who made a regular business of going out to the islands, as I tell you. The usual grounds are a great way lower down to the southward. There fish can be got at all hours, without much risk, and therefore these places are preferred. The choice spots over here among the rocks, however, not only yield the finest variety, but in far greater abundance; so that we often got in a single day, what the more timid of the craft could not scrape together in a week. In fact, we made it a matter of desperate speculation—the risk of life standing instead of labor, and courage answering for capital.

"We kept the smack in a cove about five miles higher up the coast than this; and it was our practice, in fine weather, to take advantage of the fifteen minutes' slack to push across the main channel of the Moskoe-ström, far above the pool, and then drop down upon anchorage somewhere near Otterholm, or Sandflesen, when the eddies are not so violent as elsewhere. Here we used to remain until nearly time for slack-water again, when we weighed and made for home. We never set out upon this expedition without a steady side wind for going and coming—one that we felt sure would not fail us before our return—and we seldom made a mis-calculation upon this point. Twice, during six years, we were forced to stay all night at anchor on account of a dead calm, which is a rare thing indeed just about here; and once we had to remain on the grounds nearly a week, starving to death, owing to a gale which blew up shortly after our arrival, and made the channel too boisterous to be thought of. Upon this occasion we should have been driven out to sea in spite of everything, (for the whirlpools threw us round and round so violently, that, at length, we fouled our anchor and dragged it) if it had not been that we drifted into one of the innumerable cross currents—here today and gone tomorrow—which drove us under the lee of Flimen, where, by good luck, we brought up.

"I could not tell you the twentieth part of the difficulties we encountered 'on the ground'—it is a bad spot to be in, even in good weather—but we made shift always to run the gauntlet of the Moskoe-ström itself without accident; although at times my heart has been in my mouth when we happened to be a minute or so behind or before the slack. The wind sometimes was not as strong as we though it at starting, and then we made rather less way than we could wish, while the current rendered the smack unmanageable. My eldest brother had a son eighteen years old, and I had two stout boys of my own. These would have been of great assistance at such times, in using the sweeps, as well as afterward in fishing—but, somehow, although we ran the risk ourselves, we had not the heart to let the young ones get into the danger—for, after all said and done, it *was* a horrible danger, and that is the truth.

"It is now within a few days of three years since what I am going to tell you occurred. It was on the tenth of July, 18—, a day which the people of this part of the world will never forget—for it was one in which blew the most terrible hurricane that ever came out of the heavens. And yet all the morning, and indeed until late in the afternoon, there was a gentle and steady breeze from the south-west, while the sun shone brightly, so that the oldest seaman among us could not have foreseen what was to follow.

"The three of us—my two brothers and myself—had crossed over to the islands about two o'clock P. M., and soon nearly loaded the smack with fine fish, which, we all remarked, were more plenty that day than we had ever known them. It was just seven, *by my watch*, when we weighed and started for home, so as to make the worst of the Ström at slack water, which we knew would be at eight.

"We set out with a fresh wind on our starboard quarter, and for some time spanked along at a great rate, never dreaming of danger, for indeed we saw not the slightest reason to apprehend it. All at once we were taken aback by a breeze from over Helseggen. This was most unusual—something that had never happened to us before—and I began to feel a little uneasy, without exactly knowing why. We put the boat on the wind, but could make no headway at all for the eddies, and I was upon the point of proposing to return to the anchorage, when, looking astern, we saw the whole horizon covered with a singular copper-colored cloud that rose with the most amazing velocity.

"In the meantime the breeze that had headed us off fell away, and we were dead becalmed, drifting about in every direction. This state of things, however, did not last long enough to give us time to think about it. In less than a minute the storm was upon us—in less than two the sky was entirely overcast—and what with this and the driving spray, it became suddenly so dark that we could not see each other in the smack.

"Such a hurricane as then blew it is folly to attempt describing. The oldest seaman in Norway never experienced any thing like it. We had let our sails go by the run before it cleverly took us; but, at the first puff, both our masts went by the board as if they had been sawed off—the mainmast taking with it my youngest brother, who had lashed himself to it for safety.

"Our boat was the lightest feather of a thing that ever sat upon water. It had a complete flush deck, with only a small hatch near the bow, and this hatch it had always been our custom to batten down when about to cross the Ström, by way of precaution against the chopping seas. But for this circumstance we should have foundered at once—for we lay entirely buried for some moments. How my elder brother escaped destruction I cannot say, for I never had an opportunity of ascertaining. For my part, as soon as I had let the foresail run, I threw myself flat on deck, with my feet against the narrow gunwale of the bow, and with my hands grasping a ring-bolt near the foot of the foremast. It was mere instinct that prompted me to do this—which was undoubtedly the very best thing I could have done—for I was too much flurried to think.

"For some moments we were completely deluged, as I say, and all this time I held my breath, and clung to the bolt. When I could stand it no longer I raised myself upon my knees, still keeping hold with my hands, and thus got my head clear. Presently our little boat gave herself a shake, just as a dog does in coming out of the water, and thus rid herself, in some measure, of the seas. I was now trying to get the better of the stupor that had come over me, and to collect my senses so as to see what was to be done, when I felt somebody grasp my arm. It was my elder brother, and my heart leaped for joy, for I had made sure that he was overboard—but the next moment all this joy was turned into horror—for he put his mouth close to my ear, and screamed out the word *'Moskoe-ström!'*

"No one ever will know what my feelings were at that moment. I shook from head to foot as if I had had the most violent fit of the ague. I knew what he meant by that one word well enough—I knew what he wished to make me understand. With the wind that now drove us on, we were bound for the whirl of the Ström, and nothing could save us!

"You perceive that in crossing the Ström *channel*, we always went a long way up above the whirl, even in the calmest weather, and then had to wait and watch carefully for the slack—but now we were driving right upon the pool itself, and in such a hurricane as this! 'To be sure,' I thought, 'we shall get there just about the slack—there is some little hope in that'—but in the next moment I cursed myself for being so great a fool as to dream of hope at all. I knew very well that we were doomed, had we been ten times a ninety-gun ship.

"By this time the first fury of the tempest had spent itself, or perhaps we did not feel it so much, as we scudded before it, but at all events the seas, which at first had been kept down by the wind, and lay flat and frothing, now got up into absolute mountains. A singular change, too, had come over the heavens. Around in every direction it was still as black as pitch, but nearly overhead there burst out, all at once, a circular rift of clear sky—as clear as I ever saw—and of a deep bright blue—and through it there blazed forth the full moon with a lustre that I never before knew her to wear. She lit up every thing about us with the greatest distinctness—but, oh God, what a scene it was to light up!

"I now made one or two attempts to speak to my brother—but in some manner which I could not understand, the din had so increased that I could not make him hear a single word, although I screamed at the top of my voice in his ear. Presently he shook his head, looking as pale as death, and held up one of his fingers, as if to say *'listen!'*

"At first I could not make out what he meant—but soon a hideous thought flashed upon me. I dragged my watch from its fob. It was not going. I glanced at its face by the moonlight, and then burst into tears as I flung it far away into the ocean. *It had run down at seven o'clock! We were behind the time of the slack, and the whirl of the Ström was in full fury!*

"When a boat is well built, properly trimmed, and not deep laden, the waves in a strong gale, when she is going large, seem always to slip from beneath her—which appears very strange to a landsman—and this is what is called *riding*, in sea phrase.

"Well, so far we had ridden the swells very cleverly; but presently a gigantic sea happened to take us right under the counter, and bore us with it as it rose—up—up—as if into the sky. I would not have believed that any wave could rise so high. And then down we came with a sweep, a slide, and a plunge, that made me feel sick and dizzy, as if I was falling from some lofty mountain-top in a dream. But while we were up I had thrown a quick glance around—and that one glance was all sufficient. I saw our exact position in an instant. The Moskoe-ström whirlpool was about a quarter of a mile dead ahead—but no more like the every-day Moskoe-ström, than the whirl as you now see it, is like a mill-race. If I had not know where we were, and what we had to expect, I should not have recognized the place at all.

As it was, I involuntarily closed my eyes in horror. The lids clenched themselves together as if in a spasm.

"It could not have been more than two minutes afterwards until we suddenly felt the waves subside, and were enveloped in foam. The boat made a sharp half turn to larboard, and then shot off in its new direction like a thunderbolt. At the same moment the roaring noise of the water was completely drowned in a kind of shrill shriek—such a sound as you might imagine given out by the water-pipes of many thousand steam-vessels, letting off their steam all together. We were now in the belt of surf that always surrounds the whirl; and I thought, of course, that another moment would plunge us into the abyss—down which we could only see indistinctly on account of the amazing velocity with which we were borne along. The boat did not seem to sink into the water at all, but to skim like an air-bubble upon the surface of the surge. Her starboard side was next the whirl, and on the larboard arose the world of ocean we had left. It stood like a huge writhing wall between us and the horizon.

"It may appear strange, but now, when we were in the very jaws of the gulf, I felt more composed than when we were only approaching it. Having made up my mind to hope no more, I got rid of a great deal of that terror which unmanned me at first. I suppose it was despair that strung my nerves.

"It may look like boasting—but what I tell you is truth—I began to reflect how magnificent a thing it was to die in such a manner, and how foolish it was in me to think of so paltry a consideration as my own individual life, in view of so wonderful a manifestation of God's power. I do believe that I blushed with shame when this idea crossed my mind. After a little while I became possessed with the keenest curiosity about the whirl itself. I positively felt a *wish* to explore its depths, even at the sacrifice I was going to make; and my principal grief was that I should never be able to tell my old companions on shore about the mysteries I should see. These, no doubt, were singular fancies to occupy a man's mind in such extremity—and I have often thought since, that the revolutions of the boat around the pool might have rendered me a little light-headed.

"There was another circumstance which tended to restore my self-possession; and this was the cessation of the wind, which could not reach us in our present situation—for, as you saw yourself, the belt of surf is considerably lower than the general bed of the ocean, and this latter now towered above us, a high, black, mountainous ridge. If you have never been at sea in a heavy gale, you can form no idea of the confusion of mind occasioned by the wind and spray together. They blind, deafen and strangle you, and take away all power of action or reflection. But we were now, in a great measure, rid of these annoyances—just as death-condemned felons in prison are allowed petty indulgences, forbidden them while their doom is yet uncertain.

"How often we made the circuit of the belt it is impossible to say. We careered round and round for perhaps an hour, flying rather than floating, getting gradually more and more into the middle of the surge, and then nearer and nearer to its horrible inner edge. All this time I had never let go of the ring-bolt. My brother was at the stern, holding on to a large empty water-cask which had been securely lashed under the coop of the counter, and was the only thing on deck that had not been swept overboard when the gale first took us. As we approached the brink of the pit he let go his hold upon this, and made for the ring, from which, in the agony of his terror, he endeavored to force my hands, as it was not large enough to afford us both a secure grasp. I never felt deeper grief than when I saw him attempt this act—although I knew he was a madman when he did it—a raving maniac through sheer fright. I did not care, however, to contest the point with him. I thought it could make no difference whether either of us held on at all; so I let him have the bolt, and went astern to the cask. This there was no great difficulty in doing; for the smack flew round steadily enough, and upon an even keel—only swaying to and fro, with the immense sweeps and swelters of the whirl. Scarcely had I secured myself in my new position, when we gave a wild lurch to starboard, and rushed headlong into the abyss. I muttered a hurried prayer to God, and thought all was over.

"As I felt the sickening sweep of the descent, I had instinctively tightened my hold upon the barrel, and closed my eyes. For some seconds I dared not open them—while I expected instant destruction, and wondered that I was not already in my death-struggles with the water. But moment after moment elapsed. I still lived. The sense of falling had ceased; and the motion of the vessel seemed much as it had been before while in the belt of foam, with the exception that she now lay more along. I took courage and looked once again upon the scene.

"Never shall I forget the sensations of awe, horror, and admiration with which I gazed about me. The boat appeared to be hanging, as if by magic, midway down, upon the interior surface of a funnel vast in circumference, prodigious in depth, and whose perfectly smooth sides might have been mistaken for ebony, but for the bewildering rapidity with which they spun around, and for the gleaming and ghastly radiance they shot forth, as the rays of the full moon, from that circular rift amid the clouds which I have already described, streamed in a flood of golden glory along the black walls, and far away down into the inmost recesses of the abyss.

"At first I was too much confused to observe anything accurately. The general burst of terrific grandeur was all that I beheld. When I recovered myself a little, however, my gaze fell instinctively downward. In this direction I was able to obtain an unobstructed view, from the manner in which the smack hung on the inclined surface of the pool. She was quite upon an even keel—that is to say, her deck lay in a plane parallel with that of the water—but this latter sloped at an angle of more than forty-five degrees, so that we seemed to be lying upon our beam-ends. I could not help observing, nevertheless, that I had scarcely more difficulty in maintaining my hold and footing in this situation, than if we had been upon a deal level; and this, I suppose, was owing to the speed at which we revolved.

"The rays of the moon seemed to search the very bottom of the profound gulf; but still I could make out nothing distinctly, on account of a thick mist in which everything there was enveloped, and over which there hung a magnificent rainbow, like that narrow and tottering bridge which Mussulmen say is the only pathway between Time and Eternity. This mist, or spray, was no doubt occasioned by the clashing of the great walls of the funnel, as they all met together at the bottom—but the yell that went up to the Heavens from out of that mist, I dare not attempt to describe.

"Our first slide into the abyss itself, from the belt of foam above, had carried us to a great distance down the slope; but our farther descent was by no means proportionate. Round and round we swept—not with any uniform movement—but in dizzying swings and jerks, that sent us sometimes only a few hundred feet—sometimes nearly the complete circuit of the whirl. Our progress downward, at each revolution, was slow, but very perceptible.

"Looking about me upon the wide waste of liquid ebony on which we were thus borne, I perceived that our boat was not the only object in the embrace of the whirl. Both above and below us were visible fragments of vessels, large masses of building timber and trunks of trees, with many smaller articles, such as pieces of house furniture, broken boxes, barrels and staves. I have already described the unnatural curiosity which had taken the place of my original terrors. It appeared to grow upon me as I drew nearer and nearer to my dreadful doom. I now began to watch, with a strange interest, the numerous things that floated in our company. I *must* have been delirious—for I even sought *amusement* in speculating upon the relative velocities of their several descents toward the foam below. 'This fir tree,' I found myself at one time saying, 'will certainly be the next thing that takes the awful plunge and disappears,'—and then I was disappointed to find that the wreck of a Dutch merchant ship overtook it and went down before. At length, after making several guesses of this nature, and being deceived in all—this fact—the fact of my invariable miscalculation, set me upon a train of reflection that made my limbs again tremble, and my heart beat heavily once more.

"It was not a new terror that thus affected me, but the dawn of a more exciting *hope*. This hope arose partly from memory, and partly from present observation. I called to mind the great variety of buoyant matter that strewed the coast of Lofoden, having been absorbed and then thrown forth by the Moskoe-ström. By far the greater number of the articles were shattered in the most extraordinary way—so chafed and roughened as to have the appearance of being stuck full of splinters—but then I distinctly recollected that there were *some* of them which were not disfigured at all. Now I could not account for this difference except by supposing that the roughened fragments were the only ones which had been *completely absorbed*—that the others had entered the whirl at so late a period of the tide, or, from some reason, had descended so slowly after entering, that they did not reach the bottom before the turn of the flood came, or of the ebb, as the case might be. I conceived it possible, in either instance, that they might thus be whirled up again to the level of the ocean, without undergoing the fate of those which had been drawn in more early or absorbed more rapidly. I made, also, three important observations. The first was, that as a general rule, the larger the bodies were, the more rapid their descent;—the second, that, between two masses of equal extent, the one spherical, and the other *of any other shape*, the superiority in speed of descent was with the sphere;—the third, that, between two masses of equal size, the one cylindrical, and the other of any other shape, the cylinder was absorbed the more slowly.

"Since my escape, I have had several conversations on this subject with an old school-master of the district; and it was from him that I learned the use of the words 'cylinder' and 'sphere.' He explained to me—although I have forgotten the explanation—how what I observed was, in fact, the natural consequence of the forms of the floating fragments—and showed me how it happened that a cylinder, swimming in a vortex, offered more resistance to its suction, and was drawn in with greater difficulty than an equally bulky body, of any form whatever.*

"There was one startling circumstance which went a great way in enforcing these observations, and rendering me anxious to turn them to account, and this was that, at every revolution, we passed something like a barrel, or else the broken yard or the mast of a vessel, while many of these things, which had been on our level when I first opened my eyes upon the wonders of the whirlpool, were now high up above us, and seemed to have moved but little from their original station.

"I no longer hesitated what to do. I resolved to lash myself securely to the water cask upon which I now held, to cut it loose from the counter, and to throw myself with it into the water. I attracted my brother's attention by signs, pointed to the floating barrels that came near us, and did everything in my power to make him understand what I was about to do. I thought at length that he comprehended my

* See Archimedes, "*De Incidentibus in Fluido.*"—lib. 2.

design—but, whether this was the case or not, he shook his head despairingly, and refused to move from his station by the ring-bolt. It was impossible to force him; the emergency admitted no delay; and so, with a bitter struggle, I resigned him to his fate, fastened myself to the cask by means of the lashings which secured it to the counter, and precipitated myself with it into the sea, without another moment's hesitation.

"The result was precisely what I had hoped it might be. As it is myself who now tell you this tale—as you see that I *did* escape—and as you are already in possession of the mode in which this escape was effected, and must therefore anticipate all that I have farther to say—I will bring my story quickly to conclusion. It might have been an hour, or thereabout, after my quitting the smack, when, having descended to a vast distance beneath me, it made three or four wild gyrations in rapid succession, and, bearing my loved brother with it, plunged headlong, at once and forever, into the chaos of foam below. The barrel to which I was attached sunk very little farther than half the distance between the bottom of the gulf and the spot at which I leaped overboard, before a great change took place in the character of the whirlpool. The slope of the sides of the vast funnel became momently less and less steep. The gyrations of the whirl grew, gradually, less and less violent. By degrees, the froth and the rainbow disappeared, and the bottom of the gulf seemed slowly to uprise. The sky was clear, the winds had gone down, and the full moon was setting radiantly in the west, when I found myself on the surface of the ocean, in full view of the shores of Lofoden, and above the spot where the pool of the Moskoe-ström *had been*. It was the hour of the slack—but the sea still heaved in mountainous waves from the effects of the hurricane. I was borne violently into the channel of the Ström, and in a few minutes, was hurried down the coast into the 'grounds' of the fishermen. A boat picked me up—exhausted from fatigue—and (now that the danger was removed) speechless from the memory of its horror. Those who drew me on board were my old mates and daily companions—but they knew me no more than they would have known a traveller from the spirit-land. My hair, which had been raven-black the day before, was as white as you see it now. They say too that the whole expression of my countenance had changed. I told them my story—they did not believe it. I now tell it to *you*—and I can scarcely expect you to put more faith in it than did the merry fishermen of Lofoden."

EXPOSURES

Gregory Benford

Gregory Benford is an astrophysicist who also writes fiction. To science fiction readers, he's a hard science fiction writer who is also an astronomer. The tension between the daily work of science and the avocation of writing in Benford's life has led him to write some of the finest hard sf of recent decades. Brian W. Aldiss says: "If he takes the close and narrow view of his characters—an all-too-human view, of illness, work, and marital problems—his vision of the universe in which such frail beings exist is one of vast perspectives, rather in the tradition of Stapledon and Clarke." And critic Larry McCaffery says: "Benford's work can probably best be understood as a particularly successful example of the 'modernist' branch of contemporary sf. Indeed, what may initially strike readers about his meticulously crafted, psychologically convincing, and verbally graceful fiction is the skillful manner in which he has appropriated a number of the key modernist experimental devices and applied them to a succession of familiar sf motifs and plot structures."

In Benford's view, "People build their lives around work, yet how often does the subject appear in fiction as a direct sensation, a lived experience?" Central to Benford's fiction are the characters of scientists at work. The interaction between the scientist's work and daily life is the subject of his most famous novel, *Timescape* (1980), as well as an integral part of most of his novels and stories. In an afterword to "Exposures" in his short story collection, *In Alien Flesh* (1986), Benford discusses his ideas on sf writing: "A science fiction writer is—or should be—constrained by what is, or logically might be. That can mean simple fidelity to facts. . . . To me it also means heeding the authentic, the actual, and concrete. Bad fiction uses the glossy generality; good writing needs the smattering of detail, the unrelenting busy mystery of the real. . . . For me, the only true guide is an eye for the graininess of the world, rather then the convenient, ordained maps. . . . A will toward concreteness itself brings into being the form and style appropriate to a story."

One of the really crucial things about Benford's work as a model of hard science fiction is not just that he uses well-rounded characters as vehicles of the sense of wonder, but that he is characterizing scientists in a context in which the relationship between their work and their emotional lives can be explored more fully than in literatures that won't tolerate the scientific content. "I thought," says Benford, "to reflect what the process of trawling for ideas, for insights, is like. Not necessarily the Eureka! moment, more like the quiet Oh yeah, right sensation of provisional, momentary discovery. And how it reverberates through a life." "Exposures" is a more personal, intimate view of astronomers than Latham's "The Xi Effect," and light-years from Raymond F. Jones's "The Person from Porlock" in its portrayal of a scientist at work. Benford is the first among the hard science fiction writers to have mastered and integrated Modernist techniques of characterization and use of metaphor.

Puzzles assemble themselves one piece at a time. Yesterday I began laying out the new plates I had taken up on the mountain, at Palomar. They were exposures of varying depth. In each, NGC 1097—a barred spiral galaxy about twenty megaparsecs away—hung suspended in its slow swirl.

As I laid out the plates I thought of the way our family had always divided up the breakfast chores on Sunday. On that ritual day our mother stayed in bed. I laid out the forks and knives and egg cups and formal off-white china, and then stood back in the thin morning light to survey my precise placings. Lush napkin pyramids perched on lace table cloth, my mother's favorite. Through the kitchen door leaked the mutter and clang of a meal coming into being.

I put the exposures in order according to the spectral filters used, noting the calibrated photometry for each. The ceramic sounds of Bridge Hall rang in the tiled hallways and seeped through the door of my office: footsteps, distant talk, the scrape of chalk on slate, a banging door. Examining the plates through an eye piece, I felt the galaxy swell into being, huge.

The deep exposures brought out the dim jets I was after. There were four of them pointing out of NGC 1097, two red and two blue, the brightest three discovered by Wolsencroft and Zealey, the last red one found by Lorre over at JPL. Straight lines scratched across the mottling of foreground dust and stars. No one knew what colored a jet red or blue. I was trying to use the deep plates to measure the width of the jets. Using a slit over the lens, I had stopped down the image until I could employ calibrated photometry to measure the wedge of light. Still further narrowing might allow me to measure the spectrum, to see if the blues and reds came from stars, or from excited clouds of gas.

They lanced out, two blue jets cutting through the spiral arms and breaking free into the blackness beyond. One plate, taken in that spectral spike where ionized hydrogen clouds emit, giving H II radiation, showed a string of beads buried in the curling spiral lanes. They were vast cooling clouds. Where the jets crossed the H II regions, the spiral arms were pushed outward, or else vanished altogether.

Opposite each blue jet, far across the galaxy, a red jet glowed. They, too, snuffed out the H II beads.

From these gaps in the spiral arms I estimated how far the barred spiral galaxy had turned, while the jets ate away at them: about fifteen degrees. From the velocity measurements in the disk, using the Doppler shifts of known spectral lines, I deduced the rotation rate of the NGC 1097 disk: approximately a hundred million years. Not surprising; our own sun takes about the same amount of time to circle around our galactic center. The photons which told me all these specifics had begun their steady voyage sixty million years ago, before there was a *New General Catalog of Nebulae and Clusters of Stars* to label them as they buried themselves in my welcoming emulsion. Thus do I know thee, NGC 1097.

These jets were unique. The brightest blue one dog-legs in a right angle turn and ends in silvery blobs of dry light. Its counter-jet, offset a perverse eleven degrees from exact oppositeness, continues on a warmly rose-colored path over an immense distance, a span far larger than the parent galaxy itself. I frowned, puckered my lips in concentration, calibrated and calculated and refined. Plainly these ramrod, laconic patterns of light were trying to tell me something.

But answers come when they will, one piece at a time.

I tried to tell my son this when, that evening, I helped him with his reading. Using what his mother now knowingly termed "word attack skills," he had mastered most of those tactics. The larger strategic issues of the sentence eluded him still. *Take it in phrases*, I urged him, ruffling his light brown hair, distracted, because I liked the nutmeg smell. (I have often thought that I could find my children in the dark, in a crowd, by my nose alone. Our genetic code colors the air.) He thumbed his book, dirtying a corner. Read the words between the commas, I instructed, my classroom sense of order returning. Stop at the commas, and then pause before going on, and think about what all those words mean. I sniffed at his wheatlike hair again.

I am a traditional astronomer, accustomed to the bitter cold of the cage at Palomar, the Byzantine marriage of optics at Kitt Peak, the muggy air of Lick. Through that long morning yesterday I studied the NGC 1097 jets, attempting to see with the quick eye of the theorist, "dancing on the data" as Roger Blandford down the hall had once called it. I tried to erect some rickety hypothesis that my own uncertain mathematical abilities could brace up. An idea came. I caught at it. But holding it close, turning it over, pushing terms about in an overloaded equation, I saw it was merely an old idea tarted up, already disproved.

Perhaps computer enhancement of the images would clear away some of my enveloping fog, I mused. I took my notes to the neighboring building, listening to my footsteps echo in the long arcade. The buildings at Caltech are mostly done in a pseudo-Spanish style, tan stucco with occasional flourishes of Moorish windows and tiles. The newer library rears up beside the crouching offices and classrooms, a modern extrusion. I entered the Alfred Sloan Laboratory of Physics and Mathematics, wondering for the *n*th time what a mathematical laboratory would be like, imagining Lewis Carroll in charge, and went into the new computer terminal rooms. The indices which called up my plates soon stuttered across the screen. I used a median numerical filter, to suppress variations in the background. There were standard routines to subtract particular parts of the spectrum. I called them up, averaging away noise from dust and gas and the image-saturating spikes that were foreground stars in our own galaxy. Still, nothing dramatic emerged. Illumination would not come.

I sipped at my coffee. I had brought a box of crackers from my office; and I broke one, eating each wafer with a heavy crunch. I swirled the cup and the coffee swayed like a dark disk at the bottom, a scum of cream at the vortex curling out into gray arms. I drank it. And thumbed another image into being.

This was not NGC 1097. I checked the number. Then the log. No, these were slots deliberately set aside for later filing. They were not supposed to be filled; they represented my allotted computer space. They should be blank.

Yet I recognized this one. It was a view of Sagittarius A, the intense radio source that hides behind a thick lane of dust in the Milky Way. Behind that dark obscuring swath that is an arm of our Galaxy, lies the center. I squinted. Yes: this was a picture formed from observations sensitive to the 21-centimeter wavelength line, the emission of nonionized hydrogen. I had seen it before, on exposures that looked radially inward at the Galactic core. Here was the red band of hydrogen along our line of sight. Slightly below was the well-known arm of hot, expanding gas, nine thousand light years across. Above, tinted green, was a smaller arm, a ridge of gas moving outward at 135 kilometers per second. I had seen this in seminars years ago. In the very center was the knot no more than a light year or two across, the source of the 10^{40} ergs per second of virulent energy that drove the cooker that caused all this. Still, the energy flux from our Galaxy was ten million times less than that of a quasar. Whatever the compact energy source there, it was comparatively quiet. NGC 1097 lies far to the south, entirely out of the Milky Way. Could the aim of the satellite camera have strayed so much?

Curious, I thumbed forward. The next index number gave another scan of the Sagittarius region, this time seen by the spectral emissions from outward-moving clouds of ammonia. Random blobs. I thumbed again. A formaldehyde-emission view. But now the huge arm of expanding hydrogen was sprinkled with knots, denoting clouds which moved faster, Dopplered into blue.

I frowned. No, the Sagittarius A exposures were no aiming error. These slots were to be left open for my incoming data. Someone had co-opted the space. Who? I called up the identifying codes, but there were none. As far as the master log was concerned, these spaces were still empty.

I moved to erase them. My finger paused, hovered, went limp. This was obviously high-quality information, already processed. Someone would want it. They had carelessly dumped it into my territory, but. . . .

My pause was in part that of sheer appreciation. Peering at the color-coded encrustations of light, I recalled what all this had once been like: impossibly complicated, ornate in its terms, caked with the eccentric jargon of long-dead professors, choked with thickets of atomic physics and thermodynamics, a web of complexity that finally gave forth mental pictures of a whirling, furious past, of stars burned now into cinders, of whispering, turbulent hydrogen that filled the void between the suns. From such numbers came the starscape that we knew. From a sharp scratch on a strip of film we could catch the signature of an element, deduce velocity from the Doppler shift, and then measure the width of that scratch to give the random component of the velocity, the random jigglings due to thermal motion, and thus the temperature. All from a scratch. No, I could not erase it.

When I was a boy of nine I was brow-beaten into serving at the altar, during the unendurably long Episcopal services that my mother felt we should attend. I wore the simple robe and was the first to appear in the service, lighting the candles with an awkward long device and its sliding wick. The organ music was soft and did not call attention to itself, so the congregation could watch undistracted as I fumbled with the wick and tried to keep the precarious balance between feeding it too much (so that, engorged, it bristled into a ball of orange) and the even worse embarrassment of snuffing it into a final accusing puff of black. Through the service I would alternately kneel and stand, murmuring the worn phrases as I thought of the softball I would play in the afternoon, feeling the prickly gathering heat underneath my robes. On a bad day the sweat would accumulate and a drop would cling to my nose. I'd let it hang there in mute testimony. The minister never seemed to notice. I would often slip off into decidedly untheological daydreams, intoxicated by the pressing moist heat, and miss the telltale words of the litany which signalled the beginning of communion. A whisper would come skating across the layered air and I would surface, to see the minister turned with clotted face toward me, holding the implements of his forgiving trade, waiting for me to bring the wine and wafers to be blessed. I would surge upward, swearing under my breath with the ardor only those who have just learned the words can truly muster, unafraid to be muttering these things as I snatched up the chalice and sniffed the too-sweet murky wine, fetching the plates of wafers, swearing that once the polished walnut altar rail was emptied of its upturned and strangely blank faces, once the simpering organ had ebbed into silence and I had shrugged off these robes swarming with the stench of mothballs, I would have no more of it, I would erase it.

I asked Redman who the hell was logging their stuff into my inventory spaces. He checked. The answer was: nobody. There were no recorded intrusions into those sections of the memory system. *Then look further*, I said, and went back to work at the terminal.

They were still there. What's more, some index numbers that had been free before were now filled.

NGC 1097 still vexed me, but I delayed working on the problem. I studied these new pictures. They were processed, Doppler-coded, and filtered for noise. I switched back to the earlier plates, to be sure. Yes, it was clear: these were different.

Current theory held that the arm of expanding gas was on the outward phase of an oscillation. Several hundred million years ago, so the story went, a massive explosion at the galactic center had started the expansion: a billowing, spinning doughnut of gas swelled outward. Eventually its energy was matched by the gravitational attraction of the massive center. Then, as it slowed and finally fell back toward the center, it spun faster, storing energy in rotational motion, until centrifugal forces stopped its inward rush. Thus the hot cloud could oscillate in the potential well of gravity, cooling slowly.

These computer-transformed plates said otherwise. The Doppler shifts formed a cone. At the center of the plate, maximum values, far higher than any observed before, over a thousand kilometers per second. That exceeded escape velocity from the Galaxy itself. The values tapered off to the sides, coming smoothly down to the shifts that were on the earlier plates.

I called the programming director. He looked over the displays, understanding nothing of what it meant but everything about how it could have gotten there; and his verdict was clean, certain: human error. But further checks turned up no such mistake. "Must be comin' in on the transmission from orbit," he mused. He seemed half-asleep as he punched in commands, traced the intruders. These data had come in from the new combination optical, IR, and UV 'scope in orbit, and the JPL programs had obligingly performed the routine miracles of enhancement and analysis. But the orbital staff were sure no such data had been transmitted. In fact, the 'scope had been down for inspection, plus an alignment check, for over two days. The programming director shrugged and promised to look into it, fingering the innumerable pens clipped in his shirt pocket.

I stared at the Doppler cone, and thumbed to the next index number. The cone had grown, the shifts were larger. Another: still larger. And then I noticed something more; and a cold sensation seeped into me, banishing the casual talk and mechanical-printout stutter of the terminal room.

The point of view had shifted. All the earlier plates had shown a particular gas cloud at a certain angle of inclination. This latest plate was slightly cocked to the side, illuminating a clotted bunch of minor H II regions and obscuring a fraction of the hot, expanding arm. Some new features were revealed. If the JPL program had done such a rotation and shift, it would have left the new spaces blank, for there was no way of filling them in. These were not empty. They brimmed with specific shifts, detailed spectral indices. The JPL program would not have produced the field of numbers unless the raw data contained them. I stared at the screen for a long time.

That evening I drove home the long way, through the wide boulevards of Pasadena, in the gathering dusk. I remembered giving blood the month before, in the eggshell light of the Caltech dispensary. They took the blood away in a curious plastic sack, leaving me with a small bandage in the crook of my elbow. The skin was translucent, showing the riverwork of tributary blue veins, which—recently tapped—were nearly as pale as the skin. I had never looked at that part of me before and found it tender, vulnerable, an unexpected opening. I remembered my wife had liked being stroked there when we were dating, and that I had not touched her there for a long time. Now I had myself been pricked there, to pipe brimming life into a sack, and then to some other who could make use of it.

That evening I drove again, taking my son to Open House. The school bristled with light and seemed to command the neighborhood with its luminosity, drawing families out of their homes. My wife was taking my daughter to another school, and so I was unshielded by her ability to recognize people we knew. I could never sort out their names in time to answer the casual hellos. In our neighborhood the PTA nights draw a disproportionate fraction of technical types, like me. Tonight I saw them without the quicksilver verbal fluency of my wife. They had compact cars that seemed too small for their large families, wore shoes whose casualness offset the formal, just-come-from-work jackets and slacks, and carried creamy folders of their children's accumulated work, to use in conferring with the teachers. The wives were sun-darkened, wearing crisp, print dresses that looked recently put on, and spoke with ironic turns about PTA politics, bond issues, and class sizes. In his classroom my son tugged me from board to board, where he had contributed paragraphs on wildlife. The crowning exhibit was a model of Io, Jupiter's pizza-mocking moon, which he had made from a tennis ball and thick, sulphurous paint. It hung in a box painted black and looked remarkably, ethereally real. My son had won first prize in his class for the mockup moon, and his teacher stressed this as she went over the less welcome news that he was not doing well at his reading. Apparently he arranged the plausible phrases—A, then B, then C—into illogical combinations, C coming before A, despite the instructing commas and semicolons which should have guided him. It was a minor problem, his teacher assured me, but should be looked after. Perhaps a little more reading at home, under my eye? I nodded, sure that the children of the other scientists and computer programmers and engineers did not have this difficulty, and already knew what the instructing phrase of the next century would be, before the end of this one. My son took the news matter-of-factly, unafraid, and went off to help with the cake and Kool-aid. I watched him mingle with girls whose awkwardness was lovely, like giraffes'. I remembered that his teacher (I had learned from gossip) had a mother dying of cancer, which might explain the furrow between her eyebrows that would not go away. My son came bearing cake. I ate it with him, sitting with knees slanting upward in the small chair; and quite calmly and suddenly an idea came to me and would not go away. I turned it over and felt its shape, testing it in a preliminary fashion. Underneath I was both excited and fearful and yet sure that it would survive: it was right. Scraping up the last crumbs and icing, I looked down, and saw my son had drawn a crayon design, an enormous father playing ball with a son, running and catching, the scene carefully fitted into the small compass of the plastic, throwaway plate.

The next morning I finished the data reduction on the slit-image exposures. By carefully covering over the galaxy and background, I had managed to take successive plates which blocked out segments of the space parallel to the brightest blue jet. Photometry of the resulting weak signal could give a cross section of the jet's intensity. Pinpoint calibration then yielded the thickness of the central jet zone.

The data was somewhat scattered, the error bars were larger than I liked, but still—I was sure I had it. The jet had a fuzzy halo and a bright core. The core was less than a hundred light years across, a thin filament of highly ionized hydrogen, cut like a swath through the gauzy dust beyond the galaxy. The resolute, ruler-sharp path, its thinness, its profile of luminosity: all pointed toward a tempting picture. Some energetic object had carved each line, moving at high speeds. It swallowed some of the matter in its path; and in the act of engorgement the mass was heated to incandescent brilliance, spitting UV and X-rays into an immense surrounding volume. This radiation in turn ionized the galactic gas, leaving a scratch of light behind the object, like picnickers dumping luminous trash as they pass by.

The obvious candidates for the fast-moving sources of the jets were black holes. And as I traced the slim profiles of the NGC 1097 jets back into the galaxy, they all intersected at the precise geometrical center of the barred spiral pattern.

Last night, after returning from the Open House with a sleepy boy in tow, I talked with my wife as we undressed. I described my son's home room, his artistic achievements, his teacher. My wife let slip offhandedly some jarring news. I had, apparently, misheard the earlier gossip; perhaps I had mused over some problem while she related the story to me over breakfast. It was not the teacher's mother who had cancer, but the teacher herself. I felt an instant, settling guilt. I could scarcely remember the woman's face, though it was a mere hour later. I asked why she was still working. Because, my wife explained with straightforward New England sense, it was better than staring at a wall. The chemotherapy took only a small slice of her hours. And anyway, she probably needed the money. The night beyond our windows seemed solid, flinty, harder than the soft things inside. In the glass I watched my wife take off a print dress and stretch backward, breasts thinning into crescents, her nobbed spine describing a serene curve that anticipated bed. I went over to my chest of drawers and looked down at the polished walnut surface, scrupulously rectangular and arranged, across which I had tossed the residue of an hour's dutiful parenting: a scrawled essay on marmosets, my son's anthology of drawings, his reading list, and on top, the teacher's bland paragraph of assessment. It felt odd to have called these things into being, these signs of a forward tilt in a small life, by an act of love or at least lust, now years past. The angles appropriate to cradling my children still lived in my hands. I could feel clearly the tentative clutch of my son as he attempted some upright steps. Now my eye strayed to his essay. I could see him struggling with the notion of clauses, with ideas piled upon each other to build a point, and with the caged linearity of the sentence. On the page above, in the loops of the teacher's generous flow pen, I saw a hollow rotundity, a denial of any constriction in her life. She had to go on, this schoolgirl penmanship said, to forcefully forget a gnawing illness among a roomful of bustling children. Despite all the rest, she had to keep on doing.

What could be energetic enough to push black holes out of the galactic center, up the slopes of the deep gravitational potential well? Only another black hole. The dynamics had been worked out years before—as so often happens, in another context—by William Saslaw. Let a bee-swarm of black holes orbit about each other, all caught in a gravitational depression. Occasionally, they veer close together, deforming the space-time nearby, caroming off each other like billiard balls. If several undergo these near-miss collisions at once, a black hole can be ejected from the gravitational trap altogether. More complex collisions can throw pairs of black holes in opposite directions, conserving angular momentum: jets and counter-jets. But why did NGC 1097 display two blue jets and two red? Perhaps the blue ones glowed with the phosphorescent waste left by the largest, most energetic black holes; their counter-jets must be, by some detail of the dynamics, always smaller, weaker, redder.

I went to the jutting, air-conditioned library, and read Saslaw's papers. Given a buzzing hive of black holes in a gravitational well—partly of their own making—

many things could happen. There were compact configurations, tightly orbiting and self-obsessed, which could be ejected as a body. These close-wound families could in turn be unstable, once they were isolated beyond the galaxy's tug, just as the group at the center had been. Caroming off each other, they could eject unwanted siblings. I frowned. This could explain the astonishing right-angle turn the long blue jet made. One black hole thrust sidewise and several smaller, less energetic black holes pushed the opposite way.

As the galactic center lost its warped children, the ejections would become less probable. Things would die down. But how long did that take? NGC 1097 was no younger than our own Galaxy; on the cosmic scale, a sixty-million-year difference was nothing.

In the waning of afternoon—it was only a bit more than twenty-four hours since I first laid out the plates of NGC 1097—the Operations report came in. There was no explanation for the Sagittarius A data. It had been received from the station in orbit and duly processed. But no command had made the scope swivel to that axis. Odd, Operations said, that it pointed in an interesting direction, but no more.

There were two added plates, fresh from processing. I did not mention to Redman in Operations that the resolution of these plates was astonishing, that details in the bloated, spilling clouds were unprecedented. Nor did I point out that the angle of view had tilted further, giving a better perspective on the outward-jutting inferno. With their polynomial percussion, the computers had given what was in the stream of downward-flowing data, numbers that spoke of something being banished from the pivot of our Galaxy.

Caltech is a compact campus. I went to the Athenaeum for coffee, ambling slowly beneath the palms and scented eucalyptus, and circumnavigated the campus on my return. In the varnished perspectives of these tiled hallways, the hammer of time was a set of Dopplered numbers, blue-shifted because the thing rushed toward us, a bulge in the sky. Silent numbers.

There were details to think about, calculations to do, long strings of hypothesis to unfurl like thin flags. I did not know the effect of a penetrating, ionizing flux on Earth. Perhaps it could affect the upper atmosphere and alter the ozone cap that drifts above our heedless heads. A long trail of disturbed, high-energy plasma could fan out through our benign spiral arm—odd, to think of bands of dust and rivers of stars as a neighborhood where you have grown up—churning, working, heating. After all, the jets of NGC 1097 had snuffed out the beaded H II regions as cleanly as an eraser passing across a blackboard, ending all the problems that life knows.

The NGC 1097 data was clean and firm. It would make a good paper, perhaps a letter to *Astrophysical Journal Letters*. But the rest—there was no crisp professional path. These plates had come from much nearer the Galactic center. The information had come outward at light speed, far faster than the pressing bulge, and tilted at a slight angle away from the radial vector that led to Earth.

I had checked the newest Palomar plates from Sagittarius A this afternoon. There were no signs of anything unusual. No Doppler bulge, no exiled mass. They flatly contradicted the satellite plates.

That was the key: old reliable Palomar, our biggest ground-based 'scope, showed nothing. Which meant that someone in high orbit had fed data into our satellite 'scope—exposures which had to be made nearer the Galactic center and then brought here and deftly slipped into our ordinary astronomical research. Exposures which spoke of something stirring where we could not yet see it, beyond the obscuring lanes of dust. The plumes of fiery gas would take a while longer to work through that dark cloak.

These plain facts had appeared on a screen, mute and undeniable, keyed to the data on NGC 1097. Keyed to a connection that another eye than mine could miss. Some astronomer laboring over plates of eclipsing binaries or globular clusters might well have impatiently erased the offending, multicolored spattering, not bothered to uncode the Dopplers, to note the persistent mottled red of the Galactic dust arm at the lower right, and so not known what the place must be. Only I could have made the connection to NGC 1097, and guessed what an onrushing black hole could do to a fragile planet: burn away the ozone layer, hammer the land with high-energy particles, mask the sun in gas and dust.

But to convey this information in this way was so strange, so—yes, that was the word—so alien. Perhaps this was the way they had to do it; quiet, subtle, indirect. Using an oblique analogy which only suggested, yet somehow disturbed more than a direct statement. And of course, this might be only a phrase in a longer message. Moving out from the Galactic center, they would not know we were here until they grazed the expanding bubble of radio noise that gave us away, and so their data would use what they had, views at a different slant. The data itself, raw and silent, would not necessarily call attention to itself. It had to be placed in context, beside NGC 1097. How had they managed to do that? Had they tried before? What odd logic dictated this approach? How. . . .

Take it in pieces. Some of the data I could use, some not. Perhaps a further check, a fresh look through the dusty Sagittarius arm, would show the beginnings of a ruddy swelling, could give a verification. I would have to look, try to find a bridge that would make plausible what I knew but could scarcely prove. The standards of science are austere, unforgiving—and who would have it differently? I would have to hedge, to take one step back for each two forward, to compare and suggest and contrast, always sticking close to the data. And despite what I thought I knew now, the data would have to lead, they would have to show the way.

There is a small Episcopal church, not far up Hill Street, which offers a Friday communion in early evening. Driving home through the surrounding neon consumer gumbo, musing, I saw the sign, and stopped. I had the NGC 1097 plates with me in a carrying case, ripe beneath my arm with their fractional visions, like thin sections of an exotic cell. I went in. The big oak door thumped solemnly shut behind me. In the nave two elderly men were passing woven baskets, taking up the offertory. I took a seat near the back. Idly I surveyed the people, distributed randomly like a field of unthinking stars, in the pews before me. A man came nearby and a pool of brassy light passed before me and I put something in, the debris at the bottom clinking and rustling as I stirred it. I watched the backs of heads as the familiar litany droned on, as devoid of meaning as before. I do not believe, but there is communion. Something tugged at my attention; one head turned a fraction. By a kind of triangulation I deduced the features of the other, closer to the ruddy light of the altar, and saw it was my son's teacher. She was listening raptly. I listened, too, watching her, but could only think of the gnawing at the center of a bustling, swirling galaxy. The lights seemed to dim. The organ had gone silent. *Take, eat. This is the body and blood of* and so it had begun. I waited my turn. I do not believe, but there is communion. The people went forward in their turns. The woman rose; yes, it was she, the kind of woman whose hand would give forth loops and spirals and who would dot her *i*'s with a small circle. The faint timbre of the organ seeped into the layered air. When it was time I was still thinking of NGC 1097, of how I would write the paper—fragments skittered across my mind, the pyramid of the argument was taking shape—and I very nearly missed the gesture of the elderly man at the end of my pew. Halfway to the altar rail I realized that I still carried the case of NGC 1097 exposures, crooked into my elbow, where the pressure caused a slight ache to spread: the spot where they had made the transfusion in the clinic, transferring a fraction of life, blood given. I put it beside me as I knelt. The robes of the approaching figure were cobalt blue and red, a change from the decades since I had been an acolyte. There were no acolytes at such a small service, of course. The blood would follow; first came the offered plate of wafers. Take, eat. Life calling out to life. I could feel the pressing weight of what lay ahead for me, the long roll of years carrying forward one hypothesis, and then, swallowing, knowing that I would never believe this and yet I would want it, I remembered my son, remembered that these events were only pieces, that the puzzle was not yet over, that I would never truly see it done, that as an astronomer I had to live with knowledge forever partial and provisional, that science was not final results but instead a continuing meditation carried on in the face of enormous facts—*take it in phrases*—let the sentences of our lives pile up.

THE PLANNERS

Kate Wilhelm

Kate Wilhelm is one of the most distinguished writers in sf from the 1960s (when her mature work began to appear) to the present. Her public stance, along with her husband Damon Knight, has been always for higher standards in the writing of science fiction. Both through the Milford Writing Workshops for experienced professionals and through years of teaching at the Clarion Workshops for would-be professional sf writers, she has become one of the leading personalities of the sf field. Her many stories and novels, often praised for their characterization and stylistic excellence, include more hard sf than is generally recognized, especially since she became one of the writers in the sixties and early seventies whose book titles (*The Downstairs Room*, 1968; *Abyss*, 1971; *Margaret and I*, 1971) insistently emphasized their contents as "speculative fiction." She is one of the relatively few sf writers who have consistently attempted (and often succeeded) in incorporating science fiction into the nongenre forms of the contemporary short story and novel, of which she has a sure command.

"The Planners" (1968) is one of her finest works, a winner of the Nebula Award for best story. It marks new directions for decades to come in the portrayal and characterization of the scientist in sf. From one perspective, it harks back to the scientists in Hawthorne's "Rappaccini's Daughter" and Robert Louis Stevenson's *Dr. Jekyll and Mr. Hyde* and of course, in J. G. Ballard: the literary investigations of the morality and psychology of scientists; from another it is a landmark in the subcategory of sf dealing with biological experiments in animal and human intelligence, from H. G. Wells's *The Island of Dr. Moreau* to Gordon R. Dickson's "Dolphin's Way," Daniel Keyes's "Flowers for Algernon," Vernor Vinge's "Bookworm, Run," and Pat Murphy's "Rachel in Love," among many others. Wilhelm reverses traditional moral polarities through canny management of point of view to give us a scientist who is perhaps mad, perhaps evil, and yet sympathetic. Robert A. Heinlein was reportedly an admirer of her unusual accomplishment. She succeeds in subtly linking two seeming opposites, the post-Gothic (as in Aldiss and Ballard) and hard sf.

Rae stopped before the one-way glass, stooped and peered at the gibbon infant in the cage. Darin watched her bitterly. She straightened after a moment, hands in smock pockets, face innocent of any expression what-so-goddam-ever, and continued to saunter toward him through the aisle between the cages.

"You still think it is cruel, and worthless?"

"Do you, Dr. Darin?"

"Why do you always do that? Answer my question with one of your own?"

"Does it infuriate you?"

He shrugged and turned away. His lab coat was on the chair where he had tossed it. He pulled it on over his sky-blue sport shirt.

"How is the Driscoll boy?" Rae asked.

He stiffened, then relaxed again. Still not facing her, he said, "Same as last week, last year. Same as he'll be until he dies."

The hall door opened and a very large, very homely face appeared. Stu Evers looked past Darin, down the aisle. "You alone? Thought I heard voices."

"Talking to myself," Darin said. "The committee ready yet?"

"Just about. Dr. Jacobsen is stalling with his nose-throat spray routine, as usual." He hesitated a moment, glancing again down the row of cages, then at Darin. "Wouldn't you think a guy allergic to monkeys would find some other line of research?"

Darin looked, but Rae was gone. What had it been this time: the Driscoll boy, the trend of the project itself? He wondered if she had a life of her own when she was away. "I'll be out at the compound," he said. He passed Stu in the doorway and headed toward the livid greenery of Florida forests.

The cacophony hit him at the door. There were four hundred sixty-nine monkeys on the thirty-six acres of wooded ground the research department was using. Each monkey was screeching, howling, singing, cursing, or otherwise making its presence known. Darin grunted and headed toward the compound. The Happiest Monkeys in the World, a newspaper article had called them. Singing Monkeys, a subhead announced. MONKEYS GIVEN SMARTNESS PILLS, the most enterprising paper had proclaimed. *Cruelty Charged*, added another in subdued, sorrowful tones.

The compound was three acres of carefully planned and maintained wilderness, completely enclosed with thirty-foot-high, smooth plastic walls. A transparent dome covered the area. There were one-way windows at intervals along the wall. A small group stood before one of the windows: the committee.

Darin stopped and gazed over the interior of the compound through one of the windows. He saw Heloise and Skitter contentedly picking nonexistent fleas from one another. Adam was munching on a banana; Homer was lying on his back idly touching his feet to his nose. A couple of the chimps were at the water fountain, not drinking, merely pressing the pedal and watching the fountain, now and then immersing a head or hand in the bowl of cold water. Dr. Jacobsen appeared and Darin joined the group.

"Good morning, Mrs. Bellbottom," Darin said politely. "Did you know your skirt has fallen off?" He turned from her to Major Dormouse. "Ah, Major, and how many of the enemy have you swatted to death today with your pretty little yellow rag?" He smiled pleasantly at a pimply young man with a camera. "Major, you've brought a professional peeping tom. More stories in the paper, with pictures this time?" The pimply young man shifted his position, fidgeted with the camera. The major was fiery; Mrs. Bellbottom was on her knees peering under a bush, looking for her skirt. Darin blinked. None of them had on any clothing. He turned toward the window. The chimps were drawing up a table, laden with tea things, silver, china, tiny finger sandwiches. The chimps were all wearing flowered shirts and dresses. Hortense had on a ridiculous flop-brimmed sun hat of pale green straw. Darin leaned against the fence to control his laughter.

"Soluble ribonucleic acid," Dr. Jacobsen was saying when Darin recovered, "sRNA for short. So from the gross beginnings when entire worms were trained and fed to other worms that seemed to benefit from the original training, we have come to these more refined methods. We now extract the sRNA molecule from the trained animals and feed it, the sRNA molecules in solution, to untrained specimens and observe the results."

The young man was snapping pictures as Jacobsen talked. Mrs. Whoosis was making notes, her mouth a lipless line, the sun hat tinging her skin with green. The sun on her patterned red and yellow dress made it appear to jiggle, giving her fleshy hips a constant rippling motion. Darin watched, fascinated. She was about sixty.

". . . my colleague, who proposed this line of experimentation, Dr. Darin," Jacobsen said finally, and Darin bowed slightly. He wondered what Jacobsen had said about him, decided to wait for any questions before he said anything.

"Dr. Darin, is it true that you also extract this substance from people?"

"Every time you scratch yourself, you lose this substance," Darin said. "Every time you lose a drop of blood, you lose it. It is in every cell of your body. Sometimes we take a sample of human blood for study, yes."

"And inject it into those animals?"

"Sometimes we do that," Darin said. He waited for the next, the inevitable question, wondering how he would answer it. Jacobsen had briefed them on what to answer, but he couldn't remember what Jacobsen had said. The question didn't come. Mrs. Whoosis stepped forward, staring at the window.

Darin turned his attention to her; she averted her eyes, quickly fixed her stare again on the chimps in the compound. "Yes, Mrs. uh . . . Ma'am?" Darin prompted her. She didn't look at him.

"Why? What is the purpose of all this?" she asked. Her voice sounded strangled. The pimpled young man was inching toward the next window.

"Well," Darin said, "our theory is simple. We believe that learning ability can be improved drastically in nearly every species. The learning curve is the normal, expected bell-shaped curve, with a few at one end who have the ability to learn quite rapidly, with the majority in the center who learn at an average rate, and a few at the other end who learn quite slowly. With our experiments we are able to increase the ability of those in the broad middle, as well as those in the deficient end of the curve so that their learning abilities match those of the fastest learners of any given group. . . ."

No one was listening to him. It didn't matter. They would be given the press release he had prepared for them, written in simple language, no polysyllables, no complicated sentences. They were all watching the chimps through the windows. He said, "So we gabbled the gazooka three times wretchedly until the spirit of camping fired the girls." One of the committee members glanced at him. "Whether intravenously or orally, it seems to be equally effective," Darin said, and the perspiring man turned again to the window. "Injections every morning . . . rejections, planned diet, planned parenthood, planned plans planning plans." Jacobsen eyes him suspiciously. Darin stopped talking and lighted a cigarette. The woman with the unquiet hips turned from the window, her face very red. "I've seen enough," she said. "This sun is too hot out here. May we see the inside laboratories now?"

Darin turned them over to Stu Evers inside the building. He walked back slowly to the compound. There was a grin on his lips when he spotted Adam on the far side, swaggering triumphantly, paying no attention to Hortense who was rocking back and forth on her haunches, looking very dazed. Darin saluted Adam, then, whistling, returned to his office. Mrs. Driscoll was due with Sonny at 1 P.M.

Sonny Driscoll was fourteen. He was five feet nine inches, weighed one hundred sixty pounds. His male nurse was six feet two inches and weighed two hundred twenty-seven pounds. Sonny had broken his mother's arm when he was twelve; he had broken his father's arm and leg when he was thirteen. So far the male nurse was intact. Every morning Mrs. Driscoll lovingly washed and bathed her baby, fed him, walked him in the yard, spoke happily to him of plans for the coming months, or sang nursery songs to him. He never seemed to see her. The male nurse, Johnny, was never farther than three feet from his charge when he was on duty.

Mrs. Driscoll refused to think of the day when she would have to turn her child over to an institution. Instead she placed her faith and hope in Darin.

They arrived at two-fifteen, earlier than he had expected them, later than they had planned to be there.

"The kid kept taking his clothes off," Johnny said morosely. The kid was taking them off again in the office. Johnny started toward him, but Darin shook his head. It didn't matter. Darin got his blood sample from one of the muscular arms, shot the injection into the other one. Sonny didn't seem to notice what he was doing. He never seemed to notice. Sonny refused to be tested. They got him to the chair and table, but he sat staring at nothing, ignoring the blocks, the bright balls, the crayons, the candy. Nothing Darin did or said had any discernible effect. Finally the time was up. Mrs. Driscoll and Johnny got him dressed once more and left. Mrs. Driscoll thanked Darin for helping her boy.

Stu and Darin held class from four to five daily. Kelly O'Grady had the monkeys tagged and ready for them when they showed up at the schoolroom. Kelly was very tall, very slender and red-haired. Stu shivered if she accidentally brushed him in passing; Darin hoped one day Stu would pull an Adam on her. She sat primly on her high stool with her notebook on her knee, unaware of the change that came over Stu during school hours, or, if aware, uncaring. Darin wondered if she was really a Barbie doll fully programmed to perform laboratory duties, and nothing else.

He thought of the Finishing School for Barbies where long-legged, high-breasted, stomachless girls went to get shaved clean, get their toenails painted pink, their nipples removed, and all body openings sewn shut, except for their mouths, which curved in perpetual smiles and led nowhere.

The class consisted of six black spider-monkeys who had not been fed yet. They had to do six tasks in order: 1) pull a rope; 2) cross the cage and get a stick that was released by the rope; 3) pull the rope again; 4) get the second stick that would fit into the first; 5) join the sticks together; 6) using the lengthened stick, pull a bunch of bananas close enough to the bars of the cage to reach them and take them inside where they could eat them. At five the monkeys were returned to Kelly, who wheeled them away one by one back to the stockroom. None of them had performed all the tasks, although two had gone through part of them before the time ran out.

Waiting for the last of the monkeys to be taken back to its quarters, Stu asked, "What did you do to that bunch of idiots this morning? By the time I got them, they all acted dazed."

Darin told him about Adam's performance; they were both laughing when Kelly returned. Stu's laugh turned to something that sounded almost like a sob. Darin wanted to tell him about the school Kelly must have attended, thought better of it, and walked away instead.

His drive home was through the darkening forests of interior Florida for sixteen miles on a narrow straight road.

"Of course, I don't mind living here," Lea had said once, nine years ago when the Florida appointment had come through. And she didn't mind. The house was air-conditioned; the family car, Lea's car, was air-conditioned; the back yard had a swimming pool big enough to float the Queen Mary. A frightened, large-eyed Florida girl did the housework, and Lea gained weight and painted sporadically, wrote sporadically—poetry—and entertained faculty wives regularly. Darin suspected that sometimes she entertained faculty husbands also.

"Oh, Professor Dimples, one hour this evening? That will be fifteen dollars, you know." He jotted down the appointment and turned to Lea. "Just two more today and you will have your car payment. How about that!" She twined slinky arms about his neck, pressing tight high breasts hard against him. She had to tilt her head slightly for his kiss. "Then your turn, darling. For free." He tried to kiss her; something stopped his tongue, and he realized that the smile was on the outside only, that the opening didn't really exist at all.

He parked next to an MG, not Lea's, and went inside the house where the martinis were always snapping cold.

"Darling, you remember Greta, don't you? She is going to give me lessons twice a week. Isn't that exciting?"

"But you already graduated," Darin murmured. Greta was not tall and not long-legged. She was a little bit of a thing. He thought probably he did remember her from somewhere or other, vaguely. Her hand was cool in his.

"Greta has moved in; she is going to lecture on modern art for the spring semester. I asked her for private lessons and she said yes."

"Greta Farrel," Darin said, still holding her small hand. They moved away from Lea and wandered through the open windows to the patio where the scent of orange blossoms was heavy in the air.

"Greta thinks it must be heavenly to be married to a psychologist." Lea's voice followed them. "Where are you two?"

"What makes you say a thing like that?" Darin asked.

"Oh, when I think of how you must understand a woman, know her moods and the reasons for them. You must know just what to do and when, and when to do something else . . . Yes, just like that."

His hands on her body were hot, her skin was cool. Lea's petulant voice drew closer. He held Greta in his arms and stepped into the pool where they sank to the bottom, still together. She hadn't gone to the Barbie School. His hands learned her body; then his body learned hers. After they made love, Greta drew back from him regretfully.

"I do have to go now. You are a lucky man, Dr. Darin. No doubts about yourself, complete understanding of what makes you tick."

He lay back on the leather couch staring at the ceiling. "It's always that way, Doctor. Fantasies, dreams, illusions. I know it is because this investigation is hanging over us right now, but even when things are going relatively well, I still go off on a tangent like that for no real reason." He stopped talking.

In his chair Darin stirred slightly, his fingers drumming softly on the arm, his gaze on the clock whose hands were stuck. He said, "Before this recent pressure, did you have such intense fantasies?"

"I don't think so," Darin said thoughtfully, trying to remember.

The other didn't give him time. He asked, "And can you break out of them now when you have to, or want to?"

"Oh, sure," Darin said.

Laughing, he got out of his car, patted the MG, and walked into his house. He could hear voices from the living room and he remembered that on Thursdays Lea really did have her painting lesson.

Dr. Lacey left five minutes after Darin arrived. Lacey said vague things about Lea's great promise and untapped talent, and Darin nodded sober agreement. If she had talent, it certainly was untapped so far. He didn't say so.

Lea was wearing a hostess suit, flowing sheer panels of pale blue net over a skin-tight leotard that was midnight blue. Darin wondered if she realized that she had gained weight in the past few years. He thought not.

"Oh, that man is getting impossible," she said when the MG blasted away from their house. "Two years now, and he still doesn't want to put my things on show."

Looking at her, Darin wondered how much more her things could be on show.

"Don't dawdle too long with your martini," she said. "We're due at the Ritters' at seven for clams."

The telephone rang for him while he was showering. It was Stu Evers. Darin stood dripping water while he listened.

"Have you seen the evening paper yet? That broad made the statement that conditions are extreme at the station, that our animals are made to suffer unnecessarily."

Darin groaned softly. Stu went on, "She is bringing her entire women's group out tomorrow to show proof of her claims. She's a bigwig in the SPCA, or something."

Darin began to laugh then. Mrs. Whoosis had her face pressed against one of the windows, other fat women in flowered dresses had their faces against the rest. None of them breathed or moved. Inside the compound Adam laid Hortense, then moved on to Esmeralda, to Hilda . . .

"God damn it, Darin, it isn't funny!" Stu said.

"But it is. It is."

Clams at the Ritters' were delicious. Clams, hammers, buckets of butter, a mountainous salad, beer, and finally coffee liberally laced with brandy. Darin felt cheerful and contented when the evening was over. Ritter was in Med. Eng. Lit. but he didn't talk about it, which was merciful. He was sympathetic about the stink with the SPCA. He thought scientists had no imagination. Darin agreed with him and soon he and Lea were on their way home.

"I am so glad that you didn't decide to stay late," Lea said, passing over the yellow line with a blast of the horn. "There is a movie on tonight that I am dying to see."

She talked, but he didn't listen, training of twelve years drawing out an occasional grunt at what must have been appropriate times. "Ritter is such a bore," she said. They were nearly home. "As if you had anything to do with that incredible statement in tonight's paper."

"What statement?"

"Didn't you even read the article? For heaven's sake, why not? Everyone will be talking about it . . ." She sighed theatrically. "Someone quoted a reliable source who said that within the foreseeable future, simply by developing the leads you now have, you will be able to produce monkeys that are as smart as normal human beings." She laughed, a brittle meaningless sound.

"I'll read the article when we get home," he said. She didn't ask about the statement, didn't care if it was true or false, if he had made it or not. He read the article while she settled down before the television. Then he went for a swim. The water was warm, the breeze cool on his skin. Mosquitoes found him as soon as he got out of the pool, so he sat behind the screening of the verandah. The bluish light from the living room went off after a time and there was only the dark night. Lea didn't call him when she went to bed. He knew she went very softly, closing the door with care so that the click of the latch wouldn't disturb him if he was dozing on the verandah.

He knew why he didn't break it off. Pity. The most corrosive emotion endogenous to man. She was the product of the doll school that taught that the trip down the aisle was the end, the fulfillment of a maiden's dreams; shocked and horrified to learn that it was another beginning, some of them never recovered. Lea never had. Never would. At sixty she would purse her lips at the sexual display of uncivilized animals, whether human or not, and she would be disgusted and help formulate laws to ban such activities. Long ago he had hoped a child would be the answer, but the school did something to them on the inside too. They didn't conceive, or if conception took place, they didn't carry the fruit, and if they carried it, the birth was of a stillborn thing. The ones that did live were usually the ones to be pitied more than those who fought and were defeated *in utero*.

A bat swooped low over the quiet pool and was gone again against the black of the azaleas. Soon the moon would appear, and the chimps would stir restlessly for a while, then return to deep untroubled slumber. The chimps slept companionably close to one another, without thought of sex. Only the nocturnal creatures, and the human creatures, performed coitus in the dark. He wondered if Adam remembered his human captors. The colony in the compound had been started almost twenty years ago, and since then none of the chimps had seen a human being. When it was necessary to enter the grounds, the chimps were fed narcotics in the evening to insure against their waking. Props were changed then, new obstacles added to the old conquered ones. Now and then a chimp was removed for study, usually ending up in dissection. But not Adam. He was father of the world. Darin grinned in the darkness.

Adam took his bride aside from the other beasts and knew that she was lovely. She was his own true bride, created for him, intelligence to match his own burning intelligence. Together they scaled the smooth walls and glimpsed the great world that lay beyond their garden. Together they found the opening that led to the world that was to be theirs, and they left behind them the lesser beings. And the god searched for them and finding them not, cursed them and sealed the opening so that none of the others could follow. So it was that Adam and his bride became the first man and woman and from them flowed the progeny that was to inhabit the entire world. And one day Adam said, for shame woman, seest thou that thou art naked? And the woman answered, so are you, big boy, so are you. So they covered their nakedness with leaves from the trees, and thereafter they performed their sexual act in the dark of night so that man could not look on his woman, nor she on him. And they were thus cleansed of shame. Forever and ever. Amen. Hallelujah.

Darin shivered. He had drowsed after all, and the night wind had grown chill. He went to bed. Lea drew away from him in her sleep. She felt hot to his touch. He turned to his left side, his back to her, and he slept.

"There is potential *x*," Darin said to Lea the next morning at breakfast. "We don't know where *x* is actually. It represents the highest intellectual achievement possible for the monkeys, for example. We test each new batch of monkeys that we get and sort them—*x*-1, *x*-2, *x*-3, suppose, and then we breed for more *x*-1's. Also we feed the other two groups the sRNA that we extract from the original *x*-1's. Eventually we get a monkey that is higher than our original *x*-1, and we reclassify right down the line and start over, using his sRNA to bring the others up to his level. We make constant checks to make sure we aren't allowing inferior strains to mingle with our highest achievers, and we keep control groups that are given the same training, the same food, the same sorting process, but no sRNA. We test them against each other."

Lea was watching his face with some interest as he talked. He thought he had got through, until she said, "Did you realize that your hair is almost solid white at the temples? All at once it is turning white."

Carefully he put his cup back on the saucer. He smiled at her and got up. "See you tonight," he said.

They also had two separate compounds of chimps that had started out identically. Neither had received any training whatever through the years; they had been kept isolated from each other and from man. Adam's group had been fed sRNA daily from the most intelligent chimps they had found. The control group had been fed none. The control-group chimps had yet to master the intricacies of the fountain with its ice-cold water; they used the small stream that flowed through the compound. The control group had yet to learn that fruit on the high, fragile branches could be had, if one used the telescoping sticks to knock them down. The control group huddled without protection, or under the scant cover of palm-trees when it rained and the dome was opened. Adam long ago had led his group in the construction of a rude but functional hut where they gathered when it rained.

Darin saw the women's committee filing past the compound when he parked his car. He went straight to the console in his office, flicked on a switch and manipulated buttons and dials, leading the group through the paths, opening one, closing another to them, until he led them to the newest of the compounds, where he opened the gate and let them inside. Quickly he closed the gate again and watched their frantic efforts to get out. Later he turned the chimps loose on them, and his grin grew broader as he watched the new-men ravage the old women. Some of the offspring were black and hairy, others pink and hairless, some intermediate. They grew rapidly, lined up with arms extended to receive their daily doses, stood before a machine that tested them instantaneously, and were sorted. Some of them went into a disintegration room, others out into the world.

A car horn blasted in his ears. He switched off his ignition and he got out as Stu Evers parked next to his car. "I see the old bats got here," Stu said. He walked toward the lab with Darin. "How's the Driscoll kid coming along?"

"Negative," Darin said. Stu knew they had tried using human sRNA on the boy, and failed consistently. It was too big a step for his body to cope with. "So far he has shown total intolerance to A-127. Throws it off almost instantly."

Stuart was sympathetic and noncommital. No one else had any faith whatever in Darin's own experiment. A-127 might be too great a step upward, Darin thought. The *Ateles* spider monkey from Brazil was too bright.

He called Kelly from his office and asked about the newly arrived spider monkeys they had tested the day before. Blood had been processed; a sample was available. He looked over his notes and chose one that had shown interest in the tasks without finishing any of them. Kelly promised him the prepared syringe by 1 P.M.

What no one connected with the project could any longer doubt was that those simians, and the men that had been injected with sRNA from the Driscoll boy, had actually had their learning capacities inhibited, some of them apparently permanently.

Darin didn't want to think about Mrs. Driscoll's reaction if ever she learned how they had been using her boy. Rae sat at the corner of his desk and drawled insolently, "I might tell her myself, Dr. Darin. I'll say, Sorry, Ma'am, you'll have to keep your idiot out of here; you're damaging the brains of our monkeys with his polluted blood. Okay, Darin?"

"My God, what are you doing back again?"

"Testing," she said. "That's all, just testing."

Stu called him to observe the latest challenge to Adam's group, to take place in forty minutes. Darin had forgotten that he was to be present. During the night a tree had been felled in each compound, its trunk crossing the small stream, damming it. At eleven the water fountains were to be turned off for the rest of the day. The tree had been felled at the far end of the compound, close to the wall where the stream entered, so that the trickle of water that flowed past the hut was cut off. Already the group not taking sRNA was showing signs of thirst. Adam's group was unaware of the interrupted flow.

Darin met Stu and they walked together to the far side where they would have a good view of the entire compound. The women had left by then. "It was too quiet for them this morning," Stu said. "Adam was making his rounds; he squatted on the felled tree for nearly an hour before he left it and went back to the others."

They could see the spreading pool of water. It was muddy, uninviting looking. At eleven-ten it was generally known within the compound that the water supply had failed. Some of the old chimps tried the fountain; Adam tried it several times. He hit it with a stick and tried it again. Then he sat on his haunches and stared at it. One of the young chimps whimpered pitiably. He wasn't thirsty yet, merely puzzled and perhaps frightened. Adam scowled at him. The chimp cowered behind Hortense, who bared her fangs at Adam. He waved menacingly at her, and she began picking fleas from her offspring. When he whimpered again, she cuffed him. The young chimp looked from her to Adam, stuck his forefinger in his mouth and ambled away. Adam continued to stare at the useless fountain. An hour passed. At last Adam rose and wandered nonchalantly toward the drying stream. Here and there a shrinking pool of muddy water steamed in the sun. The other chimps followed Adam. He followed the stream through the compound toward the wall that was its source. When he came to the pool he squatted again. One of the young chimps circled the pool cautiously, reached down and touched the dirty water, drew back, reached for it again, and then drank. Several of the others drank also. Adam continued to squat. At twelve-forty Adam moved again. Grunting and gesturing to several younger males, he approached the tree-trunk. With much noise and meaningless gestures, they shifted the trunk. They strained, shifted it again. The water was released and poured over the heaving chimps. Two of them dropped the trunk and ran. Adam and the other two held. The two returned.

They were still working when Darin had to leave, to keep his appointment with Mrs. Driscoll and Sonny. They arrived at one-ten. Kelly had left the syringe with the new formula in Darin's small refrigerator. He injected Sonny, took his sample, and started the tests. Sometimes Sonny cooperated to the extent of lifting one of the articles from the table and throwing it. Today he cleaned the table within ten minutes. Darin put a piece of candy in his hand; Sonny threw it from him. Patiently Darin put another piece in the boy's hand. He managed to keep the eighth piece in the clenched hand long enough to guide the hand to Sonny's mouth. When it was gone, Sonny opened his mouth for more. His hands lay idly on the table. He didn't seem to relate the hands to the candy with the pleasant taste. Darin tried to guide a second to his mouth, but Sonny refused to hold a piece a second time.

When the hour was over and Sonny was showing definite signs of fatigue, Mrs. Driscoll clutched Darin's hands in hers. Tears stood in her eyes. "You actually got him to feed himself a little bit," she said brokenly. "God bless you, Dr. Darin. God bless you!" She kissed his hand and turned away as the tears started to spill down her cheeks.

Kelly was waiting for him when the group left. She collected the new sample of blood to be processed. "Did you hear about the excitement down at the compound? Adam's building a dam of his own."

Darin stared at her for a moment. The breakthrough? He ran back to the compound. The near side this time was where the windows were being used. It seemed that the entire staff was there, watching silently. He saw Stu and edged in by him. The stream twisted and curved through the compound, less than ten inches deep, not over two feet anywhere. At one spot stones lay under it; elsewhere the bottom was of hard-packed sand. Adam and his crew were piling up stones at the one suitable place for their dam, very near their hut. The dam they were building was two feet thick. It was less than five feet from the wall, fifteen feet from where Darin and Stu shared the window. When the dam was completed, Adam looked along the wall. Darin thought the chimp's eyes paused momentarily on his own. Later he heard that nearly every other person watching felt the same momentary pause as those black, intelligent eyes sought out and held other intelligence.

". . . next thunderstorm. Adam and the flood . . ."

". . . eventually seeds instead of food . . ."

". . . his brain. Convolutions as complex as any man's."

Darin walked away from them, snatches of future plans in his ears. There was a memo on his desk. Jacobsen was turning over the SPCA investigatory committee to him. He was to meet with the university representatives, the local SPCA group, and the legal representatives of all concerned on Monday next at 10 A.M. He wrote out his daily report on Sonny Driscoll. Sonny had been on too good behavior for too long. Would this last injection give him just the spark of determination he needed to go on a rampage? Darin had alerted Johnny, the bodyguard, whoops, male nurse, for just such a possibility, but he knew Johnny didn't think there was any danger from the kid. He hoped Sonny wouldn't kill Johnny, then turn on his mother and father. He'd probably rape his mother, if that much goal-directedness ever flowed through him. And the three men who had volunteered for the injections from Sonny's blood? He didn't want to think of them at all, therefore couldn't get them out of his mind as he sat at his desk staring at nothing. Three convicts. That's all, just convicts hoping to get a parole for helping science along. He laughed abruptly. They weren't planning anything now. Not that trio. Not planning for a thing. Sitting, waiting for something to happen, not thinking about what it might be, or when, or how they would be affected. Not thinking. Period.

"But you can always console yourself that your motives were pure, that it was all for Science, can't you, Dr. Darin?" Rae asked mockingly.

He looked at her. "Go to hell," he said.

It was late when he turned off his light. Kelly met him in the corridor that led to the main entrance. "Hard day, Dr. Darin?"

He nodded. Her hand lingered momentarily on his arm. "Good night," she said, turning in to her own office. He stared at the door for a long time before he let himself out and started toward his car. Lea would be furious with him for not calling. Probably she wouldn't speak at all until nearly bedtime, when she would explode into tears and accusations. He could see the time when her tears and accusations would strike home, when Kelly's body would be a tangible memory, her words lingering in his ears. And he would lie to Lea, not because he would care actually if she knew, but because it would be expected. She wouldn't know how to cope with the truth. It would entangle her to the point where she would have to try an abortive suicide, a screaming-for-attention attempt that would ultimately tie him in tear-soaked knots that would never be loosened. No, he would lie, and she would know he was lying, and they would get by. He started the car, aimed down the long sixteen miles that lay before him. He wondered where Kelly lived. What it would do to Stu when he realized. What it would do to his job if Kelly should get nasty, eventually. He shrugged. Barbie dolls never got nasty. It wasn't built in.

Lea met him at the door, dressed only in a sheer gown, her hair loose and unsprayed. Her body flowed into his so that he didn't need Kelly at all. And he was best man when Stu and Kelly were married. He called to Rae, "Would that satisfy you?" but she didn't answer. Maybe she was gone for good this time. He parked the car outside his darkened house and leaned his head on the steering wheel for a moment before getting out. If not gone for good, at least for a long time. He hoped she would stay away for a long time.

BEEP

James Blish

James Blish was one of the leading intellectuals of the science fiction field, whose critical mind was respected, whose sharp wit was feared, whose serious approach to sf writing and criticism led Brian W. Aldiss to observe "a sense of inhuman drama is never far from his intricate surfaces," and "he was also a master of the telling detail, without which the gigantic has no meaning." In addition, Blish was a knowledgeable music critic and an amateur James Joyce scholar of some repute. Richard Ellmann, the eminent Joycean and Professor of American Literature at Oxford, mentioned to me hearing a paper of Blish's at an academic conference. Blish moved permanently to England in the sixties, where his writing was taken more seriously as contemporary literature than in the United States. His major achievements in science fiction are generally regarded as the four-volume *Cities in Flight* (1970), and *A Case of Conscience* (1958), a classic theological sf novel. His short fiction collected in *The Seedling Stars* (1957), *The Best of James Blish* (1979), and several other volumes, is also a major body of work in the modern field. His scholarly aspect is more evident in novels, such as his fantasy *Black Easter* (1968), or his historical, *Doctor Mirabilis* (1964), than in stories such as "Beep."

What is evident here is his speculative and intellectual rigor, and the intensity of his fascination with science, logic, and metaphysics. Blish presents the outline for a strictly deterministic utopia through a series of entertaining narrative devices. The wonder of the story arises from following its narrative logic to a sudden understanding and appreciation of the scale of the idea, which combines the very large and the very small, both literally and symbolically, in the beep. One of the hallmarks of classic hard sf is the embodiment of abstract and scientific ideas in concrete imagery (usually visual—in this case aural), to connect the intellectual with an emotional experience. The ability to do this regularly was one of Blish's strengths as a writer and made him a leader in the field. It is worth noting that Blish expanded this story later in his career into the novel *The Quincunx of Time* (1973), and that the longer version is disappointingly discursive. Such writers as Brian Aldiss, Ian Watson, and Bruce Sterling carry on the intellectual tradition of Blish today.

I

Josef Faber lowered his newspaper slightly. Finding the girl on the park bench looking his way, he smiled the agonizingly embarrassed smile of the thoroughly married nobody caught bird-watching, and ducked back into the paper again.

He was reasonably certain that he looked the part of a middle-aged, steadily employed, harmless citizen enjoying a Sunday break in the bookkeeping and family routines. He was also quite certain, despite his official instructions, that it wouldn't make the slightest bit of difference if he didn't. These boy-meets-girl assignments always came off. Jo had never tackled a single one that had required him.

As a matter of fact, the newspaper, which he was supposed to be using only as a blind, interested him a good deal more than his job did. He had only barely begun to suspect the obvious ten years ago when the Service had snapped him up; now, after a decade as an agent, he was still fascinated to see how smoothly the really important situations came off. The *dangerous* situations—not boy-meets-girl.

This affair of the Black Horse Nebula, for instance. Some days ago the papers and the commentators had begun to mention reports of disturbances in that area, and Jo's practiced eye had picked up the mention. Something big was cooking.

Today it had boiled over—the Black Horse Nebula had suddenly spewed ships by the hundreds, a massed armada that must have taken more than a century of effort on the part of a whole star cluster, a production drive conducted in the strictest and most fanatical kind of secrecy. . . .

And, of course, the Service had been on the spot in plenty of time. With three times as many ships, disposed with mathematical precision so as to enfilade the entire armada the moment it broke from the nebula. The battle had been a massacre, the attack smashed before the average citizen could even begin to figure out what it had been aimed at—and good had triumphed over evil once more.

Of course.

Furtive scuffings on the gravel drew his attention briefly. He looked at his watch, which said 14:58:03. That was the time, according to his instructions, when boy had to meet girl.

He had been given the strictest kind of orders to let nothing interfere with this meeting—the orders always issued on boy-meets-girl assignments. But, as usual, he had nothing to do but observe. The meeting was coming off on the dot, without any prodding from Jo. They always did.

Of course.

With a sigh, he folded his newspaper, smiling again at the couple—yes, it was the right man, too—and moved away, as if reluctantly. He wondered what would happen were he to pull away the false mustache, pitch the newspaper on the grass, and bound away with a joyous whoop. He suspected that the course of history would not be deflected by even a second of arc, but he was not minded to try the experiment.

The park was pleasant. The twin suns warmed the path and the greenery without any of the blasting heat which they would bring to bear later in the summer. Randolph was altogether the most comfortable planet he had visited in years. A little backward, perhaps, but restful, too.

It was also slightly over a hundred light-years away from Earth. It would be interesting to know how Service headquarters on Earth could have known in advance that boy would meet girl at a certain spot on Randolph, precisely at 14:58:03.

Or how Service headquarters could have ambushed with micrometric precision a major interstellar fleet, with no more preparation than a few days' buildup in the newspapers and video could evidence.

The press was free, on Randolph as everywhere. It reported the news it got. Any emergency concentration of Service ships in the Black Horse area, or anywhere else, would have been noticed and reported on. The Service did not forbid such reports for "security" reasons or for any other reasons. Yet there had been nothing to report but that (a) an armada of staggering size had erupted with no real warning from the Black Horse Nebula, and that (b) the Service had been ready.

By now, it was a commonplace that the Service was always ready. It had not had a defect or a failure in well over two centuries. It had not even had a fiasco, the alarming-sounding technical word by which it referred to the possibility that a boy-meets-girl assignment might not come off.

Jo hailed a hopper. Once inside he stripped himself of the mustache, the bald spot, the forehead creases—all the makeup which had given him his mask of friendly innocuousness.

The hoppy watched the whole process in the rear-view mirror. Jo glanced up and met his eyes.

"Pardon me, mister, but I figured you didn't care if I saw you. You must be a Service man."

"That's right. Take me to Service HQ, will you?"

"Sure enough." The hoppy gunned his machine. It rose smoothly to the express level. "First time I ever got close to a Service man. Didn't hardly believe it at first when I saw you taking your face off. You sure looked different."

"Have to, sometimes," Jo said, preoccupied.

"I'll bet. No wonder you know all about everything before it breaks. You must have a thousand faces each, your own mother wouldn't know you, eh? Don't you care if I know about your snooping around in disguise?"

Jo grinned. The grin created a tiny pulling sensation across one curve of his cheek, just next to his nose. He stripped away the overlooked bit of tissue and examined it critically.

"Of course not. Disguise is an elementary part of Service work. Anyone could guess that. We don't use it often, as a matter of fact—only on very simple assignments."

"Oh." The hoppy sounded slightly disappointed, as melodrama faded. He drove silently for about a minute. Then, speculatively: "Sometimes I think the Service must have time-travel, the things they pull. . . . Well, here you are. Good luck, mister."

"Thanks."

Jo went directly to Krasna's office. Krasna was a Randolpher. Earth-trained, and answerable to the Earth office, but otherwise pretty much on his own. His heavy, muscular face wore the same expression of serene confidence that was characteristic of Service officials everywhere—even some that, technically speaking, had no faces to wear it.

"Boy meets girl," Jo said briefly. "On the nose and on the spot."

"Good work, Jo. Cigarette?" Krasna pushed the box across his desk.

"Nope, not now. Like to talk to you, if you've got time."

Krasna pushed a button, and a toadstoollike chair rose out of the floor behind Jo. "What's on your mind?"

"Well," Jo said carefully. "I'm wondering why you patted me on the back just now for not doing a job."

"You did a job."

"I did not," Jo said flatly. "Boy would have met girl, whether I'd been here on Randolph or back on Earth. The course of true love always runs smooth. It has in all my boy-meets-girl cases, and it has in the boy-meets-girl cases of every other agent with whom I've compared notes."

"Well, good," Krasna said, smiling. "That's the way we like to have it run. And that's the way we expect it to run. But, Jo, we like to have somebody on the spot, somebody with a reputation for resourcefulness, just in case there's a snag. There almost never is, as you've observed. But—if there were?"

Jo snorted. "If what you're trying to do is to establish preconditions for the future, any interference by a Service agent would throw the eventual result farther *off* the track. I know that much about probability."

"And what makes you think that we're trying to set up the future?"

"It's obvious even to the hoppies on your own planet; the one that brought me here told me he thought the Service had time-travel. It's especially obvious to all the individuals and governments and entire populations that the Service has bailed out of serious messes for centuries, with never a single failure." Jo shrugged. "A man can be asked to safeguard only a small number of boy-meets-girl cases before he realizes, as an agent, that what the Service is safeguarding is the future children of those meetings. Ergo—the Service *knows* what those children are to be like, and has reason to want their future existence guaranteed. What other conclusion is possible?"

Krasna took out a cigarette and lit it deliberately; it was obvious that he was using the maneuver to cloak his response.

"None," he admitted at last. "We have some foreknowledge, of course. We couldn't have made our reputation with espionage alone. But we have obvious other advantages: genetics, for instance, and operations research, the theory of games, the Dirac transmitter—it's quite an arsenal, and of course there's a good deal of prediction involved in all those things."

"I see that," Jo said. He shifted in his chair, formulating all he wanted to say. He changed his mind about the cigarette and helped himself to one. "But these things don't add up to infallibility—and that's a qualitative difference, Kras. Take this affair of the Black Horse armada. The moment the armada appeared, we'll assume, Earth heard about it by Dirac, and started to assemble a counterarmada. But it takes *finite time* to bring together a concentration of ships and men, even if your message system is instantaneous.

"The Service's counterarmada was *already on hand*. It had been building there for so long and with so little fuss that nobody even noticed it concentrating until a day or so before the battle. Then planets in the area began to sit up and take notice, and be uneasy about what was going to break. But not very uneasy; the Service always wins—that's been a statistical fact for centuries. *Centuries*, Kras. Good Lord, it takes almost as long as that, in straight preparation, to pull some of the tricks we've pulled! The Dirac gives us an advantage of ten to twenty-five years in really extreme cases out on the rim of the Galaxy, but no more than that."

He realized that he had been fuming away on the cigarette until the roof of his mouth was scorched, and snubbed it out angrily. "That's a very different thing," he said, "than knowing in a general way how an enemy is likely to behave, or what kind of children the Mendelian laws say a given couple should have. It means that we've some way of reading the future in minute detail. That's in flat contradiction to everything I've been taught about probability, but I have to believe what I see."

Krasna laughed. "That's a very able presentation," he said. He seemed genuinely pleased. "I think you'll remember that you were first impressed into the Service when you began to wonder why the news was always good. Fewer and fewer people wonder about that nowadays; it's become a part of their expected environment." He stood up and ran a hand through his hair. "Now you've carried yourself through the next stage. Congratulations, Jo. You've just been promoted!"

"I have?" Jo said incredulously. "I came in here with the notion that I might get myself fired."

"No. Come around to this side of the desk, Jo, and I'll play you a little history." Krasna unfolded the desktop to expose a small visor screen. Obediently Jo rose and went around the desk to where he could see the blank surface. "I had a standard indoctrination tape sent up to me a week ago, in the expectation that you'd be ready to see it. Watch."

Krasna touched the board. A small dot of light appeared in the center of the screen and went out again. At the same time, there was a small *beep* of sound. Then the tape began to unroll and a picture clarified on the screen.

"As you suspected," Krasna said conversationally, "the Service is infallible. How it got that way is a story that started several centuries back."

II

Dana Lje—her father had been a Hollander, her mother born in the Celebes—sat down in the chair which Captain Robin Weinbaum had indicated, crossed her legs, and waited, her blue-black hair shining under the lights.

Weinbaum eyed her quizzically. The conqueror Resident who had given the girl her entirely European name had been paid in kind, for his daughter's beauty had nothing fair and Dutch about it. To the eye of the beholder, Dana Lje seemed a particularly delicate virgin of Bali, despite her Western name, clothing and assurance. The combination had already proven piquant for the millions who watched her television column, and Weinbaum found it no less charming at first hand.

"As one of your most recent victims," he said, "I'm not sure that I'm honored, Miss Lje. A few of my wounds are still bleeding. But I am a good deal puzzled as to why you're visiting me now. Aren't you afraid that I'll bite back?"

"I had no intention of attacking you personally, and I don't think I did," the video columnist said seriously. "It was just pretty plain that our intelligence had slipped badly in the Erskine affair. It was my job to say so. Obviously you were going to get hurt, since you're head of the bureau—but there was no malice in it."

"Cold comfort," Weinbaum said dryly. "But thank you, nevertheless."

The Eurasian girl shrugged. "That isn't what I came here about, anyway. Tell me, Captain Weinbaum—have you ever heard of an outfit calling itself Interstellar Information?"

Weinbaum shook his head. "Sounds like a skip-tracing firm. Not an easy business, these days."

"That's just what I thought when I first saw their letterhead," Dana said. "But the letter under it wasn't one that a private-eye outfit would write. Let me read part of it to you."

Her slim fingers burrowed in her inside jacket pocket and emerged again with a single sheet of paper. It was plain typewriter bond, Weinbaum noted automatically: she had brought only a copy with her, and had left the original of the letter at home. The copy, then, would be incomplete—probably seriously.

"It goes like this: 'Dear Miss Lje: As a syndicated video commentator with a wide audience and heavy responsibilities, you need the best sources of information available. We would like you to test our service, free of charge, in the hope of proving to you that it is superior to any other source of news on Earth. Therefore, we offer below several predictions concerning events to come in the Hercules and the so-called "Three Ghosts" areas. If these predictions are fulfilled 100 per cent—no less—we ask that you take us on as your correspondents for those areas, at rates to be agreed upon later. If the predictions are wrong in *any* respect, you need not consider us further.' "

"H'm," Weinbaum said slowly. "They're confident cusses—and that's an odd juxtaposition. The Three Ghosts make up only a little solar system, while the Hercules area could include the entire star cluster—or maybe even the whole constellation, which is a hell of a lot of sky. This outfit seems to be trying to tell you that it has thousands of field correspondents of its own, maybe as many as the government itself. If so, I'll guarantee that they're bragging."

"That may well be so. But before you make up your mind, let me read you one of the two predictions." The letter rustled in Dana Lje's hand. " 'At 03:16:10, on Year Day, 2090, the Hess-type interstellar liner *Brindisi* will be attacked in the neighborhood of the Three Ghosts system by four——' "

Weinbaum sat bolt upright in his swivel chair. "Let me see that letter!" he said, his voice harsh with repressed alarm.

"In a moment," the girl said, adjusting her skirt composedly. "Evidently I was right in riding my hunch. Let me go on reading: '—by four heavily armed vessels flying the lights of the navy of Hammersmith II. The position of the liner at that time will be at coded co-ordinates 88-A-theta-88-aleph-D and-per-se-and. It will——' "

"Miss Lje," Weinbaum said. "I'm sorry to interrupt you again, but what you've said already would justify me in jailing you at once, no matter how loudly your sponsors might scream. I don't know about this Interstellar Information outfit, or whether or not you did receive any such letter as the one you pretend to be quoting. But I can tell you that you've shown yourself to be in possession of information that only yours truly and four other men are supposed to know. It's already too late to tell you that everything you say may be held against you; all I can say now is, it's high time you clammed up!"

"I thought so," she said, apparently not disturbed in the least. "Then that liner *is* scheduled to hit those co-ordinates, and the coded time co-ordinate corresponds with the predicted Universal Time. Is it also true that the *Brindisi* will be carrying a top-secret communication device?"

"Are you deliberately trying to make me imprison you?" Weinbaum said, gritting his teeth. "Or is this just a stunt, designed to show me that my own bureau is full of leaks?"

"It could turn into that," Dana admitted. "But it hasn't, yet. Robin, I've been as honest with you as I'm able to be. You've had nothing but square deals from me up to now. I wouldn't yellow-screen you, and you know it. If this unknown outfit has this information, it might easily have gotten it from where it hints that it got it: from the field."

"Impossible."

"Why?"

"Because the information in question hasn't even reached my *own* agents in the field yet—it couldn't possibly have leaked as far as Hammersmith II or anywhere else, let alone to the Three Ghosts system! Letters have to be carried on ships, you know that. If I were to send orders by ultrawave to my Three Ghosts agent, he'd have to wait three hundred and twenty-four years to get them. By ship, he can get them in a little over two months. These particular orders have only been under way to him five days. Even if somebody has read them on board the ship that's carrying them, they couldn't possibly be sent on to the Three Ghosts any faster than they're traveling now."

Dana nodded her dark head. "All right. Then what are we left with but a leak in your headquarters here?"

"What, indeed," Weinbaum said grimly. "You'd better tell me who signed this letter of yours."

"The signature is J. Shelby Stevens."

Weinbaum switched on the intercom. "Margaret, look in the business register for an outfit called Interstellar Information and find out who owns it."

Dana Lje said, "Aren't you interested in the rest of the prediction?"

"You bet I am. Does it tell you the name of this communications device?"

"Yes," Dana said.

"What is it?"

"The Dirac communicator."

Weinbaum groaned and turned on the intercom again. "Margaret, send in Dr. Wald. Tell him to drop everything and gallop. Any luck with the other thing?"

"Yes, sir," the intercom said. "It's a one-man outfit, wholly owned by a J. Shelby Stevens, in Rico City. It was first registered this year."

"Arrest him, on suspicion of espionage."

The door swung open and Dr. Wald came in, all six and a half feet of him. He was extremely blond, and looked awkward, gentle, and not very intelligent.

"Thor, this young lady is our press nemesis, Dana Lje. Dana, Dr. Wald is the inventor of the Dirac communicator, about which you have so damnably much information."

"It's out *already*?" Dr. Wald said, scanning the girl with grave deliberation.

"It is, and lots more—*lots* more. Dana, you're a good girl at heart, and for some reason I trust you, stupid though it is to trust anybody in this job. I should detain you until Year Day, videocasts or no videocasts. Instead, I'm just going to ask you to sit on what you've got, and I'm going to explain why."

"Shoot."

"I've already mentioned how slow communication is between star and star. We have to carry all our letters on ships, just as we did locally before the invention of the telegraph. The overdrive lets us beat the speed of light, but not by much of a margin over really long distances. Do you understand that?"

"Certainly," Dana said. She appeared a bit nettled, and Weinbaum decided to give her the full dose at a more rapid pace. After all, she could be assumed to be better informed than the average layman.

"What we've needed for a long time, then," he said, "is some virtually instantaneous method of getting a message from somewhere to anywhere. Any time lag, no matter how small it seems at first, has a way of becoming major as longer and longer distances are involved. Sooner or later we must have this instantaneous method, or we won't be able to get messages from one system to another fast enough to hold our jurisdiction over outlying regions of space."

"Wait a minute," Dana said. "I'd always understood that ultrawave is faster than light."

"Effectively it is; physically it isn't. You don't understand that?"

She shook her dark head.

"In a nutshell," Weinbaum said, "ultrawave is radiation, and all radiation in free space is limited to the speed of light. The way we hype up ultrawave is to use an old application of wave-guide theory, whereby the real transmission of energy is at light speed, but an imaginary thing called "phase velocity" is going faster. But the gain in speed of transmission isn't large—by ultrawave, for instance, we get a message to Alpha Centauri in one year instead of nearly four. Over long distances, that's not nearly enough extra speed."

"Can't it be speeded further?" she said, frowning.

"No. Think of the ultrawave beam between here and Centaurus III as a caterpillar. The caterpillar himself is moving quite slowly, just at the speed of light. But the pulses which pass along his body are going forward faster than he is—and if you've ever watched a caterpillar, you'll know that that's true. But there's a physical limit to the number of pulses you can travel along that caterpillar, and we've already reached that limit. We've taken phase velocity as far as it will go.

"That's why we need something faster. For a long time our relativity theories discouraged hope of anything faster—even the high-phase velocity of a guided wave didn't contradict those theories; it just found a limited, mathematically imaginary loophole in them. But when Thor here began looking into the question of the velocity of propagation of a Dirac pulse, he found the answer. The communicator he developed does seem to act over long distances, *any* distance, instantaneously—and it may wind up knocking relativity into a cocked hat."

The girl's face was a study in stunned realization. "I'm not sure I've taken in all the technical angles," she said. "But if I'd had any notion of the political dynamite in this thing——"

"—you'd have kept out of my office," Weinbaum said grimly. "A good thing you didn't. The *Brindisi* is carrying a model of the Dirac communicator out to the periphery for a final test; the ship is supposed to get in touch with me from out there at a given Earth time, which we've calculated very elaborately to account for the residual Lorentz and Milne transformations involved in overdrive flight, and for a lot of other time phenomena that wouldn't mean anything at all to you.

"If that signal arrives here at the given Earth time, then—aside from the havoc it will create among the theoretical physicists whom we decide to let in on it—we will really have our instant communicator, and can include all of occupied space in the same time zone. And we'll have a terrific advantage over any lawbreaker who has to resort to ultrawave locally and to letters carried by ships over the long haul."

"Not," Dr. Wald said sourly, "if it's already leaked out."

"It remains to be seen how much of it has leaked," Weinbaum said. "The principle is rather esoteric, Thor, and the name of the thing alone wouldn't mean much even to a trained scientist. I gather that Dana's mysterious informant didn't go into technical details . . . or did he?"

"No," Dana said.

"Tell the truth, Dana. I know that you're suppressing some of that letter."

The girl started slightly. "All right—yes, I am. But nothing technical. There's another part of the prediction that lists the number and class of ships you will send to protect the *Brindisi*—the prediction says they'll be sufficient, by the way—and I'm keeping that to myself, to see whether or not it comes true along with the rest. If it does, I think I've hired myself a correspondent."

"If it does," Weinbaum said, "you've hired yourself a jailbird. Let's see how much mind reading J. Whatsit Stevens can do from the subcellar of Fort Yaphank."

III

Weinbaum let himself into Stevens's cell, locking the door behind him and passing the keys out to the guard. He sat down heavily on the nearest stool.

Stevens smiled the weak benevolent smile of the very old, and laid his book aside on the bunk. The book, Weinbaum knew—since his office had cleared it—was only a volume of pleasant, harmless lyrics by a New Dynasty poet named Nims.

"Were our predictions correct, Captain?" Stevens said. His voice was high and musical, rather like that of a boy soprano.

Weinbaum nodded. "You still won't tell us how you did it?"

"But I already have," Stevens protested. "Our intelligence network is the best in the Universe, Captain. It is superior even to your own excellent organization, as events have shown."

"Its results are superior, that I'll grant," Weinbaum said glumly. "If Dana Lje had thrown your letter down her disposal chute, we would have lost the *Brindisi* and our Dirac transmitter both. Incidentally, did your original letter predict accurately the number of ships we would send?"

Stevens nodded pleasantly, his neatly trimmed white beard thrusting forward slightly as he smiled.

"I was afraid so," Weinbaum leaned forward. "Do you have the Dirac transmitter, Stevens?"

"Of course, Captain. How else could my correspondents report to me with the efficiency you have observed?"

"Then why don't our receivers pick up the broadcasts of your agents? Dr. Wald says it's inherent in the principle that Dirac 'casts are picked up by *all* instruments tuned to receive them, bar none. And at this stage of the game there are so few such broadcasts being made that we'd be almost certain to detect any that weren't coming from our own operatives."

"I decline to answer that question, if you'll excuse the impoliteness," Stevens said, his voice quavering slightly. "I am an old man, Captain, and this intelligence agency is my sole source of income. If I told you how we operated, we would no longer have any advantage over your own service, except for the limited freedom from secrecy which we have. I have been assured by competent lawyers that I have every right to operate a private investigation bureau, properly licensed, upon any scale that I may choose; and that I have the right to keep my methods secret, as the so-called 'intellectual assets' of my firm. If you wish to use our services, well and good. We will provide them, with absolute guarantees on all information we furnish you, for an appropriate fee. But our methods are our own property."

Robin Weinbaum smiled twistedly. "I'm not a naïve man, Mr. Stevens," he said. "My service is hard on naïveté. You know as well as I do that the government can't allow you to operate on a free-lance basis, supplying top-secret information to anyone who can pay the price, or even free of charge to video columnists on a 'test' basis, even though you arrive at every jot of that information independently of espionage—which I still haven't entirely ruled out, by the way. If you can duplicate this *Brindisi* performance at will, we will have to have your services exclusively. In short, you become a hired civilian arm of my own bureau."

"Quite," Stevens said, returning the smile in a fatherly way. "We anticipated that, of course. However, we have contracts with other governments to consider; Erskine, in particular. If we are to work exclusively for Earth, necessarily our price will include compensation for renouncing our other accounts."

"Why should it? Patriotic public servants work for their government at a loss, if they can't work for it any other way."

"I am quite aware of that. I am quite prepared to renounce my other interests. But I do require to be paid."

"How much?" Weinbaum said, suddenly aware that his fists were clenched so tightly that they hurt.

Stevens appeared to consider, nodding his flowery white poll in senile deliberation. "My associates would have to be consulted. Tentatively, however, a sum equal to the present appropriation of your bureau would do, pending further negotiations."

Weinbaum shot to his feet, eyes wide. "You old buccaneer! You know damned well that I can't spend my entire appropriation on a single civilian service! Did it ever occur to you that most of the civilian outfits working for us are on cost-plus contracts, and that our civilian executives are being paid just a credit a year, by their own choice? You're demanding nearly two thousand credits an hour from your own government, and claiming the legal protection that the government affords you at the same time, in order to let those fanatics on Erskine run up a higher bid!"

"The price is not unreasonable," Stevens said. "The service is worth the price."

"That's where you're wrong! We have the discoverer of the machine working for us. For less than half the sum you're asking, we can find the application of the device that you're trading on—of that you can be damned sure."

"A dangerous gamble, Captain."

"Perhaps. We'll soon see!" Weinbaum glared at the placid face. "I'm forced to tell you that you're a free man, Mr. Stevens. We've been unable to show that you came by your information by any illegal method. You had classified facts in your possession, but no classified documents, and it's your privilege as a citizen to make guesses, no matter how educated.

"But we'll catch up with you sooner or later. Had you been reasonable, you might have found yourself in a very good position with us, your income as assured as any political income can be, and your person respected to the hilt. Now, however, you're subject to censorship—you have no idea how humiliating that can be, but I'm going to see to it that you find out. There'll be no more newsbeats for Dana Lje, or for anyone else. I want to see every word of copy that you file with any client outside the bureau. Every word that is of use to me will be used, and you'll be paid the statutory one cent a word for it—the same rate that the FBI pays for anonymous gossip. Everything I don't find useful will be killed without clearance. Eventually we'll have the modification of the Dirac that you're using, and when that happens, you'll be so flat broke that a pancake with a harelip could spit right over you."

Weinbaum paused for a moment, astonished at his own fury.

Stevens's clarinetlike voice began to sound in the windowless cavity. "Captain, I have no doubt that you can do this to me, at least incompletely. But it will prove fruitless. I will give you a prediction, at no charge. It is guaranteed, as are all our predictions. It is this: *You will never find that modification.* Eventually, I will give it to you, on my own terms, but you will never find it for yourself, nor will you force it out of me. In the meantime, not a word of copy will be filed with you; for, despite the fact that you are an arm of the government, I can well afford to wait you out."

"Bluster," Weinbaum said.

"Fact. Yours is the bluster—loud talk based on nothing more than a hope. I, however, *know* whereof I speak. . . . But let us conclude this discussion. It serves no purpose; you will need to see my points made the hard way. Thank you for giving me my freedom. We will talk again under different circumstances on—let me see; ah, yes, on June 9 of the year 2091. That year is, I believe, almost upon us."

Stevens picked up his book again, nodding at Weinbaum, his expression harmless and kindly, his hands showing the marked tremor of *paralysis agitans*. Weinbaum moved helplessly to the door and flagged the turnkey. As the bars closed behind him, Stevens's voice called out: "Oh, yes; and a Happy New Year, Captain."

Weinbaum blasted his way back into his own office, at least twice as mad as the proverbial nest of hornets, and at the same time rather dismally aware of his own probable future. If Stevens's second prediction turned out to be as phenomenally accurate as his first had been, Capt. Robin Weinbaum would soon be peddling a natty set of secondhand uniforms.

He glared down at Margaret Soames, his receptionist. She glared right back; she had known him too long to be intimidated.

"Anything?" he said.

"Dr. Wald's waiting for you in your office. There are some field reports, and a couple of Diracs on your private tape. Any luck with the old codger?"

"That," he said crushingly, "is Top Secret."

"Poof. That means that nobody still knows the answer but J. Shelby Stevens."

He collapsed suddenly. "You're so right. That's just what it does mean. But we'll bust him wide open sooner or later. We've *got* to."

"You'll do it," Margaret said. "Anything else for me?"

"No. Tip off the clerical staff that there's a half holiday today, then go take in a stereo or a steak or something yourself. Dr. Wald and I have a few private wires to pull . . . and unless I'm sadly mistaken, a private bottle of aquavit to empty."

"Right," the receptionist said. "Tie one on for me, Chief. I understand that beer is the best chaser for aquavit—I'll have some sent up."

"If you should return after I am suitably squiffed," Weinbaum said, feeling a little better already, "I will kiss you for your thoughtfulness. *That* should keep you at your stereo at least twice through the third feature."

As he went on through the door of his own office, she said demurely behind him, "It certainly should."

As soon as the door closed, however, his mood became abruptly almost as black as before. Despite his comparative youth—he was now only fifty-five—he had been in the service a long time, and he needed no one to tell him the possible consequences which might flow from possession by a private citizen of the Dirac communicator. If there was ever to be a Federation of Man in the Galaxy, it was within the power of J. Shelby Stevens to ruin it before it had fairly gotten started. And there seemed to be nothing at all that could be done about it.

"Hello, Thor," he said glumly. "Pass the bottle."

"Hello, Robin. I gather things went badly. Tell me about it."

Briefly, Weinbaum told him. "And the worst of it," he finished, "is that Stevens himself predicts that we won't find the application of the Dirac that he's using, and that eventually we'll have to buy it at his price. Somehow I believe him—but I can't see how it's possible. If I were to tell Congress that I was going to spend my entire appropriation for a single civilian service, I'd be out on my ear within the next three sessions."

"Perhaps that isn't his real price," the scientist suggested. "If he wants to barter, he'd naturally begin with a demand miles above what he actually wants."

"Sure, sure . . . but frankly, Thor, I'd hate to give the old reprobate even a single credit if I could get out of it." Weinbaum sighed. "Well, let's see what's come in from the field."

Thor Wald moved silently away from Weinbaum's desk while the officer unfolded it and set up the Dirac screen. Stacked neatly next to the ultraphone—a device Weinbaum had been thinking of, only a few days ago, as permanently outmoded—were the tapes Margaret had mentioned. He fed the first one into the Dirac and turned the main toggle to the position labeled START.

Immediately the whole screen went pure white and the audio speakers emitted an almost instantly end-stopped blare of sound—a *beep* which, as Weinbaum already knew, made up a continuous spectrum from about 30 cycles per second to well above 18,000 cps. Then both the light and the noise were gone as if they had never been, and were replaced by the familiar face and voice of Weinbaum's local ops chief in Rico City.

"There's nothing unusual in the way of transmitters in Stevens's offices here," the operative said without preamble. "And there isn't any local Interstellar Information staff, except for one stenographer, and she's as dumb as they come. About all we could get from her is that Stevens is 'such a sweet old man.' No possibility that she's faking it; she's genuinely stupid, the kind that thinks Betelgeuse is something Indians use to darken their skins. We looked for some sort of list or code table that would give us a line on Stevens's field staff, but that was another dead end. Now we're maintaining a twenty-four-hour Dinwiddie watch on the place from a joint across the street. Orders?"

Weinbaum dictated to the blank stretch of tape which followed: "Margaret, next time you send any Dirac tapes in here, cut that damnable *beep* off them first. Tell the boys in Rico City that Stevens has been released, and that I'm proceeding for an Order In Security to tap his ultraphone and his local lines—this is one case where I'm sure we can persuade the court that tapping's necessary. Also—and be damned sure you code this—tell them to proceed with the tap immediately and to maintain it regardless of whether or not the court O.K.s it. I'll thumbprint a Full Responsibility Confession for them. We can't afford to play pat-a-cake with Stevens—the potential is just too damned big. And oh, yes, Margaret, send the message by carrier, and send out general orders to everybody concerned not to use the Dirac again except when distance and time rule every other medium out. Stevens has already admitted that he can receive Dirac 'casts."

He put down the mike and stared morosely for a moment at the beautiful Eridanean scrollwood of his desktop. Wald coughed inquiringly and retrieved the aquavit.

"Excuse me, Robin," he said, "but I should think that would work both ways."

"So should I. And yet the fact is that we've never picked up so much as a whisper from either Stevens or his agents. I can't think of any way that could be pulled, but evidently it can."

"Well, let's rethink the problem, and see what we get," Wald said. "I didn't want to say so in front of the young lady, for obvious reasons—I mean Miss Lje, of course, not Margaret—but the truth is that the Dirac is essentially a simple mechanism in principle. I seriously doubt that there's any way to transmit a message from it which can't be detected—and an examination of the theory with that proviso in mind might give us something new."

"What proviso?" Weinbaum said. Thor Wald left him behind rather often these days.

"Why, that a Dirac transmission doesn't *necessarily* go to all communicators capable of receiving it. If that's true, then the reasons why it is true should emerge from the theory."

"I see. O.K., proceed on that line. I've been looking at Stevens's dossier while you were talking, and it's an absolute desert. Prior to the opening of the office in Rico City, there's no dope whatever on J. Shelby Stevens. The man as good as rubbed my nose in the fact that he's using a pseud when I first talked to him. I asked him what the 'J' in his name stood for, and he said, 'Oh, let's make it Jerome.' But who the man behind the pseud *is* . . ."

"Is it possible that he's using his own initials?"

"No," Weinbaum said. "Only the dumbest ever do that, or transpose syllables, or retain any connection at all with their real names. Those are the people who are in serious emotional trouble, people who drive themselves into anonymity, but leave clues strewn all around the landscape—those clues are really a cry for help, for discovery. Of course we're working on that angle—we can't neglect anything—but J. Shelby Stevens isn't that kind of case, I'm sure." Weinbaum stood up abruptly. "O.K., Thor—what's first on your technical program?"

"Well . . . I suppose we'll have to start with checking the frequencies we use. We're going on Dirac's assumption—and it works very well, and always has—that a positron in motion through a crystal lattice is accompanied by de Broglie waves which are transforms of the waves of an electron in motion somewhere else in the Universe. Thus if we control the frequency and path of the positron, we control the placement of the electron—we cause it to appear, so to speak, in the circuits of a communicator somewhere else. After that, reception is just a matter of amplifying the bursts and reading the signal."

Wald scowled and shook his blond head. "If Stevens is getting out messages which we don't pick up, my first assumption would be that he's worked out a fine-tuning circuit that's more delicate than ours, and is more or less sneaking his messages under ours. The only way that could be done, as far as I can see at the moment, is by something really fantastic in the way of exact frequency control of his positron gun. If so, the logical step for us is to go back to the beginning of our tests and rerun our diffractions to see if we can refine our measurements of positron frequencies."

The scientist looked so inexpressibly gloomy as he offered this conclusion that a pall of hopelessness settled over Weinbaum in sheer sympathy. "You don't look as if you expected that to uncover anything new."

"I don't. You see, Robin, things are different in physics now than they used to be in the twentieth century. In those days, it was always presupposed that physics was limitless—the classic statement was made by Weyl, who said that 'It is the nature of a real thing to be inexhaustible in content.' We know now that that's not so, except in a remote, associational sort of way. Nowadays, physics is a defined and self-limited science; its scope is still prodigious, but we can no longer think of it as endless.

"This is better established in particle physics than in any other branch of the science. Half of the trouble physicists of the last century had with Euclidean geometry—and hence the reason why they evolved so many recomplicated theories of relativity—is that it's a geometry of lines, and thus can be subdivided infinitely. When Cantor proved that there really is an infinity, at least mathematically speaking, that seemed to clinch the case for the possibility of a really infinite physical universe, too."

Wald's eyes grew vague, and he paused to gulp down a slug of the licorice-flavored aquavit which would have made Weinbaum's every hair stand on end.

"I remember," Wald said, "the man who taught me theory of sets at Princeton, many years ago. He used to say: 'Cantor teaches us that there are many kinds of infinities. *There* was a crazy old man!' "

Weinbaum rescued the bottle hastily. "So go on, Thor."

"Oh." Wald blinked. "Yes. Well, what we know now is that the geometry which applies to ultimate particles, like the positron, isn't Euclidean at all. It's Pythagorean—a geometry of points, not lines. Once you've measured one of those points, and it doesn't matter what kind of quantity you're measuring, you're down as far as you can go. At that point, the Universe becomes discontinuous, and no further refinement is possible.

"And I'd say that our positron-frequency measurements have already gotten that far down. There isn't another element in the Universe denser than plutonium, yet we get the same frequency values by diffraction through plutonium crystals that we get through osmium crystals—there's not the slightest difference. If J. Shelby Stevens is operating in terms of fractions of those values, then he's doing what an organist would call 'playing in the cracks'—which is certainly something you can *think* about doing, but something that's in actuality impossible to do. *Hoop.*"

"Hoop?" Weinbaum said.

"Sorry. A hiccup only."

"Oh. Well, maybe Stevens has rebuilt the organ?"

"If he has rebuilt the metrical frame of the Universe to accommodate a private skip-tracing firm," Wald said firmly, "I for one see no reason why we can't countercheck him—*hoop*—by declaring the whole cosmos null and void."

"All right, all right," Weinbaum said, grinning. "I didn't mean to push your analogy right over the edge—I was just asking. But let's get to work on it anyhow. We can't just sit here and let Stevens get away with it. If this frequency angle turns out to be as hopeless as it seems, we'll try something else."

Wald eyed the aquavit bottle owlishly. "It's a very pretty problem," he said. "Have I ever sung you the song we have in Sweden called 'Nat-og-Dag'?"

"*Hoop*," Weinbaum said, to his own surprise, in a high falsetto. "Excuse me. No. Let's hear it."

The computer occupied an entire floor of the Security building, its seemingly identical banks laid out side by side on the floor along an advanced pathological state of Peano's "space-filling curve." At the current business end of the line was a master control board with a large television screen at its center, at which Dr. Wald was stationed, with Weinbaum looking, silently but anxiously, over his shoulder.

The screen itself showed a pattern which, except that it was drawn in green light against a dark gray background, strongly resembled the grain in a piece of highly polished mahogany. Photographs of similar patterns were stacked on a small table to Dr. Wald's right; several had spilled over onto the floor.

"Well, there it is," Wald sighed at length. "And I won't struggle to keep myself from saying 'I told you so.' What you've had me do here, Robin, is to reconfirm about half the basic postulates of particle physics—which is why it took so long, even though it was the first project we started." He snapped off the screen. "There are no cracks for J. Shelby to play in. That's definite."

"If you'd said 'That's flat,' you would have made a joke," Weinbaum said sourly. "Look . . . isn't there still a chance of error? If not on your part, Thor, then in the computer? After all, it's set up to work only with the unit charges of modern physics; mightn't we have to disconnect the banks that contain that bias before the machine will follow the fractional-charge instructions we give it?"

" 'Disconnect,' he says," Wald groaned, mopping his brow reflectively. "The bias exists everywhere in the machine, my friend, because it functions everywhere on those same unit charges. It wasn't a matter of subtracting banks; we had to add one with a bias all its own, to countercorrect the corrections the computer would otherwise apply to the instructions. The technicians thought I was crazy. Now, five months later, I've proved it."

Weinbaum grinned in spite of himself. "What about the other projects?"

"All done—some time back, as a matter of fact. The staff and I checked every single Dirac tape we've received since you released J. Shelby from Yaphank, for any sign of intermodulation, marginal signals, or anything else of the kind. There's nothing, Robin, absolutely nothing. That's our net result, all around."

"Which leaves us just where we started," Weinbaum said. "All the monitoring projects came to the same dead end; I strongly suspect that Stevens hasn't risked any further calls from his home office to his field staff, even though he seemed confident that we'd never intercept such calls—as we haven't. Even our local wire tapping hasn't turned up anything but calls by Stevens's secretary, making appointments for him with various clients, actual and potential. Any information he's selling these days he's passing on in person—and not in his office, either, because we've got bugs planted all over that and haven't heard a thing."

"That must limit his range of operation enormously," Wald objected.

Weinbaum nodded. "Without a doubt—but he shows no signs of being bothered by it. He can't have sent any tips to Erskine recently, for instance, because our last tangle with that crew came out very well for us, even though we had to use the Dirac to send the orders to our squadron out there. If he overheard us, he didn't even try to pass the word. Just as he said, he's sweating us out—" Weinbaum paused. "Wait a minute, here comes Margaret. And by the length of her stride, I'd say she's got something particularly nasty on her mind."

"You bet I do," Margaret Soames said vindictively. "And it'll blow plenty of lids around here, or I miss my guess. The I.D. squad has finally pinned down J. Shelby Stevens. They did it with the voice-comparator alone."

"How does that work?" Wald said interestedly.

"Blink microphone," Weinbaum said impatiently. "Isolates inflections on single, normally stressed syllables and matches them. Standard I.D. searching technique, on a case of this kind, but it takes so long that we usually get the quarry by other means before it pays off. Well, don't stand there like a dummy, Margaret. Who is he?

" 'He,' " Margaret said, "is your sweetheart of the video waves, Miss Dana Lje."

"They're crazy!" Wald said, staring at her.

Weinbaum came slowly out of his first shock of stunned disbelief. "No, Thor," he said finally. "No, it figures. If a woman is going to go in for disguises, there are always two she can assume outside her own sex: a young boy, and a very old man. And Dana's an actress; that's no news to us."

"But—but why did she do it, Robin?"

"That's what we're going to find out right now. So we wouldn't get the Dirac modification by ourselves, eh! Well, there are other ways of getting answers besides particle physics. Margaret, do you have a pick-up order out for that girl?"

"No," the receptionist said. "This is one chestnut I wanted to see you pull out for yourself. You give me the authority, and I send the order—not before."

"Spiteful child. Send it, then, and glory in my gritted teeth. Come on, Thor—let's put the nutcracker on this chestnut."

As they were leaving the computer floor, Weinbaum stopped suddenly in his tracks and began to mutter in an almost inaudible voice.

Wald said, "What's the matter, Robin?"

"Nothing. I keep being brought up short by those predictions. What's the date?"

"M'm . . . June 9. Why?"

"It's the exact date that 'Stevens' predicted we'd meet again, damn it! Something tells me that this isn't going to be as simple as it looks."

If Dana Lje had any idea of what she was in for—and considering the fact that she was 'J. Shelby Stevens' it had to be assumed that she did—the knowledge seemed not to make her at all fearful. She sat as composedly as ever before Weinbaum's desk, smoking her eternal cigarette, and waited, one dimpled knee pointed directly at the bridge of the officer's nose.

"Dana," Weinbaum said, "this time we're going to get all the answers, and we're not going to be gentle about it. Just in case you're not aware of the fact, there are certain laws relating to giving false information to a security officer, under which we could heave you in prison for a minimum of fifteen years. By application of the statutes on using communications to defraud, plus various local laws against transvestism, pseudonymity and so on, we could probably pile up enough additional short sentences to keep you in Yaphank until you really *do* grow a beard. So I'd advise you to open up."

"I have every intention of opening up," Dana said. "I know, practically word for word, how this interview is going to proceed, what information I'm going to give you, just when I'm going to give it to you—and what you're going to pay me for it. I knew all that many months ago. So there would be no point in my holding out on you."

"What you're saying, Miss Lje," Thor Wald said in a resigned voice, "is that the future is fixed, and that you can read it, in every essential detail."

"Quite right, Dr. Wald. Both those things are true."

There was a brief silence.

"All right," Weinbaum said grimly. "Talk."

"All right, Captain Weinbaum, pay me," Dana said calmly.

Weinbaum snorted.

"But I'm quite serious," she said. "You still don't know what I know about the Dirac communicator. I won't be forced to tell it, by threat of prison or by any other threat. You see, I know for a fact that you aren't going to send me to prison, or give me drugs, or do anything else of that kind. I know for a fact, instead, that you are going to pay me—so I'd be very foolish to say a word until you do. After all, it's quite a secret you're buying. Once I tell you what it is, you and the entire service will be able to read the future as I do, and then the information will be valueless to me."

Weinbaum was completely speechless for a moment. Finally he said, "Dana, you have a heart of purest brass, as well as a knee with an invisible gunsight on it. I say that I'm *not* going to give you my appropriation, regardless of what the future may or may not say about it. I'm not going to give it to you because the way my government—and yours—runs things makes such a price impossible. Or is that really your price?"

"It's my real price . . . but it's also an alternative. Call it my second choice. My first choice, which means the price I'd settle for, comes in two parts: (a) to be taken into your service as a responsible officer; and, (b) to be married to Captain Robin Weinbaum."

Weinbaum sailed up out of his chair. He felt as though copper-colored flames a foot long were shooting out of each of his ears.

"Of all the—" he began. There his voice failed completely.

From behind him, where Wald was standing, came something like a large, Scandinavian-model guffaw being choked into insensibility.

Dana herself seemed to be smiling a little.

"You see," she said, "I don't point my best and most accurate knee at every man I meet."

Weinbaum sat down again, slowly and carefully. "Walk, do not run, to nearest exit," he said. "Women and childlike security officers first. Miss Lje, are you trying to sell me the notion that you went through this elaborate hanky-panky—beard and all—out of a burning passion for my dumpy and underpaid person?"

"Not entirely," Dana Lje said. "I want to be in the bureau, too, as I said. Let me confront you, though, Captain, with a fact of life that doesn't seem to have occurred to you at all. Do you accept as a fact that I can read the future in detail, and that that, to be possible at all, means that the future is fixed?"

"Since Thor seems able to accept it, I suppose I can too—provisionally."

"There's nothing provisional about it," Dana said firmly. "Now, when I first came upon this—uh, this gimmick—quite a while back, one of the first things that I found out was that I was going to go through the 'J. Shelby Stevens' masquerade, force myself onto the staff of the bureau, and marry you, Robin. At the time, I was both astonished and completely rebellious. I didn't want to be on the bureau staff; I liked my free-lance life as a video commentator. I didn't want to marry you, though I wouldn't have been averse to living with you for a while—say a month or so. And above all, the masquerade struck me as ridiculous.

"But the facts kept staring me in the face. I *was* going to do all those things. There were no alternatives, no fanciful 'branches of time,' no decision-points that might be altered to make the future change. My future, like yours, Dr. Wald's, and everyone else's, was fixed. It didn't matter a snap whether or not I had a decent motive for what I was going to do; I was going to do it anyhow. Cause and effect, as I could see for myself, just don't exist. One event follows another because events are just as indestructible in space-time as matter and energy are.

"It was the bitterest of all pills. It will take me many years to swallow it completely, and you too. Dr. Wald will come around a little sooner, I think. At any rate, once I was intellectually convinced that all this was so, I had to protect my own sanity. I knew that I couldn't alter what I was going to do, but the least I could do to protect myself was to supply myself with motives. Or, in other words, just plain rationalizations. That much, it seems, we're free to do; the consciousness of the observer is just along for the ride through time, and can't alter events—but it can comment, explain, invent. That's fortunate, for none of us could stand going through motions which were truly free of what we think of as personal significances.

"So I supplied myself with the obvious motives. Since I was going to be married to you and couldn't get out of it, I set out to convince myself that I loved you. Now I do. Since I was going to join the bureau staff, I thought over all the advantages that it might have over video commentating, and found that they made a respectable list. Those are my motives.

"But I had no such motives at the beginning. Actually, there are never motives behind actions. All actions are fixed. What we called motives evidently are rationalizations by the helpless observing consciousness, which is intelligent enough to smell an event coming—and, since it cannot avert the event, instead cooks up reasons for wanting it to happen."

"Wow," Dr. Wald said, inelegantly but with considerable force.

"Either 'wow' or 'balderdash' seems to be called for—I can't quite decide which," Weinbaum agreed. "We know that Dana is an actress, Thor, so let's not fall off the apple tree quite yet. Dana, I've been saving the *really* hard question for the last. That question is: *How*? How did you arrive at this modification of the Dirac transmitter? Remember, we know your background, where we didn't know that of 'J. Shelby Stevens.' You're not a scientist. There were some fairly high-powered intellects among your distant relatives, but that's as close as you come."

"I'm going to give you several answers to that question," Dana Lje said. "Pick the one you like best. They're all true, but they tend to contradict each other here and there.

"To begin with, you're right about my relatives, of course. If you'll check your dossier again, though, you'll discover that those so-called 'distant' relatives were the last surviving members of my family besides myself. When they died, second and fourth and ninth cousins though they were, their estates reverted to me, and among their effects I found a sketch of a possible instantaneous communicator based on de Broglie-wave inversion. The material was in very rough form, and mostly beyond my comprehension, because I am, as you say, no scientist myself. But I was interested; I could see, dimly, what such a thing might be worth—and not only in money.

"My interest was fanned by two coincidences—the kind of coincidences that cause-and-effect just can't allow, but which seem to happen all the same in the world of unchangeable events. For most of my adult life, I've been in communications industries of one kind or another, mostly branches of video. I had communications equipment around me constantly, and I had coffee and doughnuts with communications engineers every day. First I picked up the jargon; then, some of the procedures; and eventually a little real knowledge. Some of the things I learned can't be gotten any other way. Some other things are ordinarily available only to highly educated people like Dr. Wald here, and came to me by accident, in horseplay, between kisses, and a hundred other ways—all natural to the environment of a video network."

Weinbaum found, to his own astonishment, that the "between kisses" clause did not sit very well in his chest. He said, with unintentional brusqueness: "What's the other coincidence?"

"A leak in your own staff."

"Dana, you ought to have that set to music."

"Suit yourself."

"I can't suit myself," Weinbaum said petulantly. "I work for the government. Was this leak direct to you?"

"Not at first. That was why I kept insisting to you in person that there might be such a leak, and why I finally began to hint about it in public, on my program. I was hoping that you'd be able to seal it up inside the bureau before my first rather tenuous contact with it got lost. When I didn't succeed in provoking you into protecting yourself, I took the risk of making direct contact with the leak myself—and the first piece of secret information that came to me through it was the final point I needed to put my Dirac communicator together. When it was all assembled, it did more than just communicate. It predicted. And I can tell you why."

Weinbaum said thoughtfully, "I don't find this very hard to accept, so far. Pruned of the philosophy, it even makes some sense of the 'J. Shelby Stevens' affair. I assume that by letting the old gentleman become known as somebody who knew more about the Dirac transmitter than I did, and who wasn't averse to negotiating with anybody who had money, you kept the leak working through you—rather than transmitting data directly to unfriendly governments."

"It did work out that way," Dana said. "But that wasn't the genesis or the purpose of the Stevens masquerade. I've already given you the whole explanation of how that came about."

"Well, you'd better name me that leak, before the man gets away."

"When the price is paid, not before. It's too late to prevent a getaway, anyhow. In the meantime, Robin, I want to go on and tell you the other answer to your question about how I was able to find this particular Dirac secret, and you didn't. What answers I've given you up to now have been cause-and-effect answers, with which we're all more comfortable. But I want to impress on you that all apparent cause-and-effect relationships are accidents. There is no such thing as a cause, and no such thing as an effect. I found the secret because I found it; that event was fixed; that certain circumstances seem to explain why I found it, in the old cause-and-effect terms, is irrelevant. Similarly, with all your superior equipment and brains, you didn't find it for one reason, and one reason alone: because you didn't find it. The history of the future says you didn't."

"I pays my money and I takes no choice, eh?" Weinbaum said ruefully.

"I'm afraid so—and I don't like it any better than you do."

"Thor, what's your opinion of all this?"

"It's just faintly flabbergasting," Wald said soberly. "However, it hangs together. The deterministic universe which Miss Lje paints was a common feature of the old relativity theories, and as sheer speculation has an even longer history. I would say that, in the long run, how much credence we place in the story as a whole will rest upon her method of, as she calls it, reading the future. If it is demonstrable beyond any doubt, then the rest becomes perfectly credible—philosophy and all. If it doesn't, then what remains is an admirable job of acting, plus some metaphysics which, while self-consistent, is not original with Miss Lje."

"That sums up the case as well as if I'd coached you, Dr. Wald," Dana said. "I'd like to point out one more thing. If I can read the future, then 'J. Shelby Stevens' never had any need for a staff of field operatives, and he never needed to send a single Dirac message which you might intercept. All he needed to do was to make predictions from his readings, which he knew to be infallible; no private espionage network had to be involved."

"I see that," Weinbaum said dryly. "All right, Dana, let's put the proposition this way: *I do not believe you.* Much of what you say is probably true, but in totality I believe it to be false. On the other hand, if you're telling the whole truth, you certainly deserve a place on the bureau staff—it would be dangerous as hell *not* to have you with us—and the marriage is a more or less minor matter, except to you and me. You can have that with no strings attached; I don't want to be bought, any more than you would.

"So: if you will tell me where the leak is, we will consider that part of the question closed. I make that condition not as a price, but because I don't want to get myself engaged to somebody who might be shot as a spy within a month."

"Fair enough," Dana said. "Robin, your leak is Margaret Soames. She is an Erskine operative, and nobody's bubble-brain. She's a highly trained technician."

"Well, I'll be damned," Weinbaum said in astonishment. "Then she's already flown the coop—she was the one who first told me we'd identified you. She must have taken on that job in order to hold up delivery long enough to stage an exit."

"That's right. But you'll catch her, day after tomorrow. And you are now a hooked fish, Robin."

There was another suppressed burble from Thor Wald.

"I accept the fate happily," Weinbaum said, eying the gunsight knee. "Now, if you will tell me how you work your swami trick, and if it backs up everything you've said to the letter, as you claim, I'll see to it that you're also taken into the bureau and that all charges against you are quashed. Otherwise, I'll probably have to kiss the bride between the bars of a cell."

Dana smiled. "The secret is very simple. It's in the beep."

Weinbaum's jaw dropped. "The beep? The Dirac noise?"

"That's right. You didn't find it out because you considered the beep to be just a nuisance, and ordered Miss Soames to cut it off all tapes before sending them in to you. Miss Soames, who had some inkling of what the beep meant, was more than happy to do so, leaving the reading of the beep exclusively to 'J. Shelby Stevens'—who she thought was going to take on Erskine as a client."

"Explain," Thor Wald said, looking intense.

"Just as you assumed, every Dirac message that is sent is picked up by every receiver that is capable of detecting it. *Every* receiver—including the first one ever built, which is yours, Dr. Wald, through the hundreds of thousands of them which will exist throughout the Galaxy in the twenty-fourth century, to the untold millions which will exist in the thirtieth century, and so on. The Dirac beep is the simultaneous reception of *every one of the Dirac messages which have ever been sent, or ever will be sent.* Incidentally, the cardinal number of the total of those messages is a relatively small and of course finite number; it's far below really large finite numbers such as the number of electrons in the universe, even when you break each and every message down into individual 'bits' and count those."

"Of course," Dr. Wald said softly. "Of course! But, Miss Lje . . . how do you tune for an individual message? We tried fractional positron frequencies, and got nowhere."

"I didn't even know fractional positron frequencies existed," Dana confessed. "No, it's simple—so simple that a lucky layman like me could arrive at it. You tune individual messages out of the beep by time lag, nothing more. All the messages arrive at the same instant, in the smallest fraction of time that exists, something called a 'chronon.' "

"Yes," Wald said. "The time it takes one electron to move from one quantum-level to another. That's the Pythagorean point of time measurement."

"Thank you. Obviously no gross physical receiver can respond to a message that brief, or at least that's what I thought at first. But because there are relay and switching delays, various forms of feedback and so on, in the apparatus itself, the beep arrives at the output end as a complex pulse which has been 'splattered' along the time axis for a full second or more. That's an effect which you can exaggerate by recording the 'splattered' beep on a high-speed tape, the same way you would record any event that you wanted to study in slow motion. Then you tune up the various failure-points in your receiver, to exaggerate one failure, minimize all the others, and use noise-suppressing techniques to cut out the background."

Thor Wald frowned. "You'd still have a considerable garble when you were through. You'd have to sample the messages—"

"Which is just what I did; Robin's little lecture to me about the ultrawave gave me that hint. I set myself to find out how the ultrawave channel carries so many messages at once, and I discovered that you people sample the incoming pulses every thousandth of a second and pass on one pip only when the wave deviates in a certain way from the mean. I didn't really believe it would work on the Dirac beep, but it turned out just as well: 90 percent as intelligible as the original transmission after it came through the smearing device. I'd already got enough from the beep to put my plan in motion, of course—but now every voice message in it was available, and crystal-clear: If you select three pips every thousandth of second, you can even pick up an intelligible transmission of music—a little razzy, but good enough to identify the instruments that are playing—and that's a very close test of any communications device."

"There's a question of detail here that doesn't quite follow," said Weinbaum, for whom the technical talk was becoming a little too thick to fight through. "Dana, you say that you knew the course this conversation was going to take—yet it isn't being Dirac-recorded, nor can I see any reason why any summary of it would be sent out on the Dirac afterwards."

"That's true, Robin. However, when I leave here, I will make such a transcast myself, on my own Dirac. Obviously I will—because I've *already* picked it up, from the beep."

"In other words, you're going to call yourself up—months ago."

"That's it," Dana said. "It's not as useful a technique as you might think at first, because it's dangerous to make such broadcasts while a situation is still developing. You can safely 'phone back' details only after the given situation has gone to completion, as a chemist might put it. Once you know, however, that when you use the Dirac you're dealing with time, you can coax some very strange things out of the instrument."

She paused and smiled. "I have heard," she said conversationally, "the voice of the President of our Galaxy, in 3480, announcing the federation of the Milky Way and the Magellanic Clouds. I've heard the commander of a world-line cruiser, traveling from 8873 to 8704 along the world line of the planet Hathshepa, which circles a star on the rim of NGC 4725, calling for help across eleven million light-years—but what kind of help he was calling for, or will be calling for, is beyond my comprehension. And many other things. When you check on me, you'll hear these things too—and you'll wonder what many of them mean.

"And you'll listen to them even more closely than I did, in the hope of finding out whether or not anyone was able to understand in time to help."

Weinbaum and Wald looked dazed.

Her voice became a little more somber. "Most of the voices in the Dirac beep are like that—they're cries for help, which you can overhear decades or centuries before the senders get into trouble. You'll feel obligated to answer every one, to try to supply the help that's needed. And you'll listen to the succeeding messages and say: 'Did we—will we get there in time? Did we understand in time?'

"And in most cases you won't be sure. You'll know the future, but not what most of it means. The farther into the future you travel with the machine, the more incomprehensible the messages become, and so you're reduced to telling yourself that time will, after all, have to pass by at its own pace, before enough of the surrounding events can emerge to make those remote messages clear.

"The long-run effect, as far as I can think it through, is not going to be that of omniscience—of our consciousness being extracted entirely from the time stream and allowed to view its whole sweep from one side. Instead, the Dirac in effect simply slides the bead of consciousness forward from the present a certain distance. Whether it's five hundred or five thousand years still remains to be seen. At that point the law of diminishing returns sets in—or the noise factor begins to overbalance the information, take your choice—and the observer is reduced to traveling in time at the same old speed. He's just a bit ahead of himself."

"You've thought a great deal about this," Wald said slowly. "I dislike to think of what might have happened had some less conscientious person stumbled on the beep."

"That wasn't in the cards," Dana said.

In the ensuing quiet, Weinbaum felt a faint, irrational sense of let-down, of something which had promised more than had been delivered—rather like the taste of fresh bread as compared to its smell, or the discovery that Thor Wald's Swedish "folk song" *Nat-og-Dag* was only Cole Porter's *Night and Day* in another language. He recognized the feeling: it was the usual emotion of the hunter when the hunt is over, the born detective's professional version of the *post coitum triste*. After looking at the smiling, supple Dana Lje a moment more, however, he was almost content.

"There's one more thing," he said. "I don't want to be insufferably skeptical about this—but I want to see it work. Thor, can we set up a sampling and smearing device such as Dana describes and run a test?"

"In fifteen minutes," Dr. Wald said. "We have most of the unit in already assembled form on our big ultrawave receiver, and it shouldn't take any effort to add a high-speed tape unit to it. I'll do it right now."

He went out. Weinbaum and Dana looked at each other for a moment, rather like strange cats. Then the security officer got up, with what he knew to be an air of somewhat grim determination, and seized his fiancée's hands, anticipating a struggle.

That first kiss was, by intention at least, mostly *pro forma*. But by the time Wald padded back into the office, the letter had been pretty thoroughly superseded by the spirit. The scientist harrumphed and set his burden on the desk. "This is all there is to it," he said, "but I had to hunt all through the library to find a Dirac record with a beep still on it. Just a moment more while I make connections. . . ."

Weinbaum used the time to bring his mind back to the matter at hand, although not quite completely. Then two tape spindles began to whir like so many bees, and the end-stopped sound of the Dirac beep filled the room. Wald stopped the apparatus, reset it, and started the smearing tape very slowly in the opposite direction.

A distant babble of voices came from the speaker. As Weinbaum leaned forward tensely, one voice said clearly and loudly above the rest:

"Hello, Earth bureau. Lt. T. L. Matthews at Hercules Station NGC 6341, transmission date 13-22-2091. We have the last point on the orbit curve of your dope-runners plotted, and the curve itself points to a small system about twenty-five light-years from the base here; the place hasn't even got a name on our charts. Scouts show the home planet at least twice as heavily fortified as we anticipated, so we'll need another cruiser. We have a 'can-do' from you in the beep for us, but we're waiting as ordered to get it in the present. NGC 6341 Matthews out."

After the first instant of stunned amazement—for no amount of intellectual willingness to accept could have prepared him for the overwhelming fact itself—Weinbaum had grabbed a pencil and begun to write at top speed. As the voice signed out he threw the pencil down and looked excitedly at Dr. Wald.

"Seven months ahead," he said, aware that he was grinning like an idiot. "Thor, you know the trouble we've had with that needle in the Hercules haystack! This orbit-curve trick must be something Matthews has yet to dream up—at least he hasn't come to me with it yet, and there's nothing in the situation as it stands now that would indicate a closing time of six months for the case. The computers said it would take three more years."

"It's new data," Dr. Wald agreed solemnly.

"Well, don't stop there, in God's name! Let's hear some more!"

Dr. Wald went through the ritual, much faster this time. The speaker said:

"Nausentampen. Eddettompic. Berobsilom. Aimkaksetchoc. Sanbetogmow. Datdectamset. Domatrosmin. Out."

"My word," Wald said. "What's all that?"

"That's what I was talking about," Dana Lje said. "At least half of what you get from the beep is just as incomprehensible. I suppose it's whatever has happened to the English language, thousands of years from now."

"No, it isn't," Weinbaum said. He had resumed writing, and was still at it, despite the comparative briefness of the transmission. "Not this sample, anyhow. That, ladies and gentlemen, is code—no language consists exclusively of four-syllable words, of that you can be sure. What's more, it's a version of our code. I can't break it down very far—it takes a full-time expert to read this stuff—but I get the date and some of the sense. It's March 12, 3022, and there's some kind of a mass evacuation taking place. The message seems to be a routing order."

"But why will we be using code?" Dr. Wald wanted to know. "It implies that we think somebody might overhear us—somebody else with a Dirac. That could be very messy."

"It could indeed," Weinbaum said. "But we'll find out, I imagine. Give her another spin, Thor."

"Shall I try for a picture this time?"

Weinbaum nodded. A moment later, he was looking squarely into the green-skinned face of something that looked like an animated traffic signal with a helmet on it. Though the creature had no mouth, the Dirac speaker was saying quite clearly, "Hello, Chief. This is Thammos NGC 2287, transmission date Gor 60,

302 by my calendar, July 2, 2973 by yours. This is a lousy little planet. Everything stinks of oxygen, just like Earth. But the natives accept us and that's the important thing. We've got your genius safely born. Detailed report coming later by paw. NGC 2287 Thammos out."

"I wish I knew my New General Catalogue better," Weinbaum said. "Isn't that M 41 in Canis Major, the one with the red star in the middle? And we'll be using non-humanoids there! What *was* that creature, anyhow? Never mind, spin her again."

Dr. Wald spun her again. Weinbaum, already feeling a little dizzy, had given up taking notes. That could come later, all that could come later. Now he wanted only scenes and voices, more and more scenes and voices from the future. They were better than aquavit, even with a beer chaser.

IV

The indoctrination tape ended, and Krasna touched a button. The Dirac screen darkened, and folded silently back into the desk.

"They didn't see their way through to us, not by a long shot," he said. "They didn't see, for instance, that when one section of the government becomes nearly all-knowing—no matter how small it was to begin with—it necessarily becomes all of the government that there is. Thus the bureau turned into the Service and pushed everyone else out.

"On the other hand, those people did come to be afraid that a government with an all-knowing arm might become a rigid dictatorship. That couldn't happen and didn't happen, because the more you know, the wider your field of possible operation becomes and the more fluid and dynamic a society you need. How could a rigid society expand to other star systems, let alone other galaxies? It couldn't be done."

"I should think it could," Jo said slowly. "After all, if you know in advance what everybody is going to do . . ."

"But we don't, Jo. That's just a popular fiction—or, if you like, a red herring. Not all of the business of the cosmos is carried on over the Dirac, after all. The only events we can ever overhear are those which are transmitted as a message. Do you order your lunch over the Dirac? Of course you don't. Up to now, you've never said a word over the Dirac in your life.

"And there's much more to it than that. All dictatorships are based on the proposition that government can somehow control a man's thoughts. We know now that the consciousness of the observer is the only free thing in the Universe. Wouldn't we look foolish trying to control that, when our entire physics shows that it's impossible to do so? That's why the Service is in no sense a thought police. We're interested only in acts. We're an Event Police."

"But why?" Jo said. "If all history is fixed, why do we bother with these boy-meets-girl assignments, for instance? The meetings will happen anyhow."

"Of course they will," Krasna agreed immediately. "But look, Jo. Our interests as a government depend upon the future. We operate *as if* the future is as real as the past, and so far we haven't been disappointed: the Service is 100 per cent successful. But that very success isn't without its warnings. What would happen if we *stopped* supervising events? We don't know, and we don't dare take the chance. Despite the evidence that the future is fixed, we have to take on the role of the caretaker of inevitability. We believe that nothing can possibly go wrong . . . but we have to act on the philosophy that history helps only those who help themselves.

"That's why we safeguard huge numbers of courtships right through to contract, and even beyond it. We have to see to it that *every single person who is mentioned in any Dirac 'cast gets born.* Our obligation as Event Police is to make the events of the future possible, because those events are crucial to our society—even the smallest of them. It's an enormous task, believe me, and it gets bigger and bigger every day. Apparently it always will."

"Always?" Jo said. "What about the public? Isn't it going to smell this out sooner or later? The evidence is piling up at a terrific rate."

"Yes and no," Krasna said. "Lots of people are smelling it out right now, just as you did. But the number of new people we need in the Service grows faster—it's always ahead of the number of laymen who follow the clues to the truth."

Jo took a deep breath. "You take all this as if it were as commonplace as boiling an egg, Kras," he said. "Don't you ever wonder about some of the things you get from the beep? That 'cast Dana Lje picked up from Canes Venatici, for instance, the one from the ship that was traveling backward in time? How is that possible? What could be the purpose? Is it——"

"*Pace, pace,*" Krasna said. "I don't know and I don't care. Neither should you. That event is too far in the future for us to worry about. We can't possibly know its context yet, so there's no sense in trying to understand it. If an Englishman of around 1600 had found out about the American Revolution, he would have thought it a tragedy; an Englishman of 1950 would have a very different view of it. We're in the same spot. The messages we get from the really far future have no contexts as yet."

"I think I see," Jo said. "I'll get used to it in time, I suppose, after I use the Dirac for a while. Or does my new rank authorize me to do that?"

"Yes, it does. But, Jo, first I want to pass on to you a rule of Service etiquette that must never be broken. You won't be allowed anywhere near a Dirac mike until you have it burned into your memory beyond any forgetfulness."

"I'm listening, Kras, believe me."

"Good. This is the rule: *The date of a Serviceman's death must never be mentioned in a Dirac 'cast.*"

Jo blinked, feeling a little chilly. The reason behind the rule was decidedly tough-minded, but its ultimate kindness was plain. He said, "I won't forget that. I'll want that protection myself. Many thanks, Kras. What's my new assignment?"

"To begin with," Krasna said, grinning, "as simple a job as I've ever given you, right here on Randolph. Skin out of here and find me that cab driver—the one who mentioned time-travel to you. He's uncomfortably close to the truth; closer than you were in one category.

"Find him, and bring him to me. The Service is about to take in a new raw recruit!"

DRODE'S EQUATIONS

Richard Grant

Richard Grant is one of the younger sf writers to enter the genre with literary ambitions in the early 1980s. Like John Kessel, James Patrick Kelly, Terry Bisson, and others, his educational background is the literary humanities. After a few short stories, he devoted himself to novels, with favorable critical reception. Among his early stories is "Drode's Equations," a mathematical sf story somewhat in the mold of the *ficciones* of Jorge Luis Borges. It neatly straddles the border between the literal and the metaphorical, and comes up with an unusual solution to the intellectual problem posed. It exists in dialogue with another classic mathematical sf story, Norman Kagan's "The Mathenauts" (the title story of a Rudy Rucker anthology), in which graduate students travel literally to abstract mathematical universes by feats of mathematical imagination.

On its subtextual level, "Drode's Equations" is a story that subverts hard science fiction even while achieving it, and, as an intentional subversion of genre, is characteristic of much of the speculative fiction of recent years. Richard Grant has published an essay in which he denies the desirability of category or genre boundaries for writers. This is not a new attitude for an sf writer (it was all the rage in the sixties), but it is again characteristic of many of the best younger writers of the past and present decade. The values of hard science fiction are being called into question by a bright new generation, again. Interesting comparisons include Gene Wolfe, whose "All the Hues of Hell" establishes metaphors for hard science without stating the tenors, and John M. Ford, whose "Chromatic Aberrations" is a hybrid of hard sf and magic realism; one might contrast it to the work of Rudy Rucker, the hard sf mathematician of the cyberpunks.

When I discovered Drode's Equations one day while puttering around in the old family library, I did not realize immediately what they were. They had been written in bold ink with a scrabbly hand (Drode's? My grandfather's?) into an old, leather-backed notebook, without commentary. They caught my eye, I think, because most of the symbols they employed were unfamiliar to me. In the dim light of the library, those strange formulations scrawled across yellowed paper had an eerie, almost necromantic appearance, as if they embodied some incantation that would part the bonds of earthly phenomena. Then I recognized an archaic symbol for Time, widely used by mathematicians of the former epoch, and in a few excited seconds I knew what I had found.

Drode's Equations had been lost for so long that the idea of their ever having existed had devolved from active discussion among students of mathematics to faintly imaginative speculation by an occasional rewriter of history. The matter had fallen, in other words, into the class of such questions as Was Lord Nador the illegitimate son of King Carn? (Support your answer. 15 pts.) One of the early casualties of this descent was an accurate notion of what, exactly, the Equations were. Not so long ago I read an account of the life of old Drode, accurate for the most part, in which the author blithely averred that the Equations had "proved" Time to be an illusion, among other things. I trust that the eventual effects of Time's relentless progress—which are well known and need not be described here—will convince the author of his error. In actuality, the first thing I learned about Drode's Equations upon satisfying myself of the nature of my discovery was that they "prove"—in the naïve sense that people nowadays seem to insist upon—nothing at all.

I think I should rush to explain, before someone of genuine expertise finds me out, that I am not a mathematician myself, although I do know something of mathematics. I could excuse myself for my pretension in writing about Drode's Equations this way by arguing that I am a historian. And I suppose that by avocation by the accident of having inherited one of the most wide-ranging collections of old books in existence, I am. But the truth of the matter is that I am an expert on railways, and thus I have made a living for most of my life. That being an expert on railways does not equip one to study and understand Drode's Equations may be forcefully argued, and will receive no dissent from my quarter. My profession did, however, exert a strong influence over the history of Drode's Equations after I discovered them. For it did not take a great deal of time, spent drinking tea and scribbling in the drafty old study my father built next to the library, to realize that the depth and implications of the Equations far exceeded the reach of my workaday mind, and it was not long after this realization that I boarded the little train that leaves St. Boto on Tuesday mornings and makes the sinuous journey to Culantro. From Culantro it is an hour's carriage-ride to the Royal University. In four years or five we hope to extend rail service all the way to the University's great honeysuckle-covered fences. Unfortunately railroads, unlike mathematics, depend for progress upon a thicker tangle of factors than the breadth and reach of a single human mind.

It was autumn, and lovely, the morning I left. In order to protect the old leather notebook into which Drode's Equations had been penned, I had carefully packed it away in a little case which I carried under my arm onto the train. I entrusted this case to the safekeeping of the conductor, a whiskered young man whose courteous demeanor had made an uplifting impression on me. I must remember, I thought, to commend this young fellow to the manager of the line. In the small bag of personal items I carried to my seat was another notebook, a cheap modern one, into which I had copied the Equations in order that I might give them another turn in my mind during the train trip. I felt no doubt whatsoever that what I had found were indeed Drode's lost Equations, but I felt considerable doubt as to how valuable or important the Equations really were, beyond putting an end to a controversy that had long since been removed from the heat of discussion and been placed on a distant back burner. What I wished to do was study the Equations a while longer, while I traveled, in an effort to come to some fuller understanding myself of what manner of gift I was making to the history of ideas in our poor Kingdom, where truth and genius have never fared too well. I settled with my working notebook into my comfortable seat in the Privileged Car of the train, and peered out the window for a few minutes, imagining the pleasant journey that lay ahead.

What a fine day it was! Autumn, I think, is my favorite time of the year. The splendor of the countryside around St. Boto is of a quiet type. The hills roll rather than soar, the trees stand in crowded little clusters rather than sprouting here and there in solitary magnificence, and the fields are divided into small patches of varied coloration rather than stretching endlessly like a golden sea. My profession has obliged me to travel from one end of the real to another, and from each trip I return more contentedly to the seat of my family in this little valley. Today was especially piercing in its perfection hereabouts, it seemed to me. The air was clear and fresh and seemed almost to have taken on a discernible crisp texture I could feel even inside the train. It was as if the sharply slanting sunlight, instead of merely falling through the air to its destination on the ground, were being subtly shaped and transmuted by the almost-visible atmosphere into something more fleeting and evocative than simple brightness. My brother, a practical man, would accuse me of projecting my own passing fancy onto the hapless autumn morning. I am inclined to think, however, that one's passing fancies are often a manner of deeply-rooted response to the complex patterns and resonances in nature, which by the act of perceiving one makes a part of one's own mental makeup. Thus does the outside world, I would argue, add color and chiaroscuro to our own, apparently personal, view of things. However that may be, it cannot be disputed that it was a day of surpassing loveliness on which I set out for Culantro. It was the kind of day one might wish to prolong into eternity.

After the train had gotten well away from the station and my enjoyment of the sunlit scenery had become dulled by satiation, I pulled out and opened up the small notebook I had copied the Equations into. It took me a minute or so to fully concentrate my attention onto the figures and symbols before me. I suppose it does not take much in the way of stimulation—a stirring view from a window, for example—to totally captivate and transport my mind. By degrees, nonetheless, I was able to focus my thoughts on the matter that was literally in hand. After all, I thought, the Equations were a spectacular, if emblematic, landscape unto themselves.

I looked at them one at a time. There were three Equations altogether, evidently mutually equivalent. The last one was much simpler—by which I mean shorter and more concise—than the first two. Its significance was entirely lost on me. The others that preceded it were scarcely more comprehensible, but owing to the fact that they embodied a greater number of terms and symbols I felt that I was at least able to recognize the broad outlines of the relationships they developed. In particular, the quantity represented by the symbol I took to indicate Time was recurrent in the initial Equation, appeared once in the second, and was altogether absent from the third. I was sure this meant something, but I could not divine what. In addition, there was a constant which I believe had to do with motion, or perhaps speed, that was present in the first and last Equations but absent from the central one. Again this observation seemed pregnant with significance, albeit elusive. I scribbled absently in the margin of my notebook.

A dry sort of cough distracted my attention for a moment, and I looked across the aisle to regard the small gray man on the other side of the car. He appeared to be lost in his own cogitations, rubbing his boot against the wooden footrail in a slow, automatic pattern. I considered for a moment, also automatically, what long-term effect such boot-rubbing would have on the wood of the rail. I believe oak had been chosen as the principal wood to be used for such appurtenances in train cars, and I wondered if oak were durable enough to give sufficient years of use. Harder woods had been available, of course, but had been deemed not worth the expense. Metal was out of the question for such trivial purposes, and was difficult to winnow away from the War Ministry even for the construction of engines and tracks and the like. My young assistant was an enthusiastic advocate of the new artificial materials, the false woods and metals, but I tended to distrust them. I made a note to examine the question more fully sometime in the near future. I smiled at the old man across the aisle, who had looked up and found me gazing absently in his direction and was perhaps made uncomfortable by my stare. Then I returned to the Equations.

It is often written, and sometimes even said in conversation, that something has "leapt from the page" at someone. I have always thought this metaphor overstates the case more severely than my own thought that the autumn morning was actively altering my state of mind. When I turned my head from the old man across the aisle and looked down at the notebook in my lap, however, it certainly did seem that Drode's three Equations had acquired a new dimension to augment the flatness with which they lay upon the slightly off-white paper, just as if they were suddenly able to jump closer to my eyes. And in a way I suppose it is true that they had taken on a new dimension, for without deviating from the sloping scrawl in which I had committed them to my notebook they suddenly seemed to have become swollen with meaning. Although I realized, even at the moment, that the only change that had occurred had taken place within the confines of my own mind, I gaped at the Equations as if they had been alive and squirming on the paper below.

Suddenly I understood, or seemed to understand, something of the significance of the cryptic markings. It is difficult now to reduce to a logical arrangement the mental image that sprang upon me as if of its own accord, but the essence of what I perceived about the Equations at that moment concerned the elimination of Time in the progression from the first Equation to the last. If, as I believed, the three Equations were logically equivalent, then they must describe or formulate, in different ways, the same truth about nature, whatever that truth might be. This being the case, then this mysterious Truth (which I find myself capitalizing in my own thoughts) appears in the first Equation as something that can only be discussed by means of repeated reference to Time. And yet when we have arrived at the final Equation this Truth stands naked and unadorned by any mention of Time at all.

I considered this. I thought not about the Equations but about this elusive Truth lurking at their center. At first it would seem that the matter was so bound up with Time that it could not be stated without taking Time seriously into account. This notion squared nicely with my belief that Drode's Equations embodied some sturdy verity of nature, for I could not imagine any mortal discussion of the fundamental reality of things that did not couch itself in terms of Time slipping past us. Yet we find that in the third Equation of the series the Truth at hand is stated without so much as a tip of the hat in Time's direction. By some transcendent leap, it seemed to me, Drode's Equations had bridged the abyss between the mortal view of reality as a function of ineluctable Time and the angelic view of reality as a pure and Time-less whole.

Somehow this little epiphany leaped upon me—to return to the worn-out old metaphor—with such force that I felt myself obliged to leave off thinking of it for a while. My head swung gratefully toward the window of the train, where the delicately-colored autumn countryside was whizzing by.

I stared in a kind of wonderment at the broken patches of forest the train was passing through. The sun was nearing the top of its climb for the day, and I became conscious of its warmth on my left arm just inside the glass. The train was headed roughly west, then, I thought. I tried to place this leg of the journey on an imagined map. The old railway chart hanging behind my desk in the study appeared faintly in my mind, but I could envision only a piece of it at a time, while the surrounding sections dissolved in a tan and yellow blur. I persisted for some while at this mental game, laboring to assemble the entire map in my imagination, as it were, piecemeal.

When one area came clearly into view I would try to hold it in place, off to the side somewhere, while I conjured up an adjoining region to fasten to it. Invariably, by the time I had dreamed up the new map-section the old one would have faded to a generalized glob that floated uncertainly in space. Finally I tired of this exercise, and anyway I remembered that the only westward leg of the otherwise northerly train ride was the stretch of track at the foot of the low mountain range over which we must cross to reach Culantro. Unbidden, a distinct picture of the mountainous section of the old map formed in my mind and remained there for a few seconds, adrift and separate from the rest of the Kingdom as if it had temporarily slipped its geographical moorings and floated into a timeless netherworld.

It must be true that one's thoughts begin to wander as one ages. I returned from my mental vagary to find myself staring out the window at hilly terrain that was, indeed, starting to roll more steeply. The thought of climbing effortlessly into the mountains exhilarated me. I took a deep breath, relishing the uniqueness of the moment. The day outside was more beautiful than before.

For some reason I noticed the trees: not the trees as a body or system of things, but as individual entities. The oak trees were mostly turned to red and brown, and their leaves fluttered down in what appeared to be a light breeze, perhaps stirred by the very train on which I was riding. The smaller oaks stood almost denuded of their foliage. The maples, on the other hand, clung to their leaves with a stubborn fixity of purpose. Summer was a bit hot for maples in this part of the Kingdom, and some of the larger ones showed, in their upper leaves, the scorched battle scars of their long August campaign for survival. But the final triumph was theirs, for having outlasted the summer and the oaks they had now inherited the sunlight, which fell gracefully on their stolid branches. I made a slight bow in their direction in acknowledgment of their perseverance, and felt immediately silly for doing so.

I darted my eyes around and discovered that the old man across the aisle was watching me. Inwardly I shrugged. I had almost, but not quite, passed the stage in life of being concerned about what impression I was making on my fellow passengers. Then I considered that the old man might form an unfortunate opinion of the national railways as attracting the kind of eccentric personality that goes about nodding at passing trees, and I hastened to smile cheerfully at the old man by way of reassuring him. Then I thought perhaps a cheerful smile with no proximate cause immediately apparent might make matters worse, and I searched for something to say to round out the friendly overture.

"Marvelous weather for traveling, is it not?" I ventured. I excused myself for this triteness on grounds of expediency.

To my distinct consternation, the old man responded not by returning some mindless pleasantry as I had expected, but by turning to look out his own window, as if to determine what manner of thing was this weather that it should receive my unprompted approbation. My facial muscles were growing weary of maintaining the cheerful smile that had gotten me into this imbroglio. The old man turned around to stare pointedly at me.

"I rather fancy springtime, myself," he said. "Late springtime. Much happier season. Birth, renewal, that sort of thing. Fall's too sad, I think."

Having begun to regard the situation as ludicrous, I was mildly taken aback by this thoughtful reply. Belatedly I dropped the smile from my face and assumed what I like to think of as my philosophical expression.

"Ah," I returned, "but there's nothing sad about the cycle turning to its other side, is there? It's what makes the springtime so pleasing, after all, isn't it?"

"Hmph," the old man opined. "Wouldn't be sad if you could just stop it at fall, but next thing you've got *winter* coming along, and you know how *winter* is.

Dreadful. Like trying to enjoy the sunset without thinking how dark it's going to get straightaway. Much better in springtime, next thing you've got summer, very nice season."

I thought about this. The old man certainly seemed to have a tragic view of things. He had his point, of course; autumn was certainly fleeting. In a few weeks the leaves would be gone and the air unpleasantly cold. But there was no stopping the seasons from changing.

"Still," I offered, somewhat lamely it seemed to me, "it *is* a lovely time of the year, even if it doesn't last long. And it *is* an exceptionally nice day."

"I'm not saying it isn't," said the old man. This seemed to satisfy him as a last word upon the subject, for he turned back his head to its position of evident absorption in the intricate red-and-gold pattern of the fabric covering the seat ahead of him. I will not deny that I was relieved.

See yourself in old people, my father had told me before he himself became elderly. I tried to see myself in the old fellow across the aisle, whom I imagined to be a curmudgeonly individual who had scrimped through his life in order that he might travel, in his waning years, in the Privileged Car. Blessedly, the vision I sought eluded me. I suppose my imagination requires some more nutritive fodder to lend it the vitality to gallop away.

But what unkind and unhappy thoughts I was having, I realized. I felt a stab of dismay that made the brilliant colors of autumn seem to fade before me. As I understand is common among men of affairs, I do not like to indulge myself by giving in to abrupt changes in mood, and have become practiced in managing such things when they arise. In accordance with the advice of one of the ancient poets who still lives a sort of life in the old family library, I took solace in the study of pure mathematics.

Drode's Equations lay open and mute before me. If I expected them to leap up at me again (which, I confess, I almost palpably did) I was doomed to disappointment. Looking at them again I saw them as just so many numbers and symbols arrayed on the page of my notebook. I suppose that, having achieved a modest and speculative insight into the meaning of the Equations, I now saw them as a kind of intellectual puzzle rather than a mystical embodiment of some sublime Truth. Well, this was what I had always thought pure mathematics should be—intellectual and not mystical. I settled comfortably into the puzzle as if snuggling deeper into a leather chair, or a well-upholstered seat in the Privileged Car of a train.

Roughly I formulated the puzzle thus: how does Drode manage to overcome the need to consider Time in stating a fact or a relationship of nature that is initially propounded in such a way that Time is an important factor? Or, more succinctly, how has Drode slipped the bonds of Time? (This seemed more poetical a way of looking at it.)

The process of formulating, for myself, the puzzle of Drode's Equations seemed to relax me. I was again conscious of the sun shining warmly on my left arm, up to about four inches above the elbow. The autumn day, now sliding into early afternoon, beckoned. I yearned for the yellow fields stretching beneath the sun as I longed for a solution to the riddle in my notebook. If Drode had managed to get around the need to consider Time in stating whatever it was his Equations stated, I thought, he must have hit upon a way of looking at nature through his shrewd mathematician's eyes that was quite distinct from the usual human point of view. Whatever the phenomenon might have been that he was describing, he must have discovered a way to consider it as a *thing unto itself*, without the stretching and shading and illusory significance that Time gives to the things we perceive. For whenever we look at any aspect of nature, I thought, we see it through the highly colored lenses of our mortal minds, the most central aspect of which is that they are never still, never steady. Time rushes through us as we rush through Time. Yet here was Drode proposing a method of looking at some face of reality from which Time had been neatly refined into oblivion. Or so it seemed to me.

The sheer weight of this speculation brought me to a halt. How close was I, really, to Drode's Equations? Perhaps I had strayed onto a path of my own making, ignoring the obstruction of the underbrush until, by my own heavy-footed trodding, it was smoothed out of the way. But no, this was crediting myself too generously for insightful thinking of which I hardly thought myself capable. It could not be *me* projecting my perceptions onto the Equations. Therefore it must be that the Equations were subtly entering and shaping my thoughts. I felt a faint inward tugging, as if of memory struggling to surface, and I glanced absently leftward out the window.

The train had entered the mountains now. The ground on which the tracks were laid seemed to be a narrow ledge winding its way upward, for the scrub-covered surface fell away just outside the window and dropped vertiginously for several hundred feet. The sun had fallen slightly, making the distant contours of the terrain more sharply and starkly delineated. In this region the advent of autumn was a bit more advanced than around St. Boto. The trees had reached nearly the peak of their seasonal coloration; another week and they would be falling brown and dead to the ground. What a perfect day to be making this trip!

The young conductor with the blond whiskers stopped at my seat to ask if I would like tea.

"Tea," I said aloud. The word sounded strange and unfamiliar at first, and it was a moment before I could draw my mind away from the lure of the scenery to concentrate on the question at hand. Dimly the image of a fragrant, steaming cup came to me. "Ah, tea," I said. "By all means, thank you."

The conductor smiled a bit nervously, perhaps thinking me dotty, and turned to inquire of the old man across the aisle, but I withdrew my attention. It was a new practice, the serving of tea in the Privileged Car. When it was suggested, the idea drew criticism from some quarters as a needless expense. I had personally supported the proposal strongly, however. I argued that we should do what we reasonably could—and tea after all is not *so* expensive—to make rail travel a pleasure that will be remembered fondly by those who have paid for it. This would be my first taste of the object of my advocacy.

In a few minutes the conductor was back with a little tray that fastened onto the seat in front of me and hung a few inches above my lap. I noted with approval, before paying any mind to the things the tray held, how unobtrusively the two little clamps had been secured to the seat before me to permit the tray to be simply and easily hung. Then I regarded the tray itself, just as the conductor's hands were being withdrawn. It was made of some kind of false wood (a triumph for my young assistant!) and on it were all the things one needs for a successful bout with the tea leaves. There was a little earthware pot in which the tea, I surmised, was brewing, and a strainer with tiny reed-like crosshairs, and a good sturdy-looking mug. To the side were squat little vessels bearing thick cream and coarse sugar. Finally, there was a napkin made of the light cloth we had chosen for a variety of uses on the railway. The cloth has a cool and pleasing texture to the touch, but is inexpensive enough to dispose of when, as will inevitably happen on a train, it becomes badly soiled. As I placed this napkin loosely across my lap I considered how few people give any thought to the complexity and the unending series of small decisions involved in running a railway. Ah, but for those who are personally involved, what pleasure there is—an almost aesthetic satisfaction—in the problem correctly solved, the objective precisely attained.

I was quite smug now, with the tray suspended just above my lap, the napkin tucked in, the sun falling warmly on my left side, and the arms of my seat holding me into this little niche. I stretched out my legs until my feet rested against the little wooden footrail. With one hand I held the strainer in front of the spout of the earthware teapot while I poured a little of its contents into the mug. The tea had a dark and hearty appearance. Lifting the heavy mug to my lips I found the tea to be hot and flavorful. I decided the sugar would be unnecessary and the cream a distraction. Still holding the mug near my mouth I looked out the window at the spectacular scenery of the mountains. Everything seemed about as nice as I could imagine it possible to be. I sipped the tea beatifically.

Because I sensed that the essential perfection of the moment had stimulated my mind to an unusual sharpness, I picked up my notebook to have another look at Drode's Equations. I propped the notebook on the tray, resting its spine against the seat before me, so that I could see its open pages without interrupting my enjoyment of the tea. The Equations looked quite small. More than that, in juxtaposition with the stirring view of the mountains just a little to the left, they looked quite insignificant. Nonetheless I looked at them, the last one of them in particular. I did not concentrate on it especially. I thought, if it is true, as some modern thinkers argue, that the mind is like a machine that can be set in motion and left to follow its course without conscious supervision, then I would leave my mind to work on this third Equation while I experienced the fullness of this moment in the mountains in autumn.

The train was nearly at the top. When I say the top, of course, I mean the top of the rather small mountain over which the rails were laid. The truly large mountains stood in view around us, dwarfing our little one, dwarfing the train, its passengers, and such tiny things as three Equations in a small notebook. And yet the Equations were possibly important things, just as it was important for our Kingdom that this little railroad wend its way through the mountains. Of the importance of the passengers on this particular train I did not feel qualified to form an opinion. I remembered to enjoy my tea.

The direction the train was now taking caused the sunlight to fall on a larger part of my body than it previously had. I was beginning to grow warm. In my seat I shifted slightly. The third Equation did not seem terribly difficult, just elusive. I believed I could recognize nearly all the symbols now, recalled from the days I had studied mathematics. There were two I could not quite remember, and I could feel my mind straining to make the distant connection. I relaxed my outward self which was straining with it, and sipped more tea. The tea had cooled slightly and was at a nearly ideal temperature for drinking. It seemed to be a blend of a number of ingredients, and I wondered who had selected it to be served on the train. An excellent choice. There was a faint taste in it that I could not recognize, a taste that reminded me of something vague and forgotten. I held some of the tea in my mouth, swishing it reflectively about, and thought about my days as a student: all that effort ramming things into my memory, and now it was just as difficult to get them out again. I swallowed the tea.

The train shifted; the sun was nearly in my eyes. I was unable to make out the marks in my notebook through the sudden glare. This was fine, because I was tired of the effort of thinking of the Equations. I relaxed and had another sip of tea and felt the train stop climbing and come to a level ride. We had reached the top, I thought, watching the tea slide from one side of the mug to the other in diminishing waves of surprise. I smiled at the thought of tea surprised and looked fondly into the mug.

Chamomile, I thought, and wondered why Drode's Equations had been so puzzling. It all seemed extraordinarily clear. I saw the shimmering surface of the tea in the mug in my hand, and I felt as if I were walking on it—or better, standing on it, maintaining an impossible balance between this moment and the one that must inevitably follow. I could not move my head or avert my eyes. Although I concentrated, I could not seem to feel any awareness of being attached to my arms and legs. I was able to recognize my hand holding the mug of tea, but it seemed a thing over which I had no influence. I realized how correct I had been in imagining the sunlit air to have a distinct texture, for now I was aware of the creamy soft essence of the sunlight as it slid through me. I could feel the mountains close at hand, strong and brooding. Reality appeared to fold around the place where I was sitting, drawing my attention into its immense brightness.

I relate this series of realizations in some kind of linear order, although at the time these things were all immediately obvious, these things and something ineffable beyond them. The train had stopped, or perhaps I should say I saw through the layers of illusion that had previously caused me to think the train was in motion. My mind and the autumn afternoon were welded into a single phenomenon. I knew the bliss of unambiguity. I had understood Drode's Equations.

This thought—for it was a thought at last, after all the explosive revelations that had not been like normal thoughts at all—seemed to jolt me into a different kind of awareness. I could feel the train vibrating and clicking beneath me, the taste of tea was in my mouth, and I was overly warm in the afternoon sun. I looked at my watch but the time I read meant nothing to me. The old man was asleep across the aisle. To satisfy my urge for definite action, I took a long sip of tea from the mug. I was surprised to find it still hot, though maybe marginally below the optimal temperature for drinking. This distracted me from my enjoyment of the remainder of the mug less than the troubling feeling that I had forgotten something, that something had been on my mind that I could not quite recall. Everyone, I believe, has such feelings from time to time.

A few hours later, as it was becoming dark, the train pulled into the little station at Culantro, where a number of people were waiting. I gathered my few things and was preparing to disembark when the young conductor interrupted me to press something into my hand. It was the little case in which I had carefully laid the leather-backed notebook where Drode's Equations had been written with a scrabbly hand. I thanked the conductor, thought for a moment, handed him a modest tip, and climbed down into the chilly autumn evening.

The University, to which I had dispatched a wire as soon as my travel plans became definite, had sent a driver to meet me, and this person relieved me of the little case and my bag of personal items. As I climbed into the carriage I was still mindful of a bothersome feeling of detachment. The hour's travel over bumpy roads was unduly long and, in the deepening darkness, uneventful.

My old acquaintance on the mathematics faculty of the University was waiting for me when I arrived. I was shown into a wood-paneled parlor. It was very nice of him to have waited, I thought, but I could not summon the energy to offer more than a weary greeting in response to his kindness. He seemed to interpret my distant air as a reaction to the strenuous journey by train, for he was quick to take my bag and sit me down in a puffy armchair. I found that I was holding the little case under my arm, although I could not remember having retrieved it from the carriage driver.

"Will you have some tea?" he inquired. "Or some brandy, perhaps?"

I chose the brandy.

"It's very good to see you again," my friend told me. "We were all so excited to hear of your discovery. But I suppose you're a bit tired to talk about it just now."

With some effort I extended my arm to him with the small case clutched in my hand. He was at first bemused by my gesture, but quickly realized I was offering him this package by way of response to his mention of the "discovery." His eyes widened as he took it from me. Gently he unfastened it and drew out the old notebook.

"Ah!" he said, opening it carefully. "And here they are! Marvelous! And in Drode's own hand, unless I'm mistaken. I can barely make it out."

"It is difficult," I acknowledged, feeling the brandy doing something or other inside my head.

"Yes," he said, staring at the markings on the old paper. "Do you have any idea what it means? I must confess I'm totally baffled at a first glance."

I took another sip of the excellent brandy. "Nothing to speak of," I said. "Although there was a moment there, on the train, you know, when I thought I was beginning to understand."

"Mm," he said, eyeing the Equations thoughtfully.

The brandy swirled pleasantly inside.

High in the mountains it is a perfect autumn afternoon, clear and brilliant. The sun has just begun to drop in the sky, and its warmth falls blessedly on my arm. A taste of sweet tea with chamomile is on my tongue, and I am filled with vibrant thoughts of youth and happiness. One of my hands rests pleasantly on a soft cloth napkin, and the other holds the mug of tea that has just left my lips. The surface of the tea shimmers in the sunlight, refracting a hundred colors into my eyes. Around me is the Privileged Car of a train, a little encapsulated piece of civilization which I have helped to create and send to the top of this mountain. I have the sense of having truly arrived somewhere, of having attained a pure and final solution that is unmarred by the hedging and compromise of everyday affairs. The happiness that effulges around me is of a sort seldom glimpsed by mortal minds, for it is the happiness born of certainty that this moment will not die, that it will not break through the thin surface of the present and drown in the past.

I understand Drode's Equations.

THE WEATHER MAN

Theodore L. Thomas

Theodore L. Thomas published stories widely in the science fiction field between 1952 and the late seventies, and collaborated on two novels with Kate Wilhelm, *The Clone* (1965) and *The Year of the Cloud* (1970). He was always a competent craftsman. His best work was done for the most part for Campbell's *Astounding/ Analog*, but since he did not achieve recognition as a novelist, his shorter works are infrequently reprinted today by anthologists. This long story is perhaps his best.

Meteorology is one of the scientific disciplines that is little treated in hard sf, perhaps because it is interdisciplinary and does not yield exact predictions far in advance. Exceptions that come readily to mind include George R. Stewart's nongenre novel, *Storm* (told from the point of view of a storm); Ben Bova's novel, *The Weathermakers*; and a number of the stories of Hilbert Schenck, including "Hurricane Claude" and "The Morphology of the Kirkham Wreck"; and Thomas's "The Weather Man." Even in this era of world-building sf novels, the weather (like the social system) is often a minor factor, or ignored, just there. Yet weather control has long been a dream of science, and of science fiction of the utopian strain.

"The Weather Man" (1962) uses the venerable genre technique of extrapolating a future dominated entirely by any one facet of science and society (for good, as in H. G. Wells's "Wings Over the World" in the film *Things to Come*, or ill, as in Frederik Pohl and C. M. Kornbluth's ad agencies in *The Space Merchants*)—an approach critic Frederic Jameson has termed "world reduction." It is a special case of world-building, also subsumed under Jameson's term.

The Weather Control Board suggests a parallel to Kipling's Aerial Board of Control, in "With the Night Mail" and "As Easy as A.B.C." Thomas's big idea is that the weather on Earth could be controlled, and the controllers would rule the world. Thomas's view of politics, in the Weather Council, is notably benign for hard sf, and his woman scientist of the Weather Advisers a stronger and more rounded character than is usually found in the sf of the period. Thomas's technique is to portray the everyday world of the future in such a way that it reveals itself to the reader steadily through significant details that sometimes indicate revelations of major change. This is a story of the human meaning of science and a wonder story of technology on the largest scale. The progressive changes in point of view encourage the reader to identify with the godlike narrative voice in the end, the spirit of hard sf.

". . . And the name 'Weather Bureau' continued to be used, although the organization itself was somewhat changed in form. Thus the Weather Congress consisted of three arms. First was the political arm, the Weather Council. Second was the scientific arm, the Weather Advisors. Third was the operating arm, the Weather Bureau. All three arms were relatively independent, and each . . ."

THE COLUMBIA ENCYCLOPEDIA,
32nd Edition
Columbia University Press

Jonathan H. Wilburn opened his eyes and immediately felt the tension in the day. He lay there, puzzled, seeking the source of it. It was the start of just another day in Palermo. The street noises were normal, his apartment was quiet, and he felt good. That was it. He felt good, very good, full of vigor and strong of mind, and with the feeling that he was ready for anything that might happen.

In one movement he threw back the cover and rolled to his feet alongside the bed. Not bad for a man who had turned fifty last week. He stepped into the shower and dissolved his pajamas into a rich foam of cleansing lather. He dried and stood motionless in the center of his dressing room. The tension and the excitement were still with him. He depilated and dressed, and as he slipped into his jacket it came to him.

Sometime during the night in his sleep he had made up his mind that the time had come for him to make a move. He was fifty years old, he had carefully built a good reputation, and he had come as far as he could in the normal course of events. It was now time to push, time to take a chance. To reach the top in politics you have to take a chance.

Wilburn finished slipping into his jacket. He bared his teeth at himself in the mirror. Now he knew why the day felt different. But knowing the reason did nothing to diminish the tension. He would live with it from now on; this he knew for a certainty. He would live and work on the tips of his toes, looking for a way to seize the god of luck and give him a good ringing out.

For a quarter of a century he had moved cautiously, planning each move, insuring its success before he committed himself to it. Slowly he had climbed through the tiers of politics, the House, the Senate, the United Nations, an ambassadorship, several emergency chairmanships, and finally, the most elite of all bodies, the Weather Congress. His reputation was made, he was known as a brilliant, affable diplomat, one with high skill at bringing about agreement among other hostile Councilmen. He had built a strong following among the two hundred members in the Weather Council. But in politics as in everything else, the higher one climbs, the tougher the advancement. Wilburn suddenly came to the realization that he had not made any advancements in four years. Then came his fiftieth birthday.

Jonathan Wilburn ate breakfast with his wife that morning. Harriet was a slim woman, quietly wise in her role of the wife of a member of the Council of the Weather Congress. In one quick glance she saw that her husband was tight as a wire, and she touched the Diner and placed coffee in front of him. While he sipped it she touched out a set of onion-flavored eggs and carefully hand-basted them with the pork sauce he loved so much; she did not trust the Diner to do it right. While she worked she chatted about the news in the morning paper. Wilburn ate his breakfast, part listening, part smiling and grunting responses, and part staring into space. He kissed her good-by then, and went out and stepped on a walk.

He rode the walk through the soft Sicilian air, and then became impatient with standing still. He stepped off the walk and strode alongside, and he felt pleased at the way his legs stretched. Off in the distance he could see the dome of the main Council building, and it brought his mind back to the problem at hand. But, even as he thought it, he knew it was nothing he could reason out in advance. This was something he would have to pick up on the spur of the moment. And he would have to stay alert to recognize it when it came.

Wilburn stepped back on the walk and rode it to the Council.

He entered the Great Hall by the north stairs and walked along the east wall toward the stairs to his office. A group of sight-seers were being guided across the Great Hall by a uniformed guide, and the guide was describing the wonders of the Hall. When the guide saw Wilburn coming, he interrupted his lecture to say, "And coming toward us from our left is Councilman Wilburn of an eastern United States District of whom you have all heard and who will play such an important part in the vote today to reduce the water available to northern Australia."

The sight-seers stopped, stumbling into one another at the unexpected appearance of such a celebrity. Wilburn smiled and waved at them, and this confounded them even more, but he did not stop to talk. He knew from the guide's remarks that none of his constituents were in the group; the guide would have contrived to warn him so that he could act accordingly. Wilburn smiled to himself—an office-holder had many advantages over a mere candidate for office.

Wilburn turned to the stairs and rode up with Councilman Georges DuBois, of middle Europe. DuBois said, "I heard him. Decided yet how you are to vote on this Australian situation, Jonathan?"

"I lean toward an aye, but I don't know. Do you?"

DuBois shook his head. "I feel the same. It is a thing we should do only with the greatest of caution. It is a terrible thing to make men suffer, and even worse to do it to women and children. I don't know."

They rode in silence to the top of the stairs, and just before they parted Wilburn said, "My wife stands with me in everything *I* do, George."

DuBois looked at him thoughtfully for a moment, and then said, "Yes, I understand you. The women there are as much to blame as the men, and deserve punishment as much. Yes, that will help me if I vote aye. I will see you in Council." They nodded good-by to each other in a wordless gesture of mutual respect and understanding. DuBois was one of the thoughtful Councilmen who knew better than most the fearful responsibility carried by the political arm of the Weather Congress.

Wilburn nodded to his staff as he passed through the outer office. Once at his desk he swiftly settled down to take care of the many chores. The small pile of papers stacked neatly in the center of his desk melted away as he picked up one after another, dictated the words that disposed of it, and dropped it on another pile.

He was just finishing when a gentle masculine voice said through the speaker, "Have you time to see a friend?"

Wilburn smiled, and got up to open the door of his office for Councilman Gardner Tongareva. The two men smiled and shook hands, and Tongareva settled back deep into one of Wilburn's chairs. He was a yellow-skinned man, a Polynesian, wrinkled and old and wise. His trousers were full and short, reminiscent of the sarong worn by his ancestors. His hair was white and his face was warm and kindly. Tongareva was one of those rare men whose mere presence brought smiles to the faces of his companions and peace to their hearts. He was a man of enormous influence in the Council solely by virtue of his personality.

His district was 15–30 degrees north latitude 150–165 degrees east longitude, the same fifteen-degree-on-a-side landed area of the Earth as the District of each of the other Councilmen. But in Tongareva's case the land was vanishingly small. The only land in the entire region was Marcus Island, one square mile in area, and supporting exactly four people. This was quite a contrast with the 100 million people living in Wilburn's District of 30–45 degrees north latitude 75–90 degrees west longitude. Yet time after time when the population-weighted votes of the two hundred Councilmen were counted, it was apparent that Tongareva had swayed a large percentage of the entire globe.

Wilburn leaned back in his chair and said to Tongareva, "Have you reached a decision yet about the Australian drought?"

Tongareva nodded. "Yes, I have. I believe we have no choice but to subject them to a year's drought. Naughty children must be spanked, and for two years these people have persisted in maintaining an uneven balance of trade. What is really involved here, Jonathan, is a challenge to the supreme authority of the Weather Congress over the peoples of the world. These people in Queensland and the Northern Territory are a hardy lot. They don't really believe that we can or will chastise them by controlling their weather to their detriment. They must be punished immediately or other sections of the world will begin acting up, too. At this time a simple drought to take away their lush prosperity for a year ought to serve. Later it might become necessary to make them suffer, and none of us wants that. Yes, Jonathan, my vote will be cast in favor of the Australian drought."

Wilburn nodded soberly. He saw now that the vote almost certainly would be in favor of punishment. Most of the Councilmen seemed to feel it was necessary, but were reluctant to cause suffering. But when Tongareva stated his position as he just had, the reluctance would be put aside. Wilburn said, "I agree with you, Gardner. You have put into words the thoughts of most of us in this matter. I will vote with you."

Tongareva said nothing, but he continued to stare sharply at Wilburn. It was not a discomfiting stare; nothing Tongareva did was ever discomfiting. Tongareva said, "You are a different man this morning, my good friend. Just as you have been still a different man for the last three weeks. You have resolved whatever it is that has been disturbing you, and I am pleased. No," he raised a hand as Wilburn was about to speak, "it is quite unnecessary to discuss it. When you want me, I will be there to help you." He stood up. "And now I must go to discuss the Australian situation with some of the others." He smiled and left before Wilburn could say anything.

Wilburn stared after him, awed at the enormous ability of Tongareva to understand what he had been going through. He shook his head and gathered himself and then went out into his waiting room to talk to the dozen people who were waiting to see him.

"I'm sorry to keep you waiting," he said to all of them, "but things are hectic around the Council this morning, as I guess you know. Please forgive me for not seeing each of you alone, but we will be summoned for Council business in a few minutes. I did not want to miss the chance to see all of you for a moment or two at least. Perhaps we can get together this afternoon or tomorrow morning."

And Wilburn moved around the room shaking hands and fixing in his mind the name of each visitor. Two of them were not constituents. They were lobbyists representing the northern Australian Districts, and they launched into a tirade against the taking of any punitive action against the Districts.

Wilburn held up his hand and said, "Gentlemen, this topic may not be discussed under these circumstances. I will listen to the arguments for and against on the floor of the Council, nowhere else. That is all." He smiled and began to pass on.

The younger of the two seized his arm and turned him to face him, saying, "But, Councilman, you must listen. These poor people are being made to suffer for the acts of a few of their leaders. You cannot—"

Wilburn shrugged away from the restraining arm, stepped swiftly to the wall and pressed a button there. The lobbyist turned pale and said, "Oh, now, Councilman, I meant no harm. Please do not lodge a protest against me. Please—"

Two men in the uniform of the Weather Congress swept in the outer door. Wilburn's voice was calm and his face impassive, but his eyes glinted like ice crystals. He pointed and said to the guards, "This man grabbed my arm to try to force me to listen to his arguments on Council business. I lodge a protest against him."

It all happened so fast the rest of the visitors had difficulty recalling exactly what had happened. But the recording tapes showed, and Wilburn knew that the lobbyist would never again be allowed in the halls of the Weather Congress. The two guards softly hustled him out of the room. The other lobbyist said, "I am sorry, Councilman. I feel responsible for his conduct; he is new."

Wilburn nodded and started to speak, but a low musical chime sounded repeatedly in the room. Wilburn said to the visitors, "Please excuse me. I must go to the Council Floor now. If you wish, you may watch the proceedings from the Visitors' Auditorium. Thank you for coming up to see me, and I hope we can talk more another time." He waved and smiled and went back into his office.

Hurriedly he checked his staff to see that they were ready for the day's business. All were in position, all knew their roles in the coming debate. Wilburn then took the belt to the Floor, walking the last hundred yards out in the public hall where he could be seen. As he came to the main doors several newspapermen asked permission to approach, but he refused; he wanted to get to his desk early and start work.

He went through the doors and down the short wide hall that led to the Floor. He came out into the huge room and went down the main aisle toward his desk. A few Councilmen were already there, and as the Recorder called off Wilburn's name, they looked up and waved at him. He waved back and continued on his way to his high-seniority desk up front. He sat down and began flipping the buttons and switches that put him in touch with everything that was going on. Immediately a light glowed indicating that one of the seated Councilmen wanted to talk to him. Councilman Hardy of 165–180 west longitude 30–45 south latitude—containing most of New Zealand—said to him, "Well, Jonathan, have you talked with Tongareva yet?"

"Yes, George, I have."

"Going to vote the way he wants?"

"Yes, although I want to wait and hear what is said in opposition before I finally make up my mind. Where do you stand?"

There was a perceptible pause, then, "I will probably vote against it, unless someone expresses the extreme reluctance of the Council to vote for drought."

"Why don't you do it, George?"

"Maybe I will. Thank you, Jonathan." And he cut the circuit.

Wilburn looked around the huge chamber, and as always, he became a little awed at what he saw. It was more than the impressive array of the two hundred huge desks, the raised President's chair, the great board that showed the weather at the moment on every part of the Earth's surface, and the communications rooms set off from the main room. There was an aura about this great chamber that was felt by all the men and women who entered it, whether to work in it or simply to visit. The fate of the Earth was centered here, and had been for fifty years. From this chamber flowed the decisions that controlled the world.

The Weather Congress was the supreme body of Earth, able to bend states, nations, continents, and hemispheres to its will. What dictator, what country, could survive when no drop of rain fell for a year? Or what dictator, what country could survive when blanketed under fifty feet of snow and ice? The Weather Congress could freeze the Congo River or dry up the Amazon. It could flood the Sahara or Tierra del Fuego. It could thaw the tundra, and raise and lower the levels of the oceans at will. And here, in this chamber, all the political decisions had been made, and the chamber seemed to acquire some of the feeling that had been expressed over the last half century, from the stormy early days, to the more settled and reflective present. It was a powerful chamber, and it made its power felt by those who sat in it.

A great many Councilmen had seated themselves. Another chime sounded, and the weather requests began to be relayed to the Councilmen. The Recorder read off the requests, and his voice reached each desk through a tiny speaker. At the same time the written request flashed on the big board. In this manner the Councilmen could busy themselves with other duties while keeping an eye on the requests.

The first request, as usual, came from the Lovers of the Lowly Cactus Plant, and they wanted less rainfall and more desolation in Death Valley to keep the Barrel Cactus from becoming extinct.

Wilburn rang Tongareva's desk and said, "How many have you talked to, Gardner?"

"About forty, Jonathan. I caught a large group having a cup of coffee."

"Have you talked to Maitland?"

There was a perceptible pause. Maitland seemed always to be against anything Wilburn stood for. His District was 60–75 west longitude 30–45 north latitude, adjoining Wilburn's and including New York City and Boston. Maitland always made it plain that he considered Wilburn unfit for the position of influence he held in the Council. "No," said Tongareva, and Wilburn could see him shake his great head, "no, I did not talk to Maitland."

Wilburn signed off, and listened and watched. The president of Bolivia complained that the region around Cochabamba was running a little too cool to suit his taste. The mayor of Avigait in Greenland stated that the corn crop was ten per cent lower this year due to an extra two inches of rainfall and too much cloud cover. Wilburn nodded; there was one that should be treated seriously, and he pushed a button on his desk marked "favorable" to insure that it would be considered by the entire Council.

His phone rang. It was a constituent asking him to address the Combined Rotary Club at their annual meeting October 27th next. The clear light flashed as Wilburn's staff, monitoring and checking everything, indicated that he was free on that day. "Why, thank you, yes," said Wilburn, accepting the invitation. "I shall be grateful for the chance to talk to your group." He knew he had made no address in that region for a year, and it was high time. Probably his staff had subtly set it up in the first place.

A farmer outside of Gatrun, Libya, wanted his neighbor's water cut back so that all their crops would be the same height.

Then a conference was called among half a dozen Councilmen to discuss the order of speeches on the Australian situation. While they worked this out, Wilburn noted a request from Ceylon to be allowed to go over from rice in the inland sections to wheat, with the attendant reduction in rainfall and average temperature. He pushed the "favorable" button.

It was decided that George DuBois, of Middle Europe, should introduce the drought resolution, with appropriately reluctant language.

One George Andrews of Holtville, California, wanted to see snow fall again before he died, which would be in a few weeks now, no matter that it was July. He could not leave the semitropical environment of Holtville.

Tongareva would second the resolution, and then they would hear the Councilmen from the Australian Districts present their reasons why the punishment should not be instituted. After that they would play it by ear.

The seaport city of Stockholm requested an additional fifteen centimeters of elevation for the Baltic Sea. Kobdo, Mongolia, complained that there had been two disastrous avalanches due to the extra snow burden. And it was there that the hairs on the back of Wilburn's neck began to prickle.

He stiffened in his seat and looked around to see the source of the strange sensation. The floor bustled with activity, all of it normal. He stood up, but he could see nothing more. He saw Tongareva looking over at him. He shrugged his shoulders and sat down and stared at the barrage of lights on his desk. His skin almost crawled and the adrenaline poured into his veins and he felt wildly exhilarated. What was it? He grabbed the edge of the desk and closed his eyes and forced himself to think. He blanked out all the activity around him and forced his mind to relax and find the source of the stimulation. Australian problem? No, not that. It was . . . it was something in the weather requests. He opened his eyes, and pushed the playback button and watched the requests again.

One by one, more quickly now, they flashed on the miniature screen on his desk. Avalanches, Baltic Sea level, snow in southern California, Ceylon's rice to wheat, the Libyan farmer, the— Wait. He had it now, so he turned back to it and read it very slowly.

George Andrews of Holtville, California, wanted to see snow fall again before he died soon, and he would be unable to leave the semitropical environment of southern California. The more Wilburn stared at it, the more it seemed to have everything he needed. It had universal appeal: a dying man with a final request. It would be difficult: snow in July in southern California was unheard of; he wasn't even certain that it could be carried out. It was almost completely irrational; the Council had never bothered with such requests in the past. The more Wilburn looked at it, the more he became convinced he had found the proper cause on which to risk his career. People the world over would be behind him if he could bring it off. He remembered how it had been in the tradition of American presidents to show an occasional high concern over some unimportant individual. If he failed, he would probably be finished in politics, but that was the chance to take. And there was something about that name George Andrews, something that set off a vague, disturbing memory in the back of his mind, something that had attracted him to the request in the first place. No matter. It was time for him to call up for action all the forces he could muster.

He cut his entire staff into his circuit, and cut all others out. He said, "I am considering supporting the George Andrews request." He paused to allow the statement to sink in, smiling to himself at the shock to his staff; never had they heard of anything so wild from him. "Check out everything you can about George Andrews. Make certain that his request is bona fide and isn't some sort of trap for an innocent Councilman like me. In particular, make certain that no connection exists between George Andrews and Councilman Maitland. Check with Greenberg in the Advisors as to the chances of coming up with a solution to the problem of snow in July in southern California in an extremely restricted region. Given that answer, check with the Bureau, probably Hechmer—he's up on the sun right now—and see what the chances are of carrying it out. This must be completed in . . . just a moment." Wilburn looked around him. The weather requests had ended, and Councilman Yardley had left his desk and was walking toward the front of the Floor to assume his role as President. "You have four hours to get all the information. Go, and good luck. We will all need it this time." And Wilburn sat back. There was no time to relax, however.

Calls had piled up while he had set the investigation in motion. He began clearing them as President Yardley called the Council to order, swiftly dispensed with the old business, and then brought up the matter of the censure of Australia. Wilburn kept an ear on the transactions on the Floor as he continued to handle the incoming calls and other demands on his time. The President stated the order of the speeches for and against the drought resolution, and the Council sat back to listen. Councilman DuBois made his preliminary remarks, expressing the deep and abiding regret that the Council found it necessary in this manner to uphold the principles of the Weather Congress. It was a good speech, thought Wilburn. There could be no doubt of DuBois' sincerity, and when he solemnly stated the resolution itself, there were tears in his eyes, and his voice shook. Then the first of the Councilmen from Australia got up to argue against the resolution.

Wilburn pocketed the portable receiver, punched the button that showed he was listening via receiver, and left the floor. Many other Councilmen did the same, most of them heading for the Councilmen's Closed Restaurant where they could have a cup of coffee without having to deal with constituents, the press, lobbyists, or any of a multitude of organizations. They sipped their coffee and nibbled sweet cakes and talked. The conversation was all on the coming vote, and it was easy to see that opinion was hardening in favor of the resolution. The Councilmen talked in low voices so they could follow the trend of the arguments being made back on the floor; each Councilman had his portable receiver with him and each listened through the bone microphone behind an ear. The talk grew louder as it became apparent that the Australian Councilman was advancing nothing more than the same old arguments, don't-cause-suffering and give-us-another-chance. The vote was now almost a certainty.

Wilburn wandered back to the floor and handled some more of the day's business at his desk. He went out for more coffee, and returned. He rose to make a brief speech in favor of the resolution, expressing regret for the necessity. Then, as the arguments pro and con began to draw toward the end, the information on George Andrews began to come in.

George Andrews was one hundred and twenty-six years old with a heart condition, and the doctors had given him six weeks to live. There was no discernible connection between Andrews and Councilman Maitland. Wilburn interrupted to ask, "Who checked on that?"

"Jack Parker," was the answer, and Wilburn heard a slight chuckle, which he forgave. Jack Parker was one of the keenest investigators in the business, and Wilburn noted to himself that the staff member who had thought of putting Parker on that particular investigation was due for a bonus. At least Wilburn could now make a decision without fear of walking into a political trap of some kind. But the report continued.

"As I guess you know, Andrews came very close to being one of the most famous men in the world a hundred years ago. For a while it looked like Andrews would get credit for inventing the sessile boats, but he was finally beaten by Hans Daggensnurf. There used to be a few people around who insisted that Andrews was the real inventor all along, and that dirty politics, shrewd lawyers, unethical corporations, and filthy money combined to make a goat out of him. The name 'sessile boats' was Andrews' name for the sun boats, and the name has stuck. But then, you could never have called them Daggensnurf boats."

Wilburn remembered now, awed that his subconscious mind should have somehow alerted him to the need to check out the name George Andrews. Andrews had been the George Seldon of the automobile industry, the William Kelly of the so-called Bessemer steel process. All were forgotten men; someone else reaped the immortality. In Andrews' case, he had, according to some, been the man who invented the sun boats, those marvelous devices that made the entire Weather Congress possible. Sliding on a thin film of gaseous carbon, the sessile boats safely traversed the hell of the sun's surface, moving from place to place to stir up the activity needed to produce the desired weather. Without the sessile boats there would be no Weather Bureau staffed by lean, hard-eyed men, working the sun to produce the results called for by the Weather Council. Yes, Wilburn was lucky indeed to have dragged out his piece of ancient history just when he needed it.

The report continued, "We checked with the Weather Advisors, particularly Bob Greenberg. He says there is a fair chance they can find a way to pull snow in southern California this time of year, but he's not guaranteeing anything. One of his people has the beginnings of a new theory that might just work, and our request might be the one to test it out. But he doesn't want to be quoted on any of this. He's got a personnel problem with the genius who would do the work if our request was official. I gathered he would like for us to push it through so he could settle things one way or the other with this bright-eyed genius."

Wilburn asked, "How about the Bureau?"

"Well, we talked to Hechmer as you suggested. It is his tour on the sun right now, so he's in close touch. He says they've only got one Boat Master in the entire Bureau with enough guts and imagination, and he's having some kind of trouble at home. But Hechmer says if we come up with something special, he'll find a way to make his man produce."

Wilburn listened to many other details relating to the Andrews situation. His first assistant had added a feature of his own to the investigation, one which showed why he was such a highly paid member of Wilburn's staff. He had supervised a quiet opinion survey to find how Wilburn's constituents would react to his sponsoring a motion to grant Andrews' request. The result was predictable: If the request went through quickly and smoothly, and if the snow fell, Wilburn would be a wise, humane, and generous man. If acrimony developed in a debate and if snow did not fall, Wilburn would be a man who had blundered badly.

The report ended. Wilburn cleared his desk of all activity and took a quick look out at the floor. The debate was winding up. The Councilmen were visibly restless to get on to the voting, and it was now clear that the vote was overwhelmingly in favor of the resolution calling for a drought. Wilburn sat back to think.

But even as he sat back he knew the answer; there was really no need to make a decision here. He was going to do it. The only question was: How? And as he turned his mind to the timing of presenting his motion, he saw that here and now was the time. When better than right at the time the Council was finishing an unpleasant piece of business? He might be able to slip his motion through to help take the unpleasant taste from the mouths of the Councilmen. That was it. Wilburn sat back to wait the vote. In another ten minutes it started.

And in twenty minutes it was over. The vote in favor of the drought resolution was 192 to 8. The President lifted his gavel to adjourn the session, Wilburn stood up.

"Mr. President," he said, "we have just had to carry out a necessary but unpleasant duty. I now wish to move that the Council carry out an unnecessary but pleasant duty. I respectfully direct the attention of the honorable members to Weather Request Number 18, today's date."

He paused while the members, looking puzzled, punched the button on their desks that would play back for them the Andrews request. Wilburn waited until he saw most of the faces turned toward him in disbelief. Then he said, "I just said that our duty in this matter was unnecessary, but in a larger sense we have never had a more necessary duty in conscience to see that justice . . ." And Wilburn stated his case for Andrews. He briefly traced the history of George Andrews' career, and the debt owed him by the human race, a debt that had never been paid. As he talked, Wilburn smiled to himself at the phone calls he knew were racing from desk to desk on the Floor. "What's got into Jonathan?" "Has Wilburn lost his mind?" "Watch yourself on this one; he's up to something."

Wilburn stated the difficulty of knowing for certain whether the request was even within the realm of technological possibility. Only the Weather Advisors could tell. And even if it were possible, the Bureau might not be able to carry it out. But such considerations should not stop the Council from trying. And he concluded with an impassioned plea for this act of grace to show the world that the Council was made up of men who never lost sight of the individual.

He sat down amidst silence. Then Tongareva rose, and with soft words and gentle manner he supported the resolution, emphasizing the warmth and humanity of the motion at a time when there would be many who thought the Council too harsh. He sat down, and Maitland rose to the Floor. To Wilburn's astonishment, Maitland, too, supported the resolution. But as Wilburn listened, he understood that Maitland supported the resolution only because he saw disaster in it for Wilburn. It took nerve for Maitland to do it. He could not know what Wilburn had in mind, but Maitland was willing to trust his judgment that a mistake had been made and to try to capitalize on it.

Wilburn answered all the incoming calls from his fellow Councilmen, all of whom wanted to know if Wilburn wanted them to rise in support of the motion. Some of these were his friends, others were those who owed him a favor. To all of them Wilburn urged support in the form of a brief supporting speech. For forty minutes Councilmen bobbed up, spoke for a moment, and then sat down. When the vote came, it was one of the few unanimous votes in the history of the Council. The Australian drought was forgotten, both on the floor and on the video screens of the world. All thoughts were turned to the little town of Holtville, California.

Wilburn heard the gavel adjourn the session, and he knew he was fully committed. His fate was in the hands of others; his work was done for now, possibly forever.

But after all, if one wants to reach the top in politics, one has to take a chance.

Anna Brackney wandered up the broad steps of the Weather Advisors Building half an hour early, as usual. At the top she stopped and looked out over the city of Stockholm. It was a pretty city, sturdy under its heavy roofs, sparkling under the early morning sun, and quiet and restful. Stockholm was a fine place for the Advisors. In fact it was such an excellent choice for the kind of work the Advisors did, Anna wondered all over again how it was possible for men to have chosen it. She turned and went in.

The Maintenance Supervisor, Hjalmar Froding, directed the Polishing Machine around the lobby. He saw Anna Brackney and immediately guided the Machine to lay down a tic-tac-toe pattern in wax on the floor, and then he bowed to her. She stopped, put her finger in her mouth, and then pointed to the upper right-hand square. The Machine put an "O" on it, and then placed an "X" in the center square for Froding. The game went on until Froding had three "Xs" in a row, and the Machine triumphantly ran a straight line through them. Hjalmar Froding bowed to Anna Brackney, and she bowed to him and went on her way. She ignored the escalator and walked up the stairs, feeling pleased that she again was able to have Froding win in an unobvious manner. Anna Brackney was fond of Froding; he seldom spoke or smiled, and treated her as if she were the queen of Sweden. It was too bad some of the other men around here couldn't be guided as simply.

She had to pass through the main Weather Room on her way to her office. A great globe of the world occupied the center of the room, and it showed the weather at the moment on every part of the Earth. The globe was similar in purpose to the map in the Weather Council, but it had a few additional features. Every jet stream, density variation, inversion, every front, isobar, isallobar, isotherm, precipitation area, clouded area, and air mass showed on the globe. The globe was a mass of shifting colors, undecipherable to the untrained eye, making sense only to the mathemeteorologists who made up the technical staff of the Advisors. The curved walls of the room were covered with the instruments that made up the Weather Net, the senses of the Advisors. The entire room looked like something out of a nightmare with its seething globe and dancing lights and shimmering dials. Anna walked through without noticing with the callousness of long proximity. She headed for the private wire from the Weather Council to see if that strange request had come in yet.

The guard in the Council Communications room saluted and stepped aside for her. She went in and sat down and began to flip through the night's messages from the Council. She picked up the one that related to the imposition of a drought in northern Australia, and read it. She snorted when she finished, and said aloud to herself, "Nothing, no problem at all. A child could figure out how to bring that about." And on down the stack of messages she went.

She found it and read it carefully, and read it again. It was just as the news flashes had reported: Snow in July on a one-square-mile area in southern California. The latitude and the longitude of the area were given, and that was all there was to it. But Anna Brackney felt the excitement grow within her. Here was the nastiest problem to confront the Advisors in decades, one that probably could not be solved by standard technics. She put her finger in her mouth. Here was what she had been waiting for, the chance to prove out her theory. Now all she had to do was convince Greenberg to give her the problem. She restacked the messages and went to her office.

It was a small office measuring about eight by eight feet, but Anna Brackney still thought it too big. Her desk was in one corner facing one wall to give her the illusion of being more cramped than she really was. Anna could not stand the feeling of open spaces when she worked. There was no window, no picture on any of the walls, nothing distracting against the plain dark gray walls. Other Advisors had different ideas on the proper working environment. Some used bright splashes of color, others used woodland or ocean scenes, Greenberg had his walls covered with a black and white maze, and Hiromaka's walls were covered with nudes. Anna shuddered with disgust as she thought of it.

Instead of sitting at her desk, she stood in the middle of the small room, thinking of how she could persuade Greenberg to assign the Andrews problem to her. This would be hard. She knew that Greenberg did not like her, and she knew it was only because he was a man and she was a woman. None of the men liked her, and as a result her work never received the credit it deserved. A woman in a man's world was never allowed to be judged on the basis of her work alone. But if she could get the Andrews problem, she would show them. She would show them all.

But time was short. The Andrews problem had to be solved immediately. Sometimes the Advisors' weather programs took weeks to put into operation, and if this turned out to be one like that it would be too late. It had to be worked on and solved now to see if there was enough time. She spun on her heels and ran out of the office and down the escalator to the wide steps at the front door of the building. She would waste no time. She would meet Greenberg as he came in.

She had a ten-minute wait, and Greenberg was early at that. Anna Brackney pounced on him as he reached the top step. She said, "Dr. Greenberg, I am ready to start work immediately on the Andrews problem. I feel—"

"You've been waiting for me?" he said.

"I feel I am best equipped to solve the Andrews problem since it will call for new procedures and . . ."

"What on Earth is the Andrews problem?"

She looked at him blankly and said, "Why that's the problem that came in during the night, and I want to be the one who . . ."

"But you've nailed me out here on the steps before I've had a chance to go inside. How do I know what problems came in during the night? I haven't been upstairs yet."

"But you must know . . . you have heard of it, it's all on the news."

"There's a lot of junk on the news about our work, most of it untrue. Now why don't you wait until I get a look at it so I know what you're talking about."

They went up the escalator together in silence, he annoyed at being accosted in such a manner, and she annoyed at his obvious effort to put off doing what she wanted.

He started to go into his office first, but she said, "It's over in the Council Communications room, not in your office."

He started to retort, but thought better of it, and went on in and read the message. She said, "Now may I have it?"

"Look, damn it. This request is going to be treated like any other until we understand its ramifications. I am going to give it to Upton as I do all the others for a preliminary opinion and a recommendation as to assignment. After I have that recommendation I will decide what to do. Now don't bother me until Upton's had a look at it." He saw her mouth curve down and her eyes begin to fill. He had been through these crying sessions before, and he did not like them. "See you later," he said, and he all but ran to his office and locked the door. One thing nice at the Advisor Building. A locked door was inviolate. It meant the person inside did not want to be disturbed, and the caliber of the work was such that the wish was honored.

Anna Brackney raged back to her office. There it was again. A woman did not stand a chance around here; they refused to treat her like a man. Then she went and waited at Upton's office to explain the whole thing to him.

Upton was a portly man with an easy disposition and a mind like a razor. What's more, he understood the operation of a single-tracked mind. Anna had got out no more than half her tale of woe when he recognized that the only way to get her off his back for the day was to review the Andrews request. He sent for it, looked at it, whistled and sat down at a twenty-six-fifty computer. For half an hour he fed in data and sat back while the computer chewed and then spat out the results. The job grew, so he called in some help and soon there were three men working on the computers. In another three hours Upton swung around to Anna who had been standing behind him the entire time.

He said, "Do you have some ideas on this?"

She nodded.

"Care to tell me something about it?"

She hesitated, then said, "Well, I don't have it all yet. But I think it can be done by"—she paused and glanced at him shyly as if to see in advance whether or not he was laughing at her—"a vertical front."

Upton's jaw fell. "A ver. . . You mean a true front that is tipped perpendicular to the Earth's surface?"

She nodded, and put her finger in her mouth. Far from laughing, Upton stared at the floor for a moment, and then headed for Greenberg's office. He walked in without knocking and said to Greenberg, "There is a forty-six per cent chance of carrying out this Andrews mandate by conventional technics. And by the way, what's the matter with the Council? I've never known them to do such an idiotic thing before. What are they trying to do?"

Greenberg shook his head and said, "I don't know. I had a call asking about this from Wilburn. I've got the uncomfortable feeling that they're trying to see just what we *can* do here, sort of test us before they put some real big problem to us. They voted a drought for northern Australia yesterday, and maybe they are getting ready to put the real squeeze on some region and want to see what we can do first."

Upton said, "Drought in Australia? Well, they're getting a little tough, aren't they? That isn't like the good old easygoing Council that I know. Any difficulty with the Australian drought?"

"No. It was such a standard problem I didn't even bother to give it to you for screening. I turned it right over to Hiromaka. But there's something behind this Andrews thing, and I don't like it. We'd better find a way to carry it out."

Upton said, "Well, Brackney has an approach that's wild enough to work. Let's let her try to work out a solution, and then we can look it over and see if we feel it has a better chance to work than conventional technics."

Anna Brackney had been standing near the door. She came forward and said angrily, "What do you mean 'wild'? There's nothing wrong with it at all. You just don't want me to be the one that solves it, that's all. You just—"

"No, no, Anna," said Greenberg, "that isn't it. You'll be the one to work it out, so don't—"

"Good, I'll start right now," said Anna, and she turned and left.

The two men looked at each other. Upton shrugged his shoulders, and Greenberg raised his eyes to the ceiling, shook his head, and sighed.

Anna Brackney sat herself down in her corner and stared at the wall. It was ten minutes before she put her finger into her mouth, and another twenty minutes before she pulled out a pad and pencil and began scribbling notations. It went fast then. With her first equation set up on a small sheet of paper, she left her office to find a resident mathemeteorologist; Anna refused to use the speaker at her desk to call one of them in.

The residents were all seated at desks in one large room, and when Anna entered they all bent over as if hard at work. Ignoring their behavior, Anna went up to the desk of Betty Jepson and placed the sheet of paper on it. Anna said without any preliminaries, "Run a regression analysis on this," and her finger traced out the equation in the form $y = a_1x_1 + a_2x_2 + \ldots + a_nx_n$, "noting that n equals 46 in this case. Take the observational data from the banks of Number Eighty-three computer. I want a fit better than ninety per cent." And she turned on her heels and returned to her office.

Half an hour later she was back with another equation for Charles Bankhead, then one for Joseph Pechio. With the pattern established, she asked for the aid of a full mathemeteorologist, and Greenberg assigned Albert Kropa to her. Kropa listened to her somewhat disjointed description of what she was trying to do, and then wandered around looking over the shoulders of the residents to see what they were doing. Gradually he understood, and finally he raced to his own office and began turning out the polynomial relationships on his own.

Each equation demanded the full use of a sixteen-fifty computer and its staff under the direction of a resident, plus six hours of time to arrive at even a preliminary fit. As Anna and Kropa turned out more of the needed basic equations, it was apparent that too much time was being used in evolving each one individually. Anna broke off and spent two hours working out a method of programming a twenty-two thirty to explore the factors needed in each regression analysis. The computer began producing the required equations at the rate of one every ten minutes, so Anna and Kropa turned their attention to a method of correlating the flood of data that would descend on them when each analysis was complete. After half an hour it became apparent that they could not finish that phase of it before the data began coming in. They asked for and got two more full mathemeteorologists.

The four of them moved out to the Weather Room so they could be together as they worked. The correlating mathematics began to unfold, and all the remaining residents were called in to help with it. In another hour all the available sixteen-fifties were tied up, and Greenberg called on the University of Stockholm for the use of theirs. This held for twenty minutes, and then Greenberg called on half a dozen industrial computers in the city. But that wasn't enough. The net of computers began widening steadily out to the Continent, reaching in another two hours to the cities on the eastern seaboard of the United States. The overriding authority of the Advisors in the solving of a weather problem was absolute.

It became necessary for Upton to join the group, and when Greenberg himself took a chair at the large circle in the Weather Room there was a brief break in the work for some catcalls and some affectionately sarcastic remarks. Commitment of the Advisors was total.

Anna Brackney seemed not to notice. Her eyes were glazed and she spoke in crisp sharp sentences in contrast to her usual vague and slurred sentences. She seemed to know just a little in advance when a breakdown in the mounting flow of data was impending, and she stepped in and supplied the necessary continuity. It was fifteen hundred before Hiromaka noticed that none of them had eaten lunch. Greenberg sent for food, again at twenty-three hundred, and again at zero nine hundred.

Everyone looked terrible with sunken cheeks and rumpled clothes and great hollows under the eyes. But there was fire in the eyes of all of them, even down to the newest resident, a fire born of participation in the most complex weather problem yet to confront the Advisors.

Upton took over the task of pulling together the mathematical models relating to the planet Earth. He kept under his control the regression analysis results relating to such variables as the various possible distances of Earth from the sun; the rotational positions of the Earth relating to the sun; the shape, position, density, variation, and charge of both Van Allen radiation belts; the velocity, temperature, direction, width, and mass of fourteen hundred jet streams; the heat flow of the major ocean currents; the effect on air drift of each major land mass; the heat content of the land masses; the Coriolis effect; and superimposed over all these factors and many more, the effect of the existing and programmed weather playing over the face of the entire Earth.

Greenberg took the sun and worked with the analysis results on the movement of each sunspot; the sun's rotations; fluctuating temperatures and pressures in the photosphere, reversing layer, chromosphere, and corona; spectrum variations; and the relative output from the carbon cycle and the proton-proton chain.

Anna wandered everywhere, now looking over Upton's shoulder, now on the phone to the computers in Washington, D. C., now guiding a resident on his next chore, now inventing a new notational system to simplify feeding newly-derived mathematical models into the computers. She wandered as if in a dream, but when a question was asked or when something slowed down, her responses were far from dreamlike. Many a resident, several computer operators, and Upton himself felt the bite of one of her crisp sentences pointing out what could have been a rather obvious blunder. As time wore on and the work grew more frantic, the normally harsh lines on Anna's face softened, and she walked erect instead of with her usual slouch. Several of the mathemeteorologists, who formerly would not even have talked to her unless it was absolutely necessary, found themselves willingly turning to her for further guidance on their part of the problem.

The first partial solution was fully worked out for the first time at eleven hundred hours the next morning. It had only an eighty-one per cent fit, but that was good for the first time out; more would be coming soon. But Upton found a flaw. "No good," he said. "This solution would also increase that proposed drought in Australia by a factor of twelve. That would be nice. We pull something like that and we'll all be back reading electric meters."

The remark struck a responsive chord in the group, and the laughter spread and grew more intense. In moments every person in the Advisors Building was convulsed with violent laughter as the long strain finally took its hysterical toll. It was several minutes before the eyes were wiped and the people settled down to work again. Greenberg said, "Well, that's where our danger will be. Not necessarily in Australia, but anywhere. We've got to make sure we don't get a drastic reaction somewhere."

Anna Brackney heard him and said, "DePinza is working on a definitive analysis to insure that there can be no undesirable reaction. He'll have it in an hour." She walked off, leaving Greenberg staring after her.

It was fifteen hundred when the final set of equations was completed. The fit was ninety-four per cent, and the check-out against DePinza's analysis was one hundred and two per cent. The residents and the mathemeteorologists gathered around the large table as Greenberg considered the results. They had finished none too soon. The procedure they had worked out called for sunside operations starting three hours after the beginning of the second shift, and that went on in four hours. Greenberg rubbed the heavy stubble on his face and said, "I don't know whether to let it go or not. We could report that our procedures are untried and ought not to be used all at once."

The eyes of the group turned to Anna Brackney, but she seemed supremely unconcerned. Upton voiced what was in everyone's mind. "There's a little bit of the heart of each one of us in there." He nodded to the equations. "Since they represent the very best that we can do, I don't see how we can report that they ought not to be used. Right now those equations represent the best Advisors output; in that sense they *are* the Advisors. Both we and the people who put us here have to stand or fall on our best efforts."

Greenberg nodded, and handed the two sheets of paper to a resident and said, "Break it down to the sunside procedures and then send it up to the Weather Bureau. I hope they don't have to sweat it out the way we did." He rubbed his face. "Well, that's what we get paid for."

The resident took the sheets and went off. The others drifted away until only Greenberg and Upton were left. Upton said, "This will be quite a feather in Anna Brackney's cap. I don't know where she pulled her inspiration from."

"I don't either," said Greenberg. "But if she sticks her finger in her mouth again, I may quit the business."

Upton chuckled. "If she brings this one off, we'd better all learn to stick our fingers in our mouths."

James Eden rolled out of his bunk and stood poised on the balls of his feet. Yes, there was a faint, barely discernible chatter in the deck. Eden shook his head; the sun was rough, and it was going to be a bad day. If Base had a chatter, then the sessile boats would be hard to manage. Never knew it to fail. Try something tricky and you had to work in the worst possible conditions; try something routine, and conditions were perfect. But that was what you had to expect in the Bureau. Even the textbooks talked about it—an offshoot of an old Finagle Law.

Eden depilated and dressed, wondering what the job ahead of him would be like. They were always the last to hear anything, yet they were the ones who had to do all the dirty work. The whole Weather Congress depended on the Bureau. The Council was nothing more than a bunch of rich old fat politicians who scratched each other's backs and spent their days cooking up Big Deals. The Advisors were a bunch of nuts who sat on their duffs and read out loud all the stuff the computers figured out. But the Bureau was something else again, a fine body of dedicated men who did a job so that the planet Earth could flourish. It was good to be in the Weather Bureau—and there it was again.

Eden could not keep his thoughts away from the problem that had been nagging at him during this entire tour. He rubbed his forehead and wondered again at the perversity of women. Rebecca, black-haired and black-eyed, with warm white skin, waited for him when his tour was over, but only if he left the Bureau. He could see her now, close to him, looking deep into his eyes, the soft palm of her hand pressed against his cheek, saying, "I will not share you with any person or any thing, even your beloved Bureau. I want a complete husband. You must decide." With other women he could have laughed and picked them up and swung them around and quickly jogged them out of the mood, but not Rebecca, not Rebecca of the long black hair. Damn it!

He swung around and stepped out of his tiny cabin and headed for the mess hall. There were half a dozen men already there when he entered, and they were talking and laughing. But they stopped what they were doing and looked at him and hailed him as he came in through the door. "Hey, Jim." "About time you were rolling out." "Good to see you, boy."

Eden recognized the symptoms. They were tense, and they were talking and laughing too loud. They were relieved to have him join them. They needed somebody to lean on, and Eden pitied them a little for it. Now they would not have to make such an effort to appear normal. The others had felt the chatter in the deck, too.

Eden sat down and said, "Morning. Anything on the Board yet about the shift's work?"

The others shook their heads, and Pisca said, "Not a word. They always wait and tell us last. Everybody on the planet knows what's going on, but not us. All we get are rumors until it's time to go out and do it."

"Well," said Eden, "communication with the Bureau is not the easiest thing in the world, don't forget. We can't expect to hear everything as soon as it happens. But I sort of agree with you anyway; seems to me they could keep us posted better as things develop back on Earth."

They nodded, and then applied themselves to the breakfast. They chatted over coffee until a soft chime sounded throughout Base. They rose. It was time for the briefing, and they headed for the briefing room up at the top of the Base. Commander Hechmer was there when they walked in and took their seats. Eden watched carefully as he found a seat and sat down. In the past he had sometimes wondered if Hechmer had taken particular notice of him—an extra glance, closer attention when he asked a question, talking more to him than to the others at a briefing, little things, but important nevertheless.

Commander John H. Hechmer was a legend in the Weather Bureau at the age of forty-five years. It was he who had evolved and perfected the Pinpoint Stream technic in which a thin stream of protons could be extracted from the 4,560-degree level in a sunspot and directed against any chosen sunside part of Earth. In the days when Hechmer was the Senior Boat Master in the Bureau, great strides had been made in weather control. A fineness and detail of weather patterns on Earth had become possible that had astonished all the experts. Hechmer had even guided the Advisors, showing them the broadened scope of the Bureau's abilities. His handling of a sunboat had never been matched, and it was one of the goals in Eden's career—if he chose to stay with it—to be thought of as the man who most nearly approximated Hechmer.

Eden watched, and finally when Hechmer looked up from the table it seemed to Eden that his eyes swept the group to rest for an instant on Eden, and then they moved on. It was as if Hechmer wanted to assure himself that Eden was there. Eden could not be sure of this, but the possibility of it made him sit straighter in his chair.

Hechmer said, "Here is Phase One of the next shift's operation as received from the Advisors." He flashed the requisite portion of the page on the upright panel behind him. It took Eden one quick glance to see that it represented a substantial departure from customary procedure. Immediately he began to slump down in his seat as he lost himself in the problem of studying out how to handle it. He did not notice that Hechmer saw his instant grasp of the problem. It was a moment or two before several low whistles announced that the others had grasped it, too.

Hechmer sat quietly while they studied over the page. All of them were now thinking out how the report had to be modified to place it in useful condition for the Bureau to use. The Advisors always prided themselves on stating their solutions in clear and explicit terminology. But as a practical matter their solutions were totally unusable as received for they did not mention many of the sun conditions that the Bureau had to cope with. These are accomplishments not explained by mathematics. It was one of the quiet jokes of the Bureau to listen to the talk of an Advisor about the thoroughness of his solution and about the lack of thinking required by the Bureau, and then to ask the Advisor what he knew about "reversing granulation." No one except a working member of the Bureau could experience that strange upwelling sometimes found in the lower regions of the reversing layer.

The silence grew long. Eden's forehead was wrinkled with concentration as he tried to find some way to break into the problem. He finally saw a possible entry, and he pulled over a pad and began trying for a method of breakdown. Hechmer began to polish his own figures while the rest stared at the page on the wall as if hypnotized. It was ten minutes before another of the men finally began to make notes.

Eden sat back and looked over what he had written. With growing excitement he realized that his possible answer had never been tried before. As he looked at it more closely, though, he realized that it might not ever be done; it was a radical approach, calling for Boat performance not mentioned in the Boat specifications.

Hechmer said, "Gentlemen, we must begin. To start things off, here is my proposed answer. Pick it apart if you can."

Eden looked up at it. It was different, too, but it differed in that it called for the use of every single Boat on the sun, a thing never before needed. Hechmer's answer was to carry out the mission by sheer weight of numbers, and by this means to dig from the various levels in the sun's atmosphere the total of the streams and sheets needed to bring about the desired weather on Earth. But as he looked at it Eden began to see flaws. The streams, being taken from different parts of the sun's surface would strike the Earth and its environs at angles slightly different from those that were called for. Hechmer's answer might work, but it did not seem to have as good a chance as Eden's answer.

Hechmer said, "The main feature wrong with this plan is the wide scattering of the impinging streams. Can you think of any way to overcome that?"

Eden could not, but his mind was more occupied with his own plan. If he could be certain that the Boats could stand submersion in the sun's surface for the required length of time, there would be few problems. Oh, communication might be more difficult, but with only one Boat down there would be a much reduced need for communication; the Boat would succeed or not, and no instructions from anywhere else could help.

One of the other men was beginning to suggest the unfeasible modification of having all the Boats work closer together, a grave mistake since the Boats could not control their toruses with sufficient nicety. Eden interrupted him without thinking. "Here is a possible answer." And he dropped his page on the desk.

Hechmer continued to look at the man who had been talking, waiting politely for him to finish. The man avoided an embarrassing situation by saying, "Let's see what Jim has to offer before we go on with this one."

Hechmer slipped Eden's page into the viewer, and they all studied it. It had the advantage at least of being readily understandable, and they all began talking at once, most of them saying that it couldn't be done. "You'll lose the Boat." "Yes, and the men in it, don't forget." "Won't work even if the Boat holds up." "You can't get a Boat that deep."

Eden carefully watched Hechmer's face while he studied the plan. He saw Hechmer's eyes widen, and then narrow again, and Hechmer realized that Eden was watching him closely. For a moment the room faded from Hechmer's mind, replaced by another similar room, many years ago, when a younger and rasher Hechmer sat and anxiously watched his superior eye a new kind of plan. Hechmer said, without taking his eyes from the projected page, "Assuming the Boat can get down there, why won't this plan work?"

"Well," said the man who had stated it wouldn't work, "the streams and sheets won't necessarily emerge in the direction. . . ." But as he talked he noticed that the energy of the sunspot's field was channeled to serve as a focusing lens, and his words faded.

Hechmer nodded approval, "Glad you saw it. Anybody else? Any flaws in it once the Boat gets down and stays long enough?" The men worried at it, but could find nothing wrong, given the stated assumption. Hechmer continued, "All right, now why won't a Boat stand that kind of submersion."

One answered, "The sessile effect is not as great on the top. Burn right through."

Eden popped out, "No. Double the carbon feed to the top torus. That'll do it."

They argued for half an hour, Eden and two others defending the concept, and in the end there was no more opposition. They all worked at polishing the plan to take out as much risk as possible. By the time they finished there really was no decision for Hechmer to make. The group of Boat captains had accepted the plan, and it went without saying that Eden's Boat would be the deep Boat. There was a bare half an hour to the start of the shift, so they went to get ready.

Eden struggled into the lead suit, muttering the same curses every Boatman since the first had muttered. The Boats had ample shielding, and the suits were to provide protection only if a leak allowed in some stray radiation. But on the sun it seemed highly unlikely that a leak would allow in only a little radiation. It seemed much more likely that a leak would allow in so much of the sun's atmosphere that the men in the Boat would never know what hit them. A lead suit then would be like trying to dam a volcano with a feather. Nevertheless, lead suits were mandatory.

Entering the Boat from Base was always a tricky maneuver. The torus above the joining lock was not a permanent part of the lock, and if it moved, the full gravitational field of the sun could pull at the man, pulling his entire body down into his shoes. Eden slipped through and made the rounds of the Boat on the standard captain's inspection before he went to his chair and began the start-up procedure.

He noted the continuing roughness of the sun. First he checked the carbon supply, the material which vaporized and then in the form of a thin film protected the entire Boat from the searing heat of the sun's surface. The Boats rode the layer of vaporized carbon the way a drop of water rides a layer of vaporized water on a red-hot plate; this was the sessile effect. Next he checked the overhead torus. Here in a circular path there traveled a few ounces of protons at a velocity approaching that of light. At these velocities the few ounces of protons weighed incalculable tons and thus offset the enormous gravitational attraction of the sun itself. The same magnetic tape that supplied the field to maintain the protons in their heavy-mass state also served to maintain a polarity the same as that of the adjacent sun's surface. Hence the torus and the sun's surface repelled each other. Objects under the torus were subjected to two gravitational fields, the one from the torus almost, but not quite, canceling the sun's. As a result men worked in the Boats and in the Base in a 1-G field.

Eden ran down the entire list checking off one by one the various functioning parts of the Boat. His crew of four worked with him, each responsible for a section of the Boat. Five minutes before castoff the board was green, and at zero time on the shift they shoved off.

The Boat felt good under his hands. It leaped and surged as the sun's surface roiled and boiled, but he kept it steadily headed outward, sliding ever downhill on its thin film of carbon vapor.

"How do you ride?" he said into the intercom.

A chorus of "fines" came back, so Eden tipped the Boat a little more to increase her speed. They were on a tight schedule and they had distance to make. As always Eden felt exhilarated as their speed increased, and he did the thing he always did when he felt that way.

Carefully, he drew back one after another of the sound-deadening panels on the bulkhead next to the pilot's seat. As the eighth panel drew back he could hear it faintly, and so he drew back the ninth panel slowly, and on the tenth the roar filled the pilot's cubicle. Eden sat bathed in a thunderous roar that washed over him, shaking his body with its fury, and taking everything from his mind except the need to fight and strain and hit back. This was the direct naked roar of the sun itself that came in upon him, the thunderous concatenation of a million fission bombs detonating every infinitesimal portion of a second. Its sound and fury were mind-staggering, and a man could only let a little of it in and keep his sanity. But that little was an awesome sound, cleansing, humbling, focusing a man's attention on the powers he controlled, warning him to mind his business.

This was a thing that Eden had never told to anyone, and no one had ever told him. It was his own secret, his own way of refreshing and replenishing whatever it was that made him the man he was. He supposed that he was the only one of the pilots that did this thing, and since on this one point he did not think clearly, it never occurred to him to wonder how it came about that the only movable sound-deadening panels in the entire Boat happened to be located right alongside the pilot's seat.

For half an hour Eden guided the Boat toward its first action point, easily coping with the usual roughness of the sun's surface. He checked the operation of the inertial guidance system exactly twice as often as was required by standard operating procedure to make sure that the extra bouncing did not affect its precise operation. As they approached the action point, Eden closed the sound-deadening panels and checked in with his crew. "Four minutes to operation. What color have you?"

Back came the answer from all four points, "All green, Master." Formalities aboard the sessile Boat had started. Each man watched his own program, his fingers on the keys and his feet on the pedals, waiting for the position light. It winked on.

Out went the torpedolike capsules, down into the bowels of the sun where the carbon-nitrogen cycle raged. At a temperature of three point five million degrees the ablation head disintegrated and released into the inferno a charge of heavy nitrogen. The heavy nitrogen, appearing as it did at the end of the carbon-nitrogen cycle, disrupted the steady state conditions and produced a flood of helium that served to dampen and cool the fusion reactions in the entire region. The resultant thermal shock to the interior caused an immediate collapse followed by an incredible increase in pressure with the attendant temperature rise. The vast explosion heaved its way to the surface and became a great prominence licking its way toward the Earth and channeling huge masses of protons toward the preselected site in the vicinity of the Earth. The initial phase of the operation appeared successful.

The next hour passed in moving from site to site and planting the proper charges, now to bring about a vast electron discharge at the correct angle, now to dampen a flare, now to shift the location of a spot. On two occasions the instruments showed that the detonations did not take place at a sufficiently precise location to meet the unusual requirements for accuracy, and so subsidiary detonations had to be made. They were in constant, if difficult, communication with the other three Boats and with Base. None of the Boats was specifically aware of it, but the beginnings of the Australian drought were set in motion during the second hour out.

There was no tension aboard Eden's Boat as the time for the deep operation approached; they were all too busy. When the time came Eden merely checked out over the communication net and reduced the polarity of the magnetic field on the overhead torus. The Boat went down fast, leaving the photosphere behind. Eden kept a careful check on the temperature drop across the walls of the Boat as they fell; when the sessile effect began to diminish, he wanted to know about it. The interior walls began to heat up sooner than he expected, and once they started, the heat-up proceeded ever more rapidly. A quick check showed that the rate of heating was faster than their rate of descent; they could not reach the required depth without becoming overheated. The Boat would not withstand the temperatures that Eden had thought it would. "Too hot, too hot," he said aloud. He checked the depth; they had another half a mile to go. There was no use in even attempting to release the water where they were. It was half a mile deeper, or nothing. The plan was in jeopardy.

Eden did not really pause to make the decision. He simply drastically cut the power to the polarity-control generators to the torus, and the Boat fell like a stone toward the center of the sun. It dropped the half mile in forty seconds, the last few hundred yards in violent deceleration as Eden brought up the power level. The drop was so fast there was little additional heat-up. He hit the water releases and flung the Boat into the pattern that had been worked out, and in ten seconds the disruption was complete and a blast of Oxygen 15 was started on its way to Earth. The plan, at least, was consummated.

Eden brought up the torus power to a high level and the Boat began to rise to the relative safety of the surface. The time at the deeper level had been sufficiently short that the interior temperature of the Boat was at a tolerable 120 degrees F. The control panel showed no signs of trouble until they rose to within a thousand yards of the surface.

The steady rise slowed and drifted to a halt. The Boat sank a little and then bobbed up and down and finally found a level, and then it remained motionless. There was no way to strengthen the polarity in the torus. The instruments showed that full power flowed to the coils, and it was not enough. Eden began a check-out. He had barely started when a voice spoke in the intercom, "A portion of our right outboard coil is inoperative, Master. Possibly burned away, but I am checking further."

Eden turned his attention to the coils and soon saw the telltale reduced output. He activated all the thermocouples and other transducers in the vicinity of the coil, and in two minutes he understood what had happened. The burn-out had occurred at the point where the coil turned the corner. The sessile effect there must have been slightly less effective than elsewhere. The unexpectedly great heat had pushed past the film of carbon vapor and destroyed a portion of the titanium-molybdenum alloy wires. Full power to the coil was not enough now to increase the polarity sufficiently for the Boat to rise any farther.

Eden cut into the intercom and explained the situation to the crew. A cheerful voice responded, "Glad to hear that there is nothing seriously wrong then. It is just that we cannot move up. Is that what you make of it, Master?"

"So far, yes. Anybody have any suggestions?"

"Yes, Master. I request a leave of absence."

"Granted," said Eden. "Now put in some time on this. We've got to get up."

There was silence aboard the Boat, and the silence stretched out to twenty minutes. Eden said, "I'll try to raise Base."

For ten minutes Eden tried to reach the Base or another Boat with his long-long wave-length radio. He was about to give up when he heard a faint and garbled reply. Through the noise he could just recognize the call of the Boat mastered by Dobzhansky. He transmitted their situation, over and over, so that the other Boat could fill in missing parts of any one message. Then he listened and eventually learned that they understood and would notify Base. But as they listened to the faint retransmission all sound faded. A check of their position showed that they had drifted out of radio range, so Eden tipped the Boat and began a circle. Three quarters of the way around he picked up the signal again and listened. He heard nothing but routine communication.

One of his men said, "Fine thing. We can move in every direction with the greatest of ease except the one direction we want to go."

Base was now coming in through the other Boat, and Hechmer himself was speaking. All he had to say was, "Stand by while we see what we can do about this."

There was no levity aboard the Boat now. The Boat floated a thousand yards beneath the surface of the sun, and they began to realize that there was nothing anybody could do about it. A sharpened corner on a coil, and the Boat was helpless to return to the surface. Each man sat and stared at his instruments.

A dark-haired vision floated in front of Eden's panel, and in his mind's eye Eden could see the reproachful look on her face. This was what she meant, the black-haired Rebecca, when she said, "I will not share you with any thing." He understood, for now she would be sorry for him, trapped in a place where men had never been.

"Lost the Boat again, Master." The words jarred him. He tipped the Boat and began the circle again. The shadow of Rebecca was still on him, but suddenly he grew very annoyed. What was this? The worry of a woman to get in the way of his work? This was not for him; this was not for the Bureau. There could be no cloudiness of mind, no dichotomy of loyalty—and then he saw the way up.

As he completed the circle he checked the charts and found the nearest sunspot. It was an hour away. He came within radio range again and told Dobzhansky he was heading for the sunspot and that he would come up to the surface there. So saying he headed for it. By the most careful operation they cut their time to the spot to fifty minutes. The last ten minutes of time on the way they spent in building the speed of the Boat to the maximum obtainable. A thousand yards beneath the surface of the sun they entered the magnetic discontinuity that defined the sunspot.

They rode into it in a direction opposite to that of its rotation, and the great coils of the Boat cut across the lines of enormous magnetic force. The motion generated power, and the additional power flowed to the torus, and the Boat began to rise. It was a good spot, five thousand miles wide, and still in its prime. The Boat rode against the direction of its rotation and spiraled upward slowly as it went. It took great patience to note the fact that the Boat rose at all, but hour after hour they worked their way up and finally broke out on the indistinct surface. They rode the edges of the spot until Base came for them, and they docked the Boat and went aboard.

Eden reported to Hechmer, and they made arrangements to round off the relatively sharp corners on all coils. Most important of all, the deep technic appeared to be a success; it was added to the list of usable technics.

"Well," said Eden toward the end of the reporting session, stretching his tired muscles, "I see I'm due back on shift again in an hour. That doesn't give me much time to get rested up."

Then Hechmer said the thing that made Eden glad he had decided to stay in the Bureau. "Hm-m-m, that's right," said Hechmer, glancing up at the chronometer, "tell you what you do. You be an hour late getting back on duty."

George Andrews was very tired, and he had to work very hard to draw air into his lungs. He lay propped up on a soft bed out under the hot California sun, and his fingers plucked at the thin cover that lay over him. He was on a hilltop. Then he noticed an odd cylindrical-shaped cloud that seemed to rise from the level of the ground and reach way up through the scattered alto-cumulous clouds that dotted the blue sky. George Andrews smiled, for he could see it coming clearly now. The vertical cylinder of frothy clouds moved toward him, and he felt the chill as the leading edge touched him. He threw back the cover when the flakes began to fall so the snow could fall on him. He turned his face up to it, and it felt cold and it felt good. But more than that, he felt content.

Here was the snow he had loved so much when he was a boy. And the fact that it was here at all showed him that men had not changed much after all, for this was a foolish thing. He had no trouble with the air now; he needed none. He lay under the blanket of snow, and it was a good blanket.

Part Two

TRANSIT OF EARTH

Arthur C. Clarke

Arthur C. Clarke is the poet of technology and cosmology in modern sf. He is also as much a proponent of space travel as his peer, Robert A. Heinlein. But Clarke's influences are not Wells and Kipling, but first and foremost Olaf Stapledon, whose concerns were with philosophical immensities in space and time, and inhuman beauties. Gregory Benford has remarked, "There's more similarity between Arthur C. Clarke and Thoreau than there is between Clarke and Heinlein." For Clarke, the beauties of vistas in space are the beauties of nature, and the exploration of space is the quest for knowledge and close experience of nature, for things never before seen and felt by an individual human; and the medium through which this exploration will be achieved is technology. Technological artifacts may, in addition, be beautiful in and of themselves, interesting, mysterious, promising. Clarke, unlike Heinlein or Asimov, is also the poet of the big machine. In this he has always been a leader in hard sf, and has maintained the bond between sf and the twin communities devoted to the construction of enormous machines for scientific exploration—experimental physics and the space community—for decades. Clarke's stories tend to be about the emotional rewards of the quest for knowledge, of the wonder of huge objects and cosmic vistas (in this regard, Hilbert Schenck's "Send Me a Kiss by Wire" is Clarkeian), as opposed to the power knowledge can confer.

"Transit of Earth" is a dying-astronaut story—a form used frequently in the New Wave period, from Ballard's "Cage of Sand" to Malzberg's *Beyond Apollo* (1972) to oppose hard sf attitudes—transformed into a triumph of the hard sf attitude. It is in one sense a recasting of "The Cold Equations" from the point of view of the one dying—who recognizes the necessity of his death and nevertheless continues the quest for knowledge and consciously identifies with past heroic explorers who died. He identifies in a physical sense with his alien environment, looks forward to merging with it. Like Theodore Sturgeon's 1950 tale of a dying astronaut, "The Man Who Lost the Sea," this is a story of emotional fulfillment in a coldly beautiful place.

Testing, one, two, three, four, five . . .

Evans speaking. I will continue to record as long as possible. This is a two-hour capsule, but I doubt if I'll fill it.

That photograph has haunted me all my life; now, too late, I know why. (But would it have made any difference if I *had* known? That's one of those meaningless and unanswerable questions the mind keeps returning to endlessly, like the tongue exploring a broken tooth.)

I've not seen it for years, but I've only to close my eyes and I'm back in a landscape almost as hostile—and as beautiful—as this one. Fifty million miles sunward, and seventy-two years in the past, five men face the camera amid the antarctic snows. Not even the bulky furs can hide the exhaustion and defeat that mark every line of their bodies; and their faces are already touched by Death.

There were five of them. There were five of us, and of course we also took a group photograph. But everything else was different. We were smiling—cheerful, confident. And our picture was on all the screens of Earth within ten minutes. It was months before *their* camera was found and brought back to civilization.

And we die in comfort, with all modern conveniences—including many that Robert Falcon Scott could never have imagined, when he stood at the South Pole in 1912.

Two hours later. I'll start giving exact times when it becomes important.

All the facts are in the log, and by now the whole world knows them. So I guess I'm doing this largely to settle my mind—to talk myself into facing the inevitable. The trouble is, I'm not sure what subjects to avoid, and which to tackle head on. Well, there's only one way to find out.

The first item: in twenty-four hours, at the very most, all the oxygen will be gone. That leaves me with the three classical choices. I can let the carbon dioxide build up until I become unconscious. I can step outside and crack the suit, leaving Mars to do the job in about two minutes. Or I can use one of the tablets in the med kit.

CO_2 build-up. Everyone says that's quite easy—just like going to sleep. I've no doubt that's true; unfortunately, in my case it's associated with nightmare number one. . . .

I wish I'd never come across that damn book *True Stories of World War Two*, or whatever it was called. There was one chapter about a German submarine, found and salvaged after the war. The crew was still inside it—*two* men per bunk. And between each pair of skeletons, the single respirator set they'd been sharing. . . .

Well, at least that won't happen here. But I know, with a deadly certainty, that as soon as I find it hard to breathe, I'll be back in that doomed U-boat.

So what about the quicker way? When you're exposed to vacuum, you're unconscious in ten or fifteen seconds, and people who've been through it say it's not painful—just peculiar. But trying to breathe something that isn't there brings me altogether too neatly to nightmare number two.

This time, it's a personal experience. As a kid, I used to do a lot of skin diving, when my family went to the Caribbean for vacations. There was an old freighter that had sunk twenty years before, out on a reef, with its deck only a couple of yards below the surface. Most of the hatches were open, so it was easy to get inside, to look for souvenirs and hunt the big fish that like to shelter in such places.

Of course it was dangerous if you did it without scuba gear. So what boy could resist the challenge?

My favorite route involved diving into a hatch on the foredeck, swimming about fifty feet along a passageway dimly lit by portholes a few yards apart, then angling up a short flight of stairs and emerging through a door in the battered superstructure. The whole trip took less than a minute—an easy dive for anyone in good condition. There was even time to do some sight-seeing, or to play with a few fish along the route. And sometimes, for a change, I'd switch directions, going in the door and coming out again through the hatch.

That was the way I did it the last time. I hadn't dived for a week—there had been a big storm, and the sea was too rough—so I was impatient to get going.

I deep-breathed on the surface for about two minutes, until I felt the tingling in my finger tips that told me it was time to stop. Then I jackknifed and slid gently down toward the black rectangle of the open doorway.

It always looked ominous and menacing—that was part of the thrill. And for the first few yards I was almost completely blind; the contrast between the tropical glare above water and the gloom between decks was so great that it took quite a while for my eyes to adjust. Usually, I was halfway along the corridor before I could see anything clearly. Then the illumination would steadily increase as I approached the open hatch, where a shaft of sunlight would paint a dazzling rectangle on the rusty, barnacled metal floor.

I'd almost made it when I realized that, this time, the light wasn't getting better. There was no slanting column of sunlight ahead of me, leading up to the world of air and life.

I had a second of baffled confusion, wondering if I'd lost my way. Then I knew what had happened—and confusion turned into sheer panic. Sometime during the storm, the hatch must have slammed shut. It weighed at least a quarter of a ton.

I don't remember making a U turn; the next thing I recall is swimming quite slowly back along the passage and telling myself: Don't hurry; your air will last longer if you take it easy. I could see very well now, because my eyes had had plenty of time to become dark-adapted. There were lots of details I'd never noticed before, like the red squirrelfish lurking in the shadows, the green fronds and algae growing in the little patches of light around the portholes, and even a single rubber boot, apparently in excellent condition, lying where someone must have kicked it off. And once, out of a side corridor, I noticed a big grouper staring at me with bulbous eyes, his thick lips half parted, as if he was astonished at my intrusion.

The band around my chest was getting tighter and tighter. It was impossible to hold my breath any longer. Yet the stairway still seemed an infinite distance ahead. I let some bubbles of air dribble out of my mouth. That improved matters for a moment, but, once I had exhaled, the ache in my lungs became even more unendurable.

Now there was no point in conserving strength by flippering along with that steady, unhurried stroke. I snatched the ultimate few cubic inches of air from my face mask—feeling it flatten against my nose as I did so—and swallowed them down into my starving lungs. At the same time, I shifted gear and drove forward with every last atom of strength. . . .

And that's all I remember until I found myself spluttering and coughing in the daylight, clinging to the broken stub of the mast. The water around me was stained with blood, and I wondered why. Then, to my great surprise, I noticed a deep gash in my right calf. I must have banged into some sharp obstruction, but I'd never noticed it and even then felt no pain.

That was the end of my skin diving until I started astronaut training ten years later and went into the underwater zero-gee simulator. Then it was different, because I was using scuba gear. But I had some nasty moments that I was afraid the psychologists would notice, and I always made sure that I got nowhere near emptying my tank. Having nearly suffocated once, I'd no intention of risking it again. . . .

I know exactly what it will feel like to breathe the freezing wisp of near-vacuum that passes for atmosphere on Mars. No thank you.

So what's wrong with poison? Nothing, I suppose. The stuff we've got takes only fifteen seconds, they told us. But all my instincts are against it, even when there's no sensible alternative.

Did Scott have poison with him? I doubt it. And if he did, I'm sure he never used it.

I'm not going to replay this. I hope it's been of some use, but I can't be sure.

The radio has just printed out a message from Earth, reminding me that transit starts in two hours. As if I'm likely to forget—when four men have already died so that I can be the first human being to see it. And the only one, for exactly a hundred years. It isn't often that Sun, Earth, and Mars line up neatly like this; the last time was in 1905, when poor old Lowell was still writing his beautiful nonsense about the canals and the great dying civilization that had built them. Too bad it was all delusion.

I'd better check the telescope and the timing equipment.

The Sun is quiet today—as it should be, anyway, near the middle of the cycle. Just a few small spots, and some minor areas of disturbance around them. The solar weather is set calm for months to come. That's one thing the others won't have to worry about, on their way home.

I think that was the worst moment, watching *Olympus* lift off Phobos and head back to Earth. Even though we'd known for weeks that nothing could be done, that was the final closing of the door.

It was night, and we could see everything perfectly. Phobos had come leaping up out of the west a few hours earlier, and was doing its mad backward rush across the sky, growing from a tiny crescent to a half-moon; before it reached the zenith it would disappear as it plunged into the shadow of Mars and became eclipsed.

We'd been listening to the countdown, of course, trying to go about our normal work. It wasn't easy, accepting at last the fact that fifteen of us had come to Mars and only ten would return. Even then, I suppose there were millions back on Earth who still could not understand. They must have found it impossible to believe that *Olympus* couldn't descend a mere four thousand miles to pick us up. The Space Administration had been bombarded with crazy rescue schemes; heaven knows, we'd thought of enough ourselves. But when the permafrost under Landing Pad Three finally gave way and *Pegasus* toppled, that was that. It still seems a miracle that the ship didn't blow up when the propellant tank ruptured. . . .

I'm wandering again. Back to Phobos and the countdown.

On the telescope monitor, we could clearly see the fissured plateau where *Olympus* had touched down after we'd separated and begun our own descent. Though our friends would never land on Mars, at least they'd had a little world of their own to explore; even for a satellite as small as Phobos, it worked out at thirty square miles per man. A lot of territory to search for strange minerals and debris from space—or to carve your name so that future ages would know that you were the first of all men to come this way.

The ship was clearly visible as a stubby, bright cylinder against the dull-gray rocks; from time to time some flat surface would catch the light of the swiftly moving sun, and would flash with mirror brilliance. But about five minutes before lift-off, the picture became suddenly pink, then crimson—then vanished completely as Phobos rushed into eclipse.

The countdown was still at ten seconds when we were startled by a blast of light. For a moment, we wondered if *Olympus* had also met with catastrophe. Then we realized that someone was filming the take-off, and the external floodlights had been switched on.

During those last few seconds, I think we all forgot our own predicament; we were up there aboard *Olympus*, willing the thrust to build up smoothly and lift the ship out of the tiny gravitational field of Phobos, and then away from Mars for the long fall sunward. We heard Commander Richmond say "Ignition," there was a brief burst of interference, and the patch of light began to move in the field of the telescope.

That was all. There was no blazing column of fire, because, of course, there's really no ignition when a nuclear rocket lights up. "Lights up" indeed! That's another hangover from the old chemical technology. But a hot hydrogen blast is completely invisible; it seems a pity that we'll never again see anything so spectacular as a Saturn or a Korolov blast-off.

Just before the end of the burn, *Olympus* left the shadow of Mars and burst out into sunlight again, reappearing almost instantly as a brilliant, swiftly moving star. The blaze of light must have startled them aboard the ship, because we heard someone call out: "Cover that window!" Then, a few seconds later, Richmond announced: "Engine cutoff." Whatever happened, *Olympus* was now irrevocably headed back to Earth.

A voice I didn't recognize—though it must have been the Commander's—said "Good-by, *Pegasus*," and the radio transmission switched off. There was, of course, no point in saying "Good luck." *That* had all been settled weeks ago.

I've just played this back. Talking of luck, there's been one compensation, though not for us. With a crew of only ten, *Olympus* has been able to dump a third of her expendables and lighten herself by several tons. So now she'll get home a month ahead of schedule.

Plenty of things could have gone wrong in that month; we may yet have saved the expedition. Of course, we'll never know—but it's a nice thought.

I've been playing a lot of music, full blast—now that there's no one else to be disturbed. Even if there were any Martians, I don't suppose this ghost of an atmosphere can carry the sound more than a few yards.

We have a fine collection, but I have to choose carefully. Nothing downbeat and nothing that demands too much concentration. Above all, nothing with human voices. So I restrict myself to the lighter orchestral classics; the "New World" symphony and Grieg's piano concerto fill the bill perfectly. At the moment I'm listening to Rachmaninoff's "Rhapsody on a Theme of Paganini," but now I must switch off and get down to work.

There are only five minutes to go. All the equipment is in perfect condition. The telescope is tracking the Sun, the video recorder is standing by, the precision timer is running.

These observations will be as accurate as I can make them. I owe it to my lost comrades, whom I'll soon be joining. They gave me their oxygen, so that I can still be alive at this moment. I hope you remember that, a hundred or a thousand years from now, whenever you crank these figures into the computers. . . .

Only a minute to go; getting down to business. For the record: year, 1984; month, May; day, II, coming up to four hours thirty minutes Ephemeris Time . . . *now*.

Half a minute to contact. Switching recorder and timer to high speed. Just rechecked position angle to make sure I'm looking at the right spot on the Sun's limb. Using power of five hundred—image perfectly steady even at this low elevation.

Four thirty-two. Any moment now . . .

There it is . . . there it is! I can hardly believe it! A tiny black dent in the edge of the Sun . . . growing, growing, growing . . .

Hello, Earth. Look up at me, the brightest star in your sky, straight overhead at midnight. . . .

Recorder back to slow.

Four thirty-five. It's as if a thumb is pushing into the Sun's edge, deeper and deeper. . . . Fascinating to watch . . .

Four forty-one. Exactly halfway. The Earth's a perfect black semicircle—a clean bite out of the Sun. As if some disease is eating it away . . .

Four forty-eight. Ingress three-quarters complete.

Four hours forty-nine minutes thirty seconds. Recorder on high speed again.

The line of contact with the Sun's edge is shrinking fast. Now it's a barely visible black thread. In a few seconds, the whole Earth will be superimposed on the Sun.

Now I can see the effects of the atmosphere. There's a thin halo of light surrounding that black hole in the Sun. Strange to think that I'm seeing the glow of all the sunsets—and all the sunrises—that are taking place around the whole Earth at this very moment. . . .

Ingress complete—four hours fifty minutes five seconds. The whole world has moved onto the face of the Sun. A perfectly circular black disc silhouetted against that inferno ninety million miles below. It looks bigger than I expected; one could easily mistake it for a fair-sized sunspot.

Nothing more to see now for six hours, when the Moon appears, trailing Earth by half the Sun's width. I'll beam the recorder data back to Lunacom, then try to get some sleep.

My very last sleep. Wonder if I'll need drugs. It seems a pity to waste these last few hours, but I want to conserve my strength—and my oxygen.

I think it was Dr. Johnson who said that nothing settles a man's mind so wonderfully as the knowledge that he'll be hanged in the morning. How the hell did *he* know?

Ten hours thirty minutes Ephemeris Time. Dr. Johnson was right. I had only one pill, and don't remember any dreams.

The condemned man also ate a hearty breakfast. Cut that out . . .

Back at the telescope. Now the Earth's halfway across the disc, passing well north of center. In ten minutes, I should see the Moon.

I've just switched to the highest power of the telescope—two thousand. The image is slightly fuzzy, but still fairly good; atmospheric halo very distinct. I'm hoping to see the cities on the dark side of Earth. . . .

No luck. Probably too many clouds. A pity; it's theoretically possible, but we never succeeded. I wish . . . never mind.

Ten hours forty minutes. Recorder on slow speed. Hope I'm looking at the right spot.

Fifteen seconds to go. Recorder fast.

Damn—missed it. Doesn't matter—the recorder will have caught the exact moment. There's little black notch already in the side of the Sun. First contact must have been about ten hours forty-one minutes twenty seconds ET.

What a long way it is between Earth and Moon; there's half the width of the Sun between them. You wouldn't think the two bodies had anything to do with each other. Makes you realize just how big the Sun really is. . . .

Ten hours forty-four minutes. The Moon's exactly halfway over the edge. A very small, very clear-cut semicircular bite out of the edge of the Sun.

Ten hours forty-seven minutes five seconds. Internal contact. The Moon's clear of the edge, entirely inside the Sun. Don't suppose I can see anything on the night side, but I'll increase the power.

That's funny.

Well, well. Someone must be trying to talk to me; there's a tiny light pulsing away there on the darkened face of the moon. Probably the laser at Imbrium Base.

Sorry, everyone. I've said all my good-byes, and don't want to go through that again. Nothing can be important now.

Still, it's almost hypnotic—that flickering point of light, coming out of the face of the Sun itself. Hard to believe that, even after it's traveled all this distance, the beam is only a hundred miles wide. Lunacom's going to all this trouble to aim it exactly at me, and I suppose I should feel guilty at ignoring it. But I don't. I've nearly finished my work, and the things of Earth are no longer any concern of mine.

Ten hours fifty minutes. Recorder off. That's it—until the end of Earth transit, two hours from now.

I've had a snack and am taking my last look at the view from the observation bubble. The Sun's still high, so there's not much contrast, but the light brings out all the colors vividly—the countless varieties of red and pink and crimson, so startling against the deep blue of the sky. How different from the Moon—though that, too, has its own beauty.

It's strange how surprising the obvious can be. Everyone knew that Mars was red. But we didn't really expect the red of rust, the red of blood. Like the Painted Desert of Arizona; after a while, the eye longs for green.

To the north, there is one welcome change of color; the cap of carbon-dioxide snow on Mount Burroughs is a dazzling white pyramid. That's another surprise. Burroughs is twenty-five thousand feet above Mean Datum; when I was a boy, there weren't supposed to be any mountains on Mars. . . .

The nearest sand dune is a quarter of a mile away, and it, too, has patches of frost on its shaded slope. During the last storm, we thought it moved a few feet, but we couldn't be sure. Certainly the dunes *are* moving, like those on Earth. One day, I suppose, this base will be covered—only to reappear again in a thousand years. Or ten thousand.

That strange group of rocks—the Elephant, the Capitol, the Bishop—still holds its secrets, and teases me with the memory of our first big disappointment. We could have sworn that they were sedimentary; how eagerly we rushed out to look for fossils! Even now, we don't know what formed that outcropping. The geology of Mars is still a mass of contradictions and enigmas. . . .

We have passed on enough problems to the future, and those who come after us will find many more. But there's one mystery we never reported to Earth, or even entered in the log. . . .

The first night after we landed, we took turns keeping watch. Brennan was on duty, and woke me up soon after midnight. I was annoyed—it was ahead of time—and then he told me that he'd seen a light moving around the base of the Capitol.

We watched for at least an hour, until it was my turn to take over. But we saw nothing; whatever that light was, it never reappeared.

Now Brennan was as levelheaded and unimaginative as they come; if he said he saw a light, then he saw one. Maybe it was some kind of electric discharge, or the reflection of Phobos on a piece of sand-polished rock. Anyway, we decided not to mention it to Lunacom, unless we saw it again.

Since I've been alone, I've often awakened in the night and looked out toward the rocks. In the feeble illumination of Phobos and Deimos, they remind me of the skyline of a darkened city. And it has always remained darkened. No lights have ever appeared for me. . . .

Twelve hours forty-nine minutes Ephemeris Time. The last act's about to begin. Earth has nearly reached the edge of the Sun. The two narrow horns of light that still embrace it are barely touching. . . .

Recorder on fast.

Contact! Twelve hours fifty minutes sixteen seconds. The crescents of light no longer meet. A tiny black spot has appeared at the edge of the Sun, as the Earth begins to cross it. It's growing longer, longer. . . .

Recorder on slow. Eighteen minutes to wait before Earth finally clears the face of the Sun.

The Moon still has more than halfway to go; it's not yet reached the mid-point of its transit. It looks like a little round blob of ink, only a quarter the size of Earth. And there's no light flickering there any more. Lunacom must have given up.

Well, I have just a quarter of an hour left, here in my last home. Time seems to be accelerating the way it does in the final minutes before a lift-off. No matter; I have everything worked out now. I can even relax.

Already, I feel part of history. I am one with Captain Cook, back in Tahiti in 1769, watching the transit of Venus. Except for that image of the Moon trailing along behind, it must have looked just like this. . . .

What would Cook have thought, over two hundred years ago, if he'd known that one day a man would observe the whole Earth in transit from an outer world? I'm sure he would have been astonished—and then delighted. . . .

But I feel a closer identity with a man not yet born. I hope you hear these words, whoever you may be. Perhaps you will be standing on this very spot, a hundred years from now, when the next transit occurs.

Greetings to 2084, November 10! I wish you better luck than we had. I suppose you will have come here on a luxury liner. Or you may have been born on Mars, and be a stranger to Earth. You will know things that I cannot imagine. Yet somehow I don't envy you. I would not even change places with you if I could.

For you will remember my name, and know that I was the first of all mankind ever to see a transit of Earth. And no one will see another for a hundred years. . . .

Twelve hours fifty-nine minutes. Exactly halfway through egress. The Earth is a perfect semicircle—a black shadow on the face of the Sun. I still can't escape from the impression that something has taken a big bite out of that golden disc. In nine minutes it will be gone, and the Sun will be whole again.

Thirteen hours seven minutes. Recorder on fast.

Earth has almost gone. There's just a shallow black dimple at the edge of the Sun. You could easily mistake it for a small spot, going over the limb.

Thirteen hours eight.

Good-by, beautiful Earth.

Going, going, going. Good-by, good—

I'm O.K. again now. The timings have all been sent home on the beam. In five minutes, they'll join the accumulated wisdom of mankind. And Lunacom will know that I stuck to my post.

But I'm not sending this. I'm going to leave it here, for the next expedition—whenever that may be. It could be ten or twenty years before anyone comes here again. No point in going back to an old site when there's a whole world waiting to be explored. . . .

So this capsule will stay here, as Scott's diary remained in his tent, until the next visitors find it. But they won't find me.

Strange how hard it is to get away from Scott. I think he gave me the idea.

For his body will not lie frozen forever in the Antarctic, isolated from the great cycle of life and death. Long ago, that lonely tent began its march to the sea. Within a few years, it was buried by the falling snow and had become part of the glacier that crawls eternally away from the Pole. In a few brief centuries, the sailor will have returned to the sea. He will merge once more into the pattern of living things—the plankton, the seals, the penguins, the whales, all the multitudinous fauna of the Antarctic Ocean.

There are no oceans here on Mars, nor have there been for at least five billion years. But there is life of some kind, down there in the badlands of Chaos II, which we never had time to explore.

Those moving patches on the orbital photographs. The evidence that whole areas of Mars have been swept clear of craters, by forces other than erosion. The long-chain, optically active carbon molecules picked up by the atmospheric samplers.

And, of course, the mystery of Viking 6. Even now, no one has been able to make any sense of those last instrument readings, before something large and heavy crushed the probe in the still, cold depths of the Martian night. . . .

And don't talk to me about *primitive* life forms in a place like this! Anything that's survived here will be so sophisticated that we may look as clumsy as dinosaurs.

There's still enough propellant in the ship's tanks to drive the Mars car clear around the planet. I have three hours of daylight left—plenty of time to get down into the valleys and well out into Chaos. After sunset, I'll still be able to make good speed with the headlights. It will be romantic, driving at night under the moons of Mars. . . .

One thing I must fix before I leave. I don't like the way Sam's lying out there. He was always so poised, so graceful. It doesn't seem right that he should look so awkward now. I must do something about it.

I wonder if *I* could have covered three hundred feet without a suit, walking slowly, steadily—the way he did, to the very end.

I must try not to look at his face.

That's it. Everything shipshape and ready to go.

The therapy has worked. I feel perfectly at ease—even contented, now that I know exactly what I'm going to do. The old nightmares have lost their power.

It is true: we all die alone. It makes no difference at the end, being fifty million miles from home.

I'm going to enjoy the drive through that lovely painted landscape. I'll be thinking of all those who dreamed about Mars—Wells and Lowell and Burroughs and Weinbaum and Bradbury. They all guessed wrong—but the reality is just as strange, just as beautiful, as they imagined.

I don't know what's waiting for me out there, and I'll probably never see it. But on this starveling world, it must be desperate for carbon, phosphorus, oxygen, calcium. It can use me.

And when my oxygen alarm gives its final "ping," somewhere down there in that haunted wilderness, I'm going to finish in style. As soon as I have difficulty in breathing, I'll get off the Mars car and start walking—with a playback unit plugged into my helmet and going full blast.

For sheer, triumphant power and glory there's nothing in the whole of music to match the Toccata and Fugue in D. I won't have time to hear all of it; that doesn't matter.

Johann Sebastian, here I come.

PRIMA BELLADONNA

J. G. Ballard

J. G. Ballard is one of the two most significant contemporary English writers to emerge from the science fiction field since the 1950s (the other is Brian W. Aldiss) Of the two, Ballard is the one whose work is frequently a form of hard sf, or in dialogue with hard sf. But his style is so overtly antithetical to the transparent journalistic prose so often held up as ideal by Campbell and others, and his attitude toward science and technology so far removed from the problem-solving and faith-based assumptions of Modern science fiction, that he has most often been perceived as writing something that is not Modern science fiction at all, or is antithetical to it, and therefore irrelevant to a consideration of it. There is some truth in these assertions, but Ballard remains persistently relevant. What are we to make of his claim to being one of the few real hard sf writers today? "I feel very optimistic about science and technology," says Ballard, "and yet almost my entire fiction has been an illustration of the opposite. I show all these entropic universes with everything running down."

We choose here to reprint Ballard's first major sf story, which burst upon the scene in 1957, heralded by an enthusiastic reprint in Judith Merril's influential year's-best sf anthology. "Prima Belladonna" introduces the setting of many of Ballard's famous early stories, later collected in *Vermilion Sands* (1971). *Vermilion Sands* is a bizarre future Southern California of the mind, decadent, flamboyant, metaphorical. It is in a sense Ballard's version of Ray Bradbury's Mars. This story is Hawthorne's "Rappaccini's Daughter" transformed, an injection of Gothic sensibility and perverse sexuality into a literature (and to an audience) unprepared. During his early, fertile, genre years, until 1965 or so, Ballard continued to write in this mode, including the contents of his well-known collections *The Voices of Time* (1962), *Billenium* (1962), *Passport to Eternity* (1963), *The Terminal Beach* (1964), *The Impossible Man* (1966), and novels, including his famous disaster novels, *The Wind From Nowhere* (1962), *The Drowned World* (1962), *The Burning World* (1964), *The Crystal World* (1966). The effect on the sf field was startling: In 1965 he was proclaimed by editor Michael Moorcock as the avatar of the New Wave in England; in America, he was the subject of a series of full-scale attacks, starting with an essay by Algis Budrys in 1966—"A story by J. G. Ballard, as you know, calls for people who don't think. One begins with characters who regard the physical universe as a mysterious and arbitrary place, and who would not dream of trying to understand its actual laws"—and continuing to this day.

"Prima Belladonna" is rigorously logical, given its premises—it plays with the conventions of reading sf literally to amusing and disturbing effect. The protagonist is perfectly able to cope with the scientific side of things—it's the human element that is the problem. This is a story of abnormal psychology.

I first met Jane Ciracylides during the Recess, that world slump of boredom, lethargy and high summer which carried us all so blissfully through ten unforgettable years, and I suppose that may have had a lot to do with what went on between us. Certainly I can't believe I could make myself as ridiculous now, but then again, it might have been just Jane herself.

Whatever else they said about her, everyone had to agree she was a beautiful girl, even if her genetic background was a little mixed. The gossips at Vermilion Sands soon decided there was a good deal of mutant in her, because she had a rich patina-golden skin and what looked like insects for eyes, but that didn't bother either myself or any of my friends, one or two of whom, like Tony Miles and Harry Devine, have never since been quite the same to their wives.

We spent most of our time in those days on the wide cool balcony of my apartment off Beach Drive, drinking beer—we always kept a useful supply stacked in the refrigerator of my music shop on the street level—yarning in a desultory way and playing i-Go, a sort of decelerated chess which was popular then. None of the others ever did any work; Harry was an architect and Tony Miles sometimes sold a few ceramics to the tourists, but I usually put a couple of hours in at the shop each morning, getting off the foreign orders and turning the beer.

One particularly hot lazy day I'd just finished wrapping up a delicate soprano mimosa wanted by the Hamburg Oratorio Society when Harry phoned down from the balcony.

"Parker's Choro-Flora?" he said. "You're guilty of over-production. Come on up here. Tony and I have something beautiful to show you."

When I went up I found them grinning happily like two dogs who had just discovered an interesting tree.

"Well?" I asked. "Where is it?"

Tony tilted his head slightly. "Over there," he indicated.

I looked up and down the street, and across the face of the apartment house opposite.

"Careful," he warned me. "Don't gape at her."

I slid into one of the wicker chairs and craned my head round cautiously.

"Fourth floor," Harry elaborated slowly, out of the side of his mouth. "One left from the balcony opposite. Happy now?"

"Dreaming," I told him, taking a long slow focus on her. "I wonder what else she can do?"

Harry and Tony sighed thankfully. "Well?" Tony asked.

"She's out of my league," I said. "But you two shouldn't have any trouble. Go over and tell her how much she needs you."

Harry groaned. "Don't you realize, this one is poetic, emergent, something straight out of the primal apocalyptic sea. She's probably divine."

The woman was strolling around the lounge, re-arranging the furniture, wearing almost nothing except a large abstract metallic hat. Even in shadow the long sinuous lines of her thighs and shoulders gleamed gold and burning. She was a walking galaxy of light. Vermilion Sands had never seen anything like her.

"The approach has got to be equivocal," Harry continued, gazing into his beer. "Shy, almost mystical. Nothing urgent or grabbing."

The woman stooped down to unpack a suitcase and the metal vanes of her hat fluttered over her face. I didn't bother to remind Harry that Betty, his wife and a girl of considerable spirit, would have firmly restrained him from anything that wasn't mystical.

"She must use up about a kilowatt," I calculated. "What do you think her chemistry is?"

"Who cares," Harry said. "It doesn't matter to me if it's siliconic."

"In this heat?" I said. "She'd ignite."

The woman walked out onto the balcony, saw us staring at her, looked around for a moment and then went in again.

We sat back and looked thoughtfully at each other, like three triumvirs deciding how to divide an empire, not saying too much, and one eye watching for any chance of a double-deal.

Five minutes later the singing started.

At first I thought it was one of the azalea trios in trouble with an alkaline pH, but the frequencies were too high. They were almost out of the audible range, a thin tremolo quaver which came out of nowhere and rose up the back of the skull.

Harry and Tony frowned at me.

"Your livestock's unhappy about something," Tony told me. "Can you quieten it down?"

"It's not the plants," I told him. "Can't be."

The sound mounted in intensity, scraping the edge off my occipital bones. I was about to go down to the shop when Harry and Tony leaped out of their chairs and dived back against the wall.

"For chrissake, Steve, look out!" Tony yelled at me. He pointed wildly at the table I was leaning on, picked up a chair and smashed it down on the glass top.

I stood up and brushed the fragments out of my hair.

"What the hell's the matter?" I asked them.

Tony was looking down at the tangle of wickerwork tied round the metal struts of the table. Harry came forward and took my arm gingerly.

"That was close. You all right?"

"It's gone," Tony said flatly. He looked carefully over the balcony floor and down over the rail into the street.

"What was it?" I asked.

Harry peered at me closely. "Didn't you see it? It was about three inches from you. Emperor Scorpion, big as a lobster." He sat down weakly on a beer crate. "Must have been a sonic one. The noise has gone now."

After they'd left I cleared up the mess and had a quiet beer to myself. I could have sworn nothing had got onto the table.

On the balcony opposite, wearing a gown of shimmering ionized fiber, the golden woman was watching me.

I found out who she was the next morning. Tony and Harry were down at the beach with their wives, probably enlarging on the scorpion, and I was in the shop tuning up a Khan-Arachnid orchid with the UV lamp. It was a difficult bloom, with a normal full range of twenty-four octaves, but like all the tetracot $K_3 + 25$ C_5 A_9 chorotropes, unless it got a lot of exercise it tended to relapse into neurotic minor key transpositions which were the devil to break. And as the senior bloom in the shop it naturally affected all the others. Invariably when I opened the shop in the mornings it sounded like a madhouse, but as soon as I'd fed the Arachnid and straightened out one or two pH gradients the rest promptly took their cues from it and dimmed down quietly in their control tanks, two-time, three-four, the multi-tones, all in perfect harmony.

There were only about a dozen true Arachnids in captivity; most of the others were either mutes or grafts from dicot stems, and I was lucky to have mine at all. I'd bought the place five years earlier from an old half-deaf man called Sayers, and the day before he left he moved a lot of rogue stock out to the garbage disposal scoop behind the apartment block. Reclaiming some of the tanks, I'd come across the Arachnid, thriving on a diet of algae and perished rubber tubing.

Why Sayers had wanted to throw it away I'd never discovered. Before he came to Vermilion Sands he'd been a curator at the old Kew Conservatoire where the first choroflora had been bred, and had worked under the Director, Dr. Mandel, who as a young botanist of twenty-five had discovered the prime Arachnid in the Guiana forest. The orchid took its name from the Khan-Arachnid spider which pollinated the flower, simultaneously laying its own eggs in the fleshy ovule, guided, or as Mandel always insisted, actually mesmerized to it by the vibrations which the orchid's calyx emitted at pollination-time. The first Arachnid orchids beamed out only a few random frequencies, but by crossbreeding and maintaining them artificially at the pollination stage Mandel had produced a strain that spanned a maximum of twenty-four octaves.

Not that he's ever been able to hear them. At the climax of his life's work Mandel, like Beethoven, was stone deaf, but apparently by merely looking at a blossom he could listen to its music. Strangely, though, after he went deaf he never looked at an Arachnid.

That morning I could almost understand why. The orchid was in a vicious mood. First it refused to feed, and I had to coax it along in a fluoraldehyde flush, and then it started going ultra-sonic, which meant complaints from all the dog owners in the area. Finally it tried to fracture the tank by resonating.

The whole place was in uproar, and I was almost resigned to shutting them down and waking them all by hand individually—a back-breaking job with eighty tanks in the shop—when everything suddenly died away to a murmur.

I looked round and saw the golden-skinned woman walk in.

"Good morning," I said. "They must like you."

She laughed pleasantly. "Hello. Weren't they behaving?"

Under the black beach robe her skin was a softer, more mellow gold, and it was her eyes that held me. I could just see them under the wide-brimmed hat. Insect legs wavered delicately round two points of purple light.

She walked over to a bank of mixed ferns and stood looking at them, her ample hips cocked to one side.

The ferns reached out toward her and trebled eagerly in their liquid fluted voices.

"Aren't they sweet?" she said, stroking the fronds gently. "They need so much affection."

Her voice was low in the register, a breath of cool sand pouring, with a lilt that gave it music.

"I've just come to Vermilion Sands," she said, "and my apartment seems awfully quiet. Perhaps if I had a flower, one would be enough, I shouldn't feel so lonely."

I couldn't take my eyes off her.

"Yes," I agreed, brisk and business-like. "What about something colorful? This Sumatra Samphire, say? It's a pedigree mezzo-soprano from the same follicle as the Bayreuth Festival Prima Belladonna."

"No," she said. "It looks rather cruel."

"Or this Louisiana Lute Lily? If you thin out its SO_2 it'll play some beautiful madrigals. I'll show you how to do it."

She wasn't listening to me. Slowly her hands raised in front of her breasts so that she almost seemed to be praying; she moved toward the counter on which the Arachnid stood.

"How beautiful it is," she said, gazing at the rich yellow and purple leaves hanging from the scarlet-ribbed vibrocalyx.

I followed her across the floor and switched on the Arachnid's audio so that she could hear it. Immediately the plant came to life. The leaves stiffened and filled with color and the calyx inflated, its ribs sprung tautly. A few sharp disconnected notes spat out.

"Beautiful, but evil," I said.

"Evil?" she repeated. "No, proud." She stepped closer to the orchid and looked down into its huge malevolent head. The Arachnid quivered and the spines on its stem arched and flexed menacingly.

"Careful," I warned her. "It's sensitive to the faintest respiratory sounds."

"Quiet," she said, waving me back. "I think it wants to sing."

"Those are only key fragments," I told her. "It doesn't perform. I use it as a frequency—"

"Listen!" She held my arm and squeezed it tightly.

A low rhythmic fusion of melody had been coming from the plants around the shop, and mounting above them I heard a single stronger voice calling out, at first a thin high-pitched reed of sound that began to pulse and deepen and finally swelled into full baritone, raising the other plants in chorus about itself.

I'd never heard the Arachnid sing before and I was listening to it open-eared when I felt a glow of heat burn against my arm. I turned round and saw the woman staring intently at the plant, her skin aflame, the insects in her eyes writhing insanely. The Arachnid stretched out toward her, calyx erect, leaves like blood-red sabers.

I stepped round her quickly and switched off the argon feed. The Arachnid sank to a whimper, and around us there was a nightmarish babel of broken notes and voices toppling from high C's and L's into discord. Then only a faint whispering of leaves moved over the silence.

The woman gripped the edge of the tank and gathered herself. Her skin dimmed and the insects in her eyes slowed to a delicate wavering.

"Why did you turn it off?" she asked heavily.

"I'm sorry," I said. "But I've got ten thousand dollars worth of stock here and that sort of twelve-tone emotional storm can blow a lot of valves. Most of these plants aren't equipped for grand opera."

She watched the Arachnid as the gas drained out of its calyx, and one by one its leaves buckled and lost their color.

"How much is it?" she asked me, opening her bag.

"It's not for sale," I said. "Frankly I've no idea how it picked up those bars—"

"Will a thousand dollars be enough?" she asked, her eyes fixed on me steadily.

"I can't," I told her. "I'd never be able to tune the others without it. Anyway," I added, trying to smile, "that Arachnid would be dead in ten minutes if you took it out of its vivarium. All these cylinders and leads would look a little odd inside your lounge."

"Yes, of course," she agreed, suddenly smiling back at me. "I was stupid." She gave the orchid a last backward glance and strolled away across the floor to the long Tchaikovsky section popular with the tourists.

" 'Pathetique,' " she read off a label at random. "I'll take this."

I wrapped up the scabia and slipped the instructional booklet into the crate, keeping my eye on her all the time.

"Don't look so alarmed," she said with amusement. "I've never heard anything like that before."

I wasn't alarmed. It was just that thirty years at Vermilion Sands had narrowed my horizons.

"How long are you staying at Vermilion Sands?" I asked.

"I open at the Casino tonight," she said. She told me her name was Jane Ciracylides and that she was a specialty singer.

"Why don't you look in?" she asked, her eyes fluttering mischievously. "I come on at eleven. You may find it interesting."

I did. The next morning Vermilion Sands hummed. Jane created a sensation. After her performance 300 people swore they'd seen everything from a choir of angels taking the vocal in the music of the spheres to Alexander's Ragtime Band. As for myself, perhaps I'd listened to too many flowers, but at least I knew where the scorpion on the balcony had come from.

Tony Miles had heard Sophie Tucker singing the St. Louis Blues, and Harry the elder Bach conducting the B Minor Mass.

They came round to the shop and argued over their respective performances while I wrestled with the flowers.

"Amazing," Tony exclaimed. "How does she do it? Tell me."

"The Heidelberg score," Harry ecstased. "Sublime, absolute." He looked irritably at the flowers. "Can't you keep these things quiet? They're making one hell of a row."

They were, and I had a shrewd idea why. The Arachnid was completely out of control, and by the time I'd clamped it down in a weak saline it had blown out over $300 worth of shrubs.

"The performance at the Casino last night was nothing on the one she gave here yesterday," I told them. "The Ring of the Nibelungs played by Stan Kenton. That Arachnid went insane. I'm sure it wanted to kill her."

Harry watched the plant convulsing its leaves in rigid spasmic movements.

"If you ask me it's in an advanced state of rut. Why should it want to kill her?"

"Not literally. Her voice must have overtones that irritate its calyx. None of the other plants minded. They cooed like turtle doves when she touched them."

Tony shivered happily.

Light dazzled in the street outside.

I handed Tony the broom. "Here, lover, brace yourself on that. Miss Ciracylides is dying to meet you."

Jane came into the shop, wearing a flame yellow cocktail skirt and another of her hats.

I introduced her to Harry and Tony.

"The flowers seem very quiet this morning," she said. "What's the matter with them?"

"I'm cleaning out the tanks," I told her. "By the way, we all want to congratulate you on last night. How does it feel to be able to name your fiftieth city?"

She smiled shyly and sauntered away round the shop. As I knew she would, she stopped by the Arachnid and leveled her eyes at it.

I wanted to see what she'd say, but Harry and Tony were all around her, and soon got her up to my apartment, where they had a hilarious morning playing the fool and raiding my scotch.

"What about coming out with us after the show tonight?" Tony asked her. "We can go dancing at the Flamingo."

"But you're both married," Jane protested coyly. "Aren't you worried about your reputations?"

"Oh, we'll bring the girls," Harry said airily. "And Steve here can come along and hold your coat."

We played i-Go together. Jane said she'd never played the game before, but she had no difficulty picking up the rules, and when she started sweeping the board with us I knew she was cheating. Admittedly it isn't every day that you get a chance to play i-Go with a golden-skinned woman with insects for eyes, but nevertheless I was annoyed. Harry and Tony, of course, didn't mind.

"She's charming," Harry said, after she'd left. "Who cares? It's a stupid game anyway."

"I care," I said. "She cheats."

The next three or four days at the shop were an audio-vegetative armageddon. Jane came in every morning to look at the Arachnid, and her presence was more than the flower could bear. Unfortunately I couldn't starve the plants down below their thresholds. They needed exercise and they had to have the Arachnid to lead them. But instead of running through its harmonic scales the orchid only screeched and whined. It wasn't the noise, which only a couple of dozen people complained about, but the damage being done to their vibratory chords that worried me. Those in the 17th Century catalogues stood up well to the strain, and the moderns were immune, but the Romantics burst their calyxes by the score. By the third day after Jane's arrival I'd lost $200 worth of Beethoven and more Mendelssohn and Schubert than I could bear to think about.

Jane seemed oblivious to the trouble she was causing me.

"What's wrong with them all?" she asked, surveying the chaos of gas cylinders and drip feeds spread across the floor.

"I don't think they like you," I told her. "At least the Arachnid doesn't. Your voice may move men to strange and wonderful visions, but it throws that orchid into acute melancholia."

"Nonsense," she said, laughing at me. "Give it to me and I'll show you how to look after it."

"Are Tony and Harry keeping you happy?" I asked her. I was annoyed I couldn't go down to the beach with them and instead had to spend my time draining tanks and titrating up norm solutions, none of which ever worked.

"They're very amusing," she said. "We play i-Go and I sing for them. But I wish you could come out more often."

After another two weeks I had to give up. I decided to close the plants down until Jane had left Vermilion Sands. I knew it would take me three months to rescore the stock, but I had no alternative.

The next day I received a large order for mixed coloratura herbaceous from the Santiago Garden Choir. They wanted delivery in three weeks.

"I'm sorry," Jane said, when she heard I wouldn't be able to fill the order. "You must wish that I'd never come to Vermilion Sands."

She stared thoughtfully into one of the darkened tanks.

"Couldn't I score them for you?" she suggested.

"No, thanks," I said, laughing, "I've had enough of that already."

"Don't be silly, of course I could."

I shook my head.

Tony and Harry told me I was crazy.

"Her voice has a wide enough range," Tony said. "You admit it yourself."

"What have you got against her?" Harry asked. "She cheats at i-Go?"

"It's nothing to do with that," I said. "But her voice has a wider range than you think."

We played i-Go at Jane's apartment. Jane won ten dollars from each of us.

"I am lucky," she said, very pleased with herself. "I never seem to lose." She counted up the bills and put them away carefully in her bag, her golden skin glowing.

Then Santiago sent me a repeat query.

I found Jane down among the cafés, holding off a siege of admirers.

"Have you given in yet?" she asked me, smiling at the young men.

"I don't know what you're doing to me," I said, "but anything is worth trying."

Back at the shop I raised a bank of perennials up past their thresholds. Jane helped me attach the gas and fluid lines.

"We'll try these first," I said. "Frequencies 543-785. Here's the score."

Jane took off her hat and began to ascend the scale, her voice clear and pure. At first the Columbine hesitated and Jane went down again and drew them along with her. They went up a couple of octaves together and then the plants stumbled and went off at a tangent of stepped chords.

"Try K sharp," I said. I fed a little chlorous acid into the tank and the Columbine followed her up eagerly, the infracalyxes warbling delicate variations on the treble clef.

"Perfect," I said.

It took us only four hours to fill the order.

"You're better than the Arachnid," I congratulated her. "How would you like a job? I'll fit you out with a large cool tank and all the chlorine you can breathe."

"Careful," she told me. "I may say yes. Why don't we rescore a few more of them while we're about it?"

"You're tired," I said. "Let's go and have a drink."

"Let me try the Arachnid," she suggested. "That would be more of a challenge."

Her eyes never left the flower. I wondered what they'd do if I left them together. Try to sing each other to death?

"No," I said. "Tomorrow perhaps."

We sat on the balcony together, glasses at our elbows, and talked the afternoon away.

She told me little about herself, but I gathered that her father had been a mining engineer in Peru and her mother a dancer at a Lima vu-tavern. They'd wandered from deposit to deposit, the father digging his concessions, the mother signing on at the nearest bordello to pay the rent.

"She only sang, of course," Jane added. "Until my father came." She blew bubbles into her glass. "So you think I give them what they want at the Casino. By the way, what do you see?"

"I'm afraid I'm your one failure," I said. "Nothing. Except you."

She dropped her eyes. "That sometimes happens," she said. "I'm glad this time."

A million suns pounded inside me. Until then I'd been reserving judgment on myself.

Harry and Tony were polite, if disappointed.

"I can't believe it," Harry said sadly. "I won't. How did you do it?"

"That mystical left-handed approach, of course," I told him. "All ancient seas and dark wells."

"What's she like?" Tony asked eagerly. "I mean, does she burn, or just tingle?"

Jane sang at the Casino every night from 11 to 3, but apart from that I suppose we were always together. Sometimes in the late afternoons we'd drive out along the beach to the Scented Desert and sit alone by one of the pools, watching the sun fall away behind the reefs and hills, lulling ourselves on the heavy rose-sick air. And when the wind began to blow cool across the sand we'd slip down into the water, bathe ourselves and drive back to town, filling the streets and café terraces with jasmine and musk-rose and helianthemum.

On other evenings we'd go down to one of the quiet bars at Lagoon West, and have supper out on the flats, and Jane would tease the waiters and sing honeybirds and angelcakes to the children who came in across the sand to watch her.

I realize now that I must have achieved a certain notoriety along the beach, but I didn't mind giving the old women—and beside Jane they all seemed to be old women—something to talk about. During the Recess no one cared very much about anything, and for that reason I never questioned myself too closely over my affair with Jane Ciracylides. As I sat on the balcony with her looking out over the cool early evenings or felt her body glowing beside me in the darkness I allowed myself few anxieties.

Absurdly, the only disagreement I ever had with her was over her cheating.

I remember that I once taxed her with it.

"Do you know you've taken over $500 from me, Jane? You're still doing it. Even now!"

She laughed impishly. "Do I cheat? I'll let you win one day."

"But why do you?" I insisted.

"It's more fun to cheat," she said. "Otherwise it's so boring."

"Where will you go when you leave Vermilion Sands?" I asked her.

She looked at me in surprise. "Why do you say that? I don't think I shall ever leave."

"Don't tease me, Jane. You're a child of another world than this."

"My father came from Peru," she reminded me.

"But you didn't get your voice from him," I said. "I wish I could have heard your mother sing. Had she a better voice than yours, Jane?"

"She thought so. My father couldn't stand either of us."

That was the evening I last saw Jane. We'd changed, and in the half an hour before she left for the Casino we sat on the balcony and I listened to her voice, like a spectral fountain, pour its golden luminous notes into the air. The music remained with me even after she'd gone, hanging faintly in the darkness around her chair.

I felt curiously sleepy, almost sick on the air she'd left behind, and at 11:30, when I knew she'd be appearing on stage at the Casino, I went out for a walk along the beach and a coffee.

As I left the elevator I heard music coming from the shop.

At first I thought I'd left one of the audio switches on, but I knew the voice only too well.

The windows of the shop had been shuttered, so I got in through the passage which led from the garage courtyard round at the back of the apartment house.

The lights had been turned out, but a brilliant glow filled the shop, throwing a golden fire onto the tanks along the counters. Across the ceiling liquid colors danced in reflection.

The music I had heard before, but only in overture.

The Arachnid had grown to three times its size. It towered nine feet high out of the shattered lid of the control tank, leaves tumid and inflamed, its calyx as large as a bucket, raging insanely.

Arched forward into it, her head thrown back, was Jane.

I ran over to her, my eyes filling with light, and grabbed her arm, trying to pull her away from it.

"Jane!" I shouted over the noise. "Get down!"

She flung my hand away. In her eyes, fleetingly, was a look of shame.

While I was sitting on the stairs in the entrance Tony and Harry drove up.

"Where's Jane?" Harry asked. "Has anything happened to her? We were down at the Casino." They both turned toward the music. "What the hell's going on?"

Tony peered at me suspiciously. "Steve, anything wrong?"

Harry dropped the bouquet he was carrying and started toward the rear entrance.

"Harry!" I shouted after him. "Get back!"

Tony held my shoulder. "Is Jane in there?"

I caught them as they opened the door into the shop.

"Good God!" Harry yelled. "Let go of me, you fool!" He struggled to get away from me. "Steve, it's trying to kill her!"

I jammed the door shut and held them back.

I never saw Jane again. The three of us waited in my apartment. When the music died away we went down and found the shop in darkness. The Arachnid had shrunk to its normal size.

The next day it died.

Where Jane went to I don't know. Not long afterward the Recess ended, and the big government schemes came along and started up all the clocks and kept us too busy working off the lost time to worry about a few bruised petals. Harry told me that Jane had been seen on her way through Red Beach, and I heard recently that someone very like her was doing the nightclubs this side out of Pernambuco.

So if any of you around there keep a choro-florist's and have a Khan-Arachnid orchid, look out for a golden-skinned woman with insects for eyes. Perhaps she'll play i-Go with you, and I'm sorry to have to say it, but she'll always cheat.

TO BRING IN THE STEEL

Donald M. Kingsbury

Donald M. Kingsbury is a mathematician and science fiction writer very much of the Campbell school, who published one story as a young man in the early 1950s in *Astounding* and then did not appear again until the late seventies, when he came to prominence with four long hard sf stories, including this one. Thereafter, he turned to the novel and produced *Courtship Rite* (1982) and *The Moon Goddess and the Son* (1987), and recently the novel in Larry Niven's hard sf universe of the Man-Kzin Wars (in volume IV of the series by divers hands), "The Survivor" (1991). Kingsbury is particularly adept at building complex hard sf settings, deeply rationalized and cleverly twisted into the unexpected, to provoke his characters into illuminating modes of behavior. As interested in psychology as in the hard sciences, Kingsbury is like no one so much as Frank Herbert, the author of *Dune* (1965), whose complex and detailed investigations of how the sociology and the psychology of the characters of his world were determined by its physical characteristics. By his thorough conceptualizing and careful execution, he achieves a feeling of realism in his created worlds unusual even among hard sf writers.

What Kingsbury derives directly from Campbell is a kind of cold godlike rational approach that contrasts strongly to the humanity of his characters. It is as if the author is playing both sides, the characters versus the universe. Yet it contrasts strongly with the cold, godless affect of, say, the majority of Ballard's fiction. The Campbellian affect is of an active god (though outside and behind the story) who plays by rules, the scientific laws—the god of "The Cold Equations."

With clever allusion and careful use of specific detail, Kingsbury achieves the illusion of a whole consistent universe outside the borders of the story, one in which we as readers live for the duration, at a time later than the events portrayed. His stories have the sweep and feel of history and, like sf writers from Wells and Kipling to the present, use the historical affect to lend an epic importance to the events, but the setting is frequently a future very distant in time and space, sometimes not clearly connected to our own present. Because he is also concerned with the details of physics and math in his universe, as well as the other sciences that underpin his future world, he is in the tradition of the world-builders such as Hal Clement, Frank Herbert, and Anne McCaffrey.

"To Bring in the Steel" is one of his few short stories, and is set in the recognizably human future in San Francisco and in space on the ship *Pittsburgh*, clamped to an asteroid it carries to Earth—mining and smelting the asteroid as it hurtles homeward through the void from beyond Mars. The captain is an obsessive worthy of Bester or Ballard, who just happens to be a problem-solver (as in, say, Frank Herbert's *Under Pressure*, 1956). But the central character is a woman who, in the grand tradition, moves from personal failure to fulfillment by adopting the problem-solving ethic. Kingsbury is a master of the surprise twist and the unexpected reversal of roles, of fortune, of conventions, especially of conventional morals. Learning better is Kingsbury's usual theme; psychology and sociology are always central to his stories. His work is more authentically like classic Heinlein than any other writer to emerge in the 1970s (with the possible exception of John Varley, who has the imagery and affect perfectly down but is innocent of hard science).

I

So his ex was dead. It was like her, too—she'd used the wrong poison and died horribly. Meddrick Kell remembered the time she had been in a rage about him killing animals and had put all his shotgun shells in the fireplace thinking they'd burn gently. God, that was long ago.

The mountains of Earth erupted in his memory, striking him with giddiness. He relished the green mountains for their loneliness; they gave him the same sense of peace as did the bleak desert of an asteroid. His wife hated being alone. She was never happier than when she was partying in a fifteenth-floor penthouse with a dozen desperately elegant drunks who besotted their wit in style with Chivas Regal and Johnnie Walker. Probably it was two days of being alone that had driven her to suicide, he thought sarcastically.

Kell toasted the nude on his cabin wall with an imaginary drink—alcohol and drugs were sparingly used in puritan space villages where the members prized clearheadedness because they prized survival. "Here's to the last alimony check!"

Then he returned to the letter from his daughter. He was always astonished by Celia's typewritten prose. She was only seven years old. Two of the paragraphs described her mother's death convulsions. She might grow up to be the System's best horror-story writer if she could learn to avoid words like "eclampsia." *What the hell does "eclampsia" mean? I suppose it's all the fault of that typewriter.*

He'd never met Celia. Helen had never even sent pictures. She just cashed alimony checks. Celia was five years old before Kell received his first letter, in fat, painful child's scrawl. The fax image that had been lasered in from Earth was still glued to the wall beside his nude's left breast. It had made him laugh for days because it was so like all the women he had ever known.

Dear Daddy I want a typwreter
xxxx ooo.
LOVE Celia

Kell didn't know how to buy a gift for a girl. His only experience with children was with his older brothers, all of whom had been raised by their father in a womanless world high in the Sierra Nevada Mountains. Consequently he grappled with the idea of selecting just the right typewriter for Celia as if it were a major Asteroid Belt crisis. The choice was too vast. Finally he had given up in bafflement and ordered for her the most expensive IBM model just to be on the safe side.

You could still get cheap manual-input line printers where one knob selected the typeface and the memory was restricted to a single line, but he hadn't been sure a child could use one. What finally decided him on the IBM Vosowriter 2200 was the hard-wired program that taught children to read while it taught them to type. On top of that it included:

(1) A full screen with editing capabilities.

(2) A hook-up to a 500-page random access cartridge for manuscript revision.

(3) A dictionary with definitions and completely cross-indexed thesaurus.

(4) An auxiliary voicewriter which allowed words to be input via speech. The words appeared on the screen in BFA—Basic Phonetic Alphabet, a slightly expanded version of the long-popular Pittman Initial Teaching Alphabet, handy because it was hardly distinguishable from the Roman alphabet. A parallel program looked up the word in the magnetic bubble dictionary and replaced the phonetic spelling by the standard spelling—if the word was contained in the dictionary.

That was where Celia found words like "eclampsia," "admissibility," and "ingurgitation." But at the bottom of each of her letters was always a hand-scrawled P.S. in very short words. "I want a hole W. Shaekper drama album MGM-LM-5632."

No matter how he tried, Kell had never been able to compose a letter in reply to his daughter and so had delegated that job to his secretary. His secretary's first cute effort had been condescending, distant.

"It's too cold!"

"You're a very cold man," said his secretary with the frankness that was usual between them.

"I don't give a tinker's damn if I'm as cold as the night side of a space corpse, do it over!" Kell had growled.

"What'll I say?"

"David, if I knew what to say, I'd write it! You're an expert at smoothing out all my reports. Not only that but you've been blessed with two younger sisters. You know how the little monsters think! Ask your girlfriend, ask anybody, *just do it*."

And so the correspondence had gone on for two years as they maneuvered in from the Belt toward the orbit of Mars. This, Celia's latest letter, ended with the hand-printed line, "I want to come to Pittsburgh I want to come to Pittsburgh I want to come to Pittsburgh." Pittsburgh was the name of Kell's ship, but the name was applied loosely to the whole symbiotic spaceship-asteroid complex.

What was he going to do with her? It would be a disaster to send Celia off to his brothers, and he'd have to act quickly to keep her out of her grandmother's hands. There were boarding schools, but he didn't know anything about that way of life and didn't trust it. He should talk to a woman; they knew about such things, but he didn't know any women well enough to discuss anything that close to him.

Kell punched out the code for David's bodyphone. "David. I have an Earthside emergency going. Contact Histon McKinner in San Francisco and have him pick up Celia and take her into his personal home right now. Her mother is dead. See that he takes legal action so that I get custody."

"It's dawn at San Francisco right now. I'll take care of everything in three hours."

"Great."

Dawn in San Francisco. The fog would be red in the bay and the white stucco walls along the hillsides would be pink. *What will I do with her?*

There was no dawn on the asteroid called Pittsburgh. The spaceship that had brought them out to the Belt was leeched to the rock's surface like a great space bird of prey, its huge sunward facing mirror keeping the planetoid in darkness, its talons grasping its victim, its beak devouring her substance. The mirror soaked up energy which had been lasered 400 million kilometers across the solar system from a power station circling the sun well inside Mercury's orbit, energy which out here in this dark energy desert was used to smelt four tons of rock per second, to refine it, and to deliver three tons of waste per second to the vaporizers, where ionized slag was accelerated to eight kilometers per second and blasted out forward along the line of orbit, day after day, year after year, in thundering flame. Twelve years the beast would spiral inward. When the ship finally reached Earth its claws would be clutching the digested remains of its victim, something like 300 million tons of refined metal. Most of it had already been sold to the Japanese.

Kell thought about his daughter all during his inspection tour of the smelter. He constantly wandered over the asteroid poking into everything. He was known as the man to have around during a crisis, probably because he was so perceptive that a part of him was predicting a crisis and planning for it before it ever happened. Today he was slower than usual.

It was the Pittsburgh's second journey to the Belt. She had carried thirty-five veterans from the first trip back with her. Kell was not a veteran—he had signed on as a foreman—but that had not stopped him from rising to second in command. Small space colonies were made for village democracy. Seniority rights and absolute chains of command were not tolerated in an environment where a leader's mistakes could be lethal.

Kell had always had an answer when quick answers were needed, and so he had risen. He always had an answer because he was that engineering freak who was fascinated by obsolete technology. When he was twelve he bought a bag of iron oxide and built himself a forge in the Sierra Nevadas and learned to smelt iron. When he was fourteen he turned out a rifle barrel from his own steel on his own lathe. He blew glass and built radio receivers out of homemade vacuum tubes.

In space he was a natural. Hundreds of millions of kilometers from Earth, problems developed that could not be solved by looking up a widget in a catalog and having it flown in. Earth was a year away by the fastest ship. Kell could do things like make an electromechanical gadget that would substitute for a computer. No matter that it was five thousand times as large as it should be; it worked.

The two women he had tried to live with now shunned him. One wouldn't tell him why. The other was a girl whose relationships never lasted more than two months and who herself was mostly a hermit. No use talking to them about Celia. And the women who had babies? The rule was that no children could be brought from Earth and none born during the journey to the Belt and none born while the ship-asteroid symbiosis was being established, but that after rooms had been burrowed in the asteroid, then babies were quite acceptable.

There were eighteen children on the Pittsburgh, the eldest being four and a half. Kell doubted his popularity with their parents. Once he had made a vigorous attempt to legally limit the number of children after a baby had been found lost and injured in one of the machine shops.

No, he had no one to consult, so he consulted himself.

There were no rules about importing children once the smelter had been set up; it had just never been done. He tried to imagine what it would be like to hold Celia in his arms, but he had never held a child in his arms. He tried to imagine himself talking to her but he had never talked to a child. It would be nice to have someone around who loved him, but he had never been loved.

He tried to reach Celia through his own childhood. He remembered himself frying eggs over a wood stove in the Sierra Nevadas, and the time he had stolen an ax and gone into the woods to chop, slicing the leather off his boot toe neatly and earning a beating, and the times he saved the squeezed lemons from the garbage to give flavor to the crystalline shadow-preserved June snow that he loved to suck. But those were boy's memories that he couldn't transfer to the freefall environment of this termite colony. He had no way at all of understanding the girl his vain wife would have spoiled.

His daughter wouldn't like him. If she stayed on Earth at least she could preserve her fantasy about him. But if she stayed on Earth there might be no one who knew *how* to love her.

When he found himself not writing a report that should have been finished in five minutes, he became annoyed. There were ways of ending thoughts that lured you into an endless maze. He pulled out a black die with silver eyes that he knew was perfectly balanced because he had machined it himself. "Odds she stays," he said aloud, "evens she comes." He spun the die off the end of his thumb and it arced over until it was sucked against the ventilation screen: a six. Evens. *So she loses her illusions*, he thought cynically. It was a relief to have the decision made.

But he was vetoed.

The Pittsburgh community had evolved a simple and effective form of democracy, relevant to a group that numbered only 230. Any man could propose a law. He merely had to post it in the computer. A bulletin board might have served as well. If the lawmaker was wise he worked out the wording with three to a dozen supporting friends first. Those that the law affected were then put on a voting list. Debate followed in the form of attached comments and emendations. These were typically formulated by individuals in their spare time or by spontaneous group sessions.

If the issues were controversial a sizable body of comment would appear over a few days. Eventually a compromise version was posted and voting took place at the convenience of the individual voter. Votes were entered on a scale of one to ten, plus for a yes, minus for a no. To pass, a bill had to accumulate more than 50 percent of the eligible votes; however, any issue that polarized the community was placed on the agenda of the monthly town meeting. The vast majority of laws were passed without "going to meeting."

Kell's request to ship Celia out to the Pittsburgh had been denied by the majority. The minority who voted with Kell did not feel strongly enough about it to see that it was sent up to a meeting for debate. There was a wide consensus, cautiously stated, that Kell would not be able to properly perform the functions of a father.

Men in power are often surprised when people refuse to carry out their orders, and can be enraged when it is a simple personal request that is denied. Kell showed his rage by being more distant and by smiling more fixedly.

He had been alone all his life; he enjoyed being alone, but to be *denied* his daughter converted his state of being alone to that of exile and pain. Emotions have two faces. Love can be the peace of union and the agony of having betrayed someone you love. Hate can be the towering triumph over a crushed enemy or the rotting torture of impotence. Grief can be a sobbing relief or the longing for something that can never be.

The pain of his loneliness burned in him, demanding that he bring his daughter here to this barren place. For keeping Celia from him, the rest of them, all 229 of them, could drop like flaring torches into Sol, one by one.

He laughed.

They had given him one small out, a sop to his ego probably—a fatal error, that. He could have her—if he could find someone to take care of her. They didn't think he could do it. He smiled, not trying to force his face into pleasant lines. He smiled for himself. They didn't know how much power he really had.

On Earth the executives at Ventures Metal knew who was jockeying this orebody through the Belt and across the Mars-Earth gulf. Ventures knew who the other captains consulted when there was trouble. On Earth, where the money was, they valued this hunk of metal that when brought to port would line their vaults with more than the gross national product of many nations. So Kell felt in his bones that he could afford multimillion-dollar whims.

He would put in a requisition for a mother for his child with the same care that he might ask for a specialized machine tool. The workpersons of Pittsburgh would get the mother they had so righteously demanded. Would they get a mother!

Lisa Maria Sorenti.

He did not know her personally, and she was not even that notorious unless you followed the San Francisco Bay Area scandals, but he had once seen her in action at a wild party. Three men had fallen in love with her in the few minutes he had watched her flawless performance of the ingenue. But *he* had seen her with his own jaundiced eyes. Her only skill was an electric charm. She was dishonest. She loved to be loved. She did not like men. She was indifferent to women. She was deathly afraid of being poor when she was old. And she would do anything for money, anything.

II

The two San Francisco executives shook hands like old friends who spoke and dealt with each other often, but who just hadn't met solidly for a long time. They both wore lace shirts and short pigtails.

"Histon!"

"Roy!"

"How's Stacy?"

"She's great."

"And the kids?"

"They're great, Roy. Linda's just joined the Little League. She's a great little batter. We've got a new one. That's why I'm here. It's Meddrick Kell's girl; sweetest tyke you ever met. Linda has her out playing baseball right now. Her mother committed suicide. What's not good about it is that I'm afraid Kell has split his can."

"He never had a can to split. How's Celia taking it?"

"Do you know her?"

"Yeah, I had more dealings with her mother than I wanted. Alcoholic bitch and all that."

"Kell wants Celia shipped out."

"Unusual, but what's the problem? We have a supply ship going out."

"Pittsburgh voted him their number one no-good father. They didn't buy it."

"They know they need him! What the hell!" roared Roy.

"They'll agree to her being shipped out if he can get someone to take over as governess—but no one wants the job."

"So ship one in with Celia. Expensive, but then Kell is a billion-dollar man."

"That's what Kell thought of," said Histon morosely.

"He always had an answer. When they add up the debits and the credits, remember I hired him."

"Yeah. Now he wants you to hire Lisa Maria Sorenti. As Celia's governess."

"You're *kidding* me, Histon!"

"I told you he'd split his can."

"Wow. A nice problem."

"You know her? I know *of* her."

"I just happen to have her manager's phone number. Occasionally I give it out to hungry young men who are going into space and need a beautiful memory of Earth to come back to. We pay the bill so they'll want to come back. She's expensive. But her manager gets it all. Some women are dumb."

"She hasn't been in the news for quite some time."

"You're wrong," said Roy. "Last week she had her manager hauled in for assault and battery and then went down with tears in her eyes and bailed him out."

"I see."

"I'll show you her file in living holo." Roy went to the computer terminal. "Her manager sent me these takes to keep my memory fresh." The computer terminal began to display the pictures.

"God, what firm boobs," said Histon, staggering back.

"Nice, but look at those hips! She's a goddess!"

Histon moved his head so that he could get a better view of her tilted face. "She'll never make it as a governess."

"We could send him a bright college girl who loves children and is thrilled by space. I know one who wants to go. She's a chemist."

"Naw, I told you he's split his can. It's got to be Lisa Maria Sorenti. God, look at this one of her in the sea! He doesn't know what he's asking for. She'd blow Pittsburgh apart. I hear she wiggles, too."

"He *always* knows what he's doing. I conclude that he *wants* to blow Pittsburgh apart. If I have judged Kell correctly, he'd take deep affront at being told he doesn't qualify as a father. He's angry about that."

"What'll we do, Roy?"

"You came here just to give *me* this problem, eh?"

"Yeah."

"You bastard."

"Think you can handle it?"

"He's a youngster of thirty-three. I'm sixty-two. Therefore I am twice as smart as he is. Sure I can handle it. I'll bet you one hundred billion dollars that I can handle it."

"Great. And how's your wife?"

"Great. We're going down to Redwood City to visit the grandchildren tonight."

III

Three A.M. Hunting headlights found the shape of her car in the gloom. "That's it." And blinked out. The stocky man kissed her good night, but she had the final say before she left his Mercedes. She held on to his ears and stared into his eyes for a last minute, knowing that he could see the moonlight glowing from hers. "G'night, Punkinhead." And then she was gone.

She had a mnemonic for all of them so that she might never forget a face or a name. Her Pumpkin Head image for Mr. Pokinhet matched his constant grin and the way the silly man lighted up every time he saw her. Some of her other images were not so complimentary, and she dared not use them as endearments. Lisa Maria Sorenti envied the girls who had settled for "darling."

Like the salty skin of a lover, the flavor of the Pacific was on the air. Exhausted, she merely stood by her sports car until the Mercedes was gone, waiting for energy, listening to the whisper of her engine's flywheel. What a beautiful night.

She could remember the days of her childhood when the smog was so pervasive in the Bay Area that you couldn't even see the stars. Now, so a spaceman had told her, you could pick out the Orbital Solar Power Station that fed the San Francisco grid, always at the same point in the sky to the south, unmoving as the stars moved. But she had never been able to differentiate it from a star. Sometimes she caught a factory flowing overhead, they moved so fast.

She eased out of the parking lot on flywheel power and then kicked in the small alcohol motor when she reached the parkway that had grown up over the trail of Spanish priests. It took her twenty minutes to reach San Francisco. She wondered how different her life would be without the earthquake that had killed her mother. Actually she liked San Francisco much better now that the scars of rubble were gone. It was a more peaceful town, more open. Or maybe it only seemed more peaceful without her mother's bitching.

I hope the hell Nick's not home!

She stopped off at an all-night McDonald's for a quick twenty-five-dollar hamburger and kidded the busboy to amuse herself. She always felt comfortable in a hamburger joint when she was depressed. Some of the excitement of her first job as counter girl rubbed off on her, back from the days when her life was less complicated. She had a wry nostalgia for the post-earthquake period when people helped each other.

Her apartment house wasn't far away. It was on a hidden street with trees and a sloping hill. She smiled at their electronic doorman. "Hi, Packard." He hated to be called Tex.

"Good morning, Ms. Sorenti."

One even had to smile at the damn machines these days. They said it was because that made it easier for the pattern recognition circuits. But she suspected the companies of trying to program humans to feel that machines were cute three-year-old children. Then they'd start introducing real machine intelligence.

"Park the car. Charge the flywheel."

"Yes, ma'am." Her car moved away, driverless. "Have a good day," added the machine brightly.

She requested a key-use printout and got it. "Damn!" Nick had been home since ten-thirty. He hadn't used to spend so much time with her. She was tired, but she skipped two up elevators just to be that much longer away from him. When she arrived at her apartment, she inserted the key-card and noiselessly opened the door. She peeked in the bedroom. Yes, there he was all sprawled out in the moonlight. Suddenly she wanted a glass of milk because the kitchen was as far from the bedroom as you could get.

Lisa Maria sipped her milk in the dark, staring for a long moment at the pale whiteness of it between sips. When she needed Nick he wasn't there, he was out floating in the bars. He said he was making contacts for her. She didn't know. Half the time it was probably other women. She didn't care. Now that she was trying to figure out a way to do without him, he was always here. She felt sorry for herself.

They talk about me as if I was the strongest woman in the world, and I can't even get rid of Nick.

The thing that was sending her into an absolute panic was knowing she didn't know how to get along without him. Hamburger Queen of Market Street, that's what she was when he found her. *He* had rented that first opulent apartment where she had learned to hold court and titillate the jaded amidst her exotic array of indoor plants. *His* clever maneuverings brought her to the fringes of society and the warmth of the money that was coming in from space. It was *he* who gave her the books that had opened up those conversations between her and the great minds of California. He even read her poetry when they made love. He still did that. And wrote it. He was composing his magnum opus now that he had beaten her.

She sparred with his memory, trying to understand her trap. Nick was a cunning master of that singular conceit borne by all San Franciscans who think that their city is the only place on God's Earth where one can sin in a state of grace. He had plotted her outrageous escapades with a sure business hand, and had reaped for her the protection that went along with notoriety. "Pure sin," said San Franciscans as they laughed.

He had taught her never to talk about money, that such talk was sordid and would break the magic upon which she existed. In return she had worshipped him with the pride of a woman who *knows* that her man is not one of the suckers.

So Lisa Maria was twenty-five and didn't know how to ask a man for money. She didn't even know how much Nick charged for her. She didn't know how to pay the rent or take out a loan or buy a car. It had taken her a year to muster courage to ask someone who she should see to find out how much money she had. And six months more to comprehend that she was dimeless. She did not know if she loved Nick; she *did* know that she hated him passionately. It was easier to hate him than to hate herself.

She undressed and slipped into bed as silently as a snake in grass, but he woke up anyway, as he always did.

"Big eyes, you have a date tomorrow for lunch at the Robin's Nest. One o'clock sharp. Roy Stoerm. It's a twenty-four-hour date."

"Oh, Christ, Nick! You *know* I can't tolerate twenty-four-hour stands with strangers. I won't even have any sleep by one. And the Robin's Nest is hell-and-gone across town. Give me a break. I'll have wrinkles and I'll be dull."

"I know what I'm doing. He's from Ventures Metal. They could fill in the bay for a golf course. And he's not a stranger. He's sent you some of your best tricks. You were at one of his parties a month ago. The crew of the Glasgow."

She turned her back. *I'm going crazy.* "But I've never met *him*!"

"You will tomorrow."

I wish I was a chemist. But her mind couldn't linger over such an image long, it was too insubstantial and meaningless to her. She saw other pictures—herself welding steel beams, or punching buttons in a space factory with random flashing lights (an image borrowed from TV), or jockeying a horse, or selling hamburgers. Anything. The tears were cascading down her cheeks. For Christ's sake, anything. Anything but this body that carried man-trap scent with it wherever it went.

IV

A sarcastic *San Francisco Chronicle* journalist had once described her as the mongrel goddess who had bounced down the steps of a California pantheon after an orgy to which all the Nordic, Roman, Celtic, and Mexican deities had been invited. It was true that Lisa Maria Sorenti had Swedish and Irish and Italian and Mexican blood, and that she was illegitimate, but the rest of what the journalist said was tongue-in-cheek slander.

Her eyes had never decided whether they were Mexican or Swedish—the irises were black rimmed with ocean-foamed interiors; her hair (fresh from the hairdresser) rippled with black light as she flowed through the lunch-hour crowds like driftwood avoiding the boulders of a busy rapid. Her summer dress was Spanish moss being helplessly carried along.

I wonder if he'll like me?

The Robin's Nest had been carved out of some old brick warehouse, and skylights bathed a jungle of greenery. She spotted him immediately—he was the only man seated alone facing the door like a lion waiting beside a mouse hole. And immediately she shifted her eyes, as if to seek someone, allowing him to see her profile, letting him watch her grace as she turned to the hostess. She smiled ravishingly at the hostess, long enough for him to sip of that smile and desire it for himself. She invented a trivial conversation, punctuating it with lively gestures, exaggerated just enough to carry across the room. Only after he had had ample chance to become intoxicated did she allow herself to notice this Stoerm. She met his eyes, held his eyes for a dizzying second, then dropped hers demurely. She spoke to the hostess again, one sentence, then looked back at *him* questioningly, holding off any real reaction until the exact moment he started to rise. Then she rushed forward, delivering her warmest smile full force before she took his hand, gently, tenderly. He was only half out of his seat.

"You must be the Stoerm in my heart."

"Roy," he said, beaming.

He pulled out her chair and seated her and then sat down and appraised her while he discreetly beckoned the wine steward. Instantly she had her mnemonic for him: the Eye of the Stoerm. She could feel the power circling him lazily and the calmness within that circle. *He knows exactly what he's going to do with me.* She hated that in men, but she dared not back away into the violence of the power; she was propelled into the eye, toward closeness. She had an irrational desire to hug him, to cling to him, and that frightened her because she did not see love in his eyes.

"I'll have a Cuban Apricot," he said, "and you?"

"A Daiquiri."

"You've been in the papers again."

"Did you read *that*? That was a *horrible* story. I'm so *embarrassed*." She dropped her eyes in practiced modesty and was surprised to feel a real rush of humiliation. *Oh, God, everyone knows that my man beats me.* Hate for Nick; black hatred.

"I'm interested in your troubles."

She couldn't have spoken about them. She would have cried. But no one ever topped her or rattled her. "Tell me about your wife," she teased.

"I'm in that worst of all possible situations; my wife understands me."

She laughed. Thank God for a man who can make a woman laugh. He attempted a few more times to open her up, and she gently countered him. She was an old expert at not talking about herself, and she felt him bow graciously to superior force and begin to talk about himself. She learned a lot about his job of recruiting spacemen.

"Why don't you hire me? I'm looking for another job."

"What can you do?" he asked with a chuckle.

She hit him. Affectionately, of course.

He tried to lead her into drunkenness during the lunch conversation which went everywhere pleasant bantering could go, and nowhere, but she *never* gave up control of her body on the job—neither through drugs nor alcohol nor through reactive emotion. Once he stealthily sent a patrol through her guard to destroy the bounds she placed on her anger, and she just as deliberately ambushed the patrol with boredom. *He plays games. He's testing me.* For what purpose? *He's trying to push me into the storm to see if I'll be blown away.* When they left the table she took his arm and kept her body close to his.

In Roy's car, a small Chevrolet of the kind favored by the really rich who liked to maintain a low profile, she puzzled over this man. She could tell he liked her, but he was unusual in that he was indifferent whether she liked him or not.

She did not know where they were going. An upper-class bacchanalia, perhaps? She wondered if she was to be the hors d'oeuvre or the liqueur.

After one pit stop for fuel—an alcohol-synthigas mix—they arced over into the region of the Peninsula that was being heavily invaded by the riches pouring in from space as San Francisco established itself as the multinational capital of space enterprise. In selected areas the middle-class suburban sprawl that had grown like cancer over the Peninsula during the fifties and sixties was being replaced wholesale by the palaces of the very wealthy, leaving only the stately trees that had been planted so long ago. Even the endless winding asphalt streets were gone and the palaces were approached from under the ground through a network that rejected unidentified vehicles.

Roy Stoerm put his Chevrolet's flywheel on charge in the garage. A car could travel 100 kilometers on rotational energy, which came from space-generated electricity, before it had to cut in its ten-horsepower internal combustion engine.

They rose via elevator into a sun-gorgeous room where Roy introduced Lisa Maria to Stacy Garcia, who was an executive at Ventures Metal and wife of Histon McKinner. Stacy wore her charm with the economy of somebody who has had the languid niceties of beautiful trivia atrophied by constant use of precise authority. She was obviously staying home from work just to meet Lisa Maria. She had just as obviously never met a whore before in all her thirty-five years.

"I leave you in good hands," said Roy. "I have some business to conduct this afternoon, but I'll be back for dinner."

Stacy took her hand and gave her a grand tour. The proudest thing she owned was a jade piece given her as a gift by Han Tao Hsia, Commissar of the Red Star Space Fleet. Ventures Metal bought heavy computer-driven mining equipment from them and occasionally rented their space tugs. The Chinese had been the first to use the hybrid chemical-nuclear single-stage Earth-to-orbit freighter, forcing the Americans and then the Russians to follow their lead. Stacy Garcia was a frequent visitor to Peking and spoke fluent Cantonese.

At a den in the back, Lisa Maria met the housekeepers, two enthusiastic English Ph.D.s who maintained this palace and took care of the children, and who were trying to beat each other scripting the Great American Disc Drama when they weren't cooking and gardening and shopping and changing diapers. Stacy said with a twinkle in her eye that she sometimes babysat for them.

And then at the window overlooking the park she pointed out a small naked child running beneath the redwoods below the swimming pool. "Will you do me a favor and take care of Celia while I'm out shopping for dinner? Her mother used to let her run wild, so she bears watching, but she won't give you any trouble. My little brats are at the ballet."

"She looks adorable. I've always wanted children." That was a lie, but Lisa Maria lied easily. "It takes the right man."

"You might say that. Men make good children to practice on before you try raising some real ones. Go swimming if you want."

There were four immense redwoods, probably left over from the vanished suburbia, and ten smaller redwoods no more than six man-heights tall. Beyond that grove was a polyglot woods. She sat on the grass beside the pool, watching the girl. *Seven-year-old girls are so free. I'd love one if I could deep-freeze her on weekends.* Celia would glance up at her, but as soon as their eyes met, Celia dropped hers and busied herself with some stick or task. *Oh, she's a flirt already.* That's when Lisa Maria fell in love with Celia.

"I know that game! You don't fool me one bit! Come here."

Ten minutes later, in her own time, the child appeared in front of the strange woman. She held out one tiny finger at arm's length and let it descend so slowly that her hand trembled. "My daddy lives in a place where things fall *that* slowly," she announced. "He's going to let me live with him." And then she rushed off.

It was another half-hour before Celia delivered herself for further conversation. "Aren't you ever going swimming? I have to swim now every day to get full of the sunshine because where my daddy is the sun is all shrunk." She looked at the intruder disapprovingly. "You can't swim with your clothes on."

"If I took them off I might get caught." Lisa Maria didn't mind getting caught, but she *did* mind not knowing what the ground rules were in a game of blind man's buff. Bafflement made her very conventional.

"Last man in is a glyptodont. C'mon."

"In my best dress?"

"Nobody swims with their clothes on, *dummy*."

"Now, that's not really true."

"Oh, maybe in darker suburbia they aren't civilized," she said with impatient disdain, "but not *here*. Here you can only get caught with your clothes off if you are in the house."

I'll ruin my hairdo. But she went swimming anyway and regretted it. Celia used her shoulders as a diving board, and there were games like "spaceship docking," which consisted of Celia ramming her head as hard as she could against Lisa Maria's. It went with a ritual.

"Capowie! Bang!"

"Who's there?" *Oh, my aching head.*

"Linda."

"Linda who?"

"Linda hand with the cargo."

Eventually Roy Stoerm came to the rescue with an enormous bath towel and Celia cuddled up inside it with her new playmate, both shivering in the sunset.

Dinner was served on a long table with candelabra and gold plates, each place set with seven different kinds of knives and forks and spoons and chopsticks of some golden alloy, while the center of the table was recessed to hold the main dishes in special depressions which either heated them or refrigerated them.

The children trooped in. Stacy and Histon had four from ages seven to thirteen, and there was also Celia in an ankle-length white gown. They were remarkably disciplined, all bowing and saying hello to Lisa Maria. They didn't interrupt each other, but were ready to get a word in edgewise as soon as they found a slot. Celia was the most impatient. Once when she did interrupt Histon, she was required to get up and put a red chip in an ancient Chinese lacquered box.

It was a whole evening's mood alien to Lisa Maria until Roy made a phone call to his wife telling her that he had been detained by business. That touch put her comfortably at ease.

The eldest boy rushed out into the kitchen to fetch something that had been forgotten. The housekeepers chatted with the children. It was fashionable to hire housekeepers with Ph.D.s to train the children in the intricacies of witty table conversation and to select their Drama Discs. They were not allowed to watch TV.

As if by some signal the congregation became silent. Stacy began to say grace in a Spanish so melodious that Lisa Maria was transported in time to the tiny apartment of her scrappy grandmother, whose parents had picked tomatoes in the Imperial Valley and whose daughter was passionately anti-Catholic. The grandmother had kidnapped Lisa Maria one day when she was five and taken her to be baptized in an awesome and nameless cathedral that Lisa Maria had never been able to find again in spite of all the church collecting she did. The only Spanish she knew was the word for sin, "*pecado*."

Histon and Roy controlled the conversation, focusing on her but with the skill of film directors who were out to flatter their star and hide her wrinkles and edit her bad scenes. Stacy played script girl. Even the children, who seemed to know in their worldly way that she was a wicked lady, ad-libbed for her when she forgot her lines. *Sometimes I don't understand notoriety*, she thought. She was basking in their attention and smiling too much and drinking 10 percent faster than she should, always danger signals. *It's a trap.*

"Histon made the dessert. He won't even give *me* the recipe," complained Stacy.

"If you're stuffed, I'll take your portion," whispered Celia into Lisa Maria's ear.

V

They drank Pimpeltjens from tiny ceramic goblets after dinner, the children dispersed, the housekeepers cleaned up, and the four of them retired to the spacious room that was now starlit. They analyzed the Argentinian revolution and how a group of multinationals had banded together to put down the killing and reestablish order. Killing was bad for business. Histon and Roy chuckled over the subtleties of how the French and Socialist arms dealers had been tricked into taking a loss of over twenty-six billion dollars.

All in all, the after-dinner conversation was becoming heavy. Lisa Maria laid her head on Roy's arm and closed her eyes, hinting. Histon and his wife discreetly excused themselves and Roy took her affectionately by the shoulders for a walk through the palace and into a cozy den, where he kissed her. She understood everything now. The den's couch would swallow them and the room was private. This was Roy's night off from his wife.

"How are you doing?" he asked.

"It was a lovely evening." She held him and returned the kiss, stroking his neck under the short braid. "A nice change for me."

"I had Nick thrown in jail this afternoon. Thirty days," he said calmly as if he had been complimenting her on the smoothness of her skin.

She froze. She backed away. She stared at him.

"I said I welded him."

In the middle of her shock she felt her arm swinging—*is this me?*—to slap him viciously. "I don't want Nick hurt! He's my problem!" And she backed away, beyond arms' reach, afraid of that center of calmness which she had not even disturbed. And as she backed up she felt herself caught in the hurricane of power that circled him, then tossed wildly away on the wind. Nick was all she had. She didn't know how to get along without him. "Don't hurt him," she pleaded.

He just stared at her.

"You multinational bastards are all the same. You think you run the world!"

"We try to provide a little leadership where it is necessary."

"I want him back!" she screamed.

"I have absolutely no sympathy for Nick. He beats you. He's taken all of your money; he's stripped you bare." Stoerm opened up a report and threw it on the desk top. "I have a complete financial report on him—and you. It is not hard to find out things about you. You don't even like him."

"You want him out of the way?"

"Yes."

"Because *you* want me?"

"Yes."

"Because you're going to solve all my problems—just like Nick? *I hate you.*"

"Not like Nick. I'm going to solve all of your problems, but I'm going to give you a choice. You can go back to Nick in thirty days if that's what you want. I just want him out of the way while you make up your mind."

"The answer is *no*, you gonorrhea drip!"

"Your salary would be twenty million dollars a year."

Suddenly there was no floor under her feet. She was not sure that Roy's face was upside down or right side up or that he even had a face.

"In noninflationary terms that you can understand, Miss Hamburger Queen, that's eight hundred thousand hamburgers with french fries and coleslaw, retail."

Panic. Roy had dismissed Nick—her protector, her old man—with one blow and in the next moment he had stripped her of her free will, and she didn't want to go *there*. The mere thought terrified her. Space. Only space paid salaries like that. She was being hogtied and shanghaied into space.

"I don't want to go."

"Think of the money."

"You *bastard*!"

"You're broke now. You'll be thirty-two when you get back, still in the prime of your life, and you'll be worth one hundred and forty million dollars."

"Those women who go into space are chemists or electronic engineers or mechanics or something. I can't even get rid of Nick. Why me?"

"We have a mad spaceman out there. He's quite functional. He's worth billions to us. He has that gift for turning disaster into victory. We don't tamper with a good thing. We pamper it. He put in a requisition for you."

"So you're buying me?"

"We're offering you a contract and making it worth your while."

"A dream girl off the shelf."

"You're good at it."

"For seven years? Most guys I can't *stand* after two hours. Does he think I come with a valve in my belly button so that he can deflate me when I'm not in use?"

"It is a much more complicated situation than that. In fact it is a dangerous situation. He didn't want *you*. He wanted his daughter Celia."

"That cute kid? She's a darling."

"Those little asteroid villages are very tight. Probably the Earth hasn't seen anything like them since the New England colonists of the seventeenth century. They voted no. They told him he wasn't a qualified father. I'm sure they are right. His psych profile shows a complete blank on women and children. He grew up without women, and he has had no success with the few short relationships he has had as an adult. He abandoned his child before she was born."

"Sounds like a great guy."

"I had lunch with him once. He has a barrier personality. I don't mean he doesn't have emotions. He does. He smiles when he is filled with hate, things like that. Have you ever met these people who function perfectly in a group and have no friends? He's one of those. I think he took it hard when they wouldn't let him have even the symbol of a one-to-one relationship. They said he could have his daughter if he could find a governess. So he smiled and chose you."

"You're hiring *me* as a babysitter for that innocent girl?"

"Exactly."

"Your mind has been rotted by RPX."

"I'm not worried about Celia. Those colonies are wonderful with their children. I'm worried about the grownups."

"Because of me?"

"He wants you there to generate the hurt he can't inflict himself. And I think he chose his weapon with his usual brilliance. He's going to prove that *they* are emotionally incompetent to handle women, and that *he* is the good father. While he's tending to Celia, you'll be smashing marriages right and left and raising hell."

"You sound like a shrink right out of a Berkeley sewer."

"I'm an aerospace engineer from La Jolla who could never build ships but turned out to be handy with people."

"Men make me sick," she said. She took his hand and held it against her breast. "That's soft! How can you call that a weapon? How can I respect creatures who fall apart when they are smiled at!"

Roy laughed and pulled her body to him. There were tears in his eyes. "I'm a strong man. I've been happily married for forty years and I wouldn't trade in that woman for Nirvana, but I'm already thinking strange thoughts when I've only been with you for a few hours."

"It's not fair," she sulked, "that men are so weak!"

"Then why have you spent every waking hour for the last ten years developing your charm to the exclusion of everything else so there is nothing left of you but the charm?"

"You *bastard*! Here you are wrecking my whole life"—she was crying and horrified because they weren't fake tears—"and telling me that there is nothing behind the makeup that a man might love."

"Name ten things," he smiled.

"Ho, you think you've got me now, and I'm going to tell you everything about myself. I'm not going to tell you a damn thing! You already know too much."

"God, you have beautiful eyes!"

"The better to wreck your colony with!"

"Nope. Here's your contract. Have a lawyer check it out and make sure that it is ironclad. Notice the clause in there about wrecking colonies. You all have to deliver the steel, all of you together, to collect your monies. That's insurance we take out to assure cooperation. But *you* have a special clause. You're not allowed to do your stuff on any male in the Pittsburgh complex *except* Meddrick Kell. Or you don't get paid. See, I'm smarter than Kell. I've lived longer. He's importing what *he* sees as a deadly weapon, and so all I have to do is make sure that the weapon is going to be pointed only at him."

"What about me! What if I don't like him! He sounds like a creep!"

"Think of the money. Your mantra is money."

VI

The equatorial Free Port at Tongaro in the Pacific was the world's busiest spaceport. Lisa Maria couldn't believe it when she saw one of the eight-thousand-ton single-stage Boeing freighters sitting like a thirty-five story mushroom on the pad as it was being fueled.

The freighters were lifted by a hybrid chemical-nuclear motor that burned LOX with nuclear-heated hydrogen. The tungsten/U-233 fuel elements were manufactured and reprocessed in space, where the radioactive by-products were collected and mounted on a sail-powered basket that spiraled them into the sun. In the distance, beyond the bulk of the ship, was an electrolysis plant that manufactured LOX and LH from seawater and solar power beamed in from space.

Because Celia's father was in the mining business, Lisa Maria batted her eyes at a handsome drop-ship jockey and he took them out to see one of the drop-ships being scrapped in a flickering of cutting torches. These were perhaps the heaviest spaceships ever built by man, rivaling in weight battleships of the Yamato class, but had only one flight in them, down. The jockeys who rode them to Earth called them rafts. They were assembled crudely of massive metal in a low orbit and needed to be able to perform only two functions: to hold together while they burned off their heat shield in the atmosphere and to float when they hit the water. Sometimes they were scrapped at Tongaro and sometimes towed all the way to San Francisco or San Diego or Yokahama.

More to Lisa Maria's liking was the smaller two-stage passenger ship. The lower module was a sleek hypersonic craft that went to mach-9 on a scram-jet powered by hydrogen and air, and then circled quickly back to Tongaro to pick up another piggy-back rider for up to five trips in one day. The upper module was a compact ship backed by either a hybrid power plant or a LOX/LH power plant. She was less enthusiastic when she was taken inside. It wasn't like an airliner at all. There was no more headroom than in a car.

She could still see a patch of the Pacific through the tiny porthole when she was strapped in. *Goodbye, Earth.* Celia took her hand. She was so frightened while the countdown began that her heart was thumping in her chest.

Think of the money.

Her heart did not stop pounding all during the thundering of the rockets. That lasted no longer than the wait in a bank line. Free-fall came before she was used to the acceleration. She could see a patch of the Earth through the tiny porthole.

Woman and child were given a spartan room in the low-orbit Rockwell Station. They stayed there seven days receiving an intensive space survival course in a class of twenty new recruits. It was 10 percent theory and 90 percent training in automatic reflexes, like how to slap a patch on torn suit webbing in four seconds. The people in the course were mainly new workers. The station's primary function was to rent lofts to businesses that needed zero gravity and vacuum and unlimited power. Once Lisa Maria took Celia to visit the factory where the brains of her typewriter had been manufactured.

Five days of concentrated effort to put her space legs together finally hit Lisa Maria with the incredible gut realization that she was forever free of Nick, her great love, the man who had made a woman of her. Suddenly there was no way to stop grinning. Normally she could control her rather compulsive smile, but that fifth day any attempt to be sober resulted in a mellifluous laugh which activated so many male fantasies that she had to hide in the woman's room to calm the storm.

There she wrote a joyous love letter to Roy, teasing him about being another Nick who was only too willing to arrange her whole life for her. "After all," she penned, wishing she could use her happiness for ink, "you are keeping all *my* money in *your* bank." She had it faxed down to Earth by an operator who fell in love with her when he took the letter, and she ended the evening "on air" in the cabin of her space-survival instructor, learning how to make out in free-fall.

"Lisa Maria! Oh! Come to the window! Look. That's the *C.L. Moore*! That's *our* ship over there!" The ship was essentially a long cylinder attached to a great dish that sucked power, not from the sun, but from a point close to the sun. Celia was bouncing from floor to ceiling, from ceiling to floor. It was the seventh day.

Far away, well inside Mercury's orbit, circling twenty million kilometers from the flaming surface of Sol the Star, was a power station built by man. The sun clawed at the intruder with erupting solar flares like an angry tiger striking through his gravity bars. It was a dangerous place to be, but it was the right place to be if you wanted power—an energy flux of seventy-eight kilowatts passed through every square meter.

The power station was a strange-looking beast with a delicate appendage of radiators that spread away from the sun like a comet's tail. Mounted behind the shadow of the giant heat exchanger was a graceful laser cannon that poured gigawatts of power across the inner solar system to the birds of prey that mined the Belt. Lesser cannon fed the ships outbound from Earth's orbit. The stations themselves, deep in the sun's gravity well, were supplied by sailing ships that tacked upon a rich photon wind.

Inside the solar power station named Goliath an operations officer was making contact with the *C.L. Moore*. He was scanning with a communications laser, and every time his beam crossed the *Moore*'s parabola, the *Moore* sent out a time signal which fed into a computer on the Goliath that narrowed the scan. It wasn't a fast process. There was a sixteen-minute time lag between output and feedback, but within half an hour the communications beam was centered on the *Moore*'s receiver.

Eight minutes later the *C.L. Moore* was powered. Her drive was essentially a proton accelerator that ionized hydrogen and pushed it to 100 kilometers per second using laser energy drawn from her parabolic mirror. The cabins and freight holds and hydrogen tanks were built around the long accelerator, while the mirror was free-mounted to the starboard. If such a ship were strapped for fuel it might take two years to reach the Belt, but the normal journey took from ten to fourteen months.

The *C.L. Moore* was carrying spare parts to the Pittsburgh, and heavy machinery and thirty persons for the Osaka. Her captain was a computer. She was to return empty to Mars, refuel there and bring home a load of passengers.

Lisa Maria went stir-crazy after only five days. At first she was hyperactive and quietly hysterical. Sex with the other passengers didn't help. Counting off the days by fives on the cabin wall didn't help. Gradually she slipped into a mild catatonic depression. She wrote THINK OF THE MONEY on the wall and stared at it for hours. She hated space. Once she wrote Nick a long letter asking him to take her back but never faxed it. Celia took care of her.

Celia read her bedtime stories like Pooh Bear and when she could get her attention played Shakespeare drama discs. If she skipped a meal, Celia fed her sternly. The spaceship protein was terrible, but the fresh vegetables were juicy and at the peak of flavor.

"You have to eat if you are going to be strong enough to take care of me!"

When Lisa Maria began to come back to life, Celia put her arm around her and spent three days reading to her the classic *Planet of Magic* about the redhead Trudina and the dark Jindaram, Princesses of Zahelan, daughters of the Crimson Moon, defeated candidates for the post of High Enchantress. Their souls had been created by the Red Witch, fresh, without past lives, and the girls had been raised to introduce a new age of innocence to the Planet of Magic. But the old wizard Taslt defeated them at the Temple of T'halil because of their vanity and cleverly shipped off their souls in a silver cage to the Planet of Forgetfulness, Earth, where no one could remember their past lives and were doomed to repeat the same mistakes life after life. Of course, Trudina and Jindaram learned how to conquer their vanity after many trials and tribulations, without even knowing who they were, and finally returned to the Planet of Magic and defeated Taslt and brought on the Age of Innocence.

Lisa Maria started to smile again and wrote poetry steadily for two weeks, which she had never done before in her life. She was feeling the impact of the little girl and understanding why women and men who had children were more mature than those who didn't. Children took you back through your own childhood and gave you a fresh look at decisions you had made in innocence and forgotten about but were still using, and it showed you your own parents in a new light. She found it upsetting to see herself angry when Celia did the things that had once annoyed mother Sorenti and to be *sure* that she was *right* to be angry.

Then one evening, which wasn't any different from the spaceship day, while they were making a game of eating raw carrots together, Lisa Maria began to talk about things that she had kept secret from everybody all her life, even Nick. She didn't mind talking to Celia about the hidden feelings of a whore. She knew Celia would never grow up to be like her. In fact, Celia wanted to be a starship captain, and though she might never be because starships weren't invented yet, she would become something like that. So it was easy to talk to her. Celia just giggled or gasped or put her hand over her mouth. Then Lisa Maria read Celia a bedtime story the girl had never heard out of the favorite book of grandmother Morantes about a woman called Ruth, and their friendship solidified forever. Six months later the journey was over.

They glided in from behind, so they saw Pittsburgh's dish first. Only when they were right on top of the colony did they see the "sunrise" of the slag-jet pouring out, illuminating the shadowed face of the asteroid.

"My daddy! My daddy! You'll love my daddy. He writes better letters than I do!"

Lisa Maria thought about Daddy Kell's very very bad reputation. *I'll strangle him if he doesn't treat her right.* She wasn't worried about him. All she had to do was put on her professional hat and she could handle any man alive from sadist to fool. It wasn't going to matter whether she liked him or not.

She was worried about the women. For every job out here there were a hundred applicants thinking about the money. The women—she had seen the personnel file on the women of Pittsburgh—were so overqualified it made her sick in the pit of her stomach just to think about it. How did a woman ever get to the point where she could build and design machine tools?

She couldn't do *anything* they could do. Even the thing Lisa Maria pretended to do because it was feminine, to be an artist, was fake. She remembered her humiliation while Roy admired the glazes on her pottery, pieces she had bought in an obscure shop in Arizona while she was "doing ceramics," pieces she had lied about to her own group, to Nick, to the *San Francisco Chronicle*, to the world. Sometimes she rigged it so that she took a friend to the pottery to help her remove still warm pots from her kiln. *I can't do it!*

She thought of the money and got ready for the debarkation.

VII

When they were through the Pittsburgh's airlock Lisa Maria was wearing the personality she reserved for policemen. Celia spotted her father immediately—the nose and the half-bald head were unmistakable—but immediately she shifted her eyes, as if to seek someone, allowing him to see her profile, letting him watch her grace as she turned to Lisa Maria for emotional support. She smiled ravishingly at her governess, long enough for her father to sip of that smile and desire it for himself. Only after he had had ample chance to become intoxicated did the child allow herself to notice her father. She met his eyes, held them for a second, questioningly, holding off any real reaction until the exact moment he made a slight hand touch against the wall that told her he was going to come forward. Then she launched herself into a glide full force and stopped herself by grabbing him by the ears. She tilted his head and gazed at him. "You're my sugar daddy," she said, smiling. No one noticed Ms. Sorenti.

David showed Lisa Maria the termite digs. Pittsburgh was already old enough to be quite spacious. Each member had his own cave, and the public rooms could be quite enormous. There was jungle park, a series of large caverns filled with tropical vegetation gone slightly insane in free-fall. There was a large spherical room, laced with padded tubing, for four-sided football. The goals were at vertices of a tetrahedron. He didn't show her the working rooms, but she could feel the smelting and the blasting through the rock. The whole complex had a vibrating tone to it.

He sat down with her and took her through the laws. Smoking and drugs were forbidden. All air-seal doors were to be closed after use. She was only allowed in those areas which her key-card would open for her. The captain had absolute authority in all cases where there was no law. And so on and on.

David introduced her to many people. They seemed friendly and proud and curious and small-townish. She was warily friendly in turn. It was like deciding to eat mushrooms and having a badly edited black-and-white guidebook to go by. She was going to eat them one tiny bite at a time and watch for several days to see if she got sick before risking another bite. Somebody had been very kind and put plants in her room. It was spartan but neat.

Kell avoided her for three days. She let him. She lavished Celia with attention, especially when people were watching, but Celia soon lost herself in the labyrinth, sublimely at home; the children she adopted, the adults she adopted, and she joined one of the four-man football teams. Lisa Maria was left alone. Enough. It was time to strike.

She waited for him to return from his rounds with the patience of a spider. Before he knew she was waiting, before he could finish closing his door, she was inside, and closing the door herself. She looked him straight in the eyes without smiling.

He was damned if he was going to look away, but she could sense his fear. "Hello," he said.

She waited until the last echo of his greeting had died before she chose to ignore him. His room was messy, lived in. Socks took a minute to fall if they were dropped. They had been dropped. There were no plants. There was no beauty. The nude on the wall seemed forlornly unhappy in this place without beauty.

"Mr. Kell, I'm flattered that you think I'm worth a hundred and forty million dollars."

"I don't think anything. I wanted my daughter."

"And you just brought *me* here to educate your daughter."

"You've been good to her," he said evasively.

"And my special talents?"

"It was getting dull around here," he said in an uneasy boy's voice.

"So I'm to entertain you?"

"Entertain yourself." He was smiling and she knew he was hostile.

"So I'm to entertain you by entertaining myself?"

"I don't really care what you do."

"Mr. Kell, have we ever met before?"

"Once. At a California orgy."

"Oh, we *have* met! I knew it! Which one!" She smiled for the first time, mischievously, tauntingly.

He snorted.

"No, tell me." She batted her eyes. "Refresh my memory."

"We were at opposite ends of a large terrace with a glass roof. You were wearing a one-piece red bikini."

"One of my more modest days."

"Three men were with you. I remember one of them kissed your hand. You wore a revolting red toenail polish."

"And you never forgot a detail of it."

"They were falling in love with you. All three of them at the same time."

"And you were the fourth?"

"I was thinking what fools they were to be taken in by such superficial charm. You were there for the money."

"That's when you found out I could be bought, is it?" She was drooling venom. She turned and took the nude off the wall. "You won't need her. You've just bought yourself a hundred-and-forty-million-dollar fantasy and you're going to have to live with it. For seven years."

"Not here!"

"You can't handle me?"

"Of course not. I'll introduce you to some of our more competent Romeos." He was grinning. "We have lots of them." He hated them.

"Listen, you centimeter marvel, you don't get out of it that easily. *You* bought me."

"I don't like you any better than you like me," he snapped.

"What woman ever has?"

"Get out. I never made a deal with you."

"You don't understand something, Mr. Kell. It doesn't matter a damn whether I like you or not. It doesn't matter a damn whether you like me." Her eyes were blazing. "You bought me. I was struggling to take control of my own life. Maybe I would have made it. So I didn't. So I'm buyable. So I'm a whore. Thanks for rubbing it in with a hundred-ton stamping press!"

She watched his pain. It was interesting because it was real pain. She let him feel the knives for precisely fifteen seconds. He spoke waves of pain to her but said nothing.

"That'll teach me to wear red monokinis!" she pouted.

He didn't laugh. He was too busy feeling the pain. "Get out."

Without paying any heed to him she carefully disassembled her bitch personality, like a dressing-room makeup take-down. You had to wash under your chin and even get to the very roots of your eyebrows. A quiet sixteen-year-old country girl sat there in front of her mirror selecting a new role. It had to be worked out right down to the motions of the fingers.

For a while he didn't notice that she was smiling at him with warm adoration because the shift was too swift for him to follow. She let the smile grow, powered by her amusement. It was exactly the smile of a woman who has just been proposed to by the man she most wants to spend the rest of her life with. The embarrassed excitement in her hands was just right.

"What makes you suppose I'm going to leave? Do you think I'd come all this way for a man I didn't love?" And she let her eyes fall away so that he could see her lush eyelashes. "You've saved me from a fate worse than death. You just don't know it yet."

Cut. She switched off the lights. Pain. The visual perfection of a woman madly in love. Fade to the physical sensations of love. A tender kiss. A touch of his biceps. Slowly. Not too fast. Let him get used to it. He had become impotent, of course; they always did after that treatment. It didn't matter. Such men had to be taken apart before they would ever fit together sexually. He looked like such an incompetent creep.

She undressed, floating there in the dark, careful not to touch him physically, but careful to let the fabric of her suit brush his skin.

"I'm tired. So are you. We'll just sleep." No pressure at all to begin with. She was willing to wait days until he became used to her body before starting to turn him on erotically.

Think of the money.

Her seduction was interrupted by his work. It was interrupted by his fear. But she knew when to withdraw and when to come back. On the fifteenth evening, he brought her a flower to wear in her hair. He put it there himself and half undressed her and couldn't stop looking at her. She knew she had him hooked.

Later, when he was half asleep as men are apt to be after lovemaking, and so still that he was visibly settling in the asteroid's minute gravitic field, she snuggled up to him, chewing the flower stem. Funny, when they had offered her 140 million to keep this misanthrope happy, the job had seemed like a formidably impossible one, but now that she knew him she wasn't awed at all. If you asked him questions and listened, he answered. He was already confiding in her. Why hadn't other women succeeded? She slipped the flower behind her ear and kissed him all over the cheek. *Women are such fools! Except me.*

David was sighing over her and brushing against her by then. Secretaries had such gall. The chief rocket engineer kept turning up for carrot juice when she was in the cafeteria. And one of the married men who had a baby found excuses to visit when she was with Celia. *Men are such fools! All of them.* They approached the subject of sex like armies of crabs. She teased them. Whenever they made one of their sidewise hints, Lisa Maria lit the lights in her eyes and allowed herself to dream aloud about Kell's sensual prowess until they stopped. It was all a lie, Kell was a lousy lay, but lies never bothered her when they worked. This one kept her admirers muzzled, and of course the stories got back to Kell in the form of leers and cracks and raunchy digs, and so he became more tender and tried his best to live up to his new-found reputation. It was all boringly predictable.

At night she dreamed about being a real human being and doing the things that other women did. She'd seen them driving the rock chewers and setting a broken bone and relining furnaces and troubleshooting the comm equipment and playing a wild game of football.

One evening when Celia and her daddy and Lisa Maria were eating together in her cave-cabin, it drove her crazy to hear this child chatter on about being a starship captain. She sounded so sure of herself! It was the crack that split the rocket engine.

From some distant place in her skull she began to listen to her possessed vocal chords speak about art, using her voice. She had done thus and so with her paintings. Metal sculpturing was very satisfying, but somehow there was no greater thrill than finding a new ceramic glaze that fixed the sunset or captured the essence of a San Francisco fog. Lies, all lies, but she couldn't stop talking about it.

One week later, with the casualness that another man might offer a diamond pendant, Kell took her to an old machine shop that he had fixed up with a kiln and wheel. The kiln would cook pots in either a vacuum, an oxidizing, or a reducing mode with a computer that controlled the time-temperature profile and the amount and kind of atmosphere present.

The wheel had a magnetic frictionless bearing like in the automobile flywheels, and was made out of solid gold, so that once moving, it was difficult to slow down. Metals were not Pittsburgh's problem.

"Nobody drinks out of mugs," she said inanely.

"Make something else."

"What would I use for clay?" she said desperately.

"Ah, I had to do some research on that. But I made you up six different kinds of clay you'll have to try out, different fusing temperatures, different properties. I have the photomicrographs of the particles if that would be of any help." And he showed her the cans. He had prewetted the clay to control dust.

Thus did Lisa Maria Sorenti meet the real Meddrick Kell. She was furious. *Remind me never again to suggest anything to that man that might even remotely sound like a physical problem.* There were no Arizona craft shops to rescue her. She was caught in her lie, and since she had never had that happen before in her life, she had no handy personality to deal with it.

Her first emergency reaction was to make the lie real by transforming herself into a real potter overnight. It didn't work. The shapes that desperation produced were no better than the shapes dabbling had produced when she had her San Francisco studio. And creating a beautiful shape was only the beginning.

She became secretive. "Don't you come into my studio," she told Kell with quavering voice. "I'm the kind of artist who doesn't work well with someone watching." That bought her another week.

Finally she knew she had to face the music. She slaved over a special meal which she cooked in the cafeteria for Kell alone. She wore her best perfume and put a flower in her hair so he wouldn't know she was wearing perfume. She made up her eyes with subtle care in order to conjure an achingly beautiful image.

"You're such a nice man," she said holding his wrist. "And you're *my* old man." She let her fingers be nymphs walking in what was left of his hair. "Do you love me enough to keep a secret?"

"Yeah."

She nibbled at his ears. "I'll be mad at you if you tell *anyone*. I'll be so mad at you I'll never speak to you again."

"Not even when we have sex?" he kidded her.

"I'll *space* myself if you tell anyone!"

"Once you've told me a secret, it's not a secret anymore," he said philosophically.

She let the tears gush from her eyes. "You have to promise!"

"Aw, you know I never talk to anyone."

"I'm not a potter. I'm a fake." She held his face and made him watch her screw up and bawl so that he'd know she was vulnerably feminine and needed protection.

Lisa Maria expected some kind of emotion from him—an angry condemnation, perhaps, or maybe he'd laugh at her. But he didn't do anything. His face went blank. He shifted into what she called his "computer mode."

Pregnant pause. "When *I* lie," said his computer voice, "it is because I want something to be real that isn't. Is that why *you* lie?"

She nodded, not breathing.

"The solution is simple. Become a potter."

"But I can't," she cried. "I've tried!"

"Give me an estimate of the number of hours you've spent potting."

She thought. "Fifty."

"That doesn't qualify as a try. No one can become a potter in fifty hours. You'll *try*. I'll show you how. You have the time."

"Are you going to tell on me?"

"I'll show people the first beautiful thing you do. It took me a thousand hours to make my first iron when I was a kid, and another two thousand hours to learn how to make rifle-barrel steel."

"I've felt so incompetent since I've been here with all these amazing women."

"List for me the things that you'd like to be able to do that they do."

"Everything!" she said defiantly.

Pregnant pause. "If you mean the things they do every day, yes, that's possible for you to learn in seven years. If you mean everything they *can* do, no, that's not possible."

"Is there anything *you* can't do?"

He laughed. "Pot. And I can't write. Celia is teaching me how to write novels these days. We're working on a novel together. She says she hasn't got enough experience to write a novel, so I'm responsible for filling in her blank spots. It's killing me."

Kell set up a simple schedule for her. First she had to master her tools and materials. The goal he gave her was something she felt confident that she could do—learn to make ugly shapes that didn't blow up or crack when bisqued. She was to test her glazes on the successful pieces. A month's work, she thought. No, more like two years, he said and shrugged. Then she could begin.

He began to take her on his rounds. He gave her a stern lecture. On Earth you could go through school and get a C and be promoted. Here if you got a C you got promoted to Death. "Everything you learn to do, bring it up to full competence—or don't do it."

They were eating up the whole asteroid and refining it to metal that had to be stored in such a way that the center of gravity stayed on a line through the slag-jet. He gave her lessons in driving a rock chewer. He put her with a maintenance crew. He showed her how to operate the computer-controlled electron beam machine tools that built their spare parts. No matter how small the task he gave her, he pushed her ruthlessly until she reached full competence.

Sometimes he was too busy to bother with her for days. He left her with her pottery or with Celia. She might be with him only while he slept. Sometimes he went straight around the clock without sleeping.

She got fascinated by metalworking in gold and took lessons from a Swedish engineer who enjoyed her attention. She couldn't resist having an affair with him even though he was married; the temptation to defy Roy Stoerm and get away with it was too strong. She was risking her twenty million a year, but that gave it value in her eyes. She didn't let herself notice that she had picked the most stable and secretive man in all of Pittsburgh.

They made a golden beer stein together as a lark when Lisa Maria bemoaned the fact that it would be useless for her to throw mugs on her wheel. Inventing a beer mug that worked was hilarious. The final version sat on the air (sinking ever so slowly as things did around the asteroid) and had a pleasant inertial feel to it. A special mechanism spun the liquid so that it "fell" to the walls of the stein which when tipped created a gyroscopic resistance that caused a small scoop to throw a sip of liquid from the stein's mouth.

Gently, without any tangled emotion, her Swede withdrew from Lisa Maria, having gotten whatever it was that he wanted, to leave her alone again with Kell, feeling the hostility she felt when she had no one but him. It was dangerous to trust a man, and if you felt like trusting him he was very, very dangerous. Her Swede wasn't dangerous because she *knew* she couldn't trust him.

Wanting to trust Kell reminded her of Carl Chrisholm. Nick had introduced them and rented her to him after his wife's funeral. She was just becoming aware then that Nick was betraying her and Carl seemed so honest. He was older, rich, respected, considerate, gregarious, never dull, and a one-woman man. He took her everywhere. She liked his home, she liked his children. It was strange to love a man and not be cynical about it, to find yourself giving more than you thought you had. Glorious.

She remembered telling Nick goodbye in her mind. *I don't need you. I have*

Carl! And one evening she told Carl that she loved him and wanted to be his woman and he'd been so pleased and so loving. The next day he went out and rented a new mistress.

So to hell with Meddrick Kell. Lisa Maria replaced her Swede with David and continued to live dangerously. She had to fake it with Kell because of Stoerm's contract, but nothing in the contract said she had to trust him. She didn't like men who made you love them and all the while were planning to space you.

VIII

The emergency came suddenly, as they always do. Every eighteen days the solar power station Gilgamesh that supplied Pittsburgh passed behind the sun. Slag-jet Motor One was shut down for overhaul and Slag-jet Motor Two was fired as soon as Gilgamesh reappeared. But this time Motor Two failed within the hour after start-up.

Every available person was called on to help diagnose the trouble and get repairs operational. While the motors were not firing, the asteroid was not spiraling in toward Earth. Too many delays meant that they would reach Earth when Earth was gone and so their orbit would have to be adjusted to a much later arrival date. The consequence was extra months, perhaps an extra year in space, and grave financial fines for the crew of the Pittsburgh.

Lisa Maria was helping by tending to Kell's comforts and by running errands for him. He was pushing himself mercilessly, planning the whole operation so that all systems would be up in minimum time. She had just brought food to the command center when navigation phoned in a report.

"The single trouble we've got up here is a rock that's going to take out the mirror. The new orbit gives us a collision course. Even if Number Two started firing right now we wouldn't get out of her way in time. She's a small one, but she's got to be taken care of within the hour. Details are coming through your fax right now."

"Shit!" said Kell when he got the charts and read them.

"What's the matter now?"

"Goddamn collision. Lawson, take over. Lisa Maria, suit up. We're going to do in this rock ourselves."

"Kell, you're tired," said Lawson.

"It's okay. It'll relax me. I need a vacation from this mess. I'll be back with you in a couple of hours."

Lisa Maria followed his instant exit like his shadow, but she didn't want to go. "Are you sure I can help?"

"We have your reflexes up to speed. No problem for you."

The skintight tension suits allowed for hard work in space because they sweated like real skin. Both of them stripped and suited up almost faster than the eye could see. "What am I supposed to do?" she pleaded.

"Obey orders. Can't spare anybody else here. Don't worry. It's a picnic. A damn nuisance, but not a real problem."

Seconds later they were blasting off Pittsburgh in one of the open cockpit ships. Only then did Kell relax. "Do you know why they call these things convertibles?"

"They convert people to corpses?" she said, hanging on. Being in the center of a sphere of stars dominated by a single star was an awesome experience.

"They used to drive on the highways of California in these things. The country air feeling. The thrill of the wind in your face."

"Jesus!" said Lisa Maria, hanging on for dear life though she was strapped in. "We can laser some of these rocks out of the way. But you still have to visit them and cancel the rotation. The laser pits them on a line though the center of gravity, and the back reaction of the vaporized gases acts like a reaction jet. This rock is too big. We've got a rocket with us to do the job. A homemade sparkler, my design, lousy specific impulse, but good enough. We only need to add a quarter of a meter per second to her velocity."

"Do you ever get in collision orbits with other asteroids?"

"Naw. Our navigator is too good for that."

Once the acceleration cut out it was as if they were suspended. Within this glittering sphere she couldn't even tell whether they were mice in a toy rocket car or whether their bodies were as huge as a planet. The human mind cannot comprehend velocity or size without objects that move in relationship to each other.

"You know what they used to do in convertibles?" said Kell. "The object of the game was to run out of gas under the stars. That was an excuse to nuzzle."

"I saw the same disc. It was made in 1947. But there was a moon in the sky."

He began to caress her body.

"Get your electrically heated paws off of me!"

They both laughed inside their helmets.

Forty minutes later they decelerated and the computer brought them to rest beside their slowly tumbling rock. "How far have we gone?" she asked.

"From San Francisco to New York. And shut up. Do everything I say."

The rock was roughly twelve meters in diameter. He fixed a small rocket to its equator and they had a pinwheel flare until the rotation was stopped dead. Then he did some measurements against the stars and drilled a mount for the rocket. Meanwhile she dragged it out and brought it over. She was gliding back to the convertible when she felt an explosion throw her violently until she snapped taut against the ship line. It was all over before she could turn to see what had happened.

"Kell!" she screamed.

By reflex she pulled herself into the cockpit and sent out a radar scan for debris, asking the machine to select a human identity. It picked him up almost immediately. She ordered the convertible to "home" on him, and seconds later was pulling him out of the sky.

There was blood all over, boiling and icing, black in her headlamp. She had no time to ask whether he was dead. She was pulling out her patching equipment at the same time she was deciding what to do with the piece of rocket sticking out of him. Cut it flush to the skin or pull it out? The quickest. Pull it out. Patch instantly. Thank God he wasn't wearing a pressure suit. You couldn't decompress a tension suit unless the helmet shattered. Switch on the physiological monitor. Sudden tears. The pulse was poor, the breathing poor. He was still alive.

And the rock was still heading for a collision with the Pittsburgh mirror. But . . .

He'll die if I don't get him back.

She forgot that she had radio contact with Pittsburgh in her panic to do the right thing which, whatever it was, had to be done swifter than thought. The longer she waited to deflect the rock, the more energy it would take, and if she let it go altogether it might take more energy than Pittsburgh could bring to bear. The only rocket power available was in the convertible's motors.

Crying because Kell was dying, she nosed her vehicle against the rock. Careful! A false move and she'd only start the rock spinning. Free-fall had taught her much physics. Outside the dominating field of Earth, Newton's laws were so evident that they became built into the nervous system. Aim through the center of gravity.

Lightly does it; she was nose-heavy by about two or three thousand tons. Lock on the stars so that the gimbals of the motor will act against any spin. Set the accelerometer to stop the firing when they had changed velocity by a quarter of a meter per second. Set for minimum thrust. Fire! The motor roared to life. *God, dear God, let there be some fuel left.*

There was. She had enough fuel remaining in her tanks to take her back to the Pittsburgh in twelve hours. Kell would be long dead. Only then did she remember the radio. She was crying but she turned off the tears because she had that kind of control.

"Convertible Three to Navigation. Come in."

"Come in, Lisa Maria!"

"We've had a terrible accident. I don't know what happened. Kell's hurt, maybe dying. I can't get back." Her voice was rising into hysteria.

"Lisa, listen. I got that. I want to know something. We have a radar fix on the rock. It has moved out of collision orbit. Did you know that?"

"Yes. When the rocket blew up, I used the convertible's fuel."

"Great thinking!"

"I can't get back in time," she cried.

"Lisa. Put Kell's monitor on broadcast. Dr. Hendrick will be right on the line. Home on the Pittsburgh with whatever fuel you've got left. We're coming after you. Flat out. All the delta-vee we've got. Surgery will be set up when you get here. And you, wench, are *you* all right?"

It all went quicker than she thought it possibly could considering the fact that she was in "New York" and the ambulance was in "San Francisco." The return was a jumble of frantic memories—Kell being whisked away at a rapid glide, Celia's face in pathetic anguish: "Is my daddy dead?" and the two women who helped her desuit before she fainted, a man trying to shield her while Lawson insisted on debriefing her, a woman she hardly knew reaching out a congratulating hand. Sleep.

When she woke up, David was with her.

"How is he?"

"He's not easy to kill. Rumor has it that his blood is too cold to boil even if you spaced him. Actually, he's better. Lawson is talking about you. He thinks you've soaked up Kell through your pores. He couldn't give you a higher compliment."

"I felt so awkward."

"You didn't make a mistake and everyone knows it."

"It was just reflex."

"Spaceman's reflex."

"Is that another compliment?"

"You're going to get tired of them. Someone put in a commendation for you and everyone has voted yes already at ten on the scale."

"Well, the company is paying me twenty million dollars a year to bring in the steel and if this barge doesn't reach port we don't get paid, right?"

"Right!"

"I want to see Kell."

She found him talking into a hands-off phone about the lining of Motor Number Two. He signed off when she came in. "You're the one who can answer my questions," he said. "How did I get here?"

"I saved you."

"How come the mirror is still there?"

"I saved it."

"What did you bring me along for if you are that competent?"

"I thought the experience would do you some good, but you turned out to be as useful as a bloody corpse. Next time I won't bring you."

"Do you know what my last thought was?" he said. "I thought I had killed you and I loved you."

"Do you know what my last thought was?" she said. "I was worried sick about the mirror. I thought I might not get my hundred and forty million dollars."

She took his hand and looked at his eyes looking into hers. *I'll never tell you I love you,* she thought at him, *because then you'll hire a new mistress and I'll be unhappy again.*

GOMEZ

C. M. Kornbluth

C(yril) M. Kornbluth died suddenly at the age of thirty-five in 1958, a bit more than a month after the death of Henry Kuttner. He had begun publishing science fiction as a fourteen-year-old fan in the 1930s, a member of the same club, The Futurians, that included Isaac Asimov, James Blish, Frederik Pohl, Damon Knight, and a number of other young fans who went on to become major figures in the genre in succeeding decades. He was certainly not the least of these talents. His early work was widely published (he is said to have used eighteen or nineteen pseudonyms in the late thirties and early forties), but he first became prominent in the fifties, both for his short stories—many collected in *Thirteen O'Clock* (1970), *The Explorers* (1954), *A Mile Beyond the Moon* (1958), and *The Best of C. M. Kornbluth* (1976)—and for his novels: *Takeoff* (1952), *The Syndic* (1953), and *Not This August* (1955). He also collaborated with Judith Merril (*Outpost Mars* [1952] *and Gunner Cade* [1952]) and most prominently with Frederik Pohl (*The Space Merchants* [1953] and several others). His métier in science fiction was acerbic social criticism. Preeminently a satirist, with a dark vision of future worlds openly at odds with the bright visions of Campbell's *Astounding*, his work was devoted to examining the assumptions of Modern sf. He had a deeply embedded belief in scientific knowledge and an even deeper pessimism that individual humans, or whole societies, would misuse it; his universe is ruthless. He was the Ambrose Bierce of Modern sf.

Kornbluth's portrayal of science and scientists is at the core of "Gomez." It contrasts the joy of doing science with the threat of what the world does with the knowledge thus gained. It has the enormous respect for individualism and the individual talent at the core of hard sf wedded to the bleak suspicion (just short of pure pessimism) that politics and especially the military is the enemy of science. "Gomez" is a fascinating work to compare and contrast to Cordwainer Smith's "No, No, Not Rogov!" as an expression of the Cold War's dominance of science. Ironically, the position of the scientist in the "Free World" is eerily close to Rogov's. Taken together, these two stories represent sf's loss of faith in the ability of social institutions to relate properly to science in the atomic age that followed World War II, together with the recognition that big science was now achievable only through huge government/military funding. The age of the entrepreneurial inventor seemed over. And to top it off, Kornbluth's is the more optimistic tale of loss. The underlying faith in knowledge is reaffirmed in both Kornbluth and Smith—in the long run.

Now that I'm a cranky, constipated old man I can afford to say that the younger generation of scientists makes me sick to my stomach. Short-order fry-cooks of destruction, they hear through the little window the dim order: "Atom bomb rare, with cobalt 60!" and sing it back and rattle their stinking skillets and sling the deadly hash—just what the customer ordered, with never a notion invading their smug, too-heated havens that there's a small matter of right and wrong that takes precedence even over their haute cuisine.

There used to be a slew of them who yelled to high heaven about it. Weiner, Urey, Szilard, Morrison—dead now, and worse. Unfashionable. The greatest of them you have never heard of. Admiral MacDonald never did clear the story. He was Julio Gomez, and his story was cleared yesterday by a fellow my Jewish friends call Malach Hamovis, the Hovering Angel of Death. A black-bordered letter from Rosa advised me that Malach Hamovis had come in on runway six with his flaps down and picked up Julio at the age of 39. Pneumonia.

"But," Rosa painfully wrote, "Julio would want you to know he died not too unhappy, after a good though short life with much satisfaction——"

I think it will give him some more satisfaction, wherever he is, to know that his story at last is getting told.

It started twenty-two years ago with a routine assignment on a crisp October morning. I had an appointment with Dr. Sugarman, the head of the physics department at the University. It was the umpth anniversary of something or other—first atomic pile, the test A-bomb, Nagasaki—I don't remember what, and the Sunday editor was putting together a page on it. My job was to interview the three or four University people who were Manhattan District grads.

I found Sugarman in his office at the top of the modest physics building's square Gothic tower, brooding through a pointed arch window at the bright autumn sky. He was a tubby, jowly little fellow. I'd been seeing him around for a couple of years at testimonial banquets and press conferences, but I didn't expect him to remember me. He did, though, and even got the name right.

"Mr. Vilchek?" he beamed. "From the *Tribune*?"

"That's right, Dr. Sugarman. How are you?"

"Fine; fine. Sit down, please. Well, what shall we talk about?"

"Well, Dr. Sugarman, I'd like to have your ideas on the really fundamental issues of atomic energy, A-bomb control and so on. What in your opinion is the single most important factor in these problems?"

His eyes twinkled; he was going to surprise me. "Education!" he said, and leaned back waiting for me to register shock.

I registered. "That's certainly a different approach, doctor. How do you mean that, exactly?"

He said impressively: "Education—*technical* education—is the key to the underlying issues of our time. I am deeply concerned over the unawareness of the general public to the meaning and accomplishments of science. People underrate me—underrate *science*, that is—because they do not *understand* science. Let me show you something." He rummaged for a moment through papers on his desk and handed me a sheet of lined tablet paper covered with chicken-track handwriting. "A letter I got," he said. I squinted at the penciled scrawl and read:

October 12

Esteemed Sir:

Beg to introduce self to you the Atomic Scientist as a youth 17 working with diligence to perfect self in Mathematical Physics. The knowledge of English is imperfect since am in New-York 1 year only from Puerto Rico and due to Father and Mother poverty must wash the dishes in the restaurant. So esteemed sir excuse imperfect English which will better.

I hesitate intruding your valuable Scientist time but hope you sometime spare minutes for diligents such as I. My difficulty is with neutron cross-section absorption of boron steel in Reactor which theory I am working out. Breeder reactors demand

$$u = \frac{x}{1} + \frac{x^5}{1} + \frac{x^{10}}{1} + \frac{x^{15}}{1} + \ldots$$

for boron steel, compared with neutron cross-section absorption of

$$v = \frac{x^{2/5}}{1} + \frac{x}{1} + \frac{x^2}{1} + \frac{x^3}{1} + \ldots$$

for any concrete with which I familiarize myself. Whence arises relationship

$$v^5 = u\frac{1 - 2u + 4u^2 - 3u^2 + u^4}{1 + 3u + 4u^3 + 2u^3 + u^4}$$

indicating only a fourfold breeder gain. Intuitively I dissatisfy with this gain and beg to intrude your time to ask wherein I neglect. With the most sincere thanks.

J. Gomez
c/o Porto Bello Lunchroom
124th Street & St. Nicholas Avenue
New York, New York.

I laughed and told Dr. Sugarman appreciatively: "That's a good one. I wish our cranks kept in touch with us by mail, but they don't. In the newspaper business they come in and demand to see the editor. Could I use it, by the way? The readers ought to get a boot out of it."

He hesitated and said: "All right—if you don't use my name. Just say 'a prominent physicist.' I didn't think it was too funny myself though, but I see your point, of course. The boy may be feeble-minded—and he probably is—but he believes, like too many people, that science is just a bag of tricks which any ordinary person can acquire——"

And so on and so on.

I went back to the office and wrote the interview in twenty minutes. It took me longer than that to talk the Sunday editor into running the Gomez letter in a box on the atom-anniversary page, but he finally saw it my way. I had to retype it. If I'd just sent the letter down to the composing room as it was, we would have had a strike on our hands.

On Sunday morning, at a quarter past six, I woke up to the tune of fists thundering on my hotel-room door. I found my slippers and bathrobe and lurched blearily across the room. They didn't wait for me to unlatch. The door opened. I saw one of the hotel clerks, the Sunday editor, a frosty-faced old man and three hard-faced, hard-eyed young men. The hotel clerk mumbled and retreated and the others moved in. "Chief," I asked the Sunday editor hazily, "what's going——?"

A hard-faced young man was standing with his back to the door; another was standing with his back to the window and the third was blocking the bathroom door. The icy old man interrupted me with a crisp authoritative question snapped at the editor. "You identify this man as Vilchek?"

The editor nodded.

"Search him," snapped the old man. The fellow standing guard at the window slipped up and frisked me for weapons while I spluttered incoherently and the Sunday editor avoided my eye.

When the search was over the frosty-faced old boy said to me: "I am Rear-Admiral MacDonald, Mr. Vilchek. I'm here in my capacity as deputy director of the Office of Security and Intelligence, U.S. Atomic Energy Commission. Did you write this?" He thrust a newspaper clipping at my face.

I read, blearily:

WHAT'S SO TOUGH ABOUT A-SCIENCE?
TEENAGE POT-WASHER DOESN'T KNOW

A letter received recently by a prominent local atomic scientist points up Dr. Sugarman's complaint (see adjoining column) that the public does not appreciate how hard a physicist works. The text, complete with "mathematics" follows:

Esteemed Sir:

Beg to introduce self to you the Atomic Scientist as youth 17 working——

"Yes," I told the admiral. "I wrote it, except for the headline. What about it?"

He snapped: "The letter is purportedly from a New York youth seeking information, yet there is no address for him given. Why is that?"

I said patiently: "I left it off when I copied it for the composing room. That's *Trib.* style on readers' letters. *What* is all this about?"

He ignored the question and asked: "Where is the purported original of the letter?"

I thought hard and told him: "I think I stuck it in my pants pocket. I'll get it——" I started for the chair with my suit draped over it.

"*Hold it, mister!*" said the young man at the bathroom door. I held it and he proceeded to go through the pockets of the suit. He found the Gomez letter in the inside breast pocket of the coat and passed it to the admiral. The old man compared it, word for word, with the clipping and then put them both in his pocket.

"I want to thank you for your cooperation," he said coldly to me and the Sunday editor. "I caution you not to discuss, and above all not to publish, any account of this incident. The national security is involved in the highest degree. Good day."

He and the boys started for the door, and the Sunday editor came to life. "Admiral," he said, "this is going to be on the front page of tomorrow's *Trib.*"

The admiral went white. After a long pause he said: "You are aware that this country may be plunged into global war at any moment. That American boys are dying every day in border skirmishes. Is it to protect civilians like you who won't obey a reasonable request affecting security?"

The Sunday editor took a seat on the edge of my rumpled bed and lit a cigarette. "I know all that, admiral," he said. "I also know that this is a free country and how to keep it that way. Pitiless light on incidents like this of illegal search and seizure."

The admiral said: "I personally assure you, on my honor as an officer, that you would be doing the country a grave disservice by publishing an account of this."

The Sunday editor said mildly: "Your honor as an officer. You broke into this room without a search warrant. Don't you realize that's against the law? And I saw your boy ready to shoot when Vilchek started for that chair." I began to sweat a little at that, but the admiral was sweating harder.

With an effort he said: "I should apologize for the abruptness and discourtesy with which I've treated you. I do apologize. My only excuse is that, as I've said, this is a crash-priority matter. May I have your assurance that you gentlemen will keep silent?"

"On one condition," said the Sunday editor. "I want the *Trib.* to have an exclusive on the Gomez story. I want Mr. Vilchek to cover it, with your full co-operation. In return, we'll hold it for your release and submit it to your security censorship."

"It's a deal," said the admiral, sourly. He seemed to realize suddenly that the Sunday editor had been figuring on such a deal all along.

On the plane for New York, the admiral filled me in. He was precise and unhappy, determined to make the best of a bad job. "I was awakened at three this morning by a phone call from the chairman of the Atomic Energy Commission. *He* had been awakened by a call from Dr. Monroe of the Scientific Advisory Committee. Dr. Monroe had been up late working and sent out for the Sunday *Tribune* to read before going to sleep. He saw the Gomez letter and went off like a 16-inch rifle. The neutron cross-section absorption relationship expressed in it happens to be, Mr. Vilchek, his own work. It also happens to be one of the nation's most closely-guarded—er—atomic secrets. Presumably this Gomez stumbled on it somehow, as a janitor or something of the sort, and is feeding his ego by pretending to be an atomic scientist."

I scratched my unshaved jaw. "Admiral," I said, "you wouldn't kid me? How can three equations be a top atomic secret?"

The admiral hesitated. "All I can tell you," he said slowly, "is that breeder reactors are involved."

"But the letter said that. You mean this Gomez not only swiped the equations but knew what they were about?"

The admiral said grimly: "Somebody has been incredibly lax. It would be worth many divisions to the Soviet for their man Kapitaza to see those equations—and realize that they are valid."

He left me to chew that one over for a while as the plane droned over New Jersey. Finally the pilot called back: "E.T.A. five minutes, sir. We have landing priority at Newark."

"Good," said the admiral. "Signal for a civilian-type car to pick us up without loss of time."

"Civilian," I said.

"Of course civilian!" he snapped. "That's the hell of it. Above all we must not arouse suspicion that there is anything special or unusual about this Gomez or his letter. Copies of the *Tribune* are on their way to the Soviet now as a matter of routine—they take all American papers and magazines they can get. If we tried to stop shipment of *Tribunes* that would be an immediate give-away that there was something of importance going on."

We landed and the five of us got into a late-model car, neither drab nor flashy. One of the admiral's young men relieved the driver, a corporal with Signal Corps insignia. There wasn't much talk during the drive from Newark to Spanish Harlem, New York. Just once the admiral lit a cigarette, but he flicked it through the window after a couple of nervous puffs.

The Porto Bello Lunchroom was a store-front restaurant in the middle of a shabby tenement block. Wide-eyed, graceful, skinny little kids stared as our car parked in front of it and then converged on us purposefully. "Watch your car, mister?" they begged. The admiral surprised them—and me—with a flood of Spanish that sent the little extortionists scattering back to their stickball game in the street and their potsy layouts chalked on the sidewalks.

"Higgins," said the admiral, "see if there's a back exit." One of his boys got out and walked around the block under the dull, incurious eyes of black-shawled women sitting on their stoops. He was back in five minutes, shaking his head.

"Vilchek and I will go in," said the admiral. "Higgins, stand by the restaurant door and tackle anyone who comes flying out. Let's go, reporter. And remember that I do the talking."

The noon-hour crowd at the Porto Bello's ten tables looked up at us when we came in. The admiral said to a woman at a primitive cashier's table: "*Nueva York* Board of Health, *señora*."

"Ah!" she muttered angrily. "*Por favor, no aquí!* In back, understand? Come." She beckoned a pretty waitress to take over at the cash drawer and led us into the steamy little kitchen. It was crowded with us, an old cook and a young dishwasher. The admiral and the woman began a rapid exchange of Spanish. He played his part well. I myself couldn't keep my eyes off the kid dishwasher who somehow or other had got hold of one of America's top atomic secrets.

Gomez was seventeen, but he looked fifteen. He was small-boned and lean, with skin the color of bright Virginia tobacco in an English cigarette. His hair was straight and glossy-black and a little long. Every so often he wiped his hands on his apron and brushed it back from his damp forehead. He was working like hell, dipping and swabbing and rinsing and drying like a machine, but he didn't look pushed or angry. He wore a half-smile that I later found out was his normal relaxed expression and his eyes were far away from the kitchen of the Porto Bello Lunchroom. The elderly cook was making it clear by the exaggerated violence of his gesture and a savage frown that he resented these people invading his territory. I don't think Gomez even knew we were there. A sudden, crazy idea came into my head.

The admiral had turned to him. "*Cómo se llama, chico?*"

He started and put down the dish he was wiping. "Julio Gomez, *señor. Por qué, por favor? Qué pasa?*"

He wasn't the least bit scared.

"*Nueva York* Board of Health," said the admiral. "*Con su permiso*——" He took Gomez' hands in his and looked at them gravely, front and back, making *tsk-tsk* noises. Then, decisively: "*Vamanos, Julio. Siento mucho. Usted está muy enfermo.*" Everybody started talking at once, the woman doubtless objecting to the slur on her restaurant and the cook to losing his dishwasher and Gomez to losing time from the job.

The admiral gave them broadside for broadside and outlasted them. In five minutes we were leading Gomez silently from the restaurant. "*La lotería!*" a woman customer said in a loud whisper. "O *las mutas*," somebody said back. Arrested for policy or marihuana, they thought. The pretty waitress at the cashier's table looked stricken and said nervously: "Julio?" as we passed, but he didn't notice.

Gomez sat in the car with the half-smile on his lips and his eyes a million miles away as we rolled downtown to Foley Square. The admiral didn't look as though he'd approve of any questions from me. We got out at the Federal Building and Gomez spoke at last. He said in surprise: "This, it is not the hospital!"

Nobody answered. We marched him up the steps and surrounded him in the elevator. It would have made anybody nervous—it would have made *me* nervous—to be herded like that; everybody's got something on his conscience. But the kid didn't even seem to notice. I decided that he must be a half-wit or—there came that crazy notion again.

The glass door said "U.S. Atomic Energy Commission, Office of Security and Intelligence." The people behind it were flabbergasted when the admiral and party walked in. He turned the head man out of his office and sat at his desk, with Gomez getting the caller's chair. The rest of us stationed ourselves uncomfortably around the room.

It started. The admiral produced the letter and asked in English: "Have you ever seen this before?" He made it clear from the way he held it that Gomez wasn't going to get his hands on it.

"*Sí, seguro.* I write it last week. This is funny business. I am not really sick like you say, no?" He seemed relieved.

"No. Where did you get these equations?"

Gomez said proudly: "I work them out."

The admiral gave a disgusted little laugh. "Don't waste my time, boy. Where did you get these equations?"

Gomez was beginning to get upset. "You got no right to call me liar," he said. "I not so smart as the big physicists, *seguro*, and maybe I make mistakes. Maybe I waste the *profesor* Soohar-man his time but he got no right to have me arrest. I tell him right in letter he don't have to answer if he don't want. I make no crime and you got no right!"

The admiral looked bored. "Tell me how you worked the equations out," he said.

"Okay," said Gomez sulkily. "You know the random paths of neutron is expressed in matrix mechanics by *profesor* Oppenheim five years ago, all okay. I transform his equations from path-prediction domain to cross-section domain and integrate over absorption areas. This gives *u* series and *v* series. And from there, the *u-v* relationship is obvious, no?"

The admiral, still bored, asked: "Got it?"

I noticed that one of his young men had a shorthand pad out. He said: "Yes."

The admiral picked up the phone and said: "This is MacDonald. Get me Dr. Mines out at Brookhaven right away." He told Gomez blandly: "Dr. Mines is the chief of the A.E.C. Theoretical Physics Division. I'm going to ask him what he thinks of the way you worked the equations out. He's going to tell me that you were just spouting a lot of gibberish. And then you're going to tell me where you *really* got them."

Gomez looked mixed up and the admiral turned back to the phone. "Dr. Mines? This is Admiral MacDonald of Security. I want your opinion on the following." He snapped his fingers impatiently and the stenographer passed him his pad. "Somebody has told me that he discovered a certain relationship by taking"—he read carefully—"by taking the random paths of a neutron expressed in matrix mechanics by Oppenheim, transforming his equations from the path-prediction domain to the cross-section domain and integrating over the absorption areas."

In the silence of the room I could hear the faint buzz of the voice on the other end. And a great red blush spread over the admiral's face from his brow to his neck. The faintly buzzing voice ceased and after a long pause the admiral said slowly and softly: "No, it wasn't Fermi or Szilard. I'm not at liberty to tell you who. Can you come right down to the Federal Building Security Office in New York? I—I need your help. Crash priority." He hung up the phone wearily and muttered to himself: "Crash priority. Crash." And wandered out of the office looking dazed.

His young men stared at one another in frank astonishment. "Five years," said one, "and——"

"*Nix*," said another, looking pointedly at me.

Gomez asked brightly: "What goes on anyhow? This is damn funny business, I think."

"Relax, kid," I told him. "Looks as if you'll make out all——"

"*Nix*," said the nixer again savagely, and I shut up and waited.

After a while somebody came in with coffee and sandwiches and we ate them. After another while the admiral came in with Dr. Mines. Mines was a white-haired, wrinkled Connecticut Yankee. All I knew about him was that he'd been in mild trouble with Congress for stubbornly plugging world government and getting on some of the wrong letter-heads. But I learned right away that he was all scientist and didn't have a phony bone in his body.

"Mr. Gomez?" he asked cheerfully. "The admiral tells me that you are either a well-trained Russian spy or a phenomenal self-taught nuclear physicist. He wants me to find out which."

"Russia?" yelled Gomez, outraged. "He crazy! I am American United States citizen!"

"That's as may be," said Dr. Mines. "Now, the admiral tells me you describe the *u-v* relationship as 'obvious.' I should call it a highly abstruse derivation in the theory of continued fractions and complex multiplication."

Gomez strangled and gargled helplessly trying to talk, and finally asked, his eyes shining: "*Por favor*, could I have piece paper?"

They got him a stack of paper and the party was on.

For two unbroken hours Gomez and Dr. Mines chattered and scribbled. Mines gradually shed his jacket, vest and tie, completely oblivious to the rest of us. Gomez was even more abstracted. He *didn't* shed his jacket, vest and tie. He didn't seem to be aware of anything except the rapid-fire exchange of ideas via scribbled formulae and the terse spoken jargon of mathematics. Dr. Mines shifted on his chair and sometimes his voice rose with excitement. Gomez didn't shift or wriggle or cross his legs. He just sat and scribbled and talked in a low, rapid monotone, looking straight at Dr. Mines with his eyes very wide-open and lit up like search-lights.

The rest of us just watched and wondered.

Dr. Mines broke at last. He stood up and said: "I can't take any more, Gomez. I've got to think it over——" He began to leave the room, mechanically scooping up his clothes, and then realized that we were still there.

"Well?" asked the admiral grimly.

Dr. Mines smiled apologetically. "He's a physicist, all right," he said. Gomez sat up abruptly and looked astonished.

"Take him into the next office, Higgins," said the admiral. Gomez let himself be led away, like a sleepwalker.

Dr. Mines began to chuckle. "Security!" he said. "Security!"

The admiral rasped: "Don't trouble yourself over my decisions, if you please, Dr. Mines. My job is keeping the Soviets from pirating American science and I'm doing it to the best of my ability. What I want from you is your opinion on the possibility of that young man having worked out the equations as he claimed."

Dr. Mines was abruptly sobered. "Yes," he said. "Unquestionably he did. And will you excuse my remark? I was under some strain in trying to keep up with Gomez."

"Certainly," said the admiral, and managed a frosty smile. "Now if you'll be so good as to tell me how this completely impossible thing can have happened——?"

"It's happened before, admiral," said Dr. Mines. "I don't suppose you ever heard of Ramanujan?"

"No."

"*Srinivasa* Ramanujan?"

"*No!*"

"Oh. Well, Ramanujan was born in 1887 and died in 1920. He was a poor Hindu who failed twice in college and then settled down as a government clerk. With only a single obsolete textbook to go on he made himself a very great mathematician. In 1913 he sent some of his original work to a Cambridge professor. He was immediately recognized and called to England where he was accepted as a first-rank man, became a member of the Royal Society, a Fellow of Trinity and so forth."

The admiral shook his head dazedly.

"It happens," Dr. Mines said. "Oh, yes, it happens. Ramanujan had only one out-of-date book. But this is New York. Gomez has access to all the mathematics he could hope for and a great mass of unclassified and declassified nuclear data. And—genius. The way he puts things together . . . he seems to have only the vaguest notion of what a proof should be. He *sees* relationship as a whole. A most convenient faculty which I envy him. Where I have to take, say, a dozen painful steps from one conclusion to the next he achieves it in one grand flying leap. Ramanujan was like that too, by the way—very strong on intuition, weak on what we call 'rigor.' " Dr. Mines noted with a start that he was holding his tie, vest and coat in one hand and began to put them on. "Was there anything else?" he asked politely.

"One thing," said the admiral. "Would you say he's—he's a better physicist than you are?"

"Yes," said Dr. Mines. "Much better." And he left.

The admiral slumped, uncharacteristically, at the desk for a long time. Finally he said to the air: "Somebody get me the General Manager. No, the Chairman of the Commission." One of his boys grabbed the phone and got to work on the call.

"Admiral," I said, "where do we stand now?"

"Eh? Oh, it's you. The matter's out of my hands now since no security violation is involved. I consider Gomez to be in my custody and I shall turn him over to the Commission so that he may be put to the best use in the nation's interest."

"Like a machine?" I asked, disgusted.

He gave me both barrels of his ice-blue eyes. "Like a weapon," he said evenly.

He was right, of course. Didn't I know there was a war on? Of course I did. Who didn't? Taxes, housing shortage, somebody's cousin killed in Korea, everybody's kid brother sweating out the draft, prices skyhigh at the supermarket. Uncomfortably I scratched my unshaved chin and walked to the window. Foley Square below was full of Sunday peace, with only a single girl stroller to be seen. She walked the length of the block across the street from the Federal Building and then turned and walked back. Her walk was dragging and hopeless and tragic.

Suddenly I knew her. She was the pretty little waitress from the Porto Bello; she must have hopped a cab and followed the men who were taking her Julio away. Might as well beat it, sister, I told her silently. Julio isn't just a goodlooking kid any more; he's a military asset. The Security Office is turning him over to the policy-level boys for disposal. When that happens you might as well give up and go home.

It was as if she'd heard me. Holding a silly little handkerchief to her face she turned and ran blindly for the subway entrance at the end of the block and disappeared into it.

At that moment the telephone rang.

"MacDonald here," said the admiral. "I'm ready to report on the Gomez affair, Mr. Commissioner."

• • •

Gomez was a minor, so his parents signed a contract for him. The job-description on the contract doesn't matter, but he got a pretty good salary by government standards and a per-diem allowance too.

I signed a contract too—"Information Specialist." I was partly companion, partly historian and partly a guy they'd rather have their eyes on than not. When somebody tried to cut me out on the grounds of economy, Admiral MacDonald frostily reminded him that he had given his word. I stayed, for all the good it did me.

We didn't have any name. We weren't Operation Anything or Project Whoozis or Task Force Dinwiddie. We were just five people in a big fifteen-room house on the outskirts of Milford, New Jersey. There was Gomez, alone at the top floor with a lot of books, technical magazines and blackboards and a weekly visit from Dr. Mines. There were the three Security men, Higgins, Dalhousie and Leitzer, sleeping by turns and prowling the grounds. And there was me.

From briefing sessions with Dr. Mines I kept a diary of what went on. Don't think from that that I knew what the score was! War correspondents have told me of the frustrating life they led at some close-mouthed commands. So-and-so-many air sorties, the largest number since January 15th. Casualties a full fifteen per cent lighter than expected. Determined advance in an active sector against relatively strong enemy opposition. And so on—all adding up to nothing in the way of real information.

That's what it was like in my diary because that's all they told me. Here are some excerpts: "On the recommendation of Dr. Mines, Mr. Gomez today began work on a phase of reactor design theory to be implemented at Brookhaven National Laboratory. The work involves the setting-up of thirty-five pairs of partial differential equations . . . Mr. Gomez announced tentatively today that in checking certain theoretical work in progress at the Los Alamos Laboratory of the A.E.C. he discovered a fallacious assumption concerning neutron-spin which invalidates the conclusions reached. This will be communicated to the Laboratory . . . Dr. Mines said today that Mr. Gomez has successfully invoked a hitherto unexploited aspect of Minkowski's tensor analysis to crack a stubborn obstacle towards the control of thermonuclear reactions——"

I protested at one of the briefing sessions with Dr. Mines against this gobbledegook. He didn't mind my protesting. He leaned back in his chair and said calmly: "Vilchek, with all friendliness I assure you that you're getting everything you can understand. Anything more complex than the vague description of what's going on would be over your head. And anything more specific would give away exact engineering information which would be of use to foreign countries."

"This isn't the way they treated Bill Lawrence when he covered the atomic bomb," I said bitterly.

Mines nodded with a pleased smile. "That's it exactly," he said. "Broad principles were being developed then—interesting things that could be told without any great harm being done. If you tell somebody that a critical mass of U-235 or Plutonium goes off with a big bang, you really haven't given away a great deal. He still has millions of man-hours of engineering before him to figure out how much is critical mass, to take only one small point."

So I took his word for it, faithfully copied the communiqués he gave me and wrote what I could on the human-interest side for release some day.

So I recorded Gomez' progress with English, his taste for chicken-pot pie and rice pudding, his habit of doing his own housework on the top floor and his old-maidish neatness. "You live your first fifteen years in a tin shack, Beel," he told me once, "and you find out you like things nice and clean." I've seen Dr. Mines follow Gomez through the top floor as the boy swept and dusted, talking at him in their mathematical jargon.

Gomez worked in forty-eight-hour spells usually, and not eating much. Then for a couple of days he'd live like a human being, grabbing naps, playing catch on the lawn with one or another of the Security people, talking with me about his childhood in Puerto Rico and his youth in New York. He taught me a little Spanish and asked me to catch him up on bad mistakes in English.

"But don't you ever want to get out of here?" I demanded one day.

He grinned: "Why should I, Beel? Here I eat good, I can send money to the parents. Best, I find out what the big professors are up to without I have to wait five-ten years for damn declassifying."

"Don't you have a girl?"

He was embarrassed and changed the subject back to the big professors.

Dr. Mines drove up then, with his chauffeur who looked like a G-man and almost certainly was. As usual, the physicist was toting a bulging briefcase. After a few polite words with me, he and Julio went indoors and upstairs.

They were closeted for five hours—a record. When Dr. Mines came down I expected the usual briefing session. But he begged off. "Nothing serious," he said. "We just sat down and kicked some ideas of his around. I told him to go ahead. We've been—ah—using him very much like a sort of computer, you know. Turning him loose on the problems that were too tough for me and some of the other men. He's got the itch for research now. It would be very interesting if his forte turned out to be creative."

I agreed.

Julio didn't come down for dinner. I woke up in darkness that night when there was a loud bump overhead, and went upstairs in my pajamas.

Gomez was sprawled, fully dressed, on the floor. He'd tripped over a footstool. And he didn't seem to have noticed. His lips were moving and he stared straight at me without knowing I was there.

"You all right, Julio?" I asked, and started to help him to his feet.

He got up mechanically and said: ". . . real values of the zeta function vanish."

"How's that?"

He saw me then and asked, puzzled: "How you get in here, Beel? Is dinner-time?"

"Is four a.m., *por diós*. Don't you think you ought to get some sleep?" He looked terrible.

No; he didn't think he ought to get some sleep. He had some work to do. I went downstairs and heard him pacing overhead for an hour until I dozed off.

This splurge of work didn't wear off in forty-eight hours. For a week I brought him meals and sometimes he ate absently, with one hand, as he scribbled on a yellow pad. Sometimes I'd bring him lunch to find his breakfast untouched. He didn't have much beard, but he let it grow for a week—too busy to shave, too busy to talk, too busy to eat, sleeping in chairs when fatigue caught up with him.

I asked Leitzer, badly worried, if we should do anything about it. He had a direct scrambler-phone connection with the New York Security and Intelligence office, but his orders didn't cover anything like a self-induced nervous breakdown of the man he was guarding.

I thought Dr. Mines would do something when he came—call in an M.D., or tell Gomez to take it easy, or take some of the load off by parceling out whatever he had by the tail.

But he didn't. He went upstairs, came down two hours later and absently tried to walk past me. I headed him off into my room. "What's the word?" I demanded.

He looked me in the eye and said defiantly: "He's doing fine. I don't want to stop him."

Dr. Mines was a good man. Dr. Mines was a humane man. And he wouldn't lift a finger to keep the boy from working himself into nervous prostration. Dr. Mines liked people well enough, but he reserved his love for theoretical physics. "How important can this thing be?"

He shrugged irritably. "It's just the way some scientists work," he said. "Newton was like that. So was Sir William Rowan Hamilton——"

"Hamilton-Schmamilton," I said. "What's the sense of it? *Why* doesn't he sleep or eat?"

Mines said: "*You* don't know what it's like."

"Of course," I said, getting good and sore. "I'm just a dumb newspaper man. Tell me, Mr. Bones, what is it like?"

There was a long pause, and he said mildly: "I'll try. That boy up there is using his brain. A great chess player can put on a blindfold and play a hundred opponents in a hundred games simultaneously, remembering all the positions of his pieces and theirs and keeping a hundred strategies clear in his mind. Well, that stunt simply isn't in the same league with what Julio's doing up there.

"He has in his head some millions of facts concerning theoretical physics. He's scanning them, picking out one here and there, fitting them into new relationships, checking and rejecting when he has to, fitting the new relationships together, turning them upside-down and inside-out to see what happens, comparing them with known doctrine, holding them in his memory while he repeats the whole process and compares—and all the while he has a goal firmly in mind against which he's measuring all these things." He seemed to be finished.

For a reporter, I felt strangely shy. "What's he driving at?" I asked.

"I think," he said slowly, "he's approaching a unified field theory."

Apparently that was supposed to explain everything. I let Dr. Mines know that it didn't.

He said thoughtfully: "I don't know whether I can get it over to a layman—no offense, Vilchek. Let's put it this way. You know how math comes in waves, and how it's followed by waves of applied science based on the math. There was a big wave of algebra in the middle ages—following it came navigation, gunnery, surveying and so on. Then the renaissance and a wave of analysis—what you'd call calculus. That opened up steam power and how to use it, mechanical engineers, electricity. The wave of *modern* mathematics since say 1875 gave us atomic energy. That boy upstairs may be starting off the next big wave."

He got up and reached for his hat.

"Just a minute," I said. I was surprised that my voice was steady. "What comes next? Control of gravity? Control of personality? Sending people by radio?"

Dr. Mines wouldn't meet my eye. Suddenly he looked old and shrunken. "Don't worry about the boy," he said.

I let him go.

That evening I brought Gomez chicken-pot pie and a nonalcoholic egg nog. He drank the egg nog, said "Hi, Beel," and continued to cover yellow sheets of paper.

I went downstairs and worried.

Abruptly it ended late the next afternoon. Gomez wandered into the big first-floor kitchen looking like a starved old rickshaw coolie. He pushed his lank hair back from his forehead, said: "Beel, what is to eat——" and pitched forward on to the linoleum. Leitzer came when I yelled, expertly took Gomez's pulse, rolled him onto a blanket and threw another one over him. "It's just a faint," he said. "Let's get him to bed."

"Aren't you going to call a doctor, man?"

"Doctor couldn't do anything we can't do," he said stolidly. "And I'm here to see that security isn't breached. Give me a hand."

We got him upstairs and put him to bed. He woke up and said something in Spanish, and then, apologetically: "Very sorry, fellows. I ought to taken it easier."

"I'll get you some lunch," I said, and he grinned.

He ate it all, enjoying it heartily, and finally lay back gorged. "Well," he asked me, "what it is new, Beel?"

"What *is* new. And you should tell me. You finish your work?"

"I got it in shape to finish. The hard part is over." He rolled out of bed.

"Hey!" I said.

"I'm okay now," he grinned. "Don't write this down in your history, Beel. Everybody will think I act like a woman."

I followed him into his workroom where he flopped into an easy chair, his eyes on a blackboard covered with figures. He wasn't grinning any more.

"Dr. Mines says you're up to something big," I said.

"*Sí*. Big."

"Unified field theory, he says."

"That is it," Gomez said.

"Is it good or bad?" I asked, licking my lips. "The application, I mean."

His boyish mouth set suddenly in a grim line. "That, it is not my business," he said. "I am American citizen of the United States." He stared at the blackboard and its maze of notes.

I looked at it too—*really* looked at it for once—and was surprised by what I saw. Mathematics, of course, I don't know. But I had soaked up a very little *about* mathematics. One of the things I had soaked up was that the expressions of higher mathematics tend to be complicated and elaborate, involving English, Greek and Hebrew letters, plain and fancy brackets and a great variety of special signs besides the plus and minus of the elementary school.

The things on the blackboard weren't like that at all. The board was covered with variations of a simple expression that consisted of five letters and two symbols: a right-handed pothook and a left-handed pothook.

"What do they mean?" I asked, pointing.

"Something I made up," he said nervously. "The word for that one is 'enfields.' The other is 'is enfielded by.' "

"What's *that* mean?"

His luminous eyes were haunted. He didn't answer.

"It looks like simple stuff. I read somewhere that all the basic stuff is simple once it's been discovered."

"Yes," he said almost inaudibly. "It is simple, Beel. Too damn simple, I think. Better I carry it in my head, I think." He strode to the blackboard and erased it. Instinctively I half rose to stop him. He gave me a grin that was somehow bitter and unlike him. "Don't worry," he said. "I don't forget it." He tapped his forehead. "I *can't* forget it." I hope I never see again on any face the look that was on his.

"Julio," I said, appalled. "Why don't you get out of here for a while? Why don't you run over to New York and see your folks and have some fun? They can't keep you here against your will."

"They told me I shouldn't——" he said uncertainly. And then he got tough.

"You're damn right, Beel. Let's go in together. I get dressed up. Er—You tell Leitzer, hah?" He couldn't quite face up to the hard-boiled security man.

I told Leitzer, who hit the ceiling. But all it boiled down to was that he sincerely wished Gomez and I wouldn't leave. We weren't in the Army, we weren't in jail. I got hot at last and yelled back that we were damn well going out and he couldn't stop us. He called New York on his direct wire and apparently New York confirmed it, regretfully.

We got on the 4:05 Jersey Central, with Higgins and Dalhousie tailing us at a respectful distance. Gomez didn't notice them and I didn't tell him. He was having too much fun. He had a shine put on his shoes at Penn Station and worried about the taxi fare as we rode up to Spanish Harlem.

His parents lived in a neat three-room apartment. A lot of the furniture looked brand new, and I was pretty sure who had paid for it. The mother and father spoke only Spanish, and mumbled shyly when "*mi amigo Beel*" was introduced. I had a very halting conversation with the father while the mother and Gomez rattled away happily and she poked his ribs to point up the age-old complaint of any mother anywhere that he wasn't eating enough.

The father, of course, thought the boy was a janitor or something in the Pentagon and, as near as I could make out, he was worried about his Julio being grabbed off by a man-hungry government girl. I kept reassuring him that his Julio was a good boy, a very good boy, and he seemed to get some comfort out of it.

There was a little spat when his mother started to set the table. Gomez said reluctantly that we couldn't stay, that we were eating somewhere else. His mother finally dragged from him the admission that we were going to the Porto Bello so he could see Rosa, and everything was smiles again. The father told me that Rosa was a good girl, a very good girl.

Walking down the three flights of stairs with yelling little kids playing tag around us, Gomez asked proudly: "You not think they in America only a little time, hey?"

I yanked him around by the elbow as we went down the brownstone stoop into the street. Otherwise he would have seen our shadows for sure. I didn't want to spoil his fun.

The Porto Bello was full, and the pretty little girl was on duty as cashier at the table. Gomez got a last-minute attack of cold feet at the sight of her. "No table," he said. "We better go someplace else."

I practically dragged him in. "We'll get a table in a minute," I said.

"Julio," said the girl, when she saw him.

He looked sheepish. "Hello, Rosa. I'm back for a while."

"I'm glad to see you again," she said tremulously.

"I'm glad to see you again too——" I nudged him. "Rosa, this is my good friend Beel. We work together in Washington."

"Pleased to meet you, Rosa. Can you have dinner with us? I'll bet you and Julio have a lot to talk over."

"Well, I'll see . . . look, there's a table for you. I'll see if I can get away."

We sat down and she flagged down the proprietress and got away in a hurry.

All three of us had *arroz con pollo*—rice with chicken and lots of other things. Their shyness wore off and I was dealt out of the conversation, but I didn't mind. They were a nice young couple. I liked the way they smiled at each other, and the things they remembered happily—movies, walks, talks. It made me feel like a benevolent uncle with one foot in the grave. It made me forget for a while the look on Gomez's face when he turned from the blackboard he had covered with too-simple math.

Over dessert I broke in. By then they were unselfconsciously holding hands. "Look," I said, "why don't you two go on and do the town? Julio, I'll be at the Madison Park Hotel." I scribbled the address and gave it to him. "And I'll get a room for you. Have fun and reel in any time." I rapped his knee. He looked down and I slipped him four twenties. I didn't know whether he had money on him or not, but anything extra the boy could use he had coming to him.

"Swell," he said. "Thanks." And looked shame-faced while I looked paternal.

I had been watching a young man who was moodily eating alone in a corner, reading a paper. He was about Julio's height and build and he wore a sports jacket pretty much like Julio's. And the street was pretty dark outside.

The young man got up moodily and headed for the cashier's table. "Gotta go," I said. "Have fun."

I went out of the restaurant right behind the young man and walked as close behind him as I dared, hoping we were being followed.

After a block and a half of this, he turned on me and snarled: "Wadda you, mister? A wolf? Beat it!"

"Okay," I said mildly, and turned and walked the other way. Higgins and Dalhousie were standing there, flat-footed and open-mouthed. They sprinted back to the Porto Bello, and *I* followed *them*. But Julio and Rosa had already left.

"Tough fellows," I said to them as they stood in the doorway. They looked as if they wanted to murder me. "He won't get into any trouble," I said. "He's just going out with his girl." Dalhousie made a strangled noise and told Higgins: "Cruise around the neighborhood. See if you can pick them up. I'll follow Vilchek." He wouldn't talk to me. I shrugged and got a cab and went to the Madison Park Hotel, a pleasantly unfashionable old place with big rooms where I stay when business brings me to New York. They had a couple of adjoining singles; I took one in my own name and the other for Gomez.

I wandered around the neighborhood for a while and had a couple of beers in one of the ultra-Irish bars on Third Avenue. After a pleasant argument with a gent who thought the Russians didn't have any atomic bombs and faked their demonstrations and that we ought to blow up their industrial cities tomorrow at dawn, I went back to the hotel.

I didn't get to sleep easily. The citizen who didn't believe Russia could maul the United States pretty badly or at all had started me thinking again—all kinds of ugly thoughts. Dr. Mines who had turned into a shrunken old man at the mention of applying Gomez' work. The look on the boy's face. My layman's knowledge that present-day "atomic energy" taps only the smallest fragment of the energy locked up in the atom. My layman's knowledge that once genius has broken a trail in science, mediocracy can follow that trail.

But I slept at last, for three hours.

At four-fifteen A.M. according to my watch the telephone rang long and hard. There was some switchboard and long-distance-operator mumbo-jumbo and then Julio's gleeful voice: "Beel! Congratulate us. We got marriage!"

"Married," I said fuzzily. "You got *married*, not marriage. How's that again?"

"We got *married*. Me and Rosa. We get on the train, the taxi driver takes us to the justice of the peace, we got *married*, we go to hotel here."

"Congratulations," I said waking up. "Lots of congratulations. But you're under age, there's a waiting period——"

"Not in this state," he chuckled. "Here is no waiting periods and here I have twenty-one years if I say so."

"Well," I said. "Lots of congratulations, Julio. And tell Rosa she's got herself a good boy."

"Thanks, Beel," he said shyly. "I call you so you don't worry when I don't come in tonight. I think I come in with Rosa tomorrow so we tell her mama and my mama and papa. I call you at the hotel, I still have the piece of paper."

"Okay, Julio. All the best. Don't worry about a thing." I hung up, chuckling, and went right back to sleep.

Well, sir, it happened again.

I was shaken out of my skin by the strong, skinny hand of Admiral MacDonald. It was seven-thirty and a bright New York morning. Dalhousie had pulled a blank canvassing the neighborhood for Gomez, got panicky and bucked it up to higher headquarters.

"Where is he?" the admiral rasped.

"On his way here with his bride of one night," I said. "He slipped over a couple of state lines and got married."

"By God," the admiral said, "we've got to do something about this. I'm going to have him drafted and assigned to special duty. This is the last time——"

"*Look*," I said. "You've got to stop treating him like a chesspiece. You've got duty-honor-country on the brain and thank God for that. Somebody has to; it's your profession. But can't you get it through your head that Gomez is a kid and that you're wrecking his life by forcing him to grind out science like a machine? And I'm just a stupe of a layman, but have you professionals worried once about digging too deep and blowing up the whole shebang?"

He gave me a piercing look and said nothing.

I dressed and had breakfast sent up. The admiral and Dalhousie waited grimly until noon, and then Gomez phoned up.

"Come on up, Julio," I said tiredly.

He breezed in with his blushing bride on his arm. The admiral rose automatically as she entered, and immediately began tongue-lashing the boy. He spoke more in sorrow than in anger. He made it clear that Gomez wasn't treating his country right. That he had a great talent and it belonged to the United States. That his behavior had been irresponsible. That Gomez would have to come to heel and realize that his wishes weren't the most important things in his life. That he could and would be drafted if there were any more such escapades.

"As a starter, Mr. Gomez," the admiral snapped, "I want you to set down immediately the enfieldment matrices you have developed. I consider it almost criminal of you to arrogantly and carelessly trust to your memory alone matters of such vital importance. Here!" He thrust pencil and paper at the boy, who stood, drooping and disconsolate. Little Rosa was near crying. She didn't have the ghost of a notion as to what it was about.

Gomez took the pencil and paper and sat down at the writing-table silently. I took Rosa by the arm. She was trembling. "It's all right," I said. "They can't do a thing to him." The admiral glared briefly at me and then returned his gaze to Gomez.

The boy made a couple of tentative marks. Then his eyes went wide and he clutched his hair. "*Dios mío!*" he said. "*Está perdido! Olvidado!*"

Which means: "My God, it's lost! Forgotten!"

The admiral turned white beneath his tan. "Now, boy," he said slowly and soothingly. "I didn't mean to scare you. You just relax and collect yourself. Of course you haven't forgotten, not with that memory of yours. Start with something easy. Write down a general biquadratic equation, say."

Gomez just looked at him. After a long pause he said in a strangled voice: "*No puedo.* I can't. It too I forget. I don't think of the math or physics at all since——" He looked at Rosa and turned a little red. She smiled shyly and looked at her shoes.

"That is it," Gomez said hoarsely. "Not since then. Always before in the back of my head is the math, but not since then."

"My God," the admiral said softly. "Can such a thing happen?" He reached for the phone.

He found out that such things can happen.

Julio went back to Spanish Harlem and bought a piece of the Porto Bello with his savings. I went back to the paper and bought a car with *my* savings. MacDonald never cleared the story, so the Sunday editor had the satisfaction of bulldozing an admiral, but didn't get his exclusive.

Julio and Rosa sent me a card eventually announcing the birth of their first-born: a six-pound boy, Francisco, named after Julio's father. I saved the card and when a New York assignment came my way—it was the National Association of Dry Goods Wholesalers; dry goods are important in our town—I dropped up to see them.

Julio was a little more mature and a little more prosperous. Rosa—alas!—was already putting on weight, but she was still a pretty thing and devoted to her man. The baby was a honey-skinned little wiggler. It was nice to see all of them together, happy with their lot.

Julio insisted that he'd cook *arroz con pollo* for me, as on the night I practically threw him into Rosa's arms, but he'd have to shop for the stuff. I went along.

In the corner grocery he ordered the rice, the chicken, the garbanzos, the peppers and, swept along by the enthusiasm that hits husbands in groceries, about fifty other things that he thought would be nice to have in the pantry.

The creaking old grocer scribbled down the prices on a shopping bag and began painfully to add them up while Julio was telling me how well the Porto Bello was doing and how they were thinking of renting the adjoining store.

"Seventeen dollars, forty two cents," the grocer said at last.

Julio flicked one glance at the shopping bag and the upside-down figures. "Should be seventeen thirty-nine," he said reprovingly. "Add up again."

The grocer painfully added up again and said, "Is seventeen thirty-nine. Sorry." He began to pack the groceries into the bag.

"Hey," I said.

We didn't discuss it then or ever. Julio just said: "Don't tell, Beel." And winked.

WATERCLAP

Isaac Asimov

Isaac Asimov, after his relative withdrawal from writing sf in favor of science nonfiction in the late nineteen fifties, appeared only infrequently as a short-story writer in the field until the end of his life. Most of his sf from 1958 to 1976 is collected in a slim volume, *The Bicentennial Man* (1976); the next years' in *The Winds of Change* (1983). But he maintained a level of excellence he had reached early in his career and, although his later stories attracted perhaps less notice, they are, as a body of work, underrated.

Asimov was deeply connected to the science fiction genre and to the social community of writers and readers, and took immense pride in his position at the top of the field. Sometimes his later stories are intellectual jokes to amuse the community, slight and funny, but most often they are carefully written by a master of the form at the sustained peak of his powers, frequently more accomplished than the best-selling continuations of his early works at novel length which he wrote to satisfy his publishers and mass audience.

"Waterclap," from 1970, the only story he published that year in the sf field, is Asimov at the top of his form. The twin images of the city under the sea and the domed city on the Moon (or another location physically or chemically inhospitable to human life) are as traditional in sf as are the robot and the spaceship. It is perhaps indicative of the wide-open-spaces atmosphere of American sf that the undersea environment on Earth is seldom chosen as a setting (too close to home, maybe, for the pioneering spirit—too claustrophobic, therefore, as in British writer James White's *The Watch Below* [1966]—although not in reality any more so than the enclosed spaces of Moon colonies or spaceships large or small). Asimov, however, foresees the two cities as equal frontiers.

It is, like his classic "Nightfall," a story built around a powerful, memorable image invented to convey the horrific power of water pressure in an implosion under the sea. Asimov the hard sf writer is selling a vision of problem-solving by reason, in the classic Campbellian mold, on new frontiers.

Stephen Demerest looked at the textured sky. He kept looking at it and found the blue opaque and revolting.

Unwarily, he had looked at the Sun, for there was nothing to blank it out automatically, and then he had snatched his eyes away in panic. He wasn't blinded; just a few afterimages. Even the Sun was washed out.

Involuntarily, he thought of Ajax's prayer in Homer's *Iliad*. They were fighting over the body of Patroclus in the mist and Ajax said, "O Father Zeus, save the Achaeans out of this mist! Make the sky clear, grant us to see with our eyes! Kill us in the light, since it is thy pleasure to kill us!"

Demerest thought: Kill us in the light—

Kill us in the clear light on the Moon, where the sky is black and soft, where the stars shine brightly, where the cleanliness and purity of vacuum make all things sharp.

—Not in this low-clinging, fuzzy blue.

He shuddered. It was an actual physical shudder that shook his lanky body, and he was annoyed. He was going to die. He was sure of it. And it wouldn't be under the blue, either, come to think of it, but under the black—but a different black.

It was as though in answer to that thought that the ferry pilot, short, swarthy, crisp-haired, came up to him and said, "Ready for the black, Mr. Demerest?"

Demerest nodded. He towered over the other as he did over most of the men of Earth. They were thick, all of them, and took their short, low steps with ease. He himself had to feel his footsteps, guide them through the air; even the impalpable bond that held him to the ground was textured.

"I'm ready," he said. He took a deep breath and deliberately repeated his earlier glance at the Sun. It was low in the morning sky, washed out by dusty air, and he knew it wouldn't blind him. He didn't think he would ever see it again.

He had never seen a bathyscaphe before. Despite everything, he tended to think of it in terms of prototypes, an oblong balloon with a spherical gondola beneath. It was as though he persisted in thinking of space flight in terms of tons of fuel spewed backward in fire, and an irregular module feeling its way, spiderlike, toward the Lunar surface.

The bathyscaphe was not like the image in his thoughts at all. Under its skin, it might still be buoyant bag and gondola, but it was all engineered sleekness now.

"My name is Javan," said the ferry pilot. "Omar Javan."

"Javan?"

"Queer name to you? I'm Iranian by descent; Earthman by persuasion. Once you get down there, there are no nationalities." He grinned and his complexion grew darker against the even whiteness of his teeth. "If you don't mind, we'll be starting in a minute. You'll be my only passenger, so I guess you carry weight."

"Yes," said Demerest dryly. "At least a hundred pounds more than I'm used to."

"You're from the Moon? I thought you had a queer walk on you. I hope it's not uncomfortable."

"It's not exactly comfortable, but I manage. We exercise for this."

"Well, come on board." He stood aside and let Demerest walk down the gangplank. "I wouldn't go to the Moon myself."

"You go to Ocean-Deep."

"About fifty times so far. That's different."

Demerest got on board. It was cramped, but he didn't mind that. It might be a space module except that it was more—well, textured. There was that word again. There was the clear feeling everywhere that mass didn't matter. Mass was held up; it didn't have to be hurled up.

They were still on the surface. The blue sky could be seen greenishly through the clear thick glass. Javan said, "You don't have to be strapped in. There's no acceleration. Smooth as oil, the whole thing. It won't take long; just about an hour. You can't smoke."

"I don't smoke," said Demerest.

"I hope you don't have claustrophobia."

"Moon-men don't have claustrophobia."

"All that open—"

"Not in our cavern. We live in a"—he groped for the phrase—"a Lunar-Deep, a hundred feet deep."

"A hundred feet!" The pilot seemed amused, but he didn't smile. "We're slipping down now."

The interior of the gondola was fitted into angles but here and there a section of wall beyond the instruments showed its basic sphericity. To Javan, the instruments seemed to be an extension of his arms; his eyes and hands moved over them lightly, almost lovingly.

"We're all checked out," he said, "but I like a last-minute look-over; we'll be facing a thousand atmospheres down there." His finger touched a contact, and the round door closed massively inward and pressed against the beveled rim it met.

"The higher the pressure, the tighter that will hold," said Javan. "Take your last look at sunlight, Mr. Demerest."

The light still shone through the thick glass of the window. It was wavering now; there was water between the Sun and them now.

"The last look?" said Demerest.

Javan snickered. "Not the *last* look. I mean for the trip. . . . I suppose you've never been on a bathyscaphe before."

"No, I haven't. Have many?"

"Very few," admitted Javan. "But don't worry. It's just an underwater balloon. We've introduced a million improvements since the first bathyscaphe. It's nuclear-powered now and we can move freely by water jet up to certain limits, but cut it down to basics and it's still a spherical gondola under buoyancy tanks. And it's still towed out to sea by a mother ship because it needs what power it carries too badly to waste it on surface travel. Ready?"

"Ready."

The supporting cable of the mother ship flicked away and the bathyscaphe settled lower; then lower still, as sea water fed into the buoyancy tanks. For a few moments, caught in surface currents, it swayed, and then there was nothing. The bathyscaphe sank slowly through a deepening green.

Javan relaxed. He said, "John Bergen is head of Ocean-Deep. You're going to see him?"

"That's right."

"He's a nice guy. His wife's with him."

"She is?"

"Oh, sure. They have women down there. There's a bunch down there, fifty people. Some stay for months."

Demerest put his finger on the narrow, nearly invisible seam where door met wall. He took it away and looked at it. He said, "It's oily."

"Silicone, really. The pressure squeezes some out. It's supposed to. . . . Don't worry. Everything's automatic. Everything's fail-safe. The first sign of malfunction, any malfunction at all, our ballast is released and up we go."

"You mean nothing's ever happened to these bathyscaphes?"

"What can happen?" The pilot looked sideways at his passenger. "Once you get too deep for sperm whales, nothing can go wrong."

"Sperm whales?" Demerest's thin face creased in a frown.

"Sure, they dive as deep as half a mile. If they hit a bathyscaphe—well, the walls of the buoyancy chambers aren't particularly strong. They don't have to be, you know. They're open to the sea and when the gasoline, which supplies the buoyancy, compresses, sea water enters."

It was dark now. Demerest found his gaze fastened to the viewport. It was light inside the gondola, but it was dark in that window. And it was not the darkness of space; it was a thick darkness.

Demerest said sharply, "Let's get this straight, Mr. Javan. You are not equipped to withstand the attack of a sperm whale. Presumably you are not equipped to withstand the attack of a giant squid. Have there been any actual incidents of that sort?"

"Well, it's like this—"

"No games, please, and don't try ragging the greenhorn. I am asking out of professional curiosity. I am head safety engineer at Luna City and I am asking what precautions this bathyscaphe can take against possible collision with large creatures."

Javan looked embarrassed. He muttered, "Actually, there have been no incidents."

"Are any expected? Even as a remote possibility?"

"Anything is remotely possible. But actually sperm whales are too intelligent to monkey with us and giant squid are too shy."

"Can they see us?"

"Yes, of course. We're lit up."

"Do you have floodlights?"

"We're already past the large-animal range, but we have them, and I'll turn them on for you."

Through the black of the window there suddenly appeared a snowstorm, an inverted upward-falling snowstorm. The blackness had come alive with stars in three-dimensional array and all moving upward.

Demerest said, "What's that?"

"Just crud. Organic matter. Small creatures. They float, don't move much, and they catch the light. We're going down past them. They seem to be going up in consequence."

Demerest's sense of perspective adjusted itself and he said, "Aren't we dropping too quickly?"

"No, we're not. If we were, I could use the nuclear engines, if I wanted to waste power; or I could drop some ballast. I'll be doing that later, but for now everything is fine. Relax, Mr. Demerest. The snow thins as we dive and we're not likely to see much in the way of spectacular life forms. There are small angler fish and such but they avoid us."

Demerest said, "How many do you take down at a time?"

"I've had as many as four passengers in this gondola, but that's crowded. We can put two bathyscaphes in tandem and carry ten, but that's clumsy. What we really need are trains of gondolas, heavier on the nukes—the nuclear engines—and lighter on the buoyancy. Stuff like that is on the drawing board, they tell me. Of course, they've been telling me that for years."

"There are plans for large-scale expansion of Ocean-Deep, then?"

"Sure, why not? We've got cities on the continental shelves, why not on the deep-sea bottom? They way I look at it, Mr. Demerest, where man can go, he will go and he should go. The Earth is ours to populate and we will populate it. All we need to make the deep sea habitable are completely maneuverable 'scaphes. The buoyancy chambers slow us, weaken us, and complicate the engineering."

"But they also save you don't they? If everything goes wrong at once, the gasoline you carry will still float you to the surface. What would do that for you if your nuclear engines go wrong and you had no buoyancy?"

"If it comes to that, you can't expect to eliminate the chances of accident altogether, not even fatal ones."

"I know that very well," said Demerest feelingly.

Javan stiffened. The tone of his voice changed. "Sorry. Didn't mean anything by that. Tough about that accident."

"Yes," said Demerest. Fifteen men and five women had died. One of the individuals listed among the "men" had been fourteen years old. It had been pinned down to human failure. What could a head safety engineer say after that?

"Yes," he said.

A pall dropped between the two men, a pall as thick and as turgid as the pressurized sea water outside. How could one allow for panic and for distraction and for depression all at once? There were the Moon-Blues—stupid name—but they struck men at inconvenient times. It wasn't always noticeable when the Moon-Blues came but it made men torpid and slow to react.

How many times had a meteorite come along and been averted or smothered or successfully absorbed? How many times had a Moonquake done damage and been held in check? How many times had human failure been backed up and compensated for? How many times had accidents *not* happened?

But you don't pay off on accidents not happening. There were twenty dead—

Javan said (how many long minutes later?), "There are the lights of Ocean-Deep!"

Demerest could not make them out at first. He didn't know where to look. Twice before, luminescent creatures had flicked past the windows at a distance and with the floodlights off again, Demerest had thought them the first sign of Ocean-Deep. Now he saw nothing.

"Down there," said Javan, without pointing. He was busy now, slowing the drop and edging the 'scaphe sideways.

Demerest could hear the distant sighing of the water jets, steam-driven, with the steam formed by the heat of momentary bursts of fusion power.

Demerest thought dimly: Deuterium is their fuel and it's all around them. Water is their exhaust and it's all around them.

Javan was dropping some of his ballast, too, and began a kind of distant chatter. "The ballast used to be steel pellets and they were dropped by electromagnetic controls. Anywhere up to fifty tons of it were used in each trip. Conservationists worried about spreading rusting steel over the ocean floor, so we switched to metal nodules that are dredged up from the continental shelf. We put a thin layer of iron over them so they can still be electromagnetically handled and the ocean bottom gets nothing that wasn't sub-ocean to begin with. Cheaper, too. . . . But when we get our real nuclear 'scaphes, we won't need ballast at all."

Demerest scarcely heard him. Ocean-Deep could be seen now. Javan had turned on his floodlights and far below was the muddy floor of the Puerto Rican Trench. Resting on that floor like a cluster of equally muddy pearls was the spherical conglomerate of Ocean-Deep.

Each unit was a sphere such as the one in which Demerest was now sinking toward contact, but much larger, and as Ocean-Deep expanded—expanded—expanded, new spheres were added.

Demerest thought: They're only five and a half miles from home, not a quarter of a million.

"How are we going to get through?" asked Demerest.

The 'scaphe had made contact. Demerest heard the dull sound of metal against metal but then for minutes there had been nothing more than a kind of occasional scrape as Javan bent over his instruments in rapt concentration.

"Don't worry about that," Javan said at last, in belated answer. "There's no problem. The delay now is only because I have to make sure we fit tightly. There's an electromagnetic joint that holds at every point of a perfect circle. When the instruments read correctly, that means we fit over the entrance door."

"Which then opens?"

"It would if there were air on the other side, but there isn't. There's sea water, and that has to be driven out. *Then* we enter."

Demerest did not miss this point. He had come here on this, the last day of his life, to give that same life meaning and he intended to miss nothing.

He said, "Why the added step? Why not keep the air lock, if that's what it is, a real air lock, and have air in it at all times."

"They tell me it's a matter of safety," said Javan. "*Your* specialty. The interface has equal pressure on both sides at all times, *except* when men are moving across. This door is the weakest point of the whole system, because it opens and closes; it has joints; it has seams. You know what I mean?"

"I do," murmured Demerest. There was a logical flaw here and that meant there was a possible chink through which—but later.

He said, "Why are we waiting now?"

"The lock is being emptied. The water is being forced out."

"By air."

"Hell, no. They can't afford to waste air like that. It would take a thousand atmospheres to empty the chamber of its water, and filling the chamber with air at that density, even temporarily, is more air than they can afford to expend. Steam is what does it."

"Of course. Yes."

Javan said cheerfully, "You heat the water. No pressure in the world can stop water from turning to steam at a temperature of more than 374°C. And the steam forces the sea water out through a one-way valve."

"Another weak point," said Demerest.

"I suppose so. It's never failed yet. The water in the lock is being pushed out now. When hot steam starts bubbling out the valve, the process automatically stops and the lock is full of overheated steam."

"And then?"

"And then we have a whole ocean to cool it with. The temperature drops and the steam condenses. Once that happens, ordinary air can be let in at a pressure of one atmosphere and *then* the door opens."

"How long must we wait?"

"Not long. If there were anything wrong, there'd be sirens sounding. At least, so they say. I never heard one in action."

There was silence for a few minutes, and then there was a sudden sharp clap and a simultaneous jerk.

Javan said, "Sorry, I should have warned you. I'm so used to it I forgot. When the door opens, a thousand atmospheres of pressure on the other side forces us hard against the metal of Ocean-Deep. No electromagnetic force can hold us hard enough to prevent that last hundredth-of-an-inch slam."

Demerest unclenched his fist and released his breath. He said, "Is everything all right?"

"The walls didn't crack, if that's what you mean. It sounds like doom, though, doesn't it? It sounds even worse when I've got to leave and the air lock fills up again. Be prepared for that."

But Demerest was suddenly weary. Let's get on with it, he thought. I don't want to drag it out. He said, "Do we go through now?"

"We go through."

The opening in the 'scaphe wall was round and small; even smaller than the one through which they had originally entered. Javan went through it sinuously, muttering that it always made him feel like a cork in a bottle.

Demerest had not smiled since he entered the 'scaphe. Nor did he really smile now, but a corner of his mouth quirked as he thought that a skinny Moon-man would have no trouble.

He went through also, feeling Javan's hands firmly at his waist, helping him through.

Javan said, "It's dark in here. No point in introducing an additional weakness by wiring for lighting. But that's why flashlights were invented."

Demerest found himself on a perforated walk, its stainless metallic surface gleaming dully. And through the perforations he could make out the wavering surface of water.

He said, "The chamber hasn't been emptied."

"You can't do any better, Mr. Demerest. If you're going to use steam to empty it, you're left with that steam, and to get the pressures necessary to do the emptying that steam must be compressed to about one-third the density of liquid water. When it condenses, the chamber remains one-third full of water—but it's water at just one-atmosphere pressure. . . . Come on, Mr. Demerest."

John Bergen's face wasn't entirely unknown to Demerest. Recognition was immediate. Bergen, as head of Ocean-Deep for nearly a decade now, was a familiar face on the TV screens of Earth—just as the leaders of Luna City had become familiar.

Demerest had seen the head of Ocean-Deep both flat and in three dimensions, in black-and-white and in color. Seeing him in life added little.

Like Javan, Bergen was short and thickset; opposite in structure to the traditional (already traditional?) Lunar pattern of physiology. He was fairer than Javan by a good deal and his face was noticeably asymmetrical, with his somewhat thick nose leaning just a little to the right.

He was not handsome. No Moon-man would think he was, but then Bergen smiled and there was a sunniness about it as he held out his large hand.

Demerest placed his own thin one within, steeling himself for a hard grip, but it did not come. Bergen took the hand and let it go, then said, "I'm glad you're here. We don't have much in the way of luxury, nothing that will make our hospitality stand out, we can't even declare a holiday in your honor—but the spirit is there. Welcome!"

"Thank you," said Demerest softly. He remained unsmiling now, too. He was facing the enemy and he knew it. Surely Bergen must know it also and, since he did, that smile of his was hypocrisy.

And at that moment a clang like metal against metal sounded deafeningly and the chamber shuddered. Demerest leaped back and staggered against the wall.

Bergen did not budge. He said quietly, "That was the bathyscaphe unhitching and the waterclap of the air lock filling. Javan ought to have warned you."

Demerest panted and tried to make his racing heart slow. He said, "Javan did warn me. I was caught by surprise anyway."

Bergen said, "Well, it won't happen again for a while. We don't often have visitors, you know. We're not equipped for it and so we fight off all kinds of big wheels who think a trip down here would be good for their careers. Politicians of all kinds, chiefly. Your own case is different of course."

Is it? thought Demerest. It had been hard enough to get permission to make the trip down. His superiors back at Luna City had not approved in the first place and had scouted the idea that a diplomatic interchange would be of any use.

("Diplomatic interchange" was what they had called it.) And when he had overborne them, there had been Ocean-Deep's own reluctance to receive him.

It had been sheer persistence alone that had made his present visit possible. In what way then was Demerest's case different?

Bergen said, "I suppose you have your junketing problems on Luna City, too?"

"Very little," said Demerest. "Your average politician isn't as ambitious to travel a half-million-mile round trip as he is to travel a ten-mile one."

"I can see that," agreed Bergen, "and it's more expensive out to the Moon, of course. . . . In a way, this is the first meeting of inner and outer space. No Ocean-man has ever gone to the Moon as far as I know and you're the first Moon-man to visit a sub-sea station of any kind. No Moon-man has ever been to one of the settlements on the continental shelf."

"It's a historic meeting, then," said Demerest, and tried to keep the sarcasm out of his voice.

If any leaked through, Bergen showed no sign. He rolled up his sleeves as though to emphasize his attitude of informality (or the fact that they were very busy, so that there would be little time for visitors?) and said, "Do you want coffee? I assume you've eaten. Would you like to rest before I show you around? Do you want to wash up, for that matter, as they say euphemistically?"

For a moment, curiosity stirred in Demerest; yet not entirely aimless curiosity. Everything involving the interface of Ocean-Deep with the outside world could be of importance. He said, "How are sanitary facilities handled here?"

"It's cycled mostly; as it is on the Moon, I imagine. We can eject if we want to or have to. Man has a bad record of fouling the environment, but as the only deep-sea station, what we eject does no perceptible damage. Adds organic matter." He laughed.

Demerest filed that away, too. Matter was ejected; there were therefore ejection tubes. Their workings might be of interest and he, as a safety engineer, had a right to be interested.

"No," he said, "I don't need anything at the moment. If you're busy—"

"That's all right. We're always busy, but I'm the least busy, if you see what I mean. Suppose I show you around. We've got over fifty units here, each as big as this one, some bigger—"

Demerest looked about. Again, as in the 'scaphe, there were angles everywhere, but beyond the furnishings and equipment there were signs of the inevitable spherical outer wall. Fifty of them!

"Built up," went on Bergen, "over a generation of effort. The unit we're standing in is actually the oldest and there's been some talk of demolishing and replacing it. Some of the men say we're ready for second-generation units, but I'm not sure. It would be expensive—everything's expensive down here—and getting money out of the Planetary Project Council is always a depressing experience."

Demerest felt his nostrils flare involuntarily and a spasm of anger shot through him. It was a thrust, surely. Luna City's miserable record with the PPC must be well known to Bergen.

But Bergen went on, unnoticing. "I'm a traditionalist, too—just a little bit. This is the first deep-sea unit ever constructed. The first two people to remain overnight on the floor of an ocean trench slept here with nothing else beyond this bare sphere except for a miserable portable fusion unit to work the escape hatch. I mean the air lock, but we called it the escape hatch to begin with—and just enough controls for the purpose. Reguera and Tremont, those were the men. They never made a second trip to the bottom, either; stayed Topside forever after. Well, well, they served their purpose and both are dead now. And here we are with fifty people and with six months as the usual tour of duty. I've spent only two weeks Topside in the last year and a half."

He motioned vigorously to Demerest to follow him, slid open a door which moved evenly into a recess, and took him into the next unit. Demerest paused to examine the opening. There were no seams that he could notice between the adjacent units.

Bergen noted the other's pause and said, "When we add on our units, they're welded under pressure into the equivalent of a single piece of metal and then reinforced. We can't take chances, as I'm sure you understand, since I have been given to understand that you're the head safe—"

Demerest cut him off. "Yes," he said. "We on the Moon admire your safety record."

Bergen shrugged. "We've been lucky. Our sympathy, by the way, on the rotten break you fellows had. I mean that fatal—"

Demerest cut him off again. "Yes."

Bergen, the Moon-man decided, was either a naturally voluble man or else was eager to drown him in words and get rid of him.

"The units," said Bergen, "are arranged in a highly branched chain—three-dimensional actually. We have a map we can show you, if you're interested. Most of the end units represent living-sleeping quarters. For privacy, you know. The working units tend to be corridors as well, which is one of the embarrassments of having to live down here.

"This is our library; part of it, anyway. Not big, but it's got our records, too, on carefully indexed and computed microfilm, so that for its kind it's not only the biggest in the world, but the best and the only. And we have a special computer designed to handle the references to meet our needs exactly. It collects, selects, coordinates, weighs, then gives us the gist.

"We have another library, too, book films and even some printed volumes. But that's for amusement."

A voice broke in on Bergen's cheerful flow. "John? May I interrupt?"

Demerest started; the voice had come from behind him. Bergen said, "Annette! I was going to get you. This is Stephen Demerest of Luna City. Mr. Demerest, may I introduce my wife, Annette?"

Demerest had turned. He said stiffly, a little mechanically, "I'm pleased to meet you, Mrs. Bergen." But he was staring at her waistline.

Annette Bergen seemed in her early thirties. Her brown hair was combed simply and she wore no makeup. Attractive, not beautiful, Demerest noted vaguely. But his eyes kept returning to that waistline.

She shrugged a little. "Yes, I'm pregnant, Mr. Demerest. I'm due in about two months."

"Pardon me," Demerest muttered. "So rude of me. . . . I didn't—" He faded off and felt as though the blow had been a physical one. He hadn't expected women, though he didn't know why. He *knew* there would have to be women in Ocean-Deep. And the ferry pilot had said Bergen's wife was with him.

He stammered as he spoke. "How many women are there in Ocean-Deep, Mr. Bergen?"

"Nine at the moment," said Bergen. "All wives. We look forward to a time when we can have the normal ratio of one to one, but we still need workers and researchers primarily, and unless women have important qualifications of *some* sort—"

"They all have important qualifications of *some* sort, dear," said Mrs. Bergen. "You could keep the men for longer duty if—"

"My wife," said Bergen, laughing, "is a convinced feminist but is not above using sex as an excuse to enforce equality. I keep telling her that that is the feminine way of doing it and not the feminist way, and she keeps saying— Well, that's why she's pregnant. You think it's love, sex mania yearning for motherhood? Nothing of the sort. She's going to have a baby down here to make a philosophical point."

Annette said coolly, "Why not? Either this is going to be home for humanity or it isn't going to be. If it *is*, then we're going to have babies here, that's all. I want a baby born in Ocean-Deep. There are babies born in Luna City, aren't there, Mr. Demerest?"

Demerest took a deep breath. "*I* was born in Luna City, Mrs. Bergen."

"And well she knew it," muttered Bergen.

"And you are in your late twenties, I think?" she said.

"I am twenty-nine," said Demerest.

"And well she knew that, too," said Bergen with a short laugh. "You can bet she looked up all possible data on you when she heard you were coming."

"That is quite beside the point," said Annette. "The point is that for twenty-nine years at least children have been born in Luna City and no children have been born in Ocean-Deep."

"Luna City, my dear," said Bergen, "is longer-established. It is over half a century old; we are not yet twenty."

"Twenty years is quite enough. It takes a baby nine months."

Demerest interposed, "Are there any children in Ocean-Deep?"

"No," said Bergen. "No. Someday, though."

"In two months, anyway," said Annette Bergen positively.

The tension grew inside Demerest and when they returned to the unit in which he had first met Bergen, he was glad to sit down and accept a cup of coffee.

"We'll eat soon," said Bergen matter-of-factly. "I hope you don't mind sitting here meanwhile. As the prime unit, it isn't used for much except, of course, for the reception of vessels, an item I don't expect will interrupt us for a while. We can talk, if you wish."

"I *do* wish," said Demerest.

"I hope I'm welcome to join in," said Annette.

Demerest looked at her doubtfully, but Bergen said to him, "You'll have to agree. She's fascinated by you and by Moon-men generally. She thinks they're—uh—*you're* a new breed, and I think that when she's quite through being a Deep-woman she wants to be a Moon-woman."

"I just want to get a word in edgewise, John, and when I get that in, I'd like to hear what Mr. Demerest has to say. What do you think of us, Mr. Demerest?"

Demerest said cautiously, "I've asked to come here, Mrs. Bergen, because I'm a safety engineer. Ocean-Deep has an enviable safety record—"

"Not one fatality in almost twenty years," said Bergen cheerfully. "Only one death by accident in the C-shelf settlements and none in transit by either sub or 'scaphe. I wish I could say, though, that this was the result of wisdom and care on our part. We do our best, of course, but the breaks have been with us—"

"John," said Annette, "I really wish you'd let Mr. Demerest speak."

"As a safety engineer," said Demerest, "I can't afford to believe in luck and breaks. We cannot stop Moon-quakes or large meteorites out at Luna City, but we are designed to minimize the effects even of those. There are no excuses or there should be none for human failure. We have not avoided that on Luna City; our record recently has been"—his voice dropped—"bad. While humans are imperfect, as we all know, machinery should be designed to take that imperfection into account. We lost twenty men and women—"

"I know. Still, Luna City has a population of nearly one thousand, doesn't it? Your survival isn't in danger."

"The people on Luna City number nine hundred and seventy-two, including myself, but our survival *is* in danger. We depend on Earth for essentials. That need not always be so; it wouldn't be so right now if the Planetary Project Council could resist the temptation toward pygmy economies—"

"There, at least, Mr. Demerest," said Bergen, "we see eye to eye. We are not self-supporting either, and we could be. What's more, we can't grow much beyond our present level unless nuclear 'scaphes are built. As long as we keep that buoyancy principle, we are limited. Transportation between Deep and Top is slow; slow for men; slower still for matériel and supplies. I've been pushing, Mr. Demerest, for—"

"Yes, and you'll be getting it now, Mr. Bergen, won't you?"

"I hope so, but what makes you so sure?"

"Mr. Bergen, let's not play around. You know very well that Earth is committed to spending a fixed amount of money on expansion projects—on programs designed to expand the human habitat—and that it is not a terribly large amount. Earth's population is not going to lavish resources in an effort to expand either outer space or inner space if it thinks this will cut into the comfort and convenience of Earth's prime habitat, the land surface of the planet."

Annette broke in. "You make it sound callous of Earthmen, Mr. Demerest, and that's unfair. It's only human, isn't it, to want to be secure? Earth is overpopulated and it is only slowly reversing the havoc inflicted on the planet by the Mad Twentieth. Surely man's original home must come first, ahead of either Luna City or Ocean-Deep. Heavens, Ocean-Deep is almost *home* to me, but I can't want to see it flourish at the expense of Earth's land."

"It's not an either-or, Mrs. Bergen," said Demerest earnestly. "If the ocean and outer space are firmly, honestly, and intelligently exploited, it can only redound to Earth's benefit. A small investment will be lost but a large one will redeem itself with profit."

Bergen held up his hand. "Yes, I know. You don't have to argue with me on that point. You'd be trying to convert the converted. Come, let's eat. I tell you what. We'll eat here. If you'll stay with us overnight, or several days for that matter—you're quite welcome—there will be ample time to meet everybody. Perhaps you'd rather take it easy for a while, though."

"Much rather," said Demerest. "Actually, I want to stay here. . . . I would like to ask, by the way, why I met so few people when we went through the units."

"No mystery," said Bergen genially. "At any given time, some fifteen of our men are asleep and perhaps fifteen more are watching films or playing chess or, if their wives are with them—"

"Yes, John," said Annette.

"—And it's customary not to disturb them. The quarters are constricted and what privacy a man can have is cherished. A few are out at sea; three right now, I think. That leaves a dozen or so at work in here and you met them."

"I'll get lunch," said Annette, rising.

She smiled and stepped through the door, which closed automatically behind her.

Bergen looked after her. "That's a concession. She's playing woman for your sake. Ordinarily, it would be just as likely for me to get the lunch. The choice is not defined by sex but by the striking of random lightning."

Demerest said, "The doors between units, it seems to me, are of dangerously limited strength."

"Are they?"

"If an accident happened, and one unit was punctured—"

"No meteorites down here," said Bergen, smiling.

"Oh yes, wrong word. If there were a leak of any sort, for any reason, then could a unit or a group of units be sealed off against the full pressure of the ocean?"

"You mean, in the way that Luna City can have its component units automatically sealed off in case of meteorite puncture in order to limit damage to a single unit."

"Yes," said Demerest with a faint bitterness. "As did *not* happen recently."

"In theory, we could do that, but the chances of accident are much less down here. As I said, there are no meteorites and, what's more, there are no currents to speak of. Even an earthquake centered immediately below us would not be damaging since we make no fixed or solid contact with the ground beneath and are cushioned by the ocean itself against the shocks. So we can afford to gamble on no massive influx."

"Yet if one happened?"

"Then we could be helpless. You see, it is not so easy to seal off component units here. On the Moon, there is a pressure differential of just one atmosphere, one atmosphere inside and the zero atmosphere of vacuum outside. A thin seal is enough. Here at Ocean-Deep the pressure differential is roughly a thousand atmospheres. To secure absolute safety against that differential would take a great deal of money and you know what you said about getting money out of PPC. So we gamble and so far we've been lucky."

"And we haven't," said Demerest.

Bergen looked uncomfortable, but Annette distracted both by coming in with lunch at this moment.

She said, "I hope, Mr. Demerest, that you're prepared for Spartan fare. All our food in Ocean-Deep is prepackaged and requires only heating. We specialize in blandness and non-surprise here, and the non-surprise of the day is a bland chicken à la king, with carrots, boiled potatoes, a piece of something that looks like a brownie for dessert, and, of course, all the coffee you can drink."

Demerest rose to take his tray and tried to smile. "It sounds very like Moon fare, Mrs. Bergen, and I was brought up on that. We grow our own micro-organismic food. It is patriotic to eat that but not particularly enjoyable. We hope to keep improving it, though."

"I'm sure you *will* improve it."

Demerest said, as he ate with a slow and methodical chewing, "I hate to ride my specialty, but how secure are you against mishaps in your air-lock entry?"

"It *is* the weakest point of Ocean-Deep," said Bergen. He had finished eating, well ahead of the other two, and was half through with his first cup of coffee. "But there's got to be an interface, right? The entry is as automatic as we can make it and as fail-safe. Number one: there has to be contact at every point about the outer lock before the fusion generator begins to heat the water within the lock. What's more, the contact has to be metallic and of a metal with just the magnetic permeability we use on our 'scaphes. Presumably a rock or some mythical deep-sea monster might drop down and make contact at just the right places; but if so, nothing happens.

"Then, too, the outer door doesn't open until the steam has pushed the water out and then condensed; in other words, not till both pressure and temperature have dropped below a certain point. At the moment the outer door begins to open, a relatively slight increase in internal pressure, as by water entry, will close it again."

Demerest said, "But then, once men have passed through the lock, the inner door closes behind them and sea water must be allowed into the lock again. Can you do that gradually against the full pressure of the ocean outside?"

"Not very." Bergen smiled. "It doesn't pay to fight the ocean too hard. You have to roll with the punch. We slow it down to about one-tenth free entry but even so it comes in like a rifle shot—louder, a thunderclap, or waterclap, if you prefer. The inner door can hold it, though, and it is not subjected to the strain very often. Well, wait, you heard the waterclap when we first met, when Javan's 'scaphe took off again. Remember?"

"I remember," said Demerest. "But here is something I don't understand. You keep the lock filled with ocean at high pressure at all times to keep the outer door without strain. But that keeps the inner door at full strain. Somewhere there has to be strain."

"Yes, indeed. But if the outer door, with a thousand-atmosphere differential on its two sides, breaks down, the full ocean in all its millions of cubic miles tries to enter and that would be the end of all. If the inner door is the one under strain and it gives, then it will be messy indeed, but the only water that enters Ocean-Deep will be the very limited quantity in the lock and its pressure will drop at once. We will have plenty of time for repair, for the outer door will certainly hold a long time."

"But if both go simultaneously—"

"Then we are through." Bergen shrugged. "I need not tell you that neither absolute certainty nor absolute safety exists. You have to live with some risk and the chance of double and simultaneous failure is so microscopically small that it can be lived with easily."

"If all your mechanical contrivances fail—"

"They fail safe," said Bergen stubbornly.

Demerest nodded. He finished the last of his chicken. Mrs. Bergen was already beginning to clean up. "You'll pardon my questions, Mr. Bergen, I hope."

"You're welcome to ask. I wasn't informed, actually, as to the precise nature of your mission here. 'Fact finding' is a weasel phrase. However, I assume there is keen distress on the Moon over the recent disaster and as safety engineer you rightly feel the responsibility of correcting whatever shortcomings exist and would be interested in learning, if possible, from the system used in Ocean-Deep."

"Exactly. But, see here, if all your automatic contrivances fail safe for some reason, for any reason, you would be alive, but all your escape-hatch mechanisms would be sealed permanently shut. You would be trapped inside Ocean-Deep and would exchange a slow death for a fast one."

"It's not likely to happen but we'd *hope* we could make repairs before our air supply gave out. Besides we *do* have a manual backup system."

"Oh?"

"Certainly. When Ocean-Deep was first established and this was the only unit—the one we're sitting in now—manual controls were all we had. *That* was unsafe, if you like. There they are, right behind you—covered with friable plastic."

"In emergency, break glass," muttered Demerest, inspecting the covered setup.

"Pardon me?"

"Just a phrase commonly used in ancient fire-fighting systems. . . . Well, do the manuals still work, or has the system been covered with your friable plastic for twenty years to the point where it has all decayed into uselessness with no one noticing?"

"Not at all. It's periodically checked, as all our equipment is. That's not my job personally, but I know it is done. If any electrical or electronic circuit is out of its normal working condition, lights flash, signals sound, everything happens but a nuclear blast. . . . You know, Mr. Demerest, we are as curious about Luna City as you are about Ocean-Deep. I presume you would be willing to invite one of our young men—"

"How about a young woman?" interposed Annette at once.

"I am sure you mean yourself, dear," said Bergen, "to which I can only answer that you are determined to have a baby here and to keep it here for a period of time after birth, and that effectively eliminates you from consideration."

Demerest said stiffly, "We hope you will send men to Luna City. We are anxious to have you understand our problems."

"Yes, a mutual exchange of problems and of weeping on each other's shoulders might be of great comfort to all. For instance, you have one advantage on Luna City that I wish we could have. With low gravity and a low pressure differential, you can make your caverns take on any irregular and angular fashion that appeals to your aesthetic sense or is required for convenience. Down here we're restricted to the sphere, at least for the foreseeable future, and our designers develop a hatred for the spherical that surpasses belief. Actually it isn't funny. It breaks them down. They eventually resign rather than continue to work spherically."

Bergen shook his head and leaned his chair back against a microfilm cabinet. "You know," he continued, "when William Beebe built the first deep-sea chamber in history in the 1930s—it was just a gondola suspended from a mother ship by a half-mile cable, with no buoyancy chambers and no engines, and if the cable broke, good night, only it never did. . . . Anyway, what was I saying? Oh, when Beebe built his first deep-sea chamber, he was going to make it cylindrical; you know, so a man would fit in it comfortably. After all, a man is essentially a tall, skinny cylinder. However, a friend of his argued him out of that and into a sphere on the very sensible grounds that a sphere would resist pressure more efficiently than any other possible shape. You know who that friend was?"

"No, I'm afraid I don't."

"The man who was President of the United States at the time of Beebe's descents—Franklin D. Roosevelt. All these spheres you see down here are the great-grandchildren of Roosevelt's suggestion."

Demerest considered that briefly but made no comment. He returned to the earlier topic. "We would particularly like someone from Ocean-Deep," he said, "to visit Luna City because it might lead to a great enough understanding of the need, on Ocean-Deep's part, for a course of action that might involve considerable self-sacrifice."

"Oh?" Bergen's chair came down flat-leggedly on all fours. "How's that?"

"Ocean-Deep is a marvelous achievement; I wish to detract nothing from that. I can see where it will become greater still, a wonder of the world. *Still*—"

"Still?"

"Still the oceans are only a part of the Earth; a major part, but only a part. The deep sea is only part of the ocean. It is inner space indeed; it works inward, narrowing constantly to a point."

"I think," broke in Annette, looking rather grim, "that you're about to make a comparison with Luna City."

"Indeed I am," said Demerest. "Luna City represents outer space, widening to infinity. There is nowhere to go down here in the long run; everywhere to go out there."

"We don't judge by size and volume alone, Mr. Demerest," said Bergen. "The ocean is only a small part of Earth, true, but for that very reason it is intimately connected with over five billion human beings. Ocean-Deep is experimental but the settlements on the continental shelf already deserve the name of cities. Ocean-Deep offers mankind the chance of exploiting the whole planet—"

"Of polluting the whole planet," broke in Demerest excitedly. "Of raping it, of ending it. The concentration of human effort to Earth itself is unhealthy and even fatal if it isn't balanced by a turning outward to the frontier."

"There is nothing at the frontier," said Annette, snapping out the words. "The Moon is dead, all the other worlds out there are dead. If there are live worlds among the stars, light-years away, they can't be reached. This ocean is *living*."

"The Moon is living too, Mrs. Bergen, and if Ocean-Deep allows it, the Moon will become an independent world. We Moon-men will then see to it that other worlds are reached and made alive and, if mankind but has patience, we will reach the stars. We! We! It is only we Moon-men, used to space, used to a world in a cavern, used to an engineered environment, who could endure life in a spaceship that may have to travel centuries to reach the stars."

"Wait, wait, Demerest," said Bergen, holding up his hand. "Back up! What do you mean, if Ocean-Deep allows it? What have we to do with it?"

"You're competing with us, Mr. Bergen. The Planetary Project Commission will swing your way, give you more, give us less, because in the short term, as your wife says, the ocean is alive and the Moon, except for a thousand men, is not; because you are a half-dozen miles away and we a quarter of a million; because you can be reached in an hour and we only in three days. And because you have an ideal safety record and we have had—misfortunes."

"The last, surely, is trivial. Accidents can happen any time, anywhere."

"But the trivial can be used," said Demerest angrily. "It can be made to manipulate emotions. To people who don't see the purpose and the importance of space exploration, the death of Moon-men in accidents is proof enough that the Moon is dangerous, that its colonization is a useless fantasy. Why not? It's their excuse for saving money and they can then salve their consciences by investing part of it in Ocean-Deep instead. That's why I said the accident on the Moon had threatened the survival of Luna City even though it killed only twenty people out of nearly a thousand."

"I don't accept your argument. There has been enough money for both for a score of years."

"Not enough money. That's exactly it. Not enough investment to make the Moon self-supporting in all these years, and then they use that lack of self-support against us. Not enough investment to make Ocean-Deep self-supporting either. . . . But now they can give you enough if they cut us out altogether."

"Do you think that will happen?"

"I'm almost sure it will, unless Ocean-Deep shows a statesmanlike concern for man's future."

"How?"

"By refusing to accept additional funds. By not competing with Luna City. By putting the good of the whole race ahead of self-interest."

"Surely you don't expect us to dismantle—"

"You won't have to. Don't you see? Join us in explaining that Luna City is essential, that space exploration is the hope of mankind; that you will wait, retrench, if necessary."

Bergen looked at his wife and raised his eyebrows. She shook her head angrily. Bergen said, "You have a rather romantic view of the PPC, I think. Even if I made noble, self-sacrificing speeches, who's to say they would listen? There's a great deal more involved in the matter of Ocean-Deep than my opinion and my statements. There are economic considerations and public feeling. Why don't you relax, Mr. Demerest? Luna City won't come to an end. You'll receive funds. I'm sure of it. I tell you, I'm sure of it. Now let's break this up—"

"No, I've got to convince you one way or another that I'm serious. If necessary, Ocean-Deep must come to a halt unless the PPC can supply ample funds for both."

Bergen said, "Is this some sort of official mission, Mr. Demerest? Are you speaking for Luna City officially, or just for yourself?"

"Just for myself, but maybe that's enough, Mr. Bergen."

"I don't think it is. I'm sorry, but this is turning out to be unpleasant. I suggest that, after all, you had better return Topside on the first available 'scaphe."

"Not yet! Not yet!" Demerest looked about wildly, then rose unsteadily and put his back against the wall. He was a little too tall for the room and he became conscious of life receding. One more step and he would have gone too far to back out.

He had told them back on the Moon that there would be no use talking, no use negotiating. It was dog-eat-dog for the available funds and Luna City's destiny must not be aborted; not for Ocean-Deep; not for Earth; no, not for all of Earth, since mankind and the Universe came even before the Earth. Man must outgrow his womb and—

Demerest could hear his own ragged breathing and the inner turmoil of his whirling thoughts. The other two were looking at him with what seemed concern. Annette rose and said, "Are you ill, Mr. Demerest?"

"I am *not* ill. Sit down. I'm a safety engineer and I want to teach you about safety. Sit *down*, Mrs. Bergen."

"Sit down, Annette," said Bergen. "I'll take care of him." He rose and took a step forward.

But Demerest said, "No. Don't you move either. I have something right here. You're too naïve concerning human dangers, Mr. Bergen. You guard against the sea and against mechanical failure and you don't search your human visitors, do you? I have a weapon, Bergen."

Now that it was out and he had taken the final step, from which there was no returning, for he was now dead whatever he did, he was quite calm.

Annette said, "Oh, John," and grasped her husband's arm. "He's—"

Bergen stepped in front of her. "A weapon? Is that what that thing is? Now slowly, Demerest, slowly. There's nothing to get hot over. If you want to talk, we will talk. What is that?"

"Nothing dramatic. A portable laser beam."

"But what do you want to do with it?"

"Destroy Ocean-Deep."

"But you can't, Demerest. You know you can't. There's only so much energy you can pack into your fist and any laser you can hold can't pump enough heat to penetrate the walls."

"I know that. This packs more energy than you think. It's Moon-made and there are some advantages to manufacturing the energy unit in a vacuum. But you're right. Even so, it's designed only for small jobs and requires frequent recharging. So I don't intend to try to cut through a foot-plus of alloy steel. . . . But it will do the job indirectly. For one thing, it will keep you two quiet. There's enough energy in my fist to kill two people."

"You wouldn't kill us," said Bergen evenly. "You have no reason."

"If by that," said Demerest, "you imply that I am an unreasoning being to be somehow made to understand my madness, forget it. I have every reason to kill you and I *will* kill you. By laser beam if I have to, though I would rather not."

"What good will killing us do you? Make me understand. Is it that I have refused to sacrifice Ocean-Deep funds? I couldn't do anything else. I'm not really the one to make the decision. And if you kill me, that won't help you force the decision in your direction, will it? In fact, quite the contrary. If a Moon-man is a murderer, how will that reflect on Luna City? Consider human emotions on Earth."

There was just an edge of shrillness in Annette's voice as she joined in. "Don't you see there will be people who will say that Solar radiation on the Moon has dangerous effects? That the genetic engineering which has reorganized your bones and muscles has affected mental stability? Consider the word 'lunatic,' Mr. Demerest. Men once believed the Moon brought madness."

"I am not mad, Mrs. Bergen."

"It doesn't matter," said Bergen, following his wife's lead smoothly. "Men will say that you were; that all Moon-men are; and Luna City will be closed down and the Moon itself closed to all further exploration, perhaps forever. Is that what you want?"

"That might happen if they thought I killed you, but they won't. It will be an accident." With his left elbow, Demerest broke the plastic that covered the manual controls.

"I know units of this sort," he said. "I know exactly how it works. Logically, breaking that plastic should set up a warning flash—after all, it might be broken by accident—and then someone would be here to investigate or, better yet, the controls should lock until deliberately released to make sure the break was not merely accidental."

He paused, then said, "But I'm sure no one will come; that no warning has taken place. Your manual system is not fail-safe because in your heart you were sure it would never be used."

"What do you plan to do?" said Bergen.

He was tense and Demerest watched his knees carefully, and said, "If you try to jump toward me, I'll shoot at once, and then keep right on with what I'm doing."

"I think maybe you're giving me nothing to lose."

"You'll lose time. Let me go right on without interference and you'll have some minutes to keep on talking. You may even be able to talk me out of it. There's my proposal. Don't interfere with me and I will give you your chance to argue."

"But what do you plan to do?"

"This," said Demerest. He did not have to look. His left hand snaked out and closed a contact. "The fusion unit will now pump heat into the air lock and the steam will empty it. It will take a few minutes. When it's done, I'm sure one of those little red-glass buttons will light."

"Are you going to—"

Demerest said, "Why do you ask? You know that I must be intending, having gone this far, to flood Ocean-Deep?"

"But why? Damn it, why?"

"Because it will be marked down as an accident. Because your safety record will be spoiled. Because it will be a complete catastrophe and will wipe you out. And PPC will then turn from you, and the glamour of Ocean-Deep will be gone. *We* will get the funds; *we* will continue. If I could bring that to pass in some other way, I would, but the needs of Luna City are the needs of mankind and those are paramount."

"You will die, too," Annette managed to say.

"Of course. Once I am forced to do something like this, would I *want* to live? I'm not a murderer."

"But you will be. If you flood this unit, you will flood all of Ocean-Deep and kill everyone in it—and doom those who are out in their subs to slower death. Fifty men and women—an unborn child—"

"That is not my fault," said Demerest, in clear pain. "I did not expect to find a pregnant woman here, but now that I have, I can't stop because of that."

"But you must stop," said Bergen. "Your plan won't work unless what happens can be shown to be an accident. They'll find you with a beam emitter in your hand and with the manual controls clearly tampered with. Do you think they won't deduce the truth from that?"

Demerest was feeling very tired. "Mr. Bergen, you sound desperate. Listen— When the outer door opens, water under a thousand atmospheres of pressure will enter. It will be a massive battering ram that will destroy and mangle everything in its path. The walls of the Ocean-Deep units will remain but everything inside will be twisted beyond recognition. Human beings will be mangled into shredded tissue and splintered bone and death will be instantaneous and unfelt. Even if I were to burn you to death with the laser there would be nothing left to show it had been done, so I won't hesitate, you see. This manual unit will be smashed anyway; anything I can do will be erased by the water."

"But the beam emitter, the laser gun. Even damaged, it will be recognizable," said Annette.

"We use such things on the Moon, Mrs. Bergen. It is a common tool; it is the optical analogue of a jackknife. I could kill you with a jackknife, you know, but one would not deduce that a man carrying a jackknife, or even holding one with the blade open, was necessarily planning murder. He might be whittling. Besides, a Moon-made laser is not a projectile gun. It doesn't have to withstand an internal explosion. It is made of thin metal, mechanically weak. After it is smashed by the waterclap I doubt that it will make much sense as an object."

Demerest did not have to think to make these statements. He had worked them out within himself through months of self-debate back on the Moon.

"In fact," he went on, "how will the investigators ever know what happened in here? They will send 'scaphes down to inspect what is left of Ocean-Deep, but how can they get inside without first pumping the water out? They will, in effect, have to build a new Ocean-Deep and that would take—how long? Perhaps, given public reluctance to waste money, they might never do it at all and content themselves with dropping a laurel wreath on the dead walls of the dead Ocean-Deep."

Bergen said, "The men on Luna City will know what you have done. Surely one of them will have a conscience. The truth will be known."

"One truth," said Demerest, "is that I am not a fool. No one on Luna City knows what I planned to do or will suspect what I have done. They sent me down here to negotiate cooperation on the matter of financial grants. I was to argue and nothing more. There's not even a laser-beam emitter missing up there. I put this one together myself out of scrapped parts. . . . And it works. I've tested it."

Annette said slowly, "You haven't thought it through. Do you know what you're doing?"

"I've thought it through. I know what I'm doing. . . . And I know also that you are both conscious of the lit signal. I'm aware of it. The air lock is empty and time's up, I'm afraid."

Rapidly, holding his beam emitter tensely high, he closed another contact. A circular part of the unit wall cracked into a thin crescent and rolled smoothly away.

Out of the corner of his eye, Demerest saw the gaping darkness, but he did not look. A dankly salt vapor issued from it; a queer odor of dead steam. He even imagined he could hear the flopping sound of the gathered water at the bottom of the lock.

Demerest said, "In a rational manual unit, the outer door ought to be frozen shut now. With the inner door open, nothing ought to make the outer door open. I suspect, though, that the manuals were put together too quickly at first for that precaution to have been taken, and it was replaced too quickly for that precaution to have been added. And if I need further evidence of that, you wouldn't be sitting there so tensely if you knew the outer door wouldn't open. I need touch one more contact and the waterclap will come. We will feel nothing."

Annette said, "Don't push it just yet. I have one more thing to say. You said we would have time to persuade you."

"While the water was being pushed out."

"Just let me say this. A minute. A *minute*. I said you didn't know what you were doing. You don't. You're destroying the space program, the *space* program. There's more to space than *space*." Her voice had grown shrill.

Demerest frowned. "What are you talking about? Make sense, or I'll end it all. I'm tired. I'm frightened. I want it over."

Annette said, "You're not in the inner councils of the PPC. Neither is my husband. But I am. Do you think because I am a woman that I'm secondary here? I'm not. You, Mr. Demerest, have your eyes fixed on Luna City only. My husband has his fixed on Ocean-Deep. Neither of you know *anything*.

"Where do you expect to go, Mr. Demerest, if you had all the money you wanted? Mars? The asteroids? The satellites of the gas giants? These are all small worlds; all dry surfaces under a blank sky. It may be generations before we are ready to try for the stars and till then we'd have only pygmy real estate. Is that your ambition?

"My husband's ambition is no better. He dreams of pushing man's habitat over the ocean floor, a surface not much larger in the last analysis than the surface of the Moon and the other pygmy worlds. We of the PPC, on the other hand, want more than either of you, and if you push that button, Mr. Demerest, the greatest dream mankind has ever had will come to nothing."

Demerest found himself interested despite himself, but he said, "You're just babbling." It was possible, he knew, that somehow they had warned others in Ocean-Deep, that any moment someone would come to interrupt, someone would try to shoot him down. He was, however, staring at the only opening, and he had only to close one contact, without even looking, in a second's movement.

Annette said, "I'm not babbling. You know it took more than rocket ships to colonize the Moon. To make a successful colony possible, men had to be altered genetically and adjusted to low gravity. You are a product of such genetic engineering."

"Well?"

"And might not genetic engineering also help adjust men to greater gravitational pull? What is the largest planet of the Solar System, Mr. Demerest?"

"Jupi—"

"Yes, Jupiter. Eleven times the diameter of the Earth; forty times the diameter of the Moon. A surface a hundred and twenty times that of the Earth in area; sixteen hundred times that of the Moon. Conditions so different from anything we can encounter anywhere on the worlds the size of Earth or less that any scientist of any persuasion would give half his life for a chance to observe at close range."

"But Jupiter is an impossible target."

"Indeed?" said Annette, and even managed a faint smile. "As impossible as flying? Why is it impossible? Genetic engineering could design men with stronger and denser bones, stronger and more compact muscles. The same principles that enclose Luna City against the vacuum and Ocean-Deep against the sea can also enclose the future Jupiter-Deep against its ammoniated surroundings."

"The gravitational field—"

"Can be negotiated by nuclear-powered ships that are now on the drawing board. You don't know that but I do."

"We're not even sure about the depth of the atmosphere. The pressures—"

"The pressures! The *pressures*! Mr. Demerest, look about you. Why do you suppose Ocean-Deep was *really* built? To exploit the ocean? The settlements on the continental shelf are doing that quite adequately. To gain knowledge of the deep-sea bottom? We could do that by 'scaphe easily and we could then have spared the hundred billion dollars invested in Ocean-Deep so far.

"Don't you see, Mr. Demerest, that Ocean-Deep must mean something more than that? The purpose of Ocean-Deep is to devise the ultimate vessels and mechanisms that will suffice to explore and colonize *Jupiter*. Look about you and see the beginnings of a Jovian environment; the closest approach we can come to it on Earth. It is only a faint image of mighty Jupiter, but it's a beginning.

"Destroy this, Mr. Demerest, and you destroy any hope for Jupiter. On the other hand, let us live and we will, together, penetrate and settle the brightest jewel of the Solar System. And long before we can reach the limits of Jupiter, we will be ready for the stars, for the Earth-type planets circling them, *and* the Jupiter-type planets, too. Luna City won't be abandoned because *both* are necessary for this ultimate aim."

For the moment, Demerest had altogether forgotten about that last button. He said, "Nobody on Luna City has heard of this."

"*You* haven't. There are those on Luna City who know. If you had told them of your plan of destruction, they would have stopped you. Naturally, we can't make this common knowledge and only a few people anywhere can know. The public supports only with difficulty the planetary projects now in progress. If the PPC is parsimonious it is because public opinion limits its generosity. What do you suppose public opinion would say if they thought we were aiming toward Jupiter? What a super-boondoggle that would be in their eyes. But we continue and what money we can save and make use of we place in the various facets of Project Big World."

"Project Big World?"

"Yes," said Annette. "You know now and I have committed a serious security breach. But it doesn't matter, does it? Since we're all dead and since the project is, too."

"Wait now, Mrs. Bergen."

"If you change your mind now, don't think you can ever talk about Project Big World. That would end the project just as effectively as destruction here would. And it would end both your career and mine. It might end Luna City and Ocean-Deep, too—so now that you know, maybe it makes no difference anyway. You might just as well push that button."

"I said wait—" Demerest's brow was furrowed and his eyes burned with anguish. "I don't know—"

Bergen gathered for the sudden jump as Demerest's tense alertness wavered into uncertain introspection, but Annette grasped her husband's sleeve.

A timeless interval that might have been ten seconds long followed and then Demerest held out his laser. "Take it," he said. "I'll consider myself under arrest."

"You can't be arrested," said Annette, "without the whole story coming out." She took the laser and gave it to Bergen. "It will be enough that you return to Luna City and keep silent. Till then we will keep you under guard."

Bergen was at the manual controls. The inner door slid shut and after that there was the thunderous waterclap of the water returning into the lock.

Husband and wife were alone again. They had not dared say a word until Demerest was safely put to sleep under the watchful eyes of two men detailed for the purpose. The unexpected waterclap had roused everybody and a sharply bowdlerized account of the incident had been given out.

The manual controls were now locked off and Bergen said, "From this point on, the manuals will have to be adjusted to fail-safe. And visitors will have to be searched."

"Oh, John," said Annette. "I think people are insane. There we were, facing death for us and for Ocean-Deep; just the end of everything. And I kept thinking—I must keep calm; I mustn't have a miscarriage."

"You kept calm all right. You were magnificent. I mean, Project Big World! I never conceived of such a thing, but by—by—*Jove*, it's an attractive thought. It's wonderful."

"I'm sorry I had to say all that, John. It was all a fake, of course. I made it up. Demerest wanted me to make something up really. He wasn't a killer or destroyer; he was, according to his own overheated light, a patriot, and I suppose he was telling himself he must destroy in order to save—a common enough view among the small-minded. But he *said* he would give us time to talk him out of it and I think he was praying we would manage to do so. He wanted us to think of something that would give him the excuse to save in order to save, and I gave it to him. . . . I'm sorry I had to fool you, John."

"You didn't fool me."

"I didn't?"

"How could you? I knew you weren't a member of PPC."

"What made you so sure of that? Because I'm a woman?"

"Not at all. Because *I'm* a member, Annette, and *that's* confidential. And, if you don't mind, I will begin a move to initiate exactly what you suggested—Project Big World."

"Well!" Annette considered that and, slowly, smiled. "Well! That's not bad. Women do have their uses."

"Something," said Bergen, smiling also, "I have never denied."

WEYR SEARCH

Anne McCaffrey

Anne McCaffrey's major work in hard science fiction for three decades has been her continuing series of stories chronicling the history of the planet Pern. Originally begun under the tutelage of John W. Campbell in the late sixties, this popular exercise in hard sf world-building, complete with astrophysics and environment in the tradition of *Mission of Gravity* and *Dune,* has become the locale of many fantastic and romantic adventures, from the first book, *Dragonflight* (1968) to the most recent, *All the Weyrs of Pern* (1991). The telepathic dragons of Pern have become McCaffrey's trademark; although she has written other sf, notably *The Ship Who Sang* (1969), it is the Pern books that are automatic best-sellers today. And while they are read by hard sf fans who appreciate the world-building in the background, the mass audience undoubtedly reads them as romantic fantasies about dragons, not science fiction at all (a fact that has caused the author some dismay over the years—she vigorously, and correctly, maintains that she writes science fiction—world-building is hard work).

It is true that the stories set on Pern often have little to do with the attitudes of hard science fiction and a lot to do with the emotional bonds between humans and the dragons they ride. It is further the case that the enormous success of the series has liberated other writers both of fantasy and science fiction to pursue the direction of romantic adventure, with or without world-building, to popularity and financial success. But in genre fiction, intentions count. McCaffrey intended it as hard sf, and "Weyr Search" exists in conscious dialogue with the traditions of hard science fiction, in the lineage of *Dune*.

Intentionally or not, McCaffrey has forged a connection between world-building sf and world-building fantasy of the lineage of Tolkien's *The Lord of the Rings* and Le Guin's Earthsea. In an era when the contemporary genre fantasy was being created to a significant extent by science-fiction writers (such as Fritz Leiber) turning their talents to the creation of fantasy worlds, Pern exists as a sort of bridge between the technical rigors of hard sf and the historical, anthropological, and philological rigors of Tolkien, whose concept of the creation of a Secondary World in fantasy fiction (elucidated in his 1947 essay, "On Fairy Tales") has profoundly influenced the evolution of both fantasy and science fiction since. McCaffrey's blend, in the Pern cycle, makes her as influential on the body of sf outside hard sf as Hal Clement is on hard sf itself.

When is a legend legend? Why is a myth a myth? How old and disused must a fact be for it to be relegated to the category: Fairy tale? And why do certain facts remain incontrovertible, while others lose their validity to assume a shabby, unstable character?

Rukbat, in the Sagittarian sector, was a golden G-type star. It had five planets, plus one stray it had attracted and held in recent millennia. Its third planet was enveloped by air man could breathe, boasted water he could drink, and possessed a gravity which permitted man to walk confidently erect. Men discovered it, and promptly colonized it, as they did every habitable planet they came to and then—whether callously or through collapse of empire, the colonists never discovered, and eventually forgot to ask—left the colonies to fend for themselves.

When men first settled on Rukbat's third world, and named it Pern, they had taken little notice of the stranger-planet, swinging around its primary in a wildly erratic elliptical orbit. Within a few generations they had forgotten its existence. The desperate path the wanderer pursued brought it close to its stepsister very two hundred [Terran] years at perihelion.

When the aspects were harmonious and the conjunction with its sister-planet close enough, as it often was, the indigenous life of the wanderer sought to bridge the space gap to the more temperate and hospitable planet.

It was during the frantic struggle to combat this menace dropping through Pern's skies like silver threads, that Pern's contact with the mother-planet weakened and broke. Recollections of Earth receded further from Pernese history with each successive generation until memory of their origins degenerated past legend or myth, into oblivion.

To forestall the incursions of the dreaded Threads, the Pernese, with the ingenuity of their forgotten Yankee forebears and between first onslaught and return, developed a highly specialized variety of a life form indigenous to their adopted planet—the winged, tailed, and firebreathing dragons, named for the Earth legend they resembled. Such humans as had a high empathy rating and some innate telepathic ability were trained to make use of and preserve this unusual animal whose ability to teleport was of immense value in the fierce struggle to keep Pern bare of Threads.

The dragons and their dragonmen, a breed apart, and the shortly renewed menace they battled, created a whole new group of legends and myths.

As the menace was conquered the populace in the Holds of Pern settled into a more comfortable way of life. Most of the dragon Weyrs eventually were abandoned, and the descendants of heroes fell into disfavor, as the legends fell into disrepute.

This, then, is a tale of legends disbelieved and their restoration. Yet—how goes a legend? When is myth?

Drummer, beat, and piper, blow,
Harper, strike, and soldier, go.
Free the flame and sear the grasses
Till the dawning Red Star passes.

Lessa woke, cold. Cold with more than the chill of the everlastingly clammy stone walls. Cold with the prescience of a danger greater than when, ten full Turns ago, she had run, whimpering, to hide in the watch-wher's odorous lair.

Rigid with concentration, Lessa lay in the straw of the redolent cheese room, sleeping quarters shared with the other kitchen drudges. There was an urgency in the ominous portent unlike any other forewarning. She touched the awareness of the watch-wher, slithering on its rounds in the courtyard. It circled at the choke-limit of its chain. It was restless, but oblivious to anything unusual in the pre-dawn darkness.

The danger was definitely not within the walls of Hold Ruath. Nor approaching the paved perimeter without the Hold where relentless grass had forced new growth through the ancient mortar, green witness to the deterioration of the once stone-clean Hold. The danger was not advancing up the now little used causeway from the valley, nor lurking in the craftsmen's stony holdings at the foot of the Hold's cliff. It did not scent the wind that blew from Tillek's cold shores. But still it twanged sharply through her senses, vibrating every nerve in Lessa's slender frame. Fully roused, she sought to identify it before the prescient mood dissolved. She cast outward, towards the Pass, farther than she had ever pressed. Whatever threatened was not in Ruatha . . . yet. Nor did it have a familiar flavor. It was not, then, Fax.

Lessa had been cautiously pleased that Fax had not shown himself at Hold Ruath in three full Turns. The apathy of the craftsmen, the decaying farmholds, even the green-etched stones of the Hold infuriated Fax, self-styled Lord of the High Reaches, to the point where he preferred to forget the reason why he had subjugated the once proud and profitable Hold.

Lessa picked her way among the sleeping drudges, huddled together for warmth, and glided up the worn steps to the kitchen-proper. She slipped across the cavernous kitchen to the stable-yard door. The cobbles of the yard were icy through the thin soles of her sandals and she shivered as the predawn air penetrated her patched garment.

The watch-wher slithered across the yard to greet her, pleading, as it always did, for release. Glancing fondly down at the awesome head, she promised it a good rub presently. It crouched, groaning, at the end of its chain as she continued to the grooved steps that led to the rampart over the Hold's massive gate. Atop the tower, Lessa stared towards the east where the stony breasts of the Pass rose in black relief against the gathering day.

Indecisively she swung to her left, for the sense of danger issued from that direction as well. She glanced upward, her eyes drawn to the red star which had recently begun to dominate the dawn sky. As she stared, the star radiated a final ruby pulsation before its magnificence was lost in the brightness of Pern's rising sun.

For the first time in many Turns, Lessa gave thought to matters beyond Pern, beyond her dedication to vengeance on the murderer Fax for the annihilation of her family. Let him but come within Ruath Hold now and he would never leave.

But the brilliant ruby sparkle of the Red Star recalled the Disaster Ballads—grim narratives of the heroism of the dragon-riders as they braved the dangers of *between* to breathe fiery death on the silver Threads that dropped through Pern's skies. Not one Thread must fall to the rich soil, to burrow deep and multiply, leaching the earth of minerals and fertility. Straining her eyes as if vision would bridge the gap between peril and person, she stared intently eastward. The watch-wher's thin, whistled question reached her just as the prescience waned.

Dawnlight illumined the tumbled landscape, the unplowed fields in the valley below. Dawnlight fell on twisted orchards, where the sparse herds of milchbeasts hunted stray blades of spring grass. Grass in Ruatha grew where it should not, died where it should flourish. An odd brooding smile curved Lessa's lips. Fax realized no profit from his conquest of Ruatha . . . nor would he, while she, Lessa, lived. And he had not the slightest suspicion of the source of this undoing.

Or had he? Lessa wondered, her mind still reverberating from the savage prescience of danger. East lay Fax's ancestral and only legitimate Hold. Northeast lay little but bare and stony mountains and Benden, the remaining Weyr, which protected Pern.

Lessa stretched, arching her back, inhaling the sweet, untainted wind of morning.

A cock crowed in the stableyard. Lessa whirled, her face alert, eyes darting around the outer Hold lest she be observed in such an uncharacteristic pose. She unbound her hair, letting it fall about her face concealingly. Her body drooped into the sloppy posture she affected. Quickly she thudded down the the stairs, crossing to the watch-wher. It lurred piteously, its great eyes blinking against the growing daylight. Oblivious to the stench of its rank breath, she hugged the scaly head to her, scratching its ears and eye ridges. The watch-wher was ecstatic with pleasure, its long body trembling, its clipped wings rustling. It alone knew who she was or cared. And it was the only creature in all Pern she trusted since the day she had blindly sought refuge in its dark stinking lair to escape Fax's thirsty swords that had drunk so deeply of Ruathan blood.

Slowly she rose, cautioning it to remember to be as vicious to her as to all should anyone be near. It promised to obey her, swaying back and forth to emphasize its reluctance.

The first rays of the sun glanced over the Hold's outer wall. Crying out, the watch-wher darted into its dark nest. Lessa crept back to the kitchen and into the cheese room.

From the Weyr and from the Bowl
Bronze and brown and blue and green
Rise the dragonmen of Pern,
Aloft, on wing, seen, then unseen.

F'lar on bronze Mnementh's great neck appeared first in the skies above the chief Hold of Fax, so-called Lord of the High Reaches. Behind him, in proper wedge formation, the wingmen came into sight. F'lar checked the formation automatically; as precise as at the moment of entry to *between*.

As Mnementh curved in an arc that would bring them to the perimeter of the Hold, consonant with the friendly nature of this visitation, F'lar surveyed with mounting aversion the disrepair of the ridge defenses. The firestone pits were empty and the rock-cut gutters radiating from the pits were green-tinged with a mossy growth.

Was there even one lord in Pern who maintained his Hold rocky in observance of the ancient Laws? F'lar's lips tightened to a thinner line. When this Search was over and the Impression made, there would have to be a solemn, punitive Council held at the Weyr. And by the golden shell of the queen, he, F'lar, meant to be its moderator. He would replace lethargy with industry. He would scour the green and dangerous scum from the heights of Pern, the grass blades from its stoneworks. No verdant skirt would be condoned in any farmhold. And the tithings which had been so miserly, so grudgingly presented would, under pain of firestoning, flow with decent generosity into the Dragonweyr.

Mnementh rumbled approvingly as he vaned his pinions to land lightly on the grass-etched flagstones of Fax's Hold. The bronze dragon furled his great wings, and F'lar heard the warning claxon in the Hold's Great Tower. Mnementh dropped to his knees as F'lar indicated he wished to dismount. The bronze rider stood by Mnementh's huge wedge-shaped head, politely awaiting the arrival of the Hold lord. F'lar idly gazed down the valley, hazy with warm spring sunlight. He ignored the furtive heads that peered at the dragonman from the parapet slits and the cliff windows.

F'lar did not turn as a rush of air announced the arrival of the rest of the wing. He knew, however, when F'nor, the brown rider, his halfbrother, took the customary position on his left, a dragon-length to the rear. F'lar caught a glimpse of F'nor's boot-heel twisting to death the grass crowding up between the stones.

An order, muffled to an intense whisper, issued from within the great court, beyond the open gates. Almost immediately a group of men marched into sight, led by a heavyset man of medium height.

Mnementh arched his neck, angling his head so that his chin rested on the ground. Mnementh's many-faceted eyes, on a level with F'lar's head, fastened with disconcerting interest on the approaching party. The dragons could never understand why they generated such abject fear in common folk. At only one point in his life span would a dragon attack a human and that could be excused on the grounds of simple ignorance. F'lar could not explain to the dragon the politics behind the necessity of inspiring awe in the holders, lord and craftsman alike. He could only observe that the fear and apprehension showing in the faces of the advancing squad which troubled Mnementh was oddly pleasing to him, F'lar.

"Welcome, Bronze Rider, to the Hold of Fax, Lord of the High Reaches. He is at your service," and the man made an adequately respectful salute.

The use of the third person pronoun could be construed, by the meticulous, to be a veiled insult. This fit in with the information F'lar had on Fax; so he ignored it. His information was also correct in describing Fax as a greedy man. It showed in the restless eyes which flicked at every detail of F'lar's clothing, at the slight frown when the intricately etched sword-hilt was noticed.

F'lar noticed, in his own turn, the several rich rings which flashed on Fax's left hand. The overlord's right hand remained slightly cocked after the habit of the professional swordsman. His tunic, of rich fabric, was stained and none too fresh. The man's feet, in heavy wher-hide boots, were solidly planted, weight balanced forward on his toes. A man to be treated cautiously, F'lar decided, as one should the conqueror of five neighboring Holds. Such greedy audacity was in itself a revelation. Fax had married into a sixth . . . and had legally inherited, however unusual the circumstances, the seventh. He was a lecherous man by reputation.

Within these seven Holds, F'lar anticipated a profitable Search. Let R'gul go southerly to pursue Search among the indolent, if lovely, women there. The Weyr needed a strong woman this time; Jora had been worse than useless with Nemorth. Adversity, uncertainty: those were the conditions that bred the qualities F'lar wanted in a weyrwoman.

"We ride in Search," F'lar drawled softly, "and request the hospitality of your Hold, Lord Fax."

Fax's eyes widened imperceptibly at mention of Search.

"I had heard Jora was dead," Fax replied, dropping the third person abruptly as if F'lar had passed some sort of test by ignoring it. "So Nemorth has a new queen, hm-m-m?" he continued, his eyes darting across the rank of the ring, noting the disciplined stance of the riders, the healthy color of the dragons.

F'lar did not dignify the obvious with an answer.

"And, my Lord—?" Fax hesitated, expectantly inclining his head slightly towards the dragonman.

For a pulse beat, F'lar wondered if the man were deliberately provoking him with such subtle insults. The name of bronze riders should be as well known throughout Pern as the name of the Dragonqueen and her Weyrwoman. F'lar kept his face composed, his eyes on Fax's.

Leisurely, with the proper touch of arrogance, F'nor stepped forward, stopping slightly behind Mnementh's head, one hand negligently touching the jaw hinge of the huge beast.

"The Bronze Rider of Mnementh, Lord F'lar, will require quarters for himself. I, F'nor, brown rider, prefer to be lodged with the wingmen. We are, in number, twelve."

F'lar liked that touch of F'nor's, totting up the wing strength, as if Fax were incapable of counting. F'nor had phrased it so adroitly as to make it impossible for Fax to protest the insult.

"Lord F'lar," Fax said through teeth fixed in a smile, "the High Reaches are honored with your Search."

"It will be to the credit of the High Reaches," F'lar replied smoothly, "if one of its own supplies the Weyr."

"To our everlasting credit," Fax replied as suavely. "In the old days, many notable weyrwomen came from my Holds."

"Your Holds?" asked F'lar, politely smiling as he emphasized the plural. "Ah, yes, you are now overlord of Ruatha, are you not? There have been many from that Hold."

A strange tense look crossed Fax's face. "Nothing good comes from Ruath Hold." Then he stepped aside, gesturing F'lar to enter the Hold.

Fax's troop leader barked a hasty order and the men formed two lines, their metal-edged boots flicking sparks from the stones.

At unspoken orders, all the dragon rose with a great churning of air and dust. F'lar strode nonchalantly past the welcoming files. The men were rolling their eyes in alarm as the beasts glided above to the inner courts. Someone on the high tower uttered a frightened yelp as Mnementh took his position on that vantage point. His great wings drove phosphoric-scented air across the inner court as he maneuvered his great frame onto the inadequate landing space.

Outwardly oblivious to the consternation, fear and awe the dragons inspired, F'lar was secretly amused and rather pleased by the effect. Lords of the Holds needed this reminder that they must deal with dragons, not just with riders, who were men, mortal and murderable. The ancient respect for dragonmen as well as dragonkind must be reinstilled in modern breasts.

"The Hold has just risen from table, Lord F'lar, if . . ." Fax suggested. His voice trailed off at F'lar's smiling refusal.

"Convey my duty to your lady, Lord Fax," F'lar rejoined, noticing with inward satisfaction the tightening of Fax's jaw muscles at the ceremonial request.

"You would prefer to see your quarters first?" Fax countered.

F'lar flicked an imaginary speck from his soft wher-hide sleeve and shook his head. Was the man buying time to sequester his ladies as the old time lords had?

"Duty first," he said with a rueful shrug.

"Of course," Fax all but snapped and strode smartly ahead, his heels pounding out the anger he could not express otherwise. F'lar decided he had guessed correctly.

F'lar and F'nor followed at a slower pace through the double-doored entry with its massive metal panels, into the great hall, carved into the cliffside.

"They eat not badly," F'nor remarked casually to F'lar, appraising the remants still on the table.

"Better than the Weyr, it would seem," F'lar replied dryly.

"Young roasts and tender," F'nor said in a bitter undertone, "while the stringy, barren beasts are delivered up to us."

"The change is overdue," F'lar murmured, then raised his voice to conversational level. "A well-favored hall," he was saying amiably as they reached Fax. Their reluctant host stood in the portal to the inner Hold, which, like all such Holds, burrowed deep into stone, traditional refuge of all in time of peril.

Deliberately, F'lar turned back to the banner-hung Hall. "Tell me, Lord Fax, do you adhere to the old practices and mount a dawn guard?"

Fax frowned, trying to grasp F'lar's meaning.

"There is always a guard at the Tower."

"An easterly guard?"

Fax's eyes jerked towards F'lar, then to F'nor.

"There are always guards," he answered sharply, "on all the approaches."

"Oh, just the approaches," and F'lar nodded wisely to F'nor.

"Where else?" demanded Fax, concerned, glancing from one dragonman to the other.

"I must ask that of your harper. You do keep a trained harper in your Hold?"

"Of course. I have several trained harpers," and Fax jerked his shoulders straighter.

F'lar affected not to understand.

"Lord Fax is the overlord of six other Holds," F'nor reminded his wingleader.

"Of course," F'lar assented, with exactly the same inflection Fax had used a moment before.

The mimicry did not go unnoticed by Fax but as he was unable to construe deliberate insult out of an innocent affirmative, he stalked into the glow-lit corridors. The dragonmen followed.

The women's quarters in Fax's Hold had been moved from the traditional innermost corridors to those at cliff-face. Sunlight poured down from three double-shuttered, deep-casement windows in the outside wall. F'lar noted that the bronze hinges were well oiled, and the sills regulation spear-length. Fax had not, at least, diminished the protective wall.

The chamber was richly hung with appropriately gentle scenes of women occupied in all manner of feminine tasks. Doors gave off the main chamber on both sides into smaller sleeping alcoves and from these, at Fax's bidding, his women hesitantly emerged. Fax sternly gestured to a blue-gowned woman, her hair white-streaked, her face lined with disappointments and bitterness, her body swollen with pregnancy. She advanced awkwardly, stopping several feet from her lord. From her attitude, F'lar deduced that she came no closer to Fax than was absolutely necessary.

"The Lady of Crom, mother of my heirs," Fax said without pride or cordiality.

"My Lady—" F'lar hesitated, waiting for her name to be supplied.

She glanced warily at her lord. "Gemma," Fax snapped curtly.

F'lar bowed deeply. "My Lady Gemma, the Weyr is on Search and requests the Hold's hospitality."

"My Lord F'lar," the Lady Gemma replied in a low voice, "you are most welcome."

F'lar did not miss the slight slur on the adverb nor the fact that Gemma had no trouble naming him. His smile was warmer than courtesy demanded, warm with gratitude and sympathy. Looking at the number of women in these quarters, F'lar thought there might be one or two Lady Gemma could bid farewell without regret.

Fax preferred his women plump and small. There wasn't a saucy one in the lot. If there once had been, the spirit had been beaten out of her. Fax, no doubt, was stud, not lover. Some of the covey had not all winter long made much use of water, judging by the amount of sweet oil gone rancid in their hair. Of them all, if these were all, the Lady Gemma was the only willful one; and she, too old.

The amenities over, Fax ushered his unwelcome guests outside, and led the way to the quarters he had assigned the bronze rider.

"A pleasant room," F'lar acknowledged, stripping off gloves and wher-hide tunic, throwing them carelessly to the table. "I shall see to my men and the beasts. They have been fed recently," he commented, pointing up Fax's omission in inquiring. "I request liberty to wander through the crafthold."

Fax sourly granted what was a dragonman's traditional privilege.

"I shall not further disrupt your routine, Lord Fax, for you must have many demands on you, with seven Holds to supervise." F'lar inclined his body slightly to the overlord, turning away as a gesture of dismissal. He could imagine the infuriated expression on Fax's face from the stamping retreat.

F'nor and the men had settled themselves in a hastily vacated barrackroom. The dragons were perched comfortably on the rocky ridges above the Hold. Each rider kept his dragon in light, but alert, charge. There were to be no incidents on a Search.

As a group, the dragonmen rose at F'lar's entrance.

"No tricks, no troubles, but look around closely," he said laconically. "Return by sundown with the names of any likely prospects." He caught F'nor's grin, remembering how Fax had slurred over some names. "Descriptions are in order and craft affiliation."

The men nodded, their eyes glinting with understanding. They were flatteringly confident of a successful Search even as F'lar's doubts grew now that he had seen Fax's women. By all logic, the pick of the High Reaches should be in Fax's chief Hold—but they were not. Still, there were many large craftholds not to mention the six other High Holds to visit. All the same . . .

In unspoken accord F'lar and F'nor left the barracks. The men would follow, unobtrusively, in pairs or singly, to reconnoiter the crafthold and the nearer farmholds. The men were as overtly eager to be abroad as F'lar was privately. There had been a time when dragonmen were frequent and favored guests in all the great Holds throughout Pern, from southern Fort to high north Igen. This pleasant custom, too, had died along with other observances, evidence of the low regard in which the Weyr was presently held. F'lar vowed to correct this.

He forced himself to trace in memory the insidious changes. The Records, which each Weyrwoman kept, were proof of the gradual, but perceptible, decline, traceable through the past two hundred full Turns. Knowing the facts did not alleviate the condition. And F'lar was of that scant handful in the Weyr itself who did credit Records and Ballad alike. The situation might shortly reverse itself radically if the old tales were to be believed.

There was a reason, an explanation, a purpose, F'lar felt, for every one of the Weyr laws from First Impression to the Firestones: from the grass-free heights to ridge-running gutters. For elements as minor as controlling the appetite of a dragon to limiting the inhabitants of the Weyr. Although why the other five Weyrs had been abandoned, F'lar did not know. Idly he wondered if there were records, dusty and crumbling, lodged in the disused Weyrs. He must contrive to check when next his wings flew patrol. Certainly there was no explanation in Benden Weyr.

"There is industry but no enthusiasm," F'nor was saying, drawing F'lar's attention back to their tour of the crafthold.

They had descended the guttered ramp from the Hold into the crafthold proper, the broad roadway lined with cottages up to the imposing stone crafthalls. Silently F'lar noted moss-clogged gutters on the roofs, the vines clasping the walls. It was painful for one of his calling to witness the flagrant disregard of simple safety precautions. Growing things were forbidden near the habitations of mankind.

"News travels fast," F'nor chuckled, nodding at a hurrying craftsman, in the smock of a baker, who gave them a mumbled good day. "Not a female in sight."

His observation was accurate. Women should be abroad at this hour, bringing in supplies from the storehouses, washing in the river on such a bright warm day, or going out to the farmholds to help with planting. Not a gowned figure in sight.

"We used to be preferred mates," F'nor remarked caustically.

"We'll visit the Clothmen's Hall first. If my memory serves me right . . ."

"As it always does . . ." F'nor interjected wryly. He took no advantage of their blood relationship but he was more at ease with the bronze rider than most of the dragonmen, the other bronze riders included. F'lar was reserved in a close-knit society of easy equality. He flew a tightly disciplined wing but men maneuvered to serve under him. His wing always excelled in the Games. None ever floundered in *between* to disappear forever and no beast in his wing sickened, leaving a man in dragonless exile from the Weyr, a part of him numb forever.

"L'tol came this way and settled in one of the High Reaches," F'lar continued.

"L'tol?"

"Yes, a green rider from S'lel's wing. You remember."

An ill-timed swerve during the Spring Games had brought L'tol and his beast into the full blast of a phosphene emission from S'lel's bronze Tuenth. L'tol had been thrown from his beast's neck as the dragon tried to evade the blast. Another wingmate had swooped to catch the rider but the green dragon, his left wing crisped, his body scorched, had died of shock and phosphene poisoning.

"L'tol would aid our Search," F'nor agreed as the two dragonmen walked up to the bronze doors of the Clothmen's Hall. They paused on the threshold, adjusting their eyes to the dimmer light within. Glows punctuated the wall recesses and hung in clusters above the larger looms where the finer tapestries and fabrics were woven by master craftsmen. The pervading mood was one of quiet, purposeful industry.

Before their eyes had adapted, however, a figure glided to them, with a polite, if curt, request for them to follow him.

They were led to the right of the entrance, to a small office, curtained from the main hall. Their guide turned to them, his face visible in the wallglows. There was that air about him that marked him indefinably as a dragonman. But his face was lined deeply, one side seamed with old burnmarks. His eyes, sick with a hungry yearning, dominated his face. He blinked constantly.

"I am now Lytol," he said in a harsh voice.

F'lar nodded acknowledgment.

"You would be F'lar," Lytol said, "and you, F'nor. You've both the look of your sire."

F'lar nodded again.

Lytol swallowed convulsively, the muscles in his face twitching as the presence of dragonmen revived his awareness of exile. He essayed a smile.

"Dragons in the sky! The news spread faster than Threads."

"Nemorth has a new queen."

"Jora dead?" Lytol asked concernedly, his face cleared of its nervous movement for a second.

F'lar nodded.

Lytol grimaced bitterly. "R'gul again, huh." He stared off in the middle distance, his eyelids quiet but the muscles along his jaw took up the constant movement. "You've the High Reaches? All of them?" Lytol asked, turning back to the dragonman, a slight emphasis on "all."

F'lar gave an affirmative nod again.

"You've seen the women." Lytol's disgust showed through the words. It was a statement, not a question, for he hurried on. "Well, there are no better in all the High Reaches," and his tone expressed utmost disdain.

"Fax likes his women comfortably fleshed and docile," Lytol rattled on. "Even the Lady Gemma has learned. It'd be different if he didn't need her family's support.

Ah, it would be different indeed. So he keeps her pregnant, hoping to kill her in childbed one day. And he will. He will."

Lytol drew himself up, squaring his shoulders, turning full to the two dragonmen. His expression was vindictive, his voice low and tense.

"Kill that tyrant, for the sake and safety of Pern. Of the Weyr. Of the queen. He only bides his time. He spreads discontent among the other lords. He"—Lytol's laughter had an hysterical edge to it now—"he fancies himself as good as dragonmen."

"There are no candidates then in this Hold?" F'lar said, his voice sharp enough to cut through the man's preoccupation with his curious theory.

Lytol stared at the bronze rider. "Did I not say it?"

"What of Ruath Hold?"

Lytol stopped shaking his head and looked sharply at F'lar, his lips curling in a cunning smile. He laughed mirthlessly.

"You think to find a Torene, or a Moreta, hidden at Ruath Hold in these times? Well, all of that Blood are dead. Fax's blade was thirsty that day. He knew the truth of those harpers' tales, that Ruathan lords gave full measure of hospitality to dragonmen and the Ruathan were a breed apart. There were, you know," Lytol's voice dropped to a confiding whisper, "exiled Weyrmen like myself in that Line."

F'lar nodded gravely, unable to contradict the man's pitiful attempt at self-esteem.

"No," and Lytol chuckled softly. "Fax gets nothing from that Hold but trouble. And the women Fax used to take . . ." His laugh turned nasty in tone. "It is rumored he was impotent for months afterwards."

"Any families in the holdings with Weyr blood?"

Lytol frowned, glanced surprised at F'lar. He rubbed the scarred side of his face thoughtfully.

"There were," he admitted slowly. "There were. But I doubt if any live on." He thought a moment longer, then shook his head emphatically.

F'lar shrugged.

"I wish I had better news for you," Lytol murmured.

"No matter," F'lar reassured him, one hand poised to part the hanging in the doorway.

Lytol came up to him swiftly, his voice urgent.

"Heed what I say, Fax is ambitious. Force R'gul, or whoever is Weyrleader next, to keep watch on the High Reaches."

Lytol jabbed a finger in the direction of the Hold. "He scoffs openly at tales of the Threads. He taunts the harpers for the stupid nonsense of the old ballads and has banned from their repertoire all dragonlore. The new generation will grow up totally ignorant of duty, tradition and precaution."

F'lar was not surprised to hear that on top of Lytol's other disclosures. Yet the Red Star pulsed in the sky and the time was drawing near when they would hysterically reavow the old allegiances in fear for their very lives.

"Have you been abroad in the early morning of late?" asked F'nor, grinning maliciously.

"I have," Lytol breathed out in a hushed, choked whisper. "I have . . ." A groan was wrenched from his guts and he whirled away from the dragonmen, his head bowed between hunched shoulders. "Go," he said, gritting his teeth. And, as they hesitated, he pleaded, "*Go!*"

F'lar walked quickly from the room, followed by F'nor. The bronze rider crossed the quiet dim Hall with long strides and exploded into the startling sunlight. His momentum took him into the center of the square. There he stopped so abruptly that F'nor, hard on his heels, nearly collided with him.

"We will spend exactly the same time within the other Halls," he announced in a tight voice, his face averted from F'nor's eyes. F'lar's throat was constricted. It was difficult, suddenly, for him to speak. He swallowed hard, several times.

"To be dragonless . . ." murmured F'nor, pityingly. The encounter with Lytol had roiled his depths in a mournful way to which he was unaccustomed. That F'lar appeared equally shaken went far to dispel F'nor's private opinion that his half-brother was incapable of emotion.

"There is no other way once First Impression has been made. You know that," F'lar roused himself to say curtly. He strode off to the Hall bearing the Leathermen's device.

The Hold is barred
The Hall is bare.
  And men vanish.
The soil is barren,
The rock is bald.
  All hope banish.

Lessa was shoveling ashes from the hearth when the agitated messenger staggered into the Great Hall. She made herself as inconspicuous as possible so the Warder would not dismiss her. She had contrived to be sent to the Great Hall that morning, knowing that the Warder intended to brutalize the Head Clothman for the shoddy quality of the goods readied for shipment to Fax.

"Fax is coming! With dragonmen!" the man gasped out as he plunged into the dim Great Hall.

The Warder, who had been about to lash the Head Clothman, turned, stunned, from his victim. The courier, a farmholder from the edge of Ruatha, stumbled up to the Warder, so excited with his message that he grabbed the Warder's arm.

"How dare you leave your Hold?" and the Warder aimed his lash at the astonished holder. The force of the first blow knocked the man from his feet. Yelping, he scrambled out of reach of a second lashing. "Dragonmen indeed! Fax? Ha! He shuns Ruatha. There!" The Warder punctuated each denial with another blow, kicking the helpless wretch for good measure, before he turned breathless to glare at the clothman and the two underwarders. "How did he get in here with such a threadbare lie?" The Warder stalked to the great door. It was flung open just as he reached out for the iron handle. The ashen-faced guard officer rushed in, nearly toppling the Warder.

"Dragonmen! Dragons! All over Ruatha!" the man gibbered, arms flailing wildly. He, too, pulled at the Warder's arm, dragging the stupefied official towards the outer courtyard, to bear out the truth of his statement.

Lessa scooped up the last pile of ashes. Picking up her equipment, she slipped out of the Great Hall. There was a very pleased smile on her face under the screen of matted hair.

A dragonman at Ruatha! She must somehow contrive to get Fax so humiliated, or so infuriated, that he would renounce his claim to the Hold, in the presence of a dragonman. Then she could claim her birthright.

But she would have to be extraordinarily wary. Dragon-riders were men apart. Anger did not cloud their intelligence. Greed did not sully their judgment. Fear did not dull their reactions. Let the dense-witted believe human sacrifice, unnatural lusts, insane revel. She was not so gullible. And those stories went against her grain. Dragonmen were still human and there was Weyr blood in *her* veins. It was the same color as that of anyone else; enough of hers had been spilled to prove that.

She halted for a moment, catching a sudden shallow breath. Was this the danger she had sensed four days ago at dawn? The final encounter in her struggle to regain the Hold? No—there had been more to that portent than revenge.

The ash bucket banged against her shins as she shuffled down the low ceilinged corridor to the stable door. Fax would find a cold welcome. She had laid no new fire on the hearth. Her laugh echoed back unpleasantly from the damp walls. She rested her bucket and propped her broom and shovel as she wrestled with the heavy bronze door that gave into the new stables.

They had been built outside the cliff of Ruatha by Fax's first Warder, a subtler man than all eight of his successors. He had achieved more than all the others and Lessa had honestly regretted the necessity of his death. But he would have made her revenge impossible. He would have caught her out before she had learned how to camouflage herself and her little interferences. What had his name been? She could not recall. Well, she regretted his death.

The second man had been properly greedy and it had been easy to set up a pattern of misunderstanding between Warder and craftsmen. That one had been determined to squeeze all profit from Ruathan goods so that some of it would drop into his pocket before Fax suspected a shortage. The craftsmen who had begun to accept the skillful diplomacy of the first Warder bitterly resented the second's grasping, high-handed ways. They resented the passing of the Old Line and, even more so, the way of its passing. They were unforgiving of the insult to Ruatha; its now secondary position in the High Reaches; and they resented the individual indignities that holders, craftsmen and farmers alike, suffered under the second Warder. It took little manipulation to arrange for matters at Ruatha to go from bad to worse.

The second was replaced and his successor fared no better. He was caught diverting goods, the best of the goods at that. Fax had had him executed. His bony head still hung in the main firepit above the great Tower.

The present incumbent had not been able to maintain the Hold in even the sorry condition in which he had assumed its management. Seemingly simple matters developed rapidly into disasters. Like the production of cloth . . . Contrary to his boasts to Fax, the quality had not improved, and the quantity had fallen off.

Now Fax was here. And with dragonmen! Why dragonmen? The import of the question froze Lessa, and the heavy door closing behind her barked her heels painfully. Dragonmen used to be frequent visitors at Ruatha, that she knew, and even vaguely remembered. Those memories were like a harper's tale, told of someone else, not something within her own experience. She had limited her fierce attention to Ruatha only. She could not even recall the name of Queen or Weyrwoman from the instructions of her childhood, nor could she recall hearing mention of any queen or weyrwoman by anyone in the Hold these past ten Turns.

Perhaps the dragonmen were finally going to call the lords of the Holds to task for the disgraceful show of greenery about the Holds. Well, Lessa was to blame for much of that in Ruatha but she defied even a dragonman to confront her with her guilt. Did all Ruatha fall to the Threads it would be better than remaining dependent to Fax! The heresy shocked Lessa even as she thought it.

Wishing she could as easily unburden her conscience of such blasphemy, she ditched the ashes on the stable midden. There was a sudden change in air pressure around her. Then a fleeting shadow caused her to glance up.

From behind the cliff above glided a dragon, its enormous wings spread to their fullest as he caught the morning updraft. Turning effortlessly, he descended. A second, a third, a full wing of dragons followed in soundless flight and patterned descent, graceful and awesome. The claxon rang belatedly from the Tower and from within the kitchen there issued the screams and shrieks of the terrified drudges.

Lessa took cover. She ducked into the kitchen where she was instantly seized by the assistant cook and thrust with a buffet and a kick toward the sinks. There she was put to scrubbing grease-encrusted serving bowls with cleansing sand.

The yelping canines were already lashed to the spitrum, turning a scrawny herdbeast that had been set to roast. The cook was ladling seasonings on the carcass, swearing at having to offer so poor a meal to so many guests, and some of them high-rank. Winter-dried fruits from the last scanty harvest had been set to soak and two of the oldest drudges were scraping roots.

An apprentice cook was kneading bread; another, carefully spicing a sauce. Looking fixedly at him, she diverted his hand from one spice box to a less appropriate one as he gave a final shake to the concoction. She added too much wood to the wall oven, insuring ruin for the breads. She controlled the canines deftly, slowing one and speeding the other so that the meat would be underdone on one side, burned on the other. That the feast should be a fast, the food presented found inedible, was her whole intention.

Above in the Hold, she had no doubt that certain other measures, undertaken at different times for this exact contingency, were being discovered.

Her fingers bloodied from a beating, one of the Warder's women came shrieking into the kitchen, hopeful of refuge there.

"Insects have eaten the best blankets to shreds! And a canine who had littered on the best linens snarled at me as she gave suck! And the rushes are noxious, the best chambers full of debris driven in by the winter wind. Somebody left the shutters ajar. Just a tiny bit, but it was enough . . ." the woman wailed, clutching her hand to her breast and rocking back and forth.

Lessa bent with great industry to shine the plates.

Watch-wher, watch-wher,
In your lair,
Watch well, watch-wher!
Who goes there?

"The watch-wher is hiding something," F'lar told F'nor as they consulted in the hastily cleaned Great Hall. The room delighted to hold the wintry chill although a generous fire now burned on the hearth.

"It was but gibbering when Canth spoke to it," F'nor remarked. He was leaning against the mantel, turning slightly from side to side to gather some warmth. He watched his wingleader's impatient pacing.

"Mnementh is calming it down," F'lar replied. "He may be able to sort out the nightmare. The creature may be more senile than aware, but . . ."

"I doubt it," F'nor concurred helpfully. He glanced with apprehension up at the webhung ceiling. He was certain he'd found most of the crawlers, but he didn't fancy their sting. Not on top of the discomforts already experienced in this forsaken Hold. If the night stayed mild, he intended curling up with Canth on the heights. "That would be more reasonable than anything Fax or his Warder have suggested."

"Hm-m-m," F'lar muttered, frowning at the brown rider.

"Well, it's unbelievable that Ruatha could have fallen to such disrepair in ten short Turns. Every dragon caught the feeling of power and it's obvious the watch-wher has been tampered with. That takes a good deal of control."

"From someone of the Blood," F'lar reminded him.

F'nor shot his wingleader a quick look, wondering if he could possibly be serious in the light of all information to the contrary.

"I grant you there is power here, F'lar," F'nor conceded. "It could easily be a hidden male of the old Blood. But we need a female. And Fax made it plain, in his inimitable fashion, that he left none of the old Blood alive in the Hold the day he took it. No, no." The brown rider shook his head, as if he could dispel the lack of faith in his wingleader's curious insistence that the Search would end in Ruath with Ruathan blood.

"That watch-wher is hiding something and only someone of the Blood of its Hold can arrange that," F'lar said emphatically. He gestured around the Hall and towards the walls, bare of hangings. "Ruatha has been overcome. But she resists . . . Subtly. I say it points to the old Blood, *and* power. Not power alone."

The obstinate expression in F'lar's eyes, the set of his jaw, suggested that F'nor seek another topic.

"The pattern was well-flown today," F'nor suggested tentatively. "Does a dragonman good to ride a flaming beast. Does the beast good, too. Keeps the digestive process in order."

F'lar nodded sober agreement. "Let R'gul temporize as he chooses. It is fitting and proper to ride a firespouting beast and these holders need to be reminded of Weyr power."

"Right now, anything would help our prestige," F'nor commented sourly. "What had Fax to say when he hailed you in the Pass?" F'nor knew his question was almost impertinent but if it were, F'lar would ignore it.

F'lar's slight smile was unpleasant and there was an ominous glint in his amber eyes.

"We talked of rule and resistance."

"Did he not also draw on you?" F'nor asked.

F'lar's smile deepened. "Until he remembered I was dragon-mounted."

"He's considered a vicious fighter," F'nor said.

"I am at some disadvantage?" F'lar asked, turning sharply on his brown rider, his face too controlled.

"To my knowledge, no," F'nor reassured his leader quickly. F'lar had tumbled every man in the Weyr, efficiently and easily. "But Fax kills often and without cause."

"And because we dragonmen do not seek blood, we are not to be feared as fighters?" snapped F'lar. "Are you ashamed of your heritage?"

"I? No!" F'nor sucked in his breath. "Nor any of our wing!" he added proudly. "But there is that in the attitude of the men in this progression of Fax's that . . . that makes me wish some excuse to fight."

"As you observed today, Fax seeks some excuse. And," F'lar added thoughtfully, "there is something here in Ruatha that unnerves our noble overlord."

He caught sight of Lady Tela, whom Fax had so courteously assigned him for comfort during the progression, waving to him from the inner Hold portal.

"A case in point. Fax's Lady Tela is some three months gone."

F'nor frowned at that insult to his leader.

"She giggles incessantly and appears so addlepated that one cannot decide whether she babbles out of ignorance or at Fax's suggestion. As she has apparently not bathed all winter, and is not, in any case, my ideal, I have"—F'lar grinned maliciously—"deprived myself of her kind offices."

F'nor hastily cleared his throat and his expression as Lady Tela approached them. He caught the unappealing odor from the scarf or handkerchief she waved constantly. Dragonmen endured a great deal for the Weyr. He moved away, with apparent courtesy, to join the rest of the dragonmen entering the Hall.

F'lar turned with equal courtesy to Lady Tela as she jabbered away about the terrible condition of the rooms which Lady Gemma and the other ladies had been assigned.

"The shutters, both sets, were ajar all winter long and you should have seen the trash on the floors. We finally got two of the drudges to sweep it all into the fireplace. And then that smoked something fearful 'til a man was sent up." Lady Tela giggled. "He found the access blocked by a chimney stone fallen aslant. The rest of the chimney, for a wonder, was in good repair."

She waved her handkerchief. F'lar held his breath as the gesture wafted an unappealing odor in his direction.

He glanced up the Hall towards the inner Hold door and saw Lady Gemma descending, her steps slow and awkward. Some subtle difference about her gait attracted him and he stared at her, trying to identify it.

"Oh, yes, poor Lady Gemma," Lady Tela babbled, sighing deeply. "We are so concerned. Why Lord Fax insisted on her coming, I do not know. She is not near her time and yet . . ." The lighthead's concern sounded sincere.

F'lar's incipient hatred for Fax and his brutality matured abruptly. He left his partner chattering to thin air and courteously extended his arm to Lady Gemma to support her down the steps and to the table. Only the brief tightening of her fingers on his forearm betrayed her gratitude. Her face was very white and drawn, the lines deeply etched around mouth and eyes, showing the effort she was expending.

"Some attempt has been made, I see, to restore order to the Hall," she remarked in a conversational tone.

"Some," F'lar admitted dryly, glancing around the grandly proportioned Hall, its rafter festooned with the webs of many Turns. The inhabitants of those gossamer nests dropped from time to time, with ripe splats, to the floor, onto the table and into the serving platters. Nothing replaced the old banners of the Ruathan Blood, which had been removed from the stark brown stone walls. Fresh rushes did obscure the greasy flagstones. The trestle tables appeared recently sanded and scraped, and the platters gleamed dully in the refreshed glows. Unfortunately, the brighter light was a mistake for it was much too unflattering.

"This was such a graceful Hall," Lady Gemma murmured for F'lar's ears alone.

"You were a friend?" he asked, politely.

"Yes, in my youth," her voice dropped expressively on the last word, evoking for F'lar a happier girlhood. "It was a noble line!"

"Think you *one* might have escaped the sword?"

Lady Gemma flashed him a startled look, then quickly composed her features, lest the exchange be noted. She gave a barely perceptible shake of her head and then shifted her awkward weight to take her place at the table. Graciously she inclined her head towards F'lar, both dismissing and thanking him.

F'lar returned to his own partner and placed her at the table on his left. As the only person of rank who would dine that night at Ruath Hold, Lady Gemma was seated on his right; Fax would be beyond her. The dragonmen and Fax's upper soldiery would sit at the lower tables. No guildmen had been invited to Ruatha. Fax arrived just then with his current lady and two underleaders, the Warder bowing them effusively into the Hall. The man, F'lar noticed, kept a good distance from his overlord—as well a Warder might whose responsibility was in this sorry condition. F'lar flicked a crawler away. Out of the corner of his eye, he saw Lady Gemma wince and shudder.

Fax stamped up to the raised table, his face black with suppressed rage. He pulled back his chair roughly, slamming it into Lady Gemma's before he seated himself. He pulled the chair to the table with a force that threatened to rock the none too stable trestle-top from its supporting legs. Scowling, he inspected his goblet and plate, fingering the surface, ready to throw them aside if they displeased him.

"A roast and fresh bread, Lord Fax, and such fruits and roots as are left. Had I but known of your arrival, I could have sent to Crom for . . ."

"Sent to Crom?" roared Fax, slamming the plate he was inspecting onto the table so forcefully the rim bent under his hands. The Warder winced again as if he himself had been maimed.

"The day one of my Holds cannot support itself *or* the visit of its rightful overlord, I shall renounce it."

Lady Gemma gasped. Simultaneously the dragons roared. F'lar felt the unmistakable surge of power. His eyes instinctively sought F'nor at the lower table. The brown rider—all the dragonmen—had experienced that inexplicable shaft of exultation.

"What's wrong, Dragonman?" snapped Fax.

F'lar, affecting unconcern, stretched his legs under the table and assumed an indolent posture in the heavy chair.

"Wrong?"

"The dragons!"

"Oh, nothing. They often roar . . . at the sunset, at a flock of passing wherries, at mealtimes," and F'lar smiled amiably at the Lord of the High Reaches. Beside him his tablemate gave a squeak.

"Mealtimes? Have they not been fed?"

"Oh, yes. Five days ago."

"Oh. Five . . . days ago? And are they hungry . . . now?" Her voice trailed into a whisper of fear, her eyes grew round.

"In a few days," F'lar assured her. Under cover of his detached amusement, F'lar scanned the Hall. That surge had come from nearby. Either in the Hall or just outside. It must have been from within. It came so soon upon Fax's speech that his words must have triggered it. And the power had had an indefinably feminine touch to it.

One of Fax's women? F'lar found that hard to credit. Mnementh had been close to all of them and none had shown a vestige of power. Much less, with the exception of Lady Gemma, any intelligence.

One of the Hall women? So far he had seen only the sorry drudges and the aging females the Warder had as housekeepers. The Warder's personal woman? He must discover if that man had one. One of the Hold guards' women? F'lar suppressed an intense desire to rise and search.

"You mount a guard?" he asked Fax casually.

"Double at Ruath Hold!" he was told in a tight, hard voice, ground out from somewhere deep in Fax's chest.

"Here?" F'lar all but laughed out loud, gesturing around the sadly appointed chamber.

"Here! Food!" Fax changed the subject with a roar.

Five drudges, two of them women in brown-gray rags such that F'lar hoped they had had nothing to do with the preparation of the meal, staggered in under the emplattered herdbeast. No one with so much as a trace of power would sink to such depths, unless . . .

The aroma that reached him as the platter was placed on the serving table distracted him. It reeked of singed bone and charred meat. The Warder frantically sharpened his tools as if a keen edge could somehow slice acceptable portions from this unlikely carcass.

Lady Gemma caught her breath again and F'lar saw her hands curl tightly around the armrests. He saw the convulsive movement of her throat as she swallowed. He, too, did not look forward to this repast.

The drudges reappeared with wooden trays of bread. Burnt crusts had been scraped and cut, in some places, from the loaves before serving. As other trays were borne in, F'lar tried to catch sight of the faces of the servitors. Matted hair obscured the face of the one who presented a dish of legumes swimming in greasy liquid. Revolted, F'lar poked through the legumes to find properly cooked portions to offer Lady Gemma. She waved them aside, her face ill-concealing her discomfort.

As F'lar was about to turn and serve Lady Tela, he saw Lady Gemma's hand clutch convulsively at the chair arms. He realized that she was not merely nauseated by the unappetizing food. She was seized with labor contractions.

F'lar glanced in Fax's direction. The overlord was scowling blackly at the attempts of the Warder to find edible portions of meat to serve.

F'lar touched Lady Gemma's arm with light fingers. She turned just enough to look at F'lar from the corner of her eye. She managed a socially-correct half-smile.

"I dare not leave just now, Lord F'lar. He is always dangerous at Ruatha. And it may only be false pangs."

F'lar was dubious as he saw another shudder pass through her frame. The woman would have been a fine weyrwoman, he thought ruefully, were she but younger.

The Warder, his hands shaking, presented Fax the sliced meats. There were slivers of overdone flesh and portions of almost edible meats, but not much of either.

One furious wave of Fax's broad fist and the Warder had the plate, meats and juice, square in the face. Despite himself, F'lar sighed, for those undoubtedly constituted the only edible portions of the entire beast.

"You call this food? *You call this food?*" Fax bellowed. His voice boomed back from the bare vault of the ceiling, shaking crawlers from their webs as the sound shattered the fragile strands. "Slop! *Slop!*"

F'lar rapidly brushed crawlers from Lady Gemma who was helpless in the throes of a very strong contraction.

"It's all we had on such short notice," the Warder squealed, juices streaking down his cheeks. Fax threw the goblet at him and the wine went streaming down the man's chest. The steaming dish of roots followed and the man yelped as the hot liquid splashed over him.

"My lord, my lord, had I but known!"

"Obviously, Ruatha *cannot* support the visit of its Lord. You must renounce it," F'lar heard himself saying.

His shock at such words issuing from his mouth was as great as that of everyone else in the Hall. Silence fell, broken by the splat of falling crawlers and the drip of root liquid from the Warder's shoulders to the rushes. The grating of Fax's boot-heel was clearly audible as he swung slowly around to face the bronze rider.

As F'lar conquered his own amazement and rapidly tried to predict what to do next to mend matters, he saw F'nor rise slowly to his feet, hand on dagger hilt.

"I did not hear you correctly?" Fax asked, his face blank of all expression, his eyes snapping.

Unable to comprehend how he could have uttered such an arrant challenge, F'lar managed to assume a languid pose.

"You did mention," he drawled, "that if any of your Holds could not support itself and the visit of its rightful overlord, you would renounce it."

Fax stared back at F'lar, his face a study of swiftly suppressed emotions, the glint of triumph dominant. F'lar, his face stiff with the forced expression of indifference, was casting swiftly about in his mind. In the name of the Egg, had he lost all sense of discretion?

Pretending utter unconcern, he stabbed some vegetables onto his knife and began to munch on them. As he did so, he noticed F'nor glancing slowly around the Hall, scrutinizing everyone. Abruptly F'lar realized what had happened. Somehow, in making that statement, he, a dragonman, had responded to a covert use of the power. F'lar, the bronze rider, was being put into a position where he would *have* to fight Fax. Why? For what end? To get Fax to renounce the Hold? Incredible! But, there could be only one possible reason for such a turn of events. An exultation as sharp as pain swelled within F'lar. It was all he could do to maintain his pose of bored indifference, all he could do to turn his attention to thwarting Fax, should he press for a duel. A duel would serve no purpose. He, F'lar, had no time to waste on it.

A groan escaped Lady Gemma and broke the eye-locked stance of the two antagonists. Irritated, Fax looked down at her, fist clenched and half-raised to strike her for her temerity in interrupting her lord and master. The contraction that contorted the swollen belly was as obvious as the woman's pain. F'lar dared not look towards her but he wondered if she had deliberately groaned aloud to break the tension.

Incredibly, Fax began to laugh. He threw back his head, showing big, stained teeth, and roared.

"Aye, renounce it, in favor of her issue, if it is male . . . and lives!" he crowed, laughing raucously.

"Heard and witnessed!" F'lar snapped, jumping to his feet and pointing to his riders. They were on their feet in the instant. "Heard and witnessed!" they averred in the traditional manner.

With that movement, everyone began to babble at once in nervous relief. The other women, each reacting in her way to the imminence of birth, called orders to the servants and advice to each other. They converged towards Lady Gemma, hovering undecidedly out of Fax's range, like silly wherries disturbed from their roosts. It was obvious they were torn between their fear of their lord and their desire to reach the laboring woman.

He gathered their intentions as well as their reluctance and, still stridently laughing, knocked back his chair. He stepped over it, strode down to the meatstand and stood hacking off pieces with his knife, stuffing them, juice dripping, into his mouth without ceasing his guffawing.

As F'lar bent towards Lady Gemma to assist her out of her chair, she grabbed his arm urgently. Their eyes met, hers clouded with pain. She pulled him closer.

"He means to kill you, Bronze Rider. He loves to kill," she whispered.

"Dragonmen are not easily killed, but I am grateful to you."

"I do not want you killed," she said, softly, biting at her lip. "We have so few bronze riders."

F'lar stared at her, startled. Did she, Fax's lady, actually believe in the Old Laws?

F'lar beckoned to two of the Warder's men to carry her up into the Hold. He caught Lady Tela by the arm as she fluttered past him.

"What do you need?"

"Oh, oh," she exclaimed, her face twisted with panic; she was distractedly wringing her hands, "Water, hot. Clean cloths. And a birthing-woman. Oh, yes, we must have a birthing-woman."

F'lar looked about for one of the Hold women, his glance sliding over the first disreputable figure who had started to mop up the spilled food. He signaled instead for the Warder and peremptorily ordered him to send for the woman. The Warder kicked at the drudge on the floor.

"You . . . you! Whatever your name is, go get her from the crafthold. You must know who she is."

The drudge evaded the parting kick the Warder aimed in her direction with a nimbleness at odds with her appearance of extreme age and decrepitude. She scurried across the Hall and out the kitchen door.

Fax sliced and speared meat, occasionally bursting out with a louder bark of laughter as his inner thoughts amused him. F'lar sauntered down to the carcass and, without waiting for invitation from his host, began to carve neat slices also, beckoning his men over. Fax's soldiers, however, waited until their lord had eaten his fill.

Lord of the Hold, your charge is sure
In thick walls, metal doors and no verdure.

Lessa sped from the Hall to summon the birthing-woman, seething with frustration. So close! So close! How could she come so close and yet fail? Fax should have challenged the dragonman. And the dragonman was strong and young, his face that of a fighter, stern and controlled. He should not have temporized. Was all honor dead in Pern, smothered by green grass?

And why, oh why, had Lady Gemma chosen that precious moment to go into labor? If her groan hadn't distracted Fax, the fight would have begun and not even Fax, for all his vaunted prowess as a vicious fighter, would have prevailed against a dragonman who had her—Lessa's—support! The Hold must be secured to its rightful Blood again. Fax must not leave Ruatha, alive, again!

Above her, on the High Tower, the great bronze dragon gave forth a weird croon, his many-faceted eyes sparkling in the gathering darkness.

Unconsciously she silenced him as she would have done the watch-wher. Ah, that watch-wher. He had not come out of his den at her passing. She knew the dragons had been at him. She could hear him gibbering in panic.

The slant of the road toward the crafthold lent impetus to her flying feet and she had to brace herself to a sliding stop at the birthing-woman's stone threshold. She banged on the closed door and heard the frightened exclamation within.

"A birth. A birth at the Hold," Lessa cried.

"A birth?" came the muffled cry and the latches were thrown up on the door. "At the Hold?"

"Fax's lady and, as you love life, hurry! For if it is male, it will be Ruatha's own lord."

That ought to fetch her, thought Lessa, and in that instant, the door was flung open by the man of the house. Lessa could see the birthing-woman gathering up her things in haste, piling them into her shawl. Lessa hurried the woman out, up the steep road to the Hold, under the Tower gate, grabbing the woman as she tried to run at the sight of a dragon peering down at her. Lessa drew her into the Court and pushed her, resisting, into the Hall.

The woman clutched at the inner door, balking at the sight of the gathering there. Lord Fax, his feet up on the trestle table, was paring his fingernails with his knife blade, still chuckling. The dragonmen, in their wher-hide tunics, were eating quietly at one table while the soldiers were having their turn at the meat.

The bronze rider noticed their entrance and pointed urgently towards the inner Hold. The birthing-woman seemed frozen to the spot. Lessa tugged futilely at her arm, urging her to cross the Hall. To her surprise, the bronze rider strode to them.

"Go quickly, woman, Lady Gemma is before her time," he said, frowning with concern, gesturing imperatively towards the Hold entrance. He caught her by the shoulder and led her, all unwilling, Lessa tugging away at her other arm.

When they reached the stairs, he relinquished his grip, nodding to Lessa to escort her the rest of the way. Just as they reached the massive inner door, Lessa noticed how sharply the dragonman was looking at them—at her hand, on the birthing-woman's arm. Warily, she glanced at her hand and saw it, as if it belonged to a stranger: the long fingers, shapely despite dirt and broken nails; her small hand, delicately boned, gracefully placed despite the urgency of the grip. She blurred it and hurried on.

Honor those the dragons heed,
In thought and favor, word and deed.
Worlds are lost or worlds are saved
By those dangers dragon-braved.

Dragonman, avoid excess;
Greed will bring the Weyr distress;
To the ancient Laws adhere,
Prospers thus the Dragonweyr.

An unintelligible ululation raised the waiting men to their feet, startled from private meditations and the diversion of Bonethrows. Only Fax remained unmoved at the alarm, save that the slight sneer, which had settled on his face hours past, deepened to smug satisfaction.

"Dead-ed-ed," the tidings reverberated down the rocky corridors of the Hold. The weeping lady seemed to erupt out of the passage from the Inner Hold, flying down the steps to sink into an hysterical heap at Fax's feet. "She's dead. Lady Gemma is dead. There was too much blood. It was too soon. She was too old to bear more children."

F'lar couldn't decide whether the woman was apologizing for, or exulting in, the woman's death. She certainly couldn't be criticizing her Lord for placing Lady Gemma in such peril. F'lar, however, was sincerely sorry at Gemma's passing. She had been a brave, fine woman.

And now, what would be Fax's next move? F'lar caught F'nor's identically quizzical glance and shrugged expressively.

"The child lives!" a curiously distorted voice announced, penetrating the rising noise in the Great Hall. The words electrified the atmosphere. Every head slewed round sharply towards the portal to the Inner Hold where the drudge, a totally unexpected messenger, stood poised on the top step.

"It is male!" This announcement rang triumphantly in the still Hall.

Fax jerked himself to his feet, kicking aside the wailer at his feet, scowling ominously at the drudge. "What did you say, woman?"

"The child lives. It is male," the creature repeated, descending the stairs.

Incredulity and rage suffused Fax's face. His body seemed to coil up.

"Ruatha has a new lord!" Staring intently at the overlord, she advanced, her mien purposeful, almost menacing.

The tentative cheers of the Warder's men were drowned by the roaring of the dragons.

Fax erupted into action. He leaped across the intervening space, bellowing. Before Lessa could dodge, his fist crashed down across her face. She fell heavily to the stone floor, where she lay motionless, a bundle of dirty rags.

"Hold, Fax!" F'lar's voice broke the silence as the Lord of the High Reaches flexed his leg to kick her.

Fax whirled, his hand automatically closing on his knife hilt.

"It was heard and witnessed, Fax," F'lar cautioned him, one hand outstretched in warning, "by dragonmen. Stand by your sworn and witnessed oath!"

"Witnessed? By dragonmen?" cried Fax with a derisive laugh. "Dragonwomen, you mean," he sneered, his eyes blazing with contempt, as he made one sweeping gesture of scorn.

He was momentarily taken aback by the speed with which the bronze rider's knife appeared in his hand.

"Dragonwomen?" F'lar queried, his lips curling back over his teeth, his voice dangerously soft. Glowlight flickered off his circling knife as he advanced on Fax.

"Women! Parasites on Pern. The Weyr power is over. Over!" Fax roared, leaping forward to land in a combat crouch.

The two antagonists were dimly aware of the scurry behind them, of tables pulled roughly aside to give the duelists space. F'lar could spare no glance at the crumpled form of the drudge. Yet he was sure, through and beyond instinct sure, that she was the source of power. He had felt it as she entered the room. The dragons' roaring confirmed it. If that fall had killed her . . . He advanced on Fax, leaping high to avoid the slashing blade as Fax unwound from the crouch with a powerful lunge.

F'lar evaded the attack easily, noticing his opponent's reach, deciding he had a slight advantage there. But not much. Fax had had much more actual hand-to-hand killing experience than had he whose duels had always ended at first blood on the practice floor. F'lar made due note to avoid closing with the burly lord. The man was heavy-chested, dangerous from sheer mass. F'lar must use agility as his weapon, not brute strength.

Fax feinted, testing F'lar for weakness, or indiscretion. The two crouched, facing each other across six feet of space, knife hands weaving, their free hands, spread-fingered, ready to grab.

Again Fax pressed the attack. F'lar allowed him to close, just near enough to dodge away with a backhanded swipe. Fabric ripped under the tip of his knife. He heard Fax snarl. The overlord was faster on his feet than his bulk suggested and F'lar had to dodge a second time, feeling Fax's knife score his wherhide jerkin.

Grimly the two circled, each looking for an opening in the other's defense. Fax plowed in, trying to corner the lighter, faster man between raised platform and wall.

F'lar countered, ducking low under Fax's flailing arm, slashing obliquely across Fax's side. The overlord caught at him, yanking savagely, and F'lar was trapped against the other man's side, straining desperately with his left hand to keep the knife arm up. F'lar brought up his knee, and ducked away as Fax gasped and buckled from the pain in his groin, but Fax struck in passing. Sudden fire laced F'lar's left shoulder.

Fax's face was red with anger and he wheezed from pain and shock. But the infuriated lord straightened up and charged. F'lar was forced to sidestep quickly before Fax could close with him. F'lar put the meat table between them, circling warily, flexing his shoulder to assess the extent of the knife's slash. It was painful, but the arm could be used.

Suddenly Fax scooped up some fatty scraps from the meat tray and hurled them at F'lar. The dragonman ducked and Fax came around the table with a rush. F'lar leaped sideways. Fax's flashing blade came within inches of his abdomen, as his own knife sliced down the outside of Fax's arm. Instantly the two pivoted to face each other again, but Fax's left arm hung limply at his side.

F'lar darted in, pressing his luck as the Lord of the High Reaches staggered. But F'lar misjudged the man's condition and suffered a terrific kick in the side as he tried to dodge under the feinting knife. Doubled with pain, F'lar rolled frantically away from his charging adversary. Fax was lurching forward, trying to fall on him, to pin the lighter dragonman down for a final thrust. Somehow F'lar got to his feet, attempting to straighten to meet Fax's stumbling charge. His very position saved him. Fax overreached his mark and staggered off balance. F'lar brought his right hand over with as much strength as he could muster and his blade plunged through Fax's unprotected back until he felt the point stick in the chest plate.

The defeated lord fell flat to the flagstones. The force of his descent dislodged the dagger from his chestbone and an inch of bloody blade re-emerged.

F'lar stared down at the dead man. There was no pleasure in killing, he realized, only relief that he himself was still alive. He wiped his forehead on his sleeve and forced himself erect, his side throbbing with the pain of that last kick and his left shoulder burning. He half-stumbled to the drudge, still sprawled where she had fallen.

He gently turned her over, noting the terrible bruise spreading across her cheek under the dirty skin. He heard F'nor take command of the tumult in the Hall.

The dragonman laid a hand, trembling in spite of an effort to control himself, on the woman's breast to feel for a heartbeat . . . It was there, slow but strong.

A deep sigh escaped him for either blow or fall could have proved fatal. Fatal, perhaps, for Pern as well.

Relief was colored with disgust. There was no telling under the filth how old this creature might be. He raised her in his arms, her light body no burden even to his battleweary strength. Knowing F'nor would handle any trouble efficiently, F'lar carried the drudge to his own chamber.

Putting the body on the high bed, he stirred up the fire and added more glows to the bedside bracket. His gorge rose at the thought of touching the filthy mat of hair but nonetheless and gently, he pushed it back from the face, turning the head this way and that. The features were small, regular. One arm, clear of rags, was reasonably clean above the elbow but marred by bruises and old scars. The skin was firm and unwrinkled. The hands, when he took them in his, were filthy but well-shaped and delicately boned.

F'lar began to smile. Yes, she had blurred that hand so skillfully that he had actually doubted what he had first seen. And yes, beneath grime and grease, she was young. Young enough for the Weyr. And no born drab. There was no taint of common blood here. It was pure, no matter whose the line, and he rather thought she was indeed Ruathan. One who had by some unknown agency escaped the massacre ten Turns ago and bided her time for revenge. Why else force Fax to renounce the Hold?

Delighted and fascinated by this unexpected luck, F'lar reached out to tear the dress from the unconscious body and found himself constrained not to. The girl had roused. Her great, hungry eyes fastened on his, not fearful or expectant; wary.

A subtle change occurred in her face. F'lar watched, his smile deepening, as she shifted her regular features into an illusion of disagreeable ugliness and great age.

"Trying to confuse a dragonman, girl?" he chuckled. He made no further move to touch her but settled against the great carved post of the bed. He crossed his arms sternly on his chest, thought better of it immediately, and eased his sore arm. "Your name, girl, and rank, too."

She drew herself upright slowly against the headboard, her features no longer blurred. They faced each other across the high bed.

"Fax?"

"Dead. Your name!"

A look of exulting triumph flooded her face. She slipped from the bed, standing unexpectedly tall. "Then I reclaim my own. I am of the Ruathan Blood. I claim Ruath," she announced in a ringing voice.

F'lar stared at her a moment, delighted with her proud bearing. Then he threw back his head and laughed.

"This? This crumbling heap?" He could not help but mock the disparity between her manner and her dress. "Oh, no. Besides, Lady, we dragonmen heard and witnessed Fax's oath renouncing the Hold in favor of his heir. Shall I challenge the babe, too, for you? And choke him with his swaddling cloths?"

Her eyes flashed, her lips parted in a terrible smile.

"There is no heir. Gemma died, the babe unborn. I lied."

"Lied?" F'lar demanded, angry.

"Yes," she taunted him with a toss of her chin. "I lied. There was no babe born. I merely wanted to be sure you challenged Fax."

He grabbed her wrist, stung that he had twice fallen to her prodding.

"You provoked a dragonman to fight? To kill? *When he is on Search?*"

"Search? Why should I care about a Search? I've Ruatha as my Hold again. For ten Turns, I have worked and waited, schemed and suffered for that. What could your Search mean to me?"

F'lar wanted to strike that look of haughty contempt from her face. He twisted her arm savagely, bringing her to his feet before he released his grip. She laughed at him, and scuttled to one side. She was on her feet and out the door before he could give chase.

Swearing to himself, he raced down the rocky corridors, knowing she would have to make for the Hall to get out of the Hold. However, when he reached the Hall, there was no sign of her fleeing figure among those still loitering.

"Has that creature come this way?" he called to F'nor who was, by chance, standing by the door to the Court.

"No. Is she the source of power after all?"

"Yes, she is," F'lar answered, galled all the more. "And Ruathan Blood at that!"

"Oh ho! Does she depose the babe, then?" F'nor asked, gesturing towards the birthing-woman who occupied a seat close to the now blazing hearth.

F'lar paused, about to return to search the Hold's myriad passages. He stared, momentarily confused, at this brown rider.

"Babe? What babe?"

"The male child Lady Gemma bore," F'nor replied, surprised by F'lar's uncomprehending look.

"It lives?"

"Yes. A strong babe, the woman says, for all that he was premature and taken forcibly from his dead dame's belly."

F'lar threw back his head with a shout of laughter. For all her scheming, she had been outdone by truth.

At that moment, he heard Mnementh roar in unmistakable elation and the curious warble of other dragons.

"Mnementh has caught her," F'lar cried, grinning with jubilation. He strode down the steps, past the body of the former Lord of the High Reaches and out into the main court.

He saw that the bronze dragon was gone from his Tower perch and called him. An agitation drew his eyes upward. He saw Mnementh spiraling down into the Court, his front paws clasping something. Mnementh informed F'lar that he had seen her climbing from one of the high windows and had simply plucked her from the ledge, knowing the dragonman sought her. The bronze dragon settled awkwardly onto his hind legs, his wings working to keep him balanced. Carefully he set the girl on her feet and formed a precise cage around her with his huge talons. She stood motionless within that circle, her face toward the wedge-shaped head that swayed above her.

The watch-wher, shrieking terror, anger and hatred, was lunging violently to the end of its chain, trying to come to Lessa's aid. It grabbed at F'lar as he strode to the two.

"You've courage enough, girl," he admitted, resting one hand casually on Mnementh's upper claw. Mnementh was enormously pleased with himself and swiveled his head down for his eye ridges to be scratched.

"You did not lie, you know," F'lar said, unable to resist taunting the girl.

Slowly she turned towards him, her face impassive. She was not afraid of dragons, F'lar realized with approval.

"The babe lives. And it is male."

She could not control her dismay and her shoulders sagged briefly before she pulled herself erect.

"Ruatha is mine," she insisted in a tense low voice.

"Aye, and it would have been, had you approached me directly when the wing arrived here."

Her eyes widened. "What do you mean?"

"A dragonman may champion anyone whose grievance is just. By the time we reached Ruath Hold, I was quite ready to challenge Fax given any reasonable cause, despite the Search." This was not the whole truth but F'lar must teach this girl the folly of trying to control dragonmen. "Had you paid any attention to your harper's songs, you'd know your rights. And," F'lar's voice held a vindictive edge that surprised him, "Lady Gemma might not now lie dead. She suffered far more at that tyrant's hand than you."

Something in her manner told him that she regretted Lady Gemma's death, that it had affected her deeply.

"What good is Ruatha to you now?" he demanded, a broad sweep of his arm taking in the ruined courtyard and the Hold, the entire unproductive valley of Ruatha. "You have indeed accomplished your ends; a profitless conquest and its conqueror's death." F'lar snorted: "All seven Holds will revert to their legitimate Blood, and time they did. One Hold, one lord. Of course, you might have to fight others, infected with Fax's greed. Could you hold Ruatha against attack . . . now . . . in her decline?"

"Ruatha is mine!"

"Ruatha?" F'lar's laugh was derisive. "When you could be Weyrwoman?"

"Weyrwoman?" she breathed, staring at him.

"Yes, little fool. I said I rode in Search . . . it's about time you attended to more than Ruatha. And the object of my Search is . . . you!"

She stared at the finger he pointed at her as if it were dangerous.

"By the First Egg, girl, you've power in you to spare when you can turn a dragonman, all unwitting, to do your bidding. Ah, but never again, for now I am on guard against you."

Mnementh crooned approvingly, the sound a soft rumble in his throat. He arched his neck so that one eye was turned directly on the girl, gleaming in the darkness of the court.

F'lar noticed with detached pride that she neither flinched nor blanched at the proximity of an eye greater than her own head.

"He likes to have his eye ridges scratched," F'lar remarked in a friendly tone, changing tactics.

"I know," she said softly and reached out a hand to do that service.

"Nemorth's queen," F'lar continued, "is close to death. This time we must have a strong Weyrwoman."

"This time—the Red Star?" the girl gasped, turning frightened eyes to F'lar.

"You understand what it means?"

"There is danger . . ." she began in a bare whisper, glancing apprehensively eastward.

F'lar did not question by what miracle she appreciated the imminence of danger. He had every intention of taking her to the Weyr by sheer force if necessary. But something within him wanted very much for her to accept the challenge voluntarily. A rebellious Weyrwoman would be even more dangerous than a stupid one. This girl had too much power and was too used to guile and strategy. It would be a calamity to antagonize her with injudicious handling.

"There is danger for all Pern. Not just Ruatha," he said, allowing a note of entreaty to creep into his voice. "And *you* are needed. Not by Ruatha," a wave of his hand dismissed that consideration as a negligible one compared to the total picture. "We are doomed without a strong Weyrwoman. Without you."

"Gemma kept saying *all* the bronze riders were needed," she murmured in a dazed whisper.

What did she mean by that statement? F'lar frowned. Had she heard a word he had said? He pressed his argument, certain only that he had already struck one responsive chord.

"You've won here. Let the babe," he saw her startled rejection of that idea and ruthlessly qualified it, ". . . Gemma's babe . . . be reared at Ruatha. You have command of all the Holds as Weyrwoman, not ruined Ruatha alone. You've accomplished Fax's death. Leave off vengeance."

She stared at F'lar with wonder, absorbing his words.

"I never thought beyond Fax's death," she admitted slowly. "I never thought what should happen then."

Her confusion was almost childlike and struck F'lar forcibly. He had had no time, or desire, to consider her prodigious accomplishment. Now he realized some measure of her indomitable character. She could not have been much over ten Turns of age herself when Fax had murdered her family. Yet somehow, so young, she had set herself a goal and managed to survive both brutality and detection long enough to secure the usurper's death. What a Weyrwoman she would be! In the tradition of those of Ruathan blood. The light of the paler moon made her look young and vulnerable and almost pretty.

"You can be Weyrwoman," he insisted gently.

"Weyrwoman," she breathed, incredulous, and gazed round the inner court bathed in soft moonlight. He thought she wavered.

"Or perhaps you enjoy rags?" he said, making his voice harsh, mocking. "And matted hair, dirty feet and cracked hands? Sleeping in straw, eating rinds? You are young . . . that is, I assume you are young," and his voice was frankly skeptical. She glared at him, her lips firmly pressed together. "Is this the be-all and end-all of your ambition? What are you that this little corner of the great world is *all* you want?" He paused and with utter contempt added, "The blood of Ruatha has thinned, I see. You're afraid!"

"I am Lessa, daughter of the Lord of Ruath," she countered, stung. She drew herself erect. Her eyes flashed. "I am afraid of nothing!"

F'lar contented himself with a slight smile.

Mnementh, however, threw up his head, and stretched out his sinuous neck to its whole length. His full-throated peal rang out down the valley. The bronze communicated his awareness to F'lar that Lessa had accepted the challenge. The other dragons answered back, their warbles shriller than Mnementh's bellow. The watch-wher which had cowered at the end of its chain lifted its voice in a thin, unnerving screech until the Hold emptied of its startled occupants.

"F'nor," the bronze rider called, waving his wingleader to him. "Leave half the flight to guard the Hold. Some nearby lord might think to emulate Fax's example. Send one rider to the High Reaches with the glad news. You go directly to the Cloth Hall and speak to L'to . . . Lytol." F'lar grinned. "I think he would make an exemplary Warder and Lord Surrogate for this Hold in the name of the Weyr and the babe."

The brown rider's face expressed enthusiasm for his mission as he began to comprehend his leader's intentions. With Fax dead and Ruatha under the protection of dragonmen, particularly that same one who had dispatched Fax, the Hold would have wise management.

"She caused Ruatha's deterioration?" he asked.

"And nearly ours with her machinations," F'lar replied but having found the admirable object of his Search, he could now be magnanimous. "Suppress your exultation, brother," he advised quickly as he took note of F'nor's expression. "The new queen must also be Impressed."

"I'll settle arrangements here. Lytol is an excellent choice," F'nor said.

"Who is this Lytol?" demanded Lessa pointedly. She had twisted the mass of filthy hair back from her face. In the moonlight the dirt was less noticeable. F'lar caught F'nor looking at her with an all too easily read expression. He signaled F'nor, with a peremptory gesture, to carry out his orders without delay.

"Lytol is a dragonless man," F'lar told the girl, "no friend to Fax. He will ward the Hold well and it will prosper." He added persuasively with a quelling stare full on her, "Won't it?"

She regarded him somberly, without answering, until he chuckled softly at her discomfiture.

"We'll return to the Weyr," he announced, proffering a hand to guide her to Mnementh's side.

The bronze one had extended his head toward the watch-wher who now lay panting on the ground, its chain limp in the dust.

"Oh," Lessa sighed, and dropped beside the grotesque beast. It raised its head slowly, lurring piteously.

"Mnementh says it is very old and soon will sleep itself to death."

Lessa cradled the bestial head in her arms, scratching it behind the ears.

"Come, Lessa of Pern," F'lar said, impatient to be up and away.

She rose slowly but obediently. "It saved me. It knew me."

"It knows it did well," F'lar assured her, brusquely, wondering at such an uncharacteristic show of sentiment in her.

He took her hand again, to help her to her feet and lead her back to Mnementh. As they turned, he glimpsed the watch-wher, launching itself at a dead run after Lessa. The chain, however, held fast. The beast's neck broke, with a sickeningly audible snap.

Lessa was on her knees in an instant, cradling the repulsive head in her arms. "Why, you foolish thing, why?" she asked in a stunned whisper as the light in the beast's green-gold eyes dimmed and died out.

Mnementh informed F'lar that the creature had lived this long only to preserve the Ruathan line. At Lessa's imminent departure, it had welcomed death.

A convulsive shudder went through Lessa's slim body. F'lar watched as she undid the heavy buckle that fastened the metal collar about the watch-wher's neck. She threw the tether away with a violent motion. Tenderly she laid the watch-wher on the cobbles. With one last caress to the clipped wings, she rose in a fluid movement and walked resolutely to Mnementh without a single backward glance. She stepped calmly to the dragon's raised leg and seated herself, as F'lar directed, on the great neck.

F'lar glanced around the courtyard at the remainder of his wing which had re-formed there. The Hold folk had retreated back into the safety of the Great Hall. When his wingmen were all astride, he vaulted to Mnementh's neck, behind the girl.

"Hold tightly to my arms," he ordered her as he took hold of the smallest neck ridge and gave the command to fly.

Her fingers closed spasmodically around his forearm as the great bronze dragon took off, the enormous wings working to achieve height from the vertical takeoff. Mnementh preferred to fall into flight from a cliff or tower. Like all dragons, he tended to indolence. F'lar glanced behind him, saw the other dragonmen form the flight line, spread out to cover those still on guard at Ruatha Hold.

When they had reached a sufficient altitude, he told Mnementh to transfer, going *between* to the Weyr.

Only a gasp indicated the girl's astonishment as they hung *between*. Accustomed as he was to the sting of the profound cold, to the awesome utter lack of light and sound, F'lar still found the sensations unnerving. Yet the uncommon transfer spanned no more time than it took to cough thrice.

Mnementh rumbled approval of this candidate's calm reaction as they flicked out of the eerie *between*.

And then they were above the Weyr, Mnementh setting his wings to glide in the bright daylight, half a world away from night-time Ruatha.

As they circled above the great stony trough of the Weyr, F'lar peered at Lessa's face, pleased with the delight mirrored there; she showed no trace of fear as they hung a thousand lengths above the high Benden mountain range. Then, as the seven dragons roared their incoming cry, an incredulous smile lit her face.

The other wingmen dropped into a wide spiral, down, down while Mnementh elected to descend in lazy circles. The dragonmen peeled off smartly and dropped, each to his own tier in the caves of the Weyr. Mnementh finally completed his leisurely approach to their quarters, whistling shrilly to himself as he braked his forward speed with a twist of his wings, dropping lightly at last to the ledge. He crouched as F'lar swung the girl to the rough rock, scored from thousands of clawed landings.

"This leads only to our quarters," he told her as they entered the corridor, vaulted and wide for the easy passage of great bronze dragons.

As they reached the huge natural cavern that had been his since Mnementh achieved maturity, F'lar looked about him with eyes fresh from his first prolonged absence from the Weyr. The huge chamber was unquestionably big, certainly larger than most of the halls he had visited in Fax's procession. Those halls were intended as gathering places for men, not the habitations of dragons. But suddenly he saw his own quarters were nearly as shabby as all Ruatha. Benden was, of a certainty, one of the oldest dragonweyrs, as Ruatha was one of the oldest Holds, but that excused nothing. How many dragons had bedded in that hollow to make solid rock conform to dragon proportions! How many feet had worn the path past the dragon's weyr into the sleeping chamber, to the bathing room beyond where the natural warm spring provided ever-fresh water! But the wall hangings were faded and unraveling and there were grease stains on lintel and floor that should be sanded away.

He noticed the wary expression on Lessa's face as he paused in the sleeping room.

"I must feed Mnementh immediately. So you may bathe first," he said, rummaging in a chest and finding clean clothes for her, discards of other previous occupants of his quarters, but far more presentable than her present covering. He carefully laid back in the chest the white wool robe that was traditional Impression garb. She would wear that later. He tossed several garments at her feet and a bag of sweetsand, gesturing to the hanging that obscured the way to the bath.

He left her, then, the clothes in a heap at her feet, for she made no effort to catch anything.

Mnementh informed him that F'nor was feeding Canth and that he, Mnementh, was hungry, too. *She* didn't trust F'lar but she wasn't afraid of himself.

"Why should she be afraid of you?" F'lar asked. "You're cousin to the watch-wher who was her only friend."

Mnementh informed F'lar that he, a fully matured bronze dragon, was no relation to any scrawny, crawling, chained, and wing-clipped watch-wher.

F'lar, pleased at having been able to tease the bronze one, chuckled to himself. With great dignity, Mnementh curved down to the feeding ground.

By the Golden Egg of Faranth
By the Weyrwoman, wise and true,
Breed a flight of bronze and brown wings,
Breed a flight of green and blue.
Breed riders, strong and daring,
Dragon-loving, born as hatched,
Flight of hundreds soaring skyward,
Man and dragon fully matched.

Lessa waited until the sound of the dragonman's footsteps proved he had really gone away. She rushed quickly through the big cavern, heard the scrape of claw and the *whoosh* of the mighty wings. She raced down the short passageway, right to the edge of the yawning entrance. There was the bronze dragon circling down to the wider end of the mile-long barren oval that was Benden Weyr. She had heard of the Weyrs, as any Pernese had, but to be in one was quite a different matter.

She peered up, around, down that sheer rock face. There was no way off but by dragon wing. The nearest cave mouths were an unhandy distance above her, to one side, below her on the other. She was neatly secluded here.

Weyrwoman, he had told her. His woman? In his weyr? Was that what he had meant? No, that was not the impression she got from the dragon. It occurred to her, suddenly, that it was odd she had understood the dragon. Were common folk able to? Or was it the dragonman blood in her line? At all events, Mnementh had inferred something greater, some special rank. She remembered vaguely that, when dragonmen went on Search, they looked for certain women. Ah, certain women. She was one, then, of several contenders. Yet the bronze rider had offered her the position as if she and she, alone, qualified. He had his own generous portion of conceit, that one, Lessa decided. Arrogant he was, though not a bully like Fax.

She could see the bronze dragon swoop down to the running herdbeasts, saw the strike, saw the dragon wheel up to settle on a far ledge to feed. Instinctively she drew back from the opening, back into the dark and relative safety of the corridor.

The feeding dragon evoked scores of horrid tales. Tales at which she had scoffed but now . . . Was it true, then, that dragons did eat human flesh? Did . . . Lessa halted that trend of thought. Dragonkind was no less cruel than mankind. The dragon, at least, acted from bestial need rather than bestial greed.

Assured that the dragonman would be occupied a while, she crossed the larger cave into the sleeping room. She scooped up the clothing and the bag of cleansing sand and proceeded to the bathing room.

To be clean! To be completely clean and to be able to stay that way. With distaste, she stripped off the remains of the rags, kicking them to one side. She made a soft mud with the sweetsand and scrubbed her entire body until she drew blood from various half-healed cuts. Then she jumped into the pool, gasping as the warm water made the sweetsand foam in the lacerations.

It was a ritual cleansing of more than surface soil. The luxury of cleanliness was ecstasy.

Finally satisfied she was as clean as one long soaking could make her, she left the pool, reluctantly. Wringing out her hair she tucked it up on her head as she dried herself. She shook out the clothing and held one garment against her experimentally. The fabric, a soft green, felt smooth under her water-shrunken fingers, although the nap caught on her roughened hands. She pulled it over her head. It was loose but the darker-green overtunic had a sash which she pulled in tight at the waist. The unusual sensation of softness against her bare skin made her wriggle with voluptuous pleasure. The skirt, no longer a ragged hem of tatters, swirled heavily around her ankles. She smiled. She took up a fresh drying cloth and began to work on her hair.

A muted sound came to her ears and she stopped, hands poised, head bent to one side. Straining, she listened. Yes, there were sounds without. The dragonman and his beasts must have returned. She grimaced to herself with annoyance at this untimely interruption and rubbed harder at her hair. She ran fingers through the half-dry tangles, the motions arrested as she encountered snarls. Vexed, she rummaged on the shelves until she found, as she had hoped to, a coarse-toothed metal comb.

Dry, her hair had a life of its own suddenly, crackling about her hands and clinging to face and comb and dress. It was difficult to get the silky stuff under control. And her hair was longer than she had thought, for, clean and unmatted, it fell to her waist—when it did not cling to her hands.

She paused, listening, and heard no sound at all. Apprehensively, she stepped to the curtain and glanced warily to the sleeping room. It was empty. She listened and caught the perceptible thoughts of the sleepy dragon. Well, she would rather meet the man in the presence of a sleepy dragon than in a sleeping room. She started across the floor and, out of the corner of her eye, caught sight of a strange woman as she passed a polished piece of metal hanging on the wall.

Amazed, she stopped short, staring, incredulous, at the face the metal reflected. Only when she put her hands to her prominent cheekbones in a gesture of involuntary surprise and the reflection imitated the gesture, did she realize she looked at herself.

Why, that girl in the reflector was prettier than Lady Tela, than the clothman's daughter! But so thin. Her hands of their own volition dropped to her neck, to the protruding collarbones, to her breasts which did not entirely accord with the gauntness of the rest of her. The dress was too large for her frame, she noted with an unexpected emergence of conceit born in that instant of delighted appraisal. And her hair . . . it stood out around her head like an aureole. It wouldn't lie contained. She smoothed it down with impatient fingers, automatically bringing locks forward to hang around her face. As she irritably pushed them back, dismissing a need for disguise, the hair drifted up again.

A slight sound, the scrape of a boot against stone, caught her back from her bemusement. She waited, momentarily expecting him to appear. She was suddenly timid. With her face bare to the world, her hair behind her ears, her body outlined by a clinging fabric, she was stripped of her accustomed anonymity and was, therefore, in her estimation, vulnerable.

She controlled the desire to run away—the irrational fear. Observing herself in the looking metal, she drew her shoulders back, tilted her head high, chin up; the movement caused her hair to crackle and cling and shift about her head. She was Lessa of Ruatha, of a fine old Blood. She no longer needed artifice to preserve herself; she must stand proudly bare-faced before the world . . . and that dragonman.

Resolutely she crossed the room, pushing aside the hanging on the doorway to the great cavern.

He was there, beside the head of the dragon, scratching its eye ridges, a curiously tender expression on his face. The tableau was at variance with all she had heard of dragonmen.

She had, of course, heard of the strange affinity between rider and dragon but this was the first time she realized that love was part of that bond. Or that this reserved, cold man was capable of such deep emotion.

He turned slowly, as if loath to leave the bronze beast. He caught sight of her and pivoted completely round, his eyes intense as he took note of her altered appearance. With quick, light steps, he closed the distance between them and ushered her back into the sleeping room, one strong hand holding her by the elbow.

"Mnementh has fed lightly and will need quiet to rest," he said in a low voice. He pulled the heavy hanging into place across the opening.

Then he held her away from him, turning her this way and that, scrutinizing her closely, curious and slightly surprised.

"You wash up . . . pretty, yes, almost pretty," he said, amused condescension in his voice. She pulled roughly away from him, piqued. His low laugh mocked her. "After all, how could one guess what was under the grime of . . . ten full Turns?"

At length he said, "No matter. We must eat and I shall require your services." At her startled exclamation, he turned, grinning maliciously now as his movement revealed the caked blood on his left sleeve. "The least you can do is bathe wounds honorably received fighting your battle."

He pushed aside a portion of the drape that curtained the inner wall. "Food for two!" he roared down a black gap in the sheer stone.

She heard a subterranean echo far below as his voice resounded down what must be a long shaft.

"Nemorth is nearly rigid," he was saying as he took supplies from another drape-hidden shelf, "and the Hatching will soon begin anyhow."

A coldness settled in Lessa's stomach at the mention of a Hatching. The mildest tales she had heard about that part of dragonlore were chilling, the worst dismaying macabre. She took the things he handed her numbly.

"What? Frightened?" the dragonman taunted, pausing as he stripped off his torn and bloodied shirt.

With a shake of her head, Lessa turned her attention to the wide-shouldered, well-muscled back he presented her, the paler skin of his body decorated with random bloody streaks. Fresh blood welled from the point of his shoulder for the removal of his shirt had broken the tender scabs.

"I will need water," she said and saw she had a flat pan among the items he had given her. She went swiftly to the pool for water, wondering how she had come to agree to venture so far from Ruatha. Ruined though it was, it had been hers and was familiar to her from Tower to deep cellar. At the moment the idea had been proposed and insidiously prosecuted by the dragonman, she had felt capable of anything, having achieved, at last, Fax's death. Now, it was all she could do to keep the water from slopping out of the pan that shook unaccountably in her hands.

She forced herself to deal only with the wound. It was a nasty gash, deep where the point had entered and torn downward in a gradually shallower slice. His skin felt smooth under her fingers as she cleansed the wound. In spite of herself, she noticed the masculine odor of him, compounded not unpleasantly of sweat, leather, and an unusual muskiness which must be from close association with dragons.

She stood back when she had finished her ministration. He flexed his arm experimentally in the constricting bandage and the motion set the muscles rippling along side and back.

When he faced her, his eyes were dark and thoughtful.

"Gently done. My thanks." His smile was ironic.

She backed away as he rose but he only went to the chest to take out a clean, white shirt.

A muted rumble sounded, growing quickly louder.

Dragons roaring? Lessa wondered, trying to conquer the ridiculous fear that rose within her. Had the Hatching started? There was no watch-wher's lair to secrete herself in, here.

As if he understood her confusion, the dragonman laughed good-humoredly and, his eyes on hers, drew aside the wall covering just as some noisy mechanism inside the shaft propelled a tray of food into sight.

Ashamed of her unbased fright and furious that he had witnessed it, Lessa sat rebelliously down on the fur-covered wall seat, heartily wishing him a variety of serious and painful injuries which she could dress with inconsiderate hands. She would not waste future opportunities.

He placed the tray on the low table in front of her, throwing down a heap of furs for his own seat. There was meat, bread, a tempting yellow cheese and even a few pieces of winter fruit. He made no move to eat nor did she, though the thought of a piece of fruit that was ripe, instead of rotten, set her mouth to watering. He glanced up at her, and frowned.

"Even in the Weyr, the lady breaks bread first," he said, and inclined his head politely to her.

Lessa flushed, unused to any courtesy and certainly unused to being first to eat. She broke off a chunk of bread. It was like nothing she remembered having tasted before. For one thing, it was fresh-baked. The flour had been finely sifted, without trace of sand or hull. She took the slice of cheese he proffered her and it, too, had an uncommonly delicious sharpness. Made bold by this indication of her changed status, Lessa reached for the plumpest piece of fruit.

"Now," the dragonman began, his hand touching hers to get her attention.

Guiltily she dropped the fruit, thinking she had erred. She stared at him, wondering at her fault. He retrieved the fruit and placed it back in her hand as he continued to speak. Wide-eyed, disarmed, she nibbled, and gave him her full attention.

"Listen to me. You must not show a moment's fear, whatever happens on the Hatching Ground. And you must not let her overeat." A wry expression crossed his face. "One of our main functions is to keep a dragon from excessive eating."

Lessa lost interest in the taste of the fruit. She placed it carefully back in the bowl and tried to sort out not what he had said, but what his tone of voice implied. She looked at the dragonman's face, seeing him as a person, not a symbol, for the first time.

There was a blackness about him that was not malevolent; it was a brooding sort of patience. Heavy black hair, heavy black brows; his eyes, a brown light enough to seem golden were all too expressive of cynical emotions, or cold hauteur. His lips were thin but well-shaped and in repose almost gentle. Why must he always pull his mouth to one side in disapproval or in one of those sardonic smiles? At this moment, he was completely unaffected.

He meant what he was saying. He did not want her to be afraid. There was no reason for her, Lessa, *to* fear.

He very much wanted her to succeed. In keeping whom from overeating what? Herd animals? A newly hatched dragon certainly wasn't capable of eating a full beast. That seemed a simple enough task to Lessa. . . . Main function? *Our* main function?

The dragonman was looking at her expectantly.

"Our main function?" she repeated, an unspoken request for more information inherent in her inflection.

"More of that later. First things first," he said, impatiently waving off other questions.

"But what happens?" she insisted.

"As I was told so I tell you. No more, no less. Remember these two points. No fear, and no overeating."

"But . . ."

"You, however, need to eat. Here." He speared a piece of meat on his knife and thrust it at her, frowning until she managed to choke it down. He was about to force more on her but she grabbed up her half-eaten fruit and bit down into the firm sweet sphere instead. She had already eaten more at this one meal than she was accustomed to having all day at the Hold.

"We shall soon eat better at the Weyr," he remarked, regarding the tray with a jaundiced eye.

Lessa was surprised. This was a feast, in her opinion.

"More than you're used to? Yes, I forgot you left Ruatha with bare bones indeed."

She stiffened.

"You did well at Ruatha. I mean no criticism," he added, smiling at her reaction. "But look at you," and he gestured at her body, that curious expression crossing his face, half-amused, half-contemplative. "I should not have guessed you'd clean up pretty," he remarked. "Nor with such hair." This time his expression was frankly admiring.

Involuntarily she put one hand to her head, the hair crackling over her fingers. But what reply she might have made him, indignant as she was, died aborning. An unearthly keening filled the chamber.

The sounds set up a vibration that ran down the bones behind her ear to her spine. She clapped both hands to her ears. The noise rang through her skull despite her defending hands. As abruptly as it started, it ceased.

Before she knew what he was about, the dragonman had grabbed her by the wrist and pulled her over to the chest.

"Take those off," he ordered, indicating dress and tunic. While she stared at him stupidly, he held up a loose white robe, sleeveless and beltless, a matter of two lengths of fine cloth fastened at shoulder and side seams. "Take it off, or do I assist you?" he asked, with no patience at all.

The wild sound was repeated and its unnerving tone made her fingers fly faster. She had no sooner loosened the garments she wore, letting them slide to her feet, than he had thrown the other over her head. She managed to get her arms in the proper places before he grabbed her wrist again and was speeding with her out of the room, her hair whipping out behind her, alive with static.

As they reached the outer chamber, the bronze dragon was standing in the center of the cavern, his head turned to watch the sleeping room door. He seemed impatient to Lessa; his great eyes sparkled iridescently. His manner breathed an inner excitement of great proportions and from his throat a high-pitched croon issued, several octaves below the unnerving cry that had roused them all.

With a yank that rocked her head on her neck, the dragonman pulled her along the passage. The dragon padded beside them at such speed that Lessa fully expected they would all catapult off the ledge. Somehow, at the crucial stride, she was a-perch the bronze neck, the dragonman holding her firmly about the waist. In the same fluid movement, they were gliding across the great bowl of the Weyr to the higher wall opposite. The air was full of wings and dragon tails, rent with a chorus of sounds, echoing and re-echoing across the stony valley.

Mnementh set what Lessa was certain would be a collision course with other dragons, straight for a huge round blackness in the cliff face, high up. Magically, the beasts filed in, the greater wingspread of Mnementh just clearing the sides of the entrance.

The passageway reverberated with the thunder of wings. The air compressed around her thickly. Then they broke out into a gigantic cavern.

Why, the entire mountain must be hollow, thought Lessa, incredulous. Around the enormous cavern, dragons perched in serried ranks, blues, greens, browns and only two great bronze beasts like Mnementh, on ledges meant to accommodate hundreds. Lessa gripped the bronze neck scales before her, instinctively aware of the imminence of a great event.

Mnementh wheeled downward, disregarding the ledge of the bronze ones. Then all Lessa could see was what lay on the sandy floor of the great cavern; dragon eggs. A clutch of ten monstrous, mottled eggs, their shells moving spasmodically as the fledglings within tapped their way out. To one side, on a raised portion of the floor, was a golden egg, larger by half again the size of the mottled ones. Just beyond the golden egg lay the motionless ochre hulk of the old queen.

Just as she realized Mnementh was hovering over the floor in the vicinity of that egg, Lessa felt the dragonman's hands on her, lifting her from Mnementh's neck.

Apprehensively, she grabbed at him. His hands tightened and inexorably swung her down. His eyes, fierce and gray, locked with hers.

"Remember, Lessa!"

Mnementh added an encouragement, one great compound eye turned on her. Then he rose from the floor. Lessa half-raised one hand in entreaty, bereft of all support, even that of the sure inner compulsion which had sustained her in her struggle for revenge on Fax. She saw the bronze dragon settle on the first ledge, at some distance from the other two bronze beasts. The dragonman dismounted and Mnementh curved his sinuous neck until his head was beside his rider. The man reached up absently, it seemed to Lessa, and caressed his mount.

Loud screams and wailings diverted Lessa and she saw more dragons descend to hover just above the cavern floor, each rider depositing a young woman until there were twelve girls, including Lessa. She remained a little apart from them as they clung to each other. She regarded them curiously. The girls were not injured in any way she could see, so why such weeping? She took a deep breath against the coldness within her. Let *them* be afraid. She was Lessa of Ruatha and did not need to be afraid.

Just then, the golden egg moved convulsively. Gasping as one, the girls edged away from it, back against the rocky wall. One, a lovely blonde, her heavy plait of golden hair swinging just above the ground, started to step off the raised floor and stopped, shrieking, backing fearfully towards the scant comfort of her peers.

Lessa wheeled to see what cause there might be for the look of horror on the girl's face. She stepped back involuntarily herself.

In the main section of the sandy arena, several of the handful of eggs had already cracked wide open. The fledglings, crowing weakly, were moving towards . . . and Lessa gulped . . . the young boys standing stolidly in a semi-circle. Some of them were no older than she had been when Fax's army had swooped down on Ruath Hold.

The shrieking of the women subsided to muffled gasps. A fledgling reached out with claw and beak to grab a boy.

Lessa forced herself to watch as the young dragon mauled the youth, throwing him roughly aside as if unsatisfied in some way. The boy did not move and Lessa could see blood seeping onto the sand from dragon-inflicted wounds.

A second fledgling lurched against another boy and halted, flapping its damp wings impotently, raising its scrawny neck and croaking a parody of the encouraging croon Mnementh often gave. The boy uncertainly lifted a hand and began to scratch the eye ridge. Incredulous, Lessa watched as the fledgling, its crooning increasingly more mellow, ducked its head, pushing at the boy. The child's face broke into an unbelieving smile of elation.

Tearing her eyes from this astounding sight, Lessa saw that another fledgling was beginning the same performance with another boy. Two more dragons had emerged in the interim. One had knocked a boy down and was walking over him, oblivious to the fact that its claws were raking great gashes. The fledgling who followed its hatch-mate stopped by the wounded child, ducking its head to the boy's face, crooning anxiously. As Lessa watched, the boy managed to struggle to his feet, tears of pain streaming down his cheeks. She could hear him pleading with the dragon not to worry, that he was only scratched a little.

It was over very soon. The young dragons paired off with boys. Green riders dropped down to carry off the unacceptable. Blue riders settled to the floor with their beasts and led the couples out of the cavern, the young dragons squealing, crooning, flapping wet wings as they staggered off, encouraged by their newly acquired weyrmates.

Lessa turned resolutely back to the rocking golden egg, knowing what to expect and trying to divine what the successful boys had, or had not done, that caused the baby dragons to single them out.

A crack appeared in the golden shell and was greeted by the terrified screams of the girls. Some had fallen into little heaps of white fabric, others embraced tightly in their mutual fear. The crack widened and the wedge head broke through, followed quickly by the neck, gleaming gold. Lessa wondered with unexpected detachment how long it would take the beast to mature, considering its by no means small size at birth. For the head was larger than that of the male dragons and they had been large enough to overwhelm sturdy boys of ten full Turns.

Lessa was aware of a loud hum within the Hall. Glancing up at the audience, she realized it emanated from the watching bronze dragons, for this was the birth of their mate, their queen. The hum increased in volume as the shell shattered into fragments and the golden, glistening body of the new female emerged. It staggered out, dipping its sharp beak into the soft sand, momentarily trapped. Flapping its wet wings, it righted itself, ludicrous in its weak awkwardness. With sudden and unexpected swiftness, it dashed towards the terror-stricken girls.

Before Lessa could blink, it shook the first girl with such violence, her head snapped audibly and she fell limply to the sand. Disregarding her, the dragon leaped towards the second girl but misjudged the distance and fell, grabbing out with one claw for support and raking the girl's body from shoulder to thigh. The screaming of the mortally injured girl distracted the dragon and released the others from their horrified trance. They scattered in panicky confusion, racing, running, tripping, stumbling, falling across the sand towards the exit the boys had used.

As the golden beast, crying piteously, lurched down from the raised arena towards the scattered women, Lessa moved. Why hadn't that silly clunk-headed girl stepped aside, Lessa thought, grabbing for the wedge-head, at birth not much larger than her own torso. The dragon's so clumsy and weak she's her own worst enemy.

Lessa swung the head round so that the many-faceted eyes were forced to look at her . . . and found herself lost in that rainbow regard.

A feeling of joy suffused Lessa, a feeling of warmth, tenderness, unalloyed affection and instant respect and admiration flooded mind and heart and soul. Never again would Lessa lack an advocate, a defender, an intimate, aware instantly of the temper of her mind and heart, of her desires. How wonderful was Lessa, the thought intruded into Lessa's reflections, how pretty, how kind, how thoughtful, how brave and clever!

Mechanically, Lessa reached out to scratch the exact spot on the soft eye ridge. The dragon blinked at her wistfully, extremely sad that she had distressed Lessa.

Lessa reassuringly patted the slightly damp, soft neck that curved trustingly towards her. The dragon reeled to one side and one wing fouled on the hind claw. It hurt. Carefully, Lessa lifted the erring foot, freed the wing, folding it back across the dorsal ridge with a pat.

The dragon began to croon in her throat, her eyes following Lessa's every move. She nudged at Lessa and Lessa obediently attended the other eye ridge.

The dragon let it be known she was hungry.

"We'll get you something to eat directly," Lessa assured her briskly and blinked back at the dragon in amazement. How could she be so callous? It was a fact that this little menace had just now seriously injured, if not killed, two women.

She wouldn't have believed her sympathies could swing so alarmingly towards the beast. Yet it was the most natural thing in the world for her to wish to protect this fledgling.

The dragon arched her neck to look Lessa squarely in the eyes. Ramoth repeated wistfully how exceedingly hungry she was, confined so long in that shell without nourishment.

Lessa wondered how she knew the golden dragon's name and Ramoth replied: Why shouldn't she know her own name since it was hers and no one else's? And then Lessa was lost again in the wonder of those expressive eyes.

Oblivious to the descending bronze dragons, uncaring of the presence of their riders, Lessa stood caressing the head of the most wonderful creature on all Pern, fully prescient of troubles and glories, but most immediately aware that Lessa of Pern was Weyrwoman to Ramoth the Golden, for now and forever.

MESSAGE FOUND IN A COPY OF *FLATLAND*

Rudy Rucker

Rudy Rucker is a mathematician and writer influenced by both Lewis Carroll and Jack Kerouac: his weird variety of sf combines the nineteenth century abstract mathematical landscapes of Edwin Abbott (*Flatland: A Romance of Many Dimensions*, 1884) and C. H. Hinton (*Scientific Romances, First Series*, 1886; *Scientific Romances, Second Series*, 1902; *An Episode of Flatland*, 1907), the first writers to create imagined settings out of the spatial dimensions of mathematical conceptualizing, with the hip, paranoid, literary ethos of the beatnik underground. His stories tend toward hard sf and then bounce and veer in a variety of directions, sometimes into the range of cyberpunk. He was a fellow-traveler of Bruce Sterling and William Gibson in the early eighties and is included by Sterling in the Movement anthology *Mirrorshades* (1986). But Rucker remains an individualist: a successful popular-science writer, sometime college professor, and sf writer who careens and caroms from one sf form to another. His work is energetic and imaginative; New Wave and hard sf attitudes coexist within it.

His attitude is comic, Kerouac-hippie, his style is somewhere between Mark Twain and John Sladek. His novel *White Light* (1980) was followed by several other novels, including *Spacetime Donuts* (1981), *Software* (1982), *Wetware* (1988), and *The Hollow Earth* (1990). His short fiction tends to be intellectually demanding and abstract.

"Message Found in a Copy of *Flatland*" is an archly old-fashioned tale of a scholar trapped by his narrow-minded scholarship, a mathematical story at once a parody of the classic by Abbott and a sincere homage. There is no better example of hard science fiction making literal the abstract imagery of science and mathematics than this piece. Gregory Benford commented skeptically on the literary effectiveness of math stories: "Mathematical languages have such a wonderful aura of precision and controllability, which is why scientists are intuitively drawn to them; but they lack a quality I can only describe as human expressiveness." However, Rucker, with his broad brush strokes, manages to make his story by turns intriguing, frightening, and hilarious.

The story, which appears below, is purported to be Robert Ackley's first-person account of his strange disappearance. I am not quite sure if the account is really true . . . I rather hope, for Ackley's sake, that it is not.

I obtained the typescript of this story in a roundabout way. My friend, Gregory Gibson, was in London last year, looking for rare books. A dealer in Cheapside Street showed Gibson a copy of an early edition of Edwin Abbott's 1884 fiction, *Flatland.* The copy Gibson saw was remarkable for the fact that someone had handwritten a whole story in the margins of the book's pages. The dealer told

Gibson that the volume was brought in by a cook's helper, who had found the book in the basement of a Pakistani restaurant where he once worked.

Gibson could not afford the book's very steep purchase price, but he did obtain the dealer's permission to copy out the story written in the volume's margins. Here, without further ado, it is: the singular adventure of Robert Ackley.

All my attempts to get back through the tunnel have proven fruitless. It will be necessary for me to move on and seek another way out. Before departing, however, I will write out an account of my adventures thus far.

Until last year I had always believed Edwin Abbott's *Flatland* to be a work of fiction. Now I know better. Flatland is real. I can look up and see it as I write.

For those of my readers familiar with the book in whose margins I write, this will be startling news; for *Flatland* tells the adventures of A Square, a two-dimensional being living in a two-dimensional world. How, you may ask, could such a filmy world really exist? How could there be intelligent creatures with length and width, yet without thickness? If Flatland is real, then why am I the only living man who has touched it? Patience, dear readers. All this, and much more, will be revealed.

The scientific justification for *Flatland* is that it helps us better to understand the fourth dimension. "The fourth dimension" is a concept peculiarly linked to the late nineteenth century. In those years, mathematicians had just laid the foundations for a comprehensive theory of higher-dimensional space. Physicists were beginning to work with the notion of four-dimensional spacetime. Philosophers were using the idea of a fourth dimension to solve some of their oldest riddles. And mediums throughout Europe were coming to the conclusion that the spirits of the dead consist of four-dimensional ectoplasm. There was an immense popular interest in the fourth dimension, and *Flatland*, subtitled, "A Romance of Many Dimensions," was an immediate success.

Abbott's method was to describe a two-dimensional square's difficulties in imagining a third dimension of space. As we read of A Square's struggles, we become better able to understand our own difficulties in imagining a fourth dimension. The fourth dimension is to us, what the third dimension is to the Flatlanders.

This powerful analogy is the rarest of things: a truly new idea. I often used to ask myself where Abbott might have gotten such an idea. When Gray University granted me my sabbatical last year, I determined to go to London and look through Abbott's papers and publications. Could *Flatland* have been inspired by A.F. Möbius's *Barycentric Calculus* of 1827? Might Abbott have corresponded with C. H. Hinton, eccentric author of the 1880 essay, "What Is The Fourth Dimension?" Or is *Flatland* nothing more than the inspired reworking of certain ideas in Plato's *Republic*?

Abbott wrote many other books in his lifetime, all crashingly dull: *How to Parse, The Kernel and the Husk—Letters on Spiritual Christianity, English Lessons for English People, A Shakespearian Grammar, Parables for Children*, and so on. Except for *Flatland*, all of Abbott's books are just what one would expect from a Victorian clergyman, headmaster of the City of London School. Where did Abbott find his inspiration for *Flatland*? The answer is stranger than I could ever have imagined.

It was an unnaturally hot day in July. The London papers were full of stories about the heat-wave. One man reported that three golf-balls had exploded in the heat of his parked car. All the blackboards in a local school had cracked. Numerous pigeons had died and fallen to the sidewalks. I finished my greasy breakfast and set forth from my hotel, an unprepossessing structure not far from St. Paul's Cathedral.

My plan for the day was to visit the site of the old City of London School on

Cheapside at Milk Street. Abbott attended the school himself, and then returned as headmaster for the years 1865–1889. Under Abbott's leadership the school moved to a new building in 1882, but I had a feeling that some valuable clue to his psychology might still be found in the older building.

To my disappointment, nothing of the old building remained . . . at least nothing that I could see. Much of Cheapside was destroyed during the Blitz. Flimsy concrete and metal structures have replaced what stood there before. I came to a halt at the corner of Cheapside and Milk, utterly discouraged.

Sweat trickled down my sides. A red double-decker labored past, fouling the heavy air with its exhaust. Ugly, alien music drifted out of the little food-shops. I was jostled by men and women of every caste and color: masses of people, hot and impatient, inescapable as the flow of time.

I pushed into a wretched Pakistani snack-bar and ordered a beer. They had none. I settled for a Coke. I tried to imagine Edwin Abbott walking through this dingy space one hundred years ago.

The girl behind the counter handed me my Coke. Her skin had a fine coppery color, and her lips were like chocolate ice cream. She didn't smile, but neither did she frown. Desperate with loneliness and disorientation, I struck up a conversation.

"Have you been here long?"

"I was born in London." Her impeccable accent came as a rebuke. "My father owns this shop now for five years."

"Do you know I came all the way from America just to visit this shop?"

She laughed and looked away. A girl in a big city learns to ignore madmen.

"No, no," I insisted. "It's really true. Look . . ." I took out my dog-eared first edition of *Flatland*, this very copy in whose margins I now write. "The man who wrote this book was headmaster of a school that stood near this spot."

"What school?"

"The City School of London. They moved it to the Victoria Embankment in 1882."

"Then you should go there. Here we have only food." For some reason the sight of Abbott's book had caused her cheeks to flush an even darker hue.

"I'll save that trip for another day. Don't you want to know what the book is about?"

"I do know. It is about flat creatures who slide around in a plane."

The readiness of her response astonished me. But before I could pose another question, the girl had turned to serve another customer, a turbanned Sikh with a pockmarked face. I scanned the menu, looking for something else to order.

"Could I have some of the spicy meatballs, please?"

"Certainly."

"What's your name?"

"Deela."

She failed to ask mine, so I volunteered the information. "I'm Bob. Professor Robert Ackley of Gray University."

"And what do you profess?" She set the plate of meatballs down with an encouraging click.

"Mathematics. I study the fourth dimension, just as Abbott did. Have you really read *Flatland*?"

Deela glanced down the counter, as if fearful of being overhead. "I have not *read* it. I . . ."

The Sikh interrupted then, calling for butter on his rice. I sampled one of the meatballs. It was hot and dry as desert sand.

"Could I have another Coke, please?"

"Are you rich?" Deela whispered unexpectedly.

Was she hoping for a date with me? Well, why not? This was the longest conversation I'd had with anyone since coming to London. "I'm well-off," I said, hoping to make myself attractive. "I have a good position, and I am unmarried. Would you like to have dinner with me?"

This proposal seemed to surprise Deela. She covered her mouth with one hand and burst into high laughter. Admittedly I am no ladies' man, but this really seemed too rude to bear. I put away my book and rose to my feet.

"What do I owe you?"

"I'm sorry I laughed, Robert. You surprised me. Perhaps I will have dinner with you some day." She lowered her voice and leaned closer. "Downstairs here there is something you should see. I was hoping that you might pay to see it."

It seemed very hot and close in this little restaurant. The inclination of the Sikh's turban indicated that he was listening to our conversation. I had made a fool of myself. It was time to go. Stiffly I paid the bill and left. Only when I stepped out on the street and looked at my change did I realize that Deela had given me a note.

Robert—

Flatland is in the basement of our shop. Come back at closing time and I will show it to you. Please bring one hundred pounds. My father is ill.

Deela.

I turned and started back into the shop. But Deela made a worried face and placed her fingers on her lips. Very well, I could wait. Closing time, I noted, was ten P.M.

I spent the rest of the day in the British Museum, ferreting out obscure books on the fourth dimension. For the first time I was able to hold in my hands a copy of J.K.F. Zöllner's 1878 book, *Transcendental Physics*. Here I read how a spirit from hyperspace would be able to enter a closed room by coming in, not through walls or ceiling, but through the "side" of the room lying open to the fourth dimension.

Four-dimensional spirits . . . long sought, but never found! Smiling a bit at Zöllner's gullibility, I set his book down and reread Deela's note. *Flatland is in the basement of our shop.* What could she mean by this? Had they perhaps found Abbott's original manuscript in the ruined foundations of the old City School? Or did she mean something more literal, something more incredible, something more bizarre than spirits from the fourth dimension?

The whole time in the library, I had the feeling that someone was watching me. When I stepped back onto the street, I realized that I was indeed being followed. It was the Sikh, his obstinate turban always half a block behind me. Finally I lost him by going into a movie theater, leaving by the rear exit, and dashing into the nearest pub.

I passed a bland few hours there, drinking the warm beer and eating the stodgy food. Finally it was ten P.M.

Deela was waiting for me in the darkened shop. She let me in and locked the door behind me.

"Did you bring the money?"

The empty shop felt very private. Deela's breath was spicy and close. What had I really come for?

"Flatland," stated Deela, "is in the basement. Did you bring the money?"

I gave her a fifty-pound note. She flattened it out and held it up to examine it by the street-light. Suddenly there was a rapping at the door. The Sikh!

"Quick!" Deela took me by the arm and rushed me behind the counter and down a narrow hallway. "Down there," she said, indicating a door. "I'll get rid of him." She trotted back out to the front of the shop.

Breathless with fear and excitement, I opened the shabby door and stepped down onto the dark stairs.

The door swung closed behind me, muffling the sound of Deela's voice. She was arguing with the Sikh, though without letting him in. I moved my head this way and that, trying to make out what lay in the basement. Deela's faint voice grew shriller. There was what looked like a ball of light floating at the foot of the stairs. An oddly patterned ball of light some three feet across. I went down a few more steps to have a closer look. The thing was sort of like a huge lens, a lens looking onto . . .

Just then there came the sound of shattering glass. The Sikh had smashed his way in! The clangor of the shop's burglar alarm drowned out Deela's wild screams. Footsteps pounded close by and the door at the head of the stairs flew open.

"Come back up, Professor Ackley," called the Sikh. His voice was high and desperate. "You are in great danger."

But I couldn't tear myself away from the glowing sphere. It appeared to be an Einstein-Rosen bridge, a space-tunnel leading into another universe. The other universe seemed to contain only one thing: an endless glowing plane filled with moving forms. Flatland.

The Sikh came clattering down the stairs. My legs made a decision. I leaped forward, through the space-tunnel and into another world.

I landed on all fours . . . there was a sort of floor about a yard below the plane of Flatland. When I stood up, it was as if I were standing waist-deep in an endless, shiny lake. My fall through the Flatlanders' space had smashed up one of their houses. Several of them were nosing at my waist, wondering what I was. To my surprise, I could feel their touch quite distinctly. They seemed to have a thickness of several millimeters.

The mouth of the space-tunnel was right overhead, a dark sphere framing the Sikh's excited little face. He reached down as if to grab me. I quickly squatted down beneath the plane of Flatland and crawled away across the firm, smooth floor. The hazy, bright space shimmered overhead like an endless soap-film, effectively shielding me from the Sikh.

I could hear the sound of more footsteps on the stairs. Deela? There were cries, a gunshot, and then silence. I poked my head back up, being careful not to bump any Flatlanders. The dark opening of the space-tunnel was empty. I was safe, safe in Flatland. I rose up to my full height and surveyed the region around me.

I was standing in the middle of a "street," that is to say, in the middle of a clear path lined with Flatland houses on either side. The houses had the form of large squares and rectangles, three to five feet on a side. The Flatlanders themselves were as Abbott has described them: women are short Lines with a bright eye at one end, the soldiers are very sharp isoceles Triangles, and there are Squares, Pentagons and other Polygons as well. The adults are, on the average, about twelve inches across.

The buildings that lined my street bore signs in the form of strings of colored

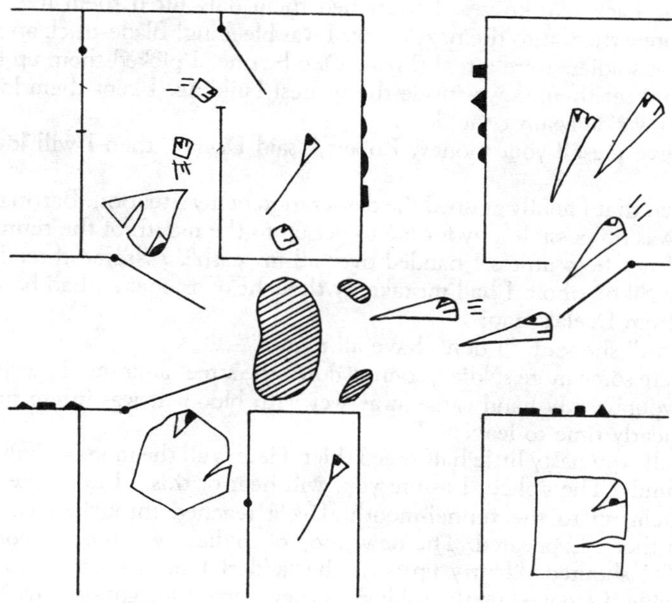

dots along their outer walls. To my right was the house of a childless Hexagon and his wife. To my left was the home of an equilateral Triangle, proud father of three little Squares. The Triangle's door, a hinged line-segment, stood ajar. One of his children, who had been playing in the street, sped inside, frightened by my appearance. The plane of Flatland cut me at the waist and arms, giving me the appearance of a large blob flanked by two smaller blobs—a weird and uncanny spectacle, to be sure.

Now the Triangle stuck his eye out of his door to study me. I could feel his excited voice vibrating the space touching my waist. Flatland seemed to be made of a sort of jelly, perhaps one-sixteenth of an inch thick.

Suddenly I heard Deela calling to me. I looked back at the dark mouth of the tunnel, floating about eight feet above the mysterious ground on which I stood. I walked towards it, staying in the middle of the street. The little line-segment doors slammed as I walked past, and I could look down at the Flatlanders cowering in their homes.

I stopped under the tunnel's mouth and looked up at Deela. She was holding a coiled-up rope-ladder.

"Do you want to come out now, Robert?" There was something cold and unpleasant about her voice.

"What happened to the Sikh?"

"He will not bother us again. How much money do you have with you?"

I recalled that so far I had only paid her half of the hundred pounds. "Don't worry, I'll give you the rest of the money." But how could she even think of money with a wonder like this to . . .

I felt a sharp pain in the small of my back, then another. I whirled around to see a platoon of two dozen Flatland soldiers bearing down on me. Two of them had stuck into my back like knives. I wrenched them out, lifted them free of their space, and threw them into the next block. I was bleeding! Blade-thick and tough-skinned, these soldiers were a real threat. One by one, I picked them up by their blunt ends and set them down inside the nearest building. I kept them locked in by propping my side against the door.

"If you give me all your money, Robert," said Deela, "then I will lower this rope-ladder."

It was then that I finally grasped the desperation of my situation. Barring Deela's help, there was no possible way for me to get up to the mouth of the tunnel. And Deela would not help unless I handed over all my cash . . . some three hundred pounds. The Sikh, whom I had mistakenly thought of as enemy, had been trying to save me from Deela's trap!

"Come on," she said. "I don't have all night."

There were some more soldiers coming down the street after me. I reached back to feel my wounds. My hand came away wet with blood. It was interesting here, but it was clearly time to leave.

"Very well, you nasty little half-breed thief. Here is all the money I have. Three hundred pounds. The police, I assure you, will hear of this." I drew the bills out and held them up to the tunnel-mouth. Deela reached through, snatched the money, and then disappeared. The new troop of soldiers was almost upon me.

"Hurry!" I shouted. "Hurry up with the ladder! I need medical attention!" Moving quickly, I scooped up the soldiers as they came. One got past my hand and stabbed me in the stomach. I grew angry, and dealt with the remaining soldiers by poking out their hearts.

When I was free to look up at the tunnel-mouth again, I saw a sight to chill the blood. It was the Sikh, eyes glazed in death, his arms dangling down towards me. I realized that Deela had shot him. I grabbed one of his hands and pulled, hoping to lift myself up into the tunnel. But the corpse slid down, crashed through Flatland, and thudded onto the floor at my feet.

"Deela!" I screamed. "For the love of God!"

Her face appeared again . . . but she was no longer holding the rope-ladder. In its stead she held a pistol. Of course it would not do to set me free. I would make difficulties. With my body already safe in this dimensional oubliette, it would be nonsense to set me free. Deela aimed her gun.

As before, I ducked below Flatland's opalescent surface and crawled for dear life. Deela didn't even bother shooting.

"Goodbye, Robert," I heard her calling. "Stay away from the tunnel or else!" This was followed by her laughter, her footsteps, the slamming of the cellar door, and then silence.

That was two days ago. My wounds have healed. The Sikh had grown stiff. I made several repellent efforts to use his corpse as a ladder or grappling-hook, but to no avail. The tunnel-mouth is too high, and I am constantly distracted by the attacks of the isoceles Triangles.

But my situation is not entirely desperate. The Flatlanders are, I have learned, edible, with a taste something like very moist smoked salmon. It takes quite a few of them to make a meal, but they are plentiful, and they are easy to catch. No matter how tightly they lock their doors, they never know when the five globs of my fingers will appear like Zöllner's spirits to snatch them away.

I have filled the margins of my beloved old *Flatland* now. It is time to move on.

Somewhere there may be another tunnel. Before leaving, I will throw this message up through the tunnel-mouth. It will lie beneath the basement stairs, and someday someone will find it.

Farewell, reader, and do not pity me. I was but a poor laborer in the vineyard of knowledge—and now I have become the Lord of Flatland.

THE COLD EQUATIONS

Tom Godwin

Tom Godwin was a Campbell writer of hard sf and science fiction adventure who began publishing stories in *Astounding* in 1953; in 1954, he wrote his most famous story, "The Cold Equations." Although he wrote on into the seventies, producing three novels and a relatively small number of stories, his generally sentimental approach to characterization did not bring him notable commercial success or popular attention—except for the enduring interest in this one story.

Here is one of the most popular and controversial hard sf stories of the last fifty years, a story that stacks the deck and then plays with the reader's emotions with carefully juxtaposed clichés that imply a *deus ex machina*—then frustrates that false expectation. It is a provocative companion piece to Philip Latham's "The Xi Effect," with which most sf readers of the period would have been familiar. Godwin's story angered many readers when it appeared in the fifties, nearly all of whom wanted the problem solved by violating some scientific principle or law. It is said that Campbell demanded the story end this way.

The point of the story, of course, is that scientific laws cannot be violated under any circumstance, and ignorance of scientific law can kill you, no matter how sincere you are. James Gunn, in his influential historical anthology, *The Road to Science Fiction* (Vol. 3, 1979), declares the story a touchstone for sf reading: "If the reader doesn't understand it or appreciate what it is trying to say about humanity and its relationship to its environment, then that reader isn't likely to appreciate science fiction. If the reader keeps objecting . . . then that reader isn't reading the story correctly." Such readers do not have the right attitude, the hard sf attitude.

If there is a universal allegory beneath the hard sf story, it is, as Hal Clement has stated, that the universe is antagonistic to life, and that only through knowledge of physical law, and adherence to it, may life survive. There is no clearer affirmation of the principle that science and scientific law rule the universe than "The Cold Equations" in all of sf, which perhaps accounts for its enduring popularity.

He was not alone.

There was nothing to indicate the fact but the white hand of the tiny gauge on the board before him. The control room was empty but for himself; there was no sound other than the murmur of the drives—but the white hand had moved. It had been on zero when the little ship was launched from the *Stardust*; now, an hour later, it had crept up. There was something in the supplies closet across the room, it was saying, some kind of a body that radiated heat.

It could be but one kind of a body—a living, human body.

He leaned back in the pilot's chair and drew a deep, slow breath, considering what he would have to do. He was an EDS pilot, inured to the sight of death, long since accustomed to it and to viewing the dying of another man with an objective lack of emotion, and he had no choice in what he must do. There could be no alternative—but it required a few moments of conditioning for even an EDS pilot to prepare himself to walk across the room and coldly, deliberately, take the life of a man he had yet to meet.

He would, of course, do it. It was the law, stated very bluntly and definitely in grim Paragraph L, Section 8, of Interstellar Regulations: *Any stowaway discovered in an EDS shall be jettisoned immediately following discovery.*

It was the law, and there could be no appeal.

It was a law not of men's choosing but made imperative by the circumstances of the space frontier. Galactic expansion had followed the development of the hyperspace drive and as men scattered wide across the frontier there had come the problem of contact with the isolated first-colonies and exploration parties. The huge hyperspace cruisers were the product of the combined genius and effort of Earth and were long and expensive in the building. They were not available in such numbers that small colonies could possess them. The cruisers carried the colonists to their new worlds and made periodic visits, running on tight schedules, but they could not stop and turn aside to visit colonies scheduled to be visited at another time; such a delay would destroy their schedule and produce a confusion and uncertainty that would wreck the complex interdependence between old Earth and new worlds of the frontier.

Some method of delivering supplies or assistance when an emergency occurred on a world not scheduled for a visit had been needed and the Emergency Dispatch Ships had been the answer. Small and collapsible, they occupied little room in the hold of the cruiser; made of light metal and plastics, they were driven by a small rocket drive that consumed relatively little fuel. Each cruiser carried four EDS's and when a call for aid was received the nearest cruiser would drop into normal space long enough to launch an EDS with the needed supplies or personnel, then vanish again as it continued on its course.

The cruisers, powered by nuclear converters, did not use the liquid rocket fuel but nuclear converters were far too large and complex to permit their installation in the EDS's. The cruisers were forced by necessity to carry a limited amount of the bulky rocket fuel and the fuel was rationed with care; the cruiser's computers determining the exact amount of fuel each EDS would require for its mission. The computers considered the course coordinates, the mass of the EDS, the mass of pilot and cargo; they were very precise and accurate and omitted nothing from their calculations. They could not, however, foresee, and allow for, the added mass of a stowaway.

The *Stardust* had received the request from one of the exploration parties stationed on Woden; the six men of the party already being stricken with the fever carried by the green *kala* midges and their own supply of serum destroyed by the tornado that had torn through their camp. The *Stardust* had gone through the usual procedure; dropping into normal space to launch the EDS with the fever serum, then vanishing again in hyperspace. Now, an hour later, the gauge was saying there was something more than the small carton of serum in the supplies closet.

He let his eyes rest on the narrow white door of the closet. There, just inside, another man lived and breathed and was beginning to feel assured that discovery of his presence would now be too late for the pilot to alter the situation. It *was* too late—for the man behind the door it was far later than he thought and in a way he would find terrible to believe.

There could be no alternative. Additional fuel would be used during the hours of deceleration to compensate for the added mass of the stowaway; infinitesimal increments of fuel that would not be missed until the ship had almost reached its destination. Then, at some distance above the ground that might be as near as a thousand feet or as far as tens of thousands of feet, depending upon the mass of ship and cargo and the preceding period of deceleration, the unmissed increments of fuel would make their absence known; the EDS would expend its last drops of fuel with a sputter and go into whistling free fall. Ship and pilot and stowaway would merge together upon impact as a wreckage of metal and plastic, flesh and blood, driven deep into the soil. The stowaway had signed his own death warrant when he concealed himself on the ship; he could not be permitted to take seven others with him.

He looked again at the telltale white hand, then rose to his feet. What he must do would be unpleasant for both of them; the sooner it was over, the better. He stepped across the control room, to stand by the white door.

"Come out!" His command was harsh and abrupt above the murmur of the drive.

It seemed he could hear the whisper of a furtive movement inside the closet, then nothing. He visualized the stowaway cowering closer into one corner, suddenly worried by the possible consequences of his act and his self-assurance evaporating.

"I said *out*!"

He heard the stowaway move to obey and he waited with his eyes alert on the door and his hand near the blaster at his side.

The door opened and the stowaway stepped through it, smiling. "All right—I give up. Now what?"

It was a girl.

He stared without speaking, his hand dropping away from the blaster and acceptance of what he saw coming like a heavy and unexpected physical blow. The stowaway was not a man—she was a girl in her teens, standing before him in little white gypsy sandals with the top of her brown, curly head hardly higher than his shoulder, with a faint, sweet scent of perfume coming from her and her smiling face tilted up so her eyes could look unknowing and unafraid into his as she waited for his answer.

Now what? Had it been asked in the deep, defiant voice of a man he would have answered it with action, quick and efficient. He would have taken the stowaway's identification disk and ordered him into the air lock. Had the stowaway refused to obey, he would have used the blaster. It would not have taken long; within a minute the body would have been ejected into space—had the stowaway been a man.

He returned to the pilot's chair and motioned her to seat herself on the boxlike bulk of the drive-control units that set against the wall beside him. She obeyed, his silence making the smile fade into the meek and guilty expression of a pup that has been caught in mischief and knows it must be punished.

"You still haven't told me," she said. "I'm guilty, so what happens to me now? Do I pay a fine, or what?"

"What are you doing here?" he asked. "Why did you stow away on this EDS?"

"I wanted to see my brother. He's with the government survey crew on Woden and I haven't seen him for ten years, not since he left Earth to go into government survey work."

"What was your destination on the *Stardust*?"

"Mimir. I have a position waiting for me there. My brother has been sending money home all the time to us—my father and mother and I—and he paid for a special course in linguistics I was taking. I graduated sooner than expected and I was offered this job on Mimir. I knew it would be almost a year before Gerry's job was done on Woden so he could come on to Mimir and that's why I hid in the closet, there. There was plenty of room for me and I was willing to pay the fine. There were only the two of us kids—Gerry and I—and I haven't seen him for so long, and I didn't want to wait another year when I could see him now, even though I knew I would be breaking some kind of a regulation when I did it."

I knew I would be breaking some kind of a regulation— In a way, she could not be blamed for her ignorance of the law; she was of Earth and had not realized that the laws of the space frontier must, of necessity, be as hard and relentless as the environment that gave them birth. Yet, to protect such as her from the results of their own ignorance of the frontier, there had been a sign over the door that led to the section of the *Stardust* that housed EDS's; a sign that was plain for all to see and heed:

UNAUTHORIZED PERSONNEL
KEEP OUT!

"Does your brother know that you took passage on the *Stardust* for Mimir?"

"Oh, yes. I sent him a spacegram telling him about my graduation and about going to Mimir on the *Stardust* a month before I left Earth. I already knew Mimir was where he would be stationed in a little over a year. He gets a promotion then, and he'll be based on Mimir and not have to stay out a year at a time on field trips, like he does now."

There were two different survey groups on Woden, and he asked, "What is his name?"

"Cross—Gerry Cross. He's in Group Two—that was the way his address read. Do you know him?"

Group One had requested the serum; Group Two was eight thousand miles away, across the Western Sea.

"No, I've never met him," he said, then turned to the control board and cut the deceleration to a fraction of a gravity; knowing as he did so that it could not avert the ultimate end, yet doing the only thing he could do to prolong that ultimate end. The sensation was like that of the ship suddenly dropping and the girl's involuntary movement of surprise half lifted her from the seat.

"We're going faster now, aren't we?" she asked. "Why are we doing that?"

He told her the truth. "To save fuel for a little while."

"You mean, we don't have very much?"

He delayed the answer he must give her so soon to ask: "How did you manage to stow away?"

"I just sort of walked in when no one was looking my way," she said. "I was practicing my Gelanese on the native girl who does the cleaning in the Ship's Supply office when someone came in with an order for supplies for the survey crew on Woden. I slipped into the closet there after the ship was ready to go and just before you came in. It was an impulse of the moment to stow away, so I could get to see Gerry—and from the way you keep looking at me so grim, I'm not sure it was a very wise impulse.

"But I'll be a model criminal—or do I mean prisoner?" She smiled at him again. "I intended to pay for my keep on top of paying the fine. I can cook and I can patch clothes for everyone and I know how to do all kinds of useful things, even a little bit about nursing."

There was one more question to ask:

"Did you know what the supplies were that the survey crew ordered?"

"Why, no. Equipment they needed in their work, I supposed."

Why couldn't she have been a man with some ulterior motive? A fugitive from justice, hoping to lose himself on a raw new world; an opportunist, seeking transportation to the new colonies where he might find golden fleece for the taking; a crackpot, with a mission—

Perhaps once in his lifetime an EDS pilot would find such a stowaway on his ship; warped men, mean and selfish men, brutal and dangerous men—but never, before, a smiling, blue-eyed girl who was willing to pay her fine and work for her keep that she might see her brother.

He turned to the board and turned the switch that would signal the *Stardust*. The call would be futile but he could not, until he had exhausted that one vain hope, seize her and thrust her into the air lock as he would an animal—or a man. The delay, in the meantime, would not be dangerous with the EDS decelerating at fractional gravity.

A voice spoke from the communicator. "*Stardust*. Identify yourself and proceed."

"Barton, EDS 34G11. Emergency. Give me Commander Delhart."

There was a faint confusion of noises as the request went through the proper channels. The girl was watching him, no longer smiling.

"Are you going to order them to come back after me?" she asked.

The communicator clicked and there was the sound of a distant voice saying, "Commander, the EDS requests—"

"Are they coming back after me?" she asked again. "Won't I get to see my brother, after all?"

"Barton?" The blunt, gruff voice of Commander Delhart came from the communicator. "What's this about an emergency?"

"A stowaway," he answered.

"A stowaway?" There was a slight surprise to the question. "That's rather unusual—but why the 'emergency' call? You discovered him in time so there should be no appreciable danger and I presume you've informed Ship's Records so his nearest relatives can be notified."

"That's why I had to call you, first. The stowaway is still aboard and the circumstances are so different—"

"Different?" the commander interrupted, impatience in his voice. "How can they be different? You know you have a limited supply of fuel; you also know the law, as well as I do: 'Any stowaway discovered in an EDS shall be jettisoned immediately following discovery.' "

There was the sound of a sharply indrawn breath from the girl. "*What does he mean?*"

"The stowaway is a girl."

"*What?*"

"She wanted to see her brother. She's only a kid and she didn't know what she was really doing."

"I see." All the curtness was gone from the commander's voice. "So you called me in the hope I could do something?" Without waiting for an answer he went on. "I'm sorry—I can do nothing. This cruiser must maintain its schedule; the life of not one person but the lives of many depend on it. I know how you feel but I'm powerless to help you. You'll have to go through with it. I'll have you connected with Ship's Records."

* * *

The communicator faded to a faint rustle of sound and he turned back to the girl. She was leaning forward on the bench, almost rigid, her eyes fixed wide and frightened.

"What did he mean, to go through with it? To jettison me . . . to go through with it—what did he mean? Not the way it sounded . . . he couldn't have. What did he mean . . . what did he really mean?"

Her time was too short for the comfort of a lie to be more than a cruelly fleeting delusion.

"He meant it the way it sounded."

"*No!*" She recoiled from him as though he had struck her, one hand half upraised as though to fend him off and stark unwillingness to believe in her eyes.

"It will have to be."

"No! You're joking—you're insane! You can't mean it!"

"I'm sorry." He spoke slowly to her, gently. "I should have told you before—I should have, but I had to do what I could first; I had to call the *Stardust*. You heard what the commander said."

"But you can't—if you make me leave the ship, I'll *die*."

"I know."

She searched his face and the unwillingness to believe left her eyes, giving way slowly to a look of dazed terror.

"You—know?" She spoke the words far apart, numb and wonderingly.

"I know. It has to be like that."

"You mean it—you really mean it." She sagged back against the wall, small and limp like a little rag doll and all the protesting and disbelief gone.

"You're going to do it—you're going to make me die?"

"I'm sorry," he said again. "You'll never know how sorry I am. It has to be that way and no human in the universe can change it."

"You're going to make me die and I didn't do anything to die for—I didn't *do* anything—"

He sighed, deep and weary. "I know you didn't, child. I know you didn't—"

"EDS." The communicator rapped brisk and metallic. "This is Ship's Records. Give us all information on subject's identification disk."

He got out of his chair to stand over her. She clutched the edge of the seat, her upturned face white under the brown hair and the lipstick standing out like a blood-red cupid's bow.

"*Now?*"

"I want your identification disk," he said.

She released the edge of the seat and fumbled at the chain that suspended the plastic disk from her neck with fingers that were trembling and awkward. He reached down and unfastened the clasp for her, then returned with the disk to his chair.

"Here's your data, Records: Identification Number T837—"

"One moment," Records interrupted. "This is to be filed on the gray card, of course?"

"Yes."

"And the time of the execution?"

"I'll tell you later."

"Later? This is highly irregular; the time of the subject's death is required before—"

He kept the thickness out of his voice with an effort. "Then we'll do it in a highly irregular manner—you'll hear the disk read, first. The subject is a girl and she's listening to everything that's said. Are you capable of understanding that?"

There was a brief, almost shocked, silence, then Records said meekly: "Sorry. Go ahead."

He began to read the disk, reading it slowly to delay the inevitable for as long as possible, trying to help her by giving her what little time he could to recover from her first terror and let it resolve into the calm of acceptance and resignation.

"Number T8374 dash Y54. Name: Marilyn Lee Cross. Sex: Female. Born: July 7, 2160. *She was only eighteen.* Height: 5-3. Weight: 110. *Such a slight weight, yet enough to add fatally to the mass of the shell-thin bubble that was an EDS.* Hair: Brown. Eyes: Blue. Complexion: Light. Blood Type: O. *Irrelevant data.* Destination: Port City, Mimir. *Invalid data—*"

He finished and said, "I'll call you later," then turned once again to the girl. She was huddled back against the wall, watching him with a look of numb and wondering fascination.

"They're waiting for you to kill me, aren't they? They want me dead, don't they? You and everybody on the cruiser wants me dead, don't you?" Then the numbness broke and her voice was that of a frightened and bewildered child. "Everybody wants me dead and I didn't *do* anything. I didn't hurt anyone—I only wanted to see my brother."

"It's not the way you think—it isn't that way, at all," he said. "Nobody wants it this way; nobody would ever let it be this way if it was humanly possible to change it."

"Then why is it! I don't understand. Why is it?"

"This ship is carrying *kala* fever serum to Group One on Woden. Their own supply was destroyed by a tornado. Group Two—the crew your brother is in—is eight thousand miles away across the Western Sea and their helicopters can't cross it to help Group One. The fever is invariably fatal unless the serum can be had in time, and the six men in Group One will die unless this ship reaches them on schedule. These little ships are always given barely enough fuel to reach their destination and if you stay aboard your added weight will cause it to use up all its fuel before it reaches the ground. It will crash, then, and you and I will die and so will the six men waiting for the fever serum."

It was a full minute before she spoke, and as she considered his words the expression of numbness left her eyes.

"Is that it?" she asked at last. "Just that the ship doesn't have enough fuel?"

"Yes."

"I can go alone or I can take seven others with me—is that the way it is?"

"That's the way it is."

"And nobody wants me to have to die?"

"Nobody."

"Then maybe— Are you sure nothing can be done about it? Wouldn't people help me if they could?"

"Everyone would like to help you but there is nothing anyone can do. I did the only thing I could do when I called the *Stardust*."

"And it won't come back—but there might be other cruisers, mightn't there? Isn't there any hope at all that there might be someone, somewhere, who could do something to help me?"

She was leaning forward a little in her eagerness as she waited for his answer.

"No."

The word was like the drop of a cold stone and she again leaned back against the wall, the hope and eagerness leaving her face. "You're sure—you *know* you're sure?"

"I'm sure. There are no other cruisers within forty light-years; there is nothing and no one to change things."

She dropped her gaze to her lap and began twisting a pleat of her skirt between her fingers, saying no more as her mind began to adapt itself to the grim knowledge. It was better so; with the going of all hope would go the fear; with the going of all hope would come resignation. She needed time and she could have so little of it. How much?

The EDS's were not equipped with hull-cooling units; their speed had to be reduced to a moderate level before entering the atmosphere. They were decelerating at .10 gravity; approaching their destination at a far higher speed than the computers had calculated on. The *Stardust* had been quite near Woden when she launched the EDS; their present velocity was putting them nearer by the second. There would be a critical point, soon to be reached, when he would have to resume deceleration. When he did so the girl's weight would be multiplied by the gravities of deceleration, would become, suddenly, a factor of paramount importance; the factor the computers had been ignorant of when they determined the amount of fuel the EDS should have. She would have to go when deceleration began; it could be no other way. When would that be—how long could he let her stay?

"How long can I stay?"

He winced involuntarily from the words that were so like an echo of his own thoughts. How long? He didn't know; he would have to ask the ship's computers. Each EDS was given a meager surplus of fuel to compensate for unfavorable conditions within the atmosphere and relatively little fuel was being consumed for the time being. The memory banks of the computers would still contain all data pertaining to the course set for the EDS; such data would not be erased until the EDS reached its destination. He had only to give the computers the new data; the girl's weight and the exact time at which he had reduced the deceleration to .10.

"Barton." Commander Delhart's voice came abruptly from the communicator, as he opened his mouth to call the *Stardust*. "A check with Records shows me you haven't completed your report. Did you reduce the deceleration?"

So the commander knew what he was trying to do.

"I'm decelerating at point ten," he answered. "I cut the deceleration at seventeen fifty and the weight is a hundred and ten. I would like to stay at point ten as long as the computers say I can. Will you give them the question?"

It was contrary to regulations for an EDS pilot to make any changes in the course or degree of deceleration the computers had set for him but the commander made no mention of the violation, neither did he ask the reason for it. It was not necessary for him to ask; he had not become commander of an interstellar cruiser without both intelligence and an understanding of human nature. He said only: "I'll have that given the computers."

The communicator fell silent and he and the girl waited, neither of them speaking. They would not have to wait long; the computers would give the answer within moments of the asking. The new factors would be fed into the steel maw of the first bank and the electrical impulses would go through the complex circuits. Here and there a relay might click, a tiny cog turn over, but it would be essentially the electrical impulses that found the answer; formless, mindless, invisible, determining with utter precision how long the pale girl beside him might live. Then five little segments of metal in the second bank would trip in rapid succession against an inked ribbon and a second steel maw would spit out the slip of paper that bore the answer.

The chronometer on the instrument board read 18:10 when the commander spoke again.

"You will resume deceleration at nineteen ten."

She looked toward the chronometer, then quickly away from it. "Is that when . . . when I go?" she asked. He nodded and she dropped her eyes to her lap again.

"I'll have the course corrections given you," the commander said. "Ordinarily I would never permit anything like this but I understand your position. There is nothing I can do, other than what I've just done, and you will not deviate from these new instructions. You will complete your report at nineteen ten. Now—here are the course corrections."

The voice of some unknown technician read them to him and he wrote them down on the pad clipped to the edge of the control board. There would, he saw, be periods of deceleration when he neared the atmosphere when the deceleration would be five gravities—and at five gravities, one hundred ten pounds would become five hundred fifty pounds.

The technician finished and he terminated the contact with a brief acknowledgment. Then, hesitating a moment, he reached out and shut off the communicator. It was 18:13 and he would have nothing to report until 19:10. In the meantime, it somehow seemed indecent to permit others to hear what she might say in her last hour.

He began to check the instrument readings, going over them with unnecessary slowness. She would have to accept the circumstances and there was nothing he could do to help her into acceptance; words of sympathy would only delay it.

It was 18:20 when she stirred from her motionlessness and spoke.

"So that's the way it has to be with me?"

He swung around to face her. "You understand now, don't you? No one would ever let it be like this if it could be changed."

"I understand," she said. Some of the color had returned to her face and the lipstick no longer stood out so vividly red. "There isn't enough fuel for me to stay; when I hid on this ship I got into something I didn't know anything about and now I have to pay for it."

She had violated a man-made law that said KEEP OUT but the penalty was not of men's making or desire and it was a penalty men could not revoke. A physical law had decreed: *h amount of fuel will power an EDS with a mass of m safely to its destination*; and a second physical law had decreed: *h amount of fuel will not power an EDS with a mass of m plus x safely to its destination.*

EDS's obeyed only physical laws and no amount of human sympathy for her could alter the second law.

"But I'm afraid. I don't want to die—not now. I want to live and nobody is doing anything to help me; everybody is letting me go ahead and acting just like nothing was going to happen to me. I'm going to die and nobody *cares*."

"We all do," he said. "I do and the commander does and the clerk in Ship's Records; we all care and each of us did what little he could to help you. It wasn't enough—it was almost nothing—but it was all we could do."

"Not enough fuel—I can understand that," she said, as though she had not heard his own words. "But to have to die for it. *Me*, alone—"

How hard it must be for her to accept the fact. She had never known danger of death; had never known the environments where the lives of men could be as fragile and fleeting as sea foam tossed against a rocky shore. She belonged on gentle Earth, in that secure and peaceful society where she could be young and gay and laughing with the others of her kind; where life was precious and well-guarded and there was always the assurance that tomorrow would come. She belonged in that world of soft winds and warm suns, music and moonlight and gracious manners and not on the hard, bleak frontier.

"How did it happen to me, so terribly quickly? An hour ago I was on the *Stardust*, going to Mimir. Now the *Stardust* is going on without me and I'm going to die and I'll never see Gerry and Mama and Daddy again—I'll never see anything again."

He hesitated, wondering how he could explain it to her so she would really understand and not feel she had, somehow, been the victim of a reasonlessly cruel injustice. She did not know what the frontier was like; she thought in terms of safe-and-secure Earth. Pretty girls were not jettisoned on Earth; there was a law against it. On Earth her plight would have filled the newscasts and a fast black Patrol ship would have been racing to her rescue. Everyone, everywhere, would have known of Marilyn Lee Cross and no effort would have been spared to save her life. But this was not Earth and there were no Patrol ships; only the *Stardust*, leaving them behind at many times the speed of light. There was no one to help her, there would be no Marilyn Lee Cross smiling from the newscasts tomorrow. Marilyn Lee Cross would be but a poignant memory for an EDS pilot and a name on a gray card in Ship's Records.

"It's different here; it's not like back on Earth," he said. "It isn't that no one cares; it's that no one can do anything to help. The frontier is big and here along its rim the colonies and exploration parties are scattered so thin and far between. On Woden, for example, there are only sixteen men—sixteen men on an entire world. The exploration parties, the survey crews, the little first-colonies—they're all fighting alien environments, trying to make a way for those who will follow after. The environments fight back and those who go first usually make mistakes only once. There is no margin of safety along the rim of the frontier; there can't be until the way is made for the others who will come later, until the new worlds are tamed and settled. Until then men will have to pay the penalty for making mistakes with no one to help them because there is no one *to* help them."

"I was going to Mimir," she said. "I didn't know about the frontier; I was only going to Mimir and *it's* safe."

"Mimir is safe but you left the cruiser that was taking you there."

She was silent for a while. "It was all so wonderful at first; there was plenty of room for me on this ship and I would be seeing Gerry so soon . . . I didn't know about the fuel, didn't know what would happen to me—"

Her words trailed away and he turned his attention to the viewscreen, not wanting to stare at her as she fought her way through the black horror of fear toward the calm gray of acceptance.

Woden was a ball, enshrouded in the blue haze of its atmosphere, swimming in space against the background of star-sprinkled dead blackness. The great mass of Manning's Continent sprawled like a gigantic hourglass in the Eastern Sea with the western half of the Eastern Continent still visible. There was a thin line of shadow along the right-hand edge of the globe and the Eastern Continent was disappearing into it as the planet turned on its axis. An hour before the entire continent had been in view, now a thousand miles of it had gone into the thin edge of shadow and around to the night that lay on the other side of the world. The dark blue spot that was Lotus Lake was approaching the shadow. It was somewhere near the southern edge of the lake that Group Two had their camp. It would be night there, soon, and quick behind the coming of night the rotation of Woden on its axis would put Group Two beyond the reach of the ship's radio.

He would have to tell her before it was too late for her to talk to her brother. In a way, it would be better for both of them should they not do so but it was not for him to decide. To each of them the last words would be something to hold and cherish, something that would cut like the blade of a knife yet would be infinitely precious to remember, she for her own brief moments to live and he for the rest of his life.

He held down the button that would flash the grid lines on the view-screen and used the known diameter of the planet to estimate the distance the southern tip of Lotus Lake had yet to go until it passed beyond radio range. It was approximately five hundred miles. Five hundred miles; thirty minutes—and the chronometer read 18:30. Allowing for error in estimating, it could not be later than 19:05 that the turning of Woden would cut off her brother's voice.

The first border of the Western Continent was already in sight along the left side of the world. Four thousand miles across it lay the shore of the Western Sea and the Camp of Group One. It had been in the Western Sea that the tornado had originated, to strike with such fury at the camp and destroy half their prefabricated buildings, including the one that housed the medical supplies. Two days before the tornado had not existed; it had been no more than great gentle masses of air out over the calm Western Sea. Group One had gone about their routine survey work, unaware of the meeting of the air masses out at sea, unaware of the force the union was spawning. It had struck their camp without warning; a thundering, roaring destruction that sought to annihilate all that lay before it. It had passed on, leaving the wreckage in its wake. It had destroyed the labor of months and had doomed six men to die and then, as though its task was accomplished, it once more began to resolve into gentle masses of air. But for all its deadliness, it had destroyed with neither malice nor intent. It had been a blind and mindless force, obeying the laws of nature, and it would have followed the same course with the same fury had men never existed.

Existence required Order and there was order; the laws of nature, irrevocable and immutable. Men could learn to use them but men could not change them. The circumference of a circle was always pi times the diameter and no science of Man would ever make it otherwise. The combination of chemical A with chemical B under condition C invariably produced reaction D. The law of gravitation was a rigid equation and it made no distinction between the fall of a leaf and the ponderous circling of a binary star system. The nuclear conversion process powered the cruisers that carried men to the stars; the same process in the form of a nova would destroy a world with equal efficiency. The laws *were*, and the universe moved in obedience to them. Along the frontier were arrayed all the forces of nature and sometimes they destroyed those who were fighting their way outward from Earth. The men of the frontier had long ago learned the bitter futility of cursing the forces that would destroy them for the forces were blind and deaf; the futility of looking to the heavens for mercy, for the stars of the galaxy swung in their long, long sweep of two hundred million years, as inexorably controlled as they by the laws that knew neither hatred nor compassion.

The men of the frontier knew—but how was a girl from Earth to fully understand? *H amount of fuel will not power an EDS with a mass of m plus x safely to its destination.* To himself and her brother and parents she was a sweet-faced girl in her teens; to the laws of nature she was *x*, the unwanted factor in a cold equation.

She stirred again on the seat. "Could I write a letter? I want to write to Mama and Daddy and I'd like to talk to Gerry. Could you let me talk to him over your radio there?"

"I'll try to get him," he said.

He switched on the normal-space transmitter and pressed the signal button. Someone answered the buzzer almost immediately.

"Hello. How's it going with you fellows now—is the EDS on its way?"

"This isn't Group One; this is the EDS," he said. "Is Gerry Cross there?"

"Gerry? He and two others went out in the helicopter this morning and aren't back yet. It's almost sundown, though, and he ought to be back right away—in less than an hour at the most."

"Can you connect me through to the radio in his 'copter?"

"Huh-uh. It's been out of commission for two months—some printed circuits went haywire and we can't get any more until the next cruiser stops by. Is it something important—bad news for him, or something?"

"Yes—it's very important. When he comes in get him to the transmitter as soon as you possibly can."

"I'll do that; I'll have one of the boys waiting at the field with a truck. Is there anything else I can do?"

"No, I guess that's all. Get him there as soon as you can and signal me."

He turned the volume to an inaudible minimum, an act that would not affect the functioning of the signal buzzer, and unclipped the pad of paper from the control board. He tore off the sheet containing his flight instructions and handed the pad to her, together with pencil.

"I'd better write to Gerry, too," she said as she took them. "He might not get back to camp in time."

She began to write, her fingers still clumsy and uncertain in the way they handled the pencil and the top of it trembling a little as she poised it between words. He turned back to the viewscreen, to stare at it without seeing it.

She was a lonely little child, trying to say her last good-by, and she would lay out her heart to them. She would tell them how much she loved them and she would tell them to not feel badly about it, that it was only something that must happen eventually to everyone and she was not afraid. The last would be a lie and it would be there to read between the sprawling, uneven lines; a valiant little lie that would make the hurt all the greater for them.

Her brother was of the frontier and he would understand. He would not hate the EDS pilot for doing nothing to prevent her going; he would know there had been nothing the pilot could do. He would understand, though the understanding would not soften the shock and pain when he learned his sister was gone. But the others, her father and mother—they would not understand. They were of Earth and they would think in the manner of those who had never lived where the safety margin of life was a thin, thin line—and sometimes not at all. What would they think of the faceless, unknown pilot who had sent her to her death?

They would hate him with cold and terrible intensity but it really didn't matter. He would never see them, never know them. He would have only the memories to remind him; only the nights to fear, when a blue-eyed girl in gypsy sandals would come in his dreams to die again—

He scowled at the viewscreen and tried to force his thoughts into less emotional channels. There was nothing he could do to help her. She had unknowingly subjected herself to the penalty of a law that recognized neither innocence nor youth nor beauty, that was incapable of sympathy or leniency. Regret was illogical—and yet, could knowing it to be illogical ever keep it away?

She stopped occasionally, as though trying to find the right words to tell them what she wanted them to know, then the pencil would resume its whispering to the paper. It was 18:37 when she folded the letter in a square and wrote a name on it. She began writing another, twice looking up at the chronometer as though she feared the black hand might reach its rendezvous before she had finished. It was 18:45 when she folded it as she had done the first letter and wrote a name and address on it.

She held the letters out to him. "Will you take care of these and see that they're enveloped and mailed?"

"Of course." He took them from her hand and placed them in a pocket of his gray uniform shirt.

"These can't be sent off until the next cruiser stops by and the *Stardust* will have long since told them about me, won't it?" she asked. He nodded and she went on, "That makes the letters not important in one way but in another way they're very important—to me, and to them."

"I know. I understand, and I'll take care of them."

She glanced at the chronometer, then back to him. "It seems to move faster all the time, doesn't it?"

He said nothing, unable to think of anything to say, and she asked, "Do you think Gerry will come back to camp in time?"

"I think so. They said he should be in right away."

She began to roll the pencil back and forth between her palms. "I hope he does. I feel sick and scared and I want to hear his voice again and maybe I won't feel so alone. I'm a coward and I can't help it."

"No," he said, "you're not a coward. You're afraid, but you're not a coward."

"Is there a difference?"

He nodded. "A lot of difference."

"I feel so alone. I never did feel like this before; like I was all by myself and there was nobody to care what happened to me. Always, before, there was Mama and Daddy there and my friends around me. I had lots of friends, and they had a going-away party for me the night before I left."

Friends and music and laughter for her to remember—and on the viewscreen Lotus Lake was going into the shadow.

"Is it the same with Gerry?" she asked. "I mean, if he should make a mistake, would he have to die for it, all alone and with no one to help him?"

"It's the same with all along the frontier; it will always be like that so long as there is a frontier."

"Gerry didn't tell us. He said the pay was good and he sent money home all the time because Daddy's little shop just brought in a bare living but he didn't tell us it was like this."

"He didn't tell you his work was dangerous?"

"Well—yes. He mentioned that, but we didn't understand. I always thought danger along the frontier was something that was a lot of fun; an exciting adventure, like in the three-D shows." A wan smile touched her face for a moment. "Only it's not, is it? It's not the same at all, because when it's real you can't go home after the show is over."

"No," he said. "No, you can't."

Her glance flicked from the chronometer to the door of the air lock then down to the pad and pencil she still held. She shifted her position slightly to lay them on the bench beside, moving one foot out a little. For the first time he saw that she was not wearing Vegan gypsy sandals but only cheap imitations; the expensive Vegan leather was some kind of grained plastic, the silver buckle was gilded iron, the jewels were colored glass. *Daddy's little shop just brought in a bare living*— She must have left college in her second year, to take the course in linguistics that would enable her to make her own way and help her brother provide for her parents, earning what she could by part-time work after classes were over. Her personal possessions on the *Stardust* would be taken back to her parents—they would neither be of much value nor occupy much storage space on the return voyage.

"Isn't it—" She stopped, and he looked at her questioningly. "Isn't it cold in here?" she asked, almost apologetically. "Doesn't it seem cold to you?"

"Why, yes," he said. He saw by the main temperature gauge that the room was at precisely normal temperature. "Yes, it's colder than it should be."

"I wish Gerry would get back before it's too late. Do you really think he will, and you didn't just say so to make me feel better?"

"I think he will—they said he would be in pretty soon." On the viewscreen Lotus Lake had gone into the shadow but for the thin blue line of its western edge and it was apparent he had overestimated the time she would have in which to talk to her brother. Reluctantly, he said to her, "His camp will be out of radio range in a few minutes; he's on that part of Woden that's in the shadow"—he indicated the viewscreen—"and the turning of Woden will put him beyond contact. There may not be much time left when he comes in—not much time to talk to him before he fades out. I wish I could do something about it—I would call him right now if I could."

"Not even as much time as I will have to stay?"

"I'm afraid not."

"Then—" She straightened and looked toward the air lock with pale resolution. "Then I'll go when Gerry passes beyond range. I won't wait any longer after that—I won't have anything to wait for."

Again there was nothing he could say.

"Maybe I shouldn't wait at all. Maybe I'm selfish—maybe it would be better for Gerry if you just told him about it afterward."

There was an unconscious pleading for denial in the way she spoke and he said, "He wouldn't want you to do that, to not wait for him."

"It's already coming dark where he is, isn't it? There will be all the long night before him, and Mama and Daddy don't know yet that I won't ever be coming back like I promised them I would. I've caused everyone I love to be hurt, haven't I? I didn't want to—I didn't intend to."

"It wasn't your fault," he said. "It wasn't your fault at all. They'll know that. They'll understand."

"At first I was so afraid to die that I was a coward and thought only of myself. Now, I see how selfish I was. The terrible thing about dying like this is not that I'll be gone but that I'll never see them again; never be able to tell them that I didn't take them for granted; never be able to tell them I knew of the sacrifices they made to make my life happier, that I knew all the things they did for me and that I loved them so much more than I ever told them. I've never told them any of those things. You don't tell them such things when you're young and your life is all before you—you're afraid of sounding sentimental and silly.

"But it's so different when you have to die—you wish you had told them while you could and you wish you could tell them you're sorry for all the little mean things you ever did or said to them. You wish you could tell them that you didn't really mean to ever hurt their feelings and for them to only remember that you always loved them far more than you ever let them know."

"You don't have to tell them that," he said. "They will know—they've always known it."

"Are you sure?" she asked. "How can you be sure? My people are strangers to you."

"Wherever you go, human nature and human hearts are the same."

"And they will know what I want them to know—that I love them?"

"They've always known it, in a way far better than you could ever put in words for them."

"I keep remembering the things they did for me, and it's the little things they did that seem to be the most important to me, now. Like Gerry—he sent me a bracelet of fire-rubies on my sixteenth birthday. It was beautiful—it must have cost him a month's pay. Yet, I remember him more for what he did the night my kitten got run over in the street. I was only six years old and he held me in his arms and wiped away my tears and told me not to cry, that Flossy was gone for just a little while, for just long enough to get herself a new fur coat and she would be on the foot of my bed the very next morning. I believed him and quit crying and went to sleep dreaming about my kitten coming back. When I woke up the next morning, there was Flossy on the foot of my bed in a brand-new white fur coat, just like he had said she would be.

"It wasn't until a long time later that Mama told me Gerry had got the pet-shop owner out of bed at four in the morning and, when the man got mad about it, Gerry told him he was either going to go down and sell him the white kitten right then or he'd break his neck."

"It's always the little things you remember people by; all the little things they did because they wanted to do them for you. You've done the same for Gerry and your father and mother; all kinds of things that you've forgotten about but that they will never forget."

"I hope I have. I would like for them to remember me like that."

"They will."

"I wish—" She swallowed. "The way I'll die—I wish they wouldn't ever think of that. I've read how people look who die in space—their insides all ruptured and exploded and their lungs out between their teeth and then, a few seconds later, they're all dry and shapeless and horribly ugly. I don't want them to ever think of me as something dead and horrible, like that."

"You're their own, their child and their sister. They could never think of you other than the way you would want them to; the way you looked the last time they saw you."

"I'm still afraid," she said. "I can't help it, but I don't want Gerry to know it. If he gets back in time, I'm going to act like I'm not afraid at all and—"

The signal buzzer interrupted her, quick and imperative.

"Gerry!" She came to her feet. "It's Gerry, now!"

He spun the volume control knob and asked: "Gerry Cross?"

"Yes," her brother answered, an undertone of tenseness to his reply. "The bad news—what is it?"

She answered for him, standing close behind him and leaning down a little toward the communicator, her hand resting small and cold on his shoulder.

"Hello, Gerry." There was only a faint quaver to betray the careful casualness of her voice. "I wanted to see you—"

"Marilyn!" There was sudden and terrible apprehension in the way he spoke her name. "What are you doing on that EDS?"

"I wanted to see you," she said again. "I wanted to see you, so I hid on this ship—"

"You *hid* on it?"

"I'm a stowaway . . . I didn't know what it would mean—"

"*Marilyn!*" It was the cry of a man who calls hopeless and desperate to someone already and forever gone from him. "What have you done?"

"I . . . it's not—" Then her own composure broke and the cold little hand gripped his shoulder convulsively. "Don't, Gerry—I only wanted to see you; I didn't intend to hurt you. Please, Gerry, don't feel like that—"

Something warm and wet splashed on his wrist and he slid out of the chair, to help her into it and swing the microphone down to her own level.

"Don't feel like that—Don't let me go knowing you feel like that—"

The sob she had tried to hold back choked in her throat and her brother spoke to her. "Don't cry, Marilyn." His voice was suddenly deep and infinitely gentle, with all the pain held out of it. "Don't cry, Sis—you mustn't do that. It's all right, Honey—everything is all right."

"I—" Her lower lip quivered and she bit into it. "I didn't want you to feel that way—I just wanted us to say good-by because I have to go in a minute."

"Sure—sure. That's the way it will be, Sis. I didn't mean to sound the way I did." Then his voice changed to a tone of quick and urgent demand. "EDS—have you called the *Stardust*? Did you check with the computers?"

"I called tht *Stardust* almost an hour ago. It can't turn back, there are no other cruisers within forty light-years, and there isn't enough fuel."

"Are you sure that the computers had the correct data—sure of everything?"

"Yes—do you think I could ever let it happen if I wasn't sure? I did everything I could do. If there was anything at all I could do now, I would do it."

"He tried to help me, Gerry." Her lower lip was no longer trembling and the short sleeves of her blouse were wet where she had dried her tears. "No one can help me and I'm not going to cry any more and everything will be all right with you and Daddy and Mama, won't it?"

"Sure—sure it will. We'll make out fine."

Her brother's words were beginning to come in more faintly and he turned the volume control to maximum. "He's going out of range," he said to her. "He'll be gone within another minute."

"You're fading out, Gerry," she said. "You're going out of range. I wanted to tell you—but I can't, now. We must say good-by so soon—but maybe I'll see you again. Maybe I'll come to you in your dreams with my hair in braids and crying because the kitten in my arms is dead; maybe I'll be the touch of a breeze that whispers to you as it goes by; maybe I'll be one of those gold-winged larks you told me about, singing my silly head off to you; maybe, at times, I'll be nothing you can see but you will know I'm there beside you. Think of me like that, Gerry; always like that and not—the other way."

Dimmed to a whisper by the turning of Woden, the answer came back:

"Always like that, Marilyn—always like that and never any other way."

"Our time is up, Gerry—I have to go now. Good—" Her voice broke in mid-word and her mouth tried to twist into crying. She pressed her hand hard against it and when she spoke again the words came clear and true:

"Good-by, Gerry."

Faint and ineffably poignant and tender, the last words came from the cold metal of the communicator:

"Good-by, little sister—"

She sat motionless in the hush that followed, as though listening to the shadow-echoes of the words as they died away, then she turned away from the communicator, toward the air lock, and he pulled the black lever beside him. The inner door of the air lock slid swiftly open, to reveal the bare little cell that was waiting for her, and she walked to it.

She walked with her head up and the brown curls brushing her shoulders, with the white sandals stepping as sure and steady as the fractional gravity would permit and the gilded buckles twinkling with little lights of blue and red and crystal. He let her walk alone and made no move to help her, knowing she would not want it that way. She stepped into the air lock and turned to face him, only the pulse in her throat to betray the wild beating of her heart.

"I'm ready," she said.

He pushed the lever up and the door slid its quick barrier between them, inclosing her in black and utter darkness for her last moments of life. It clicked as it locked in place and he jerked down the red lever. There was a slight waver to the ship as the air gushed from the lock, a vibration to the wall as though something had bumped the outer door in passing, then there was nothing and the ship was dropping true and steady again. He shoved the red lever back to close the door on the empty air lock and turned away, to walk to the pilot's chair with the slow steps of a man old and weary.

Back in the pilot's chair he pressed the signal button of the normal-space transmitter. There was no response; he had expected none. Her brother would have to wait through the night until the turning of Woden permitted contact through Group One.

It was not yet time to resume deceleration and he waited while the ship dropped endlessly downward with him and the drives purred softly. He saw that the white hand of the supplies closet temperature gauge was on zero. A cold equation had been balanced and he was alone on the ship. Something shapeless and ugly was hurrying ahead of him, going to Woden where its brother was waiting through the night, but the empty ship still lived for a little while with the presence of the girl who had not known about the forces that killed with neither hatred nor malice. It seemed, almost, that she still sat small and bewildered and frightened on the metal box beside him, her words echoing hauntingly clear in the void she had left behind her:

I didn't do anything to die for—I didn't do *anything—*

THE LAND IRONCLADS

H. G. Wells

H. G. Wells is simply the most important writer to influence—both directly, through his works, and indirectly, through the other major writers in his tradition—the course of science fiction in its formative decades. Brian W. Aldiss has called him "the Shakespeare of science fiction." The implications of Darwinian evolution and social criticism are the major themes of his works and his principal novels, *The Time Machine* (1895), *The Island of Dr. Moreau* (1896), *The Invisible Man* (1897), *The War of the Worlds* (1898), *When the Sleeper Wakes* (1899), and *The First Men in the Moon* (1901), together with five collections of short stories later combined as *The Short Stories of H. G. Wells* (1927). He was a popular and influential intellectual throughout the first half of the twentieth century, devoted to the idea of human progress.

Although he lived until 1946, he was never personally associated with genre science fiction; nonetheless many of his stories were reprinted in the early years of *Amazing Stories* as paradigms of the new kind of fiction which editor Hugo Gernsback wished to bring forth. He called himself a Scientific Romancer early in his career, and was certainly the pinnacle of that genre that preceded science fiction and existed parallel to it into the forties in the works of Olaf Stapledon, Aldous Huxley, E. Zamyatin, Karel Capek, and George Orwell (to name only the five most important writers influenced by Wells's early works). No major writer in the early decades of science fiction was so isolated as to be unaffected by Wells, and it is certainly recognized that Campbell and Heinlein as writers were particularly and enduringly immersed in his intellectual attitudes and literary techniques, and helped bring them into conventional usage in the genre.

"The Land Ironclads" (1903) is a vision of future tank warfare. It is part of a significant tradition of future war fiction that began in the 1870s and flourished between 1890 and 1914 (and continues to this day outside the genre boundaries of science fiction in such works as *The Third World War* [1978] and the recent "techno-thriller" subgenre). One of the hallmarks of this type of fiction is the invention of a new and terrible weapon. It is also, like Kipling's "With the Night Mail," part of the subgenre of "invention fiction" that thrived in the late nineteenth and early twentieth century, the age of wonderful new machines that were transforming the world for better or worse. These two genres were often combined in stories of new war machines or of the invention of "the weapon to end war."

But Wells went beyond the normal bounds of invention fiction (as he had in his earlier Scientific Romances) and future war fiction (generally set the day after tomorrow and devoted to warning the reading public of some imminent political danger in the real world) into a vision of a transformed world, in which young urban engineers conquer pastoral, chivalric warriors through science and technology. This is the story in which Wells could claim to have invented something real (as later, the bazooka was invented in the original Buck Rogers story in *Amazing*). It is specifically notable that Wells was proud of his invention, with the same attitude that Campbell later encouraged in Golden Age writers. In Wells's *Experiment in Autobiography*, he reminisces about visiting the front lines in World War I: ". . . an old notion of mine, the Land Ironclads, was being worked out at that time in the form of the Tanks, and it is absurd that my imagination was not mobilized in scheming the structure and use of these contrivances." He goes on to deplore the use of the tanks "timidly and experimentally," when they were "of immense value as a major surprise that might have ended the war."

Critic John Huntington points out (in *The Logic of Fantasy*, 1982) that "The Land Ironclads" represents a significant transition in Wells's fiction and thought, from the "artistic" (as in the time machine, Cavorite, invisibility) to the realistic. Wells here focused on the possible and the practical in his invention and envisions its use with crushing, even inhumane, logic: It solves the problem and the forces of technology win. Huntington faults the fiction because the land ironclad fails to function symbolically; it is a literal, mundane tool, murderously efficient. But in this, Wells becomes most significantly a forefather of hard sf. While this story is less aesthetically satisfying than many of his earlier fictions, it is clearly an intellectual model for the hard sf of the twentieth century.

I

The young lieutenant lay beside the war correspondent and admired the idyllic calm of the enemy's lines through his field-glass.

"So far as I can see," he said at last, "one man."

"What's he doing?" asked the war correspondent.

"Field-glass at us," said the young lieutenant.

"And this is war!"

"No," said the young lieutenant; "it's Bloch."

"The game's a draw."

"No! They've got to win or else they lose. A draw's a win for our side."

They had discussed the political situation fifty times or so, and the war correspondent was weary of it. He stretched out his limbs. "Aaai s'pose it *is*!" he yawned.

Flut!

"What was that?"

"Shot at us."

The war correspondent shifted to a slightly lower position. "No one shot at him," he complained.

"I wonder if they think we shall get so bored we shall go home?"

The war correspondent made no reply.

"There's the harvest, of course. . . ."

They had been there a month. Since the first brisk movements after the declaration of war things had gone slower and slower, until it seemed as though the whole machine of events must have run down. To begin with, they had had almost a scampering time; the invader had come across the frontier on the very dawn of the war in half-a-dozen parallel columns behind a cloud of cyclists and cavalry, with a general air of coming straight on the capital, and the defender horsemen had held him up, and peppered him and forced him to open out to outflank, and had then bolted to the next position in the most approved style, for a couple of days, until in the afternoon, bump! they had the invader against their prepared lines of defence. He did not suffer so much as had been hoped and expected: he was coming on, it seemed, with his eyes open, his scouts winded the guns, and down he sat at once without the shadow of an attack and began grubbing trenches for himself, as though he meant to sit down there to the very end of time. He was slow, but much more wary than the world had been led to expect, and he kept convoys tucked in and shielded his slow-marching infantry sufficiently well to prevent any heavy adverse scoring.

"But he ought to attack," the young lieutenant had insisted.

"He'll attack us at dawn, somewhere along the lines. You'll get the bayonets coming into the trenches just about when you can see," the war correspondent had held until a week ago.

The young lieutenant winked when he said that.

When one early morning the men the defenders sent to lie out five hundred yards before the trenches, with a view to the unexpected emptying of magazines into any night attack, gave way to causeless panic and blazed away at nothing for ten minutes, the war correspondent understood the meaning of that wink.

"What would you do if you were the enemy?" said the war correspondent, suddenly.

"If I had men like I've got now?"

"Yes."

"Take those trenches."

"How?"

"Oh—dodges! Crawl out half-way at night before moonrise and get into touch with the chaps we send out. Blaze at 'em if they tried to shift, and so bag some of 'em in the daylight. Learn that patch of ground by heart, lie all day in squatty holes, and come on nearer next night. There's a bit over there, lumpy ground, where they could get across to rushing distance—easy. In a night or so. It would be a mere game for our fellows; it's what they're made for. . . . Guns? Shrapnel and stuff wouldn't stop good men who meant business."

"Why don't *they* do that?"

"Their men aren't brutes enough; that's the trouble. They're a crowd of devitalised townsmen, and that's the truth of the matter. They're clerks, they're factory hands, they're students, they're civilised men. They can write, they can talk, they can make and do all sorts of things, but they're poor amateurs at war. They've got no physical staying power, and that's the whole thing. They've never slept in the open one night in their lives; they've never drunk anything but the purest water-company water; they've never gone short of three meals a day since they left their feeding-bottles. Half their cavalry never cocked leg over horse till it enlisted six months ago. They ride their horses as though they were bicycles—you watch 'em! They're fools at the game, and they know it. Our boys of fourteen can give their grown men points. . . . Very well——"

The war correspondent mused on his face with his nose between his knuckles.

"If a decent civilisation," he said, "cannot produce better men for war than——"

He stopped with belated politeness. "I mean——"

"Than our open-air life," said the young lieutenant.

"Exactly," said the war correspondent. "Then civilisation has to stop."

"It looks like it," the young lieutenant admitted.

"Civilisation has science, you know," said the war correspondent. "It invented and it made the rifles and guns and things you use."

"Which our nice healthy hunters and stockmen and so on, rowdy-dowdy cow-punchers and nigger-whackers, can use ten times better than—— *What's that?*"

"What?" said the war correspondent, and then seeing his companion busy with his field-glass he produced his own: "Where?" said the war correspondent, sweeping the enemy's lines.

"It's nothing," said the young lieutenant, still looking.

"What's nothing?"

The young lieutenant put down his glass and pointed. "I thought I saw something there, behind the stems of those trees. Something black. What it was I don't know."

The war correspondent tried to get even by intense scrutiny.

"It wasn't anything," said the young lieutenant, rolling over to regard the darkling evening sky, and generalised: "There never will be anything any more for ever. Unless——"

The war correspondent looked inquiry.

"They may get their stomachs wrong, or something—living without proper drains."

A sound of bugles came from the tents behind. The war correspondent slid backward down the sand and stood up. "Boom!" came from somewhere far away to the left. "Halloa!" he said, hesitated, and crawled back to peer again. "Firing at this time is jolly bad manners."

The young lieutenant was uncommunicative for a space.

Then he pointed to the distant clump of trees again. "One of our big guns. They were firing at that," he said.

"The thing that wasn't anything?"

"Something over there, anyhow."

Both men were silent, peering through their glasses for a space. "Just when it's twilight," the lieutenant complained. He stood up.

"I might stay here a bit," said the war correspondent.

The lieutenant shook his head. "There's nothing to see," he apologised, and then went down to where his little squad of sun-brown, loose-limbed men had been yarning in the trench. The war correspondent stood up also, glanced for a moment at the businesslike bustle below him, gave perhaps twenty seconds to those enigmatical trees again, then turned his face toward the camp.

He found himself wondering whether his editor would consider the story of how somebody thought he saw something black behind a clump of trees, and how a gun was fired at this illusion by somebody else, too trivial for public consumption.

"It's the only gleam of a shadow of interest," said the war correspondent, "for ten whole days.

"No," he said presently; "I'll write that other article, 'Is War Played Out?' "

He surveyed the darkling lines in perspective, the tangle of trenches one behind another, one commanding another, which the defender had made ready. The shadows and mists swallowed up their receding contours, and here and there a lantern gleamed, and here and there knots of men were busy about small fires. "No troops on earth could do it," he said. . . .

He was depressed. He believed that there were other things in life better worth having than proficiency in war; he believed that in the heart of civilisation, for all its stresses, its crushing concentrations of forces, its injustice and suffering, there lay something that might be the hope of the world; and the idea that any people, by living in the open air, hunting perpetually, losing touch with books and art and all the things that intensify life, might hope to resist and break that great development to the end of time, jarred on his civilised soul.

Apt to his thought came a file of the defender soldiers, and passed him in the gleam of a swinging lamp that marked the way.

He glanced at their red-lit faces, and one shone out for a moment, a common type of face in the defender's ranks: ill-shaped nose, sensuous lips, bright clear eyes full of alert cunning, slouch hat cocked on one side and adorned with the peacock's plume of the rustic Don Juan turned soldier, a hard brown skin, a sinewy frame, an open, tireless stride, and a master's grip on the rifle.

The war correspondent returned their salutations and went on his way.

"Louts," he whispered. "Cunning, elementary louts. And they are going to beat the townsmen at the game of war!"

From the red glow among the nearer tents came first one and then half-a-dozen hearty voices, bawling in a drawling unison the words of a particularly slab and sentimental patriotic song.

"Oh, *go* it!" muttered the war correspondent, bitterly.

II

It was opposite the trenches called after Hackbone's Hut that the battle began. There the ground stretched broad and level between the lines, with scarcely shelter for a lizard, and it seemed to the startled, just-awakened men who came crowding into the trenches that this was one more proof of that inexperience of the enemy of which they had heard so much. The war correspondent would not believe his ears at first, and swore that he and the war artist, who, still imperfectly roused, was trying to put on his boots by the light of a match held in his hand, were the victims of a common illusion. Then, after putting his head in a bucket of cold water, his intelligence came back as he towelled. He listened. "Gollys!" he said; "that's some thing more than scare firing this time. It's like ten thousand carts on a bridge of tin."

There came a sort of enrichment to that steady uproar. "Machine-guns!"

Then, "Guns!"

The artist, with one boot on, thought to look at his watch, and went to it hopping.

"Half an hour from dawn," he said. "You were right about their attacking, after all. . . ."

The war correspondent came out of the tent, verifying the presence of chocolate in his pocket as he did so. He had to halt for a moment or so until his eyes were toned down to the night a little. "Pitch!" he said. He stood for a space to season his eyes before he felt justified in striking out for a black gap among the adjacent tents. The artist coming out behind him fell over a tent-rope. It was half-past two o'clock in the morning of the darkest night in time, and against a sky of dull black silk the enemy was talking search-lights, a wild jabber of search-lights. "He's trying to blind our riflemen," said the war correspondent with a flash, and waited for the artist and then set off with a sort of discreet haste again. "Whoa!" he said, presently. "Ditches!"

They stopped.

"It's the confounded search-lights," said the war correspondent.

They saw lanterns going to and fro, near by, and men falling in to march down to the trenches. They were for following them, and then the artist began to get his night eyes. "If we scramble this," he said, "and it's only a drain, there's a clear run up to the ridge." And that way they took. Lights came and went in the tents behind, as the men turned out, and ever and again they came to broken ground and staggered and stumbled. But in a little while they drew near the crest. Something that sounded like the impact of a tremendous railway accident happened in the air above them, and the shrapnel bullets seethed about them like a sudden handful of hail. "Right-oh!" said the war correspondent, and soon they judged they had come to the crest and stood in the midst of a world of great darkness and frantic glares, whose principal fact was sound.

Right and left of them and all about them was the uproar, an army-full of magazine fire, at first chaotic and monstrous, and then, eked out by little flashes and gleams and suggestions, taking the beginnings of a shape. It looked to the war correspondent as though the enemy must have attacked in line and with his whole force—in which case he was either being or was already annihilated.

"Dawn and the dead," he said, with his instinct for headlines. He said this to himself, but afterwards by means of shouting he conveyed an idea to the artist. "They must have meant it for a surprise," he said.

It was remarkable how the firing kept on. After a time he began to perceive a sort of rhythm in this inferno of noise. It would decline—decline perceptibly, droop towards something that was comparatively a pause—a pause of inquiry. "Aren't you all dead yet?" this pause seemed to say. The flickering fringe of rifle-flashes would become attenuated and broken, and the whack-bang of the enemy's big guns two miles away there would come up out of the deeps. Then suddenly, east or west of them, something would startle the rifles to a frantic outbreak again.

The war correspondent taxed his brain for some theory of conflict that would account for this, and was suddenly aware that the artist and he were vividly illuminated. He could see the ridge on which they stood, and before them in black outline a file of riflemen hurrying down towards the nearer trenches. It became visible that a light rain was falling, and farther away towards the enemy was a clear space with men—"our men?"—running across it in disorder. He saw one of those men throw up his hands and drop. And something else black and shining loomed up on the edge of the beam-coruscating flashes; and behind it and far away a calm, white eye regarded the world. "Whit, whit, whit," sang something in the air, and then the artist was running for cover, with the war correspondent behind him. Bang came shrapnel, bursting close at hand as it seemed, and our two men were lying flat in a dip in the ground, and the light and everything had gone again, leaving a vast note of interrogation upon the light.

The war correspondent came within bawling range. "What the deuce was it? Shooting our men down!"

"Black," said the artist, "and like a fort. Not two hundred yards from the first trench."

He sought for comparisons in his mind. "Something between a big blockhouse and a giant's dish-cover," he said.

"And they were running!" said the war correspondent.

"*You'd* run if a thing like that, with a search-light to help it, turned up like a prowling nightmare in the middle of the night."

They crawled to what they judged the edge of the dip and lay regarding the unfathomable dark. For a space they could distinguish nothing, and then a sudden convergence of the search-lights of both sides brought the strange thing out again.

In that flickering pallor it had the effect of a large and clumsy black insect, an insect the size of an iron-clad cruiser, crawling obliquely to the first line of trenches and firing shots out of port-holes in its side. And on its carcass the bullets must have been battering with more than the passionate violence of hail on a roof of tin.

Then in the twinkling of an eye the curtain of the dark had fallen again and the monster had vanished, but the crescendo of musketry marked its approach to the trenches.

They were beginning to talk about the thing to each other, when a flying bullet kicked dirt into the artist's face, and they decided abruptly to crawl down into the cover of the trenches. They had got down with an unobtrusive persistence into the second line, before the dawn had grown clear enough for anything to be seen. They found themselves in a crowd of expectant riflemen, all noisily arguing about what would happen next. The enemy's contrivance had done execution upon the outlying men, it seemed, but they did not believe it would do any more. "Come the day and we'll capture the lot of them," said a burly soldier.

"Them?" said the war correspondent.

"They say there's a regular string of 'em, crawling along the front of our lines. . . . Who cares?"

The darkness filtered away so imperceptibly that at no moment could one declare decisively that one could see. The search-lights ceased to sweep hither and thither. The enemy's monsters were dubious patches of darkness upon the dark, and then no longer dubious, and so they crept out into distinctness. The war correspondent, munching chocolate absent-mindedly, beheld at last a spacious picture of battle under the cheerless sky, whose central focus was an array of fourteen or fifteen huge clumsy shapes lying in perspective on the very edge of the first line of trenches, at intervals of perhaps three hundred yards, and evidently firing down upon the crowded riflemen. They were so close in that the defender's guns had ceased, and only the first line of trenches was in action.

The second line commanded the first, and as the light grew, the war correspondent could make out the riflemen who were fighting these monsters, crouched in knots and crowds behind the transverse banks that crossed the trenches against the eventuality of an enfilade. The trenches close to the big machines were empty save for the crumpled suggestions of dead and wounded men; the defenders had been driven right and left as soon as the prow of a land ironclad had looked up over the front of the trench. The war correspondent produced his field-glass, and was immediately a centre of inquiry from the soldiers about him.

They wanted to look, they asked questions, and after he had announced that the men across the traverses seemed unable to advance or retreat, and were crouching under cover rather than fighting, he found it advisable to loan his glasses to a burly and incredulous corporal. He heard a strident voice, and found a lean and sallow soldier at his back talking to the artist.

"There's chaps down there caught," the man was saying. "If they retreat they got to expose themselves, and the fire's too straight. . . ."

"They aren't firing much, but every shot's a hit."

"Who?"

"The chaps in that thing. The men who're coming up——"

"Coming up where?"

"We're evacuating them trenches where we can. Our chaps are coming back up the zigzags. . . . No end of 'em hit. . . . But when we get clear our turn'll come. Rather! Those things won't be able to cross a trench or get into it; and before they can get back our guns'll smash 'em up. Smash 'em right up. See?" A brightness came into his eyes. "Then we'll have a go at the beggars inside," he said. . . .

The war correspondent thought for a moment, trying to realise the idea. Then he set himself to recover his field-glasses from the burly corporal. . . .

The daylight was getting clearer now. The clouds were lifting, and a gleam of lemon-yellow amidst the level masses to the east portended sunrise. He looked again at the land ironclad. As he saw it in the bleak, grey dawn, lying obliquely upon the slope and on the very lip of the foremost trench, the suggestion of a stranded vessel was very strong indeed. It might have been from eighty to a hundred feet long—it was about two hundred and fifty yards away—its vertical side was ten feet high or so, smooth for that height, and then with a complex patterning under the eaves of its flattish turtle cover. This patterning was a close interlacing of port-holes, rifle barrels, and telescope tubes—sham and real—indistinguishable one from the other. The thing had come into such a position as to enfilade the trench, which was empty now, so far as he could see, except for two or three crouching knots of men and the tumbled dead. Behind it, across the plain, it had scored the grass with a train of linked impressions, like the dotted tracings sea things leave in sand. Left and right of that track dead men and wounded men were scattered—men it had picked off as they fled back from their advanced positions in the search-light glare from the invader's lines. And now it lay with its head projecting a little over the trench it had won, as if it were a single sentient thing planning the next phase of its attack. . . .

He lowered his glasses and took a more comprehensive view of the situation. These creatures of the night had evidently won the first line of trenches and the fight had come to a pause. In the increasing light he could make out by a stray shot or a chance exposure that the defender's marksmen were lying thick in the second and third line of trenches up towards the low crest of the position, and in such of the zigzags as gave them a chance of a converging fire. The men about him were talking of guns. "We're in the line of the big guns at the crest, but they'll soon shift one to pepper them," the lean man said, reassuringly.

"Whup," said the corporal.

"Bang! bang! bang! Whir-r-r-r-r!" it was a sort of nervous jump, and all the rifles were going off by themselves. The war correspondent found himself and the artist, two idle men crouching behind a line of preoccupied backs, of industrious men discharging magazines. The monster had moved. It continued to move regardless of the hail that splashed its skin with bright new specks of lead. It was singing a mechanical little ditty to itself, "Tuf-tuf, tuf-tuf, tuf-tuf," and squirting out little jets of steam behind. It had humped itself up, as a limpet does before it crawls; it had lifted its skirt and displayed along the length of it—*feet*! They were thick, stumpy feet, between knobs and buttons in shape—flat, broad things, reminding one of the feet of elephants or the legs of caterpillars; and then, as the skirt rose higher, the war correspondent, scrutinising the thing through his glasses again, saw that these feet hung, as it were, on the rims of wheels. His thoughts whirled back to Victoria Street, Westminster, and he saw himself in the piping times of peace, seeking matter for an interview.

"Mr.—Mr. Diplock," he said; "and he called them Pedrails. . . . Fancy meeting them here!"

The marksman beside him raised his head and shoulders in a speculative mood to fire more certainly—it seemed so natural to assume the attention of the monster must be distracted by this trench before it—and was suddenly knocked backwards by a bullet through his neck. His feet flew up, and he vanished out of the margin of the watcher's field of vision. The war correspondent grovelled tighter, but after a glance behind him at a painful little confusion, he resumed his field-glass, for the thing was putting down its feet one after the other, and hoisting itself farther and farther over the trench. Only a bullet in the head could have stopped him looking just then.

The lean man with the strident voice ceased firing to turn and reiterate his point. "They can't possibly cross," he bawled. "They——"

"Bang! Bang! Bang! Bang!"—drowned everything.

The lean man continued speaking for a word or so, then gave it up, shook his head to enforce the impossibility of anything crossing a trench like the one below, and resumed business once more.

And all the while that great bulk was crossing. When the war correspondent turned his glass on it again it had bridged the trench, and its queer feet were rasping away at the farther bank, in the attempt to get a hold there. It got its hold. It continued to crawl until the greater bulk of it was over the trench—until it was all over. Then it paused for a moment, adjusted its skirt a little nearer the ground, gave an unnerving "toot, toot," and came on abruptly at a pace of, perhaps, six miles an hour straight up the gentle slope towards our observer.

The war correspondent raised himself on his elbow and looked a natural inquiry at the artist.

For a moment the men about him stuck to their position and fired furiously. Then the lean man in a mood of precipitancy slid backwards, and the war correspondent said "Come along" to the artist, and led the movement along the trench.

As they dropped down, the vision of a hillside of trench being rushed by a dozen vast cockroaches disappeared for a space, and instead was one of a narrow passage, crowded with men, for the most part receding, though one or two turned or halted. He never turned back to see the nose of the monster creep over the brow of the trench; he never even troubled to keep in touch with the artist. He heard the "whit" of bullets about him soon enough, and saw a man before him stumble and drop, and then he was one of a furious crowd fighting to get into a transverse zigzag ditch that enabled the defenders to get under cover up and down the hill. It was like a theatre panic. He gathered from signs and fragmentary words that on ahead another of these monsters had also won to the second trench.

He lost his interest in the general course of the battle for a space altogether; he became simply a modest egotist, in a mood of hasty circumspection, seeking the farthest rear, amidst a dispersed multitude of disconcerted riflemen similarly employed. He scrambled down through trenches, he took his courage in both hands and sprinted across the open, he had moments of panic when it seemed madness not to be quadrupedal, and moments of shame when he stood up and faced about to see how the fight was going. And he was one of many thousand very similar men that morning. On the ridge he halted in a knot of scrub, and was for a few minutes almost minded to stop and see things out.

The day was now fully come. The grey sky had changed to blue, and of all the cloudy masses of the dawn there remained only a few patches of dissolving fleeciness. The world below was bright and singularly clear. The ridge was not, perhaps, more than a hundred feet or so above the general plain, but in this flat region it sufficed to give the effect of extensive view. Away on the north side of the ridge, little and far, were the camps, the ordered wagons, all the gear of a big army; with officers galloping about and men doing aimless things. Here and there men were falling in, however, and the cavalry was forming up on the plain beyond the tents. The bulk of men who had been in the trenches were still on the move to the rear, scattered like sheep without a shepherd over the farther slopes. Here and there were little rallies and attempts to wait and do—something vague; but the general drift was away from any concentration. There on the southern side was the elaborate lacework of trenches and defences, across which these iron turtles, fourteen of them spread out over a line of perhaps three miles, were now advancing as fast as a man could trot, and methodically shooting down and breaking up any persistent knots of resistance. Here and there stood little clumps of men, outflanked and unable to get away, showing the white flag, and the invader's cyclist infantry was advancing now across the open, in open order, but unmolested, to complete the work of the machines. Surveyed at large, the defenders already looked a beaten army. A mechanism that was effectually ironclad against bullets, that could at a pinch cross a thirty-foot trench, and that seemed able to shoot out rifle-bullets with unerring precision, was clearly an inevitable victor against anything but rivers, precipices, and guns.

He looked at his watch. "Half-past four! Lord! What things can happen in two hours. Here's the whole blessed army being walked over, and at half-past two——

"And even now our blessed louts haven't done a thing with their guns!"

He scanned the ridge right and left of him with his glasses. He turned again to the nearest land ironclad, advancing now obliquely to him and not three hundred yards away, and then scanned the ground over which he must retreat if he was not to be captured.

"They'll do nothing," he said, and glanced again at the enemy.

And then from far away to the left came the thud of a gun, followed very rapidly by a rolling gun-fire.

He hesitated and decided to stay.

III

The defender had relied chiefly upon his rifles in the event of an assault. His guns he kept concealed at various points upon and behind the ridge ready to bring them into action against any artillery preparations for an attack on the part of his antagonist. The situation had rushed upon him with the dawn, and by the time the gunners had their guns ready for motion, the land ironclads were already in among the foremost trenches. There is a natural reluctance to fire into one's own broken men, and many of the guns, being intended simply to fight an advance of the enemy's artillery, were not in positions to hit anything in the second line of trenches. After that the advance of the land ironclads was swift. The defender-general found himself suddenly called upon to invent a new sort of warfare, in which guns were to fight alone amidst broken and retreating infantry. He had scarcely thirty minutes in which to think it out. He did not respond to the call, and what happened that morning was that the advance of the land ironclads forced the fight, and each gun and battery made what play its circumstances dictated. For the most part it was poor play.

Some of the guns got in two or three shots, some one or two, and the percentage of misses was unusually high. The howitzers, of course, did nothing. The land ironclads in each case followed much the same tactics. As soon as a gun came into play the monster turned itself almost end-on, so as to minimise the chances of a square hit, and made not for the gun, but for the nearest point on its flank from which the gunners could be shot down. Few of the hits scored were very effectual; only one of the things was disabled, and that was the one that fought the three batteries attached to the brigade on the left wing. Three that were hit when close upon the guns were clean shot through without being put out of action. Our war correspondent did not see that one momentary arrest of the tide of victory on the left; he saw only the very ineffectual fight of half-battery 96B close at hand upon his right. This he watched some time beyond the margin of safety.

Just after he heard the three batteries opening up upon his left he became aware of the thud of horses' hoofs from the sheltered side of the slope, and presently saw first one and then two other guns galloping into position along the north side of the ridge, well out of sight of the great bulk that was now creeping obliquely towards the crest and cutting up the lingering infantry beside it and below, as it came.

The half-battery swung round into line—each gun describing its curve—halted, unlimbered, and prepared for action. . . .

"Bang!"

The land ironclad had become visible over the brow of the hill, and just visible as a long black back to the gunners. It halted, as though it hesitated.

The two remaining guns fired, and then their big antagonist had swung round and was in full view, end-on, against the sky, coming at a rush.

The gunners became frantic in their haste to fire again. They were so near the war correspondent could see the expression of their excited faces through his field-glass. As he looked he saw a man drop, and realised for the first time that the ironclad was shooting.

For a moment the big black monster crawled with an accelerated pace towards the furiously active gunners. Then, as if moved by a generous impulse, it turned its full broadside to their attack, and scarcely forty yards away from them. The war correspondent turned his field-glass back to the gunners and perceived it was now shooting down the men about the guns with the most deadly rapidity.

Just for a moment it seemed splendid, and then it seemed horrible. The gunners were dropping in heaps about their guns. To lay a hand on a gun was death. "Bang!" went the gun on the left, a hopeless miss, and that was the only second shot the half-battery fired. In another moment half-a-dozen surviving artillerymen were holding up their hands amidst a scattered muddle of dead and wounded men, and the fight was done.

The war correspondent hesitated between stopping in his scrub and waiting for an opportunity to surrender decently, or taking to an adjacent gully he had discovered. If he surrendered it was certain he would get no copy off; while, if he escaped, there were all sorts of chances. He decided to follow the gully, and take the first offer in the confusion beyond the camp of picking up a horse.

IV

Subsequent authorities have found fault with the first land ironclads in many particulars, but assuredly they served their purpose on the day of their appearance. They were essentially long, narrow, and very strong steel frameworks carrying the engines, and borne upon eight pairs of big pedrail wheels, each about ten feet in diameter, each a driving wheel and set upon long axles free to swivel round a common axis. This arrangement gave them the maximum of adaptability to the contours of the ground. They crawled level along the ground with one foot high upon a hillock and another deep in a depression, and they could hold themselves erect and steady sideways upon even a steep hillside. The engineers directed the engines under the command of the captain, who had look-out points at small ports all round the upper edge of the adjustable skirt of twelve-inch iron-plating which protected the whole affair, and who could also raise or depress a conning-tower set about the portholes through the centre of the iron top cover. The riflemen each occupied a small cabin of peculiar construction, and these cabins were slung along the sides of and before and behind the great main framework, in a manner suggestive of the slinging of the seats of an Irish jaunting-car. Their rifles, however, were very different pieces of apparatus from the simple mechanisms in the hands of their adversaries.

These were in the first place automatic, ejected their cartridges and loaded again from a magazine each time they fired, until the ammunition store was at an end, and they had the most remarkable sights imaginable, sights which threw a bright little camera-obscura picture into the light-tight box in which the riflemen sat below. This camera-obscura picture was marked with two crossed lines, and whatever was covered by the intersection of these two lines, that the rifle hit. The sighting was ingeniously contrived. The rifleman stood at the table with a thing like an elaboration of a draughtsman's dividers in his hand, and he opened and closed these dividers, so that they were always at the apparent height—if it was an ordinary-sized man—of the man he wanted to kill. A little twisted strand of wire like an electric-light wire ran from this implement up to the gun, and as the dividers opened and shut the sights went up or down. Changes in the clearness of the atmosphere, due to changes of moisture, were met by an ingenious use of that meteorologically sensitive substance, catgut, and when the land ironclad moved forward the sights got a compensatory deflection in the direction of its motion. The rifleman stood up in his pitch-dark chamber and watched the little picture before him. One hand held the dividers for judging distance, and the other grasped a big knob like a door-handle. As he pushed this knob about the rifle above swung to correspond, and the picture passed to and fro like an agitated panorama. When he saw a man he wanted to shoot he brought him up to the cross-lines, and then pressed a finger upon a little push like an electric bell-push, conveniently placed in the centre of the knob. Then the man was shot. If by any chance the rifleman missed his target he moved the knob a trifle, or readjusted his dividers, pressed the push, and got him the second time.

This rifle and its sights protruded from a port-hole, exactly like a great number of other port-holes that ran in a triple row under the eaves of the cover of the land ironclad. Each port-hole displayed a rifle and sight in dummy, so that the real ones could only be hit by a chance shot, and if one was, then the young man below said "Pshaw!" turned on an electric light, lowered the injured instrument into his camera, replaced the injured part, or put up a new rifle if the injury was considerable.

You must conceive these cabins as hung clear above the swing of the axles, and inside the big wheels upon which the great elephant-like feet were hung, and behind these cabins along the centre of the monster ran a central gallery into which they opened, and along which worked the big compact engines. It was like a long passage into which this throbbing machinery had been packed, and the captain stood about the middle, close to the ladder that led to his conning-tower, and directed the silent, alert engineers—for the most part by signs. The throb and noise of the engines mingled with the reports of the rifles and the intermittent clangour of the bullet hail upon the armour. Ever and again he would touch the wheel that raised his conning-tower, step up his ladder until his engineers could see nothing of him above the waist, and then come down again with orders. Two small electric lights were all the illumination of this space—they were placed to make him most clearly visible to his subordinates; the air was thick with the smell of oil and petrol, and had the war correspondent been suddenly transferred from the spacious dawn outside to the bowels of this apparatus he would have thought himself fallen into another world.

The captain, of course, saw both sides of the battle. When he raised his head into his conning-tower there were the dewy sunrise, the amazed and disordered trenches, the flying and falling soldiers, the depressed-looking groups of prisoners, the beaten guns; when he bent down again to signal "half speed," "quarter speed," "half circle round toward the right," or what not, he was in the oil-smelling twilight of the ill-lit engine-room. Close beside him on either side was the mouth-piece of a speaking-tube, and ever and again he would direct one side or other of his strange craft to "concentrate fire forward on gunners," or to "clear out trench about a hundred yards on our right front."

He was a young man, healthy enough but by no means sun-tanned, and of a type of feature and expression that prevails in His Majesty's Navy: alert, intelligent, quiet. He and his engineers and riflemen all went about their work, calm and reasonable men. They had none of that flapping strenuousness of the half-wit in a hurry, that excessive strain upon the blood-vessels, that hysteria of effort which is so frequently regarded as the proper state of mind for heroic deeds.

For the enemy these young engineers were defeating they felt a certain qualified pity and a quite unqualified contempt. They regarded these big, healthy men they were shooting down precisely as these same big, healthy men might regard some inferior kind of nigger. They despised them for making war; despised their bawling patriotisms and their emotionality profoundly; despised them, above all, for the petty cunning and the almost brutish want of imagination their method of fighting displayed. "If they *must* make war," these young men thought, "why in thunder don't they do it like sensible men?" They resented the assumption that their own side was too stupid to do anything more than play their enemy's game, that they were going to play this costly folly according to the rules of unimaginative men. They resented being forced to the trouble of making man-killing machinery; resented the alternative of having to massacre these people or endure their truculent yappings; resented the whole unfathomable imbecility of war.

Meanwhile, with something of the mechanical precision of a good clerk posting a ledger, the riflemen moved their knobs and pressed their buttons. . . .

The captain of Land Ironclad Number Three had halted on the crest close to his captured half-battery. His lined-up prisoners stood hard by and waited for the cyclists behind to come for them. He surveyed the victorious morning through his conning-tower.

He read the general's signals. "Five and Four are to keep among the guns to the left and prevent any attempt to recover them. Seven and Eleven and Twelve, stick to the guns you have got; Seven, get into position to command the guns taken by Three. Then we're to do something else, are we? Six and One, quicken up to about ten miles an hour and walk round behind that camp to the levels near the river—we shall bag the whole crowd of them," interjected the young man. "Ah, here we are! Two and Three, Eight and Nine, Thirteen and Fourteen, space out to a thousand yards, wait for the word, and then go slowly to cover the advance of the cyclist infantry against any charge of mounted troops. That's all right. But where's Ten? Halloa! Ten to repair and get movable as soon as possible. They've broken up Ten!"

The discipline of the new war machines was businesslike rather than pedantic, and the head of the captain came down out of the conning-tower to tell his men: "I say, you chaps there. They've broken up Ten. Not badly, I think; but anyhow, he's stuck."

But that still left thirteen of the monsters in action to finish up the broken army.

The war correspondent stealing down his gully looked back and saw them all lying along the crest and talking, fluttering congratulatory flags to one another. Their iron sides were shining golden in the light of the rising sun.

V

The private adventures of the war correspondent terminated in surrender about one o'clock in the afternoon, and by that time he had stolen a horse, pitched off it, and narrowly escaped being rolled upon; found the brute had broken its leg, and shot it with his revolver. He had spent some hours in the company of a squad of dispirited riflemen, had quarrelled with them about topography at last, and gone off by himself in a direction that should have brought him to the banks of the river and didn't. Moreover, he had eaten all his chocolate and found nothing in the whole world to drink. Also, it had become extremely hot. From behind a broken, but attractive, stone wall he had seen far away in the distance the defender-horsemen trying to charge cyclists in open order, with land ironclads outflanking them on either side. He had discovered that cyclists could retreat over open turf before horsemen with a sufficient margin of speed to allow of frequent dismounts and much terribly effective sharpshooting, and he had a sufficient persuasion that those horsemen, having charged their hearts out, had halted just beyond his range of vision and surrendered. He had been urged to sudden activity by a forward movement of one of those machines that had threatened to enfilade his wall. He had discovered a fearful blister on his heel.

He was now in a scrubby gravelly place, sitting down and meditating on his pocket-handkerchief, which had in some extraordinary way become in the last twenty-four hours extremely ambigous in hue. "It's the whitest thing I've got," he said.

He had known all along that the enemy was east, west, and south of him, but when he heard land ironclads Number One and Six talking in their measured, deadly way not half a mile to the north he decided to make his own little unconditional peace without any further risks. He was for hoisting his white flag to a bush and taking up a position of modest obscurity near it until some one came along. He became aware of voices, clatter, and the distinctive noises of a body of horse, quite near, and he put his handkerchief in his pocket again and went to see what was going forward.

The sound of firing ceased, and then as he drew near he heard the deep sounds of many simple, coarse, but hearty and noble-hearted soldiers of the old school swearing with vigour.

He emerged from his scrub upon a big level plain, and far away a fringe of trees marked the banks of the river.

In the centre of the picture was a still-intact road bridge, and a big railway bridge a little to the right. Two land ironclads rested, with a general air of being long, harmless sheds, in a pose of anticipatory peacefulness right and left of the picture, completely commanding two miles and more of the river levels. Emerged and halted a few yards from the scrub was the remainder of the defender's cavalry, dusty, a little disordered and obviously annoyed, but still a very fine show of men. In the middle distance three or four men and horses were receiving medical attendance, and nearer a knot of officers regarded the distant novelties in mechanism with profound distaste. Every one was very distinctly aware of the twelve other ironclads, and of the multitude of townsmen soldiers, on bicycles or afoot, encumbered now by prisoners and captured war-gear, but otherwise thoroughly effective, who were sweeping like a great net in their rear.

"Checkmate," said the war correspondent, walking out into the open. "But I surrender in the best of company. Twenty-four hours ago I thought war was impossible—and these beggars have captured the whole blessed army! Well! Well!" He thought of his talk with the young lieutenant. "If there's no end to the surprises of science, the civilised people have it, of course. As long as their science keeps going they will necessarily be ahead of open-country men. Still. . . ." He wondered for a space what might have happened to the young lieutenant.

The war correspondent was one of those inconsistent people who always want the beaten side to win. When he saw all these burly, sun-tanned horsemen, disarmed and dismounted and lined up; when he saw their horses unskilfully led away by the singularly not equestrian cyclists to whom they had surrendered; when he saw these truncated Paladins watching this scandalous sight, he forgot altogether that he had called these men "cunning louts" and wished them beaten not four-and-twenty hours ago. A month ago he had seen that regiment in its pride going forth to war, and had been told of its terrible prowess, how it could charge in open order with each man firing from his saddle, and sweep before it anything else that ever came out to battle in any sort of order, foot or horse. And it had had to fight a few score of young men in atrociously unfair machines!

"Manhood *versus* Machinery" occurred to him as a suitable headline. Journalism curdles all one's mind to phrases.

He strolled as near the lined-up prisoners as the sentinels seemed disposed to permit, and surveyed them and compared their sturdy proportions with those of their lightly built captors.

"Smart degenerates," he muttered. "Anæmic cockneydom."

The surrendered officers came quite close to him presently, and he could hear the colonel's high-pitched tenor. The poor gentleman had spent three years of arduous toil upon the best material in the world perfecting that shooting from the saddle charge, and he was inquiring with phrases of blasphemy, natural in the circumstances, what one could be expected to do against this suitably consigned ironmongery.

"Guns," said some one.

"Big guns they can walk round. You can't shift big guns to keep pace with them, and little guns in the open they rush. I saw 'em rushed. You might do a surprise now and then—assassinate the brutes, perhaps——"

"You might make things like 'em."

"What? *More* ironmongery? Us? . . ."

"I'll call my article," meditated the war correspondent, " 'Mankind *versus* Ironmongery,' and quote the old boy at the beginning."

And he was much too good a journalist to spoil his contrast by remarking that the half-dozen comparatively slender young men in blue pyjamas who were standing about their victorious land ironclad, drinking coffee and eating biscuits, had also in their eyes and carriage something not altogether degraded below the level of a man.

THE HOLE MAN

Larry Niven

Larry Niven entered science fiction in 1964, with a new generation of writers including Ursula K. Le Guin, Roger Zelazny, Samuel R. Delany, Thomas M. Disch, and Norman Spinrad in the U.S., and Michael Moorcock, Keith Roberts, and the whole New Wave in the U.K. (which later came to dominate the sf of the sixties on both sides of the Atlantic). Of them all, he was the only one whose métier was hard science fiction, and as such he was a key figure in a generation that tried to declare the end of science fiction and the birth of speculative fiction, phoenix-like from the ashes of the genre.

Specifically, the advocates of speculative fiction wished to discard both the attitudes and affect of hard science fiction and to eliminate any necessary connection between the literature and science. Ironically, Robert A. Heinlein coined the term *speculative fiction* in his World SF Convention speech of 1941, but it never challenged the dominance of science fiction until the 1960s. During a short but intense time of passion and literary experimentation, the real action in sf was in opposition to hard science fiction, except for Larry Niven's work.

His stories of the sixties and early seventies were all hard science fiction, with the verve and action of Heinlein and Herbert combined with the fascination with science-driven plots and settings of Hal Clement. Most of his early works fit into a future history schema called "Known Space," and are collected in many volumes of his short stories, most centrally in *Neutron Star* (1968), *The Shape of Space* (1969), *All the Myriad Ways* (1971), *Tales of Known Space* (1975), *The Long ARM of Gil Hamilton* (1976), and in the novels *World of Ptavvs* (1966), *A Gift from Earth* (1968), *Ringworld* (1970), *Protector* (1973). Alone in his generation, Niven became the great hope of hard science fiction for a decade, the writer whose work was the popular focus of hard sf devotees until the next generation of hard sf writers such as Gregory Benford emerged in the seventies. Because the whole attention of younger readers had shifted in the mid-sixties, Niven's work prevented the whole New Wave controversy from becoming merely a generational argument, with the sixties children of Bester and Sturgeon replacing the fifties children of Heinlein and Campbell. Niven has continued into the nineties writing hard sf novels, as well as in collaborative works with Jerry Pournelle—*The Mote in God's Eye* (1974), *Lucifer's Hammer* (1977), *Footfall* (1985), and others.

"The Hole Man" (1973) explores the idea of a tiny quantum black hole (now a discarded bit of science but then a theoretical possibility) in a manner paradigmatic of his hard sf method. Niven sets up a dramatic situation involving characters in conflict and then proceeds to use every event to support rather large amounts of expository detail describing places, things, gadgets (including the Forward mass detector—see note to "The Singing Diamond"), and other items of speculative science. Niven's own sincere enthusiasm for neat ideas carries the day—we are to identify with the anonymous narrator, whose intense intellectual fascination with ideas represents the attitude of the story. We can even admire, intellectually, the perfect murder. That the basic science of the story is no longer "real" does not in this case lessen the impact.

One day Mars will be gone.

Andrew Lear says that it will start with violent quakes, and end hours or days later, very suddenly. He ought to know. It's all his fault.

Lear also says that it won't happen for from years to centuries. So we stay, Lear and the rest of us. We study the alien base for what it can tell us, while the center of the world we stand on is slowly eaten away. It's enough to give a man nightmares.

It was Lear who found the alien base.

We had reached Mars: fourteen of us, in the cramped bulbous life-support system of the *Percival Lowell*. We were circling in orbit, taking our time, correcting our maps and looking for anything that thirty years of Mariner probes might have missed.

We were mapping mascons, among other things. Those mass concentrations under the lunar maria were almost certainly left by good-sized asteroids, mountains of rock falling silently out of the sky until they struck with the energies of thousands of fusion bombs. Mars has been cruising through the asteroid belt for four billion years. Mars would show bigger and better mascons. They would affect our orbits.

So Andrew Lear was hard at work, watching pens twitch on graph paper as we circled Mars. A bit of machinery fell alongside the *Percival Lowell*, rotating. Within its thin shell was a weighted double lever system, deceptively simple: a Forward Mass Detector. The pens mapped its twitchings.

Over Sirbonis Palus, they began mapping strange curves.

Another man might have cursed and tried to fix it. Andrew Lear thought it out, then sent the signal that would stop the free-falling widget from rotating.

It had to be rotating to map a stationary mass.

But now it was mapping simple sine waves.

Lear went running to Captain Childrey.

Running? It was more like trapeze artistry. Lear pulled himself along by handholds, kicked off from walls, braked with a hard push of hands or feet. Moving in free fall is hard work when you're in a hurry, and Lear was a forty-year-old astrophysicist, not an athlete. He was blowing hard when he reached the control bubble.

Childrey—who *was* an athlete—waited with a patient, slightly contemptuous smile while Lear caught his breath.

He already thought Lear was crazy. Lear's words only confirmed it. "Gravity for sending signals? Dr. Lear, will you please quit bothering me with your weird ideas. I'm busy. We all are."

This was not entirely unfair. Some of Lear's enthusiasms were peculiar. Gravity generators. Black holes. He thought we should be searching for Dyson spheres: stars completely enclosed by an artificial shell. He believed that mass and inertia were two separate things: that it should be possible to suck the inertia out of a spacecraft, say, so that it could accelerate to near lightspeed in a few minutes. He was a wide-eyed dreamer, and when he was flustered he tended to wander from the point.

"You don't understand," he told Childrey. "Gravity radiation is harder to block than electromagnetic waves. Patterned gravity waves would be easy to detect. The advanced civilizations in the galaxy may all be communicating by gravity. Some of them may even be modulating pulsars—rotating neutron stars. That's where Project

Ozma went wrong: they were only looking for signals in the electromagnetic spectrum."

Childrey laughed. "Sure. Your little friends are using neutron stars to send you messages. What's that got to do with us?"

"Well, look!" Lear held up the strip of flimsy, nearly weightless paper he'd torn from the machine. "I got this over Sirbonis Palus. I think we ought to land there."

"We're landing in Mare Cimmerium, as you perfectly well know. The lander is already deployed and ready to board. Dr. Lear, we've spent four days mapping this area. It's flat. It's in a green-brown area. When spring comes next month, we'll find out whether there's life there! And everybody wants it that way except you!"

Lear was still holding the graph paper before him like a shield. "Please. Take one more circuit over Sirbonis Palus."

Childrey opted for the extra orbit. Maybe the sine waves convinced him. Maybe not. He would have liked inconveniencing the rest of us in Lear's name, to show him for a fool.

But the next pass showed a tiny circular feature in Sirbonis Palus. And Lear's mass indicator was making sine waves again.

The aliens had gone. During our first few months we always expected them back any minute. The machinery in the base was running smoothly and perfectly, as if the owners had only just stepped out.

The base was an inverted pie plate two stories high, and windowless. The air inside was breathable, like Earth's air three miles up, but with a bit more oxygen. Mars's air is far thinner, and poisonous. Clearly they were not of Mars.

The walls were thick and deeply eroded. They leaned inward against the internal pressure. The roof was somewhat thinner, just heavy enough for the pressure to support it. Both walls and roof were of fused Martian dust.

The heating system still worked—and it was also the lighting system: grids in the ceiling glowing brick red. The base was always ten degrees too warm. We didn't find the off switches for almost a week: they were behind locked panels. The air system blew gusty winds through the base until we fiddled with the fans.

We could guess a lot about them from what they'd left behind. They must have come from a world smaller than Earth, circling a red dwarf star in close orbit. To be close enough to be warm enough, the planet would have to be locked in by tides, turning one face always to its star. The aliens must have evolved on the lighted side, in a permanent red day, with winds constantly howling over the border from the night side.

And they had no sense of privacy. The only doorways that had doors in them were airlocks. The second floor was a hexagonal metal gridwork. It would not block you off from your friends on the floor below. The bunk room was an impressive expanse of mercury-filled waterbed, wall to wall. The rooms were too small and cluttered, the furniture and machinery too close to the doorways, so that at first we were constantly bumping elbows and knees. The ceilings were an inch short of six feet high on both floors, so that we tended to walk stooped even if we were short enough to stand upright. Habit. But Lear was just tall enough to knock his head if he stood up fast, anywhere in the base.

We thought they must have been smaller than human. But their padded benches seemed human-designed in size and shape. Maybe it was their minds that were different: they didn't need psychic elbow room.

The ship had been bad enough. Now this. Within the base was instant claustrophobia. It put all of our tempers on hair triggers.

Two of us couldn't take it.

• • •

Lear and Childrey did not belong on the same planet.

With Childrey, neatness was a compulsion. He had enough for all of us. During those long months aboard *Percival Lowell*, it was Childrey who led us in calisthenics. He flatly would not let anyone skip an exercise period. We eventually gave up trying.

Well and good. The exercise kept us alive. We weren't getting the healthy daily exercise anyone gets walking around the living room in a one-gravity field.

But after a month on Mars, Childrey was the only man who still appeared fully dressed in the heat of the alien base. Some of us took it as a reproof, and maybe it was, because Lear had been the first to doff his shirt for keeps. In the mess Childrey would inspect his silverware for water spots, then line it up perfectly parallel.

On Earth, Andrew Lear's habits would have been no more than a character trait. In a hurry, he might choose mismatched socks. He might put off using the dishwasher for a day or two if he were involved in something interesting. He would prefer a house that looked "lived in." God help the maid who tried to clean up his study. He'd never be able to find anything afterward.

He was a brilliant but one-sided man. Backpacking or skin diving might have changed his habits—in such pursuits you learn not to forget any least trivial thing—but they would never have tempted him. An expedition to Mars was something he simply could not turn down. A pity, because neatness is worth your life in space.

You don't leave your fly open in a pressure suit.

A month after the landing, Childrey caught Lear doing just that.

The "fly" on a pressure suit is a soft rubber tube over your male member. It leads to a bladder, and there's a spring clamp on it. You open the clamp to use it. Then you close the clamp and open an outside spigot to evacuate the bladder into vacuum.

Similar designs for women involve a catheter, which is hideously uncomfortable. I presume the designers will keep trying. It seems wrong to bar half the human race from our ultimate destiny.

Lear was addicted to long walks. He loved the Martian desert scene: the hard violet sky and the soft blur of whirling orange dust, the sharp close horizon, the endless emptiness. More: he needed the room. He was spending all his working time on the alien communicator, with the ceiling too close over his head and everything else too close to his bony elbows.

He was coming back from a walk, and he met Childrey coming out. Childrey noticed that the waste spigot on Lear's suit was open, the spring broken. Lear had been out for hours. If he'd had to go, he might have bled to death through flesh ruptured by vacuum.

We never learned all that Childrey said to him out there. But Lear came in very red about the ears, muttering under his breath. He wouldn't talk to anyone.

The NASA psychologists should not have put them both on that small a planet. Hindsight is wonderful, right? But Lear and Childrey were each the best choice for competence coupled to the kind of health they would need to survive the trip. There were astrophysicists as competent and as famous as Lear, but they were decades older. And Childrey had a thousand spaceflight hours to his credit. He had been one of the last men on the moon.

Individually, each of us was the best possible man. It was a damn shame.

The aliens had left the communicator going, like everything else in the base. It must have been hellishly massive, to judge by the thick support pillars slanting outward beneath it. It was a bulky tank of a thing, big enough that the roof had to bulge slightly to give it room. That gave Lear about a square meter of the only head room in the base.

Even Lear had no idea why they'd put it on the second floor. It would send through the first floor, or through the bulk of a planet. Lear learned that by trying it, once he knew enough. He beamed a dot-dash message through Mars itself to the Forward Mass Detector aboard *Lowell.*

Lear had set up a Mass Detector next to the communicator, on an extremely complex platform designed to protect it from vibration. The Detector produced waves so sharply pointed that some of us thought they could *feel* the gravity radiation coming from the communicator.

Lear was in love with the thing.

He skipped meals. When he ate he ate like a starved wolf. "There's a heavy point-mass in there," he told us, talking around a mouthful of food, two months after the landing. "The machine uses electromagnetic fields to vibrate it at high speed. Look—" He picked up a toothpaste tube of tuna spread and held it in front of him. He vibrated it rapidly. Heads turned to watch him around the zigzagged communal table in the alien mess. "I'm making gravity waves now. But they're too mushy because the tube's too big, and their amplitude is virtually zero. There's something very dense and massive in that machine, and it takes a hell of a lot of field strength to keep it there."

"What is it?" someone asked. "Neutronium? Like the heart of a neutron star?"

Lear shook his head and took another mouthful. "That size, neutronium wouldn't be stable. I think it's a quantum black hole. I don't know how to measure its mass yet."

I said, "A *quantum* black hole?"

Lear nodded happily. "Luck for me. You know, I was against the Mars expedition. We could get a lot more for our money by exploring the asteroids. Among other things, we might have found if there are really quantum black holes out there. But this one's already captured!" He stood up, being careful of his head. He turned in his tray and went back to work.

I remember we stared at each other along the zigzag mess table. Then we drew lots . . . and I lost.

The day Lear left his waste spigot open, Childrey had put a restriction on him. Lear was not to leave the base without an escort.

Lear had treasured the aloneness of those walks. But it was worse than that. Childrey had given him a list of possible escorts: half a dozen men Childrey could trust to see to it that Lear did nothing dangerous to himself or others. Inevitably they were the men most thoroughly trained in space survival routines, most addicted to Childrey's own compulsive neatness, least likely to sympathize with Lear's way of living. Lear was as likely to ask Childrey himself to go walking with him.

He almost never went out any more. I knew exactly where to find him.

I stood beneath him, looking up through the gridwork floor.

He'd almost finished dismantling the protective panels around the gravity communicator. What showed inside looked like parts of a computer in one spot, electromagnetic coils in most places, and a square array of pushbuttons that might have been the aliens' idea of a typewriter. Lear was using a magnetic induction sensor to try to trace wiring without actually tearing off the insulation.

I called, "How you making out?"

"No good," he said. "The insulation seems to be one hundred per cent perfect. Now I'm afraid to open it up. No telling how much power is running through there, if it needs shielding that good." He smiled down at me. "Let me show you something."

"What?"

He flipped a toggle above a dull gray circular plate. "This thing is a microphone. It took me a while to find it. I am Andrew Lear, speaking to whoever may be listening." He switched it off, then ripped paper from the Mass Indicator and showed me squiggles interrupting smooth sine waves. "There. The sound of my voice in gravity radiation. It won't disappear until it's reached the edges of the universe."

"Lear, you mentioned quantum black holes there. What's a quantum black hole?"

"Um. You know what a black hole is."

"I ought to." Lear had educated us on the subject, at length, during the months aboard *Lowell*.

When a not too massive star has used up its nuclear fuel, it collapses into a white dwarf. A heavier star—say, 1.44 times the mass of the sun and larger—can burn out its fuel, then collapse into itself until it is ten kilometers across and composed solely of neutrons packed edge to edge: the densest matter in this universe.

But a big star goes further than that. When a really massive star runs its course . . . when the radiation pressure within is no longer strong enough to hold the outer layers against the star's own ferocious gravity . . . then it can fall into itself entirely, until gravity is stronger than any other force, until it is compressed past the Schwarzchild radius and effectively leaves the universe. What happens to it then is problematical. The Schwarzchild radius is the boundary beyond which nothing can climb out of the gravity well, not even light.

The star is gone then, but the mass remains: a lightless hole in space, perhaps a hole into another universe.

"A collapsing star can leave a black hole," said Lear. "There may be bigger black holes, whole galaxies that have fallen into themselves. But there's no other way a black hole can form, *now*."

"So?"

"There was a time when black holes of all sizes could form. That was during the Big Bang, the explosion that started the expanding universe. The forces in that blast could have compressed little local vortices of matter past the Schwarzchild radius. What that left behind—the smallest ones, anyway—we call quantum black holes."

I heard a distinctive laugh behind me as Captain Childrey walked into view. The bulk of the communicator would have hidden him from Lear, and I hadn't heard him come up. He called, "Just how big a thing are you talking about? Could I pick one up and throw it at you?"

"You'd disappear into one that size," Lear said seriously. "A black hole the mass of the Earth would only be a centimeter across. No, I'm talking about things from ten-to-the-minus-fifth grams on up. There could be one at the center of the sun—"

"Eek!"

Lear was trying. He didn't like being kidded, but he didn't know how to stop it. Keeping it serious wasn't the way, but he didn't know that either. "Say ten-to-the-seventeenth grams in mass and ten-to-the-minus-eleven centimeters across. It would be swallowing a few atoms a day."

"Well, at least you know where to find it," said Childrey. "Now all you have to do is go after it."

Lear nodded, still serious. "There could be quantum black holes in asteroids. A small asteroid could capture a quantum black hole easily enough, especially if it was charged; a black hole can hold a charge, you know—"

"Ri-ight."

"All we'd have to do is check out a small asteroid with the Mass Detector. If it masses more than it should, we push it aside and see if it leaves a black hole behind."

"You'd need little teeny eyes to see something that small. Anyway, what would you do with it?"

"You put a charge on it, if it hasn't got one already, and electromagnetic fields. You can vibrate it to make gravity; then you manipulate it with radiation. I think I've got one in here," he said, patting the alien communicator.

"Ri-ight," said Childrey, and he went away laughing.

Within a week the whole base was referring to Lear as the Hole Man, the man with the black hole between his ears.

It hadn't sounded funny when Lear was telling me about it. The rich variety of the universe . . . But when Childrey talked about the black hole in Lear's Anything Box, it sounded hilarious.

Please note: Childrey did not misunderstand anything Lear had said. Childrey wasn't stupid. He merely thought Lear was crazy. He could not have gotten away with making fun of Lear, not among educated men, without knowing exactly what he was doing.

Meanwhile the work went on.

There were pools of Marsdust, fascinating stuff, fine enough to behave like viscous oil, and knee-deep. Wading through it wasn't dangerous, but it was very hard work, and we avoided it. One day Brace waded out into the nearest of the pools and started feeling around under the dust. Hunch, he said. He came up with some eroded plastic-like containers. The aliens had used the pool as a garbage dump.

We were having little luck with chemical analysis of the base materials. They were virtually indestructible. We learned more about the chemistry of the alien visitors themselves. They had left traces of themselves on the benches and on the communal waterbed. The traces had most of the chemical components of protoplasm, but Arsvey found no sign of DNA. Not surprising, he said. There must be other giant organic molecules suitable for gene coding.

The aliens had left volumes of notes behind. The script was a mystery, of course, but we studied the photographs and diagrams. A lot of them were notes on anthropology!

The aliens had been studying Earth during the first Ice Age.

None of us were anthropologists, and that was a damn shame. We never learned if we'd found anything new. All we could do was photograph the stuff and beam it up to *Lowell*. One thing was sure: the aliens had left very long ago, and they had left the lighting and air systems running and the communicator sending a carrier wave.

For us? Who else?

The alternative was that the base had been switched off for some six hundred thousand years, then come back on when something detected *Lowell* approaching Mars. Lear didn't believe it. "If the power had been off in the communicator," he said, "the mass wouldn't be in there any more. The fields have to be going to hold it in place. It's smaller than an atom; it'd fall through anything solid."

So the base power system had been running for all that time. What the hell could it be? And where? We traced some cables and found that it was under the base, under several yards of Marsdust fused to lava. We didn't try to dig through that.

The source was probably geophysical: a hole deep into the core of the planet. The aliens might have wanted to dig such a hole to take core samples. Afterward they would have set up a generator to use the temperature difference between the core and the surface.

Meanwhile, Lear spent some time tracing down the power sources in the communicator. He found a way to shut off the carrier wave. Now the mass, if there was a mass, was at rest in there. It was strange to see the Forward Mass Detector pouring out straight lines instead of drastically peaked sine waves.

We were ill-equipped to take advantage of these riches. We had been fitted out to explore Mars, not a bit of civilization from another star. Lear was the exception. He was in his element, with but one thing to mar his happiness.

I don't know what the final argument was about. I was engaged on another project.

The Mars lander still had fuel in it. NASA had given us plenty of fuel to hover while we looked for a landing spot. After some heated discussion, we had agreed to take the vehicle up and hover it next to the nearby dust pool on low thrust.

It worked fine. The dust rose up in a great soft cloud and went away toward the horizon, leaving the pond bottom covered with otherworldly junk. And more! Arsvey started screaming at Brace to back off. Fortunately Brace kept his head. He tilted us over to one side and took us away on a gentle curve. The backblast never touched the skeletons.

We worked out there for hours, being very finicky indeed. Here was another skill none of us would own to, but we'd read about how careful an archaeologist has to be, and we did our best. Traces of water had had time to turn some of the dust to natural cement, so that some of the skeletons were fixed to the rock. But we got a couple free. We put them on stretchers and brought them back. One crumbled the instant the air came hissing into the lock. We left the other outside.

The aliens had not had the habit of taking baths. We'd set up a bathtub with very tall sides, in a room the aliens had reserved for some incomprehensible ritual. I had stripped off my pressure suit and was heading for the bathtub, very tired, hoping that nobody would be in it.

I heard voices before I saw them.

Lear was shouting.

Childrey wasn't, but his voice was a carrying one. It carried mockery. He was standing between the supporting pillars. His hands were on his hips, his teeth gleamed white, his head was thrown back to look up at Lear.

He finished talking. For a time neither of them moved. Then Lear made a sound of disgust. He turned away and pushed one of the buttons on what might have been an alien typewriter keyboard.

Childrey looked startled. He slapped at his right thigh and brought the hand away bloody. He stared at it, then looked up at Lear. He started to ask a question.

He crumpled slowly in the low gravity. I got to him before he hit the ground. I cut his pants open and tied a handkerchief over the blood spot. It was a small puncture, but the flesh was puckered above it on a line with his groin.

Childrey tried to speak. His eyes were wide. He coughed, and there was blood in his mouth.

I guess I froze. How could I help if I couldn't tell what had happened? I saw a blood spot on his right shoulder, and I tore the shirt open and found another tiny puncture wound.

The doctor arrived.

It took Childrey an hour to die, but the doctor had given up much earlier. Between the wound in his shoulder and the wound in his thigh, Childrey's flesh had been ruptured in a narrow line that ran through one lung and his stomach and part of his intestinal tract. The autopsy showed a tiny, very neat hole drilled through the hipbones.

We looked for, and found, a hole in the floor beneath the communicator. It was the size of a pencil lead, and packed with dust.

"I made a mistake," Lear told the rest of us at the inquest. "I should never have touched that particular button. It must have switched off the fields that held the mass in place. It just dropped. Captain Childrey was underneath."

And it had gone straight through him, eating the mass of him as it went.

"No, not quite," said Lear. "I'd guessed it massed about ten-to-the-fourteenth grams. That only makes it ten-to-the-minus-sixth Ångstrom across, much smaller than an atom. It wouldn't have absorbed much. The damage was done to Childrey by tidal effects as it passed through him. You saw how it pulverized the material of the floor."

Not surprisingly, the subject of murder did come up.

Lear shrugged it off. "Murder with what? Childrey didn't believe there was a black hole in there at all. Neither did many of you." He smiled suddenly. "Can you imagine what the trial would be like? Imagine the prosecuting attorney trying to tell a jury what he thinks happened. First he's got to tell them what a black hole is. Then a quantum black hole. Then he's got to explain why he doesn't have the murder weapon, and where he left it, freely falling through Mars! And if he gets that far without being laughed out of court, he's still got to explain how a thing smaller than an atom could hurt anyone!"

But didn't Dr. Lear know the thing was dangerous? Could he not have guessed its enormous mass from the way it behaved?

Lear spread his hands. "Gentlemen, we're dealing with more variables than just mass. Field strength, for instance. I might have guessed its mass from the force it took to keep it there, but did any of us expect the aliens to calibrate their dials in the metric system?"

Surely there must have been safeties to keep the fields from being shut off accidentally. Lear must have bypassed them.

"Yes, I probably did, accidentally. I did quite a lot of fiddling to find out how things worked."

It got dropped there. Obviously there would be no trial. No ordinary judge or jury could be expected to understand what the attorneys would be talking about. A couple of things never did get mentioned.

For instance: Childrey's last words. I might or might not have repeated them if I'd been asked to. They were: "All right, show me! Show it to me or admit it isn't there!"

As the court was breaking up I spoke to Lear with my voice lowered. "That was probably the most unique murder weapon in history."

He whispered, "If you said that in company I could sue for slander."

"Yeah? Really? Are *you* going to explain to a jury what you think I implied happened?"

"No, I'll let you get away with it this time."

"Hell, you didn't get away scot-free yourself. What are you going to study now?

The only known black hole in the universe, and you let it drop through your fingers."

Lear frowned. "You're right. Partly right, anyway. But I knew as much about it as I was going to, the way I was going. Now . . . I stopped it vibrating in there, then took the mass of the entire setup with the Forward Mass Sensor. Now the black hole isn't in there any more. I can get the mass of the black hole by taking the mass of the communicator alone."

"Oh."

"And I can cut the machine open, see what's inside. How they controlled it. Damn it, I wish I were six years old."

"What? Why?"

"Well . . . I don't have the times straightened out. The math is chancy. Either a few years from now, or a few centuries, there's going to be a black hole between Earth and Jupiter. It'll be big enough to study. I think about forty years."

When I realized what he was implying, I didn't know whether to laugh or scream. "Lear, you can't think that something that small could absorb Mars!"

"Well, remember that it absorbs everything it comes near. A nucleus here, an electron there . . . and it's not just waiting for atoms to fall into it. Its gravity is ferocious, and it's falling back and forth through the center of the planet, sweeping up matter. The more it eats, the bigger it gets, with its volume going up as the cube of the mass. Sooner or later, yes, it'll absorb Mars. By then it'll be just less than a millimeter across—big enough to see."

"Could it happen within thirteen months?"

"Before we leave? Hmm." Lear's eyes took on a faraway look. "I don't think so. I'll have to work it out. The math is chancy . . ."

ATOMIC POWER

Don A. Stuart

John W. Campbell, Jr., took the genre of science fiction and transformed it—by his power as editor of the highest-paying market and by the force of his personality and intellect—into the kind of fiction today recognized worldwide as American science fiction. He set new standards for scientific plausibility, for prose style, and for the complex of attitudes that for decades defined "the real stuff," as opposed to some version of fantasy using science fiction devices and/or settings. Campbell's concept of science fiction was defined both by the example of what he bought and published and by the editorials he wrote for *Astounding* (later *Analog*), his magazine. At least until the late 1950s his idea of science fiction, synonymous with hard science fiction, was the dominant fashion of its day (though not by any means unchallenged by the mid-fifties). It was only in the late fifties, when the term *hard science fiction* was coined by the regular book reviewer for *Astounding*, P. Schuyler Miller, that there was a body of work in the genre and a body of influential opinion in opposition to hard science fiction.

A part of Campbell's enduring prestige is a result of his Wellsian determination to predict the future through science fiction. With a technical education from M.I.T. and Duke, Campbell knew that both atomic power and space travel were possible in the near future, if not the day after tomorrow. He wrote about them in his early editorials and he encouraged his new stable of writers to create plausible fictions about them (and often added technical information to the stories himself). The atomic bomb proved him right in a big way and gave the whole science fiction field a boost—as Campbell had confidently predicted. It was an extraordinary shock to Campbell and the field when the advent of space travel in 1957 had the opposite effect, of reducing the sf readership for a time.

Before Campbell was the editor of *Astounding*, he was one of the most popular writers of the 1930s in science fiction, both under his own name as an adventure writer of serials and stories (later published as novels and collections, e.g., *The Mightiest Machine* [1947], *The Incredible Planet* [1949], and *The Moon is Hell!* [1951]) and under the pseudonym Don A. Stuart, which he used for his more ambitious efforts (later collected in *Who Goes There?* [1948] and *Cloak of Aesir* [1952]). "Atomic Power" is a Don A. Stuart story from 1934 that combines a vision of technological and scientific progress with a horrifying scenario of disaster that could well be a precursor of Latham's in "The Xi Effect." "Atomic Power" is selling a vision and an attitude, of a human future improved by science, and of scientists and engineers as the saviors of humanity. It is interesting to note that Robert A. Heinlein became the premier Campbell writer in part because he was the best salesman of Campbell's attitudes and that as an editor, Campbell generally rejected disaster stories, although they remained a popular form in the field. The major disaster sf of the later Campbell period, such as John Wyndham's *The Day of the Triffids* (1951) and John Christopher's *The Death of Grass* (a.k.a. *No Blade of Grass*, 1956) was written in England

and became an important form there; it later became the meat of Ballard and the New Wave.

The mass of the machine crouched in hulked, latent energy, the massive conductors leading off in gleaming ruddy columns, like the pillars of some mighty temple to an unknown, evil god, pillars fluted, and capped at base and capital with great socket-clamps. Around it huge tubes glowed with a dull bluish light, so that the faces of the half-dozen students looked distorted and ghastly.

A boredly smiling engineer watched them, and the patient professor instructing them, rather bored, not overhopeful himself that he could make these students understand the wonder and the magnitude of the process going on within the great machine.

"The power," he said, really trying intensely to make them understand the grandeur of the thing, "comes, of course, from the release of the energy of atoms. It is frequently referred to as the energy of the atom, but that is an inane viewpoint to take, for in each single second, over fifty-five duodecillion atoms are destroyed. Not truly destroyed; that has not yet been done; but broken up, and the energy of the parts absorbed, and carried away by the conductors. The fuel is water—that simplest and cheapest of all substances—hydrogen and oxygen.

"Each atom," he went on, "lasts for only one million-billionth of a second before its energy is released and the parts are discharged. There is a further energy level left in these ultraminute parts that, we believe, is even greater than the energy released in breaking the parts free of each other."

So he explained the thing, and the students looked at the great machine and realized that from the streaming energy released by it came the power which cooked their food and kept them warm, for it was winter just then.

They had seen the plant and the roaring machines which had other duties, such as ventilating the great maze of subsurface tunnels, and were about to leave, when there was a sudden momentary halt in the steady throb of the great pumps. The voices of engineers rang out, cursing and excited for a few seconds. Then all went on as before for a few minutes. A new sound rose in pitch as they listened, more interested. The professor hurried them swiftly into the main power room, speaking excitedly as he did:

"You are fortunate—most fortunate. In the last eleven years, only eight times has such a thing happened. They must start the engines again!"

They hastened into the power room.

"No one knows," the instructor explained swiftly, "why these breaks occur, but once in every year or so something goes wrong, and the generators strike a bit of fuel which simply doesn't break down. No one understands why. Just that the generators stop abruptly and cannot be restarted till they are cleared of the charge contained. Perhaps some single drop of water is the cause of the trouble, a drop in no way different, save that it simply will not break.

"You are most fortunate—"

His voice was drowned by the sudden explosion of titanic discharges rushing into the generator. For scarcely a thousandth of a second it continued, before the process, restarted, backed up and stopped the discharge into it. The generator functioned perfectly.

"Most fortunate," he went on as the sound died. "The drop which caused the trouble has been ejected, the generator cleared, and now it will function for another period of a year or more unhindered, in all probability."

"What happened to the drop of water which would not break?" asked a student. "Was it saved for investigation?"

"No," replied the instructor, shrugging his shoulders. "That was done once or twice. Since then, though we of science would like it, that we might work with these strange drops, it is not done because it is so costly to dismantle and reassemble the generator. It was simply ejected. The drops which have been investigated do become susceptible after a year or two and disappear, but before that time, even high-intensity generators will not touch them, beyond reducing their outmost fringes somewhat."

"Ban" Torrence was a physicist to the core, and, like any good physicist, he was terribly concerned when perfectly sound laws of science began to have exceptions. Just now he was most worried in appearance. "Tad" Albrite, engineer, didn't seem so worried, but he was interested.

"But," objected Tad, "I don't see any vast importance in the defection of a voltmeter. You say the voltage of the cell has increased one one hundredth of a volt in a week, according to that meter. All right, what of it?"

"You yap, the thing is it hasn't increased. I measured it against a potentiometer hook-up. Now a potentiometer is a regular arm-and-pan balance for electrical voltages, as you ought to know, even if you are a civil engineer. You take a standard cell, an outside current, and standardize the thing, then substitute your unknown voltage. The system will measure a ten thousandth of a volt if you do it correctly. The point is that a potentiometer uses nothing but electrical balances. It balances a fixed current through a resistance against an electrical potential."

"The galvanometer is a magnetic device using a string, which is what you object to," said Tad.

"And when the potentiometer is balanced, the galvanometer isn't working at all, and therefore doesn't count in the circuit.

"Now by the potentiometer, the voltage of that cell last week was 1.2581. By the potentiometer this week—to-day—it is 1.2580. It has, as is quite normal, fallen one ten-thousandth of a volt. It's been doing that for a period of two months—eight weeks. That's a grand-total drop of .0008 volts. But the voltmeter in the meantime has shown a *rise* of .0003 volts.

"Now that voltmeter checks with every other one in the place; it's a five-hundred-and-forty-two-dollar standard instrument, and it's so big and massive and sensitive, I move it around on little wheels on a cart, as you see. Don't you see what I'm getting at?"

"The Leeds and Northrup Co. gypped you apparently," decided Tad judiciously.

"They didn't. I've made other tests. In the first place, that company doesn't. In the second place, it is the tiny spring that the voltage-torque is measured against that has weakened, and every single spring I can find has weakened in like amount."

"How could you determine it?"

"Now, Tad, here's the important part of it all," replied Ban very softly. "I naturally tried weighing the standard gram weights, and the springs checked—they checked absolutely right. Until I used not a gram *weight* but a gram *mass*."

Tad stared at him blankly. "What the heck's the difference?"

"Weight is the product of mass times the acceleration of gravity. Mass—is just plain mass. Mass can be measured by inertia, and that doesn't depend on gravity. So I set up a very simple little thing, so simple it couldn't go wrong—an inverted pendulum—a little lump of metal on the end of a steel spring, and I measured its period, not with an ordinary clock, but with an electric timer that didn't have a spring or pendulum in it, and—in the two months the period of that pendulum has increased, because the spring has weakened."

"Why not—they do, you know."

"Because when I measured the strength of that spring against gravity, you see," Ban said very, very softly, "it was just—as—strong—as—ever."

Tad looked at him silently for some seconds. "What in the name of blazes does that indicate?" he asked at last, explosively.

"Gravity has weakened to exactly the same extent the spring has. Every spring I have has weakened. And gravity has weakened."

"*Gravity* weakened!" gasped Albrite. "You're cockeyed—it's impossible. Why—why the whole solar system would be thrown out of gear—the astronomers would have spotted it."

"Jack Ribly will be here at two forty," replied Torrence quietly. "You know they wouldn't proclaim news like that right off, particularly because the weakening is very slight, and they do have observational errors."

"But, good Heavens, man, it—it couldn't happen."

Ban's face was suddenly drawn and tense. "Do you think for a moment, Tad, that I was quick to accept that? I've checked and counterchecked, and rechecked. And I've found out something. That's why I called you—and Jack Ribly. You're a civil engineer, and, if I'm right, you'll see the things happening soon. And Ribly's an astronomer, and he'll see them.

"You see, whatever it is that's affecting gravity, must be affecting the strength of springs in the same degree. So I tried the compressibility of liquids. Water will compress—damn little, of course, but it will—and it's changed. It compresses more. So I tried gas. That's unchanged. Pressure of gas depends solely on mass, kinetic energy, and not on intermolecular bonds. There aren't any in gas. The molecules are perfectly free to move about. In solids they're bound so tightly they can't even slide. In water they slide, but can't separate. But they have—a little.

"And the bonds are weakening. That's why springs—solids, of course—haven't the old strength. Molecular bonds are infinitesimally weaker. But the weakening is progressive. But electric and magnetic fields are untouched. So voltmeters read high. Interatomic and intra-atomic forces in general are unchanged, but everything bigger than a single molecule is different.

"I've checked it a thousand ways, Tad. I even repeated Millikan's old measurement of the mass of an electron—which measured the mass by gravitative effect on the oil droplets—and the answer was different. Magnets lift more.

"Great Heaven, Tad, the—the universe will fly to pieces!"

"What will happen?" asked Tad, awestruck now.

"Accidents—horrible accidents here on Earth first. That is, so far as we will first detect. The Sun will be retreating. The Moon flying off, too, you see, because centrifugal force is based only on mass and inertia, and it isn't weakened, but we won't notice that at first. But automobiles—they'll weigh less and less, so they won't fall apart. Men won't notice it, because they'll be getting weaker, too.

"But the inertia of the automobile will remain the same. So when they put on the brakes, the weakened material will crack. And the engines will fly to pieces as the undiminished power of the explosions blows them open. Bridges—lighter, but weaker. The wind will be strong, though. Things blowing up in the air. The air getting thinner, as it escapes against the diminishing gravity—"

"Great Heaven!" said Tad softly. Because he believed now.

The bell rang, and Ban went downstairs and opened the door. Jack Ribly was with him when he came back. He looked curiously at their solemn faces, Ban's dark, seamed face, showing his thirty-five years, but in that ageless way that made him seem eternally thirty-five. Tad Albrite looking younger than his thirty-two.

"What's up, Ban?" asked Ribly.

Swiftly Ban explained the proposition. Ribly's face worked with surprise and belief from the first second.

"Have you fellows spotted it?" Torrence asked at last.

"Yes, 'fraid of it. Didn't announce it."

"So's everybody else. Both spotted it and been afraid. What did you notice it in?"

"Our Moon first, of course. Then Mercury and Phobos and Deimos. And—Heaven help us—I didn't understand at the time, but the companion of Sirius is bluer to-night than it was a year ago!"

"I thought you said it had no intra-atomic effects; spectra are intra-atomic effects," said Albrite.

"Not in this case. Sirius' companion is so dense, the spectrum is pulled back toward the red by the intense gravitational field. The gravitational fields are weakening—even so far away as Sirius."

"Why? Why?" demanded Albrite.

The world asked, too, when it learned; when markets found pound packages of sugar and butter weighing fifteen ounces. But that was several months later. Before then, the Moon was changed. Earth began to see a smaller Moon, and a different Moon, for as the Moon circled out, the effects were cumulative, and she turned at such a rate that the face which had eternally faced Earth began to turn away, and the unseen face became visible.

And a gold merchant made a small fortune by buying gold in Brazil, using a very accurate type of pneumatic balance, and selling it in the same way in Alaska, where the centrifugal force of the Earth's spin did not cut its weight.

The three men worked together on the problem, and all over Earth other men were seeking some answer, some explanation, and some help. The diminution of weight, starting so slowly, mounted rapidly, cumulative in rate itself.

Ban Torrence did most of the work, using the figures that Ribly brought him, and the apparatus that Albrite designed. 1947 drew to a close, and 1948 began. It was a bitterly cold winter, colder than had been known before for many, many years, despite predictions that it would be a warm one.

It was February when the astronomers definitely announced that, at present rates, the winter would be everlasting, growing neither colder nor warmer, for as the Earth turned its northern hemisphere more toward the Sun, it moved away. But in the southern hemisphere, there would be rapidly increasing cold, as the two effects added, instead of subtracting.

By the last of May and early June, however, the temperature would start falling again. The report ended with that statement. "By late May or early June the temperature will again begin to fall." That was the end, because there was no other prediction. After June the temperature would fall. In February, the warmest day in New York City registered a temperature of only 42°. The coldest was −19.2°.

And still the world asked why.

The sun rose at seven thirty on March 21st. It rose much later on April 21st, for it was falling behind. Earth was no longer circling it. Earth was spiraling about it.

In late March, the three scientists had moved to Northern Mexico and established a laboratory there. It was easier to work, and much work must be done out of doors.

"Have we got anywhere at all?" Albrite demanded when they had settled again and begun a conference on advances.

"Hum-yes," decided Torrence. He glanced quizzically at Ribly. "You wouldn't believe my statement, so I won't make it. But I'll tell you something. This is about the only warm place on Earth—down in the tropics. We're in the northern hemisphere. Tropic of Cancer to the south of us."

"I still," said Albrite softly, "don't see why you didn't make a job of it and move down to the equator while you were at it."

"It's March right now, and the Sun is actually about over the equator, but it's moving north as usual, so that it'll be over the Tropic of Cancer in June—and that'll be the warmest spot on a very, very, chilly Earth. But what's the difference between the polar and equatorial diameter of the Earth?"

"I don't know—there is a difference, at that. Couple of miles, why?"

"Because the diameter of the Earth through the forty-five-degrees point is the same as the mean diameter. The poles are flattened. The equator is bulged. When gravity weakens some more, centrifugal force won't—and the thing is going to be even worse. Also—earthquakes. They'll be starting soon."

"Hmmm—that's true."

"Well, we're here. What'll we do?"

"Work—and work fast," replied Torrence. "Ever stop to think, Tad, that we'll have to use some kind of electrical generating equipment in all probability, and that we haven't time to build new, because this weakening is going on so fast that before we could spend the year so necessary normally, even if we didn't freeze first, to design and build it, it couldn't be built, because all metal would be powder? We have to use standard stuff—and the standard won't be able to stand its own centrifugal force beyond July 30th. So, friend, if we don't find the answer and start in by July to stop it—there—just isn't any use."

"Is there any?" asked Albrite hopelessly. "Trying to do something with the whole solar system!"

"Not," replied Torrence, "with the whole solar system, if my idea is right. And to do anything at all, anyway, we'll have a further little problem to meet, you see. I don't know just yet."

"Then—to work," Ribly sighed. "What must I do? Go on collecting the same old data?"

"With particular emphasis on the new nebular velocities. What's Andromeda now?"

"Minus 12," replied Ribly. "My record so far is minus 22,500. Minus means retreat. The distant constellations are showing some change, too."

It was June 10th. New York City was semideserted. Snow ten feet deep, where it wasn't drifted, blocked all the streets. Where it was drifted, which was almost everywhere, it ran forty and fifty feet deep. The few people who still lived in New York, less than five hundred thousand, moved about little; only when a boat was due to sail.

Day and night the *crunch-crack-shuff* of the icebreakers in the harbor was audible. Because the temperature had begun to drop in late May. It was −32.4 at noon, June 10th. Where the icebreakers opened the water, it steamed.

The oceans were giving up their age-old hoard of heat. Had ice only been heavier, instead of lighter, than water, the temperature would not have fallen so low, for even in the cold of space where Earth was headed now, the stored heat of the oceans would have warmed her for decades.

But ice was forming. The *Atlantic* was in port now, taking aboard passengers at five hundred dollars a head for third class, five thousand for a private room. She was a vast liner, another attempt at the "world's greatest."

And New York heard a rumor. The *Atlantic* was making her last trip—the last trip any ship would make. They were afraid of the waves. They were afraid of the winds. They were most afraid of the ice.

On June 9th there was a blizzard—an antarctic blizzard. The wind howled, and the howl mounted to a shriek. No snow fell, but the powdery stuff rose, thousands of tons of it, swept up by a wind of one-hundred-mile-an-hour velocity, with undiminished force and mass, since its inertia remained. The snow had lost weight. New York was blinded.

At seven A.M. the George Washington Bridge shrieked a new song. The fragments landed nearly a quarter of a mile down the river. At seven thirty, the older bridges failed, the Brooklyn going first. By eight fifteen there were no man-made bridges. But the wind, the snow, had sucked the heat out of the rivers, and the ice had solidified all across them, so there was a single, great ice bridge.

At ten twenty, the old Woolworth Building crashed, and on its heels came the Empire State tower. The fragments of the Empire State's tower fell over most of southeastern Manhattan.

The blizzard had died by the morning of the tenth, but there were no great towers remaining on the sky line of New York. The weakening of materials, and the titanic force of the wind, had seen to that.

And the rumor that the *Atlantic* would be the last ship to leave New York spread.

The *Atlantic* was booked by dawn of the 10th, and there were no more ships in New York harbor leaving that day, sailings scheduled the next day would not go. A crowd gathered about the sheltered dock of the *Atlantic* on the southern side of Manhattan. A wind still raged at forty-five miles an hour from the north.

Slowly the crowd grew, and the low muttering increased. Police and guards kept the lines in check till ten. The *Atlantic* was to sail at noon. At ten ten, the crowd swarmed up her gangways. Guards were killed, crushed. Men, women, and children started up the gangplanks.

Men, and some women, reached the decks and burst into the cabins. Men found and fought their way to the neighborhood of the boiler and engine rooms. At ten twenty, it was estimated there were two thousand people aboard, at ten forty, seven thousand. At eleven o'clock, at least fifteen thousand people, over a thousand tons of humanity, had got aboard.

It was like no other panic crowding. Many of those fifteen thousand were dead already, many more dying. A woman's body trampled underfoot. A girl held erect by the crowd's pressing, blood slowly oozing from her shoulder, her arm torn completely off, held perhaps in the clenched fingers of her other hand like some monstrous club, dead. A man's dismembered corpse.

For the power of human bodies is supplied by chemical combinations. These were the visible damages, there were shrieks, groans of horrible agony, for the chemical power of muscles remained undiminished, while their tensile strength declined. Literally, people tore themselves apart by the violence of their struggles.

The *Atlantic* gained no more passengers after eleven.

The officers would not sail. They might have sailed for the moment to end the deaths at the wharf, but they could not, for the ship, already filled to capacity, was overloaded. Further, she swayed slowly to the struggles of her passengers.

Then a hold, hitherto undiscovered, was broken open. Instantly a torrent of people poured in, and another five thousand came aboard the ship. A slow, grinding pressure began, and those who, finding themselves in the heated hallways, had stopped, satisfied, and blocked the entrance of more thereby, were gradually driven farther.

The captain ordered the ship to sail. The lines were cast off again, and the ship's great screws turned slowly. No human strength could hold her in now, and she broke free of the crowd at the wharf. But in the harbor, free of the crowd, she stopped again at once. The captain ordered that the crowd be forced off onto the ice shelf that they might walk home. Armed men descended toward them from the bridge.

Half a hundred shots rang out from the crowd. Three guns burst, but the captain and his officers died. The engineer died soon, and his staff was forced to obey the orders from the amateur pilot above.

The *Atlantic* weighed eighty-five thousand tons normally. Her mass remained, and she had more than her normal load aboard her now. The channels had been broken by the icebreakers, but it was wider than the actual channel, of course. And the amateur pilot had no faintest conception of the handling of an eighty-five-thousand-ton ship.

Things were not normal then. There was a forty-five-mile wind, and the ship was loaded abnormally; she was top-heavy. And she struck a great rock. Normally she would have come to instant rest, with a small ten-foot hole in her hull. The amateur pilot had the engines at half speed, and, in desperation, he had thrown them to full speed ahead, as he saw the danger, and tried to cut the wheel as though she were a motor boat.

The *Atlantic's* metal, weakened by the strange force, ripped open for two hundred and ninety-four feet. She sank in fourteen and a half seconds, and rolled on her side, off the ledge of rock, and into the deep water the amateur had almost succeeded in reaching.

Perhaps two thousand might have been saved from the part still unsubmerged. Ships were starting out after them. But the hull sloped, and some slid, for under that howling wind, ice froze in seconds. They fought, and a total of one hundred and seventy-four were saved.

And rumor had been right. The *Atlantic* was the last ship to sail from New York, for her wreck blocked the channel, and the wind howled down from the north all that day and all the next so that no well-equipped salvage ship could cut her out of the way, and for that matter it howled all the rest of the days, but that was not important. The ice in the harbor was fourteen feet thick on the morning of the 12th.

London was blocked on the 21st, Baltimore on the 22nd. And the seas of all the world steamed, and the winds, blowing over them, were warmed to some slight extent, so that New York did not have temperatures below −72 until July 3rd, when a northwest gale swept, not from the Atlantic, but all across frozen Canada, and the water in the mains fifty feet below the street froze.

Fire started that day, and ravaged unchecked, till the solid walls of stone and ice it encountered succeeded in damping it, and the wind blew it out again, as it had fanned it before.

Men had learned to be careful by that time, and no one worked even slightly harder than normal. Tens of thousands had died horribly as the automatic muscles of their hearts strained to pump the blood harder—and tore themselves to pieces.

"If," said Tad Albrite desperately, "you don't do something fairly quickly, there won't be any sense in trying. You can't get equipment to do anything in another two weeks."

Ban Torrence looked up bitterly. His eyes were tired and dead. "Will you go away? It's atomic power. I'm after it. If I get it, I can do something, and I won't need so much equipment. If I don't, I won't need any, anyway."

"Atomic power!" gasped Albrite. His voice trailed off as he said it, trailed off into hopelessness. "They've tried for decades."

Torrence motioned toward a massive piece of apparatus on one side of the laboratory. "Almost!" He sighed. "So shut up and let me work."

Albrite rose to look at the thing. Two feet long, a semicylinder. Ruddy copper bars led from it to huge electrolytic condenser banks and a bank of powerful accumulators. And to a further piece of apparatus. Silently he looked at it, then went to the closet, put on his heavy robes, and stepped out into the cold toward the observatory and Jack Ribly.

It was several hours later when he returned. Ban Torrence was fussing with his apparatus again. He looked up at their entrance.

"Hello! I wish you'd look at these blasted circuits again, Ribly, and you, too, Tad. I swear it ought to work. It almost did for a fraction of a second."

"Have you tried it again?" asked Ribly.

"No. 'Fraid it might blow up this time instead of stopping."

"Who cares? Try it," snapped Ribly.

"What ought it to do?" asked Albrite.

"Release atomic energy—not all of it, just smash the atom to parts and collect the energy of the parts. Enough, though, for what we want."

"Try it. We can't lose much," Albrite said. "What are you going to do with the power if it works? How will it help?"

"It will help. I think—I think that Earth and the solar system—just an atom in a greater universe. But they're releasing atomic energy in that greater universe—and we're the atom! If my theory's right, then I can release atomic energy myself and stop their release of *our* energy by just slightly upsetting their field, so that it passes by, harmless. Not a terrific amount of energy needed. The field would spread out from this apparatus here—if it would work—at the speed of light.

"In a second, things would be normal on Earth. In four, the Moon would start coming back. In a few minutes, the Sun's old gravity would be returned, the system balanced. Then the thing would spread till all the universe was reestablished.

"I really slightly invert their energy, so that it destroys itself. It would be a spreading sphere of neutralization, self-propagating, feeding on the thing it destroyed. I would have to add no more energy to clear all the universe we know of that force.

"You know—the force is ages old. To that superuniverse, the whole process we've been undergoing for the last months is perhaps a million billionth of a second. The thing has been going on for ages. That is why we have seen distant nebulæ rush away—to eternal destruction. The evaporation of their atomic fuel as we felt the first fringes of their power. Now we are in the heart of their release. If I can do this, I suppose they will never know what has happened.

"But I tried the thing, and the blasted thing worked for perhaps a hundredth of a second, just long enough to kick my instruments and show it worked, but not long enough to start that field.

"Shall I try again?"

"I say yes," replied Ribly.

Mutely, Tad Albrite nodded.

Ban Torrence walked over to his controls. Slowly, thoughtfully, he set up the switches. For perhaps thirty seconds of silence he waited with the last switch in his hand.

"If this works we shall be most fortunate—"

His voice was drowned by the sudden titanic discharges rushing into the generator. For scarcely a thousandth of a second it continued before the process, restarted, backed up, and stopped the discharge into it. The generator functioned perfectly.

For an infinitesimal fragment of a second, a strange nausea swept them as the wave of the counterfield drove out, swift as light, into all the universe. Ban Torrence riveted his eyes on the wall clock, the clock that had swung its pendulum with a strange lethargy, as though not interested in keeping up with time. It was ticking suddenly, with a regular, swift stroke.

"Thank Heaven—it works!" said Torrence softly. For a moment his eyes looked toward and through the mass of the machine, crouched in hulked, latent power, the massive conductors leading off in gleaming, ruddy columns. "I wonder," he went on very softly, "if, in some vaster world, they even *knew*—as this particular atom of fuel simply refused to disintegrate."

Then abruptly the scientist in him rebelled. "But why in blazes didn't it work before? I didn't change the thing in the slightest. The same fuel—water—the same generator. Just took it apart and put it back together again exactly as before. I can't see *why*."

"Was the water pure?" asked Albrite. "Maybe it wasn't—and when you took it apart the drop which caused the trouble was ejected, the generator cleared, and now it will function for another period, until another drop which can't be disintegrated hits it."

"Maybe so; somehow I doubt it. That particular drop simply wouldn't break down. I can't understand why. Just that the generator must have stopped abruptly and could not be restarted till cleared of the charge contained.

"Anyway, it's working perfectly now."

Torrence looked at it, and though he might have told those scientists of a greater world why their machines failed occasionally, since he knew much that they did not, he did not understand all that went on within an atomic generator.

Only he knew that he had restored Earth; that even now she, and her satellite, must be circling toward each other, and toward the Sun; that he had found the secret of vast power that would warm the frozen peoples and power their industry as Earth thawed out once more.

STOP EVOLUTION IN ITS TRACKS!

John T. Sladek

John T. Sladek began writing in the sf genre at the height of the New Wave. Then resident in England, he published fiction in *New Worlds* and in *Dangerous Visions*, and then several powerful satirical novels, beginning with *The Reproductive System* (1968—later *Mechasm*). He is a serious and innovative writer whose allegiance to genre conventions is nearly nonexistent, but he is a rationalist and moral satirist who despises cant and humbug, often presenting them in a darkly humorous light. *Tik-Tok* (1983), for instance, is a novel about a robot who becomes a murderer after damage to his "Asimov circuits." Sladek's stories are often absurd and surreal, but in spite of their tone, style, and affect, much of his fiction is in dialogue with genre sf, often hard sf. *The Encyclopedia of Science Fiction* characterizes him thus: "the most formally inventive, the funniest, and very nearly the most melancholy of modern U.S. sf writers, JTS has always addressed the heart of the genre, but never spoken from it."

"Stop Evolution in Its Tracks!" implies by antithesis the validity of the hard sf attitude. It is an interesting contrast in technique to James P. Hogan's "Making Light," which approaches everything from the assumed hard sf attitudes (and equates them with moral superiority), without attempting any formal innovation. This energetic and sophisticated piece succeeds by making pseudoscience into surrealism. Sladek's allegiance to reason and science is affirmed by making the opposite madness.

Creationists are seldom colorful, exuberant characters. Their name, which ought to remind us of burgeoning life, somehow calls to mind the dusty relics of another age: celluloid collars, tent meetings, barns bearing giant advertisements for laxative. For the most part, the colorful and the exuberant have deserted this unprofitable philosophy.

One exception is Professor Abner Z. Gurns, founder of the Gurns Institute for Advanced Creationist Studies. Gurns is known for other things besides creationism. There was "prayer-wars," his patented defense system employing, he claims, a crew of the lesser angels to defuse godless Soviet missiles in flight. Before that there was his attempt to translate the Bible into a virus, for innoculation of the whole world . . . And before that, his planned expedition to raise Noah's Ark, which he believed to have sunk "somewhere near the East Pole."

If Professor Gurns has a place in history, however, it will most likely be that of the father of modern creationism. Few have done as much for this controversial field as Gurns; no one has established anything remotely rivaling the Gurns Institute.

I went to interview the professor at the Institute, a cluster of modern buildings on a bluff overlooking the sturdy little town of Stove Bolt, Tennessee. The building containing Gurns's office is a no-nonsense structure of glass and steel, the kind that might pass elsewhere for a school of business administration. The only visible clue to its higher mission is the motto carved above the entrance:

WHEN ADAM DELVED AND EVE SPAN
WHO WAS THEN AN ORANGUTAN?

I waited for the professor in a bland anteroom. The only unusual note was a large framed photo on the wall. It showed ants eating a red rose. The title, I saw, was "Paths Untaken."

While I waited, I glanced through a selection of the Institute tracts ("The Great DNA Fraud"; "Fossils—God's Joke on Darwin?"). Somehow they didn't go with that disturbing photo.

I found myself trying to form a picture of my host. Based on a couple of blurry news photos, I imagined him to be a quaint fellow in a celluloid collar and rimless glasses, sporting a watchchain on his snuff-stained vest. The watch would be set to Central Standard Time.

On the contrary, Professor Abner Gurns turned out to be a boyish thirty-year-old with a crew cut and an athletic handshake. His white lab coat was open to show a sweatshirt with a picture of William Jennings Bryan (in a celluloid collar).

"I was trained as a scientist," he explained. "For years I struggled with the so-called theory of evolution, trying to make sense out of it. Heck, if it was in the textbooks, it just had to be true, right?" His boyish grin appeared.

"Well something happened one day that hit me like a ton of assorted lightning rods. It made me see that Darwin's theory of evolution is nothing but hogwash and hokum! The American public—heck, the world public!—had been deceived for a century. It was time to take off the blinders and do some real science. So I came out here and founded the Institute."

He led me into his office, where a glass wall showed the grassy bluff, and the tiny town of Stove Bolt far below. Why had he picked this place for his Institute?

"Because Stove Bolt is the place where in 1923 they held the famous Snopes Monkey Trial—the first great victory for Creationism in our century."

What was his discovery? Professor Gurns sat on the edge of his desk and explained.

"I was studying fossils night and day, spending my days at the Natural History Museum, my nights hitting the books. Trying and trying to make sense out of evolution. Then one day on my lunch hour I wandered out on the street and got knocked down by a bus. When I got up, everything seemed strange. The people were strange. I saw purple hair. I saw this short blind man wearing a derby. He was leading this tall man who played on the derby with drumsticks. I saw a dog on wheels. Then this Yellow Cab pulled up, and I looked inside—*and the whole back seat was filled with one gigantic cabbage*."

I asked the professor what all this meant to him.

"It means that nothing in the fossil world makes sense. I got more wisdom from one hairline fracture than from years of studying! I learned that we have to take fossils for what they are, and stop trying to piece them together into a story. Evolution is a fake."

He picked up a flat stone from his desk and held it in both hands. I saw that it was an ammonite, a common fossil.

"You know, Darwinists always accuse us of not studying the fossil record. That just ain't so. Speaking as a scientist, I have always been primarily interested in the fossil record—that is, the fossils themselves, and not what a bunch of Darwinists try to tell me about the fossils.

"They claim that fossils show evolution—one animal turning into another. Hogwash! There is not one fossil anywhere that shows one animal turning into another. *Every fossil you can find is perfectly still—not moving or changing at all!*"

He put down the ammonite and picked up what looked like a soup bone. "This here bone comes from one animal and one animal only, am I right? Speaking as a scientist, am I right?"

I had to agree.

"Okay, then. Anybody who tells you this here bone came from two or three animals has to be a darn fool." His eyes narrowed, and he waved the bone like a club. "A fool or an atheistic Darwinizer!"

A bell rang somewhere. He looked at his (ordinary digital wrist-) watch. "I got a lecture right now. Come along and sit in."

I followed him to the Wilberforce Auditorium, where perhaps a hundred students were seated, eager to receive his message. I sat to the side where I could watch them. They seemed a pretty typical bunch of kids, though slightly subdued.

"Speaking as a scientist," he began, "it just beats me how anybody can believe in the evolutionary fairy tale for five minutes!" There was some nervous laughter and applause.

"Evolutionists will tell you how some little old amoeba evolved itself into some bigger bug, and how that evolved itself into a fish, and so on, right up the scale until the ape evolved itself into a man. But there's two things wrong with that cockeyed story.

"In the first place, the amoebas never evolved at all. They're still here! Speaking as a scientist, I can vouch for that! I have looked down a microscope myself and seen then. They look like this."

He showed a slide of biobs. "Still the same little critturs they was when Noah marched them aboard the ark, two by two."

When the murmurs of amazement had died down, he continued: "In the second place, apes could not evolve into humans for a very simple reason: *There are no apes*. The things we call apes in zoos are nothing but men dressed up in hairy suits. I myself have visited a theatrical costume place where they rent such costumes. There they are, hairy suits *with nobody inside*."

He showed several slides: a gorilla suit hanging on a rack, a man getting into the suit, the man wearing the suit minus the head, and a gorilla. The class murmured louder, apparently angry at the duplicity of the Darwinists.

A boy wearing a DON'T BE A MONKEY'S UNCLE sweatshirt put up his hand. "Sir, how can they lie to us like that? Isn't it unconstitutional?"

"Lying breaks an even higher law, Vern," said the professor. "Not that Darwinists care about that. But let's move right along to *survival of the fittest*. Can anyone tell me what that is supposed to mean? Yes, Sue Bob?"

A girl wearing a DON'T GO APE FOR DARWIN sweatshirt stood up. "It's circular reasoning, sir. They claim the ones who survive are the fittest. Then they try to prove this by pointing to the survivors—must be fit, because they survived."

"Exactly, Sue Bob. Can anybody imagine anything more ridiculous than survival of the fittest?"

Loud laughter and some applause.

"All over the country, folks are jogging and riding bikes, going to fitness centers, all to keep fit—but do they survive? Heck no, they all die eventually, same as everyone else. The fit shall perish with the unfit. Why, old Methuselah lived a lot longer than any jogger, and we know for a fact, he never rode a bike in his life."

The professor now seemed to be in training himself. He strode back and forth energetically as he talked, he flailed his arms, pounded the lectern, and spoke at times so rapidly that it was difficult to keep notes. There are, he said, five unanswerable arguments for Creationism:

1. **The universe is one grand design.** Nucular physicists see electrons going around the atoms. (So do nuclear physicists.) Astronomers see planets and stars and stuff going round the sun. Everything goes round and round like the wheels of a watch. (This baffled many students until the professor used a large plastic model to demonstrate that watches once had wheels inside.)

The same careful planning shows up in the animal and vegetable kingdoms. A banana is easy to peel because it was made for peeling. Fish can swim, which is lucky, because they are invariably found in water. Our two ears are located on different sides of our heads to give us stereo hearing.

All of this design implies a designer—not to mention a team of draftsmen and production engineers. Butterflies and flowers come in lots of pretty colors, so a team of interior decorators are probably involved somewhere. Or take birdsong, which requires not only a composer, but an arranger, a producer, and a musician's union.

2. **You can't evolve a sow's ear into a silk purse.** In other words, there is just no way that a simple crittur can make itself complicated. You might as well expect a gas mantle to turn into a chocolate grinder. (The professor explained these items.) Life is just what you make it, not something else.

3. **The great giraffe debate.** Atheistic Darwinizers may try to claim that the giraffe went around stretching its neck up to eat leaves from the trees for a few generations, and this made its neck grow longer.

The real truth is, giraffes didn't need to stretch at all, because their necks were already so long. Besides, what about dolphins? They live in the depths of the oceans where there are no trees at all. (This puzzled me and still does. I tried to ask the professor to elaborate on it, but nearby students told me to hush my mouth.)

4. **Everything invented by the Creator has some use.** Even a duck-billed platypus proves that the Creator had a fine sense of humor. What other use could it possibly have?

5. **All of the atheistic communists in Russia believe in evolution.** Enough said.

Professor Gurns concluded his lecture by offering to thrash anyone in the room who still believed in Darwinism. That brought applause and cheers from the students.

Among the students lingering after class to ask questions was a girl student wearing an EVOLUTION—NON, MERCI sweatshirt.

"Professor, are you absolutely sure ontogeny doesn't recapitulate phylogeny?"

Gurns stood in silence for a moment, holding his large watch model. Then he said, "Darla Jeanette, I wish you would rephrase that question."

"Well they say that during pregnancy, a human fetus looks at different stages like a fish, then a frog, then . . ."

"I don't see any point in dragging in talk like that, pregnancy and fetuses," he replied. "Young girl has no need to know about that stuff, no need at all. You tend to the fossil record, and leave the pregnancies to me."

The professor then conducted me to the Deluge Lab, where a magnificent full-size replica of Noah's Ark had been constructed. After hanging up his watch model in the corner, he explained what was going on here: Creationist graduate students were packing the Ark with pairs of stuffed animals, to prove that all of the species would too fit inside.

But as in all toy arks, the giraffes seemed to be giving trouble. Researchers were climbing ladders to take measurements of two stuffed ones.

"Maybe Noah laid them down," someone suggested. "They'd fit pretty good laid down."

"But their legs spread out a lot," someone else complained.

"Maybe Noah sawed off their legs. Hey, why not? There's nothing in Genesis says they had to have all animals with legs."

"Now, now, boys and girls," said Professor Gurns. "I'm sure you can come up with a better answer than that."

Back to his office, where the professor showed me a model of the Institute, with planned future development.

"We're still *evolving*," he said, with another boyish grin. "But seriously, we need to add a few departments to fill in all the gaps. For instance, we need some professional help in classifying the fossils of sea critturs. You know, fish fossils have been found way up on mountain slopes. The only explanation is, Noah's Flood covered even the highest peaks. We aim to prove that, once we get set up with our own Department of Marine Biology. It'll go right over here. We've already got a genuine marine to run it.

"Over here will be our anatomy department, plenty of work there, too. We need to study how the leopard got his spots, how the camel got his hump, how the whale got his throat, and all like that. Then there's the whole question of Adam and Eve's navels, a subject for some serious contemplation.

"And this area will be the new department of geophysics, to help prove how the earth is flat. For that, we'll need lots of surveying equipment, maps and so on. Probably need to buy some time on a satellite and get some real clear pictures of the earth from way high up. We like to be up-to-date, you know, use the latest technological—"

Footsteps came pelting down the hall. The door banged open and a student barged in, out of breath. "Professor, come quick! The giraffe is on fire!"

As we all hurried back to the lab, the student explained. One researcher, attempting to shrink one of the stuffed giraffes slightly with a heat gun, had set it ablaze.

By the time we arrived, the fire was out, and students were opening skylights to dissipate the smoke. There was little visible damage to the animal itself. However, the great plastic model watch had melted and sagged.

As I left the Institute for Advanced Creationism, I looked out over the bluff, where students were flying kites shaped like glossy French loaves. Down below lay the town of Stove Bolt. I could just make out the little red courthouse where, more than sixty years before, the Snopes Monkey Trial had struck the first blow for Creationism. In that trial, a monkey named Snopes had been successfully prosecuted under Tennessee law for possessing an opposable thumb—a blasphemous imitation of human kind.

The Darwinists had been doing well in the trial until the very end. When the defense lawyer began his closing remarks, the jury was distracted by strange humming noises coming from within the courtroom fireplace. The humming was not like human humming, but the humming of steel rails. Finally the jury gave up all pretense of listening, and indeed the lawyer stopped speaking. All were transfixed, watching the dark hollow of the fireplace, waiting for an express train to come screaming out of the darkness and thundering through the tiny room.

THE HUNGRY GUINEA PIG

Miles J. Breuer, M.D.

The works of Miles J. Breuer, M.D., have passed out of currency, but he was a major figure in the early sf magazines from 1927 to 1942, the date of his last published story. An early collaborator with (and influence on) Jack Williamson, Breuer was noted for his fertile imagination and wide range of ideas. Unfortunately, there has never been a collection of his stories, nor has his novel, "Paradise and Iron" (1930, *Amazing Stories Quarterly*) been reprinted. This story (1930) is one of his more amusing pieces, and is one of the foundations in sf for the story of the giant creature.

Breuer, perhaps under the influence of those old-fashioned postcards of tomatoes the size of boxcars, decided to think big, but in the manner that was becoming characteristic of the emerging genre. A doctor, he introduced the everyday procedures of laboratories and lab animals, and made his humble guinea pig the monster, just by allowing it to be itself and ignoring the square-cube law. This is both amusing and may be rigorous, an effect rediscovered or recreated many times since in a spate of monster films, but also in such stories as Edward Bryant's "giANTS" and Kit Reed's "The Attack of the Giant Baby." Playing with scale is one of the major devices of science fiction. Giantism, though, remains hard sf today—see Blish's "Beanstalk" or Schenck's "Send Me A Kiss by Wire"—only so long as the square-cube law is plausibly not violated (sorry about that giant baby). Otherwise, as in the Reed story, it is satirical sf, far removed in effect from hard sf in general.

Dr. Clarence Hinkle walked reminiscently westward along Harrison Street. Things had changed. The city had grown.

"The spirit of Chicago is *growth*," thought Dr. Hinkle.

Dr. Clarence Hinkle of Dorchester, Nebraska, was a country doctor of the modern, high-caliber type. He was thoroughly scientific in his methods and made use of all the facilities that modern science offers in taking care of his prosperous farmer patients. He kept up with scientific progress by visiting conventions and taking postgraduate courses regularly. But this was the first time since his graduation that he had been back to Chicago and his alma mater. Now, after ten years of successful, satisfactory practice, he was on a pilgrimage back to old Rush. For study, yes; but also for a visit to the old places and to see old friends again.

He was especially anxious to see Parmenter. He and Parmenter had roomed together for four years, two on the South Side at the University of Chicago, and two on the West Side at Rush, in the center of the greatest aggregation of medical colleges and hospitals within the area of a square mile known to the world. Parmenter had been brilliant and eccentric. As a student he had done astonishing things in biochemistry. He had made a wild and brilliant record in the war. Hinkle had kept up a desultory correspondence with him, which had conveyed hints of some research of Parmenter's; something amazing, but without details of information. Parmenter's work had so impressed the University of Chicago that they had built him a laboratory and dispensary to work in.

Dr. Hinkle walked up Harrison Street looking for it. The huge bulk of the Cook County Hospital loomed ahead of him. Thousands of Rush graduates all over America will appreciate how he felt when he saw the old corner at Harrison and Congress Streets, with the venerable and historic building gone, and a trim, business-like new one in its place. It seemed that sacred memories and irreplaceable traditions had been desecrated. But, progress must go on. However, the old "P. & S." was also replaced by a great maze of new buildings. And there ahead was a sign: THE PARMENTER INSTITUTE. So, they had even named the clinic after him! Indeed, he must have done something.

He stopped a moment to look the building over. Two trucks piled high with heads of cabbage drew up before the side entrance. The drivers conversed as they unloaded the cabbage.

"Yesterday," Dr. Hinkle overheard one of them say, "I delivered a load of freshly cut alfalfa here. You'd think they had a lot of big animals. Funny thing for this part of town. And tomorrow we'll be bringing more stuff; wait and see."

They carried basketloads of cabbageheads up the short flight of stairs, and the porter of the building always opened the door and took the baskets from them.

"Listen!" whispered one of the truck drivers to the porter, catching him confidentially by the shoulder, "What's all these loads of green stuff for?"

"For feeding our experimental animals," replied the porter haughtily, as though he knew things they were not competent to understand.

"What sort of animals?" asked the truck driver, looking doubtfully at the building, whose windows were the same as those of the others with their small rooms.

"Guinea pigs," replied the porter.

"Guinea pigs?" The truck drivers looked blankly at each other. "What are guinea pigs?"

"Hm!" snorted the porter contemptuously. "Don't know what guinea pigs are!" He saw them every day. "A guinea pig is an animal like a rabbit; no, smaller—half as big. It looks something like a rabbit and something like a rat."

"Aw!" growled the truck driver. "He's stringin' us."

"No," replied his companion. "That's true. I saw them when I was in the hospital. The doctors use them for speerments."

An inner door opened and a white-clad attendant stood looking out of it into the hall. For a while, as the door stood open, they heard a number of short, low-pitched, whistlelike notes. Then another hand slammed the door shut, and again the hall was dark and silent. To Dr. Hinkle's mind, the sound had no resemblance whatever to the squealing of guinea pigs. The truck drivers continued to carry cabbage and to tarry inquisitively.

Dr. Hinkle walked briskly up the front steps of the Institute, and into the office. He handed his card to the girl at the information desk, stating that he had an appointment with Dr. Parmenter.

"The doctor said you were to come into the office and wait for him," she said, showing him into an adjoining room.

In Parmenter's office, a large desk was piled high with neatly arranged stacks of books and papers. Sections of bookcases filled with books, papers, and chemicals covered almost all the wall space, except where it was occupied by a great steel safe. Since there was also a safe in the business office through which he had passed, Dr. Hinkle concluded that this one held not money, but, rather, records of tremendous importance, or some sort of chemical preparation that might be dangerous in the hands of the wrong people. He sat down and waited, his eyes flitting back and forth among the titles of the medical, chemical, and biological publications.

As he sat in his chair, he could see through the open door down a long hallway. At the end of the hallway was another door; a curious door that seemed to be made of heavy planks placed horizontally, and held together with iron straps. This door was slowly pushed open, an intern emerged into the hallway, and with considerable effort tugged the door shut again and turned a heavy bolt. While it was open, Dr. Hinkle heard several more of those short, reverberating, fluty notes, like the low pipes of an organ. They were accompanied by heavy, dragging sounds, as of something tremendously heavy scraping on the floor with little short scrapes. Another intern came down the hall, and as the two met, the first one said:

"This can't go on much longer. It's got to be stopped."

The second one laughed a harsh, mirthless laugh.

"I guess we'd have stopped it already, if somebody would tell us how."

The two went back through the heavy door. Dr. Hinkle craned his neck to get a glimpse through it. In the vast half-gloom through the door, he caught a fleeting glance of a huge curved back and flanks, covered with long, straight brown hair.

"A cow? Or a bear?" he wondered in astonishment. "It's bigger than a couple of both. What in——"

Dr. Parmenter walked briskly out of a door down the hall, and seeing Hinkle in his room, hastened in. Dr. Parmenter had a worried look about him; a wrinkle in his forehead that he couldn't seem to smooth out, a wrinkle that betrayed some sort of preying anxiety. He looked much older than his country confrère, though the quondam roommates were really almost of an age. They stared wildly at each other, each surprised at the changes in the other. They gripped hands in silence for some minutes.

"Well, so this is what you're up to!" Hinkle exclaimed.

"You look like a million dollars!" Parmenter congratulated.

They sat and chatted small stuff for a while.

"You do look prosperous," Parmenter insisted. "You must be doing well."

"Oh, I've put aside a few thousand. Ten more years like these, and I could retire in modest independence."

Parmenter sighed.

"I can't seem to get ahead much financially." He paused wistfully. "You have a family?"

Hinkle nodded.

"Two boys and a girl."

"Happy dog." Parmenter had a faraway look in his eyes.

Hinkle was also looking a little thoughtful.

"The medical drudge, the traveler over country roads, the custodian of colds and stomach-aches wishes to inquire," he said earnestly, "if there is not happiness in being known all over North America; in having papers published in every scientific journal; in being invited to great conventions as an honored guest; in having a dispensary built for you and called after you—a young fellow like you? You make me feel like a moron."

Parmenter's face warmed up a little with pride.

"And a colonel during the war!" Hinkle continued. "Do you know, I'm famous back home among the common folks just because I can say I used to room with you?"

Parmenter was silent but grateful. Finally he said:

"So you got into the fracas in France, too? How did you go?"

"Oh," replied Hinkle, as though he disliked to admit it, "plodding along in a field-hospital unit. But you—" his voice rose in surprise again—"a medical man! How did you happen to go as an artillery officer? I'd think you'd want to give your country the benefit of your scientific training."

Parmenter sat straight up in his chair. His face livened up with interest.

"Scientific training!" he exclaimed. "Maybe you think you don't need scientific training in the artillery. I dare say I made better use of what scientific ability I may have in the artillery than I ever could have done as a mere medical officer. Wasn't it so in this war, that only one medical officer out of a thousand had any opportunity to do scientific work? The scientific training I got in the artillery corps has helped me to accomplish what I've done since the war."

Hinkle stared incredulously.

"If you don't think it takes *science*," Parmenter said, "to yank a four-ton gun into place in the middle of a field, and put a shell on a spot the size of a door ten miles away at the third shot—you've got another guess coming. That takes real figuring, and real accuracy in working. To come up into position one night, and by the next night to have the country for twenty miles ahead plotted into numbered squares, into any one of which you can drop a shell instantly, within ten seconds of a signal from an airplane observer—the whole medical department didn't use as much science as did our little battery of heavy field artillery. That was a glorious kickup—"

He stopped and turned his head, as several fluty whistles came faintly from within the building.

"But this is just as exciting," he continued when the eerie sound had ceased. He smiled at Hinkle's look of amazed inquiry.

"I guess I'd better show you around," he said. "I've got something here that hasn't been published yet."

"I got a peek at some ungodly thing a while ago," Hinkle remarked; "What is it—a buffalo? No; it's three times as big. A dinosaur? I never heard of any animal that would fit what I saw. Is that what makes the tooting?"

Parmenter stood enjoying his friend's amazement.

"Perhaps I'd better prepare you for the sight first. I can explain briefly in a few moments. A few years ago I got interested in ductless glands and internal secretions, and my interest eventually narrowed down to two of them about which the least is definitely known—the pituitary and the pineal bodies. I've done a lot of work on these two little brain glands and written a lot about them. Both of them are intimately concerned in body growth. You will recollect that in the pathological condition known as acromegaly, in which there is an excess of pituitary secretion supplied to the body, the limbs grow long, and tall giants are produced; and you know how stunted the individual remains in cases where the pituitary body fails to secrete adequately. Perhaps you have also followed McCord's experiments: he fed chicks with pineal glands from cattle, and they grew to three or four times the size of normal birds. Then, a couple of workers in California separated from the pituitary body a substance which they called tethelin, and which, when injected into mice, doubled their growth.

"I repeated and confirmed their work, and made large quantities of tethelin. The fact impressed me that neither the pineal experiments alone nor the pituitary experiments alone produced a well-balanced increase in the size of the experimental animals. I obtained the active principle of the pineal body, which I took the liberty of naming physein; I got it by four-day extraction with ether in the Soxhlet apparatus and recrystallization from acetone. Man, you should have seen the baskets and baskets of pituitaries and pineals from the stockyards, and all the ether and acetone we splashed. But, after all the dirty work, the half dozen bottles of gray powder that we got gave us a lot of satisfaction.

"Of course, we injected the stuff into guinea pigs. The guinea pig is always the victim. At first we used six; and six controls which received none of the tethelin-physein solution. But we soon discarded the controls, for the injected animals grew like the rising of the mercury in a thermometer. They grew so fast that we had to kill five of them when they were as big as dogs, for fear that we could not feed them. This one we kept in order to ascertain the limit of size to which it would grow. Now we have had it six months, and it is as big as—well, you'll see. It is becoming difficult to feed, and it's a rough, clumsy beast. I'd get rid of it, if I knew how——"

He was interrupted by a terrific hubbub from within the building. The whole structure shook, and there was a vast ripping and tearing. Crash after crash rent the air, followed by hollow rumbles and reverberations.

Dr. Parmenter dashed to the door and looked down the hallway. There were great cracks in the plaster, and chunks of the ceiling were raining down to the floor. The door at the end of the hall hung loose, revealing beyond it not the semigloom of a big room, but the bright daylight of outdoors; just as though a piece of the building had been torn off. A huge rattling, banging din was going on, with clouds of dust filling the air.

He started down the hall, but a shower of bricks and plaster through the wrecked doorway deterred him. Seizing Dr. Hinkle's arm, he dashed out to the street, dragging the latter with him. Hinkle was puzzled; Parmenter was pale and looked scared, but seemed to know what was going on.

Out in the street, people stood, struck motionless in the midst of their busy traffic. Fascinated, like a bird watching a serpent, they stood glued to the ground, their eyes turned toward the Institute. A moment ago the business of Harrison Street had been going monotonously along, just as it had gone for a couple of score of years. Suddenly two or three people had stopped. Some sort of queer things had appeared in a window of the Institute, horrible-looking objects, as though a monkey had jumped up on the sill. But no, the pink things were not arms and legs; each had a single huge claw at the end of it. The whole thing looked like an enormous rat's paw. The group of astonished people standing and staring at it increased momentarily.

Then the brick wall bulged outward, and a section of it as big as a room fell out on the ground in a mass of debris. A vast brown back appeared in the opening, and the thing's clumsy scratching threw layers of brick wall across the street. The enormous animal rolled out and disappeared behind the three-story signboards in the adjoining empty lot.

Dr. Hinkle and Dr. Parmenter ran across the street to watch. There was a huge commotion behind the signboards; then, with a crashing of breaking wood the whole structure of signboards went over. There were screams of people on the sidewalk who were caught beneath the falling mass, and the tinkle of glass from smashed automobile windshields. From over the flattened wreckage there gazed out at the rapidly growing crowd across the street a pair of immense, pinkish-brown eyes. They were set in a head that looked somewhat like that of an enormously magnified rabbit, though it was held down close to the ground. Behind it arched a great brown back, higher than the second-story windows, covered with long, straight brown hair, with black and white stripes and spots.

The creature looked around, jerking its head first one way and then another, apparently very much frightened. Then it moved forward a step to the accompaniment of crackling timber. The crowd surged away and disappeared frantically into buildings and around blocks, as the animal slowly started toward it. Dr. Hinkle felt a sinking sensation within him as he realized that there were injured people on the sidewalk under that mass of wreckage that crunched and crumpled under the animal's huge weight. Everywhere windows were filled with heads. In the Institute, the undamaged windows contained white-clad doctors and nurses. In the next block, an elevated train passed with a hollow, rumbling roar, and the giant guinea pig crouched down and trembled in fear.

Then it ran out into the street with short, quick steps. One could get some idea of its size from the reports of the spectators, who stated that there was barely room in the street for it to turn around in. It had started across the street, and in its efforts to get loose it caught the odor of some scraps left behind at the unloading of the cabbage trucks, for it suddenly began to turn around. Its paw caught in the window of a flat across the street, and in its efforts to get loose it wrecked a side of the building. Beds, refrigerators, and gas stoves hung out in the open air. The animal seemed very much frightened.

Dr. Hinkle and Dr. Parmenter had been carried by the crowd to the solid shelter of the Cook County receiving ward. People began to sense that the thing was dangerous, and scattered precipitately away from the scene of excitement. An Italian fruit vendor was pushing his cart westward along Harrison Street. The animal smelled the fruit and immediately became very much excited. It turned this way and that, but always there were buildings in its way. Finally it stepped up on the roof of a two-story flat on the corner. The roof caved in, and the screams of women were heard from within. In its effort to extricate itself, it made a wreck of the building. Then it hastened down a cross street in pursuit of the fruit cart.

The Italian heard its approach and stopped; he stood paralyzed by fear. The guinea pig never saw him at all; it leaped for the fruit and one accidental blow of its paw knocked him over and crushed him flat. Only a bloody, smeary, shapeless mass on the street remained to tell the tale. Parmenter, already pale and trembling, shrank back as the Italian screamed and raised his hands above his head, carried down by the giant paw. Parmenter's eyes had a cowed, beaten look in them.

The fruit on the cart made a scant mouthful for the guinea pig. It chewed very rapidly, with a side-to-side movement of its jaw. When it raised its head, its bare lower lip was visible, pale pink, and below it a group of short, white whiskers. The grinding of its teeth was audible for a block. Another train thundered along on the elevated railway, its windows crowded with curious heads. The guinea pig became frightened again, and ran swiftly westward along Harrison Street. As it ran, its feet moved beneath it, while its body was carried along smoothly rocking, as though it were on wheels. It ran very swiftly, more swiftly than the automobiles that tried to get away from it; and the people along the street had no time to get out of the way. First a child on a tricycle was swept away, and then two high-school girls disappeared under it; and when it had passed, it left behind dark smudges, as when an automobile runs over a bird. It ran three blocks west, eating up all the potatoes and vegetables, baskets and all, in front of a grocery store, and then turned north. Hinkle and Parmenter lost sight of it, noting a car filled with armed policemen in pursuit of it.

Parmenter's nerves were indeed shaken. He stared straight ahead of him and walked along like a blind man. Hinkle had to guide him and take care of him as though he were an invalid. Parmenter felt himself a murderer. All of these deaths were his fault, due directly to his efforts. Despite the fact that he was half paralyzed by remorse, he persisted in trying to follow the animal with a desperate anxiety, as though in hopes that he could yet do something to right the wrong. For a while he led Hinkle around aimlessly.

Then they heard the sound of the firing of guns, and breaking into a run, came around the block into Jefferson Square, a small, green park a couple of blocks in area. There the guinea pig was eating the shrubbery, tearing up great bundles of it with its sharp teeth. It smelled hungrily of the green grass, but was unable to get hold of the short growth with its large teeth. The bandstand and the bridge across the pond were wrecked to fragments. The police were shooting at the animal till it sounded like a battle, but it was without effect. Either its hide was so thick that the bullets did not penetrate, or else the mass of the bullets was so small that they sank into its tissues to no purpose. Once they must have struck it in a sensitive spot, for it suddenly scratched itself with a hind leg, and then went on chewing shrubbery. The police crept up closer and kept on firing; then all of a sudden the guinea pig turned around and sped up the street like lightning. Before the police re-collected themselves, it was out of sight, and the street presented a vista of overturned Fords, smashed trucks, a streetcar off the rails and crowded against a building, and tangled masses of bloody clothes. A trolley wire was emitting a string of sparks as it hung broken on the ground, and a fountain of water was hurtling out of a broken fireplug. The animal disappeared to the north; the two medical men sought it for a while and finally gave it up.

Dr. Hinkle decided that he must get his friend somewhere indoors. They succeeded in finding a taxi in the panic, and drove to Parmenter's apartment. Hinkle had to support Parmenter and put him to bed. Parmenter would not eat. He continued to groan in incoherent misery. Hinkle went out and got some evening papers.

The headlines shrieked:

MONSTER DEVASTATES WEST SIDE!
MYSTERIOUS ANIMAL SPREADS TERROR!

and so forth in their inimitable style. The reports said it was a fearful bear, bigger than an elephant or a freight engine, or that it was a prehistoric saurian miraculously come to life. They stated that it hunted people as a cat hunts mice, and that it had eaten great numbers of them, and in its savage rage had smashed buildings and vehicles. Gunfire had no effect on it, and it had in fact devoured a squad of policemen who had been sent out to kill it.

Parmenter sat up when Hinkle read some of these reports.

"The poor idiots!" he exclaimed in sudden and composed wrath. The grossly exaggerated reports seemed to have the effect of pulling him together.

"Newspapers act like a bunch of scared hens," he said contemptuously. "They're starting a real, insane panic, that's all. What do you think, Hinkle; is that guinea pig going about deliberately killing people? Is it wrecking the town out of pure spite?"

"It is quite evident," Hinkle said, "that the guinea pig is far more frightened than the people are. The deaths are mere accidents due to its clumsiness——"

"Yes," reflected Parmenter sadly. "A guinea pig has about as little brains as any animal I could have picked out. If it had been a dog, it could be careful."

"And the thing seems to be hungry," Hinkle continued. "Hunger seems to be the main cause of its destructive proclivities. It is hungry and is hunting around for food. And food is hard to find in this little ant heap."

Hinkle was correct. The whole subsequent history of the huge animal's wanderings about the city represented merely a hunt for food, and possibly a place to hide. It is doubtful if its hunger was ever satisfied, despite the vast amount of foodstuffs that it found and consumed. Certainly it paid no attention to people. The wrecking of the Lake Street Elevated Station was probably due to its efforts to find shelter. In the evening the guinea pig tried to burrow under the station and hide. The space underneath the station was too small and the steel beams too strong; and it gave up and turned away, but not until it had so bent and dislocated the steel structure that the station was a wreck and train service was interrupted. The last report of the night located it on West Washington Street. People were afraid to go to bed.

In the morning Hinkle dashed out after newspapers. The editorials corrected some of the previous day's errors about the ferocity of the giant guinea pig and called attention to the fact that it had definitely increased in size during its sixteen hours of liberty.

"If it keeps on growing bigger——?" the editor suggested, and left it as a rhetorical question.

The news items stated that during the night the guinea pig had located the vegetable market on Randolph Street, for many buildings were wrecked and their contents had vanished. The Rush Street bridge was smashed, as were the buildings at the edge of the water. And the city was beginning to go into a panic; for no efforts to stop the animal had as yet been of any avail.

The evening papers of the second day brought a new shock. Hinkle had spent the day following Parmenter about. The latter dashed this way and that, in taxicabs, surface cars, buses, and elevated trains, in frantic efforts to catch up with the animal. They did not catch sight of it all day. They arrived in Parmenter's apartment in the evening, dead tired. Parmenter was in the depths of depression. Hinkle opened a bundle of newspapers they had not had time to read.

"LAWYER'S WIDOW SUES SCIENTIST!" announced the headlines; "Mrs. Morris Koren Files Claim for Damages Against Professor Parmenter for Husband's Death. One hundred thousand dollars is demanded by the widow of the prominent attorney who was crushed in his automobile by the huge guinea pig yesterday. The plaintiff is in possession of a clear and complete chain of proofs to establish her claim——"

Parmenter sat silent and wild-eyed. Hinkle clenched his fists and swore. He thought Parmenter was suffering enough with all these deaths on his conscience. Now, to have added to it a lawsuit with its publicity, and the almost certain loss of the property he had accumulated, and the complete wrecking of his career! Parmenter gazed now this way, now that, and sat for a while with bowed head. He rose and walked back and forth. He sat down again. He said not a word. Hinkle sat and watched his friend's sufferings with a sympathy that was none the less genuine for being speechless. Before him was a broken man, in the depths of disappointment and despair. All his life Parmenter had been working, not for his own interests, but for the good of mankind. To have the people to whom he had freely given of his life and work turn against him in this unkind way was something he could neither grasp nor endure. Hinkle never saw a man change so completely in twenty-four hours.

A later edition carried the announcement of another lawsuit against Parmenter. The Chicago Wholesale Market claimed $100,000 damages for the destruction of their buildings and merchandise stock. Their evidence was also complete and flawless.

By morning, Parmenter's depression was gone. He was pale, but calm and deliberate. His lips were set in a thin line, and the angles of his jaws stood out with set muscles. He had shaken off his nervousness and a steady light shone in his eyes. His keen brain was at work as of old. Hinkle understood; no words were needed. They had been roommates for four years and knew each other's moods. Hinkle gripped his friend's hand. As eloquently as though he had said it in words, he was expressing his sympathy and joy because his friend had found his strength again despite his troubles. Troubles indeed, for the loss of life was already beyond estimate; and complete ruin for Parmenter was a certainty.

"Got to find some way of stopping the beast," Parmenter said succinctly.

"If it can be done, I know you'll do it," Hinkle replied. "Only tell me what I can do to help you."

"Stick around," said Parmenter. "That'll help." They understood each other.

Hinkle could not help admiring the sheer will power of the man. Newsboys went bawling by the window. The morning papers announced a fresh string of lawsuits, claiming a total of damages of nearly a million dollars. Parmenter paid no attention. He nodded his head and went on making notes with his pencil on the back of an envelope. He had made up his mind, and news had no further effect on him. Only once he took Hinkle's breath away with a dispassionate, impersonal reflection:

"The civil damage suits will break down of their own weight. The matter has already gone so far that it is ridiculous. It won't pay any of them to spend any money bringing it into court. But, suppose it develops into criminal proceedings?

"Well, that's all I have to expect. Science does a lot of good. But sometimes it miscalculates and does harm. Under the laws of nature, miscalculators pay the penalty of elimination."

Parmenter sat motionless most of the day. He moved once to eat mechanically, and once to receive reports by telephone from the Institute. His mind was busy, as usual.

The evening papers brought reports that the guinea pig had gotten tangled up in a trolley wire and received an electric shock which had sent it scuttling to the Lake. The wire dropped to the ground, interrupting the streetcar service of that part of the city. The guinea pig ran straight to the water. There it again smelled green forage and ran northward along Lake Shore Drive. In an hour it had devastated all the trees and shrubbery, and eaten up everything green in sight. Because it spent more time at this place, the police detachments caught up with it, and were again vainly pouring bullets at it. Again something startled it, and it ran off westward. It ran so swiftly that it was out of their sight in a few moments. For the greater part of two days they pursued it about the city in this manner, and the tale thereof is largely a repetition of what has already been said.

Parmenter hit his knee with his fist.

"We've got to stop the brute somehow, or there won't be any Chicago left. Who would have thought that a brainless, clumsy, stupid thing would have the whole city at its mercy?"

Hinkle was turning over the pages of the newspaper, scanning the editorials that were already predicting what Parmenter had foreseen, the breakdown of the damage suits. The editor stated confidently that they would never get into court.

"Better get a lawyer anyway," Hinkle suggested.

"I won't need one." Parmenter's face brightened. Did he have an idea?

There was no time to ask. A strange murmur had arisen outdoors. A rushing, rustling hum, like that of a flowing river, came from the distance. Now and then shouts rose out of the confusion. Hinkle went to the window, full of curiosity at the city's manifold noises.

He stopped for a moment. He also had a quick brain, and in an instant the meaning of the din flashed through his mind. He dashed back and caught Parmenter by the arm. With hats and coats in the other hand, he dragged Parmenter toward the back of the house.

"What's up now?" Parmenter demanded out of the depths of his preoccupation.

"A wild, raging mob!" Hinkle shouted. "The people are dancing with ferocity like a bunch of savages on the warpath. I saw clubs and guns. They probably found that there was no redress in lawsuits, and are coming after you to settle it themselves."

Parmenter still dragged back, reluctant to follow Hinkle.

"I don't care to escape," he protested. "What is the use of life in a world where there are people like that?"

Hinkle stopped a moment.

"You seem to have struck some idea for helping this city," he said sternly. "Do you want them to lay you out before you can rectify this blunder of yours?"

They were blunt, cruel words, but they worked. Parmenter straightened up.

"You're right. I've got a scheme that will work. Come on!"

They hurried through the house toward the rear door. There they stopped. There was a mob in the alley; its fierce yells greeted them as they opened the door. They shut it again and went back in.

"Now what?" asked Hinkle. It looked hopeless. The mob was closing in on all sides of the house. Parmenter stood for a moment. There was a pounding on the front stairs of numberless feet. He hurried to the front door, pulling Hinkle with him; and the two stood so that they would be behind it as it opened. The mob raged and yelled outside and blows thundered on the door.

"They don't know us from John Smith," Parmenter whispered. "Put on your hat and coat."

His plan worked perfectly. The door burst in; its fragments swung on the hinges and splinters fell over the carpet and were trampled by a dozen yelling men, who plunged violently halfway down the hall at one jump. In a moment the place was crowded. Parmenter and Hinkle waved their arms and yelled and mixed with them. No one in the mob knew what was going on anywhere except immediately about him.

They were carried on into the rooms by pressure from behind; the surge of them met the mob coming from the rear door. In a few minutes the fugitives had crowded their way out of the door and into the street. For a few moments and from a safe distance they watched the flames and the firemen. There must have been deaths in that mad stampede. Then they crept off to a downtown hotel and registered under assumed names.

Parmenter sat on the bed.

"You'd like to hear my idea?" he suggested, as though nothing had happened. Hinkle nodded his head because he was too much out of breath to speak.

"Simple," Parmenter said ironically. "The human mind is a rudimentary mechanism. To think that it took me—*me*—three days to think of it. It is so simple that I'm almost afraid to spring it at once for fear there is some flaw in it. Let me take you through the line of reasoning by which I arrived at it, clumsily, blunderingly, whereas it ought to have been a brilliant flash through mine or somebody else's brain."

He lay back relaxed on the bed, his hand over his eyes, and talked.

"I wish to analyze the situation thoroughly—on the one hand, to make sure that I am correct; on the other, to make sure that we are not passing up some good method just because nobody has thought of it.

"To stop this destruction of life and property, we've either got to *catch* the animal or *kill* it. There is no alternative, no third possibility. Is there?"

"No. Plain enough."

"They've tried to catch it. It went through the elephant chains of their trap in Lincoln Park, hardly noticing there was a trap there. Steel columns of the Elevated bend and snap under its weight. It would require weeks of special work to put together something that would really hold it. Our best bet is to kill it. Is that correct so far?"

"O.K."

"Now, what are the possible methods of killing?" He held up an envelope on which he had arranged in a column:

Poison
Disease (infection)
Starvation
Trauma (violence)

"Is there anything else?" he asked.

Hinkle thought a while and shook his head.

"These are the only known causes of death, except old age. Now, some we recognize promptly as obviously out of the question—for instance, starvation. If we wait for that, we'll starve first. Consider disease. The only available method of producing a lethal disease is by inoculating with some infection which works swiftly. But if we do that we are running the risk of its spreading its infection to the people of the city; the spread of infection might do more harm than the guinea pig is doing. Perhaps that might be considered as a hope if there wasn't something better. Now, poison——"

"It looks as though poison were your real hope," Hinkle agreed.

"Yes. *Looks* like it. The police thought so, too. They've tried poison-coated bullets, and the pig is still here. They've laid poison for it——"

"Do you think that the guinea pig has developed some sort of an immunity against poison?" Hinkle was genuinely puzzled.

"Simpler than that. There is a quantitative relationship. It takes a definite amount of poison to be fatal. Consider strychnine, for example. If you remember, it takes one one-thousandth of a grain of strychnine per pound of body weight to kill; supposing the beast only weighed a ton or two, you'd have to have a pound of strychnine. It probably weighs twenty or more tons. Where are you going to get ten or more pounds of strychnine, and how are you going to administer it?"

Hinkle sat and looked blank.

"Never thought of that," was his comment.

"Violence. Trauma. That's all that's left to us," Parmenter concluded.

"And that's out of the question," Hinkle said hopelessly. "How are you going to injure that thing?"

"To think that it's taken me three days to get the idea!" snorted Parmenter contemptuously. "If someone tried to sell you a machine as inefficient as the human brain, you'd throw it back at him. . . . Trauma! Didn't I spend two years doing exactly that in France?"

Hinkle leaped to his feet.

"Artillery!" he gasped.

Parmenter nodded.

Hinkle sat down again, the hopeful look gone out of his face.

"No use," he said. "You'll do more harm to the city with the shells than to the guinea pig."

"Say!" There was a sarcastic note in Parmenter's voice. "Do I have to tell you again that ballistics is a science? But, enough now. We'll get to work and do the arguing later."

Parmenter became a thing of intense activity. He sat at the telephone, called numbers, asked questions, gave orders with the rapidity of a machine gun. He seemed perfectly at home in it; obviously he had done it before. From the obscure hotel room he directed a miniature war. Here is some of the one-sided conversation that Hinkle heard:

"Alderman Murtha? This is Parmenter. I've worked out a plan to kill it. Authority to go ahead. Want me to explain it? All right, thanks for your confidence. We'll have it as soon as there is daylight enough to see by."

Another number:

"City engineer's office? Calling by authority of the police department. We want scale landscape maps of all the parks and plat maps of all the country from here to Clark Junction. Deliver them at once to the Fort Dearborn Hotel."

"Is this the Chief of Police? Has Alderman Murtha called you about giving me authority——? All right, thanks. Where is the animal now? South Side? Listen. Order a dozen truckloads of green stuff, cabbage, alfalfa, anything, dumped in the empty space in Jackson Park where the baseball diamonds are. Have it arrive there shortly before dawn, all piled on one big heap. Then lay a trail of the green stuff on in the direction in which the guinea pig is at the time.

"And don't forget to keep your men away from that pile of greens!"

He barked the last words out viciously. Then he called long distance. He placed several calls, asking for Colonel Hahn. Finally the Colonel answered. Parmenter talked:

"You know of our misfortune here in Chicago—that's true, but we have just now thought of it. What's the biggest field gun you can rush over here? Right now, this minute. Yes, 150's will do the business. Two batteries. At Clark Junction. A few shells nothing! We want a five-minute barrage to cover an acre! Somewhere around dawn. You're a gentleman and a soldier. A credit to the service, sir!

"Major Johnson has telegraphed to the Secretary of War and the authority will come through promptly. I have maps ready for you; send a plane to the Cicero landing field, and I'll meet it there. And two airplane observers."

He turned to Hinkle.

"Now do you get the idea?"

Hinkle slapped him on the back.

"A 150-millimeter barrage on the brute! That ought to fix him."

"Grind him up to Hamburger steak," Parmenter said grimly.

"But how will you keep from wrecking the town?"

Parmenter made a gesture of impatience.

"Not a building will be injured. The pig will be decoyed to a clear space in the park——"

"Yes, I got that idea."

"The area of dispersion for a 150-millimeter gun is about a hundred yards. That means the first shot will hit within a hundred yards of the target. They will first send over a few dummy shells, and the hits will be reported by airplane observers so that they can correct their range and angle."

"Looks dangerous anyway," Hinkle said thoughtfully. "I'm going to Milwaukee till it's over."

Of course he was not afraid. He was merely trying to carry off the situation lightly in order to encourage Parmenter. He followed Parmenter anxiously. There was little conversation during the two-hour ride to the landing field. Three military planes were already waiting there. There was a swift conference over open maps and a few minutes' drill on signals, whereupon one plane rose and sailed away into the night, bearing the maps with it to the position of the gunners. Parmenter looked after them longingly.

"It gets into your bones," he observed. "I could hardly keep myself from climbing in with him. Just think! Four miles away the huge field guns are clanking into position; motors are roaring and the line is swinging round; men are toiling in the dark. By morning there will be a semicircle of Uncle Sam's prettiest rifles pointed this way. But, we'll forget it and hunt for a telephone."

A telephone was not easy to find in Cicero at one o'clock in the morning. They finally located one in the "L" station. Parmenter called the Chief of Police.

"Where's the thing now?" he asked. "Fine. All arrangements made? Coming."

Parmenter's eyes blazed. Again he was an artillery officer.

"Jackson Park," he said to Hinkle.

There were long waits for cars at night; a change from the elevated to the surface cars; a piece in a taxi, and the elevated again. Dawn was breaking gray over the lagoon when they arrived at Jackson Park. Parmenter raced with feverish haste to the flat, empty space where a score of baseball diamonds had been laid out for the use of the public. A string of half a dozen huge trucks was thundering away from the spot. Two loaded ones were proceeding slowly; men were throwing out a trail of cabbage and alfalfa bales behind them. In the middle of the open space was a heap of green stuff, big as a huge strawstack.

Daylight was breaking rapidly. A bright orange blotch appeared out in the Lake; glorious streaks of crimson shot through the blues and grays of the water and sky; soon a glowing ball hung in a purple setting. For an instant the two medical men irresistibly admired the splendid spectacle of the sunrise. But in a moment they were interrupted by the noise of a couple of airplanes coming down in the open field. The pilots stepped out, pushing their goggles up over their helmets. Two motorcycle police came down the driveway.

The two aviators unconsciously saluted Parmenter and then grinned sheepishly, because he was not in uniform. He looked so much a soldier that their action had been a natural one.

Parmenter gave orders for one plane to taxi across the field out of the way and remain on the ground in reserve, while the other was to rise and remain in the air to direct the fire. The two motorcycle men were to locate the guinea pig and guide the bait truck toward it; and as soon as it had picked up the trail, to hurry back and notify him here at the park.

When the two motorcycles disappeared, Parmenter and Hinkle waited in nervous impatience. They walked much and talked little. The yellow of the sunbeams grew brighter, and it seemed an age before a motorcycle finally sputtered up to them.

"The pig is coming!" shouted the driver from a distance.

Parmenter threw a smoke bomb; the puff of yellow smoke was a signal to the airplane observer who, by means of his radio, notified the gunners to get ready.

"Poor pig!" thought Hinkle to himself. "The city and its police, the United States Army, motorcycles, trucks, airplanes, 150-millimeter guns, all mobilized against a poor, lost, hungry guinea pig!"

The motorcycle men stepped out long enough to tell them that the guinea pig was near Washington Park; it had sniffed a truckful of fresh alfalfa and had whirled around to seize it. The truck was demolished and the driver had not yet been recovered from the debris. Parmenter turned a shade paler and set his teeth more firmly. The guinea pig was now following along the train of alfalfa and cabbage that led directly to our heap in the park. Parmenter was silent as the motorcycle whirled around and dashed up the road.

A whining scream came from high in the air; there was a great splash on the beach which threw up sand and water and left a puff of smoke behind it. The airplane was circling around in a figure 8 between the Lake and the pile of greens. Another scream and a crash in the shrubbery, not twenty yards from the pile of greens. A third heavy thud scattered the edge of the pile of green stuff.

"Good boys!" Parmenter breathed proudly. "They can still shoot."

Hinkle admitted that it was wonderful: the guns at Clark Junction four miles away, the airplane doing figure 8's, and a shot right at the edge of the pile. A fourth shot came over and scattered the nice heap of greens all over, spreading it flat on the ground. Although the shell had been a dummy and had not exploded, nevertheless the impact of it, squarely in the middle, had scattered the cabbage and alfalfa far and wide.

"Damn!" Parmenter was annoyed. No wonder. With the greens spread over an acre, how could the guinea pig be located accurately enough to concentrate the fire properly? Someone had missed that point in the plans. They ought to have omitted that last shot.

Parmenter was swearing and shaking his fists. He started toward the scattered pile of greens on a run. Hinkle gazed dumfounded, as he began with demoniac strength to toss bales of alfalfa and heaps of cabbage back on the stack. He started over to help.

Suddenly, when Hinkle got near enough to be within earshot Parmenter whirled around, with a terrible, savage expression on his face.

"Back! Go back!" he roared.

The fierceness in his tone stopped Hinkle. He stood and stared.

"Go!" shouted Parmenter in an agonized snarl. "Go, damn you! Quick!"

Hinkle was too amazed to move.

"I wanted to help you pile it up—" he faltered.

Parmenter drew a pistol from his pocket, a hugh forty-five-caliber Army automatic, and pointed it at Hinkle.

"Now go!" he shrieked in a shrill voice. "Right now. And run! RUN!"

The command in his voice awed Hinkle. Despite the surging of a turmoil of conflicting emotions within him, he turned and ran.

"Don't stop till you reach the lagoon!" Parmenter ordered after him.

"Damn them and their mobs and lawsuits!" was the last thing Hinkle heard him growl.

He reached the lagoon and looked around. Parmenter was working feverishly, tossing greens on the rapidly growing stack.

Now there came a hubbub from the direction of the Sixty-third Street entrance, the rattle of motorcycles, shouts, the crashing of brush-wood, and an oppressive, heavy thudding. In a moment, half a dozen motorcycles drew up beside Dr. Hinkle. A hundred yards away, a huge, towering bulk loomed past. The great guinea pig thundered by, its arched brown-and-white back as high as an apartment house, crashing through shrubbery, flattening out trees, sweeping aside fences and bridges as though they had been spider webs. It skimmed along, eagerly nosing at the ground, following the trail of vegetables, piping its impatient huge, fluty whistles, ripping up lawns and driveways in frantic attempts to pick up the tiny fragments of food.

Suddenly it sighted the heap of food. It gave a gigantic leap in that direction, and ran.

"Parmenter!" shrieked Hinkle, and started out toward the busy figure of the scientist. A dozen hands seized him and jerked him back.

"Parmenter!" he moaned again, impotently.

Parmenter looked up at the yells of the motorcycle police. They were making Hinkle's ears ring with their shouts.

"Look out!"

"Come here!"

"What's the matter with you?"

Parmenter waved a light gesture to them, and calmly stepped out of the way of the gigantic rodent. The pig hungrily plunged its snout into the heap of succulent food he had prepared for it. Hinkle covered his face with his hands. The last thing he saw was Parmenter reaching out his hand to stroke the towering side of the busily feeding guinea pig.

He also recollects momentarily hearing the roar of the airplane describing figure 8's high in the air over the baseball park. Suddenly there was a long, wailing screech in the air, and a terrific roar. A volcano suddenly seemed to burst where the guinea pig had been munching. Vegetables, guinea pig, Parmenter, all disappeared in a flash. In their place was a wall of smoke, rising swiftly upward, with black fragments whirling and shooting in all directions out of it.

For five minutes, hell roared and churned and blazed out there. The din was deafening, crushing. Showers of dirt and spatters of blood reached Hinkle and the motorcycle men. Then it stopped suddenly short, leaving a strange, painful stillness, punctuated by the feeble rattle of the airplane.

Out where the baseball field had been, a hugh crater yawned. When the smoke eventually cleared out of it, there was no guinea pig. Here and there were bloody masses of something lying about the acrid, smoking earth.

For many minutes, Dr. Hinkle stood on the brink of the reeking chasm, his hat in his hand, his head bowed.

THE VERY SLOW TIME MACHINE

Ian Watson

Ian Watson is the finest young hard-science-fiction writer and one of the most acute and perceptive sf critics to emerge in England during the last two decades. His first novel, *The Embedding* (1973), was a rigorous hard sf novel about linguistics. It was followed rapidly by a string of novels and stories that were often more notable for their literary effects, political commitment, and wild imagination than for serious scientific extrapolation. They were characteristically metaphysical in their speculation. Watson was and remains a maverick outsider playing with genre conventions in science fiction, fantasy, and horror, interested in all the sciences and indeed all knowledge—and occasionally turning his attention to hard science fiction. He is a generational contemporary of Gregory Benford and holds a similar position in the U.K. to Benford's in the American field; he is a writer who brought new levels of literary technique and characterization to hard sf. But Watson has never committed himself as exclusively to hard sf as has Benford.

"The Very Slow Time Machine" (1978) is a remarkable combination of hard science ideas presented in an almost Besterian rapid-fire delivery, and an ironic examination of religious fervor and messianic metaphysics. Time-travel fiction, a standard of science fiction since H. G. Wells's famous novella in 1895, invites us to consider logical paradoxes; it is often related to mathematical sf in the kind of intellectual play offered. This is another scientific report format story, like Le Guin's "The Author of the Acacia Seeds," told from the point of view of a researcher in the world of the story, which lends verisimilitude and additional realism to this quite outrageous speculation. "The Very Slow Time Machine" is one of Watson's best pieces, and shows his command of the traditions and tropes of hard sf, but with a bad attitude. The fusion of Besterian (and Ballardian—the division into dated sections would have been read as "New Wave" in the seventies) techniques and the logic of hard science yields an unorthodox and discomfiting power to Watson's fiction. It is interesting to compare this story to Dick's "The Indefatigable Frog" or Benford's "Relativistic Effects," other treatments of the human effects of distorted time, or to Rucker's "Ms Found in a Copy of Flatland," as a story of entrapment.

(1990)

The Very Slow Time Machine—for convenience: the VSTM*—made its first appearance at exactly midday 1 December 1985 in an unoccupied space at the National Physical Laboratory. It signaled its arrival with a loud bang and a squall

* The term VSTM is introduced retrospectively in view of our subsequent understanding of the problem (2019).

of expelled air. Dr. Kelvin, who happened to be looking in its direction, reported that the VSTM did not exactly *spring* into existence instantly, but rather expanded very rapidly from a point source, presumably explaining the absence of a more devastating explosion as the VSTM jostled with the air already present in the room. Later, Kelvin declared that what he had actually seen was the *implosion* of the VSTM. Doors were sucked shut by the rush of air, instead of bursting open, after all. However, it was a most confused moment—and the confusion persisted, since the occupant of the VSTM (who alone could shed light on its nature) was not only time-reversed with regard to us, but also quite crazy.

One infuriating thing is that the occupant visibly grows saner and more presentable (in his reversed way) the more that time passes. We feel that all the hard work and thought devoted to the enigma of the VSTM is so much energy poured down the entropy sink—because the answer is going to come from him, from inside, not from us; so that we may as well just have bided our time until his condition improved (or, from his point of view, began to degenerate). And in the meantime his arrival distorted and perverted essential research at our laboratory from its course without providing any tangible return for it.

The VSTM was the size of a small caravan; but it had the shape of a huge lead sulphide, or galena, crystal—which is, in crystallographers' jargon, an octahedron-with-cube formation consisting of eight large hexagonal faces with six smaller square faces filling in the gaps. It perched precariously—but immovably—on the base square, the four lower hexagons bellying up and out towards its waist, where four more squares (oblique, vertically) connected with the mirror-image upper hemisphere, rising to a square north pole. Indeed, it looked like a kind of world globe, lopped and sheared into flat planes: and has remained very much a separate, private world to this day, along with its passenger.

All faces were blank metal except for one equatorial square facing southwards into the main body of the laboratory. This was a window—of glass as thick as that of a deep-ocean diving bell—which could apparently be opened from inside, and only from inside.

The passenger within looked as ragged and tattered as a tramp; as crazy, dirty, woebegone, and tangle-haired as any lunatic in an ancient Bedlam cell. He was apparently very old; or at any rate long solitary confinement in that cell made him seem so. He was pallid, crookbacked, skinny, and rotten-toothed. He raved and mumbled soundlessly at our spotlights. Or maybe he only mouthed his ravings and mumbles, since we could hear nothing whatever through the thick glass. When we obtained the services of a lip-reader two days later the mad old man seemed to be mouthing mere garbage, a mishmash of sounds. Or was he? Obviously no one could be expected to lip-read backwards; already Dr. Yang had suggested from his actions and gestures that the man was time-reversed. So we videotaped the passenger's mouthings and played the tape backwards for our lip-reader. Well, it was still garbage. Backwards, or forwards, the unfortunate passenger had visibly cracked up. Indeed, one proof of his insanity was that he should be trying to talk to us at all at this late stage of his journey rather than communicate by holding up written messages—as he has now begun to do. (But more of these messages later; they only begin—or, from his point of view, *cease* as he descends further into madness—in the summer of 1989.)

Abandoning hope of enlightenment from him, we set out on the track of scientific explanations. (Fruitlessly. Ruining our other, more important work. Overturning our laboratory projects—and the whole of physics in the process.)

To indicate the way in which we wasted our time, I might record that the first "clue" came from the shape of the VSTM which, as I said, was that of a lead sulphide or galena crystal. Yang emphasized that galena is used as a semiconductor in crystal rectifiers: devices for transforming alternating current into direct current. They set up a much higher resistance to an electric current flowing in one direction than another. Was there an analogy with the current of time? Could the geometry of the VSTM—or the geometry of energies circulating in its metal walls, presumably interlaid with printed circuits—effectively impede the forward flow of time, and reverse it? We had no way to break into the VSTM. Attempts to cut into it proved quite ineffective and were soon discontinued; while x-raying it was foiled, conceivably by lead alloyed in the walls. Sonic scanning provided rough pictures of internal shapes, but nothing as intricate as circuitry; so we had to rely on what we could see of the outward shape, or through the window—and on pure theory.

Yang also stressed that galena rectifiers operate in the same manner as diode valves. Besides transforming the flow of an electric current, they can also *demodulate*. They separate information out from a modulated carrier wave—as in a radio or TV set. Were we witnessing, in the VSTM, a machine for separating out "information"—in the form of the physical vehicle itself, with its passenger—from a carrier wave stretching back through time? Was the VSTM a solid, tangible analogy of a three-dimensional TV picture, played backwards?

We made many models of VSTMs based on these ideas and tried to send them off into the past, or the future—or anywhere, for that matter! They all stayed monotonously present in the laboratory, stubbornly locked to our space and time.

Kelvin, recalling his impression that the VSTM had seemed to expand outward from a point, remarked that this was how three-dimensional beings such as ourselves might well perceive a four-dimensional object first impinging on us. Thus a 4-D sphere would appear as a point and swell into a full sphere, then contract again to a point. But a 4-D octahedron-and-cube? According to our maths this shape couldn't have a regular analogue in 4-space; only a simple octahedron could. Besides, what would be the use of a 4-D time machine which shrank to a point at precisely the moment when the passenger needed to mount it? No, the VSTM wasn't a genuine four-dimensional body; though we wasted many weeks running computer programs to describe it as one, and arguing that its passenger was a normal 3-space man imprisoned within a 4-space structure—the discrepancy of one dimension between him and his vehicle effectively isolating him from the rest of the universe so that he could travel hindwards.

That he was indeed traveling hindwards was by now absolutely clear from his feeding habits (i.e., he regurgitated), though his extreme furtiveness about bodily functions, coupled with his filthy condition, meant that it took several months before we were positive, on these grounds.

All this, in turn, raised another unanswerable question: if the VSTM was indeed traveling backwards through time, precisely where did it *disappear* to, in that instant of its arrival on 1 December 1985? The passenger was hardly on an archaeological jaunt, or he would have tried to climb out.

At long last, on midsummer day 1989, our passenger held up a notice printed on a big plastic eraser slate.

CRAWLING DOWNHILL, SLIDING UPHILL!

He held this up for ten minutes, against the window. The printing was spidery and ragged; so was he.

This could well have been his last lucid moment before the final descent into madness, in despair at the pointlessness of trying to communicate with us. Thereafter it would be *downhill all the way*, we interpreted. Seeing us with all our still eager, still baffled faces, he could only gibber incoherently thenceforth like an enraged monkey at our sheer stupidity.

He didn't communicate for another three months.

When he held up his next (i.e., penultimate) sign, he looked slightly sprucer, a little less crazy (though only comparatively so, having regard to his final mumbling squalor).

THE LONELINESS! BUT LEAVE ME ALONE!
IGNORE ME TILL 1995!

We held up signs (to which, we soon realized, his sign was a response):

ARE YOU TRAVELING BACK THROUGH TIME? HOW? WHY?

We would have also dearly loved to ask: WHERE DO YOU DISAPPEAR TO ON DEC. 1 1985? But we judged it unwise to ask this most pertinent of all questions in case his disappearance was some sort of disaster; so that we would in effect be foredooming him, accelerating his mental breakdown. Dr. Franklin insisted that this was nonsense; he broke down *anyway*. Still, if we *had* held up that sign, what remorse we would have felt: because we *might* have caused his breakdown and ruined some magnificent scientific undertaking. . . . We were certain that it had to be a magnificent undertaking to involve such personal sacrifice, such abnegation, such a cutting off of oneself from the rest of the human race. This is about all we were certain of.

(1995)

No progress with our enigma. All our research is dedicated to solving it; but we keep this out of sight of him. While rotas of postgraduate students observe him round the clock, our best brains get on with the real thinking elsewhere in the building. He sits inside his vehicle, less dirty and disheveled now, but monumentally taciturn: a Trappist monk under a vow of silence. He spends most of his time rereading the same dog-eared books, which have fallen to pieces back in our past: Defoe's *Journal of the Plague Year* and *Robinson Crusoe* and Jules Verne's *Journey to the Center of the Earth*; and listening to what is presumably taped music—which he shreds from the cassettes back in 1989, flinging streamers around his tiny living quarters in a brief mad fiesta (which of course we see as a sudden frenzy of disentangling and repackaging, with maniacal speed and neatness, of tapes which have lain around, trodden underfoot, for years).

Superficially we have ignored him (and he, us) until 1995: assuming that his last sign had some significance. Having got nowhere ourselves, we expect something from him now.

Since he is cleaner, tidier, and saner now, in this year 1995 (not to mention ten years younger), we have a better idea of how old he actually is; thus some clue as to when he might have started his journey.

He must be in his late forties or early fifties—though he aged dreadfully in the last ten years, looking more like seventy or eighty when he reached 1985. Assuming that the future does not hold in store any longevity drugs (in which case he might be a century old, or more!) he should have entered the VSTM sometime between 2010 and 2025. The later date, putting him in his very early twenties if not teens, does rather suggest a "suicide volunteer" who is merely a passenger in the vehicle. The earlier date suggests a more mature researcher who played a major role in the development of the VSTM and was only prepared to test it on his own person.

Certainly, now that his madness has abated into a tight, meditative fixity of posture, accompanied by normal activities such as reading, we incline to think him a man of moral stature rather than a time-kamikaze; so we put the date of commencement of the journey around 2010 to 2015 (only fifteen to twenty years ahead) when he will be in his thirties.

Besides theoretical physics, basic space science has by now been hugely sidetracked by his presence.

The lead hope of getting man to the stars was the development of some deep-sleep or refrigeration system. Plainly this does not exist by 2015 or so—or our passenger would be using it. Only a lunatic would voluntarily sit in a tiny compartment for decades on end, ageing and rotting, if he could sleep the time away just as well, and awake as young as the day he set off. On the other hand, his life-support systems seem so impeccable that he can exist for decades within the narrow confines of that vehicle using recycled air, water, and solid matter to 100 percent efficiency. This represents no inconsiderable outlay in research and development—which must have been borrowed from another field; obviously the space sciences. Therefore the astronauts of 2015 or thereabouts require very long-term life support systems capable of sustaining them for years and decades, up and awake. What kind of space travel must they be engaged in, to need these? Well, they can only be going to the stars—the slow way; though not a *very* slow way. Not hundreds of years; but decades. Highly dedicated men must be spending many years cooped up alone in tiny spacecraft to reach Alpha Centaurus, Tau Ceti, Epsilon Eridani, or wherever. If their surroundings are so tiny, then any extra payload costs prohibitively. Now who would contemplate such a journey merely out of curiosity? No one. The notion is ridiculous—*unless* these heroes are carrying something to their destination which will then link it inexorably and instantaneously with Earth. A tachyon descrambler is the only obvious explanation. They are carrying with them the other end of a tachyon-transmission system for beaming material objects, and even living human beings, out to the stars!

So, while one half of physics nowadays grapples with the problems of reverse-time, the other half, funded by most of the money from the space vote, preempting the whole previously extant space program, is trying to work out ways to harness and modulate tachyons.

These faster-than-light particles certainly *seem* to exist; we're fairly certain of that now. The main problem is that the technology for harnessing them is needed *beforehand*, to prove that they do exist and so to work out exactly *how* to harness them.

All these reorientations of science—because of *him* sitting in his enigmatic vehicle in deliberate alienation from us, reading *Robinson Crusoe*, a strained expression on his face as he slowly approaches his own personal crack-up.

(1996)

If you were locked up in a VSTM for *x* years, would you want a calendar on permanent display—or not? Would it be consoling or taunting? Obviously his instruments are calibrated—unless it was completely fortuitous that his journey ended on 1 December 1985 at precisely midday! But can he see the calibrations? Or would he prefer to be overtaken suddenly by the end of his journey, rather than have the slow grind of years unwind itself? You see, we are trying to explain why he did not communicate with us in 1995.

Convicts in solitary confinement keep their sanity by scratching five-barred gates of days on the walls with their fingernails; the sense of time passing keeps their spirits up. But on the other hand, tests of time perception carried out on potholers who volunteered to stay below ground for several months on end show that the internal clock lags grossly—by as much as two weeks in a three-month period. Our VSTM passenger might gain a reprieve of a year—or five years!—on his total subjective journey time, by ignoring the passing of time. The potholers had no clue to night and day; but then, neither does he! Ever since his arrival, lights have been burning constantly in the laboratory; he has been under constant observation. . . .

He isn't a convict, or he would surely protest, beg to be let out, throw himself on our mercy, give us some clue to the nature of his predicament. Is he the carrier of some fatal disease—a disease so incredibly infectious that it must affect the whole human race, unless he were isolated? Which can only be isolated by a time capsule? Which even isolation on the Moon or Mars would not keep from spreading to the human race? He hardly appears to be . . .

Suppose that he had to be isolated for some very good reason, and suppose that he concurs in his own isolation (which he visibly does, sitting there reading Defoe for the *n*th time), what demands this unique dissection of one man from the whole continuum of human life and from his own time and space? Medicine, psychiatry, sociology, all the human sciences are being drawn in to the problem in the wake of physics and space science. Sitting there doing nothing, he has become a kind of funnel for all the physical and social sciences: a human black hole into which vast energy pours, for a very slight increase in our radius of understanding. That single individual has accumulated as much disruptive potential as a single atom accelerated to the speed of light—which requires all the available energy in the universe to sustain it in its impermissible state.

Meanwhile the orbiting tachyon laboratories report that they are just on the point of uniting quantum mechanics, gravitational theory, and relativity; whereupon they will at last "jump" the first high-speed particle packages over the C-barrier into a faster-than-light mode, and back again into our space. But they reported *that* last year—only to have their particle packages "jump back" as antimatter, annihilating five billion dollars' worth of equipment and taking thirty lives. They hadn't jumped into a tachyon mode at all, but had "möbiused" themselves through wormholes in the space-time fabric.

Nevertheless, prisoner of conscience (his own conscience, surely!) or whatever he is, our VSTM passenger seems nobler year by year. As we move away from his terminal madness, increasingly what strikes us is his dedication, his self-sacrifice (for a cause still beyond our comprehension), his Wittgensteinian spirituality. "Take him for all in all, he is a Man. We shall not look upon his like . . ." Again? We shall look upon his like. Upon the man himself, gaining stature every year! That's the wonderful thing. It's as though Christ, fully exonerated as Son of God, is uncrucified and his whole life reenacted before our eyes in full and certain knowledge of his true role. (Except . . . that this man's role is silence.)

(1997)

Undoubtedly he is a holy man who will suffer mental crucifixion for the sake of some great human project. Now he rereads Defoe's *Plague Year*, that classic of collective incarceration and the resistance of the human spirit and human organizing ability. Surely the "plague" hint in the title is irrelevant. It's the sheer force of spirit which beat the Great Plague of London, that is the real keynote of the book.

Our passenger is the object of popular cults by now—a focus for finer feelings. In this way his mere presence has drawn the world's peoples closer together, cultivating respect and dignity, pulling us back from the brink of war, liberating tens of thousands from their concentration camps. These cults extend from purely fashionable manifestations—shirts printed with his face, now neatly shaven in a Vandyke style; rings and worry beads made from galena crystals—through the architectural (octahedron-and-cube meditation modules) to life-styles themselves: a Zen-like "sitting quietly, doing nothing."

He's Rodin's "Thinker," the "Belvedere Apollo," and Michelangelo's "David" rolled into one for our world as the millennium draws to its close. Never have so many copies of Defoe's two books and the Jules Verne been in print before. People memorize them as meditation exercises and recite them as the supremely lucid, rational Western mantras.

The National Physical Laboratory has become a place of pilgrimage, our lawns and grounds a vast camping site—Woodstock and Avalon, Rome and Arlington all in one. About the sheer tattered degradation of his final days less is said; though that has its cultists too, its late-twentieth-century anchorites, its Saint Anthonies pole-squatting or cave-immuring themselves in the midst of the urban desert, bringing austere spirituality back to a world which appeared to have lost its soul—though this latter is a fringe phenomenon; the general keynote is nobility, restraint, quiet consideration for others.

And now he holds up a notice.

I IMPLY NOTHING. PAY NO ATTENTION TO MY PRESENCE. KINDLY GET ON DOING YOUR OWN THINGS. I CANNOT EXPLAIN TILL 2000.

He holds it up for a whole day, looking not exactly angry, but slightly pained. The whole world, hearing of it, sighs with joy at his modesty, his self-containment, his reticence, his humility. This must be the promised 1995 message, two years late (or two years early; obviously he still has a long way to come). Now he is Oracle; he is the Millennium. This place is Delphi.

The orbiting laboratories run into more difficulties with their tachyon research; but still funds pour into them, private donations too on an unprecedented scale. The world strips itself of excess wealth to strip matter and propel it over the interface between sub-light and trans-light.

The development of closed-cycle living-pods for the carriers of those tachyon receivers to the stars is coming along well, a fact which naturally raises the paradoxical question of whether his presence has in fact stimulated the development of the technology by which he himself survives. We at the National Physical Laboratory and at all other such laboratories around the world are convinced that we shall soon make a breakthrough in our understanding of time reversal—which, intuitively, should connect with that other universal interface in the realm of matter, between our world and the tachyon world—and we feel too, paradoxically, that our current research must surely lead to the development of the VSTM, which will then become so opportunely necessary to us, for reasons yet unknown. No one feels they are wasting their time. He is the Future. His presence here vindicates our every effort—even the blindest of blind alleys.

What kind of Messiah must he be, by the time he enters the VSTM? How much charisma, respect, adoration, and wonder must he have accrued by his starting point? Why, the whole world will send him off! He will be the focus of so much collective hope and worship that we even start to investigate *Psi* phenomena seriously: the concept of group mental thrust as a hypothesis for his mode of travel—as though he is vectored not through time or 4-space at all but down the waveguide of human willpower and desire.

(2001)
The millennium comes and goes without any revelation. Of course that is predictable; he is lagging by a year or eighteen months. (Obviously he can't see the calibrations on his instruments; it was his choice—that was his way to keep sane on the long haul.)

But finally, now in the autumn of 2001, he holds up a sign, with a certain quiet jubilation:

WILL I LEAVE 1985 SOUND IN WIND AND LIMB?

Quiet jubilation, because we have already (from his point of view) held up the sign in answer:

YES! YES!

We're all rooting for him passionately. It isn't really a lie that we tell him. He did leave relatively sound in wind and limb. It was just his mind that was in tatters. . . . Maybe that is inessential, irrelevant, or he wouldn't have phrased his question to refer merely to his physical body.

He must be approaching his take-off point. He's having a mild fit of tenth-year blues, first-decade anxiety, self-doubt; which we clear up for him. . . .

Why doesn't he know what shape he arrived in? Surely that must be a matter of record before he sets off. . . . *No!* Time can not be invariable, determined. Not even the Past. Time is probabilistic. He has refrained from comment for all these years so as not to unpluck the strands of time past and reweave them in another, undesirable way. A tower of strength he has been. *Ein' feste Burg ist unser Zeitgänger!* Well, back to the drawing board, and to probabilistic equations for (a) tachyon-scatter out of normal space (b) time reversal.

A few weeks later he holds up another sign, which must be his promised Delphic revelation:

I AM THE MATRIX OF MAN.

Of course! Of course! He has made himself that over the years. What else?

A matrix is a mold for shaping a cast. And indeed, out of him have men been molded increasingly since the late 1990s, such has been his influence.

Was he sent hindwards to save the world from self-slaughter by presenting such a perfect paradigm—which only frayed and tattered in the eighties when it did not matter any more; when he had already succeeded?

But a matrix is also an array of components for translating from one code into another. So Yang's demodulation of information hypothesis is revived, coupled now with the idea that the VSTM is perhaps a matrix for transmitting the "information" contained in a man across space and time (and the man-transmitter experiments in orbit redouble their efforts); with the corollary (though this could hardly be voiced to the enraptured world at large) that perhaps the passenger was *not there* at all in any real sense; and he had never been; that we merely were witnessing an experiment in the possibility of transmitting a man across the galaxy, performed on a future Earth by future science to test out the degradation factor: the decay of information—mapped from space on to time so that it could be observed by us, their predecessors! Thus the onset of madness (i.e., information decay) in our passenger, timed in years from his starting point, might set a physical limit in *light-*

years to the distance to which man could be beamed (tachyonically?). And this was at once a terrible kick in the teeth to space science—and a great boost. A kick in the teeth, as this suggested that physical travel through interstellar space must be impossible, perhaps because of Man's frailty in face of cosmic ray bombardment; and thus the whole development of intensive closed-cycle life-pods for single astronaut couriers must be deemed irrelevant. Yet a great boost too, since the possibility of a receiverless transmitter loomed. The now elderly Yang suggested that 1 December 1985 was actually a moment of lift-off to the stars. Where our passenger went then, in all his madness, was to a point in space thirty or forty light-years distant. The VSTM was thus the testing to destruction of a future man-beaming system and practical future models would only deal in distances (in times) of the order of seven or eight years. (Hence no other VSTMs had imploded into existence, hitherto.)

(2010)
I am tired with a lifetime's fruitless work; however, the human race at large is at once calmly loving—and frenetic with hope. For we must be nearing our goal. Our passenger is in his thirties now (whether a live individual, or only an epiphenomenon of a system for transmitting the information present in a human being: literally a "ghost in the machine"). This sets a limit. It sets a limit. He couldn't have set off with such strength of mind much earlier than his twenties or (I sincerely hope not) his late teens. Although the teens *are* a prime time for taking vows of chastity, for entering monasteries, for pledging one's life to a cause. . . .

(2015)
Boosted out of my weariness by the general euphoria, I have successfully put off my retirement for another four years. Our passenger is now in his middle twenties and a curious inversion in his "worship" is taking place, representing (I think) a subconscious groundswell of anxiety as well as joy. Joy, obviously, that the moment is coming when he makes his choice and steps into the VSTM, as Christ gave up carpentry and stepped out from Nazareth. Anxiety, though, at the possibility that he may pass beyond this critical point, towards infancy; ridiculous as this seems! He knows how to read books; he couldn't have taught himself to read. Nor could he have taught himself how to speak *in vitro*—and he has certainly delivered lucid, if mysterious, messages to us from time to time. The hit song of the whole world, nevertheless, this year is William Blake's "The Mental Traveller" set to sitar and gongs and glockenspiel . . .

For as he eats and drinks he grows
Younger and younger every day;
And on the desert wild they both
Wander in terror and dismay . . .

The unvoiced fear represented by this song's sweeping of the world being that he may yet evade us; that he may slide down towards infancy, and at the moment of his birth (whatever life-support mechanisms extrude to keep him alive till then!) the VSTM will implode back whence it came: sick joke of some alien superconsciousness, intervening in human affairs with a scientific "miracle" to make all human striving meaningless and pointless. Not many people feel this way openly. It isn't a popular view. A man could be torn limb from limb for espousing it in public. The human mind will never accept it; and purges this fear in a long song of joy which at once mocks and copies and adores the mystery of the VSTM.

Men put this supreme *man* into the machine. Even so, Madonna and Child does haunt the world's mind . . . and a soft femininity prevails—men's skirts are the new, soft, gracious mode of dress in the West. Yet he is now so noble, so handsome in his youth, so glowing and strong; such a Zarathustra, locked up in there.

(2018)
He can only be twenty-one or twenty-two. The world adores him, mothers him, across the unbridgeable gulf of reversed time. No progress in the Solar System, let alone on the interstellar front. Why should we travel out and away, even as far as Mars, let alone Pluto, when a revelation is at hand; when all the secrets will be unlocked here on Earth? No progress on the tachyon or negative-time fronts, either. Nor any further messages from him. But he *is* his own message. His presence alone is sufficient to express Mankind: hopes, courage, holiness, determination.

(2019)
I am called back from retirement, for he is holding up signs again: the athlete holding up the Olympic Flame.

He holds them up for half an hour at a stretch—as though we are not all eyes agog, filming every moment in case we miss something, anything.

When I arrive, the signs that he has already held up have announced:

(*Sign One*) THIS IS A VERY SLOW TIME MACHINE. (And I amend accordingly, crossing out all the other titles we had bestowed on it successively over the years. For a few seconds I wonder whether he was really naming the machine—defining it—or complaining about it! As though he'd been fooled into being its passenger on the assumption that a time machine should proceed to its destination *instanter* instead of at a snail's pace. But no. He was naming it.) TO TRAVEL INTO THE FUTURE, YOU MUST FIRST TRAVEL INTO THE PAST, ACCUMULATING HINDWARD POTENTIAL. (THIS IS CRAWLING DOWNHILL.)

(*Sign Two*) AS SOON AS YOU ACCUMULATE ONE LARGE QUANTUM OF TIME, YOU LEAP FORWARD BY THE SAME TIMESPAN *ahead* OF YOUR STARTING POINT. (THIS IS SLIDING UPHILL.)

(*Sign Three*) YOUR JOURNEY INTO THE FUTURE TAKES THE SAME TIME AS IT WOULD TAKE TO LIVE THROUGH THE YEARS IN REAL-TIME; YET YOU ALSO OMIT THE INTERVENING YEARS, ARRIVING AHEAD INSTANTLY. (PRINCIPLE OF CONSERVATION OF TIME.)

(*Sign Four*) SO, TO LEAP THE GAP, YOU MUST CRAWL THE OTHER WAY.

(*Sign Five*) TIME DIVIDES INTO ELEMENTARY QUANTA. NO MEASURING ROD CAN BE SMALLER THAN THE INDIVISIBLE ELEMENTARY ELECTRON; THIS IS ONE "ELEMENTARY LENGTH" (EL). THE TIME TAKEN FOR LIGHT TO TRAVEL ONE EL IS "ELEMENTARY TIME" (ET): I.E., 10^{-28} SECONDS; THIS IS ONE ELEMENTARY QUANTUM OF TIME. TIME CONSTANTLY LEAPS AHEAD BY THESE TINY QUANTA FOR EVERY PARTICLE; BUT, NOT BEING SYNCHRONIZED, THESE FORM A CONTINUOUS TIME-OCEAN RATHER THAN SUCCESSIVE DISCRETE "MOMENTS," OR WE WOULD HAVE NO CONNECTED UNIVERSE.

(*Sign Six*) TIME REVERSAL OCCURS NORMALLY IN STRONG NUCLEAR INTERACTIONS—I.E., IN EVENTS OF ORDER 10^{-28} SECS. THIS REPRESENTS THE "FROZEN GHOST" OF THE FIRST MOMENT OF UNIVERSE WHEN AN "ARROW OF TIME" WAS FIRST STOCHASTICALLY DETERMINED.

(*Sign Seven*) (And this is when I arrived, to be shown Polaroid photographs of the first seven signs. Remarkably, he is holding up each sign in a linear sequence from *our* point of view; a considerable feat of forethought and memory, though no less than we expect of him.) NOW, ET IS INVARIABLE & FROZEN IN; YET UNIVERSE AGES. STRETCHING OF SPACE-TIME BY EXPANSION PROPAGATES "WAVES" IN THE SEA OF TIME, CARRYING TIME-ENERGY WITH PERIOD (X) PROPORTIONAL TO THE RATE OF EXPANSION, AND TO RATIO OF TIME ELAPSED TO TOTAL TIME AVAILABLE FOR THIS COSMOS FROM INITIAL CONSTANTS. EQUATIONS FOR X YIELD A PERIOD OF 35 YEARS CURRENTLY AS ONE MOMENT OF MACROTIME WITHIN WHICH MACROSCOPIC TIME REVERSAL BECOMES POSSIBLE.

(*Sign Eight*) CONSTRUCT AN "ELECTRON SHELL" BY SYNCHRONIZING ELECTRON REVERSAL. THE LOCAL SYSTEM WILL THEN FORM A TIME-REVERSED MINICOSMOS AND PROCEED HINDWARDS TILL X ELAPSES, WHEN TIME CONSERVATION OF THE TOTAL UNIVERSE WILL PULL THE MINICOSMOS (OF THE VSTM) FORWARD INTO MESH WITH UNIVERSE AGAIN—I.E., BY 35 PLUS 35 YEARS.

"But how?" we all cried. "How do you sychronize such an infinity of electrons? We haven't the slightest idea!"

Now at least we knew when he had set off: from thirty-five years after 1985. From *next year*. We are supposed to know all this by next year! Why has he waited so long to give us the proper clues?

And he is heading for the year 2055. What is there in the year 2055 that matters so much?

(*Sign Nine*) I DO NOT GIVE THIS INFORMATION TO YOU BECAUSE IT WILL LEAD TO YOUR INVENTING THE VSTM. THE SITUATION IS QUITE OTHERWISE. TIME IS PROBABILISTIC, AS SOME OF YOU MAY SUSPECT. I REALIZE THAT I WILL PROBABLY PERVERT THE COURSE OF HISTORY AND SCIENCE BY MY ARRIVAL IN YOUR PAST (MY MOMENT OF DEPARTURE FOR THE FUTURE); IT IS IMPORTANT THAT YOU DO NOT KNOW YOUR PREDICAMENT TOO EARLY, OR YOUR FRANTIC EFFORTS TO AVERT IT WOULD GENERATE A TIME LINE WHICH WOULD UNPREPARE YOU FOR MY SETTING OFF. AND IT IS IMPORTANT THAT IT DOES ENDURE, FOR I AM THE MATRIX OF MAN. I AM THE HUMAN RACE. I AM LEGION. I SHALL CONTAIN MULTITUDES.

MY RETICENCE IS SOLELY TO KEEP THE WORLD ON TOLERABLY STABLE TRACKS SO THAT I CAN TRAVEL BACK ALONG THEM. I TELL YOU THIS OUT OF COMPASSION, AND TO PREPARE YOUR MINDS FOR THE ARRIVAL OF GOD ON EARTH.

"He's insane. He's been insane from the start."

"He's been isolated in there for some very good reason. Contagious insanity, yes."

"Suppose that a madman could project his madness—"

"He already has done that, for decades!"

"—no, I mean really project it, into the consciousness of the whole world; a madman with a mind so strong that he acted as a template, yes, a matrix for everyone else, and made them all his dummies, his copies; and only a few people stayed immune who could build this VSTM to isolate him—"

"But there isn't time to research it now!"

"What good would it do shucking off the problem for another thirty-five years? He would only reappear—"

"Without his strength. Shorn. Senile. Broken. Starved of his connections with the human race. Dried up. A mental leech. Oh, he tried to conserve his strength. Sitting quietly. Reading, waiting. But he broke! Thank God for that. It was vital to the future that he went insane."

"Ridiculous! To enter the machine next year he must already be alive! He must already be out there in the world projecting this supposed madness of his. But he isn't. We're all separate sane individuals, all free to think what we want—"

"*Are we?* The whole world has been increasingly obsessed with him these last twenty years. Fashions, religions, life-styles: the whole world has been skewed by him ever since he was born! He must have been born about twenty years ago. Around 1995. Until then there was a lot of research into him. The tachyon hunt. All that. But he only began to *obsess* the world as a spiritual figure after that. From around 1995 or 6. When he was born as a baby. Only we didn't focus our minds on his own infantile urges—because we had him here as an adult to obsess ourselves with—"

"Why should he have been born with infantile urges? If he's so unusual, why shouldn't he have been born already leeching on the world's mind—already knowing, already experiencing everything around him?"

"Yes, but the real charisma started then! All the emotional intoxication with him!"

"All the mothering. All the fear and adoration of his infancy. All the Bethlehem hysteria. Picking up as he grew and gained projective strength. We've been just as obsessed with Bethlehem as with Nazareth, haven't we? The two have gone hand in hand."

(*Sign Ten*) I AM GOD. AND I MUST SET YOU FREE. I MUST CUT MYSELF OFF FROM MY PEOPLE; CAST MYSELF INTO THIS HELL OF ISOLATION.

I CAME TOO SOON; YOU WERE NOT READY FOR ME.

We begin to feel very cold; yet we cannot feel cold. Something prevents us—a kind of malign contagious tranquility.

It is all so *right*. It slots into our heads so exactly, like the missing jigsaw piece for which the hole lies cut and waiting, that we know what he said is true; that he is growing up out there in our obseesed, blessed world, only waiting to come to us.

(*Sign Eleven*) (Even though the order of the signs was time-reversed from his point of view, there was the sense of a real dialogue now between him and us, as though we were both synchronized. Yet this wasn't because the past was inflexible, and he was simply acting out a role he knew "from history." He was really as distant from us as ever. It was the looming presence of *himself* in the real world which cast its shadow on us, molded our thoughts, and fitted our questions to his responses; and we all realized this now, as though scales fell from our eyes. We weren't guessing or fishing in the dark any longer; we were being dictated to by an overwhelming presence of which we were all conscious—and which wasn't locked up in the VSTM. The VSTM was Nazareth, the setting-off point; yet the whole world was also Bethlehem, womb of the embryonic God, his babyhood, childhood and youth combined into one synchronous sequence by his all-knowingness, with the accent on his wonderful birth that filtered through into human consciousness ever more saturatingly.)

MY OTHER SELF HAS ACCESS TO ALL THE SCIENTIFIC SPECULATIONS WHICH I HAVE GENERATED; AND ALREADY I HAVE THE SOLUTION OF THE TIME EQUATIONS. I SHALL ARRIVE SOON AND YOU SHALL BUILD MY VSTM AND I SHALL ENTER IT; YOU SHALL BUILD IT INSIDE AN EXACT REPLICA OF THIS LABORATORY, ADJACENT TO THIS LABORATORY,

SOUTHWEST SIDE. THERE IS SPACE THERE. (Indeed, it had been planned to extend the National Physical Laboratory that way, but the plans had never been taken up, because of the skewing of all our research which the VSTM had brought about.) WHEN I REACH MY TIME OF SETTING OUT, WHEN TIME REVERSES, THE PROBABILITY OF THIS LABORATORY WILL VANISH, AND THE OTHER WILL ALWAYS HAVE BEEN THE TRUE LABORATORY THAT I AM IN, INSIDE THIS VSTM. THE WASTE LAND WHERE YOU BUILD, WILL NOW BE HERE. YOU CAN WITNESS THE INVERSION; IT WILL BE MY FIRST PROBABILISTIC MIRACLE. THERE ARE HYPERDIMENSIONAL REASONS FOR THE PROBABILISTIC INVERSION, AT THE INSTANT OF TIME REVERSAL. BE WARNED NOT TO BE INSIDE THIS LABORATORY WHEN I SET OUT, WHEN I CHANGE TRACKS, FOR THIS SEGMENT OF REALITY HERE WILL ALSO CHANGE TRACKS, BECOMING IMPROBABLE, SQUEEZED OUT.

(*Sign Twelve*) I WAS BORN TO INCORPORATE YOU IN MY BOSOM; TO UNITE YOU IN A WORLD MIND, IN THE PHASE SPACE OF GOD. THOUGH YOUR INDIVIDUAL SOULS PERSIST, WITHIN THE FUSION. BUT YOU ARE NOT READY. YOU MUST BECOME READY IN 35 YEARS' TIME BY FOLLOWING THE MENTAL EXERCISES WHICH I SHALL DELIVER TO YOU, MY MEDITATIONS. IF I REMAINED WITH YOU NOW, AS I GAIN STRENGTH, YOU WOULD LOSE YOUR SOULS. THEY WOULD BE SUCKED INTO ME, INCOHERENTLY. BUT IF YOU GAIN STRENGTH, I CAN INCORPORATE YOU COHERENTLY WITHOUT LOSING YOU. I LOVE YOU ALL, YOU ARE PRECIOUS TO ME, SO I EXILE MYSELF.

THEN I WILL COME AGAIN IN 2055. I SHALL RISE FROM TIME, FROM THE USELESS HARROWING OF A LIMBO WHICH HOLDS NO SOULS PRISONER, FOR YOU ARE ALL HERE, ON EARTH.

That was the last sign. He sits reading again and listening to taped music. He is radiant; glorious. We yearn to fall upon him and be within him.

We hate and fear him too; but the Love washes over the Hate, losing it a mile deep.

He is gathering strength outside somewhere: in Wichita or Washington or Woodstock. He will come in a few weeks to reveal himself to us. We all know it now.

And then? Could we kill him? Our minds would halt our hands. As it is, we know that the sense of loss, the sheer bereavement of his departure hindwards into time will all but tear our souls apart.

And yet . . . I WILL COME AGAIN IN 2055, he has promised. And incorporate us, unite us, as separate thinking souls—if we follow all his meditations; or else he will suck us into him as dummies, as robots if we do not prepare ourselves. What then, when God rises from the grave of time, *insane*?

Surely he knows that he will end his journey in madness! That he will incorporate us all, as conscious living beings, into the matrix of his own insanity?

It is a fact of history that he arrived in 1985 ragged, jibbering, and lunatic—tortured beyond endurance by being deprived of us.

Yet he demanded, jubilantly, in 1997, confirmation of his safe arrival; jubilantly, and we lied to him and said YES! YES! And he must have believed us. (Was he already going mad from deprivation?)

If a laboratory building can rotate into the probability of that same building adjacent to itself: if time is probabilistic (which we can never prove or disprove concretely with any measuring rod, for we can never see *what has not been*, all the alternative possibilities, though they might have been), we have to wish what we know to be the truth, not to have been the truth. We can only have faith that there will be another probabilistic miracle, beyond the promised inversion of laboratories that he speaks of, and that he will indeed arrive back in 1985 calm, well-kept, radiantly sane, his mind composed. And what is this but an entrée into madness for rational beings such as us? We must perpetrate an act of madness; we must believe the world to be other than what it was—so that we can receive among us a Sane, Blessed, Loving God in 2055. A fine preparation for the coming of a mad God! For if we drive ourselves mad, believing passionately what was not true, will we not infect him with our madness, so that he is/has to be/will be/and always was mad too?

Credo quia impossible: we have to believe because it is impossible. The alternative is hideous.

Soon He will be coming. Soon. A few days, a few dozen hours. We all feel it. We are overwhelmed with bliss.

Then we must put Him in a chamber, and lose Him, and drive Him mad with loss, in the sure and certain hope of a sane and loving resurrection thirty years hence—so that He does not harrow Hell, and carry it back to Earth with Him.

THE BEAUTIFUL AND THE SUBLIME

Bruce Sterling

Bruce Sterling burst upon the sf scene in the mid-1970s with a first novel, *Involution Ocean* (1977), billed as "A Harlan Ellison Discovery," a work heavily influenced by the 1960s New Wave writers, particularly J. G. Ballard. No one expected much in the way of hard sf from him thereafter, even though his second novel, *The Artificial Kid* (1980), showed serious interest in technological speculation. It escaped general notice in the early eighties that Sterling was publishing a series of stories rich in scientific speculation and technological detail set in a future solar system swarming with humanity and aliens. Then came cyberpunk.

Sterling and his friend, Lewis Shiner, living in Austin, Texas, were visited for a summer of intense work and play by John Shirley and William Gibson. The four of them, through correspondence, through their writing, and through Bruce Sterling's one-sheet fanzine *Cheap Truth*, proclaimed a revolution, a radical reform of hard sf, a movement that is now known as *cyberpunk*. The Movement stood for political awareness and commitment, the stylistic tradition of the New Wave, a fascination with the technological nuances and surfaces of life in the future (contact lenses, running shoes, personal computers), and, most centrally, the interface between human mind and flesh and machines, especially computers. It was the next step beyond cybernetics in sf, and it was the hip, fashionable mode of the late eighties. The paradigm books are Gibson's *Neuromancer* (1984), Sterling's *Islands in the Net* (1988), and *Mirrorshades: The Cyberpunk Anthology* (1986), edited by Sterling.

Sterling also wrote *Schismatrix* (1985), the culmination of his "swarm" stories of the early eighties, one of the best hard sf novels of the decade. *Schismatrix* is in the tradition of Van Vogtian sf adventure, artfully written to a literary standard far above the general run of hard sf, jammed with plot twists and overflowing with dense speculative ideas based on real science. His stories, from pure fantasy to hard sf, are collected in *Crystal Express* (1989). "His main interest," says *The Encyclopedia of Science Fiction*, "continues to be the behavior of societies rather than individuals and the perfection of sf as a vehicle for scientific education and political debate."

"The Beautiful and the Sublime" is rooted in the sf genre, from Kipling's fascination with air travel through Ballard's fliers at Vermillion Sands, but most significantly it is in dialogue with the tradition, a challenge to hard sf. Extend your reach, it says to other writers, use the tropes of sf and the rigors of hard sf to attain sublimely new fictions.

May 30, 2070

MY DEAR MACLUHAN:

You, my friend, who know so well a lover's troubles, will understand my affair with Leona Hillis.

Since my last letter to you, I have come to know Leona's soul. Slowly, almost despite myself, I opened those reservoirs of sympathy and feeling that turn a simple liaison into something much deeper. Something that partakes of the sublime.

It is love, my dear MacLuhan. Not the appetite of the body, easily counterfeited with pills. No, it is closer to *agape*, the soaring spiritual union of the Greeks.

I know the Greeks are out of favor these days, especially Plato with his computer-like urge toward abstract intellect.

Forgive me if my sentiments take this somewhat over-Westernized expression. I can only express what I feel, simply and directly.

In other words, I am free of that sense of evanescence that poisoned my earlier commitments. I feel as if I had always loved Leona; she has a place within my soul that could never be filled by another woman.

I know it was rash of me to leave Seattle. Aksyonov was eager to have me complete the set design for his new drama. But I felt taxed and restless, and dreaded the days of draining creative effort. Inspiration comes from nature, and I had been too long pent in the city.

So, when I received Leona's invitation to her father's birthday gala in the Grand Canyon, the lure was irresistible. It combined the best of both worlds: the companionship of a charming woman, against the background of a natural wonder unrivaled for sublimity.

I left poor Aksyonov only a hasty note over the mailnet, and fled to Arizona.

And what a landscape! Great sweeping mesas, long blasted vistas in purple and rose, great gaudy sunsets reaching ethereal fingers of pure radiance halfway to the zenith! It is the opposite pole to our green, introspective Seattle; a bright yang to the drizzling yin of the Pacific Coast. The air, sharpened by sagebrush and piñon pine, seems to scrub the brain like a loofah. At once I felt my appetite return, and a new briskness lent itself to my step.

I spoke with several Arizonans about their Global Park. I found them to be sensitive and even noble people, touched to the core by the staggering beauty of their eerie landscape. They are quite modern in their sentiments, despite the large numbers of retirees—crotchety industrial-age relics. Since the draining of Lake Powell, the former floodplain of the reservoir has been opened to camping, sports, and limited development. This relieves the crowding in the Grand Canyon itself, which, under wise stewardship, is returning to a pristine state of nature.

For Dr. Hillis's celebration, Hillis Industries had hired a modern hogan, perching on the northern canyon rim. It was a broad two-story dome, wrought from native cedar and sandstone, which blended into the landscape with admirable restraint and taste. A wide cedar porch overlooked the river. Behind the dome, white-barked Ponderosa pines bordered a large rock garden.

Freed of its obnoxious twentieth-century dams, the primal Colorado raged gloriously below the cliffsides, leaping and frothing in great silted billows and surges, flinging rocks and driftwood with tigerlike abandon. In the days that followed, its hissing roar would never be far from my thoughts.

The long drowning beneath the man-made lake had added an eerie charm to these upper reaches of the great canyon. Its shale and sandstone walls were stained a viridian green. In gulfs and eddies amid the canyon's sinuous turns, old lake sediments still clung in warping slopes, clotted by the roots of cottonwoods and flowering scrub.

On the hogan porch, overlooking the cliffs, I plugged my wrist-ward into the house system and made my presence known. Also on the porch were a pair of old people. I checked their identities with my newly charged ward. But with the typical callousness of their generation, they had not plugged into the house system, and remained unknown to me.

It was with some relief, then, that I saw our old friend Mari Kuniyoshi emerge from the hogan to greet me. She and I had corresponded faithfully since her return to Osaka; mostly about her fashion business, and the latest gossip in Japanese graphic design.

I confess I never understood the magnetic attraction Mari has for so many men. My interest lies in her talent for design, and in fact I find her romances rather heartless.

My ward identified Mari's companion: her production engineer and chief technician, Claire Berger. Mari was dressed somewhat ahead of the latest taste, in a bright high-throated peach sateen jacket and subtly clinging fluted anklewrap skirt. Claire Berger wore expedition pants, a cotton trek blouse, and hiking boots. It was typical of Mari that she would use this gawky young woman as a foil.

The three of us were soon chastely sipping fruit juice under one of the porch umbrellas and admiring the view. We traded pleasantries while I waited for Mari's obvious aura of trouble to manifest itself.

It emerged that Mari's current companion, a nineteen-year-old model and aspiring actor, had become a source of friction. Also present at the Hillis birthday fete was one of Mari's older flames, the globe-trotting former cosmonaut, Friedrik Solokov. Mari had not expected Fred's appearance, though he had been traveling with Dr. Hillis for some time. Mari's model friend had sensed the rekindled rapport between Mari and Fred Solokov, and he was extravagantly jealous.

"I see," I said. "Well, at some convenient time I can take your young friend aside, for a long talk. He's an actor with ambitions, you say. Our troupe is always looking for new faces."

"My dear Manfred," she sighed, "how well you understand my little problems. You look very dashing today. I admire your ascot. What a charming effect. Did you tie it yourself or have a machine do it?"

"I confess," I said. "This ascot has prestressed molecular folds."

"Oh," said Claire Berger distantly. "Really roughing it."

I changed the subject. "How is Leona?"

"Ah. Poor Leona," Mari said. "You know how fond she is of solitude. Well, as the preparations go on, she wanders through these great desolate canyons . . . climbing crags, staring down into the mists of that fierce river. . . . Her father is not at all well." She looked at me meaningfully.

"Yes." It was well-known that old Dr. Hillis's eccentricities, even cruelties, had advanced with the years. He never understood the new society his own great work had created. It was one of those ironic strokes you're so fond of, my dear MacLuhan.

However, my Leona had paid for his reactionary stubbornness, so I failed to smile. Poor Leona, the child of the old man's age, had been raised as his industrial princess, expected to master profits and losses and quarterly reports, the blighting discipline of his grisly drudgery. In today's world, the old man might as well have trained her to be a Spanish conquistador. It's a tribute to her spirit that she's done as much for us as she has.

"Someone should be looking after her," Mari said.

"She's wearing her ward," Claire said bluntly. "She'd have to work to get lost."

"Excuse me," I said rising. "I think it's time I met our host."

I walked into the dome, where the pleasant resinous tang of last night's pine fire still clung to the cold ashes of the hearth. I admired the interior: buffalo hides and vigorous Hopi blankets with the jagged look of old computer graphics. Hexagonal skylights poured light onto a floor of rough masculine sandstone.

Following the ward's lead, I took my bags to a charming interior room on the second floor, with great braced geodesics of rough cedar, and whitewashed walls, hung with quaint agricultural tools.

In the common room downstairs, the old man had gathered with two of his elderly cronies. I was shocked to see how that famous face had aged: Dr. Hillis had become a cadaverous cheek-sucking invalid. He sat within his wheelchair, a buffalo robe over his withered legs. His friends still looked strong enough to be dangerous: crocodilian remnants from a lost age of violence and meat. The two of them had also not registered with the house system, but I tactfully ignored this bit of old-fashioned rudeness.

I joined them. "Good afternoon, Dr. Hillis. A pleasure to share this occasion with you. Thank you for having me."

"This is one of my daughter's friends," Hillis croaked. "Manfred de Kooning, of Seattle. He's an ar-tist."

"Aren't they all," said Crocodile #1.

"If that's so," I said, "we owe our happy estate to Dr. Hillis. So it's a double honor to celebrate with him."

Crocodile #2 reached into his old-fashioned business suit and produced of all things, a cigarette. He lit it and blew a lungful of cancerous reek among us. Despite myself, I had to take a half a step back. "I'm sure we'll meet again," I said. "In the meantime I should greet our hostess."

"Leona?" said Dr. Hillis, scowling. "She's not here. She's out on a private walk. With her fiancé."

I felt a sudden icy pang at this. But I could not believe that Leona had deceived me in Seattle; if she'd had a formal liaison, she would have told me. "A sudden proposal?" I hedged. "They were carried away by passion?"

Crocodile #1 smirked sourly, and I realized that I'd touched a sore spot. "Damn it," Hillis snapped, "it's not some overblown modern claptrap with ridiculous breast-beating and hair-tearing. Leona's a sensible girl with old-fashioned standards. And Dr. Somps certainly fulfills those in every degree." He glared at me as if daring me to contradict him.

Of course I did no such thing. Dr. Hillis was gravely ill; it would have been cruelty to upset a man with such a leaden look. I murmured a few noncommittal pleasantries and excused myself.

Once outside again, I quickly consulted my ward. It gave me the biographical data that Dr. Somps had placed in the house system, for the use of guests.

My rival was a man of impressive accomplishments. He had been a child prodigy possessed of profound mathematical gifts. He was now twenty-nine, two years younger than myself, and a professor of aeronautical engineering at the Tsiolkovsky Institute in Boulder, Colorado. He had spent two years in space, as a guest in the Russian station. He was the author of a textbook on wing kinematics. He was an unsurpassed expert on wind-tunnel computer simulations, as performed by the Hillis Massively Parallel Processor.

You can imagine my profound agitation at learning this, my dear MacLuhan. I imagine Leona leaning her ringleted head on the shoulder of this suave spaceman. For a moment I succumbed to rage.

Then I checked my ward, and realized that the old man had lied. The ward's locator told me that Dr. Somps was on a plateau to the west, and his companion was not Leona but his fellow cosmonaut, Fred Solokov. Leona was alone, exploring an arroyo two miles upstream, to the east!

My heart told me to rush to her side, and as always in such matters, I obeyed it.

It was a bracing hike, skirting declines and rock slides, with the sullen roar of the mighty Colorado to my right. Occasional boatloads of daredevils paddling with might and main, appeared amid the river's surges, but the trails were almost deserted.

Leona had climbed a fanglike promontory, overlooking the river. She was hidden from ground level, but my ward helped me find her. Filled with ardor, I ignored the trail and scrambled straight up the slope. At the cost of a few cactus spines, I had the pleasure of appearing suddenly, almost at her side.

I swept my broad-brimmed hat from my head. "My dear Ms. Hillis!"

Leona sat on a paisley ground cloth; she wore a loose bush jacket over a lace blouse, its white intricacy complemented by the simple lines of a calf-length Serengeti skirt. Her blue-green eyes, whose very faint protuberance seems to multiply her other charms, were red-rimmed from weeping. "Manfred!" she said, raising one hand to her lips. "You've found me despite myself."

I was puzzled. "You asked me to come. Did you imagine I'd refuse you anything?"

She smiled briefly at my galanterie, then turned to stare moodily over the savage river. "I meant this to be a simple celebration. Something to get Father out of his black mood. . . . Instead, my troubles have multiplied. Oh, Manfred, if only you knew."

I sat on the corner of the ground cloth and offered her my canteen of Apollinaris water. "You must tell me everything."

"How can I presume on our friendship?" she asked. "A kiss or two stolen backstage, a few kind words—what recompense is that? It would be best if you left me to my fate."

I had to smile at this. The poor girl equated our level of physical intimacy with my sense of obligation; as if mere physical favors could account for my devotion. She was oddly old-fashioned in that sense, with the old industrial mentality of things bought and sold. "Nonsense," I said. "I'm resolved not to leave your side until your mind is eased."

"You know I am affianced?"

"I heard the rumor," I said.

"I hate him," she said, to my vast relief. "I agreed to it in a moment of weakness. My father was so furious, and so set on the idea, that I did it for his sake, to spare him pain. He's very ill, and the chemotherapy has made him worse than ever. He's written a book—full of terrible, hateful things. It's to be released under specific conditions—upon proof of his suicide. He threatens to kill himself, to shame the family publicly."

"How horrible," I said. "And what about the gentleman?"

"Oh, Marvin Somps has been one of Father's protégés for years. Flight simulations were one of the first uses of Artificial Intelligence. It's a field that's dear to Father's heart, and Dr. Somps is brilliant at it."

"I suppose Somps worries about his funding," I said. I was never a devotee of the physical sciences, especially in their current shrunken state, but I could well imagine the agitation of Somps should his ready pool of capital dry up. Except for eccentrics like Hillis, there were few people willing to pay expensive human beings to think about such things.

"Yes, I suppose he worries," she said morosely. "After all, science is his life. He's at the airfield, up on the mesa, now. Testing some wretched machine."

For a moment I felt sorry for Somps, but I thrust the feeling aside. The man was my rival; this was love and war! I checked my ward. "I think a word with Dr. Somps is in order."

"You mustn't! Father will be furious."

I smile. "I have every respect for your father's genius. But I'm not afraid of him." I donned my hat and smoothed the brim with a quick snap of my hand. "I'll be as polite as I can, but if he needs his eyes opened, then I am the man to do it."

"Don't!" she cried, seizing my hand. "He'll disinherit me."

"What's mere pelf in the modern age?" I demanded. "Fame, glory—the beautiful and the sublime—now those are goals worth striving for!" I took her shoulders in both my hands. "Leona, your father trained you to manage his abstract riches. But you're too soulful, too much a full human being for such a mummified life."

"I like to think so," she said, her upturned eyes full of pain. "But Manfred, I don't have your talent, or the sophistication of your friends. They tolerate me for my wealth. What else do I have to offer? I haven't the taste or grace or wit of a Mari Kuniyoshi."

I felt the open ache of her exposed insecurities. It was perhaps at that moment, my dear MacLuhan, that I truly fell in love. It is easy to admire someone of grace and elegance, to have one's eye caught by the sleek drape of a skirt or by a sidelong glance across the room. In certain circles it is possible to live through an entire affair which is composed of nothing more than brittle witticisms. But the love of the spirit comes when the dark yin of the soul is exposed in the lover's sight; vanities, insecurities, those tender crevices that hold the potential of real pain.

"Nonsense," I said gently. "Even the best art is only a symptom of an inner greatness of soul. The purest art is silent appreciation of beauty. Later, calculation spoils the inner bloom to give an outer mask of sophisticated taste. But I flatter myself that I can see deeper than that."

After this, things progressed rapidly. The physical intimacies which followed were only a corollary of our inner rapport. Removing only selected articles of clothing, we followed the delightful practice of *carezza,* those embraces that enflame the mind and body, but do not spoil things with a full satisfaction.

But there was a specter at our love feast: Dr. Somps. Leona insisted that our liaison be kept secret; so I tore myself away, before others could track us with their wards and draw unwelcome conclusions.

Having arrived as an admirer, I left as a lover, determined that nothing should spoil Leona's happiness. Once on the trail again, I examined my ward. Dr. Somps was still on the tall mesa, west of the hogan.

I turned my steps in that direction, but before I had gone more than a mile I had a sudden unexpected encounter. From overhead, I heard the loud riffling of fabric wings.

I consulted my ward and looked up. It was Mari Kuniyoshi's current escort, the young model and actor, Percival Darrow. He was riding a hang glider; the machine soared with cybernetic smoothness across the banded cliff-face. He turned, spilling air, and landed on the trail before me, with an athletic bound. He stood waiting.

By the time I reached him the glider had folded itself, its prestressed folds popping and flapping into a neat orange backpack. Darrow leaned against the sun-warmed rock with a teenager's false nonchalance. He wore a sleek cream-colored flyer's jumpsuit, its elastic sleeves pushed up to reveal the brawny arms of a gymnast. His eyes were hidden by rose-colored flyer's goggles.

I was polite. "Good afternoon, Mr. Darrow. Fresh from the airfield?"

"Not that fresh," he said, a sneer wrinkling his too-perfect features. "I was floating over you half an hour ago. The two of you never noticed."

"I see," I said coldly, and walked on. He hurried after me.

"Where do you think you're going?"

"Up to the airfield, if it's any of your business," I said.

"Solokov and Somps are up there." Darrow looked suddenly desperate. "Look, I'm sorry I mentioned seeing you with Ms. Hillis. It was a bad gambit. But we both have rivals, Mr. de Kooning. And they're together. So you and I should also have an understanding. Don't you think so?"

I slowed my pace a bit. My shoes were better than his; Darrow winced as he hopped over rocks in his thin flight slippers. "What exactly do you want from me, Mr. Darrow?"

Darrow said nothing; a slow flush built up under his tanned cheeks. "Nothing from you," he said. "Everything from Mari Kuniyoshi."

I cleared my throat. "Don't say it," Darrow said, raising a hand. "I've heard it all; I've been warned away from her a dozen times. You think I'm a fool. Well, perhaps I am. But I went into this with my eyes open. And I'm not a man to stand aside politely while a rival tramples my happiness."

I knew it was rash to involve myself with Darrow, who lacked discretion. But I admired his spirit. "Percival, you're a man of my own heart," I confessed. "I like the boldness of a man who'll face even longer odds than my own." I offered my hand.

We shook like comrades. "You'll help me, then?" he said.

"Together we'll think of something," I said. "Truth to tell, I was just going to the airfield to scout out our opposition. They're formidable foes, and an ally's welcome. In the meantime it's best that we not be seen together."

"All right," Darrow said, nodding. "I already have a plan. Shall we meet tonight and discuss it?"

We agreed to meet at eight o'clock at the lodge, to plot confusion to cosmonauts. I continued down the trail, while Darrow climbed an escarpment to find a spot to launch himself.

I stopped at the hogan again to refill my canteen and enjoy a light tea. A cold shower and quick pill relieved the stresses of *carezza*. The excitement, the adventure, were doing me good. The cobwebs of sustained creative effort had been swept from my brain. You may smile, my dear MacLuhan; but I assure you that art is predicated on living, and I was now in the very thick of real life.

I was soon on my way, refreshed and groomed. An afternoon's hike and a long climb brought me to the glider grounds, an airfield atop a long-drowned mesa now known as the Throne of Adonis. Reborn from the depths of Lake Powell, it was named in consonance with the various Osirises, Vishnus, and Shivas within Grand Canyon Global Park. The hard sandstone caprock had been cleaned of sediment and leveled near one edge, with a tastefully unobtrusive light aircraft hangar, a fiberglass control tower, changing rooms, and a modest teahouse. There were perhaps three dozen flyers there, chatting and renting gliders and powered ultralights. Only two of them, Somps and Solokov, were from our party.

Solokov was his usual urbane, stocky self. He had lost some hair since I'd last seen him. Somps was a surprise. Tall, stooped, gangling, with a bladelike nose, he had coarse windblown hair and long flopping hands. They both wore flight suits; Solokov's was of modish brown corduroy, but Somps's was wrinkled day-wear from the Kosmograd space station, a garish orange with grease-stained cuffs and frayed Cyrillic mission patches.

They were muttering together over a small experimental aircraft. I stepped into sight. Solokov recognized me and nodded; Somps checked his ward and smiled briefly and distractedly.

We studied the aircraft together. It was a bizarre advanced ultralight, with four flat, paired wings, like a dragonfly's. The translucent wings were long and thin, made of gleaming lightweight film over netted struts of tough plastic. A cagelike padded rack beneath the wings would cradle the pilot, who would grip a pair of joysticks to control the flight. Behind the wings, a thick torso and long counterbalancing tail held the craft's engine.

The wings were meant to flap. It was a one-man powered ornithopter. I had never seen its like. Despite myself, I was impressed by the elegance of its design. It needed a paint job, and the wiring had the frazzled look of a prototype, but the basic structure was delightful.

"Where's the pilot?" I said.

Solokov shrugged. "I am he," he said. "My longest flight being twenty seconds."

"Why so brief?" I said, looking around. "I'm sure you'd have no lack of volunteers. I'd like a spin in it myself."

"No avionics," Somps mumbled.

Solokov smiled. "My colleague is saying that the Dragonfly has no computer on board, Mr. de Kooning." He waved one arm at the other ultralights. "These other craft are highly intelligent, which is why anyone can fly them. They are user-friendly, as they used to say. They have sonar, updraft and downdraft detection, aerofoil control, warpage control, and so forth and so forth. They almost fly themselves. The Dragonfly is different. She is seat-of-the-pants."

As you may imagine, my dear MacLuhan, this news amazed and intrigued me. To attempt to fly without a computer! One might as well eat without a plate. It then occurred to me that the effort was surely very hazardous.

"Why?" I said. "What happened to its controls?"

Somps grinned for the first time, exposing long, narrow teeth. "They haven't been invented yet. I mean, there aren't algorithms for its wing kinematics. Four wings flapping—it generates lift through vortex-dominated flow fields. You've seen dragonflies."

"Yes?" I hedged.

Solokov spread his hands. "It is a breakthrough. Machines fly through calculation of simple, fixed wings. A computer can fly any kind of traditional aircraft. But, you see, the mathematics that determine the interactions of the four moving wings—no machine can deal with such. No such programs exist. The machines cannot write them because they do not know the mathematics." Solokov tapped his head. "Only Marvin Somps knows them."

"Dragonflies use perturbations in the flow field," Somps said. "Steady-state aerodynamics theory simply can't account for dragonfly lift values. I mean, consider its major flight modes: stationary hovering, slow hovering in any direction, high-speed upward and downward flight, as well as gliding. Classic aerodynamic design can't match that." He narrowed his eyes. "The secret is unsteady separated lift flows."

"Oh," I said. I turned to Solokov. "I didn't know you grasped the mathematics, Fred."

Solokov chuckled. "No. But I took cosmonaut's pilot training, years ago. A few times we flew the primitive craft, without avionics. By feel, like riding the bicycle! The brain does not have to know, to fly. The nervous system, it has a feel. Computers fly by thinking, but they feel nothing!"

I felt a growing sense of excitement. Somps and Solokov were playing from the central truism of the modern age. Feeling—perception, emotion, intuition, and taste—these are the indefinable elements that separate humanity from the shallow logic of our modern-day intelligent environment. Intelligence is cheap, but the thrill of innate mastery is precious. Flying the Dragonfly was not a science, but an art!

I turned to Somps. "Have you tried it?"

Somps blinked and resumed his normal hangdog expression. "I don't like heights."

I made a mental note of this, and smiled. "How can you resist? I was thinking of renting a common glider here, but having seen this contraption, I feel cheated!"

Somps nodded. "My thinking exactly. Moderns . . . they like novelty. Glitter and glamour. It ought to do well if we can get it into production. Commercially, I mean." His tone wavered from resignation to defiance. I nodded encouragingly as a number of choice epithets ran through my head: money-grubbing poltroon, miserly vivisectionist, and so forth. . . .

The basic idea seemed sound. Anything with the innate elegance of Somps's aircraft had definite appeal for today's leisure society. However, it would have to be designed and promoted properly, and Somps, who struck me as something of an idiot savant, was certainly not the man for the job. You could tell just from the way he mooned over it that the machine was, in its own odd way, a labor of love. The fresh grease on his cuffs showed that Somps had spent precious hours up on the plateau, fiddling with his knobs and switches, while his bride-to-be despaired.

Such technician's dedication might have passed muster in the days of the steam engine. But in today's more humane age Somps's behavior seemed close to criminal. This head-in-the-clouds deadbeat saw my poor Leona as a convenient way to finance his pointless intellectual curiosity.

My encounter with the two ex-cosmonauts gave me much to ponder. I withdrew with polite compliments and rented one of the local hang gliders. I circled the Throne of Adonis a few times to establish my bona fides, and then flew back to the hogan.

The effect was enchanting. Cradled by the machine's slow and careful swoops and glides, one felt the majesty of an archangel. Yet I found myself wondering what it would be like without the protective shroud of computer piloting. It would be cold sweat and naked risk and a rush of adrenalin, in which the shadowed crevices far beneath one's feet would be, not an awesome panorama, but a sheer drop!

I admit I was glad to send the machine back to the mesa on its own.

Inside the hogan I enjoyed the buffet supper, carefully avoiding the reeking plates of scorched beef served to the elders. ("Barbecue," they called it. I call it murder.) I sat at a long table with Claire Berger, Percival Darrow, and several of Leona's West Coast friends. Mari herself did not make an appearance.

Leona arrived later, when machines had cleared the meal away and the younger guests had gathered round the fire. Leona and I pretended to avoid one another, but traded stolen glances in the firelight. Under the influence of the mellow light and the landscape, the talk drifted to those poles of the modern existence: the beautiful and the sublime. We made lists: the land is beautiful, the sea is sublime; day is beautiful, night is sublime; craft is beautiful, art is sublime, and so forth.

The postulate that the male is beautiful while the female is sublime provoked much heated comment. While the discussion raged, Darrow and I unstrapped our wards and left them in the common room. Anyone checking our location would see our signals there, while we actually conspired among the machines in the kitchen.

Darrow revealed his plan. He meant to accuse Solokov of cowardice, and seize his rival's glory by testing the Dragonfly himself. If necessary, he would steal the machine. Solokov had done nothing more than take a few fluttering efforts around the top of the mesa. Darrow, on the contrary, meant to fling himself into space and break the machine to his will.

"I don't think you realize the danger involved," I said.

"I've been flying since I was a kid," Darrow sneered. "Don't tell me you're spooked too."

"Those were computer-guided," I said. "This is a blind machine. It could kill you."

"Out on Big Sur we used to rig them," Darrow said. "We'd cut out the autopilot on a dare. It's simple if you find the main sensor thingamajig. It's illegal, but I've done it. Anyway, it makes it easy for you, right? If I break my neck, your Somps will look like a criminal, won't he? He'll be discredited."

"This is outrageous!" I said, but was unable to restrain a smile of admiration. There was a day when my blood ran as hot as Darrow's, and, if I no longer wore my heart on my sleeve, I could still admire the grand gesture.

"I'm going to do it anyway," Darrow insisted. "You needn't worry on my account. You're not my keeper, and it's my decision."

I thought it over. Clearly he could not be argued out of it. I could inform against him, but such a squalid betrayal was completely beneath me. "Very well," I said, clapping him on the shoulder. "How can I help?"

Our plans progressed rapidly. We then returned to the gathering and quietly resumed our wrist-wards and our places near the hearth. To my delight, I found that Leona had left a private note on my ward. We had a midnight assignation.

After the party broke up I waited in my room for her arrival. At last the welcome glow of lamplight came down the corridor. I eased the door open silently.

She wore a long nightgown, which she did not remove, but otherwise we spared outselves nothing, except for the final sating pleasure. When she left an hour later, with a last tender whisper, my nerves were singing like synthesizers. I forced myself to take two pills and waited for the ache to subside. For hours, unable to sleep, I stared at the geodesic cedar beams of the ceiling, thinking of spending days, weeks, years, with this delightful woman.

Darrow and I were up early next morning, our minds grainy and sharp with lack of sleep and a lover's adrenalin. We lurked in ambush for the unwitting Solokov as he returned from his morning jog.

We mousetrapped him badly as he prepared to go in for a much-needed shower. I stopped him, enthusing about my glider flight. Darrow then joined our conversation "accidentally" and made a number of sharp comments. Solokov was genial and evasive at first, shrugging off Darrow's insinuations. But my loud, innocent questions made things worse for poor Fred. He did his best to explain Somps's cautious testing program for the Dragonfly. But when he was forced to admit that he had only been in the air twenty seconds, the gathering crowd tittered audibly.

Things became hectic with the arrival of Crocodile #1. I had since been informed that this obnoxious old man was Craig Deakin, a medical doctor. He had been treating Dr. Hillis! Small wonder that Leona's father was near death.

Frankly, I've always had a morbid fear of doctors. The last time I was touched by an actual human doctor was when I was a small child, and I can still remember his probing fingers and cold eyes. Imagine it, my dear MacLuhan—putting your health, your very life, into the charge of a fallible human being, who may be drunk, or forgetful, or even corrupt! Thank God that medical expert-systems have made the profession almost obsolete.

Deakin entered the fray with a cutting remark toward Darrow. By now my blood was up, and I lost all patience with this sour old relic. To make things short, we created a scene, and Darrow and I got the best of it. Darrow's fiery rhetoric and my icy sarcasm made an ideal combination, and poor Solokov, gravely puzzled and embarrassed, was unwilling to fight back. As for Dr. Deakin, he simply disgraced himself. It took no skill to show him up for what he was—an arrogant, tasteless old fraud, completely out of touch with the modern world.

Solokov finally fled to the showers, and we carried the day. Deakin, still leaking venom, tottered off shortly thereafter. I smiled at the reaction of our small eavesdropping audience. They hustled out of Deakin's way as if afraid of his touch. And small wonder! Imagine it, MacLuhan—probing diseased flesh, for money! It gives you a chill.

Flushed with success, we now sought out the unsuspecting Marvin Somps.

To our surprise, our wards located Somps with Mari Kuniyoshi and her ever-present foil, Claire Berger. The three of them were watching the preparations for the evening's festivities: projection screens and an address system were being erected in the rock garden behind the hogan.

I met them first while Darrow hung back in the trees. I greeted Somps with civil indifference, then gently detached Mari from the other two. "Have you seen your Mr. Darrow recently?" I murmured.

"Why, no," she said, and smiled. "Your doing, yes?"

I shrugged modestly. "I trust things have gone well with Fred. What's he doing here, anyway?"

"Oh," she said, "old Hillis asked him to help Somps. Somps has invented some dangerous machine that no one can control. Except for Fred, of course."

I was skeptical. "Word inside was that the thing has scarcely left the ground. I had no idea Fred was the pilot. Such timidity certainly doesn't seem his style."

"He was a cosmonaut!" Mari said hotly.

"So was *he*," I said, lifting an eyebrow at Somps. In the gentle breeze Somps's lank hair was flying all over his head. He and Claire Berger were in some animated technician's shoptalk about nuts and bolts, and Somps's long hands flopped like a puppet's. In his rumpled, tasteless business suit, Somps looked the very opposite of spacefaring heroism. I smiled reassuringly. "It's not that I doubt Fred's bravery for a moment, of course. He probably distrusts Somps's design."

Mari narrowed her eyes and looked sidelong at Somps. "You think so?"

I shrugged. "They say in camp that flights have only lasted ten seconds. People were laughing about it. But it's all right. I don't think anyone knows it was Fred."

Mari's eyes flashed. She advanced on Somps. I lifted my hat and smoothed my hair, a signal to the lurking Darrow.

Somps was only too happy to discuss his obsession. "Ten seconds? Oh, no, it was twenty. I timed it myself."

Mari laughed scornfully. "Twenty? What's wrong with it?"

"We're in preliminary test mode. These are novel methods of lift production. It's a whole new class of fluid dynamic uses," Somps droned. "The testing's slow, but that's our methodical risk avoidance." He yanked an ink-stained composition book from inside his rumpled jacket. "I have some stroke cycle summaries here. . . ."

Mari looked stunned. I broke in casually. "I heard that the go-slow approach was your pilot's decision."

"What? Fred? Oh, no, he's fine. I mean, he follows orders."

Darrow ambled forward, his hands in his pockets. He was looking at almost everything except the four of us. He was so elaborately casual that I feared Mari would surely catch on. But the remark about public laughter had stung Mari's

Japanese soul. "Follows orders?" she told Somps tightly. "People are laughing. You are crushing your test pilot's face."

I took her arm. "For heaven's sake, Mari. This a commercial development. You can't expect Dr. Somps to put his plane into the hands of a daredevil."

Somps smiled gratefully. Suddenly Claire Berger burst out in his defense. "You need training and discipline for the Dragonfly. You can't just jump in and pop off like bread from a toaster! There are no computers on Marvin's flyer."

I signaled Darrow. He closed in. "Flyer?" he ad-libbed. "You're heading for the airfield, too?"

"We were just discussing Dr. Somps's aircraft," I said artlessly.

"Oh, the Ten-Second Wonder?" Darrow said, grinning. He crossed his muscular arms. "I'd certainly like a shot at that. I hear it has no computer and has to be flown by feel! Quite a challenge, eh?"

I frowned. "Don't be a fool, Percival. It's far too risky for an amateur. Besides, it's Fred Solokov's job."

"It's not his *job*," Somps mumbled. "He's doing a favor."

But Darrow overrode him. "Sounds to me like it's a bit beyond the old man. You need someone with split-second reflexes, Dr. Somps. I've flown by feel before; quite often in fact. If you want someone to take it to the limit, I'm your man."

Somps looked wretched. "You'd crash it. I need a technician, not a daredevil."

"Oh," said Darrow with withering scorn. "A *technician*. Sorry. I had the idea you needed a *flyer*."

"It's expensive," Somps said pitifully. "Dr. Hillis owns it. He financed it."

"I see," Darrow said. "A question of money." He rolled up his sleeves. "Well, if anyone needs me, I'll be on the Throne of Adonis. Or better yet, aloft." He left.

We watched him swagger off. "Perhaps you should give him a shot," I advised Somps. "We've flown together, and he really is quite good."

Somps flushed dully. On some level, I believe he suspected that he had been had. "It's not one of your glamour toys," he mumbled bitterly. "Not yet, anyway. It's my experiment and I'm doing aeronautic science. I'm not an entertainer and I'm not doing sideshow stunts for your benefit, Mr. de Kooning."

I stared at him. "No need to snap," I said coolly. "I sympathize completely. I know things would be different if you were your own man." I touched my hat. "Ladies, good day."

I rejoined Darrow, out of sight, down the trail. "You said you could talk him into it," Darrow said.

I shrugged. "It was worth a try. He was weakening for a moment there. I didn't think he'd be such a stick-in-the-mud."

"Well, now we do things my way," Darrow said. "We have to steal it." He stripped off his ward, set it on top of a handy sandstone ledge, and whacked it with a fist-sized rock. The ward whined, and its screen flared into static. "I think my ward broke," Darrow observed. "Take it in for me and plug me out of the house system, won't you? I wouldn't want anyone to try locating me with my broken ward. That would be rude."

"I still advise against stealing it," I said. "We've made both our rivals look like idiots. There's no need for high drama."

"Don't be petty, Manfred," Darrow said. "High drama is the only way to live!"

I ask you, my dear MacLuhan—who could resist a gesture like that?

That afternoon crawled by. As the celebration started in earnest, wine was served. I was nervous, so I had a glass. But after a few sips I regretted it and set it aside. Alcohol is such a sledgehammer drug. And to think that people used to drink it by the barrel and case!

Dusk arrived. There was still no sign of Darrow, though I kept checking the skies. As preparations for the outdoor banquet neared completion, corporate helicopters began arriving, disgorging their cargoes of aging bigwigs. This was, after all, a company affair; and whole hordes of retirees and cybernetic pioneers were arriving to pay tribute to Hillis.

Since they lacked the relaxed politesse of us moderns, their idea of a tribute was harried and brief. They would pack down their plates of scorched meat, swill far too much hard liquor, and listen to speeches . . . then they would check their pacemakers and leave.

A ghastly air of stuffiness descended over the hogan and its surroundings. Leona's contingent of beautiful people was soon outnumbered; pressed on all sides, they flocked together like birds surrounded by stegosaurs.

After a brief delay, a retrospective tribute to Dr. Hillis flashed onto the rock-garden's screen. We watched it politely. There were the familiar scenes, part of the folklore of our century. Young Hillis at MIT, poring over the work of Marvin Minsky and the cognitive psychologists. Hillis at Tsukuba Science City, becoming the heart and soul of the Sixth Generation Project. Hillis, the Man with a Mission, incorporating in Singapore and turning silicon to gold with a touch.

And then all that cornucopia of riches that came with making intelligence into a utility. It's so easy to forget, MacLuhan, that there was once a time when the ability to reason was *not* something that comes through wires just like electricity. When "factory" meant a place where the "blue-collar" caste went to work!

Of course Hillis was only one of a mightly host of pioneers. But as the Nobel Prize winner and the author of Structured Intellient Multiple Processing he has always been a figurehead for the industry. No, more than that; a figurehead for the age itself. There was a time, before he turned his back on the modern world, when people spoke the name Hillis in the same breath with Edison, Watt, and Marconi.

It was not at all a bad film, of its sort. It didn't tell the whole truth, of course; it was conspicuously quiet about Hillis's regrettable involvement in politics during the '40s, the EEC bribery scandal, and that bizarre episode at the Tyuratam Launch Center. But one can read about those things anywhere. Actually, I confess that I felt the loss of those glory days, which we now see, in hindsight, as the last sunset glow of the Western analytic method. Those lost battalions of scientists, technicians, engineers!

Of course, to the modern temperament, this lopsided emphasis on rational thought seems stifling. Admittedly, machine intelligence has its limits; it's not capable of those human bursts of insight that once advanced scientific knowledge by leaps and bounds. The march of science is not the methodical crawling of robots.

But who misses it? We finally have a stable global society that accommodates man's higher feelings. A world of plenty, peace, and leisure, where the beautiful and the sublime reign supreme. If the film caused me a qualm, it was a credit to our modern mastery of propaganda and public relations. Soft intuitive arts, maybe; the dark yin to the bright yang of the scientific method. But powerful arts, and, like it or not, the ones that shape our modern age.

We had advanced from soup to fish when I caught my first glimpse of Darrow. The Dragonfly emerged from the depths of the canyon in a brief frenzied arc, its four wings thrashing in the twilit air. Strangely, my first impression was not of a struggling pilot but of a poisoned bug. The thing vanished almost at once.

I must have turned pale, for I notice Mari Kuniyoshi watching me strangely. But I held my peace.

Crocodile #2 took the podium. This gentleman was another artifact of the vanished age. He'd been some kind of military bigwig, a "Pentagon chief of staff"

I think they called him. Now he was Hillis Industries' "Chief of Security," as if they needed one in this day and age. It was clear that he'd been drinking heavily. He gave a long lachrymose introduction to Hillis, droning on and on about "air force" this and "space launch" that, and Hillis's contribution to the "defense industry." I noticed then that Fred Solokov, resplendent in tie and tails, began to look noticeably offended. And who could blame him?

Hillis at last took the podium, standing erect with the help of a cane. He was applauded loudly; we were overjoyed to see Crocodile #2 go. It isn't often that you see someone with the bad taste to mention atomic weapons in public. As if sensing the scotched nerves of our Soviet friend, Hillis departed from his prepared speech and began rambling about his "latest project."

Imagine, my dear MacLuhan, the exquisite embarrassment of the moment. For as Hillis spoke, his "latest project" appeared on the fringes of camp. Darrow had mastered the machine, caught an updraft from the depths of the canyon, and was now fluttering slowly around us. Murmurs began spreading among the crowd; people began to point.

Hillis, not a gifted speaker, was painfully slow to catch on. He kept talking about the "heroic pilot" and how his Dragonfly would be airborne "sooner than we knew." The audience thought poor Hillis was making some elaborate joke, and they began laughing. Most people thought it was clever publicity. In the meantime, Darrow swooped nearer. Sensing with a model's intuition that he was the cynosure of all eyes, he began stunting.

Still avoiding the crowd, he threw the aircraft into a hover. The wings hummed audibly, their tips flapping in complex loops and circles. Slowly, he began flying backward, the craft's long tail waggling in barely controlled instability. The crowd was amazed; they cheered aloud. Hillis, frowning, squinted across the table, his drone dying into a mumble. Then he realized the truth and cried out. Crocodile #2 took his arm, and Hillis tottered backward into his nearby chair.

Dr. Somps, his long face livid, scrambled to the podium. He flung out an arm, pointing. "Stop that man!" he screeched. This provoked hysterical laughter, shading close to authentic hysteria when Darrow spun the craft twice tailfirst and caught himself at the last moment, the wings kicking up clouds of dust over the rear of the crowd. Diners, shrieking, leapt from their chairs and fled for cover. Darrow fought for height, throwing full power into the wings and blowing two tables over with a crash and spatter of tureens and cutlery. The Dragonfly shot up like a child's toy rocket.

Darrow regained control almost at once, but it was clear that the sudden lurch upward had strained one of the wings. Three of them beat smoothly at the twilit air, but the fourth, the left rear one, was out of sync. Darrow began to fall, sliding out of the sky, listing backward to his left.

He tried to throw more power into the wings again, but we all heard the painful flopping and rasping as the injured wing refused to function. At the end the craft spun about again a few feet from earth, hit a pine at the edge of our rock garden, and crashed.

That effectively ended the festivities. The crowd was horrified. A number of the more active attendees rushed to the crash site while others babbled in shock. Crocodile #2 took the microphone and began yelling for order, but he was of course ignored. Hillis, his face twisted, was hustled inside in his chair.

Darrow was pale and bloodied, still strapped into the bent ribs of the pilot's cage. He had a few scrapes, and he had managed to break his ankle. We fished him out. The Dragonfly did not look badly damaged. "The wing gave out," Darrow kept muttering stubbornly. "It was equipment failure. I was doing fine!"

Two husky sorts formed an arm-cradle for Darrow and lugged him back to the hogan. Mari Kuniyoshi hurried after him, her face pale, her hands fluttering in shock. She had a dramatic, paralyzed look.

Lights blazed from the hogan, along with the excited babbling of the crowd. The outside floodlights in the rock garden dimmed suddenly. From the clearings around us, corporate helicopters began to lift, whirring almost silently into the fragrant Arizona night.

The crowd dispersed around the damaged craft. Soon I noticed that there were only three of us left; myself, Dr. Somps, and Claire Berger. Claire shook her head. "God, it's so sad," she said.

"I'm sure he'll recover," I said.

"What, that thief?" she said. "I hope not."

"Oh. Right," I said. I examined the Dragonfly critically. "She's just a little bent, that's all. Nothing broken. She only needs a few biffs with a lug-wrench or what-have-you."

Somps glared at me. "Don't you understand? Dr. Hillis has been humiliated. And my work was the cause of it. I'd be ashamed to speak to him now, much less ask for his support."

"You still have his daughter," Claire Berger said bluntly. We both looked at her in surprise. She looked back boldly, her arms stiff at her sides.

"Right," Somps said at last. "I've been neglecting Leona. And she's so devoted to her father. . . . I think I'd better go to her. Talk to her. Do whatever I can to make this up."

"Plenty of time for that later, when things calm down," I said. "You can't just leave the Dragonfly here! The morning dew will soak her. And you don't want gawkers out here tonight—poking at her, maybe laughing. Tell you what—I'll help you carry her up to the airfield."

Somps hesitated. It did not take long, for his devotion to his machine burst all bounds. With her long wings hinged back, the Dragonfly was easy to carry. Somps and I hoisted the heavy torso to our shoulders, and Claire Berger took the tail. All the way to the mesa Somps kept up a steady monologue of self-pity and disaster. Claire did her clumsy best to cheer him up, but the man was crushed. Clearly a lifetime of silent spleen had built up, requiring just such a calamity to uncork it. Even though he sensed that I was a rival and meant him ill, he could not entirely choke back his need for sympathy.

We found some flyers at the base of the Throne of Adonis. They were curious and eager to help, so I returned to camp. Once he had the Dragonfly in her hangar and his tools at hand, I was sure that Somps would be gone for hours.

I found the camp in uproar. With amazing crassness, Crocodile #2, Hillis's security man, wanted to arrest Darrow. A furious argument broke out, for it was brutally unfair to treat Darrow as a common thief when his only crime had been a daring gesture.

To his credit, Darrow rose above this ugly allegation. He rested in a wicker peacock chair, his bandaged ankle propped on a leather hassock and his pale blond hair swept back from a bruised forehead. The craft was brilliantly designed, he said; it was only the shoddy workmanship of Hillis Industries that had put his life into danger. At various dramatic cruxes, he would lean back with a faint shudder of pain and grasp the adoring hand of Mari Kuniyoshi. No jury in the world would have touched him. All the world loves a lover, MacLuhan.

Old Dr. Hillis had retired to his rooms, shattered by the day's events. Finally, Leona broke in and settled things. She scolded Darrow and threw him out, and Mari Kuniyoshi, swearing not to leave his side, went with him. Most of the modern contingent left as well, partly as a gesture of solidarity with Darrow, partly to escape the source of embarrassment and transmute it, somewhere else, into endlessly entertaining gossip.

Poor Fred Solokov, made into the butt of jokes through absolutely no fault of his own, also stormed off. I was with the small crowd as he threw his bags into a robot chopper at midnight. "They do not treat me like this," he insisted loudly. "Hillis is mad. I thought so ever since Tyuratam. Why people admire such young vandals as Darrow these days I do not know."

Truly, I felt sorry for him. I went out of my way to shake his hand. "Sorry to see you go, Fred. I'm sure we'll meet again under better circumstances."

"Never trust women," Fred told me darkly. He paused on the running board to belt his trenchcoat, then stepped in and slammed the vacuum-sealed door. Off he went with a whir of wings. A fine man and a pleasure to know, MacLuhan. I shall have to give some thought to making things up to him.

I then hurried back to my room. With so many gone, it would now be easier for Leona and me to carry on our assignation. Unfortunately I had not had time to arrange the final details with her, And I had a lover's anxiety that she might not even arrive. The day had been a trying one, after all, and *carezza* is not a practice for harried nerves.

Still, I waited, knowing it would be a lover's crime should she arrive and find me sleeping.

At half past one I was rewarded by a dim flicker of lamplight under the door. But it passed me.

I eased the door open silently. A figure in a white nightgown was creeping barefoot around the dome's circular hall. She was too short and squat for the willowy Leona, and her trailing, loosened hair was not blond, but an unremarkable brown. It was Claire Berger.

I tied my pajamas and shuffled after her with the stealth of a medieval assassin.

She stopped, and scratched at a door with one coy forefinger. I did not need my ward to tell me this was the room of Dr. Somps. The door opened at once, and I ducked back just in time to avoid Claire's quick glance up and down the hall.

I gave the poor devils fifteen minutes. I retired to my room, wrote a note, and returned to Somps's door. It was locked, of course, but I scratched lightly and slid my note under it.

The door opened after a hurried conclave of whispers. I slipped inside. Claire was glowering, her face flushed. Somps's fists were clenched. "All right," he grated. "You have us. What is it you want?"

"What does any man want?" I said gently. "A little companionship, some open sympathy, the support of a soul mate. I want Leona."

"I thought that was it," Somps said, trembling. "She's been so different since Seattle. She never liked me, but she didn't hate me, before. I knew there was someone after her. Well, I have a surprise for you, Mr. de Kooning. Leona doesn't know this, but I've talked to Hillis and I know. He's almost bankrupt! His firm is riddled with debts!"

"Oh?" I said, interested. "So?"

"He's thrown it all away, trying to bring back the past," Somps said, the words tumbling out of him. "He's paid huge salaries to his old hangers-on and backed a hundred dud ideas. He was depending on my success to restore his fortunes. So without me, without the Dragonfly, his whole empire falls apart!" He glared at me defiantly.

"Really?" I said. "That's terrific! I always said Leona was enslaved by this nonsense. Empire indeed; why, the whole thing's a paper tiger. Why, the old fraud!" I laughed aloud. "Very well, Marvin. We're going to have it out with him right now!"

"What?" Somps said, paling.

I gave him a bracing whack on the shoulder. "Why carry on the pretense? You don't want Leona; I do. So there's a few shreds of money involved. We're talking about love, man! Our very happiness! You want some old fool to come between you and Claire?"

Somps flushed. "We were only talking."

"I know Claire better than that," I said gallantly. "She's Mari Kuniyoshi's friend. She wouldn't have stayed here just to trade technical notes."

Claire looked up, her eyes reddened. "You think that's funny? Don't ruin it for us. Please," she begged. "Don't ruin Marvin's hopes. We have enough against us as it is."

I dragged Somps out the door by main force and closed it behind me. He wrenched free and looked ready to hit me. "Listen," I hissed. "That woman is devoted to you. How dare you trample her finer feelings? Have you no sympathy, no intuition? She puts your plans above her own happiness."

Somps looked torn. He stared at the door behind him with the aspect of a man poleaxed by infatuation. "I never had time for this. I . . . I never knew it could be like this."

"Damn it, Somps, be a man!" I said. "We're having it out with the old dragon right now."

We hustled downstairs to Hillis's suite. I tried the double doors; they were open.

Groaning came from the bedroom.

My dear MacLuhan. You are my oldest and closest friend. Often we have been one another's confessors. You remember the ancient pact we swore, as mere schoolchildren, never to tell each other's mischiefs, and to hold each other's secrets silent to the grave. The pact has served us well, and many times it has eased us both. In twenty years of friendship we have never given each other cause to doubt. However, we are now adults, men steeped in life and its complications; and I'm afraid that you must bear the silent burden of my larger mischiefs with me.

I know you will not fail me, for the happiness of many people rests on your discretion. But someone must be told.

The bedroom door was locked. Somps, with an engineer's directness, knocked out its hinge pins. We rushed inside.

Dr. Hillis had fallen off the bed. A deadly litter on the bedside table told the awful truth at once. Hillis, who had been treating himself with the aid of the servile human doctor, had access to the dangerous drugs normally safely stored in machines. Using an old hand-powered hypodermic, he had injected himself with a fatally large dose of painkiller.

We tugged his frail body back into the bed. "Let me die," the old man croaked. "Nothing to live for."

"Where's his doctor?" I said.

Somps was sweating freely in his striped cotton pajamas. "I saw him leave earlier. The old man threw him out, I think."

"All bloodsuckers," Hillis said, his eyes glazed. "You can't help me. I saw to that. Let me die, I deserve to."

"We can keep him moving, maybe," Somps said. "I saw it in an old film once." It seemed a good suggestion, with our limited knowledge of medicine.

"Ignorant," Hillis muttered, as the two of us pulled his limp arms over our shoulders. "Slaves to machines! Those wards—handcuffs! I invented all that . . . I killed the scientific tradition." He began weeping freely. "Twenty-six hundred years since Socrates and then, me." He glared and his head rolled like a flower on a stalk. "Take your hands off me, you decadent weasels!"

"We're trying to help you, Doctor," Somps said, frightened and exasperated.

"Not a cent out of me, Somps," the old man raved weakly. "It's all in the book."

I then remembered what Leona had told me about the old man's book, to be published on his suicide. "Oh no," I said. "He's going to disgrace us all and disgrace himself."

"Not a penny, Somps. You failed me. You and your stupid toys. Let me go!"

We dropped him back onto the bed. "It's horrible," Somps said, trembling. "We're ruined."

It was typical of Somps that he should think of himself at a moment like that. Anyone of spirit would have considered the greater interest of society. It was unthinkable that this titan of the age should die in such squalid circumstances. It would give no one happiness, and would cause pain and disillusion to uncounted millions.

I pride myself that I rose to the challenge. My brain roared with sudden inspiration. It was the most sublime moment of my life.

Somps and I had a brief, fierce argument. Perhaps logic was not on my side, but I ground him down with the sheer passion of my conviction.

By the time I had returned with our clothes and shoes, Somps had fixed the door and disposed of the evidence of drugs. We dressed with frantic haste.

By now the old man's lips were bluish and his limbs were like wax. We hustled him into his wheelchair, wedging him in with his buffalo robe. I ran ahead, checking that we were not seen, while Somps wheeled the dying man along behind me.

Luckily there was a moon out. It helped us on the trail to the Throne of Adonis. It was a long exhausting climb, but Somps and I were men possessed.

Roseate summer dawn was touching the horizon by the time we had the Dragonfly ready and the old man strapped in. He was still breathing shallowly, and his eyelids fluttered. We wrapped his gnarled hands around the joysticks.

When the first golden rim of the sunlight touched the horizon, Somps flicked on the engine. I jammed the aircraft's narrow tail beneath my arm, braced like a lance. Then I ran forward and shoved her off into the cold air of dawn!

MacLuhan, I'm almost sure that the rushing chilly air of the descent revived him briefly. As the aircraft fell toward the roiling waters below, she began to pitch and buck like a live thing. I feel in my heart that Hillis, that seminal genius of our age, revived and fought for life in his last instants. I think he went like a hero. Some campers below saw him hit. They, too, swore he was fighting to the last.

The rest you know. They found the wreckage miles downstream, in the Global Park, next day. You may have seen Somps and myself on television. I assure you, my tears were not feigned; they came from the heart.

Our story told it as it should have happened. The insistence of Dr. Hillis that he pilot the craft, that he restore the fair name of his industries. We helped him unwillingly, but we could not refuse the great man's wishes.

I admit the hint of scandal. His grave illness was common knowledge, and the autopsy machines showed the drugs in his body. Luckily, his doctor admitted that Hillis had been using them for months to fight the pain.

I think there is little doubt in most people's minds that he meant to crash. But it is all in the spirit of the age, my dear MacLuhan. People are generous to the sublime gesture. Dr. Hillis went down fighting, struggling with a machine on the cutting edge of science. He went down defending his good name.

As for Somps and myself, the response has been noble. The mailnet has been full of messages. Some condemn me for giving in to the old man. But most thank me for helping to make his last moments beautiful.

I last saw poor Somps as he and Claire Berger were departing for Osaka. I'm afraid he still feels some bitterness. "Maybe it was best," he told me grudgingly as we shook hands. "People keep telling me so. But I'll never forget the horror of those last moments."

"I'm sorry about the aircraft," I said. "When the notoriety wears off, I'm sure it will be a great success."

"I'll have to find another backer," he said. "And then put it into production. It won't be easy. Probably take years."

"It's the yin and yang," I told him. "Once poets labored in garrets while engineers had the run of the land. Things change, that's all. If one goes against the grain, one pays the price."

My words, meant to cheer him, seemed to scald him instead. "You're so damned smug," he almost snarled. "Damn it, Claire and I build things, we shape the world, we try for real understanding! We don't just do each other's nails and hold hands in the moonlight!"

He is a stubborn man. Maybe the pendulum will one day swing his way again, if he lives as long as Dr. Hillis did. In the meantime he has a woman to stand by him and assure him that he is persecuted. So maybe he will find, in the good fight, some narrow kind of sublimity.

So, my dear MacLuhan, love has triumphed. Leona and I will shortly return to my beloved Seattle, where she will rent the suite next to my own. I feel that very soon we will take the great step of abandoning *carezza* and confronting true physical satisfaction. If all goes well then, I will propose marriage! And then, perhaps, even children.

In any case, I promise you, you will be the first to know.

Yours as always,
de K.

THE AUTHOR OF THE ACACIA SEEDS

Ursula K. Le Guin

Ursula K. Le Guin sees science fiction as "a modern, intellectualized, extravagant form of fantasy" (in her essay "Do-It-Yourself Cosmology"). The daughter of two scientists (anthropologists), she knows rigorous methodology and respects it, and knows as well the forms of the science fiction story, which she bends to her own literary goals. The science fiction story in the form of a scientific report is a venerable tradition in the field. Arthur C. Clarke used it to ironic effect in his "History Lesson," in which aliens of the future attempt to reconstruct human civilization from a Disney film, as did George P. Elliott in "Among the Dangs" (1961), in which far-future human archaeologists excavate our world and try to figure it out, getting it hilariously wrong. Michael Bishop's novella *Death and Designation Among the Asadi* (1973) is a classic of anthropological sf in report form, as is Le Guin's own book, *Always Coming Home* (1985). This one is in the form of an anthropologist's notes (although the scientist is an intelligent ant). But anthropology is not hard science, not predictive as is physics, so many readers see all anthropological sf as "soft," no matter how scientific. That is a false opposition: the opposite of hard science is nonscience—fantasy and the fantastic, even when wearing the costume of sf.

Critic Larry McCaffery, in his entertaining book of interviews with sf writers, *Across the Wounded Galaxies* (1990), has described Le Guin's science fiction as "a sophisticated blend of myth, fable, political inquiry, and metaphysical parable. A wonderful spinner of adventure tales, she also makes us take note of the codes and cultural assumptions with which we construct our present." Although it is rigorous in its method, it is precisely the complex literary positioning of her work, among the genres of fable and short story and parable, and the obvious literary ambition, together with her commitment to feminism, that have persistently made some hard sf readers uncomfortable with much of her work that is clearly and centrally in the hard sf tradition, as this story is. Her achievement in American sf is parallel to Ballard's in British sf, although she must be considered as more traditional in style and technique. Ballard, in contrast, used the cold, scientific tone and style of the medical report to powerful effect in many of his stories of the 1960s, though the clinical detachment of that tone, ironically, marked those stories as "not hard" sf to many readers. Perhaps the art of medicine and the science of anthropology have in common only that both deal intimately with the human and are therefore each suited to nontraditional sf, and very low in the hierarchy of sciences established by Campbell. Certainly Le Guin and Ballard are extremely different from each other. In the end, both are among the best and most influential sf writers of the century.

MS. FOUND IN AN ANT HILL

The messages were found written in touch-gland exudation on degerminated acacia seeds laid in rows at the end of a narrow, erratic tunnel leading off from one of the deeper levels of the colony. It was the orderly arrangement of the seeds that first drew the investigator's attention.

The messages are fragmentary, and the translation approximate and highly interpretative; but the text seems worthy of interest if only for its striking lack of resemblance to any other Ant texts known to us.

Seeds 1–13

[I will] not touch feelers. [I will] not stroke. [I will] spend on dry seeds [my] soul's sweetness. It may be found when [I am] dead. Touch this dry wood! [I] call! [I am] here!

Alternatively, this passage may be read:

[Do] not touch feelers. [Do] not stroke. Spend on dry seeds [your] soul's sweetness. [Others] may find it when [you are] dead. Touch this dry wood! Call: [I am] here!

No known dialect of Ant employs any verbal person except the third person singular and plural, and the first person plural. In this text, only the root forms of the verbs are used; so there is no way to decide whether the passage was intended to be an autobiography or a manifesto.

Seeds 14–22

Long are the tunnels. Longer is the untunneled. No tunnel reaches the end of the untunneled. The untunneled goes on farther than we can go in ten days [i.e., forever]. Praise!

The mark translated "Praise!" is half of the customary salutation "Praise the Queen!" or "Long live the Queen!" or "Huzza for the Queen!"—but the word/mark signifying "Queen" has been omitted.

Seeds 23–29

As the ant among foreign-enemy ants is killed, so the ant without ants dies, but being without ants is as sweet as honeydew.

An ant intruding in a colony not its own is usually killed. Isolated from other ants it invariably dies within a day or so. The difficulty in this passage is the word/mark "without ants," which we take to mean "alone"—a concept for which no word/mark exists in Ant.

Seeds 30–31

Eat the eggs! Up with the Queen!

There has already been considerable dispute over the interpretation of the phrase on Seed 31. It is an important question, since all the preceding seeds can be fully understood only in the light cast by this ultimate exhortation. Dr. Rosbone ingeniously argues that the author, a wingless neuter-female worker, yearns hopelessly to be a winged male, and to found a new colony, flying upward in the nuptial flight with a new Queen. Though the text certainly permits such a reading, our conviction is that nothing in the text *supports* it—least of all the text of the immediately preceding seed, No. 30: "Eat the eggs!" This reading, though shocking, is beyond disputation.

We venture to suggest that the confusion over Seed 31 may result from an ethnocentric interpretation of the word "up." To us, "up" is a "good" direction. Not so, or not necessarily so, to an ant. "Up" is where the food comes from, to be sure; but "down" is where security, peace, and home are to be found. "Up" is the scorching sun; the freezing night; no shelter in the beloved tunnels; exile; death. Therefore we suggest that this strange author, in the solitude of her lonely tunnel, sought with what means she had to express the ultimate blasphemy conceivable to an ant, and that the correct reading of Seeds 30–31, in human terms, is:

Eat the eggs! Down with the Queen!

The desiccated body of a small worker was found beside Seed 31 when the manuscript was discovered. The head had been severed from the thorax, probably by the jaws of a soldier of the colony. The seeds, carefully arranged in a pattern resembling a musical stave, had not been disturbed. (Ants of the soldier caste are illiterate; thus the soldier was presumably not interested in the collection of useless seeds from which the edible germ had been removed.) No living ants were left in the colony, which was destroyed in a war with a neighboring ant hill at some time subsequent to the death of the Author of the Acacia Seeds.

—G. D'Arbay, T. R. Bardol

ANNOUNCEMENT OF AN EXPEDITION

The extreme difficulty of reading Penguin has been very much lessened by the use of the underwater motion picture camera. On film it is at least possible to repeat, and to slow down, the fluid sequences of the script, to the point where, by constant repetition and patient study, many elements of this most elegant and lively literature may be grasped, though the nuances, and perhaps the essence, must forever elude us.

It was Professor Duby who, by pointing out the remote affiliation of the script with Low Graylag, made possible the first, tentative glossary of Penguin. The analogies with Dolphin which had been employed up to that time never proved very useful, and were often quite misleading.

Indeed it seemed strange that a script written almost entirely in wings, neck, and air should prove the key to the poetry of short-necked, flipper-winged water writers. But we should not have found it so strange if we had kept in mind the fact that penguins are, despite all evidence to the contrary, birds.

Because their script resembles Dolphin in *form*, we should never have assumed that it must resemble Dolphin in *content*. And indeed it does not. There is, of course, the same extraordinary wit and the flashes of crazy humor, the inventiveness, and the inimitable grace. In all the thousands of literatures of the Fish stock, only a few show any humor at all, and that usually of a rather simple, primitive sort; and the superb gracefulness of Shark or Tarpon is utterly different from the joyous vigor of all Cetacean scripts. The joy, the vigor, and the humor are all shared by Penguin authors; and, indeed, by many of the finer Seal *auteurs*. The temperature of the blood is a bond. But the construction of the brain, and of the womb, makes a barrier! Dolphins do not lay eggs. A world of difference lies in that simple fact.

Only when Professor Duby reminded us that penguins are birds, that they do not swim but *fly in water*, only then could the therolinguist begin to approach the sea literature of the penguin with understanding; only then could the miles of recordings already on film be restudied and, finally, appreciated.

But the difficulty of translation is still with us.

A satisfying degree of progress has already been made in Adélie. The difficulties of recording a group kinetic performance in a stormy ocean as thick as pea soup with plankton at a temperature of 31° F are considerable; but the perseverance of the Ross Ice Barrier Literary Circle has been fully rewarded with such passages as "Under the Iceberg," from the *Autumn Song*—a passage now world famous in the rendition by Anna Serebryakova of the Leningrad Ballet. No verbal rendering can approach the felicity of Miss Serebryakova's version. For, quite simply, there is no way to reproduce in writing the all-important *multiplicity* of the original text, so beautifully rendered by the full chorus of the Leningrad Ballet company.

Indeed, what we call "translations" from the Adélie—or from any group kinetic text—are, to put it bluntly, mere notes—libretto without the opera. The ballet version is the true translation. Nothing in words can be complete.

I therefore suggest, though the suggestion may well be greeted with frowns of anger or with hoots of laughter, that *for the therolinguist*—as opposed to the artist and the amateur—the kinetic sea writings of Penguin are the *least* promising field of study, and, further, that Adélie, for all its charm and relative simplicity, is a less promising field of study than is Emperor.

Emperor! I anticipate my colleagues' response to this suggestion. Emperor! The most difficult, the most remote, of all the dialects of Penguin! The language of which Professor Duby himself remarked, "The literature of the emperor penguin is as forbidding, as inaccessible, as the frozen heart of Antarctica itself. Its beauties may be unearthly, but they are not for us."

Maybe. I do not underestimate the difficulties: not least of which is the imperial temperament, so much more reserved and aloof than that of any other penguin. But, paradoxically, it is just in this reserve that I place my hope. The emperor is not a solitary, but a social bird, and while on land for the breeding season dwells in colonies, as does the Adélie; but these colonies are very much smaller and very much quieter than those of the Adélie. The bonds between the members of an emperor colony are rather personal than social. The emperor is an individualist. Therefore I think it almost certain that the literature of the emperor will prove to be composed by single authors, instead of chorally; and therefore it will be translatable into human speech. It will be a kinetic literature, but how different from the spatially extensive, rapid, multiplex choruses of sea writing! Close analysis, and genuine transcription, will at last be possible.

What! say my critics—Should we pack up and go to Cape Crozier, to the dark, to the blizzards, to the −60° cold, in the mere hope of recording the problematic poetry of a few strange birds who sit there, in the midwinter dark, in the blizzards, in the −60° cold, on the eternal ice, with an egg on their feet?

And my reply is, Yes. For, like Professor Duby, my instinct tells me that the beauty of that poetry is as unearthly as anything we shall ever find on Earth.

To those of my colleagues in whom the spirit of scientific curiosity and aesthetic risk is strong, I say, imagine it: the ice, the scouring snow, the darkness, the ceaseless whine and scream of wind. In that black desolation a little band of poets crouches. They are starving; they will not eat for weeks. On the feet of each one, under the warm belly feathers, rests one large egg, thus preserved from the mortal touch of the ice. The poets cannot hear each other; they cannot see each other. They can only feel the other's *warmth*. That is their poetry, that is their art. Like all kinetic literatures, it is silent; unlike other kinetic literatures, it is all but immobile, ineffably subtle. The ruffling of a feather; the shifting of a wing; the touch, the slight, faint, warm touch of the one beside you. In unutterable, miserable, black solitude, the affirmation. In absence, presence. In death, life.

I have obtained a sizable grant from UNESCO and have stocked an expedition. There are still four places open. We leave for Antarctica on Thursday. If anyone wants to come along, welcome!

—D. Petri

EDITORIAL—BY THE PRESIDENT OF THE THEROLINGUISTICS ASSOCIATION

What is Language?

This question, central to the science of therolinguistics, has been answered—heuristically—by the very existence of the science. Language is communication. That is the axiom on which all our theory and research rest, and from which all our discoveries derive; and the success of the discoveries testifies to the validity of the axiom. But to the related, yet not identical question, What is Art? we have not yet given a satisfactory answer.

Tolstoy, in the book whose title is that very question, answered it firmly and clearly: Art, too, is communication. This answer has, I believe, been accepted without examination or criticism by therolinguistics. For example: Why do therolinguists study only animals?

Why, because plants do not communicate.

Plants do not communicate; that is a fact. Therefore plants have no language; very well; that follows from our basic axiom. Therefore, also, plants have no art. But stay! That does *not* follow from the basic axiom, but only from the unexamined Tolstoyan corollary.

What if art is not communicative?

Or, what if some art is communicative, and some art is not?

Ourselves animals, active, predators, we look (naturally enough) for an active, predatory, communicative art; and when we find it, we recognize it. The development of this power of recognition and the skills of appreciation is a recent and glorious achievement.

But I submit that, for all the tremendous advances made by therolinguistics during the last decades, we are only at the beginning of our age of discovery. We must not become slaves to our own axioms. We have not yet lifted our eyes to the vaster horizons before us. We have not faced the almost terrifying challenge of the Plant.

If a noncommunicative, vegetative art exists, we must rethink the very elements of our science, and learn a whole new set of techniques.

For it is simply not possible to bring the critical and technical skills appropriate to the study of Weasel murder mysteries, or Batrachian erotica, or the tunnel sagas of the earthworm, to bear on the art of the redwood or the zucchini.

This is proved conclusively by the failure—a noble failure—of the efforts of

Dr. Srivas, in Calcutta, using time-lapse photography, to produce a lexicon of Sunflower. His attempt was daring, but doomed to failure. For his approach was kinetic—a method appropriate to the *communicative* arts of the tortoise, the oyster, and the sloth. He saw the extreme slowness of the kinesis of plants, and only that, as the problem to be solved.

But the problem was far greater. The art he sought, if it exists, is a noncommunicative art—and probably a nonkinetic one. It is possible that Time, the essential element, matrix, and measure of all known animal art, does not enter into vegetable art at all. The plants may use the meter of eternity. We do not know.

We do not know. All we can guess is that the putative Art of the Plant is *entirely different* from the Art of the Animal. What it is, we cannot say; we have not yet discovered it. Yet I predict with some certainty that it exists, and that when it is found it will prove to be, not an action, but a reaction: not a communication, but a reception. It will be exactly the opposite of the art we know and recognize. It will be the first *passive* art known to us.

Can we in fact know it? Can we ever understand it?

It will be immensely difficult. That is clear. But we should not despair. Remember that so late as the mid-twentieth century, most scientists, and many artists, did not believe that even Dolphin would ever be comprehensible to the human brain—or worth comprehending! Let another century pass, and we may seem equally laughable. "Do you realize," the phytolinguist will say to the aesthetic critic, "that they couldn't even read Eggplant?" And they will smile at our ignorance, as they pick up their rucksacks and hike on up to read the newly deciphered lyrics of the lichen on the north face of Pike's Peak.

And with them, or after them, may there not come that even bolder adventurer—the first geolinguist, who, ignoring the delicate, transient lyrics of the lichen, will read beneath it the still less communicative, still more passive, wholly atemporal, cold, volcanic poetry of the rocks: each one a word spoken, how long ago, by the earth itself, in the immense solitude, the immenser community, of space.

HEAT OF FUSION

John M. Ford

John M. Ford is a writer whose work is well known in the science fiction, fantasy, and horror genres. His major novel to date is a fantasy, *The Dragon Waiting* (1983), but his stories range widely, and he is a writer of both computer gaming and role-playing game scenarios. Ford is steeped in the traditions of the science fiction field and, like Poul Anderson and Isaac Asimov (to name only two of many), is occasionally drawn to the mystery and thriller. He has established a reputation as one of the finest and most complex writers of the eighties generation.

In "Heat of Fusion," Ford is advancing the literary tradition of Kornbluth's "Gomez" and Smith's "No, No, Not Rogov!" But Ford, like others in the 1980s, considers the metaphorical implications of scientific ideas, and here examines not only the character of the scientist but the metaphorical and emotional reverberations of the scientist's work. In this he is more similar to Gregory Benford (in, say, "Exposures") or Gene Wolfe in "Procreation" than to Niven, Forward, or Kingsbury. The underlying belief in the power of science (physics) and scientists (physicists) is still there. Yet he is also, and quite seriously, importing the Kafkaesque into hard sf, which alters the affect into something quite individual. The setting is minimally sketched, by allusions to airlocks and such, and by the implication (as in Kornbluth and Smith) that titanic disaster is narrowly averted. In the end, Ford's story is a challenge to the political and human-centered complacency of much contemporary hard sf. It is certainly in the tradition of "The Cold Equations."

DAY 1

I had my first fully conscious day since the accident. They tell me it has been about four days, but this will be Note #1, for completeness' sake. I feel remarkably well, for a dead man.

A. was waiting for me when I awoke, smiling brightly. He had a supply of blank notebooks and pencils for me. (Odd how, with all the shortages, we have such a huge stockpile of blank books and pencils.) In the "time remaining," I am to write down all the details of the work that my old gray head contains, so that his Project does not "slip backward."

I see I have written "his" Project. Well. It will be his, soon, since N. died in the accident. (As did I, but have not had the grace to fall down yet.)

N. is dead. And J. is dead. Y., I am told, is still "alive," though in much worse shape than I. I may be able to see her. It is something to look forward to, and I have little enough of those.

I will write the notes A. has asked for, though not necessarily the ones he wants. And separately I shall keep this notebook ("journal" is too much of a word). I don't know for whom. Myself, I suppose. As for why, see prior paragraph, last sentence.

DAY 2

While I dozed this afternoon, A. stole the notebook I had been filling for his benefit. I know it was A.; the nurse told me when I called her to search the floor for it. I hope she will not get into trouble for that.

I wondered about hiding these notes, but that is silly. Secrecy mentality. What would attract more attention than my fussing with pillows or drainpipes or loose blocks in the wall?

Even if I found one, soon enough I won't be able to move a loose block.

But they are going to play the Secrets game whether I will or not, I suppose. (I haven't seen a single soldier since the accident; what am I expected to make of that?) I'll keep this book in the pile of blank ones, well shuffled. That's enough.

I wonder what A. will make of what he has?

DAY 3

A. was not happy. I think he was furious, in fact. But I will give him this much: he controlled himself better than I had thought him capable. (Capable of?)

He did not bother with a philosophical argument, being not that much of a fool, and went straight to discussing the good of the Project. When that wore thin, he hinted that I might not be allowed to see the "recovering" Y., if I were not "cooperative."

We learn from our environments, and he has spent his Project time among the soldiers, not the scientists.

I asked him, angrily I suppose, why he had stolen my notebook. After a pause, he said that I had given it to him. "Don't you remember? Are you having trouble remembering?"

Then he looked at me with real fear. And his expression changed to

I must describe it precisely. If you have ever worked very hard at a difficult problem, one you doubt is within your capacity, and then broken it, you know the feeling that comes when the nut of solution first cracks open, the glimpse of glory within. That was A.'s look.

He went away without any books.

Perhaps he is frightened by the facts: he could not read the notes he stole because he is too poor a physicist. If all my writing to come is like that, what will become of *his* Project?

But now I know he will threaten me, and I am scared too.

DAY 4

No one came today but nurses. One said that I may be allowed to walk soon, at least to the toilet. Outstanding. Martin Luther may have had great thoughts while his bowels worked, but he wasn't using a bedpan.

I am still worried about A.'s moment of epiphany yesterday. Was it about the Project, or me? He had already held Y. over me. J. is dead.

J. is dead, and I am dead, and the living cannot threaten me.

DAY 5

I have found out A.'s scheme. What a waste of two days' fretting. One would think I had taught enough students to know that the brightest smiles come from those who have just trisected the angle.

He has started a whispering campaign that the accident was my fault. The doctors have muttered it in the halls, the nurses shake their heads as they change my bottles, A. came as close to saying it as he dared. I must finish my commentary on the Project, he said, because if I do not "erroneous impressions" may take hold.

"Erroneous impressions" is what he said. A waste of six syllables, when "lies" has only one.

DAY 6

My fault.

My fault.

I put the words on the page, and they seem to crawl from beneath the pencil, shaping themselves into countless implications but no meanings.

Presumably when the Project Final Report is written, there will be a chapter on the accident. Call it Chapter 13. And there will appear a line, to wit: He was in charge of the Principal Experimental Rig when the accident took place. It was His Fault. (This *misrepresentation* of my responsibilities will be insisted upon by A.) The line will repeat as the caption of a small and unflattering photograph of myself, Figure 13-2. 13-1 will be the standard half-page picture of the Rig, with numbered silhouettes superimposed where the others were standing.

I presume falsely, of course. There will be no such report. After the present mess is cleared up, the Project will proceed to one of two endpoints.

If it fails, there will be no one to write the report. If it succeeds, there will be no one to read it.

So this text is going to have to be as much Final Report as the Project will ever see. And epitaph enough, too, for the four of us.

DAY 7

A. came in today, falsely cheerful and a little sheepish. He asked how my "Report" was progressing. (He called it that; am I to begin dreaming true as the end approaches?) I showed him what I had for him; his delight was fake but his relief was not. I know very well that he is being driven by others, having no ability to drive himself, and I was about to feel a little sorry for him when he brought up Y. again, saying that she was *almost* able to converse, and the doctors said I was *almost* well enough to see her. (How well a corpse gets he did not explain.)

I am having second thoughts as I write: perhaps A. was ordered to use Y. as a lever against me. It was never in his nature to be deliberately cruel (his masochism, which he doubtless believes is his secret still, is more pathetic than pathological). And perhaps he is watched as he talks to me.

In which case, why do I write these secret notes to no one?

My paranoia is itself rather pathetic. I asked him if there had been memorial services for N. and J., and if not, if I might attend them, and even say a few words.

A. was, if not thunderstruck, at least surprised. He told me that, since complete dissective necropsies were required, the bodies were hardly suitable for view and had been cremated. A memorial he acknowledged as a possibility, after the "immediate problems" were settled. Then he asked to take the notebook, which I allowed, and he went away.

Of course I knew J.'s body would have been disposed of, one way or another. I wanted A., and whoever might be behind him, to be very aware that I know J. is dead, because though I do know that and threats would mean nothing, still I do not want to hear them.

As for the memorial service, tomorrow I will hold one here.

DAY 8

When J. was just a student

I let the line stand, so as to correct and amplify it. When J. had no formal credentials, so that we perceived him through a student-colored filter, I posed a question to his lecture group, one I always gave the Honors students early in the course. It involved a spinning particle, and while the answer was not complex it was tricky, in that there were several wrong answers more plausible-sounding than the correct one, and the class inevitably had to eliminate those before discerning the truth.

So when J. put his hand up first, and the others let him wave it alone, I thought he must be trapped. More fool I. Not only did he have the solution, he had reached it in a novel and elegant fashion. It was obvious that he had not simply made a lucky memorization, but *understood* the underlying theory down to its roots.

The recollection that brackets this one is of J. sitting at a test bench, holding the two pieces of an elaborate glass vacuum assembly that had somehow broken in the center. (I never did learn how that ~~acci~~ mishap occurred.) I passed by in the hall, shook my head, and went on with whatever I was doing; when I passed by again, at least half an hour later, he was still there, staring at the jagged ends of glass.

I leaned into the room and suggested he call the glassblower, whose shop was only a few doors away. Without looking up, J. said, "No need to; I've about got it now."

I let the story get about, and there was laughter at J.'s expense until I was quite as embarrassed as he was.

There are the stories; the theorist with an intuitive power that, as he learned to focus it, was at times actually frightening, who had no mind at all for experimental hardware.

They are not, I can see now, brackets but mirrors, creating an endless chain of reflections between them.

A reflector assembly.

No more today.

DAY 9

I was allowed to walk today, about four meters to the bathroom. Slow progress, in an unsmoothed curve point to point, an orderly with a death grip on my arm, but the heavy particle finally achieved the target.

Triumph.

Once there, I eliminated into cardboard containers, for the laboratory's benefit. They also received a liter or so of my exhaled breath, and of course a little blood. Ultimately I will give my all for the Project, rag and bone and hank of hair, as have J. and N. already.

I was about to write that N. would have been pleased, to know that he gave all his being. How easily the sarcasm still comes. N. loved the Project, and he loved the State, and he venerated the memory of his wife and children (while still being able to make a respectful pass at Y. one Christmas). What can I say of a man who needed to love so much?

Everything is colored by his first spring here, the first spring of the Project. N. was drafted (at least, we thought he had been drafted) to write a speech, to be delivered to all the inhabitants of the complex, about the strange dark secret in their midst. I was supposed to read this text, but A. readily accepted my deferral.

Everyone gathered in the largest common room. A. and N. sat on a dais, in their only good suits, with a few soldiers in their dress uniforms. J. and I had attended, certainly not to heckle. Maybe not to heckle. Frankly we were curious. How is a secret Project explained and still kept Secret?

Yet he did it.

N.'s speech brought up pride, and honor, and glory lost and glory regained, and on and on, and *literally* got the audience to their feet cheering for the Project, despite that they had been told not one word about what it was or what it did.

Afterward, we saw N., smiling and shaking hands and saluting (he had, as we all did, a crypto-military rank, that we might command and be commanded). He said to me "It worked, didn't it?" in the tone any of us used when looking up from the recorder or the slide rule.

The flat box I was provided today was of waxed white board, that distinctly showed the blood in my gruelly shit.

DAY 10

A. visited, hungry for more. It is tiring, and it is a dilemma. If I churn out pages for them I am too tired to think about these notes, but if A. and his masters are not kept happy I will have no peace at all.

And of course A. is not inspired but not incompetent either, and eventually he will taste what I am feeding him.

If N. were here it would be different. But N. was in Room 18. N. is dead. N. was the first of us to die, and perhaps died best.

He could take any one worker's idea of data and mathematically transform them into anyone else's mental dialect. It was N. who allowed Y. to comprehend J.'s theories, J. to puzzle out what she then constructed, and this old foolish professor to understand them both.

It was said, not really joking, that N.'s works would be bestsellers if they were not all Secret. He did, in fact, write two popular works, on physics and mathematics for young people. He dedicated them to his children, who were living then. The State press keeps them in print, and it is a fair guess that if you are reading this you read them at some time in your youth.

Unless you are a State security officer, of course.

DAY 11

At the moment of the accident, I was not in the Principal Experiment Room, Room 18, but in Room 19, the Recording and Control Room adjacent. The communicating door was open; this was against regulation but usual practice when the Rig was being operated at low energies, and the door was anyway not shielded.

Y. called to me through the open door. There was no special urgency in her voice. I took a step, then heard a chattering sound from one of the power relay cabinets behind me; as I turned, I briefly saw dials leap and pen recorders reach. Then there was a flash of light from the Rig, dazzling and warm as sunshine.

I was screened from the epicenter of flash by the bit of wall between the door and the observing window. I might have been still alive at that point; I do not know. I did not even think about it. I went to the door.

J. was standing on the platform between the B and C assemblies. Above him, a red steel flag indicated that the shutters of the C-stage reflector were fully open, at his chest level.

I entered Room 18 just as the alarm sounded. I was definitely dead then; this was well understood about the alarm system. It was supposed, correctly as it turned out, that with casualties now clearly defined, those inside (dead) could take the most efficient action to secure the area.

Y. had dropped behind a heavy desk, telephone in hand; she was spinning the crank furiously. I could not see N. J. was leaning against the C assembly, left hand clutching a pipe, right hand close to his body. As I drew close, I saw that he was holding an instrument inside the reflector cavity, and had been timing the measurement with his wristwatch.

I thought for another moment that he was alive (conscious, that is; I have already explained about the alarm), but I took another step and saw his face, half pale and half scorched, and his eyes, his empty, idiot eyes, the brain behind them washed clean of thought in a wave of particles. He stared up and away, not at me, or I think my heart should have failed. As perhaps it

Y. had abandoned the useless telephone (all its magnetic parts were scrambled) and went behind the B assembly; she called for help, and I helped her bring N. out from the small space. His clothing smoldered. There were hideous, deep black burns on his chest and neck and hands. Y. pointed at the wall, where N.'s shadow was still cast, in unburned paint.

It was Y. who locked the doors and turned off the blaring alarm. I could not think at all, not in the room with J. staring, staring at nothing, with the face of a stillborn child.

DAY 12

I was loaded into a wheelchair and taken to see Y.

She was on an entirely different level of the complex, though it did not seem any differently equipped.

A. was there, looking very pleased, with a stenographer to take notes of our conversation.

I had thought perhaps the desk protected Y. some small amount, but obviously her dose was much higher than mine. She was propped up on pillows, laced with tubes, very pale (I almost wrote "deathly"). Her voice was clear, however.

We talked about nothing much for a few minutes. I could see A. becoming impatient. (I looked for, but did not see, a stack of notebooks in the room.) I spoke to A., rather loudly, to be certain Y. was aware he was there; I believe she nodded to me.

After a little more idle talk, A. interrupted us. While we were together he said, the bastard, were there any important details of the Project that should be recorded?

Y. turned her head. The effort was visibly enormous for her. Then I did see her nod to me. "J.'s thermal data," she said, quite clearly. "The cavity readings he made on the last day."

"Were those important?" A. said. "We have them, of course, but it was thought they were only routine."

Y. coughed.

I said "We should leave you alone."

Y. whispered "Come see me again." There was blood on her lips.

I said "Of course," because it was what she wanted to hear, and then I did a stupid thing. I reached up and touched her dark hair, where it was gray at the right temple.

The hair came away in my hand.

They took me back to my room by a different route. I see they are afraid, and that does not displease me.

DAY 13

Last night Y. came to visit.

Not literally, of course. But it seemed that she was here, and it seemed that we talked, in the quiet and dark. She was young, as when we first worked together at the old University Laboratories, her hair long and dark and her almond eyes intense. I remember thinking of her as mysterious, but since I intended to solve all the mysteries of physics in a term, or two at the most, surely women would require only a summer session.

I also learned more about physics.

Now I see I have skewed your perceptions. When I say now that she was a brilliant experimenter, that she did amazing things with her hands, you will laugh in a lewd manner. That is all right. We certainly did enough of it.

But it is true that she could turn a few equations and a pencil sketch into a working bench-test rig. She could solder and drill and tap and blow glass. I saw her make waveguides out of ballpoint-pen tubing. If there was a tricky curve involved, she would twist paper clips into test shapes, using her slim hard fingers as a forming brake.

When the Project began, there were several unkind comments about Y.'s presence with myself, but I knew it (not I) must have her. And I was correct. We did not resume our other relationship; in the time between, she had gotten a husband and children, and lost them, and now there was the Project.

So we talked, last night, about things you have no context for understanding, and some that you probably do. Sunlight, and

This morning, a doctor came in, sad-eyed, to tell me that Y. was dead. He offered to take me to see her, but I said that I preferred to remember her as we had last met.

I wish now I had asked her if there were sunlight, but I will know soon enough.

I do not believe in ghosts, they are not a valid quantum phenomenon. But I imagined, as I walked so slowly to the toilet, that the irregularity beneath my slipper was a twisted paper clip.

DAY 14

A few weeks before the accident, N. came to visit me, rather late. He was a little drunk, not very, and N. was not a private drinker. He had come to show me a manuscript he had just completed. The State press had requested it long ago, for whenever the Project should be complete; "for some reason," (he said) he had written this draft.

I wonder now if he had been talking to J.

The manuscript was a pamphlet, intended for children and adult poor readers. It explained, in clear, simple language, what the Project was, why we had done it, and why it was necessary that we do it. All the eloquence of his speech to the staff, years ago, was carried over, and no little amplified by the facts he could now state; the enemy might be far away, but we could be sure that there was an enemy, and if we did not bend the laws of physics to our just and peaceful will, that enemy would certainly use them to destroy us.

That was said in such fashion that its inherent absurdity—its *redundancy*—was forgotten.

Then I read the section about the Project's effects, how they would be wholly different from anything we had known before, nothing at all to fear.

It was a naked lie, and when I looked into N.'s face I saw he knew it was a lie, and still it was a convincing lie, a pleasant and friendly lie.

Could anyone have desired to believe it more than I? I cannot think how.

I told him the booklet was very well written, which was the only truth I had loose in my head then, and I praised his ability to write for the young.

He told me that it had never been hard for him to do, that he simply wrote the piece for his children.

Then he looked at me in absolute bewilderment, and asked me who it was he had written *this* for?

DAY 15

Woke in the middle of the night, very cold, and saw J. staring at me, not living but dead and brain-dead. Wide pearly eyes with tiny uncomprehending pupils. (They are pearls that were his eyes, of his bones are radon made, Geiger counters ring his knell.)

So exquisitely ugly, like a fairy tale; he danced with the particles, and lived as one of them, until they bore his soul away and left this goggling husk.

I would live in Hell rather than see those empty eyes again. Here is Hell: I must not die now, not yet. I know now what J. was trying to do in the C cavity, and I have to see his data, on the terrible chance that he did it.

A. has the data, of course, but I dare not call him in; he must not suspect.

Maybe there is nothing there. Maybe my opinion of J. was always too high.

Oh no. This is not the time to think that.

DAY 16

These pictures that I draw are an attempt to connect points into a smooth curve, but the data will not support an honest curve. There is so little time. I could sketch in data points until my hand was too weak to move—the jewelry Y. made from solder and ceramics; the Christmas N. wrote personal sonnets to everyone he knew in the complex, had them put unsigned into our mailboxes and tried to pretend ignorance; J. wandering the halls with a chess set, playing anyone who would and never winning a single game—but would these smooth the curve, or skew it? They were people. I knew them, one of them in the Biblical sense. I cannot say I understood them, by Heisenberg's principle an it please you.

You who read this, try to understand what I cannot. The particle does not know its charge. It cannot see the outcome of its collisions. When the event is over, the patient observer may try to make some sense of the tracks left behind. Please be patient.

DAY 17

Awful tiredness today. Hands ache. Must go on maybe last entry.

Late last n. went toilet. Finished, hand hit switch, lights out.

Mirror suddenly clear. On other side sits bored soldier, smoking, solitaire. He startled as I.

Lights on quick. Back to bed.

Well it brought A. Said only for safety (mine). Maybe he believes it. Asked him for J. data.

No mirrors this room. No use burn notes now. What hell play solitaire.

DAY 18

J.'s data arrived. I read them, instead of writing, small respite. After a few pages my writing starts to look like shorthand. If u cn rd ths u cn gt gd jb phys.

There are several pages of handwritten notes, folded around a pen-recorder strip; they do not seem to have been opened and refolded. The notes describe an absurdly simple experiment, requiring eighty seconds at the C assembly. Such an elementary measurement, I understand why he did not tell the rest of us. He can hardly have believed it himself.

Yet here is the strip trace. Pure theory has mended that which was broken.

Ladies and gentlemen and the rest of you, I report the success of the Project.

I keep staring at a spike on the strip chart, twelve seconds before the experiment ends.

Twelve seconds.

Why, this is Hell, nor am I out of it.

DAY 19

Could not walk to toilet. Threw up on floor. Bloody runs too what blood Ive got. Back to bed. Tubes in again.

Pulled my hair, would it fall? Yes.

I need help.

DAY 20

I am better today, in the local-relative sense.

J. came, as I thought he would. Not the brainless idiot, but J. young and clever and full of physics and vinegar. He was holding a vacuum tube in both hands, twirling it as we talked; it was whole and without seam. He told me just what he had done with the thermocouples, taking his eighty seconds' readings; he had known that to stop before 80 seconds would ruin the whole reading.

Then Y. came in, older than before but lovely in her maturity.

Finally N. joined us, a little diffident at first, but there was still enough love in him for many men, and now, he said his children had forgiven him.

And would they forgive me? I asked.

But of course dreams always end before the desired revelation.

A. came in the morning, worried sick that I might leave his work a-dangle. He even offered to bring his stenographer if I could no longer write, a stupid offer given my speaking endurance but well-meant.

I told him what J. had been (ahem) about to discover in the C cavity. I saw his eyes widen. I told him what he would have to do, what he would need. I told him to be careful, setting the switches in Control Bank 7.

I gave him J.'s notes, with my erasures and changes (thanks given for all these identical notebooks and pencils).

When he had gone, I asked the nurses for something to eat, and they brought me some chicken stew. It tasted wonderful, even between bites of J.'s data strip.

DAY 21

Only visitor last night was my dinner. (Dessert unreadable, good.) Bad day. Nausea and worse. Death, diet, or anticipation? A. must be at work. *Must.* Theory cannot save us now. Only experiment.

DAY 22

I seem to have been granted a little strength and lucidity, here at the end. I will try to use it well. I doubt that there will be any entries to follow this one.

When the Project was first conceived, we had J., of course, and A., mistrusting each other at every step of the planning. One would suggest a name for the staff, and then the other would deliberate long and offer another, as if they were playing chess. This when we had no idea how many of the names were still alive, let alone available to us.

And—this is important—none of this distrust had anything to do with security, or even with the goals of the Project. For us, then, the goal of the Project was to do physics. We were fighting for our respective views of what (and who) made good physics.

That was all.

When I stood behind the thick glass of the Surface Station, watching the armored battery-wagons bring Y., when she stepped through the airlock, removed her heavy helmet, and looked up at the filtered sun—I swear by whatever God is left, all I thought at the time was that *now* we could test hypotheses as we were made to do.

I seem to be crying. I wonder why. It is funny. Sweet hypothesis, sweet mystery of life.

To tell another great joke: the Project was often compared (usually by A., in the presence of the soldiers) to those Projects that came before, but the analogy is very bad. They had worked in a violent but essentially untouched world, toward a goal they could never be certain was there. We worked not toward their goal—which we knew only too well was there—but toward a sort of reaction engineering which could be made to work in a world blasted to poison junk, with a barrier dropped for God's own half-life between us and our old equipment, our old materials, our old selves; a potential-barrier too high for any of the surviving particles to cross.

To that end, we—*I*—assembled J., who could theorize around junk; Y., who could build from junk; N., who could translate among all the various junks; and myself for binder. Three quarks and a gluon. Only this unit, this primary particle, could achieve the Project's purpose. That is why I assembled it, in Room 18. That much I know.

But having brought the masses together, did I intend that they react, or be kept from reacting? Heat of fusion and heat of disassociation differ only in degree, ha, ha. Perhaps I wanted both results; but Schrödinger's cat cannot be alive and dead at once. That is the essence of the paradox.

I do not know what I wanted. Thoughts are all washed away in radiation, and now there is no time to reconstruct them: a doom I now propose to visit upon the Project itself.

Tomorrow, when A. does the experiment I detailed to him, and throws a certain set of switches, and Rig, room, workers, data, yea, all which it inherit, are vanished into incandescent air, the Project will be over for a while. Not forever, because the laws of physics wait patiently for the discoverer, but perhaps long enough for the people here to know better what they want of the laws.

And time is all we can ever win against death. See how I have stolen the days.

The survivors of tomorrow's accident will search and search and never find who welded the safeties down, and set the explosives, and wired destruction into Bank 7 of the Rig controls. It could not, after all, have been a bloodless corpse bound in white linen.

But I was not dead when I did the work, four years ago, when the Project began. Maybe I knew then what I wanted, the actual few deaths instead of the hypothetical many; but if so why did I never set those switches myself?

Perhaps I still fail: A. may be a better physicist, or a better coward, than I think. One cannot do nothing and expect to triumph. To do nothing is the triumph of evil (or words to that effect).

And yet. Reactions require a moderator as well as an initiator, and there indeed was a reaction in Room 18. Because it was N., the Project's voice, who deeper than did plummet sound drowned his books, and himself, and all of us. While my beloved J., who loved Physics alone, stood in the open shutters for the twelve seconds he needed to make the Project succeed.

Fusion. Disassociation. In the end we are all heat.

Whatever I have done, I can do no more. I will let go now, as I believe Y. did, and I will see if there is sunlight. Whatever happens tomorrow, there will be a crowd of ghosts in my room, calling me to answer, and I cannot face any of them except as one myself.

DAY 23

Light. triumph

DOLPHIN'S WAY

Gordon R. Dickson

Gordon R. Dickson says: "I write philosophical fiction with a strongly thematic argument expressed within it by original mythic elements . . . these elements are embodied in a firmly-structured dramatic story." He is a master of the genre conventions of science fiction and has been known as a leading sf adventure writer since the 1950s. His major work has been the novels and stories of the "Childe Cycle," begun in the 1950s and still in progress (of which the most famous work is the novel *Dorsai!*, 1959, revised 1976), based upon a complex thesis concerning the future evolution of the human race and society. As such, his major fiction is more nearly comparable to the fiction of James Blish than to the work of his friend and sometime collaborator, Poul Anderson, though Dickson writes firmly in the Campbell (and Heinlein) tradition. Many of his more than one hundred short stories have appeared in *Astounding/Analog*, and his bent for history, friendly aliens, and pastoral settings (even on distant planets) link him to his neighbor for nearly forty years, Clifford D. Simak, who always questioned the Campbellian doctrine of human superiority. Yet, ironically, the supermen of his Dorsai books are not only humans but Scots (like Dickson, like Campbell) of the future.

"Dolphin's Way" stands halfway between Simak's "Desertion" and Kate Wilhelm's "The Planners," in the tradition of stories concerned with animal experimentation, intelligence, and communication. It shows Dickson using images of cutting-edge science (experiments with dolphin intelligence in the early sixties) and juxtaposing issues of contact with aliens constantly raised in the hard sf of the previous decades (as in Murray Leinster's "First Contact," and many others) for final ironic contrast. Harlan Ellison calls it "a story of such emotional originality that it easily commends itself to the attention of any English professor seeking a model for the perfect modern short story." Clean, precise, powerful, it is one of Dickson's finest stories.

Of course, there was no reason why a woman coming to Dolphin's Way—as the late Dr. Edwin Knight had named the island research station—should not be beautiful. But Mal had never expected such a thing to happen.

Castor and Pollux had not come to the station pool this morning. They might have left the station, as other wild dolphins had in the past—and Mal nowadays carried always with him the fear that the Willernie Foundation would seize on some excuse to cut off their funds for further research. Ever since Corwin Brayt had taken over, Mal had known this fear. Though Brayt had said nothing. It was only a feeling Mal got from the presence of the tall, cold man. So it was that Mal was out in front of the station, scanning the ocean when the water-taxi from the mainland brought the visitor.

She stepped out on the dock, as he stared down at her. She waved as if she knew him, and then climbed the stairs from the dock to the terrace in front of the door to the main building of the station.

"Hello," she said, smiling as she stopped in front of him. "You're Corwin Brayt?"

Mal was suddenly sharply conscious of his own lean and ordinary appearance in contrast to her startling beauty. She was brown-haired and tall for a girl—but these things did not describe her. There was a perfection to her—and her smile stirred him strangely.

"No," he said. "I'm Malcolm Sinclair. Corwin's inside."

"I'm Jane Wilson," she said. "*Background Monthly* sent me out to do a story on the dolphins. Do you work with them?"

"Yes," Mal said. "I started with Dr. Knight in the beginning."

"Oh, good," she said. "Then, you can tell me some things. You were here when Dr. Brayt took charge after Dr. Knight's death?"

"Mr. Brayt," he corrected automatically. "Yes." The emotion she moved in him was so deep and strong it seemed she must feel it too. But she gave no sign.

"Mr. Brayt?" she echoed. "Oh. How did the staff take to him?"

"Well," said Mal, wishing she would smile again, "everyone took to him."

"I see," she said. "He's a good research head?"

"A good administrator," said Mal. "He's not involved in the research end."

"He's not?" She stared at him. "But didn't he replace Dr. Knight, after Dr. Knight's death?"

"Why, yes," said Mal. He made an effort to bring his attention back to the conversation. He had never had a woman affect him like this before. "But just as administrator of the station, here. You see—most of our funds for work here come from the Willernie Foundation. They had faith in Dr. Knight, but when he died . . . well, they wanted someone of their own in charge. None of us mind."

"Willernie Foundation," she said. "I don't know it."

"It was set up by a man named Willernie, in St. Louis, Missouri," said Mal. "He made his money manufacturing kitchen utensils. When he died he left a trust and set up the Foundation to encourage basic research." Mal smiled. "Don't ask me how he got from kitchen utensils to that. That's not much information for you, is it?"

"It's more than I had a minute ago," she smiled back. "Did you know Corwin Brayt before he came here?"

"No." Mal shook his head. "I don't know many people outside the biological and zoological fields."

"I imagine you know him pretty well now, though, after the six months he's been in charge."

"Well—" Mal hesitated, "I wouldn't say I know him *well*, at all. You see, he's up here in the office all day long and I'm down with Pollux and Castor—the two wild dolphins we've got coming to the station, now. Corwin and I don't see each other much."

"On this small island?"

"I suppose it seems funny—but we're both pretty busy."

"I guess you would be," she smiled again. "Will you take me to him?"

"Him?" Mal awoke suddenly to the fact they were still standing on the terrace. "Oh, yes—it's Corwin you came to see."

"Not just Corwin," she said. "I came to see the whole place."

"Well, I'll take you in to the office. Come along."

He led her across the terrace and in through the front door into the air-conditioned coolness of the interior. Corwin Brayt ran the air-conditioning constantly, as if his own somewhat icy personality demanded the dry, distant coldness of a mountain atmosphere. Mal led Jane Wilson down a short corridor and through another door into a large wide-windowed office. A tall, slim, broad-shouldered man with black hair and a brown, coldly handsome face looked up from a large desk, and got to his feet on seeing Jane.

"Corwin," said Mal. "This is Miss Jane Wilson from *Background Monthly.*"

"Yes," said Corwin expressionlessly to Jane, coming around the desk to them. "I got a wire yesterday you were coming." He did not wait for Jane to offer her hand, but offered his own. Their fingers met.

"I've got to be getting down to Castor and Pollux," said Mal, turning away.

"I'll see you later then," Jane said, looking over at him.

"Why, yes. Maybe—" he said. He went out. As he closed the door of Brayt's office behind him, he paused for a moment in the dim, cool hallway, and shut his eyes. *Don't be a fool,* he told himself, *a girl like that can do a lot better than someone like you. And probably has already.*

He opened his eyes and went back down to the pool behind the station and nonhuman world of the dolphins.

When he got there, he found that Castor and Pollux were back. Their pool was an open one, with egress to the open blue waters of the Caribbean. In the first days of the research at Dolphin's Way, the dolphins had been confined in a closed pool like any captured wild animal. It was only later on, when the work at the station had come up against what Knight had called "the environmental barrier" that the notion was conceived of opening the pool to the sea, so that the dolphins they had been working with could leave or stay, as they wished.

They had left—but they had come back. Eventually, they had left for good. But strangely, wild dolphins had come from time to time to take their place, so that there were always dolphins at the station.

Castor and Pollux were the latest pair. They had showed up some four months ago after a single dolphin frequenting the station had disappeared. Free, independent—they had been most cooperative. But the barrier had not been breached.

Now, they were sliding back and forth past each other underwater utilizing the full thirty-yard length of the pool, passing beside, over and under each other, their seven-foot nearly identical bodies almost, but not quite, rubbing as they passed. The tape showed them to be talking together up in the supersonic range, eighty to a hundred and twenty kilocycles per second. Their pattern of movement in the water now was something he had never seen before. It was regular and ritualistic as a dance.

He sat down and put on the earphones connected to the hydrophones, underwater at each end of the pool. He spoke into the microphone, asking them about their movements, but they ignored him and kept on with the patterned swimming.

The sound of footsteps behind him made him turn. He saw Jane Wilson approaching down the concrete steps from the back door of the station, with the stocky, overalled, figure of Pete Adant, the station mechanic.

"Here he is," said Pete, as they came up. "I've got to get back, now."

"Thank you." She gave Pete the smile that had so moved Mal earlier. Pete turned and went back up the steps. She turned to Mal. "Am I interrupting something?"

"No." He took off the earphones. "I wasn't getting any answers, anyway."

She looked at the two dolphins in their underwater dance with the liquid surface swirling above them as they turned now this way, now that, just under it.

"Answers?" she said. He smiled a little ruefully.

"We call them answers," he said. He nodded at the two smoothly streamlined shapes turning in the pool. "Sometimes we can ask questions and get responses."

"Informative responses?" she asked.

"Sometimes. You wanted to see me about something?"

"About everything," she said. "It seems you're the man I came to talk to—not Brayt. He sent me down here. I understand you're the one with the theory."

"Theory?" he said warily, feeling his heart sink inside him.

"The notion, then," she said. "The idea that, if there is some sort of interstellar civilization, it might be waiting for the people of Earth to qualify themselves before making contact. And that test might not be a technological one like developing a faster-than-light means of travel, but a sociological one—"

"Like learning to communicate with an alien culture—a culture like that of the dolphins," he interrupted harshly. "Corwin told you this?"

"I'd heard about it before I came," she said. "I'd thought it was Brayt's theory, though."

"No," said Mal, "it's mine." He looked at her. "You aren't laughing."

"Should I laugh?" she said. She was attentively watching the dolphins' movements. Suddenly he felt sharp jealously of them for holding her attention; and the emotion pricked him to something he might not otherwise have had the courage to do.

"Fly over to the mainland with me," he said, "and have lunch. I'll tell you all about it."

"All right." She looked up from the dolphins at him at last and he was surprised to see her frowning. "There's a lot I don't understand," she murmured. "I thought it was Brayt I had to learn about. But it's you—and the dolphins."

"Maybe we can clear that up at lunch, too," Mal said, not quite clear what she meant, but not greatly caring, either. "Come on, the helicopters are around the north side of the building."

They flew a copter across to Carúpano, and sat down to lunch looking out at the shipping in the open roadstead of the azure sea before the town, while the polite Spanish of Venezuelan voices sounded from the tables around them.

"Why should I laugh at your theory?" she said again, when they were settled, and eating lunch.

"Most people take it to be a crackpot excuse for our failure at the station," he said.

Her brown arched brows rose. "Failure?" she said. "I thought you were making steady progress."

"Yes. And no," he said. "Even before Dr. Knight died, we ran into something he called the environmental barrier."

"Environmental barrier?"

"Yes." Mal poked with his fork at the shrimp in his seafood cocktail. "This work of ours all grew out of the work done by Dr. John Lilly. You read his book, *Man and Dolphin*?"

"No," she said. He looked at her, surprised.

"He was the pioneer in this research with dolphins," Mal said. "I'd have thought reading his book would have been the first thing you would have done before coming down here."

"The first thing I did," she said, "was try to find out something about Corwin Brayt. And I was pretty unsuccessful at that. That's why I landed here with the notion that it was he, not you, who was the real worker with the dolphins."

"That's why you asked me if I knew much about him?"

"That's right," she answered. "But tell me about this environmental barrier."

"There's not a great deal to tell," he said. "Like most big problems, it's simple enough to state. At first, in working with the dolphins, it seemed the early researchers were going great guns, and communication was just around the corner—a matter of interpreting the sounds they made to each other, in the humanly audible range, and above it; and teaching the dolphins human speech."

"It turned out those things couldn't be done?"

"They could. They were done—or as nearly so as makes no difference. But then we came up against the fact that communication doesn't mean understanding." He looked at her. "You and I talk the same language, but do we really understand perfectly what the other person means when he speaks to us?"

She looked at him for a moment, and then slowly shook her head without taking her eyes off his face.

"Well," said Mal, "that's essentially our problem with the dolphins—only on a much larger scale. Dolphins, like Castor and Pollux, can talk with me, and I with them, but we can't understand each other to any great degree."

"You mean intellectually understood, don't you?" Jane said. "Not just mechanically?"

"That's right," Mal answered. "We agree on denotation of an auditory or other symbol, but not on connotation. I can say to Castor—'*the Gulf Stream is a strong ocean current*' and he'll agree exactly. But neither of us really has the slightest idea of what the other really means. My mental image of the Gulf Stream is not Castor's image. My notion of 'powerful' is relative to the fact I'm six feet tall, weigh a hundred and seventy-five pounds and can lift my own weight against the force of gravity. Castor's is relative to the fact that he is seven feet long, can speed up to forty miles an hour through the water, and as far as he knows weighs nothing, since his four hundred pounds of body-weight are balanced out by the equal weight of the water he displaces. And the concept of lifting something is all but unknown to him. My mental abstraction of 'ocean' is not his, and our ideas of what a current is may coincide, or be literally worlds apart in meaning. And so far we've found no way of bridging the gap between us."

"The dolphins have been trying as well as you?"

"I believe so," said Mal. "But I can't prove it. Any more than I can really prove the dolphin's intelligence to hard-core skeptics until I can come up with something previously outside human knowledge that the dolphins have taught me. Or have them demonstrate that they've learned the use of some human intellectual process. And in these things we've all failed—because, as I believe and Dr. Knight believed, of the connotative gap, which is a result of the environmental barrier."

She sat watching him. He was probably a fool to tell her all this, but he had had no one to talk to like this since Dr. Knight's heart attack, eight months before, and he felt words threatening to pour out of him.

"We've got to learn to think like the dolphins," he said, "or the dolphins have to learn to think like us. For nearly six years now we've been trying and neither side's succeeded." Almost before he thought, he added the one thing he had been determined to keep to himself. "I've been afraid our research funds will be cut off any day now."

"Cut off? By the Willernie Foundation?" she said. "Why would they do that?"

"Because we haven't made any progress for so long," Mal said bitterly. "Or, at least, no provable progress. I'm afraid time's just about run out. And if it runs out, it may never be picked up again. Six years ago, there was a lot of popular interest in the dolphins. Now, they've been discounted and forgotten, shelved as merely bright animals."

"You can't be sure the research won't be picked up again."

"But I feel it," he said. "It's part of my notion about the ability to communicate with an alien race being the test for us humans. I feel we've got this one chance and if we flub it, we'll never have another." He pounded the table softly with his fist. "The worst of it is, I *know* the dolphins are trying just as hard to get through from their side—if I could only recognize what they're doing, how they're trying to make me understand!"

Jane had been sitting watching him.

"You seem pretty sure of that," she said. "What makes you so sure?"

He unclenched his fist and forced himself to sit back in his chair.

"Have you ever looked into the jaws of a dolphin?" he said. "They're this long." He spread his hands apart in the air to illustrate. "And each pair of jaws contains eighty-eight sharp teeth. Moreover, a dolphin like Castor weighs several hundred pounds and can move at water speeds that are almost incredible to a human. He could crush you easily by ramming you against the side of a tank, if he didn't want to tear you apart with his teeth, or break your bones with blows of his flukes." He looked at her grimly. "In spite of all this, in spite of the fact that men have caught and killed dolphins—even we killed them in our early, fumbling researches, and dolphins are quite capable of using their teeth and strength on marine enemies—no dolphin has ever been known to attack a human being. Aristotle, writing in the Fourth Century B.C., speaks of the quote gentle and kindly end quote nature of the dolphin."

He stopped, and looked at Jane sharply.

"You don't believe me," he said.

"Yes," she said. "Yes, I do." He took a deep breath.

"I'm sorry," he said. "I've made the mistake of mentioning all this before to other people and been sorry I did. I told this to one man who gave me his opinion that it indicated that the dolphin instinctively recognized human superiority and the value of human life." Mal grinned at her, harshly. "But it was just an instinct. '*Like dogs*,' he said. '*Dogs instinctively admire and love people*—' and he wanted to tell me about a dachshund he'd had, named Poochie, who could read the morning newspaper and wouldn't bring it in to him if there was a tragedy reported on the front page. He could prove this, and Poochie's intelligence, by the number of times he'd had to get the paper off the front step himself."

Jane laughed. It was a low, happy laugh; and it took the bitterness suddenly out of Mal.

"Anyway," said Mal, "the dolphin's restraint with humans is just one of the indications, like the wild dolphins coming to us here at the station, that've convinced me the dolphins are trying to understand us, too. And have been, maybe, for centuries."

"I don't see why you worry about the research stopping," she said. "With all you know, can't you convince people—"

"There's only one person I've got to convince," said Mal. "And that's Corwin Brayt. And I don't think I'm doing it. It's just a feeling—but I feel as if he's sitting in judgment upon me, and the work. I feel . . ." Mal hesitated, "almost as if he's a hatchet man."

"He isn't," Jane said. "He can't be. I'll find out for you, if you like. There're ways of doing it. I'd have the answer for you right now, if I'd thought of him as an administrator. But I thought of him as a scientist, and I looked him up in the wrong places."

Mal frowned at her, unbelievingly.

"You don't actually mean you can find out that for me?" he asked.

She smiled.

"Wait and see," she replied. "I'd like to know, myself, what his background is."

"It could be important," he said, eagerly. "I know it sounds fantastic—but if I'm right, the research with the dolphins could be important, more important than anything else in the world."

She stood up suddenly from the table.

"I'll go and start checking up right now," she said.

"Why don't you go on back to the island? It'll take me a few hours and I'll take the water-taxi over."

"But you haven't finished lunch yet," he said. "In fact you haven't even started lunch. Let's eat first, then you can go."

"I want to call some people and catch them while they're still at work," she said. "It's the time difference on these long-distance calls. I'm sorry. We'll have dinner together, will that do?"

"It'll have to," he said. She melted his disappointment with one of her amazing smiles, and went.

With her gone, Mal found he was not hungry himself. He got hold of the waiter and managed to cancel the main course of their meals. He sat and had two more drinks—not something usual for him. Then he left and flew the copter back to the island.

Pete Adant encountered him as he was on his way from the copter park to the dolphin pool.

"There you are," said Pete. "Corwin wants to see you in an hour—when he gets back, that is. He's gone over to the mainland himself."

Ordinarily, such a piece of news would have awakened the foreboding about cancellation of the research that rode always like a small, cold, metal weight inside Mal. But the total of three drinks and no lunch had anesthetized him somewhat. He nodded and went on to the pool.

The dolphins were still there, still at their patterned swimming. Or was he just imagining the pattern? Mal sat down on his chair by the poolside before the tape recorder which set down a visual pattern of the sounds made by the dolphins. He put the earphones to the hydrophones on, switching on the mike before him.

Suddenly, it struck him how futile all this was. He had gone through these same motions daily for four years now. And what was the sum total of results he had to show for it? Reel on reel of tape recording a failure to hold any truly productive conversation with the dolphins.

He took the earphones off and laid them aside. He lit a cigarette and sat gazing with half-seeing eyes at the underwater ballet of the dolphins. To call it ballet was almost to libel their actions. The gracefulness, the purposefulness of their movements, buoyed up by the saltwater, was beyond that of any human in air or on land. He thought again of what he had told Jane Wilson about the dolphin's refusal to attack their human captors, even when the humans hurt or killed them. He thought of the now-established fact that dolphins will come to the rescue of one of their own who has been hurt or knocked unconscious, and hold him up on top of the water so he would not drown—the dolphin's breathing process requiring conscious control, so that it failed if the dolphin became unconscious.

He thought of their playfulness, their affection, the wide and complex range of their speech. In any of those categories, the average human stacked up beside them looked pretty poor. In the dolphin culture there was no visible impulse to war, to murder, to hatred and unkindness. No wonder, thought Mal, they and we have trouble understanding each other. In a different environment, under different conditions, they're the kind of people we've always struggled to be. We have the technology, the tool-using capability, but with it all in many ways we're more animal than they are.

Who's to judge which of us is better, he thought, looking at their movements through the water with the slight hazy melancholy induced by the three drinks on an empty stomach. I might be happier myself, if I were a dolphin. For a second, the idea seemed deeply attractive. The endless open sea, the freedom, an end to all the complex structure of human culture on land. A few lines of poetry came back to him.

"*Come Children*," he quoted out loud to himself, "*let us away! Down and away, below . . . !*"

He saw the two dolphins pause in their underwater ballet and saw that the microphone before him was on. Their heads turned toward the microphone underwater at the near end of the pool. He remembered the following lines, and he quoted them aloud to the dolphins.

"*. . . Now my brothers call from the bay,*
Now the great winds shoreward blow,
Now the salt tides seaward flow;
Now the wild white horses play,
Champ and chafe and toss in the spray—"*

He broke off suddenly, feeling self-conscious. He looked down at the dolphins. For a moment they merely hung where they were under the surface, facing the microphone. Then Castor turned and surfaced. His forehead with its blowhole broke out into the air and then his head as he looked up at Mal. His airborne voice from the blowhole's sensitive lips and muscles spoke quacking words at the human.

"*Come, Mal*," he quacked, "*Let us away! Down and away! Below!*"

The head of Pollux surfaced beside Castor's. Mal stared at them for a long second. Then he jerked his gaze back to the tape of the recorder. There on it, was the rhythmic record of his own voice as it had sounded in the pool, and below it on their separate tracks, the tapes showed parallel, rhythms coming from the dolphins. They had been matching his speech largely in the inaudible range while he was quoting.

Still staring, Mal got to his feet, his mind trembling with a suspicion so great he hesitated to put it into words. Like a man in a daze he walked to the near end of the pool, where three steps led down into the shallower part. Here the water was only three feet deep.

"*Come, Mal!*" quacked Castor, as the two still hung in the water with their heads out, facing him. "*Let us away! Down and away! Below!*"

Step by step, Mal went down into the pool. He felt the coolness of the water wetting his pants legs, rising to his waist as he stood at last on the pool floor. A few feet in front of him, the two dolphins hung in the water, facing him, waiting.

*"The Forsaken Merman," Matthew Arnold, 1849

Standing with the water rippling lightly above his belt buckle, Mal looked at them, waiting for some sign, some signal of what they wanted him to do.

They gave him no clue. They only waited. It was up to him to go forward on his own. He sloshed forward into deeper water, put his head down, held his breath and pushed himself off underwater.

In the forefront of his blurred vision, he saw the grainy concrete floor of the pool. He glided slowly over it, rising a little, and suddenly the two dolphins were all about him—gliding over, above, around his own underwater floating body, brushing lightly against him as they passed, making him a part of their underwater dance. He heard the creaking that was one of the underwater sounds they made and knew that they were probably talking in ranges he could not hear. He could not know what they were saying, he could not sense the meaning of their movements about him, but the feeling that they were trying to convey information to him was inescapable.

He began to feel the need to breathe. He held out as long as he could, then let himself rise to the surface. He broke water and gulped air, and the two dolphin heads popped up nearby, watching him. He dove under the surface again. *I am a dolphin*—he told himself almost desperately—*I am not a man, but a dolphin, and to me all this means—what?*

Several times he dove, and each time the persistent and disciplined movements of the dolphins about him underwater convinced him more strongly that he was on the right track. He came up, blowing, at last. He was not carrying the attempt to be like them far enough, he thought. He turned and swam back to the steps at the shallow end of the pool, and began to climb out.

"*Come, Mal—let us away*!" quacked a dolphin voice behind him, and he turned to see the heads of both Castor and Pollux out of the water, regarding him with mouths open urgently.

"*Come Children—down and away*!" he repeated, as reassuringly as he could intonate the words.

He hurried up to the big cabinet of the supply locker at the near end of the pool, and opened the door of the section on skin-diving equipment. He needed to make himself more like a dolphin. He considered the air tanks and the mask of the scuba equipment, and rejected them. The dolphins could not breathe underwater any more than he could. He started jerking things out of the cabinet.

A minute or so later he returned to the steps in swimming trunks, wearing a glass mask with a snorkel tube, and swim fins on his feet. In his hand he carried two lengths of soft rope. He sat down on the steps and with the rope tied his knees and ankles together. Then, clumsily, he hopped and splashed into the water.

Lying face down in the pool, staring at the bottom through his glass faceplate, he tried to move his bound legs together like the flukes of a dolphin, to drive himself slantingly down under the surface.

After a moment or two he managed it. In a moment the dolphins were all about him as he tried to swim underwater, dolphinwise. After a little while his air ran short again and he had to surface. But he came up like a dolphin and lay on the surface filling his lungs, before fanning himself down flukefashion with his swim fins. *Think like a dolphin*, he kept repeating to himself over and over. *I am a dolphin. And this is my world. This is the way it is.*

. . . And Castor and Pollux were all about him.

The sun was setting in the far distance of the ocean when at last he dragged himself, exhausted, up the steps of the pool and sat down on the poolside. To his water-soaked body, the twilight breeze felt icy. He unbound his legs, took off his fins and mask and walked wearily to the cabinet. From the nearest compartment he took a towel and dried himself, then put on an old bathrobe he kept hanging there. He sat down in an aluminum deck chair beside the cabinet and sighed with weariness.

He looked out at the red sun dipping its lower edge in the sea, and felt a great warm sensation of achievement inside him. In the darkening pool, the two dolphins still swam back and forth. He watched the sun descending . . .

"Mal!"

The sound of Corwin Brayt's voice brought his head around. When he saw the tall, cold-faced man was coming toward him with the slim figure of Jane alongside, Mal got up quickly from his chair. They came up to him.

"Why didn't you come in to see me as I asked?" Brayt said. "I left word for you with Pete. I didn't even know you were back from the mainland until the water-taxi brought Miss Wilson out just now, and she told me."

"I'm sorry," said Mal. "I think I've run into something here—"

"Never mind telling me now." Brayt's voice was hurried and sharpened with annoyance. "I had a good deal to speak to you about but there's not time now if I'm to catch the mainland plane to St. Louis. I'm sorry to break it this way—" He checked himself and turned to Jane. "Would you excuse us, Miss Wilson? Private business. If you'll give us a second—"

"Of course," she said. She turned and walked away from them alongside the pool, into the deepening twilight. The dolphins paced her in the water. The sun was just down now, and with the sudden oncoming of tropical night, stars could be seen overhead.

"Just let me tell you," said Mal. "It's about the research."

"I'm sorry," said Brayt. "There's no point in your telling me now. I'll be gone a week and I want you to watch out for this Jane Wilson, here." He lowered his voice slightly. "I talked to *Background Monthly* on the phone this afternoon, and the editor I spoke to there didn't know about the article, or recognize her name—"

"Somebody new," said Mal. "Probably someone who didn't know her."

"At any rate it makes no difference," said Brayt. "As I say, I'm sorry to tell you in such a rushed fashion, but Willernie has decided to end its grant of funds to the station. I'm flying to St. Louis to settle details." He hesitated. "I'm sure you knew something like this was coming, Mal." Mal stared, shocked.

"It was inevitable," said Brayt coldly. "You knew that." He paused. "I'm sorry."

"But the station'll fold without the Willernie support!" said Mal, finding his voice. "You know that. And just today I found out what the answer is! Just this afternoon! Listen to me!" He caught Brayt's arm as the other started to turn away. "The dolphins have been trying to contact us. Oh, not at first, not when we experimented with captured specimens. But since we opened the pool to the sea. The only trouble was we insisted on trying to communicate by sound alone—and that's all but impossible for them."

"Excuse me," said Brayt, trying to disengage his arm.

"Listen, will you!" said Mal, desperately. "Their communication process is an incredibly rich one. It's as if you and I communicated by using all the instruments in a symphony orchestra. They not only use sound from four to a hundred and fifty kilocycles per second, they use movement, and touch—and all of it in reference to the ocean conditions surrounding them at the moment."

"I've got to go."

"Just a minute. Don't you remember what Lilly hypothecated about the dolphin's methods of navigation? He suggested that it was a multivariable method, using temperature, speed, taste of the water, position of the stars, sun and so forth, all fed into their brains simultaneously and instantaneously. Obviously, it's true, and obviously their process of communication is also a multivariable method utilizing sound, touch, position, place and movement. Now that we know this, we can go into the sea with them and try to operate across their whole spectrum of communication. No wonder we weren't able to get across anything but the most primitive exchanges, restricting ourselves to sound. It's been equivalent to restricting human communication to just the nouns in each sentence, while maintaining the sentence structure—"

"I'm very sorry!" said Brayt, firmly. "I tell you, Mal. None of this makes any difference. The decision of the Foundation is based on financial reasons. They've got just so much money available to donate, and this station's allotment has already gone in other directions. There's nothing that can be done, now."

He pulled his arm free.

"I'm sorry," he said again. "I'll be back in a week at the outside. You might be thinking of how to wind up things, here."

He turned with that, and went away, around the building toward the parking spot of the station copters. Mal, stunned, watched the tall, slim, broad-shouldered figure move off into darkness.

"It doesn't matter," said the gentle voice of Jane comfortingly at his ear. He jerked about and saw her facing him. "You won't need the Willernie funds any more."

"He told you?" Mal stared at her as she shook her head, smiling in the growing dimness. "You heard? From way over there?"

"Yes," she said. "And you were right about Brayt. I got your answer for you. He was a hatchet man—sent here by the Willernie people to decide whether the station deserved further funds."

"But we've got to have them!" Mal said. "It won't take much more, but we've got to go into the sea and work out ways to talk to the dolphins in their own mode. We've got to expand to their level of communication, not try to compress them to ours. You see, this afternoon, I had a breakthrough—"

"I know," she said. "I know all about it."

"You know?" He stared at her. "How do you know?"

"You've been under observation all afternoon," she said. "You're right. You did break through the environmental barrier. From now on it's just a matter of working out methods."

"Under observation? How?" Abruptly, that seemed the least important thing at hand. "But I have to have money," he said. "It'll take time and equipment, and that costs money—"

"No." Her voice was infinitely gentle. "You won't need to work out your own methods. Your work is done, Mal. This afternoon the dolphins and you broke the bars to communication between the two races for the first time in the history of either. It was the job you set out to do and you were part of it. You can be happy knowing that."

"Happy?" He almost shouted at her, suddenly. "I don't understand what you're talking about."

"I'm sorry." There was a ghost of a sigh from her. "We'll show you how to talk to the dolphins, Mal, if men need to. As well as some other things—perhaps." Her face lifted to him under the star-marked sky, still a little light in the west. "You see, you were right about something more than dolphins, Mal. Your idea that the ability to communicate with another intelligent race, an alien race, was a test that had to be passed before the superior species of a planet could be contacted by the intelligent races of the galaxy—that was right, too."

He stared at her. She was so close to him, he could feel the living warmth of her body, although they were not touching. He saw her, he felt her, standing before him; and he felt all the strange deep upwelling of emotion that she had released in him the moment he first saw her. The deep emotion he felt for her still. Suddenly understanding came to him.

"You mean you're not from Earth—" his voice was hoarse and uncertain. It wavered to a stop. "But you're human!" he cried desperately.

She looked back at him a moment before answering. In the dimness he could not tell for sure, but he thought he saw the glisten of tears in her eyes.

"Yes," she said, at last, slowly. "In the way you mean that—you can say I'm human."

A great and almost terrible joy burst suddenly in him. It was the joy of a man who, in the moment when he thinks he has lost everything, finds something of infinitely greater value.

"But how?" he said, excitedly, a little breathlessly. He pointed up at the stars. "If you come from some place—up there? How can you be human?"

She looked down, away from his face.

"I'm sorry," she said. "I can't tell you."

"Can't tell me? Oh," he said with a little laugh, "you mean I wouldn't understand."

"No—" Her voice was almost inaudible, "I mean I'm not allowed to tell you."

"Not allowed—" he felt an unreasoning chill about his heart. "But Jane—" He broke off fumbling for words. "I don't know quite how to say this, but it's important to me to know. From the first moment I saw you there, I . . . I mean, maybe you don't feel anything like this, you don't know what I'm talking about—"

"Yes," she whispered. "I do."

"Then—" he stared at her. "You could at least say something that would set my mind at rest. I mean . . . it's only a matter of time now. We're going to be getting together, your people and I, aren't we?"

She looked up at him out of darkness.

"No," she said, "we aren't, Mal. Ever. And that's why I can't tell you anything."

"We aren't?" he cried. "We aren't? But you came and saw us communicate—Why aren't we?"

She looked up at him for the last time, then, and told him. He, having heard what she had to say, stood still; still as a stone, for there was nothing left to do. And she, turning slowly and finally away from him, went off to the edge of the pool and down the steps into the shallow water, where the dolphins came rushing to meet her, their foamy tearing of the surface making a wake as white as snow.

Then the three of them moved, as if by magic, across the surface of the pool and out the entrance of it to the ocean. And so they continued to move off until they were lost to sight in darkness and the starlit, glinting surface of the waves.

It came to Mal then, as he stood there, that the dolphins must have been waiting for her all this time. All the wild dolphins, who had come to the station after the first two captives, were set free to leave or stay as they wanted. The dolphins had known, perhaps for centuries, that it was to them alone on Earth that the long-awaited visitors from the stars would finally come.

ALL THE HUES OF HELL

Gene Wolfe

Gene Wolfe's body of work in the science fiction field, along with that of Delany, Dick, and Le Guin's, is perhaps the most influential of any writer of the past two decades. Of them all, Wolfe is the one least interested in technology, most interested in the uses of pure science in his fiction. He remains interested in the use of the conventions, tropes, and images of genre sf, whereas the others moved away from them in the 1980s. Always one to envision the metaphorical possibilities of scientific ideas and images, Wolfe's fiction is so rich and evocative, his style so precise and complex, that much of his influence has been stylistic. His emulators, such as Paul Park, rarely embed as much science in their fiction as he does. Wolfe's characters are often not interested in, or aware of, the idea behind the story; they are more often concerned with metaphysics, or solving problems of everyday survival. He seldom uses the conventional problem-solving structure of Campbellian sf, so his stories rarely have the overt affect of hard sf. It is therefore often a challenge to the reader to perceive the scientific ideas of which the characters in the text are unaware.

"All the Hues of Hell" is a story in which theoretical physics and metaphysics combine. It has, initially, the ring of a familiar hard sf situation: three characters on a ship in space approaching an alien planet, one of them mad—or dead. Quickly the story becomes mysterious, ambiguous, and disturbing. The abstract concepts of theoretical physics are made manifest, the shadow matter (which is possibly the dark matter that makes up a significant portion of our universe) that is a feature of superstring theory is literally explored in a manner reminiscent of mathematical fictions such as *Flatland*, Norman Kagan's classic "The Mathenauts," or Greg Bear's "Tangents," all stories that take one to new places. Technical imagery, such as color enhancement, becomes freighted with rich metaphorical depth. And the powerful ending, reminiscent of the ending of Arthur C. Clarke's *2001: A Space Odyssey*, demands a reconsideration of all the previous literal and psychological coordinates of the piece. This is a big-idea story, and the scale (and meaning) increases as the plot twists and resolves.

Three with egg roll, Kyle thought. Soon four without—if this shadow world really has (oh, sacred!) life. The *Egg* was still rolling, still spinning to provide mock gravitation.

Yet the roar of the sharply angled guidance jets now seeped only faintly into the hold, and the roll was slower and slower, the feeling of weight weaker and weaker.

The *Egg* was in orbit . . . around nothing.

Or at least around nothing visible. As its spin decreased, its ports swept the visible universe. Stars that were in fact galaxies flowed down the synthetic quartz like raindrops down a canopy. Once Kyle caught sight of their mother ship; the *Shadow Show* herself looked dim and ghostly in the faint light. Of the planet they orbited, there was no trace. Polyaris screamed and took off, executing a multicolored barrel roll with outstretched wings through the empty hold; like all macaws, Polyaris doted on microgravity.

In his earphones Marilyn asked, "Isn't it pretty, Ky?" But she was admiring her computer simulation, not his ecstatic bird: an emerald forest three hundred meters high, sparkling sapphire lakes—suddenly a vagrant strip of beach golden as her hair, and the indigo southern ocean.

One hundred and twenty degrees opposed to them both, Skip answered instead, and not as Kyle himself would have. "No, it isn't." There was a note in Skip's voice that Kyle had noticed, and worried over, before.

Marilyn seemed to shrug. "Okay, darling, it's not really anything to us, less even than ultraviolet. But—"

"I can see it," Skip told her.

Marilyn glanced across the empty hold toward Kyle.

He tried to keep his voice noncommittal as he whispered to his mike. "You can see it, Skip?"

Skip did not reply. Polyaris chuckled to herself. Then silence (the utter, deadly quiet of nothingness, of the void where shadow matter ruled and writhed invisible) filled the *Egg*. For a wild instant, Kyle wondered whether silence itself might not be a manifestation of shadow matter, a dim insubstance felt only in its mass and gravity, its unseen heaviness. Galaxies drifted lazily over the ports, in a white *Egg* robbed of Up and Down. Their screens were solid sheets of deepest blue.

Skip broke the silence. "Just let me show it to you, Kyle. Allow me, Marilyn, to show you what it actually looks like."

"Because you really know, Skip?"

"Yes, because I really know, Kyle. Don't you remember, either of you, what they said?"

Kyle was watching Marilyn across the hold; he saw her shake her head. "Not all of it." Her voice was cautious. "They said so much, darling, after all. They said quite a lot of things."

Skip sounded as though he were talking to a child. "What the Life Support people said. The thing, the only *significant* thing, they did say."

Still more carefully, Marilyn asked, "And what was that, darling?"

"That one of us would die."

An island sailed across her screen, an emerald set in gold and laid upon blue velvet.

Kyle said, "That's my department, Skip. Life Support told us there was a real chance—perhaps as high as one in twenty—that one of you would die, outbound from Earth or on the trip back. They were being conservative; I would have estimated it as one in one hundred."

Marilyn murmured, "I think I'd better inform the Director."

Kyle agreed.

"And they were right," Skip said. "Kyle, I'm the one. I died on the way out. I passed away, but you two followed me."

Ocean and isle vanished from all the screens, replaced by a blinking cursor and the word DIRECTOR.

Marilyn asked, "Respiration monitor, L. Skinner Jansen."

Kyle swiveled to watch his screen. The cursor swept from side to side without any sign of inhalation or exhalation, and for a moment he was taken aback. Then Skip giggled.

Marilyn's sigh filled Kyle's receptors. "The programming wizard. What did you do, Skip? Turn down the gain?"

"That wasn't necessary. It happens automatically." Skip giggled again.

Kyle said slowly, "You're not dead, Skip. Believe me, I've seen many dead men. I've cut up their bodies and examined every organ; I know dead men, and you're not one of them."

"Back on the ship, Kyle. My former physical self is lying in the *Shadow Show*, dead."

Marilyn said, "Your physical self is right here, darling, with Ky and me." And then to the Director, "Sir, is L. Skinner Jansen's module occupied?"

The trace vanished, replaced by NEGATIVE: JANSEN 1'S MODULE IS EMPTY.

"Console," Skip himself ordered.

Kyle did not turn to watch Skip's fingers fly across the keys.

After a moment Skip said, "You see, this place—the formal name of our great republic is Hades, by the way—looks the way it does only because of the color gradiations you assigned the gravimeter data. I'm about to show you its true colors, as the expression has it."

A blaze of four-point-five, six, and seven-point-eight ten-thousandths millimeter light, Polyaris fluttered away to watch Skip. When he made no attempt to shoo her off, she perched on a red emergency lever and cocked an eye like a bright black button toward his keyboard.

Kyle turned his attention back to his screen. The letters faded, leaving only the blue southern ocean. As he watched, it darkened to sable. Tiny flames of ocher, citron, and cinnabar darted from the crests of the waves.

"See what I mean?" Skip asked. "We've been sent to bring a demon back to Earth—or maybe just a damned soul. I don't care. I'm going to stay right here."

Kyle looked across the vacant white hold toward Marilyn.

"I can't," she whispered. "I just can't, Ky. You do it."

"All right, Marilyn." He plugged his index finger into the Exchange socket, so that he sensed rather than saw the letters overlaying the hellish sea on the screens: KAPPA UPSILON LAMBDA 23011 REPORTS JANSEN 1 PSYCHOTIC. CAN YOU CONFIRM, JANSEN 2?

"Confirmed, Marilyn Jansen."

RESTRAINT ADVISED.

Marilyn said, "I'm afraid restraint's impossible as long as we're in the *Egg*, sir."

DO NOT ABORT YOUR MISSION, JANSEN 2. WILL YOU ACCEPT THE RESTRAINT OF JANSEN 1 WHEN RESTRAINT IS PRACTICAL?

"Accepted whenever practical," Marilyn said. "Meanwhile, we'll proceed with the mission."

SATISFACTORY, the Director said, and signed off.

Skip asked, "So you're going to lock me up, honeybone?"

"I hope that by the time we get back it won't be necessary. Ky, haven't you anything to give him?"

"No specifics for psychosis, Marilyn. Not here. I've got some back on the *Shadow Show*."

Skip ruffled his beard. "Sure. You're going to lock up a ghost." Across the wide hold, Kyle could see he was grinning.

Polyaris picked up the word: "Ghost! *Ghost! GHOST!*" She flapped to the vacant center of the *Egg*, posing like a heraldic eagle and watching to make certain they admired her.

The shoreline of a larger island entered their screens from the right. Its beach was ashes and embers, its forest a forest of flames.

"If we're going to make the grab, Marilyn . . ."

"You're right," she said. Courageously, she straightened her shoulders. The new life within her had already fleshed out her cheeks and swollen her breasts; Kyle felt sure that she had never been quite so lovely before. When she put on her helmet, he breathed her name (though only to himself) before he plugged into the simulation that seemed so much more real than a screen.

As a score of pink arms, Marilyn's grav beams dipped into the shadow planet's atmosphere, growing dark and heavy as they pulled up shadow fluid and gases from a lake on the island and whatever winds might ruffle it. Kyle reflected that those arms should be blue instead of black, and told the onboard assistant director to revert to the hues Marilyn had originally programmed.

Rej, the assistant director snapped.

And nothing happened. The gravs grew darker still, and the big accelerator jets grumbled at the effort required to maintain *Egg* in orbit. When Kyle glanced toward the hold, he discovered it had acquired a twelve-meter yolk as dark as the eggs Chinese bury for centuries. Polyaris was presumably somewhere in that black yolk, unable to see or feel it. He gave a shrill whistle, and she screamed and fluttered out to perch on his shoulder.

The inky simulation doubled and redoubled, swirling to the turbulence of the fresh shadow matter pumped into the *Egg* by the gravs. Generators sang the spell that kept the shadow "air" and "water" from boiling away in what was to them a high vacuum.

The grumbling of the jets rose to an angry roar.

Skip said, "You've brought Hell in here with us, honeybone. You, not me. Remember that."

Marilyn ignored him, and Kyle told him to keep quiet.

Abruptly the gravitors winked out. A hundred tons or more of the shadow world's water (whatever that might be) fell back to the surface, fully actual to any conscious entity that might be there. "Rains of frogs and fish, Polyaris," Kyle muttered to his bird. "Remember Charlie Fort?"

Polyaris chuckled, nodding.

Skip said, "Then remember too that when Moses struck the Nile with his staff, the Lord God turned the water to blood."

"You're the one who got into the crayon box, Skip. I'll call you Moses if you like, but I can hardly call you 'I Am,' after you've just assured us you're not." Kyle was following Marilyn's hunt for an example of the dominant life form, less than a tenth of his capacity devoted to Polyaris and Skip.

"You will call me *Master!*"

Kyle grinned, remembering the holovamp of an ancient film. "No, Skip. For as long as you're ill, I am the master. Do you know I've been waiting half my life to use that line?"

Then he saw it, three-quarters of a second, perhaps, after Marilyn had: an upright figure striding down a fiery beach. Its bipedal locomotion was not a complete guarantee of dominance and intelligence, to be sure; ostriches had never ruled a world and never would, no matter how big a pest they became on Mars. But—yes—those powerful forelimbs were surely GP manipulators and not mere weapons. *Now, Marilyn! Now!*

As though she had heard him, a pink arm flicked down. For an instant the shadow man floated, struggling wildly to escape, the gravitation of his shadow world countered by their gravitor; then he flashed toward them. Kyle swiveled to watch the black sphere splash (there could be no other word for it) and, under the prodding of the gravs, recoalesce. They were four.

In a moment more, their shadow man bobbed to the surface of the dark and still trembling yolk. To him, Kyle reflected, they were not there, the *Egg* was not there. To him it must seem that he floated upon a watery sphere suspended in space.

And possibly that was more real than the computer-enhanced vision he himself inhabited, a mere cartoon created from one of the weakest forces known to physics. He unplugged, and at once the *Egg*'s hold was white and empty again.

Marilyn took off her helmet. "All right, Ky, from here on it's up to you—unless you want something more from the surface?"

Kyle congratulated her and shook his head.

"Darling, are you feeling any better?"

Skip said levelly, "I'm okay now. I think that damned machine must have drugged me."

"Ky? That seems pretty unlikely."

"We should de-energize or destroy him, if we can't revise his programming."

Marilyn shook her head. "I doubt that we could reprogram him. Ky, what do you think?"

"A lot of it's hard wired, Marilyn, and can't be altered without new boards. I imagine Skip could revise my software if he put his mind to it, though it might take him quite a while. He's very good at that sort of thing."

Skip said, "And you're a very dangerous device, Kyle."

Shaking his head, Kyle broke out the pencil-thin cable he had used so often in training exercises. One end jacked into the console, the other into a small socket just above his hips. When both connections were made, he was again in the cybernetic cartoon where true matter and shadow matter looked equally real.

It was still a cartoon with colors by Skip: Marilyn's skin shone snow-white, her lips were burning scarlet, her hair like burnished brass, and her eyes blue fire; Skip himself had become a black-bearded satyr, with a terra-cotta complexion and cruel crimson lips. Kyle tightened both ferrules firmly, tested his jets, released his safety harness, and launched himself toward the center of the *Egg*, making Polyaris crow with delight.

The shadow man drifted into view as they neared the black yolk. He was lying upon what Kyle decided must be his back; on the whole he was oddly anthropomorphic, with recognizable head, neck, and shoulders. Binocular organs of vision seemed to have vanished behind small folds of skin, and Kyle would have called his respiration rapid in a human.

Marilyn asked, "How does he look, Ky?"

"Like hell," Kyle muttered. "I'm afraid he may be in shock. At least, shock's what I'd say if he were one of you. As it is, I . . ." He let the sentence trail away.

There were strange, blunt projections just above the organs that appeared to be the shadow man's ears. Absently, Kyle tried to palpate them; his hand met nothing, and vanished as it passed into the shadow man's cranium.

The shadow man opened his eyes.

Kyle jerked backward, succeeding only in throwing himself into a slow spin that twisted his cable.

Marilyn called, "What's the matter, Ky?"

"Nothing," Kyle told her. "I'm jumpy, that's all."

The shadow man's eyes were closed again. His arms, longer than a human's and more muscled than a body builder's, twitched and were still. Kyle began the minute examination required by the plan.

When it was complete, Skip asked, "How'd it go, Kyle?"

He shrugged. "I couldn't see his back. The way you've got the shadow water keyed, it's like ink."

Marilyn said, "Why don't you change it, Skip? Make it blue but translucent, the way it's supposed to be."

Skip sounded apologetic. "I've been trying to; I've been trying to change everything back. I can't, or anyway not yet. I don't remember just what I did, but I put some kind of block on it."

Kyle shrugged again. "Keep trying, Skip, please."

"Yes, please try, darling. Now buckle up, everybody. Time to rendezvous."

Kyle disconnected his cable and pulled his harness around him. After a moment's indecision, he plugged into the console as well.

If he had been unable to see it, it would have been easy to believe that *Egg*'s acceleration had no effect on the fifty-meter sphere of dark matter at its center; yet that too was mass, and the gravs whimpered like children at the strain of changing its speed and direction, their high wail audible—to Kyle at least—above the roaring of the jets. The black sphere stretched into a sooty tear. Acceleration was agony for Polyaris as well; Kyle cupped her fragile body in his free hand to ease her misery as much as he could.

Somewhere so far above the *Egg* that the gravity well of the shadow planet had almost ceased to make any difference and words like *above* held little meaning, the *Shadow Show* was unfolding to receive them, preparing itself to embed the newly fertilized *Egg* in an inner wall. For a moment Kyle's thoughts soared, drunk on the beauty of the image.

Abruptly the big jets fell silent. The *Egg* had achieved escape velocity.

Marilyn returned control of *Egg* to the assistant director. "That's it, folks, until we start guiding in. Unbuckle if you want."

Kyle tossed Polyaris toward the yolk and watched her make a happy circuit of the *Egg*'s interior.

Skip said, "Marilyn, I seem to have a little problem here."

"What is it?"

Kyle took off his harness and retracted it. He unplugged, and the yolk and its shadow man were gone. Only the chortling Polyaris remained.

"I can't get this God-damned thing off," Skip complained. "The buckle's jammed or something."

Marilyn took off her own acceleration harness and sailed across to look at it. Kyle joined them.

"Here, let me try it," Marilyn said. Her slender fingers, less nimble but more deft than Skip's, pressed the release and jiggled the locking tab; it would not pull free.

Kyle murmured, "I'm afraid you can't release Skip, Marilyn. Neither can I."

She turned to look at him.

"You accepted restraint for Skip, Marilyn. I want to say that in my opinion you were correct to do so."

She began, "You mean—"

"The Director isn't satisfied yet that Skip has recovered, that's all. Real recoveries aren't usually so quick or so—" Kyle paused, searching his dictionary file for the best word. "Convenient. This may be no more than a lucid interval. That happens, quite often. It may be no more than a stratagem."

Skip cursed and tore at the straps.

"Do you mean you can lock us . . . ?"

"No," Kyle said. "I can't. But the Director can, if in his judgment it is indicated."

He waited for Marilyn to speak, but she did not.

"You see, Marilyn, Skip, we tried very hard to prepare for every foreseeable eventuality, and mental illness was certainly one of those. About ten percent of the human population suffers from it at some point in their lives, and so with both of you on board and under a great deal of stress, that sort of problem was certainly something we had to be ready for."

Marilyn looked pale and drained. Kyle added, as gently as he could, "I hope this hasn't been too much of a shock to you."

Skip had opened the cutting blade of his utility knife and was hacking futilely at his straps. Kyle took it from him, closed it, and dropped it into one of his own storage areas.

Marilyn pushed off. He watched her as she flew gracefully across the hold, caught the pilot's-chair grab bar, and buckled herself into the seat; her eyes were shining with tears. As if sensing her distress, Polyaris perched on the bar and rubbed her ear with the side of her feathered head.

Skip muttered, "Go look at your demon, Kyle. Go anyplace but here."

Kyle asked, "Do you still think it's a demon, Skip?"

"You've seen it a lot closer up than I have. What do you think?"

"I don't believe in demons, Skip."

Skip looked calm now, but his fingers picked mechanically at his straps. "What *do* you believe in, Kyle? Do you believe in God? Do you worship Man?"

"I believe in life. Life is my God, Skip, if you want to put it like that."

"Any life? What about a mosquito?"

"Yes, any life. The mosquito won't bite me." Kyle smiled his metal smile.

"Mosquitoes spread disease."

"Sometimes," Kyle admitted. "Then they must be destroyed, the lower life sacrificed to the higher. Skip, your Marilyn is especially sacred to me now. Do you understand that?"

"Marilyn's doomed."

"Why do you say that?"

"Because of the demon, of course. I tried to tell her that she had doomed herself, but it was actually you that doomed her. You were the one who wanted him. You had to have him, you and the Director; and if it hadn't been for you, we could have gone home with a hold full of dark matter and some excuse."

"But you aren't doomed, Skip? Only Marilyn?"

"I'm dead and damned, Kyle. My doom has caught up with me. I've hit bottom. You know that expression?"

Kyle nodded.

"People talk about hitting bottom and bouncing back up. If you can bounce, that isn't the bottom. When somebody gets where I am, there's no bouncing back, not ever."

"If you're really dead, Skip, how can the straps hold you? I wouldn't think that an acceleration harness could hold a lost soul, or even a ghost."

"They're not holding me," Skip told him. "It was just that at the last moment I didn't have guts enough to let Marilyn see I was really gone. I'd loved her. I don't any more—you can't love anything or anyone except yourself where I am. But—"

"Can you get out of your seat, Skip? Is that what you're saying, that you can get out without unfastening the buckle?"

Skip nodded slowly, his dark eyes (inscrutable eyes, Kyle thought) never leaving

Kyle's face. "And I can see your demon, Kyle. I know you can't see him because you're not hooked up. But I can."

"You can see him now, Skip?"

"Not now—he's on the far side of the black ball. But I'll be able to see him when he floats around to this side again."

Kyle returned to his seat and connected the cable as he had before. The black yolk sprang into being again; the shadow man was facing him—in fact glaring at him with burning yellow eyes. He asked the Director to release Skip.

Together they drifted toward the center of the *Egg*. Kyle made sure their trajectory carried them to the side of the yolk away from the shadow man; and when the shadow man was no longer in view, he held Skip's arm and stopped them both with a tug at the cable. "Now that I know you can see him too, Skip, I'd like you to point him out to me."

Skip glanced toward the watery miniature planet over which they hovered like flies—or perhaps merely toward the center of the hold. "Is this a joke? I've told you, I can see him." A joyous blue and yellow comet, Polyaris erupted from the midnight surface, braking on flapping wings to examine them sidelong.

"That's why I need your input, Skip," Kyle said carefully. "I'm not certain the feed I'm getting is accurate. If you can apprehend shadow matter directly, I can use your information to check the simulation. Can you still see the demon? Indicate his position, please."

Skip hesitated. "He's not here, Kyle. He must be on the other side. Shall we go around and have a look?"

"The water's still swirling quite a bit. It should bring him to us before long."

Skip shrugged. "Okay, Kyle, you're the boss. I guess you always were."

"The Director's our captain, Skip. That's why we call him what we do. Can you see the demon yet?" A hand and part of one arm had floated into view around the curve of the yolk.

"No. Not yet. Do you have a soul, Kyle?"

Kyle nodded. "It's called my original monitor. I've seen a printout, though of course I didn't read it all; it was very long."

"Then when you're destroyed it may be sent here. Here comes your demon, by the way."

Kyle nodded.

"I suppose it may be put into one of these horrors. They seem more machine than human, at least to me."

"No," Kyle told him. "They're truly alive. They're shadow life, Skip, and since this one is the only example we have, just now it must be the most precious life in the universe to you, to Marilyn, and to me. Do you think he sees us?"

"He sees me," Skip said grimly.

"When I put my fingers into his brain, he opened his eyes," Kyle mused. "It was as though he felt them there."

"Maybe he did."

Kyle nodded. "Yes, possibly he did. The brain is such a sensitive mechanism that perhaps a gravitational disturbance as weak as that results in stimulation, if it is uneven. Put your hand into his head, please. I want to watch. You say he's a demon—pretend you're going to gouge out his eyes."

"You think I'm crazy!" Skip shouted. "Well, I'm telling you, you're crazy!"

Startled, Marilyn twisted in her pilot's chair to look at them.

"I've explained to you that he *sees* me," Skip said a little more calmly. "I'm not getting within his reach!"

"Touch his nose for me, Skip. Like this." Kyle lengthened one arm until his fingers seemed to brush the dark water several meters from the drifting shadow man's hideous face. "Look here, Skip. I'm not afraid."

Skip screamed.

"Have I time?" Kyle asked. He was holding the grab bar of Marilyn's control chair. In the forward port, the *Shadow Show* was distinctly visible.

"We've a few minutes yet," Marilyn told him. "And I want to know. I have to, Ky. He's the father of my child. Can you cure him?"

"I think so, Marilyn, though your correcting the simulator hues has probably helped Skip more than anything I've done thus far."

Kyle glanced appreciatively in the direction of the yolk. It was a translucent blue, as it should have been all along, and the shadow man who floated there looked more like a good-natured caricature of a human being than a demon. His skin was a dusty pinkish brown, his eyes the cheerful bright yellow of daffodils. It seemed to Kyle that they flickered for a moment as though to follow Polyaris in her flight across the hold. Perhaps a living entity of shadow matter could apprehend true matter after all—that would require a thorough investigation as soon as they were safely moored in the *Shadow Show*.

"And he can't really see shadow matter, Ky?"

Kyle shook his head. "No more than you or I can, Marilyn. He thought he could, you understand, at least on some level. On another he knew he couldn't and was faking it quite cleverly." Kyle paused, then added, "Freud did psychology a considerable disservice when he convinced people that the human mind thinks on only three levels. There are really a great many more than that, and there's no question but that the exact number varies between individuals."

"But for a while you really believed he might be able to, from what you've told me."

"At least I was willing to entertain the thought, Marilyn. Occasionally you can help people like Skip just by allowing them to test their delusional systems. What I found was that he had been taking cues from me—mostly from the direction of my eyes, no doubt. It would be wrong for you to think of that as lying. He honestly believed that when you human beings died your souls came here, to this shadow planet of a shadow system, in a shadow galaxy. And that he himself was dead."

Marilyn shook her head in dismay. "But that's insane, Ky. Just crazy."

She has never looked this lovely, Kyle thought. Aloud he said, "Mental illness is often a way of escaping responsibility, Marilyn. You may wish to consider that. Death is another, and you may wish to consider that also."

For a second Marilyn hesitated, biting her lip. "You love me, don't you, Ky?"

"Yes, I do, Marilyn. Very much."

"And so does Skip, Ky." She gave him a small, sad smile. "I suppose I'm the luckiest woman alive, or the unluckiest. The men I like most both love me, but one's having a breakdown . . . I shouldn't have started this, should I?"

"While the other is largely inorganic," Kyle finished for her. "But it's really not such a terrible thing to be loved by someone like me, Marilyn. We—"

Polyaris shrieked and shrieked again—not her shrill cry of pleasure or even her outraged squawk of pain, but the uncanny, piercing screech that signaled a prowling ocelot: Danger! *Fire!* Flood! INVASION and *CATASTROPHE!*

She was fluttering about the shadow man, and the shadow man was no longer a dusty pinkish brown. As Kyle stared, he faded to gray, then to white. His mouth opened. He crumpled, slowly and convulsively, into a fetal ball.

Horrified, Kyle turned to Marilyn. But Marilyn was self-absorbed, her hands clasping her belly. "It moved, Ky! It just moved. *I felt life!*"

OCCAM'S SCALPEL

Theodore Sturgeon

Theodore Sturgeon was one of the giants of the Golden Age, both in fantasy and science fiction. His early work was a model for the young Ray Bradbury, among others. Like Arthur C. Clarke, he came into real prominence in the 1950s with the new magazines, *Galaxy* and *The Magazine of Fantasy & Science Fiction*, which between them published a majority of his work, and with his classic novel, *More Than Human* (1953). Although his stories made clever use of science, he was never known as a hard sf writer, but rather as the finest literary craftsman of his day in the genre. Along with Alfred Bester, Sturgeon was a primary influence on the sf writers of the fifties and sixties, both as a charismatic public figure in the field, a major reviewer from the late fifties through the early seventies, and as a force for increased stylistic experimentation. His stories, collected in *Without Sorcery* (1948), *E Pluribus Unicorn* (1953), *A Way Home* (1955), *A Touch of Strange* (1958), and later volumes, are deceptively clear and direct, with none of the pyrotechnics of a Bester story (although both usually wrote about unusual, grotesque, or extraordinary people), while building toward considerable power, often with subtle resonances. In a field noted for hastily written stories, Sturgeon stood for advancing the craft of writing of science fiction (especially for improving written work by revision for the aesthetic satisfaction of the writer as opposed to changes made to editorial direction). His thumb-rule definition of sf was: a story like any other, except that it wouldn't have happened without the science fiction idea in it. His works have fallen out of print in recent years since his death in 1985, but a complete collection of his stories has been announced in eight hardcover volumes forthcoming in the mid-nineties. No one in the field has yet produced a body of short fiction superior to Sturgeon's.

Originally a Campbell writer, Sturgeon came to support the broadening term "speculative fiction" as the preferred name for the literature (note the noncategory titles of his collections, above). A lifelong outsider and bohemian, Sturgeon bridged the undergrounds of avant-garde art and science fiction fandom with penetrating and humane insight, and was regarded by his peers with something akin to worship. In differing ways, Kate Wilhelm, Gene Wolfe, and James Tiptree, Jr., have carried on the Sturgeon tradition in recent decades.

"Occam's Scalpel" is on the edge of being not sf at all. There is no better example herein of what the writers of the fifties and later meant by "speculative fiction." Strict Constructionists would rule it out. Yet it more centrally concerns science than a majority of Sturgeon's genre work: it is about scientists, about human psychology, about unconventional moral choices. Sturgeon plays with the doctrine of literality of hard sf, teases the genre reader with a non-sf explanation for the sf imagery, then allows the story to sit on the fence, both in and out of the genre. But whether in or out, it has the hard sf attitude toward knowledge, toward the universe.

Joe Triliing had a funny way of making a living. It was a good living, but of course he didn't make anything like the bundle he could have in the city. On the other hand he lived in the mountains a half mile away from a picturesque village in clean air and piney-birchy woods along with lots of mountain laurel and he was his own boss. There wasn't much competition for what he did; he had his wife and kids around all the time and more orders than he could fill. He was one of the night people and after the family had gone to bed he could work quietly and uninterruptedly. He was happy as a clam.

One night—very early morning, really—he was interrupted. *Bup-bup, bup, bup.* Knock at the window, two shorts, two longs, He froze, he whirled, for he knew that knock. He hadn't heard it for years but it had been a part of his life since he was born. He saw the face outside and filled his lungs for a whoop that would have roused them at the fire station on the village green, but then he saw the finger on the lips and let the air out. The finger beckoned and Joe Trilling whirled again, turned down a flame, read a gauge, made a note, threw a switch and joyfully but silently dove for the outside door. He slid out, closed it carefully, peered into the dark.

"Karl?"

"Shh."

There he was, edge of the woods. Joe Trilling went there and, whispering because Karl had asked for it, they hit each other, cursed, called each other the filthiest possible names. It would not be easy to explain this to an extraterrestrial; it isn't necessarily a human thing to do. It's a cultural thing. It means, I want to touch you, it means I love you; but they were men and brothers, so they hit each other's arms and shoulders and swore despicable oaths and insults, until at last even those words wouldn't do and they stood in the shadows, holding each others' biceps and grinning and drilling into each other with eyes. Then Karl Trilling moved his head sideward toward the road and they walked away from the house.

"I don't want Hazel to hear us talking," Karl said. "I don't want her or anyone to know I was here. How is she?"

"Beautiful. Aren't you going to see her at all—or the kids?"

"Yes but not this trip. There's the car. We can talk there. I really am afraid of that bastard."

"Ah," said Joe. "How is the great man?"

"Po'ly," said Karl. "But we're talking about two different bastards. The great man is only the richest man in the world, but I'm not afraid of him, especially now. I'm talking about Cleveland Wheeler."

"Who's Cleveland Wheeler?"

They got into the car. "It's a rental," said Karl. "Matter of fact, it's the second rental. I got out of the executive jet and took a company car and rented another—and then this. Reasonably sure it's not bugged. That's one kind of answer to your question, who's Cleve Wheeler. Other answers would be the man behind the throne. Next in line. Multifaceted genius. Killer shark."

"Next in line," said Joe, responding to the only clause that made any sense. "The old man is sinking?"

"Officially—and an official secret—his hemoglobin reading is four. That mean anything to you, Doctor?"

"Sure does, Doctor. Malnutritive anemia, if other rumors I hear are true. Richest man in the world—dying of starvation."

"And old age—and stubbornness—and obsession. You want to hear about Wheeler?"

"Tell me."

"Mister lucky. Born with everything. Greek coin profile. Michaelangelo muscles. Discovered early by a bright-eyed elementary school principal, sent to a private school, used to go straight to the teachers' lounge in the morning and say what he'd been reading or thinking about. Then they'd tell off a teacher to work with him or go out with him or whatever. High school at twelve, varsity track, basketball, football and high-diving—three letters for each—yes, he graduated in three years, *summa cum*. Read all the textbooks at the beginning of each term, never cracked them again. More than anything else he had the habit of success.

"College, the same thing: turned sixteen in his first semester, just ate everything up. Very popular. Graduated at the top again, of course."

Joe Trilling, who had slogged through college and medical school like a hodcarrier, grunted enviously. "I've seen one or two like that. Everybody marvels, nobody sees how easy it was for them."

Karl shook his head. "Wasn't quite like that with Cleve Wheeler. If anything was easy for him it was because of the nature of his equipment. He was like a four-hundred horsepower car moving in sixty-horsepower traffic. When his muscles were called on he used them, I mean really put it down to the floor. A very willing guy. Well—he had his choice of jobs—hell, choice of careers. He went into an architectural firm that could use his math, administrative ability, public presence, knowledge of materials, art. Gravitated right to the top, got a partnership. Picked up a doctorate on the side while he was doing it. Married extremely well."

"Mister Lucky," Joe said.

"Mister Lucky, yeah. Listen. Wheeler became a partner and he did his work and he knew his stuff—everything he could learn or understand. Learning and understanding are not enough to cope with some things like greed or unexpected stupidity or accident or sheer bad breaks. Two of the other partners got into a deal I won't bother you with—a high-rise apartment complex in the wrong place for the wrong residents and land acquired the wrong way. Wheeler saw it coming, called them in and talked it over. They said yes-yes and went right ahead and did what they wanted anyway—something that Wheeler never in the world expected. The one thing high capability and straight morals and a good education doesn't give you is the end of innocence. Cleve Wheeler was an innocent.

"Well, it happened, the disaster that Cleve had predicted, but it happened far worse. Things like that, when they surface, have a way of exposing a lot of other concealed rot. The firm collapsed. Cleve Wheeler had never failed at anything in his whole life. It was the one thing he had no practice in dealing with. Anyone with the most rudimentary intelligence would have seen that this was the time to walk away—lie down, even. Cut his losses. But I don't think these things even occurred to him."

Karl Trilling laughed suddenly. "In one of Philip Wylie's novels is a tremendous description of a forest fire and how the animals run away from it, the foxes and the rabbits running shoulder to shoulder, the owls flying in the daytime to get ahead of the flames. Then there's this beetle, lumbering along on the ground. The beetle comes to a burned patch, the edge of twenty acres of hell. It stops, it wiggles its feelers, it turns to the side and begins to walk around the fire—" He laughed again. "That's the special thing Cleveland Wheeler has, you see, under all that muscle and brain and brilliance. If he had to—and were a beetle—he wouldn't turn back and he wouldn't quit. If all he could do was walk around it, he'd start walking."

"What happened?" asked Joe.

"He hung on. He used everything he had. He used his brains and his personality and his reputation and all his worldly goods. He also borrowed and promised—and he worked. Oh, he worked. Well, he kept the firm. He cleaned out the rot and built it all up again from the inside, strong and straight this time. But it cost.

"It cost him time—all the hours of every day but the four or so he used for sleeping. And just about when he had it leveled off and starting up, it cost him his wife."

"You said he'd married well."

"He'd married what you marry when you're a young blockbuster on top of everything and going higher. She was a nice enough girl, I suppose, and maybe you can't blame her, but she was no more used to failure than he was. Only he could walk around it. He could rent a room and ride the bus. She just didn't know how—and of course with women like that there's always the discarded swain somewhere in the wings."

"How did he take that?"

"Hard. He'd married the way he played ball or took examinations—with everything he had. It did something to him. All this did things to him, I suppose, but that was the biggest chunk of it.

"He didn't let it stop him. He didn't let anything stop him. He went on until all the bills were paid—every cent. All the interest. He kept at it until the net worth was exactly what it had been before his ex-partners had begun to eat out the core. Then he gave it away. Gave it away! Sold all right and title to his interest for a dollar."

"Finally cracked, hm?"

Karl Trilling looked at his brother scornfully. "Cracked. Matter of definition, isn't it? Cleve Wheeler's goal was zero—can you understand that? What is success anyhow? Isn't it making up your mind what you're going to do and then doing it, all the way?"

"In that case," said his brother quietly, "suicide is success."

Karl gave him a long penetrating look. "Right," he said, and thought about it a moment.

"Anyhow," Joe asked, "why zero?"

"I did a lot of research on Cleve Wheeler, but I couldn't get inside his head. I don't know. But I can guess. He meant to owe no man anything. I don't know how he felt about the company he saved, but I can imagine. The man he became—was becoming—wouldn't want to owe it one damned thing. I'd say he just wanted out—but on his own terms, which included leaving nothing behind to work on him."

"Okay," said Joe.

Karl Trilling thought, *The nice thing about old Joe is that he'll wait. All these years apart with hardly any communication beyond birthday cards—and not always that—and here he is, just as if we were still together every day. I wouldn't be here if it weren't important; I wouldn't be telling him all this unless he needed to know; he wouldn't need any of it unless he was going to help. All that unsaid—I don't have to ask him a damn thing. What am I interrupting in his life? What am I going to interrupt? I won't have to worry about that. He'll take care of it.*

He said, "I'm glad I came here, Joe."

Joe said, "That's all right," which meant all the things Karl had been thinking. Karl grinned and hit him on the shoulder and went on talking.

"Wheeler dropped out. It's not easy to map his trail for that period. It pops up all over. He lived in at least three communes—maybe more, but those three were a mess when he came and a model when he left. He started businesses—all things that had never happened before, like a supermarket with no shelves, no canned music, no games or stamps, just neat stacks of open cases, where the customer took what he wanted and marked it according to the card posted by the case, with a marker hanging on a string. Eggs and frozen meat and fish and the like, and local produce were priced a flat two percent over wholesale. People were honest because they could never be sure the checkout counter didn't know the prices of everything—besides, to cheat on the prices listed would have been just too embarrassing. With nothing but a big empty warehouse for overhead and no employees spending thousands of man hours marking individual items, the prices beat any discount house that ever lived. He sold that one, too, and moved on. He started a line of organic baby foods without preservatives, franchised it and moved on again. He developed a plastic container that would burn without polluting and patented it and sold the patent."

"I've heard of that one. Haven't seen it around, though."

"Maybe you will," Karl said in a guarded tone. "Maybe you will. Anyway, he had a CPA in Pasadena handling details, and just did his thing all over. I never heard of a failure in anything he tried."

"Sounds like a junior edition of the great man himself, your honored boss."

"You're not the only one who realized that. The boss may be a ding-a-ling in many ways, but nobody ever faulted his business sense. He has always had his tentacles out for wandering pieces of very special manpower. For all I know he had drawn a bead on Cleveland Wheeler years back. I wouldn't doubt that he'd made offers from time to time, only during that period Cleve Wheeler wasn't about to go to work for anyone that big. His whole pattern is to run things his way, and you don't do that in an established empire."

"Heir apparent," said Joe, reminding him of something he had said earlier.

"Right," nodded Karl. "I knew you'd begin to get the idea before I was finished."

"But finish," said Joe.

"Right. Now what I'm going to tell you, I just want you to know. I don't expect you to understand it or what it means or what it has all done to Cleve Wheeler. I need your help, and you can't really help me unless you know the whole story."

"Shoot."

Karl Trilling shot: "Wheeler found a girl. Her name was Clara Prieta and her folks came from Sonora. She was bright as hell—in her way, I suppose, as bright as Cleve, though with a tenth of his schooling—and pretty as well, and it was Cleve she wanted, not what he might get for her. She fell for him when he had nothing—when he really wanted nothing. They were a daily, hourly joy to each other. I guess that was about the time he started building this business and that, making something again. He bought a little house and a car. He bought two cars, one for her. I don't think she wanted it, but he couldn't do enough—he was always looking for more things to do for her. They went out for an evening to some friends' house, she from shopping, he from whatever it was he was working on then, so they had both cars. He followed her on the way home and had to watch her lose control and spin out. She died in his arms."

"Oh, Jesus."

"Mister Lucky. Listen: a week later he turned a corner downtown and found himself looking at a bank robbery. He caught a stray bullet—grazed the back of his neck. He had seven months to lie still and think about things. When he got out he was told his business manager had embezzled everything and headed south with his secretary. Everything."

"What did he do?"

"Went to work and paid his hospital bill."

They sat in the car in the dark for a long time, until Joe said, "Was he paralyzed, there in the hospital?"

"For nearly five months."

"Wonder what he thought about."

Karl Trilling said, "I can imagine what he thought about. What I can't imagine is what he decided. What he concluded. What he determined to be. Damn it, there are no accurate words for it. We all do the best we can with what we've got, or try to. Or should. He *did*—and with the best possible material to start out with. He played it straight; he worked hard; he was honest and lawful and fair; he was fit; he was bright. He came out of the hospital with those last two qualities intact. God alone knows what's happened to the rest of it."

"So he went to work for the old man."

"He did—and somehow that frightens me. It was as if all his qualifications were not enough to suit both of them until these things happened to him—until they made him become what he is."

"And what is that?"

"There isn't a short answer to that, Joe. The old man has become a modern myth. Nobody ever sees him. Nobody can predict what he's going to do or why. Cleveland Wheeler stepped into his shadow and disappeared almost as completely as the boss. There are very few things you can say for certain. The boss has always been a recluse and in the ten years Cleve Wheeler has been with him he has become more so. It's been business as usual with him, of course—which means the constantly unusual—long periods of quiet, and then these spectacular unexpected wheelings and dealings. You assume that the old man dreams these things up and some high-powered genius on his staff gets them done. But it could be the genius that instigates the moves—who can know? Only the people closest to him—Wheeler, Epstein, me. And I don't know."

"But Epstein died."

Karl Trilling nodded in the dark. "Epstein died. Which leaves only Wheeler to watch the store. I'm the old man's personal physician, not Wheeler's, and there's no guarantee that I ever will be Wheeler's."

Joe Trilling recrossed his legs and leaned back, looking out into the whispering dark. "It begins to take shape," he murmured. "The old man's on the way out, you very well might be and there's nobody to take over but this Wheeler."

"Yes, and I don't know what he is or what he'll do. I do know he will command more power than any single human being on Earth. He'll have so much that he'll be above any kind of cupidity that you or I could imagine—you or I can't think in that order of magnitude. But you see, he's a man who, you might say, has had it proved to him that being good and smart and strong and honest doesn't particularly pay off. Where will he go with all this? And hypothesizing that he's been making more and more of the decisions lately, and extrapolating from that—where is he going? All you can be sure of is that he will succeed in anything he tries. That is his habit."

"What does he want? Isn't that what you're trying to figure out? What would a man like that want, if he knew he could get it?"

"I knew I'd come to the right place," said Karl almost happily. "That's it exactly. As for me, I have all I need now and there are plenty of other places I could go. I wish Epstein were still around, but he's dead and cremated."

"Cremated?"

"That's right—you wouldn't know about that. Old man's instructions. I handled it myself. You've heard of the hot and cold private swimming pools—but I bet you never heard of a man with his own private crematorium in the second sub-basement."

Joe threw up his hands. "I guess if you can reach into your pocket and pull out two billion real dollars, you can have anything you want. By the way—was that legal?"

"Like you said—if you have two billion. Actually, the county medical examiner was present and signed the papers. And he'll be there when the old man pushes off too—it's all in the final instructions. Hey—wait, I don't want to cast any aspersions on the M.E. He wasn't bought. He did a very competent examination on Epstein."

"Okay—we know what to expect when the time comes. It's afterward you're worried about."

"Right. What has the old man—I'm speaking of the corporate old man now—what has he been doing all along? What has he been doing in the last ten years, since he got Wheeler—and is it any different from what he was doing before? How much of this difference, if any, is more Wheeler than boss? That's all we have to go on, Joe, and from it we have to extrapolate what Wheeler's going to do with the biggest private economic force this world has ever known."

"Let's talk about that," said Joe, beginning to smile.

Karl Trilling knew the signs, so he began to smile a little, too. They talked about it.

II

The crematorium in the second sub-basement was purely functional, as if all concessions to sentiment and ritual had been made elsewhere, or canceled. The latter most accurately described what had happened when at last, at long long last, the old man died. Everything was done precisely according to his instructions immediately after he was certifiably dead and before any public announcements were made—right up to and including the moment when the square mouth of the furnace opened with a startling clang, a blare of heat, a flare of light—the hue the old-time blacksmiths called straw color. The simple coffin slid rapidly in, small flames exploding into being on its corners, and the door banged shut. It took a moment for the eyes to adjust to the bare room, the empty greased track, the closed door. It took the same moment for the conditioners to whisk away the sudden smell of scorched soft pine.

The medical examiner leaned over the small table and signed his name twice. Karl Trilling and Cleveland Wheeler did the same. The M.E. tore off copies and folded them and put them away in his breast pocket. He looked at the closed square iron door, opened his mouth, closed it again and shrugged. He held out his hand.

"Good night, Doctor."

"Good night, Doctor. Rugosi's outside—he'll show you out."

The M.E. shook hands wordlessly with Cleveland Wheeler and left.

"I know just what he's feeling," Karl said. "Something ought to be said. Something memorable—end of an era. Like 'One small step for man—' "

Cleveland Wheeler smiled the bright smile of the college hero, fifteen years after—a little less wide, a little less even, a great deal less in the eyes. He said in the voice that commanded, whatever he said, "If you think you're quoting the first words from an astronaut on the moon, you're not. What he said was from the ladder, when he poked his boot down. He said, 'It's some kind of soft stuff. I can kick it around with my foot.' I've always liked that much better. It was real, it wasn't rehearsed or memorized or thought out and it had to do with that moment and the next. The M.E. said good night and you told him the chauffeur was waiting outside. I like that better than anything anyone could say. I think he would, too," Wheeler added, barely gesturing, with a very strong, slightly cleft chin, toward the hot black door.

"But he wasn't exactly human."

"So they say." Wheeler half smiled and, even as he turned away, Karl could sense himself tuned out, the room itself become of secondary importance—the next thing Wheeler was to do, and the next and the one after, becoming more real than the here and now.

Karl put a fast end to that.

He said levelly, "I meant what I just said, Wheeler."

It couldn't have been the words, which by themselves might have elicited another half-smile and a forgetting. It was the tone, and perhaps the "Wheeler." There is a ritual about these things. To those few on his own level, and those on the level below, he was Cleve. Below that he was mister to his face and Wheeler behind his back. No one of his peers would call him mister unless it was meant as the herald of an insult; no one of his peers or immediate underlings would call him Wheeler at all, ever. Whatever the component, it removed Cleveland Wheeler's hand from the knob and turned him. His face was completely alert and interested. "You'd best tell me what you mean, Doctor."

Karl said, "I'll do better than that. Come." Without gestures, suggestions or explanations he walked to the left rear of the room, leaving it up to Wheeler to decide whether or not to follow. Wheeler followed.

In the corner Karl rounded on him. "If you ever say anything about this to anyone—even me—when we leave here, I'll just deny it. If you ever get in here again, you won't find anything to back up your story." He took a complex four-inch blade of machined stainless steel from his belt and slid it between the big masonry blocks. Silently, massively, the course of blocks in the corner began to move upward. Looking up at them in the dim light from the narrow corridor they revealed, anyone could see that they were real blocks and that to get through them without that key and the precise knowledge of where to put it would be a long-term project.

Again Karl proceeded without looking around, leaving go, no-go as a matter for Wheeler to decide. Wheeler followed. Karl heard his footsteps behind him and noticed with pleasure and something like admiration that when the heavy blocks whooshed down and seated themselves solidly behind them, Wheeler may have looked over his shoulder but did not pause.

"You've noticed we're alongside the furnace," Karl said, like a guided-tour bus driver. "And now, behind it."

He stood aside to let Wheeler pass him and see the small room.

It was just large enough for the tracks which protruded from the back of the furnace and a little standing space on each side. On the far side was a small table with a black suitcase standing on it. On the track stood the coffin, its corners carboned, its top and sides wet and slightly steaming.

"Sorry to have to close that stone gate that way," Karl said matter-of-factly. "I don't expect anyone down here at all, but I wouldn't want to explain any of this to persons other than yourself."

Wheeler was staring at the coffin. He seemed perfectly composed, but it was a seeming. Karl was quite aware of what it was costing him.

Wheeler said, "I wish you'd explain it to *me*." And he laughed. It was the first time Karl had ever seen this man do anything badly.

"I will. I am." He clicked open the suitcase and laid it open and flat on the little table. There was a glisten of chrome and steel and small vials in little pockets. The first tool he removed was a screwdriver. "No need to use screws when you're cremating 'em," he said cheerfully and placed the tip under one corner of the lid. He struck the handle smartly with the heel of one hand and the lid popped loose. "Stand this up against the wall behind you, will you?"

Silently Cleveland Wheeler did as he was told. It gave him something to do with his muscles; it gave him the chance to turn his head away for a moment; it gave him a chance to think—and it gave Karl the opportunity for a quick glance at his steady countenance.

He's a mensch, Karl thought. *He really is* . . .

Wheeler set up the lid neatly and carefully and they stood, one on each side, looking down into the coffin.

"He—got a lot older," Wheeler said at last.

"You haven't seen him recently."

"Here and there," said the executive, "I've spent more time in the same room with him during the past month than I have in the last eight, nine years. Still, it was a matter of minutes, each time."

Karl nodded understandingly. "I'd heard that. Phone calls, any time of the day or night, and then those long silences two days, three, not calling out, not having anyone in—"

"Are you going to tell me about the phony oven?"

"Oven? Furnace? It's not a phony at all. When we've finished here it'll do the job, all right."

"Then why the theatricals?"

"That was for the M.E. Those papers he signed are in sort of a never-never country just now. When we slide this back in and turn on the heat they'll become as legal as he thinks they are."

"Then why—"

"Because there are some things you have to know." Karl reached into the coffin and unfolded the gnarled hands. They came apart reluctantly and he pressed them down at the sides of the body. He unbuttoned the jacket, laid it back, unbuttoned the shirt, unzipped the trousers. When he had finished with this he looked up and found Wheeler's sharp gaze, not on the old man's corpse, but on him.

"I have the feeling," said Cleveland Wheeler, "that I have never seen you before."

Silently Karl Trilling responded: *But you do now*. And, *Thanks, Joey. You were dead right*. Joe had known the answer to that one plaguing question, *How should I act?*

Talk just the way he talks, Joe had said. *Be what he is, the whole time* . . .

Be what he is. A man without illusions (they don't work) and without hope (who needs it?) who has the unbreakable habit of succeeding. And who can say it's a nice day in such a way that everyone around snaps to attention and says: *Yes, SIR!*

"You've been busy," Karl responded shortly. He took off his jacket, folded it and put it on the table beside the kit. He put on surgeon's gloves and slipped the sterile sleeve off a new scalpel. "Some people scream and faint the first time they watch a dissection."

Wheeler smiled thinly. "I don't scream and faint." But it was not lost on Karl Trilling that only then, at the last possible moment, did Wheeler actually view the old man's body. When he did he neither screamed nor fainted; he uttered an astonished grunt.

"Thought that would surprise you," Karl said easily. "In case you were wondering, though, he really was a male. The species seems to be oviparous. Mammals too, but it has to be oviparous. I'd sure like a look at a female. That isn't a vagina. It's a cloaca."

"Until this moment," said Wheeler in a hypnotized voice, "I thought that 'not human' remark of yours was a figure of speech."

"No, you didn't," Karl responded shortly.

Leaving the words to hang in the air, as words will if a speaker has the wit to isolate them with wedges of silence, he deftly slit the corpse from the sternum to the pubic symphysis. For the first-time viewer this was always the difficult moment. It's hard not to realize viscerally that the cadaver does not feel anything and will not protest. Nerve-alive to Wheeler, Karl looked for a gasp or a shudder; Wheeler merely held his breath.

"We could spend hours—weeks, I imagine, going into the details," Karl said, deftly making a transverse incision in the ensiform area, almost around to the trapezoid on each side, "but this is the thing I wanted you to see." Grasping the flesh at the juncture of the cross he had cut, on the left side, he pulled upward and to the left. The cutaneous layers came away easily, with the fat under them. They were not pinkish, but an off-white lavender shade. Now the muscular striations over the ribs were in view. "If you'd palpated the old man's chest," he said, demonstrating on the right side, "you'd have felt what seemed to be normal human ribs. But look at this."

With a few deft strokes he separated the muscle fibers from the bone on a midcostal area about four inches square, and scraped. A rib emerged and, as he widened the area and scraped between it and the next one, it became clear that the ribs were joined by a thin flexible layer of bone or chitin.

"It's like baleen—whalebone," said Karl. "See this?" He sectioned out a piece, flexed it.

"My God."

III

"Now look at this." Karl took surgical sheers from the kit, snipped through the sternum right up to the clavicle and then across the lower margin of the ribs. Slipping his fingers under them, he pulled upward. With a dull snap the entire ribcage opened like a door, exposing the lung.

The lung was not pink, nor the liverish-browish-black of a smoker, but yellow—the clear bright yellow of pure sulfur.

"His metabolism," Karl said, straightening up at last and flexing the tension out of his shoulders, "is fantastic. Or was. He lived on oxygen, same as us, but he broke it out of carbon monoxide, sulfur dioxide and trioxide and carbon dioxide mostly. I'm not saying he could—I mean he had to. When he was forced to breathe what we call clean air, he could take just so much of it and then had to duck out and find a few breaths of his own atmosphere. When he was younger he could take it for hours at a time, but as the years went by he had to spend more and more time in the kind of smog he could breathe. Those long disappearances of his, and that reclusiveness—they weren't as kinky as people supposed."

Wheeler made a gesture toward the corpse. "But—what is he? Where—"

"I can't tell you. Except for a good deal of medical and biochemical details, you now know as much as I do. Somehow, somewhere, he arrived. He came, he saw, he began to make his moves. Look at this."

He opened the other side of the chest and then broke the sternum up and away. He pointed. The lung tissue was not in two discreet parts, but extended across the median line. "One lung, all the way across, though it has these two lobes. The kidneys and gonads show the same right-left fusion."

"I'll take your word for it," said Wheeler a little hoarsely. "Damn it, what *is* it?"

"A featherless biped, as Plato once described homo sap. *I* don't know what it is. I just know *that* it is—and I thought you ought to know. That's all."

"But you've seen one before. That's obvious."

"Sure. Epstein."

"Epstein?"

"Sure. The old man had to have a go-between—someone who could, without suspicion, spend long hours with him and hours away. The old man could do a lot over the phone, but not everything. Epstein was, you might say, a right arm that could hold its breath a little longer than he could. It got to him in the end, though, and he died of it."

"Why didn't you say something long before this?"

"First of all, I value my own skin. I could say reputation, but skin is the word. I signed a contract as his personal physician because he needed a personal physician—another bit of window-dressing. But I did precious little doctoring—except over the phone—and nine-tenths of that was, I realized quite recently, purely diversionary. Even a doctor, I suppose, can be a trusting soul. One or the other would call and give a set of symptoms and I'd cautiously suggest and prescribe. Then I'd get another call that the patient was improving and that was that. Why, I even got specimens—blood, urine, stools—and did the pathology on them and never realized that they were from the same source as what the medical examiner checked out and signed for."

"What do you mean, same source?"

Karl shrugged. "He could get anything he wanted—anything."

"Then—what the M.E. examined wasn't—" he waved a hand at the casket.

"Of course not. That's why the crematorium has a back door. There's a little pocket sleight-of-hand trick you can buy for fifty cents that operates the same way. This body here was inside the furnace. The ringer—a look-alike that came from God knows where; I swear to you I don't—was lying out there waiting for the M.E. When the button was pushed the fires started up and that coffin slid in—pushing this one out and at the same time drenching it with water as it came through. While we've been in here, the human body is turning to ashes. My personal private secret instructions, both for Epstein and for the boss, were to wait until I was certain I was alone and then come in here after an hour and push the second button, which would slide this one back into the fire. I was to do no investigations, ask no questions, make no reports. It came through as logical but not reasonable, like so many of his orders." He laughed suddenly. "Do you know why the old man—and Epstein too, for that matter, in case you never noticed—wouldn't shake hands with anyone?"

"I presumed it was because he had an obsession with germs."

"It was because his normal body temperature was a hundred and seven."

Wheeler touched one of his own hands with the other and said nothing.

When Karl felt that the wedge of silence was thick enough he asked lightly, "Well, boss, where do we go from here?"

Cleveland Wheeler turned away from the corpse and to Karl slowly, as if diverting his mind with an effort.

"What did you call me?"

"Figure of speech," said Karl and smiled. "Actually, I'm working for the company—and that's you. I'm under orders, which have been finally and completely discharged when I push that button—I have no others. So it really is up to you."

Wheeler's eyes fell again to the corpse. "You mean about him? This? What we should do?"

"That, yes. Whether to burn it up and forget it—or call in top management and an echelon of scientists. Or scare the living hell out of everyone on Earth by phoning the papers. Sure, that has to be decided, but I was thinking on a much wider spectrum than that."

"Such as—"

Karl gestured toward the box with his head. "What was he doing here, anyway? What has he done? What was he trying to do?"

"You'd better go on," said Wheeler; and for the very first time said something in a way that suggested diffidence. "You've had a while to think about all this, I—" and almost helplessly, he spread his hands.

"I can understand that," Karl said gently. "Up to now I've been coming on like a hired lecturer and I know it. I'm not going to embarrass you with personalities except to say that you've absorbed all this with less buckling of the knees than anyone in the world I could think of."

"Right. Well, there's a simple technique you learn in elementary algebra. It has to do with the construction of graphs. You place a dot on the graph where known data put it. You get more data, you put down another dot and then a third. With just three dots—of course, the more the better, but it can be done with three—you can connect them and establish a curve. This curve has certain characteristics and it's fair to extend the curve a little farther with the assumption that later data will bear you out."

"Extrapolation."

"Extrapolation. X axis, the fortunes of our late boss. Y axis, time. The curve is his fortunes—that is to say, his influence."

"Pretty tall graph."

"Over thirty years."

"Still pretty tall."

"All right," said Karl. "Now, over the same thirty years, another curve: change in the environment." He held up a hand. "I'm not going to read you a treatise on ecology. Let's be more objective than that. Let's just say changes. Okay: a measurable rise in the mean temperature because of CO_2 and the greenhouse effect. Draw the curve. Incidence of heavy metals, mercury and lithium, in organic tissue. Draw a curve. Likewise chlorinated hydrocarbons, hypertrophy of algae due to phosphates, incidence of coronaries . . . All right, let's superimpose all these curves on the same graph."

"I see what you're getting at. But you have to be careful with that kind of statistics game. Like, the increase of traffic fatalities coincides with the increased use of aluminum cans and plastic-tipped baby pins."

"Right. I don't think I'm falling into that trap. I just want to find reasonable answers to a couple of otherwise unreasonable situations. One is this: if the changes occurring in our planet are the result of mere carelessness—a more or less random thing, carelessness—then how come nobody is being careless in a way that benefits the environment? Strike that. I promised, no ecology lessons. Rephrase: how come all these carelessnesses promote a change and not a preservation?

"Next question: What is the direction of the change? You've seen speculative writing about 'terra-forming'—altering other planets to make them habitable by humans. Suppose an effort were being made to change this planet to suit someone else? Suppose they wanted more water and were willing to melt the polar caps by the greenhouse effect? Increase the oxides of sulfur, eliminate certain marine forms from plankton to whales? Reduce the population by increases in lung cancer, emphysema, heart attacks and even war?"

Both men found themselves looking down at the sleeping face in the coffin. Karl said softly, "Look what he was into—petrochemicals, fossil fuels, food processing, advertising, all the things that made the changes or helped the changers—"

"You're not blaming him for all of it."

"Certainly not. He found willing helpers by the million."

"You don't think he was trying to change a whole planet just so he could be comfortable in it."

"No, I don't think so—and that's the central point I have to make. I don't know if there are any more around like him and Epstein, but I can suppose this: if the changes now going on keep on—and accelerate—then we can expect them."

Wheeler said, "So what would you like to do? Mobilize the world against the invader?"

"Nothing like that. I think I'd slowly and quietly reverse the changes. If this planet is normally unsuitable to them, then I'd keep it so. I don't think they'd have to be driven back. I think they just wouldn't come."

"Or they'd try some other way."

"I don't think so," said Karl. "Because they tried this one. If they thought they could do it with fleets of spaceships and super-zap guns, they'd be doing it. No—this is their way and if it doesn't work, they can try somewhere else."

Wheeler began pulling thoughtfully at his lip. Karl said softly, "All it would take is someone who knew what he was doing, who could command enough clout and who had the wit to make it pay. They might even arrange a man's life—to get the kind of man they need."

And before Wheeler could answer, Karl took up his scalpel.

"I want you to do something for me," he said sharply in a new, commanding tone—actually, Wheeler's own. "I want you to do it because I've done it and I'll be damned if I want to be the only man in the world who has."

Leaning over the head of the casket, he made an incision along the hairline from temple to temple. Then, bracing his elbows against the edge of the box and steadying one hand with the other, he drew the scalpel straight down the center of the forehead and down on to the nose, splitting it exactly in two. Down he went through the upper lip and then the lower, around the point of the chin and under it to the throat. Then he stood up.

"Put your hands on his cheeks," he ordered. Wheeler frowned briefly (how long had it been since anyone had spoken to him that way?), hesitated, then did as he was told.

"Now press your hands together and down."

The incision widened slightly under the pressure, then abruptly the flesh gave and the entire skin of the face slipped off. The unexpected lack of resistance brought Wheeler's hands to the bottom of the coffin and he found himself face to face, inches away, with the corpse.

Like the lungs and kidneys, the eyes—eye?—passed the median, very slightly reduced at the center. The pupil was oval, its long axis transverse. The skin was pale lavender with yellow vessels and in place of a nose was a thread-fringed hole. The mouth was circular, the teeth not quite radially placed; there was little chin.

Without moving, Wheeler closed his eyes, held them shut for one second, two, and then courageously opened them again. Karl whipped around the end of the coffin and got an arm around Wheeler's chest. Wheeler leaned on it heavily for a moment, then stood up quickly and brushed the arm away.

"You didn't have to do that."

"Yes, I did," said Karl. "Would you want to be the only man in the world who'd gone through that—with nobody to tell it to?"

And after all, Wheeler could laugh. When he had finished he said, "Push that button."

"Hand me that cover."

Most obediently Cleveland Wheeler brought the coffin lid and they placed it.

Karl pushed the button and they watched the coffin slide into the square of flame. Then they left.

Joe Trilling had a funny way of making a living. It was a good living, but of course he didn't make anything like the bundle he could have made in the city. On the other hand, he lived in the mountains a half-mile away from a picturesque village, in clean air and piney-birchy woods along with lots of mountain laurel and he was his own boss. There wasn't much competition for what he did.

What he did was to make simulacra of medical specimens, mostly for the armed forces, although he had plenty of orders from medical schools, film producers and an occasional individual, no questions asked. He could make a model of anything inside, affixed to or penetrating a body or any part of it. He could make models to be looked at, models to be felt, smelled and palpated. He could give you gangrene that stunk or dewy thyroids with real dew on them. He could make one-of-a-kind or he could set up a production line. Dr. Joe Trilling was, to put it briefly, the best there was at what he did.

"The clincher," Karl told him (in much more relaxed circumstances than their previous ones; daytime now, with beer), "the real clincher was the face bit. God, Joe, that was a beautiful piece of work."

"Just nuts and bolts. The beautiful part was your idea—his hands on it."

"How do you mean?"

"I've been thinking back to that," Joe said. "I don't think you yourself realize how brilliant a stroke that was. It's all very well to set up a show for the guy, but to make him put his hands as well as his eyes and brains on it—that was the stroke of genius. It's like—well, I can remember when I was a kid coming home from school and putting my hand on a fence rail and somebody had spat on it." He displayed his hand, shook it. "All these years I can remember how that felt. All these years couldn't wear it away, all those scrubbings couldn't wash it away. It's more than a cerebral or psychic thing, Karl—more than the memory of an episode. I think there's a kind of memory mechanism in the cells themselves, especially on the hands, that can be invoked. What I'm getting to is that no matter how long he lives, Cleve Wheeler is going to feel that skin slip under his palms and that is going to bring him nose to nose with that face. No, you're the genius, not me."

"Na. You knew what you were doing. I didn't."

"Hell you didn't." Joe leaned far back in his lawn chaise—so far he could hold up his beer and look at the sun through it from the underside. Watching the receding bubbles defy perspective (because they swell as they rise), he murmured, "Karl?"

"Yuh."

"Ever hear of Occam's Razor?"

"Um. Long time back. Philosophical principle. Or logic or something. Let's see. Given an effect and a choice of possible causes, the simplest cause is always the one most likely to be true. Is that it?"

"Not too close, but close enough," said Joe Trilling lazily. "Hm. You're the one who used to proclaim that logic is sufficient unto itself and need have nothing to do with truth."

"I still proclaim it."

"Okay. Now, you and I know that human greed and carelessness are quite enough all by themselves to wreck this planet. We didn't think that was enough for the likes of Cleve Wheeler, who can really do something about it, so we constructed him a smog-breathing extraterrestrial. I mean, he hadn't done anything about saving the world for our reasons, so we gave him a whizzer of a reason if his own. Right out of our heads."

"Dictated by all available factors. Yes. What are you getting at, Joe?"

"Oh—just that our complicated hoax is simple, really, in the sense that it brought everything down to a single cause. Occam's Razor slices things down to simplest causes. Single causes have a fair chance of being right."

Karl put down his beer with a bump. "I never thought of that. I've been too busy to think of that. *Suppose we were right?*"

They looked at each other, shaken.

At last Karl said, "What do we look for now, Joe—spaceships?"

giANTS

Edward Bryant

Edward Bryant is a short-story writer whose stance from his earliest stories at the beginning of the 1970s has been stylistically ambitious. Many of his early stories were set in a colorful imagined setting hauntingly similar to Ballard's Vermillion Sands or Ray Bradbury's Mars collected in *Cinnabar* (1976). Perhaps Bryant's primary fascination has always been with the imagery of science fiction, not science. Normally he writes in modes other than hard science fiction, but in a few notable instances, including such stories as "Particle Theory" and "giANTS," his interests have coincided with hard sf.

He is of the first generation of writers influenced by the sf monster films of the fifties (these "sci-fi" films were considered just plain bad sf, powerful but inaccurate and therefore silly—later campy). So Bryant entered this territory—pioneered by Miles Breuer in early sf—filled with comical giantism created by science, and took it seriously. For one thing, Breuer and the movies are innocent of the physics of the square-cube law, but this is the point upon which Bryant's story turns. And for another, Bryant knows he's doing serious writing to rigorous standards. In the end, he's trying to satisfy the demands of hard sf and the conflicting demands of fashionable contemporary fiction outside of the genre, thus advancing the literary boundaries of hard sf. The final moment is a memorable and complex image, of which the literal meaning is obscure. This story should be considered along with Gregory Benford's work (*Timescape*, "Exposures," etc.) and Bryant's own "Particle Theory," as setting a new standard for hard sf at the beginning of the 1980s.

Paul Chavez looked from the card on the silver plate to O'Hanlon's face and back to the card. "I couldn't find the tray," she said. "Put the thing away maybe twelve years ago and didn't have time to look. Never expected to need it." Her smile folded like parchment and Chavez thought he heard her lips crackle.

He reached out and took the card. Neat black-on-white printing asserted that one Laynie Bridgewell was a bona fide correspondent for the UBC News Billings bureau. He turned the card over. Sloppy cursive script deciphered as: *Imperitive I talk to you about New Mexico Project.* "Children of electronic journalism," Chavez said amusedly. He set the card back on the plate. "I suppose I ought to see her in the drawing room—if I were going to see her, which I'm not."

"She's a rather insistent young woman," said O'Hanlon.

Chavez sat stiffly down on the couch. He plaited his fingers and rested the palms on the crown of his head. "It's surely time for my nap. Do be polite."

"Of course, Dr. Chavez," said O'Hanlon, sweeping silently out of the room, gracefully turning as she exited to close the doors of the library.

Pain simmered in the joints of his long bones. Chavez shook two capsules from his omnipresent pill case and poured a glass of water from the carafe on the walnut desk. Dr. Hansen had said it would only get worse. Chavez lay on his side on the couch and felt weary—seventy-two years' weary. He supposed he should have walked down the hall to his bedroom, but there was no need. He slept better here in the library. The hardwood panels and the subdued Mondrian originals soothed him. Endless ranks of books stood vigil. He loved to watch the windblown patterns of the pine boughs beyond the French windows that opened onto the balcony. He loved to study the colors as sunlight spilled through the leaded DNA double-helix pane Annie had given him three decades before.

Chavez felt the capsules working faster than he had expected. He thought he heard the tap of something hard against glass. But then he was asleep.

In its basics, the dream never changed.

They were there in the desert somewhere between Albuquerque and Alamogordo, all of them: Ben Peterson, the tough cop; the FBI man Robert Graham; Chavez himself; and Patricia Chavez, his beautiful, brainy daughter.

The wind, gusting all afternoon, had picked up; it whistled steadily, atonally, obscuring conversation. Sand sprayed abrasively against their faces. Even the gaunt stands of spiny cholla bowed with the wind.

Patricia had struck off on her own tangent. She struggled up the base of a twenty-foot dune. She began to slip back almost as far as each step advanced her.

They all heard it above the wind—the shrill, ululating chitter.

"What the hell is that?" Graham yelled.

Chavez shook his head. He began to run toward Patricia. The sand, the wind, securing the brim of his hat with one hand—all conspired to make his gait clumsy.

The immense antennae rose first above the crest of the dune. For a second, Chavez thought they surely must be branches of windblown cholla. Then the head itself heaved into view, faceted eyes coruscating with changing hues of red and blue. Mandibles larger than a farmer's scythe clicked and clashed. The ant paused, apparently surveying the creatures downslope.

"Look at the size of it," said Chavez, more to himself than to the others.

He heard Peterson's shout. "It's as big as a horse!" He glanced back and saw the policeman running for the car.

Graham's reflexes were almost as prompt. He had pulled his .38 Special from the shoulder holster and swung his arm, motioning Patricia to safety, yelling, "Back, get back!" Patricia began to run from the dune all too slowly, feet slipping on the sand, legs constricted by the ankle-length khaki skirt. Graham fired again and again, the gun popping dully in the wind.

The ant hesitated only a few seconds longer. The wind sleeked the tufted hair on its purplish green thorax. Then it launched itself down the slope, all six articulated legs churning with awful precision.

Chavez stood momentarily frozen. He heard a coughing stutter from beside his shoulder. Ben Peterson had retrieved a Thompson submachine gun from the auto. Gouts of sand erupted around the advancing ant. The creature never hesitated.

Patricia lost her race in a dozen steps. She screamed once as the crushing mandibles closed around her waist. She looked despairingly at her father. Blood ran from both corners of her mouth.

There was an instant eerie tableau. The tommy gun fell silent as Peterson let the muzzle fall in disbelief. The hammer of Graham's pistol clicked on a spent cylinder. Chavez cried out.

Uncannily, brutally graceful, the ant wheeled and, still carrying Patricia's body, climbed the slope. It crested the dune and vanished. Its chittering cry remained a moment more before raveling in the wind.

Sand flayed his face as Chavez called out his daughter's name over and over. Someone took his shoulder and shook him, telling him to stop it, to wake up. It wasn't Peterson or Graham.

It was his daughter.

She was his might-have-been daughter.

A concerned expression on her sharp-featured face, she was shaking him by the shoulder. Her eyes were dark brown and enormous. Her hair, straight and cut short, was a lighter brown.

She backed away from him and sat in his worn, leather-covered chair. He saw she was tall and very thin. For a moment he oscillated between dream-orientation and wakefulness. "Patricia?" Chavez said.

She did not answer.

Chavez let his legs slide off the couch and shakily sat up. "Who in the world are you?"

"My name's Laynie Bridgewell," said the young woman.

Chavez's mind focused. "Ah, the reporter."

"Correspondent."

"A semantic distinction. No essential difference." One level of his mind noted with amusement that he was articulating well through the confusion. He still didn't know what the hell was going on. He yawned deeply, stretched until a dart of pain cut the movement short, said, "Did you talk Ms. O'Hanlon into letting you up here?"

"Are you kidding?" Bridgewell smiled. "She must be a great watchdog."

"She's known me a long while. How *did* you get up here?"

Bridgewell looked mildly uncomfortable. "I, uh, climbed up."

"Climbed?"

"Up one of the pines. I shinnied up a tree to the balcony. The French doors were unlocked. I saw you inside sleeping, so I came in and waited."

"A criminal offense," said Chavez.

"They were unlocked," she said defensively.

"I meant sitting and watching me sleep. Terrible invasion of privacy. A person could get awfully upset, not knowing if another human being, a strange one at that, is secretly watching him snore or drool or whatever."

"You slept very quietly," said Bridgewell. "Very still. Until the nightmare."

"Ah," said Chavez. "It was that apparent?"

She nodded. "You seemed really upset. I thought maybe I ought to wake you."

Chavez said, "Did I say anything."

She paused and thought. "Only two words I could make out. A name—Patricia. And you kept saying 'them.' "

"That figures." He smiled. He felt orientation settling around him like familiar wallpaper in a bedroom, or old friends clustering at a departmental cocktail party. "You're from the UBC bureau in Billings?"

"I drove down this morning."

"Work for them long?"

"Almost a year."

"First job?"

She nodded. "First real job."

"You're what—twenty-one?" said Chavez.

"Twenty-two."

"Native?"

"Of Montana?" She shook her head. "Kansas."

"University of Southern California?"

Another shake. "Missouri."

"Ah," he said. "Good school." Chavez paused. "You're here on assignment?"

A third shake. "My own time."

"Ah," said Chavez again. "Ambitious. And you want to talk to me about the New Mexico Project?"

Face professionally sober, voice eager, she said, "Very much. I didn't have any idea you lived so close until I read the alumni bulletin from the University of Wyoming."

"I wondered how you found me out." Chavez sighed. "Betrayed by my alma mater . . ." He looked at her sharply. "I don't grant interviews, even if I occasionally conduct them." He stood and smiled. "Will you be wanting to use the stairs, or would you rather shinny back down the tree?"

"Who is Patricia?" said Bridgewell.

My daughter, Chavez started to say. "Someone from my past," he said.

"I lost people to the bugs," said Bridgewell quietly. "My parents were in Biloxi at the wrong time. Bees never touched them. The insecticide offensive got them both."

The pain in Chavez's joints became ice needles. He stood—and stared.

Even more quietly, Bridgewell said, "You don't have a daughter. Never had. I did my homework." Her dark eyes seemed even larger. "I don't know everything about the New Mexico Project—that's why I'm here. But I can stitch the rumors together." She paused. "I even had the bureau rent an old print of the movie. I watched it four times yesterday."

Chavez felt the disorientation return, felt exhausted, felt—damn it!—old. He fumbled the container of pain pills out of his trouser pocket, then returned it unopened. "Hungry?" he said.

"You better believe it. I had to leave before breakfast."

"I think we'll get some lunch," said Chavez. "Let's go downtown. Try not to startle Ms. O'Hanlon as we leave."

O'Hanlon had encountered them in the downstairs hall, but reacted only with a poker face. "Would you and the young lady like some lunch, Dr. Chavez?"

"Not today," said Chavez, "but thank you. Ms. Bridgewell and I are going to eat in town."

O'Hanlon regarded him. "Have you got your medicine?"

Chavez patted his trouser leg and nodded.

"And you'll be back before dark?"

"Yes," he said. "Yes. And if I'm not, I'll phone. You're not my mother. I'm older than you."

"Don't be cranky," she said. "Have a pleasant time."

Bridgewell and Chavez paused in front of the old stone house. "Why don't we take my car?" said Bridgewell. "I'll run you back after lunch." She glanced at him. "You're not upset about being driven around by a kid, are you?" He smiled and shook his head. "Okay."

They walked a hundred meters to where her car was pulled off the blacktop and hidden in a stand of spruce. It was a Volkswagen beetle of a vintage Chavez estimated to be a little older than its driver.

As if reading his thoughts, Bridgewell said, "Runs like a watch—the old kind, with hands. Got a hundred and ten thousand on her third engine. I call her Scarlett." The car's color was a dim red like dried clay.

"Do you really miss watches with hands?" said Chavez, opening the passenger-side door.

"I don't know—I guess I hadn't really thought about it. I know I don't miss slide rules."

"*I* miss hands on timepieces." Chavez noticed there were no seat belts. "A long time ago, I stockpiled all the Timexes I'd need for my lifetime."

"Does it really make any difference?"

"I suppose not." Chavez considered that as Bridgewell drove onto the highway and turned downhill.

"You love the past a lot, don't you?"

"I'm nostalgic," said Chavez.

"I think it goes a lot deeper than that." Bridgewell handled the VW like a racing Porsche. Chavez held on to the bar screwed onto the glove-box door with both hands. Balding radial tires shrieked as she shot the last curve and they began to descend the slope into Casper. To the east, across the city, they could see a ponderous dirigible-freighter settling gracefully toward a complex of blocks and domes.

"Why," she said, "are they putting a pilot fusion plant squarely in the middle of the biggest coal deposits in the country?"

Chavez shrugged. "When man entered the atomic age he opened a door into a new world. What he may eventually find in that new world no one can predict."

"Huh?" Bridgewell said. Then: "Oh, the movie. Doesn't it ever worry you—having that obsession?"

"No," said Chavez. Bridgewell slowed slightly as the road became city street angling past blocks of crumbling budget housing. "Turn left on Rosa. Head downtown."

"Where are we eating? I'm hungry enough to eat coal by-products."

"Close. We're going to the oil can."

"Huh?" Bridgewell said again.

"The Petroleum Tower. Over there." Chavez pointed at a forty-story cylindrical pile. It was windowed completely with bronze reflective panes. "The rooftop restaurant's rather good."

They left Scarlett in an underground lot and took the high-speed exterior elevator to the top of the Petroleum Tower. Bridgewell closed her eyes as the ground level rushed away from them. At the fortieth floor she opened her eyes to stare at the glassed-in restaurant, the lush hanging plants, the noontime crowd. "Who *are* these people? They all look so, uh, professional."

"They are that," said Chavez, leading the way to the maître d'. "Oil people. Uranium people. Coal people. Slurry people. Shale people. Coal gasification—"

"I've got the point," Bridgewell said. "I feel a little underdressed."

"They know me."

And so, apparently, they did. The maître d' issued orders and Bridgewell and Chavez were instantly ushered to a table beside a floor-to-ceiling window.

"Is this a perk of being maybe the world's greatest molecular biologist?"

Chavez shook his head. "More a condition of originally being a local boy. Even with the energy companies, this is still a small town at heart." He fell silent and looked out the window. The horizon was much closer than he remembered from his childhood. A skiff of brown haze lay over the city. There was little open land to be seen.

They ordered drinks.

They made small talk.

They ordered food.

"This is very pleasant," said Bridgewell, "but I'm still a correspondent. I think you're sitting on the biggest story of the decade."

"That extraterrestrial ambassadors are shortly to land near Albuquerque? That they have picked America as a way station to repair their ship?"

Bridgewell looked bemused. "I'm realizing I don't know when you're kidding."

"Am I now?"

"Yes."

"So why do you persist in questioning me?"

She hesitated. "Because I suspect you want to tell someone. It might as well be me."

He thought about that awhile. The waiter brought the garnish tray and Chavez chewed on a stick of carrot. "Why don't you tell me the pieces you've picked up?"

"And then?"

"We'll see," he said. "I can't promise anything."

Bridgewell said, "You're a lot like my father. I never knew when he was kidding either."

"Your turn," said Chavez.

The soup arrived. Bridgewell sipped a spoonful of French onion and set the utensil down. "The New Mexico Project. It doesn't seem to have anything to do with New Mexico. You wouldn't believe the time I've spent on the phone. All my vacation I ran around that state in Scarlett."

Chavez smiled a long time, finally said, "Think metaphorically. The Manhattan Project was conducted under Stagg Field in Chicago."

"I don't think the New Mexico Project has anything to do with nuclear energy," she said. "But I have heard a lot of mumbling about DNA chimeras."

"So far as I know, no genetic engineer is using recombinant DNA to hybridize creatures with all the more loathsome aspects of snakes, goats, and lions. The state of the art improves, but we're not that good yet."

"But I shouldn't rule out DNA engineering?" she said.

"Keep going."

"Portuguese is the official language of Brazil."

Chavez nodded.

"UBC's stringer in Recife has it that, for quite a while now, nothing's been coming out of the Brazilian nuclear-power complex at Xique-Xique. I mean there's *news*, but it's all through official release. Nobody's going in or out."

Chavez said, "You would expect a station that new and large to be a concern of national security. Shaking down's a long and complex process."

"Maybe." She picked the ripe olives out of the newly arrived salad and carefully placed them in a line on the plate. "I've got a cousin in movie distribution. Just real scut work so far, but she knows what's going on in the industry. She told me that the U.S. Department of Agriculture ordered a print from Warner Brothers dubbed in Portuguese and had it shipped to Brasília. The print was that movie you're apparently so concerned with—*Them!* The one about the ants mutating from radioactivity in the New Mexico desert. The one about giant ants on the rampage."

"Only a paranoid could love this chain of logic," said Chavez.

Her face looked very serious. "If it takes a paranoid to come up with this story and verify it," she said, "then that's what I am. Maybe nobody else is willing to make the jumps. I am. I know nobody else has the facts. I'm going to get them."

To Chavez, it seemed that the table had widened. He looked across the linen wasteland at her. "The formidable Formicidae family . . ." he said. "So have you got a conclusion to state?" He felt the touch of tiny legs on his leg. He felt feathery antennae tickle the hairs on his thigh. He jerked back from the table and his water goblet overturned, the water stain spreading smoothly toward the woman.

"What's wrong?" said Bridgewell. He heard concern in her voice. He slapped at his leg, stopped the motion, drew a deep breath.

"Nothing." Chavez hitched his chair closer to the table again. A waiter hovered at his shoulder, mopping the water with a towel and refilling the goblet. "Your conclusion." His voice strengthened. "I asked about your theory."

"I know this sounds crazy," said Bridgewell. "I've read about how the Argentine fire ants got to Mobile, Alabama. And I damned well know about the bees—I told you that."

Chavez felt the touch again, this time on his ankle. He tried unobtrusively to scratch and felt nothing. Just the touch. Just the tickling, chitinous touch.

"Okay," Bridgewell continued. "All I can conclude is that somebody in South America's created some giant mutant ants, and now they're marching north. Like the fire ants. Like the bees."

"Excuse me a moment," said Chavez, standing.

"Your face is white," said Bridgewell. "Can I help you?"

"No." Chavez turned and, forcing himself not to run, walked to the restroom. In a stall, he lowered his trousers. As he had suspected, there was no creature on his leg. He sat on the toilet and scratched his skinny legs until the skin reddened and he felt the pain. "Damn it," he said to himself. "Stop." He took a pill from the case and downed it with water from the row of faucets. Then he stared at himself in the mirror and returned to the table.

"You okay?" Bridgewell had not touched her food.

He nodded. "I'm prey to any number of ailments; goes with the territory. I'm sorry to disturb your lunch."

"I'm apparently disturbing yours more."

"I offered." He picked up knife and fork and began cutting a slice of cold roast beef. "I offered—so follow this through. Please."

Her voice softened. "I have the feeling this all ties together somehow with your wife."

Chavez chewed the beef, swallowed without tasting it. "Did you look at the window?" Bridgewell looked blank. "The stained glass in the library."

Her expression became mobile. "The spiral design? The double helix? I loved it. The colors are incredible."

"It's exquisite; and it's my past." He took a long breath. "Annie gave it to me for my forty-first birthday. As well, it was our first anniversary. Additionally it was on the occasion of the award. It meant more to me than the trip to Stockholm." He looked at her sharply. "You said you did your homework. How much *do* you know?"

"I know that you married late," said Bridgewell, "for your times."

"Forty."

"I know that your wife died of a freak accident two years later. I didn't follow up."

"You should have," said Chavez. "Annie and I had gone on a picnic in the Florida panhandle. We were driving from Memphis to Tampa. I was cleaning some catfish. Annie wandered off, cataloging insects and plants. She was an amateur taxonomist. For whatever reason—God only knows; I don't—she disturbed a mound of fire ants. They swarmed over her. I heard her screaming. I ran to her and dragged her away and brushed off the ants. Neither of us had known about her protein allergy—she'd just been lucky enough never to have been bitten or stung." He hesitated and shook his head. "I got her to Pensacola. Annie died in anaphylactic shock. The passages swelled, closed off. She suffocated in the car."

Bridgewell looked stricken. She started to say, "I'm sorry, Dr. Chavez. I had no—"

He held up his hand gently. "Annie was eight months pregnant. In the hospital they tried to save our daughter. It didn't work." He shook his head again, as if clearing it. "You and Annie look a bit alike—coltish, I think is the word. I expect Patricia would have looked the same."

The table narrowed. Bridgewell put her hand across the distance and touched his fingers. "You never remarried."

"I disengaged myself from most sectors of life." His voice was dispassionate.

"Why didn't you reengage?"

He realized he had turned his hand over, was allowing his fingers to curl gently around hers. The sensation was warmth. "I spent the first half of my life single-mindedly pursuing certain goals. It took an enormous investment of myself to open my life to Annie." As he had earlier in the morning when he'd first met Bridgewell, he felt profoundly weary. "I suppose I decided to take the easier course: to hold on to the past and call it good."

She squeezed his hand. "I won't ask if it's been worth it."

"What about you?" he said. "You seem to be in ferocious pursuit of your goals. Do you have a rest of your life hidden off to the side?"

Bridgewell hesitated. "No. Not yet. I've kept my life directed, very concentrated, since—since everyone died. But someday . . ." Her voice trailed off. "I still have time."

"Time," Chavez said, recognizing the sardonicism. "Don't count on it."

Her voice very serious, she said, "Whatever happens, I won't let the past dictate to me."

He felt her fingers tighten. "Never lecture someone three times your age," he said. "It's tough to be convincing." He laughed and banished the tension.

"This *is* supposed to be an interview," she said, but didn't take her hand away.

"Did you ever have an ant farm as a child?" Chavez said. She shook her head. "Then we're going to go see one this afternoon." He glanced at the food still in front of her. "Done?" She nodded. "Then let's go out to the university field station."

They stood close together in the elevator. Bridgewell kept her back to the panoramic view. Chavez said, "I've given you no unequivocal statements about the New Mexico Project."

"I know."

"And if I should tell you now that there are indeed monstrous ant mutations—creatures as large as horses—tramping toward us from the Mato Grosso?"

This time she grinned and shook her head silently.

"You think me mad, don't you?"

"I still don't know when you're kidding," she said.

"There are no giant ants," said Chavez. "Yet." And he refused to elaborate.

The field station of the Wyoming State University at Casper was thirty kilometers south, toward the industrial complex at Douglas-River Bend. Two kilometers off the freeway, Scarlett clattered and protested across the potholed access road, but delivered them safely. They crossed the final rise and descended toward the white dome and the cluster of outbuildings.

"That's huge," said Bridgewell. "Freestanding?"

"Supported by internal pressure," said Chavez. "We needed something that could be erected quickly. It was necessary that we have a thoroughly controllable internal environment. It'll be hell to protect from the snow and wind come winter, but we shouldn't need it by then."

There were two security checkpoints with uniformed guards. Armed men and women dubiously inspected the battered VW and its passengers, but waved them through when Chavez produced his identification.

"This is incredible," said Bridgewell.

"It wasn't my idea," said Chavez. "Rules."

She parked Scarlett beside a slab-sided building that adjoined the dome. Chavez guided her inside, past another checkpoint in the lobby, past obsequious underlings in lab garb who said, "Good afternoon, Dr. Chavez," and into a sterile-appearing room lined with electronic gear.

Chavez gestured at the rows of monitor screens. "We can't go into the dome today, but the entire installation is under surveillance through remotely controlled cameras." He began flipping switches. A dozen screens jumped to life in living color.

"It's all jungle," Bridgewell said.

"Rain forest." The cameras panned past vividly green trees, creepers, seemingly impenetrable undergrowth. "It's a reasonable duplication of the Brazilian interior. Now, listen." He touched other switches.

At first the speakers seemed to be crackling with electronic noise. "What am I hearing?" she finally said.

"What does it sound like?"

She listened longer. "Eating?" She shivered. "It's like a thousand mouths eating."

"Many more," Chavez said. "But you have the idea. Now, watch."

The camera eye of the set directly in front of her dollied in toward a wall of greenery wound round a tree. Chavez saw the leaves ripple, undulating smoothly as though they were the surface of an uneasy sea. He glanced at Bridgewell; she saw it too. "Is there wind in the dome?"

"No," he said.

The view moved in for a close-up. "Jesus!" said Bridgewell.

Ants. Ants covered the tree, the undergrowth, the festooned vines.

"You may have trouble with the scale," Chavez said. "They're about as big as your thumb."

The ants swarmed in efficient concert, mandibles snipping like garden shears, stripping everything green, everything alive. Chavez stared at them and felt only a little hate. Most of the emotion had long since been burned from him.

"Behold *Eciton*," said Chavez. "Driver ants, army ants, the *maripunta*, whatever label you'd like to assign."

"I've read about them," said Bridgewell. "I've seen documentaries and movies at one time or another. I never thought they'd be this frightening when they were next door."

"There is fauna in the environment too. Would you like to see a more elaborate meal?"

"I'll pass."

Chavez watched the leaves ripple and vanish, bit by bit. Then he felt the tentative touch, the scurrying of segmented legs along his limbs. He reached out and tripped a single switch; all the pictures flickered and vanished. The two of them sat staring at the opaque gray monitors.

"Those are the giant ants?" she finally said.

"I told you the truth." He shook his head. "Not yet."

"No kidding now," she said.

"The following is a deliberate breach of national security," he said, "so they tell me." He raised his hands. "So what?" Chavez motioned toward the screens. "The *maripunta* apparently are mutating into a radically different form. It's not an obvious physical change, not like in *Them!* It's not by deliberate human agency, as with the bees. It may be through accidental human action—the Brazilian double-X nuclear station is suspected. We just don't know. What we do understand is that certain internal regulators in the *maripunta* have gone crazy."

"And they're getting bigger?" She looked bewildered.

He shook his head violently. "Do you know the square-cube law? No? It's a simple rule of nature. If an insect's dimensions are doubled, its strength and the area of its breathing passages are increased by a factor of four. But the mass is multiplied by eight. After a certain point, and that point isn't very high, the insect can't move or breathe. It collapses under its own mass."

"No giant ants?" she said.

"Not yet. Not exactly. The defective mechanism in the *maripunta* is one which controls the feeding and foraging phases. Ordinarily the ants—all the millions of them in a group—spend about two weeks in a nomadic phase. Then they alternate three weeks in place in a statary phase. That's how it used to be. Now only the nomadic phase remains."

"So they're moving," said Bridgewell. "North?" She sat with hands on knees. Her fingers moved as though with independent life.

"The *maripunta* are ravenous, breeding insanely, and headed our way. The fear is that, like the bees, the ants won't proceed linearly. Maybe they'll leapfrog aboard a charter aircraft. Maybe on a Honduran freighter. It's inevitable."

Bridgewell clasped her hands; forced them to remain still in her lap.

Chavez continued, "Thanks to slipshod internal Brazilian practices over the last few decades, the *maripunta* are resistant to every insecticide we've tried."

"They're unstoppable?" Bridgewell said.

"That's about it," said Chavez.

"And that's why the public's been kept in the dark?"

"Only partially. The other part is that we've found an answer." Chavez toyed with the monitor switches but stopped short of activating them. "The government agencies with this project fear that the public will misunderstand our solution to the problem. Next year's an election year." Chavez smiled ruefully. "There's a precedence to politics."

Bridgewell glanced from the controls to his face. "You're part of the solution. How?"

Chavez decisively flipped a switch and they again saw the ant-ravaged trees. The limbs were perceptibly barer. He left the sound down. "You know my background. You were correct in suspecting the New Mexico Project had something to do with recombinant DNA and genetic engineering. You're a good journalist. You were essentially right all down the line." He looked away from her toward the screen. "I and my people here are creating giant ants."

Bridgewell's mouth dropped open slightly. "I—but you—"

"Let me continue. The purpose of the New Mexico Project has been to tinker with the genetic makeup of the *maripunta*—to create a virus-borne mutagen that will single out the queens. We've got that agent now."

All correspondent again, Bridgewell said, "What will it do?"

"At first we were attempting to readjust the ants' biological clocks and alter the nomadic phase. Didn't work; too sophisticated for what we can accomplish. So we settled for something more basic, more physical. We've altered the ants to make them huge."

"Like in *Them!*"

"Except that *Them!* was a metaphor. It stated a physical impossibility. Remember the square-cube law?" She nodded. "Sometime in the near future, bombers will be dropping payloads all across Brazil, Venezuela, the Guianas . . . anywhere we suspect the ants are. The weapon is dispersal bombs, aerosol canisters containing the viral mutagen to trigger uncontrolled growth in each new generation of ants."

"The square-cube law . . ." said Bridgewell softly.

"Exactly. We've created monsters—and gravity will kill them."

"It'll work?"

"It should." Then Chavez said very quietly, "I hope I live long enough to see the repercussions."

Bridgewell said equally quietly, "I *will* file this story."

"I know that."

"Will it get you into trouble?"

"Probably nothing I can't handle." Chavez shrugged. "Look around you at this multimillion-dollar installation. There were many more convenient places to erect it. I demanded it be built here." His smile was only a flicker. "When you're a giant in your field—and needed—the people in power tend to indulge you."

"Thank you, Dr. Chavez," she said.

"Dr. Chavez? After all this, it's still not Paul?"

"Thanks, Paul."

They drove north, back toward Casper, and watched the western photochemical sunset. The sun sank through the clouds in a splendor of reds. They talked very little. Chavez found the silence comfortable.

Why didn't you reengage?

The question no longer disturbed him. He hadn't truly addressed it. Yet it was no longer swept under the carpet. That made all the difference.

I'll get to it, he thought. Chavez stared into the windshield sun-glare and saw his life bound up in a leaded pane like an ambered insect.

Bridgewell kept glancing at him silently as she drove up the long mountain road to Chavez's house. She passed the stand of pine where she had hidden Scarlett earlier in the day and braked to a stop in front of the stone house. They each sat still for the moment.

"You'll want to be filing your story," said Chavez.

She nodded.

"Now that you know the way up my tree, perhaps you'll return to visit in a more conventional way?"

Bridgewell smiled. She leaned across the seat and kissed him on the lips. It was, Chavez thought, a more than filial kiss. "Now *I'm* not kidding," she said.

Chavez got out of the Volkswagen and stood on the flagstone walk while Bridgewell backed Scarlett into the drive and turned around. As she started down the mountain, she turned and waved. Chavez waved. He stood there and watched until the car vanished around the first turn.

He walked back to the house and found O'Hanlon waiting, arms folded against the twilight chill, on the stone step. Chavez hesitated beside her and they both looked down the drive and beyond. Casper's lights began to blossom into a growing constellation.

"Does she remind you considerably of what Patricia might have been like?" said O'Hanlon.

Chavez nodded, and then said quickly, "Don't go for easy Freud. There's more to it than that—or there may be."

A slight smile tugged at O'Hanlon's lips. "Did I say anything?"

"Well, no." Chavez stared down at the city. He said, with an attempt at great dignity. "We simply found, in a short time, that we liked each other very much."

"I thought that might be it." O'Hanlon smiled a genuine smile. "Shall we go inside? Much longer out here and we'll be ice. I'll fix some chocolate."

He reached for the door. "With brandy?"

"All right."

"And you'll join me?"

"You know I ordinarily abstain, Dr. Chavez, but—" Her smile impossibly continued. "It is rather a special day, isn't it?" She preceded him through the warm doorway.

Chavez followed with a final look at the city. Below the mountain, Casper's constellation winked and bloomed into the zodiac.

Twelve hours later, the copyrighted story by Laynie Bridgewell made the national news and the wire services.

Eighteen hours later, her story was denied by at least five governmental agencies of two sovereign nations.

Twelve days later, Paul Chavez died quietly in his sleep, napping in the library.

Twenty-two days later, squadrons of jet bombers dropped cargoes of hissing aerosol bombs over a third of the South American continent. The world was saved. For a while, anyway. The grotesquely enlarged bodies of *Eciton burchelli* would shortly litter the laterite tropical soil.

Twenty-seven days later, at night, an intruder climbed up to the balcony of Paul Chavez's house on Casper Mountain and smashed the stained-glass picture in the French doors leading into the library. No item was stolen. Only the window was destroyed.

TIME FUZE

Randall Garrett

Randall Garrett was one of the most prolific science fiction writers of the late 1950s and early 1960s, his name a fixture on the contents page of *Astounding* and his lesser stories spread throughout the other digest-size magazines, often under pseudonyms (he and Robert Silverberg on occasion wrote the entire contents of certain issues). He was facile, fast-paced, and his stories were filled with clever ideas and plot twists. He is remembered today almost exclusively for a series of stories in an alternate universe where magic is science, featuring his noble sleuth, Lord Darcy. But for nearly a decade, he was one of the characteristic sf writers of his time (he flourished from the mid-fifties to the mid-sixties), rather like Raymond F. Jones in the decade before him.

This story, from 1954, is an early work, and one of his significant contributions to hard science fiction in the subgenre of explorations of the effects of faster-than-light space travel, and the ironies and logical paradoxes it might present. Other examples include A. E. Van Vogt's "Far Centaurus" and, perhaps, Ian Watson's "The Very Slow Time Machine."

Commander Benedict kept his eyes on the rear plate as he activated the intercom. "All right, cut the power. We ought to be safe enough here."

As he released the intercom, Dr. Leicher, of the astronomical staff, stepped up to his side. "Perfectly safe," he nodded, "although even at this distance a star going nova ought to be quite a display."

Benedict didn't shift his gaze from the plate. "Do you have your instruments set up?"

"Not quite. But we have plenty of time. The light won't reach us for several hours yet. Remember, we were outracing it at ten lights."

The commander finally turned, slowly letting his breath out in a soft sigh. "Dr. Leicher, I would say that this is just about the foulest coincidence that could happen to the first interstellar vessel ever to leave the Solar System."

Leicher shrugged. "In one way of thinking, yes. It is certainly true that we will never know, now, whether Alpha Centauri A ever had any planets. But, in another way, it is extremely fortunate that we should be so near a stellar explosion because of the wealth of scientific information we can obtain. As you say, it is a coincidence, and probably one that happens only once in a billion years. The chances of any particular star going nova are small. That we should be so close when it happens is of a vanishingly small order of probability."

Commander Benedict took off his cap and looked at the damp stain in the sweatband. "Nevertheless, Doctor, it is damned unnerving to come out of ultradrive a couple of hundred million miles from the first star ever visited by man and have to turn tail and run because the damned thing practically blows up in your face."

Leicher could see that Benedict was upset; he rarely used the same profanity twice in one sentence.

They had been downright lucky, at that. If Leicher hadn't seen the star begin to swell and brighten, if he hadn't known what it meant, or if Commander Benedict hadn't been quick enough in shifting the ship back into ultradrive—Leicher had a vision of an incandescent cloud of gaseous metal that had once been a spaceship.

The intercom buzzed. The commander answered. "Yes?"

"Sir, would you tell Dr. Leicher that we have everything set up now?"

Leicher nodded and turned to leave. "I guess we have nothing to do now but wait."

When the light from the nova did come, Commander Benedict was back at the plate again—the forward one, this time, since the ship had been turned around in order to align the astronomy lab in the nose with the star.

Alpha Centauri A began to brighten and spread. It made Benedict think of a light bulb connected through a rheostat, with someone turning that rheostat, turning it until the circuit was well overloaded.

The light began to hurt Benedict's eyes even at that distance and he had to cut down the receptivity in order to watch. After a while, he turned away from the plate. Not because the show was over, but simply because it had slowed to a point beyond which no change seemed to take place to the human eye.

Five weeks later, much to Leicher's chagrin, Commander Benedict announced that they had to leave the vicinity. The ship had only been provisioned to go to Alpha Centauri, scout the system without landing on any of the planets and return. At ten lights, top speed for the ultradrive, it would take better than three months to get back.

"I know you'd like to watch it go through the complete cycle," Benedict said, "but we can't go back home as a bunch of starved skeletons."

Leicher resigned himself to the necessity of leaving much of his work unfinished, and, although he knew it was a case of sour grapes, consoled himself with the thought that he could at least get most of the remaining information from the 500-inch telescope on Luna, four years from then.

As the ship slipped into the not-quite-space through which the ultradrive propelled it, Leicher began to consolidate the material he had already gathered.

Commander Benedict wrote in the log:

> Fifty-four days out from Sol. Alpha Centauri has long since faded back into its pre-blowup state, since we have far outdistanced the light from its explosion. It now looks as it did two years ago. It—

"Pardon me, Commander," Leicher interrupted, "But I have something interesting to show you."

Benedict took his fingers off the keys and turned around in his chair. "What is it, Doctor?"

Leicher frowned at the papers in his hands. "I've been doing some work on the probability of that explosion happening just as it did, and I've come up with some rather frightening figures. As I said before, the probability was small. A little calculation has given us some information which makes it even smaller. For instance: with a possible error of plus or minus two seconds Alpha Centauri A began to explode the instant we came out of ultradrive!

"Now, the probability of that occuring comes out so small that it should happen only once in ten to the 467th seconds."

It was Commander Benedict's turn to frown. "So?"

"Commander, the entire universe is only about ten to the 17th seconds old. But to give you an idea, let's say that the chances of its happening are *once* in millions of trillions of years!"

Benedict blinked. The number, he realized, was totally beyond his comprehension—or anyone else's.

"Well, so what? Now it has happened that one time. That simply means that it will almost certainly never happen again!"

"True. But, Commander, when you buck odds like that and win, the thing to do is look for some factor that is cheating in your favor. If you took a pair of dice and started throwing sevens, one right after another—*for the next couple of thousand years*—you'd begin to suspect they were loaded."

Benedict said nothing; he just waited expectantly.

"There is only one thing that could have done it. Our ship." Leicher said it quietly, without emphasis.

"What we know about the hyperspace, or superspace, or whatever it is we move through in ultradrive is almost nothing. Coming out of it so near to a star might set up some sort of shock wave in normal space which would completely disrupt that star's internal balance, resulting in the liberation of unimaginably vast amounts of energy, causing that star to go nova. We can only assume that we ourselves were the fuze that set off that nova."

Benedict stood up slowly. When he spoke, his voice was a choking whisper. "You mean the sun—Sol—might . . ."

Leicher nodded. "I don't say that it definitely would. But the probability is that we were the cause of the destruction of Alpha Centauri A, and therefore might cause the destruction of Sol in the same way."

Benedict's voice was steady again. "That means that we can't go back again, doesn't it? Even if we're not positive, we can't take the chance."

"Not necessarily. We can get fairly close before we cut out the drive, and come in the rest of the way at sublight speed. It'll take longer, and we'll have to go on half or one-third rations, but we *can* do it!"

"How far away?"

"I don't know what the minimum distance is, but I do know how we can gauge a distance. Remember, neither Alpha Centauri B or C were detonated. We'll have to cut our drive at least as far away from Sol as they are from A."

"I see." The commander was silent for a moment, then: "Very well, Dr. Leicher. If that's the safest way, that's the only way."

Benedict issued the orders, while Leicher figured the exact point at which they must cut out the drive, and how long the trip would take. The rations would have to be cut down accordingly.

Commander Benedict's mind whirled around the monstrousness of the whole thing like some dizzy bee around a flower. What if there had been planets around Centauri A? What if they had been inhabited? Had he, all unwittingly, killed entire races of living, intelligent beings?

But, how could he have known? The drive had never been tested before. It couldn't be tested inside the Solar System—it was too fast. He and his crew had been volunteers, knowing that they might die when the drive went on.

Suddenly, Benedict gasped and slammed his fist down on the desk before him.

Leicher looked up. "What's the matter, Commander?"

"Suppose," came the answer, "Just suppose, that we have the same effect on a star when we *go into* ultradrive as we do when we come out of it?"

Leicher was silent for a moment, stunned by the possibility. There was nothing to say, anyway. They could only wait. . . .

A little more than half a light year from Sol, when the ship reached the point where its occupants could see the light that had left their home sun more than seven months before, they watched it become suddenly, horribly brighter. *A hundred thousand times brighter!*

DESERTION

Clifford D. Simak

Clifford D. Simak was one of the finest modern sf writers. Beginning his career with slam-bang intergalactic adventures in the 1930s, he became one of the most polished, sophisticated, and humane of the writers of Campbell's Golden Age in the 1940s. Algis Budrys has called him "the most charming of John W. Campbell's writers." He remained one of the most popular and respected writers in the field, publishing many award-winning stories and novels for the next fifty years, until his death in the late eighties. Robert A. Heinlein, an admirer of Simak's work, presented an encomium on the occasion of Simak's being named a Grand Master by the Science Fiction Writers of America in 1976. His notable novels include *Ring Around the Sun* (1953); *Time & Again* (1951); *Way Station* (1963); *The Goblin Reservation* (1968); *A Choice of Gods* (1972). His most famous single book, however, is the linked collection of stories from the 1940s, *City* (1952), which chronicles the future of human evolution (and that of robot intelligences, dogs, and, finally, ants) through incidents in the future history of one family, its robot servants, its dogs.

This story cycle is a revered classic of the field, and represents a literary form which was arguably the dominant long form in the genre, at least from Ray Bradbury's *The Martian Chronicles* (1951) to Robert Silverberg's *The World Inside* (1971) or Thomas M. Disch's *334* (1972), between the primacy of the magazine serial (the novel in parts) of the 1930s and 1940s (which had no other market until the paperbacks and small-press reprints of the fifties) and the full-scale novel of science fiction, which became dominant in the 1970s after twenty years of literary evolution, mainly in the form of paperback original novels expanded from magazine novellas (or combining novellas). "Desertion" ("than which there is not much better in the entire Modern Science Fiction canon"—Algis Budrys) is an episode from *City*.

The idea of shape-shifting is very old in folklore, and beguiling, but combining it with the superiority of an alien consciousness in an alien form lends it a new and science-fictional seduction. Simak invented a new mode of transcendence for the human mind and spirit in this story that, once experienced, is so nearly impossible to reject that humanity cannot. This is an elegy.

Four men, two by two, had gone into the howling maelstrom that was Jupiter and had not returned. They had walked into the keening gale—or rather, they had loped, bellies low against the ground, wet sides gleaming in the rain.

For they did not go in the shape of men.

Now the fifth man stood before the desk of Kent Fowler, head of Dome No. 3, Jovian Survey Commission.

Under Fowler's desk, old Towser scratched a flea, then settled down to sleep again.

Harold Allen, Fowler saw with a sudden pang, was young—too young. He had the easy confidence of youth, the face of one who never had known fear. And that was strange. For men in the domes of Jupiter did know fear—fear and humility. It was hard for Man to reconcile his puny self with the mighty forces of the monstrous planet.

"You understand," said Fowler, "that you need not do this. You understand that you need not go."

It was formula, of course. The other four had been told the same thing, but they had gone. This fifth one, Fowler knew, would go as well. But suddenly he felt a dull hope stir within him that Allen wouldn't go.

"When do I start?" asked Allen.

There had been a time when Fowler might have taken quiet pride in that answer, but not now. He frowned briefly.

"Within the hour," he said.

Allen stood waiting, quietly.

"Four other men have gone out and have not returned," said Fowler. "You know that, of course. We want you to return. We don't want you going off on any heroic rescue expedition. The main thing, the only thing, is that you come back, that you prove Man can live in a Jovian form. Go to the first survey stake, no farther, then come back. Don't take any chances. Don't investigate anything. Just come back."

Allen nodded. "I understand all that."

"Miss Stanley will operate the converter," Fowler went on. "You need have no fear on that particular score. The other men were converted without mishap. They left the converter in apparently perfect condition. You will be in thoroughly competent hands. Miss Stanley is the best qualified conversion operator in the Solar System. She has had experience on most of the other planets. That is why she's here."

Allen grinned at the woman and Fowler saw something flicker across Miss Stanley's face—something that might have been pity, or rage—or just plain fear. But it was gone again and she was smiling back at the youth who stood before the desk. Smiling in that prim, school-teacherish way she had of smiling, almost as if she hated herself for doing it.

"I shall be looking forward," said Allen, "to my conversion."

And the way he said it, he made it all a joke, a vast, ironic joke.

But it was no joke.

It was serious business, deadly serious. Upon these tests, Fowler knew, depended the fate of men on Jupiter. If the tests succeeded, the resources of the giant planet would be thrown open. Man would take over Jupiter as he already had taken over the other smaller planets. And if they failed—

If they failed, Man would continue to be chained and hampered by the terrific pressure, the greater force of gravity, the weird chemistry of the planet. He would continue to be shut within the domes, unable to set actual foot upon the planet, unable to see it with direct, unaided vision, forced to rely upon the awkward tractors and the televisor, forced to work with clumsy tools and mechanisms or through the medium of robots that themselves were clumsy.

For Man, unprotected and in his natural form, would be blotted out by Jupiter's terrific pressure of fifteen thousand pounds per square inch, pressure that made terrestrial sea bottoms seem a vacuum by comparison.

Even the strongest metal Earthmen could devise couldn't exist under pressure such as that, under the pressure and the alkaline rains that forever swept the planet. It grew brittle and flaky, crumbling like clay, or it ran away in little streams and puddles of ammonia salts. Only by stepping up the toughness and strength of that metal, by increasing its electronic tension, could it be made to withstand the weight of thousands of miles of swirling, choking gases that made up the atmosphere. And even when that was done, everything had to be coated with tough quartz to keep away the rain—the liquid ammonia that fell as bitter rain.

Fowler sat listening to the engines in the subfloor of the dome—engines that ran on endlessly, the dome never quiet of them. They had to run and keep on running, for if they stopped, the power flowing into the metal walls of the dome would stop, the electronic tension would ease up and that would be the end of everything.

Towser roused himself under Fowler's desk and scratched another flea, his leg thumping hard against the floor.

"Is there anything else?" asked Allen.

Fowler shook his head. "Perhaps there's something you want to do," he said. "Perhaps you—"

He had meant to say write a letter and he was glad he caught himself quick enough so he didn't say it.

Allen looked at his watch. "I'll be there on time," he said. He swung around and headed for the door.

Fowler knew Miss Stanley was watching him and he didn't want to turn and meet her eyes. He fumbled with a sheaf of papers on the desk before him.

"How long are you going to keep this up?" asked Miss Stanley and she bit off each word with a vicious snap.

He swung around in his chair and faced her then. Her lips were drawn into a straight, thin line, her hair seemed skinned back from her forehead tighter than ever, giving her face that queer, almost startling death-mask quality.

He tried to make his voice cool and level. "As long as there's any need of it," he said. "As long as there's any hope."

"You're going to keep on sentencing them to death," she said. "You're going to keep marching them out face to face with Jupiter. You're going to sit in here safe and comfortable and send them out to die."

"There is no room for sentimentality, Miss Stanley," Fowler said, trying to keep the note of anger from his voice. "You know as well as I do why we're doing this. You realize that Man in his own form simply cannot cope with Jupiter. The only answer is to turn men into the sort of things that can cope with it. We've done it on the other planets.

"If a few men die, but we finally succeed, the price is small. Through the ages men have thrown away their lives on foolish things, for foolish reasons. Why should we hesitate, then, at a little death in a thing as great as this?"

Miss Stanley sat stiff and straight, hands folded in her lap, the lights shining on her graying hair and Fowler, watching her, tried to imagine what she might feel, what she might be thinking. He wasn't exactly afraid of her, but he didn't feel quite comfortable when she was around. These sharp blue eyes saw too much, her hands looked far too competent. She should be somebody's aunt sitting in a rocking chair with her knitting needles. But she wasn't. She was the top-notch conversion unit operator in the Solar System and she didn't like the way he was doing things.

"There is something wrong, Mr. Fowler," she declared.

"Precisely," agreed Fowler. "That's why I'm sending young Allen out alone. He may find out what it is."

"And if he doesn't?"

"I'll send someone else."

She rose slowly from her chair, started toward the door, then stopped before his desk.

"Some day," she said, "you will be a great man. You never let a chance go by. This is your chance. You knew it was when this dome was picked for the tests. If you put it through, you'll go up a notch or two. No matter how many men may die, you'll go up a notch or two."

"Miss Stanley," he said and his voice was curt, "young Allen is going out soon. Please be sure that your machine—"

"My machine," she told him, icily, "is not to blame. It operates along the coordinates the biologists set up."

He sat hunched at his desk, listening to her footsteps go down the corridor.

What she said was true, of course. The biologists had set up the coordinates. But the biologists could be wrong. Just a hairbreadth of difference, one iota of digression and the converter would be sending out something that wasn't the thing they meant to send. A mutant that might crack up, go haywire, come unstuck under some condition or stress of circumstance wholly unsuspected.

For Man didn't know much about what was going on outside. Only what his instruments told him was going on. And the samplings of those happenings furnished by those instruments and mechanisms had been no more than samplings, for Jupiter was unbelievably large and the domes were very few.

Even the work of the biologists in getting the data on the Lopers, apparently the highest form of Jovian life, had involved more than three years of intensive study and after that two years of checking to make sure. Work that could have been done on Earth in a week or two. But work that, in this case, couldn't be done on Earth at all, for one couldn't take a Jovian life form to Earth. The pressure here on Jupiter couldn't be duplicated outside of Jupiter and at Earth pressure and temperature the Lopers would simply have disappeared in a puff of gas.

Yet it was work that had to be done if Man ever hoped to go about Jupiter in the life form of the Lopers. For before the converter could change a man to another life form, every detailed physical characteristic of that life form must be known—surely and positively, with no chance of mistake.

Allen did not come back.

The tractors, combing the nearby terrain, found no trace of him, unless the skulking thing reported by one of the drivers had been the missing Earthman in Loper form.

The biologists sneered their most accomplished academic sneers when Fowler suggested the coordinates might be wrong. Carefully they pointed out, the coordinates worked. When a man was put into the converter and the switch was thrown, the man became a Loper. He left the machine and moved away, out of sight, into the soupy atmosphere.

Some quirk, Fowler had suggested; some tiny deviation from the thing a Loper should be, some minor defect. If there were, the biologists said, it would take years to find it.

And Fowler knew that they were right.

So there were five men now instead of four and Harold Allen had walked out into Jupiter for nothing at all. It was as if he'd never gone so far as knowledge was concerned.

Fowler reached across his desk and picked up the personnel file, a thin sheaf of paper neatly clipped together. It was a thing he dreaded but a thing he had to do.

Somehow the reason for these strange disappearances must be found. And there was no other way than to send out more men.

He sat for a moment listening to the howling of the wind above the dome, the everlasting thundering gale that swept across the planet in boiling, twisting wrath.

Was there some threat out there, he asked himself? Some danger they did not know about? Something that lay in wait and gobbled up the Lopers, making no distinction between Lopers that were *bona fide* and Lopers that were men? To the gobblers, of course, it would make no difference.

Or had there been a basic fault in selecting the Lopers as the type of life best fitted for existence on the surface of the planet? The evident intelligence of the Lopers, he knew, had been one factor in that determination. For if the thing Man became did not have capacity for intelligence, Man could not for long retain his own intelligence in such a guise.

Had the biologists let that one factor weigh too heavily, using it to offset some other factor that might be unsatisfactory, even disastrous? It didn't seem likely. Stiff-necked as they might be, the biologists knew their business.

Or was the whole thing impossible, doomed from the very start? Conversion to other life forms had worked on other planets, but that did not necessarily mean it would work on Jupiter. Perhaps Man's intelligence could not function correctly through the sensory apparatus provided Jovian life. Perhaps the Lopers were so alien there was no common ground for human knowledge and the Jovian conception of existence to meet and work together.

Or the fault might lie with Man, be inherent with the race. Some mental aberration which, coupled with what they found outside, wouldn't let them come back. Although it might not be an aberration, not in the human sense. Perhaps just one ordinary human mental trait, accepted as commonplace on Earth, would be so violently at odds with Jovian existence that it would blast human sanity.

Claws rattled and clicked down the corridor. Listening to them. Fowler smiled wanly. It was Towser coming back from the kitchen, where he had gone to see his friend, the cook.

Towser came into the room, carrying a bone. He wagged his tail at Fowler and flopped down beside the desk, bone between his paws. For a long moment his rheumy old eyes regarded his master and Fowler reached down a hand to ruffle a ragged ear.

"You still like me, Towser?" Fowler asked and Towser thumped his tail.

"You're the only one," said Fowler.

He straightened and swung back to the desk. His hand reached out and picked up the file.

Bennett? Bennett had a girl waiting for him back on Earth.

Andrews? Andrews was planning on going back to Mars Tech just as soon as he earned enough to see him through a year.

Olson? Olson was nearing pension age. All the time telling the boys how he was going to settle down and grow roses.

Carefully, Fowler laid the file back on the desk.

Sentencing men to death. Miss Stanley had said that, her pale lips scarcely moving in her parchment face. Marching men out to die while he, Fowler, sat here safe and comfortable.

They were saying it all through the dome, no doubt, especially since Allen had failed to return. They wouldn't say it to his face, of course. Even the man or men he called before his desk and told they were the next to go wouldn't say it to him.

But he would see it in their eyes.

He picked up the file again. Bennett, Andrews, Olson. There were others, but there was no use in going on.

Kent Fowler knew that he couldn't do it, couldn't face them, couldn't send more men out to die.

He leaned forward and flipped up the toggle on the intercommunicator.

"Yes, Mr. Fowler."

"Miss Stanley, please."

He waited for Miss Stanley, listening to Towser chewing halfheartedly on the bone. Towser's teeth were getting bad.

"Miss Stanley," said Miss Stanley's voice.

"Just wanted to tell you, Miss Stanley, to get ready for two more."

"Aren't you afraid," asked Miss Stanley, "that you'll run out of them? Sending out one at a time, they'd last longer, give you twice the satisfaction."

"One of them," said Fowler, "will be a dog."

"A dog!"

"Yes, Towser."

He heard the quick, cold rage that iced her voice. "Your own dog! He's been with you all these years—"

"That's the point," said Fowler. "Towser would be unhappy if I left him behind."

It was not the Jupiter he had known through the televisor. He had expected it to be different, but not like this. He had expected a hell of ammonia rain and stinking fumes and the deafening, thundering tumult of the storm. He had expected swirling clouds and fog and the snarling flicker of monstrous thunderbolts.

He had not expected the lashing downpour would be reduced to drifting purple mist that moved like fleeing shadows over a red and purple sward. He had not even guessed the snaking bolts of lightning would be flares of pure ecstasy across a painted sky.

Waiting for Towser, Fowler flexed the muscles of his body, amazed at the smooth, sleek strength he found. Not a bad body, he decided, and grimaced at remembering how he had pitied the Lopers when he glimpsed them through the television screen.

For it had been hard to imagine a living organism based upon ammonia and hydrogen rather than upon water and oxygen, hard to believe that such a form of life could know the same quick thrill of life that humankind could know. Hard to conceive of life out in the soupy maelstrom that was Jupiter, not knowing, of course, that through Jovian eyes it was no soupy maelstrom at all.

The wind brushed against him with what seemed gentle fingers and he remembered with a start that by Earth standards the wind was a roaring gale, a two-hundred-mile-an-hour howler laden with deadly gases.

Pleasant scents seeped into his body. And yet scarcely scents, for it was not the sense of smell as he remembered it. It was as if his whole being was soaking up the sensation of lavender—and yet not lavender. It was something, he knew, for which he had no word, undoubtedly the first of many enigmas in terminology. For the words he knew, the thought symbols that served him as an Earthman would not serve him as a Jovian.

The lock in the side of the dome opened and Towser came tumbling out—at least he thought it must be Towser.

He started to call to the dog, his mind shaping the words he meant to say. But he couldn't say them. There was no way to say them. He had nothing to say them with.

For a moment his mind swirled in muddy terror, a blind fear that eddied in little puffs of panic through his brain.

How did Jovians talk? How—

Suddenly he was aware of Towser, intensely aware of the bumbling, eager friendliness of the shaggy animal that had followed him from Earth to many planets. As if the thing that was Towser had reached out and for a moment sat within his brain.

And out of the bubbling welcome that he sensed, came words.

"Hiya, pal."

Not words really, better than words. Thought symbols in his brain, communicated thought symbols that had shades of meaning words could never have.

"Hiya, Towser," he said.

"I feel good," said Towser. "Like I was a pup. Lately I've been feeling pretty punk. Legs stiffening up on me and teeth wearing down to almost nothing. Hard to mumble a bone with teeth like that. Besides, the fleas give me hell. Used to be I never paid much attention to them. A couple of fleas more or less never meant much in my early days."

"But . . . but—" Fowler's thoughts tumbled awkwardly. "You're talking to me!"

"Sure thing," said Towser. "I always talked to you, but you couldn't hear me. I tried to say things to you, but I couldn't make the grade."

"I understood you sometimes," Fowler said.

"Not very well," said Towser. "You knew when I wanted food and when I wanted a drink and when I wanted out, but that's about all you ever managed."

"I'm sorry," Fowler said.

"Forget it," Towser told him. "I'll race you to the cliff."

For the first time, Fowler saw the cliff, apparently many miles away, but with a strange crystalline beauty that sparkled in the shadow of the many-colored clouds.

Fowler hesitated. "It's a long way—"

"Ah, come on," said Towser and even as he said it he started for the cliff.

Fowler followed, testing his legs, testing the strength in that new body of his, a bit doubtful at first, amazed a moment later, then running with a sheer joyousness that was one with the red and purple sward, with the drifting smoke of the rain across the land.

As he ran the consciousness of music came to him, a music that beat into his body, that surged throughout his being, that lifted him on wings of silver speed. Music like bells might make from some steeple on a sunny, springtime hill.

As the cliff drew nearer the music deepened and filled the universe with a spray of magic sound. And he knew the music came from the tumbling waterfall that feathered down the face of the shining cliff.

Only, he knew, it was no waterfall, but an ammonia-fall and the cliff was white because it was oxygen, solidified.

He skidded to a stop beside Towser where the waterfall broke into a glittering rainbow of many hundred colors. Literally many hundred, for here, he saw, was no shading of one primary to another as human beings saw, but a clear-cut selectivity that broke the prism down to its last ultimate classification.

"The music," said Towser.

"Yes, what about it?"

"The music," said Towser, "is vibrations. Vibrations of water falling."

"But Towser, you don't know about vibrations."

"Yes, I do," contended Towser. "It just popped into my head."

Fowler gulped mentally. "Just popped!"

And suddenly, within his own head, he held a formula—the formula for a process that would make metal to withstand the pressure of Jupiter.

He stared, astounded, at the waterfall and swiftly his mind took the many colors and placed them in their exact sequence in the spectrum. Just like that. Just out of the blue sky. Out of nothing, for he knew nothing either of metals or of colors.

"Towser," he cried. "Towser, something's happening to us!"

"Yeah, I know," said Towser.

"It's our brains," said Fowler. "We're using them, all of them, down to the last hidden corner. Using them to figure out things we should have known all the time. Maybe the brains of Earth things naturally are slow and foggy. Maybe we are the morons of the universe. Maybe we are fixed so we have to do things the hard way."

And, in the new sharp clarity of thought that seemed to grip him, he knew that it would not only be the matter of colors in a waterfall or metals that would resist the pressure of Jupiter. He sensed other things, things not quite clear. A vague whispering that hinted of greater things, of mysteries beyond the pale of human thought, beyond even the pale of human imagination. Mysteries, fact, logic built on reasoning. Things that any brain should know if it used all its reasoning power.

"We're still mostly Earth," he said. "We're just beginning to learn a few of the things we are to know—a few of the things that were kept from us as human beings, perhaps because we were human beings. Because our human bodies were poor bodies. Poorly equipped for thinking, poorly equipped in certain senses that one has to have to know. Perhaps even lacking in certain senses that are necessary to true knowledge."

He stared back at the dome, a tiny black thing dwarfed by the distance.

Back there were men who couldn't see the beauty that was Jupiter. Men who thought that swirling clouds and lashing rain obscured the planet's face. Unseeing human eyes. Poor eyes. Eyes that could not see the beauty of the clouds, that could not see through the storm. Bodies that could not feel the thrill of trilling music stemming from the rush of broken water.

Men who walked alone, in terrible loneliness, talking with their tongue like Boy Scouts wigwagging out their messages, unable to reach out and touch one another's minds as he could reach out and touch Towser's mind. Shut off forever from that personal, intimate contact with other living things.

He, Fowler, had expected terror inspired by alien things out here on the surface, had expected to cower before the threat of unknown things, had steeled himself against disgust of a situation that was not of Earth.

But instead he had found something greater than Man had ever known. A swifter, surer body. A sense of exhilaration, a deeper sense of life. A sharper mind. A world of beauty that even the dreamers of the Earth had not yet imagined.

"Let's get going," Towser urged.

"Where do you want to go?"

"Anywhere," said Towser. "Just start going and see where we end up. I have a feeling . . . well, a feeling—"

"Yes, I know," said Fowler.

For he had the feeling, too. The feeling of high destiny. A certain sense of greatness. A knowledge that somewhere off beyond the horizons lay adventure and things greater than adventure.

Those other five had felt it, too. Had felt the urge to go and see, the compelling sense that here lay a life of fullness and of knowledge.

That, he knew, was why they had not returned.

"I won't go back," said Towser.

"We can't let them down," said Fowler.

Fowler took a step or two, back toward the dome, then stopped.

Back to the dome. Back to that aching, poison-laden body he had left. It hadn't seemed aching before, but now he knew it was.

Back to the fuzzy brain. Back to muddled thinking. Back to the flapping mouths that formed signals others understood. Back to eyes that now would be worse than no sight at all. Back to squalor, back to crawling, back to ignorance.

"Perhaps some day," he said, muttering to himself.

"We got a lot to do and a lot to see," said Towser. "We got a lot to learn. We'll find things—"

Yes, they could find things. Civilizations, perhaps. Civilizations that would make the civilization of Man seem puny by comparison. Beauty and, more important, an understanding of that beauty. And a comradeship no one had ever known before—that no man, no dog had ever known before.

And life. The quickness of life after what seemed a drugged existence.

"I can't go back," said Towser.

"Nor I," said Fowler.

"They would turn me back into a dog," said Towser.

"And me," said Fowler, "back into a man."

Part Three

KYRIE

Poul Anderson

Poul Anderson is one of the standard hard science fiction writers, in the tradition of Kipling, in the tradition of Campbell, in the tradition of Heinlein. He financed his honors degree in physics by writing, and has remained a writer since graduating in 1948. Distinguished as a fantasy writer—*The Broken Sword* (1954) was his first adult novel—and a mystery writer—his first mystery, *Perish by the Sword* (1959), won the Cock Robin prize—he is nevertheless principally one of the heroic figures of hard science fiction, a Campbell man whose stories have appeared in *Astounding/Analog* for five decades.

Anderson has always defended the traditions of military honor in his fiction, and devoted much of his effort to adventure plots. His many volumes of Dominic Flandry stories and novels are exemplars. But he has also turned out a number of colorful, powerful hard science fiction stories and novels, from *Brain Wave* (1954) to *The Boat of a Million Years* (1989), that are generally perceived as his major works—the most famous is probably *Tau Zero* (1970). These are marked by astronomical and physical speculation and large-scale Stapledonian vistas of time and space. Even in his swashbuckling adventure stories, he is famous for beginning with calculations of the elements of the orbit of the world to be his setting, and allowing the physics, chemistry, and biology to follow logically. He is an admirer of Hal Clement's work, and himself wrote a nonfiction book, *Is There Life on Other Worlds?* (1963), on the general subject of what kinds of life forms might inhabit what kinds of planets.

"Kyrie" is among his classic hard sf stories, one of the earliest astronomical sf tales to speculate about black holes, and the seed of many other sf stories on the topic, including Frederik Pohl's award-winning novel, *Gateway* (1977), Larry Niven's "Neutron Star" and "The Hole Man," and Jerry Pournelle's "He Fell into a Dark Hole." A deep, many-layered blending of conventional sf tropes, told in Anderson's rich prose style, "Kyrie" juxtaposes the sentimental and the coldly rational more subtly than, say, "The Cold Equations," but the message is the same. "Kyrie" is also in the lineage of Arthur C. Clarke's "The Star," and James Blish's "A Case of Conscience," of sf stories which use images of astronomy and astronomical distance to address problems of religion and metaphysics. *The Encyclopedia of Science Fiction* calls him "sf's most prolific writer of any consistent quality." If any living sf writer is the heir to Heinlein's mantle as the dean of science fiction, it is Poul Anderson.

On a high peak in the Lunar Carpathians stands a convent of St. Martha of Bethany. The walls are native rock; they lift dark and cragged as the mountainside itself, into a sky that is always black. As you approach from North-pole, flitting low to keep the force screens along Route Plato between you and the meteoroidal rain, you see the cross which surmounts the tower, stark athwart Earth's blue disc. No bells resound from there—not in airlessness.

You may hear them inside at the canonical hours, and throughout the crypts below where machines toil to maintain a semblance of terrestrial environment. If you linger a while you will also hear them calling to requiem mass. For it has become a tradition that prayers be offered at St. Martha's for those who have perished in space; and they are more with every passing year.

This is not the work of the sisters. They minister to the sick, the needy, the crippled, the insane, all whom space has broken and cast back. Luna is full of such, exiles because they can no longer endure Earth's pull or because it is feared they may be incubating a plague from some unknown planet or because men are so busy with their frontiers that they have no time to spare for the failures. The sisters wear spacesuits as often as habits, are as likely to hold a medikit as a rosary.

But they are granted some time for contemplation. At night, when for half a month the sun's glare has departed, the chapel is unshuttered and stars look down through the glaze-dome to the candles. They do not wink and their light is winter cold. One of the nuns in particular is there as often as may be, praying for her own dead. And the abbess sees to it that she can be present when the yearly mass, that she endowed before she took her vows, is sung.

Requiem aeternam dona eis, Domine,
et lux perpetua luceat eis.
Kyrie eleison, Christe eleison, Kyrie eleison.

The Supernova Sagittarii expedition comprised fifty human beings and a flame. It went the long way around from Earth orbit, stopping at Epsilon Lyrae to pick up its last member. Thence it approached its destination by stages.

This is the paradox: time and space are aspects of each other. The explosion was more than a hundred years past when noted by men on Lasthope. They were part of a generations-long effort to fathom the civilization of creatures altogether unlike us; but one night they looked up and saw a light so brilliant it cast shadows.

That wave front would reach Earth several centuries hence. By then it would be so tenuous that nothing but another bright point would appear in the sky. Meanwhile, though, a ship overleaping the space through which light must creep could track the great star's death across time.

Suitably far off, instruments recorded what had been before the outburst: incandescence collapsing upon itself after the last nuclear fuel was burned out. A jump, and they saw what happened a century ago: convulsion, storm of quanta and neutrinos, a radiation equal to the massed hundred billion suns of this galaxy.

It faded, leaving an emptiness in heaven, and the *Raven* moved closer. Fifty light-years—fifty years—inward, she studied a shrinking fieriness in the midst of a fog which shone like lightning.

Twenty-five years later the central globe had dwindled more, the nebula had expanded and dimmed. But because the distance was now so much less, everything seemed larger and brighter. The naked eye saw a dazzle too fierce to look straight at, making the constellations pale by contrast. Telescopes showed a blue-white spark in the heart of an opalescent cloud delicately filamented at the edges.

The *Raven* made ready for her final jump, to the immediate neighbourhood of the supernova.

Captain Teodor Szili went on a last-minute inspection tour. The ship murmured around him, running at one gravity of acceleration to reach the desired intrinsic velocity. Power droned, regulators whickered, ventilation systems rustled. He felt the energies quiver in his bones. But metal surrounded him, blank and comfortless. Viewports gave on a dragon's hoard of stars, the ghostly arch of the Milky Way: on vacuum, cosmic rays, cold not far above absolute zero, distance beyond imagination to the nearest human hearth-fire. He was about to take his people where none had ever been before, into conditions none was sure about, and that was a heavy burden on him.

He found Eloise Waggoner at her post, a cubbyhole with intercom connections directly to the command bridge. Music drew him, a triumphant serenity he did not recognize. Stopping in the doorway, he saw her seated with a small tape machine on the desk.

"What's this?" he demanded.

"Oh!" The woman (he could not think of her as a girl though she was barely out of her teens) started. "I . . . I was waiting for the jump."

"You were to wait at the alert."

"What have I to do?" she answered less timidly than was her wont. "I mean, I'm not a crewman or a scientist."

"You are in the crew. Special communications technician."

"With Lucifer. And he likes the music. He says we come closer to oneness with it than in anything else he knows about us."

Szili arched his brows. "Oneness?"

A blush went up Eloise's thin cheeks. She stared at the deck and her hands twisted together. "Maybe that isn't the right word. Peace, harmony, unity . . . God? . . . I sense what he means, but we haven't any word that fits."

"Hm. Well, you are supposed to keep him happy." The skipper regarded her with a return of the distaste he had tried to suppress. She was a decent sort, he supposed, in her gauche and inhibited way; but her looks! Scrawny, big-footed, big-nosed, pop eyes, and stringy dust-coloured hair—and, to be sure, telepaths always made him uncomfortable. She said she could only read Lucifer's mind, but was that true?

No. Don't think such things. Loneliness and otherness can come near breaking you out here, without adding suspicion of your fellows.

If Eloise Waggoner was really human. She must be some kind of mutant at the very least. Whoever could communicate thought to thought with a living vortex had to be.

"What are you playing, anyhow?" Szili asked.

"Bach. The Third Brandenburg Concerto. He, Lucifer, he doesn't care for the modern stuff. I don't either."

You wouldn't, Szili decided. Aloud: "Listen, we jump in half an hour. No telling what we'll emerge in. This is the first time anyone's been close to a recent supernova. We can only be certain of so much hard radiation that we'll be dead if the screenfields give way. Otherwise we've nothing to go on except theory. And a collapsing stellar core is so unlike anything anywhere else in the universe that I'm sceptical about how good the theory is. We can't sit daydreaming. We have to prepare."

"Yes, sir." Whispering, her voice lost its casual harshness.

He stared past her, past the ophidian eyes of meters and controls, as if he could penetrate the steel beyond and look straight into space. There, he knew, floated Lucifer.

The image grew in him: a fireball twenty metres across, shimmering white, red, gold, royal blue, flames dancing like Medusa locks, cometary tail burning for a hundred metres behind, a shiningness, a glory, a piece of hell. Not the least of what troubled him was the thought of that which paced his ship.

He hugged scientific explanations to his breast, though they were little better than guesses. In the multiple star system of Epsilon Aurigae, in the gas and energy pervading the space around, things took place which no laboratory could imitate. Ball lightning on a planet was perhaps analogous, as the formation of simple organic compounds in a primordial ocean is analogous to the life which finally evolves. In Epsilon Aurigae, magnetohydrodynamics had done what chemistry did on Earth. Stable plasma vortices had appeared, had grown, had added complexity, until after millions of years they became something you must needs call an organism. It was a form of ions, nuclei and force-fields. It metabolized electrons, nucleons, X rays; it maintained its configuration for a long lifetime; it reproduced; it thought.

But what did it think? The few telepaths who could communicate with the Aurigeans, who had first made humankind aware that the Aurigeans existed, never explained clearly. They were a queer lot themselves.

Wherefore Captain Szili said, "I want you to pass this on to him."

"Yes, sir." Eloise turned down the volume on her taper. Her eyes unfocused. Through her ears went words, and her brain (how efficient a transducer was it?) passed the meanings on out to him who loped alongside *Raven* on his own reaction drive.

"Listen, Lucifer. You have heard this often before, I know, but I want to be positive you understand in full. Your psychology must be very foreign to ours. Why did you agree to come with us? I don't know. Technician Waggoner said you were curious and adventurous. Is that the whole truth?

"No matter. In half an hour we jump. We'll come within five hundred million kilometers of the supernova. That's where your work begins. You can go where we dare not, observe what we can't, tell us more than our instruments would ever hint at. But first we have to verify we can stay in orbit around the star. This concerns you too. Dead men can't transport you home again.

"So. In order to enclose you within the jumpfield, without disrupting your body, we have to switch off the shield screens. We'll emerge in a lethal radiation zone. You must promptly retreat from the ship, because we'll start the screen generator up sixty seconds after transit. Then you must investigate the vicinity. The hazards to look for—" Szili listed them. "Those are only what we can foresee. Perhaps we'll hit other garbage we haven't predicted. If anything seems like a menace, return at once, warn us, and prepare for a jump back to here. Do you have that? Repeat."

Words jerked from Eloise. They were a correct recital; but how much was she leaving out?

"Very good." Szili hesitated. "Proceed with your concert if you like. But break it off at zero minus ten minutes and stand by."

"Yes, sir." She didn't look at him. She didn't appear to be looking anywhere in particular.

His footsteps clacked down the corridor and were lost.

—Why did he say the same things over? asked Lucifer.

"He is afraid," Eloise said.

—?—.

"I guess you don't know about fear," she said.

—Can you show me? . . . No, do not. I sense it is hurtful. You must not be hurt.

"I can't be afraid anyway, when your mind is holding mine."

(Warmth filled her. Merriment was there, playing like little flames over the surface of Father-leading-her-by-the-hand-when-she-was-just-a-child-and-they-went-out-one-summer's-day-to-pick-wildflowers; over strength and gentleness and

Bach and God.) Lucifer swept around the hull in an exuberant curve. Sparks danced in his wake.

—Think flowers again. Please.

She tried.

—They are like (image, as nearly as a human brain could grasp, of fountains blossoming with gamma-ray colours in the middle of light, everywhere light). But so tiny. So brief a sweetness.

"I don't understand how you can understand," she whispered.

—You understand for me. I did not have that kind of thing to love, before you came.

"But you have so much else. I try to share it, but I'm not made to realize what a star is."

—Nor I for planets. Yet ourselves may touch.

Her cheeks burned anew. The thought rolled on, interweaving its counterpoint to the marching music. —That is why I came, do you know? For you. I am fire and air. I had not tasted the coolness of water, the patience of earth, until you showed me. You are moonlight on an ocean.

"No, don't," she said. "Please."

Puzzlement: —Why not? Does joy hurt? Are you not used to it?

"I, I guess that's right." She flung her head back. "No! Be damned if I'll feel sorry for myself!"

—Why should you? Have we not all reality to be in, and is it not full of suns and songs?

"Yes. To you. Teach me."

—If you in turn will teach me— The thought broke off. A contact remained, unspeaking, such as she imagined must often prevail among lovers.

She glowered at Motilal Mazundar's chocolate face, where the physicist stood in the doorway. "What do you want?"

He was surprised. "Only to see if everything is well with you, Miss Waggoner."

She bit her lip. He had tried harder than most aboard to be kind to her. "I'm sorry," she said. "I didn't mean to bark at you. Nerves."

"We are everyone on edge." He smiled. "Exciting though this venture is, it will be good to come home, correct?"

Home, she thought: four walls of an apartment above a banging city street. Books and television. She might present a paper at the next scientific meeting, but no one would invite her to the parties afterwards.

Am I that horrible? she wondered. *I know I'm not anything to look at, but I try to be nice and interesting. Maybe I try too hard.*

—You do not with me, Lucifer said.

"You're different," she told him.

Mazundar blinked. "Beg pardon?"

"Nothing," she said in haste.

"I have wondered about an item," Mazundar said in an effort at conversation. "Presumably Lucifer will go quite near the supernova. Can you still maintain contact with him? The time dilation effect, will that not change the frequency of his thoughts too much?"

"What time dilation?" She forced a chuckle. "I'm no physicist. Only a little librarian who turned out to have a wild talent."

"You were not told? Why, I assumed everybody was. An intense gravitational field affects time just as a high velocity does. Roughly speaking, processes take place more slowly than they do in clear space. That is why light from a massive star is somewhat reddened. And our supernova core retains almost three solar masses.

Furthermore, it has acquired such a density that its attraction at the surface is, ah, incredibly high. Thus by our clocks it will take infinite time to shrink to the Schwarzschild radius; but an observer on the star itself would experience this whole shrinkage in a fairly short period."

"Schwarzschild radius? Be so good as to explain." Eloise realized that Lucifer had spoken through her.

"If I can without mathematics. You see, this mass we are to study is so great and so concentrated that no force exceeds the gravitational. Nothing can counterbalance. Therefore the process will continue until no energy can escape. The star will have vanished out of the universe. In fact, theoretically the contraction will proceed to zero volume. Of course, as I said, that will take forever as far as we are concerned. And the theory neglects quantum-mechanical considerations which come into play towards the end. Those are still not very well understood. I hope, from this expedition, to acquire more knowledge." Mazundar shrugged. "At any rate, Miss Waggoner, I was wondering if the frequency shift involved would not prevent our friend from communicating with us when he is near the star."

"I doubt that." Still Lucifer spoke, she was his instrument and never had she known how good it was to be used by one who cared. "Telepathy is not a wave phenomenon. Since it transmits instantaneously, it cannot be. Nor does it appear limited by distance. Rather, it is a resonance. Being attuned, we two may well be able to continue thus across the entire breadth of the cosmos; and I am not aware of any material phenomenon which could interfere."

"I see." Mazundar gave her a long look. "Thank you," he said uncomfortably. "Ah . . . I must get to my own station. Good luck." He bustled off without stopping for an answer.

Eloise didn't notice. Her mind was become a torch and a song. "Lucifer!" she cried aloud. "Is that true?"

—I believe so. My entire people are telepaths, hence we have more knowledge of such matters than yours do. Our experience leads us to think there is no limit.

"You can always be with me? You always will?"

—If you so wish, I am gladdened.

The comet body curvetted and danced, the brain of fire laughed low. —Yes, Eloise, I would like very much to remain with you. No one else has ever— Joy. Joy. Joy.

They named you better than they knew, Lucifer, she wanted to say, and perhaps she did. *They thought it was a joke; they thought by calling you after the devil they could make you safely small like themselves. But Lucifer isn't the devil's real name. It means only Light Bearer. One Latin prayer even addresses Christ as Lucifer. Forgive me, God, I can't help remembering that. Do You mind? He isn't Christian, but I think he doesn't need to be, I think he must never have felt sin, Lucifer, Lucifer.*

She sent the music soaring for as long as she was permitted.

The ship jumped. In one shift of world line parameters she crossed twenty-five light-years to destruction.

Each knew it in his own way, save for Eloise who also lived it with Lucifer.

She felt the shock and heard the outraged metal scream, she smelled the ozone and scorch and tumbled through the infinite falling that is weightlessness. Dazed, she fumbled at the intercom. Words crackled through: ". . . unit blown . . . back EMF surge . . . how should I know how to fix the blasted thing? . . . stand by, stand by . . ." Over all hooted the emergency siren.

Terror rose in her, until she gripped the crucifix around her neck and the mind of Lucifer. Then she laughed in the pride of his might.

He had whipped clear of the ship immediately on arrival. Now he floated in the same orbit. Everywhere around, the nebula filled space with unrestful rainbows. To him, *Raven* was not the metal cylinder which human eyes would have seen, but a lambence, the shield screen reflecting a whole spectrum. Ahead lay the supernova core, tiny at this remove but alight, alight.

—Have no fears (he caressed her). I comprehend. Turbulence is extensive, so soon after the detonation. We emerged in a region where the plasma is especially dense. Unprotected for the moment before the guardian field was re-established, your main generator outside the hull was short-circuited. But you are safe. You can make repairs. And I, I am in an ocean of energy. Never was I so alive. Come, swim these tides with me.

Captain Szili's voice yanked her back. "Waggoner! Tell that Aurigean to get busy. We've spotted a radiation source on an intercept orbit, and it may be too much for our screen." He specified coordinates. "What *is* it?"

For the first time, Eloise felt alarm in Lucifer. He curved about and streaked from the ship.

Presently his thought came to her, no less vivid. She lacked words for the terrible splendour she viewed with him: a million-kilometre ball of ionized gas where luminance blazed and electric discharges leaped, booming through the haze around the star's exposed heart. The thing could not have made any sound, for space here was still almost a vacuum by Earth's parochial standards; but she heard it thunder, and felt the fury that spat from it.

She said for him: "A mass of expelled material. It must have lost radial velocity to friction and static gradients, been drawn into a cometary orbit, held together for a while by internal potentials. As if this sun were trying yet to bring planets to birth—"

"It'll strike us before we're in shape to accelerate," Szili said, "and overload our shield. If you know any prayers, use them."

"Lucifer!" she called; for she did not want to die, when he must remain.

—I think I can deflect it enough, he told her with a grimness she had not hitherto met in him. —My own fields, to mesh with its; and free energy to drink; and an unstable configuration; yes, perhaps I can help you. But help me, Eloise. Fight by my side.

His brightness moved towards the juggernaut shape.

She felt how its chaotic electromagnetism clawed at his. She felt him tossed and torn. The pain was hers. He battled to keep his own cohesion, and the combat was hers. They locked together, Aurigean and gas cloud. The forces that shaped him grappled as arms might; he poured power from his core, hauling that vast tenuous mass with him down the magnetic torrent which streamed from the sun; he gulped atoms and thrust them backwards until the jet splashed across the heaven.

She sat in her cubicle, lending him what will to live and prevail she could, and beat her fists bloody on the desk.

The hours brawled past.

In the end, she could scarcely catch the message that flickered out of his exhaustion: —Victory.

"Yours," she wept.

—Ours.

Through instruments, men saw the luminous death pass them by. A cheer lifted.

"Come back," Eloise begged.

—I cannot. I am too spent. We are merged, the cloud and I, and are tumbling in towards the star. (Like a hurt hand reaching forth to comfort her:) Do not be afraid for me. As we get closer, I will draw fresh strength from its glow, fresh substance from the nebula. I will need a while to spiral out against that pull. But how can I fail to come back to you, Eloise? Wait for me. Rest. Sleep.

Her shipmates led her to sick bay. Lucifer sent her dreams of fire flowers and mirth and the suns that were his home.

But she woke at last, screaming. The medic had to put her under heavy sedation.

He had not really understood what it would mean to confront something so violent that space and time themselves were twisted thereby.

His speed increased appallingly. That was in his own measure; from *Raven* they saw him fall through several days. The properties of matter were changed. He could not push hard enough or fast enough to escape.

Radiation, stripped nuclei, particles born and destroyed and born again, sleeted and shouted through him. His substance was peeled away, layer by layer. The supernova core was a white delirium before him. It shrank as he approached, ever smaller, denser, so brilliant that brilliance ceased to have meaning. Finally the gravitational forces laid their full grip upon him.

—Eloise! he shrieked in the agony of his disintegration —Oh, Eloise, help me!

The star swallowed him up. He was stretched infinitely long, compressed infinitely thin, and vanished with it from existence.

The ship prowled the farther reaches. Much might yet be learned.

Captain Szili visited Eloise in sick bay. Physically she was recovering.

"I'd call him a man," he declared through the machine mumble, "except that's not praise enough. We weren't even his kin, and he died to save us."

She regarded him from eyes more dry than seemed natural. He could just make out her answer. "He is a man. Doesn't he have an immortal soul too?"

"Well, uh, yes, if you believe in souls, yes, I'd agree."

She shook her head. "But why can't he go to his rest?"

He glanced about for the medic and found they were alone in the narrow metal room. "What do you mean?" He made himself pat her hand. "I know, he was a good friend of yours. Still, his must have been a merciful death. Quick, clean; I wouldn't mind going out like that."

"For him . . . yes, I suppose so. It has to be. But—" She could not continue. Suddenly she covered her ears. "Stop! Please!"

Szili made soothing noises and left. In the corridor he encountered Mazundar. "How is she?" the physicist asked.

The captain scowled. "Not good. I hope she doesn't crack entirely before we can get her to a psychiatrist."

"Why, what is wrong?"

"She thinks she can hear him."

Mazundar smote fist into palm. "I hoped otherwise," he breathed.

Szili braced himself and waited.

"She does," Mazundar said. "Obviously she does."

"But that's impossible! He's dead!"

"Remember the time dilation," Mazundar replied. "He fell from the sky and perished swiftly, yes. But in supernova time. Not the same as ours. To us, the final stellar collapse takes an infinite number of years. And telepathy has no distance limits." The physicist started walking fast away from that cabin. "He will always be with her."

THE PERSON FROM PORLOCK

Raymond F. Jones

Raymond F. Jones was one of the frequent contributors to Campbell's *Astounding* in the forties and fifties; though his byline became infrequent after the mid-1950s, he continued to publish into the seventies. Some of his stories from that period are collected in *The Toymaker* (1951) and *The Non-Statistical Man* (1964). He is perhaps most famous, however, for one of his novels, *This Island Earth* (1952), which was made into a minor classic sf film of the same title. Many of his stories tended to reflect the proscience/antibureaucracy, anti-politician, sometimes xenophobic attitudes of Campbell's editorials; attitudes that are not readily apparent in the classic stories of the very best writers of the era (Asimov and Heinlein, Kuttner and Simak) whose work we still read, who most often tended to write in reaction to some of Campbell's attitudes, not to reflect them. But part of Jones's ecological niche as a commercial writer was to sell to *Astounding* precisely by writing stories that clearly reflected Campbell's editorials.

It was a cliché of Campbell and Golden Age sf that scientists and engineers (and sf fans) were special, the elect if you will, the agents of human progress. Devotees of sf were told by Robert A. Heinlein himself, in his famous guest of honor speech at the 1941 World SF Convention in Denver, that they were as a group the next stage in human evolution. *Slan* (1940, serial), the classic novel by A. E. Van Vogt, portrayed lonely, intellectually superior mutants surviving clandestinely in a normal human society of the future, just waiting to outbreed and supplant the ignorant and evolutionarily inferior Homo sap. The catch-phrase "fans are slans" was a powerful metaphor in sf in those days.

On the other hand, people who neither know nor do work with science are bumbling lesser creatures, perhaps actively dangerous, or even malign. Coleridge claimed he would have finished "Kubla Khan" if that clod from Porlock hadn't interrupted him and ruined his mood and concentration. Jones's story captures much of that feeling, and converts it playfully into paranoia, which is rewarded by salvation as one of the elect.

Borge, the chief engineer of Intercontinental, glanced down at the blue-backed folder in his hand. Then he looked at the strained face of Reg Stone, his top engineer.

"It's no use," said Borge. "We're canceling the project. Millen's report is negative. He finds the BW effect impossible of practical application. You can read the details yourself."

"Canceling—!" Reg Stone half rose from his chair. "But chief, you can't do that. Millen's crazy. What can he prove with only a little math and no experimental data? I'm right on the edge of success. If I could just make you see it!"

"I *have* seen it. I can't see anything that warrants our pouring out another twenty-five thousand bucks after the hundred and fifty your project has already cost the company."

"Twenty, then. Even fifteen *might* do it. Borge, if you don't let me go on with this you're passing up the biggest development of the century. Some other outfit with more guts and imagination and less respect for high-priced opinion in pretty folders is going to come through with it. Teleportation is in the bag—all we've got to do is lift it out!"

"Majestic and Carruthers Electric have both canceled their projects on it. Professor Merrill Hanford, who assisted Bots-Wellton in the original research, says that the BW effect will never be anything of more than academic interest."

"Hanford!" Reg exploded. "He's jealous because he doesn't have the brains to produce a discovery of that magnitude. Bots-Wellton himself says that his effect will eventually make it possible to eliminate all other means of freight transport and most passenger stuff except that which is merely for pleasure."

"All of which is very well," said Borge, "except that it doesn't work outside of an insignificant laboratory demonstration."

"Insignificant! The actual transfer of six milligrams of silver over a distance of ten feet is hardly insignificant. As for Millen's math, we haven't got the right tools to handle this."

"I was speaking from an engineering standpoint. Of course, the effect is of interest in a purely scientific way, but it is of no use to us. Millen's math proves it. Take this copy and see for yourself. I'm sorry, Reg, but that's the final word on it."

Reg Stone rose slowly, his big hands resting against the glass-topped desk. "I see. I'll just have to forget it then, I guess."

"I'm afraid so." Borge rose and extended his hand. "You've been working too hard on this thing. Why don't you take a couple of days off? By then we'll have your next assignment lined up. And no hard feelings over this Bots-Wellton effect business?"

"Oh, no—sure not," Reg said absently.

He strode out of the office and back to the lab where the elaborate equipment of his teleport project was strewn in chaotic piles over benches and lined up in racks and panels.

A hundred thousand dollars worth of beautiful junk, he thought. He slumped in a chair before the vast, complex panels. This cancellation was the fitting climax to the delays, misfortunes, and accidents that had dogged the project since it began.

From the first, everyone except a few members of the Engineering Committee and Reg himself had been against it. Borge considered it a waste of time and money. The other engineers referred to it as Stone's Folly.

And within Reg himself there was that smothering, frustrated, indefinable sensation which he couldn't name.

It was a premonition of failure, and there had been a thousand and one incidents to support it. From the first day, when one of his lab assistants fell and broke a precious surge amplifier, the project seemed to have been hexed. No day passed but that materials seemed mysteriously missing or blueprints turned up with the wrong specifications on them. He'd tried six incompetent junior engineers before the last one, a brilliant chap named Spence, who seemed to be the only one of the lot who knew a lighthouse tube from a stub support.

With men and materials continually snafu it was almost as if someone had deliberately sabotaged the whole project.

He caught himself up with a short, bitter laugh. The little men in white coats would be after him if he kept up that line of thought.

He passed a hand over his eyes. How tired he was! He hadn't realized until now what a tremendous peak of tension he had reached. He felt it in the faint trembling of his fingers, the pressure behind his eyeballs.

His disappointment and anger slowly settled like a vortex about Carl Millen, the consulting physicist who'd reported negatively when Borge insisted to the Engineering Committee that they get outside opinion on the practicability of BW utilization.

The cool, implacable Millen, however, could hardly be the object of anything as personal as anger. Yet, strangely enough, he had been the object of Reg Stone's friendship ever since the two of them were in engineering school together.

What each of them found in the other would have been hard to put into words, but there was some complementary view of opposite worlds which each seemed able to see through the other's eyes.

As for Millen's report on the BW project—Reg knew it had been utterly impersonal and rendered as Carl Millen saw it, though the two of them had often discussed it in heated argument in the past. But the very impersonality of Millen's point of view made the maintenance of his anger impossible for Reg.

But never in his life had he wanted anything so much as he wanted to be the one to develop the Bots-Wellton effect from a mere laboratory demonstration to a system able to transport millions of tons of freight over thousands of miles without material agent of transfer.

Now he was cut off right at the pockets. He felt at loose ends. It was a panicky feeling. For months on end he had been working at top capacity. He seemed to have suddenly dropped into a vacuum.

He debated handing in his resignation and going to some company that would let him develop the project. But who would? Majestic and Carruthers, two of the largest outfits, had pulled out, Borge had said. Who else would pick it up?

There was one other possibility, he thought breathlessly. Reg Stone could take it over!

Why not? He had a beautifully equipped backyard lab and machine shop. Tens of thousands of dollars worth of equipment from the project would have to be junked by Intercontinental. Reg felt sure Borge would let him buy it as junk.

Sure, it would be slow without the facilities of the Intercontinental labs, but it would be better than scuttling the entire project.

He suddenly glanced at the clock on the wall. He'd been sitting there without moving for over an hour. It was lunchtime. He decided to go downtown where he wouldn't meet anyone he knew, rather than eat in the company cafeteria.

He chose the Estate, a seafood restaurant three miles from the plant. As soon as he walked in he knew why he had chosen the Estate with subconscious deliberation.

He saw Carl Millen across the room. He had meant to see him. Millen always ate at the same place at the same time.

Millen spotted Reg almost simultaneously and beckoned to him.

"Sit down, Reg. You're the last person I expected to see here. What's new at your shop?"

"Not much—except Borge received a report from Carl Millen & Associates, Consulting Engineers."

Millen grinned wryly. "Did he blow his top?"

"Why did you turn in a negative report?"

"Didn't you read it? I proved the BW effect is absolutely limited by the free atomic concentration in the dispersion field. That limitation utterly forbids any mass application of the principle."

Reg was silent as the waiter brought the menus. They each ordered oysters on the half shell.

"I remember," said Reg, when the waiter had gone, "about 1925 a then very prominent aeronautical engineer wrote a learned piece proving absolutely that planes could never reach five hundred miles an hour."

Millen laughed. "Yes, and there's also the gent that proved a steamship could never carry enough fuel to get it across the Atlantic."

He stopped and looked seriously at Reg. "But for every one of those classic boners there are thousands of legitimate negative demonstrations that have saved engineering and industry untold millions. You know that as well as I do. This is one of them."

"I'll admit the first, but not the second," said Reg. "I've not read your report. I probably won't. It's faulty. It's got to be. The BW principle can be utilized somehow and I'm going to prove it."

"Just how do you propose to do that?" Millen asked, smiling gently. "Something intuitive, no doubt?"

"All right, have your fun, but come around and see me when you want to go on a quick vacation via the Stone Instantaneous Transfer Co."

"Reg, that job I talked about a year ago is still open. I could offer you Assistant Chief of Development. In a year I could let you in on a partnership. It's worth twenty thousand now, thirty later."

"I could work on the BW outside?"

Millen shook his head. "That's the only string attached. Our men haven't time for anything but customers' projects. Besides, you'd have to get used to the idea of believing in math, not intuition."

"I don't think I'd do you much good."

"You could learn, for that kind of money, couldn't you? What does that cheese factory pay you? About eight or ten?"

"Seven and a half."

"The lousy cheapskates! Three times that ought to be worth shelving your intuition in favor of math."

Reg shook his head. "There isn't that much money in the world. Solving other people's riddles for a fee is not my idea of living."

"Sometimes I think you're just a frustrated research physicist. In this business you're in for the money. It's a cinch there's no glory."

The waiter brought their orders, then.

His depression continued with Reg that evening. His three boys sensed it when he turned down a ball game. His wife, Janice, sensed it when he didn't poke his head in the kitchen on the way to his study.

After dinner, and when the boys were in bed, he told her what had happened that day.

"I don't understand why you feel so badly about the cancellation of this particular project," she said when he finished. "Others have been canceled, too."

"Because it's one of the greatest phenomena ever discovered. It's ripe for engineering application, but no one else will believe it. It's as if they deliberately try to block me in every step. All through the project it's been that way. Now this—chucking the whole business, when we've gone so far! I can't see through the reasons behind it all. Except that they just don't want it to succeed. I've got that feeling about it, and can't rid myself of it. *They want me to fail!*"

"Who does?"

"Everyone! In the drafting room. The lab technicians. The model shop. It seems as if everybody's concern with the project is simply to throw monkey wrenches in the gears."

"Oh, darling—you're just wrought up over this thing. Let's take a vacation. Let the boys go to camp this summer and go off by ourselves somewhere. You've got to have a rest."

He knew that. He'd known it for a long time, but teleportation was more important than rest. He could take care of the neuroses at his leisure, later. That's the theory he'd worked on. Now, all he had was a beautiful neurosis. It couldn't be anything else, he told himself, this absolute conviction that he was being sabotaged in his work, that others were banded against him to prevent the full development of the BW principle.

"Perhaps in a few weeks," he said. "There are some more angles about this business that I must follow up. Let's read tonight. Something fanciful, something beautiful, something faraway—"

"Coleridge," Janice laughed.

They sat by the window overlooking the garden. Their one vice of reading poetry together was something of an anachronism in a world threatened with atomic fires, but it was the single escape that Reg would allow himself from his engineering problems.

Janice began reading softly. Her voice was like music out of a past more gentle and nearer the ultimate truths than this age.

"In Xanadu did Kubla Khan
A stately pleasure-dome decree:
Where Alph, the sacred river, ran—
—that deep romantic chasm which slanted
Down the green hill athwart a cedarn cover!
A savage place! as holy and enchanted
As e'er beneath a waning moon was haunted—"

Reg suddenly stiffened and sat erect, his eyes on the distant golden cavern of the sky.

"That's it," he breathed softly. "That's just how it is—"

Janice looked up from the book, her face puzzled. "What in the world are you talking about?"

"The Person from Porlock. Remember how Coleridge wrote 'Kubla Khan'?"

"No. Who's the Person from Porlock?"

"Coleridge wrote this poem just after coming out of a dope dream. He later said that during his sleep he had produced at least two to three hundred lines. While trying to get it on paper he was interrupted by a person from the village of Porlock. When he finally got rid of the visitor, Coleridge could recall no more of his envisioned poem.

"He was furious because this self-important busybody had interrupted his work and he wrote a poem castigating the Person from Porlock and all other stupid, busy people who hamper the really industrious ones."

"And so—?"

"Don't you see? It's these Persons from Porlock who have made it impossible for me to complete my work. Borge; Millen; Dickson, the draftsman who bungled the drawings; Hansen, the model shop mechanic who boggled tolerances so badly that nothing would work. These Persons from Porlock—I wonder how many thousands of years of advancement they have cost the world!"

In the near darkness now, Janice sat staring at Reg's bitter face. Her eyes were wide and filled with genuine fear, fear of this malign obsession that had overtaken him.

"The Persons from Porlock," Reg mused, half aloud. "Wouldn't it be funny if it turned out that they were deliberately and purposely upsetting the works of other men. Suppose it were their whole object in life—"

"Reg!"

He was scarcely able to see Janice in the settling gloom, but he felt her fear. "Don't worry, Janice, I haven't gone off my rocker. I was just thinking—Sure, it's fantastic, but Coleridge was one of the world's geniuses. Perhaps he glimpsed something of a truth that no one else has guessed."

Reg went into Borge's office early the next morning. The chief engineer frowned as he saw Reg Stone. "I thought you were going to take a few days."

"I came in to ask what you are going to do with the equipment that's been built for my BW project."

"We'll store it with the miscellaneous plumbing for a while, then junk it. Why?"

"How about doing me a big favor and declaring it junk right away and letting me buy it—as junk?"

"What do you want the stuff for?"

"I want to continue the BW experiments on my own. You know, just putter around with it in my shop at home."

"Still think it will amount to something, eh?"

"Yes. That's why I'd like to buy the stuff, especially the velocitor chamber. It would take me a couple of years to build one of those on my own."

"I'd like to do it as a favor to you," said Borge, "but Bruce, the new manager, has just made a ruling that no parts or equipment may be sold to employees. It was all right during the war when the boys were outfitting their WERS stations on company time and equipment. We were on cost plus then, but too many are trying to refurnish their amateur stations now at our expense. So Bruce cut it all out."

"But that doesn't make sense with such specialized stuff as I've had built for the BW. It's no good for anything else."

"Maybe you could talk Bruce out of it. You know him."

Yes, he knew Bruce, Reg thought. A production man who, like many of his kind, considered engineers mere necessary evils. It was utterly useless to ask Bruce to make an exception to one of his own regulations.

Persons from Porlock—

Persons from Porlock—

The words echoed like a tantalizing refrain in his mind as he went downstairs toward his own lab. He knew he should forget that impossible concept, but the words were like a magic chant explaining all his misfortunes.

This huge plant and all the technological advances that had come out of it could not exist without Borge and Bruce, and the others like them. Yet, at the same time, these Persons from Porlock constituted the greatest stumbling block to modern scientific development. Every engineer in the world at some time had been stymied by one of them—an unimaginative chief, a stupid factory manager, incompetent draftsmen, model shop machinists, secretaries, expediters, administrators—

As he passed the open door of the company's technical library he spotted Dickson, his head draftsman on the BW project, sitting inside at a table. He went in.

Dickson looked up. "Hello, Reg. I wondered where you were this morning. I just heard about them junking the project. It's a devil of a tough break."

"Are you really sorry, Dickson?" said Reg.

The draftsman looked sharply. "What do you mean? Of course I hate to work on a project and see it canceled. Who wouldn't?"

"You know, looking back, it appears as if we hadn't made each one of about fifty boners, the project would have succeeded. For example, that dimension on the diameter of the focusing cavity in the assembly unit. It's the only one in the assembly that wouldn't be obvious to the model shop, and it's the only one on which you made a mistake in spite of our checking. A seven that looked like a two in your dimensioning. That made the difference between success and failure and lost us nearly four weeks while we looked for the bug in the unit."

"Reg, I've told you twenty times I'm sorry, but I can't do anything about it now. A hair on my lettering pen made just enough of a boggle of the figure so that those dopes in the model shop misread it. It was a worse two than it was a seven. They should have checked us on it even if we did miss it."

"Yeah, I know. It just seemed funny that it was that particular dimension you were drawing when the hair got on your pen."

The draftsman looked at Reg as if stunned by the unspoken implication. "If you think I did that on purpose—!"

"I didn't say that. Sure it was an accident, but why? Was it because you didn't want the thing to succeed—subconsciously?"

"Of course not! It was of no material interest to me, except, of course, as I said before I have the same enthusiasm to see a project on which I work turn out successfully as you do."

"Yeah, I suppose so. Just forget I said anything."

Reg left Dickson and walked back to the hall. Persons from Porlock—were they consciously malicious or were they mere stupid blunderers? More likely the latter, he thought, yet there must be some subconscious desire to cause failure as was the case with the mysterious accident prones so familiar to insurance companies.

The more he considered it, the less fantastic the Person from Porlock concept seemed. It was entirely possible that the genius of the poet, Coleridge, had hit upon a class of persons as definite and distinct as accident prones—and a thousand times more deadly.

There could hardly be any other explanation for the stupid blunder of Dickson in drawing the focusing cavity. He had done far more complex drawings on this project, yet that single dimension, of an extremely critical nature, had been the one to be botched.

And it meant there were others like him in the model shop because any machinist with half an eye for accuracy would have checked that figure before going ahead and shaping up the part to such critical tolerances.

He turned into the machine shop where Hansen, the machinist who'd done the job on the cavity, was working.

"Pretty nice work." He nodded toward the piece in the lathe.

"I hope the engineer thinks so," Hansen growled. "They give me plus five thousands on this thing and no minus. Next they'll want flea whiskers with zero-zero tolerance."

"You're good. That's why you get the tough ones."

"I wish the guy on the payroll desk would take note."

"But you know, there's something that's bothered me for several weeks. You remember that cavity you made for me with a one two five interior instead of a one seven five?"

Hansen turned wearily to the engineer. "Reg, I've eaten crow a hundred times over for that. I told you it looked like a two. Maybe I need my eyes examined, but it still looks that way."

"Did you have any reason for *not* wanting the cavity to work?"

"Now, look!" Hansen's anger suffused red through his face. "I'm paid to turn out screwball gadgets in this shop, not worry about whether they work or not."

"Didn't it occur to you to check that boggled figure?"

"I told you it looked all right!" Hansen turned angrily back to his lathe and resumed work.

Reg watched the mechanic for a moment, then left the shop.

The bunglers seemed to have no personal interest in their botch work, he decided. It must be something entirely subconscious as in the case of accident prones. That didn't make them any less dangerous, however. Without them on his project he would have been able by now to demonstrate the practicability of BW utilization.

But, following this line of reasoning, why couldn't the teleportation equipment be made to work now? According to all this theory the equipment he had built should have been capable of acting as a pilot model for a larger unit and it should have been able to transfer hundred pound masses at least a thousand feet. Yet, it had failed completely.

Granting that he himself was not a Person from Porlock—

But could he grant that?

Maybe the greatest blunders were his own. His failure to catch Dickson's mistake early enough, for example!

That was the one premise he could not admit, however. It led to insolvable dilemma, rendered the problem completely indeterminate. He had to assume that he was not one of the bunglers.

In that case, why did the equipment fail to work?

It meant that some of the blunders introduced by the Persons from Porlock still remained in the equipment. Remove them, and it should work!

He'd have to go over every equation, every design, every specification—point by point—compare them with the actual equipment and dig out the bugs.

He went into his own lab. He dismissed the assistants and shut the door. He sat down with the voluminous papers which he had produced in the ten months of work on the project. It was hopeless to attempt to go over the entire mass of work in short hours or days. That's what should be done, but he could cover the most vulnerable points. These lay in the routine, conventional circuits which he had left to his assistants and in whose design the draftsman and model shop had been trusted with too many details.

The first of these was the amplifier for the BW generator, whose radiation, capable of mass-modulation, carried the broken down components of the materials to be transported. The amplifier held many conventional features, though the waveform handled was radically unconventional.

It contained two stages of Class A amplification which had to be perfectly symmetrical. Reg had never made certain of the correct operation of these two stages by themselves. Spence, his junior engineer, had reported them operating correctly and Reg had taken his word on so simple a circuit.

He had no reason now to believe that anything was wrong. It was just one of those items left to a potential Person from Porlock.

He disconnected the input and output of the amplifier and hooked up a signal generator and a vacuum tube voltmeter. Point by point he checked the circuit. The positive and negative peaks were equal and a scope showed perfect symmetry, but in the second stage they weren't high enough. He wasn't getting the required soup. The output of the tube in use should have been more than sufficient to produce it.

Then he discovered the fault. The bias was wrong and the drive had been cut to preserve symmetry. Spence had simply assumed the flat tops were due to overloading.

Reg sat in silent contemplation of the alleged engineering and poured on self-recrimination for trusting Spence.

This was the reason for the apparent failure of the whole modulator circuit. Because of it, he had assumed his theory of mass modulation was faulty.

Spence was obviously one of them, he thought. That meant other untold numbers of bugs throughout the mass of equipment. During the remainder of the morning and in the afternoon he adjusted the amplifiers and got the modulator into operation. He uncovered another serious bug in an out-of-tolerance dropping resistor in the modulator. He contemplated the probability of that one defective resistor among the hundreds of thousands of satisfactory ones the plant used—the probability of its being placed in exactly that critical spot. The figure was too infinitesimal to be mere chance.

By quitting time he had the circuit as far as the mass modulator functioning fairly smoothly. He called Janice and told her he wouldn't be home until late. Then he worked until past midnight to try to get the transmission elements to accept the modulated carrier. The only result was failure and at last he went home in utter exhaustion.

The next morning, refreshed, he was filled with an unnatural exuberance, however. He had the key to the cause of his failures and he felt success was only a matter of time. If he could just get that necessary time—

The broad parking lot was dotted with infrequent cars at the early hour of the morning at which he arrived. Gail, the lab secretary, was already at her desk, however, when he walked in. She called to him, "Mr. Borge wants you to come up, Reg."

"O.K. Thanks."

He turned and went back out the door toward the chief engineer's office. This would be the new project, he thought. He strode in and Borge looked up with a brief nod.

"Sit down, Reg." The lines of Borge's face seemed to have eroded into deeper valleys in the short time since Reg had last seen him.

"I hear some things I don't like," said Borge suddenly. "About you."

"What sort of things? I haven't—"

"Dickson and Hansen have been saying you've accused them of deliberate sabotage on your project. True or not, whatever is implied by these rumors can't go on. It can wreck this shop in a month."

"I didn't accuse them of anything!" Reg flared. "I just asked if they wanted the project to fail. Of course, I didn't expect them to say that they did, but their manner showed me what I wanted to know."

"And what was that?"

Reg hesitated. This development was nothing that he had expected. How would Borge, as one of the Persons from Porlock, react to Reg's knowledge of them? Did Borge even understand his own motives? Whether he did or not, Reg could make no rational answer except the truth.

"I found that they did, subconsciously, want the project to fail. I believe this is the explanation of the numerous blunders without which my project would have been a success."

"You believe, then, that your failure is due to the . . . ah, persecutions . . . of these persons, rather than to any inherent impossibility in the project itself or your own inability to bring it off?"

"I haven't a persecution complex, if that's what you're trying to say," Reg said hotly. "Look, Borge, did you ever hear of accident prones, who plague insurance companies?"

"Vaguely. I don't know much about the subject."

"I can prove there is another kind of prone, a blunder prone, whose existence is just as definite as that of the accident prone. I call these blunder prones 'Persons from Porlock' after the one named by the poet, Coleridge, when his great poem, 'Kubla Khan,' was ruined by one of them."

"And just what do these . . . er, Persons from Porlock do?"

"They make mistakes in important work entrusted to them. They interfere with others who are doing intense and concentrated work so that trains of thought are broken and perhaps lost forever, as in the case of Coleridge. And as in my own case. I could tell of at least a hundred times when I have been deliberately interrupted at critical points of my calculations so that work had to be repeated and some points, only faintly conceived, were totally lost."

"Which couldn't have been due to your own nervous strain and overworked condition?"

"No."

"I see. These Persons of Porlock generally persecute the intelligent and superior people of the world, is that it?"

Reg's anger flared. "I'm not a psychoneurotic case and I'm not suffering from a persecution complex!"

Suddenly, cold fear washed over Reg. Borge's pattern of reason was clear, now. He would dismiss the whole matter as a neurotic complex and let Reg out of the lab. He would be blackballed with every other company in which he might have another try at BW work.

"I know you're not," Borge was saying, "but you are tired. For six years you've been turning out miracles. I hate like the devil to see you come up with something like this, Reg. Surely you must realize it's all the result of overwork and fatigue. No one is going around interfering with your work. Your mind refuses to admit defeat so it's automatically throwing it off on someone else. I'm no psychologist, but I'll bet that's close to the right answer. I want you to have Walker at the Clinic examine you. I'm willing to bet he recommends a long rest. I'll give you six months with pay if necessary. But I can't let you back in the lab unless you do this. A repetition of yesterday's performance and the whole place would be shot up. You've got to get rid of this Person from Porlock business."

The pieces of the whole puzzle locked into place with startling clarity for Reg. He knew that the last uncertainty had been removed. They were *not* random, subconsciously motivated performers. These Persons from Porlock were skillfully conscious of what they were doing. Borge could not hide the knowledge that his eyes revealed.

But *what* were they doing?

Six months—it would be too late, then. His sense of blind urgency told him that. Borge was simply showing him that there was no possible way that he could win.

He tried again. "I can't expect you to believe these things. I know it sounds fantastic. Any psychiatrist would no doubt diagnose it as a persecution complex. But I promise that no more incidents like yesterday's will take place. Give me the new assignment, but let me work on the BW just six weeks in my spare time, on my own. I'll guarantee I'll have it working in that time."

Borge shook his head. "That's the main trouble with you already—overwork. You've been pushing yourself so hard that your nerves are all shot. Anyone walking by while you are computing is such a disturbance that you think he's deliberately interfering with you. Put yourself in the care of a good doctor and let me know his report. That's the only condition upon which I can let you stay with the company. I hate to put it that way. I wish you'd try to understand for yourself—but if you won't, that's the way it's got to be."

Reg stood up, his body trembling faintly with the fury of his anger. He leaned forward across the desk. "*I know who you are!* But I warn you that I won't stop. Somehow I'm going to carry this work through, and all you and your kind can do won't stop me!"

He whirled and strode from the office, conscious of Borge's pitying glance upon his back. Conscious, too, that he was walking out for the last time.

The fury and the anger didn't last. When he got outside, he was sick with frustration as he glanced back at the plant. He had acted stupidly through the whole thing, he thought, letting them cut him off from any access to the BW equipment without a struggle.

Yet, how else could he have conducted himself? The whole thing was so fantastic at first that he couldn't have outlined a rational program to combat it.

Maybe Borge was right in one respect. He *was* devilishly tired and exhausted from the long war years of uninterrupted work. There'd been that microsearch system on which he'd spent two years at Radiation Lab. One such project as that would have sent the average engineer nuts. As soon as it was in production he'd tackled an equally tough baby in the radar fire-control equipment that had gone into fighter planes four months after he took over the project cold.

Yeah, he *was* tired—

Janice was surprised to see him, and was shocked by the pain and bewilderment on his face.

Slowly, and carefully, he explained to her what had happened. He told her how Borge had built up a case against him out of the things he'd said to Dickson and Hansen. He told her how they and Spence and the rest had sabotaged his project.

"They've got me licked," he finished. "They've done what they started out to do, knocked out the BW project."

Janice had sat quietly during his recital, only her eyes reflecting the growing terror within her.

"But, darling, why should they want to hinder the project? What possible reason could there be behind it, even if these mysterious Persons from Porlock actually existed?"

"Who knows? But it doesn't make any difference, I suppose. They're so obvious that I don't see how the world has failed to recognize them. Yet . . . you don't believe a thing I've said, do you?"

"They can't exist, Reg! Borge is right. You're tired. This notion is only something that your mind has seized upon out of Coleridge's fantasy. It has no basis in reality. Please, for my sake, take a visit to the Clinic and see if they don't advise rest and psychiatric treatment for you."

Like a cold, invisible shell, loneliness seemed to coalesce about him. There was the illusion of being cut off from all sight and sound, and he had the impression that Janice was sitting there with her lips moving, but no sound coming forth.

Illusion, of course, but the loneliness was real. It cut him off from all the world, for where was there one who would understand and believe about the Persons from Porlock? They surrounded him on every side. Wherever he turned, they stood ready to beat down his struggles for the right to work as he wished. Perhaps even Janice—

But that premise had to be denied.

"I'll let them tap my knees and my skull if it will make you happier," he said. "Maybe I'll even beg Borge to take me back if that's the way you want it. It doesn't matter any more. The BW project is dead. They killed it—but don't ever try to make me believe they don't exist."

"They don't! They don't Reg. You've got to believe that. Quit deluding yourself—"

Quite suddenly, it was beyond his endurance. He strode from the room and out into the brilliance of the day, brilliance that was like a cold, shimmering wall surrounding him, moving as he moved, surrounding but not protecting.

Not protecting from the glance of those who passed on the street nor from those who came toward him, nor those who followed after in a steady, converging stream.

He felt their presence—the Persons from Porlock—like tangible, stinging auras on every side. They surrounded him. They were out to get him.

His stride broke into a half run. How long his flight continued he never knew. It was dimming twilight when he sank, half sobbing from exhaustion, onto a park bench miles from home.

He looked about him in the gathering darkness, and somehow it seemed less evil than the light and the thousand faces of the Persons from Porlock who drifted by on every side.

If only he could drag one of them out into the open where all the world could see it and believe—that would be one way of escape from the soundless, invisible prison in which they had encased him. He had to show that they existed so that no one in the world would doubt his word again. But how?

What incontrovertible proof of their existence did he possess? What was there besides his own feelings and beliefs? He shuddered with realization that there was nothing. His knowledge, his evidence of them was of the flimsiest kind. There had to be something tangible.

But *could* there be more? Insidiously, doubts began to creep into his mind. He remembered the look in Borge's eyes, the pity and the fear in Janice's.

He rose stiffly from the park bench, cold fear driving his limbs to carry him out into the lights. If he were to remain sure of his own sanity, he had to first prove to himself beyond any doubt that the Persons from Porlock existed in actuality, not merely in his own suspicions.

There was one way by which he might be able to do this. That way lay through the report of Carl Millen and the mathematics by which he had "proved" the BW effect impossible of mass exploitation.

The math was deliberately false, Reg knew. If he proved it, confronted Millen with the fact—

He caught a taxi home. Janice met him, dry-eyed and with no questions or demands for explanations. He offered none, but went to his study and took out Millen's report. He asked Janice to brew up a pot of coffee and he began the slow weaving of a pathway through the tortuous trail of Millen's abstruse mathematical reasoning.

Sleep at last forced abandonment of his work, but he arose after a few hours and turned to the pursuit again. All through the day he kept steadily at it, and in the late afternoon he caught his first threads of what he was searching for. A thread of deliberate falsification, a beckoning toward wide paths of illogic and untruth.

It was so subtle that he passed it twice before recognizing it. Something of the intense deliberation chilled him when he realized the depths of the insinuations. It was like the devil's nine truths and a lie that he'd heard country preachers talk about when he was a boy.

This work of Carl Millen's was certainly the nine truths—and the one, black, insidious lie.

Now that he recognized it, following its development became easier until he trailed it to the final, colossal untruth that the free atomic concentration in the dispersion field made large scale application impossible.

This was it! Proof!

The triumph of his discovery swept away the exhaustion that had filled him. Let them call it a persecution complex now!

He put the report and his pile of computations in his brief case and told Janice he was going to Millen's.

As he drove with furious skill toward town he wondered what Millen's reaction would be. He could call Reg crazy, deny he was a Person from Porlock—but he could never deny the evidence of his deliberate falsifications.

The secretary told Reg that Millen was busy and would he sit down?

"Tell him it's Reg Stone, and I've found out what he tried to do in the BW report," said Reg. "I think he'll see me."

The girl glanced disapprovingly at the engineer's disheveled appearance and relayed the information. Then she nodded toward the polished, hardwood door. "He'll see you."

Reg opened the door sharply. Carl Millen looked up from behind the desk in the center of the room. His face was unsmiling.

Then Reg saw the second person in the room. Spence, his junior engineer on the BW project. The man's unexpected presence gave him a moment's uneasiness, but it would make no difference, Reg thought—since Spence was one of them, too.

"So you think you've found something in my report?" said Millen. "Pull up a chair and show me what you mean."

Reg sat down with slow deliberation, but he left his brief case closed.

"I think you know what I mean," he said. "I don't believe it's necessary to go into the details. You deliberately invented a false line of reasoning to prove the BW effect useless."

"So? And what does that prove?"

His failure to deny the accusation took Reg aback. There was no trace of surprise or consternation on Millen's face.

"It proves that you are one of them," said Reg. "One with Dickson, Hansen, Borge, and Spence here—one of those who fought to keep me from developing teleportation. I want to know why!"

Millen's face relaxed slowly. "One of your Persons from Porlock?" Amusement touched his face at the words.

"Yes."

Millen leaned forward, his almost ominous seriousness returning. "You've done a good job, Reg. Better than we hoped for a while. It looked for a time as if you weren't going to get it."

Reg stared at him. The words made no sense, but yet there was an admission here of the unknown that chilled him.

"You admit that you falsified the facts in your report? That you are one of the Persons from Porlock?"

"Yes."

The stark admission echoed in the vast silences of the room. Reg looked slowly from one face to the other.

"Who are you? What is your purpose?" he asked hoarsely.

"I'm just like you," said Millen. "I stumbled into this thing when I first opened my consulting service. Spence is the one that can tell you about it. He's the different one—your real Person from Porlock."

Reg turned to his former junior engineer. Somehow, this was what he had known since he first entered the room. Spence's face held a look of alien detachment, as if the affairs of common engineers were trivial things.

His eyes finally turned toward Reg's face and they seemed to burn with a quality of age despite the youth of his face.

"We came here a long time ago," said Spence slowly. "And now we live here and are citizens of Earth just as you are. That is our only excuse for meddling in your affairs. Our interference, however, gives you the same safety it does us."

Reg felt as if he were not hearing Spence, only seeing his lips move. "You *came* here? You are not of Earth—"

"Originally, no."

And suddenly Reg found Spence's words credible. Somehow, they removed the fantasy from the Person from Porlock concept.

"Why haven't you made yourselves known? What does all of this mean?"

"I did not come," said Spence, "but my ancestors did. They had no intention of visiting Earth. An accident destroyed their vessel and made landing here necessary. The members of the expedition were scientists and technicians, but their skill was not the kind to rebuild the ship that had brought them across space, nor were the proper materials then available on Earth.

"They became reconciled to their communication with the home planet, and knowing that the chance of being found was infinitely remote. They were skilled in the biologic sciences and managed in a generation or two to modify their physical form sufficiently to mingle undetected with Earthmen, though they kept their own group affiliation.

"From the first, they adopted a policy of noninterference, but they found living standards hardly suitable and built secret colonies where their own life and science could develop apart from that of Earthmen.

"It was one of these colonies which the drugged mind of your poet, Coleridge, was able to see in his unconsciousness, and which he began to describe in 'Kubla Khan.' My people had detected the presence of his perceptions and one of them was sent immediately to interrupt the work of recollection because they didn't want their colony revealed with such accurate description as Coleridge could make. The Person from Porlock was this disturbing emissary."

Spence smiled for the first time, briefly. "So you see, your designation of all of us as Persons from Porlock was not far from the truth."

"But why have you interfered with me? Why don't you make yourselves known and offer your advanced science to the world?"

"Surely you are sufficiently familiar with the reaction of your own people to the new and the unknown to make that last question unnecessary. We aren't concerned with advancing your science. It is progressing rapidly enough, too rapidly for your social relationships, which would benefit by some of the energy you expend on mechanical inquiries.

"In our own science we have great fields of knowledge which do not exist in yours. One is a highly specialized field of what we term prognostication logics. Your symbolic logic sciences are a brief step in that direction—very brief. We are enabled to predict the cumulative effect of events and discoveries in your culture. We take a hand in those which indicate a potential destructive to the race. We interfere to the point of preventing their development."

Reg stared at Spence. "How could my teleportation development imperil the race? Surely that was no excuse for your interference!"

"It was. It isn't obvious to you yet because you haven't come to the discovery that teleportation can be quite readily accomplished from the transmitting end without the use of terminal equipment. Further along, you would have found no receivers necessary. Everything could be done from the transmission end."

"That would have made it a thousand times more valuable!"

"Yes? Suppose the cargo to be transported was the most destructive atomic bomb your science is capable of building."

The impact of that concept burst upon Reg. "I see," he said at last, quietly. "Why did you let us produce the bomb at all?"

"We were rather divided on that question. Our computations show a high probability that you will be able to survive it, but only if a number of auxiliary implements are withheld, teleportation among others. There were some of us who were in favor of preventing the bomb's construction even with the assurance our computations give but their influence was less than that of us who know what benefits atomic energy can bring if properly utilized. As a group, we decided to let the bomb be produced."

"But the BW effect can never be utilized?"

"Not for some centuries."

Spence seemed to have said all that he was going to say, but Millen moved uneasily.

"I can never tell you how glad I am that you uncovered my math," he said. "You know the alternative if you hadn't?"

"Alternative—?" Reg looked across the desk. Then he remembered, that night, sitting in the park, seeing the shadows against the distant lights, the ghastly pursuit of imagined terrors.

"The alternative was—insanity?"

Millen nodded.

"Why? Couldn't it have been done some other way?"

Millen avoided the question. "You will never attempt to develop the BW effect now, will you?"

"No. Of course not."

"It wouldn't have been that way if Spence or some other had come to you and warned you that it wasn't to be done. You'd have laughed at him as a crackpot. Now there's no doubt in your mind."

Reg nodded slowly and cold sickness lodged in his vitals at the thought of what he had so narrowly escaped. "Yes, I see. And now I suppose I shall go back and eat crow for Borge. That is, if you will put in a good word for me with your man." He smiled wryly toward Spence.

"We have a bigger job for you," said Millen. "I still want you here."

"Doing nail puzzles and answering riddles for customers too stingy to run their own development labs? Not me!"

"Not that, exactly. We need you to take over my job. I've got something else lined up to take care of."

"What are you talking about? Take over as head of Carl Millen & Associates? That would be worse than the puzzles—desk arthritis."

"No. Who's the best man in the world today on interference with the utilization of the BW effect?"

"I don't understand you."

"You're that man. We need somebody to take charge of the whole project of BW interference. Spence has another assignment for me, but Bots-Wellton himself still needs to be worked on. Carruthers and Majestic haven't stopped their projects yet. That was only a blind to fool your company. They've got to be stopped yet. A couple of universities are working on it. It's a big job, and you're the best equipped man in the world to handle it—under Spence's direction, of course. You see, his people won't do the detail work after some of us once become trained in it. It's up to us to fry our own fish. Will you take it?"

Reg stood up and went to the window, looking down upon the street crawling with ever hopeful life. He turned back to Spence and Millen.

"How could I do anything else in the face of the drastic indoctrination and persuasion course you've given me. Sure I'll take it!"

Then he laughed softly. "Reg Stone: Person from Porlock!"

DAY MILLION

Frederik Pohl

Frederik Pohl, writer and editor, is one of the pivotal figures in the science-fiction field between the 1930s and the 1990s. Although he edited pulp science fiction magazines, *Astonishing Stories* and *Super Science Stories*, in 1940–41 before he was twenty-one, he did not become prominent until the fifties, for his novels in collaboration with C. M. Kornbluth—including the classic *The Space Merchants* (1953); for a number of powerful and satiric short stories including "The Midas Plague" (1954) and "The Tunnel Under the World" (1955); and for editing anthologies—the most innovative all-original anthologies (and the first such in paperback) of the decade were the six volumes of *Star SF* (1953–59). In 1960, Kingsley Amis, in his provocative survey of science fiction literature, *New Maps of Hell*, called Pohl "the most consistently able writer science fiction, in the modern sense, has yet produced."

In 1961, he took over the editorship of *Galaxy* and *If* for the decade, and was certainly the most important American magazine editor of the sixties, while he wrote several novels and a number of short stories, of which "Day Million" (1966) is perhaps the best. He was a public enemy of the excesses of the New Wave, but a defender of higher standards in sf writing (and of the linking of science and fiction that the New Wave denied). Satire, once the major mode in his fiction, became less salient than serious and rigorous speculation based on scientific ideas. As the 1970s opened, Pohl became an editor in mass-market publishing and in 1971 published two of his finest novellas, *The Merchants of Venus* and *The Gold at the Starbow's End*. Reaching the peak of his powers as a novelist, he published *Man Plus* (1976) and *Gateway* (1977), sweeping up major awards and becoming one of the dominant writers of the decade. He has since devoted himself to writing, publishing many novels and stories, and to peripatetic appearances throughout the science fiction world as an influential public figure (he was a founder, and remains a principal supporter, of World SF, the world organization of science fiction professionals).

Never a supporter of John W. Campbell, Jr. (who did not publish Pohl's stories), ever since his teens Pohl has remained as much a devotee of reason and of science as his teenage pal in the Futurians, Isaac Asimov. Although Pohl's chosen mode has frequently been extrapolation of politics and society, with a deep and canny bow to psychology and psychiatry, his rigorous methodology has lent an underpinning of "hardness" to much of his best fiction (especially his work since 1970) that places it rightfully beside the best of Asimov, Clarke, Herbert, and Heinlein.

"Day Million" is a virtuoso performance, a story set in a future so distant and different that we can only glimpse it in mysterious reflections and intriguing images. It is an exercise in the application of an unconventional style to the solution of a science fiction problem. What's so hard about it? The attitude is right, giving it the texture and feel of hard sf. It is written for the reader who understands the hopelessness of a universe without physical constants (Latham's "The Xi Effect"), the necessity of "The Cold Equations."

On this day I want to tell you about, which will be about ten thousand years from now, there were a boy, a girl and a love story.

Now, although I haven't said much so far, none of it is true. The boy was not what you and I would normally think of as a boy because he was a hundred and eighty-seven years old. Nor was the girl a girl, for other reasons. And the love story did not entail that sublimation of the urge to rape, and concurrent postponement of the instinct to submit, which we at present understand in such matters. You won't care much for this story if you don't grasp these facts at once. If, however, you will make the effort you'll likely enough find it jam-packed, chock-full and tip-top-crammed with laughter, tears, and poignant sentiment which may, or may not, be worthwhile. The reason the girl was not a girl was that she was a boy.

How angrily you recoil from the page! You say, who the hell wants to read about a pair of queers? Calm yourself. Here are no hot-breathing secrets of perversion for the coterie trade. In fact, if you were to see this girl you would not guess that she was in any sense a boy. Breasts, two; reproductive organs, female. Hips, callipygian; face hairless, supraorbital lobes nonexistent. You could term her female on sight, although it is true that you might wonder just what species she was a female of, being confused by the tail, the silky pelt and the gill slits behind each ear.

Now you recoil again. Cripes, man, take my word for it. This is a sweet kid, and if you, as a normal male, spent as much as an hour in a room with her you would bend heaven and Earth to get her in the sack. Dora—we will call her that; her "name" was omicron-Dibase seven-group-totter-oot S Doradus 5314, the last part of which is a color specification corresponding to a shade of green—Dora, I say, was feminine, charming and cute. I admit she doesn't sound that way. She was, as you might put it, a dancer. Her art involved qualities of intellection and expertise of a very high order, requiring both tremendous natural capacities and endless practice; it was performed in null-gravity and I can best describe it by saying that it was something like the performance of a contortionist and something like classical ballet, maybe resembling Danilova's dying swan. It was also pretty damned sexy. In a symbolic way, to be sure; but face it, most of the things we call "sexy" are symbolic, you know, except perhaps an exhibitionist's open clothing. On Day Million when Dora danced, the people who saw her panted, and you would too.

About this business of her being a boy. It didn't matter to her audiences that genetically she was male. It wouldn't matter to you, if you were among them, because you wouldn't know it—not unless you took a biopsy cutting of her flesh and put it under an electron-microscope to find the XY chromosome—and it didn't matter to them because they didn't care. Through techniques which are not only complex but haven't yet been discovered, these people were able to determine a great deal about the aptitudes and easements of babies quite a long time before they were born—at about the second horizon of cell-division, to be exact, when the segmenting egg is becoming a free blastocyst—and then they naturally helped those aptitudes along. Wouldn't we? If we find a child with an aptitude for music we give him a scholarship to Juilliard. If they found a child whose aptitudes were for being a woman, they made him one. As sex had long been dissociated from reproduction this was relatively easy to do and caused no trouble and no, or at least very little, comment.

How much is "very little"? Oh, about as much as would be caused by our own tampering with Divine Will by filling a tooth. Less than would be caused by wearing a hearing aid. Does it still sound awful? Then look closely at the next busty babe you meet and reflect that she may be a Dora, for adults who are genetically male but somatically female are far from unknown even in our own time. An accident of environment in the womb overwhelms the blueprints of heredity. The difference is that with us it happens only by accident and we don't know about it except rarely, after close study; whereas the people of Day Million did it often, on purpose, because they wanted to.

Well, that's enough to tell you about Dora. It would only confuse you to add that she was seven feet tall and smelled of peanut butter. Let us begin our story.

On Day Million, Dora swam out of her house, entered a transportation tube, was sucked briskly to the surface in its flow of water and ejected in its plume of spray to an elastic platform in front of her—ah—call it her rehearsal hall. "Oh, hell!" she cried in pretty confusion, reaching out to catch her balance and finding herself tumbled against a total stranger, whom we will call Don.

They met cute. Don was on his way to have his legs renewed. Love was the furthest thing from his mind. But when, absentmindedly taking a shortcut across the landing platform for submarines and finding himself drenched, he discovered his arms full of the loveliest girl he had ever seen, he knew at once they were meant for each other. "Will you marry me?" he asked. She said softly, "Wednesday," and the promise was like a caress.

Don was tall, muscular, bronze and exciting. His name was no more Don than Dora's was Dora, but the personal part of it was Adonis in tribute to his vibrant maleness, and so we will call him Don for short. His personality color-code, in angstrom units, was 5290, or only a few degrees bluer than Dora's 5314—a measure of what they had intuitively discovered at first sight; that they possessed many affinities of taste and interest.

I despair of telling you exactly what it was that Don did for a living—I don't mean for the sake of making money, I mean for the sake of giving purpose and meaning to his life, to keep him from going off his nut with boredom—except to say that it involved a lot of traveling. He traveled in interstellar spaceships. In order to make a spaceship go really fast, about thirty-one male and seven genetically female human beings had to do certain things, and Don was one of the thirty-one. Actually, he contemplated options. This involved a lot of exposure to radiation flux—not so much from his own station in the propulsive system as in the spillover from the next stage, where a genetic female preferred selections, and the subnuclear particles making the selections she preferred demolished themselves in a shower of quanta. Well, you don't give a rat's ass for that, but it meant that Don had to be clad at all times in a skin of light, resilient, extremely strong copper-colored metal. I have already mentioned this, but you probably thought I meant sunburned.

More than that, he was a cybernetic man. Most of his ruder parts had been long since replaced with mechanisms of vastly more permanence and use. A cadmium centrifuge, not a heart, pumped his blood. His lungs moved only when he wanted to speak out loud, for a cascade of osmotic filters rebreathed oxygen out of his own wastes. In a way, he probably would have looked peculiar to a man from the twentieth century, with his glowing eyes and seven-fingered hands. But to himself, and of course to Dora, he looked mighty manly and grand. In the course of his voyages Don had circled Proxima Centauri, Procyon and the puzzling worlds of Mira Ceti; he had carried agricultural templates to the planets of Canopus and brought back warm, witty pets from the pale companions of Aldebaran. Blue-hot or red-cool, he had seen a thousand stars and their ten thousand planets. He had, in fact, been traveling the starlanes, with only brief leaves on Earth, for pushing two centuries. But you don't care about that, either. It is people who make stories, not the circumstances they find themselves in, and you want to hear about these two people. Well, they made it. The great thing they had for each other grew and flowered and burst into fruition on Wednesday, just as Dora had promised. They met at the encoding room, with a couple of well-wishing friends apiece to cheer them on, and while their identities were being taped and stored they smiled and whispered to each other and bore the jokes of their friends with blushing repartee. Then they exchanged their mathematical analogues and went away, Dora to her dwelling beneath the surface of the sea and Don to his ship.

It was an idyll, really. They lived happily ever after—or anyway, until they decided not to bother any more and died.

Of course, they never set eyes on each other again.

Oh, I can see you now, you eaters of charcoal-broiled steak, scratching an incipient bunion with one hand and holding this story with the other, while the stereo plays d'Indy or Monk. You don't believe a word of it, do you? Not for one minute. People wouldn't live like that, you say with a grunt as you get up to put fresh ice in a drink.

And yet there's Dora, hurrying back through the flushing commuter pipes toward her underworld home (she prefers it there; has had herself somatically altered to breathe the stuff). If I tell you with what sweet fulfillment she fits the recorded analogue of Don into the symbol manipulator, hooks herself in and turns herself on . . . if I try to tell you any of that you will simply stare. Or glare; and grumble, what the hell kind of lovemaking is this? And yet I assure you, friend, I really do assure you that Dora's ecstasies are as creamy and passionate as any of James Bond's lady spies', and one hell of a lot more so than anything you are going to find in "real life." Go ahead, glare and grumble. Dora doesn't care. If she thinks of you at all, her thirty-times-great-great-grandfather, she thinks you're a pretty primordial sort of brute. You are. Why, Dora is further removed from you than you are from the australopithecines of five thousand centuries ago. You could not swim a second in the strong currents of her life. You don't think progress goes in a straight line, do you? Do you recognize that it is an ascending, accelerating, maybe even exponential curve? It takes hell's own time to get started, but when it goes it goes like a bomb. And you, you Scotch-drinking steak-eater in your relaxacizing chair, you've just barely lighted the primacord of the fuse. What is it now, the six or seven hundred thousandth-day after Christ? Dora lives in Day Million. Ten thousand years from now. Her body fats are polyunsaturated, like Crisco. Her wastes are hemodialyzed out of her bloodstream while she sleeps—that means she doesn't have to go to the bathroom. On whim, to pass a slow half hour, she can command more energy than the entire nation of Portugal can spend today, and use it to launch a weekend satellite or remold a crater on the Moon. She loves Don very much. She keeps his every gesture, mannerism, nuance, touch of hand, thrill of intercourse, passion of kiss stored in symbolic-mathematical form. And when she wants him, all she has to do is turn the machine on and she has him.

And Don, of course, has Dora. Adrift on a sponson city a few hundred yards over her head, or orbiting Arcturus fifty light-years away, Don has only to command his own symbol-manipulator to rescue Dora from the ferrite files and bring her to life for him, and there she is; and rapturously, tirelessly they love all night. Not in the flesh, of course; but then his flesh has been extensively altered and it wouldn't really be much fun. He doesn't need the flesh for pleasure. Genital organs feel nothing. Neither do hands, nor breasts, nor lips; they are only receptors, accepting and transmitting impulses. It is the brain that feels; it is the interpretation of those impulses that makes agony or orgasm, and Don's symbol-manipulator gives him the analogue of cuddling, analogue of kissing, the analogue of wild, ardent hours with the eternal, exquisite and incorruptible analogue of Dora. Or Diane. Or sweet Rose, or laughing Alicia; for to be sure, they have each of them exchanged analogues before, and will again.

Rats, you say, it looks crazy to me. And you—with your aftershave lotion and your little red car, pushing papers across a desk all day and chasing tail all night—tell me, just how the hell do you think you would look to Tiglath-pileser, say, or Attila the Hun?

CAGE OF SAND

J. G. Ballard

After the mid-sixties, J. G. Ballard's work became more experimental in style, culminating in his collection, *The Atrocity Exhibition* (1970), which was followed by a trilogy of urban disaster novels set in the present: *Crash* (1973); *Concrete Island* (1974); and *High-Rise* (1975). They explore the ways in which the technological landscape may be our own worst desires come true. For the most part, hard science fiction readers were appalled. Ballard's name became a symbol for the opposite of hard science fiction—pessimistic, experimental, nongenre, and totally unlike real sf in attitude and affect. Interviewed in the late 1970s, Ballard defended himself to the sf world. "Most of my fiction, whatever its setting may be, is not pessimistic. It's a *fiction of psychological fulfillment*. . . . All my fiction describes the merging of the self in the ultimate metaphor, the ultimate image, and that's psychologically fulfilling. It seems to me to be the only recipe for happiness we know."

In the 1980s, Ballard produced novels and stories that combined elements and images of his early style and concerns with nongenre facets of his seventies work, most significantly the autobiographical masterpiece *Empire of the Sun* (1984), *The Day of Creation* (1987), a psychological adventure novel, and *Running Wild* (1988), a dystopian murder mystery. In the 1990s, his literary reputation outside the science fiction field is that of an important living English writer. It seems clear that his literary goals diverged from those of the sf field in the later sixties so that by the seventies the majority of his writing was postmodern fiction in dialogue with genre sf; it remains so today.

Still, his stories of the early sixties form a striking and innovative part of the genre, widely influential and very much a challenge to hard science fiction. "Cage of Sand" (1962) is a story of the space age turned sour, written as real spaceflight was under construction and all astronauts were heroes, while most test rockets blew up.

The dying spaceman, from Ray Bradbury's *Martian Chronicles* through Theodore Sturgeon's "The Man Who Lost the Sea," was one of the conventional tragic figures in the sf of the fifties (and beyond—see Arthur C. Clarke's "Transit of Earth"). The dead spaceman in satellite orbit was also a similar figure, from James E. Gunn's "The Cave of Night." Ballard stripped the imagery of its associations with the wonders of space, and transformed it into a symbol of the inhumanity of space travel and the coldness of the inimical universe: his mountains of Martian sand burying Cape Canaveral are complex, symbolic, and link this landscape to his Vermillion Sands. He also stripped it of romanticism and optimism, and used the minutiae of real-life space programs for verisimilitude. He thus violated nearly all of the attitudes and conventions of Campbellian sf, while remaining quite faithful to many of the details of real space engineering and technology. Ironically, it is the Ballardian strain of sf that seems to predict the boring and dehumanizing aspects of the governmental space programs of the sixties and beyond, and even such tragedies as the *Challenger* disaster.

The ironies of the ending constitute a psychological fulfillment that is as powerful as a problem solved—but also a radically different mode of discourse from conventional hard sf. The characters in this form are *a priori* not in a position to deal with the problem, and are controlled by their own powerful psychological obsessions, which are brought to the fore by the set premise of the story. This is not merely nongenre sf; it is a radical departure from the baseline of hard sf: by constantly alluding to conventional images of sf (while transforming them), it calls the whole traditional sf enterprise into doubt by making solutions impossible. This is actually the vision of the entropic universe that underlies hard sf pushed to its extreme, different in execution but not in kind from, say, Latham's "The Xi Effect."

At sunset, when the vermilion glow reflected from the dunes along the horizon fitfully illuminated the white faces of the abandoned hotels, Bridgman stepped onto his balcony and looked out over the long stretches of cooling sand as the tides of purple shadow seeped across them. Slowly, extending their slender fingers through the shallow saddles and depressions, the shadows massed together like gigantic combs, a few phosphorescing spurs of obsidian isolated for a moment between the tines, and then finally coalesced and flooded in a solid wave across the half-submerged hotels. Behind the silent facades, in the tilting sand-filled streets which had once glittered with cocktail bars and restaurants, it was already night. Halos of moonlight beaded the lamp standards with silver dew, and draped the shuttered windows and slipping cornices like a frost of frozen gas.

As Bridgman watched, his lean bronzed arms propped against the rusting rail, the last whorls of light sank away into the cerise funnel withdrawing below the horizon, and the first wind stirred across the dead Martian sand. Here and there miniature cyclones whirled about a sandspur, drawing off swirling feathers of moon-washed spray, and a nimbus of white dust swept across the dunes and settled in the dips and hollows. Gradually the drifts accumulated, edging toward the former shoreline below the hotels. Already the first four floors had been inundated, and the sand now reached up to within two feet of Bridgman's balcony. After the next sandstorm he would be forced yet again to move to the floor above.

"Bridgman!"

The voice cleft the darkness like a spear. Fifty yards to his right, at the edge of the derelict sandbreak he had once attempted to build below the hotel, a square stocky figure wearing a pair of frayed cotton shorts waved up at him. The moonlight etched the broad sinewy muscles of his chest, the powerful bowed legs sinking almost to their calves in the soft Martian sand. He was about forty-five years old, his thinning hair close-cropped so that he seemed almost bald. In his right hand he carried a large canvas holdall.

Bridgman smiled to himself. Standing there patiently in the moonlight below the derelict hotel, Travis reminded him of some long-delayed tourist arriving at a ghost resort years after its extinction.

"Bridgman, are you coming?" When the latter still leaned on his balcony rail, Travis added, "The next conjunction is tomorrow."

Bridgman shook his head, a rictus of annoyance twisting his mouth. He hated the bimonthly conjunctions, when all seven of the derelict satellite capsules still orbiting the Earth crossed the sky together. Invariably on these nights he remained in his room, playing over the old memo-tapes he had salvaged from the submerged chalets and motels further along the beach (the hysterical "This is Mamie Goldberg,

62955 Cocoa Boulevard, I really wanna protest against this crazy evacuation . . ." or resigned "Sam Snade here, the Pontiac convertible in the back garage belongs to anyone who can dig it out"). Travis and Louise Woodward always came to the hotel on the conjunction nights—it was the highest building in the resort, with an unrestricted view from horizon to horizon—and would follow the seven converging stars as they pursued their endless courses around the globe. Both would be oblivious of everything else, which the wardens knew only too well, and they reserved their most careful searches of the sand sea for these bimonthly occasions. Invariably Bridgman found himself forced to act as lookout for the other two.

"I was out last night," he called down to Travis. "Keep away from the northeast perimeter fence by the Cape. They'll be busy repairing the track."

Most nights Bridgman divided his time between excavating the buried motels for caches of supplies (the former inhabitants of the resort area had assumed the government would soon rescind its evacuation order) and disconnecting the sections of metal roadway laid across the desert for the wardens' jeeps. Each of the squares of wire mesh was about five yards wide and weighed over three hundred pounds. After he had snapped the lines of rivets, dragged the sections away, and buried them among the dunes he would be exhausted, and spend most of the next day nursing his strained hands and shoulders. Some sections of the track were now permanently anchored with heavy steel stakes, and he knew that sooner or later they would be unable to delay the wardens by sabotaging the roadway.

Travis hesitated, and with a noncommittal shrug disappeared among the dunes, the heavy toolbag swinging easily from one powerful arm. Despite the meager diet which sustained him, his energy and determination seemed undiminished—in a single night Bridgman had watched him dismantle twenty sections of track and then loop together the adjacent limbs of a crossroad, sending an entire convoy of six vehicles off into the wastelands to the south.

Bridgman turned from the balcony, then stopped when a faint tang of brine touched the cool air. Ten miles away, hidden by the lines of dunes, was the sea, the long green rollers of the middle Atlantic breaking against the red Martian strand. When he had first come to the beach five years earlier there had never been the faintest scent of brine across the intervening miles of sand. Slowly, however, the Atlantic was driving the shore back to its former margins. The tireless shoulder of the Gulf Stream drummed against the soft Martian dust and piled the dunes into grotesque rococo reefs which the wind carried away into the sand sea. Gradually the ocean was returning, reclaiming its great smooth basin, sifting out the black quartz and Martian obsidian which would never be wind-borne and drawing these down into its deeps. More and more often the stain of brine would hang on the evening air, reminding Bridgman why he had first come to the beach and removing any inclination to leave.

Three years earlier he had attempted to measure the rate of approach, by driving a series of stakes into the sand at the water's edge, but the shifting contours of the dunes carried away the colored poles. Later, using the promontory at Cape Kennedy, where the old launching gantries and landing ramps reared up into the sky like derelict pieces of giant sculpture, he had calculated by triangulation that the advance was little more than thirty yards per year. At this rate—without wanting to, he had automatically made the calculation—it would be well over five hundred years before the Atlantic reached its former littoral at Cocoa Beach. Though discouragingly slow, the movement was nonetheless in a forward direction, and

Bridgman was happy to remain in his hotel ten miles away across the dunes, conceding toward its time of arrival the few years he had at his disposal.

Later, shortly after Louise Woodward's arrival, he had thought of dismantling one of the motel cabins and building himself a small chalet by the water's edge. But the shoreline had been too dismal and forbidding. The great red dunes rolled on for miles, cutting off half the sky, dissolving slowly under the impact of the slate-green water. There was no formal tideline, but only a steep shelf littered with nodes of quartz and rusting fragments of Mars rockets brought back with the ballast. He spent a few days in a cave below a towering sand reef, watching the long galleries of compacted red dust crumble and dissolve as the cold Atlantic stream sluiced through them, collapsing like the decorated colonnades of a baroque cathedral. In the summer the heat reverberated from the hot sand as from the slag of some molten sun, burning the rubber soles from his boots, and the light from the scattered flints of washed quartz flickered with diamond hardness. Bridgman had returned to the hotel grateful for his room overlooking the silent dunes.

Leaving the balcony, the sweet smell of brine still in his nostrils, he went over to the desk. A small cone of shielded light shone down over the tape recorder and rack of spools. The rumble of the wardens' unsilenced engines always gave him at least five minutes' warning of their arrival, and it would have been safe to install another lamp in the room—there were no roadways between the hotel and the sea, and from a distance any light reflected onto the balcony was indistinguishable from the corona of glimmering phosphors which hung over the sand like myriads of fireflies. However, Bridgman preferred to sit in the darkened suite, enclosed by the circle of books on the makeshift shelves, the shadow-filled air playing over his shoulders through the long night as he toyed with the memo-tapes, fragments of a vanished and unregretted past. By day he always drew the blinds, immolating himself in a world of perpetual twilight.

Bridgman had easily adapted himself to his self-isolation, soon evolved a system of daily routines that gave him the maximum of time to spend on his private reveries. Pinned to the walls around him were a series of huge whiteprints and architectural drawings, depicting various elevations of a fantastic Martian city he had once designed, its glass spires and curtain walls rising like heliotropic jewels from the vermilion desert. In fact, the whole city was a vast piece of jewelry, each elevation brilliantly visualized but as symmetrical, and ultimately as lifeless, as a crown. Bridgman continuously retouched the drawings, inserting more and more details, so that they almost seemed to be photographs of an original.

Most of the hotels in the town—one of a dozen similar resorts buried by the sand which had once formed an unbroken strip of motels, chalets, and five-star hotels thirty miles to the south of Cape Kennedy—were well stocked with supplies of canned food abandoned when the area was evacuated and wired off. There were ample reservoirs and cisterns filled with water, apart from a thousand intact cocktail bars six feet below the surface of the sand. Travis had excavated a dozen of these in search of his favorite vintage bourbon. Walking out across the desert behind the town one would suddenly find a short flight of steps cut into the annealed sand and crawl below an occluded sign announcing THE SATELLITE BAR OR THE ORBIT ROOM into the inner sanctum, where the jutting deck of a chromium bar had been cleared as far as the diamond-paned mirror freighted with its rows of bottles and figurines. Bridgman would have been glad to see them left undisturbed.

The whole trash of amusement arcades and cheap bars on the outskirts of the beach resorts were a depressing commentary on the original spaceflights, reducing them to the level of monster sideshows at a carnival.

Outside his room, steps sounded along the corridor, then slowly climbed the stairway, pausing for a few seconds at every landing. Bridgman lowered the memo-tape in his hand, listening to the familiar tired footsteps. This was Louise Woodward, making her invariable evening ascent to the roof ten stories above. Bridgman glanced to the timetable pinned to the wall. Only two of the satellites would be visible, between 12:25 and 12:35 A.M., at an elevation of 62 degrees in the southwest, passing through Cetus and Eridanus, neither of them containing her husband. Although the sighting was two hours away, she was already taking up her position, and would remain there until dawn.

Bridgman listened wanly to the feet recede slowly up the stairwell. All through the night the slim pale-faced woman would sit out under the moonlit sky, as the soft Martian sand her husband had given his life to reach sifted around her in the dark wind, stroking her faded hair like some mourning mariner's wife waiting for the sea to surrender her husband's body. Travis usually joined her later, and the two of them sat side by side against the elevator house, the frosted letters of the hotel's neon sign strewn around their feet like the fragments of a dismembered zodiac, then at dawn made their way down into the shadow-filled streets to their aeries in the nearby hotels.

Initially Bridgman often joined their nocturnal vigil, but after a few nights he began to feel something repellent, if not actually ghoulish, about their mindless contemplation of the stars. This was not so much because of the macabre spectacle of the dead astronauts orbiting the planet in their capsules, but because of the curious sense of unspoken communion between Travis and Louise Woodward, almost as if they were celebrating a private rite to which Bridgman could never be initiated. Whatever their original motives, Bridgman sometimes suspected that these had been overlayed by other, more personal ones.

Ostensibly, Louise Woodward was watching her husband's satellite in order to keep alive his memory, but Bridgman guessed that the memories she unconsciously wished to perpetuate were those of herself twenty years earlier, when her husband had been a celebrity and she herself courted by magazine columnists and TV reporters. For fifteen years after his death—Woodward had been killed testing a new lightweight launching platform—she had lived a nomadic existence, driving restlessly in her cheap car from motel to motel across the continent, following her husband's star as it disappeared into the eastern night, and had at last made her home at Cocoa Beach in sight of the rusting gantries across the bay.

Travis's real motives were probably more complex. To Bridgman, after they had known each other for a couple of years, he had confided that he felt himself bound by a debt of honor to maintain a watch over the dead astronauts for the example of courage and sacrifice they had set him as a child (although most of them had been piloting their wrecked capsules for fifty years before Travis's birth), and that now they were virtually forgotten he must single-handedly keep alive the fading flame of their memory. Bridgman was convinced of his sincerity.

Yet later, going through a pile of old news magazines in the trunk of a car he excavated from a motel port, he came across a picture of Travis wearing an aluminum pressure suit and learned something more of his story. Apparently Travis had at one time been himself an astronaut—or rather, a would-be astronaut. A test pilot for one of the civilian agencies setting up orbital relay stations, his nerve had failed him a few seconds before the last "hold" of his countdown, a moment of pure unexpected funk that cost the company some five million dollars.

Obviously it was his inability to come to terms with this failure of character, unfortunately discovered lying flat on his back on a contour couch two hundred feet above the launching pad, which had brought Travis to Kennedy, the abandoned Mecca of the first heroes of astronautics.

Tactfully Bridgman had tried to explain that no one would blame him for this failure of nerve—less his responsibility than that of the selectors who had picked him for the flight, or at least the result of an unhappy concatenation of ambiguously worded multiple-choice questions (crosses in the wrong boxes, some heavier to bear and harder to open than others! Bridgman had joked sardonically to himself). But Travis seemed to have reached his own decision about himself. Night after night, he watched the brilliant funerary convoy weave its gilded pathway toward the dawn sun, salving his own failure by identifying it with the greater, but blameless, failure of the seven astronauts. Travis still wore his hair in the regulation "Mohican" cut of the spaceman, still kept himself in perfect physical trim by the vigorous routines he had practiced before his abortive flight. Sustained by the personal myth he had created, he was now more or less unreachable.

"Dear Harry, I've taken the car and deposit box. Sorry it should end like—"

Irritably, Bridgman switched off the memo-tape and its recapitulation of some thirty-year-old private triviality. For some reason he seemed unable to accept Travis and Louise Woodward for what they were. He disliked this failure of compassion, a nagging compulsion to expose other people's motives and strip away the insulating sheaths around their naked nerve strings, particularly as his own motives for being at Cape Kennedy were so suspect. Why was *he* there, what failure was *he* trying to expiate? And why choose Cocoa Beach as his penitential shore? For three years he had asked himself these questions so often that they had ceased to have any meaning, like a fossilized catechism or the blunted self-recrimination of a paranoiac.

He had resigned his job as the chief architect of a big space development company after the large government contract on which the firm depended, for the design of the first Martian city-settlement, was awarded to a rival consortium. Secretly, however, he realized that his resignation had marked his unconscious acceptance that despite his great imaginative gifts he was unequal to the specialized and more prosaic tasks of designing the settlement. On the drawing board, as elsewhere, he would always remain earthbound.

His dreams of building a new Gothic architecture of launching ports and controls gantries, of being the Frank Lloyd Wright and Le Corbusier of the first city to be raised outside Earth, faded forever, but left him unable to accept the alternative of turning out endless plans for low-cost hospitals in Ecuador and housing estates in Tokyo. For a year he had drifted aimlessly, but a few color photographs of the vermilion sunsets at Cocoa Beach and a news story about the recluses living on in the submerged motels had provided a powerful compass.

He dropped the memo-tape into a drawer, making an effort to accept Louise Woodward and Travis on their own terms, a wife keeping watch over her dead husband and an old astronaut maintaining a solitary vigil over the memories of his lost comrades-in-arms.

The wind gusted against the balcony window, and a light spray of sand rained across the floor. At night dust storms churned along the beach. Thermal pools isolated by the cooling desert would suddenly accrete like beads of quicksilver and erupt across the fluffy sand in miniature tornadoes.

• • •

Only fifty yards away, the dying cough of a heavy diesel cut through the shadows. Quickly Bridgman turned off the small desk light, grateful for his meanness over the battery packs plugged into the circuit, then stepped to the window.

At the leftward edge of the sand break, half-hidden in the long shadows cast by the hotel, was a large tracked vehicle with a low camouflaged hull. A narrow observation bridge had been built over the bumpers directly in front of the squat snout of the engine housing, and two of the beach wardens were craning up through the Plexiglas windows at the balconies of the hotel, shifting their binoculars from room to room. Behind them, under the glass dome of the extended driving cabin, were three more wardens, controlling an outboard spotlight. In the center of the bowl a thin mote of light pulsed with the rhythm of the engine, ready to throw its powerful beam into any of the open rooms.

Bridgman hid back behind the shutters as the binoculars focused upon the adjacent balcony, moved to his own, hesitated, and passed to the next. Exasperated by the sabotaging of the roadways, the wardens had evidently decided on a new type of vehicle. With their four broad tracks, the huge squat sand cars would be free of the mesh roadways and able to rove at will through the dunes and sand hills.

Bridgman watched the vehicle reverse slowly, its engine barely varying its deep bass growl, then move off along the line of hotels, almost indistinguishable in profile among the shifting dunes and hillocks. A hundred yards away, at the first intersection, it turned toward the main boulevard, wisps of dust streaming from the metal cleats like thin spumes of steam. The men in the observation bridge were still watching the hotel. Bridgman was certain that they had seen a reflected glimmer of light, or perhaps some movement of Louise Woodward's on the roof. However reluctant to leave the car and be contaminated by the poisonous dust, the wardens would not hesitate if the capture of one of the beachcombers warranted it.

Racing up the staircase, Bridgman made his way to the roof, crouching below the windows that overlooked the boulevard. Like a huge crab, the sand car had parked under the jutting overhang of the big department store opposite. Once fifty feet from the ground, the concrete lip was now separated from it by little more than six or seven feet, and the sand car was hidden in the shadows below it, engine silent. A single movement in a window, or the unexpected return of Travis, and the wardens would spring from the hatchways, their long-handled nets and lassos pinioning them around the neck and ankles. Bridgman remembered one beachcomber he had seen flushed from his motel hideout and carried off like a huge twitching spider at the center of a black rubber web, the wardens with their averted faces and masked mouths like devils in an abstract ballet.

Reaching the roof, Bridgman stepped out into the opaque white moonlight. Louise Woodward was leaning on the balcony, looking out toward the distant, unseen sea. At the faint sound of the door creaking she turned and began to walk listlessly around the roof, her pale face floating like a nimbus. She wore a freshly ironed print dress she had found in a rusty spin dryer in one of the launderettes, and her streaked blond hair floated out lightly behind her on the wind.

"Louise!"

Involuntarily she started, tripping over a fragment of the neon sign, then moved backward toward the balcony overlooking the boulevard.

"Mrs. Woodward!" Bridgman held her by the elbow, raised a hand to her mouth before she could cry out. "The wardens are down below. They're watching the hotel. We must find Travis before he returns."

Louise hesitated, apparently recognizing Bridgman only by an effort, and her eyes turned up to the black marble sky. Bridgman looked at his watch; it was almost 12:35. He searched the stars in the southwest.

Louise murmured, "They're nearly here now, I must see them. Where is Travis, he should be here?"

Bridgman pulled at her arm. "Perhaps he saw the sand car. Mrs. Woodward, we should leave."

Suddenly she pointed up at the sky, then wrenched away from him and ran to the rail. "There they are!"

Fretting, Bridgman waited until she had filled her eyes with the two companion points of light speeding from the western horizon. These were Merril and Pokrovski—like every schoolboy he knew the sequences perfectly, a second system of constellations with a more complex but far more tangible periodicity and precession—the Castor and Pollux of the orbiting zodiac, whose appearance always heralded a full conjunction the following night.

Louise Woodward gazed up at them from the rail, the rising wind lifting her hair off her shoulders and entraining it horizontally behind her head. Around her feet the red Martian dust swirled and rustled, silting over the fragments of the old neon sign, a brilliant pink spume streaming from her long fingers as they moved along the balcony ledge. When the satellites finally disappeared among the stars along the horizon, she leaned forward, her face raised to the milk-blue moon as if to delay their departure, then turned back to Bridgman, a bright smile on her face.

His earlier suspicions vanishing, Bridgman smiled back at her encouragingly. "Roger will be here tomorrow night, Louise. We must be careful the wardens don't catch us before we see him."

He felt a sudden admiration for her, at the stoical way she had sustained herself during her long vigil. Perhaps she thought of Woodward as still alive, and in some way was patiently waiting for him to return? He remembered her saying once, "Roger was only a boy when he took off, you know, I feel more like his mother now," as if frightened how Woodward would react to her dry skin and fading hair, fearing that he might even have forgotten her. No doubt the death she visualized for him was of a different order than the mortal kind.

Hand in hand, they tiptoed carefully down the flaking steps, jumped down from a terrace window into the soft sand below the windbreak. Bridgman sank to his knees in the fine silver moon dust, then waded up to the firmer ground, pulling Louise after him. They climbed through a breach in the tilting palisades, then ran away from the line of dead hotels looming like skulls in the empty light.

"Paul, wait!" Her head still raised to the sky, Louise Woodward fell to her knees in a hollow between two dunes, with a laugh stumbled after Bridgman as he raced through the dips and saddles. The wind was now whipping the sand off the higher crests, flurries of dust spurting like excited wavelets. A hundred yards away, the town was a fading film set, projected by the camera obscura of the sinking moon. They were standing where the long Atlantic seas had once been ten fathoms deep, and Bridgman could scent again the tang of brine among the flickering whitecaps of dust, phosphorescing like shoals of animalcula. He waited for any sign of Travis.

"Louise, we'll have to go back to the town. The sandstorms are blowing up, we'll never see Travis here."

They moved back through the dunes, then worked their way among the narrow alleyways between the hotels to the northern gateway to the town. Bridgman found a vantage point in a small apartment block, and they lay down looking out below a window lintel into the sloping street, the warm sand forming a pleasant cushion. At the intersections the dust blew across the roadway in white clouds, obscuring the warden's beach car parked a hundred yards down the boulevard.

Half an hour later an engine surged, and Bridgman began to pile sand into the interval in front of them. "They're going. Thank God!"

Louise Woodward held his arm. "Look!"

Fifty feet away, his white vinyl suit half-hidden in the dust clouds, one of the wardens was advancing slowly toward them, his lasso twirling lightly in his hand. A few feet behind was a second warden, craning up at the windows of the apartment block with his binoculars.

Bridgman and Louise crawled back below the ceiling, then dug their way under a transom into the kitchen at the rear. A window opened onto a sand-filled yard, and they darted away through the lifting dust that whirled between the buildings.

Suddenly, around a corner, they saw the line of wardens moving down a side street, the sand car edging along behind them. Before Bridgman could steady himself a spasm of pain seized his right calf, contorting the gastrocnemius muscle, and he fell to one knee. Louise Woodward pulled him back against the wall, then pointed at a squat, bowlegged figure trudging toward them along the curving road into town.

"Travis—"

The toolbag swung from his right hand, and his feet rang faintly on the wire-mesh roadway. Head down, he seemed unaware of the wardens hidden by a bend in the road.

"Come on!" Disregarding the negligible margin of safety, Bridgman clambered to his feet and impetuously ran out into the center of the street. Louise tried to stop him, and they had covered only ten yards before the wardens saw them. There was a warning shout, and the spotlight flung its giant cone down the street. The sand car surged forward, like a massive dust-covered bull, its tracks clawing at the sand.

"Travis!" As Bridgman reached the bend, Louise Woodward ten yards behind, Travis looked up from his reverie, then flung the toolbag over one shoulder and raced ahead of them toward the clutter of motel roofs protruding from the other side of the street. Lagging behind the others, Bridgman again felt the cramp attack his leg, broke off into a painful shuffle. When Travis came back for him Bridgman tried to wave him away, but Travis pinioned his elbow and propelled him forward like an attendant straight-arming a patient.

The dust swirling around them, they disappeared through the fading streets and out into the desert, the shouts of the beach wardens lost in the roar and clamor of the baying engine. Around them, like the strange metallic flora of some extraterrestrial garden, the old neon signs jutted from the red Martian sand—SATELLITE MOTEL, PLANET BAR, MERCURY MOTEL. Hiding behind them, they reached the scrub-covered dunes on the edge of the town, then picked up one of the trails that led away among the sand reefs. There, in the deep grottoes of compacted sand which hung like inverted palaces, they waited until the storm subsided. Shortly before dawn the wardens abandoned their search, unable to bring the heavy sand car onto the disintegrating reef.

Contemptuous of the wardens, Travis lit a small fire with his cigarette lighter, burning splinters of driftwood that had gathered in the gullies. Bridgman crouched beside it, warming his hands.

"This is the first time they've been prepared to leave the sand car," he remarked to Travis. "It means they're under orders to catch us."

Travis shrugged. "Maybe. They're extending the fence along the beach. They probably intend to seal us in forever."

"What?" Bridgman stood up with a sudden feeling of uneasiness. "Why should they? Are you sure? I mean, what would be the point?"

Travis looked up at him, a flicker of dry amusement on his bleached face. Wisps of smoke wreathed his head, curled up past the serpentine columns of the grotto to the winding interval of sky a hundred feet above. "Bridgman, forgive me saying so, but if you want to leave here, you should leave now. In a month's time you won't be able to."

Bridgman ignored this, and searched the cleft of dark sky overhead, which framed the constellation Scorpio, as if hoping to see a reflection of the distant sea. "They must be crazy. How much of this fence did you see?"

"About eight hundred yards. It won't take them long to complete. The sections are prefabricated, about forty feet high." He smiled ironically at Bridgman's discomfort. "Relax, Bridgman. If you do want to get out, you'll always be able to tunnel underneath it."

"I don't want to get out," Bridgman said coldly. "Damn them, Travis, they're turning the place into a zoo. You know it won't be the same with a fence all the way around it."

"A corner of Earth that is forever Mars." Under the high forehead, Travis's eyes were sharp and watchful. "I see their point. There hasn't been a fatal casualty now—" he glanced at Louise Woodward, who was strolling about in the colonnades "—for nearly twenty years, and passenger rockets are supposed to be as safe as commuters' trains. They're quietly sealing off the past, Louise and I and you with it. I suppose it's pretty considerate of them not to burn the place down with flamethrowers. The virus would be a sufficient excuse. After all, we are probably the only reservoirs left on the planet." He picked up a handful of red dust and examined the fine crystals with a somber eye. "Well, Bridgman, what are you going to do?"

His thoughts discharging themselves through his mind like frantic signal flares, Bridgman walked away without answering.

Behind them, Louise Woodward wandered among the deep galleries of the grotto, crooning to herself in a low voice to the sighing rhythms of the whirling sand.

The next morning they returned to the town, wading through the deep drifts of sand that lay like a fresh fall of red snow between the hotels and stores, coruscating in the brilliant sunlight. Travis and Louise Woodward made their way toward their quarters in the motels further down the beach. Bridgman searched the still, crystal air for any signs of the wardens, but the sand car had gone, its tracks obliterated by the storm.

In his room he found their calling card.

A huge tide of dust had flowed through the French windows and submerged the desk and bed, three feet deep against the rear wall. Outside the sand break had been inundated, and the contours of the desert had completely altered, a few spires of obsidian marking its former perspectives like buoys on a shifting sea. Bridgman spent the morning digging out his books and equipment, dismantled the electrical system and its batteries and carried everything to the room above. He would have moved to the penthouse on the top floor, but his lights would have been visible for miles.

Settling into his new quarters, he switched on the tape recorder, heard a short clipped message in the brisk voice which had shouted orders at the wardens the previous evening. "Bridgman, this is Major Webster, deputy commandant of Cocoa Beach Reservation. On the instructions of the Anti-Viral Subcommittee of the UN General Assembly we are now building a continuous fence around the beach area. On completion no further egress will be allowed, and anyone escaping will be immediately returned to the reservation. Give yourself up now, Bridgman, before—"

Bridgman stopped the tape, then reversed the spool and erased the message, staring angrily at the instrument. Unable to settle down to the task of rewiring the room's circuits, he paced about, fiddling with the architectural drawings propped against the wall. He felt restless and hyperexcited, perhaps because he had been trying to repress, not very successfully, precisely those doubts of which Webster had now reminded him.

He stepped onto the balcony and looked out over the desert, at the red dunes rolling to the windows directly below. For the fourth time he had moved up a floor, and the sequence of identical rooms he had occupied were like displaced images of himself seen through a prism. Their common focus, that elusive final definition of himself which he had sought for so long, still remained to be found. Timelessly the sand swept toward him, its shifting contours, approximating more closely than any other landscape he had found to complete psychic zero, enveloping his past failures and uncertainties, masking them in its enigmatic canopy.

Bridgman watched the red sand flicker and fluoresce in the steepening sunlight. He would never see Mars now, and redress the implicit failure of talent, but a workable replica of the planet was contained within the beach area.

Several million tons of the Martian topsoil had been ferried in as ballast some fifty years earlier, when it was feared that the continuous firing of planetary probes and space vehicles, and the transportation of bulk stores and equipment to Mars, would fractionally lower the gravitational mass of the Earth and bring it into a tighter orbit around the Sun. Although the distance involved would be little more than a few millimeters, and barely raise the temperature of the atmosphere, its cumulative effects over an extended period might have resulted in a loss into space of the tenuous layers of the outer atmosphere, and of the radiological veil which alone made the biosphere habitable.

Over a twenty-year period a fleet of large freighters had shuttled to and from Mars, dumping the ballast into the sea near the landing grounds of Cape Kennedy. Simultaneously the Russians were filling in a small section of the Caspian Sea. The intention had been that the ballast should be swallowed by the Atlantic and Caspian waters, but all too soon it was found that the microbiological analysis of the sand had been inadequate.

At the Martian polar caps, where the original water vapor in the atmosphere had condensed, a residue of ancient organic matter formed the topsoil, a fine sandy loess containing the fossilized spores of the giant lichens and mosses which had been the last living organisms on the planet millions of years earlier. Embedded in these spores were the crystal lattices of the viruses which had once preyed on the plants, and traces of these were carried back to Earth with the Kennedy and Caspian ballast.

A few years afterward a drastic increase in a wide range of plant disease was noticed in the southern states of America and in the Kazakhstan and Turkmenistan republics of the Soviet Union. All over Florida there were outbreaks of blight and mosaic disease, orange plantations withered and died, stunted palms split by the roadside like dried banana skins, manila grass stiffened into paper spears in the summer heat. Within a few years the entire peninsula was transformed into a desert. The swampy jungles of the Everglades became bleached and dry, the rivers' cracked husks strewn with the gleaming skeletons of crocodiles and birds, the forests petrified.

The former launching ground at Kennedy was closed, and shortly afterward the Cocoa Beach resorts were sealed off and evacuated, billions of dollars of real estate were abandoned to the virus. Fortunately never virulent to animal hosts, its influence was confined to within a small radius of the original loess which had borne it, unless ingested by the human organism, when it symbioted with the bacteria in the gut flora, benign and unknown to the host, but devastating to vegetation thousands of miles from Kennedy if returned to the soil.

Unable to rest despite his sleepless night, Bridgman played irritably with the tape recorder. During their close escape from the wardens he had more than half-hoped they would catch him. The mysterious leg cramp was obviously psychogenic. Although unable to accept consciously the logic of Webster's argument, he would willingly have conceded to the *fait accompli* of physical capture, gratefully submitted to a year's quarantine at the Parasitological Cleansing Unit at Tampa, and then returned to his career as an architect, chastened but accepting his failure.

As yet, however, the opportunity for surrender had failed to offer itself. Travis appeared to be aware of his ambivalent motives; Bridgman noticed that he and Louise Woodward had made no arrangements to meet him that evening for the conjunction.

In the early afternoon he went down into the streets, ploughed through the drifts of red sand, following the footprints of Travis and Louise as they wound in and out of the side streets, finally saw them disappear into the coarser, flintlike dunes among the submerged motels to the south of the town. Giving up, he returned through the empty, shadowless streets, now and then shouted up into the hot air, listening to the echoes boom away among the dunes.

Later that afternoon he walked out toward the northeast, picking his way carefully through the dips and hollows, crouching in the pools of shadow whenever the distant sounds of the construction gangs along the perimeter were carried across to him by the wind. Around him, in the great dust basins, the grains of red sand flittered like diamonds. Barbs of rusting metal protruded from the slopes, remnants of Mars satellites and launching stages which had fallen onto the Martian deserts and then been carried back again to Earth. One fragment which he passed, a complete section of hull plate like a concave shield, still carried part of an identification numeral, and stood upright in the dissolving sand like a door into nowhere.

Just before dusk he reached a tall spur of obsidian that reared up into the tinted cerise sky like the spire of a ruined church, climbed up among its jutting cornices and looked out across the intervening two or three miles of dunes to the perimeter. Illuminated by the last light, the metal grilles shone with a roseate glow like fairy portcullises on the edge of an enchanted sea. At least half a mile of the fence had been completed, and as he watched, another of the giant prefabricated sections was cantilevered into the air and staked to the ground. Already the eastern horizon was cut off by the encroaching fence, the enclosed Martian sand like the gravel scattered at the bottom of a cage.

Perched on the spur, Bridgman felt a warning tremor of pain in his calf. He leaped down in a flurry of dust, without looking back made off among the dunes and reefs.

Later, as the last baroque whorls of the sunset faded below the horizon, he waited on the roof for Travis and Louise Woodward, peering impatiently into the empty moon-filled streets.

Shortly after midnight, at an elevation of 35 degrees in the southwest, between Aquila and Ophiuchus, the conjunction began. Bridgman continued to search the streets, and ignored the seven points of speeding light as they raced toward him from the horizon like an invasion from deep space. There was no indication of their convergent orbital pathways, which would soon scatter them thousands of miles apart, and the satellites moved as if they were always together, in the tight configuration Bridgman had known since childhood, like a lost zodiacal emblem, a constellation detached from the celestial sphere and forever frantically searching to return to its place.

"Travis! Confound you!" With a snarl, Bridgman swung away from the balcony and moved along to the exposed section of rail behind the elevator head. To be avoided like a pariah by Travis and Louise Woodward forced him to accept that he was no longer a true resident of the beach and now existed in a no-man's-land between them and the wardens.

The seven satellites drew nearer, and Bridgman glanced up at them cursorily. They were disposed in a distinctive but unusual pattern resembling the Greek letter *chi*, a limp cross, a straight lateral member containing four capsules more or less in line ahead—Connolly, Tkachev, Merril, and Maiakovski—bisected by three others forming with Tkachev an elongated **Z**—Pokrovski, Woodward, and Brodisnek. The pattern had been variously identified as a hammer and sickle, an eagle, a swastika, and a dove, as well as a variety of religious and runic emblems, but all these were being defeated by the advancing tendency of the older capsules to vaporize.

It was this slow disintegration of the aluminum shells that made them visible—it had often been pointed out that the observer on the ground was looking, not at the actual capsule, but at a local field of vaporized aluminum and ionized hydrogen peroxide gas from the ruptured altitude jets now distributed within half a mile of each of the capsules. Woodward's, the most recently in orbit, was a barely perceptible point of light. The hulks of the capsules, with their perfectly preserved human cargoes, were continually dissolving, and a wide fan of silver spray opened out in a phantom wake behind Merril and Pokrovski (1998 and 1999), like a double star transforming itself into a nova in the center of a constellation. As the mass of the capsules diminished they sank into a closer orbit around the Earth, would soon touch the denser layers of the atmosphere and plummet to the ground.

Bridgman watched the satellites as they moved toward him, his irritation with Travis forgotten. As always, he felt himself moved by the eerie but strangely serene spectacle of the ghostly convoy endlessly circling the dark sea of the midnight sky, the long-dead astronauts converging for the ten-thousandth time upon their brief rendezvous and then setting off upon their lonely flight paths around the perimeter of the ionosphere, the tidal edge of the beachway into space which had reclaimed them.

How Louise Woodward could bear to look up at her husband he had never been able to understand. After her arrival he once invited her to the hotel, remarking that there was an excellent view of the beautiful sunsets, and she had snapped back bitterly: "Beautiful? Can you imagine what it's like looking up at a sunset when your husband's spinning around through it in his coffin?"

This reaction had been a common one when the first astronauts had died after failing to make contact with the launching platforms in fixed orbit. When these new stars rose in the west an attempt had been made to shoot them down—there was the unsettling prospect of the skies a thousand years hence, littered with orbiting refuse—but later they were left in this natural graveyard, forming their own monument.

Obscured by the clouds of dust carried up into the air by the sandstorm, the satellites shone with little more than the intensity of second-magnitude stars, winking as the reflected light was interrupted by the lanes of stratocirrus. The wake of diffusing light behind Merril and Pokrovski which usually screened the other capsules seemed to have diminished in size, and he could see both Maiakovski and Brodisnek clearly for the first time in several months. Wondering whether Merril or Pokrovski would be the first to fall from orbit, he looked toward the center of the cross as it passed overhead.

With a sharp intake of breath, he tilted his head back. In surprise he noticed that one of the familiar points of light was missing from the center of the group. What he had assumed to be an occlusion of the conjoint vapor trails by dust clouds was simply due to the fact that one of the capsules—Merril's, he decided, the third of the line ahead—had fallen from its orbit.

Head raised, he sidestepped slowly across the roof, avoiding the pieces of rusting neon sign, following the convoy as it passed overhead and moved toward the eastern horizon. No longer overlayed by the wake of Merril's capsule, Woodward's shone with far greater clarity, and almost appeared to have taken the former's place, although he was not due to fall from orbit for at least a century.

In the distance somewhere an engine growled. A moment later, from a different quarter, a woman's voice cried out faintly. Bridgman moved to the rail, over the intervening rooftops saw two figures silhouetted against the sky on the elevator head of an apartment block, then heard Louise Woodward call out again. She was pointing up at the sky with both hands, her long hair blown about her face, Travis trying to restrain her. Bridgman realized that she had misconstrued Merril's descent, assuming that the fallen astronaut was her husband. He climbed onto the edge of the balcony, watching the pathetic tableau on the distant roof.

Again, somewhere among the dunes, an engine moaned. Before Bridgman could turn around, a brilliant blade of light cleaved the sky in the southwest. Like a speeding comet, an immense train of vaporizing particles stretching behind it to the horizon, it soared toward them, the downward curve of its pathway clearly visible. Detached from the rest of the capsules, which were now disappearing among the stars along the eastern horizon, it was little more than a few miles off the ground.

Bridgman watched it approach, apparently on a collision course with the hotel. The expanding corona of white light, like a gigantic signal flare, illuminated the rooftops, etching the letters of the neon signs over the submerged motels on the outskirts of the town. He ran for the doorway, as he raced down the stairs saw the glow of the descending capsule fill the somber streets like a hundred moons. When he reached his room, sheltered by the massive weight of the hotel, he watched the dunes in front of the hotel light up like a stage set. Three hundred yards away the low camouflaged hull of the wardens' beach car was revealed poised on a crest, its feeble spotlight drowned by the glare.

With a deep metallic sigh, the burning catafalque of the dead astronaut soared overhead, a cascade of vaporizing metal pouring from its hull, filling the sky with incandescent light. Reflected below it, like an expressway illuminated by an aircraft's spotlights, a long lane of light several hundred yards in width raced out into the desert toward the sea. As Bridgman shielded his eyes, it suddenly erupted in a tremendous explosion of detonating sand. A huge curtain of white dust lifted into the air and fell slowly to the ground. The sounds of the impact rolled against the hotel, mounting in a sustained crescendo that drummed against the windows. A series of smaller explosions flared up like opalescent fountains. All over the desert fires flickered briefly where fragments of the capsule had been scattered. Then the noise subsided, and an immense glistening pall of phosphorescing gas hung in the air like a silver veil, particles within it beading and winking.

Two hundred yards away across the sand was the running figure of Louise Woodward, Travis twenty paces behind her. Bridgman watched them dart in and out of the dunes, then abruptly felt the cold spotlight of the beach car hit his face and flood the room behind him. The vehicle was moving straight toward him, two of the wardens, nets and lassos in hand, riding the outboard.

Quickly Bridgman straddled the balcony, jumped down into the sand, and raced toward the crest of the first dune. He crouched and ran on through the darkness as the beam probed the air. Above, the glistening pall was slowly fading, the particles of vaporized metal sifting toward the dark Martian sand. In the distance the last echoes of the impact were still reverberating among the hotels of the beach colonies further down the coast.

Five minutes later he caught up with Louise Woodward and Travis. The capsule's impact had flattened a number of the dunes, forming a shallow basin some quarter of a mile in diameter, and the surrounding slopes were scattered with the still glowing particles, sparkling like fading eyes. The beach car growled somewhere four or five hundred yards behind him, and Bridgman broke off into an exhausted walk. He stopped beside Travis, who was kneeling on the ground, breath pumping into his lungs. Fifty yards away Louise Woodward was running up and down, distraughtly gazing at the fragments of smoldering metal. For a moment the spotlight of the approaching beach car illuminated her, and she ran away among the dunes. Bridgman caught a glimpse of the inconsolable anguish in her face.

Travis was still on his knees. He had picked up a piece of the oxidized metal and was pressing it together in his hands.

"Travis, for God's sake tell her! This was Merril's capsule, there's no doubt about it! Woodward's still up there."

Travis looked up at him silently, his eyes searching Bridgman's face. A spasm of pain tore his mouth, and Bridgman realized that the barb of steel he clasped reverently in his hands was still glowing with heat.

"Travis!" He tried to pull the man's hands apart, the pungent stench of burning flesh gusting into his face, but Travis wrenched away from him. "Leave her alone, Bridgman! Go back with the wardens!"

Bridgman retreated from the approaching beach car. Only thirty yards away, its spotlight filled the basin. Louise Woodward was still searching the dunes. Travis held his ground as the wardens jumped down from the car and advanced toward him with their nets, his bloodied hands raised at his sides, the steel barb flashing like a dagger. At the head of the wardens, the only one unmasked, was a trim, neat-featured man with an intent, serious face. Bridgman guessed that this was Major Webster, and that the wardens had known of the impending impact and hoped to capture them, and Louise in particular, before it occurred.

Bridgman stumbled back toward the dunes at the edge of the basin. As he neared the crest he trapped his foot in a semicircular plate of metal, sat down, and freed his heel. Unmistakably it was part of a control panel, the circular instrument housings still intact.

Overhead the pall of glistening vapor had moved off to the northeast, and the reflected light was directly over the rusting gantries of the former launching site at Cape Kennedy. For a few fleeting seconds the gantries seemed to be enveloped in a sheen of silver, transfigured by the vaporized body of the dead astronaut, diffusing over them in a farewell gesture, his final return to the site from which he had set off to his death a century earlier. Then the gantries sank again into their craggy shadows, and the pall moved off like an immense wraith toward the sea, barely distinguishable from the star glow.

Down below Travis was sitting on the ground surrounded by the wardens. He scuttled about on his hands like a frantic crab, scooping handfuls of the virus-laden sand at them. Holding tight to their masks, the wardens maneuvered around him, their nets and lassos at the ready. Another group moved slowly toward Bridgman.

Bridgman picked up a handful of the dark Martian sand beside the instrument panel, felt the soft glowing crystals warm his palm. In his mind he could still see the silver-sheathed gantries of the launching site across the bay, by a curious illusion almost identical with the Martian city he had designed years earlier. He watched the pall disappear over the sea, then looked around at the other remnants of Merril's capsule scattered over the slopes. High in the western night, between Pegasus and Cygnus, shone the distant disk of the planet Mars, which for both himself and the dead astronaut had served for so long as a symbol of unattained ambition. The wind stirred softly through the sand, cooling this replica of the planet which lay passively around him, and at last he understood why he had come to the beach and been unable to leave it.

Twenty yards away Travis was being dragged off like a wild dog, his thrashing body pinioned in the center of a web of lassos. Louise Woodward had run away among the dunes toward the sea, following the vanished gas cloud.

In a sudden access of refound confidence, Bridgman drove his fist into the dark sand, buried his forearm like a foundation pillar. A flange of hot metal from Merril's capsule burned his wrist, bonding him to the spirit of the dead astronaut.

"Merril!" he cried exultantly as the wardens' lassos stung his neck and shoulders. "We made it!"

THE PSYCHOLOGIST WHO WOULDN'T DO AWFUL THINGS TO RATS

James Tiptree, Jr.

James Tiptree, Jr., was the pseudonym of Alice B. Sheldon, a writer who spent most of her life working for the Central Intelligence Agency and other secret agencies of the U.S. government before becoming an experimental psychologist in the late sixties, and bursting into the science fiction field with one of the most important and influential careers of the seventies, her most productive decade. She was a technician who was always determined to learn more and exercise her skills as a writer. Her reputation is based upon her short fiction, collected in *Ten Thousand Light Years from Home* (1973), *Warm Worlds and Otherwise* (1975), *Starsongs of an Old Primate* (1978), *Out of the Everywhere and Other Extraordinary Visions* (1981), etc. She continued to write at a reduced pace in the 1980s, when she produced her second and best novel, *Brightness Falls from the Air* (1985), until her death (a widely publicized suicide) in 1987.

She was a complex and mysterious individual, who never appeared in public but was nevertheless a public figure in the sf field (in contrast to the pseudonymous Cordwainer Smith, who remains mysterious even after two decades of posthumous biographical investigation by fans and scholars).

The closest parallel to her work in impact, in attitude, in attention to craft and art, is Theodore Sturgeon's writing of the 1950s. Like Sturgeon, when she erred, it was in the direction of too much passionate sentiment. She was associated with raising the feminist consciousness of the sf field in the seventies, but was rarely considered as hard sf (too much sentiment, not enough science and technology). She was obsessed with the theme and the imagery of the alien, biologically and emotionally. Yet at least one of her stories, "The Girl Who Was Plugged In" (1973, one of her several award-winners), is acknowledged by William Gibson as one of the sources of cyberpunk. Ironically, her affect was closest to the hard sf attitude in those of her stories that most clearly revealed her fascination, perhaps her obsession, with death. She certainly felt that the universe was a formidable antagonist.

This story is in a sense a companion piece to Wilhelm's "The Planners," about being a working scientist in a laboratory, facing moral choices, but replacing the fantasizing of Wilhelm's piece with a drunken, dreamlike supernatural phantasmagoria at the center of this story, reminiscent of a Keatsian visit to Faerie. Tiptree's story is another milestone in the characterization of the scientist, invoking the gothic, Hawthorne strain. Here the rich subjectivity of the individual is juxtaposed to the mechanistic model of research in the physical sciences. Tiptree continually challenged the idea of the coldness of the universe, portraying that coldness as a negative aspect of human character rather than an affect existing somehow in external reality—until her last stories. *Crown of Stars* (1988) gathers most of her final tales, suicide-filled and full of the idea of honorable death. She was a deeply moral writer, even when embracing death.

This story is a counterpoint to "The Cold Equations," while portraying its affect ironically, and may be taken as representative of the movement by many of the newer writers in 1970s sf away from the hard sf affect into the fantastic.

He comes shyly hopeful into the lab. He is unable to suppress this childishness which has deviled him all his life, this tendency to wake up smiling, believing for an instant that today will be different.

But it isn't; is not.

He is walking into the converted cellars which are now called animal laboratories by this nationally respected university, this university which is still somehow unable to transmute its nationwide reputation into adequate funding for research. He squeezes past a pile of galvanized Skinner boxes and sees Smith at the sinks, engaged in cutting off the heads of infant rats. Piercing squeals; the headless body is flipped onto a wet furry pile on a hunk of newspaper. In the holding cage beside Smith the baby rats shiver in a heap, occasionally thrusting up a delicate muzzle and then burrowing convulsively under their friends, seeking to shut out Smith. They have previously been selectively shocked, starved, subjected to air blasts and plunged in ice water; Smith is about to search the corpses for appropriate neuroglandular effects of stress. He'll find them, undoubtedly. *Eeeeeee—Ssskrick!* Smith's knife grates, drinking life.

"Hello, Tilly."

"Hi." He hates his nickname, hates his whole stupid name: Tilman Lipsitz. He would go nameless through the world if he could. If it even could be something simple, Moo or Urg—anything but the absurd high-pitched syllables that have followed him through life: Tilly Lipsitz. He has suffered from it. Ah well. He makes his way around the pile of Purina Lab Chow bags, bracing for the fierce clamor of the rhesus. Their Primate Room is the ex-boiler room, really; these are tenements the university took over. The rhesus scream like sirens. Thud! Feces have hit the grill again; the stench is as strong as the sound. Lipsitz peers in reluctantly, mentally apologizing for being unable to like monkeys. Two of them are not screaming, huddled on the steel with puffy pink bald heads studded with electrode jacks. Why can't they house the creatures better, he wonders irritably for the nth time. In the trees they're clean. Well, cleaner, anyway, he amends, ducking around a stand of somebody's breadboard circuits awaiting solder.

On the far side is Jones, bending over a brightly lighted bench, two students watching mesmerized. He can see Jones's fingers tenderly roll the verniers that drive the probes down through the skull of the dog strapped underneath. Another of his terrifying stereotaxes. The aisle of cages is packed with animals with wasted fur and bloody heads. Jones swears they're all right, they eat; Lipsitz doubts this. He has tried to feed them tidbits as they lean or lie blear-eyed, jerking with wire terrors. The blood is because they rub their heads on the mesh; Jones, seeking a way to stop this, has put stiff plastic collars on several.

Lipsitz gets past them and has his eye rejoiced by the lovely hourglass-shaped ass of Sheila, the brilliant Israeli. Her back is turned. He observes with love the lily waist, the heart-lobed hips that radiate desire. But it's his desire, not hers; he knows that. Sheila, wicked Sheila; she desires only Jones, or perhaps Smith, or even Brown or White—the muscular large hairy ones bubbling with professionalism, with cheery shop talk. Lipsitz would gladly talk shop with her. But somehow his talk is different, uninteresting, is not in the mode. Yet he too believes in "the organism," believes in the miraculous wiring diagram of life; he is naively impressed by the complexity, the intricate interrelated delicacies of living matter. Why is he so reluctant to push metal into it, produce lesions with acids or shock? He has this unfashionable yearning to learn by appreciation, to tease out the secrets with only his eyes and mind. He has even the treasonable suspicion that other procedures might be more efficient, more instructive. But what other means are there? Probably none, he tells himself firmly. Grow up. Look at all they've discovered with the knife. The cryptic but potent centers of the amygdalas, for example. The subtle limbic homeostats—would we ever have known about these? It is a great knowledge. Never mind that its main use seems to be to push more metal into human heads, my way is obsolete.

"Hi, Sheila."

"Hello, Tilly."

She does not turn from the hamsters she is efficiently shaving. He takes himself away around the mop stand to the coal-cellar dungeon where he keeps his rats—sorry, his experimental subjects. His experimental subjects are nocturnal rodents, evolved in friendly dark warm burrows. Lipsitz has sensed their misery, suspended in bright metal and Plexiglas cubes in the glare. So he has salvaged and repaired for them a stack of big old rabbit cages and put them in this dark alcove nobody wanted, provoking mirth among his colleagues.

He has done worse than that, too. Grinning secretly, he approaches and observes what has been made of his latest offering. On the bottom row are the cages of parturient females, birthing what are expected to be his experimental and control groups. Yesterday those cages were bare wire mesh, when he distributed to them the classified section of the Sunday *Post.* Now he sees with amazement that they are solid cubic volumes of artfully crumpled and plastered paper strips. Fantastic, the labor! Nests; and all identical. Why has no one mentioned that rats as well as birds can build nests? How wrong, how painful it must have been, giving birth on the bare wire. The little mothers have worked all night, skillfully constructing complete environments beneficient to their needs.

A small white muzzle is pointing watchfully at him from a paper crevice; he fumbles in his pocket for a carrot chunk. He is, of course, unbalancing the treatment, his conscience remonstrates. But he has an answer; he has carrots for them all. Get down, conscience. Carefully he unlatches a cage. The white head stretches, bright-eyed, revealing sleek black shoulders. They are the hooded strain.

"Have a carrot," he says absurdly to the small being. And she does, so quickly that he can barely feel it, can barely feel also the tiny razor slash she has instantaneously, shyly given his thumb before she whisks back inside to her babies. He grins, rubbing the thumb, leaving carrots in the other cages. A mother's monitory bite, administered to an ogre thirty times her length. Vitamins, he thinks, enriched environments, that's the respectable word. Enriched? No, goddamn it. What it is is something approaching sane unstressed animals—experimental subjects, I mean. Even if they're so genetically selected for tameness they can't survive in the feral state, they're still rats. He sees he must wrap something on his thumb; he is ridiculously full of blood.

Wrapping, he tries not to notice that his hands are crisscrossed with old bites. He is a steady patron of the antitetanus clinic. But he is sure that they don't really mean ill, that he is somehow accepted by them. His colleagues think so too, somewhat scornfully. In fact Smith often calls him to help get some agonized creature out and bring it to his electrodes. Judas-Lipsitz does, trying to convey by the warmth of his holding hands that somebody is sorry, is uselessly sorry. Smith explains that his particular strain of rats is bad; a bad rat is one that bites psychologists; there is a constant effort to breed out this trait.

Lipsitz has tried to explain to them about animals with curved incisors, that one must press the hand into the biter's teeth. "It can't let go," he tells them. "You're biting yourself on the rat. It's the same with cats' claws. Push, they'll let go. Wouldn't you if somebody pushed his hand in your mouth?"

For a while he thought Sheila at least had understood him, but it turned out she thought he was making a dirty joke.

He is giving a rotted Safeway apple to an old male named Snedecor whom he has salvaged from Smith when he hears them call.

"Li-i-ipsitz!"

"Tilly? R. D. wants to see you."

"Yo."

R. D. is Professor R. D. Welch, his department head and supervisor of his grant. He washes up, makes his way out and around to the front entrance stairs. A myriad guilts are swirling emptily inside him; he has violated some norm, there is something wrong with his funding, above all he is too slow, too slow. No results yet, no columns of data. Frail justifying sentences revolve in his head as he steps into the clean bright upper reaches of the department. Because he is, he feels sure, learning. Doing something, something appropriate to what he thinks of as science. But what? In this glare he (like his rats) cannot recall. Ah, maybe it's only another hassle about parking space, he thinks as he goes bravely in past R. D.'s high-status male secretary. I can give mine up. I'll never be able to afford that transmission job anyway.

But it is not about parking space.

Doctor Welch has a fat file folder on his desk in Exhibit A position. He taps it expressionlessly, staring at Lipsitz.

"You are doing a study of, ah, genetic influences on, ah, tolerance of perceptual novelty."

"Well, yes . . ." He decides not to insist on precision. "You remember, Doctor Welch, I'm going to work in a relation to emotionalism, too."

Emotionalism, in rats, is (a) defecating and (b) biting psychologists. Professor Welch exhales troubledly through his lower teeth, which Lipsitz notes are slightly incurved. Mustn't pull back.

"It's so unspecific," he sighs. "It's not integrated with the overall department program."

"I know," Lipsitz says humbly. "But I do think it has relevance to problems of human learning. I mean, why some kids seem to shy away from new things." He jacks up his technical vocabulary. "The failure of the exploration motives."

"Motives don't *fail*, Lipsitz."

"I mean, conditions for low or high expression. Neophobia. Look, Doctor Welch. If one of the conditions turns out to be genetic we could spot kids who need help."

"Um'mmm."

"I could work in some real learning programs in the high tolerants, too," Lipsitz adds hopefully. "Contingent rewards, that sort of thing."

"Rat learning . . ." Welch lets his voice trail off. "If this sort of thing is to have any relevance it should involve primates. Your grant scarcely extends to that."

"Rats can learn quite a lot, sir. How about if I taught them word cues?"

"Doctor Lipsitz, rats do not acquire meaningful responses to words."

"Yes, sir." Lipsitz is forcibly preventing himself from bringing up the totally unqualified Scotswoman whose rat knew nine words.

"I do wish you'd go on with your brain studies," Welch says in his nice voice, giving Lipsitz a glowing scientific look. Am I biting myself on him? Lipsitz wonders. Involuntarily he feels himself empathize with the chairman's unknown problems.

As he gazes back, Welch says encouragingly, "You could use Brown's preparations; they're perfectly viable with the kind of care you give."

Lipsitz shudders awake; he knows Brown's preparations. A "preparation" is an animal spread-eagled on a rack for vivisection, dosed with reserpine so it cannot cry or struggle but merely endures for days or weeks of pain. Guiltily he wonders if Brown knows who killed the bitch he had left half dissected and staring over Easter. Pull yourself together, Lipsitz.

"I am so deeply interested in working with the intact animal, the whole organism," he says earnestly. That is his magic phrase; he has discovered that "the whole organism" has some fetish quality for them, from some far-off line of work; very fashionable in the abstract.

"Yes." Balked, Welch wreathes his lips, revealing the teeth again. "Well. Doctor Lipsitz, I'll be blunt. When you came on board we felt you had a great deal of promise. *I* felt that, I really did. And your teaching seemed to be going well, in the main. In the main. But your research; no. You seem to be frittering away your time and funds—and our space—on these irrelevancies. To put it succinctly, our laboratory is not a zoo."

"Oh, no, sir!" cried Lipsitz, horrified.

"What are you actually doing with those rats? I hear all kinds of idiotic rumors."

"Well, I'm working up the genetic strains, sir. The coefficient of homozygosity is still very low for meaningful results. I'm cutting it as fine as I can. What you're probably hearing about is that I am giving them a certain amount of enrichment. That's necessary so I can differentiate the lines." What I'm really doing is multiplying them, he thinks queasily; he hasn't had the heart to deprive any yet.

Welch sighs again; he *is* worried, Lipsitz thinks, and finding himself smiling sympathetically stops at once.

"How long before you wind this up? A week?"

"A week!" Lipsitz almost bleats, recovers his voice. "Sir, my test generation is just neonate. They have to be weaned, you know. I'm afraid it's more like a month."

"And what do you intend to do after this?"

"After this!" Lipsitz is suddenly fecklessly happy. So many, so wondrous are the things he wants to learn. "Well, to begin with I've seen a number of behaviors nobody seems to have done much with—I mean, watching my animals under more . . . more naturalistic conditions. They, ah, they emit very interesting responses. I'm struck by the species-specific aspect—I mean, as the Brelands said, we may be using quite unproductive situations. For example, there's an enormous difference between the way Rattus and Cricetus—that's hamsters—behave in the open field, and they're both *rodents*. Even as simple a thing as edge behavior—"

"*What* behavior?" Welch's tone should warn him, but he plunges on, unhappily aware that he has chosen an insignificant example. But he loves it.

"Edges. I mean the way the animal responds to edges and the shape of the environment. I mean it's basic to living and nobody seems to have explored it. They used to call it thigmotaxis. Here, I sketched a few." He pulls out a folded sheet,* pushes it at Welch. "Doesn't it raise interesting questions of arboreal descent?"

Welch barely glances at the drawings, pushes it away.

"Doctor Lipsitz. You don't appear to grasp the seriousness of this interview. All right. In words of one syllable, you will submit a major project outline that we can justify in terms of this department's program. If you can't come up with one such, regretfully we have no place for you here."

*See illustration.

EDGE BEHAVIORS OF RATTUS RATTUS
(Lipsitz' sketches)

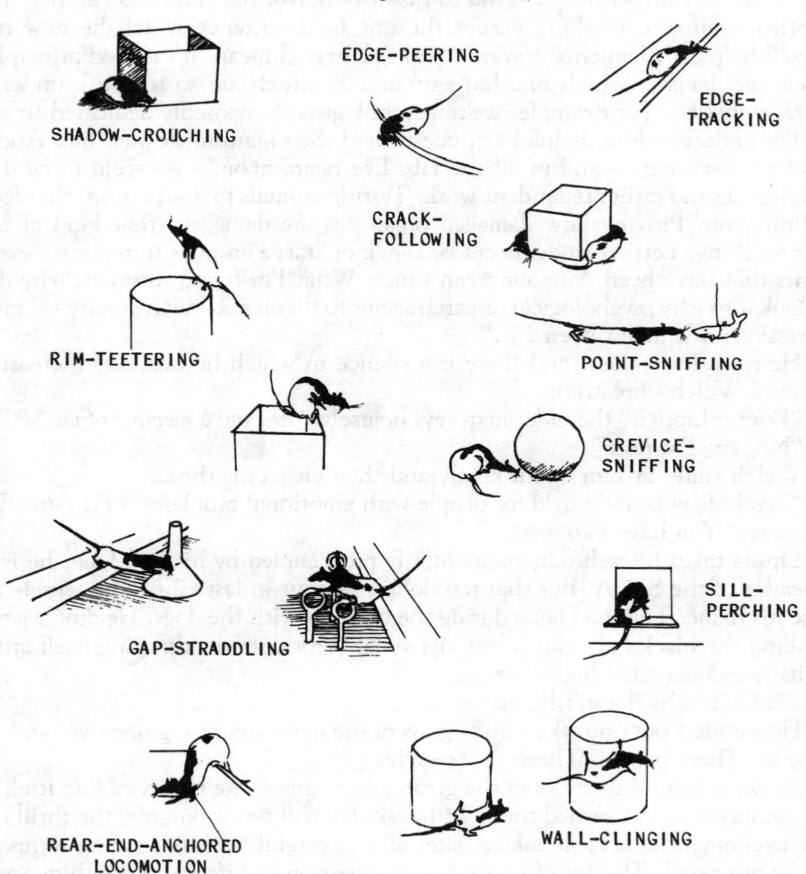

Appendix III, Figure 18. Examples of Thigmotaxic Responses
Drawings by Raccoona Sheldon

Lipsitz stares at him, appalled.

"A major project . . . I see. But . . ." And then something comes awake, something is rising in him. Yes. Yes, yes, of course there are bigger things he can tackle. Bigger questions—that means people. He's full of such questions. All it takes is courage.

"Yes, sir," he says slowly, "There are some major problems I have thought of investigating."

"Good," Welch says neutrally. "What are they?"

"Well, to start with . . ." And to his utter horror his mind has emptied itself, emptied itself of everything except the one fatal sentence which he now hears himself helplessly launched toward. "Take us here. I mean, it's a good principle to attack problems to which one has easy access, which are so to speak under our noses, right? So. For example, we're psychologists. Supposedly dedicated to some kind of understanding, helpful attitude toward the organism, toward life. And yet all of us down here—and in all the labs I've heard about—we seem to be doing such hostile and rather redundant work. Testing animals to destruction, that fellow at Princeton. Proving how damaged organisms are damaged, that kind of engineering thing. Letting students cut or shock or starve animals to replicate experiments that have been done umpteen times. What I'm trying to say is, why don't we look into why psychological research seems to involve so much cruelty—I mean, aggression? We might even . . ."

He runs down then, and there is a silence in which he becomes increasingly aware of Welch's breathing.

"Doctor Lipsitz," the older man says hoarsely, "*are you a member of the SPCA?*"

"No, sir, I'm not."

Welch stares at him unblinkingly and then clears his throat.

"Psychology is not a field for people with emotional problems." He pushed the file away. "You have two weeks."

Lipsitz takes himself out, momentarily preoccupied by his lie. True, he is not a *member* of the SPCA. But that ten dollars he sent in last Christmas, surely they have his name. That had been during the business with the dogs. He flinches now, recalling the black Labrador puppy, its vocal cords cut out, dragging itself around on its raw denervated haunches.

Oh God, why doesn't he just quit?

He wanders out onto the scruffy grass of the main campus, going over and over it again. These people. These . . . people.

And yet behind them loom the great golden mists, the reality of Life itself and the questions he has earned the right to ask. He will never outgrow the thrill of it. The excitement of *actually asking*, after all the careful work of framing terms that can be answered. The act of putting a real question to Life. And watching, reverently, excited out of his skin as Life condescends to tell him yes or no. My animals, my living works of art (of which you are one), do thus and so. Yes, in this small aspect you have understood Me.

The privilege of knowing how, painfully, to frame answerable questions, answers which will lead him to more insights and better questions as far as his mind can manage and his own life lasts. It is what he wants more than anything in the world to do, always has.

And these people stand in his way. Somehow, some way, he must pacify them. He must frame a project they will buy.

He plods back toward the laboratory cellars, nodding absently at students, revolving various quasi-respectable schemes. What he really wants to do is too foggy to explain yet; he wants to explore the capacity of animals to *anticipate*, to gain some knowledge of the wave-front of expectations that they must build up, even in the tiniest heads. He thinks it might even be useful, might illuminate the labors of the human infant learning its world. But that will have to wait. Welch wouldn't tolerate the idea that animals have mental maps. Only old crazy Tolman had been allowed to think that, and he's dead.

He will have to think of something with Welch's favorite drive variables. What are they? And lots of statistics, he thinks, realizing he is grinning at a really pretty girl walking with that cow Polinski. Yes, why not use students? Something complicated with students—that doesn't cost much. And maybe sex differentials, say, in perception—or is that too far out?

A wailing sound alerts him to the fact that he has arrived at the areaway. A truck is off-loading crates of cats, strays from the pound.

"Give a hand, Tilly! Hurry up!"

It's Sheila, holding the door for Jones and Smith. They want to get these out of sight quickly, he knows, before some student sees them. Those innocent in the rites of pain. He hauls a crate from the tailboard.

"There's a female in here giving birth," he tells Sheila. "Look." The female is at the bottom of a mess of twenty emaciated struggling brutes. One of them has a red collar.

"Hurry up, for Christ's sake." Sheila waves him on.

"But . . ."

When the crates have disappeared inside he does not follow the others in but leans on the railing, lighting a cigarette. The kittens have been eaten, there's nothing he can do. Funny, he always thought that females would be sympathetic to other females. Shows how much he knows about Life. Or is it that only certain types of people empathize? Or does it have to be trained in, or was it trained out of her? Mysteries, mysteries. Maybe she is really compassionate somewhere inside, toward something. He hopes so, resolutely putting away a fantasy of injecting Sheila with reserpine and applying experimental stimuli.

He becomes aware that the door has been locked from the inside; they have all left through the front. It's getting late. He moves away too, remembering that this is the long holiday weekend. Armistice Day. Would it were—he scoffs at himself for the bathos. But he frowns, too; long weekends usually mean nobody goes near the lab. Nothing gets fed or watered. Well, three days—not as bad as Christmas week.

Last Christmas week he had roused up from much-needed sleep beside a sky-high mound of term papers and hitchhiked into town to check the labs. It had been so bad, so needless. The poor brutes dying in their thirst and hunger, eating metal, each other. Great way to celebrate Christmas.

But he will have to stop that kind of thing, he knows. Stop it. Preferably starting now. He throws down the cigarette stub, quickens his stride to purposefulness. He will collect his briefcase of exam papers from the library where he keeps it to avoid the lab smell and get on home and get at it. The bus is bound to be jammed.

Home is an efficiency in a suburban high-rise. He roots in his moldy fridge, carries a sandwich and ale to the dinette that is his desk. He has eighty-one exams to grade; junior department members get the monster classes. It's a standard multiple-choice thing, and he has a help—a theatrically guarded manila template he can lay over the sheets with slots giving the correct response. By just running down them he sums an arithmetical grade. Good. Munching, he lays out the first mimeoed wad.

But as he starts to lay it on the top page he sees—oh, no!—somebody has scrawled instead of answering Number 6. It's that fat girl, that bright bum Polinsky.

And she hasn't marked answers by 7 or 8 either. Damn her fat female glands; he squints at the infantile uncials: "I won't mark this because its smucky! Read it, Dr. Lipshitz." She even has his name wrong.

Cursing himself, he scrutinizes the question. "Fixed versus variable reinforcement is called a—" Oh yes, he remembers that one. Bad grammar on top of bad psychology. Why can't they dump these damn obsolete things? Because the office wants grade intercomparability for their records, that's why. Is Polinsky criticizing the language or the thought? Who knows. He leafs through the others, sees more scribbles. Oh, shit, they know I read them. They all know I don't mark them like I should. Sucker.

Grimly masticating the dry sandwich, he starts to read. At this rate he is working, he has figured out, for seventy-five cents an hour.

By midnight he isn't half through, but he knows he ought to break off and start serious thought about Welch's ultimatum. Next week all his classes start Statistical Methods; he won't have time to blow his nose, let alone think creatively.

He gets up for another ale, thinking, Statistical Methods, brrr. He respects them, he guesses. But he is incurably sloppy-minded, congenitally averse to ignoring any data that don't fit the curve. Factor analysis, multivariate techniques—all beautiful; why is he troubled by this primitive visceral suspicion that somehow it ends up proving what the experimenter wanted to show? No, not that, really. Something about qualities as opposed to quantities, maybe? That some statistically insignificant results *are* significant, and some significant ones . . . aren't? Or just basically that we don't know enough yet to use such ultraprecise weapons. That we should watch more, maybe. Watch and learn more and figure less. All right, call me St. Lipsitz.

Heating up a frozen egg roll, he jeers at himself for superstition. Face facts, Lipsitz. Deep down you don't really believe dice throws are independent. Psychology is not a field for people with personality problems.

Ignoring the TV yattering through the wall from next door, he sits down by the window to think. Do it, brain. Come up with the big one. Take some good testable hypothesis from somebody in the department, preferably something that involves electronic counting of food pellets, bar presses, latencies, defecations. And crank it all into printed score sheets with a good Fortran program. But what the hell are they all working on? Reinforcement schedules, cerebral deficits, split brain, God knows only that it seems to produce a lot of dead animals. "The subjects were sacrificed." They insist on saying that. He has been given a lecture when he called it "killing." Sacrificed, like to a god. Lord of the Flies, maybe.

He stares out at the midnight streets, thinking of his small black-and-white friends, his cozy community in the alcove. Nursing their offspring, sniffing the monkeys, munching apples, dreaming ratly dreams. He likes rats, which surprises him. Even the feral form, Rattus rattus itself; he would like to work with wild ones. Rats are vicious, they say. But people know only starving rats. Anything starving is "vicious." Beloved beagle eats owner on fourth day.

And his rats are, he blushingly muses, affectionate. They nestle in his hands, teeteringly ride his shoulder, display humor. If only they had fluffy tails, he thinks. The tail is the problem. People think squirrels are cute. They're only overdressed rats. Maybe I could do something with the perceptual elements of "cuteness," carry on old Tinbergen's work?

Stop it.

He pulls himself up; this isn't getting anywhere. A terrible panorama unrolls before his inner eye. On the one hand the clean bright professional work he should be doing, he with those thousands of government dollars invested in his doctorate, his grant—and on the other, what he is really doing. His cluttered alcove full of irregular rodents, his tiny, doomed effort to . . . what? To live amicably and observantly with another species? To understand trivial behaviors? Crazy. Spending all his own money, saving everybody's cripples—God, half his cages aren't even experimentally justifiable!

His folly. Suddenly it sickens him. He stands up, thinking, It's a stage you go through. I'm a delayed adolescent. Wake up, grow up. They're only animals. Get with it.

Resolve starts to form in him. Opening another ale can, he lets it grow. This whole thing is no good, he knows that. So what if he does prove that animals learn better if they're treated differently—what earthly use is that? Don't we all know it anyway? Insane. Time I braced up. All right. Ale in hand, he lets the resolve bloom.

He will go down there and clean out the whole mess, right now.

Kill all his rats, wipe the whole thing off. Clear the decks. That done, he'll be able to think; he won't be locked into the past.

The department will be delighted, Doctor Welch will be delighted. Nobody believed his thing was anything but a waste of time. All right, Lipsitz. Do it. Now, tonight.

Yes.

But first he will have something analgesic, strengthening. Not ale, not a toke. That bottle of—what is it, absinthe?—that crazy girl gave him last year. Yes, here it is back of the roach-killer he never used either. God knows what it's supposed to do, it's wormwood, something weird.

"Fix me," he tells it, sucking down a long licorice-flavored draft. And goes out, bottle in pocket.

It has, he thinks, helped. He is striding across the campus now; all the long bus ride his resolve hasn't wavered. A quiet rain is falling. It must be two in the morning, but he's used to the spooky empty squares. He has often sneaked down here at odd hours to water and feed the brutes. The rain is moving strange sheens of shadow on the old tenement block, hissing echoes of the lives that swirled here once. At the cellar entrance he stops for another drink, finds the bottle clabbered with carrot chunks. Wormwood and Vitamin C, very good.

He dodges down and unlocks, bracing for the stench. The waste cans are full—cats that didn't make it, no doubt. Inside is a warm rustling reek.

When he finds the light, a monkey lets out one eerie whoop and all sounds stop. Sunrise at midnight; most of these experimental subjects are nocturnal.

He goes in past the crowded racks, his eye automatically checking levels in the hundreds of water bottles. Okay, okay, all okay . . . What's this? He stops by Sheila's hamster tier. A bottle is full to the top. But there's a corpse by the wire, and the live ones look bedraggled. Why? He jerks up the bottle. Nothing comes out of the tube. It's blocked. Nobody has checked it for who knows how long. Perishing of thirst in there, with the bottle full.

He unblocks it, fishes out the dead, watches the little beasts crowd around. How does Sheila report this? Part of an experimental group was, uh, curtailed. On impulse he inserts some carrots too, inserts more absinthe into himself. He knows he is putting off what he has come here to do.

All right, get at it.

He stomps past a cage of baby rabbits with their eyes epoxyed shut, somebody's undergraduate demonstration of perceptual learning, and turns on the light over the sinks. All dirty with hanks of skin and dog offal. Why the hell can't they clean up after themselves? We are scientists. Too lofty. He whooshes with the power hose, which leaks. Nobody cares enough even to bring a washer. He will bring one. No, he won't! He's going to be doing something different from here on in.

But first of all he has to get rid of all this. Sacrifice his subjects. His ex-subjects. Where's my ether?

He finds it back of the mops, has another snort of the cloudy liquor to fortify himself while he sets up his killing jars. He has evolved what he thinks is the decentest way: an ether pad under a grill to keep their feet from being burned by the stuff.

The eight jars are in a row on the sink. He lifts down a cage of elderly females, the grandmothers of his present group. They cluster at the front, trustfully expectant. Oh God; he postpones murder long enough to give them some carrot, deals out more to every cage in the rack so they'll have time to eat. Tumult of rustling, hopping, munching.

All right. He goes back to the sink and pours in the ether, keeping the lids tight. Then he reaches in the holding cage and scoops up a soft female in each hand. Quick: He pops them both in one jar, rescrews the lid. He has this fatuous belief that the companionship helps a little. They convulse frantically, are going limp before he has the next pair in theirs. Next. Next. Next . . . It takes five minutes to be sure of death.

This will be, he realizes, a long night.

He lifts down another cage, lifts up his bottle, leaning with his back to the jars to look at his rack, his little city of rats. My troops. My pathetic troops. An absinthe trip flashes through his head of himself leading his beasts against his colleagues, against the laughing pain-givers. Jones having his brain reamed by a Dachshund pup. A kitten in a surgical smock shaving Sheila, wow. Stop it!

His eye has been wandering over the bottom cages. The mothers have taken the goodies in to their young; interesting to see what goes on in there, maybe if he used infrared—stop that, too. A lab is not a zoo. Down in one dark back cage he can see the carrot is still there. Where's Snedecor, the old brain-damaged male? Why hasn't he come for it? Is the light bothering him?

Lipsitz turns off the top lights, goes around to the side to check. Stooping, he peers into the gloom. Something funny down there—good grief, the damn cage is busted, it's rotted through the bottom. Where's old Sneddles?

The ancient cage rack has wheels. Lipsitz drags one end forward, revealing Stygian darkness behind. In prehistoric times there was a coal chute there. And there's something back here now, on the heap of bags by the old intake.

Lipsitz frowns, squints; the lab lights behind him seem to be growing dim and gaseous. The thing—the thing has black and white patches. Is it moving?

He retreats to the drainboard, finds his hand on the bottle. Yes. Another short one. What's wrong with the lights? The fluorescents have developed filmy ectoplasm, must be chow dust. This place is a powder keg. The monkeys are still as death, too. That's unusual. In fact everything is dead quiet except for an odd kind of faint clicking, which he realizes is coming from the dark behind the rack. An animal. Some animal has got out and been living back there, that's all it is.

All right, Lipsitz: Go see.

But he delays, aware that the absinthe has replaced his limbs with vaguer, dreamlike extensions. The old females on the drainboard watch him alertly; the dead ones in the jars watch nothing. All his little city of rats has stopped moving, is watching him. Their priest of pain. This is a temple of pain, he thinks. A small shabby dirty one. Maybe its dirt and squalor are better so, more honest. A charnel house shouldn't look pretty, like a clean kitchen. All over the country, the world, the spotless knives are slicing, the trained minds devising casual torments in labs so bright and fair you could eat off their floors. Auschwitz, Belsen were neat. With flowers. Only the reek of pain going up to the sky, the empty sky. But people don't think animals' pain matters. They didn't think my people's pain mattered either, in the death camps a generation back. It's all the same, endless agonies going up unheard from helpless things. And all for what?

Maybe somewhere there is a reservoir of pain, he muses. Waiting to be filled. When it is full, will something rise from it? Something created and summoned by torment? Inhuman, an alien superthing . . . He knows he is indulging drunkenness. The clicking has grown louder.

Go and look at the animal, Lipsitz.

He goes, advances on the dark alcove, peering down, hearing the click-click-click. Suddenly he recognizes it: the tooth-click a rat makes in certain states of mind. Not threatening at all, it must be old Sneddles in there. Heartened, he pulls a dim light bulb forward on its string—and sees the thing plain, while the lab goes unreal around him.

What's lying back there among the Purina bags is an incredible whorl—a tangle of rat legs, rat heads, rat bodies, rat tails intertwined in a great wheellike formation, *joined* somehow abnormally rat to rat—a huge rat pie, heaving, pulsing, eyes reflecting stress and pain. Quite horrible, really; the shock of it is making him fight for breath. And it is not all laboratory animals; he can see the agouti coats of feral rats mixed in among it. Have wild rats come in here to help form this gruesome thing?

And at that moment, hanging to the light bulb, he knows what he is seeing. He has read in the old lore, the ancient grotesque legends of rat and man.

He is looking at a Rat King.

Medieval records were full of them, he recalls dimly. Was it Württemberg? "*They are monstrously Joynt, yet Living . . . It can by no way be Separated, and screamed much in the Fyre.*" Apparitions that occurred at times of great attack on the rats. Some believed that the rat armies had each their king of this sort, who directed them. And they were sometimes connected to or confused with King Rats of still another kind: gigantic animals with eyes of fire and gold chains on their necks.

Lipsitz stares, swaying on the light cord. The tangled mass of the Rat King remains there clicking faintly, pulsing, ambiguously agonized among the sacks. His other hand seems to be holding the bottle; good. He takes a deep pull, his eyes rolling to fix the ghastliness, wondering what on earth he will do. "I can't," he mumbles aloud, meaning the whole thing, the whole bloody thing. "*I can't . . .*"

He can do his own little business, kill his animals, wind up his foolishness, get out. But he cannot—can not—be expected to cope with this, to abolish this revenant from time, this perhaps supernatural horror. For which he feels obscurely, hideously to blame. It's my fault, I . . .

He realizes he is weeping thinly, his eyes are running. Whether it's for the animals or himself he doesn't know; he knows only that he can't stand it, can't take any of it any more. And now *this*.

"No!" Meaning, really, the whole human world. Dizzily he blinks around at the jumbled darkness, trying to regain his wits, feeling himself a random mote of protesting life in an insignificant fool-killer. Slowly his eyes come back to the monstrous, pitiable rat pie. It seems to be weakening; the click has lost direction. His gaze drifts upward, into the dark shadows.

—And he is quite unsurprised, really, to meet eyes looking back. Two large round animal eyes deep in the darkness, at about the level of his waist, the tapetums reflecting pale vermilion fire.

He stares; the eyes shift right, left, calmly in silence, and then the head advances. He sees the long wise muzzle, the vibrissae, the tuned shells of the ears. Is there a gold collar? He can't tell; but he can make out the creature's forelimbs now, lightly palping the bodies or body of the Rat King. And the tangled thing is fading, shrinking away. It was perhaps its conjoined forces which strove and suffered to give birth to this other—the King himself.

"Hello," Lipsitz whispers idiotically, feeling no horror any more but emotion of a quite other kind. The big warm presence before him surveys him. Will he be found innocent? He licks his lips; they have come at last, he thinks. They have risen; they are going to wipe all this out. Me, too? But he does not care; a joy he can't possibly control rises in him as he sees gold glinting on the broad chest fur. He licks his dry lips again, swallows.

"Welcome. Your Majesty."

The Beast-King makes no response; the eyes leave him and go gravely toward the aisles beyond. Involuntarily Lipsitz backs aside. The King's vibrissae are fanning steadily, bringing the olfactory news, the quiet tooth-click starts. When the apparition comes forward a pace Lipsitz is deeply touched to see the typical half hop, the ratly carriage. The King's coat is lustrous gray-brown, feral pelage. Of course. It is a natural male, too; he smiles timidly, seeing that the giant body has the familiar long hump, the heavy rear-axle loading. Is old Snedecor translated into some particle of this wonder? The cellar is unbreathing, hushed except for the meditative click-click from the King.

"You, you are going to . . ." Lipsitz tries but is struck dumb by the sense of something happening all around him. Invisible, inaudible—but tangible as day. An emergence, yes! In the rooms beyond they are emerging, coming out from the score upon score of cages, boxes, pens, racks, shackles and wires—all of them emerging, coming to the King. All of them, blinded rabbits, mutilated hamsters, damaged cats and rats and brain-holed rhesus quietly knuckling along, even the paralyzed dogs moving somehow, coming toward their King.

And at this moment Lipsitz realizes the King is turning too, the big brown body is wheeling, quite normally away from him, going away toward the deeper darkness in the end of the coal bay. They are leaving him!

"Wait!" He stumbles forward over the dead rat pie; he cannot bear to lose this. "Please . . ."

Daring all, he reaches out and touches the flank of the magical beast, expecting he knows not what. The flank is warm, is solid! The King glances briefly back at him, still moving away. Boldly Lipsitz strides closer, comes alongside, his hand now resting firmly on the withers as they go.

But they are headed straight at what he knows is only wall, though he can see nothing. The cellar ends there. No matter—he will not let go of the magic, no, and he steps out beside the moving King, thinking, I am an animal, too!—And finds at the last instant that his averted, flinching head is moving through dark nothing, through a blacker emptiness where the King is leading—they are going, going out.

Perhaps an old sewer, he thinks, lurching along beside the big benign presence, remembering tales of forgotten tunnels under this old city, into which the new subway has bored. Yes, that's what it must be. He is finding he can see again in a pale ghostly way, can now walk upright. His left hand is tight on the shoulders of the calmly pacing beast, feeling the living muscles play beneath the fur, bringing him joy and healing. Where are the others?

He dares a quick look back and sees them. They are coming. The dim way behind is filled with quiet beasts, moving together rank on rank as far as he can sense, animals large and small. He can hear their peaceful rustling now. And they are not only the beasts of his miserable lab, he realizes, but a torrent of others—he has glimpsed goats, turtles, a cow, raccoon, skunks, an opossum and what appeared as a small monkey riding on a limping spaniel. Even birds are there, hopping and fluttering above!

My God, it is everything, he thinks. It is Hamlin in reverse; all the abused ones, the gentle ones, are leaving the world. He risks another glance back and thinks he can see a human child too and maybe an old person among the throng, all measuredly, silently moving together in the dimness. An endless host going, going out at last, going away. And he is feeling their emanation, the gentleness of it, the unspeaking warmth. He is happier than he has been ever in his life.

"You're taking us away," he says to the King-Beast beside him. "The ones who can't cut it. We're all leaving for good, isn't that it?"

There is no verbal answer; only a big-stemmed ear swivels to him briefly as the King goes gravely on. Lipsitz needs no speech, no explanation. He simply walks alongside letting the joy rise in him. Why had it always been forbidden to be gentle? he wonders. Did they really see it as a threat, to have hated us so? But that is all over now, all over and gone, he is sure, although he has no slightest idea where this may be leading, this procession into chthonian infinity. For this moment it is enough to feel the silent communion, the reassurance rising through him from his hand on the flank of the great spirit-beast. The flank is totally solid; he can feel all the workings of life; it is the body of a real animal. But it is also friendship beyond imagining; he has never known anything as wonderful as this communion, not sex or sunsets or even the magic hour on his first bike. It is as if everything is all right now, will be all right forever—griefs he did not even know he carried are falling from him, leaving him light as smoke.

Crippled, he had been; crippled from the years of bearing it, not just the lab, the whole thing. Everything. He can hardly believe the relief. A vagrant thought brushes him: Who will remain? If there is anything to care for, to be comforted, who will care? He floats it away, concentrating on the comfort that emanates from the strange life at his side, the myth-beast ambling in the most ordinary way through this dark conduit, which is now winding down, or perhaps up and down, he cannot tell.

The paving under his feet looks quite commonplace, damp and cracked. Beside him the great rat's muscles bunch and stretch as each hind leg comes under; he glances back and smiles to see the King's long ring-scaled tail curve right, curve left, carried in the relaxed-alert mode. No need for fluffy fur now. He is, he realizes, going into mysteries. Inhuman mysteries, perhaps. He doesn't care. He is among his kind. Where they are going he will go. Even to inhumanity, even alone.

But he is not, he realizes as his eyes adapt more and more, alone after all! A human figure is behind him on the far side of the King, quietly threading its way forward, overtaking him. A girl—is it a girl? Yes. He can scarcely make her out, but as she comes closer still he sees with growing alarm that it is a familiar body—it could be, oh God, it is! Sheila.

Not *Sheila*, here! No, no.

But light-footed, she has reached him, is walking even with him, stretching out her hand, too, to touch the moving King.

And then to his immense, unspeakable relief he sees that she is of course not Sheila—how could it be? Not Sheila at all, only a girl of the same height, with the same dove-breasted close-coupled curves that speak to his desire, the same heavy dark mane. Her head turns toward him across the broad back of the King, and he sees that although her features are like Sheila's, the face is wholly different, open, informed with innocence. An Eve in this second morning of the world. Sheila's younger sister, perhaps, he wonders dazedly, seeing that she is looking at him now, that her lips form a gentle smile.

"Hello," he cannot help whispering, fearful to break the spell, to inject harsh human sound into his progress. But the spell does not break; indeed, the girl's face comes clearer. She puts up a hand to push her hair back, the other firmly on the flank of the King.

"Hello." Her voice is very soft but in no way fragile. She is looking at him with the eyes of Sheila, but eyes so differently warmed and luminous that he wants only to gaze delighted as they pass to whatever destination; he is so overwhelmed to meet a vulnerable human soul in those lambent brown eyes. A soul? he thinks, feeling his unbodied feet step casually, firmly on the way to eternity, perhaps. What an unfashionable word. He is not religious, he does not believe there are any gods or souls, except as a shorthand term denoting—what?—compassion or responsibility, all that. And so much argument about it all, too; his mind is momentarily invaded by a spectral horde of old debating scholars, to whom he had paid less than no attention in his classroom days. But he is oddly prepared now to hear the girl recite conversationally, "There is no error more powerful in leading feeble minds astray from the straight path of virtue than the supposition that the soul of brutes is of the same nature as our own."

"Descartes," he guesses.

She nods, smiling across the big brown shape between them. The King's great leaflike ears have flickered to their interchange, returned to forward hold.

"He started it all, didn't he?" Lipsitz says, or perhaps only thinks. "That they're robots, you can do anything to them. Their pain doesn't count. But we're animals, too," he added somberly, unwilling to let even a long-dead philosopher separate him from the flow of this joyous River. Or was it that? A faint disquiet flicks him, is abolished.

She nods again; the sweet earnest woman-face of her almost kills him with love. But as he stares the disquiet flutters again; is there beneath her smile a transparency, a failure of substance—even a sadness, as though she was moving to some inexorable loss? No; it is all right. It is.

"Where are we going, do you know?" he asks, against some better judgment. The King-Beast flicks an ear; but Lipsitz must know, now.

She smiles, unmistakably mischievous, considering him.

"To where all the lost things go," she says. "It's very beautiful. Only . . ." She falls silent.

"Only what?" He is uneasy again, seeing she has turned away, is walking with her small chin resolute. Dread grows in him, cannot be dislodged. The moments of simple joy are past now; he fears that he still has some burden. It is perhaps a choice? Whatever it is, it's looming around him or in him as they go—an impending significance he wishes desperately to avoid. It is not a thinning out nor an awakening; he clutches hard at the strong shoulders of the King, the magical leader, feels his reassuring warmth. All things are in the lotus . . . But loss impends.

"Only what?" he asks again, knowing he must and must not. Yes; he is still there, is moving with them to the final refuge. The bond holds. "The place where lost things go is very beautiful, only what?"

"Do you really want to know?" she asks him with the light of the world in her face.

It *is* a choice, he realizes, trembling now. It is not for free, it's not that simple. But can't I just stop this, just go on? Yes, he can—he knows it. Maybe. But he hears his human voice persist.

"Only *what?*"

"Only it isn't real," she says. And his heart breaks.

And suddenly it is all breaking, too—a fearful thin wave of emptiness slides through him, sends him stumbling, his handhold lost. "No! Wait!" He reaches desperately; he can feel them still near him, feel their passage all around. "Wait . . ." He understands now, understands with searing grief that it really is the souls of things, and perhaps himself that are passing, going away forever. They have stood it as long as they can and now they are leaving. The pain has culminated in this, that they leave us—leave me, leave me behind in a clockwork Cartesian world in which nothing will mean anything forever.

"Oh, wait," he cries in dark nowhere, unable to bear the loss, the still-living comfort, passing away. *Only it isn't real*, what does that mean? Is it the choice, that the reality is that I must stay behind and try, and try?

He doesn't know, but can only cry, "No, please take me! Let me come, too!" staggering after them through unreality, feeling them still there, still possible, ahead, around. It is wrong; he is terrified somewhere that he is failing, doing wrong. But his human heart can only yearn for the sweetness, for the great benevolent King-Beast so surely leading, to feel again their joy. "Please, I want to go with you—"

—And yes! For a last instant he has it; he touches again the warmth and life, sees the beautiful lost face that was and wasn't Sheila—they are there! And he tries with all his force crazily to send himself after them, to burst from his skin, his life if need be—only to share again that gentleness. "*Take* me!"

But it is no good—he can't; they have vanished and he has fallen kneeling on dank concrete, nursing his head in empty shaking hands. It was in vain, and it was wrong. Or was it? his fading thought wonders as he feels himself black out. Did something of myself go too, fly to its selfish joy? He does not know.

. . . And will never know, as he returns to sodden consciousness, makes out that he is sprawled like a fool in the dirt behind his rat cages with the acid taste of wormwood sickly in his mouth and an odd dryness and lightness in his heart.

What the hell had he been playing at? That absinthe is a bummer, he thinks, picking himself up and slapping his clothes disgustedly. This filthy place, what a fool he'd been to think he could work here. And these filthy rats. There's something revolting back here on the floor, too. Leave it for posterity; he drags the rack back in place.

All right, get this over. Humming to himself, he turns the power hose on the messy floor, gives the stupid rats in their cages a blast too for good measure. There are his jars—but whatever had possessed him, trying to kill them individually like that? Hours it would take. He knows a simpler way if he can find a spare garbage can.

Good, here it is. He brings it over and starts pulling out cage after cage, dumping them all in together. Nests, babies, carrots, crap and all. Shrieks, struggling. Tough tit, friends. The ether can is almost full; he pours the whole thing over the crying mess and jams on the lid, humming louder. The can walls reverberate with teeth. Not quite enough gas, no matter.

He sits down on it and notices that a baby rat has run away hiding behind his shoe. Mechanical mouse, a stupid automaton. He stamps on its back and kicks it neatly under Sheila's hamster rack, wondering why Descartes has popped into his thoughts. There is no error more powerful—Shit with old D., let's think about Sheila. There is no error more powerful than the belief that some cunt can't be had. Somehow he feels sure that he will find that particular pussy-patch wide open to him any day now. As soon as his project gets under way.

Because he has an idea. (That absinthe wasn't all bad.) Oh yes. An idea that'll pin old Welch's ears back. In fact it may be too much for old Welch, too, quotes, commercial. Well, fuck old Welch, this is one project somebody will buy, that's for sure. Does the Mafia have labs? Ho ho, far out.

And fuck students too, he thinks genially, wrestling the can to the entrance, ignoring sounds from within. No more Polinskis, no more shit, teaching is for suckers. My new project will take care of that. Will there be a problem getting subjects? No—look at all the old walking carcasses they sell for dogfood. And there's a slaughterhouse right by the freeway, no problem at all. But he *will* need a larger lab.

He locks up, and briskly humming the rock version of "Anitra's Dance," he goes out into the warm rainy dawnlight, reviewing in his head the new findings on the midbrain determinants of motor intensity.

It should be no trick at all to seat some electrodes that will make an animal increase the intensity of whatever it's doing. Like say, *running*. Speed it right up to max, run like it never ran before regardless of broken legs or what. What a natural! Surprising someone else hasn't started already.

And just as a cute hypothesis, he's pretty sure he could seal the implants damn near invisibly; he has a smooth hand with flesh. Purely hypothetical, of course. But suppose you used synthetics with, say, acid-release. That would be hard to pick up on X rays. H'mmm.

Of course, he doesn't know much about horses, but he learns fast. Grinning, he breaks into a jog to catch the lucky bus that has appeared down the deserted street. He has just recalled a friend who has a farm not fifty miles away. Wouldn't it be neat to run the pilot project using surplus Shetland ponies?

IN THE YEAR 2889

Jules Verne

Jules Verne is one of the four nineteenth-century writers (with Mary Shelley, Edgar Allan Poe, and H. G. Wells) without whose work science fiction would not exist today. Before he ever wrote one of his imaginary voyages, he wrote a long article on Poe for a leading French magazine, *Musée des Familles*, noting particularly Poe's use of science for verisimilitude. Verne's voyages to the Moon, to the center of the earth, under the sea, around the world in the fabulously rapid time of eighty days, all use advanced technology based on exact and real contemporary science. He, and his audience, had a taste and a patience for exposition and explanation to an extent now out of fashion in literature, although expository detail has remained an integral, essential element of hard science fiction. In addition, he was an essential founder of the optimistic attitude in the literature that science will take you places, do things, solve problems. Verne became rich and famous for his novels in the extraordinary voyage genre, one of the vigorous precursors of sf.

It is the fiction of Jules Verne that most influenced Hugo Gernsback, always a devotee of extensive expository detail, in the years before he decided to declare the birth of a new genre in 1926. Clearly, one of Gernsback's prime motives was didactic—one need only glance at Gernsback's own fiction, for instance his novel, *Ralph 124C 41+ (1925)*, a forest of exposition, with only a nod to plot and characterization. It is the moral sentiment and didactic enthusiasm of Verne, whom Gernsback reprinted often in the early issues of *Amazing Stories*, that encouraged early genre sf writers in the tendency to create a juvenile literature, thrilling wonder stories for boys and young men.

Worth noting is the fact that Verne's later works, in the 1880s and later, are darker in mood and progressively less optimistic about science and technology. But these novels, from *The Begum's Fortune* (1880) to *Master of the World* (1904), were eclipsed by the continuing popularity of his earlier works. Verne always stressed his scientific accuracy, a hallmark of the hard sf attitude, though modern devotees of hard sf never tire of pointing out that he was often ignorant of one or another scientific principle (for instance, there is only a moment of zero gee in *From Earth to the Moon* in the space capsule, although there is free fall outside it). This same attitude leads to critiques of Herbert's failure in forgetting to provide a source for the air on the planet Dune. This stance is descended from Verne's own criticism of H. G. Wells as second-rate because he "invents" science, whereas Verne represented himself as adhering to the known.

Verne's loosely structured novels form the overwhelming majority of his influential work. Verne's short fiction was occasional and minor, but we include this slight but charming piece to mark his place. Jules Verne, *sine qua non*.

Little though they seem to think of it, the people of this twenty-ninth century live continually in fairyland. Surfeited as they are with marvels, they are indifferent in presence of each new marvel. To them all seems natural. Could they but duly appreciate the refinements of civilization in our day; could they but compare the present with the past, and so better comprehend the advance we have made! How much fairer they would find our modern towns, with populations amounting sometimes to 10,000,000 souls; their streets 300 feet wide, their houses 100 feet in height; with a temperature the same in all seasons; with their lines of aërial locomotion crossing the sky in every direction! If they would but picture to themselves the state of things that once existed, when through muddy streets rumbling boxes on wheels, drawn by horses—yes, by horses!—were the only means of conveyance. Think of the railroads of the olden time, and you will be able to appreciate the pneumatic tubes through which to-day one travels at the rate of 100 miles an hour. Would not our contemporaries prize the telephone and the telephote more highly if they had not forgotten the telegraph?

Singularly enough, all these transformations rest upon principles which were perfectly familiar to our remote ancestors, but which they disregarded. Heat, for instance, is as ancient as man himself; electricity was known 3000 years ago, and steam 1100 years ago. Nay, so early as ten centuries ago it was known that the differences between the several chemical and physical forces depend on the mode of vibration of the etheric particles, which is for each specifically different. When at last the kinship of all these forces was discovered, it is simply astounding that 500 years should still have to elapse before men could analyze and describe the several modes of vibration that constitute these differences. Above all, it is singular that the mode of reproducing these forces directly from one another, and of reproducing one without the others, should have remained undiscovered till less than a hundred years ago. Nevertheless, such was the course of events, for it was not till the year 2792 that the famous Oswald Nier made this great discovery.

Truly was he a great benefactor of the human race. His admirable discovery led to many another. Hence is sprung a pleiad of inventors, its brightest star being our great Joseph Jackson. To Jackson we are indebted for those wonderful instruments—the new accumulators. Some of these absorb and condense the living force contained in the sun's rays; others, the electricity stored in our globe; others again, the energy coming from whatever source, as a waterfall, a stream, the winds, etc. He, too, it was that invented the transformer, a more wonderful contrivance still, which takes the living force from the accumulator, and, on the simple pressure of a button, gives it back to space in whatever form may be desired, whether as heat, light, electricity, or mechanical force, after having first obtained from it the work required. From the day when these two instruments were contrived is to be dated the era of true progress. They have put into the hands of man a power that is almost infinite. As for their applications, they are numberless. Mitigating the rigors of winter, by giving back to the atmosphere the surplus heat stored up during the summer, they had revolutionized agriculture. By supplying motive power for aërial navigation, they have given to commerce a mighty impetus. To them we are indebted for the continuous production of electricity without batteries or dynamos, of light without combustion or incandescence, and for an unfailing supply of mechanical energy for all the needs of industry.

Yes, all these wonders have been wrought by the accumulator and the transformer. And can we not to them also trace, indirectly, this latest wonder of all, the great "Earth Chronicle" building in 253d Avenue, which was dedicated the other day? If George Washington Smith, the founder of the Manhattan "Chronicle," should come back to life today, what would he think were he to be told that this palace of marble and gold belongs to his remote descendant, Fritz Napoleon Smith, who, after thirty generations have come and gone, is owner of the same newspaper which his ancestor established!

For George Washington Smith's newspaper has lived generation after generation, now passing out of the family, anon coming back to it. When, 200 years ago, the political center of the United States was transferred from Washington to Centropolis, the newspaper followed the government and assumed the name of Earth Chronicle. Unfortunately, it was unable to maintain itself at the high level of its name. Pressed on all sides by rival journals of a more modern type, it was continually in danger of collapse. Twenty years ago its subscription list contained but a few hundred thousand names, and then Mr. Fritz Napoleon Smith bought it for a mere trifle, and originated telephonic journalism.

Every one is familiar with Fritz Napoleon Smith's system—a system made possible by the enormous development of telephony during the last hundred years. Instead of being printed, the Earth Chronicle is every morning spoken to subscribers, who, in interesting conversations with reporters, statesmen, and scientists, learn the news of the day. Furthermore, each subscriber owns a phonograph, and to this instrument he leaves the task of gathering the news whenever he happens not to be in a mood to listen directly himself. As for purchasers of single copies, they can at a very trifling cost learn all that is in the paper of the day at any of the innumerable phonographs set up nearly everywhere.

Fritz Napoleon Smith's innovation galvanized the old newspaper. In the course of a few years the number of subscribers grew to be 85,000,000 and Smith's wealth went on growing, till now it reaches the almost unimaginable figure of $10,000,000,000. This lucky hit has enabled him to erect his new building, a vast edifice with four *façades*, each 3,250 feet in length, over which proudly floats the hundred-starred flag of the Union. Thanks to the same lucky hit, he is to-day king of newspaperdom; indeed, he would be king of all the Americans, too, if Americans could ever accept a king. You do not believe it? Well, then, look at the plenipotentiaries of all nations and our own ministers themselves crowding about his door, entreating his counsels, begging for his approbation, imploring the aid of his all-powerful organ. Reckon up the number of scientists and artists that he supports, of inventors that he has under his pay.

Yes, a king is he. And in truth his is a royalty full of burdens. His labors are incessant, and there is no doubt at all that in earlier times any man would have succumbed under the overpowering stress of the toil which Mr. Smith has to perform. Very fortunately for him, thanks to the progress of hygiene, which, abating all the old sources of unhealthfulness, has lifted the mean of human life from 37 up to 52 years, men have stronger constitutions now than heretofore. The discovery of nutritive air is still in the future, but in the meantime men to-day consume food that is compounded and prepared according to scientific principles, and they breathe an atmosphere freed from the microorganisms that formerly used to swarm in it; hence they live longer than their forefathers and know nothing of the innumerable diseases of olden times.

Nevertheless, and notwithstanding these considerations, Fritz Napoleon Smith's mode of life may well astonish one. His iron constitution is taxed to the utmost by the heavy strain that is put upon it. Vain the attempt to estimate the amount of labor he undergoes; an example alone can give an idea of it. Let us then go about with him for one day as he attends to his multifarious concernments.

What day? That matters little; it is the same every day. Let us then take at random September 25th of this present year 2889.

This morning Mr. Fritz Napoleon Smith awoke in very bad humor. His wife having left for France eight days ago, he was feeling disconsolate. Incredible though it seems, in all the ten years since their marriage, this is the first time that Mrs. Edith Smith, the professional beauty, has been so long absent from home; two or three days usually suffice for her frequent trips to Europe. The first thing that Mr. Smith does is to connect his phonotelephote, the wires of which communicate with his Paris mansion. The telephote! Here is another of the great triumphs of science in our time. The transmission of speech is an old story; the transmission of images by means of sensitive mirrors connected by wires is a thing but of yesterday. A valuable invention indeed, and Mr. Smith this morning was not niggard of blessings for the inventor, when by its aid he was able distinctly to see his wife notwithstanding the distance that separated him from her. Mrs. Smith, weary after the ball or the visit to the theater the preceding night, is still abed, though it is near noontide at Paris. She is asleep, her head sunk in the lace-covered pillows. What? She stirs? Her lips move. She is dreaming perhaps? Yes, dreaming. She is talking, pronouncing a name—his name—Fritz! The delightful vision gave a happier turn to Mr. Smith's thoughts. And now, at the call of imperative duty, light-hearted he springs from his bed and enters his mechanical dresser.

Two minutes later the machine deposited him all dressed at the threshold of his office. The round of journalistic work was now begun. First he enters the hall of the novel-writers, a vast apartment crowned with an enormous transparent cupola. In one corner is a telephone, through which a hundred Earth Chronicle *littérateurs* in turn recount to the public in daily installments a hundred novels. Addressing one of these authors who was waiting his turn, "Capital! Capital! my dear fellow," said he, "your last story. The scene where the village maid discusses interesting philosophical problems with her lover shows your very acute power of observation. Never have the ways of country folk been better portrayed. Keep on, my dear Archibald, keep on! Since yesterday, thanks to you, there is a gain of 5000 subscribers."

"Mr. John Last," he began again, turning to a new arrival, "I am not so well pleased with your work. Your story is not a picture of life; it lacks the elements of truth. And why? Simply because you run straight on to the end; because you do not analyze. Your heroes do this thing or that from this or that motive, which you assign without ever a thought of dissecting their mental and moral natures. Our feelings, you must remember, are far more complex than all that. In real life every act is the resultant of a hundred thoughts that come and go, and these you must study, each by itself, if you would create a living character. 'But,' you will say, 'in order to note these fleeting thoughts one must know them, must be able to follow them in their capricious meanderings.' Why, any child can do that, as you know. You have simply to make use of hypnotism, electrical or human, which gives one a two-fold being, setting free the witness-personality so that it may see, understand, and remember the reasons which determine the personality that acts. Just study yourself as you live from day to day, my dear Last. Imitate your associate whom I was complimenting a moment ago. Let yourself be hypnotized. What's that? You have tried it already? Not sufficiently, then, not sufficiently!"

Mr. Smith continues his round and enters the reporters' hall. Here 1500 reporters, in their respective places, facing an equal number of telephones, are communicating to the subscribers the news of the world as gathered during the night. The organization of this matchless service has often been described. Besides his telephone, each reporter, as the reader is aware, has in front of him a set of commutators, which enable him to communicate with any desired telephotic line. Thus the subscribers not only hear the news but see the occurrences. When an incident is described that is already past, photographs of its main features are transmitted with the narrative. And there is no confusion withal. The reporters' items, just like the different stories and all the other component parts of the journal, are classified automatically according to an ingenious system, and reach the hearer in due succession. Furthermore, the hearers are free to listen only to what specially concerns them. They may at pleasure give attention to one editor and refuse it to another.

Mr. Smith next addresses one of the ten reporters in the astronomical department—a department still in the embryonic stage, but which will yet play an important part in journalism.

"Well, Cash, what's the news?"

"We have phototelegrams from Mercury, Venus, and Mars."

"Are those from Mars of any interest?"

"Yes, indeed. There is a revolution in the Central Empire."

"And what of Jupiter?" asked Mr. Smith.

"Nothing as yet. We cannot quite understand their signals. Perhaps ours do not reach them."

"That's bad," exclaimed Mr. Smith, as he hurried away, not in the best of humor, toward the hall of the scientific editors. With their heads bent down over their electric computers, thirty scientific men were absorbed in transcendental calculations. The coming of Mr. Smith was like the falling of a bomb among them.

"Well, gentlemen, what is this I hear? No answer from Jupiter? Is it always to be thus? Come, Cooley, you have been at work now twenty years on this problem, and yet——"

"True enough," replied the man addressed. "Our science of optics is still very defective, and though our mile-and-three-quarter telescopes——"

"Listen to that, Peer," broke in Mr. Smith, turning to a second scientist. "Optical science defective! Optical science is your speciality. But," he continued, again addressing William Cooley, "failing with Jupiter, are we getting any results from the moon?"

"The case is no better there."

"This time you do not lay the blame on the science of optics. The moon is immeasurably less distant than Mars, yet with Mars our communication is fully established. I presume you will not say that you lack telescopes?"

"Telescopes? Oh no, the trouble here is about—inhabitants!"

"That's it," added Peer.

"So, then, the moon is positively uninhabited?" asked Mr. Smith.

"At least," answered Cooley, "on the face which she presents to us. As for the opposite side, who knows?"

"Ah, the opposite side! You think, then," remarked Mr. Smith, musingly, "that if one could but——"

"Could what?"

"Why, turn the moon about-face."

"Ah, there's something in that," cried the two men at once. And indeed, so confident was their air, they seemed to have no doubt as to the possibility of success in such an undertaking.

"Meanwhile," asked Mr. Smith, after a moment's silence, "have you no news of interest to-day?"

"Indeed we have," answered Cooley. "The elements of Olympus are definitely settled. That great planet gravitates beyond Neptune at the mean distance of 11,400,799,642 miles from the sun, and to traverse its vast orbit takes 1311 years, 294 days, 12 hours, 43 minutes, 9 seconds."

"Why didn't you tell me that sooner?" cried Mr. Smith. "Now inform the reporters of this straightway. You know how eager is the curiosity of the public with regard to these astronomical questions. That news must go into to-day's issue."

Then, the two men bowing to him, Mr. Smith passed into the next hall, an enormous gallery upward of 3200 feet in length, devoted to atmospheric advertising. Every one has noticed those enormous advertisements reflected from the clouds, so large that they may be seen by the populations of whole cities or even of entire countries. This, too, is one of Mr. Fritz Napoleon Smith's ideas, and in the Earth Chronicle building a thousand projectors are constantly engaged in displaying upon the clouds these mammoth advertisements.

When Mr. Smith to-day entered the sky-advertising department, he found the operators sitting with folded arms at their motionless projectors, and inquired as to the cause of their inaction. In response, the man addressed simply pointed to the sky, which was of a pure blue. "Yes," muttered Mr. Smith, "a cloudless sky! That's too bad, but what's to be done? Shall we produce rain? That we might do, but is it of any use? What we need is clouds, not rain. Go," said he, addressing the head engineer, "go see Mr. Samuel Mark, of the meteorological division of the scientific department, and tell him for me to go to work in earnest on the question of artificial clouds. It will never do for us to be always thus at the mercy of cloudless skies!"

Mr. Smith's daily tour through the several departments of his newspaper is now finished. Next, from the advertisement hall he passes to the reception chamber, where the ambassadors accredited to the American government are awaiting him, desirous of having a word of counsel or advice from the all-powerful editor. A discussion was going on when he entered. "Your Excellency will pardon me," the French Ambassador was saying to the Russian, "but I see nothing in the map of Europe that requires change. 'The North for the Slavs?' Why, yes, of course; but the South for the Latins. Our common frontier, the Rhine, it seems to me, serves very well. Besides, my government, as you must know, will firmly oppose every movement, not only against Paris, our capital, or our two great prefectures, Rome and Madrid, but also against the kingdom of Jerusalem, the dominion of Saint Peter, of which France means to be the trusty defender."

"Well said!" exclaimed Mr. Smith. "How is it," he asked, turning to the Russian ambassador, "that you Russians are not content with your vast empire, the most extensive in the world, stretching from the banks of the Rhine to the Celestial Mountains and the Kara-Korum, whose shores are washed by the Frozen Ocean, the Atlantic, the Mediterranean, and the Indian Ocean? Then, what is the use of threats? Is war possible in view of modern inventions—asphyxiating shells capable of being projected a distance of 60 miles, an electric spark of 90 miles, that can at one stroke annihilate a battalion; to say nothing of the plague, the cholera, the yellow fever, that the belligerents might spread among their antagonists mutually, and which would in a few days destroy the greatest armies?"

"True," answered the Russian; "but can we do all that we wish? As for us Russians, pressed on our eastern frontier by the Chinese, we must at any cost put forth our strength for an effort toward the west."

"Oh, is that all? In that case," said Mr. Smith, "the thing can be arranged. I will speak to the Secretary of State about it. The attention of the Chinese government shall be called to the matter. This is not the first time that the Chinese have bothered us."

"Under these conditions, of course——" And the Russian ambassador declared himself satisfied.

"Ah, Sir John, what can I do for you?" asked Mr. Smith as he turned to the representative of the people of Great Britain, who till now had remained silent.

"A great deal," was the reply. "If the Earth Chronicle would but open a campaign on our behalf——"

"And for what object?"

"Simply for the annulment of the Act of Congress annexing to the United States the British islands."

Though, by a just turn-about of things here below, Great Britain has become a colony of the United States, the English are not yet reconciled to the situation. At regular intervals they are ever addressing to the American government vain complaints.

"A campaign against the annexation that has been an accomplished fact for 150 years!" exclaimed Mr. Smith. "How can your people suppose that I would do anything so unpatriotic?"

"We at home think that your people must now be sated. The Monroe Doctrine is fully applied; the whole of America belongs to the Americans. What more do you want? Besides, we will pay for what we ask."

"Indeed!" answered Mr. Smith, without manifesting the slightest irritation. "Well, you English will ever be the same. No, no, Sir John, do not count on me for help. Give up our fairest province, Britain? Why not ask France generously to renounce possession of Africa, that magnificent colony the complete conquest of which cost her the labor of 800 years? You will be well received!"

"You decline! All is over then!" murmured the British agent sadly. "The United Kingdom falls to the share of the Americans; the Indies to that of——"

"The Russians," said Mr. Smith, completing the sentence.

"Australia——"

"Has an independent government."

"Then nothing at all remains for us!" sighed Sir John, downcast.

"Nothing?" asked Mr. Smith, laughing. "Well, now, there's Gibraltar!"

With this sally the audience ended. The clock was striking twelve, the hour of breakfast. Mr. Smith returns to his chamber. Where the bed stood in the morning a table all spread comes up through the floor. For Mr. Smith, being above all a practical man, has reduced the problem of existence to its simplest terms. For him, instead of the endless suites of apartments of the olden time, one room fitted with ingenious mechanical contrivances is enough. Here he sleeps, takes his meals, in short, lives.

He seats himself. In the mirror of the phonotelephote is seen the same chamber at Paris which appeared in it this morning. A table furnished forth is likewise in readiness here, for notwithstanding the difference of hours, Mr. Smith and his wife have arranged to take their meals simultaneously. It is delightful thus to take breakfast *tête-à-tête* with one who is 3000 miles or so away. Just now, Mrs. Smith's chamber has no occupant.

"She is late! Woman's punctuality! Progress everywhere except there!" muttered Mr. Smith as he turned the tap for the first dish. For like all wealthy folk in our day, Mr. Smith has done away with the domestic kitchen and is a subscriber to the Grand Alimentation Company, which sends through a great network of tubes to subscribers' residences all sorts of dishes, as a varied assortment is always in readiness. A subscription costs money, to be sure, but the *cuisine* is of the best, and the system has this advantage, that it does away with the pestering race of the *cordons-bleus*. Mr. Smith received and ate, all alone, the *hors-d'œuvre, entrées, rôti*, and *legumes* that constituted the repast. He was just finishing the dessert when Mrs. Smith appeared in the mirror of the telephote.

"Why, where have you been?" asked Mr. Smith through the telephone.

"What! You are already at the desert? Then I am late," she exclaimed, with a winsome *naïveté*. "Where have I been, you ask? Why, at my dress-maker's. The hats are just lovely this season! I suppose I forgot to note the time, and so am a little late."

"Yes, a little," growled Mr. Smith; "so little that I have already quite finished breakfast. Excuse me if I leave you now, but I must be going."

"Oh certainly, my dear; good-by till evening."

Smith stepped into his air-coach, which was in waiting for him at a window. "Where do you wish to go, sir?" inquired the coachman.

"Let me see; I have three hours," Mr. Smith mused. "Jack, take me to my accumulator works at Niagara."

For Mr. Smith has obtained a lease of the great falls of Niagara. For ages the energy developed by the falls went unutilized. Smith, applying Jackson's invention, now collects this energy, and lets or sells it. His visit to the works took more time than he had anticipated. It was four o'clock when he returned home, just in time for the daily audience which he grants to callers.

One readily understands how a man situated as Smith is must be beset with requests of all kinds. Now it is an inventor needing capital; again it is some visionary who comes to advocate a brilliant scheme which must surely yield millions of profit. A choice has to be made between these projects, rejecting the worthless, examining the questionable ones, accepting the meritorious. To this work Mr. Smith devotes every day two full hours.

The callers were fewer to-day than usual—only twelve of them. Of these, eight had only impracticable schemes to propose. In fact, one of them wanted to revive painting, an art fallen into desuetude owing to the progress made in color-photography. Another, a physician, boasted that he had discovered a cure for nasal catarrh! These impracticables were dismissed in short order. Of the four projects favorably received, the first was that of a young man whose broad forehead betokened his intellectual power.

"Sir, I am a chemist," he began, "and as such I come to you."

"Well!"

"Once the elementary bodies," said the young chemist, "were held to be sixty-two in number; a hundred years ago they were reduced to ten; now only three remain irresolvable, as you are aware."

"Yes, yes."

"Well, sir, these also I will show to be composite. In a few months, a few weeks, I shall have succeeded in solving the problem. Indeed, it may take only a few days."

"And then?"

"Then, sir, I shall simply have determined the absolute. All I want is money enough to carry my research to a successful issue."

"Very well," said Mr. Smith. "And what will be the practical outcome of your discovery?"

"The practical outcome? Why, that we shall be able to produce easily all bodies whatever—stone, wood, metal, fibers——"

"And flesh and blood?" queried Mr. Smith, interrupting him. "Do you pretend that you expect to manufacture a human being out and out?"

"Why not?"

Mr. Smith advanced $100,000 to the young chemist, and engaged his services for the Earth Chronicle laboratory.

The second of the four successful applicants, starting from experiments made so long ago as the nineteenth century and again and again repeated, had conceived the idea of removing an entire city all at once from one place to another. His special project had to do with the city of Granton, situated, as everybody knows, some fifteen miles inland. He proposes to transport the city on rails and to change it into a watering-place. The profit, of course, would be enormous. Mr. Smith, captivated by the scheme, bought a half-interest in it.

"As you are aware, sir," began applicant No. 3, "by the aid of our solar and terrestrial accumulators and transformers, we are able to make all the seasons the same. I propose to do something better still. Transform into heat a portion of the surplus energy at our disposal; send this heat to the poles; then the polar regions, relieved of their snow-caps, will become a vast territory available for man's use. What think you of the scheme?"

"Leave your plans with me, and come back in a week. I will have them examined in the meantime."

Finally, the fourth announced the early solution of a weighty scientific problem. Every one will remember the bold experiment made a hundred years ago by Dr. Nathaniel Faithburn. The doctor, being a firm believer in human hibernation—in other words, in the possibility of our suspending our vital functions and of calling them into action again after a time—resolved to subject the theory to a practical test. To this end, having first made his last will and pointed out the proper method of awakening him; having also directed that his sleep was to continue a hundred years to a day from the date of his apparent death, he unhesitatingly put the theory to the proof in his own person. Reduced to the condition of a mummy, Dr. Faithburn was coffined and laid in a tomb. Time went on. September 25th, 2889, being the day set for his resurrection, it was proposed to Mr. Smith that he should permit the second part of the experiment to be performed at his residence this evening.

"Agreed. Be here at ten o'clock," answered Mr. Smith; and with that the day's audience was closed.

Left to himself, feeling tired, he lay down on an extension chair. Then, touching a knob, he established communication with the Central Concert Hall, whence our greatest *maestros* send out to subscribers their delightful successions of accords determined by recondite algebraic formulas. Night was approaching. Entranced by the harmony, forgetful of the hour, Smith did not notice that it was growing dark. It was quite dark when he was aroused by the sound of a door opening. "Who is there?" he asked, touching a commutator.

Suddenly, in consequence of the vibrations produced, the air became luminous.

"Ah! you, Doctor?"

"Yes," was the reply. "How are you?"

"I am feeling well."

"Good! Let me see your tongue. All right! Your pulse. Regular! And your appetite?"

"Only passably good."

"Yes, the stomach. There's the rub. You are over-worked. If your stomach is out of repair, it must be mended. That requires study. We must think about it."

"In the meantime," said Mr. Smith, "you will dine with me."

As in the morning, the table rose out of the floor. Again, as in the morning, the *potage*, *rôti*, *ragoûts*, and *legumes* were supplied through the food-pipes. Toward the close of the meal, phonotelephotic communication was made with Paris. Smith saw his wife, seated alone at the dinner-table, looking anything but pleased at her loneliness.

"Pardon me, my dear, for having left you alone," he said through the telephone. "I was with Dr. Wilkins."

"Ah, the good doctor!" remarked Mrs. Smith, her countenance lighting up.

"Yes. But, pray, when are you coming home?"

"This evening."

"Very well. Do you come by tube or by air-train?"

"Oh, by tube."

"Yes; and at what hour will you arrive?"

"About eleven, I suppose."

"Eleven by Centropolis time, you mean?"

"Yes."

"Good-by, then, for a little while," said Mr. Smith as he severed communication with Paris.

Dinner over, Dr. Wilkins wished to depart. "I shall expect you at ten," said Mr. Smith. "To-day, it seems, is the day for the return to life of the famous Dr. Faithburn. You did not think of it, I suppose. The awakening is to take place here in my house. You must come and see. I shall depend on your being here."

"I will come back," answered Dr. Wilkins.

Left alone, Mr. Smith busied himself with examining his accounts—a task of vast magnitude, having to do with transactions which involve a daily expenditure of upward of $800,000. Fortunately, indeed, the stupendous progress of mechanic art in modern times makes it comparatively easy. Thanks to the Piano Electro-Reckoner, the most complex calculations can be made in a few seconds. In two hours Mr. Smith completed his task. Just in time. Scarcely had he turned over the last page when Dr. Wilkins arrived. After him came the body of Dr. Faithburn, escorted by a numerous company of men of science. They commenced work at once. The casket being laid down in the middle of the room, the telephote was got in readiness. The outer world, already notified, was anxiously expectant, for the whole world could be eyewitnesses of the performance, a reporter meanwhile, like the chorus in the ancient drama, explaining it all *viva voce* through the telephone.

"They are opening the casket," he explained. "Now they are taking Faithburn out of it—a veritable mummy, yellow, hard, and dry. Strike the body and it resounds like a block of wood. They are now applying heat; now electricity. No result. These experiments are suspended for a moment while Dr. Wilkins makes an examination of the body. Dr. Wilkins, rising, declares the man to be dead. 'Dead!' exclaims every one present. 'Yes,' answers Dr. Wilkins, 'dead!' 'And how long has he been dead?' Dr. Wilkins makes another examination. 'A hundred years,' he replies."

The case stood just as the reporter said. Faithburn was dead, quite certainly dead! "Here is a method that needs improvement," remarked Mr. Smith to Dr. Wilkins, as the scientific committee on hibernation bore the casket out. "So much for that experiment. But if poor Faithburn is dead, at least he is sleeping," he continued. "I wish I could get some sleep. I am tired out, Doctor, quite tired out! Do you not think that a bath would refresh me?"

"Certainly. But you must wrap yourself up well before you go out into the hall-way. You must not expose yourself to cold."

"Hall-way? Why, Doctor, as you well know, everything is done by machinery here. It is not for me to go to the bath; the bath will come to me. Just look!" and he pressed a button. After a few seconds a faint rumbling was heard, which grew louder and louder. Suddenly the door opened, and the tub appeared.

Such, for this year of grace 2889, is the history of one day in the life of the editor of the Earth Chronicle. And the history of that one day is the history of 365 days every year, except leap-years, and then of 366 days—for as yet no means has been found of increasing the length of the terrestrial year.

SURFACE TENSION

James Blish

James Blish was one of the most literate men, one of the sharpest critical minds, one of the ablest writers, ever to devote himself to science fiction. His four-volume *Spenglerian Cities in Flight* (published in one volume in 1970) is a classic work, as is his *A Case of Conscience* (1958). Brian W. Aldiss comments on Blish in his magisterial history of sf, *Trillion Year Spree*: "Science fiction readers, on the whole, thrive on multiple units and gigantic objects like galaxies. These, Blish could provide. He was also a master of the telling detail, without which the gigantic has no meaning."

His background in microbiology, however, led him into one of the most extraordinary imaginative leaps in modern science fiction. Obviously, in a multiplicity of alien worlds, the environment would so often be deadly hostile to normal human life that most worlds would be excluded from human habitation. In a future universe the wholesale changing of planetary environments to make them suitable for human life (terraforming) is almost certainly impractical. Thus Blish speculated upon genetic engineering so extreme that alien worlds might be sown with human seed in strange forms appropriate to the environment—but still human in mind and spirit, if not in physique. So he wrote this classic story, about the struggles and triumphs of microhumans, who live out their lives in a watery world but aspire to travel in space. This is a completely new vision of the conquest of space and the spread of humanity to a multiplicity of worlds.

Microcosmic sf has a long, rich history, from the microscopic world of Fitz-James O'Brien's "The Diamond Lens" (1858) to the subatomic world of Ray Cummings's *The Girl in the Golden Atom* (1921) and many pulp stories particularly in the Gernsback era, to Richard Matheson's *The Shrinking Man* (1956) and Robert L. Forward's *Dragon's Egg* (1980). Because of the geometric constraints of the virtually two-dimensional biological world Blish created, it strongly resembles the two-dimensional mathematical world of Abbott's *Flatland*, revisited in this volume by Rudy Rucker in "Message. . . ." Blish's speculations about genetic engineering remain, however, unique and provocative even in this subcategory.

I

Dr. Chatvieux took a long look over the microscope, leaving la Ventura with nothing to do but look out at the dead landscape of Hydrot. Waterscape, he thought, would be a better word. The new world had shown only one small, triangular continent, set amid endless ocean; and even the continent was mostly swamp.

The wreck of the seed-ship lay broken squarely across the one real spur of rock Hydrot seemed to possess, which reared a magnificent twenty-one feet above sea level. From this eminence, la Ventura could see forty miles to the horizon across a flat bed of mud. The red light of the star Tau Ceti, glinting upon thousands of small lakes, pools, ponds, and puddles, made the watery plain look like a mosaic of onyx and ruby.

"If I were a religious man," the pilot said suddenly, "I'd call this a plain case of divine vengeance."

Chatvieux said: "Hmn?"

"It's as if we've been struck down for—is it *hubris*, arrogant pride?"

"Well, is it?" Chatvieux said, looking up at last. "I don't feel exactly swollen with pride at the moment. Do you?"

"I'm not exactly proud of my piloting," la Ventura admitted. "But that isn't quite what I meant. I was thinking about why we came here in the first place. It takes arrogant pride to think that you can scatter men, or at least things like men, all over the face of the Galaxy. It takes even more pride to do the job—to pack up all the equipment and move from planet to planet and actually make men suitable for every place you touch."

"I suppose it does," Chatvieux said. "But we're only one of several hundred seed-ships in this limb of the Galaxy, so I doubt that the gods picked us out as special sinners." He smiled dryly. "If they had, maybe they'd have left us our ultraphone, so the Colonization Council could hear about our cropper. Besides, Paul, we try to produce men adapted to Earthlike planets, nothing more. We've sense enough—humility enough, if you like—to know that we can't adapt men to Jupiter or to Tau Ceti."

"Anyhow, we're here," la Ventura said grimly. "And we aren't going to get off. Phil tells me that we don't even have our germ-cell bank any more, so we can't seed this place in the usual way. We've been thrown onto a dead world and dared to adapt to it. What are the panatropes going to do—provide built-in water wings?"

"No," Chatvieux said calmly. "You and I and the rest of us are going to die, Paul. Panatropic techniques don't work on the body, only on the inheritance-carrying factors. We can't give you built-in water wings, any more than we can give you a new set of brains. I think we'll be able to populate this world with men, but we won't live to see it."

The pilot thought about it, a lump of cold collecting gradually in his stomach. "How long do you give us?" he said at last.

"Who knows? A month, perhaps."

The bulkhead leading to the wrecked section of the ship was pushed back, admitting salty, muggy air, heavy with carbon dioxide. Philip Strasvogel, the communications officer, came in, tracking mud. Like la Ventura, he was now a man without a function, but it did not appear to bother him. He unbuckled from around his waist a canvas belt into which plastic vials were stuffed like cartridges.

"More samples, Doc," he said. "All alike—water, very wet. I have some quicksand in one boot, too. Find anything?"

"A good deal, Phil. Thanks. Are the others around?"

Strasvogel poked his head out and hallooed. Other voices rang out over the mudflats. Minutes later, the rest of the survivors were crowding into the panatrope deck: Saltonstall, Chatvieux's senior assistant; Eunice Wagner, the only remaining ecologist; Eleftherios Venezuelos, the delegate from the Colonization Council; and Joan Heath, a midshipman whose duties, like la Ventura's and Strasvogel's, were now without meaning.

Five men and two women—to colonize a planet on which standing room meant treading water.

They came in quietly and found seats or resting places on the deck, on the edges of tables, in corners.

Venezuelos said: "What's the verdict, Dr. Chatvieux?"

"This place isn't dead," Chatvieux said. "There's life in the sea and in the fresh water, both. On the animal side of the ledger, evolution seems to have stopped with the crustacea; the most advanced form I've found is a tiny crayfish, from one of the local rivulets. The ponds and puddles are well stocked with protozoa and small metazoans, right up to a wonderfully variegated rotifer population—including a castle-building rotifer like Earth's *Floscularidae*. The plants run from simple algae to the thalluslike species."

"The sea is about the same," Eunice said, "I've found some of the larger simple metazoans—jellyfish and so on—and some crayfish almost as big as lobsters. But it's normal to find saltwater species running larger than freshwater."

"In short," Chatvieux said, "we'll survive here—if we fight."

"Wait a minute," la Ventura said. "You've just finished telling me that we wouldn't survive. And you were talking about us, not about the species, because we don't have our germ-cell banks any more. What's—"

"I'll get to that in a moment," Chatvieux said. "Saltonstall, what would you think of taking to the sea? We came out of it once; maybe we could come out of it again."

"No good," Saltonstall said immediately. "*I* like the idea, but I don't think this planet ever heard of Swinburne, or Homer, either. Looking at it as a colonization problem, as if we weren't involved ourselves, I wouldn't give you a credit for *epi oinopa ponton*. The evolutionary pressure there is too high, the competition from other species is prohibitive; seeding the sea would be the last thing we attempt. The colonists wouldn't have a chance to learn a thing before they were destroyed."

"Why?" la Ventura said. The death in his stomach was becoming hard to placate.

"Eunice, do your seagoing Coelenterates include anything like the Portuguese man-of-war?"

The ecologist nodded.

"There's your answer, Paul," Saltonstall said. "The sea is out. It's got to be fresh water, where the competing creatures are less formidable and there are more places to hide."

"We can't compete with a jellyfish?" la Ventura asked, swallowing.

"No, Paul," Chatvieux said. "The panatropes make adaptations, not gods. They take human germ-cells—in this case, our own, since our bank was wiped out in the crash—and modify them toward creatures who can live in any reasonable environment. The result will be manlike and intelligent. It usually shows the donor's personality pattern, too.

"*But we can't transmit memory.* The adapted man is worse than a child in his new environment. He has no history, no techniques, no precedents, not even a language. Ordinarily the seeding teams more or less take him through elementary school before they leave the planet, but we won't survive long enough for that. We'll have to design our colonists with plenty of built-in protections and locate them in the most favorable environment possible, so that at least some of them will survive the learning process."

The pilot thought about it, but nothing occurred to him which did not make the disaster seem realer and more intimate with each passing second. "One of the new creatures can have my personality pattern, but it won't be able to remember being me. Is that right?"

"That's it. There may be just the faintest of residuums—panatropy's given us some data which seem to support the old Jungian notion of ancestral memory. But we're all going to die on Hydrot, Paul. There's no avoiding that. Somewhere we'll leave behind people who behave as we would, think and feel as we would, but who won't remember la Ventura, or Chatvieux, or Joan Heath—or Earth."

The pilot said nothing more. There was a gray taste in his mouth.

"Saltonstall, what do you recommend as a form?"

The panatropist pulled reflectively at his nose. "Webbed extremities, of course, with thumbs and big toes heavy and thornilke for defense until the creature has had a chance to learn. Book-lungs, like the arachnids, working out of intercostal spiracles—they are gradually adaptable to atmosphere-breathing, if it ever decides to come out of the water. Also I'd suggest sporulation. As an aquatic animal, our colonist is going to have an indefinite life span, but we'll have to give it a breeding cycle of about six weeks to keep its numbers up during the learning period; so there'll have to be a definite break of some duration in its active year. Otherwise it'll hit the population problem before it's learned enough to cope with it."

"Also, it'll be better if our colonists could winter inside a good hard shell," Eunice Wagner added in agreement. "So sporulation's the obvious answer. Most microscopic creatures have it."

"Microscopic?" Phil said incredulously.

"Certainly," Chatvieux said, amused. "We can't very well crowd a six-foot man into a two-foot puddle. But that raises a question. We'll have tough competition from the rotifers, and some of them aren't strictly microscopic. I don't think your average colonist should run under 25 microns, Saltonstall. Give them a chance to slug it out."

"I was thinking of making them twice that big."

"Then they'd be the biggest things in their environment," Eunice Wagner pointed out, "and won't ever develop any skills. Besides, if you make them about rotifer size, it'll give them an incentive for pushing out the castle-building rotifers.

"They'll be able to take over the castles as dwellings."

Chatvieux nodded. "All right, let's get started. While the panatropes are being calibrated, the rest of us can put our heads together on leaving a record for these people. We'll microengrave the record on a set of corrosion-proof metal leaves, of a size our colonists can handle conveniently. Some day they may puzzle it out."

"Question," Eunice Wagner said. "Are we going to tell them they're microscopic? I'm opposed to it. It'll saddle their entire early history with a gods-and-demons mythology they'd be better off without."

"Yes, we are," Chatvieux said; and la Ventura could tell by the change in the tone of his voice that he was speaking now as their senior. "These people will be of the race of men, Eunice. We want them to win their way back to the community of men. They are not toys, to be protected from the truth forever in a freshwater womb."

"I'll make that official," Venezuelos said, and that was that.

And then, essentially, it was all over. They went through the motions. Already they were beginning to be hungry. After la Ventura had had his personality pattern recorded, he was out of it. He sat by himself at the far end of the ledge, watching Tau Ceti go redly down, chucking pebbles into the nearest pond, wondering morosely which nameless puddle was to be his Lethe.

He never found out, of course. None of them did.

Old Shar set down the heavy metal plate at last, and gazed instead out the window of the castle, apparently resting his eyes on the glowing green-gold obscurity of the summer waters. In the soft fluorescence which played down upon him, from the Noc dozing impassively in the groined vault of the chamber, Lavon could see that he was in fact a young man. His face was so delicately formed as to suggest that it had not been many seasons since he had first emerged from his spore.

But of course there had been no real reason to expect an old man. All the Shars had been referred to traditionally as "old" Shar. The reason, like the reasons for everything else, had been forgotten, but the custom had persisted; the adjective at least gave weight and dignity to the office.

The present Shar belonged to the generation XVI, and hence would have to be at least two seasons younger than Lavon himself. If he was old, it was only in knowledge.

"Lavon, I'm going to have to be honest with you," Shar said at last, still looking out of the tall, irregular window. "You've come to me for the secrets of the metal plates, just as your predecessors did to mine. I can give some of them to you—but for the most part, I don't know what they mean."

"After so many generations?" Lavon asked, surprised. "Wasn't it Shar III who first found out how to read them? That was a long time ago."

The young man turned and looked at Lavon with eyes made dark and wide by the depths into which they had been staring. "I can read what's on the plates, but most of it seems to make no sense. Worst of all, the plates are incomplete. You didn't know that? They are. One of them was lost in a battle during the final war with the Eaters, while these castles are still in their hands."

"What am I here for, then?" Lavon said. "Isn't there anything of value on the remaining plates? Do they really contain 'the wisdom of the Creators' or is that another myth?"

"No. No, that's true," Shar said slowly, "as far as it goes."

He paused, and both men turned and gazed at the ghostly creature which had appeared suddenly outside the window. Then Shar said gravely, "Come in, Para."

The slipper-shaped organism, nearly transparent except for the thousands of black-and-silver granules and frothy bubbles which packed its interior, glided into the chamber and hovered, with a muted whirring of cilia. For a moment it remained silent, probably speaking telepathically to the Noc floating in the vault, after the ceremonious fashion of all the protos. No human had ever intercepted one of these colloquies, but there was no doubt about their reality: humans had used them for long-range communications for generations.

Then the Para's cilia buzzed once more. Each separate hairlike process vibrated at an independent, changing rate; the resulting sound waves spread through the water, intermodulating, reinforcing or canceling each other. The aggregate wave-front, by the time it reached human ears, was recognizable human speech.

"We are arrived, Shar and Lavon, according to the custom."

"And welcome," said Shar. "Lavon, let's leave this matter of the plates for a while, until you hear what Para has to say; that's a part of the knowledge Lavons must have as they come of age, and it comes before the plates. I can give you some hints of what we are. First Para has to tell you something about what we aren't."

Lavon nodded, willingly enough, and watched the proto as it settled gently to the surface of the hewn table at which Shar had been sitting. There was in the entity such a perfection and economy of organization, such a grace and surety of movement, that he could hardly believe in his own new-won maturity. Para, like all the protos, made him feel not, perhaps, poorly thought-out, but at least unfinished.

"We know that in this universe there is logically no place for man," the gleaming now immobile cylinder upon the table droned abruptly. "Our memory is the common property to all our races. It reaches back to a time when there were no such creatures as men here. It remembers also that once upon a day there were men here, suddenly, and in some numbers. Their spores littered the bottom; we found the spores only a short time after our season's Awakening, and in them we saw the forms of men slumbering.

"Then men shattered their spores and emerged. They were intelligent, active. And they were gifted with a trait, a character, possessed by no other creature in this world. Not even the savage Eaters had it. Men organized us to exterminate the Eaters and therein lay the difference. Men had initiative. We have the word now, which you gave us, and we apply it, but we still do not know what the thing is that it labels."

"You fought beside us," Lavon said.

"Gladly. We would never have thought of that war by ourselves, but it was good and brought good. Yet we wondered. We saw that men were poor swimmers, poor walkers, poor crawlers, poor climbers. We saw that men were formed to make and use tools, a concept we still do not understand, for so wonderful a gift is largely wasted in this universe, and there is no other. What good are tool-useful members such as the hands of men? We do not know. It seems plain that so radical a thing should lead to a much greater rulership over the world than has, in fact, proven to be possible for men."

Lavon's head was spinning. "Para, I had no notion that you people were philosophers."

"The protos are old," Shar said. He had again turned to look out the window, his hands locked behind his back. "They aren't philosophers, Lavon, but they are remorseless logicians. Listen to Para."

"To this reasoning there could be but one outcome," the Para said. "Our strange ally, Man, was like nothing else in this universe. He was and is ill fitted for it. He does not belong here; he has been—adopted. This drives us to think that there are other universes besides this one, but where these universes might lie, and what their properties might be, it is impossible to imagine. We have no imagination, as men know."

Was the creature being ironic? Lavon could not tell. He said slowly: "Other universes? How could that be true?"

"We do not know," the Para's uninflected voice hummed. Lavon waited, but obviously the proto had nothing more to say.

Shar had resumed sitting on the windowsill, clasping his knees, watching the come and go of dim shapes in the lighted gulf. "It is quite true," he said. "What is written on the remaining plates makes it plain. Let me tell you now what they say.

"*We were made*, Lavon. We were made by men who are not as we are, but men who were our ancestors all the same. They were caught in some disaster, and they made us here in our universe—so that, even though they had to die, the race of men would live."

Lavon surged up from the woven spyrogrya mat upon which he had been sitting. "You must think I'm a fool!" he said sharply.

"No. You're our Lavon; you have a right to know the facts. Make what you like of them." Shar swung his webbed toes back into the chamber. "What I've told you may be hard to believe, but it seems to be so; what Para says backs it up. Our unfitness to live here is self-evident. I'll give you some examples:

"The past four Shars discovered that we won't get any further in our studies until we learn how to control heat. We've produced enough heat chemically to show that even the water around us changes when the temperature gets high enough. But there we're stopped."

"Why?"

"Because heat produced in open water is carried off as rapidly as it's produced. Once we tried to enclose that heat, and we blew up a whole tube of the castle and killed everything in range; the shock was terrible. We measured the pressures that were involved in that explosion, and we discovered that no substance we know could have resisted them. Theory suggests some stronger substances—*but we need heat to form them*!

"Take our chemistry. We live in water. Everything seems to dissolve in water, to some extent. How do we confine a chemical test to the crucible we put it in? How do we maintain a solution at one dilution? I don't know. Every avenue leads me to the same stone door. We're thinking creatures, Lavon, but there's something drastically wrong in the way we think about this universe we live in. It just doesn't seem to lead to results."

Lavon pushed back his floating hair futilely. "Maybe you're thinking about the wrong results. We've had no trouble with warfare, or crops, or practical things like that. If we can't create much heat, well, most of us don't miss it; we don't need any. What's the other universe supposed to be like, the one our ancestors lived in? Is it any better than this one?"

"I don't know," Shar admitted. "It was so different that it's hard to compare the two. The metal plates tell a story about men who were traveling from one place to another in a container that moved by itself. The only analogy I can think of is the shallops of diatom shells that our youngsters used to sled along the thermocline; but evidently what's meant is something much bigger.

"I picture a huge shallop, closed on all sides, big enough to hold many people—maybe twenty or thirty. It had to travel for generations through some kind of space where there wasn't any water to breathe, so that the people had to carry their own water and renew it constantly. There were no seasons; no yearly turnover; no ice forming on the sky, because there wasn't any sky in a closed shallop; no spore formation.

"Then the shallop was wrecked somehow. The people in it knew they were going to die. They made us, and put us here, as if we were their children. Because they had to die, they wrote their story on the plates, to tell us what had happened. I suppose we'd understand it better if we had the plate Shar III lost during the war, but we don't."

"The whole thing sounds like a parable," Lavon said, shrugging. "Or a song. I can see why you don't understand it. What I can't see is why you bother to try."

"Because of the plates," Shar said. "You've handled them yourself, so you know that we've nothing like them. We have crude, impure metals we've hammered out, metals that last for a while and then decay. But the plates shine on and on, generation after generation. They don't change; our hammers and graving tools break against them; the little heat we can generate leaves them unharmed. Those plates weren't formed in our universe—and that one fact makes every word on them important to me. Someone went to a great deal of trouble to make those plates indestructible to give them to us. Someone to whom the word 'stars' was important enough to be worth fourteen repetitions, despite the fact that the word doesn't seem to mean anything. I'm ready to think that if our makers repeated the word even twice on a record that seems likely to last forever, it's important for us to know what it means."

"All these extra universes and huge shallops and meaningless words—I can't say that they don't exist, but I don't see what difference it makes. The Shars of a few generations ago spent their whole lives breeding better crops for us, and showing us how to cultivate them instead of living haphazardly off bacteria. That was work worth doing. The Lavons of those days evidently got along without the metal plates, and saw to it that the Shars did, too: Well, as far as I'm concerned, you're welcome to the plates, if you like them better than crop improvement—but I think they ought to be thrown away."

"All right," Shar said, shrugging. "If you don't want them, that ends the traditional interview. We'll go our—"

There was a rising drone from the tabletop. The Para was lifting itself, waves of motion passing over its cilia, like the waves which went across the fruiting stalks of the fields of delicate fungi with which the bottom was planted. It had been so silent that Lavon had forgotten it; he could tell from Shar's startlement that Shar had, too.

"This is a great decision," the waves of sound washing from the creature throbbed. "Every proto has heard it and agrees with it. We have been afraid of these metal plates for a long time, afraid that men would learn to understand them and to follow what they say to some secret place, leaving the protos behind. Now we are not afraid."

"There wasn't anything to be afraid of," Lavon said indulgently.

"No Lavon before you had said so," Para said. "We are glad. We will throw the plates away."

With that, the shining creature swooped toward the embrasure. With it, it bore away the remaining plates which had been resting under it on the tabletop, suspended delicately in the curved tips of its supple cilia. With a cry, Shar plunged through the water toward the opening.

"Stop, Para!"

But Para was already gone, so swiftly that he had not even heard the call. Shar twisted his body and brought up one shoulder against the tower wall. He said nothing. His face was enough. Lavon could not look at it for more than an instant.

The shadows of the two men moved slowly along the uneven cobbled floor. The Noc descended toward them from the vault, its single thick tentacle stirring the water, its internal light flaring and fading irregularly. It, too, drifted through the window after its cousin, and sank slowly away toward the bottom. Gently its living glow dimmed, flickered, winked out.

II

For many days, Lavon was able to avoid thinking much about the loss. There was always a great deal of work to be done. Maintenance of the castles, which had been built by the now-extinct Eaters rather than by human hands, was a never-ending task. The thousand dichotomously bracing wings tended to crumble, especially at their bases where they sprouted from each other, and no Shar had yet come forward with a mortar as good as the rotifer-spittle which had once held them together. In addition, the breaking through of windows and the construction of chambers in the early days had been haphazard and often unsound. The instinctive architecture of the rotifers, after all, had not been meant to meet the needs of human occupants.

And then there were the crops. Men no longer fed precariously upon passing bacteria; now there were the drifting mats of specific water-fungi, rich and nourishing, which had been bred by five generations of Shars. These had to be tended constantly to keep the strains pure, and to keep the older and less intelligent species of the protos from grazing on them. In this latter task, to be sure, the more intricate and farseeing proto types cooperated, but men were needed to supervise.

There had been a time, after the war with the Eaters, when it had been customary to prey upon the slow-moving and stupid diatoms, whose exquisite and fragile glass shells were so easily burst, and who were unable to learn that a friendly voice did not necessarily mean a friend. There were still people who would crack open a diatom when no one else was looking, but were regarded as barbarians, to the puzzlement of the protos. The blurred and simpleminded speech of the gorgeously engraved plants had brought them into the category of pets—a concept which the protos were utterly unable to grasp, especially since men admitted that diatoms on the half-frustrule were delicious.

Lavon had had to agree, very early, that the distinction was tiny. After all, humans did eat the desmids, which differed from the diatoms only in three particulars: their shells were flexible, they could not move, and they did not speak. Yet to Lavon, as to most men, there did seem to be some kind of distinction, whether the protos could see it or not, and that was that. Under the circumstances he felt that it was a part of his duty, as a leader of men, to protect the diatoms from the occasional poachers who browsed upon them, in defiance of custom, in the high levels of the sunlit sky.

Yet Lavon found it impossible to keep himself busy enough to forget that moment when the last clues to Man's origin and destination had been seized and borne away into dim space.

It might be possible to ask Para for the return of the plates, explain that a mistake had been made. The protos were creatures of implacable logic, but they respected Man, and might reverse their decision if pressed—

We are sorry. The plates were carried over the bar and released in the gulf. We will have the bottom there searched, but . . .

With a sick feeling he could not repress, Lavon knew that when the protos decided something was worthless, they did not hide it in some chamber like old women. They threw it away—efficiently.

Yet despite the tormenting of his conscience, Lavon was convinced that the plates were well lost. What had they ever done for man, except to provide Shars with useless things to think about in the late seasons of their lives? What the Shars themselves had done to benefit Man, here, in the water, in the world, in the universe, had been done by direct experimentation. No bit of useful knowledge ever had come from the plates. There had never been anything in the plates but things best left unthought. The protos were right.

Lavon shifted his position on the plant frond, where he had been sitting in order to overlook the harvesting of an experimental crop of blue-green, oil-rich algae drifting in a clotted mass close to the top of the sky, and scratched his back gently against the coarse bole. The protos were seldom wrong, after all. Their lack of creativity, their inability to think an original thought, was a gift as well as a limitation. It allowed them to see and feel things at all times as they were—not as they hoped they might be, for they had no ability to hope, either.

"La-von! Laa-vah-on!"

The long halloo came floating up from the sleepy depths. Propping one hand against the top of the frond, Lavon bent and looked down. One of the harvesters was looking up at him, holding loosely the adze with which he had been splitting free the glutinous tetrads of the algae.

"Up here. What's the matter?"

"We have the ripened quadrant cut free. Shall we tow it away?"

"Tow it away," Lavon said, with a lazy gesture. He leaned back again. At the same instant, a brilliant reddish glory burst into being above him, and cast itself down toward the depths like mesh after mesh of the finest-drawn gold. The great light which lived above the sky during the day, brightening or dimming according to some pattern no Shar ever had fathomed, was blooming again.

Few men, caught in the warm glow of that light, could resist looking up at it—especially when the top of the sky itself wrinkled and smiled just a moment's climb or swim away. Yet, as always, Lavon's bemused upward look gave back nothing but his own distorted, bobbling reflection, and a reflection of the plant on which he rested.

Here was the upper limit, the third of the three surfaces of the universe.

The first surface was the bottom, where the water ended.

The second surface was the thermocline, the invisible division between the colder waters of the bottom and the warm, light waters of the sky. During the height of the warm weather, the thermocline was so definite a division as to make for good sledding and for chilly passage. A real interface formed between the cold, denser bottom waters and the warm reaches above, and maintained itself almost for the whole of the warm season.

The third surface was the sky. One could no more pass through that surface than one could penetrate the bottom, nor was there any better reason to try. There the universe ended. The light which played over it daily, waxing and waning as it chose, seemed to be one of its properties.

Toward the end of the season, the water gradually grew colder and more difficult to breathe, while at the same time the light became duller and stayed for shorter periods between darknesses. Slow currents started to move. The high waters turned chill and began to fall. The bottom mud stirred and smoked away, carrying with it the spores of the fields of fungi. The thermocline tossed, became choppy, and melted away. The sky began to fog with particles of soft silt carried up from the bottom, the walls, the corners of the universe. Before very long, the whole world was cold, inhospitable, flocculent with yellowing dying creatures.

Then the protos encysted; the bacteria, even most of the plants and, not long afterward, men, too, curled up in their oil-filled amber shells. The world died until the first tentative current of warm water broke the winter silence.

"La-von!"

Just after the long call, a shining bubble rose past Lavon. He reached out and poked it, but it bounded away from his sharp thumb. The gas-bubbles which rose from the bottom in late summer were almost invulnerable—and when some especially hard blow or edge did penetrate them, they broke into smaller bubbles which nothing could touch, and fled toward the sky, leaving behind a remarkably bad smell.

Gas. There was no water inside a bubble. A man who got inside a bubble would have nothing to breathe.

But, of course, it was impossible to penetrate a bubble. The surface tension was too strong. As strong as Shar's metal plates. As strong as the top of the sky.

As strong as the top of the sky. And above that—once the bubble was broken—a world of gas instead of water? Were all worlds bubbles of water drifting in gas?

If it were so, travel between them would be out of the question, since it would be impossible to pierce the sky to begin with. Nor did the infant cosmology include any provisions for bottoms for the worlds.

And yet some of the local creatures did burrow *into* the bottom, quite deeply, seeking something in those depths which was beyond the reach of Man. Even the surface of the ooze, in high summer, crawled with tiny creatures for which mud was a natural medium. Man, too, passed freely between the two countries of water which were divided by the thermocline, though many of the creatures with which he lived could not pass that line at all, once it had established itself.

And if the new universe of which Shar had spoken existed at all, it had to exist beyond the sky, where the light was. Why could not the sky be passed, after all? The fact that bubbles could be broken showed that the surface skin that formed between water and gas wasn't completely invulnerable. Had it ever been tried?

Lavon did not suppose that one man could butt his way through the top of the sky, any more than he could burrow into the bottom, but there might be ways around the difficulty. Here at his back, for instance, was a plant which gave every appearance of continuing beyond the sky: its uppermost fronds broke off and were bent back only by a trick of reflection.

It had always been assumed that the plants died where they touched the sky. For the most part, they did, for frequently the dead extension could be seen, leached and yellow, the boxes of its component cells empty, floating imbedded in the perfect mirror. But some were simply chopped off, like the one which sheltered him now. Perhaps that was only an illusion, and instead it soared indefinitely into some other place—some place where men might once have been born, and might still live . . .

The plates were gone. There was only one other way to find out.

Determinedly, Lavon began to climb toward the wavering mirror of the sky. His thorn-thumbed feet trampled obliviously upon the clustered sheaves of fragile stippled diatoms. The tulip-heads of Vortae, placid and murmurous cousins of Para, retracted startledly out of his way upon coiling stalks, to make silly gossip behind him.

Lavon did not hear them. He continued to climb doggedly toward the light, his fingers and toes gripping the plant bole.

"Lavon! Where are you going? Lavon!"

He leaned out and looked down. The man with the adze, a doll-like figure, was beckoning to him from a patch of blue-green retreating over a violet abyss. Dizzily he looked away, clinging to the bole; he had never been so high before. Then he began to climb again.

After a while, he touched the sky with one hand. He stopped to breathe. Curious bacteria gathered about the base of his thumb where blood from a small cut was fogging away, scattered at his gesture, and wriggled mindlessly back toward the dull red lure.

He waited until he no longer felt winded, and resumed climbing. The sky pressed down against the top of his head, against the back of his neck, against his shoulders. It seemed to give slightly, with a tough, frictionless elasticity. The water here was intensely bright, and quite colorless. He climbed another step, driving his shoulders against that enormous weight.

It was fruitless. He might as well have tried to penetrate a cliff.

Again he had to rest. While he panted, he made a curious discovery. All around the bole of the water plant, the steel surface of the sky curved upward, making a kind of sheath. He found that he could insert his hand into it—there was almost enough space to admit his head as well. Clinging closely to the bole, he looked up into the inside of the sheath, probing with his injured hand. The glare was blinding.

There was a kind of soundless explosion. His whole wrist was suddenly encircled in an intense, impersonal grip, as if it were being cut in two. In blind astonishment, he lunged upward.

The ring of pain traveled smoothly down his upflung arm as he rose, was suddenly around his shoulders and chest. Another lunge and his knees were being squeezed in the circular vine. Another—

Something was horribly wrong. He clung to the bole and tried to gasp, but there was—nothing to breathe.

The water came streaming out of his body, from his mouth, his nostrils, the spiracles in his sides, spurting in tangible jets. An intense and fiery itching crawled over the entire surface of his body. At each spasm, long knives ran into him, and from a great distance he heard more water being expelled from his book-lungs in an obscene, frothy sputtering.

Lavon was drowning.

With a final convulsion, he kicked away from the splintery bole, and fell. A hard impact shook him; and then the water, which had clung to him so tightly when he had first attempted to leave it, took him back with cold violence.

Sprawling and tumbling grotesquely, he drifted down and down and down, toward the bottom.

III

For many days, Lavon lay curled insensibly in his spore, as if in the winter sleep. The shock of cold which he had felt on reentering his native universe had been taken by his body as a sign of coming winter, as it had taken the oxygen-starvation of his brief sojourn above the sky. The spore-forming glands had at once begun to function.

Had it not been for this, Lavon would surely have died. The danger of drowning disappeared even as he fell, as the air bubbled out of his lungs and readmitted the life-giving water. But for acute desiccation and third degree sunburn, the sunken universe knew no remedy. The healing amnionic fluid generated by the spore-forming glands, after the transparent amber sphere had enclosed him, offered Lavon his only chance.

The brown sphere was spotted after some days by a prowling amoeba, quiescent in the eternal winter of the bottom. Down there the temperature was always an even 4°, no matter what the season, but it was unheard of that a spore should be found there while the high epilimnion was still warm and rich in oxygen.

Within an hour, the spore was surrounded by scores of astonished protos, jostling each other to bump their blunt eyeless prows against the shell. Another hour later, a squad of worried men came plunging from the castles far above to press their own noses against the transparent wall. Then swift orders were given.

Four Para grouped themselves about the amber sphere, and there was a subdued explosion as the trichocysts which lay embedded at the bases of their cilia, just under the pellicle, burst and cast fine lines of a quickly solidifying liquid into the water. The four Paras thrummed and lifted, tugging.

Lavon's spore swayed gently in the mud and then rose slowly, entangled in the web. Nearby, a Noc cast a cold pulsating glow over the operation—not for the Paras, who did not need the light, but for the baffled knot of men. The sleeping figure of Lavon, head bowed, knees drawn up to its chest, revolved with an absurd solemnity inside the shell as it was moved.

"Take him to Shar, Para."

The young Shar justified, by minding his own business, the traditional wisdom with which his hereditary office had invested him. He observed at once that there was nothing he could do for the encysted Lavon which would not be classifiable as simple meddling.

He had the sphere deposited in a high tower room of his castle, where there was plenty of light and the water was warm, which should suggest to the hibernating form that spring was again on the way. Beyond that, he simply sat and watched, and kept his speculations to himself.

Inside the spore, Lavon's body seemed rapidly to be shedding its skin, in long strips and patches. Gradually, his curious shrunkenness disappeared. His withered arms and legs and sunken abdomen filled out again.

The days went by while Shar watched. Finally he could discern no more changes, and, on a hunch, had the spore taken up to the topmost battlements of the tower, into the direct daylight.

An hour later, Lavon moved in his amber prison.

He uncurled and stretched, turned blank eyes up toward the light. His expression was that of a man who had not yet awakened from a ferocious nightmare. His whole body shone with a strange pink newness.

Shar knocked gently on the wall of the spore. Lavon turned his blind face toward the sound, life coming into his eyes. He smiled tentatively and braced his hands and feet against the inner wall of the shell.

The whole sphere fell abruptly to pieces with a sharp crackling. The amnionic fluid dissipated around him and Shar, carrying away with it the suggestive odor of a bitter struggle against death.

Lavon stood among the bits of shell and looked at Shar silently. At last he said: "Shar—I've been beyond the sky."

"I know," Shar said gently.

Again Lavon was silent. Shar said, "Don't be humble, Lavon. You've done an epoch-making thing. It nearly cost you your life. You must tell me the rest—all of it."

"The rest?"

"You taught me a lot while you slept. Or are you still opposed to useless knowledge?"

Lavon could say nothing. He no longer could tell what he knew from what he wanted to know. He had only one question left, but he could not utter it. He could only look dumbly into Shar's delicate face.

"You have answered me," Shar said, even more gently. "Come, my friend; join me at my table. We will plan our journey to the stars."

It was two winter sleeps after Lavon's disastrous climb beyond the sky that all work on the spaceship stopped. By then, Lavon knew that he had hardened and weathered into that temporarily ageless state a man enters after he has just reached his prime; and he knew also that there were wrinkles engraved upon his brow, to stay and to deepen.

"Old" Shar, too, had changed, his features losing some of their delicacy as he came into his maturity. Though the wedge-shaped bony structure of his face would give him a withdrawn and poetic look for as long as he lived, participation in the plan had given his expression a kind of executive overlay, which at best gave it a masklike rigidity, and at worst coarsened it somehow.

Yet despite the bleeding away of the years, the spaceship was still only a hulk. It lay upon a platform built above the tumbled boulders of the sandbar which stretched out from one wall of the world. It was an immense hull of pegged wood, broken by regularly spaced gaps through which the raw beams of the skeleton could be seen.

Work upon it had progressed fairly rapidly at first, for it was not hard to visualize what kind of vehicle would be needed to crawl through empty space without losing its water. It had been recognized that the sheer size of the machine would enforce a long period of construction, perhaps two full seasons; but neither Shar nor Lavon had anticipated any serious snag.

For that matter, part of the vehicle's apparent incompleteness was an illusion. About a third of its fittings were to consist of living creatures, which could not be expected to install themselves in the vessel much before the actual takeoff.

Yet time and time again, work on the ship had had to be halted for long periods. Several times whole sections needed to be ripped out, as it became more and more evident that hardly a single normal, understandable concept could be applied to the problem of space travel.

The lack of the history plates, which the Para steadfastly refused to deliver up, was a double handicap. Immediately upon their loss, Shar had set himself to reproduce them from memory; but unlike the more religious of his people, he had never regarded them as holy writ, and hence had never set himself to memorizing them word by word. Even before the theft, he had accumulated a set of variant translations of passages presenting specific experimental problems, which were stored in his library, carved in wood. But most of these translations tended to contradict each other, and none of them related to spaceship construction, upon which the original had been vague in any case.

No duplicates of the cryptic characters of the original had ever been made, for the simple reason that there was nothing in the sunken universe capable of destroying the originals, nor of duplicating their apparently changeless permanence. Shar remarked too late that through simple caution they should have made a number of verbatim temporary records—but after generations of green-gold peace, simple caution no longer covers preparation against catastrophe. (Nor, for that matter, did a culture which had to dig each letter of its simple alphabet into pulpy waterlogged wood with a flake of stonewort, encourage the keeping of records in triplicate.)

As a result, Shar's imperfect memory of the contents of the history plates, plus the constant and millennial doubt as to the accuracy of the various translations, proved finally to be the worst obstacle to progress on the spaceship itself.

"Men must paddle before they can swim," Lavon observed belatedly, and Shar was forced to agree with him.

Obviously, whatever the ancients had known about spaceship construction, very little of that knowledge was usable to a people still trying to build its first spaceship from scratch. In retrospect, it was not surprising that the great hulk still rested incomplete upon its platform above the sand boulders, exuding a musty odor of wood steadily losing its strength, two generations after its flat bottom had been laid down.

The fat-faced young man who headed the strike delegation was Phil XX, a man two generations younger than Lavon, four younger than Shar. There were crow's-feet at the corners of his eyes, which made him look both like a querulous old man and like an infant spoiled in the spore.

"We're calling a halt to this crazy project," he said bluntly. "We've slaved our youth away on it, but now that we're our own masters, it's over, that's all. Over."

"Nobody's compelled you," Lavon said angrily.

"Society does; our parents do," a gaunt member of the delegation said. "But now we're going to start living in the real world. Everybody these days knows that there's no other world but this one. You oldsters can hang on to your superstitions if you like. We don't intend to."

Baffled, Lavon looked over at Shar. The scientist smiled and said, "Let them go, Lavon. We have no use for the fainthearted."

The fat-faced young man flushed. "You can't insult us into going back to work. We're through. Build your own ship to no place!"

"All right," Lavon said evenly. "Go on, beat it. Don't stand around here orating about it. You've made your decision and we're not interested in your self-justifications. Good-by."

The fat-faced young man evidently still had quite a bit of heroism to dramatize which Lavon's dismissal had short-circuited. An examination of Lavon's stony face, however, convinced him that he had to take his victory as he found it. He and the delegation trailed ingloriously out the archway.

"Now what?" Lavon asked when they had gone. "I must admit, Shar, that I would have tried to persuade them. We do need the workers, after all."

"Not as much as they need us," Shar said tranquilly. "How many volunteers have you got for the crew of the ship?"

"Hundreds. Every young man of the generation after Phil's wants to go along. Phil's wrong about that segment of the population, at least. The project catches the imagination of the very young."

"Did you give them any encouragement?"

"Sure," Lavon said. "I told them we'd call on them if they were chosen. But you can't take that seriously! We'd do badly to displace our picked group of specialists with youths who have enthusiasm and nothing else."

"That's not what I had in mind, Lavon. Didn't I see a Noc in your chambers somewhere? Oh, there he is, asleep in the dome. Noc!"

The creature stirred its tentacles lazily.

"Noc, I've a message," Shar called. "The protos are to tell all men that those who wish to go to the next world with the spaceship must come to the staging area right away. Say that we can't promise to take everyone, but that only those who help us build the ship will be considered at all."

The Noc curled its tentacles again and appeared to go back to sleep. Actually, of course, it was sending its message through the water in all directions.

IV

Lavon turned from the arrangement of speaking-tube megaphones which was his control board and looked at the Para. "One last try," he said. "Will you give us back the plates?"

"No, Lavon. We have never denied you anything before, but this we must."

"You're going with us though, Para. Unless you give us the knowledge we need, you'll lose your life if we lose ours."

"What is one Para?" the creature said. "We are all alike. This cell will die; but the protos need to know how you fare on this journey. We believe you should make it without the plates."

"Why?"

The proto was silent. Lavon stared at it a moment, then turned deliberately back to the speaking tubes. "Everyone hang on," he said. He felt shaky. "We're about to start. Tol, is the ship sealed?"

"As far as I can tell, Lavon."

Lavon shifted to another megaphone. He took a deep breath. Already the water seemed stifling, though the ship hadn't moved.

"Ready with one-quarter power. One, two, three, go."

The whole ship jerked and settled back into place again. The raphe diatoms along the under hull settled into their niches, their jelly treads turning against broad endless belts of crude leather. Wooden gears creaked, stepping up the slow power of the creatures, transmitting it to the sixteen axles of the ship's wheels.

The ship rocked and began to roll slowly along the sandbar. Lavon looked tensely through the mica port. The world flowed painfully past him. The ship canted and began to climb the slope. Behind him, he could feel the electric silence of Shar, Para, the two alternate pilots, as if their gaze were stabbing directly through his body and on out the port. The world looked different, now that he was leaving it. How had he missed all this beauty before?

The slapping of the endless belts and the squeaking and groaning of the gears and axles grew louder as the slope steepened. The ship continued to climb, lurching. Around it, squadrons of men and protos dipped and wheeled, escorting it toward the sky.

Gradually the sky lowered and pressed down toward the top of the ship.

"A little more work from your diatoms, Tanol," Lavon said. "Boulder ahead." The ship swung ponderously. "All right, slow them up again. Give us a shove from your side, Than—no, that's too much—there, that's it. Back to normal; you're still turning us! Tanol, give us one burst to line us up again. Good. All right, steady drive on all sides. Won't be long now."

"How can you think in webs like that?" the Para wondered behind him.

"I just do, that's all. It's the way men think. Overseers, a little more thrust now; the grade's getting steeper."

The gears groaned. The ship nosed up. The sky brightened in Lavon's face. Despite himself, he began to be frightened. His lungs seemed to burn, and in his mind he felt his long fall through nothingness toward the chill slap of water as if he were experiencing it for the first time. His skin itched and burned. Could he go up *there* again? Up there into the burning void, the great gasping agony where no life should go?

The sandbar began to level out and the going became a little easier. Up here, the sky was so close that the lumbering motion of the huge ship disturbed it. Shadows of wavelets ran across the sand. Silently, the thick-barreled bands of blue-green algae drank in the light and converted it to oxygen, writhing in their slow mindless dance just under the long mica skylight which ran along the spine of the ship. In the hold, beneath the latticed corridor and cabin floors, whirring Vortae kept the ship's water in motion, fueling themselves upon drifting organic particles.

One by one, the figures wheeling about the ship outside waved arms or cilia and fell back, coasting down the slope of the sandbar toward the familiar world, dwindling and disappearing. There was at last only one single Euglena, half-plant cousin of the protos, forging along beside the spaceship into the marches of the shallows. It loved the light, but finally it, too, was driven away into cooler, deeper waters, its single whiplike tentacle undulating placidly as it went. It was not very bright, but Lavon felt deserted when it left.

Where they were going, though, none could follow.

Now the sky was nothing but a thin, resistant skin of water coating the top of the ship. The vessel slowed, and when Lavon called for more power, it began to dig itself in among the sandgrains.

"That's not going to work," Shar said tensely. "I think we'd better step down the gear ratio, Lavon, so you can apply stress more slowly."

"All right," Lavon agreed. "Full stop, everybody. Shar, will you supervise gear-changing, please?"

Insane brilliance of empty space looked Lavon full in the face just beyond his big mica bull's-eye. It was maddening to be forced to stop here upon the threshold of infinity; and it was dangerous, too. Lavon could feel building in him the old fear of the outside. A few moments more of inaction, he knew with a gathering coldness at the pit of his stomach, and he would be unable to go through with it.

Surely, he thought, there must be a better way to change gear-ratios than the traditional one, which involved dismantling almost the entire gear-box. Why couldn't a number of gears of different sizes be carried on the same shaft, not necessarily all in action all at once, but awaiting use simply by shoving the axle back and forth longitudinally in its sockets? It would still be clumsy, but it could be worked on orders from the bridge and would not involve shutting down the entire machine—and throwing the new pilot into a blue-green funk.

Shar came lunging up through the trap and swam himself a stop.

"All set," he said. "The big reduction gears aren't taking the strain too well, though."

"Splintering?"

"Yes. I'd go it slow at first."

Lavon nodded mutely. Without allowing himself to stop, even for a moment, to consider the consequences of his words, he called: "Half power."

The ship hunched itself down again and began to move, very slowly indeed, but more smoothly than before. Overhead, the sky thinned to complete transparency. The great light came blasting in. Behind Lavon there was an uneasy stir. The whiteness grew at the front ports.

Again the ship slowed, straining against the blinding barrier. Lavon swallowed and called for more power. The ship groaned like something about to die. It was now almost at a standstill.

"More power," Lavon called out.

Once more, with infinite slowness, the ship began to move. Gently, it tilted upward.

Then it lunged forward and every board and beam in it began to squall.

"Lavon! Lavon!"

Lavon started sharply at the shout. The voice was coming at him from one of the megaphones, the one marked for the port at the rear of the ship.

"Lavon!"

"What is it? Stop your damn yelling."

"I can see the top of the sky! From the *other* side, from the top side! It's like a big sheet of metal. We're going away from it. We're above the sky, Lavon, we're above the sky!"

Another violent start swung Lavon around toward the forward port. On the outside of the mica, the water was evaporating with shocking swiftness, taking with it strange distortions and patterns made of rainbows.

Lavon saw Space.

* * *

It was at first like a deserted and cruelly dry version of the bottom. There were enormous boulders, great cliffs, tumbled, split, riven, jagged rocks going up and away in all directions.

But it had a sky of its own—a deep blue dome so far away that he could not believe it, let alone compute, what its distance might be. And in this dome was a ball of white fire that seared his eyeballs.

The wilderness of rock was still a long way away from the ship, which now seemed to be resting upon a level, glistening plain. Beneath the surface-shine, the plain seemed to be made of sand, nothing but familiar sand, the same substance which had heaped up to form a bar in Lavon's own universe, the bar along which the ship had climbed. But the glassy, colorful skin over it—

Suddenly Lavon became conscious of another shout from the megaphone banks. He shook his head savagely and asked. "What is it now?"

"Lavon, this is Than. What have you gotten us into? The belts are locked. The diatoms can't move them. They aren't faking, either; we've rapped them hard enough to make them think we are trying to break their shells, but they still can't give us more power."

"Leave them alone," Lavon snapped. "They can't fake; they haven't enough intelligence. If they say they can't give you more power, they can't."

"Well, then, you get us out of it," Than's voice said frightenedly.

Shar came forward to Lavon's elbow. "We're on a space-water interface, where the surface tension is very high," he said softly. "This is why I insisted on our building the ship so that we could lift the wheels off the ground whenever necessary. For a long while I couldn't understand the reference of the history plates to 'retractable landing gear,' but it finally occurred to me that the tension along a space-water interface—or, to be more exact, a space-mud interface—would hold any large object pretty tightly. If you order the wheels pulled up now, I think we'll make better progress for a while on the belly-treads."

"Good enough," Lavon said. "Hello below—up landing gear. Evidently the ancients knew their business after all, Shar."

Quite a few minutes later, for shifting power to the belly-treads involved another setting of the gear box, the ship was crawling along the shore toward the tumbled rock. Anxiously, Lavon scanned the jagged, threatening wall for a break. There was a sort of rivulet off toward the left which might offer a route, though a dubious one, to the next world. After some thought, Lavon ordered his ship turned toward it.

"Do you suppose that thing in the sky is a 'star'?" he asked. "But there were supposed to be lots of them. Only one is up there—and one's plenty for *my* taste."

"I don't know," Shar admitted. 'But I'm beginning to get a picture of the way the universe is made, I think. Evidently our world is a sort of cup in the bottom of this huge one. This one has a sky of its own; perhaps it, too, is only a cup in the bottom of a still huger world, and so on and on without end. It's a hard concept to grasp, I'll admit. Maybe it would be more sensible to assume that all the worlds are cups in this one common surface, and that the great light shines on them all impartially."

"Then what makes it seem to go out every night, and dim even in the day during winter?" Lavon demanded.

"Perhaps it travels in circles, over first one world, then another. How could I know yet?"

"Well, if you're right, it means that all we have to do is crawl along here for a while, until we hit the top of the sky of another world," Lavon said. "Then we dive in. Somehow it seems too simple, after all our preparations."

Shar chuckled, but the sound did not suggest that he had discovered anything funny. "Simple? Have you noticed the temperature yet?"

Lavon had noticed it, just beneath the surface of awareness, but at Shar's remark he realized that he was gradually being stifled. The oxygen content of the water, luckily, had not dropped, but the temperature suggested the shallows in the last and worst part of the autumn. It was like trying to breathe soup.

"Than, give us more action from the Vortae," Lavon called. "This is going to be unbearable unless we get more circulation."

It was all he could do now to keep his attention on the business of steering the ship.

The cut or defile in the scattered razor-edged rocks was a little closer, but there still seemed to be many miles of rough desert to cross. After a while, the ship settled into a steady, painfully slow crawling, with less pitching and jerking than before, but also with less progress. Under it, there was now a sliding, grinding sound, rasping against the hull of the ship itself, as if it were treadmilling over some coarse lubricant whose particles were each as big as a man's head.

Finally Shar said, "Lavon, we'll have to stop again. The sand this far up is dry, and we're wasting energy using the treads."

"Are you sure we can take it?" Lavon asked, gasping for breath. "At least we are moving. If we stop to lower the wheels and change gears again, we'll boil."

"We'll boil if we don't," Shar said calmly. "Some of our algae are already dead and the rest are withering. That's a pretty good sign that we can't take much more. I don't think we'll make it into the shadows, unless we do change over and put on some speed."

There was a gulping sound from one of the mechanics. "We ought to turn back," he said raggedly. "We were never meant to be out here in the first place. We were made for the water, not this hell."

"We'll stop," Lavon said, "but we're not turning back. That's final."

The words made a brave sound, but the man had upset Lavon more than he dared to admit, even to himself. "Shar," he said, "make it fast, will you?"

The scientist nodded and dived below.

The minutes stretched out. The great white globe in the sky blazed and blazed. It had moved down the sky, far down, so that the light was pouring into the ship directly in Lavon's face, illuminating every floating particle, its rays like long milky streamers. The currents of water passing Lavon's cheek were almost hot.

How could they dare go directly forward into that inferno? The land directly under the "star" must be even hotter than it was here!

"Lavon! Look at Para!"

Lavon forced himself to turn and look at his proto ally. The great slipper had settled to the deck, where it was lying with only a feeble pulsation of its cilia. Inside, its vacuoles were beginning to swell, to become bloated, pear-shaped bubbles, crowding the granulated protoplasm, pressing upon the dark nuclei.

"This cell is dying," Para said, as coldly as always. "But go on—go on. There is much to learn, and you may live, even though we do not. Go on."

"You're . . . for us now?" Lavon whispered.

"We have always been for you. Push your folly to its uttermost. We will benefit in the end, and so will Man."

The whisper died away. Lavon called the creature again, but it did not respond.

There was a wooden clashing from below, and then Shar's voice came tinnily from one of the megaphones. "Lavon, go ahead! The diatoms are dying, too, and then we'll be without power. Make it as quickly and directly as you can."

Grimly, Lavon leaned forward. "The 'star' is directly over the land we're approaching."

"It is? It may go lower still and the shadows will get longer. That's our only hope."

Lavon had not thought of that. He rasped into the banked megaphones. Once more, the ship began to move.

It got hotter.

Steadily, with a perceptible motion, the "star" sank in Lavon's face. Suddenly a new terror struck him. Suppose it should continue to go down until it was gone entirely? Blasting though it was now, it was the only source of heat. Would not space become bitter cold on the instant—and the ship an expanding, bursting block of ice?

The shadows lengthened menacingly, stretched across the desert toward the forward-rolling vessel. There was no talking in the cabin, just the sound of ragged breathing and the creaking of the machinery.

Then the jagged horizon seemed to rush open upon them. Stony teeth cut into the lower rim of the ball of fire, devoured it swiftly. It was gone.

They were in the lee of the cliffs. Lavon ordered the ship turned to parallel the rock-line; it responded heavily, sluggishly. Far above, the sky deepened steadily from blue to indigo.

Shar came silently up through the trap and stood beside Lavon, studying that deepening color and the lengthening of the shadows down the beach toward their world. He said nothing, but Lavon knew that the same chilling thought was in his mind.

"Lavon."

Lavon jumped. Shar's voice had iron in it. "Yes?"

"We'll have to keep moving. We must make the next world, wherever it is, very shortly."

"How can we dare move when we can't see where we're going? Why not sleep it over—if the cold will let us?"

"It will let us." Shar said. "It can't get dangerously cold up here. If it did, the sky—or what we used to think of as the sky—would have frozen over every night, even in summer. But what I'm thinking about is the water. The plants will go to sleep now. In our world that wouldn't matter; the supply of oxygen is enough to last through the night. But in this confined space, with so many creatures in it and no source of fresh water, we will probably smother."

Shar seemed hardly to be involved at all, but spoke rather with the voice of implacable physical laws.

"Furthermore," he said, staring unseeingly out at the raw landscape, "the diatoms are plants, too. In other words, we must stay on the move for as long as we have oxygen and power—and pray that we make it."

"Shar, we had quite a few protos on board this ship once. And Para there isn't quite dead yet. If he were, the cabin would be intolerable. The ship is nearly sterile of bacteria, because all the protos have been eating them as a matter of course and there's no outside supply of them, any more than there is for oxygen. But still and all there would have been some decay."

Shar bent and tested the pellicle of the motionless Para with a probing finger. "You're right, he's still alive. What does that prove?"

"The Vortae are also alive; I can feel the water circulating. Which proves it wasn't the heat that hurt Para. *It was the light.* Remember how badly my skin was affected after I climbed beyond the sky? Undiluted starlight is deadly. We should add that to the information on the plates."

"I still don't see the point."

"It's this. We've got three or four Noc down below. They were shielded from the light, and so must be alive. If we concentrate them in the diatom galleys, the dumb diatoms will think it's still daylight and will go on working. Or we can concentrate them up along the spine of the ship, and keep the algae putting out oxygen. So the question is: which do we need more, oxygen or power? Or can we split the difference?"

Shar actually grinned. "A brilliant piece of thinking. We'll make a Shar of you yet, Lavon. No, I'd say that we can't split the difference. There's something about daylight, some quality, that the light Noc emits doesn't have. You and I can't detect it, but the green plants can, and without it they don't make oxygen. So we'll have to settle for the diatoms—for power."

Lavon brought the vessel away from the rocky lee of the cliff, out onto the smoother sand. All trace of direct light was gone now, although there was still a soft, general glow on the sky.

"Now, then," Shar said thoughtfully, "I would guess that there's water over there in the canyon, if we can reach it. I'll go below and arrange—"

Lavon gasped, "What's the matter?"

Silently, Lavon pointed, his heart pounding.

The entire dome of indigo above them was spangled with tiny, incredibly brilliant lights. There were hundreds of them, and more and more were becoming visible as the darkness deepened. And far away, over the ultimate edge of the rocks, was a dim red globe, crescented with ghostly silver. Near the zenith was another such body, much smaller, and silvered all over . . .

Under the two moons of Hydrot, and under the eternal stars, the two-inch wooden spaceship and its microscopic cargo toiled down the slope toward the drying little rivulet.

V

The ship rested on the bottom of the canyon for the rest of the night. The great square doors were thrown open to admit the raw, irradiated, life-giving water from outside—and the wriggling bacteria which were fresh food.

No other creatures approached them, either with curiosity or with predatory intent, while they slept, though Lavon had posted guards at the doors. Evidently, even up here on the very floor of space, highly organized creatures were quiescent at night.

But when the first flush of light filtered through the water, trouble threatened.

First of all, there was the bug-eyed monster. The thing was green and had two snapping claws, either one of which could have broken the ship in two like a spyrogyra straw. Its eyes were black and globular, on the ends of short columns, and its long feelers were as thick as a plant bole. It passed in a kicking fury of motion, however, never noticing the ship at all.

"Is that—a sample of the kind of life we can expect in the next world?" Lavon whispered. Nobody answered, for the very good reason that nobody knew.

After a while, Lavon risked moving the ship forward against the current, which was slow but heavy. Enormous writhing worms whipped past them. One struck the hull a heavy blow, then thrashed on obliviously.

"They don't notice us," Shar said. "We're too small, Lavon, the ancients warned us of the immensity of space, but even when you see it, it's impossible to grasp. And all those stars—can they mean what I think they mean? It's beyond thought, beyond belief!"

"The bottom's sloping," Lavon said, looking ahead intently. "The walls of the canyon are retreating, and the water's becoming rather silty. Let the stars wait, Shar; we're coming toward the entrance of our new world."

Shar subsided moodily. His vision of space had disturbed him, perhaps seriously. He took little notice of the great thing that was happening, but instead huddled worriedly over his own expanding speculations. Lavon felt the old gap between their two minds widening once more.

Now the bottom was tilting upward again. Lavon had no experience with delta-formation, for no rivulets left his own world, and the phenomenon worried him. But his worries were swept away in wonder as the ship topped the rise and nosed over.

Ahead, the bottom sloped away again, indefinitely, into glimmering depths. A proper sky was over them once more, and Lavon could see small rafts of plankton floating placidly beneath it. Almost at once, too, he saw several of the smaller kinds of protos, a few of which were already approaching the ship—

Then the girl came darting out of the depths, her features distorted with terror. At first she did not see the ship at all. She came twisting and turning lithely through the water, obviously hoping only to throw herself over the ridge of the delta and into the savage streamlet beyond.

Lavon was stunned. Not that there were men here—he had hoped for that—but at the girl's single-minded flight toward suicide.

"What—"

Then a dim buzzing began to grow in his ears, and he understood.

"Shar! Than! Tanol!" he bawled. "Break out crossbows and spears! Knock out all the windows!" He lifted a foot and kicked through the big port in front of him. Someone thrust a crossbow into his hand.

"Eh? What's happening?" Shar blurted.

"*Eaters!*"

The cry went though the ship like a galvanic shock. The rotifers back in Lavon's own world were virtually extinct, but everyone knew thoroughly the grim history of the long battle man and proto had waged against them.

The girl spotted the ship and paused, stricken by despair at the sight of the new monster. She drifted with her own momentum, her eyes alternately fixed hypnotically upon the ship and glancing back over her shoulder, toward where the buzzing snarled louder and louder in the dimness.

"Don't stop!" Lavon shouted. "This way, this way! We're friends! We'll help!"

Three great semitransparent trumpets of smooth flesh bored over the rise, the many thick cilia of their coronas whirring greedily. Dicrans—the most predacious of the entire tribe of Eaters. They were quarreling thickly among themselves as they moved, with the few blurred, presymbolic noises which made up their "language."

Carefully, Lavon wound the crossbow, brought it to his shoulder, and fired. The bolt sang away through the water. It lost momentum rapidly, and was caught by a stray current which brought it closer to the girl than to the Eater at which Lavon had aimed.

He bit his lip, lowered the weapon, wound it up again. It did not pay to underestimate the range; he would have to wait until he could fire with effect. Another bolt, cutting through the water from a side port, made him issue orders to cease firing.

The sudden irruption of the rotifers decided the girl. The motionless wooden monster was strange to her and had not yet menaced her—but she must have known what it would be like to have three Dicrans over her, each trying to grab away from the other the biggest share. She threw herself toward the big port. The Eaters screamed with fury and greed and bored after her.

She probably would not have made it, had not the dull vision of the lead Dicran made out the wooden shape of the ship at the last instant. It backed off, buzzing, and the other two sheered away to avoid colliding with it. After that they had another argument, though they could hardly have formulated what it was that they were fighting about. They were incapable of saying anything much more complicated than the equivalent of "Yaah," "Drop dead," and "You're another."

While they were still snarling at each other, Lavon pierced the nearest one all the way through with an arablast bolt. It disintegrated promptly—rotifers are delicately organized creatures despite their ferocity—and the remaining two were at once involved in a lethal battle over the remains.

"Than, take a party out and spear me those two Eaters while they're still fighting," Lavon ordered. "Don't forget to destroy their eggs, too. I can see that this world needs a little taming."

The girl shot through the port and brought up against the far wall of the cabin, flailing in terror. Lavon tried to approach her, but from somewhere she produced a flake of stonewort chipped to a nasty point. He sat down on the stool before his control board and waited while she took in the cabin, Lavon, Shar, the pilot, the senescent Para.

At last she said: "Are—you—the gods from beyond the sky?"

"We're from beyond the sky, all right," Lavon said. "But we're not gods. We're human beings, like yourself. Are there many humans here?"

The girl seemed to assess the situation very rapidly, savage though she was. Lavon had the odd and impossible impression that he should recognize her. She tucked the knife back into her matted hair—ah, Lavon thought, that's a trick I may need to remember—and shook her head.

"We are few. The Eaters are everywhere. Soon they will have the last of us." Her fatalism was so complete that she actually did not seem to care.

"And you've never cooperated against them? Or asked the protos to help?"

"The protos?" She shrugged. "They are as helpless as we are against the Eaters. We have no weapons which kill at a distance, like yours. And it is too late now for such weapons to do any good. We are too few, the Eaters too many."

Lavon shook his head emphatically. "You've had one weapon that counts all along. Against it, numbers mean nothing. We'll show you how we've used it. You may be able to use it even better than we did, once you've given it a try."

The girl shrugged again. "We have dreamed of such a weapon now and then, but never found it. I do not think that what you say is true. What is this weapon?"

"Brains," Lavon said. "Not just one brain, but brains. Working together. Cooperation."

"Lavon speaks the truth," a weak voice said from the deck.

The Para stirred feebly. The girl watched it with wide eyes. The sound of the

Para using human speech seemed to impress her more than the ship or anything else it contained.

"The Eaters can be conquered," the thin, buzzing voice said. "The protos will help, as they helped in the world from which we came. They fought this flight through space, and deprived Man of his records; but Man made the trip without the records. The protos will never oppose men again. I have already spoken to the protos of this world and have told them what Man can dream, Man can do, whether the protos wish it or not.

"Shar, your metal records are with you. They were hidden in the ship. My brothers will lead you to them.

"This organism dies now. It dies in confidence of knowledge, as an intelligent creature dies. Man has taught us this. There is nothing that knowledge . . . cannot do. With it, men . . . have crossed . . . have crossed space . . ."

The voice whispered away. The shining slipper did not change, but something about it was gone. Lavon looked at the girl; their eyes met.

"We have crossed space," Lavon repeated softly.

Shar's voice came to him across a great distance. The young-old man was whispering: "But *have* we?"

"As far as I'm concerned, yes," said Lavon.

NO, NO, NOT ROGOV!

Cordwainer Smith

Cordwainer Smith was the pseudonym of Paul Linebarger, a mysterious and colorful figure who was an expert on psychological warfare (he wrote a standard text) and spent his career in the intelligence community. He went to college with L. Ron Hubbard, the famous pulp science fiction writer who later invented Scientology, and they published in the same literary magazine. There was apparently some real competitiveness in Linebarger, for he wrote an entire book manuscript (never published) in the late 1940s on the science of mental health. In typical hard sf fashion, both Linebarger and Hubbard were trying to raise psychology to the status of a "real" science.

Nearly all of Smith's science fiction takes place in a consistent future history, "The Instrumentality of Mankind," comprising many stories and one novel, *Norstrilia* (1975). The series chronicles events in the millennia-long struggle between the human Instrumentality and the Underpeople, intelligent animals biologically transformed into humanlike forms. A devout High Anglican, Smith built complex levels of religious allegory into his series.

As is evident from the foregoing, he was not characteristically a hard sf writer, but he did occasionally explore hard sf territory, although always in a highly ornamented style at the furthest remove from the traditional unornamented prose of scientific reportage normally identified with the "hard stuff."

"No, No, Not Rogov!" is his only sf story set in contemporary times. It is in the mode of invention fiction, but is set in the Soviet Union during the 1940s and beyond. It explores the work of science under totalitarian political conditions, a subject that Linebarger knew well. The setting reflects the ambiguous attitude toward the linkage of the military and scientific establishments that has characterized postatomic bomb sf. The political/psychological portraits may be assumed to be accurate. It is also a link between the present and his visionary future of the Instrumentality.

The portrayal of experimental science is a chilling parallel to Tiptree's "The Psychologist Who Wouldn't Do Awful Things to Rats," and the portrait of the scientist as a partly willing political prisoner is an ironic contrast to Kornbluth's "Gomez." It is a work that explodes into something visionary and transcendent and shows Cordwainer Smith's distinctive and unusual voice in sf.

That golden shape on the golden steps shook and fluttered like a bird gone mad—like a bird imbued with an intellect and a soul, and, nevertheless, driven mad by ecstasies and terrors beyond human understanding—ecstasies drawn momentarily down into reality by the consummation of superlative art. A thousand worlds watched.

Had the ancient calendar continued this would have been A.D. *13,582. After defeat, after disappointment, after ruin and reconstruction, mankind had leapt among the stars.*

Out of meeting inhuman art, out of confronting nonhuman dances, mankind had made a superb esthetic effort and had leapt upon the stage of all the worlds.

The golden steps reeled before the eyes. Some eyes had retinas. Some had crystalline cones. Yet all eyes were fixed upon the golden shape which interpreted The Glory and Affirmation of Man *in the Inter-World Dance Festival of what might have been* A.D. *13,582.*

Once again mankind was winning the contest. Music and dance were hypnotic beyond the limits of systems, compelling, shocking to human and inhuman eyes. The dance was a triumph of shock—the shock of dynamic beauty.

The golden shape on the golden steps executed shimmering intricacies of meaning. The body was gold and still human. The body was a woman, but more than a woman. On the golden steps, in the golden light, she trembled and fluttered like a bird gone mad.

I

The Ministry of State Security had been positively shocked when they found that a Nazi agent, more heroic than prudent, had almost reached N. Rogov.

Rogov was worth more to the Soviet armed forces than any two air armies, more than three motorized divisions. His brain was a weapon, a weapon for the Soviet power.

Since the brain was a weapon, Rogov was a prisoner.

He didn't mind.

Rogov was a pure Russian type, broad-faced, sandy-haired, blue-eyed, with whimsy in his smile and amusement in the wrinkles of the tops of his cheeks.

"Of course I'm a prisoner," Rogov used to say. "I am a prisoner of State service to the Soviet peoples. But the workers and peasants are good to me. I am an academician of the All Union Academy of Sciences, a major general in the Red Air Force, a professor in the University of Kharkov, a deputy works manager of the Red Flag Combat Aircraft Production Trust. From each of these I draw a salary."

Sometimes he would narrow his eyes at his Russian scientific colleagues and ask them in dead earnest, "Would I serve capitalists?"

The affrighted colleagues would try to stammer their way out of the embarrassment, protesting their common loyalty to Stalin or Beria, or Zhukov, or Molotov, or Bulganin, as the case may have been.

Rogov would look very Russian: calm, mocking, amused. He would let them stammer.

Then he'd laugh.

Solemnity transformed into hilarity, he would explode into bubbling, effervescent, good-humored laughter. "Of course I could not serve the capitalists. My little Anastasia would not let me."

The colleagues would smile uncomfortably and would wish that Rogov did not talk so wildly, or so comically, or so freely.

Even Rogov might wind up dead.

Rogov didn't think so.

They did.

Rogov was afraid of nothing.

Most of his colleagues were afraid of each other, of the Soviet system, of the world, of life, and of death.

Perhaps Rogov had once been ordinary and mortal like other people and full of fears.

But he had become the lover, the colleague, the husband of Anastasia Fyodorovna Cherpas.

Comrade Cherpas had been his rival, his antagonist, his competitor, in the struggle for scientific eminence in the daring Slav frontiers of Russian science. Russian science could never overtake the inhuman perfection of German method, the rigid intellectual and moral discipline of German teamwork, but the Russians could and did get ahead of the Germans by giving vent to their bold, fantastic imaginations. Rogov had pioneered the first rocket launchers of 1939. Cherpas had finished the job by making the best of the rockets radiodirected.

Rogov in 1942 had developed a whole new system of photomapping. Comrade Cherpas had applied it to color film. Rogov, sandy-haired, blue-eyed, and smiling, had recorded his criticisms of Comrade Cherpas's naïveté and unsoundness at the top-secret meetings of Russian scientists during the black winter nights of 1943. Comrade Cherpas, her butter-yellow hair flowing down like living water to her shoulders, her unpainted face gleaming with fanaticism, intelligence, and dedication, would snarl her own defiance at him, deriding his Communist theory, pinching at his pride, hitting his intellectual hypotheses where they were weakest.

By 1944 a Rogov-Cherpas quarrel had become something worth traveling to see.

In 1945 they were married.

Their courtship was secret, their wedding a surprise, their partnership a miracle in the upper ranks of Russian science.

The emigré press had reported that the great scientist, Peter Kapitza, once remarked, "Rogov and Cherpas, there is a team. They're Communists, good Communists; but they're better than that! They're *Russian*, Russian enough to beat the world. Look at them. That's the future, our Russian future!" Perhaps the quotation was an exaggeration, but it did show the enormous respect in which both Rogov and Cherpas were held by their colleagues in Soviet science.

Shortly after their marriage strange things happened to them.

Rogov remained happy. Cherpas was radiant.

Nevertheless, the two of them began to have haunted expressions, as though they had seen things which words could not express, as though they had stumbled upon secrets too important to be whispered even to the most secure agents of the Soviet State Police.

In 1947 Rogov had an interview with Stalin. As he left Stalin's office in the Kremlin, the great leader himself came to the door, his forehead wrinkled in thought, nodding, "Da, da, da."

Even his own personal staff did not know why Stalin was saying "Yes, yes, yes," but they did see the orders that went forth marked ONLY BY SAFE HAND, and TO BE READ AND RETURNED, NOT RETAINED, and furthermore stamped FOR AUTHORIZED EYES ONLY AND UNDER NO CIRCUMSTANCES TO BE COPIED.

Into the true and secret Soviet budget that year by the direct personal order of a noncommittal Stalin an item was added for "Project Telescope." Stalin tolerated no inquiry, brooked no comment.

A village which had had a name became nameless.

A forest which had been opened to the workers and peasants became military territory.

Into the central post office in Kharkov there went a new box number for the *village of Ya. Ch.*

Rogov and Cherpas, comrades and lovers, scientists both and Russians both, disappeared from the everyday lives of their colleagues. Their faces were no longer seen at scientific meetings. Only rarely did they emerge.

On the few times they were seen, usually to and from Moscow at the time the All Union budget was made up each year, they seemed smiling and happy. But they did not make jokes.

What the outside world did not know was that Stalin in giving them their own project, granting them a paradise restricted to themselves, had seen to it that a snake went with them in the paradise. The snake this time was not one, but two personalities—Gausgofer and Gauck.

Stalin died.

Beria died too—less willingly.

The world went on.

Everything went into the forgotten village of Ya. Ch. and nothing came out.

It was rumored that Bulganin himself visited Rogov and Cherpas. It was even whispered that Bulganin said as he went to the Kharkov airport to fly back to Moscow, "It's big, big, big. There'll be no cold war if they do it. There won't be any war of any kind. We'll finish capitalism before the capitalists can ever begin to fight. If they do it. If they do it." Bulganin was reported to have shaken his head slowly in perplexity and to have said nothing more but to have put his initials on the unmodified budget of Project Telescope when a trusted messenger next brought him an envelope from Rogov.

Anastasia Cherpas became a mother. Their first boy looked like his father. He was followed by a little girl. Then another little boy. The children didn't stop Cherpas's work. They had a large dacha and trained nursemaids took over the household.

Every night the four of them dined together.

Rogov, Russian, humorous, courageous, amused.

Cherpas, older, more mature, more beautiful than ever but just as biting, just as cheerful, just as sharp as she had ever been.

But then the other two, the two who sat with them across the years of all their days, the two colleagues who had been visited upon them by the all-powerful word of Stalin himself.

Gausgofer was a female: bloodless, narrow-faced, with a voice like a horse's whinny. She was a scientist and a policewoman, and competent at both jobs. In 1917 she had reported her own mother's whereabouts to the Bolshevik Terror Committee. In 1924 she had commanded her father's execution. He had been a Russian German of the old Baltic nobility and he had tried to adjust his mind to the new system, but he had failed. In 1930 she had let her lover trust her a little too much. He had been a Romanian Communist, very high in the Party, but he had whispered into her ear in the privacy of their bedroom, whispered with the tears pouring down his face; she had listened affectionately and quietly and had delivered his words to the police the next morning.

With that she had come to Stalin's attention.

Stalin had been tough. He had addressed her brutally. "Comrade, you have some brains. I can see you know what Communism is all about. You understand loyalty. You're going to get ahead and serve the Party and the working class, but is that all you want?" He had spat the question at her.

She had been so astonished that she gaped.

The old man had changed his expression, favoring her with leering benevolence. He had put his forefinger on her chest. "Study science, Comrade. Study science. Communism plus science equals victory. You're too clever to stay in police work."

Gausgofer took a reluctant pride in the fiendish program of her German namesake, the wicked old geographer who made geography itself a terrible weapon in the Nazi anti-Soviet struggle.

Gausgofer would have liked nothing better than to intrude on the marriage of Cherpas and Rogov.

Gausgofer fell in love with Rogov the moment she saw him.

Gausgofer fell in hate—and hate can be as spontaneous and miraculous as love—with Cherpas the moment she saw *her*.

But Stalin had guessed that too.

With the bloodless, fanatic Gausgofer he had sent a man named B. Gauck.

Gauck was solid, impassive, blank-faced. In body he was about the same height as Rogov. Where Rogov was muscular, Gauck was flabby. Where Rogov's skin was fair and shot through with the pink and health of exercise, Gauck's skin was like stale lard, greasy, gray-green, sickly even on the best of days.

Gauck's eyes were black and small. His glance was as cold and sharp as death. Gauck had no friends, no enemies, no beliefs, no enthusiasm. Even Gausgofer was afraid of him.

Gauck never drank, never went out, never received mail, never sent mail, never spoke a spontaneous word. He was never rude, never kind, never friendly, never really withdrawn: he couldn't withdraw any more than the constant withdrawal of all his life.

Rogov had turned to his wife in the secrecy of their bedroom soon after Gausgofer and Gauck came and had said, "Anastasia, is that man sane?"

Cherpas intertwined the fingers of her beautiful, expressive hands. She who had been the wit of a thousand scientific meetings was now at a loss for words. She looked up at her husband with a troubled expression. "I don't know, Comrade . . . I just don't know . . ."

Rogov smiled his amused Slavic smile. "At the least then I don't think Gausgofer knows either."

Cherpas snorted with laughter and picked up her hairbrush. "That she doesn't. She really doesn't know, does she? I'll wager she doesn't even know to whom he reports."

That conversation had receded into the past. Gauck, Gausgofer, the bloodless eyes and the black eyes—they remained.

Every dinner the four sat down together.

Every morning the four met in the laboratory.

Rogov's great courage, high sanity, and keen humor kept the work going.

Cherpas's flashing genius fueled him whenever the routine overloaded his magnificent intellect.

Gausgofer spied and watched and smiled her bloodless smiles; sometimes, curiously enough, Gausgofer made genuinely constructive suggestions. She never understood the whole frame of reference of their work, but she knew enough of the mechanical and engineering details to be very useful on occasion.

Gauck came in, sat down quietly, said nothing, did nothing. He did not even smoke. He never fidgeted. He never went to sleep. He just watched.

The laboratory grew and with it there grew the immense configuration of the espionage machine.

In theory what Rogov had proposed and Cherpas seconded was imaginable. It consisted of an attempt to work out an integrated theory for all the electrical and radiation phenomena accompanying consciousness and to duplicate the electrical functions of mind without the use of animal material.

The range of potential products was immense.

The first product Stalin had asked for was a receiver, if possible, capable of tuning in the thoughts of a human mind and of translating those thoughts into either a punch-tape machine, an adapted German Hellschreiber machine, or phonetic speech. If the grids could be turned around and the brain-equivalent machine could serve not as a receiver but as a transmitter, it might be able to send out stunning forces which would paralyze or kill the process of thought.

At its best, Rogov's machine would be designed to confuse human thought over great distances, to select human targets to be confused, and to maintain an electronic jamming system which would jam straight into the human mind without the requirement of tubes or receivers.

He had succeeded—in part. He had given himself a violent headache in the first year of work.

In the third year he had killed mice at a distance of ten kilometers. In the seventh year he had brought on mass hallucinations and a wave of suicides in a neighboring village. It was this which impressed Bulganin.

Rogov was now working on the receiver end. No one had ever explored the infinitely narrow, infinitely subtle bands of radiation which distinguished one human mind from another, but Rogov was trying, as it were, to tune in on minds far away.

He had tried to develop a telepathic helmet of some kind, but it did not work. He had then turned away from the reception of pure thought to the reception of visual and auditory images. Where the nerve ends reached the brain itself he had managed over the years to distinguish whole pockets of microphenomena, and on some of these he had managed to get a fix.

With infinitely delicate tuning he had succeeded one day in picking up the eyesight of their second chauffeur and had managed, thanks to a needle thrust in just below his own right eyelid, to "see" through the other man's eyes as the other man, all unaware, washed their Zis limousine 1,600 meters away.

Cherpas had surpassed his feat later that winter and had managed to bring in an entire family having dinner over in a nearby city. She had invited B. Gauck to have a needle inserted into his cheekbone so that he could see with the eyes of an unsuspecting spied-on stranger. Gauck had refused any kind of needles, but Gausgofer had joined in the work.

The espionage machine was beginning to take form.

Two more steps remained. The first step consisted of tuning in on some remote target, such as the White House in Washington or the NATO Headquarters outside of Paris. The machine itself could obtain perfect intelligence by eavesdropping on the living minds of people far away.

The second problem consisted of finding a method of jamming those minds at a distance, stunning them so that the subject personnel fell into tears, confusion, or sheer insanity.

Rogov had tried, but he had never gotten more than thirty kilometers from the nameless village of Ya. Ch.

One November there had been seventy cases of hysteria, most of them ending in suicide, down in the city of Kharkov several hundred kilometers away, but Rogov was not sure that his own machine was doing it.

Comrade Gausgofer dared to stroke his sleeve. Her white lips smiled and her watery eyes grew happy as she said in her high, cruel voice, "*You* can do it, Comrade. You can do it."

Cherpas looked on with contempt. Gauck said nothing.

The female agent Gausgofer saw Cherpas's eyes upon her, and for a moment an arc of living hatred leapt between the two women.

The three of them went back to work on the machine.

Gauck sat on his stool and watched them.

The laboratory workers never talked very much and the room was quiet.

It was the year in which Eristratov died that the machine made a breakthrough. Eristratov died after the Soviet and People's democracies had tried to end the cold war with the Americans.

It was May. Outside the laboratory the squirrels ran among the trees. The leftovers from the night's rain dripped on the ground and kept the earth moist. It was comfortable to leave a few windows open and to let the smell of the forest into the workshop.

The smell of their oil-burning heaters and the stale smell of insulation, of ozone and the heated electronic gear was something with which all of them were much too familiar.

Rogov had found that his eyesight was beginning to suffer because he had to get the receiver needle somewhere near his optic nerve in order to obtain visual impressions from the machine. After months of experimentation with both animal and human subjects he had decided to copy one of their last experiments, successfully performed on a prisoner boy fifteen years of age, by having the needle slipped directly through the skull, up and behind the eye. Rogov had disliked using prisoners, because Gauck, speaking on behalf of security, always insisted that a prisoner used in experiments had to be destroyed in not less than five days from the beginning of the experiment. Rogov had satisfied himself that the skull-and-needle technique was safe, but he was very tired of trying to get frightened unscientific people to carry the load of intense, scientific attentiveness required by the machine.

Rogov recapitulated the situation to his wife and to their two strange colleagues.

Somewhat ill-humored, he shouted at Gauck, "Have you ever known what this is all about? You've been here years. Do you know what we're trying to do? Don't you ever want to take part in the experiments yourself? Do you realize how many years of mathematics have gone into the making of these grids and the calculation of these wave patterns? Are you good for anything?"

Gauck said, tonelessly and without anger, "Comrade Professor, I am obeying orders. You are obeying orders too. I've never impeded you."

Rogov almost raved. "I know you never got in my way. We're all good servants of the Soviet State. It's not a question of loyalty. It's a question of enthusiasm. Don't you ever want to glimpse the science we're making? We are a hundred years or a thousand years ahead of the capitalist Americans. Doesn't that excite you? Aren't you a human being? Why don't you take part? Will you understand me when I explain it?"

Gauck said nothing: he looked at Rogov with his beady eyes. His dirty-gray face did not change expression. Gausgofer exhaled loudly in a grotesquely feminine sigh of relief, but she too said nothing. Cherpas, her winning smile and her friendly eyes looking at her husband and two colleagues, said, "Go ahead, Nikolai. The comrade can follow if he wants to."

Gausgofer looked enviously at Cherpas. She seemed inclined to keep quiet, but then had to speak. She said, "Do go ahead, Comrade Professor."

Said Rogov, "*Kharosho*, I'll do what I can. The machine is now ready to receive minds over immense distances." He wrinkled his lip in amused scorn. "We may even spy into the brain of the chief rascal himself and find out what Eisenhower is planning to do today against the Soviet people. Wouldn't it be wonderful if our machine could stun him and leave him sitting addled at his desk?"

Gauck commented, "Don't try it. Not without orders."

Rogov ignored the interruption and went on. "First I receive. I don't know what I will get, who I will get, or where they will be. All I know is that this machine will reach out across all the minds of men and beasts now living and it will bring the eyes and ears of a single mind directly into mine. With the new needle going directly into the brain it will be possible for me to get a very sharp fixation of position. The trouble with that boy last week was that even though we knew he was seeing something outside of this room, he appeared to be getting sounds in a foreign language and did not know enough English or German to realize where or what the machine had taken him to see."

Cherpas laughed. "I'm not worried. I saw then it was safe. You go first, my husband. If our comrades don't mind—?"

Gauck nodded.

Gausgofer lifted her bony hand breathlessly up to her skinny throat and said, "Of course, Comrade Rogov, of course. You did *all* the work. You *must* be the first."

Rogov sat down.

A white-smocked technician brought the machine over to him. It was mounted on three rubber-tired wheels and it resembled the small X-ray units used by dentists. In place of the cone at the head of the X-ray machine there was a long, incredibly tough needle. It had been made for them by the best surgical-steel craftsmen in Prague.

Another technician came up with a shaving bowl, a brush, and a straight razor. Under the gaze of Gauck's deadly eyes he shaved an area four centimeters square on the top of Rogov's head.

Cherpas herself then took over. She set her husband's head in the clamp and used a micrometer to get the skullfittings so tight and so clear that the needle would push through the dura mater at exactly the right point.

All this work she did deftly with kind, very strong fingers. She was gentle, but she was firm. She was his wife, but she was also his fellow scientist and his fellow colleague in the Soviet State.

She stepped back and looked at her work. She gave him one of their own very special smiles, the secret gay smiles which they usually exchanged with each other only when they were alone. "You won't want to do this every day. We're going to have to find some way of getting into the brain without using this needle. But it won't hurt you."

"Does it matter if it does hurt?" said Rogov. "This is the triumph of all our work. *Bring it down.*"

Gausgofer looked as though she would like to be invited to take part in the experiment, but she dared not interrupt Cherpas. Cherpas, her eyes gleaming with attention, reached over and pulled down the handle, which brought the tough needle to within a tenth of a millimeter of the right place.

Rogov spoke very carefully. "All I felt was a little sting. You can turn the power on now."

Gausgofer could not contain herself. Timidly she addressed Cherpas. "May *I* turn on the power?"

Cherpas nodded. Gauck watched. Rogov waited. Gausgofer pulled down the bayonet switch.

The power went on.

With an impatient twist of her hand, Anastasia Cherpas ordered the laboratory attendants to the other end of the room. Two or three of them had stopped working and were staring at Rogov, staring like dull sheep. They looked embarrassed and then they huddled in a white-smocked herd at the other end of the laboratory.

The wet May wind blew in on all of them. The scent of forest and leaves was about them.

The three watched Rogov.

Rogov's complexion began to change. His face became flushed. His breathing was so loud and heavy they could hear it several meters away. Cherpas fell on her knees in front of him, eyebrows lifted in mute inquiry.

Rogov did not dare nod, not with a needle in his brain. He said through flushed lips, speaking thickly and heavily, "Do—not—stop—now."

Rogov himself did not know what was happening. He thought he might see an American room, or a Russian room, or a tropical colony. He might see palm trees, or forests, or desks. He might see guns or buildings, washrooms or beds, hospitals, homes, churches. He might see with the eyes of a child, a woman, a man, a soldier, a philosopher, a slave, a worker, a savage, a religious one, a Communist, a reactionary, a governor, a policeman. He might hear voices; he might hear English, or French, or Russian, Swahili, Hindu, Malay, Chinese, Ukrainian, Armenian, Turkish, Greek. He did not know.

Something strange was happening.

It *seemed* to him that he had left the world, that he had left time. The hours and the centuries shrank up as the meters and the machine, unchecked, reached out for the most powerful signal which any humankind had transmitted. Rogov did not know it, but the machine had conquered time.

The machine reached the dance, the human challenger, and the dance festival of the year that was not A.D. 13,582, but which might have been.

Before Rogov's eyes the golden shape and the golden steps shook and fluttered in a ritual a thousand times more compelling than hypnotism. The rhythms meant nothing and everything to him. This was Russia, this was Communism. This was his life—indeed it was his soul acted out before his very eyes.

For a second, the last second of his ordinary life, he looked through flesh-and-blood eyes and saw the shabby woman whom he had once thought beautiful. He saw Anastasia Cherpas, and he did not care.

His vision concentrated once again on the dancing image, this woman, those postures, that dance!

Then the sound came in—music which would have made a Tchaikovsky weep, orchestras which would have silenced Shostakovich or Khachaturian forever, so much did it surpass the music of the twentieth century.

The people-who-were-not-people between the stars had taught mankind many arts. Rogov's mind was the best of its time, but his time was far, far behind the time of the great dance. With that one vision Rogov went firmly and completely mad. He became blind to the sight of Cherpas, Gausgofer, and Gauck. He forgot the village of Ya. Ch. He forgot himself. He was like a fish, bred in stale fresh water, which is thrown for the first time into a living stream. He was like an insect emerging from the chrysalis. His twentieth-century mind could not hold the imagery and the impact of the music and the dance.

But the needle was there and the needle transmitted into his mind more than his mind could stand.

The synapses of his brain flicked like switches. The future flooded into him.

He fainted. Cherpas leapt forward and lifted the needle. Rogov fell out of the chair.

It was Gauck who got the doctors. By nightfall they had Rogov resting comfortably and under heavy sedation. There were two doctors, both from the military headquarters. Gauck had obtained authorization for their services by dint of a direct telephone call to Moscow.

Both the doctors were annoyed. The senior one never stopped grumbling at Cherpas.

"You should not have done it, Comrade Cherpas. Comrade Rogov should not have done it either. You can't go around sticking things into brains. That's a medical problem. None of you people are doctors of medicine. It's all right for you to contrive devices with the prisoners, but you can't inflict things like this on Soviet scientific personnel. I'm going to get blamed because I can't bring Rogov back. You heard what he was saying. All he did was mutter, 'That golden shape on the golden steps, that music, that me is a true me, that golden shape, that golden shape, I want to be with that golden shape,' and rubbish like that. Maybe you've ruined a first-class brain forever—" He stopped himself short as though he had said too much. After all, the problem was a security problem and apparently both Gauck and Gausgofer represented the security agencies.

Gausgofer turned her watery eyes on the doctor and said in a low, even, unbelievably poisonous voice, "Could *she* have done it, Comrade Doctor?"

The doctor looked at Cherpas, answering Gausgofer. "How? You were there. I wasn't. *How* could she have done it? *Why* should she do it? You were there."

Cherpas said nothing. Her lips were compressed tight with grief. Her yellow hair gleamed, but her hair was all that remained, at that moment, of her beauty. She was frightened and she was getting ready to be sad. She had no time to hate foolish women or to worry about security; she was concerned with her colleague, her lover, her husband, Rogov.

There was nothing much for them to do except to wait. They went into a large room and tried to eat.

The servants had laid out immense dishes of cold sliced meat, pots of caviar, and an assortment of sliced breads, pure butter, genuine coffee, and liquors.

None of them ate much.

They were all waiting.

At 9:15 the sound of rotors beat against the house.

The big helicopter had arrived from Moscow.

Higher authorities took over.

The higher authority was a deputy minister, a man by the name of V. Karper.

Karper was accompanied by two or three uniformed colonels, by an engineer civilian, by a man from the headquarters of the Communist Party of the Soviet Union, and by two doctors.

They dispensed with the courtesies. Karper merely said, "You are Cherpas. I have met you. You are Gausgofer. I have seen your reports. You are Gauck."

The delegation went into Rogov's bedroom. Karper snapped, "Wake him."

The military doctor who had given him sedatives said, "Comrade, you mustn't—"

Karper cut him off. "Shut up." He turned to his own physician, pointed at Rogov. "Wake him up."

The doctor from Moscow talked briefly with the senior military doctor. He too began shaking his head. He gave Karper a disturbed look. Karper guessed what he might hear. He said, "Go ahead. I know there is some danger to the patient, but I've got to get back to Moscow with a report."

The two doctors worked over Rogov. One of them asked for his bag and gave Rogov an injection. Then all of them stood back from the bed.

Rogov writhed in his bed. He squirmed. His eyes opened, but he did not see them. With childishly clear and simple words Rogov began to talk: ". . . that golden shape, the golden stairs, the music, take me back to the music, I want to be with the music, I really am the music . . ." and so on in an endless monotone.

Cherpas leaned over him so that her face was directly in his line of vision. "My darling! My darling, wake up. This is serious."

It was evident to all of them that Rogov did not hear her, because he went on muttering about golden shapes.

For the first time in many years Gauck took the initiative. He spoke directly to the man from Moscow, Karper. "Comrade, may I make a suggestion?"

Karper looked at him. Gauck nodded at Gausgofer. "We were both sent here by orders of Comrade Stalin. She is senior. She bears the responsibility. All I do is double-check."

The deputy minister turned to Gausgofer. Gausgofer had been staring at Rogov on the bed; her blue, watery eyes were tearless and her face was drawn into an expression of extreme tension.

Karper ignored that and said to her firmly, clearly, commandingly, "What do you recommend?"

Gausgofer looked at him very directly and said in a measured voice, "I do not think that the case is one of brain damage. I believe that he has obtained a communication which he must share with another human being and that unless one of us follows him there may be no answer."

Karper barked, "Very well. But what do we do?"

"Let *me* follow—into the machine."

Anastasia Cherpas began to laugh slyly and frantically. She seized Karper's arm and pointed her finger at Gausgofer. Karper stared at her.

Cherpas slowed down her laughter and shouted at Karper, "The woman's mad. She has loved my husband for many years. She had hated my presence, and now she thinks that she can save him. She thinks that she can follow. She thinks that he wants to communicate with her. That's ridiculous. I will go myself!"

Karper looked about. He selected two of his staff and stepped over into a corner of the room. They could hear him talking, but they could not distinguish the words. After a conference of six or seven minutes he returned.

"You people have been making serious security charges against each other. I find that one of our finest weapons, the mind of Rogov, is damaged. Rogov's not just a man. He is a Soviet project." Scorn entered his voice. "I find that the senior security officer, a policewoman with a notable record, is charged by another Soviet scientist with a silly infatuation. I disregard such charges. The development of the Soviet State and the work of Soviet science cannot be impeded by personalities. Comrade Gausgofer will follow. I am acting tonight because my own staff physician says that Rogov may not live and it is very important for us to find out just what has happened to him and why."

He turned his baneful gaze on Cherpas. "You will not protest, Comrade. Your mind is the property of the Russian State. Your life and your education have been paid for by the workers. You cannot throw these things away because of personal sentiment. If there is anything to be found Comrade Gausgofer will find it for both of us."

The whole group of them went back into the laboratory. The frightened technicians were brought over from the barracks. The lights were turned on and the windows were closed. The May wind had become chilly.

The needle was sterilized.

The electronic grids were warmed up.

Gausgofer's face was an impassive mask of triumph as she sat in the receiving chair. She smiled at Gauck as an attendant brought the soap and the razor to shave a clean patch on her scalp.

Gauck did not smile back. His black eyes stared at her. He said nothing. He did nothing. He watched.

Karper walked to and fro, glancing from time to time at the hasty but orderly preparation of the experiment.

Anastasia Cherpas sat down at a laboratory table about five meters away from the group. She watched the back of Gausgofer's head as the needle was lowered. She buried her face in her hands. Some of the others thought they heard her weeping, but no one heeded Cherpas very much. They were too intent on watching Gausgofer.

Gausgofer's face became red. Perspiration poured down the flabby cheeks. Her fingers tightened on the arm of her chair.

Suddenly she shouted at them, "*That golden shape on the golden steps.*"

She leapt to her feet, dragging the apparatus with her.

No one had expected this. The chair fell to the floor. The needle holder, lifted from the floor, swung its weight sidewise. The needle twisted like a scythe in Gausgofer's brain. Neither Rogov nor Cherpas had ever expected a struggle within the chair. *They did not know that they were going to tune in on* A.D. *13,582.*

The body of Gausgofer lay on the floor, surrounded by excited officials.

Karper was acute enough to look around at Cherpas.

She stood up from the laboratory table and walked toward him. A thin line of blood flowed down from her cheekbone. Another line of blood dripped down from a position on her cheek, one and a half centimeters forward of the opening of her left ear.

With tremendous composure, her face as white as fresh snow, she smiled at him. "I eavesdropped."

Karper said, "What?"

"I eavesdropped, eavesdropped," repeated Anastasia Cherpas. "I found out where my husband has gone. It is not somewhere in this world. It is something hypnotic beyond all the limitations of our science. We have made a great gun, but the gun has fired upon us before we could fire it. You may think you will change my mind, Comrade Deputy Minister, but you will not.

"I know what has happened. My husband is never coming back. And I am not going any further forward without him.

"Project Telescope is finished. You may try to get someone else to finish it, but you will not."

Karper stared at her and then turned aside.

Gauck stood in his way.

"What do you want?" snapped Karper.

"To tell you," said Gauck very softly, "to tell you, Comrade Deputy Minister, that Rogov is gone as she says he is gone, that she is finished if she says she is finished, that all this is true. I know."

Karper glared at him. "How do you know?"

Gauck remained utterly impassive. With superhuman assurance and perfect calm he said to Karper, "Comrade, I do not dispute the matter. I know these people, though I do not know their science. Rogov is done for."

At last Karper believed him. Karper sat down in a chair beside a table. He looked up at his staff. "Is it possible?"

No one answered.

"I ask you, is it possible?"

They all looked at Anastasia Cherpas, at her beautiful hair, her determined blue eyes, and the two thin lines of blood where she had eavesdropped with small needles.

Karper turned to her. "What do we do now?"

For an answer she dropped to her knees and began sobbing, "No, no, not Rogov! No, no, not Rogov!"

And that was all that they could get out of her. Gauck looked on.

On the golden steps in the golden light, a golden shape danced a dream beyond the limits of all imagination, danced and drew the music to herself until a sigh of yearning, yearning which became a hope and a torment, went through the hearts of living things on a thousand worlds.

Edges of the golden scene faded raggedly and unevenly into black. The gold dimmed down to a pale gold-silver sheen and then to silver, last of all to white. The dancer who had been golden was now a forlorn white-pink figure standing, quiet and fatigued, on the immense white steps. The applause of a thousand worlds roared in upon her.

She looked blindly at them. The dance had overwhelmed her too. Their applause could mean nothing. The dance was an end in itself. She would have to live, somehow, until she danced again.

IN A PETRI DISH UPSTAIRS

George Turner

George Turner is the dean of Australian sf writers, a serious Australian novelist who turned to science fiction writing in the late 1970s after establishing a reputation as a fearsome and knowledgeable critic of the genre. His bent is Campbellian, but his execution is contoured by deeply held moral convictions and his life as a contemporary novelist. Ursula K. Le Guin's work of the sixties and seventies is perhaps the most important influence on his science fiction writing (as Stanislaw Lem is on his criticism), but his roots lie deep in decades of reading the genre before he began writing sf. His first sf novel, *Beloved Son* (1978), involves interstellar travel, a postholocaust civilization in the twenty-first century, and genetic engineering—this last has remained one of the principal concerns of his fiction in recent works such as *The Sea and Summer* (1987—a.k.a. *Drowning Towers*), *Brain Child* (1991), and *The Destiny Makers* (1993). His future societies have a satisfying complexity, portraying class conflict and economic disparities in a gritty, realistic fashion absent from most American sf.

"In a Petri Dish Upstairs" is set at an earlier time in the same future world as *Beloved Son* and its sequels, *Vaneglory* (1981) and *Yesterday's Men* (1983). Turner considers a situation similar to that in Ing's "Down and Out on Ellfive Prime": a human satellite culture evolving in nearby space environments with a need to break free of the domination of groundlings. But while American sf sees space as simply the new frontier, Turner, the Australian, envisions it as an alien place with a strange and different culture, one with its own moral imperatives and structures—as he envisions the future on Earth as operating under other moral structures different from ours today.

Evolution has always been one of the underlying ideas of hard sf, and so sf has developed a spectrum of conventional isolated environments (the space colony, the generational spaceship, the domed city), all images of enclosed worlds where evolution may be isolated and examined. The latest of these is "cyberspace," the internal world of computer space, posited by William Gibson in his cyberpunk fiction (see "Johnny Mnemonic"). Other interesting comparisons and contrasts include Asimov's "Waterclap" (both the space colony and the domed city under the sea), and Heinlein's "It's Great to Be Back" (space colonies as the next step in the evolution of human society).

When, some fifty years after the Plagues and The Collapse, Alastair Dunwoodie put the first Solar Power Station into synchronous orbit over Melbourne Town—that is, some 38,000 kilometers above it—no warning angel tapped his shoulder to whisper, "You have created a fresh culture and rung the knell of an old one."

It would have been told to mind its own celestial business. With solar power now gathered by the immense space mirrors and microbeamed to Earth for network distribution, the Golden Age was appreciably closer. With a Station in Heaven, all was right with the world.

Remarkably soon there were seventeen Power Stations in orbit above strategic distribution points around the world, sufficient for the needs of a planet no longer crawling with the famined, resource-consuming life of the Twentieth Century. The Plagues and The Collapse and yet less pleasant events had thinned the problem.

Dunwoodie was a builder, not a creator; his ideas had been mooted in the 1970s, some eight years before, but had not come to fruition when The Collapse intervened. It was, however, notable that even in those days, when social studies of crowding and isolation had been to the fore, nobody seemed to have considered what changes might occur among the first people to live out their lives in a steel cylinder in space.

And not for a further eighty years after the launching did the Custodian of Public Safety of Melbourne Town begin to consider it—when, for the first time in three generations, an Orbiter proposed to visit Earth. When he had arrived at the vagueness of a possible decision, he visited the Mayor.

"Do you mean to give a civic reception for this brat?"

The Mayor of Melbourne Town was unenthusiastic. "It's an event, of sorts. A reception will let Orbiter vanity preen while it keeps the Town's society belles from claiming they weren't allowed to meet him. I hear he's a good looking lad."

The Custodian seemed uninterested in that.

The Mayor asked at last, "But why? After three generations they send a youngster—nineteen, I believe—to visit. What do they want? Why a boy?"

"A boy on a man's errand, you think?"

The Mayor's expression asked, *Why are you wasting my time?* and he waited for explanation.

The Custodian went at it obliquely. "The Global Ethic," he said, "the Ethic of Non-Interference—do you ever question it?"

The Mayor was a very young man, the Custodian an old and dangerously experienced one. The Mayor went sharply on guard but his expression remained as bland as his answer: "Why should I? It works."

The Custodian's authority outweighed the Mayor's—Mayoral duties were social rather than gubernatorial—but he had no overt power to punish. But advancement could be blocked or privilege curtailed without open defiance of the Ethic as it operated on Departmental levels.

The Custodian surprised him. "You should, James; you should question continuously. Particularly morals, conventions, habits, regulations—and ethics. The older and more ingrained, the more questionable."

Stiffly, "Those are matters for Global League delegates."

The Custodian grinned like a friendly skull. "You needn't be so damned careful; I want your help, not your scalp. Review some facts." He flicked a raised finger. "First: the Power Stations as originally flown were rotated about the long axis to afford peripheral gravity." Another finger. "Second: when the final Stations were flown, the seventeen formed themselves into the Orbital League." Third finger. "Then they made unreasonable demands for luxuries, surplus wealth, cultural artifacts and civic privilege under threat of throttling down the power beams. That was seventy years back."

"School is a year or two behind me," said the Mayor coldly, "but basic history remains familiar."

"I'm selecting facts, not lecturing." Fourth finger. "So the Global Council of the time authorized use of a remote-action energy blind, a—call it a weapon—

whose existence had not been publicly known. The Orbiters threatened our microbeams, so *we* blinded the internal power systems of Station One from a single projector in Melbourne Town. After a week of staling air, falling temperature and fouling water they cried quits and—" fifth finger "—the Orbital League has made no such further error since."

"So for once the Ethic was ignored."

"Oh, but it wasn't. We took suitable action, harming no one seriously, to preserve the status quo. That was all."

The Mayor said, "It was *not* all. The Stations had been earning extra revenue with their null-g factories—perfect ball bearings, perfectly formed crystals and so on. Earth stopped buying, limiting Orbiter income to the Power Charter allocation. That was reprisal and un-Ethical."

"Earth protected herself against wealthy Stations accumulating the means of further blackmail."

The Mayor was contemptuous. "Semantic drivel."

"It was a Council decision. Do you dispute it?"

"Yes," said the Mayor and waited for an ax to fall.

"Good, good, good! So you see, the bloody Ethic means whatever you need it to mean."

The Mayor retained caution. "Most realize that, privately. Still, it works."

"Because *laissez faire* has become part of our cultural mentality. But what of the cultural mentality Upstairs?"

"Well, we know they have developed non-Terrene conventions and behavior. There's been little physical contact since they cut themselves off."

"Quite so."

Silence dragged while the Mayor wondered had he said more than he knew. What the Orbiters had done was to stop the rotation of the Stations and give themselves over to a null-g existence. When you thought of it, why not? To live in utter physical freedom, to fly, to leap, to glide, to dispose for ever of the burden of the body . . . the wonder was that they had waited so long to grasp delight.

It followed that the first generation born in space was cut off from Earth. Once muscle structure and metabolism had settled into null-g conditions, exposure to gravity became inconceivable, possibly disastrous . . . ahh!

"This young man, this Peter Marrian—how will he deal with weight? Power-assist harness?"

"I must tell you about that," said the Custodian. "You'll be fascinated . . ."

The no-nonsense Orbiters preserved no fairy tales from their Earthly heritage but they had formulated a few austere anecdotes for the very young. One concerned a supervirile Orbiter who married a Terrene heiress and brought her home to live in orbit.

Peter heard the tale when he was not quite three and already absorbing Orbiter lore with a mind the commune nurses noted, in their giggly fashion, as destined for Upper Crust privilege.

"—then, when he'd defeated all the schemes of the rich girl's wicked father, he joined with her in a church as they do Downstairs. Then he brought her to the Station with all her riches and the Commune Fathers awarded him such extra privileges that he lived happily ever after."

It did not occur to him then (or later, for that matter) to ask how *she* lived ever after. His interest was in the early part of the story, which told how the young Orbiter became big and powerful in order to face the monstrous Terrene weapon, Gravity. Now, how was that accomplished?

He spat at the nurses who said he would understand when he was older. They had no idea, for they were only thirdwomen and not educated beyond their needs, and such rearing facilities did not then exist. But soon would.

Such facilities, *all* facilities, cost money. The Commune's only money-wealth was the cynically limited income derived from the Power Charter, kept at a "reasonable minimum." The Orbiters were welcome to pride and null-g freedom—at a suitably cheap rate.

The first generation had tried blackmail and learned a rapid lesson.

The second generation had reasoned that conditions were humiliating rather than unbearable—and in fact provided much which Earth could not—and could be endured until better opportunity offered. The important thing was to acquire money with which to buy—well, facilities.

By the third generation the Commune Fathers had grown longer sighted and the first cheeseparingly sequestered funds were being transformed into a huge centrifuge at about the time young Peter asked his question. Cutting gravity and so cutting culturally loose from Earth had been a fine gesture but there could be advantage in a squad of Orbiters who could move comfortably on Earth's surface. And recommencing rotation was out of the question for the older folk.

"I hate it!"—shrieked and repeated to exhaustion—was the reaction of Peter, aged four, to his first experience of the centrifuge. Even the fiddling 0.2 g was outrage to a physique which had come to terms with mass and inertia but knew nothing of weight, nor wished to.

On the second day, after a bout of desperate clinging to the doorgrip, he was allowed out after ten minutes, bellowing, while the thirdwomen giggled at his aggressiveness. It would be a useful trait in the future planned for him.

After a fortnight of systematic lengthening of his daily accustomization—allowing internal organs to realign gently to a vertically weighted structure—increase of the g factor began. His rages evolved into arrogant self-confidence as the psychlinicians worked with cold devotion on the boy's emotional fabric.

At age six he lived most of his day in the centrifuge, a series of belts round the internal circumference of the Station and large enough to accommodate a considerable cadre now that a method had been established. With his weight at 0.5 g (he was the only one as yet on the fastest belt) he looked forward, under psychological prodding, to greater conquests. Signs of muscular shape, as distinct from subcutaneous muscular structure, were discernible.

The Commune Fathers allotted him the personal name of "Marrian"—a joke of sorts, and their first mistake.

"Since the Orbiters set aside wedlock and the family system, second names have been allotted on a descriptive basis, focusing on job or personal attributes. What does Marrian describe?"

The Mayor had been, as promised, fascinated by the facts but more intrigued by the Custodian's possession of them. "I'm sure I don't know, and I know even less how you came by this knowledge. You have excellent informants."

"If you mean spies," the Custodian said comfortably, "say spies. I haven't any really. Only shuttle pilots and a few delivery agents visit the Stations, but their tattle and observations add up to this and that."

"So they penetrated the nurseries to learn bedtime stories and discovered the centrifuge nobody else knows about—and didn't, er, *tattle* even to their best friends?"

"Well, they told *me*."

"They thought bedtime stories worth a custodial report, these most unofficial agents?"

"Perhaps I should admit to some literary license in fleshing out the picture." The Mayor, played with, shrugged and was silent. "Am I so inept? Must I tell the truth?"

Administrative secrets can be slippery, but curiosity had carried the Mayor too far for retreat. "It would help," he said coldly and the Custodian's instant grin warned him that he shared the pool with a shark.

"The Power Stations talk to each other. I listen. I don't hear deadly secrets, for they aren't stupid. Only occasional indiscretions and errors come my way. It has taken fifteen years to form a picture from scraps."

"They talk in clear?"

"By line of sight laser."

The Mayor saw appalling involvements opening but the hook was in his jaws. "Transceivers would be shielded, and you can't tap into a laser beam undetected."

"Who can't?"

It was not really a shock, only one more privacy violated by nameless men. The Custodian offered a spin-off comment: "The intention of the Ethic is preserved by continuous distortion of the letter."

"Semantics!" But the repetition was halfhearted.

"The price of language. Now you know some secrets. There's a price on those also."

"Which I pay at once?"

"There is an action to be taken and I must not be implicated. Public Safety must not seem interested in Orbiter affairs. Less obvious people are needed—like those uniformless couriers of yours who fix giddy-gossipy eyes on Town affairs and keep you informed of the social fluxes you so gently do not seem to guide."

The Mayor said uncomfortably, "I rarely interfere—"

"But how could you? The Ethic, the Ethic! But I want to share your knowledge of everything Peter Marrian does on Earth and every word he speaks here."

"My boys aren't equipped—"

"They will be. Sensitized clothing and sound crystals at the roots of the hair. They'll be walking audio-cameras."

"This is all you want?"

"For the moment."

There it was, the—no, not "veiled threat," but . . . that phrase the pre-Collapsers had used . . . the "rain check" taken out on him. "Am I to know what we are looking for?"

"The reason for Peter Marrian's visit."

A part of the Mayor's very considerable intelligence had been worrying at the question since first mention of the name and had reached a conclusion. He thought, In for a credit in for a bust, and said, "But we know that, don't we?"

The Custodian smiled, at last like a man rather than a skull. "We do?"

"The Orbiters, if what formal communication we have with them is a reliable guide, have developed lazy habits of speech. They drop unnecessary final consonants, like *g* and *f* and *h*—sendin, mysel, strengt. Peter Marrian's name refers to his job, but has been misunderstood. Peter Marrying."

The Custodian laughed like a madman. "Do you imagine they'd waste resources preparing a brat to come Downstairs to get married? They don't even recognize marriage."

"But we do. And isn't that the whole point of the bedtime story?"

The Custodian calmed abruptly. "You'll do. It took me several years to realize that. The reason for it all?"

"Money. If you can't earn it, marry it. All Orbiter property is, I believe, communal."

"Good, good. And so?"

"This visit is, perhaps, exploratory, perhaps the opening move in an Orbiter campaign for . . ." He trailed off. "For what?"

The Custodian stood to go. "That is what I asked the Global Council to consider. They are still considering. Meanwhile it is up to you and me to see that Peter Marryin, however often best man, is never the groom."

It was unfortunately true that the Custodian's information derived mainly from Orbiter indiscretions and errors. Much escaped him entirely; much was filled in only after the affair was over.

He did not know, for instance, that Peter Marryin's face was not wholly his own. Orbiter technicians, observing the TV shows of Melbourne Town's entertainment idols (whom they despised utterly) with special attention to those who brought the young groveling in ill-concealed sexual hysteria, spent two years designing the face; surgeons spent a further two creating it. The result was coldly calculated to turn the heads and raise the blood pressures of a prognosticated 90 percent of Melbourne Town females between the ages of thirteen and thirty—a carnally desirable young lout with something for everybody and a dedication to its use.

Such thoroughness would have scared the Custodial wits out of him, more so if he had realized that the target had been narrowed to this one city on Earth.

Peter should have gone to Earth when he was eighteen, in that era an ideal age for a beginner at wiving, but the Commune Fathers were a committee and had fallen into the committee traps of indecision, vacillation and name-calling without in nearly twelve months selecting a plump enough fly for their spider.

There were too many possibilities. One of the more disastrous outcomes of the planetary Ethic of Non-Interference had seen economic expertise, enhanced by psychelectronics, carve obese fortunes out of the reindustrialized planet; young heiresses were available in a wealthy world where small families were still the cautious habit of a species which had once already come within an ace of starving itself to death.

The Commune bickerings had ended with the death of old Festus Grant, right under their feet, in Melbourne Town. In wonderment they totaled the fabulous holdings—Rare Metals Research, Lunar Constructions, Ecological Rehabilitation and Exploitation, Monopole Ramjets, Mini-Shuttles Corporation, Sol-Atmos Research and Reclamation and more, more, more—the list rang louder bells for them than all the Jesus Cult cathedrals in history.

And all—all—all went to Claire Grant, only child of the dead widower.

The haste with which they groomed, briefed and dispatched the casually confident Peter was worse than indecent; it was comic and contemptible. And thorough.

At nineteen the boy had all the traditional Orbiter contempt for Earthworms, amplified by the hundreds of teleplays he had been forced to watch in order to become familiar with customs, speech idioms and etiquette. (He still did not really understand their drama; third generation Orbiters were unable to comprehend the preoccupations and philosophies of people not reared in a steel tube.) He had also an instilled awareness of being a cultural hero in embryo, the bedtime-story-boy who lived happily ever after in a swagger of privilege.

By Terrene standards he was paranoid (by Orbiter standards arrogant) but had been coached in adapting his responses to an Earthworm norm. The coaching, brilliant in its fashion, allowed insufficiently for unpredictable encounters (encounters were rarely unpredictable in an Orbiter tube) and the shuttle was scarcely spaceborne before his furies stirred to Earthworm insolence.

The pilot was a jokey type, all bonhomie and loud mouth, saying, "You'll find old Earth heavy going, feller," and laughing madly at his obscure pun based on an idiom not in use Upstairs—one which sounded to Peter like a mannerless criticism. And: "Watch the women, boy! They'll *weight* for you to *fall* for them. Get it? *Weight* for you to—"

"I get it, thank you. Now mind your own damn business and watch your disgustin tongue."

"Hey, now!"

The copilot dug him in the ribs to shut him up and grinned sympathetically at Peter, who interpreted the grin as zoological observation of the freak from Upstairs and returned a glare of rage. The copilot shrugged, adding fuel to a conviction of insulting pity.

The fool at the landing field, who mocked his strength by offering to carry his luggage, was saved from assault only by a memory of teleplays showing the planetary obsession with menialism—free intelligences actually *offering* service! He relinquished the bags with contempt and began to focus his accelerating dislike for things Terrene on the unfortunate girl he had been reared to meet. *She* was responsible for the shame and insult he must bear in the course of duty.

In his anger he forgot even his irrational fear that Earth gravity would be mysteriously different from his experience in the centrifuge—that "real" weight would be something else. By the time he noticed that it was not he had calmed sufficiently to go through the mental balancing routine laid down for him by the Orbiter psychlinicians.

It was an excellent routine, devised by men who knew more about his mind than he ever could. By evening he was ready—"debonair" was the word he favored—to face the Reception at the Town Hall, the first in line of the haunts of the rich bitches. The Grant had better be there; he was not in dawdling mood.

It was the Mayor, now, who sat in the Custodian's office; the audio-crystals and the transcripts Englished from them were politically too touchy to risk outside a secured area. The tape they had heard had been prepared from a crystal lodged at the root of a hair on the head of a shuttle copilot. How the Mayor had achieved that, far outside his sphere of authority, the Custodian had the good taste not to ask; he was certain that this young man would go far and successfully.

"An unpleasant little shit," he said.

The Mayor (who, if age were the only factor, could have been the Custodian's great-grandson) was beginning to feel at home with the old exhibitionist. "I think that the Orbiters are what we have made them."

"Yes. Be properly glum about it."

"If he looks like bringing off a marriage—"

The Custodian said harshly, "He won't."

"But if?"

"Very well—if?"

"We might engineer small events, derogatory to his self-esteem, to push him past his restraints, allow him to erupt in public scenes which will make him socially unacceptable. Then we could look down our official noses and send him back Upstairs with a complaint of his behavior."

The Custodian laughed and asked, "Are you ambitious?"

"In two years I will be thirty and no longer eligible for minor civil office. If I am not selected for a further Supervisory career I must fall back on commerce. The last Mayor of Melbourne Town is now a factory hand. This youth-decade in Social Administration can be a trap for the unprepared."

"I wouldn't worry too much."

They understood each other exactly.

But they did not understand Orbiters at all. Deny how they might, they shared in the recesses of their minds the common opinion that Oribiters were peculiar, backward and hardly to be taken seriously. In a perilously easygoing culture the problems of underdogs—their sense of grievance and drive, not for equality but for revenge—were little comprehended on realistic levels.

Nor did either understand the drive for achievement latent in a moneyed nonentity. They had thought, when assessing the field, that Peter would certainly be snatched up by the glamour crowd, and little Cinderella Claire lost in the crush.

The hall was crowded. Not, of course, that one cared a damn for the barbarian Orbiters or their peculiar tribalisms, but one was justified in observing a Social Curiosity.

Among the crowd Festus Grant's daughter was strung taut, breathless at her own projected daring, at what she intended to do tonight. When this ball was over she would be the envy of the smart set, even a center of scandal, but for once she would have shone as "the girl who dared."

She was a social nobody and knew it. She would, at age nineteen in a year's time, attain her majority and control of the greatest fortune in Australasia, but that meant nothing to the Pleasured Classes; after a certain number of millions money became an environment rather than a possession and simple quantity no ground for eminence.

That she was intelligent, good-hearted and socially more willing than able counted not at all against her plain features, washed-out eyes and too-plump figure. The physical defects could have been surgically corrected but among the Pleasured Classes this was Not Done; the struggling masses might falsify and pretend but One Was Above That.

Worse, she lacked taste. She was wickedly overdressed—with too much jewelry, a too blatantly fantastic hair arrangement, a dress too brightly red and too ornate and—and without the subtlety of choice which could subtract and adjust and transform her into what she wished to be.

All she had was useless money. She was accustomed to the attentions of men who pursued her prospects rather than herself and, as one who could buy any number of husbands, despised men who could be bought.

She danced with one of them to pass the time. *He* would not appear until just before the Protocol Dance, the fourth. While the eager young man found her unresponsive, in her mind she rehearsed her move. As the richest heiress present (and this was a point of etiquette wherein money *did* count) she would automatically take place next to the Lady Mayoress and be the second person presented. If *He* had been married, some wealthy matron would have been in the place of opportunity; it paid to know the rules and to be prepared to use them.

Color and sound died as the orchestrator left the keyboard, and she rid herself of the eager young man.

When at last *He* arrived—he was anticlimactic.

Secretly she had hoped against common sense for something strange, exotic (so, secretly, had they all), an outworld fantastication of dress, an oddity of manner or unexpectedness of appearance—

—anything but the too-ordinary pale and slender young man, in commonplace

Terrene attire, who hesitated at the door as if taken with yokel surprise at the spectacle of Melbourne Town's Pleasured Class frozen in the half-bow and half-curtsy of welcoming protocol, then came uncertainly down the hall, guided by the traditional Visitor's Escort of Police Controller and Aide, whose dress uniforms outshone him utterly.

He was a mistake, a nothing. Her scandalous resolution lapsed; he was not worth it.

Then he came close. The escort fell back as he halted the correct four paces from the Mayor. At least, she thought, he had been coached in the observances. The Mayor stepped forward and the Orbiter lifted his face to the light.

Disappointment vanished before the most vitally handsome man she had ever seen. He was the epitome, the gathering, the expression of every media star and public idol who had ever roused her fantasies. He was The Orbiter—unearthly.

She scarcely heard the formal exchange; she ached to have done with it and with the visitor's formal round of the floor with the Lady Mayoress, so that she . . .

Peter bowed to the Lady Mayoress as the introduction was made, but the matron did not offer her arm.

They talked.

With the orchestrator's hands poised, waiting, over the keys—they talked.

Claire was furious. The woman was waiving the protocol of the first dance. Orbiters might be socially backward, but this was diplomatic insult.

Then the Mayoress took a pace back, terminating the exchange, and still the orchestrator waited on the Mayor's signal.

Claire saw a faint uncertainty in the Orbiter's fixed smile and knew that this was the moment. A public prank became an act of rescue.

She stepped quickly forward and he, perceiving the movement, half turned to her. She made the formal half-curtsy, knew she did it awkwardly and cared not a damn for that, and asked with a clarity that shivered to the doors of the hall,

"May I request the Protocol Dance?"

There was a stillness. She saw fury on the Mayor's face, instantly veiled. She sensed rather than heard an intake of half a thousand breaths—and realized the meaning of the disregarded dance, the substitution of formal chat. Gently the Protocol Dance had been passed over in consideration of a visitor who in a weightless community could never have learned the Viennese waltz.

Through the petrification of her shame she heard the voice that could have charmed demons: "Why, thank you," and felt the slender fingers take hers. Lifted from the curtsy, she gazed into the smile that had been sculpted for her to gaze into. He said, "I shall be charmed, Miss Grant." But it was she who was charmed that unbelievably he knew her name, and it was she who triumphed over Mayor and Mayoress, escort and orchestrator and all the Pleasured Class as he added, "I have taken delight in learnin your ballroom antics."

While he cursed the Freudian slip behind his plastic smile she treasured it as the needed oddity, the otherworldiness that made him truly a visitor to Earth.

If Claire Grant and Peter Marryin made a less than graceful couple, the swishing of tongues outmaneuvered was balm to the ugly duckling's waltzing ego.

Sensitized areas on the couriers' jackets did not make the best of cameras. Subject to crumpling and difficult to aim with accuracy, two of them yet caught Claire's expression at different times during the ball.

"She's in an enchantment," said the Mayor.

"She's on heat," said the Custodian, to whom romance had suddenly become a dirty word. "He's had brat's luck."

"Or good preparation."

"Meaning what?"

The Mayor ran back through the audiotapes. "This."

Peter's voice murmured in midair, "Ugly ducklin? What is that? You have charm."

"You don't mean that." She was coy, ecstatic, flirtatious and pleading all at once. ("Thank sanity we don't stay young," the Custodian muttered.)

Peter's ghostvoice said, "I do mean it. Men appreciate charm in a woman."

"They appreciate money in a woman."

"I don' understan you."

"You don't understand money?"

"Intellectually I do, but not as an attraction. We don' use money Upstairs."

Then he talked of other things as though money were of no interest.

"Neat," the Custodian agreed. "Made his point and left it at that. Even stuck to the truth."

"But not to the truth behind the truth. He has been very well prepared."

"Fortunately, so have we."

The Custodian was wrong about that. On his fourth day on Earth Peter Marryin proposed to the infatuated, richest girl in Melbourne Town, was accepted by her and married to her (with housekeeper and maid for witnesses) by public data-record plug-in, a terminal of which was, quite naturally, located in her late father's study.

Capture and consolidation took something under fifteen minutes, whereas the Custodian had relied on an Engagement, a Round of Gaiety and a Splendid Society Wedding for time in which to generate a dozen subtle interferences. Against Peter's precision and speed no bugging system could do more than record the outwitting of science and power.

The Mayor was silently amused at the old man's raging against defeat. The backward barbarians Upstairs had foreseen opposition and surveillance and designed a lightning campaign to outflank both. He began to respect the barbarians.

But the old man stamped and raved in gutter language that stripped away the cool superiority of his public persona. It was altogether too humanizing. Embarrassing.

The Mayor raised his voice to drown the performance. "She's under age. The marriage can be annulled."

The Custodian snarled at him, "Only if her guardians demand it. Do you think they give a damn while they control the money in trust?"

"There might be means to persuade one of them—"

The Custodian calmed suddenly. "All right, you're trying. But we can't do it. Undue influence? Try and prove it! Even the newscasts are squalling 'the star-struck love story' a bare hour after the event, telling the world romance is alive and throbbing. Public opinion will see interference as bias against Orbiters. Nobody gives a damn for Orbiters but everybody loves lovers, and bias will be elevated into accusations of racialism or exoticism or some bloody pejorative coinage. And if interference were traced to me—" He shuddered.

And certainly not to me, thought the Mayor, who now had an assured future to protect.

The "star-struck lovers" honeymooned brilliantly around the Earth for a month before Mr. and Mrs. Peter Marryin left for the Power Station.

A structure two thousand meters long and five hundred in diameter, floating below a battery of thousand-meter solar mirrors, is immense by any standard, but nothing looks big in space until you are close enough to be dwarfed and awed. Dwarfed and awed Claire Marryin surely was, gasping at her beautiful husband's ambience of marvels.

She had never been in space. (After all, who had, save those whose work took them there? Nobody would *need* the stars for generations yet.) So she played with null-g, bruising herself a little and laughing at her own clumsiness, while Peter fumed and was darling enough not to show it. When the shuttle entered the vast lock in the Station's anal plate (they actually called it that, she found, with a smothered laugh) she calmed down and set herself to be a stately matron of eighteen, worthy of a wonderful man.

From the passage opening on the interior of the Station they came quite suddenly—he guiding her, at times a little roughly, because Orbiters made their topology connective at any angle instead of in terms of up and down—to a platform from which was displayed the whole panorama of the Power Station.

She looked along a huge tube whose walls were checkered with little square boxes which she only slowly recognized as dwellings, grouped around larger boxes which were community buildings and surrounded by neat squares and circles of lush green. In the gravitational center of the tube hung a great disk whose visible face seemed to be nearly all window glass and which occupied perhaps a third of the inner diameter. But it was nearly a thousand meters distant and did not at a glance seem so big, any more than the boxes two hundred meters below and above—*around, away*—seemed large enough for dwellings.

She clapped her hands and cried out, "It's like a toyland!"

"Toylan!" On his face an expression she had not seen there before—anger, revulsion, contempt—slipped into bleak control. He said stiffly, "Your toylan is the home of a fine an proud people," and led her to the conveyor belt while she held back tears for her stupidity. Then it seemed he remembered that these were new and fabulous sights for her and set himself to be kind, and within minutes she was asking shy questions, trying not to have them foolish ones.

"The disk? The factory, we call it. It's empty."

She asked timidly, "But why?" and thought he considered carefully before he answered.

"It was part of the original Station, a complex for the manufacture of artifacs which could be perfectly formed only in null-g conditions. But the Station grew too rich for the comfort of Earth an an embargo was placed on our goods. The factories have stood empty for more than seventy years."

"But that's unfair!"

"Yes!" The one word, with again the blank look of emotion repressed.

So there was a tiny cloud of resentment of her Earth. Best to ignore, allow it time to disperse. There was much to exclaim at here; for instance, she had not expected moving streetways, with railings. There were, in fact, railings everywhere. Strange for dwellers in free-fall, free flight.

"There are free jump areas," he told her, "above roof level. There people may break their bones as they please. Once you take off you can' slow down or change direction, an in collision no weight doesn' mean no inertia. So in public places you ride an hang on, for the sake of others."

There was a touch of explanation-to-the-child-mind about that, and some impatience as he said, "I suppose you busy Terrenes don' think about such things."

Her loving tongue babbled, "Why should we, dear? It isn't our way of life."

She did not know she had just told a paranoid hero that Orbiter affairs were not considered interesting. Or that were it not for her nearing nineteenth birthday and the Grant industrial holdings he could have wished her dead. The stupid, yammering bitch!

The Station observed a twenty-four hour routine for metabolic stability, and that "night" Peter played host. Claire understood that social customs must alter and evolve in a closed community and that personal contacts might come uneasily until she found her niche, but the function left her bewildered.

The "party" was held on the lawns surrounding their "house"—their living-box—like a green pool. The box itself existed for privacy; in the weatherless Station life was conducted in public.

There was nothing for her to do. A fleshy, shapeless woman appeared, requisitioned by Peter, to prepare snack dishes, and Claire's attempts to talk to her were balked upon grunted variations of "I'm only thirdwoman an don' know those things," making it plain that she was there to work and wanted only to get on with it.

What was a thirdwoman? A junior wife? But the Orbiters did not marry. They had some manner of temporary liaison for early child care but she, Claire, was uniquely the only *wife* on the Station. She could not question this clod but later must ask Peter.

At eight o'clock the major lights dimmed throughout the tube. Street lamps remained and some free-floating clusters of colored globes and rods and planes that she found restful to watch. The Orbiters' artificial night had its own soft charm.

Nothing else did. The guests arrived in male and female groups, never mixed. They congratulated Peter on his bride—and hesitated over the word or pronounced it with a sly grin or could not recall it until reminded. They seemed to regard the marriage as a triumphant joke.

After they had congratulated Peter they stared uninhibitedly at her. When Peter introduced them, most seemed not to know what to say to her; the men in particular seemed resentful at being expected to make conversation at all.

Even the women, grouped together and apart from the men, seemed interested in her only as an exotic display piece. And well, she thought, might they stare! Plain on Earth, here she was a beauty. These shapeless females, all flesh and rounded tubes of muscleless limb, were like talking grubs. She swore she would exercise, go daily to the centrifuge and *never* let herself fall victim to null-g.

The men were as bad as their women, pipestem roly-polies; Peter alone looked like a real human being. And even he, she thought with a touch of dispirited spite, was no physical match for a real Terrene man.

Perhaps in her isolation and disappointment she had drunk too much, and had become afraid of vertigo in weightlessness, for she showed no more than a dumb resentment when a massive pudding of a woman dragged her into a disapproving group to hiss at her, "Stop tryin to talk to the men. Sexes mix in private!"

Even Peter seemed only occasionally to recall her presence. The "party" dragged interminably and she did not remember going to bed.

She woke to a hangover and a furious Peter dressing with compressed lips. She scarcely believed she heard him mutter, "Drunken bitch!"

Over coffee she gathered courage to ask what a thirdwoman might be and he snapped at her, "A bloody servan, trained for that an nothin else."

The words were plain but she did not understand the threat in his eyes.

He said, "I'm goin out. Stay here. Don' leave the house. I'll be an hour."

Desolate and uncomprehending, she drifted through the living-box, with its neatness, its compactness, its accessories to comfortable living. To efficient living, she amended; the Orbiters were not a comfortable people. She recalled the ill manners of last night, the resentment scarcely repressed, the smiles that were silent laughter.

And was suddenly afraid. And as suddenly more afraid that it was too late for that.

Peter returned within the hour, in more cheerful mood, ready to kiss and play. She responded with silly relief, as if a smile could cancel ill will already delivered. He had "pulled strings," he told her, made an arrangement which only her special circumstances could justify.

"The Psychlinic will take you immediately."

She fled from his arms, too affronted for fear. "I'm not ill, Peter!"

"No, no!" He laughed, soothing and conciliating and as handsome as all hell and temptation. "It's a teachin group. It isn' fair to toss you unprepared into our ways and customs so I've arranged an implant, a rundown of all the special social conditions, etiquettes, things you need to know so as not to stub a social toe every time you step out."

She cried a soft "O-oh!" for a gift without price. Much of her education had been by psycho-implant and she knew what was involved. He had given her a ticket to painless knowledge she would have been months in achieving.

And a man who could command the time of a Psychlinic was no mean husband.

The clinic was absurdly old-fashioned, its "chair" a cocoon of electrodes and leads and handles to be gripped and precision clamps and heaven knew what else. On Earth the whole thing was done with a single helmet and a hypodermic.

Perhaps her amusement showed, for the Psychlinician explained, in a tone stiff with nonapology, that the Station used its original equipment, that there was no money for new models from Downstairs.

Claire said with her friendliest smile, "Then I shall buy it for you," and sat herself firmly in his ancient chair.

An unreadable expression came and went as he said, "Why, I'm sure you will."

It might be their mode of thanks, but it lacked gratitude. She felt a mild numbness in her thighs, shifted slightly to ease it and realized that the whole buttock was losing sensation.

In sudden, frightened anger she cried out, "You've used a penetrant narcotic! In the chair seat!"

He said bluntly, "Yes," and winced as her voice rose to screaming pitch.

"That's treatment for dangerous criminals and violent lunatics. I'm not—I'm not—"

He said forcefully, "Sit back an shut up!"

And, since that was the nature of the drug, she obeyed. In the few minutes of mental freedom left her she peered into hellmouth.

What they did with her occupied several days. They fed her the acclimatization material, of course, since she was to dwell here permanently and not be a clumsy nuisance. Then came the establishing of submissive reactions, no simple job on a mind accustomed to freedoms which to the Orbiters seemed sheer anarchy. Only then could they begin the deep probing necessary to planning the personality split. When that was done they designed and imprinted the controlled schizophrenic balance that could be tipped either way with proper triggering. It was necessary that a superficially "normal" personality be available if Melbourne Town should send an envoy who would demand to talk with her when the inevitable questions came to be asked.

Aside from that, the Psychlinic found her a fascinating study; relaxation viewing of Terrene teleplays had not prepared them for the revealed truths of Earthworm culture.

"Effete and decaden," said the Chief, "floatin over realities and never seein them. Gravity or no gravity, it's we who are the strong. *We* are the human future."

On her nineteenth birthday a healthy and self-possessed, if unwontedly serious, Claire Marryin contacted her guardians by visiphone and made her wishes known. They argued against the control of immense wealth being taken out of Terrene hands; they pleaded, stormed and stalled until she threatened to settle the matter by simple deed of transfer. She behaved throughout with polite but weary stubborness.

The Commune Fathers of Power Station One became the administrators of the Grant interests.

"That," noted the Mayor, "makes them owners of just eight and one quarter percent of Melbourne Town and unhealthily concerned in mining estate and development from Mars to the solar corona."

"It was expected," said the Custodian, "but what will they do with it? We know better now than to guess at Orbital thinking."

What they did was unexpected in its naïveté. They tried to play the market. They not only lost a great deal of money but wreaked some small havoc with those lesser Grant holdings they chose for their experiments in finance.

"Economic stability is threatened," said the Custodian, with a perfectly straight face. "It is time to return their visit."

The seventeen Spokesmen of the seventeen Station Commune Councils were in session on Station One when a delivery receivals clerk chattered over intercom that the Custodian of Public Safety of Melbourne Town was in the anal corridor and demanding entry.

"How large is his party?"

"He is alone, Alastair Father."

"Delay him five minutes, then escort him here yourself."

"Yes, Alastair Father." The clerk returned to the corridor where the lean and lined and very patrician old man took his ease without benefit of handhold, as to the manner born. In a Terrene that seemed obscurely insolent, as did the silent waiting for the clerk to speak.

"I am to escort you to the Father, but firs there are matters I mus atten to. I won' be—"

The Custodian delivered arrogance with a polite smile. "I am sure you have nothing more important on your hands than my visit."

The clerk said, "That's as may be," and turned toward his office. *Snotty Downstairs bastard!* Orbiter insularity overcame him. "Stationhans don' take orders from Terrenes."

"Pity," said the Custodian equably. The clerk withdrew, wondering was that a subtle Terrene threat.

Alastair First Father, who had been Alastair Dunwoodie, swept them out of the room like children. Before his immense prestige the communards made no attempt to argue but sought invisibility in the nearest dwellings. All, that is, save the inevitable youngest-promoted, still inclined to display intransigence rather than sense.

"Refuse him! Sen him about his business!"

"He is about his business." The First Father urged him toward the door. "It is too soon to invite reprisals, an I am curious to see Charles again."

"Charles! You know him?"

"We were friens once. Now, go!"

The youngest-promoted went, bemusedly reckoning the Father's age.

Were friens? It was an uncommonly wistful thought for Alastair. And now? Loyalties had come between. He punched an intercom number and said, "There's a Terrene envoy here. Prepare Claire Thirdwoman."

The Chief Psychlinician dispatched his Physical Training Authority, Peter Marryin, to the hydroponic garden where the girl would be making the daily harvest of fruit and vegetables, a faintly stupid smile on her face. She was plump now, and losing shape, but seemed contented enough; it had been necessary to repress most of her emotional reaction-strength in order not to blur the edges between personalities by creating a too-obtrusive secondary.

The code phrase which brought her original persona to life was cruel to the point of obscenity but served its purpose of reaching deep into the preconscious. Peter, who had never conceived of her as more than a means to an end, gave no thought to brutality and outrage as he said distinctly into her ear, "Peter Marryin loves Claire Grant."

The young Charles had worked in space and knew the rules of null-g movement, and the old Charles had wisely spent fifty hours in the shuttles reconditioning himself before facing Alastair. He would not lose face through physical incompetence.

He even managed to inject a hint of swagger into his slide-and-shuffle entry into the Council Hall where the old man stood alone at the head of the long table with its—yes, seventeen chairs. All present and correct—then hurriedly got rid of while impudent clerk obstructed.

He said, "You're showing your age, Alastair," and gave his skull grin. "Old as God and no doubt twice as crafty."

Alastair flowed to greet him in a movement which seemed to glide him, upright, down the length of the room, making Charles's swagger mere bumptiousness, and held out his hand. "Well, ol frien!"

The Custodian returned the grip gently and allowed himself a bare sentence of old affection: "I have always remembered you, Alastair." Then, as they measured each other with uncertain and wary smiles, "I bring not peace but a sword."

Alastair, too, had been a Cultist in the old days. "To set man agains his father an daughter agains her mother? Not on the Stations, Charles. Our conception of relationships does not allow internecine frictions."

"Not Terrene against Orbiter, those brothers on Earth and in Heaven?"

"The chance of brotherhood is gone by."

As simply as that the lines of battle were drawn.

They sat at the table, using the bodybelts that allowed movement and gesture without reactive floating, and the Custodian launched his attack directly.

"The Governance of Australasia suggests—" he laid the lightest of stresses on the verb, "—that a Committee of Advice be appointed to guide your financial handling of the Grant holdings."

"There are no Grant holdins. I suppose you mean the Orbital League holdins brought to the Communes by Claire Thirdwoman."

So the whole League was in it; not really news. The final words penetrated less swiftly, then shockingly.

"Thirdwoman! Alastair, that's slavery!"

The First Father smiled thinly. "What could she be good for but manual labor an childbearin? Your children of wealth learn nothin useful to an Orbiter. I assure you she is not discontented."

"I want to see her!"

"You shall."

"Good." *Some double-dealing there? Be watchful.* "Now, the holdings—"

"No Committee of Advice, Charles!"

"You're amateurs. You'll go broke."

"Our economists are learnin. We buy expert advice now from Earth. Terrene's have little that can' be bought, includin allegiance."

"I know damned well what you buy. I also know that your first attempts to deal in millions caused a minor recession in Melbourne Town. If you succeed in bringing down the whole Grant empire there'll be economic chaos."

"We aren' stupid."

"But you are inexperienced. We must protect ourselves."

"No Committee, Charles!"

"It is already set up."

"*Un*set it. We won' obey it." The Custodian's expression gave him pause. "The Ethic, Charles! You can' interfere." The skull grin threatened to engulf him. "*What have you done, Charles?*"

As the declaration of love unlocked the sleeping persona, Claire burst from within herself like an emerging butterfly. Life flooded her face; her lips parted and smiled, her spoiling body straightened and she looked into her lover's eyes with an instant's joy that faded into apprehension and loathing.

He had seen it all before, was turning away when she asked, "What do they want now?" and answered over his shoulder, "Firs Father wans you. There's a Terrene envoy here."

Envoy! Hope was immediately quenched. No envoy could free her. In a moment they would give her the injection and tell her what to say and do and there she would be, gabbling that she was happy and had no desire to leave the Station, that everyone was so kind and that she had fulfilment here such as Earth could never offer and more and more gushing, lying rubbish.

She asked, "Why should I bother?"

"What?"

"What's the use? I don't want to see him, to tell force-fed lies and build myself more unhappiness."

He faced her furiously. "Listen, girl! You're an Orbiter and what Firs Father says, you do."

In the rare periods of personality release, such as the visiphone communications with bankers and inquiring relatives, her hatred had been born in the schizophrenic hell of the submission drugs. During the long weeks of thirdwoman regression her subconscious mind had been conjuring powers of viciousness the little Claire Grant could never have roused from her psyche. Now, in these moments of hyper-euphoria, between the awakening and the drugging, she was uniquely herself, undrugged and unregressed—a creature of misery and rage.

She said, with a menace he did not hear because in his thinking it could not be there, "Don't talk to me like that."

"Come on; don' waste my time."

She goaded, "Your time is nothing to me."

"Bitch!" He put out a grasping hand and she struck it away, hissing, "Don't touch me, you filth!"

It was stunning. No woman spoke to a man like that, *no* woman. Nor would a man dare use such words to Peter the Culture Hero. And she had struck his hand! Outraged self-love rose like a scald in the throat and his fingers hooked into claws.

She said, making sure of him, "If you touch me I'll kill you."

She needed to kill someone, and who better than the man who had married for her money the girl who despised fortune hunters? As his hands reached for her she casually took one in hers, dragged the arm straight and kicked him in the elbow, breaking it to the obbligato of his screaming. It was easy. Orbiters knew little about aggression or defense; both were difficult or embarrassingly ludicrous in null-g.

The screaming unleashed joy in her and she knew that she *would* kill him. Others in the street had heard him and heads were turning but they could not save him. She, Claire Thirdwoman, slave, dupe and Earthworm, was about to murder the Culture Hero before their eyes.

They could not realize how simple it was for her. A year of null-g had made her competent in the leaps and anglings of free-fall, and her Earthworm musculature made it possible for her to achieve takeoff speeds and endure landing collisions no Orbiter could match. Even her centrifuge-reared "husband" was not her equal.

She caught his arm and he shrieked again, and hooked her foot under the moving-way guide rail. Figures now leapt toward her, too late. Taking him by wrist and smashed elbow she flung him, howling, against the wall of a dwelling twenty meters away. He hit it face forward, sprawling like a spider, and she launched herself after him, turning in midair to strike with her feet at his spine, and heard it crack.

She had her moment of murderer's ecstasy, sexual, blood-deep, complete. Let the surgeons and biochemists revive and rebuild him (as they would), but she had cleansed herself of shame and hatred.

Then reaction set in and with a crippling weariness of spirit she turned to defend herself . . .

"Done?" the Custodian echoed. "I have set up a Committee of Advice. Nothing else."

"Unacceptable."

"But there are, of course, alternatives."

"Which are?"

"One is that you should reassign the League holdings to Claire Grant and return her to Earth."

The First Father laughed, but uneasily because the breathtaking impudence of the demand spoke of threat behind threat. "You're out of your min."

"We can take the money from you, you know."

"Not by way of Claire. She gave it to us. I feel you will have a record, verbal and written, of the whole transaction."

"I have, Alastair. And an expert psychological report on her speech and behavior patterns during the exchanges with her administrators, showing a ninety percent certainty that she was under submission drugs. I can recommend that the Marketing Court freeze your assets while the transfer is re-examined."

"You can' prove druggin."

"You don't deny it?"

"Or admit it."

The Custodian felt less regret for that old friendship. Neither was the same man he had been eighty years ago, and both were centenarians, patterns of biochemistry and geriatric technique, with interests and loyalties eight decades divergent. He found himself caring not a damn for Alastair's needs so long as Melbourne Town survived. The perilous honesty of chauvinism at least left him unrepentant of hard hitting.

"You'd have to kill the girl to prevent me getting the truth. Would you do that, Alastair?"

The First Father's smile was deep winter. "No. I don' wan the Global Council puttin a military prize crew aboard my Station."

They came from all sides, angling up toward her. Almost lethargically she struck with her feet at the first comer, a squealing firstwoman spitting anti-Terrene rage, and used her mass to change direction and clutch at the jump-halting rail on a dwelling roof. The rest fell into a confusion of collisions and reachings for any anchored mass. Their babbling anger and shock sounded ridiculous; they lived such ordered lives that in emergency they flapped and fluttered. If they caught her they would kick and hit and pinch and threaten but in the end she would still be thirdwoman in the hydroponic garden. And Peter reconstructed. And nothing changed.

Then why not let them take her? There was no freedom.

For an instant, looking upward, she saw where, five hundred meters away across the diameter of the cylinder, final freedom lay, and reflexively launched herself toward it.

At once she knew she had been stupid, that it was better to live. There could always be the unexpected, the reversal of fortune. In panic she began to struggle, but what Peter had told her was true: once in free-fall you cannot stop or slow down or change direction.

Her launch had been deadly accurate, a simple straight line with no gravity-fed trajectory for miscalculation.

The end of Claire Thirdwoman, crying and clawing for the inaccessible sides, was entry into the twenty-meter maw of the Station disposal unit, the vast mouth that could swallow machine complexes or obsolescent building units without the need for laborious dismemberment. She died at once as the heat units sensed her, felt nothing as the grinders shredded her contemptuously in a spurt of gears and in seconds was a mist of molecules expanding into invisibility in pressureless space.

In a right little, tight little island in the sky there is small precedent for announcing the neodeath of a local hero and the dissolution of his killer. Inexperience blurted out the news breathlessly in front of the Earthworm stranger.

For the second time during the affair the Custodian exploded in ranting fury, cursing Orbiter and Terrene stupidity alike, reducing himself to manic gutter level, until he saw that the First Father watched him with the bleak care of a duelist who sees advantage.

He checked himself abruptly. In an access of intuition, even some residual affection, he pondered the needs and frustrations the Orbiters had brought on themselves when they sought the pastures of heaven by casting away weight.

He said, "We need truth, Alastair, both of us. Neither was ready to move; now we must."

The First Father bowed his head. Concealing a smile? At any event, he made no attempt to argue. In minutes the Custodian knew all he needed, including the business of the League meeting his advent had dispersed—the secret buying of weapons, offensive and defensive, from men on the five continents Downstairs who would sell honor, history and the future for money.

That was bad enough. Worse was that the First Father did not fear him.

Feeling all his years, he sat down with the other old man—friend, enemy and game player—to plan a fresh tomorrow.

Emotion subsided; perspectives revived; Claire's death became a tactical weapon each sought to grasp. They circled, testing defenses, until a confident Alastair made the first lunge.

"Charles, you can no more risk investigation of this affair than I can."

The Custodian sighed inwardly. It had been, he supposed, inevitable that Alastair, despite his remoteness from the social psychology of the Earthworm, should recognize that.

Still, he must try. "*You* certainly cannot. Your League is no danger to Terrene culture yet, but this last year holds the proof that you will be. Some day. Even soon." He added easily, "You will be stopped, of course."

Too late; that hand was already lost. "How, Charles? How will Earth explain retributive action a secon time? Attemp it and I, *I*, will tell the story of how Claire Marryin died. I will tell the trut, all the trut. And your Earthworms will discover how their precious Ethic has created a poverty-stricken ghetto in the sky, but one that intens to kick the Ethic to pieces rather than continue as the unseen slaveys of some Victorian servan quarters in the attic Upstairs. Revenge on us may be swif but public scrutiny of the Ethic *and* of its manipulators will be pitiless. It will be the end of the Ethic."

The Custodian had seen from the beginning that he was caught. It was not easy even to go down fighting. He said lightly, "But everybody questions the Ethic in his heart. It is an elaboration of good manners, pointless in essence but providing a permanent framework of behavior for discussion without bloodshed."

Alastair laughed at him. "It mus be one of the great jokes of history that Earth has based its firs planetary culture on good manners, then created an offshoot with none. An a better joke that the collapse of a lie nobody believes in could plunge you into cultural anarchy. All your international relationships balance on it. You won' take the risk."

Of course he, and Earth, would not. Bluntness now would serve as well as anything. "What do you want?"

"To be rid of you."

That was unexpected; he said nothing at all but waited for Alastair to continue.

"You can' blow us out of the sky. Too un-Ethical and too revealin. But you can pay us to go away. And we'll go." He grinned with sudden savagery. "Like the classic barbarians on the Imperial borders."

That was staggering. The Custodian groped for words, any words to stall for thought. "The power supplies—"

"Automated platforms to replace the Stations. The plans are ready. Ten years from keel to full operation."

That was worth a sour laugh in return. "We've had automation plans of our own for the past twenty years. The problem has been what to do with you. Now you tell me you'll go away. Where to? Let me guess at your view of the matter."

He ruminated.

Alastair said, "There's somethin you should see. Come along."

They floated out of the hall to a moving-way which carried them up the curve of the hull, through little nests of the living-boxes and the lawns and gardens in their patterns of cultivated brilliance. All growing things were a passion of Orbiters. Their natural art form, perhaps? They could have chosen more coldly and worse.

He said, "I think I have it. The basic need was money. First for armaments in case Earth did indeed become provoked into violence by the demands you would some day make. Second for *material* to implement whatever design you have in mind. Behind this is a determination to cut loose from Earth once and for all. The cultures have diverged to the point where neither understands the other or needs the other. Cultures which don't understand each other despise each other, have no use for each other, no matter how they pretend otherwise. Am I doing well?"

"Very well."

They left the moving-way and Alastair opened a door. Inside was nothing at all, an empty room.

"Total isolation breeds its own neuroses, Charles. Our psychologists set up this room years ago. People come here to soothe their tensions, pacify their resentments, defuse their aggressions."

He touched switches; the room became black dark. A slit twenty meters wide glimmered faintly in the floor, opened like a vast eye, and gazed at the stars.

The Custodian understood only vaguely. "The galaxy means little to me, but for you it has come to have psychological significance. Is this where you will go?"

"Eventually. Not yet. It is a long dream."

"And now?"

"Firs, Jupiter. You can pay us to mine the satellites and the atmosphere."

The Custodian knew he should have foreseen it but the politician in him asked, "Why should we?"

"Because in a century or so you will have another population-an-resources crisis Downstairs, and you can use somebody to prepare the alternatives for you. By then we will be wealthy enough an self-sufficien to engage the universe on our own terms. There are eighty thousan people in the Stations now; we mus plan for a million. Ten Mother Islands and a hundred minin scows for a start. The resources out there will cover your nex dozen population explosions; you'll find us a good bargain. And what remains of the Ethic can seek virtue in Non-Interference with our cultural destiny."

"The impudence of it all is breathtaking. All I need do is lay the idea before the Global Council and they'll collapse like cards before your diplomatic acumen! It will need more than a silver tongue to sway them."

"Let the Ethic sway them!"

The Custodian swallowed a sound like a smothered laugh. "Blackmail, Alastair!"

"But mos Ethical, Charles, within the Terrene meanin of the word. By the way, did you know that the original twentieth-century intention in suggestin space platforms was to establish free colonies in space?"

"Was it indeed?"

"Indeed. I have always said that we learned nothin from The Collapse. We've simply taken a little longer to arrive where they wished to go anyway."

Several hours later, when the Custodian was preparing to return home, the First Father glanced fortuitously overhead to where, across the diameter, a disposal gang loaded a day's garbage into the vent, and felt a twinge of guilt.

The Custodian, following his gaze, wondered aloud if everything was recycled.

"Not quite everythin."

"No? Oh, yes, of course, that— Tragic business; tragic . . ." He was busy formulating his approach to the Global Council.

The version retailed to the Mayor was perhaps a little slanted. He was impressed. "You know, we'll be well rid of them."

"For the time being."

The Mayor's eyebrows rose.

"Nothing ends, James. Alastair First Father is quite aware that as Lords of the Solar System one day they'll come home again—as barbarians at the ancient gates. But you and I won't be around to worry over that."

WITH THE NIGHT MAIL

Rudyard Kipling

Rudyard Kipling is one of the major literary figures influencing the flowering of science fiction in the twentieth century. H. G. Wells was the great imaginative force behind Scientific Romance from 1895 to at least the 1920s, but Rudyard Kipling was the most popular English language writer of his day, and it is not Wellsian but Kiplingesque storytelling and attitudes that dominated the Golden Age of sf and its descendants. Even though he wrote very little actual sf—"With the Night Mail" (1905) is his single most important story of this kind—fantastic elements abound in his fiction. The recent (1992) publication of a volume of *Kipling's Science Fiction* laden with encomiums from such diverse sf writers as Jerry Pournelle, Gene Wolfe, and John Brunner only confirms his enduring appeal and influence. In his introduction John Brunner points out that Kipling uses the historic present tense, in his day an unusual usage in English, which became part of the arsenal of sf writers.

While Robert A. Heinlein certainly borrowed techniques liberally from the fiction of H. G. Wells, the affect of his classic stories is markedly from Kipling. Certain devices from this story—in particular the imaginary future advertisements, news reports, and letters to the editor that accompanied its first publication—turned up in some of Heinlein's future history stories. Poul Anderson and Gordon R. Dickson, to name only two others among many, also acknowledge a debt to Kipling.

In fact the whole complex of attitudes about the manly virtues of military service in sf is more a legacy of Kipling's poetry and fiction than of any other body of work. It is possibly the coincidence of World War II with Campbell's Golden Age (when many of the most influential stories of Robert A. Heinlein were first published), followed by the dreary Cold War, that has kept the link between hard science fiction and Kiplingesque military sf strong.

"With the Night Mail" is Kipling's sociological speculation based upon the invention of a new machine and a new technology to support it. It is an interesting contrast to H. G. Wells's story of another machine in "The Land Ironclads." It is worth noting that the name of one of Hugo Gernsback's other magazines, published in the 1920s before he founded *Amazing Stories*, was *Science and Invention* (partly devoted to wonderful inventions and partly to fiction). This Kipling story idealizes ship captains and crews, military discipline, and civil service all at once: a hierarchal, paramilitary air postal service controls communications and rules the world of the future, for the benefit of all. The story was so popular, in the day of the competition between the airplane and the airship for the future of the air, that Kipling also wrote a sequel, "As Easy as A. B. C." in 1912; "With the Night Mail" was also reprinted and published alone in an illustrated hardcover volume in 1909.

At nine o'clock of a gusty winter night I stood on the lower stages of one of the G. P. O. outward mail towers. My purpose was a run to Quebec in "Postal Packet 162 or such other as may be appointed"; and the Postmaster-General himself countersigned the order. This talisman opened all doors, even those in the despatching-caisson at the foot of the tower, where they were delivering the sorted Continental mail. The bags lay packed close as herrings in the long grey underbodies which our G. P. O. still calls "coaches." Five such coaches were filled as I watched, and were shot up the guides to be locked on to their waiting packets three hundred feet nearer the stars.

From the despatching-caisson I was conducted by a courteous and wonderfully learned official—Mr. L. L. Geary, Second Despatcher of the Western Route—to the Captains' Room (this wakes an echo of old romance), where the mail captains come on for their turn of duty. He introduces me to the captain of "162"—Captain Purnall, and his relief, Captain Hodgson. The one is small and dark; the other large and red; but each has the brooding sheathed glance characteristic of eagles and aeronauts. You can see it in the pictures of our racing professionals, from L. V. Rautsch to little Ada Warrleigh—that fathomless abstraction of eyes habitually turned through naked space.

On the notice-board in the Captains' Room, the pulsing arrows of some twenty indicators register, degree by geographical degree, the progress of as many homeward-bound packets. The word "Cape" rises across the face of a dial; a gong strikes: the South African mid-weekly mail is in at the Highgate Receiving Towers. That is all. It reminds one comically of the traitorous little bell which in pigeon-fanciers' lofts notifies the return of a homer.

"Time for us to be on the move," says Captain Purnall, and we are shot up by the passenger-lift to the top of the despatch-towers. "Our coach will lock on when it is filled and the clerks are aboard." . . .

"No. 162" waits for us in Slip E of the topmost stage. The great curve of her back shines frostily under the lights, and some minute alteration of trim makes her rock a little in her holding-down slips.

Captain Purnall frowns and dives inside. Hissing softly, "162" comes to rest as level as a rule. From her North Atlantic Winter nose-cap (worn bright as diamond with boring through uncounted leagues of hail, snow, and ice) to the inset of her three builtout propeller-shafts is some two hundred and forty feet. Her extreme diameter, carried well forward, is thirty-seven. Contrast this with the nine hundred by ninety-five of any crack liner, and you will realize the power that must drive a hull through all weathers at more than the emergency speed of the *Cyclonic*!

The eye detects no joint in her skin plating save the sweeping hair-crack of the bow-rudder—Magniac's rudder that assured us the dominion of the unstable air and left its inventor penniless and half-blind. It is calculated to Castelli's "gull-wing" curve. Raise a few feet of that all but invisible plate three-eighths of an inch and she will yaw five miles to port or starboard ere she is under control again. Give her full helm and she returns on her track like a whip-lash. Cant the whole forward—a touch on the wheel will suffice—and she sweeps at your good direction up or down. Open the complete circle and she presents to the air a mushroom-head that will bring her up all standing within a half-mile.

"Yes," says Captain Hodgson, answering my thought, "Castelli thought he'd discovered the secret of controlling aeroplanes when he'd only found out how to steer dirigible balloons. Magniac invented his rudder to help war-boats ram each other; and war went out of fashion and Magniac he went out of his mind because he said he couldn't serve his country any more. I wonder if any of us ever know what we're really doing."

"If you want to see the coach locked you'd better go aboard. It's due now," says Mr. Geary. I enter through the door amidships. There is nothing here for display. The inner skin of the gas-tanks comes down to within a foot or two of my head and turns over just short of the turn of the bilges. Liners and yachts disguise their tanks with decoration, but the G.P.O. serves them raw under a lick of grey official paint. The inner skin shuts off fifty feet of the bow and as much of the stern, but the bow-bulkhead is recessed for the lift-shunting apparatus as the stern is pierced for the shaft-tunnels. The engine-room lies almost amidships. Forward of it, extending to the turn of the bow tanks, is an aperture—a bottomless hatch at present—into which our coach will be locked. One looks down over the coamings three hundred feet to the despatching-caisson whence voices boom upward. The light below is obscured to a sound of thunder, as our coach rises on its guides. It enlarges rapidly from a postage-stamp to a playing-card; to a punt and last a pontoon. The two clerks, its crew, do not even look up as it comes into place. The Quebec letters fly under their fingers and leap into the docketed racks, while both captains and Mr. Geary satisfy themselves that the coach is locked home. A clerk passes the way-bill over the hatch-coaming. Captain Purnall thumb-marks and passes it to Mr. Geary. Receipt has been given and taken. "Pleasant run," says Mr. Geary, and disappears through the door which a foot-high pneumatic compressor locks after him.

"A-ah!" sighs the compressor released. Our holding-down clips part with a tang. We are clear.

Captain Hodgson opens the great colloid underbody porthole through which I watch over-lighted London slide eastward as the gale gets hold of us. The first of the low winter clouds cuts off the well-known view and darkens Middlesex. On the south edge of it I can see a postal packet's light ploughing through the white fleece. For an instant she gleams like a star ere she drops toward the Highgate Receiving Towers. "The Bombay Mail," says Captain Hodgson, and looks at his watch. "She's forty minutes late."

"What's our level?" I ask.

"Four thousand. Aren't you coming up on the bridge?"

The bridge (let us ever praise the G. P. O. as a repository of ancientest tradition!) is represented by a view of Captain Hodgson's legs where he stands on the Control Platform that runs thwart-ships overhead. The bow colloid is unshuttered and Captain Purnall, one hand on the wheel, is feeling for a fair slant. The dial shows 4300 feet.

"It's steep to-night," he mutters, as tier on tier of cloud drops under. "We generally pick up an easterly draught below three thousand at this time o' the year. I hate slathering through fluff."

"So does Van Cutsem. Look at him huntin' for a slant!" says Captain Hodgson. A fog-light breaks cloud a hundred fathoms below. The Antwerp Night Mail makes her signal and rises between two racing clouds far to port, her flanks blood-red in the glare of Sheerness Double Light. The gale will have us over the North Sea in half-an-hour, but Captain Purnall lets her go composedly—nosing to every point of the compass as she rises.

"Five thousand—six, six thousand eight hundred"—the dip-dial reads ere we find the easterly drift, heralded by a flurry of snow at the thousand-fathom level. Captain Purnall rings up the engines and keys down the governor on the switch before him. There is no sense in urging machinery when Æolus himself gives you good knots for nothing. We are away in earnest now—our nose notched home on our chosen star. At this level the lower clouds are laid out, all neatly combed by the dry fingers of the East. Below that again is the strong westerly blow through which we rose. Overhead, a film of southerly drifting mist draws a theatrical gauze across the firmament. The moonlight turns the lower strata to silver without a stain except where our shadow underruns us. Bristol and Cardiff Double Lights (those statelily inclined beams over Severnmouth) are dead ahead of us; for we keep the Southern Winter Route. Coventry Central, the pivot of the English system, stabs upward once in ten seconds its spear of diamond light to the north; and a point or two off our starboard bow The Leek, the great cloud-breaker of Saint David's Head, swings its unmistakable green beam twenty-five degrees each way. There must be half a mile of fluff over it in this weather, but it does not affect The Leek.

"Our planet's overlighted if anything," says Captain Purnall at the wheel, as Cardiff-Bristol slides under. "I remember the old days of common white verticals that 'ud show two or three hundred feet up in a mist, if you knew where to look for 'em. In really fluffy weather they might as well have been under your hat. One could get lost coming home then, an' have some fun. Now, it's like driving down Piccadilly."

He points to the pillars of light where the cloud-breakers bore through the cloud-floor. We see nothing of England's outlines: only a white pavement pierced in all directions by these manholes of variously coloured fire—Holy Island's white and red—St. Bee's interrupted white, and so on as far as the eye can reach. Blessed be Sargent, Ahrens, and the Dubois brothers, who invented the cloud-breakers of the world whereby we travel in security!

"Are you going to lift for The Shamrock?" asks Captain Hodgson. Cork Light (green, fixed) enlarges as we rush to it. Captain Purnall nods. There is heavy traffic hereabouts—the cloud-bank beneath us is streaked with running fissures of flame where the Atlantic boats are hurrying Londonward just clear of the fluff. Mail-packets are supposed, under the Conference rules, to have the five-thousand-foot lanes to themselves, but the foreigner in a hurry is apt to take liberties with English air. "No. 162" lifts to a long-drawn wail of the breeze in the fore-flange of the rudder and we make Valencia (white, green, white) at a safe 7000 feet, dipping our beam to an incoming Washington packet.

There is no cloud on the Atlantic, and faint streaks of cream round Dingle Bay show where the driven seas hammer the coast. A big S. A. T. A. liner (*Société Anonyme des Transports Aëriens*) is diving and lifting half a mile below us in search of some break in the solid west wind. Lower still lies a disabled Dane: she is telling the liner all about it in International. Our General Communication dial has caught her talk and begins to eavesdrop. Captain Hodgson makes a motion to shut it off but checks himself. "Perhaps you'd like to listen," he says.

"*Argol* of St. Thomas," the Dane whimpers. "Report owners three starboard shaft collar-bearings fused. Can make Flores as we are, but impossible further. Shall we buy spares at Fayal?"

The liner acknowledges and recommends inverting the bearings. The *Argol* answers that she has already done so without effect, and begins to relieve her mind about cheap German enamels for collar-bearings. The Frenchman assents cordially, cries "*Courage, mon ami*," and switches off.

Their lights sink under the curve of the ocean.

"That's one of Lundt & Bleamers' boats," says Captain Hodgson. "Serves 'em right for putting German compos in their thrust-blocks. *She* won't be in Fayal to-night! By the way, wouldn't you like to look round the engine-room?"

I have been waiting eagerly for this invitation and I follow Captain Hodgson from the control-platform, stooping low to avoid the bulge of the tanks. We know that Fleury's gas can lift anything, as the world-famous trials of '89 showed, but its almost indefinite powers of expansion necessitate vast tank room. Even in this thin air the lift-shunts are busy taking out one-third of its normal lift, and still "162" must be checked by an occasional downdraw of the rudder or our flight would become a climb to the stars. Captain Purnall prefers an overlifted to an underlifted ship; but no two captains trim ship alike. "When *I* take the bridge," says Captain Hodgson, "you'll see me shunt forty per cent. of the lift out of the gas and run her on the upper rudder. With a swoop upward instead of a swoop downward, *as* you say. Either way will do. It's only habit. Watch our dip-dial! Tim fetches her down once every thirty knots as regularly as breathing."

So is it shown on the dip-dial. For five or six minutes the arrow creeps from 6700 to 7300. There is the faint "szgee" of the rudder, and back slides the arrow to 6000 on a falling slant of ten or fifteen knots.

"In heavy weather you jockey her with the screws as well," says Captain Hodgson, and, unclipping the jointed bar which divides the engine-room from the bare deck, he leads me on to the floor.

Here we find Fleury's Paradox of the Bulk-headed Vacuum—which we accept now without thought—literally in full blast. The three engines are H. T. & T. assisted-vacuo Fleury turbines running from 3000 to the Limit—that is to say, up to the point when the blades make the air "bell"—cut out a vacuum for themselves precisely as over-driven marine propellers used to do. "162's" Limit is low on account of the small size of her nine screws, which, though handier than the old colloid Thelussons, "bell" sooner. The midships engine, generally used as a reinforce, is not running; so the port and starboard turbine vacuum-chambers draw direct into the return-mains.

The turbines whistle reflectively. From the low-arched expansion-tanks on either side the valves descend pillarwise to the turbine-chests, and thence the obedient gas whirls through the spirals of blades with a force that would whip the teeth out of a power-saw. Behind, is its own pressure held in leash or spurred on by the lift-shunts; before it, the vacuum where Fleury's Ray dances in violet-green bands and whirled turbillons of flame. The jointed U-tubes of the vacuum-chamber are pressure-tempered colloid (no glass would endure the strain for an instant) and a junior engineer with tinted spectacles watches the Ray intently. It is the very heart of the machine—a mystery to this day. Even Fleury who begat it and, unlike Magniac, died a multi-millionaire, could not explain how the restless little imp shuddering in the U-tube can, in the fractional fraction of a second, strike the furious blast of gas into a chill greyish-green liquid that drains (you can hear it trickle) from the far end of the vacuum through the eduction-pipes and the mains back to the bilges. Here it returns to its gaseous, one had almost written sagacious, state and climbs to work afresh. Bilge-tank, upper tank, dorsal-tank, expansion-chamber, vacuum, main-return (as a liquid), and bilge-tank once more is the ordained cycle. Fleury's Ray sees to that; and the engineer with the tinted spectacles sees to Fleury's Ray. If a speck of oil, if even the natural grease of the human finger touch the hooded terminals, Fleury's Ray will wink and disappear and must be laboriously built up again. This means half a day's work for all hands and an expense of one hundred and seventy-odd pounds to the G. P. O. for radium-salts and such trifles.

"Now look at our thrust-collars. You won't find much German compo there. Full-jewelled, you see," says Captain Hodgson as the engineer shunts open the top of a cap. Our shaft-bearings are C. M. C. (Commercial Minerals Company) stones, ground with as much care as the lens of a telescope. They cost £37 apiece. So far we have not arrived at their term of life. These bearings came from "No. 97," which took them over from the old *Dominion of Light* which had them out of the wreck of the *Perseus* aeroplane in the years when men still flew wooden kites over oil engines!

They are a shining reproof to all low-grade German "ruby" enamels, so-called "boort" facings, and the dangerous and unsatisfactory alumina compounds which please dividend-hunting owners and turn skippers crazy.

The rudder-gear and the gas lift-shunt, seated side by side under the engine-room dials, are the only machines in visible motion. The former sighs from time to time as the oil plunger rises and falls half an inch. The latter, cased and guarded like the U-tube aft, exhibits another Fleury Ray, but inverted and more green than violet. Its function is to shunt the lift out of the gas, and this it will do without watching. That is all! A tiny pump-rod wheezing and whining to itself beside a sputtering green lamp. A hundred and fifty feet aft down the flat-topped tunnel of the tanks a violet light, restless and irresolute. Between the two, three white-painted turbine-trunks, like eel-baskets laid on their side, accentuate the empty perspectives. You can hear the trickle of the liquefied gas flowing from the vacuum into the bilge-tanks and the soft *gluck-glock* of gas-locks closing as Captain Purnall brings "162" down by the head. The hum of the turbines and the boom of the air on our skin is no more than a cotton-wool wrapping to the universal stillness. And we are running an eighteen-second mile.

I peer from the fore end of the engine-room over the hatch-coamings into the coach. The mail-clerks are sorting the Winnipeg, Calgary, and Medicine Hat bags; but there is a pack of cards ready on the table.

Suddenly a bell thrills; the engineers run to the turbine-valves and stand by; but the spectacled slave of the Ray in the U-tube never lifts his head. He must watch where he is. We are hard-braked and going astern; there is language from the Control Platform.

"Tim's sparking badly about something," says the unruffled Captain Hodgson. "Let's look."

Captain Purnall is not the suave man we left half an hour since, but the embodied authority of the G. P. O. Ahead of us floats an ancient, aluminum-patched, twin-screw tramp of the dingiest, with no more right to the 5000-foot lane than has a horse-cart to a modern road. She carries an obsolete "barbette" conning-tower—a six-foot affair with railed platform forward—and our warning beam plays on the top of it as a policeman's lantern flashes on the area sneak. Like a sneak-thief, too, emerges a shock-headed navigator in his shirt-sleeves. Captain Purnall wrenches open the colloid to talk with him man to man. There are times when Science does not satisfy.

"What under the stars are you doing here, you skyscraping chimney-sweep?" he shouts as we two drift side by side. "Do you know this is a Mail-lane? You call yourself a sailor, sir? You ain't fit to peddle toy balloons to an Esquimaux. Your name and number! Report and get down, and be——!"

"I've been blown up once," the shock-headed man cries, hoarsely, as a dog barking. "I don't care two flips of a contact for anything *you* can do, Postey."

"Don't you, sir? But I'll make you care. I'll have you towed stern first to Disko and broke up. You can't recover insurance if you're broke for obstruction. Do you understand *that?*"

Then the stranger bellows: "Look at my propellers! There's been a wulli-wa down below that has knocked us into umbrella-frames! We've been blown up about forty thousand feet! We're all one conjuror's watch inside! My mate's arm's broke;

my engineer's head's cut open; my Ray went out when the engines smashed; and . . . and . . . for pity's sake give me my height, Captain! We doubt we're dropping."

"Six thousand eight hundred. Can you hold it?" Captain Purnall overlooks all insults, and leans half out of the colloid, staring and snuffing. The stranger leaks pungently.

"We ought to blow into St. John's with luck. We're trying to plug the fore-tank now, but she's simply whistling it away," her captain wails.

"She's sinking like a log," says Captain Purnall in an undertone. "Call up the Banks Mark Boat, George." Our dip-dial shows that we, keeping abreast the tramp, have dropped five hundred feet the last few minutes.

Captain Purnall presses a switch and our signal beam begins to swing through the night, twizzling spokes of light across infinity.

"That'll fetch something," he says, while Captain Hodgson watches the General Communicator. He has called up the North Banks Mark Boat, a few hundred miles west, and is reporting the case.

"I'll stand by you," Captain Purnall roars to the lone figure on the conning-tower.

"Is it as bad as that?" comes the answer. "She isn't insured. She's mine."

"Might have guessed as much," mutters Hodgson. "Owner's risk is the worst risk of all!"

"Can't I fetch St. John's—not even with this breeze?" the voice quavers.

"Stand by to abandon ship. Haven't you *any* lift in you, fore or aft?"

"Nothing but the midship tanks, and they're none too tight. You see, my Ray gave out and——" he coughs in the reek of the escaping gas.

"You poor devil!" This does not reach our friend. "What does the Mark Boat say, George?"

"Wants to know if there's any danger to traffic. Says she's in a bit of weather herself, and can't quit station. I've turned in a General Call, so even if they don't see our beam some one's bound to help—or else we must. Shall I clear our slings? Hold on! Here we are! A Planet liner, too! She'll be up in a tick!"

"Tell her to have her slings ready," cries his brother captain. "There won't be much time to spare . . . Tie up your mate," he roars to the tramp.

"My mate's all right. It's my engineer. He's gone crazy."

"Shunt the lift out of him with a spanner. Hurry!"

"But I can make St. John's if you'll stand by."

"You'll make the deep, wet Atlantic in twenty minutes. You're less than fifty-eight hundred now. Get your papers."

A Planet liner, east bound, heaves up in a superb spiral and takes the air of us humming. Her underbody colloid is open and her transporter-slings hang down like tentacles. We shut off our beam as she adjusts herself—steering to a hair—over the tramp's conning-tower. The mate comes up, his arm strapped to his side, and stumbles into the cradle. A man with a ghastly scarlet head follows, shouting that he must go back and build up his Ray. The mate assures him that he will find a nice new Ray all ready in the liner's engine-room. The bandaged head goes up wagging excitedly. A youth and a woman follow. The liner cheers hollowly above us, and we see the passengers' faces at the saloon colloid.

"That's a pretty girl. What's the fool waiting for now?" says Captain Purnall.

The skipper comes up, still appealing to us to stand by and see him fetch St. John's. He dives below and returns—at which we little human beings in the void cheer louder than ever—with the ship's kitten. Up fly the liner's hissing slings; her underbody crashes home and she hurtles away again. The dial shows less than 3000 feet.

The Mark Boat signals we must attend to the derelict, now whistling her death-song, as she falls beneath us in long sick zigzags.

"Keep our beam on her and send out a General Warning," says Captain Purnall, following her down.

There is no need. Not a liner in air but knows the meaning of that vertical beam and gives us and our quarry a wide berth.

"But she'll drown in the water, won't she?" I ask.

"Not always," is his answer. "I've known a derelict up-end and sift her engines out of herself and flicker round the Lower Lanes for three weeks on her forward tanks only. We'll run no risks. Pith her, George, and look sharp. There's weather ahead."

Captain Hodgson opens the underbody colloid, swings the heavy pithing-iron out of its rack which in liners is generally cased as a smoking-room settee, and at two hundred feet releases the catch. We hear the whir of the crescent-shaped arms opening as they descend. The derelict's forehead is punched in, starred across, and rent diagonally. She falls stern first, our beam upon her; slides like a lost soul down that pitiless ladder of light, and the Atlantic takes her.

"A filthy business," says Hodgson. "I wonder what it must have been like in the old days?"

The thought had crossed my mind, too. What if that wavering carcass had been filled with the men of the old days, each one of them taught (*that* is the horror of it!) that after death he would very possibly go for ever to unspeakable torment?

And scarcely a generation ago, we (one knows now that we are only our fathers re-enlarged upon the earth), *we*, I say, ripped and rammed and pithed to admiration.

Here Tim, from the Control Platform, shouts that we are to get into our inflators and to bring him his at once.

We hurry into the heavy rubber suits—the engineers are already dressed—and inflate at the air-pump taps. G. P. O. inflators are thrice as thick as a racing man's "flickers," and chafe abominably under the armpits. George takes the wheel until Tim has blown himself up to the extreme of rotundity. If you kicked him off the c. p. to the deck he would bounce back. But it is "162" that will do the kicking.

"The Mark Boat's mad—stark ravin' crazy," he snorts, returning to command. "She says there's a bad blow-out ahead and wants me to pull over to Greenland. I'll see her pithed first! We wasted half an hour fussing over that dead duck down under, and now I'm expected to go rubbin' my back all round the Pole. What does she think a Postal packet's made of? Gummed silk? Tell her we're coming on straight, George."

George buckles him into the Frame and switches on the Direct Control. Now under Tim's left toe lies the port-engine Accelerator; under his left heel the Reverse, and so with the other foot. The lift-shunt stops stand out on the rim of the steering-wheel where the fingers of his left hand can play on them. At his right hand is the midships engine lever ready to be thrown into gear at a moment's notice. He leans forward in his belt, eyes glued to the colloid, and one ear cocked toward the General Communicator. Henceforth he is the strength and direction of "162," through whatever may befall.

The Banks Mark Boat is reeling out pages of A. B. C. Directions to the traffic at large. We are to secure all "loose objects"; hood up our Fleury Rays; and "on no account to attempt to clear snow from our conning-towers till the weather abates." Under-powered craft, we are told, can ascend to the limit of their lift, mail-packets to look out for them accordingly; the lower lanes westward are pitting very badly, "with frequent blow-outs, vortices, laterals, etc."

Still the clear dark holds up unblemished. The only warning is the electric skin-tension (I feel as though I were a lace-maker's pillow) and an irritability which the gibbering of the General Communicator increases almost to hysteria.

We have made eight thousand feet since we pithed the tramp and our turbines are giving us an honest two hundred and ten knots.

Very far to the west an elongated blur of red, low down, shows us the North Banks Mark Boat. There are specks of fire round her rising and falling—bewildered planets about an unstable sun—helpless shipping hanging on to her light for company's sake. No wonder she could not quit station.

She warns us to look out for the back-wash of the bad vortex in which (her beam shows it) she is even now reeling.

The pits of gloom about us begin to fill with very faintly luminous films—wreathing and uneasy shapes. One forms itself into a globe of pale flame that waits shivering with eagerness till we sweep by. It leaps monstrously across the blackness, alights on the precise tip of our nose, pirouettes there an instant, and swings off. Our roaring bow sinks as though that light were lead—sinks and recovers to lurch and stumble again beneath the next blow-out. Tim's fingers on the lift-shunt strike chords of numbers—1:4:7:—2:4:6:—7:5:3, and so on; for he is running by his tanks only, lifting or lowering her against the uneasy air. All three engines are at work, for the sooner we have skated over this thin ice the better. Higher we dare not go. The whole upper vault is charged with pale krypton vapours, which our skin friction may excite to unholy manifestations. Between the upper and lower levels—5000 and 7000, hints the Mark Boat—we may perhaps bolt through if . . . Our bow clothes itself in blue flame and falls like a sword. No human skill can keep pace with the changing tensions. A vortex has us by the beak and we dive down a two-thousand foot slant at an angle (the dip-dial and my bouncing body record it) of thirty-five. Our turbines scream shrilly; the propellers cannot bite on the thin air; Tim shunts the lift out of five tanks at once and by sheer weight drives her bullet-wise through the maelstrom till she cushions with a jar on an up-gust, three thousand feet below.

"*Now* we've done it," says George in my ear. "Our skin-friction, that last slide, has played Old Harry with the tensions! Look out for laterals, Tim; she'll want some holding."

"I've got her," is the answer. "Come *up*, old woman."

She comes up nobly, but the laterals buffet her left and right like the pinions of angry angels. She is jolted off her course four ways at once, and cuffed into place again, only to be swung aside and dropped into a new chaos. We are never without a corposant grinning on our bows or rolling head over heels from nose to midships, and to the crackle of electricity around and within us is added once or twice the rattle of hail—hail that will never fall on any sea. Slow we must or we may break our back, pitch-poling.

"Air's a perfectly elastic fluid," roars George above the tumult. "About as elastic as a head sea off the Fastnet, ain't it?"

He is less than just to the good element. If one intrudes on the Heavens when they are balancing their volt-accounts; if one disturbs the High Gods' market rates by hurling steel hulls at ninety knots across tremblingly adjusted electric tensions, one must not complain of any rudeness in the reception. Tim met it with an unmoved countenance, one corner of his under lip caught up on a tooth, his eyes fleeting into the blackness twenty miles ahead, and the fierce sparks flying from his knuckles at every turn of the hand. Now and again he shook his head to clear the sweat trickling from his eyebrows, and it was then that George, watching his chance, would slide down the life-rail and swab his face quickly with a big red handkerchief. I never imagined that a human being could so continuously labour and so collectedly think as did Tim through that Hell's half-hour when the flurry was at its worst. We were dragged hither and yon by warm or frozen suctions, belched up on the tops of wulli-was, spun down by vortices and clubbed aside by laterals under a dizzying rush of stars in the company of a drunken moon. I heard the rushing click of the midship-engine-lever sliding in and out, the low growl of the lift-shunts, and, louder then the yelling winds without, the scream of the bow-rudder gouging into any lull that promised hold for an instant. At last we began to claw up on a cant, bow-rudder and port-propeller together; only the nicest balancing of tanks saved us from spinning like the rifle-bullet of the old days.

"We've got to hitch to windward of that Mark Boat somehow," George cried.

"There's no windward," I protested feebly, where I swung shackled to a stanchion. "How can there be?"

He laughed—as we pitched into a thousand foot blow-out—that red man laughed beneath his inflated hood!

"Look!" he said. "We must clear those refugees with a high lift."

The Mark Boat was below and a little to the sou'west of us, fluctuating in the centre of her distraught galaxy. The air was thick with moving lights at every level. I take it most of them were trying to lie head to wind, but, not being hydras, they failed. An under-tanked Moghrabi boat had risen to the limit of her lift, and, finding no improvement, had dropped a couple of thousand. There she met a superb wulli-wa, and was blown up spinning like a dead leaf. Instead of shutting off she went astern and, naturally, rebounded as from a wall almost into the Mark Boat, whose language (our G. C. took it in) was humanly simple.

"If they'd only ride it out quietly it 'ud be better," said George in a calm, while we climbed like a bat above them all. "But some skippers *will* navigate without enough lift. What does that Tad-boat think she is doing, Tim?"

"Playin' kiss in the ring," was Tim's unmoved reply. A Trans-Asiatic Direct liner had found a smooth and butted into it full power. But there was a vortex at the tail of that smooth, so the T. A. D. was flipped out like a pea from off a finger-nail, braking madly as she fled down and all but over-ending.

"Now I hope she's satisfied," said Tim. "I'm glad I'm not a Mark Boat . . . Do I want help?" The General Communicator dial had caught his ear. "George, you may tell that gentleman with my love—love, remember, George—that I do not want help. Who *is* the officious sardine-tin?"

"A Rimouski drogher on the look-out for a tow."

"Very kind of the Rimouski drogher. This postal packet isn't being towed at present."

"Those droghers will go anywhere on a chance of salvage," George explained. "We call 'em kittiwakes."

A long-beaked, bright steel ninety-footer floated at ease for one instant within hail of us, her slings coiled ready for rescues, and a single hand in her open tower. He was smoking. Surrendered to the insurrection of the airs through which we tore our way, he lay in absolute peace. I saw the smoke of his pipe ascend untroubled ere his boat dropped, it seemed, like a stone in a well.

We had just cleared the Mark Boat and her disorderly neighbours when the storm ended as suddenly as it had begun. A shooting-star to northward filled the sky with the green blink of a meteorite dissipating itself in our atmosphere.

Said George: "That may iron out all the tensions." Even as he spoke, the conflicting winds came to rest; the levels filled; the laterals died out in long, easy swells; the air-ways were smoothed before us. In less than three minutes the covey round the Mark Boat had shipped their power-lights and whirred away upon their businesses.

"What's happened?" I gasped. The nerve-storm within and the volt-tingle without had passed: my inflators weighed like lead.

"God, He knows!" said Captain George soberly. "That old shooting-star's skin-friction has discharged the different levels. I've seen it happen before. Phew! What a relief!"

We dropped from ten to six thousand and got rid of our clammy suits. Tim shut off and stepped out of the Frame. The Mark Boat was coming up behind us. He opened the colloid in that heavenly stillness and mopped his face.

"Hello, Williams!" he cried. "A degree or two out o' station, ain't you?"

"May be," was the answer from the Mark Boat. "I've had some company this evening."

"So I noticed. Wasn't that quite a little draught?"

"I warned you. Why didn't you pull out north? The east-bound packets have."

"Me? Not till I'm running a Polar consumptives' sanatorium boat. I was squinting through a colloid before you were out of your cradle, my son."

"I'd be the last man to deny it," the captain of the Mark Boat replies softly. "The way you handled her just now—I'm a pretty fair judge of traffic in a volt-hurry—it was a thousand revolutions beyond anything even I've ever seen."

Tim's back supples visibly to this oiling. Captain George on the c. p. winks and points to the portrait of a singularly attractive maiden pinned up on Tim's telescope bracket above the steering-wheel.

I see. Wholly and entirely do I see!

There is some talk overhead of "coming round to tea on Friday," a brief report of the derelict's fate, and Tim volunteers as he descends: "For an A. B. C. man young Williams is less of a high-tension fool than some. . . . Were you thinking of taking her on, George? Then I'll just have a look round that port-thrust—seems to me it's a trifle warm—and we'll jog along."

The Mark Boat hums off joyously and hangs herself up in her appointed eyrie. Here she will stay a shutterless observatory; a life-boat station; a salvage tug; a court of ultimate appeal-cum-meteorological bureau for three hundred miles in all directions, till Wednesday next when her relief slides across the stars to take her buffeted place. Her black hull, double conning-tower, and ever-ready slings represent all that remains to the planet of that odd old word authority. She is responsible only to the Aerial Board of Control—the A. B. C. of which Tim speaks so flippantly. But that semi-elected, semi-nominated body of a few score of persons of both sexes, controls this planet. "Transportation is Civilisation," our motto runs. Theoretically, we do what we please so long as we do not interfere with the traffic *and all it implies*. Practically, the A. B. C. confirms or annuls all international arrangements and, to judge from its last report, finds our tolerant, humorous, lazy little planet only too ready to shift the whole burden of public administration on its shoulders.

I discuss this with Tim, sipping maté on the c. p. while George fans her along over the white blur of the Banks in beautiful upward curves of fifty miles each. The dip-dial translates them on the tape in flowing freehand.

Tim gathers up a skein of it and surveys the last few feet, which record "162's" path through the volt-flurry.

"I haven't had a fever-chart like this to show up in five years," he says ruefully.

A postal packet's dip-dial records every yard of every run. The tapes then go to the A. B. C., which collates and makes composite photographs of them for the instruction of captains. Tim studies his irrevocable past, shaking his head.

"Hello! Here's a fifteen-hundred-foot drop at fifty-five degrees! We must have been standing on our heads then, George."

"You don't say so," George answers. "I fancied I noticed it at the time."

George may not have Captain Purnall's catlike swiftness, but he is all an artist to the tips of the broad fingers that play on the shunt-stops. The delicious flight-curves come away on the tape with never a waver. The Mark Boat's vertical spindle of light lies down to eastward, setting in the face of the following stars. Westward, where no planet should rise, the triple verticals of Trinity Bay (we keep still to the Southern route) make a low-lifting haze. We seem the only thing at rest under all the heavens; floating at ease till the earth's revolution shall turn up our landing-towers.

And minute by minute our silent clock gives us a sixteen-second mile.

"Some fine night," says Tim, "we'll be even with that clock's Master."

"He's coming now," says George, over his shoulder. "I'm chasing the night west."

The stars ahead dim no more than if a film of mist had been drawn under unobserved, but the deep air-boom on our skin changes to a joyful shout.

"The dawn-gust," says Tim. "It'll go on to meet the Sun. Look! Look! There's the dark being crammed back over our bows! Come to the after-colloid. I'll show you something."

The engine-room is hot and stuffy; the clerks in the coach are asleep, and the Slave of the Ray is ready to follow them. Tim slides open the aft colloid and reveals the curve of the world—the ocean's deepest purple—edged with fuming and intolerable gold. Then the Sun rises and through the colloid strikes out our lamps. Tim scowls in his face.

"Squirrels in a cage," he mutters. "That's all we are. Squirrels in a cage! He's going twice as fast as us. Just you wait a few years, my shining friend, and we'll take steps that will amaze you. *We'll* Joshua you!"

Yes, that is our dream: to turn all earth into the Vale of Ajalon at our pleasure. So far, we can drag out the dawn to twice its normal length in these latitudes. But some day—even on the Equator—we shall hold the Sun level in his full stride.

Now we look down on a sea thronged with heavy traffic. A big submersible breaks water suddenly. Another and another follows with a swash and a suck and a savage bubbling of relieved pressures. The deep-sea freighters are rising to lung up after the long night, and the leisurely ocean is all patterned with peacock's eyes of foam.

"We'll lung up, too," says Tim, and when we return to the c. p. George shuts off, the colloids are opened, and the fresh air sweeps her out. There is no hurry. The old contracts (they will be revised at the end of the year) allow twelve hours for a run which any packet can put behind her in ten. So we breakfast in the arms of an easterly slant which pushes us along at a languid twenty.

To enjoy life, and tobacco, begin both on a sunny morning half a mile or so above the dappled Atlantic cloud-belts and after a volt-flurry which has cleared and tempered your nerves. While we discussed the thickening traffic with the superiority that comes of having a high level reserved to ourselves, we heard (and I for the first time) the morning hymn on a Hospital boat.

She was cloaked by a skein of ravelled fluff beneath us and we caught the chant before she rose into the sunlight. "*Oh, ye Winds of God*," sang the unseen voices: "*bless ye the Lord! Praise Him and magnify Him for ever*!"

We slid off our caps and joined in. When our shadow fell across her great open platforms they looked up and stretched out their hands neighbourly while they sang. We could see the doctors and the nurses and the white-button-like faces of the cot-patients. She passed slowly beneath us, heading northward, her hull, wet with the dews of the night, all ablaze in the sunshine. So took she the shadow of a cloud and vanished, her song continuing. *"Oh, ye holy and humble men of heart, bless ye the Lord! Praise Him and magnify Him for ever."*

"She's a public lunger or she wouldn't have been singing the *Benedicite*; and she's a Greenlander or she wouldn't have snow-blinds over her colloids," said George at last. "She'll be bound for Frederikshavn or one of the Glacier sanatoriums for a month. If she was an accident ward she'd be hung up at the eight-thousand-foot level. Yes—consumptives."

"Funny how the new things are the old things. I've read in books," Tim answered, "that savages used to haul their sick and wounded up to the tops of hills because microbes were fewer there. We hoist 'em into sterilized air for a while. Same idea. How much do the doctors say we've added to the average life of a man?"

"Thirty years," says George with a twinkle in his eye. "Are we going to spend 'em all up here, Tim?"

"Flap ahead, then. Flap ahead. Who's hindering?" the senior captain laughed, as we went in.

We held a good lift to clear the coastwise and Continental shipping; and we had need of it. Though our route is in no sense a populated one, there is a steady trickle of traffic this way along. We met Hudson Bay furriers out of the Great Preserve, hurrying to make their departure from Bonavista with sable and black fox for the insatiable markets. We overcrossed Keewatin liners, small and cramped; but their captains, who see no land between Trepassy and Blanco, know what gold they bring back from West Africa. Trans-Asiatic Directs we met, soberly ringing the world round the Fiftieth Meridian at an honest seventy knots; and white-painted Ackroyd & Hunt fruiters out of the south fled beneath us, their ventilated hulls whistling like Chinese kites. Their market is in the North among the northern sanatoria where you can smell their grape-fruit and bananas across the cold snows. Argentine beef boats we sighted too, of enormous capacity and unlovely outline. They, too, feed the northern health stations in icebound ports where submersibles dare not rise.

Yellow-bellied ore-flats and Ungava petrol-tanks punted down leisurely out of the north, like strings of unfrightened wild duck. It does not pay to "fly" minerals and oil a mile farther than is necessary; but the risks of transhipping to submersibles in the icepack off Nain or Hebron are so great that these heavy freighters fly down to Halifax direct, and scent the air as they go. They are the biggest tramps aloft except the Athabasca grain-tubs. But these last, now that the wheat is moved, are busy, over the world's shoulder, timber-lifting in Siberia.

We held to the St. Lawrence (it is astonishing how the old water-ways still pull us children of the air), and followed his broad line of black between its drifting ice-blocks, all down the Park that the wisdom of our fathers—but every one knows the Quebec run.

We dropped to the Heights Receiving Towers twenty minutes ahead of time, and there hung at ease till the Yokohama Intermediate Packet could pull out and give us our proper slip. It was curious to watch the action of the holding-down clips all along the frosty river front as the boats cleared or came to rest. A big Hamburger was leaving Pont Levis and her crew, unshipping the platform railings, began to sing "Elsinore"—the oldest of our chanteys. You know it of course:

Mother Rugen's tea-house on the Baltic—
  Forty couple waltzing on the floor!
And you can watch my Ray,

For I must go away
  And dance with Ella Sweyn at Elsinore!

Then, while they sweated home the covering-plates:

Nor-Nor-Nor-Nor-
West from Sourabaya to the Baltic—
  Ninety knot an hour to the Skaw!
Mother Rugen's tea-house on the Baltic
  And a dance with Ella Sweyn at Elsinore!

The clips parted with a gesture of indignant dismissal, as though Quebec, glittering under her snows, were casting out these light and unworthy lovers. Our signal came from the Heights. Tim turned and floated up, but surely then it was with passionate appeal that the great tower arms flung open—or did I think so because on the upper staging a little hooded figure also opened her arms wide toward her father?

In ten seconds the coach with its clerks clashed down to the receiving-caisson; the hostlers displaced the engineers at the idle turbines, and Tim, prouder of this than all, introduced me to the maiden of the photograph on the shelf. "And by the way," said he to her, stepping forth in sunshine under the hat of civil life, "I saw young Williams in the Mark Boat. I've asked him to tea on Friday."

AERIAL BOARD OF CONTROL

Lights

No changes in English Inland lights for week ending Dec. 18th.

CAPE VERDE—Week ending Dec. 18. Verde inclined guide-light changes from 1st proximo to triple flash—green white green—in place of occulting red as heretofore. The warning light for Harmattan winds will be continuous vertical glare (white) on all oases of trans-Saharan N. E. by E. Main Routes.

INVERCARGIL (N. Z.)—From 1st prox.: extreme southerly light (double red) will exhibit white beam inclined 45 degrees on approach of Southerly Buster. Traffic flies high off this coast between April and October.

TABLE BAY—Devil's Peak Glare removed to Simonsberg. Traffic making Table Mountain coastwise keep all lights from Three Anchor Bay at least two thousand feet under, and do not round to till East of E. shoulder Devil's Peak.

SANDHEADS LIGHT—Green triple vertical marks new private landing-stage for Bay and Burma traffic only.

SNAEFELL JOKUL—White occulting light withdrawn for winter.

PATAGONIA—No summer light south Cape Pilar. This includes Staten Island and Port Stanley.

C. NAVARIN—Quadruple fog flash (white), one minute intervals (new).

EAST CAPE—Fog flash—single white with single bomb, 30 sec. intervals (new).

MALAYAN ARCHIPELAGO—Lights unreliable owing eruptions. Lay from Cape Somerset to Singapore direct, keeping highest levels.

For the Board:

CATTERTHUN
ST. JUST
VAN HEDDER } *Lights.*

Casualties

Week ending Dec. 18th.

SABLE ISLAND—Green single barbette-tower freighter, number indistinguishable, up-ended, and fore-tank pierced after collision, passed 300-ft. level 2 P.M. Dec. 15th. Watched to water and pithed by Mark Boat.

N. F. BANKS—Postal Packet 162 reports *Halma* freighter (Fowey—St. John's) abandoned, leaking after weather, 46° 15′ N. 50° 15′ W. Crew rescued by Planet liner *Asteroid*. Watched to water and pithed by Postal Packet, Dec. 14th.

KERGUELEN, MARK BOAT reports last call from *Cymena* freighter (Gayer Tong Huk & Co.) taking water and sinking in snow-storm South McDonald Islands. No wreckage recovered. Messages and wills of crew at all A. B. C. offices.

FEZZAN—T. A. D. freighter *Ulema* taken ground during Harmattan on Akakus Range. Under plates strained. Crew at Ghat where repairing Dec. 13th.

BISCAY, MARK BOAT reports *Carducci* (Valandingham Line) slightly spiked in western gorge Point de Benasque. Passengers transferred *Andorra* (Fulton Line). Barcelona Mark Boat salving cargo Dec. 12th.

ASCENSION, MARK BOAT—Wreck of unknown racing-plane, Parden rudder, wire-stiffened xylonite vans, and Harliss engine-seating, sighted and salved 7° 20′ S. 18° 41′ W. Dec. 15th. Photos at all A. B. C. offices.

Missing

No answer to General Call having been received during the last week from following overdues, they are posted as missing:

Atlantis, W. 17630	Canton—Valparaiso
Audhumla W. 889	Stockholm—Odessa
Berenice, W. 2206	Riga—Vladivostock
Draco, E. 446	Coventry—Puntas Arenas
Tontine, E. 3068	C. Wrath—Ungava
Wu-Sung, E. 41776	Hankow—Lobito Bay

General Call (all Mark Boats) out for:

Jane Eyre, W. 6990	Port Rupert—City of Mexico
Santander, W. 5514	Gobi Desert—Manila
V. Edmundsun, E. 9690 . . .	Kandahar—Fiume

Broke for Obstruction, and Quitting Levels

VALKYRIE (racing plane), A. J. Hartley owner, New York (twice warned).
GEISHA (racing plane), S. van Cott owner, Philadelphia (twice warned).
MARVEL OF PERU (racing plane), J. X. Peixoto owner, Rio de Janeiro (twice warned).

For the Board:

LAZAREFF
MCKEOUGH } *Traffic.*
GOLDBLATT

NOTES

High-Level Sleet

The Northern weather so far shows no sign of improvement. From all quarters come complaints of the unusual prevalence of sleet at the higher levels. Racing-planes and digs alike have suffered severely—the former from unequal deposits of half-frozen slush on their vans (and only those who have "held up" a badly balanced plane in a cross-wind know what that means), and the latter from loaded bows and snow-cased bodies. As a consequence, the Northern and North-western upper levels have been practically abandoned, and the high fliers have returned to the ignoble security of the Three, Five, and Six hundred foot levels. But there remain a few undaunted sun-hunters who, in spite of frozen stays and ice-jammed connecting-rods, still haunt the blue empyrean.

Bat-Boat Racing

The scandals of the past few years have at last moved the yachting world to concerted action in regard to "bat" boat racing.

We have been treated to the spectacle of what are practically keeled racing-planes driven a clear five foot or more above the water, and only eased down to touch their so-called "native element" as they near the line. Judges and starters have been conveniently blind to this absurdity, but the public demonstration off St. Catherine's Light at the Autumn Regattas has borne ample, if tardy, fruit. In the future the "bat" is to be a boat, and the long-unheeded demand of the true sportsman for "no daylight under mid-keel in smooth water" is in a fair way to be conceded. The new rule severely restricts plane area and lift alike. The gas compartments are permitted both fore and aft, as in the old type, but the water-ballast central tank is rendered obligatory. These things work, if not for perfection, at least for the evolution of a sane and wholesome *waterborne* cruiser. The type of rudder is unaffected by the new rules, so we may expect to see the Long-Davidson make (the patent on which has just expired) come largely into use henceforward, though the strain on the sternpost in turning at speeds over forty miles an hour is admittedly very severe. But bat-boat racing has a great future before it.

Crete and the A. B. C.

The story of the recent Cretan crisis, as told in the A. B. C. *Monthly Report*, is not without humour. Till the 25th October Crete, as all our planet knows, was the sole surviving European repository of "autonomous institutions," "local self-government," and the rest of the archaic lumber devised in the past for the confusion of human affairs. She has lived practically on the tourist traffic attracted by her annual pageants of Parliaments, Boards, Municipal Councils, etc., etc. Last summer the islanders grew wearied, as their premier explained, of "playing at being savages for pennies," and proceeded to pull down all the landing-towers on the island and shut off general communication till such time as the A. B. C. should annex them. For side-splitting comedy we would refer our readers to the correspondence between the Board of Control and the Cretan premier during the "war." However, all's well that ends well. The A. B. C. have taken over the administration of Crete on normal lines; and tourists must go elsewhere to witness the "debates," "resolutions," and "popular movements" of the old days. The only people to suffer will be the Board of Control, which is grievously overworked already. It is easy enough to condemn the Cretans for their laziness; but when one recalls the large, prosperous, and presumably public-spirited communities which during the last few years have deliberately thrown themselves into the hands of the A. B. C., one cannot be too hard upon St. Paul's old friends.

CORRESPONDENCE

Skylarking on the Equator

TO THE EDITOR: Only last week, while crossing the Equator (W. 26-15), I became aware of a furious and irregular cannonading some fifteen or twenty knots S. 4 E. Descending to the 500 ft. level, I found a party of Transylvanian tourists engaged in exploding scores of the largest pattern atmospheric bombs (A. B. C. standard) and, in the intervals of their pleasing labours, firing bow and stern smoke-ring swivels. This orgie—I can give it no other name—went on for at least two hours, and naturally produced violent electric derangements. My compasses, of course, were thrown out, my bow was struck twice, and I received two brisk shocks from the lower platform-rail. On remonstrating, I was told that these "professors" were engaged in scientific experiments. The extent of their "scientific" knowledge may be judged by the fact that they expected to produce (I give their own words) "a little blue sky" if "they went on long enough." This in the heart of the Doldrums at 450 feet! I have no objection to any amount of blue sky in its proper place (it can be found at the 4000 level for practically twelve months out of the year), but I submit, with all deference to the educational needs of Transylvania, that "skylarking" in the centre of a main-travelled road where, at the best of times, electricity literally drips off one's stanchions and screw blades, is unnecessary. When my friends had finished, the road was seared, and blown, and pitted with unequal pressure-layers, spirals, vortices, and readjustments for at least an hour. I pitched badly twice in an upward rush—solely due to these diabolical throw-downs—that came near to wrecking my propeller. Equatorial work at low levels is trying enough in all conscience without the added terrors of scientific hooliganism in the Doldrums.

Rhyl. J. VINCENT MATHEN

[We entirely sympathize with Professor Mathen's views, but till the Board sees fit to further regulate the Southern areas in which scientific experiments may be conducted, we shall always be exposed to the risk which our correspondent describes. Unfortunately, a chimera bombinating in a vacuum is, nowadays, only too capable of producing secondary causes.—*Editor*.]

Answers to Correspondents

VIGILANS—The Laws of Auroral Derangements are still imperfectly understood. Any overheated motor may of course "seize" without warning; but so many complaints have reached us of accidents similar to yours while shooting the Aurora that we are inclined to believe with Lavalle that the upper strata of the Aurora Borealis are practically one big electric "leak," and that the paralysis of your engines was due to complete magnetization of all metallic parts. Low-flying planes often "glue up" when near the Magnetic Pole, and there is no reason in science why the same disability should not be experienced at higher levels when the Auroras are "delivering" strongly.

INDIGNANT—On your own showing, you were not under control. That you could not hoist the necessary N. U. C. lights on approaching a traffic-lane because your electrics had short-circuited is a misfortune which might befall any one. The A. B. C., being responsible for the planet's traffic, cannot, however, make allowance for this kind of misfortune. A reference to the Code will show that you were fined on the lower scale.

PLANISTON—(1) The Five Thousand Kilometre (overland) was won last year by L. V. Rautsch; R. M. Rautsch, his brother, in the same week pulling off the Ten Thousand (oversea). R. M.'s average worked out at a fraction over 500 kilometres per hour, thus constituting a record. (2) Theoretically, there is no limit to the lift of a dirigible. For commercial and practical purposes 15,000 tons is accepted as the most manageable.

PATERFAMILIAS—None whatever. He is liable for direct damage both to your chimneys and any collateral damage caused by fall of bricks into garden, etc.,

etc. Bodily inconvenience and mental anguish may be included, but the average courts are not, as a rule, swayed by sentiment. If you can prove that his grapnel removed *any* portion of your roof, you had better rest your case on decoverture of domicile (see Parkins *v.* Duboulay). We sympathize with your position, but the night of the 14th was stormy and confused, and—you may have to anchor on a stranger's chimney yourself some night. *Verbum sap!*

ALDEBARAN—(1) War, as a paying concern, ceased in 1967. (2) The Convention of London expressly reserves to every nation the right of waging war so long as it does not interfere with the traffic *and all that implies*. (3) The A. B. C. was constituted in 1949.

L. M. D.—(1) Keep her full head-on at half power, taking advantage of the lulls to speed up and creep into it. She will strain much less this way than in quartering across a gale. (2) Nothing is to be gained by reversing into a following gale, and there is always risk of a turn-over. (3) The formulae for stun'sle brakes are uniformly unreliable, and will continue to be so as long as air is compressible.

PEGAMOID—(1) Personally we prefer glass or flux compounds to any other material for winter work nose-caps as being absolutely non-hygroscopic. (2) We cannot recommend any particular make.

PULMONAR—(1) For the symptoms you describe, try the Gobi Desert Sanatoria. The low levels of most of the Saharan Sanatoria are against them except at the outset of the disease. (2) We do not recommend boarding-houses or hotels in this column.

BEGINNER—On still days the air above a large inhabited city being slightly warmer—*i.e.*, thinner—than the atmosphere of the surrounding country, a plane drops a little on entering the rarefied area, precisely as a ship sinks a little in fresh water. Hence the phenomena of "jolt" and your "inexplicable collisions" with factory chimneys. In air, as on earth, it is safest to fly high.

EMERGENCY—There is only one rule of the road in air, earth, and water. Do you want the firmament to yourself?

PICCIOLA—Both Poles have been overdone in Art and Literature. Leave them to Science for the next twenty years. You did not send a stamp with your verses.

NORTH NIGERIA—The Mark Boat was within her right in warning you off the Reserve. The shadow of a low-flying dirigible scares the game. You can buy all the photos you need at Sokoto.

NEW ERA—It is not etiquette to overcross an A. B. C. official's boat without asking permission. He is one of the body responsible for the planet's traffic, and for that reason must not be interfered with. You, presumably, are out on your own business or pleasure, and must leave him alone. For humanity's sake don't try to be "democratic."

EXCORIATED—All inflators chafe sooner or later. You must go on till your skin hardens by practice. Meantime vaseline.

REVIEW

The Life of Xavier Lavalle
(Reviewed by Réné Talland. École Aëronautique, Paris)

Ten years ago Lavalle, "that imperturbable dreamer of the heavens," as Lazareff hailed him, gathered together the fruits of a lifetime's labour, and gave it, with well-justified contempt, to a world bound hand and foot to Barald's Theory of Vertices and "compensating electric nodes." "They shall see," he wrote—in that immortal postscript to *The Heart of the Cyclone*—"the Laws whose existence they derided written in fire *beneath* them."

"But even here," he continues, "there is no finality. Better a thousand times my conclusions should be discredited than that my dead name should lie across the threshold of the temple of Science—a bar to further inquiry."

So died Lavalle—a prince of the Powers of the Air, and even at his funeral Céllier jested at "him who had gone to discover the secrets of the Aurora Borealis."

If I choose thus to be banal, it is only to remind you that Céllier's theories are to-day as exploded as the ludicrous deductions of the Spanish school. In the place of their fugitive and warring dreams we have, definitely, Lavalle's Law of the Cyclone which he surprised in darkness and cold at the foot of the overarching throne of the Aurora Borealis. It is there that I, intent on my own investigations, have passed and re-passed a hundred times the worn leonine face, white as the snow beneath him, furrowed with wrinkles like the seams and gashes upon the North Cape; the nervous hand, integrally a part of the mechanism of his flighter; and above all, the wonderful lambent eyes turned to the zenith.

"Master," I would cry as I moved respectfully beneath him, "what is it you seek to-day?" and always the answer, clear and without doubt, from above: "The old secret, my son!"

The immense egotism of youth forced me on my own path, but (cry of the human always!) had I known—if I had known—I would many times have bartered my poor laurels for the privilege, such as Tinsley and Herrera possess, of having aided him in his monumental researches.

It is to the filial piety of Victor Lavalle that we owe the two volumes consecrated to the ground-life of his father, so full of the holy intimacies of the domestic hearth. Once returned from the abysms of the utter North to that little house upon the outskirts of Meudon, it was not the philosopher, the daring observer, the man of iron energy that imposed himself on his family, but a fat and even plaintive jester, a farceur incarnate and kindly, the co-equal of his children, and, it must be written, not seldom the comic despair of Madame Lavalle, who, as she writes five years after the marriage, to her venerable mother, found "in this unequalled intellect whose name I bear the abandon of a large and very untidy boy." Here is her letter:

"Xavier returned from I do not know where at midnight, absorbed in calculations on the eternal question of his Aurora—*la belle Aurore*, whom I begin to hate. Instead of anchoring—I had set out the guide-light above our roof, so he had but to descend and fasten the plane—he wandered, profoundly distracted, above the town with his anchor down! Figure to yourself, dear mother, it is the roof of the mayor's house that the grapnel first engages! That I do not regret, for the mayor's wife and I are not sympathetic; but when Xavier uproots my pet araucaria and bears it across the garden into the conservatory I protest at the top of my voice. Little Victor in his night-clothes runs to the window, enormously amused at the parabolic flight without reason, for it is too dark to see the grapnel, of my prized tree. The Mayor of Meudon, thunders at our door in the name of the Law, demanding, I suppose, my husband's head. Here is the conversation through the megaphone—Xavier is two hundred feet above us:

" 'Mons. Lavalle, descend and make reparation for outrage of domicile. Descend, Mons. Lavalle!'

"No one answers.

" 'Xavier Lavalle, in the name of the Law, descend and submit to process for outrage of domicile.'

"Xavier, roused from his calculations, comprehending only the last words: 'Outrage of domicile? My dear mayor, who is the man that has corrupted thy Julie?'

"The mayor, furious, 'Xavier Lavalle——'

"Xavier, interrupting: 'I have not that felicity. I am only a dealer in cyclones!'

"My faith, he raised one then! All Meudon attended in the streets, and my Xavier, after a long time comprehending what he had done, excused himself in a thousand apologies. At last the reconciliation was effected in our house over a supper at two in the morning—Julie in a wonderful costume of compromises, and I have her and the mayor pacified in bed in the blue room."

And on the next day, while the mayor rebuilds his roof, her Xavier departs anew for the Aurora Borealis, there to commence his life's work. M. Victor Lavalle tells us of that historic collision (*en plane*) on the flank of Hecla between Herrera, then a pillar of the Spanish school, and the man destined to confute his theories and lead him intellectually captive. Even through the years, the immense laugh of Lavalle as he sustains the Spaniard's wrecked plane, and cries: "Courage! *I* shall not fall till I have found Truth, and I hold *you* fast!" rings like the call of trumpets. This is that Lavalle whom the world, immersed in speculations of immediate gain, did not know nor suspect—the Lavalle whom they adjudged to the last a pedant and a theorist.

The human, as apart from the scientific, side (developed in his own volumes) of his epoch-making discoveries is marked with a simplicity, clarity, and good sense beyond praise. I would specially refer such as doubt the sustaining influence of ancestral faith upon character and will to the eleventh and nineteenth chapters, in which are contained the opening and consummation of the Tellurionical Records extending over nine years. Of their tremendous significance be sure that the modest house at Meudon knew as little as that the Records would one day be the planet's standard in all official meteorology. It was enough for them that their Xavier—this son, this father, this husband—ascended periodically to commune with powers, it might be angelic, beyond their comprehension, and that they united daily in prayers for his safety.

"Pray for me," he says upon the eve of each of his excursions, and returning, with an equal simplicity, he renders thanks "after supper in the little room where he kept his barometers."

To the last Lavalle was a Catholic of the old school, accepting—he who had looked into the very heart of the lightnings—the dogmas of papal infallibility, of absolution, of confession—of relics great and small. Marvellous—enviable contradiction!

The completion of the Tellurionical Records closed what Lavalle himself was pleased to call the theoretical side of his labours—labours from which the youngest and least impressionable planeur might well have shrunk. He had traced through cold and heat, across the deeps of the oceans, with instruments of his own invention, over the inhospitable heart of the polar ice and the sterile visage of the deserts, league by league, patiently, unweariedly, remorselessly, from their ever-shifting cradle under the magnetic pole to their exalted death-bed in the utmost ether of the upper atmosphere—each one of the Isoconical Tellurions—Lavalle's Curves, as we call them to-day. He had disentangled the nodes of their intersections, assigning to each its regulated period of flux and reflux. Thus equipped, he summons Herrera and Tinsley, his pupils, to the final demonstration as calmly as though he were ordering his flighter for some mid-day journey to Marseilles.

"I have proved my thesis," he writes. "It remains now only that you should witness the proof. We go to Manila to-morrow. A cyclone will form off the

Pescadores S. 17 E. in four days, and will reach its maximum intensity twenty-seven hours after inception. It is there I will show you the Truth."

A letter heretofore unpublished from Herrera to Madame Lavalle tells us how the Master's prophecy was verified.

I will not destroy its simplicity or its significance by any attempt to quote. Note well, though, that Herrera's preoccupation throughout that day and night of superhuman strain is always for the Master's bodily health and comfort. "At such a time," he writes, "I forced the Master to take the broth"; or "I made him put on the fur coat as you told me." Nor is Tinsley (see pp. 184, 85) less concerned. He prepares the nourishment. He cooks eternally, imperturbably, suspended in the chaos of which the Master interprets the meaning. Tinsley, bowed down with the laurels of both hemispheres, raises himself to yet nobler heights in his capacity of a devoted *chef*. It is almost unbelievable! And yet men write of the Master as cold, aloof, self-contained. Such characters do not elicit the joyous and unswerving devotion which Lavalle commanded throughout life. Truly, we have changed very little in the course of the ages! The secrets of earth and sky and the links that bind them, we felicitate ourselves we are on the road to discover; but our neighbours' heart and mind we misread, we misjudge, we condemn—now as ever. Let all, then, who love a man read these most human, tender, and wise volumes.

MISCELLANEOUS

WANTS

REQUIRED IMMEDIATELY, FOR East Africa, a thoroughly competent Plane and Dirigible Driver, acquainted with Petrol Radium and Helium motors and generators. Low-level work only, but must understand heavy-weight digs.

MOSSAMEDES TRANSPORT ASSOC.
84 Palestine Buildings, E. C.

MAN WANTED — DIG DRIVER for Southern Alps with Saharan summer trips. High levels, high speed, high wages.

Apply M. SIDNEY
Hotel San Stefano, Monte Carlo.

FAMILY DIRIGIBLE. A COMPETENT, steady man wanted for slow speed, low level Tangye dirigible. No night work, no sea trips. Must be member of the Church of England, and make himself useful in the garden.

M. R.,
The Rectory, Gray's Barton, Wilts.

COMMERCIAL DIG, CENTRAL and Southern Europe. A smart, active man for a L. M. T. Dig. Night work only. Headquarters London and Cairo. A linguist preferred.

BAGMAN
Charing Cross Hotel, W. C. (urgent.)

FOR SALE — A BARGAIN — SINGLE Plane, narrow-gauge vans, Pinke motor. Restayed this autumn. Hansen air-kit, 38 in. chest, 15½ collar. Can be seen by appointment.

N. 2650, This office.

The Bee-Line Bookshop

BELT'S WAY-BOOKS, giving town lights for all towns over 4,000 pop. as laid down by A. B. C.

THE WORLD. Complete 2 vols. Thin Oxford, limp back. 12s. 6d.

BELT'S COASTAL ITINERARY. Shore Lights of the World. 7s. 6d.

THE TRANSATLANTIC AND MEDITERRANEAN TRAFFIC LINES. (By authority of the A.B.C.) Paper, 1s. 6d.; cloth, 2s. 6d. Ready Jan. 15.

ARCTIC AEROPLANING. Siemens and Galt. Cloth, bds. 3s. 6d.

LAVALLE'S HEART OF THE CYCLONE, with supplementary charts. 4s. 6d.

RIMINGTON'S PITFALLS IN THE AIR, and Table of Comparative Densities. 3s. 6d.

ANGELO'S DESERT IN A DIRIGIBLE. New edition, revised. 5s. 9d.

VAUGHAN'S PLANE RACING IN CALM AND STORM. 2s. 6d.

VAUGHAN'S HINTS TO THE AIRMATEUR. 1s.

HOFMAN'S LAWS OF LIFT AND VELOCITY. With diagrams, 3s. 6d.

DE VITRE'S THEORY OF SHIFTING BALLAST IN DIRIGIBLES. 2s. 6d.

SANGER'S WEATHERS OF THE WORLD. 4s.

SANGER'S TEMPERATURES AT HIGH ALTITUDES. 4s.

HAWKIN'S FOG AND HOW TO AVOID IT. 3s.

VAN ZUYLAN'S SECONDARY EFFECTS OF THUNDERSTORMS. 4s. 6d.

DAHLGREN'S AIR CURRENTS AND EPIDEMIC DISEASES. 5s. 6d.

REDMAYNE'S DISEASE AND THE BAROMETER. 7s. 6d.

WALTON'S HEALTH RESORTS OF THE GOBI AND SHAMO. 3s. 6d.

WALTON'S THE POLE AND PULMONARY COMPLAINTS. 7s. 6d.

MUTLOW'S HIGH LEVEL BACTERIOLOGY. 7s. 6d.

HALLIWELL'S ILLUMINATED STAR MAP, with clockwork attachment, giving apparent motion of heavens, boxed, complete with clamps for binnacle, 36 inch size, only £2. 2. 0. (Invaluable for night work.) With A.B.C. certificate, £3. 10s. 0d.

Zalinski's Standard Works:
PASSES OF THE HIMALAYAS, 5s.
PASSES OF THE SIERRAS, 5s.
PASSES OF THE ROCKIES, 5s.
PASSES OF THE URALS, 5s.
The four boxed, limp cloth, with charts, 15s.

GRAY'S AIR CURRENTS IN MOUNTAIN GORGES, 7s. 6d.

A. C. BELT & SON, READING

SAFETY WEAR FOR AERONAUTS

Flickers! Flickers! Flickers!

High Level Flickers

"He that is down need fear no fall"
Fear not! You will fall lightly as down!

¶ Hansen's air-kits are down in all respects. Tremendous reductions in prices previous to winter stocking. Pure para kit with cellulose seat and shoulder-pads, weighted to balance. Unequalled for all drop-work.

Our trebly resilient heavy kit is the *ne plus ultra* of comfort and safety.

Gas-buoyed, waterproof, hail-proof, non-conducting Flickers with pipe and nozzle fitting all types of generator. Graduated tap on left hip.

Hansen's Flickers Lead the Aerial Flight
197 Oxford Street

The new weighted Flicker with tweed or cheviot surface cannot be distinguished from the ordinary suit till inflated.

Flickers! Flickers! Flickers!

APPLIANCES FOR AIR PLANES

What

"SKID"

was to our forefathers on the ground,

"PITCH"

is to their sons in the air.

The popularity of the large, unwieldy, slow, expensive Dirigible over the light, swift, Plane is mainly due to the former's immunity from pitch.

Collison's forward-socketed Air Van renders it impossible for any plane to pitch. The C.F S. is automatic, simple as a shutter, certain as a power hammer, safe as oxygen. Fitted to any make of plane.

COLLISON
186 Brompton Road
Workshops, Chiswick

LUNDIE & MATHERS
Sole Agts for East'n Hemisphere

Starters and Guides

Hotel, club, and private house plane-starters, slips and guides affixed by skilled workmen in accordance with local building laws.

Rackstraw's forty-foot collapsible steel starters with automatic release at end of travel —prices per foot run, clamps and crampons included. The safest on the market.

Weaver & Denison
Middleboro

AIR PLANES AND DIRIGIBLES

C.M.C.

Our Synthetical Mineral

BEARINGS

are chemically and crystallogically identical with the minerals whose names they bear. Any size, any surface.

Diamond, Rock-Crystal, Agate and Ruby Bearings—cups, caps and collars for the higher speeds.

For tractor bearings and spindles—Imperative.

For rear propellers—Indispensable.

For all working parts—Advisable.

Commercial Minerals Co.
107 Minories

Resurgam!

IF YOU HAVE NOT CLOTHED YOURSELF IN A

Normandie Resurgam

YOU WILL PROBABLY NOT BE INTERESTED IN OUR NEXT WEEK'S LIST OF AIR-KIT.

Resurgam Air-Kit Emporium

HYMANS & GRAHAM
1198
Lower Broadway, New York

Remember!

¶ It is now nearly a generation since the Plane was to supersede the Dirigible for all purposes.

¶ TO-DAY *none* of the Planet's freight is carried *en plane.*

¶ Less than two per cent. of the Planet's passengers are carried *en plane.*

We design, equip and guarantee Dirigibles for all purposes.

Standard Dig Construction Company
MILLWALL and BUENOS AYRES

BAT-BOATS

Flint & Mantel

Southampton

FOR SALE

at the end of Season the following Bat-Boats:

GRISELDA, 65 knt., 42 ft., 430 (nom.) Maginnis Motor, under-rake rudder.
MABELLE, 50 knt., 40 ft., 310 Hargreaves Motor, Douglas' lock-steering gear.
IVEMONA, 50 knt., 35 ft., 300 Hargreaves (Radium accelerator), Miller keel and rudder.

The above are well known on the South Coast as sound, wholesome knockabout boats, with ample cruising accommodation. *Griselda* carries spare set of Hofman racing vans and can be lifted three foot clear in smooth water with ballast-tank swung aft. The others do not lift clear of water, and are recommended for beginners.

Also, by private treaty, racing B. B. *Tarpon* (76 winning flags) 120 knt., 60 ft.; Long-Davidson double under-rake rudder, new this season and unstrained. 850 nom. Maginnis motor, Radium relays and Pond generator. Bronze breakwater forward, and treble reinforced forefoot and entry. Talfourd rockered keel. Triple set of Hofman vans, giving maximum lifting surface of 5327 sq. ft.

Tarpon has been lifted *and held* seven feet for two miles between touch and touch.

Our Autumn List of racing and family Bats ready on the 9th January.

AIR PLANES AND STARTERS

Hinks's Moderator

¶ Monorail overhead starter for family and private planes up to twenty-five foot over all

Absolutely Safe

Hinks & Co., Birmingham

J. D. ARDAGH

I AM NOT CONCERNED WITH YOUR 'PLANE AFTER IT LEAVES MY GUIDES, BUT *TILL THEN* I HOLD MYSELF PERSONALLY RESPONSIBLE FOR YOUR LIFE SAFETY, AND COMFORT. MY HYDRAULIC BUFFER-STOP *CANNOT* RELEASE TILL THE MOTORS ARE WORKING UP TO BEARING SPEED, THUS SECURING A SAFE AND GRACEFUL FLIGHT WITHOUT PITCHING.

Remember our motto, *"Upward and Outward,"* and do not trust yourself to so-called "rigid" guide-bars

J. D. ARDAGH, BELFAST AND TURIN

ACCESSORIES AND SPARES | ACCESSORIES AND SPARES

CHRISTIAN WRIGHT & OLDIS

ESTABLISHED 1924

Accessories and Spares

Hooded Binnacles with dip-dials automatically recording change of level (illuminated face).

All heights from 50 to 15,000 feet . . . £2 10 0
With Aerial Board of Control certificate . . . £3 11 0

Foot and Hand Foghorns; Sirens toned to any club note; with air-chest belt-driven from motor £6 8 0

Wireless installations syntonised to A.B.C. requirements, in neat mahogany case, hundred mile range £3 3 0

Grapnels, mushroom-anchors, pithing-irons, winches, hawsers, snaps, shackles and mooring ropes, for lawn, city, and public installations.

Detachable under-cars, aluminum or stamped steel.

Keeled under-cars for planes: single-action detaching-gear, turning car into boat with one motion of the wrist. Invaluable for sea trips.

Head, side, and riding lights (by size) Nos. 00 to 20 A.B.C. Standard. Rockets and fog-bombs in colours and tones of the principal clubs (boxed).

A selection of twenty . . . £2 17 6
International night-signals (boxed) . . . £1 11 6

Spare generators guaranteed to lifting power marked on cover (prices according to power).

Wind-noses for dirigibles—Pegamoid, cane-stiffened, lacquered cane or aluminum and flux for winter work.

Smoke-ring cannon for hail storms, swivel mounted, bow or stern.

Propeller blades: metal, tungsten backed; papier-maché; wire stiffened; ribbed Xylonite (Nickson's patent); all razor-edged (price by pitch and diameter).

Compressed steel bow-screws for winter work.

Fused Ruby or Commercial Mineral Co. bearings and collars. Agate-mounted thrust-blocks up to 4 inch.

Magniac's bow-rudders—(Lavalle's patent grooving).

Wove steel beltings for outboard motors (non-magnetic).

Radium batteries, all powers to 150 h.p. (in pairs).

Helium batteries, all powers to 300 h.p. (tandem).

Stun'sle brakes worked from upper or lower platform.

Direct plunge-brakes worked from lower platform only, loaded silk or fibre, wind-tight.

Catalogues free throughout the Planet

THE LONGEST SCIENCE FICTION STORY EVER TOLD

Arthur C. Clarke

Arthur C. Clarke, like Isaac Asimov, has had a lifelong commitment to logic and rationality, has written many impressive works of popular science (principally about space travel, astronomy, and the oceans), and a fair number of humorous sf stories. Hard sf humor, invented in its modern form by L. Sprague De Camp, Anthony Boucher, Henry Kuttner, and Fredric Brown in the late thirties and early forties, flourished in the fifties. Clarke joined the tradition with a series of stories collected in *Tales From the White Hart* (1957), full of clever notions and (occasionally bad) jokes following the lead of L. Sprague de Camp and Fletcher Pratt's *Tales from Gavagan's Bar* (1953).

A certain element of clever scientific puzzles and games has always been present in hard science fiction, the legacy perhaps of Lewis Carroll, or of math classes and their word problems. And logic problems of all sorts are the meat of hard science fiction. They can make such lovely, surprising plot twists. Rod Serling took this kind of story, sometimes derived from the fantasy of John Collier and sometimes from this type of sf, and made clever plotting an essential element of his own "Twilight Zone."

This tiny entertainment, an example of the short short story (of which form Fredric Brown, Asimov, and Clarke are masters), is a gem by one of the greats of hard sf. It is the humorous translation of a recursive series—which is theoretically infinite—from mathematics into prose. It is both a visual pun and an intellectual joke, perhaps the scientist's version of the concrete poem.

Dear Mr. Jinx:
I'm afraid your idea is not at all original. Stories about writers whose work is always plagiarized even *before* they can complete it go back at least to H. G. Wells's "The Anticipator." About once a week I receive a manuscript beginning:

> Dear Mr. Jinx:
> I'm afraid your idea is not at all original. Stories about writers whose work is always plagiarized even *before* they can complete it go back at least to H. G. Wells's "The Anticipator." About once a week I receive a manuscript beginning:
>
> > Dear Mr. Jinx:
> > I'm afraid your idea is not . . .
> >
> > Better luck next time!
> > Sincerely,
> > Morris K. Mobius
> > Editor, *Stupefying Stories*
>
> Better luck next time!
> Sincerely,
> Morris K. Mobius
> Editor, *Stupefying Stories*.

Better luck next time!
Sincerely,
Morris K. Mobius
Editor, *Stupefying Stories*.

THE PI MAN

Alfred Bester

Alfred Bester published fourteen science fiction stories between 1939 and 1942, mostly in Campbell's magazines. He left the field to work in comics and then in radio drama, returned to sf in 1950 and published only twelve more short stories and two novels before 1960. Those novels—*The Demolished Man* (1953) and *The Stars My Destination* (1956)—and those few stories made him for many the premier science fiction writer of that decade. In fact, in the 1970s, *The Stars My Destination* was still generally considered the best sf novel ever written. His 1950s work was symbolic of the new styles of sf championed by *Galaxy* and *The Magazine of Fantasy & Science Fiction*; none of his stories appeared in *Astounding*.

"The one word most symbolic of science fiction is, of course, 'extrapolation,' " he said in his collection, *Starlight* (1976), and defined it as "The continuation of a trend, either increasing, decreasing, or steady-state, to its culmination in the future. The only constraint is the limit set by the logic of the universe." Note that he does not mention science. This is not exactly what Campbell meant when he used the term *extrapolation*, and Bester's usage is slippery enough to permit much more of the fantastic (and little or no overt science). Elsewhere, he said, "I'm not much interested in extrapolating science and technology; I merely use extrapolation as a means of putting people into new quandaries which produce colorful pressures and conflicts." His example was enormously influential. Nearly every ambitious young sf writer of the sixties, certainly all the New Wave writers, from Brian W. Aldiss to Samuel R. Delany, from Michael Moorcock to Roger Zelazny, revered his work. Twenty years ago, it would have been surprising that any of his books be out of print, as they all are today.

Bester championed psychiatry, when hard sf ranked it with voodoo and religion. He was pyrotechnic, self-consciously literary, artificial, and brilliant, and utterly rejected the style and affect of hard sf. His fiction was lurid, brash, full of plot twists, coincidence, colorful special effects in imagery and even typography. "I've always been obsessed with patterns, rhythms, and tempi, and I always feel my stories in those terms. It's this pattern obsession that compels me to experiment with typography. I'm trying very hard to develop a technique of blending the sight, sound, and context of words into dramatic patterns. I want to make the eye, ear, and mind of the reader merge into a whole that is bigger than the sum of its parts." Reading should be "a total sensory and intellectual experience," he said. He was a string of firecrackers thrown into the sf crowd of the 1950s. Everyone applauded. "If you want to get a sense of how groovy it could have been to be alive and young and living in New York in the fifties, read Bester's sf," William Gibson said recently.

One of the dozen from the fifties is "The Pi Man," a mathematical sf story that plays jazz riffs on statistics. Of science, there is less here than meets the eye. Bester claims it is "extrapolating my obsession with patterns . . . The story explores an outré but logically possible exaggeration of environment on a contemporary man." But there are constant nuggets of knowledge and information. The basic technique, of charming the reader with fast talk, street wisdom, and an exaggerated character is borrowed to a large extent from Heinlein. And it was the field that revered Heinlein that made Bester a star in the fifties. Herein lie the roots of the contemporary diversity in science fiction, and the roots of the need, after a decade of Bester, to find a name, "hard science fiction," for the best old fashioned kind in the early 1960s.

How to say? How to write? When sometimes I can be fluent, even polished, and then, *reculer pour mieux sauter*, patterns take hold of me. Push. Compel.

```
                    Sometimes

            I           I           I
                am      am      am
                    3.14159 +
            from        from        from
        this            other           that
    space               space               space

                    Othertimes not
```

I have no control, but I try anyways.

I wake up wondering who, what, when, where, why?

Confusion result of biological compensator born into my body which I hate. Yes, birds and beasts have biological clock built in, and so navigate home from a thousand miles away. I have biological compensator, equalizer, responder to unknown stresses and strains. I relate, compensate, make and shape patterns, adjust rhythms, like a gridiron pendulum in a clock, but this is an unknown clock, and I do not know what time it keeps. Nevertheless I must. I am force. Have no control over self, speech, love, fate. Only to compensate.

Quae nocent docent. Translation follows: Things that injure teach. I am injured and have hurt many. What have we learned? However. I wake up the morning of the biggest hurt of all wondering which house. Wealth, you understand. Damme! Mews cottage in London, villa in Rome, penthouse in New York, rancho in California. I awake. I look. Ah! Layout familiar. Thus:

```
Foyer
      Bedroom
         Bath            T
         Bath            e
      Living Room        r
Kitchen                  r
      Dressing Room      a
         Bedroom         c
              T e r r a c e
```

So. I am in penthouse in New York, but that bath-bath-back-to-back. Pfui! All rhythm wrong. Pattern painful. Why have I never noticed before? Or is this sudden awareness result of phenomenon elsewhere? I telephone to janitor-mans downstairs. At that moment I lose my American-English. Damn nuisance. I'm compelled to speak a compost of tongues, and I never know which will be forced on me next.

"*Pronto. Ecco mi. Signore Marko. Miscusi tanto*—"

Pfui! Hang up. Hate the garbage I must sometimes speak and write. This I now write during period of AmerEng lucidity, otherwise would look like goulash. While I wait for return of communication, I shower body, teeth, hairs, shave face, dry everything, and try again. *Voilà!* Ye Englishe, she come. Back to invention of Mr. A. G. Bell and call janitor again.

"Good morning, Mr. Lundgren. This is Peter Marko. Guy in the penthouse. Right. Mr. Lundgren, be my personal rabbi and get some workmen up here this morning. I want those two baths converted into one. No, I mean it. I'll leave five thousand dollars on top of the icebox. Yes? Thanks, Mr. Lundgren."

Wanted to wear grey flannel this morning but compelled to put on sharkskin. Damnation! Black Power has peculiar side effects. Went to spare bedroom (see diagram) and unlocked door which was installed by the Eagle Safe Company—Since 1904—Bank Vault Equipment—Fireproof Files & Ledger Trays—Combinations changed. I went in.

Everything broadcasting beautifully, up and down the electromagnetic spectrum. Radio waves down to 1,000 meters, ultraviolet up into the hard X-rays and the 100 Kev (one hundred thousand electron volts) gamma radiation. All interrupters innn-tt-errrr-up-ppp-t-ingggg at random. I'm jamming the voice of the universe at least within this home, and I'm at peace. Dear God! To know even a moment of peace!

So. I take subway to office in Wall Street. Limousine more convenient but chauffeur too dangerous. Might become friendly, and I don't dare have friends anymore. Best of all, the morning subway is jam-packed, mass-packed, no patterns to adjust, no shiftings and compensations required. Peace.

In subway car I catch a glimpse of an eye, narrow, bleak, grey, the property of an anonymous man who conveys the conviction that you've never seen him before and will never see him again. But I picked up that glance and it tripped an alarm in the back of my mind. He knew it. He saw the flash in my eyes before I could turn away. So I was being tailed again. Who, this time? U.S.A.? U.S.S.R.? Interpol? Skip-Tracers, Inc.?

I drifted out of the subway with the crowd at City Hall and gave them a false trail to the Woolworth Building in case they were operating double-tails. The whole theory of the hunters and the hunted is not to avoid being tailed, no one can escape that; the thing to do is give them so many false leads to follow up that they become overextended. Then they may be forced to abandon you. They have a man-hour budget; just so many men for just so many operations.

City Hall traffic was out of sync, as it generally is, so I had to limp to compensate. Took elevator up to tenth floor of bldg. As I was starting down the stairs, I was suddenly seized by something from out there, something bad. I began to cry, but no help. An elderly clerk emerge from office wearing alpaca coat, gold spectacles, badge on lapel identify: *N. N. Chapin.*

"Not him," I plead with nowhere. "Nice mans. Not N. N. Chapin, please."

But I am force. Approach. Two blows, neck and gut. Down he go, writhing. I trample spectacles and smash watch. Then I'm permitted to go downstairs again. It was ten-thirty. I was late. Damn! Took taxi to 99 Wall Street. Driver's pattern smelled honest; big black man, quiet and assured. Tipped him fifty dollars. He raise eyebrows. Sealed one thousand in envelope (secretly) and sent driver back to bldg.

to find and give to N. N. Chapin on tenth floor. Did not enclose note: "From your unknown admirer."

Routine morning's work in office. I am in arbitrage, which is simultaneous buying and selling of moneys in different markets to profit from unequal price. Try to follow simple example: Pound sterling is selling for $2.79½ in London. Rupee is selling for $2.79 in New York. One rupee buys one pound in Burma. See where the arbitrage lies? I buy one rupee for $2.79 in New York, buy one pound for rupee in Burma, sell pound for $2.79½ in London, and I have made ½ cent on the transaction. Multiply by $100,000, and I have made $250 on the transaction. Enormous capital required.

But this is only crude example of arbitrage; actually the buying and selling must follow intricate patterns and have perfect timing. Money markets are jumpy today. Big Boards are hectic. Gold fluctuating. I am behind at eleven-thirty, but the patterns put me ahead $57,075.94 by half-past noon, Daylight Saving Time.

57075 makes a nice pattern but that 94¢! Iych! Ugly. Symmetry above all else. Alas, only 24¢ hard money in my pockets. Called secretary, borrowed 70¢ from her, and threw sum total out window. Felt better as I watched it scatter in space, but then I caught her looking at me with delight. Very dangerous. Fired girl on the spot.

"But why, Mr. Marko? Why?" she asked, trying not to cry. Darling little thing. Pale-faced and saucy, but not so saucy now.

"Because you're beginning to like me."

"What's the harm in that?"

"When I hired you, I warned you not to like me."

"I thought you were putting me on."

"I wasn't. Out you go."

"But why?"

"Because I'm beginning to like you."

"Is this some new kind of pass?"

"God forbid!"

"Well you don't have to worry," she flared. "I despise you."

"Good. Then I can go to bed with you."

She turned crimson and opened her mouth to denounce me, the while her eyes twinkled at the corners. A darling girl, whatever her name was. I could not endanger her. I gave her three weeks' salary for a bonus and threw her out. *Punkt.* Next secretary would be a man, married, misanthropic, murderous; a man who could hate me.

So, lunch. Went to nicely balanced restaurant. All chairs filled by patrons. Even pattern. No need for me to compensate and adjust. Also, they give me usual single corner table which does not need guest to balance. Ordered nicely patterned luncheon:

Martini Martini
Croque M'sieur Roquefort
Salad
Coffee

But so much cream being consumed in restaurant that I had to compensate by drinking my coffee black, which I dislike. However, still a soothing pattern.

$x^2 + x + 41$ = prime number. Excuse, please. Sometimes I'm in control and see what compensating must be done . . . tick-tock-tick-tock, good old gridiron pendulum . . . other times is force on me from God knows where or why or how or even if there is a God. Then I must do what I'm compelled to do, blindly, without motivation, speaking the gibberish I speak and think, sometimes hating it like what I do to poor mans Mr. Chapin. Anyway, the equation breaks down when x = 40.

The afternoon was quiet. For a moment I thought I might be forced to leave for Rome (Italy) but whatever it was adjusted without needing my two ($0.02) cents. ASPCA finally caught up with me for beating my dog to death, but I'd contributed $5,000.00 to their shelter. Got off with a shaking of heads. Wrote a few graffiti on posters, saved a small boy from a clobbering in a street rumble at a cost of sharkskin jacket. Drat! Slugged a maladroit driver who was subjecting his lovely Aston-Martin to cruel and unusual punishment. He was, how they say, "grabbing a handful of second."

In the evening to ballet to relax with all the beautiful Balanchine patterns; balanced, peaceful, soothing. Then I take a deep breath, quash my nausea, and force myself to go to *The Raunch*, the West Village creepsville. I hate *The Raunch*, but I need a woman and I must go where I hate. That fair-haired girl I fired, so full of mischief and making eyes at me. So, *poisson d'avril*, I advance myself to *The Raunch*.

Chaos. Blackness. Cacophony. My vibes shriek. 25 Watt bulbs. Ballads of Protest. Against L. wall sit young men with pubic beards, playing chess. Badly. *Exempli gratia*:

1	P—Q4	Kt—KB3
2	Kt—Q2	P—K4
3	P X P	Kt—Kt5
4	P—KR3	Kt—K6

If White takes the knight, Black forces mate with Q-R5ch. I didn't wait to see what the road-company Capablancas would do next.

Against R. wall is bar, serving beer and cheap wine mostly. There are girls with brown paper bags containing toilet articles. They are looking for a pad for the night. All wear tight jeans and are naked under loose sweaters. I think of Herrick (1591–1674): *Next, when I lift mine eyes and see/That brave vibration each way free/ Oh, how that glittering taketh me!*

I pick out the one who glitters the most. I talk. She insult. I insult back and buy hard drinks. She drink my drinks and snarl and hate, but helpless. Her name is Bunny and she has no pad for tonight. I do not let myself sympathize. She is a dyke; she does not bathe, her thinking patterns are jangles. I hate her and she's safe; no harm can come to her. So I maneuvered her out of Sink City and took her home to seduce by mutual contempt, and in the living room sat the slender little paleface secretary, recently fired for her own good.

She sat there in my penthouse, now minus one (1) bathroom, and with $1,997.00 change on top of the refrigerator. Oi! Throw $6.00 into kitchen Dispos-All (a Federal offense) and am soothed by the lovely 1991 remaining. She sat there, wearing a pastel thing, her skin gleaming rose-red from embarrassment, also red for danger. Her saucy face was very tight from the daring thing she thought she was doing. *Gott bewahre!* I like that.

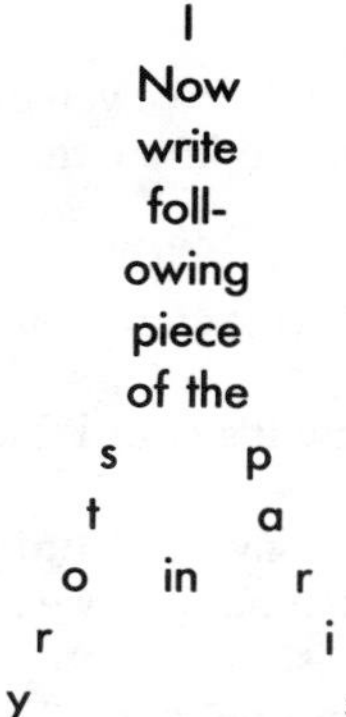

Address: 49bis Avenue Hoche, Paris, 8 eme, France

Forced to go there by what happened in the U.N., you understand. It needed extreme compensation and adjustment. Almost, for a moment, I thought I would have to attack the conductor of the *Opéra Comique*, but fate was kind and let me off with nothing worse than indecent exposure, and I was able to square it by founding a scholarship at the Sorbonne. Didn't someone suggest that fate was the square root of minus one?

Anyway, back in New York it is my turn to denounce the paleface but suddenly my AmerEng is replaced by a dialect out of a B-picture about a white remittance man and a blind native girl on a South Sea island who find redemption together while she plays the ukulele and sings gems from Lawrence Welk's Greatest Hits.

"Oh-so," I say. "Me-fella be ve'y happy ask why you-fella invade 'long my apa'tment, 'cept me' now speak pidgin. Ve'y emba'ss 'long me."

"I bribed Mr. Lundgren," she blurted. "I told him you needed important papers from the office."

The dyke turned on her heel and bounced out, her brave vibration each way free. I caught up with her in front of the elevator, put $101 into her hand, and tried to apologize. She hated me more so I did a naughty thing to her vibration and returned to the living room.

"What's she got?" the paleface asked.

My English returned. "What's your name?"

"Good Lord! I've been working in your office for two months and you don't know my name? You really don't?"

"No."

"I'm Jemmy Thomas."

"Beat it, Jemmy Thomas."

"So that's why you always called me 'Miss Uh.' You're Russian?"

"Half."

"What's the other half?"

"None of your business. What are you doing here? When I fire them they stay fired. What d'you want from me?"

"You," she said, blushing fiery.

"Will you for God's sake get the hell out of here."

"What did she have that I don't?" paleface demanded. Then her face crinkled. "Don't? Doesn't? I'm going to Bennington. They're strong on aggression but weak on grammar."

"What d'you mean, you're going to Bennington?"

"Why, it's a college. I thought everybody knew."

"But *going?*"

"Oh. I'm in my junior year. They drive you out with whips to acquire practical experience in your field. You ought to know that. Your office manager—I suppose you don't know her name, either."

"Ethel M. Blatt."

"Yes. Miss Blatt took it all down before you interviewed me."

"What's your field?"

"It used to be economics. Now it's you. How old are you?"

"One hundred and one."

"Oh, come on. Thirty? They say at Bennington that ten years is the right difference between men and women because we mature quicker. Are you married?"

"I have wives in London, Paris, and Rome. What is this catechism?"

"Well, I'm trying to get something going."

"I can see that, but does it have to be me?"

"I know it sounds like a notion." She lowered her eyes, and without the highlight of their blue, her pale face was almost invisible. "And I suppose women are always throwing themselves at you."

"It's my untold wealth."

"What are you, blasé or something? I mean, I know I'm not staggering, but I'm not exactly repulsive."

"You're lovely."

"Then why don't you come near me?"

"I'm trying to protect you."

"I can protect me when the time comes. I'm a Black Belt."

"The time is now, Jemmy Thompson."

"Thomas."

"Walk, not run, to the nearest exit, Jemmy Thomas."

"The least you could do is offend me the way you did that hustler in front of the elevator."

"You snooped?"

"Sure I snooped. You didn't expect me to sit here on my hands, did you? I've got my man to protect."

I had to laugh. This spunky little thing march in, roll up her sleeves and set to work on me. A wonder she didn't have a pot roast waiting in the oven and herself waiting in the bed.

"Your man?" I ask.

"It happens," she said in a low voice. "I never believed it, but it happens. You fall in and out of love and affairs, and each time you think it's real and forever. And then you meet somebody and it isn't a question of love anymore. You just know that he's your man, and you're stuck with him, whether you like it or not." She burst out angrily. "I'm stuck, dammit! Stuck! D'you think I'm enjoying this?"

She looked at me through the storm; violet eyes full of youth and determination and tenderness and fear. I could see she too was being forced and was angry and afraid. And I knew how lonely I was, never daring to make friends, to love, to share. I could fall into those violet eyes and never come up. I looked at the clock. 2:30 A.M. Sometimes quiet at this hour. Perhaps my AmerEng would stay with me a while longer.

"You're being compelled, Jemmy," I said. "I know all about that. Something inside you, something you don't understand, made you take your dignity in both hands and come after me. You don't like it, you don't want to, you've never begged in your life, but you had to. Yes?"

She nodded.

"Then you can understand a little about me. I'm compelled, too."

"Who is she?"

"No, no. Not forced to beg from a woman; compelled to hurt people."

"What people?"

"Any people; sometimes strangers, and that's bad; other times people I love, and that's not to be endured. So now I no longer dare love. I must protect people from myself."

"I don't know what you're talking about. Are you some kind of psychotic monster?"

"Yes, played by Lon Chaney, Jr."

"If you can joke about it, you can't be all that sick. Have you seen a shrink?"

"No. I don't have to. I know what's compelling me." I looked at the clock again. Still a quiet time. Please God the English would stay with me a while longer. I took off my jacket and shirt. "I'm going to shock you," I said, and showed her my back, crosshatched with scars. She gasped.

"Self-inflicted," I told her. "Because I permitted myself to like a man and become friendly with him. This is the price I paid, and I was lucky that he didn't have to. Now wait here."

I went into the master bedroom where my heart's shame was embalmed in a silver case hidden in the right-hand drawer of my desk. I brought it to the living room. Jemmy watched me with great eyes.

"Five years ago a girl fell in love with me," I told her. "A girl like you. I was lonely then, as always, so instead of protecting her from me, I indulged myself and tried to love her back. Now I want to show you the price *she* paid. You'll loathe me for this, but I must show you. Maybe it'll save you from—"

I broke off. A flash had caught my eye—the flash of lights going on in a building down the street; not just a few windows, a lot. I put on my jacket, went out on the terrace, and watched. All the illuminated windows in the building three down from me went out. Five-second eclipse. On again. It happened in the building two down and then the one next door. The girl came to my side and took my arm. She trembled slightly.

"What is it?" she asked. "What's the matter? You look so grim."

"It's the Geneva caper," I said. "Wait."

The lights in my apartment went out for five seconds and then came on again.

"They've located me the way I was nailed in Geneva," I told her.

"They? Located?"

"They've spotted my jamming by d/f."

"What jamming?"

"The full electromagnetic spectrum."

"What's dee eff?"

"Radio direction-finder. They used it to get the bearing of my jamming. Then they turned off the current in each building in the area, building by building, until the broadcast stopped. Now they've pinpointed me. They know I'm in this house, but they don't know which apartment yet. I've still got time. So. Good night, Jemmy. You're hired again. Tell Ethel Blatt I won't be in for a while. I wish I could kiss you good-bye, but safer not."

She clamped her arms around my neck and gave me an honest kiss. I tried to push her away.

She clung like The Old Man of the Sea. "You're a spy," she said. "I'll go to the chair with you."

"I wish to heaven I only was a spy. Good-bye, my love. Remember me."

A great mistake letting that slip. It happen, I think, because my speech slip, too. Suddenly forced to talk jumble again. As I run out, the little paleface kick off her sandals so she can run, too. She is alongside me going down the fire stairs to the garage in the basement. I hit her to stop, and swear Swahili at her. She hit back and swear gutter, all the time laughing and crying. I love her for it, so she is doomed. I will ruin her like all the rest.

We get into car and drive fast. I am making for 59th Street bridge to get off Manhattan Island and head east. I own plane in Babylon, Long Island, which is kept ready for this sort of awkwardness.

"*J'y suis, J'y reste* is not my motto," I tell Jemmy Thomas, whose French is as uncertain as her grammar, an endearing weakness. "Once Scotland Yard trapped me with a letter. I was receiving special mail care of General Delivery. They mailed me a red envelope, spotted me when I picked it up, and followed me to No. 13 Mayfair Mews, London W.1., Telephone, Mayfair 7711. Red for danger. Is the rest of you as invisible as your face?"

"I'm not invisible," she said, indignant, running hands through her streaky fair hair. "I tan in the summer. What is all this chase and escape? Why do you talk so funny and act so peculiar? In the office I thought it was because you're a crazy Russian. Half crazy Russian. Are you sure you're not a spy?"

"Only positive."

"It's too bad. A Commie 007 would be utter blissikins."

"Yes, I know. You see yourself being seduced with vodka and caviar."

"Are you a being from another world who came here on a UFO?"

"Would that scare you?"

"Only if it meant we couldn't make the scene."

"We couldn't anyway. All the serious side of me is concentrated on my career. I want to conquer the earth for my robot masters."

"I'm only interested in conquering you."

"I am not and have never been a creature from another world. I can show you my passport to prove it."

"Then what are you?"

"A compensator."

"A what?"

"A compensator. Like a clock pendulum. Do you know dictionary of Messrs Funk & Wagnalls? Edited by Frank H. Vizetelly, Litt.D., LL.D.? I quote: One who or that which compensates, as a device for neutralizing the influence of local attraction upon a compass-needle, or an automatic apparatus for equalizing—Damn!"

Litt.D. Frank H. Vizetelly does not use that word. It is my own because roadblock now faces me on 59th Street bridge. I should have anticipated. Should have sensed patterns, but too swept up with this inviting girl. Probably there are roadblocks on all exits leading out of this $24 island. Could drive off bridge, but maybe Bennington College has also neglected to teach Jemmy Thomas how to swim. So. Stop car. Surrender.

"*Kamerad,*" I pronounce. "Who you? John Birch?"

Gentlemans say no.

"White Supremes of the World, Inc.?"

No again. I feel better. Always nasty when captured by lunatic fringers.

"U.S.S.R.?"

He stare, then speak. "Special Agent Hildebrand. FBI," and flash his identification which no one can read in this light. I take his word and embrace him in gratitude. FBI is safe. He recoil and wonder if I am fag. I don't care. I kiss Jemmy

Thomas, and she open mouth under mine to mutter, "Admit nothing. Deny everything. I've got a lawyer."

I own thirteen lawyers, and two of them can make any court tremble, but no need to call them. This will be standard cross-examination; I know from past experience. So let them haul me off to Foley Square with Jemmy. They separate us. I am taken to Inquisition Room.

Brilliant lights; the shadows arranged just so; the chairs placed just so; mirror on wall probably one-way window with observers outside; I've been through this so often before. The anonymous man from the subway this morning is questioning me. We exchange glances of recognition. His name is R. Sawyer. The questions come.

"Name?"

"Peter Marko."

"Born?"

"Lee's Hill, Virginia."

"Never heard of it."

"It's a very small town, about thirty miles north of Roanoke. Most maps ignore it."

"You're Russian?"

"Half, by descent."

"Father Russian?"

"Yes. Eugene Alexis Markolevsky."

"Changed his name legally?"

"Shortened it when he became a citizen."

"Mother?"

"Vera Broadhurst. English."

"You were raised in Lee's Hill?"

"Until ten. Then Chicago."

"Father's occupation?"

"Teacher."

"Yours, financier?"

"Arbitrageur. Buying and selling money on the open market."

"Known assets from identified bank deposits, three million dollars."

"Only in the States. Counting overseas deposits and investments, closer to seventeen million."

R. Sawyer shook his head, bewildered. "Marko, what the hell are you up to? I'll level with you. At first we thought espionage, but with your kind of money— What are you broadcasting from your apartment? We can't break the code."

"There is no code, only randomness so I can get a little peace and some sleep."

"Only what?"

"Random jamming. I do it in all my homes. Listen, I've been through this so often before, and it's difficult for people to understand unless I explain it my own way. Will you let me try?"

"Go ahead." Saywer was grim. "You better make it good. We can check everything you give us."

I take a breath. Always the same problem. The reality is so strange that I have to use simile and metaphor. But it was 4:00 A.M. and maybe the jumble wouldn't interrupt my speech for a while. "Do you like to dance?"

"What the hell . . ."

"Be patient. I'm trying to explain. You like to dance?"

"I used to."

"What's the pleasure of dancing? It's people making rhythms together—patterns, designs, balances. Yes?"

"So?"

"And parades. Masses of men and music making patterns. Team sports, also. Action patterns. Yes?"

"Marko, if you think I'm going to—"

"Just listen, Sawyer. Here's the point. I'm sensitive to patterns on a big scale; bigger than dancing or parades, more than the rhythms of day and night, the seasons, the glacial epochs."

Sawyer stared. I nodded. "Oh yes, people respond to the 2/2 of the diurnal-nocturnal rhythms, the 4/4 of the seasons, the great terra-epochs. They don't know it, but they do. That's why they have sleep-problems, moon-madness, sun-hunger, weather-sensitivity. I respond to these local things, too, but also to gigantic patterns, influences from infinity."

"Are you some kind of nut?"

"Certainly. Of course. I respond to the patterns of the entire galaxy, maybe universe; sight and sound; and the unseen and unheard. I'm moved by the patterns of people, individually and demographically; hostility; generosity, selfishness, charity, cruelties and kindnesses, groupings and whole cultures. And I'm compelled to respond and compensate."

"How a nut like you ever made seventeen mill—How do you compensate?"

"If a child hurts itself, the mother responds with a kiss. That's compensation. Agreed? If a man beats a horse you beat *him*. You boo a bad fight. You cheer a good game. You're a cop, Sawyer. Don't the victim and murderer seek each other to fulfill their pattern?"

"Maybe in the past; not today. What's this got to do with your broadcasts?"

"Multiply that compensation by infinity and you have me. I must kiss and kick. I'm driven. I must compensate in a pattern I can't see or understand. Sometimes I'm compelled to do extravagant things, other times I'm forced to do insane things; talk gibberish, go to strange places, perform abominable acts, behave like a lunatic."

"What abominable acts?"

"Fifth amendment."

"But what about those broadcasts?"

"We're flooded with wave emissions and particles, sometimes in patterns, sometimes garbled. I feel them all and respond to them the way a marionette jerks on strings. I try to neutralize them by jamming, so I broadcast at random to get a little peace."

"Marko, I swear you're crazy."

"Yes, I am, but you won't be able to get me committed. It's been tried before. I've even tried myself. It never works. The big design won't permit it. I don't know why, but the big design wants me to go on as a Pi Man."

"What the hell are you talking about? What kind of pie?"

"Not pee-eye-ee-man. Pee-eye-man. Pi. Sixteenth letter in the Greek alphabet. It's the relation of the circumference of a circle to its diameter. 3.14159+. The series goes on into infinity. It's transcendental and can never be resolved into a finite pattern. They call extrasensory perception Psi. I call extrapattern perception Pi. All right?"

He glared at me, threw my dossier down, sighed, and slumped into a chair. That made the grouping wrong, so I had to shift. He cocked an eye at me.

"Pi Man," I apologized.

"All right," he said at last. "We can't hold you."

"They all try but they never can."

"Who try?"

"Governments, police, counterintelligence, politicals, lunatic fringe, religious sects . . . They track me down, hoping they can nail me or use me. They can't. I'm part of something much bigger. I think we all are, only I'm the first to be aware of it."

"Are you claiming you're a superman?"

"Good God! No! I'm a damned man . . . a tortured man, because some of the patterns I must adjust to are outworld rhythms like nothing we ever experience on earth . . . 29/51 . . . 108/303 . . . tempi like that, alien, terrifying, agony to live with."

He took another deep breath. "Off the record, what's this about abominable acts?"

"That's why I can't have friends or let myself fall in love. Sometimes the patterns turn so ugly that I have to make frightful sacrifices to restore the design. I must destroy something I love."

"This is sacrifice?"

"Isn't it the only meaning of sacrifice, Sawyer? You give up what's dearest to you."

"Who to?"

"The Gods. The Fates. The Big Pattern that's controlling me. From where? I don't know. It's too big a universe to comprehend, but I have to beat its tempo with my actions and reactions, emotions and senses, to make the patterns come out even, balanced in some way that I don't understand. The pressures that

whipsaw
me
back and
and turn
forth me
and into
back the
and transcendental
forth 3.14159 +
and maybe I talk too much to R. Sawyer and the
patterns pronounce: PI MAN, IT IS NOT PERMITTED.

So. There is darkness and silence.

"The other arm now," Jemmy said firmly. "Lift."

I am on my bed, me. Thinking upheaved again. Half (½) into pyjamas; other half (½) being wrestled by paleface girl. I lift. She yank. Pyjamas now on, and it's my turn to blush. They raise me prudish in Lee's Hill.

"Pot roast done?" I ask.

"What?"

"What happened?"

"You pooped out. Keeled over. You're not so cool."

"How much do you know?"

"Everything. I was on the other side of that mirror thing. Mr. Sawyer had to let you go. Mr. Lundgren helped lug you up to the apartment. He thinks you're stoned. How much should I give him?"

"*Cinque lire. No. Parla Italiano, gentile signorina?*"

"Are you asking me do I speak Italian? No."

"*Entschuldigen Sie, bitte. Sprechen Sie Deutsch?*"

"Is this your patterns again?"

I nod.

"Can't you stop?"

After stopovers in Greece and Portugal, Ye Englishe finally returns to me. "Can you stop breathing, Jemmy?"

"Is it like that, Peter? Truly?"

"Yes."

"When you do something . . . something bad . . . do you know why? Do you know exactly what it is somewhere that makes you do it?"

"Sometimes yes. Other times no. All I know is that I'm compelled to respond."

"Then you're just the tool of the universe."

"I think we all are. Continuum creatures. The only difference is, I'm more sensitive to the galactic patterns and respond violently. So why don't you get the hell out of here, Jemmy Thomas?"

"I'm still stuck," she said.

"You can't be. Not after what you heard."

"Yes, I am. You don't have to marry me."

Now the biggest hurt of all. I have to be honest. I have to ask, "Where's the silver case?"

A long pause. "Down the incinerator."

"Do you . . . Do you know what was in it?"

"I know what was in it."

"And you're still here?"

"It was monstrous what you did. Monstrous!" Her face suddenly streaked with mascara. She was crying. "Where is she now?"

"I don't know. The checks go out every quarter to a numbered account in Switzerland. I don't want to know. How much can the heart endure?"

"I think I'm going to find out, Peter."

"Please don't find out." I make one last effort to save her. "I love you, paleface, and you know what that can mean. When the patterns turn cruel, you may be the sacrifice."

"Love creates patterns, too." She kissed me. Her lips were parched, her skin was icy, she was afraid and hurting, but her heart beat strong with love and hope. "Nothing can crunch us now. Believe me."

"I don't know what to believe anymore. We're part of a world that's beyond knowing. What if it turns out to be too big for love?"

"All right," she said composedly. "We won't be dogs in the manger. If love is a little thing and has to end, then let it end. Let all little things like love and honor and mercy and laughter end, if there's a bigger design beyond."

"But what's bigger? What's beyond? I've asked that for years. Never an answer. Never a clue."

"Of course. If we're too small to survive, how can we know? Move over."

Then she is in bed with me, the tips of her body like frost while the rest of her is hot and evoking, and there is such a consuming burst of passion that for the first time I can forget myself, forget everything, abandon everything, and the last thing I think is: God damn the world. God damn the universe. God damn GGG-o-dddddd

RELATIVISTIC EFFECTS

Gregory Benford

Gregory Benford, an astrophysicist specializing in plasma physics, grew up a science fiction fan and began to write fiction as a hobby in 1965. Some of his early work was written in collaboration with Gordon Eklund (their story, "If the Stars Are Gods," won a Nebula Award in 1975; it was expanded in 1977 into a novel of the same title). In the mid-seventies he began to write his own fiction more consistently and revised his first novel, *Deeper Than the Darkness* (1970) as *The Stars in Shroud* (1976). His next novel, *In the Ocean of Night* (1977), is generally regarded as his first mature work, followed by *Timescape* (1980), his most famous novel and widely regarded as the best hard-science-fiction novel of recent decades, a milestone in using more rounded characterization and social detail than was previously attempted in hard sf. Brian Aldiss (in *Trillion Year Spree*) comments on Benford's early work, "The interest in anthropological roots, in language and its limitations, and in the curious division of the human brain between thought and feeling, characterizes not merely Benford's work but much of the sf of the seventies."

Since the 1970s, Benford had been a staunch and articulate defender of hard science fiction, both as a public personality in the sf field and in essays and articles, speaking with the force of experience as a working scientist and as perhaps the most respected hard sf writer of his generation. He is now regarded as the central figure of the generation after Larry Niven in hard science fiction.

Often linked particularly with the tradition of Stapledon and Arthur C. Clarke, Benford after 1980 began to incorporate more of the technical influences of wider reading in Modernist American fiction into his work. A Southerner himself, Benford found the stories of William Faulkner a particularly rich repository, and mined "The Bear" for the novel *Against Infinity* (1983), and *As I Lay Dying* for the story "To the Storming Gulf" (1985). Faulkner had a real command of the history of the South and its psychological implications. If much of sf is a mythic retelling of American history, what makes Benford's borrowing from Faulkner particularly valuable to sf is that he is borrowing a subtle synthesis of the history of the South along with it. American history has a good deal to do with what hard sf is about, and the history of the South is a neglected area which nonetheless has many psychological resonances. Benford set out to exploit them in the eighties, then continued on to develop his Clarkeian future history (begun in *In the Ocean of Night*) in *Across the Sea of Suns* (1984), *Great Sky River* (1987), and *Tides of Light* (1989).

His body of work in the 1980s is the most stylistically advanced, varied, and sophisticated hard science fiction, the first to have successfully integrated many conventional stylistic features of contemporary literary fiction, especially a more psychologically rounded characterization, into hard science fiction.

"Relativistic Effects" shows that Benford can manipulate the tropes and conventions of genre sf and at the same time make the people of the distant future seem human and sympathetic, regardless of their bizarre circumstances. Here is the classic enclosed world of the spaceship traveling faster than the speed of light; the physics of the situation makes the life of these people different in quite specific ways that are metaphorically suggestive but grounded in a serious attempt to portray a rigorous, literal situation in conformance with what relativity predicts. It is interesting to compare this story to Poul Anderson's novel, *Tau Zero* (1970), and to Edward Bryant's "Particle Theory," other stories that investigate some of the rich metaphorical possibilities of certain elements of physics.

They came into the locker room with a babble of random talk, laughter, and shouts. There was a rolling bass undertone, gruff and raw. Over it the higher feminine notes ran lightly, warbling, darting.

The women had a solid, businesslike grace to them, doing hard work in the company of men. There were a dozen of them and they shed their clothes quickly and efficiently, all modesty forgotten long ago, their minds already focused on the job to come.

"You up for this, Nick?" Jake asked, yanking off his shorts and clipping the input sockets to his knees and elbows. His skin was red and callused from his years of linked servo work.

"Think I can handle it," Nick replied. "We're hitting pretty dense plasma already. There'll be plenty of it pouring through the throat." He was big but he gave the impression of lightness and speed, trim like a boxer, with broad shoulders and thick wrists.

"Lots of flux," Jake said. "Easy to screw up."

"I didn't get my rating by screwing up 'cause some extra ions came down the tube."

"Yeah. You're pretty far up the roster, as I remember," Jake said, eyeing the big man.

"Uh-huh. Number one, last time I looked," Faye put in from the next locker. She laughed, a loud braying that rolled through the locker room and made people look up. "Bet 'at's what's botherin' you, uh, Jake?"

Jake casually made an obscene gesture in her general direction and went on. "You feelin' OK, Nick?"

"What you think I got, clenchrot?" Nick spat out with sudden ferocity. "Just had a cold, is all."

Faye said slyly, "Be a shame to prang when you're so close to winnin', movin' on up." She tugged on her halter and arranged her large breasts in it.

Nick glanced at her. Trouble was, you work with a woman long enough and after a while, she looked like just one more competitor. Once he'd thought of making a play for Faye—she really did look fairly good sometimes—but now she was one more sapper who'd elbow him into a vortex if she got half a chance. Point was, he never gave her—or anybody else—a chance to come up on him from some funny angle, throw him some unexpected momentum. He studied her casual, deft movements, pulling on the harness for the connectors. Still, there was something about her. . . .

"You get one more good run," Faye said slyly, "you gonna get the promotion. 'At's what I'd say."

"What matters is what they say upstairs, on A deck."

"Touchy, touchy, tsk tsk," Jake said. He couldn't resist getting in a little dig.

Nick knew. Not when Jake knew it might get Nick stirred up a little. But the larger man stayed silent, stolidly pulling on his neural hookups.

Snick, the relays slide into place and Nick feels each one come home with a percussive impact in his body, he never gets used to that no matter that it's been years he's been in the Main Drive crew. When he really sat down and thought about it he didn't like this job at all, was always shaky before coming down here for his shift. He'd figured that out at the start, so the trick was, he didn't think about it, not unless he'd had too much of that 'ponics-processed liquor, the stuff that was packed with vitamin B and C and wasn't supposed to do you any damage, not even leave the muggy dregs and ache of a hangover, only of course it never worked quite right because nothing on the ship did anymore. If he let himself stoke up on that stuff he'd gradually drop out of the conversation at whatever party he was, and go off into a corner somewhere and somebody'd find him an hour or two later staring at a wall or into his drink, reliving the hours in the tube and thinking about his dad and the grandfather he could only vaguely remember. They'd both died of the ol' black creeping cancer, same as eighty percent of the crew, and it was no secret the Main Drive was the worst place in the ship for it, despite all the design specs of fifty-meter rock walls and carbon-steel bulkheads and lead-lined hatches. A man'd be a goddamn fool if he didn't think about that, sure, but somebody had to do it or they'd all die. The job came down to Nick from his father because the family just did it, that was all, all the way back to the first crew, the original bridge officers had decided that long before Nick was born, it was the only kind of social organization that the sociometricians thought could possibly work on a ship that had to fly between stars, they all knew that and nobody questioned it any more than they'd want to change a pressure spec on a seal. You just didn't, was all there was to it. He'd learned that since he could first understand the church services, or the yearly anniversary of the Blowout up on the bridge, or the things that his father told him, even when the old man was dying with the black crawling stuff eating him from inside, Nick had learned that good—

"God, this dump is gettin' worse every—lookit 'at." Faye pointed.

A spider was crawling up a bulkhead, inching along on the ceramic smoothness.

"Musta got outta Agro," somebody put in.

"Yeah, don't kill it. Might upset the whole damn biosphere, an' they'd have our fuckin' heads for it."

A murmur of grudging agreement.

"Lookit 'at dumb thing," Jake said. "Made it alla way up here, musta come through air ducts an' line feeds an' who knows what." He leaned over the spider, eyeing it. It was a good three centimeters across and dull gray. "Pretty as sin, huh?"

Nick tapped in sockets at his joints and tried to ignore Jake. "Yeah."

"Poor thing. Don't know where in hell it is, does it? No appreciation for how important a place this is. We're 'bout to see a whole new age start in this locker room, soon's Nick here gets his full score. He'll be the new super an' we'll be—well, hell, we'll be like this li'l spider here. Just small and havin' our own tiny place in the big design of Nick's career, just you think how it's gonna—"

"Can the shit," Nick said harshly.

Jake laughed.

There was a tight feeling in the air. Nick felt it and figured it was something about his trying to get the promotion, something like that, but not worth bothering about. Plenty of time to think about it, once he had finished this job and gotten on up the ladder. Plenty of time then.

The gong rang brassily and the men and women finished suiting up. The minister came in and led them in a prayer for safety, the same as every other shift. Nothing different, but the tension remained. They'd be flying into higher plasma densities, sure, Nick thought. But there was no big deal about that. Still, he murmured the prayer along with the rest. Usually he didn't bother. He'd been to church services as usual, everybody went, it was unthinkable that you wouldn't, and anyway he'd never get any kind of promotion if he didn't show his face reg'lar, hunch on up to the altar rail and swallow that wafer and the alky-laced grape juice that went sour in your mouth while you were trying to swallow it, same as a lot of the talk they wanted you to swallow, only you did, you got it down because you had to and without asking anything afterward either, you bet, 'cause the ones who made trouble didn't get anywhere. So he muttered along, mouthing the familiar litany without thinking. The minister's thin lips moving, rolling on through the archaic phrases, meant less than nothing. When he looked up, each face was pensive as they prepared to go into the howling throat of the ship.

Nick lies mute and blind and for a moment feels nothing but the numb silence. It collects in him, blotting out the dim rub of the snouts which cling like lampreys to his nerves and muscles, pressing embrace that amplifies every movement, and—

—*spang*—

—he slips free of the mooring cables, a rush of sight-sound-taste-touch washes over him, so strong and sudden a welter of sensations that he jerks with the impact. He is servo'd to a thing like an eel that swims and flips and dives into a howling dance of protons. The rest of the ship is sheltered safely behind slabs of rock. But the eel is his, the eel is *him*. It shudders and jerks and twists, skating across sleek strands of magnetic plains. To Nick, it is like swimming.

The torrent gusts around him and he feels its pinprick breath. In a blinding orange glare Nick swoops, feeling his power grow as he gets the feel of it. His shiny shelf is wrapped in a cocoon of looping magnetic fields that turn the protons away, sending them gyrating in a mad gavotte, so the heavy particles cannot crunch and flare against the slick baked skin. Nick flexes the skin, supple and strong, and slips through the magnetic turbulence ahead. He feels the magnetic lines of force stretch like rubber bands. He banks and accelerates.

Streams of protons play upon him. They make glancing collisions with each other but do not react. The repulsion between them is too great and so this plasma cannot make them burn, cannot thrust them together with enough violence. Something more is needed or else the ship's throat will fail to harvest the simple hydrogen atoms, fail to kindle it into energy.

There— In the howling storm Nick sees the blue dots that are the keys, the catalyst: carbon nuclei, hovering like sea gulls in an updraft.

Split-image phosphors gleam, marking his way. He swims in the streaming blue-white glow, through a murky storm of fusing ions. He watches plumes of carbon nuclei striking the swarms of protons, wedding them to form the heavier nitrogen nuclei. The torrent swirls and screams at Nick's skin and in his sensors he sees and feels and tastes the lumpy, sluggish nitrogen as it finds a fresh incoming proton and with the fleshy smack of fusion the two stick, they hold, they wobble like raindrops—falling—merging—ballooning into a new nucleus, heavier still: oxygen.

But the green pinpoints of oxygen are unstable. These fragile forms split instantly. Jets of new particles spew through the surrounding glow—neutrinos, ruddy photons of light, and slower, darker, there come the heavy daughters of the marriage: a swollen, burnt-gold cloud of a bigger variety of nitrogen.

Onward the process flies. Each nucleus collides millions of times with the others in a fleck-shot swirl like glowing snowflakes. All in the space of a heartbeat. Flakes ride the magnetic field lines. Gamma rays flare and sputter among the blundering motes like fitful fireflies. Nuclear fire lights the long roaring corridor that is the ship's main drive. Nick swims, the white-hot sparks breaking over him like foam. Ahead he sees the violet points of gravid nitrogen and hears them crack into carbon plus an alpha particle. So in the end the long cascade gives forth the carbon that catalyzed it, carbon that will begin again its life in the whistling blizzard of protons coming in from the forward maw of the ship. With the help of the carbon, an interstellar hydrogen atom has built itself up from mere proton to, finally, an alpha particle—a stable clump of two neutrons and two protons. The alpha particle is the point of it all. It flees from the blurring storm, carrying the energy that fusion affords. The ruby-rich interstellar gas is now wedded, proton to proton, with carbon as the matchmaker.

Nick feels a rising electric field pluck at him. He moves to shed his excess charge. To carry a cloak of electrons here is fatal. Upstream lies the chewing gullet of the ramscoop ship, where the incoming protons are sucked in and where their kinetic power is stolen from them by the electric fields. There the particles are slowed, brought to rest inside the ship, their streaming energy stored in capacitors.

A cyclone shrieks behind him. Nick swims sideways, toward the walls of the combustion chamber. The nuclear burn that flares around him is never pure, cannot be pure because the junk of the cosmos pours through here, like barley meal laced with grains of granite. The incoming atomic rain spatters constantly over the fluxlife walls, killing the organic superconductor strands there.

Nick pushes against the rubbery magnetic fields and swoops over the mottled yellow-blue crust of the walls. In the flickering lightning glow of infrared and ultraviolet he sees the scaly muck that deadens the magnetic fields and slows the nuclear burn in the throat. He flexes, wriggles, and turns the eel-like form. This brings the electron beam gun around at millimeter range. He fires. A brittle crackling leaps out, onto the scaly wall. The tongue bites and gouges. Flakes roast off and blacken and finally bubble up like tar. The rushing proton currents wash the flakes away, revealing the gunmetal blue beneath. Now the exposed superconducting threads can begin their own slow pruning of themselves, life casting out its dead. Their long organic chain molecules can feed and grow anew. As Nick cuts and turns and carves he watched the spindly fibers coil loose and drift in eddies. Finally they spin away into the erasing proton storm. The dead fibers sputter and flash where the incoming protons strike them and then with a rumble in his acoustic pickup coils he sees them swept away. Maintenance.

Something tugs at him. He sees the puckered scoop where the energetic alpha particles shoot by. They dart like luminous jade wasps. The scoop sucks them in. Inside they will be collected, drained of energy, inducing megawatts of power for the ship, which will drink their last drop of momentum and cast them aside, a wake of broken atoms.

Suddenly he spins to the left—*Jesus, how can*—he thinks—and the scoop fields lash him. A megavolt per meter of churning electrical vortex snatches at him. It is huge and quick and relentless to Nick (though to the ship it is a minor ripple in its total momentum) and magnetic tendrils claw at his spinning, shiny surfaces. The scoop opening is a plunging, howling mouth. Jets of glowing atoms whirl by him, mocking. The walls near him counter his motion by increasing their magnetic fields. Lines of force stretch and bunch.

How did this—is all he has time to think before a searing spot blooms nearby. His presence so near the scoop has upset the combination rates there. His eyes widen. If the reaction gets out of control it can burn through the chamber vessel, through the asteroid rock beyond, and spike with acrid fire into the ship, toward the life dome.

A brassy roar. The scoop sucks at his heels. Ions run white-hot. A warning knot strikes him. Tangled magnetic ropes grope for him, clotting around the shiny skin.

Panic squeezes his throat. Desperately he fires his electron beam gun against the wall, hoping it will give him a push, a fresh vector—

Not enough. Orange ions blossom and swell around him—

Most of the squad was finished dressing. They were tired and yet the release of getting off work brought out an undercurrent of celebration. They ignored Nick and slouched out of the locker room, bound for families or assignations or sensory jolts of sundry types. A reek of sweat and fatigue diffused through the sluggishly stirring air. The squad laughed and shouted old jokes to each other. Nick sat on the bench with his head in his hands.

"I . . . I don't get it. I was doin' pretty well, catchin' the crap as it came at me, an' then somethin' grabbed . . ."

They'd had to pull him out with a robot searcher. He'd gone dead, inoperative, clinging to the throat lining, fighting the currents. The surges drove the blood down into your gut and legs, the extra g's slamming you up against the bulkhead and sending big dark blotches across your vision, purple swarms of dots swimming everywhere, hollow rattling noises coming in through the transducer mikes, nausea, the ache spreading through your arms—

It had taken three hours to get him back in, and three more to clean up. A lot of circuitry was fried for good, useless junk. The worst loss was the high-grade steel, all riddled with neutrons and fissured by nuclear fragments. The ship's foundry couldn't replace that, hadn't had the rolling mill to even make a die for it in more than a generation. His neuro index checked out okay, but he wouldn't be able to work for a week.

He was still in a daze and the memory would not straighten itself out in his mind. "I dunno, I . . ."

Faye murmured, "Maybe went a li'l fast for you today."

Jake grinned and said nothing.

"Mebbe you could, y'know, use a rest. Sit out a few sessions." Faye cocked her head at him.

Nick looked at both of them and narrowed his eyes. "That wasn't a mistake of mine, was it? Uh? No mistake at all. Somebody—" He knotted a fist.

"Hey, nothin' you can prove," Jake said, backing away. "I can guarantee that, boy."

"Some bastard, throwin' me some extra angular when I wasn't lookin', I oughta—"

"Come on, Nick, you got no proof 'a those charges. You know there's too much noise level in the throat to record what ever'body's doin'." Faye grinned without humor.

"Damn." Nick buried his face in his hands. "I was *that* close, so damned near to gettin' that promotion—"

"Yeah. Tsk tsk. You dropped points back there for sure, Nick, burnin' out a whole unit that way an' gettin—"

"Shut it. Just shut it."

Nick was still groggy and he felt the anger build in him without focus, without resolution. These two would make up some neat story to cover their asses, same as everybody did when they were bringing another member of the squad down a notch or two. The squad didn't have a lot of love for anybody who looked like they were going to get up above the squad, work their way up. That was the way it was, jobs were hard to change, the bridge liked it stable, said it came out better when you worked at a routine all your life and—

"Hey, c'mon, let's get our butts down to the Sniffer," Faye said. "No use jawin' 'bout this, is 'ere? I'm gettin' thirsty after all that, uh, work."

She winked at Jake. Nick saw it and knew he would get a ribbing about this for weeks. The squad was telling him he had stepped out of line and he would just have to take it. That was just the plain fact of it. He clenched his fists and felt a surge of anger.

"Hey!" Jake called out. "This damn spider's still tryin' to make it up this wall." He reached out and picked it up in his hand. The little gray thing struggled against him, legs kicking.

"Y'know, I hear there're people over in Comp who keep these for pets," Faye said. "Could be one of theirs."

"Creepy li'l thing," Nick said.

"You get what you can," Faye murmured. "Ever see a holo of a dog?"

Nick nodded. "Saw a whole movie about this one, it was a collie, savin' people an' all. Now that's a pet."

They all stared silently at the spider as it drummed steadily on Jake's hand with its legs. Nick shivered and turned away. Jake held it firmly, without hurting it, and slipped it into a pocket. "Think I'll take it back before Agro busts a gut lookin' for it."

Nick was silent as the three of them left the smells of the locker room and made their way up through the corridors. They took a shortcut along an undulating walkway under the big observation dome. Blades of pale blue light shifted like enormous columns in the air, but they were talking and only occasionally glanced up.

The vast ship of which they were a part was heading through the narrow corridor between two major spiral galaxies. On the right side of the dome the bulge of one galaxy was like a whirlpool of light, the points of light like grains of sand caught in a vortex. Around the bright core, glowing clouds of the spiral arms wended their way through the flat disk, seeming to cut through the dark dust clouds like a river slicing through jungle. Here and there black towers reared up out of the confusion of the disk, where masses of interstellar debris had been heaved out of the galactic plane, driven by collisions between clouds, or explosions of young stars.

There were intelligent, technological societies somewhere among those drifting stars. The ship had picked up their transmissions long ago—radio, UV, the usual—and had altered course to pass nearby.

The two spirals were a binary system, bound together since their birth. For most of their history they had stayed well apart, but now they were brushing within a galactic diameter of each other. Detailed observations in the last few weeks of ship's time—all that was needed to veer and swoop toward the twinned disks—had shown that this was the final pass: the two galaxies would not merely swoop by and escape. The filaments of gas and dust between them had created friction over the billions of years past, eroding their orbital angular momentum. Now they would grapple fatally.

The jolting impact would be spectacular: shock waves, compression of the gas in the galactic plane, and shortly thereafter new star formation, swiftly yielding an increase in the supernova rate, a flooding of the interstellar medium with high energy particles. The rain of sudden virulent energy would destroy the planetary environments. The two spirals would come together with a wrenching suddenness, the disks sliding into each other like two saucers bent on destruction, the collision effectively occurring all over the disks simultaneously in an explosive flare of X-ray and thermal brems-strahlung radiation. Even advanced technologies would be snuffed out by the rolling, searing tide.

The disks were passing nearly face-on to each other. In the broad blue dome overhead the two spirals hung like cymbals seen on edge. The ship moved at extreme relativistic velocity, pressing infinitesimally close to light speed, passing through the dim halo of gas and old dead stars that surrounded each galaxy. Its speed compressed time and space. Angles distorted as time ran at a blinding pace outside, refracting images. Extreme relativistic effects made the approach visible to the naked eye. Slowly, the huge disks of shimmering light seemed to swing open like a pair of doors. Bright tendrils spanned the gap between them.

Jake was telling a story about two men in CompCatynch section, rambling on with gossip and jokes, trying to keep the talk light. Faye went along with it, putting in a word when Jake slowed. Nick was silent.

The ship swooped closer to the disks and suddenly across the dome streaked red and orange bursts. The disks were twisted, distorted by their mutual gravitational tugs, wrenching each other, twins locked in a tightening embrace. The planes of stars rippled, as if a huge wind blew across them. The galactic nuclei flared with fresh fires: ruby, orange, mottled blue, ripe gold. Stars were blasted into the space between. Filaments of raw, searing gas formed a web that spanned the two spirals. This was the food that fed the ship's engines. They were flying as near to the thick dust and gas of the galaxies as they could. The maw of the ship stretched outward, spanning a volume nearly as big as the galactic core. Streamers of sluggish gas veered toward it, drawn by the onrushing magnetic fields. The throat sucked in great clouds, boosting them to still higher velocity.

The ship's hull moaned as it met denser matter.

Nick ignores the babble from Jake, knowing it is empty foolishness, and thinks instead of the squad, and how he would run it if he got the promotion: They had to average five thousand cleared square meters a week, minimum, that was a full ten percent of the whole ship's throat, minus of course the lining areas that were shut down for full repair, call that one thousand square meters on the average, so with the other crews operating on forty-five-hour shifts they could work their way through and give the throat a full scraping in less than a month, easy, even allowing for screwups and malfs and times when the radiation level was too high for even the suits to screen it out. You had to keep the suits up to 99 plus percent operational or you caught hell from upstairs, but the same time they came at you with their specifications reports and never listened when you told them about the delays, that was your problem not theirs and they said so every chance they got, that bunch of blowhard officers up there, descended from the original ship's bridge officers who'd left Earth generations back with every intention of returning after a twelve-year round trip to Centauri, only it hadn't worked, they didn't count on the drive freezing up in permanent full-bore thrust, the drive locked in and the deceleration components slowly getting fried by the increased neutron flux from the reactions, until when they finally could taper off on the forward drive the decelerators were finished, beyond repair, and then the ship had nothing to do but drive on, unable to stop or even turn the magnetic gascatchers off, because once you did that the incoming neutral atoms would be a sleet of protons and neutrons that'd riddle everybody within a day, kill them all. So the officers had said they had to keep going, studying, trying to figure a way to rebuild the decelerators, only nobody ever did, and the crew got older and they flew on, clean out of the galaxy, having babies and quarrels and finally after some murders and suicides and worse, working out a stable social structure in a goddamn relativistic runaway, officers' sons and daughters becoming officers themselves, and crewmen begetting crewmen again, down through five generations now in the creaky old ship that had by now flown through five million years of outside-time, so that there was no purpose or dream of returning Earthside anymore, only names attached to pictures and stories, and the same jobs to do every day, servicing the weakening stanchions and struts, the flagging motors, finding replacements for every little doodad that fractured, working because to stop was to die, all the time with officers to tell you what new scientific experiment they'd thought up and how maybe this time it would be the answer, the clue to getting back to their own galaxy—a holy grail beloved of the first and second generations that was now, even under high magnification, a mere mottled disk of ruby receding pinprick lights nobody alive had ever seen up close. Yet there was something in what the bridge officers said, in what the scientific mandarins mulled over, a point to their lives here—

"Let's stop in this'n," Jake called, interrupting Nick's muzzy thoughts, and he followed them into a small inn. Without his noticing it they had left the big observation dome. They angled through a tight, rocky corridor cut from the original asteroid that was the basic body of the whole starship.

Among the seven thousand souls in the ten-kilometer-wide-starship, there were communities and neighborhoods and bars to suit everyone. In this one there were thick veils of smoky euphorics, harmless unless you drank an activating potion. Shifts came and went, there were always crowds in the bar, a rich assortment of faces and ages and tongues. Techs, metalworkers, computer jockeys, manuals, steamfitters, muscled grunt laborers. Cadaverous and silent alesoakers, steadily pouring down a potent brown liquid. Several women danced in a corner, oblivious, singing, rhyming as they went.

Faye ordered drinks and they all three joined in the warm feel of the place. The euphorics helped. It took only moments to become completely convinced that this was a noble and notable set of folk. Someone shouted a joke. Laughter pealed in the close-packed room.

Nick saw in this quick moment an instant of abiding grace: how lovely it was when Faye forgot herself and laughed fully, opening her mouth so wide you could see the whole oval cavern with its ribbed pink roof and the arching tongue alive with tension. The heart-stopping blackness at the back led down to depths worth a lifetime to explore, all revealed in a passing moment like a casual gift: a momentary and incidental beauty that eclipsed the studied, long-learned devices of women and made them infinitely more mysterious.

She gave him a wry, tossed-off smile. He frowned, puzzled. Maybe he had never paid adequate attention to her, never sensed her dimensions. He strained forward to say something and Jake interrupted his thoughts with, "Hey there, look. Two bridgies."

And there were. Two bridge types, not mere officers but scientists; they wore the sedate blue patches on their sleeves. Such people seldom came to these parts of the ship; their quarters, ordained by time, nestled deep in the rock-lined bowels of the inner asteroid.

"See if you can hear what they're sayin'," Faye whispered.

Jake shrugged. "Why should I care?

Faye frowned. "Wanna be a scuzzo dope forever?"

"Aw, stow it," Jake said, and went to get more beer.

Nick watched the scientist nearest him, the man, lift the heavy champagne bottle and empty it. Have to hand it to bioponics, he thought. They keep the liquor coming. The crisp golden foil at the head would be carefully collected, reused; the beautiful heavy hollow butts of the bottles had doubtless been fondled by his own grandfather. Of celebration there was no end.

Nick strained to hear.

"Yes, but the latest data shows definitely there's enough mass, no question."

"Maybe, maybe," said the other. "Must say I never thought there'd be enough between the clusters to add up so much—"

"But there *is*. No doubt of it. Look at Fenetti's data, clear as the nose on your face. Enough mass density between the clusters to close off the universe's geometry, to reverse the expansion."

Goddamn, Nick thought. They're talking about the critical mass problem. Right out in public.

"Yes. My earlier work seems to have been wrong."

"Look, this opens possibilities."

"How?"

"The expansion has to stop, right? So after it does, and things start to implode back, the density of gas the ship passes through will get steadily greater—right?"

Jesus, Nick thought, the eventual slowing down of the universal expansion, billions of years—

"Okay."

"So we'll accelerate more, the relativistic rate will get bigger—the whole process outside will speed up, as we see it."

"Right."

"Then we can sit around and watch the whole thing play out. I mean, shipboard time from now to the implosion of the whole universe, I make it maybe only three hundred years."

"That short?

"Do the calculation."

"Ummm. Maybe so, if we pick up enough mass in the scoop fields. This flyby we're going through, it helps, too."

"Sure it does. We'll do more like it in the next few weeks. Look, we're getting up to speeds that mean we'll be zooming by a galaxy every *day*."

"Uh-huh. If we can live a couple more centuries, shipboard time, we can get to see the whole shebang collapse back in on itself."

"Well, look, that's just a preliminary number, but I think we might make it. In this generation."

Faye said, "Jeez, I can't make out what they're talkin' about."

"I can," Nick said. It helped to know the jargon. He had studied this as part of his program to bootstrap himself up to a better life. You take officers, they could integrate the gravitational field equations straight off, or tell how a galaxy was evolving just by looking at it, or figure out the gas density ahead of the ship just by squinting at one of the X-ray bands from the detectors. They *knew*. He would have to know all of that too, and more. So he studied while the rest of the squad slurped up the malt.

He frowned. He was still stunned, trying to think it through. If the total mass between the clusters of galaxies was big enough, that extra matter would provide enough gravitational energy to make the whole universe reverse its expansion and fall backward, inward, given enough time . . .

Jake was back. "Too noisy in 'ere," he called. "Fergit the beers, bar's mobbed. Let's lift 'em."

Nick glanced over at the scientists. One was earnestly leaning forward, her face puffy and purplish, congested with the force of the words she was urging into the other's ear. He couldn't make out any more of what they were saying; they had descended into quoting mathematical formulas to each other.

"Okay," Nick said.

They left the random clamor of the bar and retraced their steps, back under the observation dome. Nick felt a curious elation.

Nick knows how to run the squad, knows how to keep the equipment going even if the voltage flickers, he can strip down most suits in under an hour using just plain rack tools, been doing it for forty years, all those power tools around the bay, most of the squad can't even turn a nut on a manifold without it has to be pneumatic *rrrrtt* quick as you please nevermind the wear on the lubricants lost forever that nobody aboard can synthesize, tools seize up easy now, jam your fingers when they do, give you a hand all swole up for a week, and all the time the squad griping 'cause they have to birddog their own stuff, breadboard new ones if some piece of gear goes bad, complaining 'cause they got to form and fabricate their own microchips, no easy replacement parts to just clip in the way you read about the way it was in the first generation, and God help you if a man or woman on the crew gets a fatal injury working in the throat crew, 'cause then your budget is docked for the cost of keeping 'em frozen down, waiting on cures that'll never come just like Earth will never come, the whole planet's been dead now a million years prob'ly, and the frozen corpses on board running two percent of the energy budget he read somewhere, getting to be more all the time, but then he thinks about that talk back in the bar and what it might mean, plunging on until you could see the whole goddamn end of the universe—

"Gotta admit we got you that time, Nick," Jake says as they approach the dome, "smooth as glass I come up on you, you're so hard workin' you don't see nothin', I give you a shot of extra spin, *man* your legs fly out you go wheelin' away—"

Jake starts to laugh.

—and livin' in each other's hip pockets like this the hell of it was you start to begrudge ever' little thing, even the young ones, the kids cost too, not that he's against them, hell, you got to keep the families okay or else they'll be slitting each other's throats inside a year, got to remember your grandfather who was in the Third Try on the decelerators, they came near to getting some new magnets in place before the plasma turbulence blew the whole framework away and they lost it, every family's got some ancestor who got flung down the throat and out into nothing, the kids got to be brought up rememberin' that, even though the little bastards do get into the bioponic tubes and play pranks, they got not a lot to do 'cept study and work, same as he and the others have done for all their lives, average crewman lasts two hundred years or so now, all got the best biomed (goddamn lucky they were shippin' so much to Centauri), bridge officers maybe even longer, get lots of senso augmentation to help you through the tough parts, and all to keep going, or even maybe get ahead a little like this squad boss thing, he was *that* close an' they took it away from him, small-minded bastards scared to shit he might make, what was it, fifty more units of rec credit than they did, not like being an officer or anything, just a job-jockey getting ahead a little, wanting just a scrap, and they gigged him for it and now this big mouth next to his ear is goin' on, puffing himself up in front of Faye, Faye who might be worth a second look if he could get her out of the shadow of this loudmouthed secondrate—

Jake was in the middle of a sentence, drawling on. Nick grabbed his arm and whirled him around.

"Keep laughin', you slimy bastard, just keep—"

Nick got a throat hold on him and leaned forward. He lifted, pressing Jake against the railing of the walkway. Jake struggled but his feet left the floor until he was balanced on the railing, halfway over the twenty-meter drop. He struck out with a fist but Nick held on.

"Hey, hey, vap off a li'l," Faye cried.

"Yeah—look—you got to take it—as it comes," Jake wheezed between clenched teeth.

"You two done me an' then you laugh an' don't think I don't know you're, you're—" He stopped, searching for words and not finding any.

Globular star clusters hung in the halo beyond the spirals. They flashed by the ship like immense chandeliers of stars. Odd clumps of torn and twisted gas rushed across the sweep of the dome overhead. Tortured gouts of sputtering matter were swept into the magnetic mouth of the ship. As it arched inward toward the craft it gave off flashes of incandescent light. These were stars being born in the ship-driven turbulence, the compressed gases, collapsing into firefly lives before the ship's throat swallowed them. In the flicker of an eyelid on board, a thousand years of stellar evolution transpired on the churning dome above.

The ship had by now carved a swooping path through the narrow strait between the disks. It had consumed banks of gas and dust, burning some for power, scattering the rest with fresh ejected energy into its path. The gas would gush out, away from the galaxies, unable to cause the ongoing friction that drew the two together. This in turn would slow their collision, giving the glittering worlds below another million years to plan, to discover, to struggle upward against the coming catastrophe. The ship itself, grown vast by relativistic effects, shone in the night skies of a billion worlds as a fiercely burning dot, emitting at impossible frequencies, slicing through kiloparsecs of space with its gluttonous magnetic throat, consuming.

"Be easy on him, Nick," Faye said softly.

Nick shook his head. "Naw. Trouble with a guy like this is, he got nothin' to do but piss on people. Hasn't got per . . . perspective."

"Stack it, Nick," Faye said.

Above them, the dome showed briefly the view behind the ship, where the reaction engines poured forth the raw refuse of the fusion drives. Far back, along their trajectory, lay dim filaments, wisps of ivory light. It was the Local Group, the cluster of galaxies that contained the Milky Way, their home. A human could look up, extend a hand, and a mere thumbnail would easily cover the faint smudge that was in fact a clump of spirals, ellipticals, dwarfs and irregular galaxies. It was a small part of the much larger association of galaxies, called the Local Supercluster. The ship was passing now beyond the fringes of the Local Supercluster, forging outward through the dim halo of random glimmering-galaxies which faded off into the black abyss beyond. It would be a long voyage across that span, until the next supercluster was reached: a pale blue haze that ebbed and flowed before the nose of the ship, liquid light distorted by relativity. For the moment the glow of their next destination was lost in the harsh glare of the two galaxies. The disks yawned and turned around the ship, slabs of hot gold and burnt orange, refracted, moving according to the twisted optical effects of special relativity. Compression of wavelengths and the squeezing of time itself made the disks seem to open wide, immense glowing doors swinging in the vacuum, parting to let pass this artifact that sped on, riding a tail of forking, sputtering, violet light.

Nick tilted the man back farther on the railing. Jake's arms fanned the air and his eyes widened.

"Okay, okay, you win," Jake grunted.

"You going upstairs, tell 'em you scragged me."

"Ah . . . okay."

"Good. Or else somethin' might, well, happen." Nick let Jake's legs down, back onto the walkway.

Faye said, "You didn't have to risk his neck. We would've cleared it for you if you'd—"

"Yeah, sure," Nick said sourly.

"You bastard, I oughta—"

"Yeah?"

Jake was breathing hard, his eyes danced around, but Nick knew he wouldn't try anything. He could judge a thing like that. Anyway, he thought, he'd been right, and they knew it. Jake grimaced, shook his head. Nick waved a hand and they walked on.

"Y'know what your trouble is, Nick?" Jake said after a moment. "Yer like this spider here."

Jake took the spider out of his jumpsuit pocket and held up the gray creature. It stirred, but was trapped.

"Wha'cha mean?" Nick asked.

"You got no perspective on the squad. Don't know what's really happenin'. An' this spider, he dunno either. He was down in the locker room, he didn't appreciate what he was in. I mean, that's the center of the whole damn ship right there, the squad."

"Yeah. So?"

"This spider, he don't appreciate how far he'd come from Agro. You either, Nick. You don't appreciate how the squad helps you out, how you oughta be grateful to them, how mebbe you shouldn't keep pushin' alla time."

"Spider's got little eyes, no lens to it," Nick said. "Can't see farther than your hand. Can't see those stars up there. I can, though."

Jake sputtered, "Crap, relative to the spider you're—"

"Aw, can it," Nick said.

Faye said, "Look, Jake, maybe you stop raggin' him alla time, he—"

"No, he's got a point there," Nick said, his voice suddenly mild. "We're all tryin' to be reg'lar folks in the ship, right? We should keep t'gether."

"Yeah. You push too hard."

Sure, Nick thought. Sure I do. And the next thing I'm gonna push for is Faye, take her clean away from you.

• • •

—the way her neck arcs back when she laughs, graceful in a casual way he never noticed before, a lilting note that caught him, and the broad smile she had, but she was solid too, did a good job in the blowback zone last week when nobody else could handle it, red gases flaring all around her, good woman to have with you, and maybe he'd need a lot of support like that, because he knows now what he really wants: to be an officer someday, it wasn't impossible, just hard, and the only way is by pushing. All this scratching around for a little more rec credits, maybe some better food, that wasn't the point, no, there was something more, the officers keep up the promotion game 'cause we've got to have something to keep people fretting and working, something to take our minds off what's outside, what'll happen if—no, *when*—the drive fails, where we're going, only what these two don't know is that we're not bound for oblivion in a universe that runs down into blackness, we're going on to see the reversal, we get to hear the recessional, galaxies, peeling into the primordial soup as they compress back together and the ship flies faster, always faster as it sucks up the dust of time and hurls itself further on, back to the crunch that made everything and will some day—hell, if he can stretch out the years, right in his own lifetime!—press everything back into a drumming hail of light and mass, now *that's* something to live for—

Faye said pleasantly, "Just think how much good we did back there. Saved who knows how many civilizations, billions of living creatures, gave them a reprieve."

"Right," Jake said, his voice distracted, still smarting over his defeat.

Faye nodded and the three of them made their way up an undulating walkway, heading for the bar where the rest of the squad would be. The ship thrust forward as the spiral galaxies dropped behind now, Doppler reddened into dying embers.

The ship had swept clean the space between them, postponed the coming collision. The scientists had seen this chance, persuaded the captain to make the slight swerve that allowed them to study the galaxies, and in the act accelerate the ship still more. The ship was now still closer to the knife-edge of light speed. Its aim was not a specific destination, but rather to plunge on, learning more, studying the dabs of refracted lights beyond, struggling with the engines, forging on as the universe wound down, as entropy increased, and the last stars flared out. It carried the cargo meant for Centauri—the records and past lives of all humanity, a library for the colony there. If the drives held up, it would carry them forward until the last tick of time.

Nick laughed. "Not that they'll know it, or ever give a—" He stopped. He'd been going to say *ever give a Goddamn about who did it*, but he knew how Faye felt about using the Lord's name in vain.

"Why, sure they will," Faye said brightly. "We were a big, hot source of all kinds of radiation. They'll know it was a piece of technology."

"Big lights in the sky? Could be natural."

"With a good spectrometer—"

"Yeah, but they'll never be sure."

She frowned. "Well, a ramscoop exhaust looks funny, not like a star or anything."

"With the big relativistic effect factored in, our emission goes out like a searchlight. One narrow little cone of scrambled-up radiation, Dopplered forward. So they can't make us out the whole time. Most of 'em 'd see us for just a few years, tops," Nick said.

"So?"

"Hard to make a scientific theory about somethin' that happens once, lasts a little while, never repeats."

"Maybe."

"They could just as likely think it was something unnatural. Supernatural. A god or somethin'."

"Huh. Maybe." Faye shrugged. "Come on. Let's get 'nother drink before rest'n rec hours are over."

They walked on. Above them the great knives of light sliced down through the air, ceaselessly changing, and the humans kept on going, their small voices indomitable, reaching forward, undiminished.

MAKING LIGHT

James P. Hogan

James P. Hogan, with Robert L. Forward and Charles Sheffield, was a leader in the new generation of hard sf writers in the early 1980s. At the same moment when Gregory Benford (and slightly later, Greg Bear) raised the literary standards of hard sf with their novels and stories, Hogan entered the field as if it were 1939 or 1949 and he had just discovered Heinlein and Asimov, Campbell and *Astounding*. This was in certain ways a great step backward, and shows a strong reaction on the part of a significant portion of the reading audience against the fashionable literary sf of the day (not, we hasten to add, against the hard sf but against the "speculative fiction"). Generally uninterested in reading in the contemporary field, Hogan in particular set about reinventing it from the forties onward, in novels filled with ideas and technology—such as *Inherit the Stars* (1977), *The Genesis Machine* (1978), *The Two Faces of Tomorrow* (1979), *Thrice in Time* (1980), and *Code of the Lifemaker* (1983)—that made him one of the more popular writers of the decade.

He has published very few short stories (collected in *Minds, Machines & Evolution* [1988]); the novel is his natural métier. This little hard sf satire skewers one of the favorite targets of the techie community: bureaucracy and governmental regulation of science—as Mr. Spock would say, "it is illogical." Regularly presented as the enemies of science and reason since the 1940s, the politician and the bureaucrat had become, in the 1980s, stock stereotype villains of *Analog*-type stories. Hogan, who writes for scientists and engineers and not for the more literary segments of the sf community, represents that community's feelings and prejudices through his fiction as much as any sf writer of the eighties. This story represents that strain of hard sf descended from Raymond F. Jones's "The Person From Porlock." While it is intended to entertain by preaching to the converted, there seems to be an endless appetite among devotees of hard sf for amusements of this sort. And one must acknowledge that it seems easy enough and clever enough to the nonliterary aspiring writer of sf that in each decade it encourages new writers from the scientific and engineering community to enter the field, as Hogan has remarked he did, with the attitude that "I can do that and do it better." This is one of the ways in which hard sf continues to attract new writers today.

In his spacious office atop the Headquarters Building of the Celestial Construction Company Inc., the General Operations Director hummed to himself as he sat at his desk and scanned over Contract 15,000,000,000 B.C. The contract document was brief and straightforward and called for the creation of a standard Mark IV universe—plenty of light; the usual suns, planets, and moons; a few firmaments here and there with birds and animals on the land; fish-filled waters around the land. There was an attached schedule for accessories, spares for renewable resources, and some supporting services. Deadline for the contract was seven days—a piece of cake, the GOD told himself. Design Engineering Department's final proposal for the bid lay to one side of the desk in the form of a bulky folder that constituted the Works Order Review Document. Until final approvals were granted, the WORD would be all that existed of the universe . . . but it was a beginning.

What promised to make this project a little different from the previous Mark IV's, and somewhat more interesting, was the optional extra that Design Engineering had tagged on in the *Appendix* section of the proposal: *people*. Unlike the species that made up the usual mix of Mark IV animal forms, which simply consumed resources and multiplied until they achieved a balance with the environment, the people would have the capacity to harness fire, make tools, and generally think about how they could be better off. This would produce an awareness of needs and the motivation to do something about satisfying them. Eventually the people would discover that, as their numbers and their demands increased, they would no longer be able to satisfy their needs with the resources that came readily to hand. At that point, the computer simulations indicated, they could simply give up, they could fight over what they had until it ran out and then be obliged to give up anyway, or they could develop the intellectual potential inherent in their design and apply it to discovering the progression of newer resources hidden around them like the successively more challenging, but at the same time more rewarding, clues of a treasure hunt. The way out of the maze lay in the third alternative.

Wood, growing all over the surface of the planets, would be the most obvious fuel following the taming of fire, but it would not prove adequate for long. It would, however, enable the more easily mined metal ores—conveniently scattered on top of the crusts or not very far below—to be smelted and exploited to make the tools necessary for digging deeper to the coal. Coal would enable an industrial base to be set up for producing machines suitable for drilling and processing oil, which in turn would yield the more highly concentrated fuels essential for aircraft and rudimentary space vehicles. The scientific expertise that would emerge during this phase would be the key to unlocking nuclear energy from crustal uranium, and the fission technologies thus brought into being would pave the way into fusion—initially using the deuterium from the special-formula oceans premixed for the purpose—and hence out to the stars and on to the advanced methods that would render resources effectively infinite for the lifetime of the universe. On planets set up for them in that way and with brains that ought to be capable of figuring the rest out for themselves, the people would have a fair chance of winning the game.

What the purpose of the game was, Design Engineering hadn't said. The GOD suspected that it was more for their own amusement than anything else, but he hadn't objected since he was quite curious himself to find out how the people would handle the situation. A modicum of applied precognition could no doubt have revealed that, but somehow it would have spoiled things.

He was still browsing over the last page of the contract when the phone rang with a peal of rising and falling chimes. It was Gabriel, the Vice President of Manufacturing. He sounded worried. "It's proposal number fifteen billion B.C.," he said. "I think we might have problems."

The GOD frowned. "I was just going through it. Looks fine to me. What's the problem?"

"Somebody from Equal Employment Opportunities Creation has been onto the Legal Department. They're objecting to DE's proposal for the people on the grounds that it would discriminate unfairly against the animals. I think we ought to get the department heads together to talk about it. How are you fixed?"

"Pretty clear for the next few millennia. When did you want to do it?"

"How about right now, while the large conference and congregation room's free?"

"Sure. Get the others over and I'll see you there in, say, ten minutes."

"Leave it to me."

The GOD replaced the phone, slipped the contract document inside the WORD folder, tucked the folder under his arm as he stood up from the desk, and began walking toward the door. Outside in the corridor he paused to pat the pockets of his suit and found he was out of holy smokes, so he made a slight detour to get a pack from the machine by the ascension and descension elevators.

"The EEOC says that we can't endow one species with that kind of intelligence," the Head of the Legal Department explained across the gilt-edged conference table a quarter of an hour later. "Doing so would confer such a devastating advantage that the animals would be guaranteed permanent second-class status with no opportunity to compete, which would constitute an infringement of rights."

"And we've been looking into some of the other implications," another of the lawyers added. "The people would eventually assume a uniquely dominant role. That could set us up for an antitrust suit."

All heads turned toward the Chief Design Engineer.

"Well, we can't take the intelligence away from the people," he objected. "The physiques that we've specified don't give them any other means of survival. They'd have no chance. Then we'd still be in trouble with EEOC but with everything the other way around." He threw his hands out impatiently. "And besides, it would defeat the purpose of the whole exercise. It was the addition of intelligence that was going to make this project more interesting.

"Why not make *all* the species equally intelligent?" somebody suggested.

The CDE shook his head. "We planned the ecology so that the animals would do most of the work for the people in the early phases and provide a lot of their food. If we made them equally intelligent, the situation would qualify as slavery and exploitation. We'd never get it past the Justice Department."

"And on top of that they'd all become eligible for education, sickness benefits, and retirement pensions," the CDE's assistant pointed out. "HEW would never accept the commitment. They couldn't handle the load."

That was true, the GOD admitted as he thought about it. Already the Department of Harps, Eternity-pensions, and Wings had insisted that all guarantees of benefits be deleted from the proposal. And that had been just on account of the projected numbers of people, never mind all the animals. "So why can't we change things so the people don't have to depend on the animals at all?" he asked, at last looking up. "Let's make them strong enough to do all the work themselves, and have them just eat plants."

"Not that easy," the CDE answered, shaking his head dubiously. "They'd have to be at least the size of elephants on an input of vegetable protein. Then food-gathering would become such a problem that they'd never have any time left over for mental development, which puts us back to square one." He thought for a second or two, then added, "Though it might work if we redesigned the food chain somehow."

The GOD looked over at the Head of Research. "What do you say to that?" he asked.

The scientist didn't appear too happy as he pinched his nose and reflected upon the question. "We'd have to figure it out again all the way down to the bacteria," he replied after a while. "You're talking about a complete redesign, not just a few modifications. Setting up a whole new ecology and running it through the simulator is a long job. I don't think we could finish before the closing date on the bid, and that doesn't allow for having to rewrite the proposal from scratch. If we could use the new Infallible Biological Modeler we might have had a chance, but we can't. It's not up and running yet."

"I thought the IBM was supposed to have been installed last week," the GOD said, sounding surprised.

"It was, but the systems angelists haven't handed it over yet," the Research Chief replied. "They're not through exorcizing the bugs."

The GOD frowned down at the table in front of him. "Hell," he muttered irritably.

"Er . . . we don't say that here," Gabriel reminded him politely.

"Oh, of course." The GOD made an apologetic gesture and then cast his eyes around the table. "Does anyone else have any suggestions?" he invited. No one had. He sighed in resignation, then looked at the Chief Design Engineer. "I'm sorry, Chief, but it sounds as if we're stuck. I guess there's no choice but to drop the extras and revert to a standard Mark IV."

"No people?" The CDE sounded disappointed.

"No people," the GOD confirmed. "It was a nice thought, but it's out of the question on the timescale of this contract. Keep working on it with Research, and maybe you'll have it all figured out in time for the next bid, huh?" The CDE nodded glumly. The meeting ended shortly thereafter, and the Vice President of Sales went back to his office to begin drafting a revised *Appendix* section to be delivered to the customer by winged messenger. So the project wasn't going to be so interesting after all, the GOD reflected with a pang of regret as he collected his papers. But at least that meant there was less risk of overrunning on time and incurring penance clauses.

The Chief Design Engineer was on the phone shortly after lunch on the following day. "Have you heard?" he asked. He sounded distressed.

"Heard what?" the GOD answered.

"Feathers, Aviation, and Aquatics have been onto our legal people. They're trying to tell us that our birds and fish aren't safe."

"That's ridiculous! They're the same ones as we've always used. What's wrong with our birds and fish?"

"According to FAA regulations, all flight-control and navigation systems have to be duplicated," the CDE said. "Our birds only have a single nervous system. Also, we're allowing them to fly over water without inflatable life jackets."

The GOD was completely taken aback. "What's gotten into them?" he demanded. "They've never complained about anything like that before."

"They've never really bothered to check the regulations before, but the controversy over the people has attracted their attention to this project," the CDE told him. "Our legal people think they're all at it—all the angelcies are brushing the dust off manuals they've never looked at before and going through them with magnifying glasses. We could be in for some real hassles."

The GOD groaned. "But what do they want us to do? We can't go loading the birds up with all kinds of duplicated junk. Their power-weight ratios are critically balanced. They'd never get off the ground."

"I know that. But all the same it's regulations, and the FAA won't budge. They also say we have to fit bad-weather landing aids."

The GOD's patience snapped abruptly. "They don't fly in bad weather," he yelled. "They just sit in the trees. If they don't fly, why do they need aids for landing? It'd be like putting life jackets on the camels."

"I know, I know, I know. But that's what the book says, and that's all the FAA's interested in."

"Can we do it?" the GOD asked when he had calmed down a little.

"Only with the penguins, the ostriches, and the others that walk. I called the FAA guy a couple of minutes ago and told him that the only way we could equip all the birds for bad-weather landing was by making them all walk. He said that sounded fine."

"I've never heard of anything so stupid! What's the point of having birds at all if they're only allowed to walk? We can't have planets with walking birds all over the place. The competition would die laughing."

"I know all that. I'm just telling you what the guy said."

A few seconds of silence went by. Then the GOD asked, "What's wrong with the fish?"

"The shallow-water species don't have coastal radar."

Pause.

"Is this some kind of joke?"

"I wish it were. They're serious all right."

The GOD shook his head in disbelief and slumped back in his chair. "Maybe we might just have to go along without birds and shallow-water fish this time," he said at last. "Would the rest still work?"

"I'm not so sure it would," the CDE replied. "The birds were supposed to spread seeds around to produce enough vegetation to support the herbivores. If we reduce the quotas of herbivores, we'd have to cut back on the carnivores, too. And without the birds to keep down the insects, we'd have the Forestry Cherubim on our backs for endangering the trees. With the trees in trouble and no shallow-water fish to clean up the garbage from the rivers, the whole ecosystem would break down. None of the animal species would be able to support themselves."

The GOD sighed and wrestled with the problem in his head. The CDE himself had precipitated the current crisis by introducing the idea of people in the first place, but there would be nothing to be gained by starting rounds of recriminations and accusations at this point, he thought. What was important was to get the proposal into an acceptable form before the closing date for the bid. "The only thing I can think of is that if the animals become unable to support themselves, we'll have to put them all on welfare. If I call HEW and see if I can fix it, would that solve the problem?"

"Well . . . yeah, I guess it would . . . if you can fix it." The CDE didn't sound too hopeful.

The GOD phoned the HEW Director a few minutes later and explained the situation. Would HEW accept a commitment to supplying welfare support for the animals?

"No way!" was the emphatic reply.

"What in he—heaven's name do you expect us to do?" the GOD demanded, shouting in exasperation. "How can we meet anybody's regulations when they always conflict with somebody else's?"

"That's not our problem," the HEW Director stated bluntly. "Sorry."

Another meeting was called early the next morning to discuss the quandary. After all avenues had been explored, there seemed only one solution that would avoid all the conflicts: an azoic universe. *All* forms of living organisms would have to be deleted from the proposal. The meeting ended on a note of somber resignation.

• • •

The Environmental Protection Angel was on the line later that afternoon. Her voice was shrill and piercing, grating on the GOD's nerves. "Without any plants at all, the levels of carbon dioxide, nitrogen oxides, and sulfur compounds from volcanic activity would exceed the permitted limits. The proposal as it stands is quite unacceptable. We would not be able to issue operating licenses for the volcanoes."

"But the limits were set to safeguard only living organisms!" the GOD thundered. "We've scrapped them—all of them. There *aren't any* living organisms to be safeguarded."

"There is no clause in the regulations which specifically exempts lifeless planets," the EPA told him primly. It was too much.

"What kind of lunatics are you?" the GOD raged into the phone. "You don't need a specific exemption. What do you need protective regulations for when there isn't anything to be protected? How stupid can you get? Any idiot could see that it doesn't apply here—any of it. You're out of your mind."

"I'm simply doing my job, and I don't expect personal insults," came the reply. "The standards are quite clear, and they must be met. Good day." The line went dead.

The GOD conveyed the news to Design Engineering, who discussed it with Research. Without the volcanoes there wouldn't be enough planetary outgassing to form the atmospheres and oceans. Okay, the atmospheres and oceans would have to go. But the volcanoes were also intended to play a role in relieving the structural stresses and thermal buildups in the planetary crusts. How could that be taken care of without any volcanoes? Only by having more earthquakes to make up the difference, the CDE declared. The GOD told him to revise the proposal by deleting the volcanoes and making the crustal formations more earthquake-prone. Everybody agreed that the problem appeared at last to have been solved.

The Department of Highlands, Undulations, and Deserts called the GOD a day later with an objection. "I'm dreadfully sorry, old chap, but we seem to have run into a bit of a problem," the man from HUD told him. "You see, the mountain ranges you've proposed don't quite come up to the standards set out in our building codes for the increased level of seismic activity. We'd have no choice but to condemn them as unsafe, I'm afraid."

"What if we do away with the mountains, then?" the GOD growled sullenly.

"That would be perfectly satisfactory as far as we're concerned, but I rather suspect that you might still have a problem in getting it passed by the Occupational Safety and Health Angelcy. All those fissures opening up and landslides going on all over the place . . . it would be a bit hazardous for the animals, wouldn't it?"

"But we've already gotten rid of the animals," the GOD pointed out. "There won't be any."

"I see your point," the man from HUD agreed amiably, "but it is still in the jolly old rules. You know how finicky those OSHA types can be. Just a friendly word in your ear. Frightfully sorry and all that."

The GOD was past arguing.

Design Engineering's response was to make the planets completely inactive. There would be no mountains, no fluid interiors, no mobile plates—in fact, no tectonic processes of any kind. The planets would be simply featureless balls of solid rock that could never by any stretch of the imagination be considered potentially hazardous to any living thing, whether one existed or not.

The Great Accounting Overseer didn't like it. "What do you need them for?"

a GAO minion challenged a day later. "They don't serve any useful purpose at all. They're just a needless additional expense on the cost budget. Why not get rid of them completely?"

"They've got a point," the CDE admitted when the GOD went over to Engineering to talk about it. "I guess the only reason we put them in is because that's the way we've always done it. Yeah . . . I reckon we should strike them out. No planets."

But the Dispenser of Energy wasn't happy about the idea of a universe consisting of nothing but stars. "It might be budgeted to last for billions of years, but it's still finite nevertheless," an assistant of the DOE declared in a call to the GOD. "We are trying to encourage a policy of conservation, you know. This idea of having billions of stars just pouring out all that energy into empty space with none of it being used for anything at all . . . well, it would be terribly wasteful and inefficient. I don't think we could possibly approve something like that."

"But it's just as we've always done it," the GOD protested. "The planets never used more than a drop in the ocean. The difference isn't worth talking about."

"Quantitatively, yes, but I'm talking about a difference in principle," the DOE assistant replied. "The waste was high in the earlier projects, but at least there was a reason in principle. This time there isn't any, and that does make a difference. We couldn't give this universe an approval stamp. Sorry."

A day later Design Engineering had come up with a way to conserve the energy: Instead of being concentrated into masses sufficiently dense to sustain fusion reactions and form stars, the stellar material would be dispersed evenly throughout space as clouds of dust and gas in which the small amount of free energy that remained would be conserved through an equilibrium exchange between radiation and matter. The DOE was satisfied with that. Unfortunately the EPA was not; the clouds of dust and gas would exceed the pollution limits.

With two days to go before the closing date for the bid, the GOD called all the department heads and senior technical staff members together to discuss the situation. The ensuing meeting went on all through the night. After running calculations through the computers several times, they at last came up with a solution they were sure had to be acceptable to everybody. Sales forwarded a revised final proposal to the customer, and the company waited nervously for the responses. Miraculously the phone on the GOD's desk didn't ring once all through the next day. The proposal was approved, and the final contract was awarded.

Out at the construction site, Gabriel watched despondently as the project at last got under way. All that was left of the original plan was a pinpoint of exotic particles of matter, radiation, space, and time, all compressed together at a temperature of billions of degrees. The bizarre particles fell apart into protons, neutrons, electrons, muons, neutrinos, and photons, which after a while began clustering together through the radiation fluid as he watched. After the grandeur of the previous projects he had witnessed, the sight was depressing. "I guess we just write this one off, forget all about it, and file it away," he murmured to the GOD, who was standing next to him. "It's not much to look at, is it? I can't see this even getting a mention in the report to the stockholders." He turned his head to find that the GOD's eyes were twinkling mischievously. "What's funny?" he asked, puzzled.

The GOD tipped his yellow hard-hat to the back of his head and grinned in a conspiratorial kind of way as he scratched his forehead. "Don't worry about it," he said quietly. "We've worked out a new method. It'll all come out just the way we planned . . . everything."

Gabriel blinked at him in astonishment. "What are you talking about? How do you mean, *everything*? You don't mean the stars, the planets, the oceans, the mountains . . ." His voice trailed away as he saw the GOD nodding.

"And the birds, and the fish, and the animals, all the way through to the people," the GOD told him confidently. "It'll turn out just the way we planned it in the original proposal."

Gabriel shook his head, nonplussed. "But . . . how?" He gestured at the expanding fireball, in which traces of helium and a few other light nuclei were beginning to appear. "How could it all come out of *that?*"

The GOD chuckled. "The research people developed some things called 'Laws of Physics' that they buried inside it. The angelcies will never find them. But they're in there, and they'll make it all happen just the way we planned. We ran the numbers through the IBM last night, and they work. You wait and see."

Gabriel looked over his shoulder at the site supervisor's hut and then gazed back at the embryo universe with a new interest and respect. "I was going to go inside for a coffee," he said. "But this sounds interesting. I think I'll hang around a little longer. I don't want to miss this."

The GOD smiled. "Oh, that's okay—you go get your coffee," he said. "There's plenty of time yet."

THE LAST QUESTION

Isaac Asimov

Isaac Asimov used the figure of the robot often in his most memorable science fiction of the 1950s, culminating in his famous novels, *The Caves of Steel* (1954) and *The Naked Sun* (1957). His famous "Three Laws" of robotics were generally accepted by all sf writers by 1950. But by the early fifties, a new image from contemporary science was emerging in sf that began to push the ambulatory humanoid machines aside: the big computers—huge thinking machines, each one bigger and better than the previous generation, that might someday equal or surpass the capabilities of the human brain. The evolution of pure machine intelligence (as opposed to robot "men") became a recurring theme in science fiction, growing in strength over the decades until it became a central concern of much of the literature in the 1980s, especially among the cyberpunks.

At the start of the Golden Age, Robert A. Heinlein's Hamilton Felix in *Beyond This Horizon* had said that the real job of humanity and science is to confront the ultimate metaphysical questions. But in the 1950s John W. Campbell was not interested in metaphysical stories that suggested a machine's superiority to a human, so Asimov published this innovative, uncharacteristic work (1956) in a minor market, *Science Fiction Quarterly*.

The evolution of thinking machines was an enduring theme in the fiction of Isaac Asimov; he wrote several stories about Multivac, the ultimate computer, including "The Life and Times of Multivac" earlier in this book, and the current story. As late as 1990 he claimed "The Last Question" was his favorite of all his own stories. "It was an idea which excited me and which I was sure had never been done before." From the humanoid robots of his early stories, to the huge computers of his fifties work, to the (again) humanoids of his last robot novels, advances in machine intelligence fascinated him, were the springboard for some of his finest flights of speculation. In this uncharacteristically Stapledonian story, the hugest scale in time and space is compressed and distilled, physics yields to metaphysics, creation occurs.

The last question was asked for the first time, half in jest, on May 21, 2061, at a time when humanity first stepped into the light. The question came about as a result of a five-dollar bet over highballs, and it happened this way:

Alexander Adell and Bertram Lupov were two of the faithful attendants of Multivac. As well as any human beings could, they knew what lay behind the cold, clicking, flashing face—miles and miles of face—of that giant computer. They had at least a vague notion of the general plan of relays and circuits that had long since grown past the point where any single human could possibly have a firm grasp of the whole.

Multivac was self-adjusting and self-correcting. It had to be, for nothing human could adjust and correct it quickly enough or even adequately enough. So Adell and Lupov attended the monstrous giant only lightly and superficially, yet as well as any men could. They fed it data, adjusted questions to its needs and translated the answers that were issued. Certainly they, and all others like them, were fully entitled to share in the glory that was Multivac's.

For decades Multivac had helped design the ships and plot the trajectories that enabled man to reach the Moon, Mars and Venus, but past that, Earth's poor resources could not support the ships. Too much energy was needed for the long trips. Earth exploited its coal and uranium with increasing efficiency, but there was only so much of each.

But slowly Multivac learned enough to answer deeper questions more fundamentally, and on May 14, 2061, what had been theory became fact.

The energy of the Sun was stored, converted and utilized directly on a planet-wide scale. All Earth turned off its burning coal, its fissioning uranium, and flipped the switch that connected all of it to a small station, one mile in diameter, circling the Earth at half the distance of the Moon. All Earth ran by invisible beams of sunpower.

Seven days had not sufficed to dim the glory of it, and Adell and Lupov finally managed to escape from the public function and to meet in quiet where no one would think of looking for them, in the deserted underground chambers, where portions of the mighty, buried body of Multivac showed. Unattended, idling, sorting data with contented lazy clickings, Multivac too had earned its vacation and the boys appreciated that. They had no intention, originally, of disturbing it.

They had brought a bottle with them, and their only concern at the moment was to relax in the company of each other and the bottle.

"It's amazing when you think of it," said Adell. His broad face had lines of weariness in it, and he stirred his drink slowly with a glass rod, watching the cubes of ice slur clumsily about. "All the energy we can possibly ever use for free. Enough energy, if we wanted to draw on it, to melt all Earth into a big drop of impure liquid iron and still never miss the energy so used. All the energy we could ever use, forever and forever and forever."

Lupov cocked his head sideways. He had a trick of doing that when he wanted to be contrary, and he wanted to be contrary now, partly because he had had to carry the ice and glassware. "Not forever," he said.

"Oh, hell, just about forever. Till the sun runs down, Bert."

"That's not forever."

"All right, then. Billions and billions of years. Twenty billion maybe. Are you satisfied?"

Lupov put his fingers through his thinning hair as though to reassure himself that some was still left and sipped gently at his drink. "Twenty billion years isn't forever."

"Well, it will last our time, won't it?"

"So would the coal and uranium."

"All right, but now we can hook up each individual spaceship to the Solar Station, and it can go to Pluto and back a million times without ever worrying about fuel. You can't do *that* on coal and uranium. Ask Multivac if you don't believe me."

"I don't have to ask Multivac. I know that."

"Then stop running down what Multivac's done for us," said Adell, blazing up. "It did all right."

"Who says it didn't? What I say is that a sun won't last forever. That's all I'm saying. We're safe for twenty billion years; but then what?" Lupov pointed a slightly shaky finger at the other. "And don't say we'll switch to another sun."

There was silence for a while. Adell put his glass to his lips only occasionally, and Lupov's eyes slowly closed. They rested.

Then Lupov's eyes snapped open. "You're thinking we'll switch to another sun when ours is done, aren't you?"

"I'm not thinking."

"Sure you are. You're weak on logic, that's the trouble with you. You're like the guy in the story who was caught in a sudden shower and ran to a grove of trees and got under one. He wasn't worried, you see, because he figured when one tree got wet through, he would just get under another one."

"I get it," said Adell. "Don't shout. When the sun is done, the other stars will be gone too."

"Darn right they will," muttered Lupov. "It all had a beginning in the original cosmic explosion, whatever that was, and it'll all have an end when all the stars run down. Some run down faster than others. Hell, the giants won't last a hundred million years. The Sun will last twenty billion years and maybe the dwarfs will last a hundred billion for all the good they are. But just give us a trillion years and everything will be dark. Entropy has to increase to maximum, that's all."

"I know all about entropy," said Adell, standing on his dignity.

"The hell you do."

"I know as much as you do."

"Then you know everything's got to run down someday."

"All right. Who says it won't?"

"You did, you poor sap. You said we had all the energy we needed, forever. You said 'forever.' "

It was Adell's turn to be contrary. "Maybe we can build things up again someday," he said.

"Never."

"Why not? Someday."

"Ask Multivac."

"Never."

"*You* ask Multivac. I dare you. Five dollars says it can't be done."

Adell was just drunk enough to try, just sober enough to be able to phrase the necessary symbols and operations into a question which, in words, might have corresponded to this: Will mankind one day, without the net expenditure of energy, be able to restore the sun to its full youthfulness even after it had died of old age?

Or maybe it could be put more simply like this: How can the net amount of entropy of the Universe be massively decreased?

Multivac fell dead and silent. The slow flashing of lights ceased, the distant sounds of clicking relays ended.

Then, just as the frightened technicians felt they could hold their breath no longer, there was a sudden springing to life of the teletype attached to that portion of Multivac. Five words were printed: INSUFFICIENT DATA FOR MEANINGFUL ANSWER.

"No bet," whispered Lupov. They left hurriedly.

By next morning, the two, plagued with throbbing heads and cottony mouths, had forgotten the incident.

Jerrodd, Jerrodine and Jerrodette I and II watched the starry picture in the visiplate change as the passage through hyperspace was completed in its nontime lapse. At once the even powdering of stars gave way to the predominance of a single bright marble disk, centered.

"That's X-23," said Jerrodd confidently. His thin hands clamped tightly behind his back and the knuckles whitened.

The little Jerrodettes, both girls, had experienced the hyperspace passage for the first time in their lives and were self-conscious over the momentary sensation of inside-outness. They buried their giggles and chased one another wildly about their mother, screaming, "We've reached X-23—we've reached X-23—we've—"

"Quiet, children," said Jerrodine sharply. "Are you sure, Jerrodd?"

"What is there to be but sure?" asked Jerrodd, glancing up at the bulge of featureless metal just under the ceiling. It ran the length of the room, disappearing through the wall at either end. It was as long as the ship.

Jerrodd scarcely knew a thing about the thick rod of metal except that it was called a Microvac; that one asked it questions if one wished; that if one did not, it still had its task of guiding the ship to a preordered destination; of feeding on energies from the various Sub-galactic Power Stations; of computing the equations for the hyperspatial jumps.

Jerrodd and his family had only to wait and live in the comfortable residence quarters of the ship.

Someone had once told Jerrodd that the "ac" at the end of "Microvac" stood for "automatic computer" in ancient English, but he was on the edge of forgetting even that.

Jerrodine's eyes were moist as she watched the visiplate. "I can't help it. I feel funny about leaving Earth."

"Why, for Pete's sake?" demanded Jerrodd. "We had nothing there. We'll have everything on X-23. You won't be alone. You won't be a pioneer. There are over a million people on the planet already. Good Lord, our great-grandchildren will be looking for new worlds because X-23 will be overcrowded." Then, after a reflective pause, "I tell you, it's a lucky thing the computers worked out interstellar travel the way the race is growing."

"I know, I know," said Jerrodine miserably.

Jerrodette I said promptly, "Our Microvac is the best Microvac in the world."

"I think so too," said Jerrodd, tousling her hair.

It *was* a nice feeling to have a Microvac of your own, and Jerrodd was glad he was part of his generation and no other. In his father's youth, the only computers had been tremendous machines taking up a hundred square miles of land. There was only one to a planet. Planetary ACs they were called. They had been growing in size steadily for a thousand years and then, all at once, came refinement. In place of transistors had come molecular valves so that even the largest Planetary AC could be put into a space only half the volume of a spaceship.

Jerrodd felt uplifted, as he always did when he thought that his own personal Microvac was many times more complicated than the ancient and primitive Multivac that had first tamed the Sun, and almost as complicated as Earth's Planetary AC (the largest) that had first solved the problem of hyperspatial travel and had made trips to the stars possible.

"So many stars, so many planets," sighed Jerrodine, busy with her own thoughts. "I suppose families will be going out to new planets forever, the way we are now."

"Not forever," said Jerrodd with a smile. "It will all stop someday, but not for billions of years. Many billions. Even the stars run down, you know. Entropy must increase."

"What's entropy, Daddy?" shrilled Jerrodette II.

"Entropy, little sweet, is just a word which means the amount of running down of the Universe. Everything runs down, you know, like your little walkie-talkie robot, remember?"

"Can't you just put in a new power unit, like with my robot?"

"The stars *are* the power units, dear. Once they're gone, there are no more power units."

Jerrodette I at once set up a howl. "Don't let them, Daddy. Don't let the stars run down."

"Now look what you've done," whispered Jerrodine, exasperated.

"How was I to know it would frighten them?" Jerrodd whispered back.

"Ask the Microvac," wailed Jerrodette I. "Ask him how to turn the stars on again."

"Go ahead," said Jerrodine. "It will quiet them down." (Jerrodette II was beginning to cry also.)

Jerrodd shrugged. "Now, now, honeys. I'll ask Microvac. Don't worry, he'll tell us."

He asked the Microvac, adding quickly, "Print the answer."

Jerrodd cupped the strip of thin cellufilm and said cheerfully, "See now, the Microvac says it will take care of everything when the time comes, so don't worry."

Jerrodine said, "And now, children, it's time for bed. We'll be in our new home soon."

Jerrodd read the words on the cellufilm again before destroying it: INSUFFICIENT DATA FOR MEANINGFUL ANSWER.

He shrugged and looked at the visiplate. X-23 was just ahead.

VJ-23X of Lameth stared into the black depths of the three-dimensional, small-scale map of the galaxy and said, "Are we ridiculous, I wonder, in being so concerned about the matter?"

MQ-17J of Nicron shook his head. "I think not. You know the galaxy will be filled in five years at the present rate of expansion."

Both seemed in their early twenties; both were tall and perfectly formed.

"Still," said VJ-23X, "I hesitate to submit a pessimistic report to the Galactic Council."

"I wouldn't consider any other kind of report. Stir them up a bit. We've got to stir them up."

VJ-23X sighed. "Space is infinite. A hundred billion galaxies are there for the taking. More."

"A hundred billion is *not* infinite and it's getting less infinite all the time. Consider! Twenty thousand years ago mankind first solved the problem of utilizing stellar energy, and a few centuries later, interstellar travel became possible. It took mankind a million years to fill one small world and then only fifteen thousand years to fill the rest of the galaxy. Now the population doubles every ten years—"

VJ-23X interrupted. "We can thank immortality for that."

"Very well. Immortality exists and we have to take it into account. I admit it has its seamy side, this immortality. The Galactic AC has solved many problems for us, but in solving the problems of preventing old age and death, it has undone all its other solutions."

"Yet you wouldn't want to abandon life, I suppose."

"Not at all," snapped MQ-17J, softening it at once to, "Not yet. I'm by no means old enough. How old are you?"

"Two hundred twenty-three. And you?"

"I'm still under two hundred.—But to get back to my point. Population doubles every ten years. Once this galaxy is filled, we'll have filled another in ten years. Another ten years and we'll have filled two more. Another decade, four more. In a hundred years, we'll have filled a thousand galaxies. In a thousand years, a million galaxies. In ten thousand years, the entire known Universe. Then what?"

VJ-23X said, "As a side issue, there's a problem of transportation. I wonder how many sunpower units it will take to move galaxies of individuals from one galaxy to the next."

"A very good point. Already mankind consumes two sunpower units per year."

"Most of it's wasted. After all, our own galaxy alone pours out a thousand sunpower units a year and we only use two of those."

"Granted, but even with a hundred-percent efficiency, we only stave off the end. Our energy requirements are going up in a geometric progression even faster than our population. We'll run out of energy even sooner than we run out of galaxies. A good point. A very good point."

"We'll just have to build new stars out of interstellar gas."

"Or out of dissipated heat?" asked MQ-17J sarcastically.

"There may be some way to reverse entropy. We ought to ask the Galactic AC."

VJ-23X was not really serious, but MQ-17J pulled out his AC contact from his pocket and placed it on the table before him.

"I've half a mind to," he said. "It's something the human race will have to face someday."

He stared somberly at his small AC contact. It was only two inches cubed and nothing in itself, but it was connected through hyperspace with the great Galactic AC that served all mankind. Hyperspace considered, it was an integral part of the Galactic AC.

MQ-17J paused to wonder if someday in his immortal life he would get to see the Galactic AC. It was on a little world of its own, a spiderwebbing of force beams holding the matter within which surges of sub-mesons took the place of the old clumsy molecular valves. Yet despite its subetheric workings, the Galactic AC was known to be a full thousand feet across.

MQ-17J asked suddenly of his AC contact, "Can entropy ever be reversed?"

VJ-23X looked startled and said at once, "Oh, say, I didn't really mean to have you ask that."

"Why not?"

"We both know entropy can't be reversed. You can't turn smoke and ash back into a tree."

"Do you have trees on your world?" asked MQ-17J.

The sound of the Galactic AC startled them into silence. Its voice came thin and beautiful out of the small AC contact on the desk. It said: THERE IS INSUFFICIENT DATA FOR A MEANINGFUL ANSWER.

VJ-23X said, "See!"

The two men thereupon returned to the question of the report they were to make to the Galactic Council.

Zee Prime's mind spanned the new galaxy with a faint interest in the countless twists of stars that powdered it. He had never seen this one before. Would he ever see them all? So many of them, each with its load of humanity. But a load that was almost a dead weight. More and more, the real essence of men was to be found out here, in space.

Minds, not bodies! The immortal bodies remained back on the planets, in suspension over the eons. Sometimes they roused for material activity but that was growing rarer. Few new individuals were coming into existence to join the incredibly mighty throng, but what matter? There was little room in the Universe for new individuals.

Zee Prime was roused out of his reverie upon coming across the wispy tendrils of another mind.

"I am Zee Prime," said Zee Prime. "And you?"

"I am Dee Sub Wun. Your galaxy?"

"We call it only the galaxy. And you?

"We call ours the same. All men call their galaxy their galaxy and nothing more. Why not?"

"True. Since all galaxies are the same."

"Not all galaxies. On one particular galaxy the race of man must have originated. That makes it different."

Zee Prime said, "On which one?"

"I cannot say. The Universal AC would know."

"Shall we ask him? I am suddenly curious."

Zee Prime's perceptions broadened until the galaxies themselves shrank and became a new, more diffuse powdering on a much larger background. So many hundreds of billions of them, all with their immortal beings, all carrying their load of intelligences with minds that drifted freely through space. And yet one of them was unique among them all in being the original galaxy. One of them had, in its vague and distant past, a period when it was the only galaxy populated by man.

Zee Prime was consumed with curiosity to see this galaxy and he called out: "Universal AC! On which galaxy did mankind originate?"

The Universal AC heard, for on every world and throughout space, it had its receptors ready, and each receptor lead through hyperspace to some unknown point where the Universal AC kept itself aloof.

Zee Prime knew of only one man whose thoughts had penetrated within sensing distance of Universal AC, and he reported only a shining globe, two feet across, difficult to see.

"But how can that be all of Universal AC?" Zee Prime had asked.

"Most of it," had been the answer, "is in hyperspace. In what form it is there I cannot imagine."

Nor could anyone, for the day had long since passed, Zee Prime knew, when any man had any part of the making of a Universal AC. Each Universal AC designed and constructed its successor. Each, during its existence of a million years or more, accumulated the necessary data to build a better and more intricate, more capable successor, in which its own store of data and individuality would be submerged.

The Universal AC interrupted Zee Prime's wandering thoughts, not with words, but with guidance. Zee Prime's mentality was guided into the dim sea of galaxies, and one in particular enlarged into stars.

A thought came, infinitely distant but infinitely clear. "THIS IS THE ORIGINAL GALAXY OF MAN."

But it was the same after all, the same as any other, and Zee Prime stifled his disappointment.

Dee Sub Wun, whose mind had accompanied the other, said suddenly, "And is one of these stars the original star of Man?"

The Universal AC said, "MAN'S ORIGINAL STAR HAS GONE RED GIANT. IT IS NOW A WHITE DWARF."

"Did the men upon it die?" asked Zee Prime, startled and without thinking.

The Universal AC said, "A NEW WORLD, AS IN SUCH CASES, WAS CONSTRUCTED FOR THEIR PHYSICAL BODIES IN TIME."

"Yes, of course," said Zee Prime, but a sense of loss overwhelmed him even so. His mind released its hold on the original galaxy of Man, let it spring back and lose itself among the blurred pin points. He never wanted to see it again.

Dee Sub Wun said, "What is wrong?"

"The stars are dying. The original star is dead."

"They must all die. Why not?"

"But when all energy is gone, our bodies will finally die, and you and I with them."

"It will take billions of years."

"I do not wish it to happen even after billions of years. Universal AC! How may stars be kept from dying?"

Dee Sub Wun said in amusement, "You're asking how entropy might be reversed in direction."

And the Universal AC answered: "THERE IS AS YET INSUFFICIENT DATA FOR A MEANINGFUL ANSWER."

Zee Prime's thoughts fled back to his own galaxy. He gave no further thought to Dee Sub Wun, whose body might be waiting on a galaxy a billion light-years away, or on the star next to Zee Prime's own. It didn't matter.

Unhappily Zee Prime began collecting interstellar hydrogen out of which to build a small star of his own. If the stars must someday die, at least some could yet be built.

Man considered with himself, for in a way, Man, mentally, was one. He consisted of a trillion, trillion, trillion ageless bodies, each in its place, each resting quiet and incorruptible, each cared for by perfect automatons, equally incorruptible, while the minds of all the bodies freely melted one into the other, indistinguishable.

Man said, "The Universe is dying."

Man looked about at the dimming galaxies. The giant stars, spendthrifts, were gone long ago, back in the dimmest of the dim far past. Almost all stars were white dwarfs, fading to the end.

New stars had been built of the dust between the stars, some by natural processes, some by Man himself, and those were going too. White dwarfs might yet be crashed together and of the mighty forces so released, new stars built, but only one star for every thousand white dwarfs destroyed, and those would come to an end too.

Man said, "Carefully husbanded, as directed by the Cosmic AC, the energy that is even yet left in all the Universe will last for billions of years."

"But even so," said Man, "eventually it will all come to an end. However it may be husbanded, however stretched out, the energy once expended is gone and cannot be restored. Entropy must increase forever to the maximum."

Man said, "Can entropy not be reversed? Let us ask the Cosmic AC."

The Cosmic AC surrounded them but not in space. Not a fragment of it was in space. It was in hyperspace and made of something that was neither matter nor energy. The question of its size and nature no longer had meaning in any terms that Man could comprehend.

"Cosmic AC," said Man, "how may entropy be reversed?"

The Cosmic AC said, "THERE IS AS YET INSUFFICIENT DATA FOR A MEANINGFUL ANSWER."

Man said, "Collect additional data."

The Cosmic AC said, "I WILL DO SO. I HAVE BEEN DOING SO FOR A HUNDRED BILLION YEARS. MY PREDECESSORS AND I HAVE BEEN ASKED THIS QUESTION MANY TIMES. ALL THE DATA I HAVE REMAINS INSUFFICIENT."

"Will there come a time," said Man, "when data will be sufficient or is the problem insoluble in all conceivable circumstances?"

The Cosmic AC said, "NO PROBLEM IS INSOLUBLE IN ALL CONCEIVABLE CIRCUMSTANCES."

Man said, "When will you have enough data to answer the question?"

The Cosmic AC said, "THERE IS AS YET INSUFFICIENT DATA FOR A MEANINGFUL ANSWER."

"Will you keep working on it?" asked Man.

The Cosmic AC said, "I WILL."

Man said, "We shall wait."

The stars and galaxies died and snuffed out, and space grew black after ten trillion years of running down.

One by one Man fused with AC, each physical body losing its mental identity in a manner that was somehow not a loss but a gain.

Man's last mind paused before fusion, looking over a space that included nothing but the dregs of one last dark star and nothing besides but incredibly thin matter, agitated randomly by the tag ends of heat wearing out, asymptotically, to the absolute zero.

Man said, "AC, is this the end? Can this chaos not be reversed into the Universe once more? Can that not be done?"

AC said, "THERE IS AS YET INSUFFICIENT DATA FOR A MEANINGFUL ANSWER."

Man's last mind fused and only AC existed—and that in hyperspace.

Matter and energy had ended and with it space and time. Even AC existed only for the sake of the one last question that it had never answered from the time a half-drunken computer technician ten trillion years before had asked the question of a computer that was to AC far less than was a man to Man.

All other questions had been answered, and until this last question was answered also, AC might not release his consciousness.

All collected data had come to a final end. Nothing was left to be collected.

But all collected data had yet to be completely correlated and put together in all possible relationships.

A timeless interval was spent in doing that.

And it came to pass that AC learned how to reverse the direction of entropy.

But there was now no man to whom AC might give the answer to the last question. No matter. The answer—by demonstration—would take care of that too.

For another timeless interval AC thought how best to do this. Carefully AC organized the program.

The consciousness of AC encompassed all of what had once been a Universe and brooded over what was now Chaos. Step by step, it must be done.

And AC said, "LET THERE BE LIGHT!"

And there was light—

THE INDEFATIGABLE FROG

Philip K. Dick

Philip K. Dick, to the astonishment of many traditional science fiction readers, emerged in the 1970s as perhaps the most important living sf writer in the eyes of literary critics and a preponderance of readers worldwide outside the United States. His most famous novels include *Solar Lottery* (1955), *Time Out of Joint* (1959), *The Man in the High Castle* (1962), *Martian Time-Slip* (1964), *The Three Stigmata of Palmer Eldritch* (1965), *Ubik* (1969), *Flow My Tears, The Policeman Said* (1974), *Valis* (1981). Dick was fascinated by the surfaces and images of technology, and was more taken with philosophical ideas and the nature of reality than with science and its rigorous methodology. He was also a humorist. His closest relations among science fiction writers when he began to write in the fifties were A. E. van Vogt (for his huge, ambitious, metaphysical ideas in endless profusion and combination) and Henry Kuttner (for his stylish play with the tropes and clichés of science fiction—a future world filled with talking appliances and strange shifts in reality, more Carrollian than Campbellian). By the 1960s, the influence of Kurt Vonnegut, Jr.—especially of *The Sirens of Titan* (1959)—became prominent, both in the sentiment and politics of, for example, *The Man in the High Castle*, and *Dr. Bloodmoney, Or How We Got Along After the Bomb* (1965), and in the structure and constant shifting of point-of-view characters, then quite unusual in sf novels. Of all American science fiction writers of the fifties through the early eighties, Dick's work is most amenable to the reading protocols of postmodern critics, and his reputation has only increased since his death in 1982, the year of the classic sf film *Bladerunner*, based on Dick's novel *Do Androids Dream of Electric Sheep* (1968).

We include "The Indefatigable Frog," an early story, because it shows Dick playing with a mathematical and philosophical idea (like Richard Grant three decades later), using it to parody the character of his scientists. Dick's fiction was often in opposition to the rest of the genre, especially to the attitudes of most hard science fiction. This is, in fact, one of the rare occasions in his work when science is at the center of the story. It is also in the tradition of Breuer's "The Hungry Guinea Pig" and might, as well, be in reaction to the rash of low-budget science fiction creature movies of the early 1950s which often used small animals as sf creatures (made huge or alien by special effects—see Bryant's "giANTS"). At heart, though, it is a funny story about Zeno's paradox, part of the subgenre of mathematical and scientific play stories like Rucker's "Message Found in a Copy of *Flatland*" or John Sladek's "Stop Evolution in Its Tracks!" that subvert the idea that experimental science can be useful in settling theoretical or philosophical questions.

"Zeno was the first great scientist," Professor Hardy stated, looking sternly around his classroom. "For example, take his paradox of the frog and the well. As Zeno showed, the frog will never reach the top of the well. Each jump is half the previous jump; a small but very real margin always remains for him to travel."

There was silence, as the afternoon Physics 3-A Class considered Hardy's oracular utterance. Then, in the back of the room, a hand slowly went up.

Hardy stared at the hand in disbelief. "Well?" he said. "What is it, Pitner?"

"But in Logic we were told the frog *would* reach the top of the well. Professor Grote said—"

"The frog will not!"

"Professor Grote says he will."

Hardy folded his arms. "In this class the frog will never reach the top of the well. I have examined the evidence myself. I am satisfied that he will always be a small distance away. For example, if he jumps—"

The bell rang.

All the students rose to their feet and began to move towards the door. Professor Hardy stared after them, his sentence half finished. He rubbed his jaw with displeasure, frowning at the horde of young men and women with their bright, vacant faces.

When the last of them had gone, Hardy picked up his pipe and went out of the room into the hall. He looked up and down. Sure enough, not far off was Grote, standing by the drinking fountain, wiping his chin.

"Grote!" Hardy said. "Come here!"

Professor Grote looked up, blinking, "What?"

"Come here." Hardy strode up to him. "How dare you try to teach Zeno? He was a scientist, and as such he's my property to teach, not yours. Leave Zeno to me!"

"Zeno was a philosopher." Grote stared up indignantly at Hardy. "I know what's on your mind. It's that paradox about the frog and the well. For your information, Hardy, the frog will easily get out. You've been misleading your students. Logic is on my side."

"Logic, bah!" Hardy snorted, his eyes blazing. "Old dusty maxims. It's obvious that the frog is trapped forever, in an eternal prison and can never get away!"

"He will escape."

"He will not."

"Are you gentlemen quite through?" a calm voice said. They turned quickly around. The Dean was standing quietly behind them, smiling gently. "If you are through, I wonder if you'd mind coming into my office for a moment." He nodded towards his door. "It won't take too long."

Grote and Hardy looked at each other. "See what you've done?" Hardy whispered, as they filed into the Dean's office. "You've got us into trouble again."

"You started it—you and your frog!"

"Sit down, gentlemen." The Dean indicated two stiff-backed chairs. "Make yourselves comfortable. I'm sorry to trouble you when you're so busy, but I do wish to speak to you for a moment." He studied them moodily. "May I ask what is the nature of your discussion this time?"

"It's about Zeno," Grote murmured.

"Zeno?"

"The paradox about the frog and the well."

"I see." The Dean nodded. "I see. The frog and the well. A two-thousand-year-old saw. An ancient puzzle. And you two grown men stand in the hall arguing like a—"

"The difficulty," Hardy said, after a time, "is that no one has ever performed the experiment. The paradox is a pure abstraction."

"Then you two are going to be the first to lower the frog into his well and actually see what happens."

"But the frog won't jump in conformity to the conditions of the paradox."

"Then you'll have to make him, that's all. I'll give you two weeks to set up control conditions and determine the truth of this miserable puzzle. I want no more wrangling, month after month. I want this settled, once and for all."

Hardy and Grote were silent.

"Well, Grote," Hardy said at last, "let's get it started."

"We'll need a net," Grote said.

"A net and a jar." Hardy sighed. "We might as well be at it as soon as possible."

The "Frog Chamber," as it got to be called, was quite a project. The University donated most of the basement to them, and Grote and Hardy set to work at once, carrying parts and materials downstairs. There wasn't a soul who didn't know about it before long. Most of the science majors were on Hardy's side; they formed a Failure Club and denounced the frog's efforts. In the philosophy and art departments there was some agitation for a Success Club, but nothing ever came of it.

Grote and Hardy worked feverishly on the project. They were absent from their classes more and more of the time, as the two weeks wore on. The Chamber itself grew and developed, resembling more and more a long section of sewer pipe running the length of the basement. One end of it disappeared into a maze of wires and tubes: at the other there was a door.

One day when Grote went downstairs there was Hardy already, peering into the tube.

"See here," Grote said, "we agreed to keep hands off unless both of us were present."

"I'm just looking inside. It's dark in there." Hardy grinned. "I hope the frog will be able to see."

"Well, there's only one way to go."

Hardy lit his pipe. "What do you think of trying out a sample frog? I'm itching to see what happens."

"It's too soon." Grote watched nervously as Hardy searched about for his jar. "Shouldn't we wait a bit?"

"Can't face reality, eh? Here, give me a hand."

There was a sudden sound, a scraping at the door. They looked up. Pitner was standing there, looking curiously into the room, at the elongated Frog Chamber.

"What do you want?" Hardy said. "We're very busy."

"Are you going to try it out?" Pitner came into the room. "What are all the coils and relays for?"

"It's very simple," Grote said, beaming. "Something I worked out myself. This end here—"

"I'll show him," Hardy said. Hardy said. "You'll only confuse him. Yes, we were about to run the first trial frog. You can stay, boy, if you want." He opened the jar and took a damp frog from it. "As you can see, the big tube has an entrance and an exit. The frog goes in the entrance. Look inside the tube, boy. Go on."

Pitner peered into the open end of the tube. He saw a long black tunnel. "What are the lines?"

"Measuring line. Grote, turn it on."

The machinery came on, humming softly. Hardy took the frog and dropped him into the tube. He swung the metal door shut and snapped it tight. "That's so the frog won't get out again, at this end."

"How big a frog were you expecting?" Pitner said. "A full-grown man could get into that."

"Now watch." Hardy turned the gas cock up. "This end of the tube is warmed. The heat drives the frog up the tube. We'll watch through the window."

They looked into the tube. The frog was sitting quietly in a little heap, staring sadly ahead.

"Jump, you stupid frog," Hardy said. He turned the gas up.

"Not so high, you maniac!" Grote shouted. "Do you want to stew him?"

"Look!" Pitner cried. "There he goes."

The frog jumped. "Conduction carries the heat along the tube bottom," Hardy explained. "He has to keep on jumping to get away from it. Watch him go."

Suddenly Pitner gave a frightened rattle. "My God, Hardy. The frog has shrunk. He's only half as big as he was."

Hardy beamed. "That is the miracle. You see, at the far end of the tube there is a force field. The frog is compelled to jump towards it by the heat. The effect of the field is to reduce animal tissue to its proximity. The frog is made smaller the farther he goes."

"Why?"

"It's the only way the jumping span of the frog can be reduced. As the frog leaps he diminishes in size, and hence each leap is proportionally reduced. We have arranged it so that the diminution is the same as in Zeno's paradox."

"But where does it all end?"

"That," Hardy said, "is the question to which we are devoted. At the far end of the tube there is a photon beam which the frog would pass through, if he ever got that far. If he could reach it, he would cut off the field."

"He'll reach it," Grote muttered.

"No. He'll get smaller and smaller, and jump shorter and shorter. To him, the tube will lengthen more and more, endlessly. He will never get there."

They glared at each other. "Don't be so sure," Grote said.

They peered through the window into the tube. The frog had gone quite a distance up. He was almost invisible, now, a tiny speck no larger than a fly, moving imperceptibly along the tube. He became smaller. He was a pin point. He disappeared.

"Gosh," Pitner said.

"Pitner, go away," Hardy said. He rubbed his hands together. "Grote and I have things to discuss."

He locked the door after the boy.

"All right," Grote said. "You designed this tube. What became of the frog?"

"Why, he's still hopping, somewhere in a sub-atomic world."

"You're a swindler. Some place along that tube the frog met with misfortune."

"Well," Hardy said. "If you think that, perhaps you should inspect the tube personally."

"I believe I will. I may find a—trap door."

"Suit yourself," Hardy said, grinning. He turned off the gas and opened the big metal door.

"Give me the flashlight," Grote said. Hardy handed him the flashlight and he crawled into the tube, grunting. His voice echoed hollowly. "No tricks, now."

Hardy watched him disappear. He bent down and looked into the end of the tube. Grote was half-way down, wheezing and struggling. "What's the matter?" Hardy said.

"Too tight. . . ."

"Oh?" Hardy's grin broadened. He took his pipe from his mouth and set it on the table. "Well, maybe we can do something about that."

He slammed the metal door shut. He hurried to the other end of the tube and snapped the switches. Tubes lit up, relays clicked into place.

Hardy folded his arms. "Start hopping, my dear frog," he said. "Hop for all you're worth."

He went to the gas sock and turned it on.

It was very dark. Grote lay for a long time without moving. His mind was filled with drifting thoughts. What was the matter with Hardy? What was he up to? At last he pulled himself on to his elbows. His head cracked against the roof of the tube.

It began to get warm. "Hardy!" His voice thundered around him, loud and panicky. "Open the door. What's going on?"

He tried to turn around in the tube, to reach the door, but he couldn't budge. There was nothing to do but go forward. He began to crawl, muttering under his breath. "Just wait, Hardy. You and your jokes. I don't see what you expect to—"

Suddenly the tube leaped. He fell, his chin banging against the metal. He blinked. The tube had grown; now there was more than enough room. And his clothing! His shirt and pants were like a tent around him.

"Oh, heavens," Grote said in a tiny voice. He rose to his knees. Laboriously he turned around. He pulled himself back through the tube the way he had come, towards the metal door. He pushed against it, but nothing happened. It was now too large for him to force.

He sat for a long time. When the metal floor under him became too warm he crawled reluctantly along the tube to a cooler place. He curled himself up and stared dismally into the darkness. "What am I going to do," he asked himself.

After a time a measure of courage returned to him. "I must think logically. I've already entered the force field once, therefore I'm reduced in size by one-half. I must be about three feet high. That makes the tube twice as long."

He got out the flashlight and some paper from his immense pocket and did some figuring. The flashlight was almost un-manageable.

Underneath him the floor became warm. Automatically he shifted, a little up the tube to avoid the heat. "If I stay here long enough," he murmured, "I might be—"

The tube leaped again, rushing off in all directions. He found himself floundering in a sea of rough fabric, choking and gasping. At last he struggled free.

"One and a half feet," Grote said, staring around him. "I don't dare move any more, not at all."

But when the floor heated under him he moved some more. "Three-quarters of a foot." Sweat broke out on his face. "Three-quarters of one foot." He looked down the tube. Far, far down at the end was a spot of light, the photon beam crossing the tube. If he could reach it, if only he could reach it, if only he could reach it!

He mediated over his figures for a time. "Well," he said at last, "I hope I'm correct. According to my calculations I should reach the beam of light in about nine hours and thirty minutes, if I keep walking steadily." He took a deep breath and lifted the flashlight to his shoulder.

"However," he murmured, "I may be rather small by that time. . . ." He started walking, his chin up.

Professor Hardy turned to Pitner. "Tell the class what you saw this morning."

Everyone turned to look. Pitner swallowed nervously. "Well, I was downstairs in the basement. I was asked in to see the Frog Chamber. By Professor Grote. They were going to start the experiment."

"What experiment do you refer to?"

"The Zeno one," he explained nervously. "The frog. He put the frog in the tube and closed the door. And then Professor Grote turned on the power."

"What occurred?"

"The frog started to hop. He got smaller."

"He got smaller, you say. And then what?"

"He disappeared."

Professor Hardy sat back in his chair. "The frog did not reach the end of the tube, then?"

"No."

"That's all." There was a murmuring from the class. "So you see, the frog did not reach the end of the tube, as expected by my colleague, Professor Grote. He will never reach the end. Alas, we shall not see the unfortunate frog again."

There was a general stir. Hardy tapped with his pencil. He lit his pipe and puffed calmly, leaning back in his chair. "This experiment was quite an awakener to poor Grote, I'm afraid. He has had a blow of some unusual proportion. As you may have noticed, he hasn't appeared for his afternoon classes. Professor Grote, I understand, has decided to go on a long vacation to the mountains. Perhaps after he has had time to rest and enjoy himself, and to forget—"

Grote winced. But he kept on walking. "Don't get frightened," he said to himself. "Keep on."

The tube jumped again. He staggered. The flashlight crashed to the floor and went out. He was alone in the enormous cave, an immense void that seemed to have no end, no end at all.

He kept walking.

After a time he began to get tired again. It was not the first time. "A rest wouldn't do any harm." He sat down. The floor was rough under him, rough and uneven. "According to my figures it will be more like two days, or so. Perhaps a little longer. . . ."

He rested, dozing a little. Later on he began to walk again. The sudden jumping of the tube had ceased to frighten him; he had grown accustomed to it. Sooner or later he would reach the photon beam and cut through it. The force field would go off and he would resume his normal size. Grote smiled a little to himself. Wouldn't Hardy be surprised to—

He stubbed his toe and fell, headlong into the blackness around him. A deep fear ran through him and he began to tremble. He stood up, staring around him.

Which way?

"My God," he said. He bent down and touched the floor under him. Which way? Time passed. He began to walk slowly, first one way, then another. He could make out nothing, nothing at all.

Then he was running, hurrying through the darkness, this way and that, slipping and falling. All at once he staggered. The familiar sensation: he breathed a sobbing sigh of relief. He was moving in the right direction! He began to run again, calmly, taking deep breaths, his mouth open. Then once more the staggering shudder as he shrank down another notch; but he was going the right way. He ran on and on.

And as he ran the floor became rougher and rougher. Soon he was forced to stop, falling over boulders and rocks. Hadn't they smoothed the pipe down? What had gone wrong with the sanding, the steel wool—

"Of course," he murmured. "Even the surface of a razor blade . . . if one is small. . . ."

He walked ahead, feeling his way along. There was a dim light over everything, rising up from the great stones around him, even from his own body. What was it? He looked at his hands. They glittered in the darkness.

"Heat," he said. "Of course. Thanks, Hardy." In the half light he leaped from stone to stone. He was running across an endless plain of rocks and boulders, jumping like a goat, from crag to crag. "Or like a frog," he said. He jumped on, stopping once in a while for breath. How long would it be? He looked at the size of the great blocks of ore piled up around him. Suddenly a terror rushed through him.

"Maybe I shouldn't figure it out," he said. He climbed up the side of one towering cliff and leaped across to the other side. The next gulf was even wider. He barely made it, gasping and struggling to catch hold.

He jumped endlessly, again and again. He forgot how many times.

He stood on the edge of a rock and leaped.

Then he was falling, down, down, into the cleft, into the dim light. There was no bottom. On and on he fell.

Professor Grote closed his eyes. Peace came over him, his tired body relaxed.

"No more jumping," he said, drifting down, down. "A certain law regarding falling bodies . . . the smaller the body the less the effect of gravity. No wonder bugs fall so lightly . . . certain characteristics. . . ."

He closed his eyes and allowed the darkness to take him over, at last.

"And so," Professor Hardy said, "we can expect to find that this experiment will go down in science as—"

He stopped, frowning. The class was staring towards the door. Some of the students were smiling, and one began to laugh. Hardy turned to see what it was.

"Shades of Charles Fort," he said.

A frog came hopping into the room.

Pitner stood up. "Professor," he said excitedly. "This confirms a theory I've worked out. The frog became so reduced in size that he passed through the spaces—"

"What?" Hardy said. "This is another frog."

"—through the spaces between the molecules which form the floor of the Frog Chamber. The frog would then drift slowly to the floor, since he would be proportionally less affected by the law of acceleration. And leaving the force field, he would regain his original size."

Pitner beamed down at the frog as the frog slowly made his way across the room.

"Really," Professor Hardy began. He sat down at his desk weakly. At that moment the bell rang, and the students began to gather their books and papers together. Presently Hardy found himself alone, staring down at the frog. He shook his head. "It can't be," he murmured. "The world is full of frogs. It can't be the same frog."

A student came up to the desk. "Professor Hardy—"

Hardy looked up.

"Yes? What is it?"

"There's a man outside in the hall wants to see you. He's upset. He has a blanket on."

"All right," Hardy said. He sighed and got to his feet. At the door he paused, taking a deep breath. Then he set his jaw and went out into the hall.

Grote was standing there, wrapped in a red-wool blanket, his face flushed with excitement. Hardy glanced at him apologetically.

"We still don't know!" Grote cried.

"What?" Hardy murmured. "Say, er, Grote—"

"We still don't know whether the frog would have reached the end of the tube. He and I fell out between the molecules. We'll have to find some other way to test the paradox. The Chamber's no good."

"Yes, true," Hardy said. "Say, Grote—"

"Let's discuss it later," Grote said. "I have to get to my classes. I'll look you up this evening."

And he hurried off down the hall clutching his blanket.

CHROMATIC ABERRATION

John M. Ford

John M. Ford is equally adept at fantasy and science fiction, but is known more for the variety and richness of his works than for his rigorous use of science. He is impatient, it seems, with conventional approaches; in such stories as this one, he applies the techniques of and exploits a conventional setting of the school of magic realism to embody the idea of paradigm shifts (from contemporary philosophy of science). He is also writing an "alternate universe" sf story.

The idea of shifts in the basic physical nature of reality have been part of the playing field of hard sf from Campbell's "Atomic Power" and Latham's "The Xi Effect." In contemporary works such as Benford's "Relativistic Effects," on the one hand, and Grant's "Drode's Equations" on the other, a writer can draw from hard sf tradition—up to, for instance, Poul Anderson's novel, *Tau Zero* (1970)—or from Borges and Nabokov (and perhaps Philip K. Dick). But the stories of the seventies and eighties generally used the reality shifts as metaphors of dislocation or alienation. Ford takes a new tack.

"Chromatic Aberration" depends upon the reader's knowledge external to the story of the concept of paradigm shifts (a concept invented in the seventies by Thomas Kuhn—those synthetic scientific insights into the physical nature of reality that contour our whole notion of how the universe operates—Newtonian physics, Einsteinian relativity, Quantum physics, each one yielding greater knowledge). It does not literally deal with them in the story.

It also demands, by implication, some familiarity with the tradition of "alternate universe" sf—which is usually not hard sf. This tradition, currently very much in fashion, uses the rigorous methods of hard sf to create a setting in the past or present (infrequently in the future) in which some important event caused history to branch off in a direction that did not (will not) lead to our contemporary reality. Since this need not involve either science or technology, this has become as useful to writers out of the genre as in, resulting in a blurring of genre boundaries. There have been a number of popular best-sellers based on, for instance, the Germans and Japanese having won World War II, such as Len Deighton's *SS-GB* (1978), that are not intended as works in the genre, as well as the genre classic, *The Man in the High Castle* (1962), by Philip K. Dick. And there are romances and mysteries and stories in other genres that use the device nowadays. What we have here is a story at the very fringe of science fiction that teases at genre definition, yet plays by the rules as Ford perceives them.

The end of the ancient world can be precisely fixed in space and time. It took place in the central square of the capital city, before the steps of the Great Hall of Justice, in an area twenty meters by twenty-five that had been especially cleared of wire and debris. It occurred at noon, six days after the rocket attack on the Veterans'

Hospital. The sky was clear, hard like glass, a few dense clouds trapped stationary in its substance. The sun was low, it being early spring, and the shadow of the Justice Hall fell sharp as a sundial's gnomon with its point in White Birch Street. Six military aircraft flew over just then, in a perfect triangle, one followed by two followed by three, splintering the solid atmosphere with noise and contrails. Had their pilots looked down at that moment, they would have seen the city as an ordered field of white blocks mated to black parallelograms, dissected by the gray lines of streets. From that height, it was a vision not too different from the city before the revolution (I speak here only in the grossest physical sense). The geometry of a city is not destroyed by war or time, but only eroded, as memory is never completely erased, but only decays, a word here, a library there. All fires had been extinguished in the six days, and only one small one lit, there before the steps of Justice. The ancient world declined that morning in the autumn glow of a bayonet heated in a brazier, and it stopped that noon in a long moist hiss.

The ancient world having stood its correction, the modern one began in a long dance of stately measures: the eradication of monuments to ancient events, dates, persons, the reform of the currency, the restructuring of the system of national health.

It was in the early afternoon, when the sun had just moved below the peak of the Justice Hall, bathing the square and all who knelt there in coolness, that the leaders of the revolutionary forces made the announcement that was both a reform and a revelation: the Declaration of the Modern Spectrum. It had been established through careful historical analysis that the colors used by the ancients were, like so many ancient things, untrue to life, a fraud perpetrated by the rulers on the ruled. As the laborer toiled for money, believing that it had value, as he prayed to the saints, believing that they had power, so he said that the sky was such a color, grass another, blood another, not knowing that he was caught in a trap of perception. Finally (so ran the Declaration) our eyes had been opened, we could perceive the true colors of the world.

It was said by indifferent foreign observers (and I use the term in an ironic sense) that color is immutable, a matter of wavelengths and retinal stimuli. Through this (again you will pardon the term) blindness, these ancient relics showed only that they did not understand the nature of revolution, which is to revise all things, to remake the soul. If there are modern colors—as we now know that there are—perhaps they were truly not seen before: The ancient patterns blinded the eye to them, even as the modern pattern extends the range of vision, so that now we can actually see the sky, the grass, the blood.

My senses tell me that you still do not understand. Very well, I shall try to illustrate, to illuminate in modern color what ancient color distorted and shadowed. Some will call these tales fantastical and unreal: yet I say to you that the revolution itself was once only a dream in the minds of modern people: and I say moreover that the ancient world, for all its ingenuity of repair and destruction, was driven by a dream of the identical substance. Before all mechanism is the dream of mechanism, and all machines have their ghosts. This endures, no matter what.

These words summarize the credo of the revolution: What was true then, is not true now. These words summarize the credo of revolution. Thus by the subtraction of a single three-letter word is a declarative fact made into a platitude. Yet is the platitude any less valid? Can we not therefore say that the word *the* was unnecessary, that its meaning was overdetermined? Surely so. Suppose we broaden the analysis to the credo itself: subtract the word true, in fact, subtract it twice. What was then, is not now. Just as meaningful, just as valid. And the word was used twice! Are we then to assume that truth can be extracted from any statement without altering its essential meaning? Continue the process: What was, is not. Something is wrong here: we have reduced the statement by half, and suffered no loss in value. This is a puzzle worthy of study, but I have no time to continue the analysis now, the immediate matter must be turned to, but please, do not forget.

The first color described in the Modern Spectrum is redor. It is a strong, heraldic tincture, without taint or compromise. Redor is the principal color of our flag; the monuments to those slain in the revolution are draped upon the Anniversary of Victory in silk dyed redor in the thread.

The revolution was entering its final hours. All the major buildings of the capital city were under the control of the modern forces. Small units of soldiers went from door to door, spreading the news of the victory and seeking out the few ancient fighters who remained in hiding. These units were armed, both for protection against unstable ancients and because the immediate correction of certain individuals had been decreed by the common will and for the common good.

One such unit was moving along White Birch Street, in the direction of the central square. The namesake trees that lined the street on both sides, spaced at exact seven-meter intervals, were still bare with the season. Many had been badly damaged by gunfire or other accidents of war. The soldiers passed the Institute for Famine Research, which had been renovated early in the revolution, and the National Theatre, which was sealed. They passed a small park to the left, a promenade to the right, and then entered the Hospital for War Veterans. It was known that many of the aged and crippled residents of the Hospital remained loyal to the ancient regime; but no corrections were planned. The Hospital was, at last report, quiet and in good order.

This report, as so many in war, was seriously out of date.

The soldiers went up a shallow ramp and passed through broad doors to reach the Hospital's main entrance hall, which was tiled, double-vaulted, with murals of parkland scenes on its walls. The main desk, of bronze and oak, was just ahead; to the right, an ornate stairway enclosed a brass-cage elevator. It was at this intersection that they were attacked by the patients. Some were armed with surgical tools, some with crutches and artificial limbs, some with only their hands. The soldiers were young and brave, but surprised, surrounded. The ancients were military veterans, hardened to wounding, and what they did to the soldiers (as what they had done to the doctors and nurses committed to their care) does not bear detailed recounting. Soon the patients proceeded from the Hospital and onto White Birch Street, armed with the soldiers' weapons, armed with ancient fury.

By reports, they hesitated and milled for some minutes. Many were from the provinces, unfamiliar with the pattern of the city. Others had been wounded in ancient wars, and had spent many years knowing only the levels, lifts, and corridors of the Hospital. The openness of streets, of sky, the lack of understandable landmarks and well-remembered doors, must have confounded them. It might have been possible to have saved them, even then, but the ancient wheel of destruction had great momentum once it was turning.

It is said by some that they began to cry for justice; if this is so, then the tragedy is doubled. Others report that persons who seemed able-bodied, either malingerers or convalescents near full healing, shouted commands that imposed an order and direction on the patients. Whatever the cause, they began to move—in good order, as the soldiers they had been, not a rabble, not a mob—past the Hospital gates, to White Birch Street, and then to the right toward the Great Hall of Justice.

The Hall dominates the square. To the left as one faces it is the Exposition Park, which was once public grazeland and was later used for fairs and public displays. To the right was, at one time, the Basilica of the Apostles, a domed cruciform building whose promenade was lined with life-size statues of the Twelve Collaborationists. The statues had, however, been renovated in one of the first revolutionary incidents, and the fragments allowed to remain as a symbol of either rebel atrocity or the inevitable triumph of the revolution. (A few bits were secretly removed by the ancients, through powerless dust is all that they were.) Both the Basilica and the promenade have been removed without trace since modern times began, but at that moment they existed, one solidly, one only halfway in memory.

At that moment the Great Hall of Justice was occupied by one hundred seventeen revolutionary militia under the command of one rebel Colonel (formerly a Lieutenant of the national guard) and a Modernization Officer (formerly a waiter at the Regency Hotel). The defenders were ranked on the steps, behind barbed wire, armed with rifles and two tripod-mounted machine guns in sandbagged emplacements.

There is no doubt that the revolutionaries fired the first shots, single shots from individual rifles. They had no communication of the incident at the Hospital, and at long range of engagement they could not identify the dress of the approaching force. (Some of the patients also wore pieces of their former uniform, an ancient custom of remembrance, adding to the confusion, further underscoring the self-destructive essence of the ancient world.) The patients returned fire. And then it was war, and there was no recourse.

The patients advanced, under fire. The took losses; they inflicted them. And then, just as the two sides were close enough for recognition, the patients charged.

The revolutionary forces could now see who was attacking them. It is said that some of the old and young soldiers were related by blood; this is true in spirit if not in fact. But the modern forces knew their duty was to defend the Great Hall of Justice, and this they did. They fired, and fired, as many of the attackers and not a few of their own number fell. Uniforms and bandages were stained with blood and bone and brain. Flesh limbs and wooden ones were shattered. The wire was crossed in the traditional manner: by using men, dead or about to be, as bridges. The sound of guns in the long moment of that charge has been compared to hammering, to forging, to bells, and stone broke like crockery; but no one who was there can recall a single cry of pain, nor of triumph, not one human sound at all. Only the guns, and the stones, until all the sound stopped, and the last charge of the ancient world was over. The last old soldier had fallen barely an arm's reach from the defending line.

There was, in the remaining seven days of the ancient world, discussion of a memorial to these people, who died in the pursuance of their faith, but on reflection it was seen that modern children, on seeing the monument, would ask why it was there, who it memorialized, what they had done: and there were no longer any answers to these questions. Instead, a scroll was prepared, bearing the names of the patients; then the paper was thrust into a brazier alight on the steps of the Great Hall of Justice. It burned with a redor flame.

In the course of examining the bodies for the preparation of the roster, it was discovered that one-seventh of them had died not of wounds but of heart failure in the charge; and one in four was blind. Are you moved, despite the futility? I am.

Words are inadequate (the poor craftsman curses his tools) to describe the loveliness of our coastal regions, but words are what I have available. From the Western Delta to Fox Point Light is a map distance of seven hundred forty kilometers, the major landmarks being, in order west to east, Guise Inlet, Nine Wreck Head, Paradise Shoals, and the Great Palisade. The actual distance cannot even be estimated, as the shore is looped and involuted with inlets, coves, and pools. A thousand things have hidden along that shore in ancient times: smugglers, pirates, hermits from time, though all are gone now. The coast is rocky, and swept by wind and water, and life there can be hard, yet when the sun is low through mist, or the moon looks palely upon a quiet sea, one might never look upon another scene, and still be content to live in those memories.

Angeyel, the second modern hue, is a delicate color, of great beauty in deep concentration; but it is best appreciated in subdued light, as the strong light of full day tends to wash it out, to destroy it.

There was a woman who lived by a tidal pool, who though she had no formal training had made the study of the pool's creatures her life. A few of the older folk in the town knew the woman's name, but they never used it. She was called Sea Angel, after a variety of small shrimp that she found especially beautiful and fascinating, and bred in dishes, and made into a delicately flavored soup.

The water and her garden gave her food, and she sold rare shells washed up on the shore to buy books and equipment for her work. She had a fine optical microscope, and many hundreds of prepared and fixed slides, racked and elaborately catalogued. There was only one other thing that she desired, and on certain nights a small boat would cross the pool from the fishing town on the other side, and return only with the morning.

One of those who made this late voyage was called Knotsmith, because of the fineness of his craft in weaving nets. Sea Angel was delighted by the skill of his strong slender fingers, and Knotsmith in turn admired her studies by the pool, for he was in fact of modern mind, and early on became a leader of the revolution.

Knotsmith often asked Sea Angel to join in the modern movement, but she, not understanding, would only laugh and say "I am an uneducated water-widow who knows nothing of these matters. I live in the drops of water beneath my strong glasses; I live within shells from the strand."

The battles of the revolution did not reach Knotsmith's village or Sea Angel's pool. Knotsmith made the night voyage rarely now, kept away by the needs of the war; but when he did return Sea Angel was pleased to see him, and tell him of her discoveries in salt water. Once he brought her a book from a distant nation, describing the very tiniest of water life, creatures Sea Angel's microscope could not reveal: he told her that in the modern world she would have the device for this perception, and any other equipment she might desire.

Sea Angel smiled and thanked Knotsmith for the book, and placed it on her shelves with the other books, and files, and specimens, but to his sorrow she still did not understand, did not take the lesson that the modern world could see things the ancients could not. She saw still in the ancient manner, which is to say, she could not see at all, but felt her way blindly through halls of memory.

On a night not long before the final triumph of the revolution, Knotsmith came to Sea Angel's house by the water. She saw that his wrists were puffy and sore, discolored from scratching them.

Sea Angel scraped at Knotsmith's swollen skin with a small knife, then spread the scrapings upon a glass slide and examined them through her microscope.

"You have been fishing in strange waters," she said.

"What—do you mean?" Knotsmith asked.

"The itching is caused by mites in your flesh. From their form I am certain that they are sea mites, but they are a kind I have never seen before. Where have you woven your nets, Knotsmith?"

Knotsmith said "The modern world is wide," and would say no more. Sea Angel spread a balm on his wrists, and turned the lantern down.

Knotsmith departed earlier than his custom, rowing back across the pool well before dawn. When the lantern on his boat was only a flicker on the dark water, Sea Angel put out her own boat, a gift from a fisherman friend, fastened on the small motor her shell-money had purchased, and went out to sea.

Just at dawn she saw a ship. It mounted cranes, and its deck was piled with crates. Atop its pilothouse was a curious bristling of metal rods, bright in the rising sun. Sea Angel looked through her binoculars, and saw that it flew the flag of a nation half the world away.

Then she turned her attention away from the ship, and lowered her sampling bottles into the sea. She opened a tin, and cast a handful of her namesake shrimp on the water, then shook out her small fishing net. If the mites were in the water here, if she could catch a fish she was almost certain to find them.

She put on a broad-brimmed hat to shade her eyes from the blinding sun, and sat quite still, the net in her hands, watching her bait. A little while later, she heard the sound of motors; it did not come from the freight vessel, and she turned to look.

A fishing boat was approaching, but alone, not part of the fleet. Men in uniforms stood on the rail, their guns out; and in the prow stood Knotsmith, in a uniform with metal on his shoulder and his sleeve. Sea Angel watched as the boat drew close to the freighter, pulled alongside and was drawn fast.

Idly curious, she looked again through her binoculars, and saw Knotsmith going aboard the freighter. After him went a soldier, carrying a bundle of a peculiar color.

There was a ripple on the water, and Sea Angel cast her net; she brought up a pair of small fish, that landed flopping on the bottom of her boat. She lowered them gently into a bucket of water, started her boat's motor and turned toward her pool and her house, the boats all forgotten.

It did not take long for her to find the unusual sea mites in swabbings from the fishes' gills. She sat down with her notebooks, describing the discovery in detail.

As she was writing, a slip of paper she had used as a placemarker fluttered to the floor. She picked it up, struck by its color. It was a note of modern currency, given to her by Knotsmith. Enblu, he had called the shade. It was just the color of the bundle the soldier had carried aboard the ship. She put it back in the notebook and thought no more of it.

After some time, she heard a weary splash from her bucket with the fish in it. "I am sorry, I entirely forgot you," she said, picked up the bucket and carried it back to the shore of the pool.

The fishing boat was just coming to the shore. The crates from the freighter were stacked on its deck. Knotsmith had jumped over the rail and was wading through the shallows toward Sea Angel; some of the soldiers came after him.

Sea Angel reached into the bucket, took hold of the slippery, squirming fish. "Thank you, fish," she said, "find your way home safely," and cast them in a long low arc out toward deep water. They splashed, and leaped, and were gone.

"Sea Angel," said Knotsmith, the rest of his words trailing away as a boat vanishing into fog.

"Good day, Knotsmith. I know now where you have been weaving your nets."

Knotsmith looked down at the water eddying around his boots. The soldiers behind him stopped short.

"Of all the greetings you might have spoken," Knotsmith said, "I wish you had chosen any other than that."

"I don't understand," said Sea Angel.

"That is the difficulty," Knotsmith said, "you do not, you have never understood, and now your speech repairs me. . . ." He made a gesture, and the soldiers moved toward Sea Angel. "You have committed a terrible and ancient error," Knotsmith said, "and you must stand corrected."

"I am sorry that I do not understand," Sea Angel said, "but there are things which I know—" and she broke away from the soldiers and ran for the sea, flying from the strand like a bright leaping fish. But Knotsmith spoke an order, and the soldiers fired with revolutionary precision, and Sea Angel fell dead on the shore, neither quite in the sea nor out.

The soldiers set fire to the house, and then they and the man who led them got into their boat and went back across the pool, the first time that anyone had ever sailed from Sea Angel's shore at twilight.

In the morning there came several small boats from the town, but the fire had been thorough, and the night tide had come and gone. The books and files were scattered, the slides for the microscope smashed to powder, the knowledge all disordered, and there was nothing to take back or preserve or remember, only traces left for the imaginations of those such as I.

Lie of the ground is important militarily, both for its direct physical effect on combat and the supplying of combat, and for its function as a framework for the conduct of the war. River lines, defensible passes, the possession of hills and encirclement of cities: these are the syntax that structures the speech of guns. And when the guns have spoken their part, it will be the rivers and the passes, the hills and the cities, that column and paragraph the memories of those who were there. It is the ordered vision that persists.

The next modern color is known as lowgre. It is a strong, deep color, a color for arms and armor. It is the color of the uniform worn by all soldiers in the modern army.

The General of the Fourth Brigade of Armor had first seen war as a boy, smuggling ammunition and medicine to the rebels in the hills. He was a small boy, and wiry, dressed in uniform trousers with the legs rolled up, sneakers, and a shapeless army blanket; all of these he stole from the depots of the national guard. The blanket served him as overcoat and sunshade and tent, as carryall bag and camouflage. The hill country was a language he spoke fluently, as anyone living among an enemy must use the enemy's language in the prescribed manner, especially when one has dangerous things to say. At the first step of a sentry he could throw himself to the ground, the blanket settling upon him, and become invisible, a patch of moss or an overgrown boulder upon the hillside. There was a saying among the rebel fighters: "Never shoot the earth, it's friendly." The boy, and the others like him, may have given rise to this proverb, or perhaps it was an expression of solidarity with the land, or more mundanely a warning against wasting precious ammunition.

Due no doubt to these early habits, the boy who would become the General of the Fourth Brigade never adopted the habit of uniform dress. He would wear military clothing, which is after all utilitarian, but old, odd, mismatched pieces, sometimes from the ancients' uniform. He was the despair of his training leaders, and later his supply controllers, and in the ancient forces would surely have ended in prison or disgrace, just for the look of him. But modern times were dawning, and the great leader within the poor costume was recognized and allowed to develop.

For he was indeed one of those whom soldiers will follow, though it be to death, or utter annihilation; and even in ancient times it was understood that this power is not made or created, it simply is.

When he was a colonel of the revolutionary forces—no longer rebels, but a genuine army, in a true war—he led a surprise assault on a stronghold of the national guard, striking like lightning at daybreak, using trucks and motorcycles as if they were tanks and planes. The garrison surrendered in less than an hour.

The commander of the guard camp was a strutting small General who wore a black tunic hung with his shining minor medals. He was brought to the Colonel with his tunic and trousers unbuttoned, with a rope around his neck. The little General knew that he must stand corrected, and he did not argue for his life: he asked only that his soldiers not be killed outright.

This was a brave and noble thing to say, though without understanding. When the Colonel heard it, he ordered the rope taken from the camp commander's neck, and that the General stand his correction by gunfire. It was an ancient custom that there was a difference.

The Colonel's men gave him the General's fine black tunic as a prize of war. He removed the medals and put it on; the General had been a small man, but the Colonel was slender. The sound of the correction was loud in the camp, drowning out small cries that came from closed rooms: for though the Colonel had insisted that the defenders not be repaired, information was required. Balance was required. The repair of human beings is terrible to watch, but it brings information, and balance. And many of those repaired need no more suffer to watch anything.

When the leaders of the revolutionary forces heard the story of the capture, and saw the Colonel in his black coat, they knew that they were in the presence of, not a man, but a legend: "Since you are wearing a General's stars," they said, "you had best be a General." And in the next moment, there was a Fourth Brigade of Armor, and the Colonel was its General, though the entire armored contingent of the revolutionary forces was two old automobiles with boiler plates welded to them.

This would change.

In the last weeks of the last campaign of the revolution, the Fourth Brigade had twenty tanks and fifty armored cars and support vehicles, and the General was still wearing his black coat to lead them. Then the leaders of forces called the General in for a conference, and gave him a uniform, well-tailored to his measurements. It was colored lowgre, of course, in strong and striking value, almost as dramatic as the tunics the leaders themselves wore.

"The revolution is nearly over," the leaders said. "The image we cast now will be the image that shall remain with us in modern times. This uniform is part of that image. You see that we all wear them; this one has been made for you to wear."

"I've never needed such a thing," the General said.

"There are other needs besides your own," the leaders said. "Think of the soldiers who follow you."

"They gave me this coat," said the General.

"And is it the coat they follow," said the most astute of the leaders, "or you?"

"You aren't people who bear arguing with," the General said, and without another word took the new uniform and put it on.

The General's aide-de-camp, a woman of the city where the General had been born, saw him on his return to the Brigade and said "That is a fine new uniform."

"Your perceptions have always been accurate," said the General, and no more was spoken of the matter.

The Fourth Brigade of Armor was on the move, ordered from its camp near the city of the General's birth to the capital, along the roads and half-roads, through the woods and glades. The General was at the head of his columns, as always, dressed in his new uniform.

In the General's eyes, there was a movement, in the heavy growth to the side of the trails. "Look there," he said, and pointed.

"At what, sir?" said his aide.

"I saw a boy," the General said, "wearing a blanket on his back."

The aide looked into the brush. She was sharp-eyed, having herself been a scout for the revolutionary forces when only a child. "I see nothing," she said. "It could have been an animal."

"Yes, it could have been," said the General, and pointed ahead, the signal for the column to proceed.

Not long afterward the General waved his vehicle to a halt. "Look, look now," he said.

"I see nothing," his aide said.

"Could it not have been a boy?" said the General, "in sneakers, and pieces of a captured uniform?"

"The people of this area are all modern of thought," said the aide, "but if you wish me to take a patrol, I will do so."

"No," the General said, "your perceptions have always been accurate. We shall continue to the capital, as ordered."

In only a few more minutes the General stood up in his vehicle, pointing and staring into the trees and the moss and stones he knew as well as he knew the words for trees and moss and stones. "There again—there again! Crouching against the soil—do you see?"

The aide hesitated. Then she said, "What might I see, sir . . . if I were to look in the right place?"

The General looked at his aide, and smiled faintly. "Give the orders to button up," he said. "We're going into the brush."

And the Fourth Brigade wheeled to the right, plunging into the rough country, the half-roads and possibilities of roads, through the gullies and roots and pale thick mist. Every soldier of the Fourth knew that their orders were to move to the capital. Every soldier of the Fourth followed the General without a moment's pause.

The going was difficult; indeed, this was the same terrain in which the revolutionary forces (during their days as rebels) had so often ambushed the national guard. But the General led them through as if he were leading close friends on a tour of his home. Which, of course, he was.

"General," the aide said gently, and offered him a sip of tea from her flask.

The General drank, without taking his eyes from the country. "I see where he has gone," he said. "Through here, and over that large rock, and vaulting between those trees so as to leave no footprint nor ground scent. . . . Yes, I see very clearly now."

The aide waited for a little while. The Fourth Brigade was becoming dispersed, and a support vehicle broke an axle and had to be abandoned. Still the soldiers of the Fourth pressed on after the General's lead.

Finally the aide opened her mouth to speak: but instead her eyes widened, and in place of whatever she might have been about to say, she said "Commandos, sir. Ahead, to the right. Commandos of the national guard."

And then, before anyone could say anything more, there was the pop of gunfire and the rainlike rustling of bullets through the leaves, and the Fourth Brigade of Armor was at war with the ancient army. Had things been one way, the Fourth might have been lost, its great vehicles immobilized by the terrain amid the swarm of commando troopers; but this was the General's land and way of war, and things were not that way but another. Again he transformed the equipment under his command into what he needed, using his tanks and cars as if they were bunkers and helicopters, and in the space of half an hour the guardsmen who had been on their way to brutalize the General's home city as of ancient times were themselves alive only in history.

The Fourth Brigade cheered its General upon the field of victory. And then a strange thing happened. The General looked down, into the face of one of the dead ancients, and said "Do I not know this man? Was he not a rebel with me, in the hills, when we were young?"

"He wears the uniform of the national guard commandos," said the aide, pointing at the dead man's black tunic. The General nodded and turned away, saying "Certainly he does. Come, now, we may be needed at the capital."

The Fourth Brigade reached the capital city in good time, encountering no resistance. When the column was in sight of the downtown buildings, a messenger from the revolutionary leaders approached the General.

"There is terrible news, General," the messenger said. "A team of commandos from the national guard has attacked your home city; there are reports of grave atrocities."

"How can this be?" said the General's aide.

The messenger said "They attacked from out of the hill country. The press has been notified; they are going there to report the horror to the world. The ancients have hurt themselves badly by this."

The General looked past the messenger. He seemed to see something very clearly, though the aide saw only the buildings of the capital. "Come with me," he said, and they left the Fourth Brigade to rest, and followed the messenger back to the headquarters of the revolution.

The aide waited in a bare room while the General spoke to the leaders in their inner chambers. She was used to the open air, and felt uncertain in the windowless room; she felt as if she were in an empty, dead cell, surrounded by busy cells crowded with unknown machineries. When the General came out again, he took his aide gently by the arm—this startled her, as he had never touched her in any fashion before this—and led her out of the headquarters. In one direction was the city, in the other the forest where the Fourth Brigade was encamped.

The General pointed toward the encampment. "Do you see a boy?" he said, "a boy in sneakers, with a blanket on his back, who runs through the hill country as only a rebel hill boy can know how to run?"

"No, sir," said the aide, in an uneven voice.

"If the boy were not so dressed . . . if he wore another sort of uniform, would you see him then?"

"Sir, I see no boy," said the aide, nearly in tears because she did not understand.

"You do not see the boy, and your perceptions have always been accurate," the General said, "therefore the boy does not exist. . . . Yet still I see him."

And with that the General of the Fourth Brigade of Armor drew his pistol, pressed its muzzle to his chin, and splashed his brains into the clear, clear sky.

There is a statue of the General in the city where he was born, the city that he saved. An ancient library was renovated to make space for it; bits of the rubble are still preserved by the citizens. The statue is not large, though it stands upon a high plinth: the figure is in fact exactly the size of the General in life. It is important that art should tell the truth.

The General stands with his knees slightly bent and his arm outstretched, his metal finger pointing forward. The statue is all one color, the General's face and hands, his boots and weapons, all the lowgre of his uniform. The pose is dynamic, yet very natural.

Everyone knows what the figure illustrates: the General is leading his brigade forward to victory. But no one asks what his finger is pointing at. Even the children do not ask what it is that the General sees.

And perhaps it is best that they do not.

Truth, it was said in the most ancient times, is an absolute. The later ancients, troubled by the ease with which the absolute would shift on the plate under the stab of their forks, swung to the opposite asymptote, deciding that truth was a purely relative condition, dependent on external factors that entirely evaded quantitative measurement. But with modern study, the same study that gave us the reality of color, we know that truth is discoverable to any desired precision, in any number of its parameters, except for the parameter used to take the measurement: as a physicist would say, we may know the position by rendering the velocity unknowable through the detector's impact, or know the velocity at the cost of the position. It then simply becomes a question of deciding which part of your subject's nature is of no importance, and then (figuratively speaking, of course) beating it out of the population.

The fourth shade of new light, enblu, is a moral color, a color of truth and straightforward dealing. Our currency is enblu, and the greatest care is taken to ensure that its inks are of the truest, clearest hues possible to modern technologies.

The Controller of the Currency reached within his coat, producing a large bronze key. "This is the only key to the counting room," he said, unlocked the wired-glass door, and entered. After him came two of the leaders of the revolution, and four counting clerks in smocks and gloves.

Around them was downward lighting, soft so as to spare the clerks' eyes, and steel tables covered with neat stacks of freshly cut notes. Through the floor was a gentle thrum, transmitted from the coin-minting floor below; a high whine penetrated from the printing presses a few rooms away. There were neatly pigeonholed forms and tools and office supplies around the walls, and white-surfaced tallyboards, neatly gridded, neatly written upon in cleanly erasable marker.

"All of the notes pass through this room?" one of the leaders said.

"Every one," said the Controller of the Currency. "The ancient problem of diversion has been reduced to the vanishing point through our redesign of the system of corridors and locked doors."

"Vanishing point?" said the other leader. "What precisely does that mean? A tiny amount, or zero?"

The Controller of the Currency picked up a pen and drew a figure on one of the tally boards, like an elongated S. "The integral," he said lightly. "A quantity smaller than measurement allows, but a quantity nonetheless." The Controller had been a mathematician, in the ancient world.

"What sort of nonsense is that?" said the leaders, who were modern men. "Either all the notes are accounted for, or they are not."

The clerks looked uncertain.

The Controller said "We count. We check. We count many times; when the blank paper is delivered, when the serial-numbering apparatus is started and stopped, when the notes are cut, in this room where they are stacked and bundled. We are even researching a method of weighing the ink before and after the presses are operated, though variations in humidity make this unreliable." He did not mention the spectroanalysis machines, which, being calibrated to the ancient colors, had been removed from the office and were undergoing torture until they should tell the truth.

"And?"

"And still we are people. Still there is a possibility of errors going unchecked, regardless of the number of checks. As I say, vanishingly small—"

"I believe I understand," said a leader. "You are imposing a mathematical abstraction upon the reality."

"I am saying," the Controller said firmly, "that errors are never zero. Zero is itself a mathematical abstraction, that can never be imposed upon reality."

"Have there been corrections? You may ask for them, you know. If you like, we will authorize you a standing repairman."

"A clerk stood corrected some weeks ago, for removing a few notes in his clothing," said the Controller. "He was not a clever thief, however, and his correction merely stopped a known loss. We have, as I told you earlier today, no known losses. That is the problem."

"It is time we moved on," said one of the leaders of the revolution to the other. Then he said to the Controller, "We will accept that you are trying to solve the problem of missing notes. This plan of weighing ink sounds promising; if you require humidity-controlling equipment, you know the proper channels of approach."

The Controller led the leaders from the building. The Currency Office was an almost painfully rectilinear structure, everything in it—work cubicles, tables, pigeonholes, the empty spaces where the spectrographs had been—being built to the space-efficient perpendicular; the staircases came closest to rebellion, but only to the extent of forty-five degrees. The revolutionary leaders went out the square doors, down the square steps, walking with square shoulders and a precisely parallel gait. Then the Controller returned to the counting room, where the clerks were still standing at attention, cubical beads of sweat on their flat foreheads. The Controller erased the sign of the integral from the tally board and said to the clerks, "You may begin now."

The clerks completed their counting in the early afternoon. The Controller of the Currency thanked them, locked away their tally reports, and saw them out of the Treasury building. Then he admitted a second set of clerks, who repeated the counting process on the same stacks of notes. Long after dark he locked these out as well, and then compared the two sets of reports himself. Nothing was missing, of course. The Controller sighed. Nothing could be missing, he thought, resting his face in his hands. His eyes hurt so much. Still his mathematician's soul rebelled at absolutes; and he knew well enough that no absolute would satisfy the leaders anyway.

The Controller was not an economist, but he understood the leaders' concern. The ancient world had nearly destroyed itself playing games of paper wealth, creating a system no nation could stabilize but any could capsize; mutually assured fiscal destruction. The modern world had to make certain that its currency could not be used as a weapon by the forces of reaction. That was the leaders' concern.

It was the Controller's concern as well; he hoped that the leaders knew this. Halfway between sunset and dawn he locked the door to the counting room and walked home, enblu afterimages burning his eyes.

Early the following day, another leader of the revolution arrived at the Treasury. "Does the currency travel of its own volition?" he said. "It does not. You must stop this hemorrhage of our economic lifeblood." As he spoke, he knotted a skein of cord in his slender fingers.

"What is blood?" said the Controller wearily. "Only seawater."

The leader gripped the cord in his hands. "You do not seem to understand our concern," he said to the Controller.

"Perhaps I do not," the Controller replied, and though the leader continued to talk, the Controller did not hear him.

Eventually the leader left, and the first shift of counting clerks was replaced by the second, and finally the Controller was left all alone in the Treasury building, looking at a piece of paper from the teleprinter in his office.

The paper called for the Treasury to transfer several hundred ounces of the ancient metal locked in its basement vaults to an account in a distant nation, in exchange for some of the enblu notes that lived in numerical symbiosis with the metal, balanced on the other side of an equal sign.

Tomorrow, he knew, the leaders would ask him to again examine the procedures of accounting, to discover how so many of the notes could have found their way to that other nation.

The Controller of the Currency did not know how the notes escaped, and he had tried, tried very hard, to trace their route. Nor did he know who it was that possessed the notes, but desired the ancient metal more. He had, more than once, asked the modern leaders if they would suspend the exchanges, draw a stroke through the equation; they would not. They told him he did not understand.

And, being no economist, he did not. He sat in the counting room, all quiet and alone, seeing no more than an ancient could. The minting and printing presses were all shut down, and the stillness droned in his ears, like a pounding heart buried beneath the floorboards.

A note fluttered up from the counting table, and was caught in a draft of air: it flew past the back of the Controller's hand, its edge flicking along his skin. The crisp paper cut him, and he bled.

The Controller flexed his hand. The film of blood smeared, and his sweat entered the cut, making it burn with salt; in the fire there was light, and clarity.

Large industrial fans were mounted on the minting floors for relief from the heat of work. The Controller of the Currency moved two of these into the note-counting room. He locked the door behind himself and switched the fans to their highest speed.

Notes stirred, as if awakening from a sleep; they arose, they flew, beating their sharp wings upon the turbulent air.

The Controller of the Currency watched the rising storm, feeling a joy he had thought lost to him forever. He began to undress, hurrying, fumbling as a boy eager to be a boy no longer, and as frightened. He threw his clothing into the wind, and then he threw himself.

He was struck by flying paper, and was cut, and bled, and the wetness upon his body (of blood and ink and other things) made the notes adhere, so that the Controller grew scales, was leafed as a tree, as the leafy man of ancient legend. He became dizzy with the loss of blood, and nearly fell, but the wind bore him up. Notes covered his face, and there was darkness, a blindness the color of wealth and as finely engraved as the surface of human skin. He could not see, but sometimes one has seen enough. Sometimes.

The sheath of currency stiffened, grew heavy. As it brought him finally down, the Controller knew that he was now one with it, inseparable: They would never disengage him from his work now . . . they would never complete their count, unless it numbered him in the telling.

To organize and record large quantities of data before the printing press, the extreme ancients created what they called Memory Palaces: furnished rooms of the mind in which each fixture, each detail, recalled some fact. The palace builder could at liberty walk through his creation, into the room where (say) the philosophies of sunlight and reflection were archived, a long bright gallery open to the sky along the solar path of the equinoxes, and in every sill and stela read a line of the accumulated text.

This seems illogical, which combined with its ancientness is to say insane, to the modern; but this is because we are immersed in the printed word. Movable type is a sort of standard builder's brick for knowledge, that anyone may use to brick thoughts up in lasting fashion, for everyone. This was the failing of the Memory Palace, truth to tell: only the proprietor had access. No one else could enter, no matter how much light they might have brought, how blinding the glow they held.

Continuing along the spectrum, we come now, suddenly and lightly, to eindi. This is a trivial color, a color of the fashionable moment. Some have said that modern times have no place for eindi, but this is shortsighted. Humanity's concerns are not all grand in scope: to ignore our trivialities is to deny a crucial part of that humanity. Some portion of each of us is colored eindi: it is part of our spectrum.

At the end of the Night Physician's rounds, when she was nearly overcome with weariness, she would climb five flights of stairs, past the operating theatres, the examining suites, the patient rooms, to the hospital solarium, a long, rectangular room with skylights and long windows. From there she would look into the eastern distance, toward the soft line of dawn. As she stood in the unlit room, among the night-shapes of tables and chairs and plants, the dawnglow seemed to bathe her in coolness, quench her hot grainy eyes, as a man in the heat of sunlight might be soothed by shadowfall. She never sat down; but sometimes she would drift into something like sleep, standing up, eyes open, until an edge of sun showed itself and dazzled her, or an orderly wanting to sneak a cigarette came in and, seeing her, hurried out again.

Then, stirred again into slow motion, she would go back down the stairs—never the elevator—and sign herself and her equipment out of the building, put a woolen serape over her hospital tunic (whatever the weather, though the mornings were always cool) and board a shuttle bus, one of those that endlessly courses the city, day and night, like the motion of those small memories of distant pains and pleasures, that are invisible until they appear to transport one away with them.

The Night Physician's apartment was in a new building, gray and blank, its walls constructed at oblique angles so that something kept the eye from banal madness. The apartment was very clean, though books and papers and medical journals littered it; this litter was not confusion, but the Night Physician's method of keeping information accessible. She would make a small meal, read a journal while eating, and then retire to her heavy-curtained bedroom, whose soft deep carpets had never known another footstep than her own.

On a particular morning the Night Physician's reverie was interrupted by a man's voice saying "Do you think the dawn is so beautiful because it is so brief, so evanescent?"

The Night Physician turned. A man sat in one of the solarium armchairs. He was dressed in linen, and his eyes were sunken and his cheeks were darkly hollow. The Night Physician looked around for someone else the man in linen might have been speaking to, but there was no one else. "Who are you?" she said.

"A patient here," said the man in linen. "Who are you?"

"A physician here," the Night Physician said. "Patients should not be here at this hour."

"Ah, but I am a very special patient," said the man in linen. "I will never leave this building . . . not alive, I mean."

"This is a certainty? You have been told?"

"As certain as the sunrise. It was sunrise we were discussing. Do you agree, it is the dawn's death in daylight that makes it so exquisite a phenomenon?"

"If you are a patient, you should not be here," the Night Physician said, "and my work here is over, and I must be going home."

"I shall be here again," the man in linen said.

And he was, for the next several nights, speaking of death and dawn in the same short breath. The Night Physician considered calling the orderlies to replace the man in linen in his room, in his bed, but she never did. Properly he should not have been in the solarium, but he was causing no disturbance to the hospital by being there.

She had the vague, curious feeling that if she were to call for orderlies, they would arrive to find her alone in the solarium, looking at an empty chair. At least, she had this feeling at first; with each night that passed, the reality, the palpability, of the man in linen became more apparent.

Yet he was a disturbance, a source of disorder, in a place that should know no disorder. The instruments on a surgical tray are always laid out in a certain fashion; when the fingers reach for a hemostat they do not find a sponge. The controls of the anesthesia equipment always turn in the same way. Dosages are specified in common units, in common terminology. It is well to be ruthless about certain things.

She examined hospital records, to see who he might be; but without knowing his name, or at least his ailment, there was no way of being certain. The staff must know, she thought, but she was the Night Physician, and as such had little contact with them.

In the hours between her work and her silent trips home, the Night Physician moved through the hospital corridors and chambers as, when a student, she had probed the connections and organs of her dissection cadaver. In the basement was the hyperbaric chamber, brought dismantled from its country of origin and reassembled plate and bolt and valve according to detailed written instructions, its purpose to drive out the terrible anaerobic infections of the wild country (which eat flesh alive, and induce visions) with pure oxygen under high pressure, drowning alien life in the substance of life. Here also was the radiology unit, where invisible energy was used to search and renovate.

On the first floor were the file and record rooms, neat racks of little spaces where every patient in the hospital's history was preserved from admission to treatment to departure (by whatever means), a four-dimensional cross-section of the universe. There was also a laboratory with every instrument of research, even spectrometers; health care being a priority of the modern government, the hospital's machines were the first to be tortured.

On the second floor were the examination and treatment suites, equipped for minor surgery, including ophthalmic laser and electric cautery. Neither of these tools was used for enucleation (that is, the renovation of an eye for the good of the patient), that being done with a small scalpel with a curved blade. The knife was not heated for such use, though of course it had been sterilized, in the hissing autoclave.

The third, fourth, and fifth floors housed patients, in their rooms, in their beds, by day in the light that pleases the eye open to receive it, by night in the darkness that blankets all pain, that even those without eyes can feel.

It was on the eleventh night (the fifteenth in absolute terms, since she had rounds only five days in seven) that she threw her serape over his shoulders and led him down the stairs and out of the hospital. And so her bedroom knew a second set of footsteps, though they made no sound.

When she awoke, the man in linen was gone. She did not see him that night, or the next, but on the one following he appeared, and with only the smallest exchange of words he again wore her serape from the hospital.

On the third such morning, the Night Physician said "Why do you do this?"

"It is merely a thing I wish to know, before I depart forever," said the man in linen.

"Surely you must have known it before this."

"But not with you. Not with . . ."

"Yes?"

"All of us are different."

There was a silence.

"I wonder if I have proven adequate," the Night Physician said. "I am very tired, at the conclusion of my rounds."

"You are more than adequate," said the man in linen. "You are all that I had hoped you might be."

"Still, there is something I would like to know, while you are still here," said the Night Physician. "Would you meet me before my rounds begin, while I am still fresh?"

The man hesitated, then said "Of course. But I have a roommate at the hospital—"

"I know of a room that will be empty," said the Night Physician, and gave him the number. "I will trust you to be there tonight."

"I am a committed man," he said. "What else have I but trust?"

That afternoon the Night Physician's clock awoke her hours before her usual arising time. The man in linen was gone, the print of his head on the pillow still warm. The Night Physician dressed and packed her equipment, and then went to the hospital, where she spent the late afternoon in the office of patient records.

Not long after dark, the man in linen was sitting on the edge of the bed in an empty hospital room. There was a tap at the door, and he smiled and said "I told you I was trustworthy."

Two muscular orderlies entered the room, and before the man in linen could do anything the orderlies stripped off his tunic, pinned him down to the bed, and fastened straps around his wrists and ankles. The man protested. The orderlies ignored him and went out of the room without having spoken a word.

The Night Physician entered, placed her kit on the bedside table and began to unpack her tools. The man in linen began to wail and moan. "Others have called out," said the Night Physician. "These rooms are quite proof against sound."

"What are you going to do?"

"I am the Night Physician," she said, "you know that, and you know what it is that I do on my rounds. You said when first we met that you were one of my patients."

"A lie," shouted the man in linen.

"You are a trustworthy man." She took the rubber mask and the small steel bottle from her bag. "What else do you have, in your hopeless condition?"

"No, no! I did it because—"

"I know why you did it. I think many of my patients have desired to do it. You are only the first to find the courage."

"But I am not one of your patients," the man in linen cried, "it was a lie, I am not, I am not!"

"You have become one," said the Night Physician, pressing down the rubber mask over the face of the man on the bed. "Do you not know that some diseases are contagious?"

The man in linen strained at the straps that bound him to the bed, and might have broken free, for they were designed for persons in a weakened state, from disease, or recent repair; but they held, and soon he ceased to struggle.

The Night Physician removed the mask and went on to the completion of her rounds. Then she slowly climbed the steps to the solarium and waited, alone, for the first light of morning to fall softly upon her, as upon I or you.

Tell what was in the past, the saying goes, and what is in the present will surely make sense. Yet if the ancients saw their world through compound prisms of lies—as we know that they did—then what shall we say that past was? Is not the sitter a part of the portrait, the occupant of the house a component of the home?

The last of the new shades, the distant end of the accurate wavelengths, is goviolet. Goviolet is the color of our hopes, our dreams, our imaginations of tomorrow. It is not a color that lends itself to commonplace uses—an article of clothing, the wall of a room—because of this quality of reflecting not what is, but what could be.

The Artillerist and the Architect had grown up in nearby houses, in a part of the capital of moderate prosperity—enough to insulate their families from both the agonies and the corruptions of the ancient world. They attended the same school, used the same playground, even (through one of those complicated circumstances of linkage that bears no investigation) found themselves at the same large family functions, identically bored.

As children, their play was a curious reversal of their later careers: for it was the young Artillerist who built fortresses, of blocks or sand or snow, and the young Architect who found ingenious ways to bring them down.

Their fascinations were the world and one another. Their families did not disapprove; this is not one of those stories. It was commonly thought that they would, in time, form a linkage. The young people may or may not have thought this themselves: it is true that they went together on the search for secret things, but they did not ever reach the brightest dark place.

And when they parted company, one to study construction at the university and the other to enter the Engineering Academy of the national guard, it was not with a thought of meeting again, or of not meeting: it was the evening of the day and that was all.

But of course they did meet again, or there would be no story.

The first time was during an inter-university competition, a ritual of the ancients believed to enhance learning through formal conflict. There were sporting events, tests of computational skill (as if anything were proven by the position of a ball on a field or the rapid working out of equations with solutions already known) . . . and, in the case that concerns us, a battle between the Engineer cadets and the students of Architecture.

The battle took place in the Exposition Park, directly across the city square from the Basilica of the Apostles and diagonally adjacent to the Great Hall of Justice. The Architects were given a large fresh hen's egg, and a certain quantity of materials to construct a defense around it: the Engineers had a quantity of explosives and other materiel to attack the bunker, and break the egg.

The bunker the students built was a squat pyramid of earth and wood and wire, the goal egg buried within it. The cadets' devices reached and arched and crouched around the pyramid, fencings of destructive potential.

The field was cleared. The audience became quiet. Then a pistol was fired into the air, circuits were closed, the attack began. Sprays of pellets scarified the pyramid; jets of flame and molten metal chewed into it; a wave of liquid fire engulfed it, burning the inner wooden scaffoldings to crumbling charcoal so that the earth heaved and subsided. Oily smoke obscured vision of the scene, and for long minutes there were only flashes and sounds in a dark cloud.

Then the battlefield fell silent, and the smoke cleared. The students and the cadets moved in, to count the dead.

Under close supervision to avoid any trickery, an Architect—our Architect—moved a set of baffles and in moments exposed the egg. This clever design drew applause. The Architect lifted the egg in a gloved hand, and displayed it unbroken.

"But it is hard-cooked," the Architect announced. "The bunker was designed so that the heat of the first attacks cooked it, hardening it against shock."

The applause rose at this ingenious tactic. Then quite suddenly, there was a whistling, screaming sound from high overhead, rising in pitch with the approach of the source in a descending catenary of fire.

Some of the people on the field beneath the screaming missile dove for cover; some stood entirely still. Before there was time for any considered action, the missile struck the ground with a small pop.

Only a pop, for the device was only a length of cardboard tube with tin fins notched to whistle through the air.

From behind a greenskeeper's pavilion at the edge of the Park there came an Artillerist—our Artillerist—carrying a pail. She dumped water over the fizzling skyrocket. Then she pointed at the egg, which was still in the hand of the Architect. But his fingers had closed upon it, very hard.

"It's broken," she said, which it surely was. "We win."

The audience began to laugh, and to applaud. The team of architecture students began to protest. Then our Architect was stopped still by the shock of recognition, and he entirely forgot his surroundings and ran to embrace the Artillerist.

In the years that followed this incident, the two would cross paths many more times. This might have been considered unusual in those ancient times, when little was understood of the dynamics of history. It is possible that this particular dynamic was responsible for the Architect's modernization of spirit; whatever the precise cause, it is true that he began to hold revolutionary views, and fell therefore into deep disfavor with the powerful ancients who had once been pleased to purchase his services.

It happened one day that the Architect was in the National Library, in the great vaulted Hall of Maps, and heard a step behind himself. He turned, expecting one cannot say what, and saw the Artillerist, who now wore the uniform of a Colonel of the national guard.

The Hall of Maps was memorable for its surface detail. The walls had vertical wainscot of book-matched, strongly figured oak, and above that the arched ceiling was hexagonally tessellated, a decorative brass boss in the center of each cell. The map cases that filled the chamber were also hexagonal, for closest-ordered packing. The map librarians disapproved of this arrangement, as it defied standard grid numbering for the location of a particular tube. It introduced, they said, a fifty percent error. Yet the meticulous grandeur of the Hall, and the tactile satisfaction of the hexagonal wooden map tubes in their carefully carpentered racks, overrode such delicate objections. Besides, the mystery extended only to the boxes. A map, once uncased and unrolled, is either the one you are seeking or it is not: the batteryworks near Fox Point Light are not going to pretend that they are a hill-country forest. Maps are not given to irony.

The Artillerist looked at the diagrams spread out before the Architect, and said "The Great Hall of Justice is a fine building."

"It is a parody-Palladian heap without a single line in proportion," said the Architect, "but it is strong and defensible."

"It may be built of stone, but if charges were to be placed here and here and here"—she indicated locations on the elevation drawings—"it would become so uncertain of support that it would have to be abandoned."

"Wrappings of wire would ablate your charges."

"Shaped charges would turn your wire into molten cutting torches."

"You would never reach the steps to plant them, given only a few soldiers upon these steps."

"Those steps are too shallow for effective ranked fire, and the statuary in the square—especially the figures of the Apostles—create many blind fields. What do you mean to do with this information?"

"I will take it into the hills," said the Architect, "where there are people who will know what use to make of it . . . for whom the nation's justice is already so uncertain of support that it must be abandoned."

The Artillerist was silent for a little while. "You should not have told me that last," she said, "for it will be very difficult for me to keep it silent."

"I do not care if you keep it silent," said the Architect. "It is a thing that needs speaking."

"Nevertheless, I shall say nothing."

"I do not care."

"That is not the truth," said the Artillerist. "The truth is that there is nothing in the world that you do not care about, in one way or another."

"I built houses in the hills, for the wealthy and powerful," said the Architect, very softly, "and they are beautiful houses, and they shall all be destroyed in the times to come."

The Artillerist said "One cannot make an omelet without breaking an egg."

The two of them touched hands, and then the Architect gathered up his papers and left the Artillerist alone in the library hall, and that too was the end of a day. It was, though neither of them knew it, the last day of the wholly ancient world.

They did not see one another again for all the years of the revolution. That is to say, they never saw one another face to face; but from time to time the Artillerist would examine a revetment or empty bolt-hole that had resisted her efforts to an exceptional degree, and the Architect would walk through the broken and smoldering renovation of a modern construction, and they were in each other's presence.

In the course of the war, the Architect became an advisor and confidant to the leaders of the revolution, in a curious modern version of his old relations with the ancients. He was asked by the leaders to help plan the modern housing and public buildings that would be raised once the ancient world was dust. So it happened that in the last hours of the revolution the Architect was in the capital city, examining what had survived the fighting and what had not. He was in White Birch Street, with his pad and his pencil, when he saw a face at a window; and as on another battlefield he was taken in his depths by recognition.

The Architect walked up the ramp to the building, which was strangely empty of life and wildly littered for a hospital. He approached the main desk, which was untenanted, turned right, climbed the stairs encircling the elevator. He knew the layout of this building exactly; he knew the plan of every major structure in the city. He went through the seventh door on the right-hand side of the hallway, and found the Artillerist.

She was sitting up in bed, near the window. She wore a linen tunic, buttoned at the shoulder, and her lower body was wrapped in cotton sheets. "You will pardon me for not getting up," she said, through lips that the ancients with their inaccurate vision would have called colorless.

"Let me help you," said the Architect.

"Not much chance of that now," said the Artillerist, but she allowed him to move her into a wheeled chair, and when he began to weep at the sight of what the sheets had hidden, she said "Triumph of construction over assault. Else I'd not be here."

There was the sound of gunfire from the city square, and the Artillerist added "But the assault was potent too, or I'd be elsewhere. You've noticed all my roommates have gone." She rubbed her eyes, though they were only tired with looking from the window; a small folding binocular was upon the sill. Blindness produces a bitter depression, all the more when it is blindness caused by war, for the last image, the last deeply burnt memory, is of the bayonet and the enemy who holds it.

Then there was a whistling from the sky outside, and the building shook. The lighting failed, windows broke, beams fell. The smells of plaster dust and ozone mixed with those of disinfectant and old wounds.

"Is this how it ends?" said the Architect, who could predict a building's whole fate from an echo down its corridors.

"Must you hold me so tight, is that your idea of reliving history? Besides, those are no work of mine. If those had been my rockets we'd be omelets by now."

The Architect eased the Artillerist in her chair down the quaking flights to the ground floor. In the lobby, amid the mess, the Artillerist gripped the wheels of the chair. "Listen," she said. "The firing from the Plaza has stopped. And do you hear the whistling? Not my artillery, but rebel—"

"We must hurry," said the Architect. "The ceiling will give way under another impact."

"The second salvo should arrive just now," said the Artillerist, and rolled herself away from her companion.

Both of them were right. Plaster and metal and wood fell. The Architect was blinded by dust and smoke; when his vision cleared, the Artillerist had disappeared. He called to her, and listened through ringing ears, but heard no answer; then he saw her hand, protruding from a heap of debris. The Architect had been here before, many times; it had been a long war. He knew when there was hope and when not, and there was not, and he could not bear to touch the hand knowing this. He staggered from the building.

He felt hard body blows, and supposed that he must have been deafened, since he had not heard the shots. He looked up at the soldiers, and was confused for a moment, then realized that his uniform was covered with plaster and splinters, unrecognizable. The soldiers had misperceived him, fired upon the fallen ancient dust, the bits of broken Apostles.

He turned to go back into the building, wanting now to hold the Artillerist's hand, but he felt more bullets strike him, and his legs would no longer hold him up.

"Was there ever such a love as this?" the Architect cried out, and in his voice there was the terrible sound of a soul that knows it has lived too long, if only by a few minutes. And then the story—all the stories—were over.

You will understand that I am no longer young, and if my tales seem vague and discursive, it is only from a desire to present all the information necessary in the most usable fashion. Of all the changes modern times have brought, I think perhaps the most important is the insistence upon diagrammatic clarity in the arts, the presentation of clear moral truths, rather than murky pools in which the patron must fish blindly for meanings. This ancient tactic led to acts of outright madness, such as the reading of secret messages from texts, say, in the last word before a line break, or the first word after. Such people might stare until they burned the eyes from their heads: and would that be unjust, unmerited, undeserved?

It was this lack of emotional clarity that caused the ancients to repair others for what they had lost in themselves, to renovate that which they found empty, to wander the streets hollow-eyed, looking for the place where their former joy had been concealed. To frame one more story, it was as if, having refused to pay the piper who lured their rats away, their children were taken from them as well.

But modern vision shows us that the children were never gone at all. They were there, in front of everyone—but reflecting a light of colors that ancient eyes simply could not detect. The empty places were filled with light unknown. The joy was before them, but they were blind to it.

Blindness is not just blindness, you see. You see, you see, you see, you see, you see.

THE SNOWBALL EFFECT

Katherine MacLean

Katherine MacLean represents the leading edge of those sf writers who have applied the methodologies and principles of the hard sciences to "soft sciences" such as anthropology, psychology, and sociology, to make them predictive, to find their laws, to make them solve problems. This was generally done with a condescending affect in the Campbell era and yet it produced a stream of sf that grew into serious treatment of those sciences in the works of Chad Oliver in the 1950s, and flourished in the works of Ursula K. Le Guin and Michael Bishop in recent decades. MacLean's collection, *The Diploids* (1962), contains many of the best of her early stories. Kingsley Amis called her "an excellent woman writer" and singled out two of her stories for extended discussion in *New Maps of Hell*. She published little in the 1960s, returning at the end of the decade with award-winning stories and a novel about psi powers, *The Missing Man* (1975).

"The Snowball Effect" is one of her famous (and typical) pieces. A sociologist is challenged to make his science do something real and so he does. It is a satire on social engineering that has the humorous attitude of real scientists doing a postmortem on an insufficiently, rigorously imagined, and comically failed experiment. Behind it is the moral position shared between writer and audience that doing science can be dangerous and should be left to real scientists, not amateurs. It inhabits the same part of the genre as John Sladek's "Stop Evolution in Its Tracks" and James P. Hogan's "Making Light": although the tone is different, the underlying attitudes about science are the same. It also coexists recognizably alongside the mainstream of hard sf stories from Heinlein and Asimov to Bob Shaw's "Light of Other Days": one big idea that changes the world is examined from the point of view of the hard sf attitude.

"All right," I said, "what is sociology good for?"

Wilton Caswell, Ph.D., was head of my Sociology Department, and right then he was mad enough to chew nails. On the office wall behind him were three or four framed documents in Latin, but I didn't care at that moment if he papered the walls with his degrees. I had been appointed Dean and President to see to it that the University made money. I had a job to do, and I meant to do it.

He bit off each word with great restraint: "Sociology is the study of social institutions, Mr Halloway."

I tried to make him understand my position. "Look, it's the big-money men who are supposed to be contributing to the support of this college. To them, sociology sounds like socialism—nothing can sound worse than that—and an institution is where they put Aunt Maggy when she began collecting Wheaties in a stamp album. We can't appeal to them that way. Come on now." I smiled condescendingly, knowing it would irritate him. "What are you doing that's worth anything?"

He glared at me, his white hair bristling and his nostrils dilated like a war-horse about to whinny. I can say one thing for them—these scientists and professors always keep themselves well under control. He had a book in his hand and I was expecting him to throw it, but he spoke instead:

"This department's analysis of institutional accretion, by the use of open-system mathematics, has been recognized as an outstanding and valuable contribution to—"

The words were impressive, whatever they meant, but this still didn't sound like anything that would pull in money. I interrupted, "Valuable in what way?"

He sat down on the edge of his desk thoughtfully, apparently recovering from the shock of being asked to produce something solid for his position, and ran his eyes over the titles of the books that lined his office walls.

"Well, sociology has been valuable to business in initiating worker efficiency and group motivation studies, which they now use in management decisions. And, of course, since the Depression, Washington has been using sociological studies of employment, labour, and standards of living as a basis for its general policies of—"

I stopped him with both hands raised. "Please, Professor Caswell! That would hardly be a recommendation. Washington, the New Deal and the present Administration are somewhat touchy subjects to the men I have to deal with. They consider its value debatable, if you know what I mean. If they got the idea that sociology professors are giving advice and guidance—No, we have to stick to brass tacks and leave Washington out of this. What, specifically, has the work of this specific department done that would make it as worthy to receive money as—say, a heart-disease research fund?"

He began to tap the corner of his book absently on the desk, watching me. "Fundamental research doesn't show immediate effects, Mr. Halloway, but its value is recognized."

I smiled and took out my pipe. "All right, tell me about it. Maybe I'll recognize its value."

Professor Caswell smiled back tightly. He knew his department was at stake. The other departments were popular with donors and pulled in gift money by scholarships and fellowships, and supported their professors and graduate students by research contracts with the Government and industry. Caswell had to show a way to make his own department popular—or else.

He laid down his book and ran a hand over his ruffled hair. "Institutions—organizations, that is"—his voice became more resonant; like most professors, when he had to explain something he instinctively slipped into his platform lecture mannerisms, and began to deliver an essay—"have certain tendencies built into the way they happen to have been organized, which cause them to expand or contract without reference to the needs they were founded to serve."

He was becoming flushed with the pleasure of explaining his subject. "All through the ages, it has been a matter of wonder and dismay to men that a simple organization—such as a church to worship in, or a delegation of weapons to a warrior class merely for defence against an outside enemy—will either grow insensately and extend its control until it is a tyranny over their whole lives, or, like other organizations set up to serve a vital need, will tend to repeatedly dwindle and vanish, and have to be painfully rebuilt.

"The reason can be traced to little quirks in the way they were organized, a matter of positive and negative power feedbacks. Such simple questions as 'Is there a way a holder of authority in this organization can use the power available to him to increase his power?' provide the key. But it still could not be handled until the complex questions of interacting motives and long-range accumulations of minor effects could somehow be simplified and formulated. In working on the problem, I found that the mathematics of open system, as introduced to biology by Ludwig von Bertalanffy and George Kreezer, could be used as a base that would enable me to develop a specifically social mathematics, expressing the human factors of intermeshing authority and motives in simple formulas.

"By these formulations, it is possible to determine automatically the amount of growth and period of life of any organization. The U.N., to choose an unfortunate example, is a shrinker-type organization. Its monetary support is not in the hands of those who personally benefit by its governmental activities, but, instead, in the hands of those who would personally lose by any extension and encroachment of its authority on their own. Yet by the use of formula analysis—"

"That's theory," I said. "How about proof?"

"My equations are already being used in the study of limited-size Federal corporations. Washington—"

I held up my palm again. "Please, not that nasty word again. I mean, where else has it been put into operation? Just a simple demonstration, something to show that it works, that's all."

He looked away from me thoughtfully, picked up the book and began to tap it on the desk again. It had some unreadable title and his name on it in gold letters. I got the distinct impression again that he was repressing an urge to hit me with it.

He spoke quietly. "All right. I'll give you a demonstration. Are you willing to wait six months?"

"Certainly, if you can show me something at the end of that time."

Reminded of time, I glanced at my watch and stood up.

"Could we discuss this over lunch?" he asked.

"I wouldn't mind hearing more, but I'm having lunch with some executors of a millionaire's will. They have to be convinced that by 'furtherance of research into human ills' he meant that the money should go to research fellowships for postgraduate biologists at the University, rather than to a medical foundation."

"I see you have your problems, too," Caswell said, conceding me nothing. He extended his hand with a chilly smile. "Well, good afternoon, Mr. Halloway. I'm glad we had this talk."

I shook hands and left him standing there, sure of his place in the progress of science and the respect of his colleagues, yet seething inside because I, the President and Dean, had boorishly demanded that he produce something tangible.

My job isn't easy. For a crumb of favourable publicity and respect in the newspapers and an annual ceremony in a silly costume, I spend the rest of the year going hat in hand, asking politely for money at everyone's door, like a well-dressed panhandler, and trying to manage the University on the dribble I get. As far as I was concerned, a department had to support itself or be cut down to what student tuition pays for, which is a handful of overcrowded courses taught by an assistant lecturer. Caswell had to make it work or get out.

But, the more I thought about it, the more I wanted to hear what he was going to do for a demonstration.

At lunch, three days later, while we were waiting for our order, he opened a small notebook. "Ever hear of feedback effects?"

"Not enough to have it clear."

"You know the snowball effect, though."

"Sure, start a snowball rolling downhill and it grows."

"Well, now—" He wrote a short line of symbols on a blank page and turned the notebook around for me to inspect it. "Here's the formula for the snowball process. It's the basic general growth formula—covers everything."

It was a row of little symbols arranged like an algebra equation. One was a concentric spiral going up, like a cross-section of a snowball rolling in snow. That was a growth sign.

I hadn't expected to understand the equation, but it was almost as clear as a sentence. I was impressed and slightly intimidated by it. He had already explained enough so that I knew that, if he was right, here was the growth of the Catholic Church and the Roman Empire, the conquests of Alexander and the spread of the smoking habit and the change and rigidity of the unwritten law of styles.

"Is it really as simple as that?" I asked.

"You notice," he said, "that when it becomes too heavy for the cohesion strength of snow it breaks apart. Now, in human terms—"

The chops and mashed potatoes and peas arrived.

"Go on," I urged.

He was deep in the symbology of human motives and the equations of human behaviour in groups. After running through a few different types of grower- and shrinker-type organizations, we came back to the snowball, and decided to run the test by making something grow.

"You add the motives," he said, "and the equation will translate them into organization."

"How about a good selfish reason for the ins to drag others into the group—some sort of bounty on new members, a cut of their membership fee?" I suggested uncertainly, feeling slightly foolish. "And maybe a reason why the members would lose if any of them resigned, and some indirect way they could use to force each other to stay in."

"The first is the chain-letter principle," he nodded. "I've got that. The other. . . ." He put the symbols through some mathematical manipulation so that a special grouping appeared in the middle of the equation. "That's it."

Since I seemed to have the right idea, I suggested some more, and he added some, and juggled them around in different patterns. We threw out a few that would have made the organization too complicated, and finally worked out an idyllically simple and deadly little organization set-up where joining had all the temptation of buying a sweepstakes ticket, going in deeper was as easy as hanging around a race track, and getting out was like trying to pull free from a Malayan thumb-trap. We put our heads closer together and talked lower, picking the best place for the demonstration.

"Abington?"

"How about Watashaw? I have some student sociological surveys of it already. We can pick a suitable group from that."

"This demonstration has got to be convincing. We'd better pick a little group that no one in his right mind would expect to grow."

"There should be a suitable club—"

"Ladies," said the skinny female chairman of the Watashaw Sewing Circle. "Today we have guests." She signalled for us to rise, and we stood up, bowing to polite applause and smiles. "Professor Caswell, and Professor Smith." (My alias.) "They are making a survey of the methods and duties of the clubs of Watashaw."

We sat down to another ripple of applause and slightly wider smiles, and then the meeting of the Watashaw Sewing Circle began. In five minutes I began to feel sleepy.

There were only about thirty people there, and it was a small room, not the halls of Congress, but they discussed their business of collecting and repairing second-hand clothing for charity with the same endless boring parliamentary formality.

I pointed out to Caswell the member I thought would be the natural leader, a tall, well-built woman in a green suit, with conscious gestures and a resonant, penetrating voice, and then went into a half-doze while Caswell stayed awake beside me and wrote in his notebook. After a while the resonant voice roused me to attention for a moment. It was the tall woman holding the floor over some collective dereliction of the club. She was being scathing.

I nudged Caswell and murmured, "Did you fix it so that a shover has a better chance of getting into office than a nonshover?"

"I think there's a way they could find for it," Caswell whispered back, and went to work on his equation again. "Yes, several ways to bias the elections."

"Good. Point them out tactfully to the one you select. Not as if she'd use such methods, but just as an example of the reason why only *she* can be trusted with initiating the change. Just mention all the personal advantages an unscrupulous person could have."

He nodded, keeping a straight and sober face as if we were exchanging admiring remarks about the techniques of clothes repairing, instead of conspiring.

After the meeting, Caswell drew the tall woman in the green suit aside and spoke to her confidentially, showing her the diagram of organization we had drawn up. I saw the responsive glitter in the woman's eyes and knew she was hooked.

We left the diagram of organization and our typed copy of the new by-laws with her and went off soberly, as befitted two social-science experimenters. We didn't start laughing until our car passed the town limits and began the climb for University Heights.

If Caswell's equations meant anything at all, we had given that sewing circle more growth drives than the Roman Empire.

Four months later I had time out from a very busy schedule to wonder how the test was coming along. Passing Caswell's office, I put my head in. He looked up from a student research paper he was correcting.

"Caswell, about that sewing club business—I'm beginning to feel the suspense. Could I get an advance report on how it's coming?"

"I'm not following it. We're supposed to let it run the full six months."

"But I'm curious. Could I get in touch with that woman—what's her name?"

"Searles. Mrs. George Searles."

"Would that change the results?"

"Not in the slightest. If you want to graph the membership rise, it should be going up in a log curve, probably doubling every so often."

I grinned. "If it's not rising, you're fired."

He grinned back. "If it's not rising, you won't have to fire me—I'll burn my books and shoot myself."

I returned to my office and put in a call to Watashaw.

While I was waiting for the phone to be answered, I took a piece of graph paper and ruled it off into six sections, one for each month. After the phone had rung in the distance for a long time, a servant answered with a bored drawl:

"Mrs. Searles' residence."

I picked up a red gummed star and licked it.

"Mrs. Searles, please."

"She's not in just now. Could I take a message?"

I placed the star at the thirty line in the beginning of the first section. Thirty members they'd started with.

"No, thanks. Could you tell me when she'll be back?"

"Not until dinner. She's at the meetin'."

"The sewing club?" I asked.

"No, *sir*, not that thing. There isn't any sewing club any more, not for a long time. She's at the Civic Welfare meeting."

Somehow I hadn't expected anything like that.

"Thank you," I said and hung up, and after a moment noticed I was holding a box of red gummed stars in my hand. I closed it and put it down on top of the graph of membership in the sewing circle. No more members. . . .

Poor Caswell. The bet between us was ironclad. He wouldn't let me back down on it even if I wanted to. He'd probably quit before I put through the first slow move to fire him. His professional pride would be shattered, sunk without a trace. I remembered what he said about shooting himself. It had seemed funny to both of us at the time, but. . . . What a mess that would make for the University.

I had to talk to Mrs. Searles. Perhaps there was some outside reason why the club had disbanded. Perhaps it had not just died.

I called back. "This is Professor Smith," I said, giving the alias I had used before. "I called a few minutes ago. When did you say Mrs. Searles will return?"

"About six-thirty or seven o'clock."

Five hours to wait.

And what if Caswell asked me what I had found out in the meantime? I didn't want to tell him anything until I had talked it over with that woman Searles first.

"Where is this Civic Welfare meeting?"

She told me.

Five minutes later, I was in my car, heading for Watashaw, driving considerably faster than usual and keeping a careful watch for highway-patrol cars as the speedometer climbed.

The town meeting-hall and theatre was a big place, probably with lots of small rooms for different clubs. I went in through the centre door and found myself in the huge central hall where some sort of rally was being held. A political-type rally—you know, cheers and chants, with bunting already down on the floor, people holding banners, and plenty of enthusiasm and excitement in the air. Someone was making a speech up on the platform. Most of the people there were women.

I wondered how the Civic Welfare League could dare hold its meeting at the same time as a political rally that could pull its members away. The group with Mrs. Searles was probably holding a shrunken and almost memberless meeting somewhere in an upper room.

There probably was a side door that would lead upstairs.

While I glanced around, a pretty girl usher put a printed bulletin in my hand, whispering, "Here's one of the new copies." As I attempted to hand it back, she retreated. "Oh, you can keep it. It's the new one. Everyone's supposed to have it. We've just printed up 6000 copies to make sure there'll be enough to last."

The tall woman on the platform had been making a driving, forceful speech about some plans for rebuilding Watashaw's slum section. It began to penetrate my mind dimly as I glanced down at the bulletin in my hands.

"Civic Welfare League of Watashaw. The United Organization of Church and Secular Charities." That's what it said. Below began the rules of membership.

I looked up. The speaker, with a clear, determined voice and conscious, forceful gestures, had entered the home stretch of her speech, an appeal to the civic pride of all citizens of Watashaw.

"With a bright and glorious future—potentially without poor and without uncared-for ill—potentially with no ugliness, no vistas which are not beautiful—the best people in the best-planned town in the country—jewel of the United States."

She paused and then leaned forward intensely, striking her clenched hand on the speaker's stand with each word for emphasis.

"All we need is more members. Now, get out there and recruit!"

I finally recognized Mrs. Searles, as an answering sudden blast of sound half deafened me. The crowd was chanting at the top of its lungs: "Recruit! Recruit!"

Mrs. Searles stood still at the speaker's table and behind her, seated in a row of chairs, was a group that was probably the board of directors. It was mostly women, and the women began to look vaguely familiar, as if they could be members of the sewing circle.

I put my lips close to the ear of the pretty usher while I turned over the stiff printed bulletin on a hunch. "How long has the League been organized?" On the back of the bulletin was a constitution.

She was cheering with the crowd, her eyes sparkling. "I don't know," she answered between cheers. "I only joined two days ago. Isn't it wonderful?"

I went into the quiet outer air and got into my car with my skin prickling. Even as I drove away, I could hear them. They were singing some kind of organization song with the tune of "Marching through Georgia."

Even at the single glance I had given it, the constitution looked exactly like the one we had given the Watashaw Sewing Circle.

All I told Caswell when I got back was that the sewing circle had changed its name and the membership seemed to be rising.

Next day, after calling Mrs. Searles, I placed some red stars on my graph for the first three months. They made a nice curve, rising steeply as it reached the fourth month. They had picked up their first increase in membership simply by amalgamating with all the other types of charity organizations in Watashaw, changing the club name with each fusion, but keeping the same constitution—the constitution with the bright promise of advantages as long as there were always new members being brought in.

By the fifth month, the League had added a mutual baby-sitting service and had induced the local school board to add a nursery school to the town service, so as to free more women for League activity. But charity must have been completely organized by then, and expansion had to be in other directions.

Some real-estate agents evidently had been drawn into the whirlpool early, along with their ideas. The slum improvement plans began to blossom and take on a tinge of real-estate planning later in the month.

The first day of the sixth month, a big two-page spread appeared in the local paper of a mass meeting which had approved a full-fledged scheme for slum clearance of Watashaw's shack-town section, plus plans for rehousing, civic building, and re-zoning. And good prospects for attracting some new industries to the town, industries which had already been contacted and seemed interested by the privileges offered.

And, with all this, an arrangement for securing and distributing to the club members *alone* most of the profit that would come to the town in the form of a rise in the price of building sites and a boom in the building industry. The profit-distributing arrangement was the same one that had been built into the organization plan for the distribution of the small profits of membership fees and honorary promotions. It was becoming an openly profitable business. Membership was rising more rapidly now.

By the second week of the sixth month, news appeared in the local paper that the club had filed an application to incorporate itself as the Watashaw Mutual Trade and Civic Development Corporation, and all the local real-estate promoters had finished joining *en masse*. The Mutual Trade part sounded to me as if the Chamber of Commerce was on the point of being pulled in with them, ideas, ambitions and all.

I chuckled while reading the next page of the paper, on which a local politician was reported as having addressed the club with long flowery oration on their enterprise, charity and civic spirit. He had been made an honorary member. If he allowed himself to be made a *full member* with its contractual obligations and its lures, if the politicians went into this, too. . . .

I laughed, filing the newspaper with the other documents on the Watashaw test. These proofs would fascinate any businessman with the sense to see where his bread was buttered. A businessman is constantly dealing with organizations, including his own, and finding them either inert, cantankerous, or both. Caswell's formula could be a handle to grasp them with. Gratitude alone would bring money into the University in car-load lots.

The end of the sixth month came. The test was over and the end reports were spectacular. Caswell's formulas were proven to the hilt.

After reading the last newspaper reports, I called him up.

"Perfect, Wilt, *perfect*! I can use this Watashaw thing to get you so many fellowships and scholarships and grants for your department that you'll think it's snowing money!"

He answered somewhat uninterestedly, "I've been busy working with students on their research papers and marking tests—not following the Watashaw business at all, I'm afraid. You say the demonstration went well and you're satisfied?"

He was definitely putting on a chill. We were friends now, but obviously he was still peeved whenever he was reminded that I had doubted that his theory could work. And he was using its success to rub my nose in the realization that I had been wrong. A man with a string of degrees after his name is just as human as anyone else. I had needled him pretty hard that first time.

"I'm satisfied," I acknowledged. "I was wrong. The formulas work beautifully. Come over and see my file of documents on it if you want a boost for your ego. Now let's see the formula for stopping it."

He sounded cheerful again. "I didn't complicate that organization with negatives. I wanted it to *grow*. It falls apart naturally when it stops growing for more than two months. It's like the great stock boom before an economic crash. Everyone in it is prosperous as long as the prices must keep going up and new buyers come into the market, but they all know what would happen if it stopped growing. You remember, we built in as one of the incentives that the members know they are going to lose if membership stops growing. Why, if I tried to stop it now, they'd cut my throat."

I remembered the drive and frenzy of the crowd in the one early meeting I had seen. They probably would.

"No," he continued. "We'll just let it play out to the end of its tether and die of old age."

"When will that be?"

"It can't grow past the female population of the town. There are only so many women in Watashaw, and some of them don't like sewing."

The graph on the desk before me began to look sinister. Surely Caswell must have made some provision for—

"You underestimate their ingenuity," I said into the phone. "Since they wanted to expand, they didn't stick to sewing. They went from general charity to social welfare schemes to something that's pretty close to an incorporated government. The name is now the Watashaw Mutual Trade and Civic Development Corporation, and they're filing an application to change it to Civic Property Pool and Social Dividend, membership contractual, open to all. That social dividend sounds like a Technocrat climbed on the band wagon, eh?"

While I spoke, I carefully added another red star to the curve above the thousand-member level, checking with the newspaper that still lay open on my desk. The curve was definitely some sort of log curve now, growing more rapidly with each increase.

"Leaving out practical limitations for a moment, where does the formula say it will stop?" I asked.

"When you run out of people to join it. But, after all, there are only so many people in Watashaw. It's a pretty small town."

"They've opened a branch office in New York," I said carefully into the phone, a few weeks later.

With my pencil, very carefully, I extended the membership curve from where it was then.

After the next doubling, the curve went almost straight up and off the page.

Allowing for a lag of contagion from one nation to another, depending on how much their citizens intermingled, I'd give the rest of the world about twelve years.

There was a long silence while Caswell probably drew the same graph in his own mind. Then he laughed weakly. "Well, you asked me for a demonstration."

That was as good an answer as any. We got together and had lunch in a bar, if you can call it lunch. The movement we started will expand by hook or by crook, by seduction or by bribery or by propaganda or by conquest, but it will expand. And maybe a total world government will be a fine thing—until it hits the end of its rope in twelve years or so.

What happens then, I don't know.

But I don't want anyone to pin that on me. From now on, if anyone asks me, I've never heard of Watashaw.

THE MORPHOLOGY OF THE KIRKHAM WRECK

Hilbert Schenck

Hilbert Schenck is a retired professor of ocean engineering whose work in science fiction has characteristically been about the interactions of humanity with weather and with the oceans. His stories are as influenced by the books of Edward Rowe Snow, the popular chronicler of the New England seacoast (where most of his stories are set), as by the hard sf tradition. *The Encyclopedia of Science Fiction* characterizes his stories thusly: "their intensities are fluent, grounded and scientifically competent." Their closest relative in emotional range is the fiction of James Tiptree, Jr. They began appearing in the late 1970s; his first novel, *At the Eye of the Ocean* (1980), and story collection, *Wave Rider* (1980), marked out his territory, which was further explored in subsequent novels such as *A Rose For Armageddon* (1982) and *Chronosequence* (1988). His novella *Steam Bird* (1982) is an alternate universe hard sf story which is an amusing portrayal of the world of fandom (in this case, of steam engine buffs).

This particular story is both historically accurate and wildly imaginative. There really was such a hurricane, and the late-nineteenth-century New England seacoast has several heroic rescues of legendary and improbable bravery, including the story of Chase as reported by Snow. What does science do when faced with the impossible? It waits for new data. What does hard sf do? It invents; in this case, alien observers, who make it all a bit more plausible. Something like it happened—but it was too implausible without the fiction. For one with the hard science fiction attitude.

This is one of the most striking tricks in sf literature. What it accomplishes, of course, is to substitute a rational sf explanation for the explanation that would certainly have been more acceptable in the late nineteenth century than mere coincidental success against great statistical odds—teleological intervention. For some, unusual happenings become quite implausible without the explanation of divine intervention, and the substitution of a science fictional rationale affirms the scientific worldview cleverly here. Thus science supplants superstition, and the allegory underlying hard science fiction is affirmed once again. It is an interesting case of the replacement principle at work. Schenk is underrated as one of the most accomplished writers of the hard sf affect.

The Riches of the Commonwealth
Are free strong minds, and hearts of health;
And more to her than gold or grain,
The cunning hand and cultured brain.

—Robert B. Thomas,
The Old Farmers Almanack,
1892, William Ware and Company,
Boston, Mass.

When the three-masted schooner *H. P. Kirkham* stranded on Rose and Crown Shoal southeast of Nantucket Island on January 19, 1892, the Coskata Life Saving Crew, led by Keeper Walter Chase, responded. The ensuing rescue attempt involved alterations in the local time flow of magnitudes never before observed within this continuum. Evolutionary physical forces were changed beyond the control of time-using peoples, and a fundamental question was introduced into the information matrix of this continuum, having, apparently, no resolution.

Time-using societies had always recognized the possibility that energy-users might attain significant mastery of time manipulation. Indeed, even occasional members of Keeper Chase's world group had, under the impetus of some violent or emotional event, been able to perform some limited and simple feats of time engineering, usually associated with mood and incentive control of others in the immediate situation. What became evident when the *Kirkham* stranded was that extreme-value probability theory could not set a limit on such activity by an energy-user totally motivated and having what Keeper Chase's peoples would incorrectly call a high level of "psychic" ability but what in fact is simply the ability to make information transfers within an altered time domain.

The northern gale blew shrieking along the back of Great Point, driving the spume off the wave tops and over the bitter beach. The patrolman crouched behind a sand hill, hunched to keep an occasional swirl of snow out of his collar, staring dully out at the white and gray sea. The wind had built up through the night, and now the shreds of dawn were blowing south over Nantucket, and the wind spoke continuously of urgent death.

The beach patrol, a hulking dark figure, turned to put the blast behind him and started back toward the station, where watchers in the cupola could relieve him in the light of day. It was twelve degrees above zero, with the wind gusting over forty.

Inside the Coskata Station the dark, shadowed paneling glowed faintly pink, reflecting the luminous brilliance of a huge coal stove in the center of the big common room. Nyman was cookie that week, and the wheatcakes were piling up on the cookstove in the small galley under the stairs. Four men sat silent, waiting for their breakfast, not trying to speak against the whines and rattles of the wind gusts. Yet they clearly heard the telephone tinkle in the cupola. A moment later, Surfman Eldridge appeared at the top of the stairs. "Skipper? It's Joe Remsen at Sankaty Light."

Keeper Walter Chase rose in the dark glow of the station, a giant, almost seven feet tall; his huge shadow startlingly flew up to obscure the walls and ceiling as he moved in front of the ruddy stove and up the stairs.

And Surfman Perkins, toying with his coffee mug, listening to the wind snapping and keening around the station, knowing that dawn calls from the lighthouse meant only one thing, suddenly realized for the first time in his life that he might die. He coughed, sharp barks of sound contrasting with the heavy, measured tread of Keeper Chase mounting the two flights to the cupola.

"Walter Chase here. Is that you, Joe?"

"Walter!" An urgent tone. Chase sensed that time was beginning to run away from him. "Masts on Bass Rip. We saw a flare last night late, but couldn't tell where. She's leaning some. Seems steady, but it's awful far to tell."

"What's her true bearing, Joe?"

"Just about due east from us. That would put her on the north end of Bass Rip."

Keeper Chase consulted a chart and compared angles. He looked out over the station pointer with powerful glasses. "Joe, I can't make her out. She *has* to be further out. We've got forty feet here and I could sure see her if she was laying on Bass Rip. She's got to be on Rose and Crown. South end from your bearing."

A pause. "Well . . . I don't know, Walter. I doubt we'd see her so clear that far. She may have lost her topmasts."

There was no point in arguing. Chase knew the wreck was fifteen miles out, on Rose and Crown Shoal. A sudden gust blew through the stout government sashes and swirled its chill into the cupola. The little tower rattled and shook. Walter Chase looked out at the ragged dawn, across at Eldridge, then down at the phone. "Joe, hang on. I'm getting the surfboat ready. We'll haul to the backside and launch there. I'll be back to you before I leave the station." Chase rose, ducking his head instinctively in the small room, and slowly climbed down the ladder, his mind fragmenting, working the launch, estimating the tide rips, laying beside the stranded vessel. "Eat quick!" shouted Walter Chase down the stairs. "We got a wreck on Rose and Crown!"

The difficulty in predicting improbable, time-controlling events by energy-users stems from these people's unlikely and illogical motivations and perception. One might assume that Keeper Chase's need to "defeat" the seas of the Nantucket South Shoals flowed from some sense of vengeance or hatred on his part resulting from the loss of a loved parent or a woman in some sea disaster. In fact, Keeper Chase suffered no such loss. Distant family members had, through the years, died on various whaling and trading voyages, but they were only names to Keeper Chase with little emotional attachment. Yet where the winter storms easily broke and ruined other capable men, for Keeper Chase the natural variation of wind and sea, so implacable and daunting to most of Chase's world group, only resonated with his self-image. In essence, Chase did not strongly believe in the "God" concepts so typical of energy users, but he strongly believed in a "Devil"—that is, the continual temptation of his world group by easy choices and safe paths. Keeper Chase saw the variability of the ocean as a natural test of behavior, as a kind of "Devil's assistant." That this naive motivation coupled with his great physical strength and the urgent and marginal situation at the stranded *Kirkham* should have produced such an unprecedented control over time flow cannot now be understood. Keeper Chase's meaning and purpose in this continuum thus remains inexplicable, as in fact he himself was to realize.

Surfman Flood ducked around the corner of the station, finally relieved of the wind blast at his back. He saw the stable door was open, and in the dim interior, Perkins and Gould were fastening a long wooden yoke across the neck of the silent ox. Harness bells tinkled, sound pinpoints in the rush and scream of the wind. Flood's heart seemed hollow. "Where's it at?" he asked at the door.

Josiah Gould peered from under his slicker hat. "Rose and Crown."

Flood sighed. "Fifteen miles downwind."

"Ayeh. Better get some breakfast."

Flood pushed open the station door and felt the relative warmth and stillness of the dark interior suck at his resolve. Nyman was steadily lifting forkfuls of flapjack into his mouth, alternating with steaming coffee from a huge cup in his left hand. Across the table was Flood's place set with a heaping meal.

"We got some rowin' to do, George. Better feed your face quick," said John Nyman. As they ate, rapidly and silently, the two wide doors of the apparatus room opened on the other side of the station, and swirls and draughts of chill rushed everywhere. They heard the shouts and tinkles as the stolid ox was backed over the sills and the harness lashings connected to the surfboat cart.

"Gawd, John, hits just awful on the beach!"

Nyman grinned and winked in the dark, chilling room. "The govinmint only pays you to go out, George," he said quoting the old wheeze. "You got to get back any way you can."

"Fifteen miles to windward! Hell's delight, we won't row a hundred yards in this smother!"

They heard Keeper Chase's deep voice in the apparatus room as the creak of the wheels signaled the surfboat's movement out into the wild dawn. He came into the common room and looked at the two men. "You fellers follow across the neck when you're finished and bring back the ox. I'm going to call Joe Remsen at Sankaty and have him order a tug from Woods Hole. We hain't going to row very far in this blow after we get them fellers off the wreck."

"Amen," said Surfman Flood under his breath. The wind was penetrating everywhere in the station, and the commotion was restless and insistent.

Walter Chase climbed back up into the cupola and cranked the phone magneto.

"Sankaty Light, Keeper Remsen."

"Joe, Walter Chase again. We'll be launching pretty quick. Can you still see her out there?"

"Hang on . . . yep. No change in her heel, as far as I can tell."

"Joe, will you call the town and have them telegraph Woods Hole for a tug. I think this storm's got another day to run, and we just hain't going to row back against it."

"Walter, I'll do my best . . . Them salvage fellows . . . they're hardly what you'd call heroes, you know."

Walter Chase grinned in the dark tower, which was suddenly shaking like a wet terrier. "Rats, vultures, buzzards, and skunks is what I usually hear them called, Joe. But we'll get back. Listen, Joe, I'm taking a line and drail. Might be some squeteague in those shallows in this rough weather."

But Joe Remsen made no sudden answer. He had rowed in the surfboat with Walter Chase under old Captain Pease when the Coskata Station had opened eight years before. Together they had worked the wreck of the infamous brig *Merriwa*, manned by a crew of New York City thugs who attempted to shoot up the station soon after they were landed. Walter Chase and an ax handle had secured the pistols, and then he and Joe had gone with them, now drunk as lords, to town in Wallace Adams' catboat. And Joe Remsen, feeling the tough and solid tower of Sankaty Light vibrate as a thin scream of icy air pierced the solid masonry, smiled in spite of himself, remembering the lunch at the American House. One of the drunken hoodlums had shoved his hand under a waitress's dress, and she had let him have a full tray of food plumb in the face. Back to back, he and Walter Chase had fought the six of them, chairs flying, crockery smashing everywhere. Joe Remsen's throat had a catch. He had to say something. "Walter . . . old friend, take care . . . God bless."

The walk across the neck took only a few blustery minutes, and Walter Chase met Nyman and Flood midway in that walk leading the ox home. Chase strode through the tidal cut between two high dunes, and the full wind caught his slicker and blew it suddenly open so that for a moment he seemed impossibly huge in the gray, fitful light. The surfboat lay above high water, and the men around it huddled together, their backs against the cutting wind.

Surfman Jesse Eldridge was number one in the Coskata crew. He walked, hunched and stolid, to Walter Chase. "It's going to be a tough launch, Skipper. Them waves are running almost along the beach," he shouted.

Chase nodded. "We're getting some lee from Point Rip, Jesse, but we'll have to launch across them, hold her head to the east. Otherwise, we'll be back ashore before we know it." They watched the breaking curls running toward them from the north.

Nyman and Flood came back, and the men, three on a side, began to shift the surfboat into the backwash. The wind blustered at them. "We got to go quick . . . when we go, boys!" shouted Walter Chase.

The blow was slightly west of north, but the waves were running directly south and meeting the beach at a sharp angle. "Take her out about nor'east!" shouted Walter Chase. "Ready . . . Now, jump to it!"

The six men lifted the boat by its gunwales and ran into the waves. A large group had passed and now the nearshore was a confused and choppy mess. The leading surfmen, Cathcart and Perkins, were almost up to their waists, and over the sides they vaulted, lifting and dropping their oars in the rowlocks. Now Gould and Nyman scrambled in, then Eldridge and Flood. Walter Chase pushed the surfboat out alone, deeper in, and now a curl appeared more from the east than the others and slapped the surfboat's bow to port back towards shore. Walter Chase moved his right hand forward along the starboard gunwale and pulled sharply. The twenty-three-foot boat gave a hop and her bow shifted eastward again. Then Chase was gracefully over the stern and the men were rowing strongly while he put out the long steering oar. They were clear of the shore break and moving into deeper water. Yet even here the waves were huge, rolling by under the boat and now and again breaking unexpectedly under the keel or beside them as they pulled together.

George Flood, cheerful and round-faced, was rowing port oar next to Jesse Eldridge. "Say, Skipper," he shouted up at Walter Chase. "I'm sure glad your ma never stinted you food. We must have been in a fathom of water before you climbed in."

Walter Chase thought a moment. "Actually, George, I hain't all that big, as Chases go," he boomed. "My great-uncle Reuben Chase was harpooner with Cap'n Grant on the *Niger*, and he went over seven feet. They claimed he could play a bull walrus or a whale on a harpoon line like you or I would a blue or striped bass." Chase paused, then . . . " 'Course, that would be a *small* whale, you understand."

Josiah Gould, seated directly ahead of Eldridge, lifted his head, his huge mustache blowing every which way. "Hain't that awful!" he yelled. "He's not just taking us out here to catch our death from pee-nu-monia, but now we're going to listen to more of them Chase family lies, too!"

Flood grinned over his shoulder and shouted back. "Them's not exactly lies, Josiah. Them's what's called 'artistic license.' "

Walter Chase looked benignly at Flood, his small eyes bright and his sideburns wild and full in the whipping wind. "I wisht I had your education, George. It's a plain wonder how you fellers with schooling can call one single thing by so many names. Now my daddy always said there was just three kinds: plain lies; mean, dirty, awful lies; and what's in the *Congressional Record*."

Gould and Nyman looked sideways at each other, winking. If they could get Skipper Chase going on them "govinmint fellers," it would be a short and cheerful run to Rose and Crown.

But the wind was worse. They were completely clear of any lee from Great Point. Even Chase's huge voice would be torn away and mutilated. "We're . . . far enough . . . out! Get . . . the sail up!" The four stern oarsmen continued to row, now more northerly into the teeth of the blasting wind. Cathcart and Perkins brought their oars inboard and wrestled the sail, tied in a tight bundle, out from under the thwarts and up into the wind. With Gould's and Nyman's help they finally stepped the mast and then unfurled and dropped the small lateen rig. It caught and filled with a snap, and Walter Chase wrenched the steering oar so hard to port that it described a long arc between the water and the steering notch in the transom. The boat darted off. Eldridge manned the sheet, and the other men huddled on the floorboards, their heads hunched inside the thick issue sweaters and stiff slickers.

Chase, at the steering oar, and Eldridge, on the stern thwart, had their heads close together; and now, running with the wind on the stern quarter, they could suddenly speak less stridently.

"I'm going to head for the lightship south of Great Round Shoal, Jesse," said Walter Chase, his arms in constant motion. "If it comes on to blow worse, we'll just have to go on board her. If we decide to keep going, we'll lay off sou'east and run down to Rose and Crown."

Eldridge was silent, then: "When do you figure we decide, Skipper?"

Chase looked at the jagged seas, whitecaps everywhere to the horizon. "Much beyond the Bass Rip line, we could never fetch the lightship. This lugger hain't much to windward."

The two men looked out ahead as the surfboat, heavily driven, wallowed and yawed and fought the pull of Walter Chase and his tough hickory steering oar.

Now they were three miles out, and looking south, Walter Chase saw that Bass Rip was clear and that the wreck was certainly on Rose and Crown. "We got to decide, Jesse," said Walter Chase.

Surfman Eldridge looked down at his high gum-rubber boots and nodded. "It hain't got worse, Skipper."

Chase's small eyes glittered. "Let out the sail, Jesse," he said, and the surfboat bounced and slapped and rolled, but now it was better, for the waves were astern. Off they dashed southeast, surfing down the long rollers in the deep water, then struggling up the shifting water hills. Between the Bass Rip line and McBlair's Shoal, Walter Chase first saw the masts of the wreck. She was at the south end of Rose and Crown, probably in that one-fathom spot there, and leaning to the south perhaps twenty degrees. He headed a bit more southerly and they left the choppy white smother of McBlair's Shoal behind.

Now the three masts were clearly visible. The vessel lay roughly east and west with her stern to Nantucket. She had struck and then bilged, and now the waves were breaking cleanly over her. They had driven the hull over to starboard so that a spectacular line of surf would suddenly appear all along her port side that canted up to face the seas. They were too far away to count the men, but Chase could see dark forms in the ratlines. He peered intently at the wreck. Was it shifting now? It was a bad stranding! If she were facing the seas, even quartering, but broadside they were wrenching her. And the tide was coming. The seas would enlarge and she'd be hit even harder. Chase peered and peered at the wreck, and the surfboat drove along the line made by his eyes.

Chase Two was aware of the *H.P. Kirkham* in a total sense. She was not going to stay together any longer. Chase Two detected unbalanced forces within the ship-sand-wind-water field matrix. He penetrated the force structure around the *Kirkham*, but there was no TIME! The surfboat was running down the seas. The *Kirkham* was twisting as the combers, steepened and shortened by the shoal, boarded her with shuddering blows. Chase Two clinched, and time flowed more slowly. The waves moved like molasses. The shocks were stretched out, and he could trace the force imbalances. SLOWER! He could not speed the finite duration of impulses flowing between his billions of neural cells, but he could slow time and process data that way. Fiercely he clinched. Time, he realized, could be traded for information. He saw the *Kirkham* completely, and yet simultaneously in every relevant detail. The mizzenmast was shaky, split. Not much had shown on the mast's surface, but now the stick was resonating with the wind, and the splitting was worse. It would soon bring down the main and foremast, and the men as well.

There was no solution within the energy matrix alone, and neither time nor information domains extended directly into the energy system. The mast would have to be replaced.

Chase Two stooped like a hawk down the *Kirkham's* time line. He saw her leave Rose and Crown Shoal and flow backwards to Halifax and leave her lading. Then faster, backwards to other voyages in her brief year of life. Now the masts were out and the hull was coming apart on the stocks of a boatyard near the tiny town of Liverpool on the south coast of Nova Scotia. The masts suddenly grew branches, and in a twinkling, Chase Two watched a French timber cruiser looking up at a tall pine deep in the Nova Scotia forests. The cruiser turned to his associate, the shipyard boss's young son on his first wood-buying trip into the woods. "By gar, dat's one fine tree, eh?"

The young man nodded. It was the tallest in the area. But now Chase Two showed the Frenchman something he had not seen before, that other time. The tree had been struck by lightning. The scar was grown over, but you could just make it out curling from the top and disappearing around the trunk.

"Look," said the timber cruiser. "Dat tree been struck. We walk around." And on the other side they saw the faint scar traveling down to the ground. "Risky, dose ones," said the Frenchman in a superior way. "Hmmmmm." And as he looked around, Chase Two showed him a shorter but perfectly branched mast tree on the other side of the clearing, and the French cruiser pointed and smiled. "Not so beeg, dat one, but plenty tough, I teenk."

And back down the time line, Chase Two dropped like a stone. He saw the new mizzen erected on the Liverpool ways, then, faster and faster, the loading and unloading and movement until the *Kirkham* again struck on Rose and Crown Shoal, bilged, and lay through the stormy night with her men in her rigging.

When Keeper Chase learned that informational and temporal entropy flows could be interchanged, his power to influence events grew at an unprecedented pace. In the course of replacing the *Kirkham's* mast, Keeper Chase solved a variety of hydrodynamic and structural problems of extreme complexity and entirely by inspection and processing of data. Much more significant, he dealt surely with the philosophical and practical problems of time-information interchange and realized that if time flow could be slowed, it could be controlled in other ways. His ability to arrest time flow within his local region was now so pronounced that a detectable chronologic entropy gradient existed within the entire continuum.

The surfboat blew down on the stricken schooner from the north, heading directly for her battered port side, where white spume flew up twenty feet or more when a big wave took her full on.

"You bow men," shouted Walter Chase. "Get the anchor ready." The positioning had to be done correctly the first time. There would be no clawing back up from the schooner's lee to reanchor if they did it badly. Walter Chase watched the choppy, surging space shorten between the surfboat and the schooner. The current was running to the northeast with the wind a bit west of north and the waves about from due north. He decided to anchor upwind of the vessel's stern and then lay back south and easterly to come under the mainmast and her center ratlines, where the crew was now clustered.

Chase's small eyes gleamed in the gray, dull light. He watched the distance shorten and the schooner widen and her masts grow up and, in them, the men now clearly seen.

"Watch your head, Jesse!" shouted Walter Chase. "We're rounding up now!" He put the steering oar hard over, and again it formed a bow of iron-hard hickory, arched against the forces that drove the boat halfway around, heeling and wallowing wildly until it faced the screaming wind and sharp seas. "Anchor over!" shouted Walter Chase, then, "Oars out, all of you!"

They were up on the thwarts holding her head against the wind as she slipped back with Perkins paying out the anchor line over a smooth, maple cleat. The surfboat lay on her tether about southeast, and Walter Chase guided her back and back until they were a few yards from the schooner and just beyond where the big rollers broke and shuddered the vessel all along her length. The surge was ten feet or more. The surfboat lay down in a trough, and they could look up and see several feet of the schooner's side, then up until they were above the rail and a great wave was sliding out from under them and creaming white and lovely over the vessel's port rail in a burst of foam and a sound of roaring and groaning that made Walter Chase flinch his cheek muscles, for he knew how weak the schooner was.

Chase cupped his hands and bellowed directly into the wind. "Perkins, throw them the heaving stick."

Perkins heard and readied the stick and its loops of line. The surge picked the surfboat up, and as they came level with the schooner's rail, Perkins hurled the stick into the rigging, with the thin line paying smoothly out behind in a graceful arc. One of the crew crawled up the ratlines to where the stick was entangled in the shrouds and turned toward the surfboat.

"You . . . bend a line on that! Use your topsail clew line." The roar of Walter Chase's voice flew downwind, and in moments, the clew line was fast to the stick, and back it came, hand by hand, through the smother to Perkins, who bent it on the same cleat as the anchor warp.

The other end of the clew line was in the hands of the sailor and two others who had crawled over to join him. Walter Chase shouted again. "Tie that line to a shroud, you men!"

They stared stupidly at him, and sudden spray flew up in their faces. Walter Chase turned back to Perkins. "Start to haul in on that slowly. You rowers, ease us toward her side."

But the schooner's crew had waited long enough, and they, or three of them, began to pull fiercely on the clew line themselves. Walter Chase felt the boat jerk roughly toward the schooner and begin a deep roll broadside in a trough. He crammed the steering oar violently over and spun around, pointing at the schooner. "Stop hauling! Stop, I say! Make your end fast. If you make one more pull on that line, we'll cut it!" And as he spoke, Chase pulled a big clasp knife from his slicker pocket and opened the blade with a snick that pierced the duller voice of the gale. Then he passed the big silver knife forward to Perkins, who brandished it above the clew line. The men on the schooner saw the great dark figure with the knife and heard the huge voice driven down by the wind, and they tied off the line and huddled, dully watching the Coskata crew, using both rope and oars, begin to move toward the wreck.

Suddenly the schooner shuddered and inexplicably rolled to windward. She came almost upright and then went back over to starboard, stopping her breathtaking swing at the same list as before. The mizzen gaff snapped off and fell, thudding against its mast on the way down. The schooner began another roll to port, and Perkins looked directly at the men in the ratlines, and his eyes and theirs met. He remembered a Sunday six years ago when, after church, he and his mother had driven in the wagon over to Little Mioxes Pond where, everyone said, a large vessel had blown ashore. They had spent the day with hundreds of others watching the men in the rigging, too weak to grasp the lines shot over the vessel by the surfside crew, falling one after another into the raging sea. The vessel had stranded well out so the crew were only small black figures and they did not move very much when they fell, but Perkins never after that time shot another crow or grackle with the .22 Winchester pump that his mother had saved for a year to buy him. Even if they were just birds, they fell the same way, black against the far sky. And now these men were about to fall, blackly still, but he would see their eyes clearly this time.

"Gawd help us, Skipper! She'll shake her sticks out!" shouted Perkins in a choking, coughing voice, strident with terror.

Walter Chase had followed that roll with bright, keen eyes. She could not withstand much more of that! "No!" he said sharply.

Chase Three surveyed the flow field under the wreck and processed the observations. He clamped intensely on the time flow, and the *Kirkham* was motionless in a sea of stationary fluid and a sky of stationary wind. He explored the flow characteristics of the near shores in every particular, considering the special character of the *Kirkham's* fields of forces. The current, shifting clockwise during the flood as it did in the area, had undermined the sand bed on which the *Kirkham* lay. But worse, the current, now running more and more counter to the wind, was moving the hull as well.

Chase Three considered how the force and energy relationships could be corrected. The wind was beyond manipulation, deriving as it did from such a disparate mass of variables as to make significant time-based alteration impractical. But the flows of gravity and wind-driven water were another matter. As Chase Three studied these fields of flow, he gradually realized that the natural relationships allowed a bifurcation within the viscosity functions. There were at least two flow-field configurations that had equal probability, and most important, either could exist with no change in total energy level within the continuum. The present field system allowed a strong easterly current to move in over the shoal against the *Kirkham*, but with the alternate field the flow would be slightly damped and diverted more northerly, and the wind force on the schooner would be sufficient to hold her against the sand and damp the roll forces.

Since there was no energy gradient involved, Chase Three immediately altered the continuum to the new flow field, this information gradient being offset by the altered time flow in the local area. The *Kirkham* shuddered but did not roll again.

With his introduction of the Chase Field into the information matrix of our continuum, Keeper Chase was reaching the peak of his astonishing powers. That any alternate description of the fluid-dynamic field existed was not even known, and that Keeper Chase should have found a solution at equal energies was quite marvelous. He did not, when utilizing time-information entropy balances to make the shift, consider that these same laws govern the development and evolution of galactic and supra-galactic motion and that the field shift must occur there as well. Thus Keeper Chase, in addition to sustaining an extraordinary temporal gradient within the continuum, had now inadvertently but irrevocably altered the way in which the energy universe would develop. Those time-using peoples who existed outside the gradient now convened and considered the immediate situation. We too could work within altered time, but the randomness of what was occurring put us beyond normal information transfer procedures. The storm on the Nantucket South Shoals had spawned a gradient storm in time itself. If the rescue attempt should become unlikely within any statistically allowed alternate energy structure, we would have to consider Keeper Chase's reaction to that perception and what an impossible but certainly powerful reaction by Keeper Chase to breach the energy-time-information barriers would cause within these boundaries.

Perkins, bent in a fit of coughing, saw that the schooner was stationary again. "Cathcart," shouted Walter Chase. "Bend a bowline in our painter and get ready to heave it over."

Now they edged closer, hanging like a lunging pony against the whipping anchor line. "Throw!" shouted Chase and the line flew across. "One man at a time," shouted Chase down the screaming wind to the schooner. "Put that bight around your waist."

A large, hulking Negro who had caught the painter passed it to a smaller figure, evidently the cabin boy. The youngster put the line over his head and waited, staring frozenly into the wind.

"Now . . ." and Chase's voice boomed under and around the wind's cry. "When I say jump, you come! You hear!"

The boy nodded, staring out at the marching lines of water foaming towards them.

"Cathcart, haul us in a bit . . . Now, steady, boys!" The surfboat was caught by a comber and lifted, up and up, and the wave was pushing the boat toward the schooner. They were on the peak and the curl was slipping past.

"JUMP!"

The boy flung himself off the ratlines, his legs flailing. Cathcart and Perkins handed in the painter as he fell, thudding, into the space between the bow and center thwarts. "Ease that bow line quick!" shouted Walter Chase, and the surfboat lay off to the east before an early break could turn them over at the schooner's rail.

The boy looked up from the floorboards, his ankle hurting, his teeth chattering; and over him loomed a gigantic figure, sideburns wild and blustery, eyes small and intensely bright, beacons against the wild gray sky. "We count six more, son. Have you lost anyone yet?"

Somehow the boy was able to speak. "No, sir. Seven in all. The cap'n—the cap'n ain't so well. We—we been in the rigging since eight last night. Gawd, it's . . ."

"What ship?" asked George Flood, turning suddenly around.

"*H.P. Kirkham*," said the boy. "From Halifax with fish. Bound to New York."

Walter Chase stood up. "Let's get the next one. You starboard rowers, bring us in slow. Cathcart, bring her head in."

Each time, they approached the *Kirkham* and waited for the proper wave to lift them up and slide the boat close. Then a black tumbling figure would come down into the surfboat every which way, limp with fear and exhaustion and dazed by the sudden, unexpected hope.

Now there were three left and the surfboat rolled more heavily and more water slopped over the gunwales. "Sir," shouted the cabin boy. "I think the cap'n's coming next. They're going to have to sort o' throw him."

Walter Chase peered at the three figures in the ratlines. The wind had slackened a bit and it seemed brighter. He could see an old man, conscious but unable to hold his head up, supported and held against the ratlines by a huge Negro and another big man in bulky clothes. "Josiah, Johnny . . . get ready to help when this fellow comes across."

The center rowers shipped oars and waited. Cathcart carefully pulled them in, a bit at a time. Then he cleated the clew line and hurled the painter back across the foamy gap. They put the loop over the old man's head and shoulders. The boat was rising. "Get ready!" shouted Walter Chase to the three men. "Now!"

The two men threw the captain feet first into the boat. He came down crossways, catching John Nyman across the cheek with his fist as he fell. His head thumped a thwart and he slumped, a bundle of rags, into the bottom of the boat.

Walter Chase quickly knelt and lifted the old man's head. "Keeper Walter Chase. Coskata Life Saving Station. Can you understand me, Captain?"

The old man, his whiskers white with frost and brown with frozen tobacco juice and spittle, stared back unseeing. "Aye. Captain McCloud, master, *H. P. Kirkham* out of Nova Scotia. Thank God . . ."

Chase's eyes pierced the old man's own eyes, and he nodded. "Captain McCloud, we cannot save your vessel. She is breaking up and this storm will grow worse by nightfall."

"I know," said McCloud and his head fell forward and his eyes shut and he shivered in cold and pain and despair. Then . . . "This bloody, foul, awful coast!" His eyes briefly lost their dullness. "Worse than Scotland! Worse than the Channel! These rotting shoals stick out so bleeding far . . . God Almighty . . ." The effort exhausted him. He did not speak again.

The next man was the first mate, hard, grizzled; Cockney-tough enough to sit up after his jump and stare at the young, slender Perkins, bent over in a fit of coughing. "Well, you blokes don't look like bloody much, but you bloomin' well know your business out here!"

And on their final surge up over the schooner's rail the huge black crewman flew between the great and little boats with a sudden grace, and he, like the mate, sat up immediately and peered about from huge white eyes. But he said nothing.

"Now, lads," boomed Walter Chase, as the surfboat lay off easterly, bobbing and pitching in the smother like a logy cork. "Oars out. We got to clear this shallows afore the wind comes on. Lively now."

The four stern oarsmen pulled mightily while Perkins and Cathcart heaved on the anchor warp. Slowly they moved to windward, their efforts sending rivers of sweat inside the heavy sweaters and slickers in the twelve-degree, forty-knot blast.

"Anchor up, Skipper!" shouted Cathcart while Perkins suddenly bent double, both hands over his mouth.

Walter Chase looked back, his side whiskers black spikes, his huge slicker masking the *Kirkham*. He hated to give the gale an inch, but to get past her stern to the west would be a near thing, and the wind was rising again. He put the steering oar over and they fell off on a big soft wave to starboard. "Pull, boys, we got to stay ahead of these combers."

They rowed eastward, then more southerly and cleared the *Kirkham*'s smashed and sagging bow by forty feet. Walter Chase put his oar to starboard and they pulled under the schooner's lee. It was easier there. The schooner was acting as a breakwater, taking the big ones before they reached the surfboat, and they pulled strongly to the west, the wind hard and vicious on their starboard quarter and the sea confused and breaking everywhere, an endless mouth filled with shifting teeth.

But once beyond the schooner's length it was impossible. Chase put her more toward the south, taking the wind on the beam with the current still northeast and running those great, curling rips in the very shallow spots.

"Jesse," said Walter Chase, leaning forward. "We got to clear this shoal afore the high tide this afternoon. Them rollers'll start to break and we couldn't lay at anchor. And the wind's making up again. Them clouds are coming back."

Jesse Eldridge only nodded. He was pulling too hard to talk. They were moving southeast, but only barely. The *Kirkham* was close behind them, and the surfboat was slopping about, taking splash on every wave.

Walter Chase looked at the men they had rescued. His little bright eyes fixed on the first mate and the Negro, their heads buried in coats against the chill. "You fellers. Yank that sail and mast out of there and pitch it over the side. Our sailing days are done!"

The men moved slowly, as best they could, helped by a hand from this or that rower, and finally the outfit went over the side in a piecemeal fashion, trailing astern and finally pulling loose.

George Flood looked up and winked at Walter Chase. "Skipper," he panted, "how you going to explain throwing that valuable govinmint property over the side to the inspector?"

Walter Chase, at that moment fighting a great, half-breaking wave that threatened to broach the surfboat, suddenly winked a gleaming eye back. "George, I'll just tell that feller that we met this here bureaucrat adrift on his very own desk looking for Washington, D.C., and we just plumb did the Christian thing and loaned him our sail."

Charles Cathcart, leaning intently forward as he pulled, burst into a roar of laughter. "Hell's fire, Skipper! They'd just say you didn't get him to fill in the right forms."

Perkins's oar trailed astern, and he leaned over the side, vomiting and coughing great, deep, sharp barks above the gale. Cathcart reached towards him, and the surfboat lost way and began to bounce and shift southerly into the troughs. Walter Chase looked piercingly at his men. They *must* clear the shoal now. It would only get worse.

Chase Four entered Perkins's continuity of self-awareness. The boy was sick, probably pneumonia, for his lungs were very wet. He was beaten. The cockney mate's praise had got him through the anchor recover, but now he was completely involved with his cough and nausea.

Chase Four dropped down Perkins's time line seeking a point that would reverberate with the *Kirkham* rescue. . . .

Each year on the last day of July along the islands, the life-saving crews return from a two-month off-duty period to a ten-month routine of patrols and watches. On that night the previous summer, the Coskata crew had produced their usual party. They had hired a banjo and violin from town, asked their wives, relatives, friends, and suppliers to the festive evening, and cleared out the dark apparatus room of its large gear. Colored streamers hung from the suspended life car, and festoons of buoys made arches beneath which the dancers turned. The girls, slim and pretty in ankle-length dresses, puffed sleeves, and swinging hair ringlets, smiled at the tall men in their government blue. Before the light went, they trooped outside to the breeches buoy training tower, and the girls climbed, one above the other up the ladder, and all looked back smiling while George Flood pressed his Kodak button and gave a happy shout.

But the prettiest there was Abigail Coffin with Roland Perkins. When the others returned in the dusk to the laughter and screech of the fiddler's bow, he caught her arm. "Let's go look at the ocean, Abby," he said. She was the nicest girl in the town, always smiling, her eyes so bright and full; and as they walked away from the station, Perkins could barely breathe, his chest was so full of love and hope. "Abby . . . could I . . . would you . . . ?" and he leaned toward her and brought his other arm up behind her back.

Chase Four did not wait for the sharp and hurtful reaction; he had skimmed by it once. Instead, he showed Abby Coffin that Roland Perkins was actually a fine, handsome boy. As she looked at him, she realized how sensitive and brave he would always be, how good and gentle his thoughts were toward her. She turned her face upward and they kissed. Later, under a bright moon, she said breathlessly, "Yes, you can touch me there, Roland."

Perkins, his coughing fit mastered, nodded at Cathcart and began to row strongly. Walter Chase urged them on. "We got to make some depth, boys." Perkins, grinning to himself, pulled and pulled. He knew they would get these men back. Chase was too good a boatman to fail, whatever the wind. They would all get government medals. And he thought of Abby and the medal and how she would hold him when he told her. Slowly the surfboat left the *Kirkham* behind.

George Flood's eyes popped open. "Look back quick, Skipper!" he shouted. Walter Chase spun around. In that instant, the *Kirkham* was dissolving. Her foremast was halfway down, with her main following. The taut and snapping shrouds ripped the quarter-boards completely off the starboard side, and the deck buckled in several large pieces. The mizzen fell, and before it struck the water, the entire hull had disappeared. She had gone like smoke in a gale. Flood looked up at Walter Chase. "Dang lucky we didn't wait for another cup of coffee at the station, Skipper!" he shouted.

Walter Chase, fighting the steering oar continually in the heavy and confused seas, still stared back at the unchecked rollers now streaming over the *Kirkham*'s last berth. They had taken the last man off less than an hour before. His eyes narrowed and he wondered about the rescue. Everything was so damn near, so chancy.

The Coskata crew rowed and rowed on Rose and Crown Shoal. Sometimes the boat moved west and sometimes it paused and pitched. Noon was past and the sky had darkened again. The wind was rising with the tide, but they were slowly getting into deeper water, into the twelve-fathom channel that cut aimlessly between Rose and Crown and Bass Rip. The waves were longer and not so steep, but the wind was too heavy. They were hardly moving and the men were exhausted. And the current had revolved almost due easterly and was actually setting them back away from Nantucket. This would have to do for now.

"Cathcart! We got to anchor. Handy now!" They lay back with the winds hammering their starboard quarter, all the scope they could muster laid out to their biggest anchor. The men slumped over their shipped oars while Walter Chase shoved the steering oar this way and that, using the current run to steer his boat up and over the combers. The wind was building again, and its scream and slash was icy and terrible. Jesse Eldridge, hunched in a nest of sweaters and slicker, looked up at Walter Chase. "Skipper, we didn't even make a mile in three hours. You think that tug'll get out here?"

"I figure he will as long as he thinks there might be some loot on the schooner, Jesse," said Walter Chase. He sensed, in fact, that the tug would not come into these wild shoals. Bitterly he thought of the wonderful strength of her cross-compound steam engine driving that big powerful screw. Yellow, rotten cowards!

What was the point of even building such a vessel if you could not find men to man it? The surfboat jumped and tugged at the snapping anchor line, while the crew bailed as the spume and spray came in on them with every wave. Perkins and Cathcart gently tended the anchor line, wrapping it in rags, shifting it a few inches now and then to relieve the chafing.

The sky grew darker as the afternoon wore on and the wind built up again. There was so much agitation and violent activity, so many unexpected swoops and thumps, so many waves that appeared from odd directions and with surprising steepness.

Chase pulled and fought the oar, staring out at the screaming bowl of energy around him while a coldness and fierceness steadied his heart and mind. He would bring these men home, all of them. Nothing anywhere was more important than that. The tug, the lifesaving service, the men at their desks in Washington and Boston, the sea and its commerce, the life cars and motor-driven surfboats, the rescues of the past and future, men adrift on the seas of the world and foundering forever in the gales and currents along the coasts, meant nothing beside these few in the Coskata surfboat. He focused his great strength on this single purpose and found a balance between the forces of the storm and his own resolve. They pitched and waited in the freezing blast for the tide to turn.

Dusk comes early to Nantucket in January, and it was almost dark by the time the surfboat had swung clockwise on her tether and now lay a bit west of south. Chase knew they had to go whenever the tide could drive them, and he shouted and joshed the men. Tiredly they put out oars, pulled up the anchor, then struggled off to the west. Chase used his rowers to hold a northerly set, counting on the southeast current to give them a general westerly direction. They took plenty of slop with the waves on their starboard bow, and Chase urged the *Kirkham*'s mate and her black crewman to bailing. The boat moved into deeper water, and as the night came on, Chase suddenly saw, on the very rim of his world, the tiny, flashing point of Sankaty Light.

"Hey, boys!" he shouted. "There's old Sankaty and Joe Remsen having fried bluefish for supper with a bit of Medford rum and lime in hot water."

"Dang me, Skipper," said George Flood, "I wouldn't mind the rum, but Joe can keep the bluefish."

"George," said Walter Chase shaking his head sadly, "I can't make out how you fellers can call yourselves Nantucketers when you like that awful, smelly cod better'n a little fried blue."

This discussion, which ebbed and flowed at the station depending on who was cook that week, somehow cheered Jesse Eldridge immensely. "Walter," he said, loudly and firmly, "even them rich Boston summer folk won't give a nickel a pound for blues. You know that as well as I do."

Chase leaned on the oar and turned them a bit more northerly, staring off at the lighthouse. He roared with laughter. "Jesse, them Boston folk smack their lips over three-day boiled cabbage and corn beef, flaked cod that would turn a hog's stomach, and fin and haddy so hard it would break a shark's jaw. Hell's delight, they wouldn't even *notice* a nice hot little blue laying in a nest of parsley, new potatoes, and melted butter."

They rowed on and on toward the light, and the men turned now and then to stare at the pinpoint, so bright and yet so tiny against the black swirl of wind. When they turned back to where the *Kirkham* had been, they saw answering bright and tiny spots in Walter Chase's eyes somehow reflecting and focusing Sankaty.

By ten that night the wind was blowing a three-quarter gale, and the current was rotating to the northeast. They could not go against it, and Walter Chase ordered the anchor down again. Now the wind, filled with a fitful snow, was bitter, and the men slumped against each other, their sweat drying coldly under their clothes, their heads nodding. Chase continually worked the steering oar, roused the men as they drifted off into frozen sleep, ordered the bow crewmen to watch the chafing of the line, and continually rotated his head seeking the great seas moving in the dark. They suddenly appeared as dim, faintly phosphorescent mountains that dashed out of and into the dark at terrifying speeds.

In the intense and shouting dark, the seas loomed huge and unsuspected. There was a wildness about them, a wholly random cruelty. The storm had blown for two days and unusual current motions had been set going. Walter Chase's head swiveled back and forth. He sensed the movement, the surge and backflow. The chill ate at his bones, but his own cold resolve was more arctic still.

Chase Five examined the lumpy and stationary sea. He then examined the rate of change of the water profiles. This was a deadly business! The circulation due to wind stress had rotated the current further than usual to the east. This set up a possible amplification with the flow between Bass Rip and McBlair's Shoal. There was a statistical possibility of one or more resonant occurrences that night! Yet they were still relatively unlikely. No! Chase Five clamped the time flow even tighter and increased the gradient. Within minutes a resonance would actually occur! The wave would build at the north end of Rose and Crown, receiving energy from the cross flow and a sudden wind gust stress. It would break in a mile-long line just north of them and reach them cresting at eighteen feet. The chance of their staying upright was one in three. The chance of their not swamping was . . . nil!

Chase Five, within the theoretical bounds set by entropy flow requirements, stopped time utterly. The continuum waited as Chase Five's neural interconnections achieved a higher level of synthesis. He saw a single possibility. If this resonant wave was unlikely enough . . . yes . . . that was it! Extreme value probability theory could be modified within the time domain, providing that no significantly less likely event was occurring at that instant in the energy continuum. He could lower the expectation and make the wave more unlikely without interaction within the energy domain. Furthermore, it was not just the wave itself that was unlikely, but the wave interpreted by Chase Five, himself a most unlikely event.

That was it! He changed the probabilities, and the wave, instead of building towards its terrifying height, received its new energies at slightly different times and . . . No!

The wave was suddenly building again! Chase Five sensed some other manipulation. Staggered, he clamped tightly on the time flow and asked his first question: "Who?"

When Keeper Chase modified the laws of extreme value probability within the continuum, he forced us time-using observers to become participants in his struggle with the storm. While highly unlikely events occur infrequently, they exercise a hugely disproportionate effect on the evolution of the continuum. Just as a coastline on Keeper Chase's world will lie unchanged for a hundred years, to be altered drastically by a single unlikely storm lasting a few hours, so the improbable but possible events in the evolution of stellar and information systems often determine the long-term character of huge volumes of energy and temporal space. We could not, then, allow such essential probabilities to be manipulated at the whim of energy storms and energy-users. Thus we intervened and canceled the change. Keeper Chase detected us at once and asked his first question. We decided to answer him . . . almost totally.

* * *

Chase Five received the full brunt of the information dump. Like the sky falling in from every angle, the answer to his question flowed faster than thought into his mind. It was an implosion of data, a total, sudden awareness of the continuum, of time and energy and information and their interactions. Of worlds and stars, creatures and spaces, hidden truths and intricate insights.

Chase Five was staggered. He clamped on the time flow and tried to organize it all. Like a swimmer, thrown deeply into the dark blue of the deep ocean, he fought and rose toward the light of day, moving through a boundless mass of data. Yet what was happening? Why was he so deeply involved with these others? How did the *Kirkham*, one in ten thousand among such schooners, and these men, a few among millions, come to be at the center of all this? Chase Five assimilated the focal points of the continuum, but he did not yet understand himself or the nature of his adversaries. Clamping and clamping on the time stream, he desperately asked his second question:

"God?"

Irony, in the sense understood by those in Keeper Chase's world group, is not a normal component of time-using organizations and duties. Yet Keeper Chase's second question to us achieved the exact essence of that special quality. For if there was a single conscious entity within the entire continuum at the moment who qualified as "God," in the sense of Keeper Chase's question, it was Keeper Chase himself. We could not determine how large an information excess Keeper Chase could tolerate, but his confusion seemed to offer us an opportunity. We responded with the remaining information that we had withheld the first time: we showed Keeper Chase how the continuum was organized within its various aspects and, finally, the nature of consciousness within this organization and its relationship with the information, time, and energy aspects of the whole.

The second dump of information was not as extensive, but far more staggering. For Chase Five finally saw himself within the total continuum. He saw the circularity and hermetic nature of his activity at the *Kirkham*, the unlikely, really senseless character of the rescue and how unimportant, really meaningless were the men now barely alive in the wet and pitching boat. Good Lord, what was the point anyway? His control wavered and time began to slip. The wind moved back towards its own natural pace. The seas became more independent. . . .

Now wait! Chase Five, in his puzzlement and despair, still processed data. And suddenly he saw the fallacy, the problem with their attacks against him. He steadied and clamped time. Yes! Yes, of course! He was stronger! The circularity didn't matter! What mattered was *only* the event! Everything led to that. And the more *unlikely* it was, the more *essential* it became. Yes! He, Walter Chase, Keeper of the Coskata Life Saving Station, was exactly and completely his own justification. And now Chase Five struck back at them. Masterful in his total control of information, gigantic astride the interlaced worlds of energy and time, he stated his third and final question. But because he completely dominated the continuum in all its aspects, he no longer asked. For he knew with complete certainty that none of them could deny what he stated.

"I am central to the evolution of the continuum. My control and my improbability are proof of that!"

At once the growing wave received its various inputs in harmless and likely sequences and passed under the Coskata boat as a huge but almost unnoticed roller. And with that, the storm on the Nantucket South Shoals began to die. For it, like all storms, had to obey the laws of probabilities, and after two harsh days, it was moving off and softening as it went.

Walter Chase, the steering oar now inboard as the wind slackened, saw that dawn and the new tide were coming together. "All right, boys! This time we'll get there!" he shouted. In came the anchor and off they went, the great seas cresting no longer, the wind lessening, and the temperature rising as snow squalls came and went, gray against a dull dawn.

On and on they rowed, and Walter Chase now became aware that Perkins looked odd. His eyes were shining, liquid and bright, and his cheeks were much too red and also shining strangely. The boy rowed as strongly as any, but Chase watched him with more and more concern.

"Perkins," shouted Walter Chase, "see if that mate from the *Kirkham* can relieve you for a while."

But Perkins was thinking of Abby on the beach. She would probably be there when they came in, for her brother was in the surfside crew and he would have told her that they were out. "I'm okay, Skipper," he said in a voice that Chase could barely hear. Chase peered through the snow at the rowers. Perkins was very sick. Perkins must . . .

Chase Six realized that Perkins was dying. The boy's level of consciousness integration had slipped drastically. Desperate, Chase Six plummeted down Perkins's time line seeking solutions everywhere. But the lessening of the storm had sapped his abilities. He could no longer clamp on time or integrate his hard-won information to tasks like this. Yet his very agony gave him the control to achieve the data that crushed, and crushed again, his hopes. How tenuous and marvelous self-awareness was in the continuum! How delicate, beyond yet embedded within the energy system, linked with loops of information, operating within and yet outside of time. Perkins had driven himself, and been driven by Chase, beyond reintegration. And yet Perkins was filled with joy! Within himself, Chase Six finally wept. And as he did, his powers fled away in an unending stream like the fog of a harsh night evaporating as the morning sun pierced through and through it.

Keeper Chase's great time-based powers failed as the emergency abated. Unable to maintain the temporal gradient without the urgency of the storm, he could no longer retrieve or even sustain his vast information resource in any practical sense. Yet he had defeated us and dominated the continuum at almost every moment of his adventure. Staggered after his second question and the implications of our answers, he went on to his final and greatest feat. He dared us to prove that he was not an essential evolutionary force within the continuum. Since such a determination would require understanding of other continuums, if such exist, and that necessary understanding would involve an information entropy gradient so vast that it could not even be theoretically sustained, he effectively blocked all further intervention.

But in the end he could not save his youngest crewman. He learned that conscious self-awareness is the most improbable and delicate balance of all within the continuum. Even his great strengths could not bring Surfman Perkins back from the temporal disintegration toward which he had slipped. If the energy-users of Keeper Chase's world group understood how novel and tenuous such consciousness actually is, they would surely behave far differently than they do.

The actual effects of his alterations within the continuum will only become evident in distant times and through much statistical activity on our part. But his greatest effect was the introduction of his third question, to which we may never have a complete or satisfactory answer. Of course, the so-called heroes of Keeper Chase's world group always have this as their primary purpose—that is, the introduction of central and intractable questions.

At a little after nine in the morning of the twenty-first of January, the Coskata boat was sighted through the fading snow from the bluffs of Siasconset, eight miles south of the shore they had left the day before. Soon the entire community was out on the beach, silently watching the surfboat moving toward them, steered by Walter Chase standing at the stern.

The 'Sconset schoolteacher, a young, thin man who had spent two years reading literature at Harvard College, ran up the bluff, a dozen children behind him. As he topped the rise, the thin sun suddenly pierced the damp air and illuminated the tiny boat and its huge captain, looming back even a half mile out.

"Godfreys mighty!" exclaimed the young man to no one in particular. "It's Captain Ahab himself!" for he believed that literature and life were contiguous.

"Naw, tain't," said Widow Tilton. "Hit's Skipper Chase and the Coskata surfboat." She turned to stare at the young man and laughed. "Hit's the only red surfboat around. Skipper painted it red after the Muskeget boat was almost lost in the ice last December, 'cause no one could see it. They wrote from Boston. Said it was nonregulation. Skipper Chase, he wrote back. Don't remember all he wrote, but there was something in his letter about them desk navigators whose experience with ice amounted to sucking it out of their whiskey and sodas at lunch."

The schoolteacher had been only half listening, but now he turned and grinned at Widow Tilton. "He said that to them, did he?" The young man stared again at the approaching boat and then ran down the sand hill. "Come on, boys!" he shouted back at his class. "Let's help get this boat up!"

The Coskata boat grounded silently in a long swell, and a huge crowd waded into the backwash and pulled her up the slick sand. Everyone tried to help the men get out, yet still no one cheered. Instead, soft and kind words flew everywhere, and joy and comfort seemed to warm the very beach.

Walter Chase boomed at the Macy boys to get their oxen and haul the boat up to the dunes. Then he turned and saw Perkins helped and held by Abby Coffin. The boy could no longer speak. Chase smiled at the girl. "Abby, don't take him home. Get him to your sister-in-law's house here in 'Sconset and put him to bed. Get him warm, quick as you can!"

But Abby knew. She could see the emptiness in Roland Perkins's eyes, his fevered cheeks. She wept, so full of grief and pride and love that she could not speak either. But always afterwards she remembered how sharp and yet sad Skipper Chase's eyes had been when he spoke to her and how completely he dominated the beach in those moments at the end of the rescue.

"Isaiah!" shouted Walter Chase. The youngster dashed up, beaming all over his face, so proud that Skipper Chase had picked him out of the great crowd.

"Yessir, Skipper!" He grinned.

"How's that hoss of yours, Isaiah?" said Walter Chase, and now he grinned too.

"Fastest hoss on Nantucket, Skipper," replied the boy promptly. "She'll win at the summer fair for sure!"

"Well, you climb aboard that nag and hustle for town. Find my wife and tell her we got back safe. Then find the rest of them. You know where the crew's folks live?"

The boy nodded and dashed off. Everyone was now moving up the beach toward the village. Each crewman of the *Kirkham* or man of Coskata was surrounded by residents helping them along, throwing coats or blankets over their shoulders, talking at them about the impossible miracle of the rescue.

Captain McCloud of the *Kirkham* staggered along between his huge black crewman and the Widow Tilton, herself well over six feet and two hundred and fifty pounds. Suddenly the old man pitched forward on his knees, pulling the weakened Negro down with him. "Dear God!" he shouted. "Thank Thee for this deliverance! Thank Thee for sparing Thy humble servants. Thank Thee . . ."

Widow Tilton pulled the old man to his feet and, looking back, saw Walter Chase, huge against the dull sun, his tiny eyes like daytime stars. "You better not worry about thanking God, mister," she suddenly said loudly. "It was Skipper Chase got you back here, and don't ever forget that!"

"Walter." It was his uncle beside him. "When they said you was coming in, I put on a gallon of coffee. Come on. Why, man, you're shaking like a leaf!"

Indeed, Walter Chase suddenly was shaking. He could not stop it, and he let his uncle lead him over the dune and down to the little house with its roaring driftwood-filled fire and the huge blackened pot of powerful coffee.

"Uncle," said Walter Chase as he sipped from a huge mug, "I'm shaking so damn much I've got to drink this outside."

He opened the door and stepped back into the narrow, rutted 'Sconset street just as Joe Remsen, sharp in his blue uniform and issue cap, driving the dapper black and gold-trimmed buggy of the Light House Service, pulled by a smart, high-stepping bay, whirled around the corner and pulled up short in a cloud of dust.

"God in Heaven, Walter!" shouted Joe Remsen. "You all did get back!"

Walter Chase, his huge hands still shaking continuously in the thin, cold morning, looked smiling up at his old friend. "Joe, that's just the handsomest one-hoss outfit on the island," he said simply.

"Walter, they say she came apart less than an hour after you got them off! I saw her masts go down at noon yesterday from the tower!"

Walter Chase stretched suddenly and stared, quite piercingly, back at Joe Remsen. "Well," he said, "we didn't need her after the crew got off, did we, Joe?"

At the time his old friend thought Walter Chase was joking, and he laughed out loud. But thinking back on that moment in later years, he realized that Walter Chase had meant what he said. The *Kirkham* had been allowed to collapse because she somehow wasn't *needed* any more. Yet he never asked about it again, but only wondered.

Joe Remsen climbed down from the buggy and shook his head. "We figured you were goners. That damn tug went as far as Great Point and then turned back last night. Too blamed rough, they said, the rotten cowards! By God, Walter, there won't never be another rescue like this one! You better believe that! They're going to build that canal one of these days. Them gasoline engines'll get better and they'll put them in the surfboats. God Almighty, you took seven of them off. Not one lost. Twenty-six hours out in that smother! It's a miracle! Why, man, you moved heaven and earth . . ."

The hot coffee drained its warmth through Walter Chase, and suddenly he felt drowsy. "Joe, we never did try a drail for squeteague out there. Just too blamed busy the whole time . . ."

And the two old friends grinned and chuckled at each other in the winter sunlight on a 'Sconset street.

TANGENTS

Greg Bear

Greg Bear looks at this moment to be the most successful of all the younger hard sf writers of the 1980s. He seems to have taken a place in the perceptions of hard sf readers in the lineal descent from Clarke and Clement through Niven and Benford to the present generation. He is married to Astrid Anderson, the daughter of Poul Anderson and is a past President of the Science Fiction Writers of America. Like Clarke and Benford in particular, he is often drawn to speculative ideas on the largest scale, in the philosophical tradition of Olaf Stapledon, but with a characteristically genre-writer's devotion to plot logic and character. He has not been afraid to experiment in his short fiction, and was included by Bruce Sterling in the influential *Mirrorshades: The Cyberpunk Anthology*, but his public allegiance is to hard sf, not "the Movement." Uncharacteristically, he trained not as a scientist but as an artist, and his first notable sf publications were cover illustrations in the 1970s.

Bear's stories and novels began to appear in the late seventies, but it was with his story "Blood Music" (expanded into a novel in 1985) and his collection *The Wind From a Burning Woman* (1983) that he first came into prominence, and rapidly thereafter he produced an impressive list of hard sf novels—*Eon* (1985), *The Forge of God* (1987), *Eternity* (1987), and *Queen of Angels* (1990)—that catapulted him into the first ranks of hard sf writers.

"Tangents" is the title story from his second collection of stories (1989). It is a fascinating mathematical tale, in the direct line from Abbott's *Flatland* (and a companion piece to Rucker's "Message Found in a Copy of *Flatland*"). It is a hard sf story, in which the characters solve problems, go places, do things. Bear's clever and accomplished use of genre materials and stereotypes (the isolated scientific genius, the mathematical wunderkind, the prejudiced political and scientific establishment) combine beautifully and powerfully with his translation of abstract mathematical concepts into literal images. It is also an interesting contrast to Philip K. Dick's "The Indefatigable Frog," in its attitude toward the science and math, and Kuttner's classic "Mimsy Were the Borogoves," wherein Carrollian games and logical paradoxes are privileged over the literal use of scientific knowledge to solve problems.

The nut-brown boy stood in the California field, his Asian face shadowed by a hard hat, his short, stocky frame clothed in a T-shirt and a pair of brown shorts. He squinted across the hip-high grass at the spraddled old two-story ranch house, and then he whistled a few bars from a Haydn piano sonata. Out of the upper floor of the house came a man's high, frustrated "bloody hell!" and the sound of a fist slamming on a solid surface. Silence for a minute. Then, more softly, a woman's question: "Not going well?"

"No. I'm swimming in it, but I don't see it."

"The encryption?" the woman asked timidly.

"The tesseract. If it doesn't gel, it isn't aspic."

The boy squatted in the grass and listened.

"And?" the woman encouraged.

"Ah, Lauren, it's still cold broth."

The conversation stopped. The boy lay back in the grass, aware he was on private land. He had crept over the split-rail and brick-pylon fence from the new housing project across the road. School was out, and his mother—adoptive mother—did not like him around the house all day. Or at all.

He closed his eyes and imagined a huge piano keyboard and himself dancing on the keys, tapping out the Oriental-sounding D-minor scale, which suited his origins, he thought. He loved music.

He opened his eyes and saw the thin, graying lady in a tweed suit leaning over him, staring down with her brows knit.

"You're on private land," she said.

He scrambled up and brushed grass from his pants. "Sorry."

"I thought I saw someone out here. What's your name?"

"Pal," he replied.

"Is that a name?" she asked querulously.

"Pal Tremont. It's not my real name. I'm Korean."

"Then what's your real name?"

"My folks told me not to use it anymore. I'm adopted. Who are you?"

The gray woman looked him up and down. "My name is Lauren Davies," she said. "You live near here?"

He pointed across the fields at the close-packed tract homes.

"I sold the land for those homes ten years ago," she said. "I don't normally enjoy children trespassing."

"Sorry," Pal said.

"Have you had lunch?"

"No."

"Will a grilled cheese sandwich do?"

He squinted at her and nodded.

In the broad, red-brick and tile kitchen, sitting at an oak table with his shoulders barely rising above the top, he ate the mildly charred sandwich and watched Lauren Davies watching him.

"I'm trying to write about a child," she said. "It's difficult. I'm a spinster and I don't know children well."

"You're a writer?" he asked, taking a swallow of milk.

She sniffed. "Not that anyone would know."

"Is that your brother, upstairs?"

"No," she said. "That's Peter. We've been living together for twenty years."

"But you said you're a spinster—isn't that someone who's never married or never loved?" Pal asked.

"Never married. And never you mind. Peter's relationship to me is none of your concern." She put together a tray with a bowl of soup and a tuna-salad sandwich. "His lunch," she said. Without being asked, Pal trailed up the stairs after her.

"This is where Peter works," Lauren explained. Pal stood in the doorway, eyes wide. The room was filled with electronics gear, computer terminals, and industrial-gray shelving with odd cardboard sculptures sharing each level, along with books and circuit boards. She put the lunch tray on top of a cart, resting precariously on a box of floppy disks.

"Still having trouble?" she asked a thin man with his back turned toward them.

The man turned around on his swivel chair, glanced briefly at Pal, then at the lunch, and shook his head. The hair on top of his head was a rich, glossy black; on the close-cut sides, the color changed abruptly to a bright, fake-looking white. He had a small, thin nose and large green eyes. On the desk before him was a computer monitor. "We haven't been introduced," he said, pointing to Pal.

"This is Pal Tremont, a neighborhood visitor. Pal, this is Peter Tuthy. Pal's going to help me with that character we discussed."

Pal looked at the monitor curiously. Red and green lines went through some incomprehensible transformation on the screen, then repeated.

"What's a tesseract?" Pal asked, remembering the words he had heard through the window as he stood in the field.

"It's a four-dimensional analog of a cube. I'm trying to find a way to teach myself to see it in my mind's eye," Tuthy said. "Have you ever tried that?"

"No," Pal admitted.

"Here," Tuthy said, handing him the spectacles. "As in the movies."

Pal donned the spectacles and stared at the screen. "So?" he said. "It folds and unfolds. It's pretty—it sticks out at you, and then it goes away." He looked around the workshop. "Oh, wow!" In the east corner of the room a framework of aluminum pipes—rather like a plumber's dream of an easel—supported a long, disembodied piano keyboard mounted in a slim, black case. The boy ran to the keyboard. "A Tronclavier! With all the switches! My mother had me take piano lessons, but I'd rather learn on this. Can you play it?"

"I toy with it," Tuthy said, exasperated. "I toy with all sorts of electronic things. But what did you see on the screen?" He glanced up at Lauren, blinking. "I'll eat the food, I'll eat it. Now please don't bother us."

"He's supposed to be helping *me*," Lauren complained.

Peter smiled at her. "Yes, of course. I'll send him downstairs in a little while."

When Pal descended an hour later, he came into the kitchen to thank Lauren for lunch. "Peter's a real flake. He's trying to see certain directions."

"I know." Lauren said, sighing.

"I'm going home now." Pal said. "I'll be back, though . . . if it's all right with you. Peter invited me."

"I'm sure that it will be fine," Lauren replied dubiously.

"He's going to let me learn the Tronclavier." With that, Pal smiled radiantly and exited through the kitchen door.

When she retrieved the tray, she found Peter leaning back in his chair, eyes closed. The figures on the screen patiently folded and unfolded, cubes continuously passing through one another.

"What about Hockrum's work?" she asked.

"I'm on it," Peter replied, eyes still closed.

Lauren called Pal's adoptive mother on the second day to apprise them of their son's location, and the woman assured her it was quite all right. "Sometimes he's a little pest. Send him home if he causes trouble—but not right away! Give me a rest," she said, then laughed nervously.

Lauren drew her lips together tightly, thanked her and hung up.

Peter and the boy had come downstairs to sit in the kitchen, filling up paper with line drawings. "Peter's teaching me how to use his program," Pal said.

"Did you know," Tuthy said, assuming his highest Cambridge professorial tone, "that a cube, intersecting a flat plane, can be cut through a number of geometrically different cross sections?"

Pal squinted at the sketch Tuthy had made. "Sure," he said.

"If shoved through the plane, the cube can appear, to a two-dimensional creature living on the plane—let's call him a Flatlander—to be either a triangle, a rectangle, a trapezoid, a rhombus, or a square. If the two-dimensional being observes the cube being pushed through all the way, what he sees is one or more of these objects growing larger, changing shape suddenly, shrinking, and disappearing."

"Sure," Pal said, tapping his sneakered toe. "It's easy. Like in that book you showed me."

"And a sphere pushed through a plane would appear to the hapless Flatlander first as an *invisible* point (the two-dimensional surface touching the sphere, tangential), then as a circle. The circle would grow in size, then shrink back to a point and disappear again." He sketched the stick figures, looking in awe at the intrusion.

"Got it," Pal said. "Can I play with the Tronclavier now?"

"In a moment. Be patient. So what would a tesseract look like, coming into our three-dimensional space? Remember the program, now—the pictures on the monitor."

Pal looked up at the ceiling. "I don't know," he said, seeming bored.

"Try to think," Tuthy urged him.

"It would . . ." Pal held his hands out to shape an angular object. "It would look like one of those Egyptian things, but with three sides . . . or like a box. It would look like a weird-shaped box, too, not square."

"And if we turned the tesseract around?"

The doorbell rang. Pal jumped off the kitchen chair. "Is that my mom?"

"I don't think so," Lauren said. "More likely it's Hockrum." She went to the front door to answer. She returned with a small, pale man behind her. Tuthy stood and shook the man's hand. "Pal Tremont, this is Irving Hockrum," he introduced, waving his hand between them. Hockrum glanced at Pal and blinked a long, not-very-mammalian blink.

"How's the work coming?" he asked Tuthy.

"It's finished," Tuthy said. "It's upstairs. Looks like your savants are barking up the wrong logic tree." He retrieved a folder of papers and printouts and handed them to Hockrum.

Hockrum leafed through the printouts.

"I can't say this makes me happy," he said. "Still, I can't find fault. Looks like the work is up to your usual brilliant standards. I just wish you'd had it to us sooner. It would have saved me some grief—and the company quite a bit of money."

"Sorry," Tuthy said nonchalantly.

"Now I have an important bit of work for you. . . ." And Hockrum outlined another problem. Tuthy thought it over for several minutes and shook his head.

"Most difficult, Irving. Pioneering work there. It would take at least a month to see if it's even feasible."

"That's all I need to know for now—whether it's feasible. A lot's riding on this, Peter." Hockrum clasped his hands together in front of him, looking even more pale and worn than when he had entered the kitchen. "You'll let me know soon?"

"I'll get right on it," Tuthy said.

"Protégé?" he asked, pointing to Pal. There was a speculative expression on his face, not quite a leer.

"No, a friend. He's interested in music," Tuthy said. "Damned good at Mozart, in fact."

"I help with his tesseracts," Pal asserted.

"Congratulations," Hockrum said. "I hope you don't interrupt Peter's work. Peter's work is important."

Pal shook his head solemnly. "Good," Hockrum said, and then left the house to take the negative results back to his company.

Tuthy returned to his office, Pal in train. Lauren tried to work in the kitchen, sitting with fountain pen and pad of paper, but the words wouldn't come. Hockrum always worried her. She climbed the stairs and stood in the doorway of the office. She often did that; her presence did not disturb Tuthy, who could work under all sorts of conditions.

"Who was that man?" Pal was asking Tuthy.

"I work for him." Tuthy said. "He's employed by a very big electronics firm. He loans me most of the equipment I use here—the computers, the high-resolution monitors. He brings me problems and then takes my solutions back to his bosses and claims he did the work."

"That sounds stupid," Pal said. "What kind of problems?"

"Codes, encryptions. Computer security. That was my expertise, once."

"You mean, like fencerail, that sort of thing?" Pal asked, face brightening. "We learned some of that in school."

"Much more complicated, I'm afraid," Tuthy said, grinning. "Did you ever hear of the German 'Enigma,' or the 'Ultra' project?"

Pal shook his head.

"I thought not. Don't worry about it. Let's try another figure on the screen now." He called up another routine on the four-space program and sat Pal before the screen. "So what would a hypersphere look like if it intruded into our space?"

Pal thought a moment. "Kind of weird."

"Not really. You've been watching the visualizations."

"Oh, in *our* space. That's easy. It just looks like a balloon, blowing up from nothing and then shrinking again. It's harder to see what a hypersphere looks like when it's real. Reft of us, I mean."

"Reft?" Tuthy said.

"Sure. Reft and light. Dup and owwen. Whatever the directions are called."

Tuthy stared at the boy. Neither of them had noticed Lauren in the doorway. "The proper terms are *ana* and *kata*," Tuthy said. "What does it look like?"

Pal gestured, making two wide swings with his arms. "It's like a ball, and it's like a horseshoe, depending on how you look at it. Like a balloon stung by bees, I guess, but it's smooth all over, not lumpy."

Tuthy continued to stare, then asked quietly, "You actually see it?"

"Sure," Pal said. "Isn't that what your program is supposed to do—make you see things like that?"

Tuthy nodded, flabbergasted.

"Can I play the Tronclavier now?"

Lauren backed out of the doorway. She felt she had eavesdropped on something momentous but beyond her. Tuthy came downstairs an hour later, leaving Pal to pick out Telemann on the keyboard. He sat at the kitchen table with her. "The program works," he said. "It doesn't work for me, but it works for him. He's a bloody natural." Tuthy seldom used such language. He was clearly awed. "I've just been showing him reverse-shadow figures. There's a way to have at least a sensation of seeing something rotated through the fourth dimension. Those hollow masks they use at Disneyland . . . seem to reverse in and out, depending on the lighting? Crater pictures from the moon—resemble hills instead of holes? That's what Pal calls the reversed images—hills and holes."

"And what's special about them?"

"Well, if you go along with the game and make the hollow faces seem to reverse and poke out at you, that is similar to rotating them in the fourth dimension. The features seem to reverse left and right—right eye becomes left eye, and so on. He caught on right away, and then he went off and played Haydn. He's gone through all my sheet music. The kid's a genius."

"Musical, you mean?"

He glanced directly at her and frowned. "Yes, I suppose he's remarkable at that, too. But spatial relations—coordinates and motion in a higher dimension. . . . Did you know that if you take a three-dimensional object and rotate it in the fourth dimension, it will come back with left-right reversed? There is no fixed left-right in the fourth dimension. So if I were to take my hand—" He held up his right hand, "and lift it *dup*—or drop it *owwen*, it would come back like this?" He held his left hand over his right, balled the right up into a fist, and snuck it away behind his back.

"I didn't know that," Lauren said. "What are *dup* and *owwen*?"

"That's what Pal calls movement along the fourth dimension. *Ana* and *kata* to purists. Like up and down to a Flatlander, who only comprehends left and right, back and forth."

She thought about the hands for a moment. "I still can't see it," she said.

"Neither can I," Tuthy admitted. "Our circuits are just too hardwired, I suppose."

Pal had switched the Tronclavier to a cathedral organ and wah-guitar combination and was playing variations on Pergolesi.

"Are you going to keep working for Hockrum?" Lauren asked. Tuthy didn't seem to hear her.

"It's remarkable," he murmured. "The boy just walked in here. You brought him in by accident. Remarkable."

"Do you think you can show me the direction—point it out to me?" Tuthy asked the boy three days later.

"None of my muscles move that way," he replied. "I can see it, in my head, but . . ."

"What is it like, seeing it? That direction?"

Pal squinted. "It's a lot bigger. Where we live is sort of stacked up with other places. It makes me feel lonely."

"Why?"

"Because I'm stuck here. Nobody out there pays any attention to us."

Tuthy's mouth worked. "I thought you were just intuiting those directions in your head. Are you telling me you're actually *seeing* out there?"

"Yeah. There's people out there, too. Well, not people, exactly. But it isn't my eyes that see them. Eyes are like muscles—they can't point those ways. But the head—the brain, I guess—can."

"Bloody hell," Tuthy said. He blinked and recovered. "Excuse me. That's rude. Can you show me the people . . . on the screen?"

"Shadows, like we were talking about."

"Fine. Then draw the shadows for me."

Pal sat down before the terminal, fingers pausing over the keys. "I can show you, but you have to help me with something."

"Help you with what?"

"I'd like to play music for them—out there. So they'll notice us."

"The people?"

"Yeah. They look really weird. They stand on us, sort of. They have hooks in our world. But they're tall . . . high dup. They don't notice us because we're so small, compared with them."

"Lord, Pal, I haven't the slightest idea how we'd send music out to them. . . . I'm not even sure I believe they exist."

"I'm not lying," Pal said, eyes narrowing. He turned his chair to face a "mouse" perched on a black ruled pad and used it to sketch shapes on the monitor. "Remember, these are just shadows of what they look like. Next I'll draw the dup and owwen lines to connect the shadows."

The boy shaded the shapes to make them look solid, smiling at his trick but explaining it was necessary because the projection of a four-dimensional object in normal space was, of course, three dimensional.

"They look like you take the plants in a garden and give them lots of arms and fingers . . . and it's kind of like seeing things in an aquarium," Pal explained.

After a time, Tuthy suspended his disbelief and stared in open-mouthed wonder at what the boy was re-creating on the monitor.

"I think you're wasting your time, that's what I think," Hockrum said. "I needed that feasibility judgment by today." He paced around the living room before falling as heavily as his light frame permitted into a chair.

"I *have* been distracted," Tuthy admitted.

"By that boy?"

"Yes, actually. Quite a talented fellow."

"Listen, this is going to mean a lot of trouble for me. I guaranteed the judgment would be made by today. It'll make me look bad." Hockrum screwed up his face in frustration. "What in hell are you doing with that boy?"

"Teaching him, actually. Or rather, he's teaching me. Right now, we're building a four-dimensional cone, part of a speaker system. The cone is three dimensional—the material part—but the magnetic field forms a fourth-dimensional extension."

"Did you ever think how it looks, Peter?"

"It looks very strange on the monitor, I grant you—"

"I'm talking about you and the boy."

Tuthy's bright, interested expression fell slowly into long, deep-lined dismay. "I don't know what you mean."

"I know a lot about you, Peter. Where you come from, why you had to leave. . . . It just doesn't look good."

Tuthy's face flushed crimson.

"Keep him away," Hockrum advised.

Tuthy stood. "I want you out of this house," he said quietly. "Our relationship is at an end."

"I swear," Hockrum said, his voice low and calm, staring up at Tuthy from under his brows, "I'll tell the boy's parents. Do you think they'd want their kid hanging around an old—pardon the expression—queer? I'll tell them if you don't get the feasibility judgment made. I think you can do it by the end of this week—two days. Don't you?"

"No, I don't think so." Tuthy said softly. "Leave."

"I know you're here illegally. There's no record of you entering the country. With the problems you had in England, you're certainly not a desirable alien. I'll pass word to the INS. You'll be deported."

"There isn't time to do the work," Tuthy said.

"Make time. Instead of 'educating' that kid."

"Get out of here."

"Two days, Peter."

Over dinner, Tuthy explained to Lauren the exchange he had had with Hockrum. "He thinks I'm buggering Pal. Unspeakable bastard. I will never work for him again."

"I'd better talk to a lawyer, then," Lauren said. "You're sure you can't make him . . . happy, stop all this trouble?"

"I could solve his little problem for him in just a few hours. But I don't want to see him or speak to him again."

"He'll take your equipment away."

Tuthy blinked and waved one hand through the air helplessly. "Then we'll just have to work fast, won't we? Ah, Lauren, you were a fool to bring me over here. You should have left me to rot."

"They ignored everything you did for them," Lauren said bitterly. She stared through the kitchen window at the overcast sky and woods outside. "You saved their hides during the war, and then . . . they would have shut you up in prison."

The cone lay on the table near the window, bathed in morning sun, connected to both the minicomputer and the Tronclavier. Pal arranged the score he had composed on a music stand before the synthesizer. "It's like a Bach canon," he said, "but it'll play better for them. It has a kind of counterpoint or over-rhythm that I'll play on the dup part of the speaker."

"Why are we doing this, Pal?" Tuthy asked as the boy sat down to the keyboard.

"You don't belong here, really, do you, Peter?" Pal asked. Tuthy stared at him.

"I mean, Miss Davies and you get along okay—but do you belong *here*, now?"

"What makes you think I don't belong?"

"I read some books in the school library. About the war and everything. I looked up *Enigma* and *Ultra*. I found a fellow named Peter Thornton. His picture looked like you but younger. The books made him seem like a hero."

Tuthy smiled wanly.

"But there was this note in one book. You disappeared in 1965. You were being prosecuted for something. They didn't even mention what it was you were being prosecuted for."

"I'm a homosexual," Tuthy said quietly.

"Oh. So what?"

"Lauren and I met in England, in 1964. They were going to put me in prison, Pal. We liked—love each other, so she smuggled me into the U.S. through Canada."

"But you're a homosexual. They don't like women."

"Not at all true, Pal. Lauren and I like each other very much. We could talk. She told me her dreams of being a writer, and I talked to her about mathematics and about the war. I nearly died during the war."

"Why? Were you wounded?"

"No. I worked too hard. I burned myself out and had a nervous breakdown. My lover . . . a man . . . kept me alive throughout the forties. Things were bad in England after the war. But he died in 1963. His parents came in to settle the estate, and when I contested the settlement in court, I was arrested." The lines on his face deepened, and he closed his eyes for a long moment. "I suppose I don't really belong here."

"I don't either. My folks don't care much. I don't have too many friends. I wasn't even born here, and I don't know anything about Korea."

"Play," Tuthy said, his face stony. "Let's see if they'll listen."

"Oh, they'll listen," Pal said. "It's like the way they talk to each other."

The boy ran his fingers over the keys on the Tronclavier. The cone, connected with the keyboard through the minicomputer, vibrated tinnily. For an hour, Pal paged back and forth through his composition, repeating passages and creating variations. Tuthy sat in a corner, chin in hand, listening to the mousy squeaks and squeals produced by the cone. *How much more difficult to interpret a four-dimensional sound,* he thought. *Not even visual clues.* Finally the boy stopped and wrung his hands, then stretched his arms. "They must have heard. We'll just have to wait and see." He switched the Tronclavier to automatic playback and pushed the chair away from the keyboard.

Pal stayed until dusk, then reluctantly went home. Tuthy stood in the office until midnight, listening to the tinny sounds issuing from the speaker cone. There was nothing more he could do. He ambled down the hall to his bedroom, shoulders slumped.

All night long the Tronclavier played through its preprogrammed selection of Pal's compositions. Tuthy lay in bed in his room, two doors down from Lauren's room, watching a shaft of moonlight slide across the wall. *How far would a four-dimensional being have to travel to get here?*

How far have I come to get here?

Without realizing he was asleep, he dreamed, and in his dream a wavering image of Pal appeared, gesturing with both arms as if swimming, eyes wide. *I'm okay,* the boy said without moving his lips. *Don't worry about me. . . . I'm okay. I've been back to Korea to see what it's like. It's not bad, but I like it better here. . . .*

Tuthy awoke sweating. The moon had gone down, and the room was pitch-black. In the office, the hypercone continued its distant, mouse-squeak broadcast.

Pal returned early in the morning, whistling disjointed selections from Mozart's Fourth Violin Concerto. Lauren opened the front door for him, and he ran upstairs to join Tuthy. Tuthy sat before the monitor, replaying Pal's sketch of the four-dimensional beings.

"Do you see them now?" he asked the boy.

Pal nodded. "They're closer. They're interested. Maybe we should get things ready, you know—be prepared." He squinted. "Did you ever think what a four-dimensional footprint would look like?"

Tuthy considered this for a moment. "That would be most interesting," he said. "It would be solid."

On the first floor, Lauren screamed.

Pal and Tuthy almost tumbled over each other getting downstairs. Lauren stood in the living room with her arms crossed above her bosom, one hand clamped over her mouth. The first intrusion had taken out a section of the living-room floor and the east wall.

"Really clumsy," Pal said. "One of them must have bumped it."

"The music," Tuthy said.

"What in *hell* is going on?" Lauren queried, her voice starting as a screech and ending as a roar.

"You'd better turn the music off," Tuthy elaborated.

"Why?" Pal asked, face wreathed in an excited smile.

"Maybe they don't like it."

A bright, filmy blue blob rapidly expanded to a diameter of a yard beside Tuthy, wriggled, froze, then just as rapidly vanished.

"That was like an elbow," Pal explained. "One of its arms. I think it's trying to find out where the music is coming from. I'll go upstairs."

"Turn it off!" Tuthy demanded.

"I'll play something else." The boy ran up the stairs. From the kitchen came a hideous hollow crashing, then the sound of vacuum being filled—a reverse pop, ending in a hiss—followed by a low-frequency vibration that set their teeth on edge.

The vibration caused by a four-dimensional creature *scraping* across their three-dimensional "floor." Tuthy's hands shook with excitement.

"Peter!" Lauren bellowed, all dignity gone. She unwrapped her arms and held clenched fists out as if she were ready to exercise or start boxing.

"Pal's attracted visitors," Tuthy explained.

He turned toward the stairs. The first four steps and a section of floor spun and vanished. The rush of air nearly drew him down the hole.

After regaining his balance, he kneeled to feel the precisely cut, concave edge. Below was the dark basement.

"Pal!" Tuthy called out. "Turn it *off*!"

"I'm playing something new for them," Pal shouted back. "I think they like it."

The phone rang. Tuthy was closest to the extension at the bottom of the stairs and instinctively reached out to answer. Hockrum was on the other end, screaming.

"I can't talk now—" Tuthy said. Hockrum screamed again, loud enough for Lauren to hear. Tuthy abruptly hung up. "He's been fired, I gather," he said. "He seemed angry." He stalked back three paces and turned, then ran forward and leapt the gap to the first intact step. "Can't talk." He stumbled and scrambled up the stairs, stopping on the landing. "Jesus," he said, as if something had suddenly occurred to him.

"He'll call the government," Lauren warned.

Tuthy waved that off. "I know what's happening. They're knocking chunks out of three-space, into the fourth. The fourth dimension. Like Pal says: clumsy brutes. They could kill us!"

Sitting before the Tronclavier, Pal happily played a new melody. Tuthy approached and was abruptly blocked by a thick green column, as solid as rock and with a similar texture. It vibrated and described an arc in the air. A section of the ceiling a yard wide was kicked out of three-space. Tuthy's hair lifted in the rush of wind. The column shrunk to a broomstick, and hairs sprouted all over it, writhing like snakes.

Tuthy edged around the hairy broomstick and pulled the plug on the Tronclavier. A cage of zeppelin-shaped brown sausages encircled the computer, spun, elongated to reach the ceiling, the floor, and the top of the monitor's table, and then pipped down to tiny strings and was gone.

"They can't see too clearly here," Pal said, undisturbed that his concert was over. Lauren had climbed the outside stairs and stood behind Tuthy. "Gee, I'm sorry about the damage."

In one smooth, curling motion, the Tronclavier and cone and all the wiring associated with them were peeled away as if they had been stick-on labels hastily removed from a flat surface.

"Gee," Pal said, his face suddenly registering alarm.

Then it was the boy's turn. He was removed more slowly, with greater care.

The last thing to vanish was his head, which hung suspended in the air for several seconds.

"I think they liked the music," he said with a grin.

Head, grin and all, dropped away in a direction impossible for Tuthy or Lauren to follow. The room sucked air through the open door, then quietly sighed back to normal.

Lauren stood her ground for several minutes, while Tuthy wandered through what was left of the office, passing his hand through mussed hair.

"Perhaps he'll be back," Tuthy said. "I don't even know . . ." But he didn't finish. *Could a three-dimensional boy survive in a four-dimensional void, or whatever lay dup—or owwen?*

Tuthy did not object when Lauren took it upon herself to call the boy's foster parents and the police. When the police arrived, he endured the questions and accusations stoically, face immobile, and told them as much as he knew. He was not believed; nobody knew quite what to believe. Photographs were taken.

It was only a matter of time, Lauren told him, until one or the other or both of them were arrested. "Then we'll make up a story," he said. "You'll tell them it was my fault."

"I will *not*," Lauren said. "But where *is* he?"

"I'm not positive," Tuthy said. "I think he's all right, however."

"How do you know?"

He told her about the dream.

"But that was before," she said.

"Perfectly allowable in the fourth dimension," he explained. He pointed vaguely up, then down, then shrugged.

On the last day, Tuthy spent the early morning hours bundled in an overcoat and bathrobe in the drafty office, playing his program again and again, trying to visualize *ana* and *kata*. He closed his eyes and squinted and twisted his head, intertwined his fingers and drew odd little graphs on the monitors, but it was no use. His brain was hardwired.

Over breakfast, he reiterated to Lauren that she must put all the blame on him.

"Maybe it will all blow over," she said. "They have no case. No evidence . . . nothing."

All blow over, he mused, passing his hand over his head and grinning ironically. *How over, they'll never know.*

The doorbell rang. Tuthy went to answer it, and Lauren followed a few steps behind.

Putting it all together later, she decided that subsequent events happened in the following order:

Tuthy opened the door. Three men in gray suits, one with a briefcase, stood on the porch. "Mr. Peter Tuthy?" the tallest asked.

"Yes," Tuthy acknowledged.

A chunk of the doorframe and wall above the door vanished with a roar and a hissing pop. The three men looked up at the gap. Ignoring what was impossible, the tallest man returned his attention to Tuthy and continued, "Sir, it's our duty to take you into custody. We have information that you are in this country illegally."

"Oh?" Tuthy said.

Beside him, an irregular, filmy blue blob grew to a length of four feet and hung in the air, vibrating. The three men backed away. In the middle of the blob, Pal's head emerged, and below that, his extended arm and hand. Tuthy leaned forward to study this apparition. Pal's fingers waggled at him.

"It's fun here," Pal said. "They're friendly."

"I believe you," Tuthy said calmly.

"Mr. Tuthy," the tallest man valiantly persisted, though his voice was a squeak.

"Won't you come with me?" Pal asked.

Tuthy glanced back at Lauren. She gave him a small fraction of a nod, barely understanding what she was assenting to, and he took Pal's hand. "Tell them it was all my fault," he said again.

From his feet to his head, Peter Tuthy was peeled out of this world. Air rushed in. Half of the brass lamp to one side of the door disappeared. The INS men returned to their car with damp pants and embarrassed, deeply worried expressions, and without any further questions. They drove away, leaving Lauren to contemplate the quiet.

She did not sleep for three nights, and when she did sleep, Tuthy and Pal visited her and put the question to her.

Thank you, but I prefer it here, she replied.

It's a lot of fun, the boy insisted. *They like music.*

Lauren shook her head on the pillow and awoke. Not very far away, there was a whistling, tinny kind of sound, followed by a deep vibration. To her, it sounded like applause.

She took a deep breath and got out of bed to retrieve her notebook.

JOHNNY MNEMONIC

William Gibson

William Gibson is the avatar of cyberpunk, whose novel *Neuromancer* (1984) took the sf field by storm and made him one of the big names of sf. He occupies a central position in that decade as J. G. Ballard did in the 1960s, as a nexus of controversy and attention. "A lot of what I've written so far," said Gibson in an interview, "is a conscious reaction to what I felt sf—especially American sf—had become by the time I started writing in the late seventies. In fact, I felt I was writing so far outside the mainstream that my highest goal was to become a minor cult figure, a sort of lesser Ballard. . . . Some of my resistance had to do with a certain didactic, right-wing stance that I associated with a lot of hard sf, but mainly it was a more generalized angle of attack [against genre sf]."

Furthermore he said, "I'm not interested in producing the kind of literalism most readers associate with sf. This may be a suicidal admission, but most of the time I don't know what I'm talking about when it comes to the scientific or logical rationales that supposedly underpin my books. Apparently, though, part of my skill lies in my ability to convince people otherwise. Some of the sf writers who are actually working scientists do know what they are talking about; but for the rest of us, to present a whole world that doesn't exist and make it seem real, we have to more or less pretend we're polymaths. *That's just the act of all good writing*." One can readily see why Benford, Brin, and many others were up in arms about Gibson and cyberpunk in the eighties, and, on the other hand, why postmodern writers such as Kathy Acker and publications from *The Village Voice* to *Vogue* have picked up the banner of cyberpunk. *Neuromancer*, and the stories collected in *Burning Chrome* (1986), are the pure essence of "the Movement." With his cohort Bruce Sterling, Gibson remains the spokesman for the attitudes and images of cyberpunk, although they no longer see it as a movement. "I'm looking for images that supply a certain atmosphere. Right now science and technology seem to be very useful sources. But I'm more interested in the *language* of, say, computers than I am in the technicalities." Although by 1987 Sterling and Gibson had declared the Movement dead, the imagery and the name as a marketing term survive as a major influence on the sf of the 1990s. Brian Aldiss has observed that Gibson's "emphasis on surface style, which continually manifests itself in Gibson's work through sparkling visual one-liners, is reminiscent of Bester and Delany, as is the portrait of a society glimpsed from its heights and its Stygian depths." Gibson himself has also acknowledged such diverse influences as William S. Burroughs and James Tiptree, Jr.'s "The Girl Who Was Plugged In."

Gibson's immense popularity among sf readers is rooted in his ability to intuit and portray intimate connections of mind and technology in a plausible fashion. This is especially powerful in a decade where many sf readers for the first time were using home computers and connecting directly by modem to the computers of others through vast networks, and playing sophisticated video games with characters whom they might identify with on the screen—as in the films *Tron* (1982), and *Bladerunner* (1982), the twin sources whose imagery has perhaps overwhelmed Gibson's works as the prime influence on later cyberpunk fictions. Gibson himself did not own a computer until after he wrote his essential cyberpunk corpus.

"My sf *is* realistic in that I write about what I see around me," Gibson says. The conventional setting of cyberpunk fiction is a future world dominated by computer technology, massive cartels, and cyberspace, an artificial universe created through the linkup of tens of millions of machines. This is the world of "Johnny Mnemonic." It is one of the stories that introduced a new affect into the hard sf dialogue in the genre.

I put the shotgun in an Adidas bag and padded it out with four pairs of tennis socks, not my style at all, but that was what I was aiming for: If they think you're crude, go technical; if they think you're technical, go crude. I'm a very technical boy. So I decided to get as crude as possible. These days, though, you have to be pretty technical before you can even aspire to crudeness. I'd had to turn both those twelve-gauge shells from brass stock, on a lathe, and then load them myself; I'd had to dig up an old microfiche with instructions for hand-loading cartridges; I'd had to build a lever-action press to seat the primers—all very tricky. But I knew they'd work.

The meet was set for the Drome at 2300, but I rode the tube three stops past the closest platform and walked back. Immaculate procedure.

I checked myself out in the chrome siding of a coffee kiosk, your basic sharp-faced Caucasoid with a ruff of stiff, dark hair. The girls at Under the Knife were big on Sony Mao, and it was getting harder to keep them from adding the chic suggestion of epicanthic folds. It probably wouldn't fool Ralfi Face, but it might get me next to his table.

The Drome is a single narrow space with a bar down one side and tables along the other, thick with pimps and handlers and an arcane array of dealers. The Magnetic Dog Sisters were on the door that night, and I didn't relish trying to get out past them if things didn't work out. They were two meters tall and thin as greyhounds. One was black and the other white, but aside from that they were as nearly identical as cosmetic surgery could make them. They'd been lovers for years and were bad news in a tussle. I was never quite sure which one had originally been male.

Ralfi was sitting at his usual table. Owing me a lot of money. I had hundreds of megabytes stashed in my head on an idiot/savant basis, information I had no conscious access to. Ralfi had left it there. He hadn't, however, come back for it. Only Ralfi could retrieve the data, with a code phrase of his own invention. I'm not cheap to begin with, but my overtime on storage is astronomical. And Ralfi had been very scarce.

Then I'd heard that Ralfi Face wanted to put out a contract on me. So I'd arranged to meet him in the Drome, but I'd arranged it as Edward Bax, clandestine importer, late of Rio and Peking.

The Drome stank of biz, a metallic tang of nervous tension. Muscle-boys scattered through the crowd were flexing stock parts at one another and trying on thin, cold grins, some of them so lost under superstructures of muscle graft that their outlines weren't really human.

Pardon me. Pardon me, friends. Just Eddie Bax here, Fast Eddie the Importer, with his professionally nondescript gym bag, and please ignore this slit, just wide enough to admit his right hand.

Ralfi wasn't alone. Eighty kilos of blond California beef perched alertly in the chair next to his, martial arts written all over him.

Fast Eddie Bax was in the chair opposite them before the beef's hands were off the table. "You black belt?" I asked eagerly. He nodded, blue eyes running an automatic scanning pattern between my eyes and my hands. "Me, too," I said. "Got mine here in the bag." And I shoved my hand through the slit and thumbed the safety off. Click. "Double twelve-gauge with the triggers wired together."

"That's a gun," Ralfi said, putting a plump, restraining hand on his boy's taut blue nylon chest. "Johnny has an antique firearm in his bag." So much for Edward Bax.

I guess he'd always been Ralfi Something or Other, but he owed his acquired surname to a singular vanity. Built something like an overripe pear, he'd worn the once-famous face of Christian White for twenty years—Christian White of the Aryan Reggae Band, Sony Mao to his generation, and final champion of race rock. I'm a whiz at trivia.

Christian White: classic pop face with a singer's high-definition muscles, chiseled cheekbones. Angelic in one light, handsomely depraved in another. But Ralfi's eyes lived behind that face, and they were small and cold and black.

"Please," he said, "let's work this out like businessmen." His voice was marked by a horrible prehensile sincerity, and the corners of his beautiful Christian White mouth were always wet. "Lewis here," nodding in the beefboy's direction, "is a meatball." Lewis took this impassively, looking like something built from a kit. "You aren't a meatball, Johnny."

"Sure I am, Ralfi, a nice meatball chock-full of implants where you can store your dirty laundry while you go off shopping for people to kill me. From my end of this bag, Ralfi, it looks like you've got some explaining to do."

"It's this last batch of product, Johnny." He sighed deeply. "In my role as broker—"

"Fence," I corrected.

"As broker, I'm usually very careful as to sources."

"You buy only from those who steal the best. Got it."

He sighed again. "I try," he said wearily, "not to buy from fools. This time, I'm afraid, I've done that." Third sigh was the cue for Lewis to trigger the neural disruptor they'd taped under my side of the table.

I put everything I had into curling the index finger of my right hand, but I no longer seemed to be connected to it. I could feel the metal of the gun and the foam-padded tape I'd wrapped around the stubby grip, but my hands were cool wax, distant and inert. I was hoping Lewis was a true meatball, thick enough to go for the gym bag and snag my rigid trigger finger, but he wasn't.

"We've been very worried about you, Johnny. Very worried. You see, that's Yakuza property you have there. A fool took it from them, Johnny. A dead fool."

Lewis giggled.

It all made sense then, an ugly kind of sense, like bags of wet sand settling around my head. Killing wasn't Ralfi's style. Lewis wasn't even Ralfi's style. But he'd got himself stuck between the Sons of the Neon Chrysanthemum and something that belonged to them—or, more likely, something of theirs that belonged to someone else. Ralfi, of course, could use the code phrase to throw me into idiot savant, and I'd spill their hot program without remembering a single quarter tone. For a fence like Ralfi, that would ordinarily have been enough. But not for the Yakuza. The Yakuza would know about Squids, for one thing, and they wouldn't want to worry about one lifting those dim and permanent traces of their program out of my head. I didn't know very much about Squids, but I'd heard stories, and

I made it a point never to repeat them to my clients. No, the Yakuza wouldn't like that; it looked too much like evidence. They hadn't got where they were by leaving evidence around. Or alive.

Lewis was grinning. I think he was visualizing a point just behind my forehead and imagining how he could get there the hard way.

"Hey," said a low voice, feminine, from somewhere behind my right shoulder, "you cowboys sure aren't having too lively a time."

"Pack it, bitch," Lewis said, his tanned face very still. Ralfi looked blank.

"Lighten up. You want to buy some good free base?" She pulled up a chair and quickly sat before either of them could stop her. She was barely inside my fixed field of vision, a thin girl with mirrored glasses, her dark hair cut in a rough shag. She wore black leather, open over a T-shirt slashed diagonally with stripes of red and black. "Eight thou a gram weight."

Lewis snorted his exasperation and tried to slap her out of the chair. Somehow he didn't quite connect, and her hand came up and seemed to brush his wrist as it passed. Bright blood sprayed the table. He was clutching his wrist white-knuckle tight, blood trickling from between his fingers.

But hadn't her hand been empty?

He was going to need a tendon stapler. He stood up carefully, without bothering to push his chair back. The chair toppled backward, and he stepped out of my line of sight without a word.

"He better get a medic to look at that," she said. "That's a nasty cut."

"You have no idea," said Ralfi, suddenly sounding very tired, "the depths of shit you have just gotten yourself into."

"No kidding? Mystery. I get real excited by mysteries. Like why your friend here's so quiet. Frozen, like. Or what this thing here is for," and she held up the little control unit that she'd somehow taken from Lewis. Ralfi looked ill.

"You, ah, want maybe a quarter-million to give me that and take a walk?" A fat hand came up to stroke his pale, lean face nervously.

"What I want," she said, snapping her fingers so that the unit spun and glittered, "is work. A job. Your boy hurt his wrist. But a quarter'll do for a retainer."

Ralfi let his breath out explosively and began to laugh, exposing teeth that hadn't been kept up to the Christian White standard. Then she turned the disruptor off.

"Two million," I said.

"My kind of man," she said, and laughed. "What's in the bag?"

"A shotgun."

"Crude." It might have been a compliment.

Ralfi said nothing at all.

"Name's Millions. Molly Millions. You want to get out of here, boss? People are starting to stare." She stood up. She was wearing leather jeans the color of dried blood.

And I saw for the first time that the mirrored lenses were surgical inlays, the silver rising smoothly from her high cheekbones, sealing her eyes in their sockets. I saw my new face twinned there.

"I'm Johnny," I said. "We're taking Mr. Face with us."

He was outside, waiting. Looking like your standard tourist tech, in plastic zoris and a silly Hawaiian shirt printed with blowups of his firm's most popular microprocessor; a mild little guy, the kind most likely to wind up drunk on sake in a bar that puts out miniature rice crackers with seaweed garnish. He looked like the kind who sing the corporate anthem and cry, who shake hands endlessly with the bartender. And the pimps and the dealers would leave him alone, pegging him as innately conservative. Not up for much, and careful with his credit when he was.

The way I figured it later, they must have amputated part of his left thumb, somewhere behind the first joint, replacing it with a prosthetic tip, and cored the stump, fitting it with a spool and socket molded from one of the Ono-Sendai diamond analogs. Then they'd carefully wound the spool with three meters of monomolecular filament.

Molly got into some kind of exchange with the Magnetic Dog Sisters, giving me a chance to usher Ralfi through the door with the gym bag pressed lightly against the base of his spine. She seemed to know them. I heard the black one laugh.

I glanced up, out of some passing reflex, maybe because I've never got used to it, to the soaring arcs of light and the shadows of the geodesics above them. Maybe that saved me.

Ralfi kept walking, but I don't think he was trying to escape. I think he'd already given up. Probably he already had an idea of what we were up against.

I looked back down in time to see him explode.

Playback on full recall shows Ralfi stepping forward as the little tech sidles out of nowhere, smiling. Just a suggestion of a bow, and his left thumb falls off. It's a conjuring trick. The thumb hangs suspended. Mirrors? Wires? And Ralfi stops, his back to us, dark crescents of sweat under the armpits of his pale summer suit. He knows. He must have known. And then the joke-shop thumbtip, heavy as lead, arcs out in a lightning yo-yo trick, and the invisible thread connecting it to the killer's hand passes laterally through Ralfi's skull, just above his eyebrows, whips up, and descends, slicing the pear-shaped torso diagonally from shoulder to rib cage. Cuts so fine that no blood flows until synapses misfire and the first tremors surrender the body to gravity.

Ralfi tumbled apart in a pink cloud of fluids, the three mismatched sections rolling forward onto the tiled pavement. In total silence.

I brought the gym bag up, and my hand convulsed. The recoil nearly broke my wrist.

It must have been raining; ribbons of water cascaded from a ruptured geodesic and spattered on the tile behind us. We crouched in the narrow gap between a surgical boutique and an antique shop. She'd just edged one mirrored eye around the corner to report a single Volks module in front of the Drome, red lights flashing. They were sweeping Ralfi up. Asking questions.

I was covered in scorched white fluff. The tennis socks. The gym bag was a ragged plastic cuff around my wrist. "I don't see how the hell I missed him."

"'Cause he's fast, so fast." She hugged her knees and rocked back and forth on her bootheels. "His nervous system's jacked up. He's factory custom." She grinned and gave a little squeal of delight. "I'm gonna get that boy. Tonight. He's the best, number one, top dollar, state of the art."

"What you're going to get, for this boy's two million, is my ass out of here. Your boyfriend back there was mostly grown in a vat in Chiba City. He's a Yakuza assassin."

"Chiba. Yeah. See, Molly's been Chiba, too." And she showed me her hands, fingers slightly spread. Her fingers were slender, tapered, very white against the polished burgundy nails. Ten blades snicked straight out from their recesses beneath her nails, each one a narrow, double-edged scalpel in pale blue steel.

• • •

I'd never spent much time in Nighttown. Nobody there had anything to pay me to remember, and most of them had a lot they paid regularly to forget. Generations of sharpshooters had chipped away at the neon until the maintenance crews gave up. Even at noon the arcs were soot-black against faintest pearl.

Where do you go when the world's wealthiest criminal order is feeling for you with calm, distant fingers? Where do you hide from the Yakuza, so powerful that it owns comsats and at least three shuttles? The Yakuza is a true multinational, like ITT and Ono-Sendai. Fifty years before I was born the Yakuza had already absorbed the Triads, the Mafia, the Union Corse.

Molly had an answer: You hide in the Pit, in the lowest circle, where any outside influence generates swift, concentric ripples of raw menace. You hide in Nighttown. Better yet, you hide *above* Nighttown, because the Pit's inverted, and the bottom of its bowl touches the sky, the sky that Nighttown never sees, sweating under its own firmament of acrylic resin, up where the Lo Teks crouch in the dark like gargoyles, black-market cigarettes dangling from their lips.

She had another answer, too.

"So you're locked up good and tight, Johnny-san? No way to get that program without the password?" She led me into the shadows that waited beyond the bright tube platform. The concrete walls were overlaid with graffiti, years of them twisting into a single metascrawl of rage and frustration.

"The stored data are fed in through a modified series of microsurgical contraautism prostheses." I reeled off a numb version of my standard sales pitch. "Client's code is stored in a special chip; barring Squids, which we in the trade don't like to talk about, there's no way to recover your phrase. Can't drug it out, cut it out, torture it. I don't *know* it, never did."

"Squids? Crawly things with arms?" We emerged into a deserted street market. Shadowy figures watched us from across a makeshift square littered with fish heads and rotting fruit.

"Superconducting quantum interference detectors. Used them in the war to find submarines, suss out enemy cyber systems."

"Yeah? Navy stuff? From the war? Squid'll read that chip of yours?" She'd stopped walking, and I felt her eyes on me behind those twin mirrors.

"Even the primitive models could measure a magnetic field a billionth the strength of geomagnetic force; it's like pulling a whisper out of a cheering stadium."

"Cops can do that already, with parabolic microphones and lasers."

"But your data's still secure." Pride in profession. "No government'll let their cops have Squids, not even the security heavies. Too much chance of interdepartmental funnies; they're too likely to watergate you."

"Navy stuff," she said, and her grin gleamed in the shadows. "Navy stuff. I got a friend down here who was in the navy, name's Jones. I think you'd better meet him. He's a junkie, though. So we'll have to take him something."

"A junkie?"

"A dolphin."

He was more than a dolphin, but from another dolphin's point of view he might have seemed like something less. I watched him swirling sluggishly in his galvanized tank. Water slopped over the side, wetting my shoes. He was surplus from the last war. A cyborg.

He rose out of the water, showing us the crusted plates along his sides, a kind of visual pun, his grace nearly lost under articulated armor, clumsy and prehistoric. Twin deformities on either side of his skull had been engineered to house sensor units. Silver lesions gleamed on exposed sections of his gray-white hide.

Molly whistled. Jones thrashed his tail, and more water cascaded down the side of the tank.

"What is this place?" I peered at vague shapes in the dark, rusting chain link and things under tarps. Above the tank hung a clumsy wooden framework, crossed and recrossed by rows of dusty Christmas lights.

"Funland. Zoo and carnival rides. 'Talk with the War Whale.' All that. Some whale Jones is. . . ."

Jones reared again and fixed me with a sad and ancient eye.

"How's he talk?" Suddenly I was anxious to go.

"That's the catch. Say 'hi,' Jones."

And all the bulbs lit simultaneously. They were flashing red, white, and blue.

```
RWBRWBRWB
RWBRWBRWB
RWBRWBRWB
RWBRWBRWB
RWBRWBRWB
```

"Good with symbols, see, but the code's restricted. In the navy they had him wired into an audiovisual display." She drew the narrow package from a jacket pocket. "Pure shit, Jones. Want it?" He froze in the water and started to sink. I felt a strange panic, remembering that he wasn't a fish, that he could drown. "We want the key to Johnny's bank, Jones. We want it fast."

The lights flickered, died.

"Go for it, Jones!"

```
    B
BBBBBBBBB
    B
    B
    B
```

Blue bulbs, cruciform.

Darkness.

"Pure! It's *clean*. Come on, Jones."

```
WWWWWWWWW
WWWWWWWWW
WWWWWWWWW
WWWWWWWWW
WWWWWWWWW
```

White sodium glare washed her features, stark monochrome, shadows cleaving from her cheekbones.

```
R   RRRRR
R   R
RRRRRRRRR
    R   R
RRRRR   R
```

The arms of the red swastika were twisted in her silver glasses. "Give it to him," I said. "We've got it."

Ralfi Face. No imagination.

Jones heaved half his armored bulk over the edge of his tank, and I thought the metal would give way. Molly stabbed him overhand with the Syrette, driving the needle between two plates. Propellant hissed. Patterns of light exploded, spasming across the frame and then fading to black.

We left him drifting, rolling languorously in the dark water. Maybe he was dreaming of his war in the Pacific, of the cyber mines he'd swept, nosing gently into their circuitry with the Squid he'd used to pick Ralfi's pathetic password from the chip buried in my head.

"I can see them slipping up when he was demobbed, letting him out of the navy with that gear intact, but how does a cybernetic dolphin get wired to smack?"

"The war," she said. "They all were. Navy did it. How else you get 'em working for you?"

"I'm not sure this profiles as good business," the pirate said, angling for better money. "Target specs on a comsat that isn't in the book—"

"Waste my time and you won't profile at all," said Molly, leaning across his scarred plastic desk to prod him with her forefinger.

"So maybe you want to buy your microwaves somewhere else?" He was a tough kid, behind his Mao-job. A Nighttowner by birth, probably.

Her hand blurred down the front of his jacket, completely severing a lapel without even rumpling the fabric.

"So we got a deal or not?"

"Deal," he said, staring at his ruined lapel with what he must have hoped was only polite interest. "Deal."

While I checked the two recorders we'd bought, she extracted the slip of paper I'd given her from the zippered wrist pocket of her jacket. She unfolded it and read silently, moving her lips. She shrugged. "This is it?"

"Shoot," I said, punching the RECORD studs of the two decks simultaneously.

"Christian White," she recited, "and his Aryan Reggae Band."

Faithful Ralfi, a fan to his dying day.

Transition to idiot-savant mode is always less abrupt than I expect it to be. The pirate broadcaster's front was a failing travel agency in a pastel cube that boasted a desk, three chairs, and a faded poster of a Swiss orbital spa. A pair of toy birds with blown-glass bodies and tin legs were sipping monotonously from a Styrofoam cup of water on a ledge beside Molly's shoulder. As I phased into mode, they accelerated gradually until their Day-Glo-feathered crowns became solid arcs of color. The LEDs that told seconds on the plastic wall clock had become meaningless pulsing grids, and Molly and the Mao-faced boy grew hazy, their arms blurring occasionally in insect-quick ghosts of gesture. And then it all faded to cool gray static and an endless tone poem in an artificial language.

I sat and sang dead Ralfi's stolen program for three hours.

The mall runs forty kilometers from end to end, a ragged overlap of Fuller domes roofing what was once a suburban artery. If they turn off the arcs on a clear day, a gray approximation of sunlight filters through layers of acrylic, a view like the prison sketches of Giovanni Piranesi. The three southernmost kilometers roof Nighttown. Nighttown pays no taxes, no utilities. The neon arcs are dead, and the geodesics have been smoked black by decades of cooking fires. In the nearly total darkness of a Nighttown noon, who notices a few dozen mad children lost in the rafters?

We'd been climbing for two hours, up concrete stairs and steel ladders with perforated rungs, past abandoned gantries and dust-covered tools. We'd started in what looked like a disused maintenance yard, stacked with triangular roofing segments. Everything there had been covered with that same uniform layer of spraybomb graffiti: gang names, initials, dates back to the turn of the century. The graffiti followed us up, gradually thinning until a single name was repeated at intervals. LO TEK. In dripping black capitals.

"Who's Lo Tek?"

"Not us, boss." She climbed a shivering aluminum ladder and vanished through a hole in a sheet of corrugated plastic. " 'Low technique, low technology.' " The plastic muffled her voice. I followed her up, nursing my aching wrist. "Lo Teks, they'd think that shotgun trick of yours was effete."

An hour later I dragged myself up through another hole, this one sawed crookedly in a sagging sheet of plywood, and met my first Lo Tek.

"'S okay," Molly said, her hand brushing my shoulder. "It's just Dog. Hey, Dog."

In the narrow beam of her taped flash, he regarded us with his one eye and slowly extruded a thick length of grayish tongue, licking huge canines. I wondered how they wrote off tooth-bud transplants from Dobermans as low technology. Immunosuppressives don't exactly grow on trees.

"Moll." Dental augmentation impeded his speech. A string of saliva dangled from his twisted lower lip. "Heard ya comin'. Long time." He might have been fifteen, but the fangs and a bright mosaic of scars combined with the gaping socket to present a mask of total bestiality. It had taken time and a certain kind of creativity to assemble that face, and his posture told me he enjoyed living behind it. He wore a pair of decaying jeans, black with grime and shiny along the creases. His chest and feet were bare. He did something with his mouth that approximated a grin. "Bein' followed, you."

Far off, down in Nighttown, a water vendor cried his trade.

"Strings jumping, Dog?" She swung her flash to the side, and I saw thin cords tied to eyebolts, cords that ran to the edge and vanished.

"Kill the fuckin' light!"

She snapped it off.

"How come the one who's followin' you's got no light?"

"Doesn't need it. That one's bad news, Dog. Your sentries give him a tumble, they'll come home in easy-to-carry sections."

"This a *friend* friend, Moll?" He sounded uneasy. I heard his feet shift on the worn plywood.

"No. But he's mine. And this one," slapping my shoulder, "he's a friend. Got that?"

"Sure," he said, without much enthusiasm, padding to the platform's edge, where the eyebolts were. He began to pluck out some kind of message on the taut cords.

Nighttown spread beneath us like a toy village for rats; tiny windows showed candlelight, with only a few harsh, bright squares lit by battery lanterns and carbide lamps. I imagined the old men at their endless games of dominoes, under warm, fat drops of water that fell from wet wash hung out on poles between the plywood shanties. Then I tried to imagine him climbing patiently up through the darkness in his zoris and ugly tourist shirt, bland and unhurried. How was he tracking us?

"Good," said Molly. "He smells us."

* * *

"Smoke?" Dog dragged a crumpled pack from his pocket and prized out a flattened cigarette. I squinted at the trademark while he lit it for me with a kitchen match. Yiheyuan filters. Beijing Cigarette Factory. I decided that the Lo Teks were black marketeers. Dog and Molly went back to their argument, which seemed to revolve around Molly's desire to use some particular piece of Lo Tek real estate.

"I've done you a lot of favors, man. I want that floor. And I want the music."

"You're not Lo Tek. . . ."

This must have been going on for the better part of a twisted kilometer, Dog leading us along swaying catwalks and up rope ladders. The Lo Teks leech their webs and huddling places to the city's fabric with thick gobs of epoxy and sleep above the abyss in mesh hammocks. Their country is so attenuated that in places it consists of little more than holds for hands and feet, sawed into geodesic struts.

The Killing Floor, she called it. Scrambling after her, my new Eddie Bax shoes slipping on worn metal and damp plywood, I wondered how it could be any more lethal than the rest of the territory. At the same time I sensed that Dog's protests were ritual and that she already expected to get whatever it was she wanted.

Somewhere beneath us, Jones would be circling his tank, feeling the first twinges of junk sickness. The police would be boring the Drome regulars with questions about Ralfi. What did he do? Who was he with before he stepped outside? And the Yakuza would be settling its ghostly bulk over the city's data banks, probing for faint images of me reflected in numbered accounts, securities transactions, bills for utilities. We're an information economy. They teach you that in school. What they don't tell you is that it's impossible to move, to live, to operate at any level without leaving traces, bits, seemingly meaningless fragments of personal information. Fragments that can be retrieved, amplified . . .

But by now the pirate would have shuttled our message into line for blackbox transmission to the Yakuza comsat. A simple message: Call off the dogs or we wideband your program.

The program. I had no idea what it contained. I still don't. I only sing the song, with zero comprehension. It was probably research data, the Yakuza being given to advanced forms of industrial espionage. A genteel business, stealing from Ono-Sendai as a matter of course and politely holding their data for ransom, threatening to blunt the conglomerate's research edge by making the product public.

But why couldn't any number play? Wouldn't they be happier with something to sell back to Ono-Sendai, happier than they'd be with one dead Johnny from Memory Lane?

Their program was on its way to an address in Sydney, to a place that held letters for clients and didn't ask questions once you'd paid a small retainer. Fourth-class surface mail. I'd erased most of the other copy and recorded our message in the resulting gap, leaving just enough of the program to identify it as the real thing.

My wrist hurt. I wanted to stop, to lie down, to sleep. I knew that I'd lose my grip and fall soon, knew that the sharp black shoes I'd bought for my evening as Eddie Bax would lose their purchase and carry me down to Nighttown. But he rose in my mind like a cheap religious hologram, glowing, the enlarged chip on his Hawaiian shirt looming like a reconnaissance shot of some doomed urban nucleus.

So I followed Dog and Molly through Lo Tek heaven, jury-rigged and jerry-built from scraps that even Nighttown didn't want.

The Killing Floor was eight meters on a side. A giant had threaded steel cable back and forth through a junkyard and drawn it all taut. It creaked when it moved, and it moved constantly, swaying and bucking as the gathering Lo Teks arranged themselves on the shelf of plywood surrounding it. The wood was silver with age, polished with long use and deeply etched with initials, threats, declarations of passion. This was suspended from a separate set of cables, which lost themselves in darkness beyond the raw white glare of the two ancient floods suspended above the Floor.

A girl with teeth like Dog's hit the Floor on all fours. Her breasts were tattooed with indigo spirals. Then she was across the Floor, laughing, grappling with a boy who was drinking dark liquid from a liter flask.

Lo Tek fashion ran to scars and tattoos. And teeth. The electricity they were tapping to light the Killing Floor seemed to be an exception to their overall aesthetic, made in the name of . . . ritual, sport, art? I didn't know, but I could see that the Floor was something special. It had the look of having been assembled over generations.

I held the useless shotgun under my jacket. Its hardness and heft were comforting, even though I had no more shells. And it came to me that I had no idea at all of what was really happening, or of what was supposed to happen. And that was the nature of my game, because I'd spent most of my life as a blind receptacle to be filled with other people's knowledge and then drained, spouting synthetic languages I'd never understand. A very technical boy. Sure.

And then I noticed just how quiet the Lo Teks had become.

He was there, at the edge of the light, taking in the Killing Floor and the gallery of silent Lo Teks with a tourist's calm. And as our eyes met for the first time with mutual recognition, a memory clicked into place for me, of Paris, and the long Mercedes electrics gliding through the rain to Notre Dame; mobile greenhouses, Japanese faces behind the glass, and a hundred Nikons rising in blind phototropism, flowers of steel and crystal. Behind his eyes, as they found me, those same shutters whirring.

I looked for Molly Millions, but she was gone.

The Lo Teks parted to let him step up onto the bench. He bowed, smiling, and stepped smoothly out of his sandals, leaving them side by side, perfectly aligned, and then he stepped down onto the Killing Floor. He came for me, across that shifting trampoline of scrap, as easily as any tourist padding across synthetic pile in any featureless hotel.

Molly hit the Floor, moving.

The Floor screamed.

It was miked and amplified, with pickups riding the four fat coil springs at the corners and contact mikes taped at random to rusting machine fragments. Somewhere the Lo Teks had an amp and a synthesizer, and now I made out the shapes of speakers overhead, above the cruel white floods.

A drumbeat began, electronic, like an amplified heart, steady as a metronome.

She'd removed her leather jacket and boots; her T-shirt was sleeveless, faint telltales of Chiba City circuitry traced along her thin arms. Her leather jeans gleamed under the floods. She began to dance.

She flexed her knees, white feet tensed on a flattened gas tank, and the Killing Floor began to heave in response. The sound it made was like a world ending, like the wires that hold heaven snapping and coiling across the sky.

He rode with it, for a few heartbeats, and then he moved, judging the movement of the Floor perfectly, like a man stepping from one flat stone to another in an ornamental garden.

He pulled the tip from his thumb with the grace of a man at ease with social gesture and flung it at her. Under the floods, the filament was a refracting thread of rainbow. She threw herself flat and rolled, jackknifing up as the molecule whipped past, steel claws snapping into the light in what must have been an automatic rictus of defense.

The drum pulse quickened, and she bounced with it, her dark hair wild around the blank silver lenses, her mouth thin, lips taut with concentration. The Killing Floor boomed and roared, and the Lo Teks were screaming their excitement.

He retracted the filament to a whirling meter-wide circle of ghostly polychrome and spun it in front of him, thumbless hand held level with his sternum. A shield.

And Molly seemed to let something go, something inside, and that was the real start of her mad-dog dance. She jumped, twisting, lunging sideways, landing with both feet on an alloy engine block wired directly to one of the coil springs. I cupped my hands over my ears and knelt in a vertigo of sound, thinking Floor and benches were on their way down, down to Nighttown, and I saw us tearing through the shanties, the wet wash, exploding on the tiles like rotten fruit. But the cables held, and the Killing Floor rose and fell like a crazy metal sea. And Molly danced on it.

And at the end, just before he made his final cast with the filament, I saw something in his face, an expression that didn't seem to belong there. It wasn't fear and it wasn't anger. I think it was disbelief, stunned incomprehension mingled with pure aesthetic revulsion at what he was seeing, hearing—at what was happening to him. He retracted the whirling filament, the ghost disk shrinking to the size of a dinner plate as he whipped his arm above his head and brought it down, the thumbtip curving out for Molly like a live thing.

The Floor carried her down, the molecule passing just above her head; the Floor whiplashed, lifting him into the path of the taut molecule. It should have passed harmlessly over his head and been withdrawn into its diamond-hard socket. It took his hand off just behind the wrist. There was a gap in the Floor in front of him, and he went through it like a diver, with a strange deliberate grace, a defeated kamikaze on his way down to Nighttown. Partly, I think, he took that dive to buy himself a few seconds of the dignity of silence. She'd killed him with culture shock.

The Lo Teks roared, but someone shut the amplifier off, and Molly rode the Killing Floor into silence, hanging on now, her face white and blank, until the pitching slowed and there was only a faint pinging of tortured metal and the grating of rust on rust.

We searched the Floor for the severed hand, but we never found it. All we found was a graceful curve in one piece of rusted steel, where the molecule went through. Its edge was bright as new chrome.

We never learned whether the Yakuza had accepted our terms, or even whether they got our message. As far as I know, their program is still waiting for Eddie Bax on a shelf in the back room of a gift shop on the third level of Sydney Central-5. Probably they sold the original back to Ono-Sendai months ago. But maybe they did get the pirate's broadcast, because nobody's come looking for me yet, and it's been nearly a year. If they do come, they'll have a long climb up through the dark, past Dog's sentries, and I don't look much like Eddie Bax these days. I let Molly take care of that, with a local anesthetic. And my new teeth have almost grown in.

I decided to stay up here. When I looked out across the Killing Floor, before he came, I saw how hollow I was. And I knew I was sick of being a bucket. So now I climb down and visit Jones, almost every night.

We're partners now, Jones and I, and Molly Millions, too. Molly handles our business in the Drome. Jones is still in Funland, but he has a bigger tank, with fresh seawater trucked in once a week. And he has his junk, when he needs it. He still talks to the kids with his frame of lights, but he talks to me on a new display unit in a shed that I rent there, a better unit than the one he used in the navy.

And we're all making good money, better money than I made before, because Jones's Squid can read the traces of anything that anyone ever stored in me, and he gives it to me on the display unit in languages I can understand. So we're learning a lot about all my former clients. And one day I'll have a surgeon dig all the silicon out of my amygdalae, and I'll live with my own memories and nobody else's, the way other people do. But not for a while.

In the meantime it's really okay up here, way up in the dark, smoking a Chinese filtertip and listening to the condensation that drips from the geodesics. Real quiet up here—unless a pair of Lo Teks decide to dance on the Killing Floor.

It's educational, too. With Jones to help me figure things out, I'm getting to be the most technical boy in town.

WHAT CONTINUES, WHAT FAILS . . .

David Brin

David Brin came into prominence in sf in the 1980s with several award-winning hard sf novels, including *Startide Rising* (1983), *The Uplift War* (1987), and *Earth* (1990). A working physicist as well as a part-time professional writer, Brin rapidly became a spokesman for hard sf on the convention circuit. William Gibson described a particularly vociferous mid-eighties panel discussion as composed of cyberpunks versus "the hard sf 'Killer *Bs*'—Brin, Bear, and Benford—who have their own identity, their own dress code," thus giving the sf field a new image of the conflict between science and art—the new old guard of hard sf doesn't dress hip, write hip. The implication of literary conservatism is appropriate here; Brin is of the old school of Campbellian hard sf, adept at storytelling manipulation and stock characterization in the colorful mode of Robert A. Heinlein—clever, facile, slick, entertaining, with a clear and usually unornamented prose style. His thriving career is proof that there is still a large and enthusiastic audience for science fiction that incorporates few of the literary changes and devices that have entered the field in the last three decades. He is the most important writer of hard sf to enter the field in the 1980s.

Brin writes comparatively few short stories. "What Continues, What Fails" is uncharacteristic Brin, with no male characters, set in a distant future society that reminds one of the atmospheres of, say, James Tiptree, Jr., or John Varley. Brin here ironically incorporates much of the sensibility of the feminist writers of the 1970s and, as does Godwin with the romanticism of the fifties, contrasts it to the coldness of scientific law and the enormity of astronomical scale. As in Le Guin's "Nine Lives," questions of identity, and questions of the unchanging human heart, reverberate through the story.

Black, as deep as night is black between the stars.

Deeper than that. Night isn't really black, but a solemn, utter shade of red.

As black, then, as Tenembro Nought, which drinks all color, texture, substance from around it, giving back only its awful depth of presence.

But no. She had found redness of an immeasurably profound hue, emerging from that awful pit in space. Not even the singularity was pure enough to typify true blackness. Nor was Isola's own dark mood, for that matter—although, since the visitors' arrival, she had felt smothered, robbed of illumination.

In comparison, a mere ebony luster of skin and hair seemed too pallid to dignify with the name, "black." Yet, those traits were much sought after on Pleasence World, one of many reasons a fetch ship had come all this way to claim the new life within her.

The fetus might know blackness, Isola thought, laying a hand over her curved abdomen, feeling a stirring there. She purposely used cool, sterile terms, never calling it "baby," or a personalized "she." Anyway, when is a fetus's sensory innervation up to "knowing" anything at all? Can one who has never seen light comprehend blackness?

Leaning toward the dimly illuminated field-effect mirror, Isola touched its glass-smooth, silky-cool, pseudo-surface. Peering at her own reflection, she found at last what she was looking for.

That's it. Where light falls, never to emerge again.

She brought her face closer still, centring on one jet pupil, an inky well outlined by a dark iris—the universe wherein she dwelt.

"It is said nothing escapes from inside a black hole, but that isn't quite so."

Mikaela was well into her lecture when Isola slipped into the theater, late but unrepentant. A brief frown was her partner's only rebuke for her tardiness. Mikaela continued without losing a beat.

"In this universe of ours, the rules seem to allow exceptions even to the finality of great noughts . . ."

Isola's vision adapted and she discreetly scanned the visitors—six space travellers whose arrival had disrupted a quiet, monastic research routine. The guests from Pleasence World lounged on pseudo-life chaises overlooking Mikaela and the dais. Each sleek-furred settee was specially tuned to the needs of its occupant. While the three humans in the audience made little use of their couch amenities—only occasionally lifting fleshy tubes to infuse endorphin-laced oxygen; the squat, toadlike Vorpal and pair of slender Butins had already hooked up for full breathing symbiosis.

Well, they must have known they were coming to a rude outpost station, built with only a pair of humans in mind. Isola and Mikaela had not expected guests until a few months ago, when the decelerating starship peremptorily announced itself, and made its needs known.

Those needs included use of Isola's womb.

"Actually, there are countless misconceptions about gravitational singularities, especially the massive variety formed in the recoil of a supernova. One myth concerns the possibility of communicating across a black hole's event horizon, to see what has become of all the matter which left this universe so violently and completely, long ago."

Mikaela turned with a flourish of puffy sleeves toward the viewing tank. Winking one eye, she called up a new image to display in midair, above the dais. Brilliance spilled across Mikaela's fair skin and the visitors' multi-hued faces, causing several to flinch involuntarily. Isola smiled.

Titanic fields enveloped and deformed a tortured sun, dragging long shreds of its substance toward a spinning, flattened, whirlpool—a disc so bright it searingly outshone the unfortunate nearby star.

"Until now, most investigations of macro black holes have concentrated on showy cases like this one—the Cygnus A singularity—which raises such ferocious tides on a companion sun as to tear it apart before our eyes. In galactic cores, greedy mega holes can devour entire stellar clusters. No wonder most prior expeditions were devoted to viewing noughts with visible accretion discs. Besides, their splashy radiance made them easy to find."

Isola watched the victim star's tattered, stolen essence spiral into the planate cyclone, which brightened painfully despite attenuation by the viewing software. Shimmering, lambent stalks traced magnetically directed plasma beams, jetting from the singularity north and south. As refulgent gas swirled inward, jostling and heating, it suddenly reached an inner lip—the edge of a black circle, tiny in diameter but awesome in conclusiveness. The Event Horizon.

Spilling across that boundary, the actinic matter vanished abruptly, completely. Once over the edge it was no longer part of reality. Not *this* reality, anyway.

Mikaela had begun her lecture from a basic level, since some of the visitors weren't cosmogonists. One of these, Jarlquin, the geneticist from Pleasence, shifted on her chaise. At some silent order, a pseudo-life assistant appeared to massage her shoulders. Petite, even for a starfarer, Jarlquin glanced toward Isola, offering a conspiratorial smile. Isola pretended not to notice.

"Most massive noughts don't have stars as close neighbours, nor gas clouds to feed them so prodigiously and make them shine." Closing one eye again, Mikaela sent another command. In a flickered instant, the ostentatious display of stellar devouring was replaced by serene quiet. Cool, untroubled constellations spanned the theatre. Tenembro Nought was a mere ripple in one quadrant of the starry field, unnoticed by the audience until Mikaela's pointer drew attention to its outlines. A lenslike blur of distortion, nothing more.

"Solitary macro-singularities like Tenembro are far more common than their gaudy cousins. Standing alone in space, hungry, but too isolated to draw in more than a rare atom or meteoroid, they are also harder to find. Tenembro Nought was discovered only after detecting the way it bent light from faraway galaxies.

"The black hole turned out to be perfect for our needs, and only fifty-nine years, shiptime, from the colony on Kalimarn."

Under Mikaela's mute guidance, the image enlarged. She gestured towards a corner of the tank where a long, slender vessel could be seen, decelerating into orbit around the cold dimple in space. From the ship's tail emerged much smaller ripples, which also had the property of causing starlight to waver briefly. The distortion looked similar—though on a microscopic scale—to that caused by the giant nought itself. This was no coincidence.

"Once in orbit, we began constructing research probes. We converted our ship's drive to make tailored micro-singularities . . ."

At that moment, a tickling sensation along her left eyebrow told Isola that a datafeed was queued with results from her latest experiment. She closed that eye with a trained squeeze denoting ACCEPT. Implants along the inner lid came alight, conveying images in crisp focus to her retina. Unlike the digested pap in Mikaela's presentation, what Isola saw was in real time . . . or as "real" as time got, this near a macro black hole.

More rippling images of constellations. She subvocally commanded a shift to graphic mode; field diagrams snapped over the starry scene, showing Tenembro's mammoth, steepening funnel in space-time. An uneven formation of objects—minuscule in comparison—skimmed toward glancing rendezvous with the great nought's eerily bright-black horizon. Glowing traceries depicted one of the little objects as another space-funnel. Vastly smaller, titanically narrower, it too possessed a center that was severed from this reality as if amputated by the scalpel of God.

". . . with the objective of creating ideal conditions for our instruments to peer down . . ."

Columns of data climbed across the scene under Isola's eyelid. She could already tell that this experiment wasn't going any better than the others. Despite all their careful calculations, the camera probes still weren't managing to straddle between the giant and dwarf singularities at the right moment, just when the black discs touched. Still, she watched that instant of grazing passage, hoping to learn something—

The scene suddenly shivered as Isola's belly gave a churning lurch, provoking waves of nausea. She blinked involuntarily and the image vanished.

The fit passed, leaving her short of breath, with a prickle of perspiration on her face and neck. Plucking a kerchief from her sleeve, Isola dabbed her brow. She lacked the will to order the depiction back. Time enough to go over the results later, with full-spectrum facilities.

This is getting ridiculous, Isola brooded. She had never imagined, when the requisition-request came, that a simple clonal pregnancy would entail so many inconveniences!

". . . taking advantage of a loophole in the rules of our cosmos, which allow for a slightly offset boundary when the original collapstar possessed either spin or charge. This offset from perfection is one of the features we hope to exploit . . ."

Isola felt a sensation of being watched. She shifted slightly. From her nearby pseudo-life chaise, Jarlquin was looking at Isola again, with a measuring expression.

She might have the courtesy to feign attention to Mikaela's presentation, Isola thought, resentfully. *Jarlquin seems more preoccupied with my condition than I am.*

The Pleasencer's interest was understandable, after having come so far just for the present contents of Isola's womb. *My anger with Jarlquin has an obvious source. Its origin is the same as my own.*

An obsession with beginnings had brought Isola to this place on the edge of infinity.

How did the universe begin?

Where did it come from?

Where do I come from?

It was ironic that her search would take her to where creation ended. For while the expanding cosmos has no "outer edge," as such, it does encounter a sharp boundary at the rim of a black hole.

Isola remembered her childhood, back on Kalimarn, playing in the yard with toys that made pico-singularities on demand, from which she gained her first experience examining the warped mysteries of succinct event horizons. She recalled the day these had ceased to be mere dalliances, or school exercises in propulsion engineering, when they instead became foci for exaltation and wonder.

The same equations that describe an expanding universe also tell of a gravity trough's collapse. Explosion, implosion . . . the only difference lay in reversing time's arrow. We are, in effect, living inside a gigantic black hole!

Her young mind marvelled at the implications.

Everything within is aleph. Aleph is cut off from contact with that which is not aleph. Or that which came before aleph. Cause and effect, forever separated.

As I am separated from what brought me into being.

As I must separate from what I bring into being . . .

The foetus kicked again, setting off twinges, unleashing a flood of symbiotic bonding hormones. One side effect came as a sudden wave of unasked-for sentimentality. Tears filled Isola's eyes, and she could not have made image-picts even if she tried.

Jarlquin had offered drugs to subdue these effects—to make the process "easier." Isola did not want it eased. This could be her sole act of biological creation, given the career she had chosen. The word, "motherhood," might be archaic nowadays, but it still had connotations. She wanted to experience them.

It was simple enough in conception.

Back in the 18th century, a physicist, John Mitchell, showed that any large enough lump of matter might have an escape velocity greater than the speed of light. Even luminous waves should not be able to escape. When John Wheeler, two hundred years later, performed the same conjuring trick with mass *density*, the name "black hole" was coined.

Those were just theoretical exercises. What actually happens to a photon that tries to climb out of singularity? Does it behave like a rocket, slowing down under gravity's insistent drag? Coming to a halt, then turning to plummet down again?

Not so. Photons move at a constant rate, one single speed, no matter what reference frame you use. Unless physically blocked or diverted, light slows for no one.

But tightly coiled gravity does strange things. It changes *time*. Gravitation can make light pay a toll for escaping. Photons lose energy not by slowing down, but by stretching redder, ever redder as they rise from a space-time well, elongating to microwave lengths, then radio, and onward. Theoretically, on climbing to the event horizon of a black hole, any light wave has reddened down to nothing.

Nothing emerges. Nothing—travelling at the speed of light. In a prim, legalistic sense, that nothing *is* still light.

Isola spread her traps, planning tight, intersecting orbits. She lay in a web designed to ambush nothing . . . to peer down into nowhere.

"You know, I never gave it much thought before. The whole thing seemed such a bother. Anyway, I always figured there'd be plenty of time later, after we finished our project."

Mikaela's non-sequitur came by complete surprise. Isola looked up from the chart she had been studying. Across the breakfast table, her colleague wore an expression that seemed outwardly casual, but studied. Thin as frost.

"Plenty of time for what?" Isola asked.

Mikaela lifted a cup of *port'tha* to her lips. "You know . . . procreation."

"Oh." Isola did not know what to say. Ever since the visitor-ship announced itself, her partner had expressed nothing but irritation over havoc to their research schedules. Of late her complaints had been replaced with pensive moodiness. *So this is what she's been brooding about*, Isola realized. To give herself a moment, she held out her own cup for the pseudo-life servitor to refill. Her condition forbade drinking *port'tha*, so she made do with tea.

"And what have you concluded?" she asked, evenly.

"That I'd be foolish to waste this opportunity."

"Opportunity?"

Mikaela shrugged. "Look, Jarlquin came all this way hoping to requisition your clone. You could have turned her down—"

"Mikaela, we've gone over this so many times . . ." But Isola's partner cut her off, raising one hand, placatingly.

"That's all right. I now see you were right to agree. It's a great honor. Records of your clone-line are on file throughout the sector."

Isola sighed. "My ancestresses were explorers and star messengers. So, many worlds in the region would have—"

"Exactly. It's all a matter of available information! Pleasence World had data on you, but not on a seminatural variant like me, born on Kalimarn of Kalimarnese stock. For all we know, I might have what Jarlquin's looking for, too."

Isola nodded earnestly. "I'm sure of that. Do you mean you're thinking—"

"—of getting tested?" Mikaela watched Isola over the rim of her cup. "Do you think I should?"

Despite her continuing reservations over having been requisitioned in the first place, Isola felt a surge of enthusiasm. The notion of sharing this experience—this unexpected experiment in motherhood—with her only friend gave her strange pleasure. "Oh, yes! They'll jump at the chance. Of course . . ." She paused.

"What?" Mikaela asked, tension visible in her shoulders.

Isola had a sudden image of the two of them, waddling about the station, relying utterly on drones and pseudo-life servitors to run errands and experiments. The inconvenience alone would be frightful. Yet, it would only add up to a year or so, altogether. She smiled ironically. "It means our guests would stay longer. And you'd have to put up with Jarlquin—"

Mikaela laughed. A hearty laugh of release. "Yeah, dammit. That is a drawback!"

Relieved at the lifting of her partner's spirits, Isola grinned too. They were in concord again. She had missed the old easiness between them, which had been under strain since that first surprise message disrupted their hermits' regime. *This will put everything right,* she hoped. *We'll have years to talk about a strange, shared experience after it's all over.*

The best solutions are almost always the simplest.

Within a sac of amniotic fluid, a play is acted out according to a script. The script calls for proteins, so amino acids are lined up by ribosomes to play their roles. Enzymes appear at the proper moment. Cells divide and jostle for position. The code demands they specialize, so they do. Subtle forces of attraction shift them into place, one by one.

It is a script that has been played before.

A script designed to play again.

The pair of nano-draughts—each weighing just a million tons—hovered within a neutral gravity tank. Between the microscopic wells of darkness, a small recording device peered into one of the tiny singularities. Across the room, screens showed only the color black.

Special fields kept each nought from self-destructing—either through quantum evaporation or by folding space round itself like a blanket and disappearing. Other beams of force strained to hold the two black holes apart, preventing gravity from slamming them together uncontrollably.

It was an unstable situation. But Isola was well practiced. Seated on a soft chaise to support her overstrained back, she used subtle machines to manipulate the two funnels of sunken metric toward each other. The outermost rims of their spacetime wells merged. Two microscopic black spheres—the event horizons themselves—lay centimeters apart, ratcheting closer by the second, as Isola let them slowly draw together.

Tides tugged at the camera, suspended between, and at the fibre-thin cable leading from the camera to her recorders. Peering into one of those pits of blackness, the mini-telescope saw nothing. That was only natural.

Nothing could escape from inside a black hole.

A special kind of nothing, though. Nothing that had formerly been light, before being stretched down to true nothingness in the act of climbing that steep slope.

The two funnels merged closer still. The microscopic black balls drew nearer.

Light trying to escape a black hole is reddened to nonexistence. Nevertheless, virtual light can theoretically escape one nought, only to be sucked into the other. There, it starts blue-shifting exponentially, as gravity yanks it down again.

Between one event horizon and the other, the light doesn't "officially" exist. Not in the limiting case. Yet ideally, there should be a flow.

They had not believed her on Kalimarn. Until one day she showed them it was possible, for the narrowest of instants, to tap the virtual stream. To squeeze between the red-shifted and blue-shifted segments. To catch the briefest glimpse—

It happened too fast to follow with human eyes. One moment two black spheres were inching microscopically toward each other with the little, doomed instrumentality tortured and whining between them. The next instant, in a sudden flash, all contents of the tank combined and vanished. Space-time backlash set the reinforced vacuum chamber rocking—a side effect of that final stroke which severed forever all contact between the noughts and this cosmos where they'd been made. In the instant it took Isola to blink, they were gone, leaving behind the neatly severed end of fiber cable.

Gone, but not forgotten. In taking the camera with them, the singularities had given it the moment it needed. The moment when "nothing" was no longer nothing but merely a deep red.

And red is visible . . .

This was what had won her funding to seek out a partner and come here to Tenembro Nought. For if it was possible to look inside a micro-hole, why not a far bigger one that had been born in the titanic self-devouring of a star? So far, she and Mikaela hadn't yet succeeded in that part of the quest. Their research at the micro end, however, kept giving surprising and wonderful results.

Isola checked to make sure all the secrets of the vanished nano-nought had been captured during that narrow instant, and were safely stored in memory. Its rules. Its nature as a cosmos all its own. She had varied the formation recipe again, and wondered what physics would be revealed this time.

Before she could examine the snapshot of a pocket universe, however, her left eyelid twitched and came alight with a reminder. Time for her appointment. Damn.

But Jarlquin had shown Isola how much more pleasant it was to be on time.

The temperature of the universe is just under three degrees, absolute. It has chilled considerably, in the act of expanding over billions of years, from fireball to cosmos. Cooling in turn provoked changes in state. Delicately balanced forces shifted as the original heat diffused, allowing protons to form from quarks, then electrons to take orbit around them, producing that wonder, Hydrogen. Later rebalancings caused matter to gather, forming monstrous swirls. Many of these eddies coalesced and came alight spectacularly—all because the rules allowed it.

Because the rules *required* it.

Time processed one of those lights—by those selfsame rules—until it finished burning and collapsed, precipitating a fierce explosion and ejection of its core from the universe.

Tenembro Nought sat as a fossil relic of that banishment. A scar, nearly healed, but palpable.

All of this had come about according to the rules.

"We've liberated ourselves from Darwin's Curse, but it still comes down to the same thing."

The visitor made a steeple of her petite hands, long and narrow, with delicate fingers like a surgeon's. Her lips were full and dyed a rich mauve hue. Faint ripples passed across her skin as pores opened and closed rhythmically. A genetic graft, Isola supposed. Probably some Vorpal trait inserted into Jarlquin's genome before she was even conceived.

Fortunately, laws limit the gene trade, Isola thought. *All they can ask of me is a simple cloning.*

Over Jarlquin's shoulder, through the window of the lounge, Isola saw the starscape and realized Smolin Cluster was in view. Subvocally, she ordered the magni-focus pane to enlarge one quadrant for her eye only. Flexing gently, imperceptibly by other visitors across the room, the window sent Isola a scene of suns like shining grains. One golden pinpoint—Pleasence Star—shone soft and stable. Its kind, by nature's laws, would last eons and never become a nought.

"You see," Jarlquin continued, blithely ignorant of Isola's distraction. "Although we've pierced much of the code of Life, and reached a truce of sorts with Death, the fundamental rule's the same. That is successful which continues. And what continues most successfully is that which not only lives, but multiplies."

Why is she telling me this? Isola wondered, sitting in a gently vibrating non-life chair across from Jarlquin. Did the biologer-nurturist actually care what her subject thought? Isola had agreed to disrupt her research and donate a clone, for the genetic benefit of Pleasence World. Wasn't that enough?

I ought to be flattered. Tenembro Nought may be "close" to their world by interstellar standards, still, how often does a colony send a ship so far, just to collect one person's neonate clone?

Oh, the visitors had also made a great show of scrutinizing their work here, driving Mikaela to distraction with their questions. The pair of Butins were physicists and exuded enthusiasm along with their pungent, blue perspiration. But Jarlquin had confided in Isola. They would never have been approved to come all this way if not also to seek her seed. To treasure and nurture it, and take it home with them.

As I was taken from my own parent, who donated an infant duplicate to Kalimarn as her ship swept by. We are a model in demand, it seems.

The reasons were clear enough, in abstract. In school she had learned about the interstellar economy of genes, which prevented the catastrophe of inbreeding and spread the boon of diversity. But tidal surges of hormone and emotion had not been in her syllabus. Isola could not rightly connect abstractions with events churning away below her sternum. They seemed as unrelated as a sonnet and a table.

Two pseudo-life servitors entered—no doubt called when Jarlquin winked briefly a moment ago—carrying hot beverages on a tray. The blank-faced, bipedal protoplasmoids were as expressionless as might be expected of beings less than three days old . . . and destined within three more to slip back into the vat from which they'd been drawn. One servant poured for Isola as it had been programmed to do, with uncomplaining perfection no truly living being could have emulated.

"You were speaking of multiplication," Isola prompted, lest Jarlquin lose her train of thought and decide to launch into another recital of the wonders of Pleasence. The fine life awaiting Isola's clone.

"Ah?" Jarlquin pursed her lips, tasting the tea. "Yes, multiplication. Tell me, as time goes on, who populates the galaxies? Obviously, those who disperse and reproduce. Even though we aren't *evolving* in the old way—stressed by death and natural selection—a kind of selection is still going on."

"Selection."

"Indeed, selection. For traits appropriate to a given place and time. Consider what happened to those genes which, for one reason or another, kept individuals from leaving Beloved Earth during the first grand waves of colonization. Are descendants of those individuals still with us? Do those genes persist, now that Earth is gone?"

Isola saw Jarlquin's point. The impulsive drive to reproduce sexually had ebbed from humanity—at least in this sector. She had heard things were otherwise, spinward of galactic West and in the Magellanics. Nevertheless, certain models of humanity seemed to spread and thrive, while other types remained few, or disappeared.

"So it's been in other races we've formed symbioses with. Planets and commonwealths decide what kinds of citizens they need and requisition clones or new variants, often trading with colonies many parsecs away. Nowadays you can be successful at reproduction without ever even planning to."

Isola realized Jarlquin must know her inside and out. Not that her ambivalence was hard to read.

To become a mother, she thought. *I am about to . . . give birth. I don't even know what it means, but Jarlquin seems to envy me.*

"Whatever works," the Pleasencer continued, sipping her steaming tea. "That law of nature, no amount of scientific progress will ever change. If you have what it takes to reproduce, and pass on those traits to your offspring, then *they* will likely replicate as well, and your kind will spread."

What came before? And what came before that?

As a very little girl, back on Kalimarn, she had seen how other infants gleefully discovered a way to drive parents and guardians to distraction with the game of "Why." It could start at any moment, given the slightest excuse to ask that first, guileless question. Any adult who innocently answered with an explanation was met with the same simple, efficient rejoinder—another "why?" Then another . . . Used carefully, deliciously, it became an inquisition guaranteed to provoke either insanity or pure enlightenment by the twentieth repetition. More often the former.

To be different, Isola modified the exercise.

What caused that? she asked. Then—*What caused the cause?* and so on.

She soon learned how to dispense quickly with preliminaries. The vast, recent ages of space travel and colonization were quickly dealt with, as was the Dark Climb of man, back on old Beloved Earth. Recorded history was like a salad, archaeology an aperitif. Neanderthals and dinosaurs offered adult bulwarks, but she would not be distracted. Under pestering inquiry, the homeworld unformed, its sun unravelled into dust and gas, which swirled backward in time to be absorbed by reversed supernovas. Galaxies unwound. Starlight and cold matter fell together, compressing into universal plasma as the cosmos shrank toward its origins. By the time her poor teachers had parsed existence to its debut epoch—the first searing day, its earliest, actinic minute, down to micro-fractions of a second—Isola felt a sense of excitement like no story book or fairy tale could provide.

Inevitably, instructors and matrons sought refuge in the singularity. The Great Singularity. Before ever really grasping their meaning, Isola found herself stymied by pat phrases like "quantum vacuum fluctuation" and "boundary-free existence," at which point relieved adults smugly refused to admit of any prior cause.

It was a cop-out of the first order. Like when they told her how unlikely it was she would ever meet her true parent—the one who had brought her into being—no matter how far she travelled or how long she lived.

> Subtle chemical interactions cause cells to migrate and change, taking up specialties and commencing to secrete new chemicals themselves. Organs form and initiate activity. All is done according to a code.
>
> It is the code that makes it so.

Isola took her turn in the control chamber, relieving Mikaela at the end of her shift. Even there, one was reminded of the visitors. Just beyond the crystal-covered main aperture, Isola could make out the long, narrow ship from Pleasence, tugged by Tenembro's tides so that its crew quarters lay farthest from the singularity. The implosion chamber dangled towards the great hole in space.

"Remember when they came into orbit?" Mikaela asked, pointing toward the engine section. "How they pulsed their drive noughts at a peculiar pitch?"

"Yes." Isola nodded, wishing for once that Mikaela were not all business, but would actually talk to her. Something was wrong.

"Yes, I remember. The nano-holes collapsed quickly, emitting stronger spatial backwash than I'd seen before."

"That's right," Mikaela said without meeting Isola's eyes. "By creating metric-space ahead of themselves at a faster rate, they managed a steeper deceleration. Their engineer—the Vorpal, I'q'oun—gave me their recipe." Mikaela laid a data-sliver on the console. "You might see whether it's worth inserting some of their code into our next probe."

"Mmm." Isola felt reluctant. A debt for useful favours might disturb the purity of her irritation with these visitors. "I'll look into it," she answered noncommittally.

Although she wanted to search Mikaela's eyes, Isola thought it wiser not to press matters. The level of tension between them, rather than declining since that talk over breakfast, had risen sharply soon after. Something must have happened. *Did she ask Jarlquin to be tested?* Isola wondered. *Or could I have said something to cause offense?*

Mikaela clearly knew she was behaving badly and it bothered her. To let emotion interfere with work was a sign of unskilled selfing. The fair-skinned woman visibly made an effort to change tacks.

"How's the . . . you know, coming along?" she asked, gesturing vaguely toward Isola's midriff.

"Oh, well, I guess. All considered."

"Yeah?"

"I . . . feel strange though," Isola confided, hoping to draw her partner out. "As if my body were doing something it understood that's totally beyond *me*, you know?" She tapped herself on the temple. "Then, last night, I dreamt about a man. You know, a male? We had some on Kalimarn, you know. It was very . . . odd." She shook her head. "Then there are these mood swings and shifts of emotion I never imagined before. It's quite an experience."

To Isola's surprise, a coldness seemed to fill the room. Mikaela's visage appeared locked, her expression as blank as pseudo-life.

"I'll bet it is."

There was a long, uncomfortable silence. This episode had disrupted their planned decade of research, but now there was more to it than that. A difference whose consequences seemed to spiral outward, pushing the two of them apart, cutting communication. Isola suddenly knew that her friend had gone to Jarlquin, and what the answer had been.

If asked directly, Mikaela would probably claim indifference, that it didn't matter, that procreation had not figured in her plans, anyway. Nevertheless, it must have been a blow. Her eyes lay impenetrable under twin hoods.

"Well. Good night, then." The other woman's voice was ice. She nodded, turning to go.

"Good night," Isola called after her. The portal shut silently.

Subtle differences in heritage—that was all this was about. It seemed so foolish and inconsequential. After all, what was biological reproduction on the cosmological scale of things? Would any of this matter a million years from now?

One good thing about physics—its rules could be taken apart in fine, separable units, examined, and superposed again to make good models of the whole. Why was this so for the cosmos, but not for conscious intellects? *I'll be glad when this is over*, Isola told herself.

She went to the Suiting Room, to prepare for going outside. Beyond another crystal pane, Tenembro Nought's glittering blackness seemed to distort a quarter of the universe, a warped, twisted, tortured tract of firmament.

There was a vast contrast between the scale human engineers worked with—creating pico, nano, and even micro singularities by tricks of quantum bookkeeping—and a monster like Tenembro, which had been crushed into existence, or pure *non*-existence, by nature's fiercest explosion. Yet, in theory, it was the same phenomenon. Once matter had been concentrated to such density that space wraps around itself, what remains is but a hole.

The wrapping could sometimes even close off the hole. Ripples away from such implosions gave modern vessels palpable waves of spacetime to skim upon, much as their ancestors' crude ships rode the pulsing shock-fronts of antimatter explosions. The small black holes created in a ship's drive lasted for but an instant. Matter "borrowed" during that brief moment was compressed to superdensity and then vanished before the debt came due, leaving behind just a fossil field and spacial backwash to surf upon.

No origin to speak of. No destiny worth mentioning, That was how one of Isola's fellow students had put it, back in school. It was glib and her classmate had been proud of the aphorism. To Isola, it had seemed too pat, leaving unanswered questions.

Her spacesuit complained as pseudo-life components stretched beyond programmed parameters to fit her burgeoning form. Isola waited patiently until the flesh-and-metal concatenation sealed securely. Then, feeling big and awkward, she pushed through the exit port—a jungle of overlapping lock-seal leaves—and stepped out upon the station platform, surrounded by the raw vacuum of space.

Robotic servitors gathered at her ankles jostling to be chosen for the next one-way mission. Eagerness to approach the universal edge was part of their programming—as it appeared to be in hers.

Even from this range, Isola felt Tenembro Nought's tides tugging at fine sensors in her inner ears. The fetus also seemed to note that heavy presence. She felt it turn to orient along the same direction as the Visitor Ship, feet toward the awful blankness with its crown of twisted stars.

Let's get on with it, she thought, irritated by her sluggish mental processes. Isola had to wink three times to finally set off a flurry of activity. Well-drilled, her subordinates prepared another small invasion force, designed to pierce what logically could not be pierced. To see what, by definition, could not be seen.

The color of the universe had once been blue. Blue-violet of a purity that was essential. Primal. At that time the cosmos was too small to allow any other shade. There was only room for short, hot light.

Then came expansion, and a flow of time. These, plus subtle rules of field and force, wrought inexorable reddening on photons. By the time there were observers to give names to colors, the vast bulk of the universe was redder than infra-red.

None of this mattered to Tenembro Nought. By then, it was a hole. A mystery. Although some might search for color in its depths, it could teach the universe a thing or two about futiginal darkness.

For all intents and purposes, its color was black.

* * *

"I thought these might intrigue you," Jarlquin told her that evening.

There was no way to avoid the visitor—not without becoming a hermit and admitting publicly that something was bothering her. Mikaela was doing enough sulking for both of them, so Isola attended to her hosting duties in the station lounge. This time, while the other visitors chatted near the starward window, the nurturist from Pleasence held out toward Isola several jagged memory lattices. They lay in her slender hand like fragments of ancient ice.

Isola asked, "What are they?"

"Your ancestry," Jarlquin replied with a faint smile. "You might be interested in what prompted us to requisition your clone."

Isola stared at the luminous crystals. This data must have been prepared long ago: enquiries sent to her home world and perhaps beyond. All must have been accomplished before their ship even set sail. It bespoke a long view on the part of folk who took their planning seriously.

She almost asked—*"How did you know I'd want these?"* Perhaps on Pleasence they didn't consider it abnormal, as they had on Kalimarn, to be fascinated by origins.

"Thank you," she told the visitor instead, keeping an even tone.

Jarlquin nodded with an enigmatic smile. "Contemplate continuity."

"I shall."

In school, young Isola had learned there were two major theories of True Origin—how everything began in that first, fragmentary moment.

In both cases the result, an infinitesimal fraction of a second after creation, was a titanic explosion. In converting from the first "seed" of false vacuum to a grapefruit-sized ball containing all the mass-energy required to form a universe, there occurred something called *Inflation*. A fundamental change of state was delayed just long enough for a strange, negative version of gravity to take hold, momentarily driving the explosion even faster than allowed by lightspeed.

It was a trick, utilizing a clause in creation's codebook that would never again be invoked. The conditions would no longer exist—not in *this* universe—until final collapse brought all galaxies and stars and other ephemera together once more, swallowing the sum into one Mega Singularity, bringing the balance sheet back to zero.

That was how some saw the universe, as just another borrowing. The way a starship briefly "borrows" matter without prior existence, in order to make small black holes whose collapse and disappearance repays the debt again. So the entire universe might be thought of as a *loan*, on a vastly larger scale.

What star voyagers did on purpose, crudely, with machines, Creation had accomplished insensately but far better, by simple invocation of the Laws of Quantum Probability. Given enough time, such a fluctuation was bound to occur, sooner or later, according to the rules.

But this theory of origin had a flaw. In what context did one mean ". . . given enough time . . ."? How could there have been time before the universe itself was born? What clocks measured it? What observers noted its passage?

Even if there was a context . . . even if this borrowing was allowed under the rules . . . where did the rules *themselves* come from?

Unsatisfied, Isola sought a second theory of origins.

Black.

Within her eye's dark iris, the pupil was black. So was her skin.

It had not always been so.

She looked from her reflection to a row of images projected in the air nearby. Her ancestresses. Clones, demi-clones and variants going back more than forty generations. Only the most recent had her rich ebony flesh tone. Before that, shades had varied considerably around a dark theme. But other similarities ran true.

A certain line of jaw . . .

An arching of the brows . . .

A reluctant pleasure in the smile . . .

Women Isola had never known or heard of, stretched in diminishing rows across the room. Part of a continuity.

Further along, she found troves of data from still earlier times. There appeared images of *fathers* as well as mothers, fascinating her and vastly complicating the branchings of descent. Yet it remained possible to note patterns, moving up the line. Long after all trace of "family" resemblance vanished, she still saw consistent motifs, those Jarlquin had spoken of.

Five fingers on each clasping hand . . .

Two eyes, poised to catch subtleties . . .

A nose to scent . . . a brain to perceive . . .

A persistent will to continue . . .

This was not the only design for making thinking beings, star travellers, successful colonizers of galaxies. There were also Butins, Vorpals, Leshi and ten score other models which, tried and tested by harsh nature, now thrived in diversity in space. Nevertheless, this was a successful pattern. It endured.

Life stirred beneath Isola's hand. Her warm, tumescent belly throbbed, vibrating not just her skin and bones, but membranes, deep within, that she had never expected to have touched by another. Now at least there was a context to put it all in. Her ancestors' images nourished some deep yearning. The poignancy of what she'd miss—the chance to know this living being soon to emerge from her own body—was now softened by a sense of continuity.

It reassured her.

There was a certain beauty in the song of DNA.

Perched in orbit, circling a deep well.

A well with a rim from which nothing escapes.

Micro-noughts, spiralling toward that black boundary, seem cosmically, comically, out of scale with mighty Tenembro, star-corpse, gate-keeper, universal scar. What they lack in width, they make up for in depth just as profound. Wide or narrow, each represents a one-way tunnel to oblivion.

Is it crazy to ask if oblivions come in varieties, or differ in ways that matter?

Rules were a problem of philosophical dimensions when Isola first studied origins.

Consider the ratio of electric force to gravity. If this number had been infinitesimally higher, stars would never grow hot enough within their bowels to form and then expel heavy nuclei—those, like carbon and oxygen—needed for life. If the ratio were just a fraction *lower*, stars would race through brief conflagrations too quickly for planets to evolve. Take the ratio a little farther off in either direction, and there would be no stars at all.

The universal rules of Isola's home cosmos were rife with such fine-tuning. Numbers which, had they been different by even one part in a trillion, would not have allowed subtleties like planets or seas, sunsets and trees.

Some called this evidence of design. Master craftsmanship. Creativity. Creator.

Others handled the coincidence facilely. "If things were different," they claimed, "there would be no observers to note the difference. So it's no surprise that we, who exist, observe around us the precise conditions needed for existence!

"Besides, countless *other* natural constants seem to have nothing special about their values. Perhaps it's just a matter of who is doing the calculating!"

Hand-waving, all hand-waving. Neither answer satisfied Isola when she delved into true origins. Creationists, Anthropicists, they all missed the point.

Everything has to come from somewhere. Even a creator. Even coincidence.

Mikaela barely spoke to her anymore. Isola understood. Her partner could not help feeling rejected. The worlds had selected against her. In effect, the universe had declared her a dead end.

Isola felt, illogically, that it must be *her* fault. She should have found a way to console her friend. *It must be strange to hear you'll be the last in your line.*

Yet, what could she say?

That it's also strange to know your line will continue, but out of reach, out of sight? Beyond all future knowing?

The experiments continued. Loyal camera probes were torn apart by tides, or aged to dust in swirling back-flows of time near Tenembro's vast event horizon. Isola borrowed factors from the visitors' ship-drive. She tinkered with formulas for small counterweight black holes, and sent the new micro-singularities peeling off on ever-tighter trajectories toward the great nought's all-devouring maw.

Cameras maneuvered to interpose themselves between one nothing and another. During that brief, but time-dilated instant, as two wells of oblivion competed to consume them, the machines tried to take pictures.

Pictures of nothing, and all.

"To pass the time, I've been tinkering with your pseudo-life tanks," Jarlquin announced proudly one evening. "Your servitor fabricants ought to last as long as nine days now, before having to go back into the vat."

The visitor was obviously pleased with herself, finding something useful to do while Isola gestated. Jarlquin puttered, yet her interest remained focused on a product more subtle than anything she herself would ever design. Unskilled, but tutored by a billion years of happenstance, Isola prepared that product for delivery.

The second theory of origins had amazed her.

It was not widely talked about in Kalimarn's academies, where savants preferred notions of Quantum Fluctuation. After all, Kalimarn served as banking world for an entire cluster. No doubt the colonists *liked* thinking of the universe as something out on loan.

Nevertheless, in her academy days, Isola had sought other explanations.

We might have come from somewhere else! she realized one evening, when her studies took her deeply into frozen archives. The so-called "crackpot" theories she found there did not seem so crazy. Their mathematics worked just as well as models of quantum usury.

When a black hole is created after a supernova explosion, the matter that collapses into it doesn't just vanish. According to the equations, it goes . . . "elsewhere." To another spacetime. A continuum completely detached from ours.

Each new black hole represents another universe! A new creation.

The implication wasn't hard to translate in the opposite direction.

Our own cosmos may have had its start with a black hole that formed in some earlier cosmos!

The discovery thrilled her. It appalled Isola that none of her professors shared her joy.

"Even if true," one of them had said. "It's an unanswerable, unrewarding line of enquiry. By the very nature of the situation, we are cut off, severed from causal contact with that earlier cosmos. Given that, I prefer simpler hypotheses."

"But think of the implications!" she insisted. "Several times each year, new macro-black holes are created in supernovas—"

"Yes? So?"

"—What's more, at any moment across this galaxy alone, countless starships generate innumerable *micro*-singularities, just to surf the payback wave when they collapse. Each of these "exhaust" singularities becomes a universe too!"

The savant had smiled patronizingly. "Shall we play god, then? Try to take responsibility in some way for our creations?" The old woman's tone was supercilious. "This argument's almost as ancient as debating angels on pinheads. Why don't you transfer to the department of archaic theology?"

Isola would not be put off, nor meekly accept conventional wisdom. She eventually won backing to investigate the quandaries that consumed her. Much later, Jarlquin told her this perseverance was in part inherited. Some colonies had learned to cherish tenacity like hers. Though sometimes troublesome, the trait often led to profit and art. It was a major reason Pleasence World had sent a fetch ship to Tenembro Nought.

They cared little about the specific truths Isola pursued. They wanted the trait that drove her to pursue.

> Cells differentiate according to patterns laid down in the codes. Organs form which would—by happenstance—provide respiration, circulation, cerebration . . .
>
> In one locale, cells even begin preparing for future reproduction. New eggs align themselves in rows, then go dormant. Within each egg lay copies of the script.
>
> Even this early, the plan lays provisions for the next phase.

Normally, a pseudo-life incubator would have taken over during her final weeks. But the nurturist, Jarlquin, wanted none of that. Pseudo-life was but a product. Its designs, no matter how clever, came out of theory and mere generations of practice, while Isola's womb was skilled from trial and error successes stretching back several galactic rotations. So Isola waddled, increasingly awkward and inflated, wondering how her ancestors ever managed.

Every one of them made it. Each managed to get someone else started.

It was a strange consolation, and she smiled, sardonically. *Maybe I'm starting to think like Jarlquin!*

She no longer went outside to conduct experiments. Using her calculations, Mikaela fine-tuned the next convoy sent to skim Tenembro's vast event horizon, while Isola went back to basics in the laboratory.

> *What mystery is movement—distinguishing one location from another? In some natures, all points correspond—instantaneous, coincidental. Uninteresting.*
>
> *What riddle, then, is* change—*one object* evolving *into another? Some worlds disallow this. Though they contain multitudes, all things remain the same.*
>
> *Is a reality cursed which suffers entropy? Or is it consecrated?*

Once more a flash. Two micro-singularities fell together, carrying a tiny holo-camera with them to oblivion. In the narrow moment of union, the robot took full-spectrum readings of one involute realm. The results showed Isola a mighty, but flawed, kingdom.

The amount of mass originally used to form the nought mattered at this end—determining its gravitational pull and event horizon. But on the other side, beyond the constricted portal of the singularity, it made little difference. Whether a mere million tons had gone into the black hole or the weight of a thousand suns, it was the act of geometric transformation that counted. Instants after the nought's formation, inflation had turned it into a macrocosm. A fiery ball of plasma exploding in its own context, in a reference frame whose dimensions were all perpendicular to those Isola knew. Within that frame, a wheel of time marked out events, just as it did in Isola's universe—only vastly speeded up from her point of view.

Energy—or something like what she'd been taught to call "energy"—drove the expansion, and traded forms with substances that might vaguely be called "matter." Forces crudely akin to electromagnetism and gravity contested over nascent particles that in coarse ways resembled quarks and leptons. Larger concatenations tried awkwardly to form.

But there was no rhythm, no symmetry. The untuned orchestra could not decide what score to play. There was no melody.

In the speeded-up reference frame of the construct-cosmos, her sampling probe had caught evolution of a coarse kind. Like a pseudo-life fabrication too long out of the vat, the universe Isola had set out to create lurched toward dissipation. The snapshot showed no heavy elements, no stars, no possibility of self-awareness. How could there be? All the rules were wrong.

Nevertheless, the wonder of it struck Isola once more. To make universes!

Furthermore, she was getting better. Each new design got a little farther along than the one before it. Certainly farther than most trash cosmos spun off as exhaust behind starships. At the rate she was going, in a million years some descendant of hers might live to create a cosmos in which crude galaxies formed.

If only we could solve the problem of looking down Tenembro, she thought.

That great black ripple lay beyond the laboratory window, crowned by warped stars. It was like trying to see with the blind spot in her eye. There was a tickling notion that something lay there, but forever just out of reach.

To Isola, it felt like a dare. A challenge.

What strange rules must reign in there! She sighed. *Weirdness beyond imagination . . .*

Isola's gut clenched. The laboratory blurred as waves of painful constriction spasmed inside her. The chaise grew arms which held on, keeping her from falling, but they could not stop Isola from trying to double over, gasping.

Such pain . . . I never knew . . .

Desperately, she managed a faint moan.

"Jar . . . Jarlquin . . ."

She could only hope the room monitor would interpret it as a command. For the next several minutes, or hours, or seconds, she was much too distracted to try again.

It is a narrow passage, fierce and tight and terrible. Forces stretch and compress to the limit, almost bursting. What continues through suffers a fiery, constricted darkness.

Then a single point of light. An opening. Release!

Genesis.

They watched the fetch ship turn and start accelerating. Starlight refracted through a wake of disturbed space. If any of the multitude of universes created by its drive happened, by sheer chance, to catch a knack for self-existence, no one in *this* cosmos would ever know.

Isola's feelings were a murky tempest, swirling from pain to anaesthesia. A part of her seemed glad it was over, that she had her freedom back. Other, intense voices cried out at the loss of her captivity. All the limbs and organs she had possessed a year ago were still connected, yet she ached with a sense of dismemberment. Jarlquin had carefully previewed all of this. She had offered drugs. But Isola's own body now doped her quite enough. She sensed flowing endorphins start the long process of adjustment. Beyond that, artificial numbing would have robbed the colors of her pain.

The fetch ship receded to a point, leaving behind Tenembro's cavity of twisted metric, its dimple in the great galactic wheel. Ahead, Pleasence Star beckoned, a soft, trustworthy yellow.

Isola blessed the star. To her, its glimmer would always say—*You continue. Part of you goes on.*

She went on to bless the ship, the visitors, even Jarlquin. What had been taken from her would never have existed without their intervention, their "selection." Perhaps, like universes spun off behind a star-drive, you weren't meant to know what happened to your descendants. Even back in times when parents shared half their lives with daughters and sons, did any of them ever really know what cosmos lay behind a child's eye?

Unanswerable questions were Isola's metier. In time, she might turn her attention to these. If she got another chance, in a better situation. For now, she had little choice but to accept the other part of Jarlquin's prescription. Work was an anodyne. It would have to do.

"They're gone," she said, turning to her friend.

"Yes, and good riddance."

In Mikaela's pale eyes, Isola saw something more than sympathy for her pain. Something transcendent glimmered there.

"Now I can show you what we've found," Mikaela said, as if savouring the giving of a gift.

"What we . . ." Isola blinked. "I don't understand."

"You will. Come with me and see."

Tenembro was black. But this time Isola saw a different sort of blackness.

Tenembro's night fizzed with radio echoes, reddened heat of its expansion, a photon storm now cool enough to seem dark to most eyes, but still a blaze across immensity.

Tenembro's blackness was relieved by sparkling pinpoints, whitish blue and red and yellow. Bright lights like shining dust, arrayed in spiral clouds.

Tenembro Universe shone with galaxies, turning in stately splendour. Now and then, a pinwheel island brightened as some heavy sun blared exultantly, seeding well-made elements through space, leaving behind a scar.

"But . . ." Isola murmured, shaking her head as she contemplated the holistic sampling—their latest panspectral snapshot. "It's *our* universe! Does the other side of the wormhole emerge somewhere else in our cosmos?"

There were solutions to the equations which allowed this. Yet she had been so sure Tenembro would lead to another creation. Something special . . .

"Look again," Mikaela told her. "At beta decay in this isotope . . . And here, at the fine structure constant . . ."

Isola peered at the figures, and inhaled sharply. There *were* differences. Subtle, tiny differences. It was another creation after all. They had succeeded! They had looked down the navel of a macro singularity and seen . . . everything.

The still-powerful tang of her pain mixed with a heady joy of discovery. Disoriented by so much emotion, Isola put her hand to her head and leaned on Mikaela, who helped her to a chaise. Breathing deeply from an infusion tube brought her around.

"But . . ." she said, still gasping slightly. ". . . the rules are so close to ours!"

Her partner shook her head. "I don't know what to make of it either. We've been trying for years to design a cosmos that would hold together, and failed to get even close. Yet here we have one that occurred by natural processes, with no conscious effort involved—"

Mikaela cut short as Isola cried out an oath, staring at the pseudo-life chaise, then at a waiter-servitor that shambled in carrying drinks, a construct eight days old and soon to collapse from unavoidable buildup of errors in its program. Isola looked back at the holographic image of Tenembro's universe, then at Mikaela with a strange light in her eyes.

"It . . . *has* to be that way," she said, hoarse-voiced with awe. "Oh, don't you see? We're pretty smart. We can make life of sorts, and artificial universes. But we're new at both activities, while nature's been doing both for a very long time!"

"I . . ." The pale woman shook her head. "I don't see . . ."

"Evolution! Life never *designs* the next generation. Successful codes in one lifetime get passed on to the next, where they are sieved yet again, and again, adding refinements along the way. As Jarlquin said—whatever works, continues!"

Mikaela swallowed. "Yes, I see. But universes . . ."

"Why not for universes too?"

Isola moved forward to the edge of the chaise, shrugging aside the arms that tried to help her.

"Think about all the so-called laws of nature. In the "universes" we create in lab, these are almost random, chaotically flawed or at least simplistic, like the codes in pseudo-life."

She smiled ironically. "But Tenembro Universe has rules as subtle as those reigning in our own cosmos. Why not? Shouldn't a child resemble her mother!"

What came before me?

How did I come to be?

Will something of me continue after I am gone?

Isola looked up from her notepad to contemplate Tenembro Nought. This side—the deceptively simple black sphere with its star-tiara. Not a scar, she had come to realize, but an umbilicus. Through such narrow junctures, the Home Cosmos kept faint contact with its daughters.

If this was possible for universes, Isola felt certain something could be arranged for her, as well. She went back to putting words down on the notepad. She did not have to speak, just will them, and the sentences wrote themselves.

My dear child, these are among the questions that will pester you, in time. They will come to you at night and whisper, troubling your sleep.

Do not worry much, or hasten to confront them. They are not ghosts, come to haunt you. Dream sweetly. There are no ghosts, just memories.

It wasn't fashionable what she was attempting—to reach across the parsecs and make contact. At best it would be tenuous, this communication by long-distance letter. Yet, who had better proof that it was possible to build bridges across a macrocosm?

You have inherited much that you shall need, she went on reciting. *I was just a vessel, passing on gifts I received, as you will pass them on in turn, should selection also smile on you.*

Isola lifted her head. Stars and nebulae glittered beyond Tenembro's dark refraction, as they did in that universe she had been privileged to glimpse through the dark nought—the offspring firmament that so resembled this one.

As DNA coded for success in life-forms, so did *rules* of nature—fields and potentials, the finely balanced constants—carry through from generation to generation of universes, changing subtly, varying to some degree, but above all programmed to prosper.

Black holes are eggs. That was the facile metaphor. *Just as eggs carry forward little more than chromosomes, yet bring about effective chickens, all a singularity has to carry through is* rules. *All that follows is but consequence.*

The implications were satisfying.

There is no mystery where we come from. Those cosmos whose traits lead to forming stars of the right kind—stars which go supernova, then collapse into great noughts—those are the cosmos which have "young." Young that carry on those traits, or else have no offspring of their own.

It was lovely to contemplate, and coincidentally also explained why she was here to contemplate it!

While triggering one kind of birth, by collapsing inward, supernovas also seed through space the elements needed to make planets, and beings like me.

At first, that fact would seem incidental, almost picayune.

Yet I wonder if somehow that's not selected for, as well. Perhaps it is how universes evolve self-awareness. Or even . . .

Isola blinked, and smiled ruefully to see she had been subvocalizing all along, with the notepad faithfully transcribing her disordered thoughts. Interesting stuff, but not exactly the right phrases to send across light years to a little girl.

Ah, well. She would write the letter many times before finishing the special antenna required for its sending. By the time the long wait for a reply was over, her daughter might have grown up and surpassed her in all ways.

I hope so, Isola thought. *Perhaps the universe, too, has some heart, some mind somewhere, which can feel pride. Which can know its offspring thrive, and feel hope.*

Someday, in several hundred billion years or so, long after the last star had gone out, the great crunch, the Omega, would arrive. All the ash and cinders of those galaxies out there—and the quarks and leptons in her body—would hurtle together then to put *fini* on the long epic of this singularity she dwelled within, paying off a quantum debt incurred so long ago.

By then, how many daughter universes would this one have spawned? How many cousins must already exist in parallel somewhere, in countless perpendicular directions?

There is no more mystery where we come from. Had she really thought that, only a few moments ago? For a brief time she had actually been *satiated.* But hers was not a destiny to ever stop asking the next question.

How far back does the chain stretch? Isola wondered, catching the excitement of a new wonder. *If our universe spawns daughters, and it came, in turn, from an earlier mother, then how far back can it be traced?*

Trillions of generations of universes, creating black holes which turn into new universes, each spanning trillions of years? All the way back to some crude progenitor universe? To the simplest cosmos possible with rules subtle enough for reproduction, I suppose.

From that point forward, selection would have made improvements each generation. But in the crude beginning . . .

Isola thought about the starting point of this grand chain. If laws of nature could evolve, just like DNA, mustn't there exist some more *basic* law, down deep, that let it all take place? Could theologians then fall back on an ultimate act of conscious Creation after all, countless mega creations ago? Or was that first universe, primitive and unrefined, a true, primeval accident?

Either answer begged the question. Accident or Creation . . . in what context? In what setting? What conditions held sway *before* that first ancestor universe, that forerunner genesis, allowing it to start?

Her letter temporarily forgotten, with mere galaxies as backdrop, Isola began sketching outlines of a notion of a plan.

Possible experiments.

Ways to seek what might have caused the primal cause.

What had been before it all began.

MAMMY MORGAN PLAYED THE ORGAN; HER DADDY BEAT THE DRUM

Michael F. Flynn

Michael Flynn is one of the most prominent of the writers to emerge from *Analog* in the late 1980s and early nineties. His novel, *The Country of the Blind* (1990) and his collection, *The Nanotech Chronicles* (1991), as well as his nonfiction articles on psychohistory, have established him as a writer to watch. A statistician by profession, in his fiction Flynn is interested in technology and the people who work with it. So he's a perfect match for the traditional image of the hard sf writer, of the contemporary sort one finds in *Analog* two decades after Campbell. His fiction is full of confidence in the ability of logic and scientific training to solve human problems, perhaps a bit superior in that knowledge—the latest evolutionary stage descended from the *Astounding* group of the forties whose fans identified with *Slan*; his first published story was "Slan Libh" (1984). He is constantly experimenting with styles and technical tricks in his writing and seems not yet to have fully hit his stride.

This story is a clever amalgam of the ghost story and sf, plausibly updating the discredited experiments in spiritualism of the nineteenth and early twentieth century as well as investigating the psychology of the scientist and the physics of ghosts. It is Flynn's interest in the psychology of his central character, over and above the climactic scientific discovery, that shows a deepening in human concerns still not typical of the *Analog* story of recent decades. Still, note that physics is the privileged science in this story, and that, too, is a foundation of the *Analog* school of today.

I

An idle breeze was all it was. It was all it could have been.

Hilda Schenckweiler raised her head and looked around the business office. A sound? The old library building creaked at night, as its century-old foundation snuggled deeper into the soil. It popped and groaned with voices that went unnoticed during the bustle of the day, but which caught the attention during the still evenings. And the other librarians told certain stories, absurd stories on the face of them, that became more uncertain and less absurd as the night deepened. She laid aside the correspondence she had been answering and sat very still.

Yes, definitely a sound. But what? A soft, sliding sound, like the breath of a sleeping child. Familiar; but that nagging sort of familiarity that defied recognition. A shuddery feeling crawled like spiders up the back of her head and she brushed instinctively at her hair.

The sound seemed to come from behind her. She rose from her seat, hesitated a moment, then walked to the doorway that led to Interlibrary Loan. The illumination spilling from the business office spread a fan of light into the darkened work areas, teasing the dim shapes of tables and arching doorways from the shadows. Her own shadow, elongated and angular, was a spear thrusting into the shrouded gloom. Open doorways were cave mouths along the left hand wall. Directly ahead, across the workroom, the entrance to Acquisitions & Processing was a blacker rectangle, barely discernible in the stray light from the desk behind her.

She held her breath and listened. It was a quiet, almost casual sound. It seemed somehow idle, diffident.

The clock in the boardroom next door began to chime. Seven notes spaced in slow cadence. She caught her lower lip between her teeth and backed away from the yawning mouths of the dark doorways. When she bumped into the desk her heart froze for an instant. Without taking her eyes off the open workroom door, she probed behind herself with her right hand.

And knocked over the pencil cup. Pencils, pens, and paper clips clattered to the floor, and Hilda watched as, in slow motion, a gum eraser bounced soundlessly out the door and into the workroom, where it lay neatly centered in the wedge of light.

Her heart timed the long seconds that followed. With every beat she became more certain that someone—something—would emerge from one of the doorways.

But no one came to pick the eraser up. No shadow fell across the doorway. And, after another minute had passed, she realized that the sounds had stopped.

Slowly, she untensed, releasing a breath she hadn't known she was holding. Alone at night in a large building . . . It was easy to get spooked. She had been warned about it when she had volunteered for the overtime. The building was too dark. There were no windows in the business office to admit the streetlights or the moonlight or the comforting sounds of evening traffic.

She stepped boldly into the darkened workroom. Darker shadows limned huge and silent shapes that she knew—*she knew!*—were book racks and furniture. Yet, behind the veils of darkness she could imagine—things.

She turned left and glanced inside the boardroom. Shadows of tree branches played black lightning across the window. A reflected street lamp glimmered in the surface of the broad, polished conference table, like the moon on a midnight pond. The Empress Maria Theresa stared back primly from her portrait on the wall.

Hilda left the boardroom, closing the door carefully behind her, and continued across the Interlibrary Loan workroom. The floorboards complained beneath the carpeting. As she passed the entrance to Cataloguing, a blue-green flash teased the corner of her eye. A flashbulb? An electrical short? She stood in the entrance peering at the dim shapes looming in the darkness.

Nothing.

No flash. No sparks. Yet, she had seen something. She was sure of it. She groped for the wall switch and the overhead fluorescents flickered on. Squinting her eyes against the sudden illumination, Hilda took a careful step into the room. To her right was the huge, incongruous brick fireplace, a reminder of a time long ago when this had been a public reading room. (Reading in those days had been a serious business, conducted in comfortable, quiet surroundings.) To her left was the long work table with the scissors and the paste and the Dewey reference books. Backed against the far wall stood the row of five-foot high wooden catalogues. She saw nothing out of place.

But, when she turned to go, she froze. The fireplace was flanked by two doors: the one she had just come in and another on the farther side. Between the other door and the fireplace itself stood two, small, nine-drawer cabinets, one atop the other. The center drawer of the top cabinet hung halfway out.

She approached it with tentative steps, circling around to her left. That was what the sound had been. The familiar sound of card drawers opening and closing. That was all it had been.

Except that she was alone in the building.

A damp cold enveloped her and her breath was mist in the suddenly frigid air. Hilda wrapped her body tightly in her arms and the sigh of an old wind ran up her spine. Someone was watching her. Someone behind her. She felt it. She could feel the eyes on the back of her head; twin spots like the pressure of two fingertips where her neck joined her skull. It was not a menacing feeling, exactly. She felt no menace, but a cold disinterest that was far more chilling than any threat could be. Her breathing was loud and hoarse in her ears. She did not want to turn around. She did *not* want to turn around. She . . .

Felt a hand run through her hair.

And screamed.

And when she did turn, she saw there was no one behind her, after all. Nobody. So it must have been a breeze. What else could it have been?

II

"What else?" Leo Reissman asked. "A hysterical reaction," he told her, "brought on by the isolation and the dark. The human mind is a strange and wonderful thing. The neural impulses that we interpret as sights or sounds can be triggered without any external input. By a migraine, for example." He folded his hands across his vest and beamed at the two women. He wondered if this might be the case that would make his reputation; restore his respectability in the department. Odd—to chase over half a country in search of the bizarre, then to find it, almost literally, in his own backyard. More likely, though, it was nothing. Another false alarm. Night fears of the sort he was already too familiar with.

"I saw what I saw," Hilda Schenckweiler insisted, twisting her hands together. "The drawer was open. That was no hallucination. I shoved it closed myself. The rest of it. The sound. The light. The cold. I don't know. But that drawer was open."

"Ah, but what was the significance of its being open?" he asked. "Perhaps it had been hanging open the whole while."

The director was sitting behind her desk, turning Leo's business card over and over in her hands. She looked up at him. "Everything is properly put away when the library closes."

Leo shrugged. "Carelessness does happen," he reminded them.

"It's not the first time," said Hilda suddenly. Leo looked at her with surprise; the director, with annoyance. She flushed. "I mean odd things happening at night, not carelessness."

Leo raised his eyebrows. "Indeed?"

"It is very eerie sitting in the old building at night," the director told him, and Leo wondered briefly why she insisted on answering for her librarian. "We've all gotten 'the willies' at one time or another, Doctor . . ." She glanced briefly at the business card she was twisting in her hand. "Doctor Reissman. That doesn't mean there is anything, well, supernatural taking place."

Leo blinked and lifted his head. "Oh, dear. I should think not!" he said.

The director seemed confused. She looked at Hilda. "But the patrolman said that he would send around a man who . . . Hilda, how did he put it?"

"A man who has had experience with this sort of phenomenon," Hilda quoted carefully.

"He said that?" Leo chuckled. "Oh, Sam was just being mysterious. That's his nature. I helped him out once with a little problem he had, but there was nothing supernatural about it. I don't believe in the supernatural."

"But . . ." The director flicked her finger against his business card. "Aren't you a psychic?"

"What? Oh, *that's* why you're confused." He gestured toward the business card. "If you would read it again?" he suggested.

The director frowned at him; frowned at the card. "Physicist," she read. She looked up at Leo. "Physicist?"

Leo smiled at them again. "Certainly. Nothing supernatural about physics, I assure you."

"I don't understand," Hilda said to him as they stood together at the entrance to the Cataloguing Room. "Why would a physicist be interested in ghosts?"

Leo studied the layout of the room from the doorway. Yes, there was the catalogue, nestled between the fireplace and the other doorway. The accused looked innocent enough. Hardly the sort of thing to frighten a librarian.

Yet, hardly the sort of thing to open and close of itself on a dark, lonely night.

Probably just a case of nerves, he told himself. Nerves and fright accounted for more apparitions than anything physical. That was the problem with this sort of thing. It was often a struggle to establish whether anything had happened at all. And most often of all, he knew with a glum satisfaction, nothing *had* happened. That would explain so much. It was an answer he hungered for with an intensity that sometimes frightened him. If it *were* true, then he was most assuredly alone; but he would know, at last, why he was alone.

"Ghosts?" he answered her at last, though with more force than he had intended. "There are no such things as ghosts." Something harsh must have come out in his voice, because Hilda backed away from him.

"Then, do you think I'm crazy? That I imagined it all?"

"I didn't say that," he assured her. "Perhaps you did see something. But if you did, then it was something real, made of matter and energy, not a ghost." He shrugged his shoulders and pushed his hands into his pants pockets. "No, I don't believe in ghosts," he continued. "But I don't believe that the edge of the universe or the inside of the nucleus are the only frontiers of physics, either. There are still discoveries to be made in the odd nooks and crannies of the workaday world." He turned his mouth up. "Other physicists study quarks. I study quirks."

She smiled tentatively at his joke.

"I think," he continued, "that what you saw was a natural phenomenon that has never been properly studied. Like *Kugelblitz*. That was once dismissed as folklore, too." He realized abruptly that they were both still standing in the doorway, like two kids afraid to enter a haunted house. "Well," he said, rubbing his hands, "shall we get started?"

He crossed the room and began examining the card catalogue. It was a very old, dark wood cabinet about three feet by three feet, and it sat atop a second, similar cabinet. The dark wood shone from decades of rubbing hands. Leo touched the little brass fingerhook on the front of one of the drawers and it slid easily in and out. "Was this the drawer?" He wondered if the drawers could slide by themselves. From traffic vibrations, perhaps. Unlikely, but . . . Experimentally, he shook the heavy, wooden unit, but it did not budge and the drawers stayed put.

"No," he heard her say. "The one I saw was the center drawer, second row; but I heard the sounds for several minutes. More than the one drawer might have moved."

Or none, Leo thought. He turned and saw with surprise that Hilda was still standing in the doorway. "Aren't you coming in?" he asked.

She hugged herself and shook her head. "I'm frightened."

"There's no need to be frightened."

He had meant to comfort her; but—unexpectedly—she flared up at him. "What do you know about it? You weren't there!"

"I—" Memories bubbled beneath his thoughts. The birds blackening the sky. The half-heard fragment of a word. Lying awake sweat-soaked in the heart of the night. He pressed his teeth into his lower lip. "I've studied a fair number of snugs," he said finally.

"Snugs?"

"SNGs. Standard Nighttime Ghosts." He found quick refuge in the jargon. "The acronym is less semantically loaded. If you use the word 'ghost,' you make assumptions about what the phenomenon is."

She turned up her mouth. "And if you use the acronym, you make assumptions about what it *isn't*."

"I'm sorry," he told her. "I never meant to sound patronizing. Whether your snug was a real phenomenon or not, your fright certainly was."

"Don't trivialize it!" She hunched over her folded arms. "My fright was more than just a 'real phenomenon.' It was something I *felt*. That I still feel."

"Would it help," he asked quietly after a moment, "if I told you that I know exactly how you felt?"

Hilda raised her head and studied him for a few moments. Her mouth parted slightly and Leo was afraid that she would ask him how he knew how she felt; but she said nothing. Finally, she unfolded her arms and stepped into the room. As she approached the catalogue, she side-stepped to her left and pointed to a file drawer. "That's the one I saw open."

Leo sucked in his breath. She had walked *desail*. . . . The Dundrum Effect? If so, how to test it? As casually as he could, he walked to the fireplace and pretended to look up the flue. He pulled his head out. "Ms. Schenckweiler," he said "would you come over here a moment?"

She gave him a frown. "What is it?" He watched her turn and take a step and . . .

"There! You're doing it again!"

She stopped and looked around herself with a bewildered expression. "What?"

"Just now, and earlier, when you walked toward the catalogue, you turned—right about there." He pointed to a spot half a meter in front of the catalogue. "As if you were stepping around an obstacle."

Hilda stared at the empty air, then she turned wide eyes on him. "Obstacle?" she said. Her voice rose in pitch and she took a hasty step backward away from The Spot. "Do you mean the ghost is still there?" Her hand sought her mouth.

Dammit, now I've frightened her. Leo raised his hands, palms out. "Now don't—" He stopped himself. He had almost said *don't be frightened*. "It's a common experience. I call it the Dundrum Effect, after the Irish village where Conway first described it. I believe that it is due to a sort of 'peripheral vision' that some especially sensitive people possess. Perhaps a sense much as the blind develop, when they can 'feel' the presence of a wall or of another person."

She lowered her hand slowly. "It does help a little."

"Eh? What does?"

"Your dry-as-dust explanations. You make it sound so ordinary. That . . . takes the edge off." She kept staring at The Spot.

Dry-as-dust? Leo grunted. He took a tape measure and a small notebook from his jacket pocket and measured The Spot's location from several benchmarks around the room. He entered the figures in the notebook. "SNGs," he told her as he worked, "generally recur within well-defined loci. So, it is always there, even if it is not always manifest."

"What do you mean?" Hilda responded. "They don't move?"

Leo was kneeling on the floor. He released the button on the tape measure and the steel strip snaked back into the spool. He rocked back on his heels and considered her question. "Well, not exactly," he said. "Some are mobile. . . . That is, some do move. But they move along well defined trajectories; always repeating the same actions."

"I see," she said. "Like an obsessive-compulsive personality disorder."

He cocked his head. "Actually, more like a stuck record. Don't jump to the conclusion that snugs have a personality to be 'compelled'; or that they are even 'conscious,' in some sense. Those are some of the assumptions we make when we say 'ghosts.' When you think about it, the ocean tides show the same sort of 'compulsive' behavior."

"How do you *know* that your 'snugs' don't have self-awareness? Aren't they the spirits of the dead?"

Leo hesitated a moment. He rubbed his left hand absently with his right. *The flutter of birds blackening the sky. The faint echo of an unheard voice.* He took a deep breath and buried the memories that threatened to break surface. "I don't know that they are. Carpenter's Conjecture is that souls and ghosts are equivalent entities; but that has never been proven. Back in 1906, a Boston physician named MacDougall weighed six people on platform scales as they were dying, and recorded a weight loss of ten to forty grams at the moment of death. So it would seem that *something* physical leaves the body at death. However, no one has ever repeated the experiment under proper controls, so we cannot be sure. The weights MacDougall recorded are about the same as for the snugs I've measured; but the similarity of mass may be coincidence. There may be snugs that are not souls; and souls that are not snugs. And even if there is a connection of some sort, the snug may be nothing more than a . . . a holographic recording of the soul, lacking volition or awareness."

Hilda leaned forward and waved her hand tentatively through the air above The Spot. "I . . . don't feel anything."

Leo rose and brushed at his pants. "No, you wouldn't. Snugs have extremely low density. About a tenth of a milligram per cubic centimeter. You could walk right through them and never notice. Go ahead. Take a step forward."

She looked at him and hesitated. "Go ahead," he urged her. "It can't hurt you."

She closed her eyes and took three abrupt steps. Then she opened her eyes and slowly unclenched her fists. "Nothing." She looked at him. "No feeling of avoidance."

"Exactly. The Dundrum Effect only occurs when you don't consciously think about where you're walking."

"I didn't feel a thing," she said.

"I told you snugs have low density."

Hilda laughed a short, high-pitched laugh that caused Leo to give her an uncertain look.

"What is it?"

"The old proof that ghosts are invisible. You've never seen one, have you? Then that proves that they're invisible!"

III

The director stopped him as he passed through the business office on his way out.

"May I see you for a moment?" She stood in the doorway to the secretary's office. Leo shifted the overcoat draped across his arm and glanced toward the hall door where Hilda Schenckweiler waited for him.

"Certainly," he said.

"Hilda, you may wait for Doctor Riessman downstairs."

Leo followed the director through the secretary's office and left into the librarian's office. He noticed a fireplace in the corner, the twin to the one in the Cataloguing Room, and surmised that these two offices had been built from a second reading room, a mirror-image of the one on the other side of the building. The director sat behind her desk, leaning forward in her chair, elbows planted on the desktop. Leo waited for her to say what she intended to say.

"This 'investigation' of yours needn't last long."

He was not sure if she was making a forecast, expressing an opinion, or giving an order. Leo had heard the quotation marks in her voice. "I will try to be expeditious," he said.

She picked up a pencil from her desk and twisted it in her fingers. "I doubt that there is any more to this incident than simple hysteria."

"Most of the cases that I have examined," he said carefully, "have turned out to be nothing more than wild imagination. A few have been deliberate hoaxes."

The director tapped the eraser end of the pencil on her desk blotter. "I don't believe Hilda would deliberately hoax anyone."

Something about her voice pricked Leo's curiosity. "But . . ." he probed.

The woman sat back and brushed a hand at her hair. "It is really not my place to say. . . ."

But you'll say it anyway.

"Hilda *has* had a few problems in her life recently. Her mother, you understand. She had to put her in a home. She has been seeing a psychiatrist about it."

"Seeing a psychiatrist is not—"

She broke him off with a flip of her hand. "I know that, Doctor. I know that. These days it is almost a status symbol. But—" She paused in thought. "What I am trying to say is that the Library Ghost is an old tradition with the staff here. Every time a new girl is scheduled to work evenings, she is told all sorts of stories. You know the kind I mean. Well, the old building is genuinely creepy at night, and you do hear sounds and feel light drafts. Someone with, well, with an uncertain imagination, may magnify them into—who knows what?" She laid the pencil down; picked it up again.

Leo nodded curtly. "I understand Ms. Schenckweiler may not have seen anything. That is certainly a possibility that I will keep in mind." He straightened his overcoat and turned to go.

The director's voice stopped him at the door. "It will all turn out to be a hyperactive imagination. You'll see."

He turned and looked at her. Her fingers were twisting and turning the pencil. Leo locked eyes with her for a moment. Then he nodded. "More than likely," he told her.

Hilda was waiting for him when the elevator doors chimed open on the first floor lobby. She took him firmly by the arm and guided him toward the front door, past the odd-looking flag in its glass display case. "The First Stars and Stripes of the

United Colonies—July 8, 1776." It resembled the Betsy Ross flag, save that the stripes were in the canton and the stars were in the fly. Leo waved his rumpled, felt fedora toward the rear door. "But, my car . . ." he started to say.

"I thought you told me you wanted a tour of the grounds outside."

Leo didn't remember saying that at all. He looked at her and opened his mouth, but then thought better of it. There was a crease on her forehead, above her nose, and her face had a tight, closed-in expression. He shrugged. Whatever it was she wanted to tell him, he would learn in due time. So, he followed her lead. Outside was a bracing October afternoon, and a walk around the building would do him no harm.

They stepped out into a swirl of wind; red and gold leaves chattered in their faces. Leo clamped his hand firmly to his head to keep his hat from flying off. The sidewalk was bounded on the left by the "new" annex and on the right by a brick wall retaining the bank of a grassy knoll. The wind, trapped in the pocket, struggled to escape.

Leo strode briskly forward, out of the whirlwind. At the point where the sidewalk cascaded down flights of steps to Church Street, he turned and faced the building. The library grounds occupied the entire block of Church Street between Fifth and Sixth. The original building, a dark brick Carnegie-style structure, sat atop the crest of the knoll in the center of the block. Attached to its east face and extending to the corner at Fifth, was the annex that now housed the Circulating Collection. Behind the two loomed the massive, tree-shrouded, stone knob of Mount Jefferson.

A side path branched off the sidewalk and wound west toward the old building. *The original entrance*, Leo surmised, studying the arched portal with its decorative scrollwork. *They don't make 'em like that anymore.* It was sealed up now; the old, grand staircase was a platform for shrubbery planters. *Too bad.* The old building *looked* like a library. Its facade was distinctive; not like the anonymous structures they put up nowadays. Stone benches were spotted here and there about the grounds. Leo wondered if anyone ever used them.

Hilda was waiting for him at the point where the sidewalk forked. Beside her, atop the grassy knoll, was an odd-looking stone structure. It was flat, like a table or a bench; but it was too low for the one and too wide for the other. And it was surrounded by a wrought iron fence. Leo frowned at it. He felt he should know what it was; that, in another setting, it would be instantly recognizable. "What is that?" he asked her.

Hilda turned her head. "What, this? Why, it's only Billy."

The surprise in her voice was overdone. *She wanted me to see this*, he thought. *It's why she led me out this way.* Leo hunched his shoulders against the wind and walked up the side path and around on the grass to look down on the object.

It was a flat-topped sepulcher. A grave.

Of course. Instantly recognizable; but not something that one would expect to find sitting beside the town library's main entrance. Leo knelt and brushed away the dirt and leaves that obscured the horizontal slab. *William M. Parsons, Esq.*, he read. *Born May 6, 1701. Died December 22, 1752. He rocked Easton in her cradle and watched of her infant footsteps with paternal solicitude.* He ran his fingers across the slab. The stone was cold and rough. Old. It was strange to think that this grave was nearly a quarter century old when certain men had pledged their lives and fortunes at Philadelphia.

He looked up and saw that Hilda had joined him. "This is a grave," he said, which was stupid because she knew it was a grave. "A grave on the library grounds. Why did no one mention this earlier?"

Hilda rubbed her palms together against the chill. She glanced briefly at the windows overlooking them. "The director thought it would be best not to bring it up."

"Why ever not?" He stood and brushed at his trousers.

"Because she doesn't want any sensationalism attached to the library. She doesn't want us on the cover of the *National Enquirer.*"

He grunted. *Then why did you insist on leading me right to it?* He wanted to ask her straight out, but something in her face made him hesitate. Some deep-seated worry that gnawed within her. Best to approach the issue sideways. If at all. What did Hilda Schenckweiler's state of mind have to do with his investigation? Perhaps nothing. Perhaps everything. He remembered what the director had told him just before he left. Then he wondered if Hilda might have waited outside the office and overheard the comments. Showing him the grave might be nothing more than an act of defiance on her part. "I can appreciate her fears; but I really do need all the facts of your case."

"My case." She gestured toward the sepulcher. "Parsons was the city's founder. He did the surveying and laid out the plots for Thomas Penn." She gazed toward the far corner of the building; at the Cataloguing Room windows. "Do you think that he was doing late night research or something?"

Leo laughed. "No, I don't know that he has anything to do with what happened last night; but, then I don't know that he hasn't, either. Unless I have all the data, I cannot decide what is important and what is not."

Hilda glanced again at the oversize windows of the Librarian's Office, and Leo turned and saw the slat of a venetian blind flick closed.

"Is there anything else you haven't told me?"

Hilda took a deep breath. "Follow me."

The second grave was less elaborate. It was little more than a rock surrounded by an iron rail situated in the little park on the west side of the driveway. The rock was about two feet high and was worn and pitted. Leo thought it looked a bit like a meteor. A large concavity on its top had collected a pool of stagnant rain water, in which floated a brown, curled leaf.

Elizabeth Bell Morgan, stated the small plaque. *"Mammy Morgan" Died October 16, 1839. Aged about 79 years.* Leo grunted. He squinted at the plaque. "Mammy Morgan. Is that the same Mammy Morgan—"

"That the hill was named after? Of course. How many Mammy Morgans do you suppose there were?"

"Just asking." He shaded his eyes and looked south across the rooftops. From Mount Jefferson, Mammy Morgan's Hill was a motley of orange and gold and red in the October-lit distance. "Who was she? When I moved out here, Magruder took me around and showed me all the sights; but they're only names to me."

Hilda folded her arms against the chill. "I suppose you could call her a foundress of our library. Her donations of money and law books helped get the library started back in 1811."

"Law books? She was a lawyer? Wasn't that unusual for a woman back then?"

Hilda shook her head. "She wasn't a lawyer, but she was probably better educated than most of the lawyers in town. She was born and raised a Quaker in Philadelphia, but her parents sent her to school in Europe. She had fallen in love with a soldier boy and they hoped to 'cure' her. That was before the Revolution. She came here later, in 1793, when the yellow fever epidemic swept Philadelphia. Her husband set her and the children up in a hotel on the hill—" she gestured toward the south "—then he went back to Philadelphia, and wound up in a mass grave."

"What? Why on earth would he go back?"

"Why? He was a doctor. That's what doctors do during epidemics. History is full of forgotten, everyday heroes like Abel Morgan. Afterwards, the Widow Morgan bought the hotel and ran it for fifty years. She had a fine collection of books from her European studies and her favorite pastime was reading law."

Leo chuckled. "Light reading, eh?"

Hilda scowled. "It beats soap operas. She kept her law books on a bench in the hotel's public room. Her neighbors kept asking for her opinions on disputes, so she began to 'dispense law,' as she put it."

"Like Judge Roy Bean," said Leo. "The Law South of the Lehigh."

She turned her mouth up. "Without the arbitrary hangings. She was a woman. She ruled so wisely that people seldom appealed their cases to the regular courts. The Germans began to call her *Die Mommie*. When she died, the funeral procession stretched over two miles, from here all the way to Lachenour Heights. The Indian corn mill—" she gestured toward the tombstone "—was added later."

"One of your folk heroes, I see. But there's more to the story," he prodded. "Isn't there?"

Hilda rubbed her arms and looked at the stone. "You know how people are. An educated woman, living alone, supporting herself. Especially in those days. The local bar tried especially hard to discredit her, spreading malicious stories about her character and about goings-on in her hotel. Some people said . . . Well, they said she was a witch."

He looked at her. "A witch."

She look back. "Nonsense of course. But people love to spread malicious rumors. There was a children's rhyme: *'Mammy Morgan played the organ/Her daddy beat the drum.'* It was no more than rhyme play on her name; but some tried to make it sound as if she was involved in powwow magic."

Leo pursed his lips. "So, there are two graves on the library grounds, then."

Hilda cocked her head. "Follow me," she said.

Leo stared at the indentation in the northeast section of the library's driveway. "Eighty-eight?" he asked incredulously.

"There's a vault under there," Hilda told him.

"Eighty-eight bodies?" He still couldn't believe it. He looked around: at the buildings, the parking lot. There was an old man sitting on one of the park benches, reading a book. Children were playing in the dead-end of Sixth Street. The rocky knob behind him rose steeply into a whispering shroud of trees. "What is this, a cemetery?"

"Yes."

He gave her a sharp glance. "Are you serious?"

"Quite serious," she replied tartly. "You might as well know it all. When they started construction on the library in 1901, the cheapest land available was the old German Reformed Cemetery, on this hilltop. There were five hundred fourteen bodies in it then, and they exhumed them all."

Leo's breath caught in his throat. Digging up hundreds of rotted corpses . . . The gaping skulls; the bones fleshed out in tatters . . . What was it like to turn over the earth and find . . . No, he was letting his imagination get the better of him. The bodies—the "remains"—would have been in coffins, and the coffins would have been largely intact. Most of them, anyway. He took a deep breath and glanced at Hilda. "What . . . What did they do with them all?" he asked huskily.

She gave him a quizzical look. "Reusing old cemeteries was fairly common around the turn of the last century. People weren't as uptight about 'disturbing the dead' as they are now. The city wrote letters to all the relatives and descendants they could locate, asking them to come and claim the remains. Most of them were reburied elsewhere." Her eyes dropped to the concavity in the asphalt. "All but these eighty-eight. They were put in new wooden caskets and buried together in a large underground cavern."

"I see. And were there any, ah, unusual events reported during the construction?"

"She said I shouldn't tell you."

Leo looked at her. "The director."

"Yes. But . . ." She shrugged heavily. "What's the point? You can look it up in our own archives. It was never kept secret. There were even newspaper features about it over the years." She pointed toward the end of the driveway. "The people who lived along North Fifth claimed they saw moving lights at night; and—" She paused and made a face. "A headless woman."

Leo stifled a sudden laugh. The lights were a possibility; but the headless woman was too much. Too Gothic. Although, he reminded himself, this part of Pennsylvania had been heavily settled by Germans, so Gothic images might be expected. He studied the row houses along North Fifth Street at the end of the driveway. The site of the vault would have been clearly visible back then. "You're not pulling my leg, are you?" Some people thought it was great fun to try to fool him with tall tales. Hilda didn't seem the type, but you never knew.

"Of course I'm not," she said. "But I can't answer for the local residents a hundred years ago. *They* may have been pulling every leg in sight. You know the German sense of humor. The next night, people came from all over town, hoping to see 'die shpooken'; but nothing happened. Then, after everyone left, the locals claimed the ghosts came back."

Leo smiled. "You're right. It sounds like they were having some fun."

"I'm sure they were; because no one reported anything unusual in the midsixties."

"Oh? What happened then?"

"That's when the annex was built." She gestured toward the newer building. "The weight of the construction equipment broke the vault open. Caskets disintegrated and there were bones and skulls rolling all over."

It took him by surprise. Death images clawed their way to the surface of his mind. Whitened skeletons robed in rotted, worm-eaten flesh. Hanks of colorless hairs; eyeless sockets. *Gonna roll them bones.* He sucked in his breath. "My God! That's terrible!"

"Yes, it sounds like a scene from a bad horror movie, doesn't it?"

Leo mopped his brow against the chill autumn air. "But for one difference."

"What's that?"

"In the movies, that sort of scene is always a prelude to something grisly and horrible. But in the real world, when you 'disturb the dead,' nothing supernatural happens."

One side of the parking lot opened onto the park by Sixth Street; the other was bounded by the wooded knob of rock—private property, Hilda told him. A castellated stone wall marched along the backside of the grounds, from the stone knob all the way across the dead end of Sixth. Gravel crunched beneath their feet as they walked together toward his car.

They stopped beside his car and Leo fished in his pocket for his keys. Hilda glanced toward the library building. "Do you think you can explain what happened to me last night?"

There was an odd tightness to her voice and Leo studied her as he juggled the car keys in his hand. "I don't know," he replied honestly. "We don't have all the answers. We never will."

"Oh," she said and fell silent.

He paused with his keys out and gazed across the roof of his car. Leafy branches reached up and over the stone wall. In the distance he could see the trees and houses covering the slopes of College Hill. He frowned. There was something wrong with the vista. Foreground and background; but no middleground. "What's on the other side of that wall," he asked.

"Nothing."

"Eh?" He froze, knowingly dreading what she would say next.

"Unless you count 120 feet of air as something."

Leo glanced from her to the wall and back. There was a sudden void in his chest. He knew what she meant. He knew. He pocketed his keys and walked slowly to the back end of the lot. Every step was torture, but he had to see for himself. When he reached the wall, he craned his neck and looked down without leaning over.

A heavily shrubbed, rocky cliff dropped in a near vertical line to the black asphalt ribbon of Bushkill Street. Toy cars hummed below across his field of vision. Farther west, the slope was more gentle and ribbed with trees growing out of the side of the hill; but here, at the east edge of the parking lot, it was a straight drop. *A stumble, Falling, falling. Leo! Hands grabbing. Bushes torn out by their roots.* The scene below seemed to turn slowly counterclockwise. He backed away and stared at the comforting solidity of the rocky knob that capped Mount Jefferson. It added, he judged, another thirty feet; and the drop-off was just as sheer. The high dive platform.

Hilda joined him. "It's a long way to fall, isn't it?"

Leo started. What macabre impulse had prompted her to say that? "Not really," he said. "It would only take about three seconds to reach the bottom. It would be over with quickly."

"Three seconds?" she said. "Long enough to realize what was happening to you." She braced her hands on the top of the wall and leaned over. Leo gasped and grabbed her by the arm.

"Hey!"

"Don't do that!" She pulled her arm from his grasp. "What's the matter with you?"

"I . . . don't like heights," he said. His heart was pumping heavily. *Long enough to know.*

She gave him an odd look; but stepped away from the wall and folded her arms. "It's getting cold. I'd better get back inside."

"All right."

"I'm sorry. Did I make you nervous, leaning out like that?"

"No. Yes." Some people had no grasp of physics; no conception of the forces that could kill them. Their knowledge of force and motion came from Hollywood movies and television shows. Not more than a few meters away, the planetary mass was waiting to smash her like a bug onto a windshield; and she leaned out over the wall and dared it.

They walked together back to his car and Leo fumbled again with his keys. A cliff. He hadn't known that the library backed so close to the cliff.

"Do you think anyone could survive?"

"What?" He looked at Hilda. "Survive what?"

She was gazing toward the back end of the parking lot. "A fall. Off the cliff. You said it would only take three seconds to reach the bottom."

Good Lord! He refused to turn and look with her. "It's not how long you fall that matters," he told her. "It's how fast you're moving when you hit. Freefalling a hundred and twenty feet, under gravitational acceleration . . ." He thought it through, doing the calculations in traditional units so she would understand. Numbers were a comforting abstraction, hiding the reality of the drop; the terror of the fall. "You would hit the ground traveling eighty-eight feet per second. That's roughly sixty miles an hour."

She looked at the wall. "Oh." She thought for a moment. "It would be horrible to die like that, to *watch* it happening to you. Can you imagine what it would be like to know that you were going to die?"

Branches snapping; shrubs uprooted; stones clattering loose beneath flailing hands. Leo gave a backward glance at the wall. "But it would be so much worse to remember afterward."

He sat in the car after she left him and let the engine idle, grumbling and complaining in its mechanical way about the mild chill. He glanced around while he waited for the car to warm up. The old building, the annex, the park, the depression in the driveway. Everywhere but that awful drop behind him. Hilda's remarks. So thoughtless; so callous. Gallows humor. He fought to expel it from his mind. He concentrated on the problem at hand. The haunt. If it was a haunt.

So, the library was built on deconsecrated ground. And there's the body of the town's founder, who watched over it all his life—and maybe longer. And the body of a woman who was certainly not a witch, but who loved to read books. And the bodies of eighty-eight poor souls thrown into a common grave and later spilled all over like a game of pick-up sticks.

Yes, this could be an interesting case. If only there hadn't been a cliff.

IV

Hilda felt the director watching over her shoulder as she wound the roll of graph paper into a tube. She wished the other woman would not stand so close and hunched her shoulders as she strapped a rubber band around the tube.

"What is all that?" asked the director.

"I told you. It's a strip recorder for the thermocouples. Leo . . . Dr. Reissman asked me to bring the tracings in today." She put the graph paper into her purse and snapped it shut.

"Does that mean he's finished?" The director's lips pressed together as she surveyed the equipment set up around the room. "I don't like my library cluttered up this way."

"I don't know. I'll ask him."

The director muttered something.

"What did you say?"

"I said he was a crazy old coot. Wasting his time—and ours—on this foolishness."

"He isn't that old."

The director looked at her. "Nor that crazy, I suppose."

"He's nice," Hilda told her. "A gentleman. Maybe a little stuffy. And shy because he's stuffy. And he's afraid of heights." She hefted the purse and slung it over her shoulder. "I think he is very sad about something, an old hurt. Sometimes, when he doesn't know anyone is watching, he forgets to smile."

"Does he." The director made a moue with her lips. "Well, he's kept this business out of the newspapers. I'll grant him that. But what has he discovered after two weeks? People have been seeing and hearing and feeling things in this library for years. You weren't the first to hear card drawers sliding. Or the first to feel a hand in your hair." The director's hand made a half-conscious move toward her own coiffure.

"I know. I've talked to Andy and Barbara Lynn and some of the others who used to work here. They would tell each other ghost stories whenever any of them had to work late."

The director cracked a smile. "I imagine half the night-time experiences here have been because of those stories."

"And the other half?" Hilda asked.

The director's face went hard. "It was just a manner of speaking."

Leaving the library, Hilda felt her car bounce through the depression in the driveway. She had driven over that spot hundreds of times before. Now, every time she did so, she remembered what lay under it. Restlessly, perhaps?

She thought for a moment about the thermocouples that Leo had installed around the Cataloguing Room. Physical evidence, he had told her. *Our first priority is to establish whether the phenomenon is internal or external.* A fancy way he had of hinting that it might have all been in her mind. It was easier to believe that than to believe that ghosts might be real. . . . *From ghosties and ghoulies and long-leggéd beasties and things that go bump in the night, Good Lord, deliver us.* If ghosts were real, what else might be? What horrors might lurk in the shadows around us?

Yet, what if it *had* all been in her mind? In many ways, that was even more frightening, because that would mean it was herself and not reality that was cracking. *The breakdown of the universe I can deal with.* The other was a road she had no desire to travel. She had already seen what lay at the end of it.

She tightened her grip on the steering wheel; and, when she turned right onto Fifth, she cut much harder than she needed to.

The college had perched atop the hill overlooking a bend of the Bushkill Creek since 1826, and its older buildings had had ample time to acquire the customary mantle of ivy. Cliffs dropped to the Bushkill on two sides of the campus, while city streets and residential housing hemmed it in on the east and north. Hilda found herself a parking place on McCartney close by the campus gate. When she entered, she encountered the marquis, himself.

"Lafayette, I am here," she told the statue.

A passing student showed her the way to the physics building, where the department secretary told her which office was Dr. Reissman's and said she could go inside and wait. "It isn't as if there were anything worth stealing in there," she said with a sniff.

Hilda found Leo's office cluttered, but neat. One entire wall was taken up by shelves stuffed with books and technical journals arranged according to some obscure logic. On one shelf sat a black box with a set of funny-looking lenses. A cable connected it to a computer on a side table. A plain wooden desk facing the far wall was stacked high with papers, each stack held in place by machinists' blocks of various shapes.

She lifted the paperweight from one of the stacks and saw that on top was a typewritten manuscript: "On Possible Mechanisms for a Thermophotonic Effect," by Leo M. Reissman, Ph.D. Paper-clipped to it was a handwritten note: *Sorry, Leo, but the referees just couldn't buy it.* Beneath that paper she found another: "Frequency and Duration of SNG Sightings, with Reference to Boltzmann Statistics." This time the attached note read: *Is this a joke?*

Hilda replaced the papers and paperweight and wandered idly around the office. A small, framed snapshot sat on the right hand corner of the desk. She picked it up and looked at it. Two teenaged boys—identical twins—dressed in scout uniforms smiled back at her. They had their arms around each other's shoulders and they looked like younger versions of the physicist. Leo's sons? The twin smiles frozen in time gave her no answer.

She set the snapshot down and peered into the corner between the bookshelves and the desk. A dollhouse? She bent over and lifted it. Yes, a dollhouse. The plastic kind, made with snap-together panels. Cheap. Not like the one her grandfather had built for her in his workshop. (Sometimes she wondered what had ever happened to it. Why did the adult always yearn for the treasures that the teenager spurned?) She studied the dollhouse she held. Each room was filled with a clear, gelatin-like plastic. Now what—?

"What would a grown man want with a dollhouse in his office, right?"

The voice behind her made her jump and she nearly dropped the toy. She turned and saw Leo standing in the doorway. "L—Dr. Reissman. You startled me."

"I'm sorry." He waved a hand toward the chair beside the desk. "Have a seat, Ms. Schenckweiler. I hadn't expected you so soon."

Hilda sat holding the dollhouse in her lap. She looked at it dumbly for a moment, then she made an exasperated sound in her throat and started to get up; but Leo took it from her.

"Never mind. I'll put it back." He gave the toy an affectionate glance. "This is my main claim to fame, you know."

"A dollhouse?"

He cocked his head at her. "Oh, yes. You wouldn't know, would you? It's why the college keeps me around in my dotage. They're hoping for another apple to rap me on the head and reflect credit on them—presumably for granting me a spot under their tree. You see, I once devised a reliable and inexpensive method for projecting holographs. That was my field of specialization before I took up more arcane realms. Lasers and holography." He placed the dollhouse on the desk, with the open back facing Hilda. "Lasers and holography," he repeated to himself. He opened and closed the front door of the dollhouse. "Watch this."

He stepped to the bookcase, where he pressed something on the black box. Ghostly shapes flickered inside the rooms. Near-solid images of furniture and wallpaper appeared. Hilda leaned forward. Why, that was marvelous! He was projecting three-dimensional pictures of the furnishings into each room.

Leo tapped some buttons on the computer console, and the furniture in the living room changed style and color. The phantom wallpaper became a new shape and pattern. Hilda gasped.

He turned the unit off and the furnishings winked out. "What do you think of it?"

"I think it's very clever. Delightful. I wish I had known about this before I redecorated my house. I've always found it difficult to visualize an entire room from a sample swatch of wallpaper or carpeting. Decorators and architects must love this."

"They do, but that is just one application. I understand that some enterprising individuals in California are attempting a holographic motion picture." Leo lifted the dollhouse from the table. "Patent royalties and tenure," he said. "Those are what grant me the freedom to pursue my somewhat unorthodox investigations. Well . . ." He returned the dollhouse to its cranny. "Enough of my checkered past. What do you have for me?"

Crackpots. Hilda told herself, did not invent clever and useful gadgets. Leo thought that ghosts were real—or, at least, that there was a reality that people called "ghosts"—and Leo was a serious and practical scientist. She took the rolls of graph paper from her purse. "I put fresh rolls into the recorders and reset the timers the way you showed me. Was that all right?"

"Oh, certainly. Certainly." He rubbed his hands together briskly. "Now, which one is the chart for The Spot?"

She handed it to him and he pulled off the rubber band and unrolled it like a papyrus scroll. He studied it silently for a few minutes; then he chuckled to himself. "Yes. Yes." He rapped the paper with his fingernail. "Excellent."

"What is it?"

He spread the sheet across the table. "Look here," he pointed. "And here." Hilda bent over the chart and stared at the wriggling pen line.

"There's your snug," he told her. "See those jogs in the plot? Those are temperature drops."

She shook her head. The wriggling line was just a wriggling line. The jog his finger pointed to looked no different to her than any of the other random ups and downs; only a trifle deeper. "I don't see anything. Why is that so important?"

He looked at her and blinked his eyes. "Why, it proves that there is something physical happening at that location. Something that caused the temperature to fall abuptly. It wasn't in your head."

"I never thought it was." *Liar.* The untightening she felt deep within herself belied that. *Oh, Mother* . . . She ran her finger along the graph. The sharp spikes were icicles, sudden bursts of cold. Real, physical cold; measured not by a shivering librarian, but by an inanimate instrument. *Not crazy. Not crazy.* Who ever said that objectivity was dehumanizing?

"I don't understand. What does the temperature have to do with the gh—ah, 'snug.' "

Leo pulled a small rule from his shirt pocket and measured the slopes of the lines. "When a snug lights up," he said, "it uses energy. My guess is that it converts the thermal energy in the air directly to photons, somehow tapping the 'high energy tail' of the Maxwell-Boltzmann thermal distribution. The only spirit involved is Maxwell's Demon. Ah . . ." He looked up at her and flushed. "I'm doing it again. Lecturing. You see, air molecules are not all the same. . . . Well, let's say that they are not all the same 'temperature.' That's close enough. There is a random distribution of temperatures. Some air molecules are 'warmer'; and—"

"Wait a minute! Are you trying to tell me that ghosts are a lot of hot air?"

His flush deepened. "No, I am trying *not* to tell you that, because I have heard it too often from my colleagues here." He hung his head and entered the numbers into a small desk calculator. "A thermocouple converts heat energy into electricity. Why can there not be a similar mechanism—a natural mechanism—that converts heat into light? It needn't be too energetic. The brightest snug I've ever measured has had an output of less than twenty watts. Regardless . . ." He raised his head again and looked at her. "If a snug uses the high end of the thermal energy curve to energize itself, the temperature of the surrounding air will naturally drop. When the dew point is reached, the moisture in the air will condense, so you would feel 'cold and clammy' and the snug will be shrouded in fog. So, you see . . ." He spread his hands. ". . . the traditional descriptions of ghosts matches physical theory quite well. Even to the extent that 'shrouded ghosts' are more commonly seen in the British Isles, where the dew point is high."

Leo blinked at the calculator display. "The temperature drops in the library averaged about 3.4°C per minute. That would make your snug's power output . . ." His fingers danced on the keypad. ". . . around five watts. Durations ranged from a few seconds to five minutes."

Hilda ran her finger along the plot trace. "It was real. That's all that matters."

He hunched over the rule, measuring the distances between icicles. "Mean recurrence rate . . . 2,460 minutes, plus or minus a trivial amount that could be instrument error. Let's see . . . Forty-one hours. Hunh." He put the end of the rule in his mouth and chewed on it. "Diurnally out of synch. That's interesting."

Hilda raised her head and looked at him. "What? You mean the ghost reappears every two days? I don't believe it! More people would have seen it."

"Not every two days. Forty-one hours. That would be . . . Got it! It's a harmonic of the lunar month! One-sixteenth. So, each appearance would be seven hours earlier in the day than the previous one." He stopped and blinked at her. "Oh. Why haven't more people seen it? Think. Most of the night-time events would take place on weekends or holidays or in the wee hours of the morning, when no one was around to see them. And more than half the occurrences would be during daylight or early evening when the building lights would be on. A five-watt snug doesn't make much of a flash and the vast majority of the events would be too brief to notice. You were lucky that night, to have experienced such a long-lasting event."

Lucky? She supposed that, from Leo's viewpoint, she had been. But he hadn't been there. He hadn't experienced that horrid feeling. "What about the cold?" she asked, to avoid thinking about it. "Or the fog? People would notice that, even during the day. Especially in the summer."

"Would they? In an air-conditioned building? Or would they think it was a draft? Most thermoluminescent events would be very short; a few seconds, perhaps. Boltzmann statistics. The longer the event, the less frequently it occurs. Now, a 'bright' twenty-watt snug would trigger a drop of, say, ten degree celcius per minute. That's a maximum, without convection or anything. So if the snug 'lit up' for two seconds, you would experience a local temperature drop of at most one-third of a degree. Who would notice? And the Library Snug is much dimmer than that. It only shows up on my trace because of the sensitivity of the instruments."

"Then it probably won't happen to me again," she said.

Leo sighed. "Probably not," he said with regret. "Reproducibility is such a problem in this field. Oh." He looked into her eyes and, surprised, she turned her face away. "It was a frightening experience, wasn't it?" His eyes grew distant. "Frightening," he repeated to himself. "I could prepare a schedule for you of the snug's expected reappearances. There is no way of telling beforehand whether an event will fall in the longer-lived tail of the distribution; but you can schedule your late night work to avoid them."

"That would be nice. Thank you."

"Meanwhile . . ." He pulled a calendar appointment book from his shirt pocket and flipped quickly through the pages. "You first sensed the snug, when? The 9th, wasn't it?"

"Yes. It was seven at night." She shivered. "I still remember the chimes."

"Uh huh. And the last event on the strip recorder was, hmm . . ." He ran his eye down the chart on his desk. "Six P.M. on the 21st."

"Hey!" she said. "That means there was one today, doesn't it?" She closed her eyes and counted the hours on the clockface. "At 11 A.M.!" She gasped. "I was in the room then!"

Leo was still studying his calendar. "Didn't notice anything, right?"

"I—No."

He waved a pencil at the graph. "Daytime. Short duration. If you weren't looking straight at it, you wouldn't know anything had happened. Even if you were, the overhead lights would probably have masked it. Here we go. The next one is at 4 A.M. the day after tomorrow." He shook his head. "Too soon. We won't be ready in time. It'll have to be 9 P.M. on the 26th." He penciled a notation on his calendar and put it back in his shirt pocket. He reached behind himself to the desk, where he found a small booklet, which he opened.

"Ready? Ready for what?"

He picked up his telephone and flipped through the booklet. "I have a friend in aerospace engineering who doesn't think I'm too crazy," he told her. "He has some computer imaging equipment he will let me borrow, if I'm not too explicit about why I want it. I'll tell him it's for a holographic experiment. He'll know I'm lying, but that will cover him with his chairman."

"You want to take its picture. The ghost."

"The snug. Of course. More than just a visual picture. With modern image enhancement techniques I can study the snug at virtually every wavelength and obtain a pretty thorough electromagnetic footprint."

"You want to set up all this equipment in the Cataloguing Room? The director won't be happy about that."

"She won't care," Leo predicted. "Not too much, anyway. The 26th is a Sunday. No one will be around to be scandalized."

"Well, I'll ask her," she said uncertainly.

Leo smiled. "Tell her I will continue to pester her if she does not let us do this experiment."

Hilda looked at her watch. "Look at the time!" she said. "I've got to be going. I suppose your wife will be waiting supper for you."

"My wife?" Leo seemed puzzled, as if wondering whether he had forgotten if he had one. Then he blinked and said, "Oh, no. I am not married. I never have been."

"Oh," She pointed toward the desk. "I thought those were your sons."

"Sons?" He twisted his head to see where she was pointing. "Ah." He gazed at the picture for a long time before answering. "That picture was taken many years ago," he said finally. "A great many years ago. I am the one on the left." He stared at the snapshot a while longer before adding, "Harry and I did everything together. Read the same books, saw the same movies, earned the same merit badges." He smiled slightly, his head cocked in reminiscence. "Dated the same girl. You never saw one of us without the other. We dressed alike. We even thought alike. Sometimes he would answer a question before I even asked it."

"Where is he now?"

Leo sighed and turned his back on the picture. "Dead."

"Oh. I'm sorry."

Leo shrugged. "It was a long time ago." He made a ball of his hands, twisted his fingers together.

"I'm sorry," she repeated, unable to think of anything else worth saying.

Leo studied his hands. "It was the only thing we never did together."

V

He hadn't thought about Harry in a long time. Leo rinsed his mouth and spat into the sink. He put his toothbrush back in the rack; then he leaned forward and studied his own face in the mirror. It would have been Harry's face, too, he decided. They would never have grown too different. He tried not to think about reality; about what Harry's face must look like now, after all these years below the ground. Decay. Rot. Worms. He shuddered and turned out the bathroom light and went to bed.

And lay there unable to sleep. It was too hot with the covers on; too cold with them off. The dark and the quiet blanketed him. Far away, he could hear a faint, intermittent knocking. Only his own pulse in his ears. He had established that long ago, after innumerable and futile trips to his apartment door, peering through the spyhole at empty hallways. Only his own pulse, audible now that the world was hushed. He closed his eyes and tried to empty his mind.

As he relaxed into the borderland of sleep, the voices began.

Fragments. Soft, random syllables, chopped off, with long pauses in between. Seldom a complete word. Never anything that made sense. *Wonder-*, whispered a voice. And *Waysdi-*. Leo strained to hear the message, knowing there was none. *Beewith-* and *Verythi-*. The voices were without tone or inflection—not masculine, not feminine—bursting like shells in the silence of his mind.

Insensibly he drifted out of the borderland and the popcorn voices were stilled. As he lay there in the quiet he became gradually aware that someone was watching him. He was lying on his side and behind him was the wall and between the bed and the wall stood . . . something.

It watched him as he lay there. He knew how tall it was: five foot eight. He could feel its height. It was black and featureless, with not even eyes to break its seamless shadow. Utterly silent, with no whisper of breath; its gaze, neither threatening nor benevolent, but an implacable dispassion. It watched without feeling or interest.

Leo knew he had to see it; to confront it. He gathered his will from a dozen scattered points and rolled over on his back and opened his eyes. . . .

And awoke lying on his side in the darkness.

He contemplated the fact that he had dreamed about dreaming, and wondered if, even now, he was awake; because, if so, he had awoken into his dream, into the same dark bedroom, curled into the same position.

With the same monstrous feeling of being watched.

He twisted around and stared into the darkness between the bed and the wall, and there was nothing there save the darkness itself. Unless . . . was there, within the darkness, a deeper shadow, somehow solid? He could feel its inexorable presence pressing on his skin, brushing the small hairs of his neck and arms.

Leo opened his mouth to speak, but the words came out as a flaccid cry, a low pitched moan that lacked the will to scream. He woke with a gasp and groped for the bedside lamp and turned it on, fearful that, this once, there would be a shadow its light would not dispel.

But, of course, there was not.

He sat up in his bed, with his back braced against his pillows and listened to the hammer of his heart. Resolutely, his eyes sought out the familiar landmarks of his room. The chest. The hairbrush. The tie thrown across the chairback. Simple, ordinary objects. Anchors to reality. Comforting in their everyday intimacy. Slowly, his pulse stilled and he lay back down again. There was no need to check the thermocouple. He had disconnected it a long time ago. In all the years, there had never been a quiver on it.

He went to sleep with the light on; something he had not done since he was a boy.

The next morning, Leo's nightmare faded as he installed the equipment. That was the best therapy. Concentrate on the task at hand. Lose yourself in the details of a routine task; let the mind idle in neutral while the subconscious sorts things out. He started to hum.

Hilda picked up the loose end of a cable. "Where do you want this?"

"Here, give it to me. It goes in the computer port."

A *complete physical record*, he thought. At last, he would have a complete physical record. Electromagnetic, sound, temperature and relative humidity. Everything. Let Magruder argue with that, if he could!

Leo stopped humming and grimaced. He probably would. What did physical evidence mean? There had been too many photographs of "flying saucers" and "Martian faces" and "Loch Ness monsters." Mistaken identity. Wishful thinking. Even outright hoaxes. Magruder wouldn't accuse him of hoaxing the department. At least, not aloud.

He set his jaw. This would be no blurred, half-focused snapshot. This was the best equipment NASA could buy.

"What's wrong?"

"Eh?" He looked up from his wiring and saw Hilda watching him. "What do you mean?"

"Well, you looked so happy there for a while. Then, all of a sudden, you were the face of gloom."

He twisted his smile. "I was just thinking about some of my colleagues; how they won't accept my findings, in spite of everything."

"I don't understand. They're scientists. They'll have to believe you if you show them the evidence."

Leo wiped his hands on a rag. He set the camera atop its tripod and screwed it in place. "You don't know scientists. If they already believe a thing is impossible, they'll refuse even to look at the evidence. If I had Magruder here and he saw the snug for himself, he would still refuse to believe it. A trick, he'd say. An illusion. He might even find a stage magician who could duplicate everything that happened. As if any phenomenon that *could* be duplicated by hoax must therefore always be a hoax." He smiled sadly and looked into the distance. "I am an embarrassment to them. They think I am so far around the bend, that I cannot even see the bend anymore." He picked up a screwdriver. "They took away my freshman classes this year. I'm professor emeritus, now. E-meritus. That means 'without merit.'" He laughed at his own joke.

"And can you see it?" she asked.

"Can I what?"

"See the bend."

He paused and looked at her with raised eyebrows. Hilda had her hands half-raised and clenched at waist level. "As clearly as anyone else," he told her. He bent again over his work. Why was Hilda so concerned with *his* mental health? "You see, I don't have a problem with snugs—hell, with 'ghosts.' There is a class of phenomenon that needs explaining, that's all. I have no vested interest in the nature of the explanation. The problem with unbelievers is that they are believers, too."

"What do you mean?"

He grunted. "They can't just disbelieve. They've got to disbelieve in a certain way. Orthodox disbelief! Talk with an atheist some time; you'll never get a clearer vision of the fundamentalist God. God, they'll tell you, wouldn't play games with fossils or light waves just to trick us into thinking that the universe was older than six thousand years. Now, *Loki* might very well do that, or *Raven*; but those aren't the gods that they disbelieve in."

"You don't really believe that—"

"That the physical universe was created in 4004 B.C.?" He made a face. "Of course not. Although the date does approximate the creation of our *cultural* universe. No, I was merely using it as an example, to show how even unbelievers hold certain unquestionable beliefs. My colleagues have a mental image of the *sort* of ghosts they do not believe in, and if someone like me comes along with a different paradigm—a materialistic one, unconnected with magic or superstition . . . Why, they'll denounce it as rank heresy! I try to talk about a mechanism for the thermophotonic effect and they'll argue that spells and pentagrams violate conservation of energy. I try to describe the frequency and duration of certain odd events and they'll point out that mediums and spiritualists are frauds. I wonder if there might not be *something* that needs explaining and they'll bring up crystals and pyramid power." He tossed the screwdriver to the table. It banged and rolled and dropped to the floor. Leo made a face. "Sorry," he said. "Even we nut cases can grow exasperated with the stupidity of others."

" 'What am I doing in here with all these crazy people?' "

Leo chuckled. "Yes, exactly." But he looked at her and saw she wasn't smiling. "What's wrong?"

She folded her arms under her breasts and hunched over. She studied the equipment on the table. "I wasn't making a joke," she told the oscilloscope.

Leo stood quietly with the cable in his hand and waited.

Hilda unfolded her arms and lightly touched the knobs on the scope. "You would think that when a person's mind goes, she wouldn't recognize mental illness in others. But it isn't like that at all." She turned and looked him in the eye. "My mother and I were very close." She said it as a challenge. "Especially after Father died. We were the kind of mother and daughter who dressed alike and went places together. I look like her—I mean, I look like she did when she was younger. There isn't a trace of my father anywhere in my face. Even after I was grown, we did things together. I thought she was just so wonderful, and I wanted to be just like her."

"Then . . . ?"

She looked away, at the card catalogue, at the racks of books. "Then something happened inside her head. I don't know what it was. The doctors didn't know what it was. They talked about strokes and lithium imbalance and I don't know what else. But they didn't know anything, really. What it all came down to was that she wasn't my mother anymore. She was a stranger who saw things, who heard things. Sometimes the voices talked to her; and she talked back. Twice, she left my apartment while I was at work and wandered around the neighborhood. After a while, I couldn't deal with it any more and I—" Her hands clenched again. "I had her committed. When I went back the first time to visit her, she gave me the most heartbreakingly open and bewildered look and asked me why she was in there with all those crazy people."

Leo saw a tear in the corner of her eye. "It was probably the best thing you could have done," he said slowly. "I mean, the professionals would know how to—"

"You don't understand." She shook her head slowly. "When I visit the . . . place where she lives now . . . when I look at her, I see myself, only older. *I wanted to grow up to be just like her!*"

"Oh." Leo bent over and plugged the cable into the computer.

"So I've got to know, Doctor Reissman. I've got to know, am I starting to see things, too?"

He straightened and looked at her. Hilda's lower lip was almost white from the pressure of her teeth. "I told you you weren't. I showed you the traces on the temperature records. You saw something real."

She shook her head. "You showed me some lines on a chart. They could have meant anything. I don't understand things like that. I'm not a technical person. I just want to know if I can believe you. Or are you a nut case, too?"

Leo wiped his palms on his pants legs. *What can I tell her? That I hear voices? That things visit me in the night?* He touched the computer with his forefinger, rubbing it along the top of the case. "The mind can see and hear things that aren't real. I'll grant you that. I think it happens to everyone at some time or another. The signals are blocked or scrambled or misinterpreted. But it doesn't matter what I am. Because this—" He rapped the computer with his knuckles. "This will only see a picture if there are photons; it will only record a voice if there are sound waves."

Hilda flexed her fingers, brushed at the sleeves of her blouse. "Then we'll let the machines tell us if we're sane," she said; but Leo pretended he hadn't heard.

VI

The ticking of the clock in the boardroom next door was a steady, distant metronome. *Funny*, Hilda thought. She had never realized how loud it was; unless its sound was magnified by the evening stillness, or by her imagination. She glanced to her right, where Leo sat quietly in the other chair studying the instruments that he had racked on the table before him. *How can he wait so calmly?* she wondered. He reached out to the oscilloscope and turned one of its knobs an infinitesimal fraction to the right. Hilda thought he had turned it to the left just a short while ago; so perhaps he was not as calm as he appeared. That made her feel fractionally better.

"How much longer?" she asked.

Leo pushed his sleeve up. "Five minutes. That is one minute less than the last time you asked."

Hilda blushed. She was acting like a fidgety schoolgirl. Yet the waiting was, in many ways, worse than the unexpected apparition of a fortnight or so past. Surprise could be numbing; but anticipation amplified everything, until the nerve endings stuck out a foot beyond the skin, and the least little event exploded on the senses.

In five—no, four—minutes, a ghost would appear. Or not. And she was afraid of either outcome, though in different ways. The unknown; or the known-too-well. Unless it was not fear, but another emotion entirely, that trembled in her body.

Leo rose and walked to the doorway, where he turned off the overhead lights. The room went dark, except for the dim green glow of his instruments and scopes. "We will be better able to see it with our own eyes," he said, "if the room is darkened."

Hilda turned from him and hunched herself in her chair. She clenched and unclenched her hands. The glow from Leo's instruments teased the corners of her eyes. She stared into the darkness, toward The Spot, waiting. "How much—"

"Sh!"

Dim shapes emerged from the black as her vision adjusted to the room. There was the work bench, the fireplace, and, yes, the old card catalogue. The only sounds were her own breath and the faint electrical hum of the equipment.

It seemed as if an endless time went by. Then a light winked in the air, as brief as a firefly on a summer's eve; a spark that was gone before it was even seen. Leo rose and walked toward the light switch. Hilda expelled her breath. "Was that it?"

Leo turned the lights back on. He returned to the instrument table and leaned over the scope. He pressed a button. "Yes," he said.

"Why, that was hardly anything at all." She felt peeved; as if the ghost had let her down. All that anticipation. All that buildup. It seemed anticlimactic. Only a fleeting glimmer in the dark. No sliding drawers. No hand in her hair. No piercing cold. She clasped her hands together. Had she imagined everything, after all?

She watched over Leo's shoulder as he replayed the apparition on his computer screen. She saw the spark flash again—a digitized memory of it. Leo froze the display and the screen showed a featureless smear of white. Not what she had ever imagined a ghost should look like. Yet, the instruments *had* recorded something.

Leo scowled and advanced the record one frame at a time. Forward. Backward. Forward, again. Hilda could not decide what he was looking for. The whiteness wasn't there, then it was, then it wasn't. Like a light that had turned on and off.

When she leaned forward to see better, she placed her hand on his shoulder, and he jerked as if electrocuted. Hilda backed away from him. He gave her a distant, preoccupied look and turned back to the screen without speaking. His fingers made clacking sounds on the keyboard.

Finally, he sighed. "Here, look at this," he said.

Hilda stepped cautiously to his side. She did not know why he was so edgy, but she did not want to disturb him. "What is it?"

"I have enhanced the signal to show greater detail."

The freeze frame showed the same featureless blob she had seen before. She shook her head. "I don't see anything."

Leo made a sound in his throat. "Look more carefully. See the way it narrows into a head? And those dark spots near the top. Those must be eyes, wouldn't you say?"

"No. It's just a white smear."

"It's not only white. The spectral analysis shows some blue with some overtones of green. Auroral effects from the excitation of di-atomic nitrogen and monatomic oxygen."

"If you say so," she said doubtfully.

"I have had more practice than you at image interpretation. Let me refine the image further." He again bent over the keyboard and the NASA equipment did whatever it was that it did. The image on the screen changed colors. Vertical wipes passed through it, changed it. The edges became sharper. The suggestion of contour emerged.

"There is a face there. I know it." Leo hit the keys several more times and features solidified out of the smoky shape. "There! There! Do you see it now?"

"I see a woman in a billowy gown," she said slowly. The balloon shape could be a hoop skirt. The halo could be a bonnet. And, yes, if she concentrated on it long enough, she could see the pits of eyes and the shadow of a long straight nose. She looked at Leo. Had the image been there in the shape all the time, waiting to be evoked by the computer; or had Leo, for some reason of his own, imposed an image upon it—an electronic Michelangelo creating a digital *Madonna*? She couldn't know. She couldn't. If you worried at it long enough, could your heart not find any form at all buried in formlessness? Weren't there bestiaries in ink blots; menageries in the clouds?

Leo straightened with a satisfied look on his face. "That proves it, wouldn't you say?" Hilda started to answer, but realized that he was not talking to her. "A human face couldn't be a coincidence. There must be a connection between ghosts and the souls of the dead." He folded his arms and studied the woman on the screen. "I wonder who she was? One of the women in the vault? Or Mammy Morgan herself?" He pulled out a chair and sat down and began scratching rapidly in his notebook. "I should be able to excite the ghost artificially. Increase its brightness and duration. With a laser, perhaps. The matrix appears to be a hologram of some sort; the light is naturally coherent. Yes. With a laser, I can amplify the signal; make contact." The point of his pencil snapped against the notebook page and he looked at it dumbly.

Ghost. He had said "ghost." Hilda wondered what had become of snugs. She realized suddenly that Leo was never going to settle the reality of her ghost or the stability of her mind. Everything he said or did could be colored by his own yearnings for . . . What? Vindication? Respectability? Something else? She had been foolish to rely on this old man and his facade of scientific objectivity. No amount of gadgetry could ever quiet her doubts, because the doubts had grown inside herself, where no instrument could reach.

"I could bring my own laser over. The projector. Create an excited state directly in the heart of the ghost." He flipped the pages on his notebook. "Damn!" He ran his finger down a column of figures. "The next two apparitions will be during the daylight on weekdays. Well, I've waited this long; I can wait a short while longer." He drummed his fingers on the table. Then he looked at her as if he had suddenly recalled her presence.

"Your director would be very upset if this equipment were still sitting here tomorrow morning. We must break it down and store it for a few days. Is there a room here in the library I can use?"

"Yes," she said. "There's a place in back of the closed stacks."

"Good. Good." He nodded. "Would you help me set it up again on Friday after the library closes? The next nighttime appearance is twelve o'clock that night."

"Midnight," she said without checking the calendar. "All Hallows' Eve."

The next five days passed slowly. A climax, Hilda thought (and a climax was coming, she knew) should not come after an intermission. There should not be such a lapse in which to think and doubt and wonder. The days seemed pointlessly spent; idle time. She discussed Leo's experiment with the director, who listened in prim disapproval, but did not forbid it. For whatever reason, Hilda said nothing of her doubts regarding Leo himself.

She read all she could about ghosts. Not the sensational things, the kinds of reports that smacked of showmanship and the need to be noticed; but the quietly understated tales of casual, everyday haunts. Most haunts, she discovered, did not involve grisly and horrible events. Instead, they were almost matter-of-fact. The sound of a ball bouncing down the hallway, when there was no such ball. A shadow on a wall, when there was nothing to cast it. They were almost comforting in their ordinariness. The Irish ghost scholar, Dr. Michael MacLiammoir, wrote that "it is the unbeliever who feels the greatest fear of ghosts; for the believer knows that they are harmless."

She made it a point to be in the Cataloguing Room on the occasion of both the predicted daytime events. She was not sure why, or what she expected to see—

which was nothing in the first case and (maybe) a brief spark in the second—but she could not wait out the days doing nothing.

Then, finally, it was the night of Leo's experiment. Hilda drove to the library at 10:00 P.M. Midnight, he had said; but, of course, he would need time to set up his equipment. The downtown was empty when she drove through; her tires hissed on abandoned streets. Stone veterans of Antietam and Gettysburg gazed down from their monument in Center Square. It was a ghost-lit night. Black clouds streaked a silver-dollar moon. The wind shivered naked tree branches against the sky.

She turned onto Church and drove past the darkened library. A single light broke the black facade; the director's office, she noted with surprise. Why tonight, of all nights, had the director stayed to watch? Hilda turned right into the driveway and drove all the way to the rear parking lot. Her headlight beams cut across the night, picking out the colorless shapes of two other cars and, briefly, a solitary figure standing by the back wall.

When she cut her engine, she could hear the muted rush of the wind through the trees. She shivered. It was a cold sound, a lonely sound. Autumn was, in many ways, a colder time than winter. She unbuckled herself and got out of the car. The slam of the door closing behind her echoed in the nighttime silence. She peered toward the wall, where she had seen the figure, and saw Leo already approaching. His overcoat, unbuttoned, flapped in the breeze; and he held his hat in place with his left hand. The smile that cut his face tightened his skin like a drum.

"Well," he said. "Tonight is the night."

And that simply had to be true, because it could mean anything.

"All Hallows' Eve," she told Leo as they reconnected the monitors, "was the old Celtic New Year. New Year's Day began at sunset on the last day of October. The Celts believed that the spirits of those who had died during the year would roam the night, trying to occupy the bodies of the living. People dressed themselves in frightening costumes to scare the spirits off."

Leo grunted as he strung the cables. "I know that. It's all myth, though. Superstition. The dead go walking all year 'round, not just tonight."

There was no possible reply to a remark like that. And he had said it in so reasonable a tone. Still, if he was right that the recurrent, spontaneous light flashes were the souls of the dead, they did indeed go a-walking all year round. Every two days in the library work room.

If there was any connection at all. She thought it was remarkable that, as she had come to think of the flashes as simple, physical events, Leo had gone the other way. Rather suddenly, it seemed to her. Between her visit to his office and their first test on the 26th. Something had happened to him over that weekend. Make contact, he had said after that first test. Contact with what? A flashbulb? A holographic recording? Leo was not setting up an experiment, she suddenly realized; he was conducting a seance. Not with trumpets or tambourines, though; there would be no holding hands in the dark. This was a modern seance, with all the modern, electronic conveniences.

She watched him hunched over his work. His lips were drawn tight against his teeth and his hand trembled very slightly. *What was he thinking?* she wondered. She was not sure she wanted to know.

Everything was ready by 11:40, and the last few minutes seemed to drag by as slowly as they had five days before. Leo had rigged his laser to a photoelectric cell so that it would fire the instant the ghost appeared. The idea, he explained, was not to destroy the entity, but to amplify it through a kind of supercharging. Hilda did not understand what he said about energy levels and transitions and the like. She assumed that, in this one arena, at least, he was a competent gladiator.

She was not concerned with whether the ghost would appear. It would, and that was all there was to it. The Sun rose and set; the Moon ran through her phases; and the library ghost would make its regular appearance. As simply and predictably as that. And didn't that predictability argue against its being a 'person'? People always took you by surprise. Consider her mother, or even Leo. Things happened; people changed. Only the natural world ran forever in a predictable rut. "The stars in their courses . . ." So, it might not be a ghost as she had always thought of ghosts, as hauntings by the unquiet dead. It might be, as Leo had once told her, a stuck, holographic record. But that did not bother her. It wasn't *what* it was that mattered, but only *that* it was. It was that knowledge that made her safe within her own skull.

The director appeared in the doorway, bearing a tray. She carried it to the work table against the east wall and set it down. "I thought you might want some coffee," she said.

Leo raised his head. "What? Who . . . ? Oh. No. No coffee. Thank you." He ducked back into his work.

"I'll have a cup," Hilda said quietly.

The director poured from a portable electric pot into two china cups and handed one to Hilda.

"Thank you." Hilda sipped from the hot liquid. "Why are you here?" she asked bluntly.

The director shrugged. "Who can resist putting her beliefs to the test? Tonight is the *dénoument*, isn't it? Tonight will settle things once and for all."

Hilda glanced at Leo. "Some things."

The director followed her glance. She raised her own cup to her lips. "Yes. Well."

Leo turned out the lights and they waited quietly in the dark while the clock crept toward midnight. Hilda could hear the hushed sounds of breathing, and, occasionally, the sharp tink of a cup against its saucer. The director had said nothing more after the first brief sentences. She stood in the shadows beside Hilda, thin and proper and faintly disapproving, and asked no questions. Hilda resisted the urge to cross the room and sit beside Leo. Instead, she leaned back against the work table. "Soon, now," Leo's voice announced from the gloom.

When the clock in the boardroom struck, Hilda jerked and leaned forward, peering into the dark. She held her breath as the soft chimes rang a slow, leaking drip of sound.

It happened suddenly on the tenth ring. A brightness flickered on the far side of the room and, simultaneously, a ruby-red beam of light, straight as a steel rod, pierced its heart. In an instant, a phosphorescent sphere bloomed in the darkened room. It was white with a tinge of blue around its edges. It throbbed like a soap-bubble heart.

Hilda shivered in the sudden cold. Her breath made puffs of steam that glowed in the pale light emanating from the ghost. Campfire-shadows writhed on the walls. Hilda heard the director's coffee cup shatter on the floor; she saw Leo stand and lean across his table.

"Can you hear me?" Leo asked.

The pearly ball of light stretched and twisted like an amoeba.

"Can you take a message? For Harry? I must speak with him!"

The ghost pulsated and danced in the air.

The director grabbed her by the sleeve. "Do you see it?" she demanded. "Do you see it?"

Hilda disengaged her sleeve from the curled fingers. "Of course, I see it."

"Oh, it's wonderful! It's so wonderful!"

She turned and looked at the woman. The director's face was a crescent moon in the ghostly light. "Why?" she asked her. "Why is it so wonderful?"

"Don't you see? It means we go on. It means we don't end when we die!"

Across the room, Leo shouted question at the light. Hilda backed away from her companions. Were they both mad? The apparition was an iridescent soap bubble floating in the air. A strange thing, yes, a beautiful thing; but only a thing, as incapable of silent witness as it was of answering questions. Was she the only one who saw nothing more? Were they blind; or she?

The world was an enigma, a conundrum that everyone solved to their own contentment; and in the end, each person's world was as impenetrably individual as her mother's. The ghost was a perfect mirror, reflecting whatever images each imagination could project. The director saw eternal life glowing in the room. Harry saw a channel to his dead brother. She saw . . .

A light. Only a light. Mystery, but no magic.

Leo gave a shout and twisted something on his control panel. The instruments hummed louder and the ruby light brightened. The ghost waxed, shimmering with a thousand colors. Streamers of azure and crimson roiled through it. Silver bubbles drifted from the center toward the edge and fell back inward. The surface twitched and spasmed. Frost appeared on the window panes of the room, on the work tables. The cold bit into Hilda and her teeth chattered.

Then the ghost fell in on itself like a collapsing star. For just an instant, Hilda thought she saw it coalesce into a slim, fine-featured woman; then it shattered into a billion twinkling lights that exploded soundlessly into the corners of the room, dying like fireworks in the nighttime sky.

The room fell dark.

Hilda sucked in a breath. Beside her, she heard the director's soft "Amen." The hum of the equipment was the only other sound. The cold slowly faded; the frost dripped from the windows. The laser cast a small, red spot on the card catalogue. Abruptly, it, too, vanished. Across the room, she heard Leo sob.

Hilda hit the light switch and saw Leo slumped in his chair with his face in his hands. She went to him and put a gentle hand on his shoulder. "Leo?"

He turned a face toward her. "He'll never come back," he said. "He'll never come back to me." He pushed her hand away, rose, and staggered from the room.

"Who?" That was the director. The question was flat, unemotional. Hilda turned around and saw the same hard face she had always known. There was no trace of her earlier exaltation. "Who will never come back?"

Hilda sighed and hugged herself. Who? Everyone. Anyone. Leo's brother. Her mother. All the strangers we once thought we knew. "Harry," she said aloud. "Leo's twin brother, Harry."

The director pressed her lips together. "Of course, he won't. His brother is dead. I talked to his chairman. He told me that Doctor Reissman's brother had died while they were on a boy scout hike. He stumbled off a cliff in the dark." She shook her head. "Tragic. I imagine twins are very close."

Hilda felt the blood drain from her. "Off of a cliff? Oh, God!" And she turned and bolted from the room.

When she burst from the library's back door into the cold of the night, the wind bit through her blouse like a knife. It tore her hair loose and sent it streaming. It sucked the breath from her open mouth. She remembered what she had said to Leo that first day. *A long way to fall. Time enough to know.* How cruel her words must have been! But she hadn't known. How could she have known?

Time enough for a gulping breath; then she turned and ran to the parking lot. Halfway across the flat asphalt surface, she skidded to a halt. Leo was standing atop the stone wall at the east end, where the drop was nearly shear. She did not want to startle him; so she walked slowly to his side and waited for him to notice her.

He was staring down into the black depths. Above, the Moon glowed cold behind racing clouds. Hilda shivered in the icy wind.

"You should go back inside," he said after a moment. "You'll catch pneumonia."

"You will, too."

He shook his head. "I won't be standing here long enough for it to matter."

"Please, Leo. Harry can't want that."

He turned his head and looked at her. His cheeks drooped, pulling his mouth down. "He must."

"Why?" She forced her voice to remain as quiet and as reasonable as his. She wanted to shout, to scream at him. Calm, she told herself. Stay calm.

"Why? So we can be together, like we always were. Like we were meant to be."

She knew then that there was a third sort of fear. She knew that Leo would die unless she saved him, and she did not know if she could do it. Caring was not enough. She had not been able to save her own mother.

"You can't mean that." Did you argue with the suicidal? Did logic convince them? If not logic, what?

"I knew it the moment it happened." He spoke in a quiet, distant voice. "I woke up in the middle of the night, and I knew that something had happened to him. I roused the scoutmaster and told him that Harry was gone, that he needed help." He sighed and studied the cloud-shrouded sky. "It was just growing light when we found him. He was at the bottom of a hundred-foot cliff. He had gone off to take a leak away from the camp, turned the wrong way in the dark, and walked off the edge. When I closed my eyes I could picture every step he had taken. I could remember his hands flailing wildly, grasping vainly for handholds as he fell. Fingers breaking against the rocks." He looked again at the rocks below him.

"He was still alive," he continued. "If he had been dead already, it might not have hurt so much. But he was still alive. I saw him move an arm. It took an hour for them to find another way to the bottom. I sat at the top of the cliff and watched. Harry opened his eyes and he saw me up there looking down; and, for an instant, I saw myself seeing him. Then he closed his eyes and he didn't move again. A few minutes later, every bird in the forest took wing and circled above, blackening the sky, screeching. I knew that Harry had died. There was always a link of some sort, a channel that joined us; and someone had just . . . hung up the extension. That's as clearly as I can explain it. I could call out, but no one would ever answer again. I have never been happy since that moment."

"It must have been terrible." She thought her words were shallow, inadequate; but it did not matter. He continued as if she had not spoken at all.

"A few years later, I thought I heard a whisper over our private line. A few words spoken in the darkness as I fell asleep. I thought Harry was trying to reach me. To tell me something important. I tried to listen; but the harder I concentrated, the more elusive the words were. They were . . . 'peripheral' sounds. Every night, before I went to bed, I prayed that Harry would come back. But I had read 'The Monkey's Paw' and sometimes I was afraid that my prayers would be answered.

Teenaged boys don't like to cry; but I cried. I cried. Then, one night, while I was in college, he did come back. Or he tried to."

Hilda took a deep breath and hunched over. She knew she shouldn't try to grab him. If she did, he would pull away and fall; and she would never be able to hang onto him. "What happened?" Behind her, she could hear the library door open and footsteps clicking on the asphalt. She knew that the director had followed them—after first stopping sensibly for her overcoat. Without turning, Hilda gestured with her hand, and she heard the other woman leave, to—sensibly—call the rescue squad.

"I was asleep," Leo said. "I was in my dormitory room asleep when I felt him standing beside my bed. The prickling at the back of my head woke me up and, for a moment, I thought I had dreamed it. Then, I realized that I could still feel the presence beside me. I stared toward it, but I could see nothing. I tried to raise my arm to reach out, but I was paralyzed. I felt nothing over the channel Harry and I had shared—only a vast indifference—so I knew that, though he was trying to come back to me, he was unable to make it through all the way."

"Did it . . . Did you . . ." She let her breath out. "I know the feeling."

He nodded slowly. "Yes, so you told me. That was when I knew that ghosts were souls. When you told me that you had felt the same thing. That could not have been coincidence."

"But that mightn't mean that at all. You told me so yourself."

"I did. I *wanted* apparitions to be false, or that they not be souls. I needed to believe that."

"You never were objective about it."

He shook his head and studied the darkness below him. "If ghosts were real and they were souls, then why had Harry never come back to me?"

There was nothing she could answer to that. "What changed your mind?"

"Last Friday night, my haunt returned. I knew it wasn't real—I had settled that years ago—but I knew your library ghost was real. And that didn't make any sense. Why the library ghost and not Harry? I had to know."

How paper-thin was the barrier between thought and unreality. The slightest thing—a stroke, a psychic trauma—rips it through. She recalled that Leo used his laser to project images. What had they really seen in the workroom tonight? Did even Leo know? "I was close to my mother, too," she told him. "We could have been twins, too; except for the age."

He looked at her. "Your mother is still alive."

She avoided his gaze. "But I treated her as if she were dead. Your brother is dead, but you treat him as if he were alive. You won't let him go."

He turned and faced the drop once more. "I can't."

"How many years has it been?"

"A great many."

"It's too long ago to matter any more."

He turned a tear-stained face to her. He looked older than at any other time she had seen him. "It will always matter. If I had gotten up with him, he would never have died."

So, that was it. Hilda felt like crying herself. "Or you might both have died. You can't torture yourself over things that might have been."

"Can't I? My brother is dead, and it was my fault. Now, my career is finished; my colleagues laugh at me. Why should I not take this one last step? It is such a small one."

"Because *I* don't want you to!" She cried it, shouted it into the night.

"Eh?" He gave her an astonished look.

She was angry with him, for what he had done to her and to her life; and for what he had done to himself. "Do you think I want to go through the rest of my life with the same load of guilt you've been carrying; always rerunning this night and asking myself what I could have done differently? Blaming myself."

He looked stricken. "But . . . But you mustn't blame yourself," he said. "You can not be responsible for what I do."

She held her breath, willing him to see the connection. She could not tell him; he had to tell himself. He stood there for two long breaths, studying her. The seconds seemed to stretch out forever. Then he nodded. "Yes. I see." He glanced once more at the abyss below him; then he stepped down onto the solidity of the parking lot. He began to shake. Hilda closed her eyes briefly and said a prayer of thanks. She opened her arms and he stepped into them and laid his head on her shoulder and wept. "There," she said. "It's all right now." She patted him on the back. "It's all right."

"I would have jumped," he said. "I would have."

"I know. It's all right, now."

"No, it is not all right," he said after a long silence. "I'm frightened of what I yet might do." He shook his head. "I'm not happy. I won't be any time soon; but I think, perhaps, I can see happiness from here."

After a few moments, he disengaged himself. He rubbed his hand over his face and turned back to the wall. Hilda held one hand out to him, but he only approached the wall and gazed over its edge. The tears still coated his cheeks. Hilda watched him, her arms half-raised toward him, her hands clenched. The wind was bitterly cold. Winter was coming. All tears were ice; and winter must be brave.

BOOKWORM, RUN!

Vernor Vinge

Vernor Vinge is a mathematician living in California who has been writing hard sf for thirty years and slowly gaining a reputation as one of the significant talents in the field. Virtually unnoticed in the 1960s and '70s, his novels and stories have sometimes been spaced years apart, so that although he entered the field at nearly the same time as Larry Niven, his work was known for years only to a comparatively small circle of specialists. The last ten years have been his most productive period, featuring his collection *True Names* (1987) and his three best novels to date, *The Peace War* (1984), *Marooned in Realtime* (1986), and *A Fire Upon the Deep* (1992). He is now widely popular and seems likely to be one of the major hard sf writers of the 1990s.

Vinge began writing stories during the final years of Campbell's career at *Analog*, including "Bookworm, Run." This is an early combination of animal intelligence experiments with computers, particularly artificial intelligence programs. It is interesting to compare this story to Daniel Keyes's classic, "Flowers for Algernon," in its treatment of enhanced intelligence and its problems, and to contrast it to Kate Wilhelm's portrayal of unsuccessful experiments with chimpanzees in "The Planners." The theme is persistent during the last thirty years in sf, down to Pat Murphy's recent Nebula Award-winning "Rachel in Love." Even more interesting, perhaps, is the implication that the super chimp is a metaphor for the adolescent sf fan, bright but imprisoned by seemingly benign social institutions, looking forward to a life of service to the military/industrial complex.

They knew what he'd done.

Norman Simmons cringed, his calloused black fingers grasped "Tarzan of the Apes" so tightly that several pages ripped. Seeing what he had done, Norman shut the book and placed it gently on his desk. Then, almost shaking with fear, he tried to roll himself into a ball small enough to escape detection. Gradually he relaxed, panting; Kimball Kinnison would never refuse to face danger. There must be a way out. He knew several routes to the surface. If no one saw him . . .

They'd be hunting for him; and when they caught him, he would die.

He was suddenly anxious to leave the prefab green aluminum walls of his room and school—but what should he take? He pulled the sheet off his bed and spread it on the floor. Norman laid five or six of his favorite books on the sheet, scuttled across the room to his closet, pulled out an extra pair of red and orange Bermuda shorts, and tossed them on top of the books. He paused, then added a blanket, his portable typewriter, his notebook, and a pencil. Now he was equipped for any contingency.

Norman wrapped the sheet tightly about his belongings and dragged the makeshift sack to the door. He opened the door a crack, and peeked out. The passageway was empty. He cautiously opened the door wide and stepped down onto the bedrock floor of the tunnel. Then he dragged the sheet and its contents over the doorsill. The bag dropped the ten inches which separated the aluminum floor of his room from the tunnel. The typewriter landed with a muffled clank. Norman glanced anxiously around the corner of the room, up the tunnel. The lights were off in the Little School. It was Saturday and his teachers' day off. The Lab was closed, too, which was unforeseen good luck, since the aloof Dr. Dunbar was usually there at this time.

He warily circled about a nearby transport vehicle. *Model D-49 Food Cargo Carrier, Army Transport Mark XIXe. Development Contract D-49f1086-1979. First deliveries, January, 1982 . . . RESTRICTED Unauthorized use of RESTRICTED materials is punishable by up to 10 years imprisonment, $10,000 fine, or both: Maintenance Manual: Chapter I, Description . . . The Mark XIXe is a medium speed transport designed to carry loads of less than fifteen tons through constricted areas, such as mine tunnels or storage depots. The "e" modification of the Mark XIX indicates the substitution of a 500-hp Bender fusion power source for the Wankel engine originally intended for use with the XIX. As the Bender pack needs only the natural water vapor in the air for fuel, it is an immense improvement over any other power source. This economy, combined with the tape programmed auto-pilot, make the XIXe one of . . .* Norman shook his head, trying to cut off the endless flow of irrelevant information that came to mind. With practice, he was sure that he would eventually be able to pick out just the data he needed to solve problems, but in the meantime the situation was often very confusing.

The passage he was looking for was between the 345th and 346th fluorescent tube—counting from his room; it was on the left side of the tunnel. Norman began running, at the same time pulling the sack behind him. This was an awkward position for him and he was soon forced to a walk. He concentrated on counting the lighting tubes that were hung from the roof of the tunnel. Each fluorescent cast harsh white light upon the walls of the tunnel, but between the tubes slight shadows lingered. The walls of the passage were streaky with whorls almost like wood or marble, but much darker and grayish-green. As he walked a slight draft of fresh air from faraway air regenerators ruffled the hair on his back.

Norman finally turned to face the left wall of the passage and stopped—343–344–345. The liquid streaks of pyrobole and feldspar appeared the same here as in any other section of the tunnel. Taking another step, Norman stood at the darkest point between the two lights. He carefully counted five hand-widths from the point where the wall blended into the floor. At this spot he cupped his hands and shouted into the wall: "Why does the goodwife like Dutch Elm disease for tea?"

The wall replied, "I don't know, I just work here."

Norman searched his memory, looking for one piece of information among the billions. "Well, find out before her husband does."

There was no reply. Instead, a massive section of bedrock swung noiselessly out of the wall, revealing another tunnel at right-angles to Norman's.

He hurried into it, then paused and glanced back. The huge door had already shut. As he continued up the new tunnel, Norman was careful to count the lights. When he came to number 48, he again selected a place on the wall and shouted some opening commands. The new tunnel was slanted steeply upward, as were the next three passages which Norman switched to. At last he reached the spot in the sixth tunnel which contained the opening to the surface. He paused, feeling both relief and fear: Relief because there weren't any secret codes and distances to remember after this; fear because he didn't know what or who might be waiting for him on the other side of this last door. What if they were just hiding there to shoot him?

Norman took a deep breath and shouted: "There are only 3,456,628 more shopping days till Christmas."

"So?" came the muffled reply.

Norman thought: *NSA (National Security Agency) cryptographic (code) analysis organization. Report Number 36390-201. MOST SECRET. (Unauthorized use of MOST SECRET materials is punishable by death.): "Mathematical Analysis of Voice and Electronic Pass Codes," by Melvin M. Rosseter, RAND contract 748970-1975. Paragraph 1: Consider L, an m by n matrix (rectangular array—arrangement) of (n times m) elements (items) formed by the Vrevik product . . .* Norman screamed shrilly. In his haste, he had accepted the wrong memories. The torrent of information, cross-references and explanatory notes, was almost as overwhelming as his experience the time he foolishly decided to learn all about plasma physics.

With an effort he choked off the memories. But now he was getting desperate. He had to come up with the pass code, and fast.

Finally, "So avoid the mash. Shop December 263."

A large section of the ceiling swung down into the tunnel. Through the opening, Norman could see the sky. But it was gray, not blue like the other time! Norman had not realized that a cloudy day could be so dreary. A cold, humid mist oozed into the tunnel from the opening. He shuddered, but scrambled up the inclined plane which the lowered ceiling section formed. The massive trapdoor shut behind him.

The air seemed still, but so cold and wet. Norman looked around. He was standing atop a large stony bluff. Scrub trees and scraggly brush covered most of the ground, but here and there large sections of greenish, glacier-scoured bedrock were visible. Every surface glistened with a thin layer of water. Norman sneezed. It had been so nice and warm the last time. He peered out over the lower land and saw fog. It was just like the description in the "Adventures of the Two and the Three." The fog hung in the lower land like some tenuous sea, filling rocky fjords in the bluff. Trees and bushes and boulders seemed to lurk mysteriously within it.

This mysterious quality of the landscape gave Norman new spirit. He was a bold adventurer setting out to discover new lands.

He was also a hunted animal.

Norman found the small footpath he remembered, and set off across the bluff. The wet grass tickled his feet and his hair was already dripping. His books and typewriter were getting an awful beating as he dragged them over the rough ground.

He came to the edge of the bluff. The grass gave way to a bedrock shelf overlooking a drop of some fifty feet. Over the years, winter ice had done its work. Sections of the face of the cliff had broken off. Now the rubble reached halfway up the cliff, almost like a carelessly strewn avalanche of pebbles except that each rock weighed many tons. The fog worked in and out among the boulders and seemed to foam up the side of the cliff.

Norman crept to the edge of the cliff and peered over. Five feet below was a ledge about ten inches wide. The ledge slanted down. At its lower end it was only seven feet above the rocks. He went over, clinging to the cliff with one hand, and grasping the sack which lay on the ground above him with the other. Norman had not realized how slimy the rocks had become in the wet air. His hand slipped and he fell to the ledge below. The sack was jerked over the edge, but he kept his hold on it. The typewriter in the sack hit the side of the cliff with a loud clang.

He collected his wits and crawled to the lower part of the ledge. Here he again went over, but was very careful to keep a firm grip. He let go and landed feet first on a huge boulder directly below. The sack crashed down an instant later. Norman clambered over the rocks and soon had descended to level ground.

Nearby objects were obscured by the fog. It was even colder and damper than above. The fog seemed to enter his mouth and nose and draw away his warmth. He paused, then started in the direction that he remembered seeing the airplane hangar last time. Soon he was ankle deep in wet grass.

After about one hundred yards, Norman noticed a darkness to his left. He turned and approached it. Gradually the form of a light plane was defined. Soon he could clearly see the Piper Cub. *Four place, single-jet aircraft; maximum cargo weight, 1200 pounds; minimum runway for takeoff with full load, 90 yards; maximum speed, 250 miles per hour.* Its wings and fuselage shone dully in the weak light. Norman ran up to the Cub, clambered over the struts, and pulled himself into the cabin. He settled his sack in the copilot's seat and slammed the door. The key had been left in the ignition: someone had been extremely careless.

Norman inspected the controls of the little aircraft. Somehow his fear had departed, and specific facts now came easily to mind. He saw that there was an autopilot on the right-hand dash, but it was of a simple-minded variety and could handle only cruising flight.

He reached down and felt the rudder pedals with his feet. By bracing his back against the seat he could touch the pedals and at the same time hold the steering wheel. Of course, he would not be able to see out very easily, but there really wasn't very much to see.

He had to get across the border fast and this airplane was probably the only way.

He turned the starter and heard the fuel pumps and turbines begin rotating. Norman looked at the dash. What was he supposed to do next? He pushed the button marked FLASH and was rewarded with a loud *ffumpf* as the jet engine above the wing ignited. He twisted the throttle. The Cub crawled across the field, picking up speed. It bounced and jolted over the turf.

. . . Throttle to full, keeping stick forward . . . until you are well over stall speed (35 miles per hour for a 1980 Cub) . . . pull back gently on the stick, being careful to remain over . . . (35 miles per hour) . . .

He craned his neck, trying to get a view ahead. The ride was becoming smooth. The cub was airborne! Still nothing but fog ahead. For an instant the mist parted, revealing a thirty-foot Security fence barely fifty yards away. He had to have altitude!

. . . Under no circumstances should high angle-of-attack (climb) maneuvers be attempted without sufficient air speed . . .

Instructions are rarely the equal of actual experience, and now Norman was going to learn the hard way. He pushed at the throttle and pulled back hard on the stick. The little aircraft nosed sharply upward, its small jet engine screaming. The air speed fell and with it the lifting power of the wings. The Cub seemed to pause for an instant suspended in the air, then fell back. Jet still whining, the nose came down and the plane plunged earthwards.

Imagine a plate of spaghetti—no sauce or meatballs. O.K., now picture an entire room filled with such food. This wormy nightmare gives you some idea of the complexity of the First Security District, otherwise known as the Labyrinth. By analogy each strand of spaghetti is a tunnel segment carved through bedrock. The Labyrinth occupied four cubic miles under the cities of Ishpeming and Negaunee in the Upper Peninsula of Michigan. Without the power of controlled nuclear fusion such a maze could never have been made. Each tunnel was connected to several others by a random system of secret hatches, controlled by voice and electronic codes. Truly the First Security District was the most spy-proof volume in the solar system. The Savannah plant, the CIA, Soviet IKB, and the entire system of GM factories could have co-existed in it without knowledge of each other. As a matter of fact, thirty-one different Security projects, laboratories, and military bases existed in the Labyrinth with their coordinates listed in a single filing computer—and there's the rub . . .

"Because he's been getting straight A's," Dr. William Dunbar finished.

Lieutenant General Alvin Pederson, Commander of the First Security District, looked up from the computer console with a harried expression on his face. The two men were alone in the chamber containing the memory bank of United States Government Files Central, usually referred to as Files Central or simply Files. Behind the console were racks of fiber glass, whose orderly columns and rows filled most of the room. At the base of each rack, small lasers emitted modulated and coherent light; as the light passed through the fibers, it was altered and channeled by subtle impurities in the glass. Volume for volume, the computer was ten thousand times better than the best cryogenic models. Files Central contained all the information, secret and otherwise, possessed by the U.S.—including the contents of the Library of Congress, which managed to fill barely ten per cent of Files' capacity. The fact that Pederson kept his office here rather than at Continental Air Defense Headquarters, which occupied another part of the Labyrinth, indicated just how important the functions of Files were.

Pederson frowned. He had better things to do than listen to every overwrought genius that wanted to talk to him, though Dunbar usually spoke out only when he had something important to say. "You'd better start at the beginning, Doctor."

The mathematician began nervously. "Look. Norman has never had any great interest in his schoolwork. We may have given the chimp high intelligence with this brain-computer combination, but he has the emotional maturity of a nine-year-old human. Norman is bright, curious—and *lazy*; he would rather read science fiction than study history. His schoolwork has always been poorly and incompletely done—until six weeks ago. Since then he has spent virtually no time on real studying. At the same time he has shown a complete mastery of the factual information in his courses. It's almost as if he had an eidetic memory of *facts that were never presented to him*. As if . . ."

Dunbar started on a different tack. "General, you know how much trouble we had coordinating the chimp's brain with his computer in the first place. On the one hand you have an African chimpanzee, and on the other an advanced optical computer which theoretically is superior even to Files here. We wanted the chimp's brain to cooperate with the computer as closely as the different parts of a human brain work together. This meant that the computer had to be programmed to operate the way the chimp's mind did. We also had to make time-lapse corrections, because the chimp and the computer are not physically together. All in all, it was a terrifically complicated job. It makes the Economic Planning Programs look like setting up Fox and Geese on a kid's Brain Truster kit." Seeing the other's look of impatience, Dunbar hurried on. "Anyway, you remember that we needed to use the Files computer, just to program *our* computer. And the two machines had to be electronically connected."

The scientist came abruptly to the point, "If by some accident or mechanical failure, the link between Files and Norman *were never cut*, then . . . then the chimp would have complete access to U. S. Files."

Pederson's preoccupation with other matters disappeared. "If that's so, we've got one hell of a problem. And it would explain a lot of other things. Look." He shoved a sheet of paper at Dunbar. "As a matter of routine, Files announces how much information it has supplied to queries during every twenty-four-hour period. Actually it's sort of a slick gimmick to impress visitors with how efficient and useful Files is, supplying information to twenty or thirty different agencies at once. Up until six weeks ago the daily reading hung around ten to the tenth bits per day. During the next ten days it climbed to over ten to the twelfth—then to ten to the fourteenth. We couldn't hunt down the source of the queries and most of the techs thought the high readings were due to mechanical error.

"Altogether, Files has supplied almost ten to the fifteenth bits to—someone. And that, Doctor, is equal to the total amount of information contained in Files. It looks as if your monkey has programmed himself with all the information the U.S. possesses."

Pederson turned to the query panel, typed two questions. A tape reel by the desk spun briefly, stopped. Pederson pointed to it. "Those are the coordinates of your lab. I'm sending a couple men down to pick up your simian friend. Then I'm sending some more men to wherever his computer is."

Pederson looked at the tape reel expectantly, then noticed the words gleaming on a readout screen above the console:

The coordinates you request are not On File.

Pederson lunged forward and typed the question again, carefully. The message on the screen didn't even flicker:

The coordinates you request are not On File.

Dunbar leaned over the panel. "It's true, then," he said hoarsely, for the first time believing his fears. "Probably Norman thought we would punish him if we found out he was using Files."

"We would," Pederson interrupted harshly.

"And since Norman could use information On File, he could also *erase* information there. We hardly ever visit the tunnel where his computer was built, so we haven't noticed until now that he had erased its coordinates."

Now that he knew an emergency really existed, Dunbar seemed calm. He continued inexorably, "And if Norman was this fearful of discovery, then he probably had Files advise him when you tried to find the location of his computer. My lab is only a couple hundred feet below the surface—and he surely knows how to get out."

The general nodded grimly. "This chimp seems to be one step ahead of us all the way." He switched on a comm, and spoke into it. "Smith, send a couple men over to Dunbar's lab . . . Yeah, I've got the coordinates right here." He pressed another switch and the reel of tape spun, transmitting its magnetic impressions to a similar reel at the other end of the hookup. "Have them grab the experimental chimp and bring him down here to Files Central. Don't hurt him, but be careful—you know how bright he is." He cut the circuit and turned back to Dunbar.

"If he's still there, we'll get him; but if he's already made a break for the surface, there's no way we can stop him now. This place is just too decentralized." He thought for a second, then turned back to the comm and gave more instructions to his aide.

"I've put in a call to Sawyer AFB to send some airborne infantry over here. Other than that, we can only watch."

A TV panel brightened, revealing a view from one of the hidden surface cameras. The scene was misty, and silent except for an occasional dripping sound.

Several minutes passed; then a superbly camouflaged and counter-balanced piece of bedrock in the center of their view swung down, and a black form in orange Bermuda shorts struggled out of the ground, dragging a large white sack. The chimp shivered, then moved off, disappearing over the crest of the bluff.

Pederson's hands were pale white, clenched in frustration about the arms of his chair. Although the First Security District was built under Ishpeming, its main entrances were fifteen miles away at Sawyer Armed Forces Base. There were only three small and barely accessible entrances in the area where Norman had escaped. Fortunately for the chimpanzee, his quarters had been located near one of them. The area which contained these entrances belonged to the Ore REclamation Service, a government agency charged with finding more efficient methods of low-grade ore refining. (With the present economic situation, it was a rather superfluous job since the current problem was to get *rid* of the ore on hand rather than increase production.) All this indirection was designed to hide the location of the First Security District from the enemy. But at the same time it made direct control of the surface difficult.

A shrill sound came from the speaker by the TV panel. Dunbar puzzled, "Sounds almost like a light jet."

Pederson replied, "It probably is. The ORES people maintain a small office up there for appearances' sake, and they have a Piper Cub . . . *Could that chimp fly one!*"

"I doubt it, but I suppose if he were desperate enough he would try anything."

Smith's voice interrupted them, "General, our local infiltration radar has picked up an aircraft at an altitude of fifteen feet. Its present course will take it into the Security fence." The buzzing became louder. "The pilot is going to stall it out! It's in a steep climb . . . eighty feet, one hundred. It's stalled!"

The buzzing whine continued for a second and then abruptly ceased.

The typewriter departed through the front windshield at great speed. Norman Simmons came to in time to see his dog-eared copy of "Galactic Patrol" disappear into the murky water below. He made a wild grab for the book, missed it, and received a painful scratch from shards of broken windshield. All that remained of his belongings was the second volume of the Foundation series and the blanket which somehow had been draped half in and half out of the shattered window. The bottom edge of the blanket swung gently back and forth just a couple of inches above the water. The books he could do without; they really had only sentimental value. Since he had learned the Trick, there was no need to physically possess any books. But in the cold weather he was sure to need the blanket; he carefully retrieved it.

Norman pushed open a door, and climbed onto the struts of the Cub for a look around. The plane had crashed nose first into a shallow pond. The jet had been silenced in the impact, and the loudest sound to be heard now was his own breathing. Norman peered into the fog. How far was he from "dry" land? A few yards away he could see swamp vegetation above the still surface of the water; beyond that, nothing but mist. A slight air current eased the gloom. There! For an instant he glimpsed dark trees and brush about thirty yards away.

Thirty yards, through cold and slimy water. Norman's lips curled back in revulsion as he stared at the oily liquid. Maybe there was an aerial route, like Tarzan used. He glanced anxiously up, looking for some overhanging tree branch or vine. No luck. He would have to go *through* the water. Norman almost cried in despair at the thought. Suffocating visions of death by drowning came to mind. He imagined all the creatures with pointy teeth and ferocious appetites that might be lurking in the seemingly placid water: piranhas to strip his bones and—no, they were tropical fish, but something equally deadly. If he could only pretend that it were clear, ankle-deep water.

Dal swam silently toward the moonlit palms and palely gleaming sands just five hundred yards away. Five hundred yards, he thought exultantly, to freedom, to his own kind. The enemy could never penetrate the atoll's camouflage . . . He didn't notice a slight turbulence, the swift emergence of a leathery tentacle from the water. But he fought desperately as he felt it tighten about his leg. Dal's screams were bubbly gurglings inaudible above the faint drone of the surf, as he was hauled effortlessly into the depths and sharp, unseen teeth . . .

For a second his control lapsed, and the fictional incident slipped in. In the comfort of his room, the death of Dal had been no more than the pleasantly chilling end of a villain; here it was almost unbearable. Norman extended one foot gingerly into the water, and quickly drew it back. He tried again, this time with both feet. Nothing bit him and he cautiously lowered himself into the clammy water. The swamp weeds brushed gently against his legs. Soon he was holding the strut with one hand and was neck deep in water. The mass of weeds had slowly been compressed as he descended and now just barely supported his weight, even though he had not touched bottom. He released his grip on the strut and began moving toward shore. With one hand he attempted to keep his blanket out of the water while with the other he paddled. Norman glanced about for signs of some hideous tentacle or fin, saw nothing but weeds.

He could see the trees on the shore quite clearly now, and the weeds at his feet seemed backed by solid ground. Just a few more yards—Norman gasped with relief as he struggled out of the water. He noticed an itching on his legs and arms. There had been blood-drinkers in the water after all, but fortunately small ones. He paused to remove the slugs from his body.

Norman sneezed violently and inspected his blanket. Although the mists had made it quite damp, he wrapped it around himself. Only after he was more or less settled did he notice the intermittent thrumming sound coming through the trees on his left. It sounded like the transport vehicles back in the tunnels, or like the automobiles that he had heard and seen on film.

Norman scrambled through the underbrush in the direction of the noises. Soon he came to a dilapidated four-lane asphalt highway. Every minute or so, a car would appear out of the mist, travel through his narrow range of vision, and disappear into the mist again.

MOST SECRET. *(Unauthorized use of* MOST SECRET *materials is punishable by death.)* He had to get to Canada or they would kill him for sure. He knew millions, *billions* of things labeled MOST SECRET. Nearly all were unintelligible. The rest were usually boring. A very small percentage were interesting, like something out of an adventure story. And some were horrifying bits of nightmare couched in cold, matter-of-fact words. But all were labeled MOST SECRET, and his access to them was certainly unauthorized. If only he had known beforehand the consequences of Memorizing It All. It had been so easy to do, and so useful, but it was also a deadly, clinging gift.

Now that the airplane had crashed, he had to find some other way to get to Canada. Maybe one of these cars could take him some place where he would have better luck in his attempt. For some reason, the idea didn't trigger warning memories. Blissfully unaware that a talking chimpanzee is not a common sight in the United States, Norman started down the embankment to the shoulder of the highway, and in the immortal tradition of the hitchhiker in "Two for the Road," stuck out his thumb.

Three minutes passed; he clutched the blanket more tightly to himself as his teeth began to chatter. In the distance he heard the thrum of an approaching vehicle. He stared eagerly in the direction of the sound. Within fifteen seconds, a sixty-ton ore carrier emerged from the fog and lumbered toward him. Norman jumped up and down in a frenzy, waving and shouting. The blanket gave him the appearance of a little Amerind doing a particularly violent rain dance. The huge truck rolled by him at about thirty-five miles per hour. Then when it was some forty yards away, the driver slammed on the brakes and the doughy rollagon tires bit into asphalt.

Norman ran joyfully toward the cab, not noticing the uncared-for condition of the starboard ore cranes, the unpainted and dented appearance of the cab, or the wheezy putputting of the Wankel rotary engine—all signs of dilapidation which would have been unthinkable four years before.

He stopped in front of the cab door and was confronted by a pair of cynical, bloodshot eyes peering at him over a three-day growth of beard. "Who . . . Whash are you?" (The condition of the driver would have been unthinkable four years ago, too.)

"My name's Norman—Jones." Norman slyly selected an alias. He resolved to act dull, too, for he knew that most chimps were somewhat stupid, and couldn't speak clearly without the special operations he had had. (In spite of his memory and intelligence, Norman had an artificial block against ever completely realizing his uniqueness.) "I want to go to"—he searched his memory—"Marquette."

The driver squinted and moved his head from side to side as if to get a better view of Norman. "Say, you're a monkey."

"No," Norman stated proudly, forgetting his resolution, "I'm a chimpanzee."

"A talkin' monkey," the driver said almost to himself. "You could be worth plen . . . wherezhu say you wanna go . . . Marquette? Sure, hop in. That's where I'm takin' this ore."

Norman clambered up the entrance ladder into the warm cab. "Oh, thanks a lot."

The ore carrier began to pick up speed. The highway had been blasted through greenish bedrock, but it still made turns and had to climb over steep hills.

The driver was expansive, "Can't wait to finish this trip. This here is my las' run, ya know. No more drivin' ore fer the government an' its 'Public Works Projects.' I know where to get a couple black market fusion packs, see? Start my own trucking line. No one'll ever guess where I get my power." He swerved to avoid a natural abutment of greenish rock that appeared out of the mist, and decided that it was time to turn on his fog lights. His mind wandered back to prospects of future success, but along a different line. "Say, you like to talk, Monkey? You could make me a lot of money, ya know: 'Jim Traly an' His Talkin' Monkey.' Sounds good, eh?"

With a start, Norman realized that he was listening to a drunk. The driver's entire demeanor was almost identical to that of the fiend's henchman in "The Mores of the Morgue." Norman had no desire to be a "talkin' monkey" for the likes of Traly, whose picture he now remembered in Social Security Records. The man was listed as an unstable, low competence type who might become violent if frustrated.

As the ore carrier slowed for a particularly sharp turn, Norman decided that he could endure the cold of the outside for a few more minutes. He edged to the door and began to pull at its handle. "I think I better get off now, Mr. Traly."

The ore carrier slowed still more as the driver lunged across the seat and grabbed Norman by one of the purple suspenders that kept his orange Bermuda shorts up. A full grown chimpanzee is a match for most men, but the driver weighed nearly three hundred pounds and Norman was scared stiff. "You're shtaying right here, see?" Traly shouted into Norman's face, almost suffocating the chimpanzee in alcohol vapor. The driver transferred his grip to the scruff of Norman's neck as he accelerated the carrier back to cruising speed.

"Crashed in a shallow swamp just beyond the Security fence, sir." The young Army captain held a book up to the viewer. "This copy of Asimov was all that was left in the cabin, but we dredged up some other books and a typewriter from the water. It's only about five feet deep there."

"But where did the chim . . . the pilot go?" Pederson asked.

"The pilot, sir?" The captain knew what the quarry was but was following the general's line. "We have a man here from Special Forces who's a tracker, sir. He says that the pilot left the Cub and waded ashore. From there, he tracked him through the brush to the old Ishpeming-Marquette road. He's pretty sure that the . . . um . . . pilot hitched a ride in the direction of Marquette." The captain did not mention how surprised the lieutenant from Special Forces had been by the pilot's tracks. "He probably left the area about half an hour ago, sir."

"Very well, Captain. Set up a guard around the plane; if anyone gets nosy, tell them that ORES has asked you to salvage their crashed Cub. Fly everything you found in the cabin and swamp back to Sawyer and have it sent down here to Files Central."

"Yes, sir."

Pederson cut the connection and began issuing detailed instructions to his chief aide over another circuit. Finally he turned back to Dunbar. "That chimp is not going to remain one step ahead of us for very much longer. I've alerted all the armed forces in the Upper Peninsula to start a search, with special concentration on Marquette. It's lucky that we have permission to conduct limited maneuvers there or I might have an awful time just getting permission to station airbornes over the city.

"And now we can take a little time to consider ways of catching this Norman Simmons, rather than responding spastically to *his* initiative."

Dunbar said quickly, "In the first place, you can cut whatever connection there is between Files and Norman's computer."

Pederson grinned. "Good enough. That was mixed in with the rest of the instructions I've given Smith. If I remember right, the two computers were connected by a simple copper cable, part of the general cable net that was installed interweaving with the tunnel system. It should be a simple matter to cut the circuit where the cable enters the Files room."

The general thought for a moment. "The object now is to catch the chimp, discover the location of the chimp's computer, or both. Down here we can't do anything directly about the chimp. But the computer has to be in contact with Norman Simmons. Could we trace these emanations?"

Dunbar blinked. "You know that better than I, General. The Signal Corps used our experiment to try a *quote* entirely new concept in communications *unquote*. They supplied all the comm equipment, even the surgical imbeds for Norman. And they are playing it pretty cozy with the technique. Whatever it is, it goes through almost anything, does not travel faster than light, and can handle several billion bits per second. It might even be ESP, if what I've read about telepathy is true."

Pederson looked sheepish. "I do recognize the 'new concept' you mention. I just never connected the neutri . . . this technique with your project. But I should have known; we have only one way to broadcast through solid rock as if it were vacuum. Unfortunately, with the devices we have now, there's no way of getting a directional bearing on such transmissions. With enough time and as a last resort we might be able to jam them, though."

Now it was Dunbar's turn to make a foolish suggestion. "Maybe if a thorough search of the tunnels were made, we could find the—"

Pederson grimaced. "Bill, you've been here almost three years. Haven't you realized how complicated the Labyrinth is? The maze is composed of thousands of tunnel segments spread through several cubic miles of bedrock. It's simply too complex for a blind search—and there's only one set of blueprints," he jerked a thumb at the racks of fiber glass. "Even for routine trips, we have to make out tapes to plug into the transport cars down there. If we hadn't put his quarters close to ground level, so you could take him for walks on the surface, Norman would still be wandering around the Labyrinth, even though he knows what passages to take.

"About twice a day I ride over to Continental Air Defense Headquarters. It takes about half an hour and the trip is more tortuous than a swoopride at a carnival. CAD HQ could be just a hundred yards from where we're sitting, or it could be two miles—in any direction. For that matter, I don't really know where *we* are right now. But then," he added with a sly smile, "neither do the Russki or Han missilemen. I'm sorry, Doctor, but it would take years of random searching to find the computer."

And Dunbar realized that he was right. It was general policy in the First Security District to disperse experiments and other installations as far as possible through the tunnel maze. So it had been with Norman's computer. With its own power source the computer needed no outside assistance to function.

The scientist remembered its strange appearance, resting like a huge jewel in a vacant tunnel—where? It was a far different sight from the appearance of Files. Norman's computer had the facets of a cut gem, although this had been a functional rather than an aesthetic necessity. Dunbar remembered the multicolor glows that appeared near its surface; further in, the infinite reflections and subtle refractions of microcomponent flaws in the glass blended into a mysterious flickering, hinting at the cheerful though immature intelligence that was Norman Simmons. This was the object which had to be found.

Dunbar broke out of his reverie. He started on a different tack. "Really, General, I don't quite see how this situation can be quite as desperate as you say. Norman isn't going to sell secrets to the Reds; he's as loyal as a human child could be—which is a good deal more than most adults, because he can't rationalize disloyalty so easily. Besides, you know that we were eventually going to provide him with large masses of data, anyway. The goal of this whole project is to test the possibility of giving humans an encyclopedic mental grasp. He just saw how much the information could help him, and how much easier it could be obtained than by study, and he pushed the experiment into its next phase. He shouldn't be punished or hurt because of that. This situation is really no one's fault."

Pederson snapped back, "Of course, it's no one's fault; that's just the hell of it. When no one is to blame for something, it means that the situation is fundamentally beyond human control. To me, your whole project is taking control away from people and giving it to *others*. Here an experimental animal, a chimpanzee, has taken the initiative away from the U. S. Government—don't laugh, or so help me—" The general made a warning gesture. "Your chimp is more than a co-ordinator of information; he's also *smarter* than he was before. *What're the humans we try this on going to be like?*"

Pederson calmed himself with a deliberate effort. "Never mind that now. The important thing is to find Simmons, since he appears to be the only one who," Pederson groaned, "knows where his brains are. So let's get practical. Just what can we expect from him? How easy is it for him to correlate information in his memory?"

Dunbar considered. "I guess the closest analogy between his mind and a normal one is to say that he has an eidetic memory—and a *very* large one. I imagine that when he first began using the information he was just swamped with data. Everything he saw stimulated a deluge of related memories. As his subconscious became practiced, he probably remembered only information that was pertinent to a problem. Say that he saw a car, and wondered what year and make it was. His subconscious would hunt through his copy of Files—at very high speed—and within a tenth of a second Norman would 'remember' the information he had just wondered about.

"However, if for some reason he suddenly wondered what differential equations were, it would be a different matter, because he couldn't *understand* the information presented, and so would have to wade through the same preliminary material that every child must in order to arrive at high-school math. But he could do it very much faster, because of the ease with which he could pick different explanations from different texts. I imagine he could get well into calculus from where he is now in algebra with a couple hours of study."

"In other words, the longer he has this information, the more dangerous he'll be."

"Uh, yes. However, there *are* a couple things on our side. First, it's mighty cold and damp on the surface, for Norman at least. He is likely to be very sick in a few hours. Second, if he travels far enough away from the First Security District, he will become mentally disoriented. Although Norman doesn't know it—unless he has specifically considered the question—he could never get much farther than fifteen miles away and remain sane. Norman's mind is a very delicate balance between his organic brain and the hidden computer. The co-ordination is just as subtle as that of different nerve paths in the human brain. The information link between the two has to transmit more than a billion bits of information per second. If Norman gets beyond a certain point, the time lapse involved in transmission between him and the computer will upset the co-ordination. It's something like talking by radio with a spacecraft; beyond a certain distance it is difficult or impossible to maintain a meaningful conversation. When Norman goes beyond a certain point it will be impossible for him to think coherently."

Dunbar was struck by an unrelated idea. He added, "Say, I can see one reason why this could get sticky. What if Norman got picked up by foreign agents? That would be the biggest espionage coup in the history of man."

Pederson smiled briefly. "Ah, the light dawns. Yes, some of the information this Simmons has could mean the death of almost everyone on Earth, if it were known to the wrong people. Other secrets would *merely* destroy the United States.

"Fortunately, we're fairly sure that the Red's domestic collapse has reduced their overseas enterprises to about nil. As I remember it, there are only one or two agents in all of Michigan. Thank God for small favors."

Boris Kuchenko scratched and was miserable. A few minutes before, he had been happily looking forward to receiving his weekly unemployment check and then spending the afternoon clipping articles out of the *NATO Armed Forces Digest* for transmission back to Moscow. And now this old coot with his imperious manner was trying to upset everything. Kuchenko turned to his antagonist and tried to put on a brave front. "I am sorry, Comrade, but I have my orders. As the ranking Soviet agent in the Upper Peninsu—"

The other snapped back, "Ranking agent, nothing! You were never supposed to know this, Kuchenko, but you are a cipher, a stupid dummy used to convince U. S. Intelligence that the USSR has given up massive espionage. If only I had some decent agents here in Marquette, I wouldn't have to use idiots like you."

Ivan Sliv was an honest-to-God, effective Russian spy. Behind his inconspicuous middle-aged face lurked a subtle mind. Sliv spoke five languages and had an excellent grasp of engineering, mathematics, geography, and history—*real* history, not State-sponsored fairy tales. He could make brilliantly persuasive conversation at a cocktail party or commit a political murder with equal facility. Sliv was the one really in charge of espionage in the militarily sensitive U.P. area. He and other equally talented agents concentrated on collecting information from Sawyer AFB and from the elusive First Security District.

The introduction of Bender's fusion pack had produced world-wide depression, and the bureaucracies of Russia had responded to this challenge with all the resiliency of a waterlogged pretzel. The Soviet economic collapse had been worse than that of any other major country. While the U.S. was virtually recovered from the economic depression caused by the availability of unlimited power, counter-revolutionary armies were approaching Moscow from the West *and* the East. Only five or ten ICBM bases remained in Party hands. But the Comrades had been smart in one respect. If you can't win by brute force, it is better to be subtle. Thus the planetary spy operations were stepped up, as was a very secret project housed in a system of caves under the Urals. Sliv's mind shied away from that project—he was one of the few to know of it, and that knowledge must never be hinted at.

Sliv glared at Kuchenko. "Listen, you fat slob: I'm going to explain things once more, if possible in words of one syllable. I just got news from Sawyer that some Amie superproject has backfired. An experimental animal has escaped from their tunnel network and half the soldiers in the U.P. are searching for it. They think it's here in Marquette."

Kuchenko paled, "A war virus test? Comrade, this could be—" the fat Soviet agent boggled at the possibilities.

Sliv swore. "No, no, no! The Army's orders are to *capture*, not destroy the thing. We are the only agents that are in Marquette now, or have a chance to get in past the cordon that's sure to be dropped around the city. We'll split up and—" He stopped and took conscious notice of the buzzing sound that had been building up over the last several minutes. He walked quickly across the small room and pushed open a badly cracked window. Cold air seemed to ooze into the room. Below, the lake waters splashed against the pilings of the huge automated pier which incidentally contained this apartment. Sliv pointed into the sky and snapped at the bedraggled Kuchenko, "See? The Amie airbornes have been over the city for the last five minutes, at least. We've got to get going, man!"

But Boris Kuchenko was a man who liked his security. He miserably inspected his dirty fingernails, and began, "I really don't know if this is the right thing, Comrade. We—"

The fog had disappeared, only to be replaced by a cold drizzle. Jim Traly guided the ore carrier through Marquette to the waterfront. Even though drunk, he maintained a firm grip on Norman's neck. The carrier turned onto another street, and Norman got his first look at Lake Superior. It was so gray and cold; beyond the breakwater the lake seemed to blend with the sullen hue of the sky. The carrier turned again. They were now moving parallel to the water along a row of loading piers. In spite of the rollagons, the carrier dipped and sagged as they drove over large potholes in the substandard paving material. The rain had collected in these depressions and splashed as they drove along. Traly apparently recognized his destination. He slowed the carrier and moved it to the side of the street.

Traly opened his door and stepped down, dragging Norman behind him. With difficulty the chimpanzee kept his balance and did not land on his head. The drunk driver was muttering to himself, "Las' time I drive this trash. They can pick up the inventories themselves. Good riddance." He kicked a rollagon. "Just wait till I get some Bender fusion packs. I'll show 'em. C'mon, you." He gave Norman a jerk, and began walking across the street.

The waterfront was almost deserted. Traly was heading for what appeared to be the only operating establishment in the area: a tavern. The bar had a rundown appearance. The "aluminum" trim around the door had long since begun to rust, and the memory cell for the bar's sky sign suffered from amnesia so that it now projected into the air:

The D-unk PuT pavern

Traly entered the bar, pulling Norman in close behind. Once the fluorescents had probably lighted the place well, but now only two or three in a far corner were operating.

He pulled Norman around in front of him and seemed eager to announce his discovery of the "talkin' monkey." Then he noticed that the bar was almost empty. No one was sitting at any of the tables, although there were half empty glasses of beer left on a few of them. Four or five men and the barkeeper were engaged in an intense discussion at the far end of the room. "Where is everybody?" Traly was astonished.

The barkeeper looked up. "Jimmy! Right at lunch President Langley came on TV an' said that the government was going to let us buy as many Bender fusion boxes as we want. You could go out an' buy one right now for twenty-five bucks. When everybody heard that, why they just asked themselves what they were doin' sittin' around in a bar when they could have a job an' even be in business for themselves. Not much profit for me this afternoon, but I don't care. I know where I can get some junk copters. Fit 'em out with Bender packs and start a tourist service. You know: See the U.P. with Don Zalevsky." The bartender winked.

Traly's jaw dropped. He forgot Norman. "You really mean that there's no more black market where we can get fusion boxes?"

One of the customers, a short man with a protuberant beak and a bald pate, turned to Traly. "What do you need a black market for when you can go out an' buy a Pack for twenty-five dollars? Well, will you look at that: Traly's disappointed. Now you can do whatcher always bragging about, go out and dig up some fusion boxes and go into business." He turned back to the others.

"And we owe it all to President Langley's fizical and economic policies. Bender's Pack coulda destroyed our nation. Instead we only had a little depression, an' look at us now. Three years after the invention, the economy's on an even keel enough to let us buy as many power packs as we want."

Someone interrupted, "You got rocks in your head, buddy. The government closed down most of the mines so the oil corporations would have a market to make plastics for; we get to produce just enough ore up here so no one starves. Those 'economic measures' have kept us all hungry. If the government had only let us buy as many Packs as we wanted and not interfered with free competition, there wouldna been no depression or nothing."

From the derisive remarks of the other customers, this appeared to be a minority opinion. The Beak slammed his glass of beer down and turned to his opponent. "You know what wouldna happened if there wasn't no 'interference'?" He didn't wait for an answer. "Everybody woulda gone out an' bought Packs. All the business in the U.S. woulda gone bankrupt, 'cause anyone with a Bender and some electric motors would hardly need to buy any regular goods, except food. It wouldn't been a depression, it woulda been just like a jungle. As it is, we only had a short period of adjustment," he almost seemed to be quoting, "an' now we're back on our feet. We got power to burn; those ore buckets out in the bay can fly through the air and space, and we can take the salt out of the water and—"

"Aw, you're jus' repeating what Langley said in his speech."

"Sure I am, but it's true." Another thought occurred to him. "And *now* we don't even need Public Works Projects."

"Yeah, no more Public Works Projects," Traly put in, disappointed.

"There wouldn't have been no need for PWP if it wasn't for Langley and his loony ideas. My old man said the same thing about Roosevelt." The dissenter was outnumbered but voluble.

Norman had become engrossed in the argument. In fact he was so interested that he had forgotten his danger. Back in the District he had been made to learn some economics as part of his regular course of study—and, of course, he could remember considerably more about the subject. Now he decided to make his contribution. Traly had loosened his grip; the chimpanzee easily broke the hold and jumped to the top of the counter. "This man," he pointed to the Beak, "is right, you know. The Administration's automatic stabilizers and discretionary measures prevented total catastro—"

"What is *this*, Jimmy?" The bartender broke the amazed silence that greeted Norman's sudden action.

"That's what I've been trying to tell you guys. I picked up this monkey back in Ishpeming. He's like a parrot, only better. Jus' listen to him. I figure he could be worth a lot of money."

"Thought you were going into the trucking business, Jimmy."

Traly shrugged, "This could be a lot greener."

"That's no parrot-talk," the Beak opined. "The monkey's *really* talking. He's smart like you and me."

Norman decided that he had to trust someone. "Yes I am, yes I am! And I need to get into Canada. Otherwise—"

The door to the Drunk Pup Tavern squeaked as a young man in brown working clothes pushed it halfway open. "Hey, Ed, all of you guys. There's a bunch of big Army copters circling the bay, and GI's all over. It doesn't look like any practice maneuver." The man was panting as if he had run several blocks.

"Say, let's see that," moved the Beak. He was informally seconded. Even the bartender seemed ready to leave. Norman started. *They* were still after him, and they were close. He leaped off the counter and ran through the half-open door, right by the knees of the young man who had made the announcement. The man stared at the chimpanzee and made a reflex grab for him. Norman evaded the snatch and scuttled down the street. Behind him, he heard Traly arguing with the man about, "Letting my talking monkey escape."

He had dropped his blanket when he jumped onto the counter. Now the chill drizzle made him regret the loss. Soon he was damp to the skin again, and the water splashed his forearms and legs as he ran through spots where water had collected in the tilted and cracked sections of sidewalk. All the shops and dives along the street were closed and boarded up. Some owners had left in such disgust and discouragement that they had not bothered even to pull in their awnings. He stopped under one such to catch his breath and get out of the rain.

Norman glanced about for some sign of airborne infantrymen, but as far as he could see, the sky was empty of men and aircraft. He examined the awning above him. For several years the once green plastic fabric had been subjected alternately to baking sun and rotting rain. It was cheap plastic and now it hung limp, the gray sky visible through the large holes in the material. Norman looked up, got an idea. He backed away from the awning and then ran toward it. He leaped and caught its rusting metal frame. The shade sagged even more, but held. He eased himself over the frame and rested for an instant on the top; then pulled himself onto the windowsill of a second-story apartment.

Norman looked in, saw nothing but an old bed and a closet with one lonely hanger. He caught the casing above the window and swung up. It was almost like being Tarzan. (Usually, Norman tended to identify himself with Tarzan rather than with the Lord-of-the-Jungle's chimpanzee flunkies.) He caught the casing with his toes, pushed himself upwards until he could grasp the edge of the flat roof. One last heave and he was lying on the tar-and-gravel roofing material. In places where the tar had been worn away, someone had sprayed plastite, but more time had passed and that "miracle construction material" had deteriorated, too.

The roofs provided scant cover from observation. Fifty feet away, Norman saw the spidery black framework of a radio tower mounted on the roof of another building. It was in good repair; probably it was a government navigation beacon. Norman sneezed several times, violently. He crawled warily across the roof toward the tower. The buildings were separated by a two-foot alley which Norman easily swung across.

He arrived at the base of the tower. Its black plastic members gleamed waxily in the dull light. As with many structures built after 1980, Hydrocarbon Products Administration regulations dictated that it be constructed with materials deriving from the crippled petroleum and coal industries, Norman remembered. In any case, the intricate framework provided good camouflage. Norman settled himself among the girders and peered out across Marquette.

There were hundreds of them! In the distance, tiny figures in Allservice green were walking through the streets, inspecting each building. Troop carriers and airtanks hung above them. Other airtanks patrolled some arbitrary perimeter about the city and bay. Norman recognized the setup as one of the standard formations for encirclement and detection of hostile forces. With confident foreknowledge he looked up and examined the sky above him. Every few seconds a buckrogers fell out of the apparently empty grayness. After a free fall of five thousand feet, the airborne infantrymen hit their jets just two or three hundred feet above the city. Already, more than twenty of them were posted over the various intersections.

The chimpanzee squinted, trying to get a clearer view of the nearest buckrogers. Images seen through the air behind and below the soldier seemed to waver. This and a faint screaming sound was the only indication of the superheated air shot from the Bender powered thermal element in the soldier's back pack. The infantryman's shoulders seemed lopsided. On more careful inspection Norman recognized that this was due to a GE fifty-thousand line reconnaissance camera strapped to the soldier's upper arm and shoulder. The camera's eight-inch lens gaped blackly as the soldier turned (rotated?) in the chimp's direction.

Norman froze. He knew that every hyper-resolution picture was being transmitted back to Sawyer AFB where computers and photo-interp teams analyzed them. Under certain conditions just a clear footprint or the beady glint of Norman's eyes within the maze of girders would be enough to bring a most decisive—though somewhat delayed—reaction.

As the buckrogers turned away, Norman sighed with relief. But he knew that he wouldn't remain safe for long. Sooner or later—most likely sooner—they would be able to trace him. And then . . . With horror he remembered once again some of the terrible bits of information that hid in the vast pile he knew, remembered the punishments for unauthorized knowledge. *He had to escape them!* Norman considered the means, both fictional and otherwise, that had been used in the past to elude pursuers. In the first place, he recognized that some outside help was needed, or he could never escape from the country. Erik Satanssen, he remembered, always played the double agent, gaining advantages from both sides right up to the denouement. Or take Slippery Jim DiGriz . . . the point was there are always some loopholes even in the most mechanized of traps. What organization would have a secret means of getting across Lake Superior into Canada? The Reds, of course!

Norman stopped fiddling with his soaked supenders, and looked up. That was the pat answer, in some stories: Pretend to side up with the baddies just long enough to get out of danger and expose them at the same time. Turning around, he gazed at the massive automated pier jutting out into the bay. At its root were several fourth-class apartments—and in one of them was the only Soviet agent in the Upper Peninsula! Norman remembered more about Boris Kuchenko. What sort of government would employ a slob like that as a spy? He racked his memory but could find no other evidence of espionage in the U.P. area.

Many tiny details seemed to crystallize into an idea. It was just like in some stories where the hero appears to pull his hunches out of the thin air. Norman *knew*, without any specific reason, that the Soviets were not as incapacitated as they seemed. Stark, Borovsky, Ivanov were smart boys, much smarter than the so-called Bumpkinov incompetents they had replaced. If Stark had been in power in the first place, the Soviet Union might have survived Bender's invention without losing more than a few outlying SSR's. As it was the Party bosses controlled only the area immediately around Moscow and some "hardened" bases in the Urals. Somehow Norman felt that, if all the mental and physical resources of the rulers had been used against the counter-revolutionaries, the Reds' position would have to be better. Borovsky and Ivanov especially, were noted for devious, back-door victories. Something smelled about this spy business.

If Kuchenko was more than he seemed, there might be a way out even yet. If he could trick the Reds into thinking he was a stupe or a traitor, they might take him to some hideout in Canada. He knew they would be interested in him and his knowledge; that was his passport and his peril. They must never know the things *he* knew. And then later, in Canada, maybe he could expose the Russian spies and gain forgiveness.

The nearest buckrogers was now facing directly away from Norman's tower. The chimpanzee moved away from the tower, hurried to the edge of the roof, and swung himself over. Now he was out of the line of sight of the infantryman. He reached the ground and scampered across the empty street. Soon he was padding along the base of the huge auto pier. Finally he reached the point where the street was swallowed by the enclosed portion of the pier. Norman ran into the dimness; at least he was out of the rain now. Along the side of the inner wall was a metal grid stairway. The chimp clambered up the stairs, found himself in the narrow corridor serving the cheap apartments which occupied what otherwise would have been dead space in the warehouse pier. He paused before turning the doorknob.

". . . Move fast!" The knob was snatched from his fingers, as someone on the other side pulled the door open. Norman all but fell into the room. "What the hell!" The speaker slammed the door shut behind the chimpanzee. Norman glanced about the room, saw Boris Kuchenko frozen in the act of wringing his hands. The other man spun Norman around, and the chimpanzee recognized him as one Ian Sloane, civilian employee No. 36902u at Sawyer AFB; so the hunch had been right! The Reds *were* operating on a larger scale than the government suspected.

Norman assumed his best conspiratorial air. "Good morning, gentlemen . . . or should I say Comrades?"

The older man, Sloane, kept a tight grip on his arm. A look of surprise and triumph and oddly—fear, was on his face. Norman decided to go all the way with the double-agent line. "I'm here to offer my services, uh, Comrades. Perhaps you don't know quite what and who I am . . ." He looked around expectantly for some sign of curiosity. Sloane—that was the only name Norman could remember, but it couldn't be his real one—gazed at him attentively, but kept a tight grip on his arm. Seeing that he was going to get no response, Norman continued less confidently. "I . . . I know who you are. Get me out of the country and you'll never regret it. You must have some way of escaping—at the very least some hiding place." He noticed Boris Kuchenko glance involuntarily at a spot in the ceiling near one of the walls. There was an ill-concealed trap hacked raggedly out of the ceiling. It hardly seemed the work of a master spy.

At last Sloane spoke. "I think we can arrange your escape. And I am sure that we will not regret it."

His tone made Norman realize how naïve his plan had been. These agents would get the information and secrets from him or they would destroy him, and there was no real possibility that he would have any opportunity to create a third, more acceptable alternative. The fire was much hotter than the frying pan, and fiction was vaporized by reality. He was in trouble.

Pfft.

The tiny sound came simultaneously with a pinprick in his leg. The curtains drawn before the window jerked slightly. A faint greenish haze seemed to hang in the air for an instant, then disappeared. He scratched his leg with his free hand and dislodged a black pellet. Then he knew that the photointerpretation group at Sawyer had finally found his trail. They knew exactly where he was, and now they were acting. They had just fired at least two PAX cartridges into the room, one of which had failed to go off. The little black object was a cartridge of that famous nerve gas.

During the Pittsburgh Bread Riots back in '81, screaming mobs, the type that dismember riot police, had been transformed into the most docile groups by a few spoken commands and a couple of grams of PAX diffused over the riot area. The stuff wasn't perfect, of course; in about half a per cent of the population there were undesirable side effects such as pseudo-epilepsy and permanent nerve damage; another half per cent weren't affected by normal dosages at all. But the great majority of people immediately lost all power to resist outside suggestion. He felt Sloane's grip loosening.

Norman pulled away and spoke to both men. "Give me a boost through that trap door."

"Yes, sir." The two men agreeably formed a stirrup and raised the chimpanzee toward the ceiling. As they did, Norman suddenly wondered why the gas had not affected him. *Because I'm not all here!* He answered himself with an almost hysterical chuckle. The gas could only affect the part of him that was physically present. And, though that was a very important part, he still retained some of his own initiative.

As Norman pushed open the trap, there was a splintering crash from the window as a buckrogers in full battle gear came hurtling feet first into the room. With a spastic heave, the chimp drew himself into the darkness above. From below he heard an almost plaintive, "Halt!" then Sloane's formerly menacing voice; "We'll go quietly, Officer."

Norman picked himself up and began running. The way was dimly lit from windows mounted far above. Now that his eyes were adjusted, he could see bulky crates around him and above him. He looked down, and gasped, for he could see crates below him, too. He seemed suspended. Then Norman remembered. In the dim light it wasn't too evident, but the floor and ceiling of this level were composed of heavy wire mesh. From a control board somewhere in the depths of the building, roller segments in the mesh could be turned on, and the bulkiest crates could be shuttled about the auto pier like toys. When in operation the pier could handle one million tons of merchandise a day; receiving products from trucks, storing them for a short time, and then sliding them into the holds of superfreighters. This single pier had been expected to bring the steel industry to Marquette, thus telescoping the mining and manufacturing complexes into one. Perhaps after the Recovery it would fulfill its promise, but at the moment it was dead and dark.

Norman zigzagged around several crates, scampered up an incline. Behind him he could hear the infantrymen, shed of their flying gear, scrambling through the trap door.

They would never believe his honesty now that he had been seen consorting with the communists. Things did indeed look dark—he complimented himself on this pun delivered in the midst of danger—but he still had some slim chance of escaping capture and the terrible punishment that would be sure to follow. He had one undetonated PAX cartridge. Apparently its relatively gentle impact with his flesh had kept it from popping. Perhaps not all the soldiers were wearing the antiPAX nose filters—in which case he might be able to commandeer a helicopter. It was a wild idea, but the time for cautious plans was past.

The pier seemed to extend forever. Norman kept moving. He had to get away; and he was beginning to feel very sick. Maybe it was some effect of the gas. He ran faster, but even so he felt a growing terror. His mind seemed to be dissolving, disintegrating. Could *this* be the effect of PAX? He groped mentally for some explanation, but somehow he was having trouble remembering the most obvious things, while at the same time extraneous memories were swamping him more completely than they had for weeks. He should know what the source of the danger was, but somehow . . . *I'm not all here!* That was the answer! But he couldn't understand what its significance was anymore. He no longer could form rational plans. Only one goal remained—to get away from the things that were stalking him. The dim gray glow far ahead now seemed to offer some kind of safety. If he could only reach it. Intelligence was deserting him, and chaos was creeping in.

Faster!

3,456,628 more shopping days until Christmas . . . Latitude 40.9234°N, Longitude 121.3018°W: Semi-hardened Isis missile warehouse; 102 megatons total . . . Latitude 95.00160°N, Longitude 87.4763°W: Cluster of three Vega class Submarine Launched Ballistic Missiles; 35 megatons total . . . depth 105.4 fathoms . . . Allserv IFF codes as follows: I. 398547 . . . 436344 . . . 51 . . . "Hey, let me out!" . . . *Master of jungle poised, knife ready as . . . the nature of this rock formation was not realized until the plutonist theory of Bender's . . . New Zealand Harbor Defense of Wellington follows: Three antisubmarine detection rings at 10° 98 miles from . . . REO factory depot Boise, Idaho contains 242,925 million-hp consumer fusion packs; inventory follows.* Cold gray light shining in the eyes. And I must escape or . . . "*die with a stake driven through his heart," the professor laughed.* STOP or you'll fall; MOVE or you'll die; escape escape escape seascape orescape3scape5scape2pecape4ea1aoop30 68913501011213-1010001010110000101010100001111010101—

The chimpanzee crouched frozen and glared madly at the soft gray light coming through the window.

The tiny black face looked up from the starched white of the pillow and stared dazedly at the ceiling. Around the bed hung the glittering instruments of the SOmatic Support unit. Short of brain tissue damage, the SOS could sustain life in the most terribly mangled bodies. At the moment it was fighting pneumonia, TB, and polio in the patient on the bed.

Dunbar sniffed. The medical ward of the Labyrinth used all the latest procedures—gone was the antiseptic stink of earlier years. The germicidals used were a very subtle sort—and only a shade different from antipersonnel gases developed in the '60's and '70's. William Dunbar turned to Pederson, the only other human in the room. "According to the doctors, he'll make it." Dunbar gestured to the unconscious chimp. "And his reactions to those questions you asked him under truth drug indicate that no great damage has been done to his 'amplified personality.' "

"Yeah," Pederson replied, "but we won't know whether he responded truthfully until I have these co-ordinates for his computer checked out." He tapped the sheet of paper on which he had scrawled the numbers Norman had called off. "For all we know, he may be immune to truth drug in the same way he is to PAX."

"No, I think he probably told the truth, General. He is, after all, in a very confused state.

"Now that we know the location of his computer, it should be an easy matter to remove the critical information from it. When we try the invention on a man we can be much more careful with the information initially presented."

Pederson stared at him for a long moment. "I suppose you know that I've always opposed your project."

"Uh, yes," said Dunbar, startled, "though I can't understand why you do."

Pederson continued, apparently without noticing the other's answer, "I've never quite been able to convince my superiors of the dangers inherent in the things you want to do. I think I can convince them now and I intend to do everything in my power to see that your techniques are never tried on a human, or for that matter, on any creature."

Dunbar's jaw dropped. "But why? We *need* this invention! Nowadays there is so much knowledge in so many different areas that it is impossible for a man to become skilled in more than two or three of them. If we don't use this invention, most of that knowledge will sit in electronic warehouses waiting for insight and correlations that will never occur. The human-computer symbiosis can give man the jump on evolution and nature. Man's intellect can be ex—"

Pederson swore. "You and Bender make a pair, Dunbar; both of you see the effects of your inventions with narrow utopian blinders. But yours is by far the most dangerous of the two. Look what this one chimpanzee has done in under six hours—escaped from the most secure post in America, eluded a large armed force, and deduced the existence of an espionage net that we had completely overlooked. Catching him was more an *accident* than anything else. If he had had time to think about it, he probably would have deduced that distance limit and found some way to escape us that really would have worked. And this is what happens with an experimental *animal*! His intelligence has increased steadily as he developed a firmer command of his information banks. We captured him more or less by chance, and unless we act fast while he's drugged, we won't be able to hold him.

"*And you want to try this thing on a man, who's starting out at a much higher level of intelligence!*

"Tell me, Doctor, who are you going to give godhood to first, hm-m-m? If your choice is wrong, the product will be more satanic than divine. It will be a devil that we cannot possibly beat except with the aid of some fortuitous accident, for we can't outthink that which, by definition, is smarter than we. The slightest instability on the part of the person you choose would mean the death or *domestication* of the entire human race."

Pederson relaxed, his voice becoming calmer. "There's an old saw, Doctor, that the only truly dangerous weapon is a man. By that standard, you have made the only advance in weaponry in the last one hundred thousand years!" He smiled tightly. "It may seem strange to you, but I oppose arms races and I intend to see that you don't start one."

William Dunbar stared, pale-faced, entertaining a dream and a nightmare at the same time. Pederson noted the scientist's expression with some satisfaction.

This tableau was interrupted by the buzzing of the comm. Pederson accepted the call. "Yes," he said, recognizing Smith's features on the screen.

"Sir, we just finished with those two fellows we picked up on the auto pier," the aide spoke somewhat nervously. "One is Boris Kuchenko, the yuk we've had spotted all along. The other is Ivan Sliv, who's been working for the last nine months as a code man at Sawyer under the name of Ian Sloane. We didn't suspect him at all before. Anyway, we gave both of them a deep-probe treatment, and then erased their memories of what's happened today, so we could release them and use them as tracers."

"Fine," replied Pederson.

"They've been doing the darndest things, those spies." Smith swallowed, "But that isn't what this call is about."

"Oh?"

"Can I talk? Are you alone?"

"Never mind, say it."

"Sir, this Sliv is really a top man. Some of his memories are under blocks that I'm sure the Russkies' never thought we could break. Sir—he knows of a project the Sovs are running in an artificial cave system under the Urals. They've taken a dog and wired it—wired it into a computer. Sliv has heard the dog talk, just like Dunbar's chimp. Apparently this is the big project they're pouring their resources into to the exclusion of all others. In fact, one of Sliv's main duties was to detect and obstruct any similar project here. When all the bugs have been worked out, Stark, or one of the other Red chiefs, is going to use it on himself and—"

Pederson turned away from the screen, stopped listening. He half noticed Dunbar's face, even paler than before. He felt the same sinking, empty sensation he had four years before when he had heard of Bender's fusion pack. Always it was the same pattern: The invention, the analysis of the dangers, the attempt at suppression, and then the crushing knowledge that no invention can really be suppressed and that the present case is no exception. Invention came after invention, each with greater changes. Bender's Pack would ultimately mean the dissolution of central collections of power, of cities—but Dunbar's invention meant an increased *capability* for invention.

Somewhere under the Urals slept a very smart son of a bitch indeed . . .

And so he must choose between the certain disaster of having a Russian dictator with superhuman intelligence, and the probable disaster involved in beating the enemy to the punch.

He knew what the decision must be; as a practical man he must adapt to changes beyond his control, must plan for the safest possible handling of the unavoidable.

. . . For better or worse, the world would soon be unimaginably different.

Appendix
Another Path Through the Book

In one phase of this book's gestation, it was to be divided into sections according to the manner in which science was used in the story. This appendix gives an alternate order from the table of contents in which to enjoy the stories. Hard science fiction—the part of sf that takes science as its central subject—is sf's center. What we bring to you is an anthology of sf stories in which science plays a crucial role and is in the foreground. Of course, one can find science in many different aspects of the science fiction story, and so this book is an attempt to reveal many of the varied ways in which science is manifest in science fiction.

I. Stories using the imagery of science and technology (as you read these stories, you will notice that these writers use scientific and technological images in quite different ways, which was of course the point):

Arthur C. Clarke's "Transit of Earth"
Poul Anderson's "Kyrie"
Nathaniel Hawthorne's "Rappaccini's Daughter"
J. G. Ballard's "Prima Belladonna"
John Sladek's "Stop Evolution in Its Tracks!"
William Gibson's "Johnny Mnemonic"
Philip Latham's "The Xi Effect."

II. Stories in which science and technology are central to who and what the characters are include:

James Tiptree, Jr.'s "The Psychologist Who Would Not Do Awful Things to Rats"
Gregory Benford's "Exposures"
John M. Ford's "Heat of Fusion"
Greg Bear's "Tangents"
C. M. Kornbluth's "Gomez"
Cordwainer Smith's "No, No, Not Rogov!"
Vernor Vinge's "Bookworm, Run!"
Hilbert Schenck's "Send Me a Kiss By Wire"
Alfred Bester's "The Pi Man."

III. Stories in "built worlds," created by the author's extrapolation from today's science and technology include:

Anne McCaffrey's "Weyr Search"
George Turner's "In a Petri Dish Upstairs"
Rudy Rucker's "Message Found in a Copy of *Flatland*"

Gregory Benford's "Relativistic Effects"
Raymond Z. Gallun's "Davy Jones' Ambassador"
Gene Wolfe's "All the Hues of Hell"
Donald M. Kingsbury's "To Bring in the Steel."

IV. Stories in which science and technology shaped the literary point of view include:
Ursula K. Le Guin's "Author of the Acacia Seeds"
Henry Kuttner's and C.L. Moore's "Mimsy Were the Borogoves"
Kate Wilhelm's "The Planners"
James P. Hogan's "Making Light"
Gordon Dickson's "Dolphin's Way"
John M. Ford's "Chromatic Aberration"
Isaac Asimov's "Nightfall"
Gene Wolfe's "Procreation."

V. Stories in which the pacing was controlled, shaped, or distorted by the scientific and technological content include:
Ian Watson's "The Very Slow Time Machine"
Arthur C. Clarke's "The Longest Science Fiction Story Ever Told"
Frederik Pohl's "Day Million"
Isaac Asimov's "The Last Question"
Hilbert Schenck's "Morphology of the Kirkham Wreck."

VI. Stories created around one big scientific idea include:
Bob Shaw's "Light of Other Days"
Edward Bryant's "giANTS"
Don A. Stuart's "Atomic Power"
Philip K. Dick's "The Indefatigable Frog."

VII. Stories built around the problem-solving science fiction plot include:
Larry Niven's "The Hole Man"
Edgar Allen Poe's "A Descent Into the Maelström"
Katherine MacLean's "The Snowball Effect"
Hal Clement's "Proof."

While we did not, in the end, opt for this organization of the book, the reader may wish to read these stories in groups, exploring the ways in which science manifests itself in hard sf through the various aspects of fiction.